STEPHEN COONTS
Three Great Novels

Stephen Coots is the author of six *New York Times* bestselling novels, the first of which was the classic flying tale *Flight of the Intruder,* which spent more than six months on the top of the *New York Times* bestseller list. His novels have been published around the world and have been translated into more than a dozen languages. He was honoured by the U.S. Naval Institute with its Author of the Year award in 1986. His latest novel is *America.* He is also the editor of an anthology of true flying stories, *War in the Air.* He lives with his wife, Deborah, in Highlands, Maryland.

Also by Stephen Coonts

America

Flight of the Intruder

Final Flight

The Minotaur

Under Siege

The Red Horseman

The Intruders

Edited by Stephen Coonts

Combat

War in the Air

Stephen Coonts

Fortunes of War
Cuba
Hong Kong

ORION

First published in Great Britain in 2001 by Orion Books
an imprint of The Orion Publishing Group
Orion House, 5 Upper St Martin's Lane, London WC2H 9EA

A CIP catalogue record for this book
is available from the British Library

ISBN 0 75284 7589 (hardback)
ISBN 0 75284 7597 (trade paperback)

Typeset by Deltatype Ltd, Birkenhead, Merseyside

Printed and bound in Great Britain by
Clays Ltd, St Ives plc

Contents

For Larry and Craig

Fortunes of War

To Deborah

Acknowledgements

The author solicited technical advice from experts for various portions of this book. For their kindness, the author wishes to thank publicly Ray A. Crockett, Charles G. Wilson, and Captain Sam Sayers, USN Ret. A special tip of the flight helmet goes to Colonel Bob Price, USMC Ret., and his colleagues, the test pilots at Lockheed-Martin, who watched the author fly the F-22 cockpit concept demonstrator and didn't laugh.

1

The two telephone company vans moved along the traffic-choked boulevard beside the Imperial Palace at a snail's pace, precisely the speed at which everyone drove. Traffic in Tokyo this June morning was heavy, as usual. Reeking exhaust fumes rose from the packed roadways into the warm, hazy air in shimmering waves.

In the lead van, the driver kept his eyes strictly on the traffic. The driver was in his mid-twenties, and he looked extraordinarily fit in his telephone company one-piece jumper. He wore a blue company billed cap over short, carefully groomed hair. Concentrating fiercely on the traffic around him, he drove with both hands on the steering wheel.

The passenger in the lead van was a few years older than the driver. He, too, wore a one-piece blue jumper and billed cap, both of which sported the company logo. This man examined with sharp, intelligent eyes the stone wall that surrounded the palace grounds.

Between the fifteen-foot wall and the boulevard was a centuries-old moat that still contained water. Atop the wall was a green tangle of trees and shrubs, seemingly impenetrable. There were actually two moats, an outer moat and an inner one, but here and there they had been permanently bridged. In many places, they had just been filled in. Here in the heart of Tokyo, the remaining hundred-foot-wide expanses of water populated with ducks and lined with people were stunning, inviting, an inducement to contemplation.

The passenger of the lead van paid little attention to the open water or the crowds. He was interested in police cars and palace security vehicles, and he mentioned every one he saw to the driver. Occasionally, he checked his watch.

When the two vans had completely circled the royal compound, the man in the cargo area of the lead van spoke a few words into a handheld radio, listened carefully to the reply, then nodded at the man in the passenger seat, who was looking at him. That man patted the driver on the arm twice.

In a few seconds, the vans turned into a service entrance. The inner moat had been filled in here, and the vehicles went through a narrow gate in the wall to a courtyard. A uniformed security officer in a glassed-in guardhouse watched the vehicles park. There were two armed officers by the gate and two by the door of the building. All four of them watched the passenger get out of the lead vehicle and walk over to the guardhouse.

The security officer's little window was already open, apparently for ventilation.

The passenger gave a polite bow, just a head bob. 'We are the telephone repairmen. They told us to come this morning.'

'Identity cards, please.'

The passenger passed them over.

'Yes. I have you on the list.' The officer gave the cards back.

'Where should we park?'

'Near the door.' He gestured vaguely. 'There should be no conflicts. How long will your repairs take?'

'I don't know. We will have to inspect the failure, ensure we have the proper equipment to repair it.'

'You must be out of the palace by four o'clock.'

'And if we cannot fix it by then?'

'You will have to call the Imperial Household Agency, describe the problem, and make an appointment to return.'

'I understand. First, we must diagnose the problem. We have some test equipment to take inside.'

The security officer nodded and gestured to the two armed policemen standing near the door.

It took a bit to get the vans parked and unloaded. One of the security officers went over and spoke for a moment to the man in the guardhouse while the telephone men checked their equipment. The four men each hoisted a share. One of the security officers held the door open for them, and another followed them inside.

'I will show you where the problem is,' he told the four, then took the lead. 'The agency has a telephone technician on the staff. If you wish, I will have him summoned and he can tell you what he learned when he examined the system.'

'We may have to do that,' the man who had been the passenger in the lead van said. 'We will look first.'

They went up a staircase to the second floor and down a long corridor. They were inside an equipment room when the garroting wire went over the guard's head, startling him. The wire bit deeply into his neck before he could make a sound. He was struggling against the wire when one of the men, now in front of him, seized his head and twisted it so violently that his neck snapped.

The repairmen took the guard's weight as he went limp. They placed the body in a corner of the room, out of sight of anyone who might come to the door, open it, and look in. The murder had taken no more than sixty seconds.

The men picked up their equipment. Outside in the hallway, the passenger from the van ensured the door was completely shut and latched.

Their rubber-soled shoes made no noise as the four men walked the marble corridors deeper and deeper into the huge palace.

The bubbling, laughing children circled about the empress with carefree abandon. They giggled deliciously as they danced around her arm in arm on the manicured green lawn, among the shrubs and flowers growing riot in lush beds, under a bright sun shining down from a gentle blue sky, while temple bells chimed in the distance. Stately, measured, the bells proclaimed the beauty of an ordered universe.

Emperor Naruhito was probably the only person to pay any attention to the chiming temple bells, which he thought the perfect musical accompaniment to the informal lawn ceremony in front of him. The children's bright, traditional dress contrasted sharply with the deep green grass and captured the eye as they circled around the empress, who was wearing a silk ivory-colored kimono trimmed with exquisite organdy. The other adults were removed a pace or two, ceding center stage to the empress and the happy children. The photographers shooting the scene stationed themselves ever so slightly out of the way. They were dressed in nondescript clothing, rarely moved, and, in the finest tradition of their profession, managed to fade into the scene almost like shadows.

The natural world certainly had an innocent charm that human affairs lacked, the emperor mused bitterly. For weeks now he had been brooding upon the current political situation. The new prime minister, Atsuko Abe, seemed bent on forcing the nation onto a new course, a course that Emperor Naruhito regarded with a growing sense of horror.

The Japanese political situation had been drifting to the right for years, the emperor thought as he watched the empress and the children. He reviewed the sequence yet again, trying to make sense of an avalanche of events that seemed beyond human control.

Each government since the great bank collapse had lasted a short while, then was swept from office and replaced by one even more reactionary. As the emperor saw it, the problem was that politicians were not willing to tell the Japanese people the truth. Their island nation was small, overpopulated, and lacked natural resources. The prosperity of the post-World War II era was built on turning imported raw materials into manufactured products and selling them to the American market at prices American manufacturers could not compete with. Japan's price advantage rested on low labor costs, which eventually disappeared. Sky-high real estate and hyperinflated stock values fell sickeningly as Japan's economic edge evaporated. The government propped up the overextended banking system for a while, but finally it collapsed, nearly bankrupting the government. Then tensions in the

Mideast rose to the flash point and the Arabs cut off the sale of oil to force the developed world to pressure Israel.

The oil was flowing once again, but the damage was done. Japan found it could not afford Mideast oil at any price. The yen was essentially worthless, the banking system in ruins, huge industrial enterprises couldn't pay their bills, and disillusioned workers had been laid off in droves.

Maybe the Japanese were doomed. The emperor had moments when cold anxieties seized his heart, and he had one such now.

Perhaps they were all doomed. To be led into the outer darkness by a poisonous ultranationalist like Atsuko Abe, a demagogue preaching against the evils of foreign values and foreign institutions while extolling the virtues of the ancient Japanese nation — was this the Japanese destiny? Was this what the nation had come to?

Ah . . . Japan, ancient yet young, fertile yet pure and unspoiled, home for the select of mankind, the Japanese.

If that Japan had ever existed, it was long gone, yet today Abe waved the racial memory like a flag before a dispirited, once-proud people betrayed by everything they trusted. Betrayed, Abe claimed, by Western democracy. Betrayed by bureaucrats. Betrayed by captains of industry . . . betrayed by capitalism, an import from a foreign culture . . .

Japan, Abe thundered, had been betrayed by a people who refused to hold its values dear, the Japanese. *They* were guilty. And they would have to pay the price.

All of this was political rhetoric. It inflamed half-wits and foreigners and gave newspapers much to editorialize about, but it was only hot air, spewed by Abe and his friends to distance themselves from other, more traditional politicians, and to win votes, which it did. Only when he was firmly ensconced in the prime minister's office, with the reins of power in his hands, did Atsuko Abe begin to discuss his true agenda with his closest allies.

Friends of the emperor whispered to him of Abe's ambitions, because they were deeply troubled. Abe's proclamations, they said, were more than rhetoric. He fully intended to make Japan a world power, to do 'whatever was required.'

Naruhito, always conscious of the fact that the post-World War II constitution limited the throne to strictly ceremonial duties, held his tongue. Still, the burden of history weighed oppressively upon him.

A personal letter from the president of the United States shattered Naruhito's private impasse. 'I am deeply concerned,' the President said, 'that the Japanese government is considering a military solution to aggravating regional and economic problems, a solution that will rupture the peace of the region and may well trigger worldwide conflagration. Such a calamity would have enormous, tragic implications for every human on this planet. As heads of state, we owe our countrymen and our fellow citizens of the planet our best efforts to ensure such an event never occurs.'

There was more. Naruhito read the letter with a sense of foreboding. The president of the United States knew more about the political situation in Japan than he, the emperor, did. Obviously, the president got better information.

Near the end of the letter, the president said, 'We believe the Abe administration plans an invasion of Siberia to secure a permanent, stable oil supply. The recent appeals of the indigenous Siberian people for Japanese aid in their revolt against the Russians are a mere pretext orchestrated by the Abe government. I fear such an invasion might trigger a world war, the like of which this planet has never seen. A third world war, one more horrible than any conflict yet waged by man, may bring civilization to a tragic end, throwing the world into a new dark age, one from which our species may never recover.'

Here, in writing, were the words that expressed the horror the emperor felt as he observed the domestic political situation. Even though he lacked the specific information that the president of the United States had, Naruhito also felt that he was watching the world he knew slide slowly and inexorably toward a horrible doom.

'I am writing you personally,' the president concluded, 'to ask for your help. We owe it to mankind to preserve the rule of law for future generations. Our worldwide civilization is not perfect; it is a work in progress, made better by every person who obeys the laws and works for his daily bread, thereby contributing to the common good. Civilization is the human heritage, the birthright of all who will come after us.'

Naruhito asked the prime minister to call.

Although the emperor had met Atsuko Abe on several occasions since he had become prime minister, he had never before had the opportunity to speak privately with him. Always, there were aides around, functionaries, security people. This time, it was just the two of them, in the emperor's private study.

After the polite preliminaries, the emperor mentioned the letter and gave Abe a copy to read.

Atsuko Abe was unsure how to proceed or just what to say. A private audience with the emperor was an extraordinary honor, one that left him somewhat at a loss for words. Yet this letter . . . He knew the Americans had spies – spies and political enemies were everywhere.

'Your Highness, we are at a critical juncture in our nation's history,' Atsuko Abe said, feeling his way. 'The disruption of our oil supply was the final straw. It wrecked the economy. Japan is in ruins; millions are out of work. We must repair the damage and ensure it never happens again.'

'Is it true?' the emperor asked, waving the letter. 'Is your government planning an invasion of Siberia?'

11

'Your Excellency, we have received a humanitarian appeal from the native Siberian people, who are seeking to throw off the Russian yoke. Surely you have been briefed on this development. The justice of their situation is undeniable. Their appeal is quite compelling.'

'You are evasive, sir. Now is the time for speaking the blunt truth, not polite evasion.'

Abe was astounded. Never had he seen the emperor like this, nor imagined he could be like this.

'The time has come for Japan to assume its rightful place in the world,' the prime minister said.

'Which is?'

'A superpower,' Abe said confidently. He stared boldly at the emperor, who averted his eyes from the challenge on Abe's face.

Then, ashamed, he forced himself to look the prime minister in the eye. 'Is it true?' the emperor asked obstinately. 'Does Japan plan to invade Siberia?'

'Our hour has come,' Abe replied firmly. 'We are a small island nation, placed by the gods beside a growing Chinese giant. We *must* have oil.'

'But you have signed an agreement with the Russians! They will sell us oil.'

'That, Your Excellency, is precisely the problem. As long as we are buying Russian oil, we are at their mercy. *Japan must have its own resources.*'

The son of an industrialist, Atsuko Abe had spent the first two decades of his adult life in the Japanese Self-Defense Force, the military. Although he was selected for flag rank, he left at an early age and obtained a post in the defense ministry. There Abe made friends with politicians across the spectrum, rose in influence, won promotion after promotion. Finally, he left the bureaucracy and ran for a seat in the Diet, which he won handily. He had been there for almost ten years, surfing the political riptides that surged through the capital.

He was ready now, at sixty-two years of age. *This* was his moment.

The emperor refused to look away. '*Our* hour? How dare you? This nation has never been in a shadow. Our way of life is honorable; we have kept faith with our ancestors. Our nation has made mistakes in the past, for which our people have paid dearly, but our honor is unstained. We need no hour of conquest, no triumph of violence, no blood on our hands.'

'You are born to your position,' Abe said bitterly. 'What do you know of struggle, of triumph?'

The emperor fought to maintain his composure. 'Russia has nuclear weapons, which the Russians might use to defend themselves. Have you the right to risk the very life of this nation?'

'We are in a grave crisis, Your Excellency.'

'Don't patronize me, Prime Minister.'

Abe bowed. When he straightened, he said, 'Forgive me, Excellency. The

12

fact you do not know is that Japan also is a nuclear power. I am convinced that Russia will not risk nuclear war to retain a wasteland that has never earned her a single yen of profit.'

The emperor sat stunned. 'Japan has nuclear weapons?' he whispered. 'Yes.'

'How? How were these weapons developed and manufactured?'

'With the greatest secrecy. Obviously.' The manufacture of these weapons was Abe's greatest triumph, a program reluctantly agreed to by politicians watching their world collapse, then accomplished under a security blanket worthy of Joseph Stalin.

'The government did this without the consent of the Diet? Without the knowledge and consent of the Japanese people? In violation of the constitution and the laws?'

Abe merely bowed his head.

'What if you are wrong about Russia?' the emperor demanded. 'Answer me that. What if Russia retaliates with nuclear weapons?'

'The risk is as great for Russia as it is for Japan, and Russia has less at stake.'

'They may not see the equation as you do, Prime Minister.'

Abe said nothing.

The emperor was too astonished to go further. The man is mad, he thought. The prime minister has gone completely mad.

After a bit, the emperor recovered his voice sufficiently to ask, 'What do you suggest I tell the president of the United States in answer to his letter?'

Abe made an irritated gesture. 'Ignore it. No answer is necessary, Your Excellency. The president does not know his place.'

Naruhito shook his head ponderously from side to side. 'My grandfather, Hirohito, received a letter from President Roosevelt on the eve of World War Two, pleading for peace. Hirohito did not answer that letter. He refused to intervene with the government. All my life, I have wondered how history might have been different had my grandfather spoken up for what he believed.'

'Emperor Hirohito believed that the government was acting in the nation's best interests.'

'Perhaps he did. I am not convinced that your government is now.'

Abe shook himself. He had come too far, endured too much. He faced the emperor like a sumo wrestler. 'The government must speak for you, and the nation, which are the same. *That* is the law.'

'Do not speak to me of law. Not after what you have told me.'

Abe pounded his chest. 'You reign, I *rule*. That is the Japanese way.'

Abe took several deep breaths to compose himself. 'If you will give me a copy of the letter, I will have the foreign minister prepare a reply.'

The emperor didn't seem to hear. He continued, thinking aloud: 'In this era of nuclear, biological, and chemical weapons, war is obsolete. It is no longer a viable political option. The nation that plunges headlong into war in the twenty-first century will, I fear, merely be committing national suicide. *Death*, sir, is most definitely not Japan's destiny. Death is final and eternal, whether it comes slowly, from natural causes, or swiftly, in a spectacular blaze of glory. *Life*, sir, must be our business. *Life* is our concern.'

Before Abe could think of a polite reply, the emperor added softly, 'You carry a very heavy burden, Prime Minister. You carry the hopes and dreams of every Japanese alive today and those of our honored ancestors. You literally carry Japan upon your back.'

'Your Excellency, I am aware of my responsibilities,' Atsuko Abe retorted, as politely as he could. He struggled to keep a grip on his temper. 'Keenly aware,' he added through clenched teeth.

'In your public speeches that I have read, sir, you speak as if Japan's destiny were as obvious as the rising sun on a clear morning,' Emperor Naruhito said without rancor. 'I suggest you consult the representatives of the people in the Diet before you make any major commitments.'

He could think of nothing else to say to this fool facing him . . .

'Follow the law,' the emperor added. That was always excellent advice, but . . .

'The Japanese are a great people,' the emperor told the prime minister, to fill the silence. 'If you keep faith with them, they will have faith in you.'

Abe forced his head down in a gesture of respect. The skin on his head was tan, the hair cropped short.

Naruhito could stand no more of this scoundrel. He rose stiffly, bowed, and walked from the room.

That had been two days ago.

Naruhito had forsaken his ceremonial, almost-mystical position as head of state to speak the truth as he believed it, for the good of the nation. He had never done that before, but Abe . . . advocating the unthinkable. . . telling the emperor to his face what his duty was – never in his life had Naruhito been so insulted. The memory of Abe's words still burned deeply.

He had written a letter to the president of the United States, written it by hand because he did not wish to trust a secretary.

The truth was bitter: He could not affect events.

The children were singing now, led by Naruhito's wife, Masako. A flush of warmth went through the emperor as he regarded her, his dearly beloved wife, his empress, singing softly, leading the children.

Truly, he loved life. Loved his wife, his people, his nation . . . *this* Japanese nation. His life, the nation's life, they were all bound up together, one and inseparable. A profound sense of loss swept over him. Time *is* running out . . .

Captain Shunko Kato stood concealed by a curtain at a second-floor window in the Imperial Palace, watching the ceremony on the lawn below. Behind him stood the other three erstwhile telephone repairmen, *his* men, standing motionless, seemingly at perfect ease. They weren't, Kato knew. He could feel the tension, tight as a violin string. Military discipline held them motionless, silent, each man in communion only with his thoughts.

The sunlight coming through the window made a lopsided rectangle on the floor. Kato looked at the sunlit floor, the great frame that held the window, the hedge, the lawn, the people, the bold, brazen sky above . . .

He was seeing all this for the last time. Ah, but to dwell on his personal fate was unworthy. Kato brushed the thought away and concentrated on the figures before him on the lawn.

There was the emperor, shorter than the average Japanese male at five feet four, erect, carrying a tummy. Surrounding the group were security officers in civilian clothes – most of these men had their backs to the ceremony.

Kato retreated a few inches. He ensured he was concealed by the shadow of the drape, hidden from the observation of anyone on the lawn who might look at this window. Satisfied, he scanned the security guards quickly, taking in their state of alertness at a glance; then he turned his attention back to the royal party.

The emperor stood slightly in front of a group of officials, watching the empress and the children, seemingly caught up in the simple ritual. No doubt he was. He certainly had nothing else to worry about. The emperor, Kato was sure, was quite oblivious to the desperation that had ravaged so many lives since the bank collapse. How could it be otherwise? The emperor certainly didn't move in ordinary circles.

Yet the man must read newspapers, occasionally watch television. How could he miss the corruption of the politicians, the bribes, the influence peddling, the stench of scandal after scandal? Could he not see the misery of the common people, always loyal, always betrayed?

He never spoke out against corruption, avarice, greed. Never. And never condemning, he silently approved.

Kato felt his chest swelling with indignation. Oh, that they called such a man 'Son of Heaven!' An extraordinary obscenity.

The empress was saying good-bye to the children. The ceremony was ending.

Kato turned, surveyed his men. Still wearing the blue jumpers and caps of the telephone company, they were as fit as professional athletes, lean, with ropy muscles and easy, fluid movements. Kato had trained them, hardened them, made them soldiers in the Bushido tradition. In truth, he was proud of them, and now that pride showed on his face. The men looked back at him with faces that were also unable to conceal their emotion.

'For Japan,' he said softly, just loudly enough for them to hear.

'For Japan.' Their lips moved soundlessly, for he had told them to make no sound. Still, the reply echoed in Kato's ears.

'Banzai,' he mouthed.

'Banzai!' The silent reply lashed his soul.

The security guards escorted the emperor and empress toward the door of the Imperial Palace. One of them held it open for the emperor, who always preceded his wife by two paces. The security men did not enter the hallway; they remained outside. The entire palace was inside a security zone.

Inside the building, away from other eyes, the emperor paused to let Masako reach his side. She flashed him a grin, a very un-Japanese gesture, but then she had spent years in the United States attending college before their marriage. He dearly enjoyed seeing her grin, and he smiled his pleasure.

She took his arm and leaned forward, so that her lips brushed his cheek. His smile broadened.

Arm in arm, they walked down the hall to the end, then turned right.

Four men stood silently, waiting. They blocked the hallway.

The emperor stopped.

One of the men moved noiselessly to position himself behind the royal couple, but the others did not give way. Nor, the emperor noted with surprise, did they bow. Not even the tiniest bob.

Naruhito looked from face to face. Not one of the men broke eye contact.

'Yes?' he said finally.

'Your wife may leave, Your Excellency,' said one of the men. His voice was strong, even, yet not loud.

'Who are you?' asked the emperor.

'I am Captain Shunko Kato of the Japanese Self-Defense Force.' Kato bowed deeply from the waist, but none of the other men moved a muscle. 'These enlisted men are under my command.'

'By whose authority are you here?'

'By our own.'

Naruhito felt his wife's hand tighten on his arm. He looked again from face to face, waiting for them to look away as a gesture of respect. None of them did.

'Why are you here?' the emperor asked finally. He realized that time was on his side, not theirs, and he wished to draw this out as long as possible.

Kato seemed to read his thoughts. 'We are here for Japan,' Kato said crisply, then added, 'The empress must leave now.'

Naruhito could read the inevitable in their faces. Although the thought did not occur to Captain Kato, Naruhito had as much courage as any man there. He turned toward the empress.

'You must go, dear wife.'

16

She stared into his face, panic-stricken. Both her hands clutched his arm in a fierce grip.

He leaned toward her and whispered, 'We have no choice. Go, and know I love you.'

She tore her eyes from him and swept them around the group, looking directly into the eyes of each man. Three of them averted their gaze.

Then she turned and walked back toward the lawn.

From a decorative table nearby, Kato took a samurai sword, which the emperor had not previously noticed. With one swift motion, the officer withdrew the blade from the sheath.

'For Japan,' he said, grasping the handle with both hands.

The sword was very old, the emperor noticed. Hundreds of years old. His heart was audibly pounding in his ears. He looked again at each face. They were fanatics.

Resigned, Emperor Naruhito sank to his knees. He would not let them see him afraid. Thank heavens his hands were not trembling. He closed his eyes and cleared his thoughts. Enough of these zealots. He thought of his wife and his son and daughter.

The last thing he heard was the slick whisper of the blade whirring through the air.

Masako walked slowly toward the door where just seconds ago she and her husband had entered the palace. Every step was torture, agony...

The men were assassins.

Masako, in her horror, had sensed it the moment she saw them. They had no respect; their faces registered extraordinary tension – not like loyal subjects meeting their emperor and his wife, but like assassins.

She knew her nation's history, of course, knew how assassins had plagued rulers and politicians in times of turmoil, how they always murdered *for Japan* – as if their passionate patriotism could excuse the blood, could excuse slashing the life from men who had little or no control over the events that fired the murderers – then atoned for their crimes in orgies of ritual suicide.

The bloody melodrama was terrible theater, yet most Japanese loved it, reveled in it, were inspired by it. Ancient racial memories were renewed with flowing fresh red blood. New sacrifices propitiated savage urges ... and mesmerized the audience.

Patriotic murder was sadistic, Masako thought, an obscene perversion that surfaced when the world pressed relentlessly in upon the Japanese, as it had in the 1930s, as it had in December 1941, as it apparently was...

Now?

She could scarcely place one foot in front of another.

Oh, Naruhito, beloved husband, that we should have to face this ... and I should not be at your side ...

She turned and hurried back toward her husband. Toward the evil that awaited them both.

She ran, the length of her stride constrained by her skirt.

Just before she reached the corner, she heard the singing of the sword and then the sickening *thunk* as it bit into flesh.

She turned the corner in time to see her husband's head rolling along the floor and his upright torso toppling forward.

She saw no more. Despite her pain – or perhaps because of it – she passed out, collapsed in a heap.

Shunko Kato did not look again at the emperor's corpse. There was little time, and staring at the body of a man who had failed Japan would be wasting it.

He arranged a letter on the table where the sword had rested. The letter was written in blood, the blood of each man there, and they had all signed it.

For Japan.

Kato knelt and drew his knife. He looked at his chief NCO, who was standing beside him, his pistol in his hand. 'Banzai,' he said.

'Banzai.'

Kato stabbed the knife to the hilt in his own stomach.

The sergeant raised his pistol and shot Kato in the back of the head. Blood and brains flew from the captain's head. The sound of the shot made a stupendous thunderclap in the hallway. In the silence that followed, he could hear the tinny sound of the spent cartridge skittering across the floor.

Air escaping from the captain's body made an audible sound, but the sergeant was paying no attention.

He looked at his comrades. They, too, had their pistols out.

Brave men, doing what had to be done.

The sergeant took a deep breath, then raised the barrel of his pistol to his own head. The others did the same. The sergeant inadvertently squeezed his eyes shut just before he pulled the trigger.

2

'Captain Kato and his men were all dead when the security men got there,' Takeo Yahiro told the prime minister, Atsuko Abe. 'Apparently they committed suicide after they beheaded the emperor. The empress was the only person alive — she was passed out on the floor.'

Abe's astonishment showed on his face. 'The emperor was beheaded in the presence of his wife?'

'It would seem so, sir. She was lying on the floor in a faint when the security officers came upon the scene.'

Abe shook his head, trying to make the nightmare easier to endure. To assassinate a powerful official for political reasons was certainly not unheard of in Japan, but to do so in the presence of his wife . . . the *empress*? He had never heard of such a thing.

What would the public think?

'Captain Kato left a letter under the sword scabbard, sir, a letter written in blood. It gave the reasons for his actions.'

The prime minister was still fixated upon the presence of the empress at the murder scene. With his eyes closed, he asked, 'Did the assassins touch the empress?'

'I do not know, sir. Perhaps the doctors —'

'Has the press gotten this detail?'

Takeo Yahiro spoke softly, yet with assurance. 'No, sir. I took the liberty of refusing to allow any press release until senior officials were notified.'

Abe breathed deeply through his nose, considering, before he finally opened his eyes. He nodded almost imperceptibly, a mere fraction of an inch.

'Very well, Yahiro. Inflaming the public will not accomplish anything. A tragedy, a horrible tragedy . . .'

'There was a letter, sir. The assassins were disciples of Mishima.'

'Ahh . . .' said the prime minister, then fell silent, thinking.

Yukio Mishima had been an ultranationalist, a zealot. Unfortunately he had also been a writer, a novelist, one with a flaming passion for the brutal, bloody gesture. Thirty-eight years ago he and four followers stormed into Japan's military headquarters in downtown Tokyo, barricaded themselves in

19

the office of the commanding general, and called for the military to take over the nation. That didn't happen, of course, but Mishima was not to be denied. He removed his tunic and plunged a sword into his belly; then one of his disciples lopped off his head before killing himself, as well. The whole thing was neatly and tidily done in the grand samurai tradition. Mishima seared a bold political statement into the national conscience in a way impossible to ignore. And, incidentally, there was no one left alive for the authorities to punish – except for a few people on a minor trespass charge.

In the years since Mishima had become a cult figure. His ultranationalistic, militarist message was winning new converts every day, people who were finally coming to understand that they had an absolute duty to fulfill the nation's destiny, to uphold its honor.

'Public dissemination of the fact that the empress was a witness to her husband's assassination would accomplish nothing,' Abe said.

'The empress may mention it, sir.'

'She never speaks to the press without clearing her remarks with the Imperial Household Agency. She has suffered a terrible shock. When she recovers, she will understand that to speak of her presence at the murder scene would not be in the national interest.'

'Yes, sir. I will call the agency immediately.'

The prime minister merely nodded – Yahiro was quite reliable – then moved on.

'Prince Hirohito must be placed on the throne. In a matter of hours. Ensure that the ancient ceremony is scrupulously observed – the nation's honor demands it. He must receive the imperial and state seals and the replicas of the Amaterasu treasures.' The actual treasures – a mirror, a sword, and a crescent-shaped jewel – could be traced back to the Shinto sun goddess, Amaterasu, from whom the imperial family was descended, so they were too precious to be removed from their vault.

'Arrange it, please, Yahiro.'

'Yes, Prime Minister. By all means.'

'The senior ministers will all attend. The empress may attend if the doctors think she is strong enough.'

The prime minister was almost overcome by the historic overtones of the moment and was briefly unable to speak. *The emperor was dead.* A new emperor was waiting to be enthroned.

He shook his head, trying to clear his thoughts. So much to be done . . .

'Clear my calendar and send for a speechwriter,' the prime minister told the aide. 'And the protocol officer. We must declare a period of national mourning, notify the foreign embassies – all of that – then set up a state funeral. Heads of government from all over the world will undoubtedly attend, so there is much planning to do.'

'Yes, sir.'

'Ensure that a copy of Captain Kato's letter is given to the press. The public is entitled to know the reason for this great calamity.'

'Yes, sir.'

'We are on the cusp of history, Yahiro. We must strive to measure up to the vastness of our responsibilities. Future generations will judge us critically.'

Yahiro pondered that remark as he went out of the office, but only for a few seconds. He was a busy man.

Prime Minister Abe waited until the door closed on Yahiro; then he opened the door to the conference room that adjoined his office and went in. Two men in uniform were sitting at the large table. Small teacups sat on the table before them.

One of the men was chief of the Japanese Self-Defense Force. The other was his deputy.

The two soldiers looked expectantly at Abe's face.

'It is done.'

The soldiers straightened in their chairs, looked at one another.

'His wife was with him ... She saw it.'

'A bad omen,' one said. Careful planning, dedicated men, and then this horrible slipup.

'We'll try to keep the public from learning that fact,' Abe said. He made a gesture of irritation. 'We must move on. There is much to be done.'

The generals got to their feet, then bowed. 'For Japan,' the chief of staff said softly.

When Masako awoke, she was in her bed in the royal residence, a Western-style home on the grounds of the Imperial Palace. A physician and nurse were in attendance. The nurse was taking her pulse; the doctor was writing something.

She closed her eyes. The scene came back so vividly she opened them again, focused on the ceiling.

The nurse whispered to the doctor; the doctor came to check her head. He pressed on her forehead, which was sore. Apparently, she had hit it when she had fallen.

'Please leave me alone,' she asked.

It took a while, with much bowing by the nurse, but eventually the professionals left the room and closed the door behind them.

Masako kept her eyes open. She was afraid of what she might see if she closed them.

They killed him.

She wondered if she was going to cry.

When it became apparent that she was not, she sat up in bed, examined her sore head in a mirror. Yes, she had fallen on her forehead, which sported a vicious bruise. She fingered the place, felt the pain as she pressed, savored it.

They killed him! A shy, gentle man, a figurehead with no power. Murdered. For reasons that would be specious, ridiculous. For reasons that would interest only an insane fanatic, *they killed him.*

She felt empty, as if all life had been taken from her. She was only an unfeeling shell, a mere observer of this horrible tragedy that this woman named Masako was living through.

She sat upon the bed, unwilling to move. Scenes of her life with Naruhito flashed through her mind, raced along, but finally they were gone and the tree outside had thrown the room in shadow, and she was merely alone, in an empty room, with her husband dead.

In Washington, D.C., the president of the United States was getting ready for bed. He was going to bed alone, as usual, because his wife was at a soiree somewhere in Georgetown, playing the First Lady role to the hilt. The president was chewing two antiacid tablets when he picked up the ringing telephone and mumbled, 'Uumpf.'

'Mr. President, the emperor of Japan was assassinated in the Imperial Palace about two hours ago. The report is that he was beheaded.' The voice was that of Jack Innes, national security adviser. He would have been called about this matter by the duty officers in the White House situation room.

'Who did it?'

'Apparently a junior officer in the military and three enlisted men. They got into the palace by posing as telephone repairmen. Lopped off the emperor's head with a four-hundred-year-old samurai sword. Then they committed suicide.'

'All of them?'

'All four. The officer stabbed himself in the gut; then someone shot him in the head. The three enlisted apparently shot themselves.'

'Jesus!'

'Yes, sir.'

'Right-wing group?'

'Apparently they were followers of some right-wing cult, Mishima something. They left a letter written in blood, full of bullshit about Japan's destiny and national glory.'

'Have we received any answer from the emperor to my letter?' the president asked.

'Not to my knowledge, sir. I'll check with the Tokyo embassy and the State Department.'

'Do we even know if he received it?'

'It was delivered to the Japanese government by our ambassador. That is all we know for certain.'

'We are fast running out of options.'

'We should know more in the morning, Mr President.'

'When you know more, wake me up.'

'Yes, sir.'

President David Herbert Hood cradled the instrument and lay down on his bed. He was very tired. It seemed that he was always in that condition these days.

So Naruhito was dead. Murdered.

And the letter had accomplished nothing.

The president, Jack Innes, and the secretary of state had sweated for three days over the wording in that letter. After careful consideration, they had decided not to mention the fact that the United States had a secret military protocol with Russia promising military aid if Russia's borders were ever violated. The protocol was three years old, negotiated and signed as an inducement to Russia's fledgling democratic government to speed up the pace of nuclear disarmament. Even he, David Herbert Hood, had personally told the Russian president that the secret protocol was a solemn promise: 'Russian territory is as sacred as the boundaries of the United States.'

Well, a promise is a promise, but whether the promise would be honored was a different matter entirely.

The president got out of bed and went to the window. He stood there looking at the lights of Washington. After a bit, he sank into a chair and rubbed his head. He had spent the last twenty years in politics and he had seen his share of unexpected disasters. Most of the time, he had learned, the best thing to do was nothing at all.

Yes, nothing was usually best. The Japanese had another crisis on their hands, and the Japanese were going to have to solve it.

He should get some sleep.

The news from the far side of the Pacific had been getting steadily worse for years. Democracy in Russia had been a mixed blessing. Freed at last from Communist tyranny and mismanagement, the Russians soon found they lacked the ability to create a stable government. Corruption and bribery were endemic everywhere, in every occupation and walk of life. A dying man couldn't see a doctor without bribing the receptionist. Apparently, the only people doing well in the post-Communist era were the criminals. Ethnic minorities all over Russia had seized this moment to demand self-government, their own enclaves. If the Russian government didn't get a grip soon, a new dictator was inevitable.

In the United States, the public didn't want to hear bad news from overseas. The recent crisis in the Mideast had doubled the price of oil, here and around the world, a harbinger of shortages to come. Still, America had oil, so it didn't suffer as badly as Japan did. And the oil was flowing again. All in all, life in America was very, very good. And David Herbert Hood had the extreme good fortune to be riding the crest of the wave, presiding at the world's greatest party. His popularity was at a historic high; the nation was prosperous and at peace ... He would go into the history books with a smile on his face, children would read his biography in grade school for the next century, at least, and ... Japan was about to invade Siberia.

The president stared gloomily at the lights out there in the night. He had this feeling that, for some reason just beyond the edge of the light, mankind had been enjoying a rare interlude of prosperity and peace. They certainly hadn't earned it.

The emperor ... murdered. My God! The man was the benign symbol of all that was best in the Japanese culture. And they cut off his head!

Captain Jiro Kimura sat on the small balcony of his flat, staring between apartment and office buildings at Mount Fuji and drinking a beer. Although he was looking at Fuji, in his mind's eye he saw Pikes Peak, stark, craggy, looming high into the blue Colorado sky. 'The Peak of Pike,' his fellow cadets had called it, back when they were students at the U.S. Air Force Academy.

It was in his second or third year that three of his friends convinced themselves, and him, that they should run up the mountain. And back down. They tried it the second weekend in September, a Pikes Peak marathon, thirteen miles up and thirteen down.

Jiro Kimura smiled at the memory. What studs they had been back then, whippet-lean, tough as sole leather, ready to conquer the world! They actually made it to the top of the mountain and back down. Still, the last few miles going up, the pace was not what anyone would call a run. Not above twelve thousand feet!

Although that weekend had been almost twelve years ago, Jiro could recall the faces of those boys as if it were yesterday. He could see Frank Truax's shy, toothy grin; Joe Layfield's freckles and jug ears; Ben Franklin Garcia's white teeth flashing in his handsome brown face.

Garcia had died six years ago in an F-16 crash, somewhere in Nevada. They said his engine flamed out and, rather than ejecting, he tried to stretch a glide. That sure sounded like Ben Garcia, 'the pride of Pecos, Texas,' as they called him back then. He had been tough and smart, with something to prove, something Jiro Kimura could never quite put a finger on. Well, Ben was gone now, gone to wherever it is God sends those driven men when they finally fall to earth.

Truax was somewhere in the states flying C-141s, and Layfield was getting a master's degree in finance.

And Jiro Kimura was flying Japan's top-secret fighter plane, the new Zero.

His wife, Shizuko, came out onto the balcony with another beer. 'Colonel Cassidy will be here soon,' she said, a gentle reminder that he might wish to dress in something besides a T-shirt and shorts.

Jiro smiled his thanks.

24

Bob Cassidy. He had been a major back then, a young fighter pilot at the Academy for a tour. He had been commander of Jiro's cadet squadron. He took a liking to the Japanese youngster, who had nowhere to go for weekends or holidays, so he took him home.

Cassidy was married then, to Sweet Sabrina, as he always called her. Never just Sabrina, always with the adjective before her name, and always with a smile. Sweet Sabrina ... with the long brown hair and a ready smile ...

She and the boy died in a car wreck two years after Jiro graduated. Cassidy never remarried.

He should have married again, Jiro Kimura told himself, and he involuntarily glanced through the open door at Shizuko, busy within.

Perhaps Cassidy had never found another woman who measured up to Sweet Sabrina. Perhaps ...

Ah, if only he could go back. If only he could go back and relive those days, go back to the patio in Cassidy's yard with Truax and Garcia and Layfield, with Sweet Sabrina serving cold beer to boys not yet twenty-one while Bob Cassidy pretended not to notice, someone tuning the radio to the station called 'The Peak' because it played all the top hits.

Just one day ... that wouldn't be asking too much. A hot day, in the high eighties or low nineties, so the sweat on your skin would evaporate as fast as it appeared, a hot, high, dry day, with that Colorado sun warming your face and a faint scent of juniper in the air and the shady side of Pikes Peak purple in the afternoon.

Jiro missed those days.

He missed those people. Or most of them, anyway. He certainly didn't miss Major Tarleton, the physics professor, whose two uncles had died in the western Pacific, 'fighting the Japs.' That was the way he'd phrased it, wasn't it, while staring at Jiro as if he had personally ordered the attack on Pearl Harbor? There had been others, too, officers and enlisted, who went out of their way to let him know they didn't appreciate the fact that a Japanese soldier was training at the U.S. Air Force Academy.

Tarleton had been more than prejudiced – he had tried to ruin Jiro's academic career, gave him a failing grade for quiz after quiz, even though every answer was correct. Afraid, alone, Jiro endured in silence. Then Tarleton accused him of cheating on an exam. An ice-cold Bob Cassidy called the young cadet into his office, grilled him until he had it all.

The following Monday morning, Tarleton was gone, and Jiro heard no more about the alleged honor code violation.

Cassidy was like that. He would risk everything to save one scared kid.

Jiro Kimura took another drag at the beer and stared with unseeing eyes at the snowcapped cone of Fuji.

Maybe what he missed was America.

He wiped the tears from his eyes.

They had never asked who his father was, what he did, how much money he had. Not once. They took him for who he was, what he was. And they made him one of them.

Cassidy was a colonel now, the Air Force liaison officer at the U.S. embassy in Tokyo. He was still trim, still grinned, although maybe not as readily as he used to when Sweet Sabrina was alive.

He worked too hard now. Jiro was sure of that. Good colonels work a lot more than captains, and Cassidy was a good one. In fact, he was one of the best.

Back then some of the guys had called him 'Hopalong' behind his back. Or 'Butch.' They had to explain the references to Jiro. He never did understand exactly how nicknames were derived or bestowed, although he did acquire the American taste for them. Still, for him, Cassidy was always Cassidy.

Or Bob. How American! 'Use my first name. That shows that you like me.'

Jiro was in the bedroom changing clothes when he heard the knock on the door and the sounds of Shizuko greeting Cassidy.

'Oh, Colonel, so good to see you.' Shizuko's English was not so good, but Cassidy had never had too much trouble understanding it.

'Have you heard the news? About the emperor?' Cassidy's voice was hard, very concerned.

'What news?' He could hear the worry in Shizuko's voice.

'He was assassinated. They just announced it.'

Shizuko said something that Jiro didn't hear, then several seconds later he heard the sound of the television announcer.

He quickly finished dressing and hurried into the living room. It was a small room, about a third the size of the one Cassidy used to have in Colorado Springs. Jiro shook his head, annoyed that that irrelevant thought should distract him at a time like this.

He said hello to Cassidy, who gave a tiny bow while remaining intent on the television.

'Sit, Colonel. Bob. Please.'

Cassidy knew some Japanese, apparently enough to follow the television announcer without too much difficulty.

Shizuko hid her face in her hands.

'Perhaps this isn't a good evening . . .' Cassidy began, but Jiro waved him into silence.

They sat on the mats in front of the television as the last of the afternoon light faded from the sky. It was completely dark when Jiro turned off the set and Shizuko went into the small Pullman-style kitchen to make dinner.

Cassidy was about six feet tall, a wiry man with a runner's build. Tonight he wore civilian clothes, dark slacks and a beige short-sleeve shirt. He had blue eyes, thinning sandy-colored hair, and a couple of chipped teeth, which

26

had been that way for years. A cheap watch on his left wrist was his only jewelry.

'Beer?'

'Sure.'

'Good to see you, Bob.' Kimura spoke like an American, Cassidy thought, with fluent, unaccented English.

'When I heard the news on the radio, I almost turned around and went home,' Cassidy told his host. 'Thought you and Shizuko might want some privacy. But I figured that these get-together times are so hard to arrange that . . .'

'Yeah. I needed to talk to you. This assassination is not good.' Jiro Kimura thought for several seconds, then shook his head. 'Not good. Japan is on a strange, dangerous road.'

Cassidy looked around the apartment, accepted the offered beer. Kimura turned on a radio, played with the dial until he got music, then resumed his seat just across from his guest.

'They are preparing to move the planes to forward bases,' Jiro said. 'We are packing everything, crating all the support gear, all the special tools, spare engines, parts, tires, everything.'

'You mean bases outside of Japan?'

'Yes.'

Robert Cassidy sat in silence, digesting Kimura's comment. Finally, he sipped his beer, then waited expectantly for his host to decide what else he wanted to say. For some reason, at that moment he recalled Jiro as he had first known him, a lost, miserable doolie at the U.S. Air Force Academy. A more forlorn kid, Cassidy had never met.

Of course, the Japanese had sent their very best to the United States as an exchange student. Jiro finished second in his class, with a 3.98 grade point average – in aeronautical engineering. The first person in the class was a black girl from Georgia with a 180 IQ. After graduation, she didn't spend a day in uniform; she went on to get a Ph.D. in physics on the Air Force's dime. The last Cassidy heard, she was doing fusion research at the Lawrence Livermore Laboratory.

Jiro became a first-rate fighter pilot – for Japan. Now he was flying an airplane that had been developed in the utmost secrecy. Until Kimura mentioned the new Zero to him six months ago, Cassidy had not known of the plane. Judging by the startled reaction his report caused in Washington when he sent it in, no one there knew about it, either. Since then he had received a blizzard of requests from Washington for further information on the new plane, and he had had just two further conversations with Jiro.

The first occurred when he invited the Kimuras to dinner in Tokyo. Jiro didn't mention his job during the course of the evening. Cassidy couldn't bring himself to ask a question.

It was obvious that Jiro had wrestled with his conscience long and hard before he violated the Japanese security regs the first time.

Cassidy decided that the next move was up to Jiro. If he wanted to tell the U.S. government Japanese secrets, Cassidy would convey the information. But he would not ask.

Last month he and Jiro had attended a baseball game together. In the isolation of a nearly empty upper deck of the stadium, Jiro discussed in general terms the dimensions of the Japanese military buildup that had been under way for at least five years. Some of that information Cassidy knew from other sources; some was new. He merely listened, asked questions only to clarify, then wrote a detailed report that evening when he got home. That afternoon Jiro had been short on specifics.

Whatever internal battle Jiro was fighting then was apparently over now. Tonight he met Cassidy's gaze. 'The new Zero is the most advanced fighter on earth. Very maneuverable, stealthy, good range, speed, easy to fly. Very sophisticated radar and computer, GPS' – this was the global positioning system – 'all the goodies. And it has Athena.'

'I don't know what that is,' Cassidy said.

'Athena is, or was, the American project code name for some very advanced stealth technology, an active ECM protection system. Somehow Japan acquired the technology, which had almost died in the United States due to a lack of development funds.'

Cassidy nodded. American spending on research and development of military technology had slowed to a trickle since the end of the Cold War.

Jiro continued. 'Athena arrived here just when the government was looking to spend serious money on developing a military tech edge. They latched onto Athena and made it the centerpiece of the new Zero.'

'Explain to me how it works.'

When Jiro didn't immediately reply, Cassidy added, 'You know you don't have to tell me anything, Jiro. I didn't ask you for anything.'

'I know! I want to tell you, Bob.' Jiro Kimura searched for words. He stood and went out on the balcony. Cassidy followed.

'I was born in this country. I live here. But America is also my home. Do you understand?'

'I think so.'

'I have two homes, two peoples. I will tell you what I can, and you must pass it on in great secrecy. If the Japanese find out I have even spoken of these matters, I will be in serious trouble.'

'Up to your ass in it, kiddo. I understand.'

'The world is too small for loyalties based on race. Or nationality.'

'That is sort of an advanced idea, but I'll grant you –'

'Just don't think less of me because I need to tell you these things. I don't ever want to fight against Americans.'

He was facing Cassidy now, looking straight into his eyes. 'Do you see how it is, Bob?'

'Yeah, kid. I see.'

Jiro rested his forearms on the balcony railing and looked between the high-rises at the white ghost of Fuji, just visible against the late-evening sky. 'Athena is active ECM.' ECM meant electronic countermeasures. 'It detects enemy radar transmissions, then radiates on the same frequency from antennas all over the plane to cancel out the incoming transmissions. Uses a small super-cooled computer.'

'Uh-huh.'

Jiro Kimura could see from the look on Cassidy's face that he had no appreciation of the advantage that Athena conferred on the plane it protected. 'What Athena does, Bob, is make the Zero invisible to radar.'

Cassidy's eyebrows went up.

'Low-observable – stealth – technology began when designers tried to minimize the radar return by altering the shape of the craft. Then designers used radar-absorbent materials to the maximum extent practicable. Athena is stealth technology a generation beyond shapes and materials, which, as you know, limit the performance and capabilities of a stealth aircraft.

'The Zero is a conventional aircraft made of composites – a damn big engine, gas tanks stuck everywhere, vectored thrust, boundary layer control on a fixed wing, really extraordinary performance. It's got all the electronic goodies to help its pilot find the enemy and kill him. Athena hides it.'

'Sounds like a hell of a plane.'

'It is that, Bob, one hell of a fighter plane. It can do simply unbelievable things in the air, and the brass wants us to use it as a straight and level interceptor. Find the enemy, launch missiles, fly home to an instrument approach. Sounds like something a bunch of brass-hatted desk pilots thought up from the safety of a corner office, huh?'

'Well, if you have enough missiles . . .'

'There are never enough.'

'How many Zeros are there?'

'About a hundred. The number is classified and no one mentions it. I have been trying to count nosewheels, so to speak.'

After a bit, the American colonel asked, 'So where is the Japanese government planning on using these things?'

'Russia, I think. But no one had confirmed that.'

'When?'

'Soon. Very soon.'

'Abe is very nationalistic, advocates a larger role for the military in Japanese life. What do the folks in uniform think of all this?'

'Most of them like Abe, like what he is saying. The officers seem to be with him almost to a man.' Jiro paused to gather his thoughts. 'The Japanese have much more respect for authority than Americans. They like being part of a large, organized society. It fits them somehow. The American concept of individual freedom . . .' He shook his head negatively and shrugged.

'What about the Mishima disciples?' These ultra-right-wing nationalists were back in the news again, claiming converts in the military and civil service.

'Mishima was a fanatic zealot, a fossil, a relic of a bygone age. Everybody knows that. But he preached a return to the noble-warrior concept, the samurai spirit, and that still fascinates a lot of Japanese.'

Bob Cassidy rubbed his face hard, then said, 'I guess I have trouble taking Mishima, Abe, this samurai warrior shit – I have trouble taking any of that seriously. All that testosterone ranting and posturing . . . man, that crap went out everywhere else when gunpowder came in. There is no such thing as a noble death in the nuclear age. The very term is an oxymoron. Didn't Hiroshima and Nagasaki teach the Japanese that?'

A grimace crossed Jiro's face. 'Bob, you're talking to the converted,' he said. 'My morals were corrupted in Colorado Springs years ago. I'm just trying to explain.'

'The only noble death is from old age,' Cassidy continued, 'but you gotta get there to get it, amigo. That's getting harder and harder to do these days.'

Shizuko came out of the kitchen carrying a large dish.

'Thanks, Jiro.'

'I wish Shizuko and I were back in Colorado Springs, Bob, sitting on your patio with Sweet Sabrina.'

'We can't ever go back,' Cassidy told him. 'When the song is over, it's over. I know. I wanted to go back so badly, I almost died.'

In the middle of dinner, Jiro said, 'The United States is going to have to take a stand, Bob. Atsuko Abe and his friends are crazy, but I don't think they are crazy enough to strap on the United States.'

'I hope to God you're right.'

Shizuko acted as if she didn't understand the English words.

'What if *you* aren't?' Cassidy asked in a small voice.

Jiro pretended he hadn't heard.

Bob Cassidy's thoughts went to Sweet Sabrina. It was good, he thought, to be with someone who remembered her fondly.

The U.S. ambassador to Japan was Stanley P. Hanratty, who owned a string of automobile dealerships around Cleveland and Akron. He was balding, overweight, and smart. His middle initial stood for Philip, a name he hated, yet he thought his name looked too informal without a middle name or initial or something, so he used the *P*.

Stanley P. had spent twenty-seven years of his life getting to Japan. He started out selling used cars, mortgaged his house and soul to acquire a used-car sales lot, and then a second, and a third, finally a new car dealership, then another and another and another.

He was arranging the financing on the second dealership when he made his first big political contribution. Occasionally men from humble backgrounds have large ambitions, and Hanratty did: he wanted someday to be an ambassador to a big country.

For years, he listened to windy speeches, shook hands, wrote checks, and watched the political hopefuls come and go. By the time he had eight dealerships, he was giving to political parties in a six-figure way. Finally, he was rewarded with an ambassadorship.

Stanley P. had never forgotten the conversation when one of the members of the new president's transition team called him about the position.

'The president-elect would like to send your name to the Senate. Mr. Hanratty, he wants you *on his team*.'

'Guinea-Bis what? How did you say that?'

'Bissau. It's in Africa, I think.'

'North or south of the equator?'

'Well, sir, I don't know. I seem to recall that it's on the west side of the continent, but don't hold me to that.'

Through the years, Stanley P. had invested a lot of money in his quest, so he didn't hesitate. With feeling, he said, 'You tell the president-elect that I'm honored he thought of me. I'll be delighted to serve his administration anywhere he wants.'

After he hung up the telephone, he looked the place up in an atlas.

U.S. ambassador to Guinea-Bissau!

In Guinea-Bissau, Hanratty did more than luxuriate in the ambassador's quarters of the embassy, which in truth were not all that luxurious; he studiously applied himself to learning the business of diplomacy. He attacked the State Department's paper-flow charts and the ins and outs of Bissauan politics with the same common sense, drive, and determination that he used to sell cars. He made shrewd evaluations of local politicians and wrote clear, concise, accurate reports. He didn't once blame conditions in Guinea-Bissau on United States foreign policy, an attitude that State Department professionals found both unusual and refreshing. He also proved to have an extraordinary quality that endeared him to policy makers in Washington: if given instructions, he followed them to the letter.

After he correctly predicted that a military coup would occur in Guinea-Bissau if a certain person won an election, Hanratty was named ambassador to a nation in the Middle East endangered by fundamentalist Islamic zealots. He performed superbly there, too, so when the U.S. ambassador to Japan dropped dead of a heart attack, the secretary of state was relieved that he could send Stanley P. Hanratty to the American embassy in Tokyo.

Hanratty had been in Tokyo for thirteen months when the emperor was

31

assassinated. During his habitual sixteen-hour workdays, he had become expert in the myriad aspects of U.S.–Japanese relations and made many friends in key places. This evening, just hours after the emperor's murder, with the world still in shock, he was sitting in his office with the television on, putting the finishing touches on a private letter to the secretary of state, when he heard the knocking on the door.

'Come in,' he called loudly, because the doors were thick and heavy.

'Mr Ambassador, I wonder if I might have a few moments of your time?'

'Colonel Cassidy, please come in.'

Stanley P. liked the Air Force attaché, who occasionally dropped by to inform him firsthand of developments in the Japanese military that he would eventually read about weeks later in secret CIA summaries. The senior CIA officer, on the other hand, never told him anything. It was almost as if that gentleman thought the ambassador couldn't be trusted with sensitive information, which frosted Stanley P. a little.

'It's been a long day, Colonel. How about a drink?'

'Thank you, sir. I'll have whatever you're having.'

Stanley P. removed a bottle of bourbon and two glasses from his lower desk drawer. He poured a shot in each glass and passed one to Cassidy.

'I've been speculating, Colonel. Speculating with no information. Speculate with me a little.'

Cassidy sipped the whiskey.

'Do you think it's possible that a faction, shall we say, in the Japanese government might have had a hand in the emperor's assassination?'

'I had dinner this evening with an officer in the Japanese Self-Defense Force, the air arm, and he said the officers are with Abe almost to a man. They think he's going to save the nation.'

'The killers were soldiers, I believe.'

'That's what the government is telling the press. I suppose some high official might have enlisted some zealots to undertake a suicide mission. There is historical precedence, as I recall.'

'There is precedent by the page,' the ambassador admitted. He concentrated on savoring the golden liquid.

'The assassination is going down pretty hard with the guy on the street,' the colonel said. 'I rode the train back to Tokyo. The people in the subways and trains seem pretty upset.'

'Murder is a filthy business,' the ambassador muttered.

'This officer I had dinner with tonight . . . he told me some things that he shouldn't have. Perhaps the news of the assassination made him feel that . . . Oh, I don't know!'

Cassidy brushed the thought away, unwilling to try to analyze his friend or make polite excuses for him. Jiro did what Jiro felt he had to do. 'The Japanese have developed, manufactured, and put in service about one hundred new, highly capable fighter planes.' The colonel weighed his words.

'They are more capable than anything in our inventory, according to my source.'

'How good is your source?'

'Beyond reproach. One hundred percent credible.'

The ambassador poured himself another drink, offered more to the colonel, who refused. Cassidy could see his and the ambassador's reflections in the window glass. Beyond the reflections were the lights of Tokyo.

'The thing my source confided in me that I believe you should know, sir, is this: His squadron is packing for deployment in the near future.'

'Deployment where?'

'Russia, he thought.'

'The appeal for Japanese help by the native minorities – there was a television broadcast about them last night. According to the government, they are the racial cousins of the Japanese.' The ambassador channel-surfed with his television remote. He had picked up more than a smattering of the language.

'Perhaps they will just move your source's squadron to another base here in Japan,' Stanley P. suggested to Cassidy.

'That is possible, sir. My source didn't think so, though. He thinks the squadron is going a lot farther than that.'

3

When Masataka Okada returned to his office after lunch everyone in the department was watching television – a day after Emperor Naruhito's assassination, the television types were still microanalyzing the implications. Okada's office was fairly large by Japanese standards, about ten feet by ten feet, but all the walls above waist level were glass. Apparently the architect believed that the best way to keep spies in line was to let them watch one another.

Okada had spent the morning decoding the message from an agent with the code name of Ten, or Ju in Japanese. Alas, it was forbidden to input messages this highly classified into the computer, so the work had to be done by hand.

He had completed the decoding, a tedious task, then did the translation and typed the result before lunch. Now he removed the file from his personal safe and read the translation again.

The message was important, no question.

Very important. In fact, Masataka Okada suspected that the future of both Japan and Russia hinged on the contents of this two-page message from Agent Ju. Of course, Okada had no idea who Ju actually was, but he obviously had access to the very top leadership in the Russian army. He also had access to the contents of the safes of the top leadership, because some of this information could have come only from official documents.

Boiled down, the message was that the last of the guidance systems had been removed from the Russians' submarine-based ballistic missiles. The Russians had finished removing the guidance systems from their land-based ICBMs last year; their tactical nuclear warheads had been removed from service and destroyed five years ago.

Russia was no longer a nuclear power.

Okada knew that the United States had secretly insisted upon nuclear disarmament as the price of the massive foreign aid needed by the current, elected regime to solidify its hold on power. That fact came from intercepted American diplomatic traffic. The United States hadn't even briefed its allies.

Well, the secret had certainly been well kept, even in Russia. Not a

34

whisper of this earth-shattering development had appeared anywhere in the public press in Russia or Western Europe: Okada would have seen it mentioned in the agency's press summaries if it had been. Part of the reason was that only the top echelon of military commanders in Russia knew that *all* the guidance systems had been removed in a series of maintenance programs nominally designed to test and return to service every system in the inventory.

Disarmament was such a political hot potato that the Russian government had kept it a secret from its own people.

By some tangled loop of Kremlin logic, this course of action made perfect sense. As long as no one outside the upper echelons of government knew that the nuclear weapons delivery systems were no longer operational, no one lost face, and no one lost votes. The domestic political crises never materialized. And as long as no one outside Russia knew, the missiles continued to deter potential aggressors, just as they always had. Deterrence *was* the function of ICBMs, wasn't it?

Now the Japanese knew. And the Russian government didn't know they knew.

That is, the Japanese would know as soon as Masataka Okada signed the routing slip and sent the message to his superior officer, the head of Asian intelligence for the Japanese Intelligence Agency.

From Okada's boss, the news would go to the head of the agency, who would take it to the prime minister, Atsuko Abe.

What Atsuko Abe would make of this choice tidbit was a matter to speculate darkly about. Masataka Okada did just that now as he chewed on a fingernail. Abe's national-destiny speeches leapt to mind, as did the secret military buildup that had been going on in Japan for the last five years. And now there was the assassin's letter, written in blood, which had been leaked to the newspapers by someone in the prosecutor's office investigating the assassination. The letter demanded that the military take over the government and lead Japan to glory. Okada's friends and acquaintances – indeed, the whole nation – could talk of little else. Amazingly, the ritual suicides of the emperor's killers had given the ultranationalistic, militaristic views of the Mishima sect a mainstream legitimacy that they had never before enjoyed.

Watching this orgy of twisted patriotism gave Okada chills.

What would be the consequences to Japan if military force was used against Russia?

Okada well knew that there would be consequences, mostly unpredictable and, he feared, mostly negative. He certainly didn't share Abe's faith in Japan's destiny.

Okada's father's first wife died at Hiroshima under the mushroom cloud. He was a son of the second wife, who had been severely burned at Hiroshima but had survived. As a boy, he had examined his mother's scars as she bathed. When he was ten she died of leukemia – another victim of the bomb. Forty years had passed since then, but he could still close his eyes and see how the flesh on her back had been burned, literally cooked, by the thermal pulse of the explosion.

He fumbled for his cigarettes, lit one, and tried to forget his mother's back as he inhaled deeply, savoring the smoke.

What if . . .

What if this message merely reported that some of the guidance systems had been removed?

Masataka Okada scrutinized the message carefully. Well, it would be easy enough to write another translation. If he deleted this third sentence, changed this phrase, added a sentence or two at the bottom, he could make it appear that the Russians were still years away from complete disarmament.

His superiors would catch him eventually.

Or would they?

It wasn't like the head of the agency was going to Moscow any time soon for a personal chat with Agent Ju.

The other people in the office were still intently watching the television set.

I must be going mad. Crazy. The pressure is getting to me. The first rule, the very first rule, is never, ever put anything in writing that creates the least suspicion. Leave no tracks.

But what I'm contemplating is not espionage; it's sabotage.

He intertwined his fingers and twisted until the pain brought tears to his eyes.

At some point, a man must make a stand.

This is insane! You are merely buying time.

Okada scrolled a sheet of paper into his typewriter, glanced yet again at the backs of his colleagues, and began to type.

You are buying time at the cost of your own life, fool. No one will care. Not a single, solitary soul will care one iota.

After two lines, he stopped and stared at the words he had written.

This wouldn't work.

Ju was certain to send follow-up reports; indeed, he might have already sent other reports on this subject. It was probable that he had. Both previous and future reports might be given to another cryptographer to decode. It was just a stroke of good fortune that Okada had been handed this particular message.

He took the sheet of paper from the typewriter and inserted another.

The best way to discount the message wasn't to change the facts related, but to change the way they were related. Okada knew his boss, Toshihiko Ayukawa. The man had an uncanny ability to separate gold from dross. Intelligence agencies inevitably gathered huge amounts of dross: idle rumors, wild speculations, inaccurate gossip, outright lies, and, worst of all, disinformation passed as truth.

Through the years, Okada had become a connoisseur of intelligence reports. As he had first typed it, Agent Ju's report seemed to be pure gold – it contained eloquent facts, lots of them, crammed into as few words as possible, yet the source for each fact was carefully related. What if the style was changed, not too much, but just enough?

It would be dicey – the message would have to appear to someone who knew Ju's style to be indubitably his, yet the tone had to be wrong – not clearly wrong, just subtly wrong, enough to create a shadow of doubt about the truth of the facts related in the mind of a knowledgeable reader. The tone would be the lie.

God knows, Toshihiko Ayukawa was a knowledgeable reader!

Okada lit another cigarette. He flexed his fingers.

His colleagues were still glued to the television in the common area.

He took a last drag, put the cigarette in an ashtray to smolder, and began to type quickly.

The thought shot through his head that Ayukawa might ask another cryptographer to decode the original of this message again.

True, he might, if he thought Okada had done a sloppy job.

And if he did that, Okada would be in more trouble than he could handle.

He would just have to rely on his reputation, that's all. He was the best. The boss damn well knew it.

Oh well, every man's fate was in the hands of the gods. They would write a man's life as they chose.

His fingers flew over the keyboard.

When he finished the message, he read it over carefully. He had it the way he wanted it.

He put the fake message into the official envelope and signed the routing slip in the box provided for the cryptographer.

The people outside were still watching television, milling around, talking. No one seemed to be looking his way.

Okada held the copy of the real message under his desk and folded it carefully. He then slipped the small square of paper into a sock.

He took the envelope in his hand, weighing it one last time. When he walked out of this office with this envelope in his hand, he was irrevocably committed.

He swayed slightly as the enormity of what he had done pressed down upon him. He had to struggle to draw a breath.

Ayukawa knew Ju's work. This fake message might stand out like a police emergency light on a dark night.

If so, Masataka Okada was doomed.

His eye fell upon the old photo of his family that stood on the back of his desk. It was perched precariously there, almost ready to fall on the floor, shoved out of the way when he made room for the usual books and files and reports that seemed to grow like mushrooms on his desk. That picture must be at least ten years old. His daughter was grown now, with a baby of her own. His son was in graduate school.

What would they look like with their skin black and smoking and hanging in putrid ribbons from their backs? From their faces?

Masataka Okada took a firm grip on the envelope and walked out of his office.

At six that evening, Okada's superior officer, Toshihiko Ayukawa, got around to opening the classified security envelope containing the decoded message from Agent Ju. He'd had a feeling when this message first came in that it might be very important, but he had spent the afternoon in meetings and was just now getting to the red-hot matters awaiting his attention in his office. It was a wonder his desk hadn't melted, with a belligerent China, civil unrest in Siberia, and riots in the streets of Hong Kong. Yet the assassination of the emperor and the coming state funeral took precedence over everything.

'No,' he had told the agency director, 'we have no indication whatever that any Asian power had anything to do with the emperor's murder.'

As Ayukawa read the message, he frowned. It sounded like Ju, cited the proper codes, yet ... He read it through again slowly, his mind racing.

He looked at the envelope for the signature of the cryptographer. Okada.

Then he called his confidential assistant, Sushi Maezumi. He held up the envelope where Sushi could see it.

'Why did you give this to Okada?'

The assistant looked at the signature, then his face fell. 'I apologize, sir. I forgot.'

'I had another copy of this message for decoding.' Ayukawa consulted his ledger. He believed in keeping his operation strictly compartmentalized. It was unfortunate that the aide had to know that he occasionally handed out duplicates of the messages to be decoded and translated, but unless he had the time to do everything himself – and he didn't – he had to delegate. The use of duplicates allowed him to check on the competency of his staff. And their loyalty. And if the message was important, he would have two versions to compare, for they were never exactly the same.

'Number three four oh nine,' Ayukawa said. 'Where is it?'

'Here, sir.' Sushi removed the envelope from the bottom of the pile.

Ayukawa ripped it open and scanned the message. He didn't even bother to compare this with Okada's short story.

'You disobeyed my order. I told you not to give any sensitive item to Okada without my express approval.'

'I forgot, sir.'

The avoidance of direct confrontation was one of the pillars on which Japanese society rested. Ayukawa had little use for that social more. 'That's no excuse,' he said bluntly to his aide, who blanched. 'My instructions must be obeyed to the letter. *Always.* I am the officer responsible, not you. And you know that we have a mole in this agency . . . But enough – we'll discuss it later. Go see if Okada is still in the building. Now, quickly.'

Speechless after this verbal hiding, Sushi Maezumi shot from the office as if he had been scalded.

In the Shinjuku district neon lights tinted the skins of visitors red, green, blue, orange, and yellow, all in succession, as they moved from one garishly lit storefront to the next. Beyond the light was the night, but here there was life. Here there was sex.

This was Tokyo's French Quarter, only more so, a concentration of adult bookstores, peep shows, porno palaces, and nightclubs, with here and there a whorehouse for the terminally conventional. The whorehouses ranged from bordellos specializing in cheap quickies to geisha houses where the evening's entertainment might cost thousands of dollars.

The crowds were an inherent part of the district's attraction. A visitor could blend into the mass of humanity and become an anonymous voyeur, savoring sexual pleasures denied by social convention, which is the very essence of pornography.

Masataka Okada moved easily through the swarms of people. He enjoyed the sexual tension, a release from the extraordinary, heart-attack stress he had experienced that day, as he did every day. The flashing lights and weird colors, highlighted on the men's white shirts, seemed to draw him and everyone else into the fantasy world of pleasure.

Okada bought two square cakes of fried shark meat from a sidewalk vendor. The heat of the evening and closeness of the crowd made the smell of the cooking fat and fish particularly pungent.

He walked on, adrift in this sea of people. The lights and heat and smells engulfed him.

Somewhere on this planet there might be an occupation more stressful than that of a spy, but it would be difficult to imagine what it would be. A spy played a deadly game, was always onstage, spent every waking moment waiting for the ax to fall. In the beginning it had been easier for Masataka Okada, but now, as the full implications of his choices became increasingly clear, just getting through each day became more and more difficult. Every gesture, every word, every unspoken nuance had to be examined for a sinister meaning. Any slip would be fatal, so every choice came laden with stress.

The truth of the matter was that Masataka Okada was burning out. He was nearing the end of his string.

As he strolled and watched the crowd this evening, his thoughts turned to

World War II. Every Japanese had to come to grips with World War II in some personal way. Every living person had lost family members in that holocaust – grandfathers, fathers, brothers, uncles, cousins, mothers, aunts, grandmothers – all gone, like smoke, as if they had never been. Yet they *had* been; they *had* lived, and they had been cut down.

About 2.1 million Japanese had perished in that war, over 6 million Chinese and, however the apologists dressed it up, the fact remained that the war in the Pacific had begun with Japan's full-scale assault on China in 1937. Once blood had been drawn, Japan's doom became inevitable: the rape of Nanking, Pearl Harbor, the Bataan death march, the firebombing of Japanese cities, Okinawa, the obliteration of Hiroshima and Nagasaki – it was a litany of human suffering as horrific as any event the species had yet endured.

Okada had long ago made up his mind who was responsible for that suicidal course of events: Japan's government, and its people, for governments do not act in a vacuum. When you thought about it dispassionately, you had to question the sanity of the persons responsible. A crowded island nation about the size of California willingly had sought total war with the most powerful nation on earth, one with twice its population and *ten* times its industrial capacity.

And so, in a tragedy written in blood, an entire generation of young men had been sacrificed on the altar of war; the treasure of the nation – accumulated through the centuries – had been squandered, every family ripped asunder, the homeland devastated, laid waste.

All that was history, the dead past. As long ago and far away as the Mejii restoration, as the first shogun . . . and yet it wasn't. The war had scarred them all.

An hour's strolling back and forth through the neighborhood brought Okada to a small peep parlor. With a long last look in a window at the reflections of the people behind him, he paid his admission and went inside.

The foyer was dimly lit. Sound came from hidden speakers: Japanese music, adenoidal wailing above a twanging string instrument – just noise.

From the foyer, one entered a long hallway, each side of which was lined with doors. Small red bulbs in the ceiling illuminated the very air, which was almost an impenetrable solid: swirling cigarette smoke, the smell of perspiration, and something sickeningly sweet – semen.

The walls seemed to close in; it was almost impossible to breathe.

An attendant was in the hall, a small man in a white shirt with no collar. His teeth were so misshapen that his lips were twisted into a permanent sneer. A smoldering cigarette hung from one corner of his mouth. He looked at Okada with dead eyes and lifted his fingers, signaling numbers.

Thirty-two.

Okada looked for that number on a door. It was beyond the attendant. He turned sideways in the narrow hallway to get by the attendant. As he did so, the man behind him opened a door. For a few seconds, Okada and the attendant were isolated in a tiny space in the hallway, isolated from all other human eyes.

In that brief moment, Okada pressed the message into the attendant's hand.

He found booth 32, opened the door, and entered.

There were ten of them waiting for him to come home, but Masataka Okada didn't know that. They were arranged in two circles, the first of which covered the possible approach routes to the apartment building, and the second of which covered the entrances. Two men were in the apartment with his wife, waiting.

The man in the subway station saw him first, waited until he was out of sight, then reported the contact on his handheld radio.

Okada was nervous, wary. The sensations of Shinjuku had been wasted upon him tonight. He hadn't been able to get the message from Ju off his mind, couldn't stop thinking about the murder of the emperor, couldn't stop thinking about his mother's scarred back. Despite being keyed up and alert, he didn't see the man in the subway.

A block later, he did spot the man watching the side entrance to the building where he lived. This man was in a parked car, and he made the mistake of looking around. When he saw Okada, he looked away, but too late.

Masataka Okada kept walking toward the entrance as his mind raced.

They had come. Finally. They were here for him!

His wife . . . she was upstairs. Fortunately, she knew absolutely nothing about his spying, not even that he did it. So there was nothing she could tell them.

It shouldn't have to end like this. Really, it shouldn't.

He had done his best. He didn't want future generations of Japanese to go through what his parents had endured, and he had had the courage to act on his convictions. Now it was time to pay the piper.

Well, the Americans had the message from Ju, as well as all the others, all the copies of documents that he had made and passed on detailing the secret arms contracts and the buildup of the military that had been going on for the last seven years. They knew, and Abe didn't know they knew.

Abe would find out, if these men managed to arrest him. They would get the truth from him one way or the other. Okada had no illusions on that score. They would use any means necessary to make him talk; there was just too much at stake.

The dark doorway of the building loomed in front of him.

If he walked through that door, they had him. Some of them might be inside just now, waiting to grab him, throw him to the floor, and slap handcuffs on him.

Even if they let him go up to the apartment, they would come for him there. They would never let him leave the building.

These thoughts zipped through his head in the time it took for him to take just one step toward the doorway.

He would not go in.

He turned right, down the sidewalk, and began to walk briskly.

Glancing back over his shoulder, he saw the man in the car looking his way and holding a radio mike in front of his mouth.

Even though he knew he shouldn't, Masataka Okada began to run.

He had had a good life, and he didn't want to give it up. Those fools who killed the emperor, committing hara-kari, voluntarily ended the only existence they would ever have. Ah, was life so worthless that a man should throw it away, as if it didn't matter?

He darted into the street and managed to avoid an oncoming bus. He made it to the sidewalk on the other side and swerved into an alley. Down the alley a ways was a brick wall, which Okada climbed over with much huffing and puffing, severely skinning his ankle.

He found himself inside a cemetery. The headstones and little temples looked weird in the reflected half-light of the city, sinister. *This* was Japan's future – he saw it in a horrible revelation: a nation of tombstones and funeral temples, ashes in urns, a nation of the dead.

Sobbing, Okada threaded his way through all this masonry and crawled across the wall on the other side. His ankle hurt like fire, but the collapse of his world and his vision of the future hurt worse.

His wife ... what would she think? Oh, how he had abandoned her, poor, loyal woman.

He was now in another alley, this one lined with little wooden houses, relics of old Japan. He thought about stealing a bicycle but couldn't bring himself to do it.

At the end of the alley was a street. Although he was severely winded already, he managed to work himself into a trot. As he rounded the corner, he met a man running the other way. Fortune favored Okada – he reacted first and got his hands up, bowling the other man over as he went by.

He didn't look back, just ran. Alas, his gait was a hell-bent stagger, his lungs tearing at him as he gasped futilely, unable to get enough oxygen.

Ahead was a subway station. If he could catch a train, he could get off anywhere, could lose himself in Tokyo, perhaps even make his way to the American embassy.

Those Americans, they said that someday this might happen. He had refused to believe, even when he knew they spoke the truth.

He was close to passing out from the exertion, almost unable to think. He smoked several packs of cigarettes a day, had done so for years, and he never exercised.

Okada could hear footsteps pounding the pavement behind him.

There – the stairs into the subway! He ran down them, grabbed the turnstile, and leapt over.

More stairs. He took them two at a time.

He could hear the running feet behind him, closer and closer, but he used the last of his energy, forcing himself to run even though he could scarcely breathe and was having difficulty seeing. Spots swam before his eyes.

A train was coming.

If they catch me . . .

The train was still moving at a pretty good clip when Masataka Okada did a swan dive off the platform, right in front of it.

4

He could see it above him, at least two miles up, a flashing silver shape in the vast, deep blue. Jiro Kimura used the handhold on the canopy bow to hold himself upright against the G forces. He grunted, kept his muscles tense so that he would not pass out, fought to keep his eyes on that flashing silver plane so far above.

If he lost sight of that plane, it might take several seconds to reacquire it, seconds he could ill afford to lose. The other pilot was undoubtedly looking down at him, watching him twist and turn, waiting for an opening when he could come swooping down with his gun blazing – like an angel of doom. Or the bloody Red Baron. To kill.

Jiro Kimura knew all of that because he knew the other pilot. His name was Sasai. He was just twenty-four, rarely smiled, and never made the same mistake twice. This was only Sasai's third one-on-one flight, but he was learning quickly.

Just now, Kimura wanted to make Sasai think that he had an opening when he really didn't.

Kimura rocked his wings violently from side to side, first one way and then the other. He was also feeding in forward stick, unloading the plane and accelerating, but Sasai couldn't see that from two miles above. All he could see were the wings rocking, as if Kimura had momentarily lost sight and was futilely trying to find his opponent.

Sasai turned to arc in behind Kimura and put his nose down, committing himself.

Kimura waited for several seconds, maybe four, then lit the afterburner and pulled his nose up. The G felt good, solid, as the horizon fell away. Jiro Kimura loved to fly, and this morning he acknowledged that fact to himself, again, for the thousandth time. To fly a state-of-the-art fighter plane in an endless blue sky, to have someone to yank and bank with and try to outwit, then to go home and think about how it had been while planning to do it again tomorrow – what had life to offer that could possibly be sweeter?

When he was vertical, Kimura spun around his longitudinal axis until his wings were perpendicular to Sasai's flight path; then he pulled his nose over to lead Sasai, who was now frantically trying to evade the trap. Because he was slower, Kimura could turn more quickly than the descending plane, could bring his gun to bear first.

Jiro Kimura pulled the trigger on the stick.

'You're dead, Sasai,' Kimura said on the radio, trying to keep the satisfaction out of his voice. 'Let's break it off and go home.'

Sasai rendezvoused on Kimura, who consulted his GPS display, then set a course for base. They were over the Sea of Japan above a broken layer of low clouds. Kimura checked his fuel, verified his course on the wet compass, then stretched. The silver airplanes, the sun high in the blue vault overhead, the sea below, the clouds and distant haze – if heaven was like this, he was ready.

If Shizuko could go, too, of course.

He felt guilty that he was contemplating paradise without Shizuko. Then he felt silly that he was even thinking these thoughts.

Well, maybe it wasn't silly. Real combat seemed to be coming, almost like a terrible storm just over the horizon that no one wanted to acknowledge. We make plans, for next week, next month, next year, while refusing to acknowledge that our safe, secure little world is about to disintegrate.

Jiro looked across the invisible river of air flowing between the planes and saw Sasai in his cockpit. He was looking Jiro's way. They stared at each other's helmeted figures for a moment; then Jiro looked away.

Kimura was the senior officer, and leader, of his flight. Then came Ota, Miura, and Sasai. They would fly together as a unit whenever possible.

Alas, Sasai was green, inexperienced. He knew how to use the new Zero fighter as an interceptor, utilizing the radar, GPS, computer, and all the rest of it, but he didn't know how to dogfight, to fight another aircraft when it was out of the interception parameters.

Neither Ota nor Miura was particularly skilled at the craft, either. The colonels and generals insisted that Zero pilots be well trained in the use of the state-of-the art weapons system, that they know it cold and practice constantly, so all their training had been in using the aircraft's system to acquire the target, then fire missiles when the target came within range.

'What will you do,' Kimura asked the three pilots on his team, 'if the enemy attacks you as you are taking off?'

His junior wingmen looked slightly stunned, as if the possibility had never occurred to them. Their superior officers, none of whom were combat veterans, reasoned that the plane's electronic suite was the heart of the weapons system, the technological edge that made the new Zero the best fighter on earth: the airframe, engine, and wings existed merely to take the system to a point in space where it could be employed against the enemy. The never-voiced assumption almost seemed to be that the enemy would fly along straight and level while the Japanese pilots locked them up with radar, stepped the computer into attack, and watched the missiles ripple off the racks and streak away for the kill.

The senior officer in the air arm had been quoted as saying, 'Dogfighting is obsolete. We have put a gun in the Zero for strafing, not shooting at other airplanes.' Indeed, the heads-up display – HUD – did not feature a lead-computing gunsight.

Jiro Kimura didn't think air-to-air combat would be quite that easy. Whenever they were not running practice intercepts, he had been dogfighting with his flight members. They didn't get to do this often; still, they were learning quickly – even Sasai.

They should be able to handle the Russians.

Ah yes, the Russians. This morning at the weekly intelligence briefing, the wing commander had given them the word: Siberia, two weeks from now. 'Study the Russian air force and be ready to destroy it.'

'Two weeks?' someone had murmured, incredulous.

'No questions. This information is highly classified. The day is almost upon us and we must be ready.'

Jiro raised his helmet visor and used the back of his glove to swab the perspiration from his eyes. After checking the cockpit altitude, he removed his oxygen mask and used the glove to wipe his face dry.

He snapped the mask back into place and lowered his visor.

'It will be a quick war,' Ota had predicted. 'In two days they will have nothing left to fly. The MiGs, even the Sukhoi-27s, will go down like ducks.'

Jiro Kimura said nothing. There was nothing to say. Whatever was going to happen would happen. Words would not change it.

Still, after he had suited up in his flight gear, before he and Sasai went out on the mat to preflight their planes, he had called Bob Cassidy at the American embassy in Tokyo. Just a short chat, an invitation to dinner a week from now, and a comment about an alumni letter Jiro had received from the Air Force Academy in Colorado Springs.

He dismissed Russia and Cassidy from his mind so he could concentrate on the task at hand. The clouds ahead over Honshu looked solid, so he and Sasai were going to have to make an instrument approach. Jiro signaled his wingman to make a radio frequency change to air traffic control; then he called the controller.

Three men were waiting for Bob Cassidy when he came out of the back entrance to the embassy. At least he thought there were three – he arrived at that number several minutes later – but there might have been more.

As he walked along the sidewalk, they followed him, keeping well back – one behind, one on the other side of the street, and one in a car creeping along a block behind. The guy in the car was the one he wasn't sure of for several minutes.

This was a first. Cassidy had never before been openly followed.

He wondered about the timing. Why now?

The one behind him on his side of the street was about medium height for a Japanese, wearing glasses and some sort of sport coat. His stride proclaimed his fitness.

The one across the street was balding and short. He wore slacks and a dark pullover shirt. Cassidy couldn't see the driver of the car.

If there were three men he knew about, how many were there that he didn't?

Undecided as to how he should handle this, he walked the route he always took toward his apartment. When he'd reported to the embassy fifteen months ago, he'd had the choice of sharing an apartment inside the embassy compound or finding his own apartment 'on the economy.' He chose the latter. Without children in school or a wife who wanted to socialize with other Americans, it was an easy choice.

These men had been waiting for him. They must know where he lived, the route he usually took to get there. They must have followed him in the past and he just hadn't paid attention.

Well, maybe his conversation with Jiro had made him apprehensive, so that was why he was looking now. Actually, he admitted to himself, he felt guilty. Jiro shouldn't have talked out of school.

Oh, he was glad he had, but still . . . Cassidy felt guilty.

A block from home, just before turning a corner, he paused to look at the reflection in a slab of marble siding on a store. The balding man was visible, and, just turning the far corner, the car.

Bob Cassidy went into his apartment building. He collected his mail at the lobby mailbox, then rode the elevator to his floor and unlocked the door to his apartment. He didn't turn on the light.

He sat in the evening twilight, looking out the window, trying to decide what to do.

They must be monitoring the telephones at the base, or at the embassy.

Jiro was the only member of the Japanese military who had ever told Cassidy anything classified. Oh, as air attaché, he routinely talked to Japanese military men, many of whom were personal friends. A dozen of his contacts even held flag rank. The things these soldiers told him were certainly not secrets. He collected common, everyday 'this is how we do it' stuff, the filler that military attachés all over the world gather and send home for their own militaries to analyze. Finding out the things that the Japanese didn't want the Americans to know was the job of another agency, the CIA.

So did the tail mean the Japanese knew that Jiro had talked?

One of Cassidy's fears was that his report of the conversation with Jiro had been compromised – that is, passed right back to the Japanese. Alas, the United States had suffered through too many spy scandals in the last twenty years. Bitter, disappointed men seemed all too willing to sell out their colleagues and their country for money. God knows, the Japanese certainly had enough money.

He would have to report being tailed to the embassy security officer; perhaps he should do that now, and ask him if anyone else had reported being followed. He picked up the telephone and held it in his hand, but he didn't dial. This phone was probably tapped, too. If he called embassy security and reported the tail, it would look like he had something to hide.

He went to the window and stood looking at the Tokyo skyline, or what little he could see of it from a fifth-floor window. He checked his watch. Two hours.

He was supposed to meet Jiro in two hours. Jiro had mentioned Colorado Springs when he called earlier that day. Two days ago, when Cassidy had dinner at the Kimuras', he and Jiro had agreed that the mention of that city would be the code for a meet at a site they agreed upon then.

The code had been Jiro's idea. Cassidy had a bad taste in his mouth about the whole thing. Neither one of them was a trained spy; they were in over their heads. They were going to compromise themselves. Even if they didn't, Cassidy had this feeling deep down that this episode was going to cost him a close friend.

He turned his mind back to the problem at hand.

Jiro had called, and a plainclothes tailing team had been waiting when he left the embassy compound.

Perhaps they were monitoring all the calls from Kimura's base and had intercepted this one, then decided to check to see if Kimura was meeting people he had no good reason to meet.

Or maybe they were onto Kimura.

Maybe they knew he had spilled some secrets to the Americans. Maybe they were trying to rope in Kimura's U.S. contact.

Maybe, maybe, maybe . . .

Cassidy changed into civilian clothes while he mulled the problem over, then went into the kitchen and got a beer from the refrigerator.

Hanging on the wall was a photo of himself at the controls of an F-16. The plane was high, over thirty thousand feet, brilliantly lit by the sun, against a sky so blue it was almost black. Cassidy stood sipping beer as he looked at the photo. What he saw in his mind's eye was not the F-16, but the new Zero.

He had actually seen it. Last week. From a hill near the Japanese air base at Niigata. He had hiked up carrying a video camera in a hard case on a strap over his shoulder. He had videotaped the new fighters taking off and landing. Although the base was six miles away, on the climb-out and approach they came within a half mile of where he was standing.

He had also gotten some still pictures with a 35-mm camera from just under the glide path. He had driven into a noise-saturated neighborhood beside the base and snapped the photos from the driver's seat of his car as the planes went overhead.

The CIA had sent him a gadget to play with as the new Zero flew over, a device that resembled a portable cassette player and could pass for one on casual examination. It did, however, have a three-foot-long antenna that he had to dangle out the window.

Cassidy did all this high-tech spying in plain sight. Only one person had paid any attention to him, a youngster on a tricycle, who sat on the sidewalk four feet away and watched him fiddle with the cassette player and antenna as the jets flew over.

He remembered the sense of relief that came over him when he was finished. He had started the car and slipped it into gear while he took one last careful look around to see if anyone was watching.

It was amazing, when you stopped to think about it. The Japanese designed, manufactured, and tested the ultimate fighter plane, one invisible to radar, put it into squadron service, and the United States knew nothing about it – didn't even know it existed, until one of the pilots sought out the U.S. air attaché at the American embassy and told him.

Perhaps, Cassidy thought as he looked out the window to see if the tails were still waiting, the Japanese are too far from war. As it has for Americans, war for them has become an abstraction, an event of the historical past that students read about in school – dates, treaties, forgotten battles with strange names. War is no longer the experience of a whole people, the defining event of an entire generation. Today the only people with combat experience are a few professional soldiers, like Cassidy.

As a young man, he had flown in the Gulf War – he even shot down a MiG – and he dropped some bombs in Bosnia. His recollections of those days seemed like something remembered from an old B movie, bits and pieces of a past that was fragmentary, fading, irrelevant.

Today war is sold as a video game, Cassidy decided. Shoot at the bad guys and they fall down. If the score is too low, put in another coin and play the game again. You can't get hurt. You can't get . . . *dead*! All you can lose are a few coins.

Cassidy had to make a decision.

Kimura had called, had wanted to see him. The tails were out there. If he didn't go to the meet, Kimura was safe, for the time being anyway, and he would not learn what Kimura wanted the American government to know. On the other hand, if he went, he might be followed, despite his best efforts, and Kimura might wind up in prison, or worse. Hell, Cassidy might wind up in prison, which would really be a unique capstone for his Air Force career.

Jiro seemed to have a lot of faith in the U.S. government, Cassidy mused. Cassidy had long ago lost his. Still, Jiro had to do what he thought right. Indeed, he had an obligation to do so. That *is* what they teach at the Air Force Academy, isn't it?

He finished the beer, tossed the empty can into the trash. He belched.

Okay, Jiro. Ready or not, here I come.

Bob Cassidy was standing near the large incense burner at the Asakusa Temple when he saw Jiro Kimura buy a bundle of incense sticks. He lit them at one of the two nearby braziers, then tossed them into the large burner. Cassidy went over and the two stood in the crowd, waving the holy smoke over their hair and face.

'I was followed,' Cassidy said in a low voice, 'but I think I lost them.'

'Me, too. I've been riding the subways for an hour. Sorry I'm late.'

'They've tapped the phones at the embassy or your base.'

'Probably both places,' Jiro said under his breath. 'They are very efficient.' He led the way to the water fountain, where he helped himself to a dipper, filled it with water, and sipped it.

'God only knows what you'll catch drinking out of that. You'll probably shit for a week. Your damn teeth are gonna fall out.'

'Uh-huh.' Jiro handed the dipper to the person behind him, then moved on. Few Japanese spoke English, so Cassidy's remarks didn't disturb anyone.

Jiro went into the Buddhist temple and tossed some coins into the offertory. He moved forward to the rail and prayed while Cassidy hung back.

At the door, he moved over beside Cassidy.

'It's Siberia. Our wing commander told us this morning in a secret intel briefing. In two weeks, he said.'

'He has a timetable?'

'Yes. We were told to be ready to tackle the Russian air force and destroy it.'

'Did he say why you are going?'

'Just what I've told you. Cryptic as hell, isn't it?'

Cassidy walked with Kimura out of the temple. They stood for a moment on the steps watching the people around the incense burner.

'Happy, aren't they?' Cassidy said.

Kimura didn't answer. He went back into the temple, to the fortune drawers on the right side of the altar.

'I may not see you before you go,' said Cassidy, who had followed Jiro back into the temple.

'You won't. Ten to one, when we go in tomorrow, they'll close the base, lock us up. It's a miracle they didn't think of that today.'

'Maybe they wanted to see who you would talk to.'

'Maybe,' Jiro muttered. He put a hundred-yen coin in the offering slot and picked up a large aluminum tube. He shook it, then turned it upside down and examined the opening. The head of a stick was just visible there. He pulled it out. 'Seventy-six,' he said, and put the stick back into the tube.

'I'm trying to tell you, amigo. They may already have burned you.'

'I wish to Christ we were back in the Springs.'

The sudden shift of subject threw Bob Cassidy. 'Those were good times,' he said, because he could think of nothing else to say.

'With Sweet Sabrina,' Jiro said. He opened drawer number seventy-six and took out a sheet of paper. He closed the drawer, moved a couple of steps back, then glanced at the paper.

'Yeah,' Cassidy said. He had a lump in his throat.

Jiro didn't seem to notice. He folded up the paper and put it in his pocket. 'We'll meet again someday. In this life or the next.'

' "This life or the next," ' Cassidy echoed. The words gave him goose bumps – the cadets at the Academy used to say that to one another on graduation day.

He pointed toward Jiro's pocket, the paper from the drawer. 'Was your fortune good?'

'No.'

Cassidy snorted. 'That stuff is crap.'

'Yeah.'

'A racket for the monks, to get money from suckers.'

'I gotta go, Bob.'

'Hey, man.'

'*Vaya con Dios.*'

'You, too.'

Jiro Kimura turned and walked out of the temple. He kept going without looking back.

Bob Cassidy felt helpless. He was losing Jiro, too. Sabrina, little Robbie, now Jiro . . .

'This life or the next, Jiro.' A tear trickled down his cheek. He wiped it away angrily. He was losing everything.

The next morning Jiro went straight to the office of his commanding officer and knocked. When he was admitted, he told the colonel that he had been followed the previous night.

'I have no idea who that man was, sir, but I wish to make a report so that the incident may be investigated. I have never before been followed – that I know about anyway.'

The colonel was surprised. He apparently had not been told that Kimura was a suspicious character, Jiro concluded, or else he should be on the stage professionally. It was with a sense of relief that Jiro described the man in the train station.

'Perhaps this man wasn't really following you, Captain. Perhaps you are too suspicious.'

'Sir, that is possible. But I wish you would report the incident so that the proper authorities may investigate. In light of what the wing commander said yesterday . . .'

'Yes. Indeed. I will make a report, Captain Kimura. This incident should be investigated. Japan is filled with foreigners who cannot be trusted.'

On that illogical note, Jiro was dismissed.

And he was right about the base closure. Just before noon, the colonel called an officers' meeting and made the announcement that all officers and enlisted were confined to the base until further notice.

5

The first person in Russia to learn that Japan planned to invade Siberia was Janos Ilin, who heard the news an hour after the American national security adviser, Jack Innes, told the Russian ambassador to the United States.

Ilin got the news from a FIS officer in the Russian embassy in Washington. The FIS officer had much less bureaucracy to work through, so his news arrived in Moscow first.

Ilin was at his desk in the Foreign Intelligence Service – which had replaced the old KGB – building in Dzerzhinsky Square. He read the translation of the encrypted message completely and carefully, laid it on his desk, cleaned his glasses, lit an American cigarette, then read it again.

Janos Ilin was not a Communist. He wasn't anything. He was old enough and wise enough to know that the reason Russia was a sewer was because Russians lived there. In his fifty-five years on earth he had come to believe that in their heart of hearts, most Russians were selfish, lazy peasants who hated anyone with a ruble more than they had.

From Ilin's office window, looking above the tops of the buildings across the square, he could see the onion spires of the Kremlin.

These were the days of Kalugin, who now ruled the tattered remnants of the czars' empire. In truth, the empire that the Communists had inherited and held with grim determination for seventy-five years was now irretrievably gone; only Russia and Siberia remained. Still, Russia and Siberia were huge beyond imagination. In towns and villages and isolated cottages out in the vastness of the steppe, the long grass prairies, and the boreal and subarctic forests, Kalugin was just a name, a photo or flickering image on the television. Life went on pretty much as it had since the death of Stalin, when the secret police stopped dragging people away. The winters were still long and fierce, work hard, food scarce, vodka too plentiful.

Kalugin fought his way to the top, promising to restore Russia's glory and build an economic system that worked. His plan was to legitimize the vast criminal enterprises that were actually feeding, clothing, and housing a significant percentage of the population, and making the people who ran them rich beyond the dreams of avarice.

Kalugin was one of those rich ones. He could orate long and loudly on the glory of Mother Russia, and he had never paid a ruble in taxes. Now he was in the Kremlin, surrounded by men just like him.

Janos Ilin took a deep breath and sighed. War again. Against Mother Russia.

Now we find out what Kalugin is made of, he thought.

He finished his cigarette before he went to see the minister.

Washington, D.C. was overcast and dreary in the rain. The soldier at the wheel of the government sedan had little to say, which was just as well because Bob Cassidy was whacked from jet lag. He felt as if he hadn't slept in a week. His eyes burned, his skin itched, and he was desperate for a long, hot shower and a bed. Alas, it was six in the evening here and his orders were to proceed directly to the Pentagon. The driver had been waiting for him when he got off the plane at Dulles Airport.

He rode along for a while watching traffic, then leaned back in the seat and closed his eyes. He hadn't slept a wink on the all-night flight from Tokyo to Seattle, nor on the cross-continent flight to Dulles. He hated airliners, hated the claustrophobia brought on by being shoehorned into too small a seat. But that was past. He felt himself relaxing as he enjoyed the motion of the car, the rhythm of the wipers.

'We're here, Colonel. Sir! We're here.'

Cassidy levered himself erect and looked around. The soldier was parked outside the main entrance, and he was offering Cassidy a security badge. 'You need to show this to the security guard inside, sir.'

'You'll wait for me?'

'Yes, sir. I have your luggage. I'll wait right here.'

Cassidy took the security badge and climbed from the car. He paused to straighten his tie – he was wearing a civilian suit – then marched for the main entrance. The rain was still falling, a medium drizzle.

Inside, one of the security guards led him along endless gray corridors, up stairs, along more corridors. He was completely disoriented within two minutes. Once, through an open door, he saw a window that appeared to be on an outside wall, but he wasn't sure.

Finally, he arrived at a decorated corridor, one with blue paint and original artwork on the walls, carpet on the floor.

The security guard led him into a reception area, introduced him to a Marine Corps lieutenant colonel, who asked him to take a seat for a minute. The marine disappeared into an office. In minutes, he was back. 'It will be just a few minutes before the chairman can see you, Colonel. Could I offer you a soft drink or a cup of coffee?'

'Coffee would be perfect. Black, thank you.'

The headline in the newspaper on the table screamed at him: SECRET MILITARY PROTOCOL WITH RUSSIA REVEALED. Under the headline, smaller type said, 'President committed U.S. to defense of Russia. Key congressional leaders approved secret pact.'

Tired as he was, Cassidy picked up the paper and read the story. When the marine returned with a paper cup full of steaming black fluid, Cassidy sipped gratefully as he finished the story. The marine waited patiently.

'Do you have a room where I could wash my face and brush this suit?'

'The general will see you in just a few minutes, sir. Believe me, you don't have to put on the dog for him. He knows you just got off the plane.'

They made small talk for several minutes; then the telephone buzzed. Thirty seconds later, Cassidy was shaking hands with the chairman of the Joint Chiefs, General Stanford Tuck.

The marine aide left the room and pulled the door closed behind him.

They sat in leather chairs facing each other, on the same side of the large desk. 'I'm sorry for the short notice, Colonel. Things are happening quickly, which is par for the course around here. I don't know just what they told you at the embassy in Tokyo, so let me summarize. It appears that Japan will invade Siberia in the very near future.'

Cassidy just nodded. Apparently the bigwigs believed Jiro's tale.

Tuck continued: 'We project that Japan's new Zero fighter will destroy Russia's air force within a week, if the Russians are willing to keep sending their planes up to get shot down. Due to the dearth of decent roads in Siberia and the vast distances involved, both sides are going to have to rely on air transport for all their food, fuel, and ammo. Baldly, the side with air superiority will win.'

Tuck's gray eyes held Cassidy transfixed.

'It is doubtful if the United States will take sides in this regional conflict,' the general continued.

'I saw the story on the military protocol in the paper.'

Tuck gestured at the heavens. 'We are toying with the idea of loaning Russia a dozen of our best fighters to take on the Zeros. That's where you come in.'

'What kind of airplanes, sir?'

'F-22 Raptors.'

'These will be American airplanes?'

'No. We are going to sell or trade them to the Russians. These will be Russian airplanes, and the Russians will hire qualified American civilians to fly them. They just don't know it yet.'

'When will they know it?'

'We'll bring this subject up after the shooting starts. You understand?'

Cassidy shook his head. 'No, sir. I don't pretend to understand any of it.'

'A refreshing attitude. I'm not sure I understand much of it, either. Still, if we decide to go through with this proposal, your job, Colonel, would be to command the Russian F-22 squadron.'

Cassidy just stared. This trip to Washington had occurred on two hours' notice. No reason given, just a summons to be on the afternoon plane. He had speculated all the way across the Pacific, which was one reason he hadn't had any sleep. He had concluded that the folks in the Pentagon wanted to ensure they had everything he knew about the new Japanese Zero fighter. He certainly hadn't suspected this.

It occurred to him to ask, 'Why me, sir?'

Stanford Tuck thought that a logical question. He said, 'You know as much about Asia as any senior flight officer, and you are F-22-qualified, so we won't have to waste weeks teaching you how to fly the darn thing. Amazingly enough, when we put our criteria into the idiot box, your name was at the head of the very short list that popped out.'

'I don't know what to say, sir.'

'Don't say anything. That's normally best.' The general smiled.

'I'll have to think about it, sir. This is right out of the blue. I'm not sure I could do the job.'

Cassidy looked tired, the general thought.

'As you might suspect, there are political complications,' the general continued, 'so there are some serious wrinkles. The political types think we are skirting dangerously close to the abyss if we have a serving U.S. officer in combat against a friendly power, so you'll have to retire from the Air Force.'

'Well, I –'

'Another is that the Air Force chief of staff doesn't want any of his active duty F-22 pilots resigning to accept commissions in the Russian air force. I think he's afraid of starting a precedent.'

The general's eyes solidified, like water freezing. 'He didn't want to lose you, either, but he didn't have a choice. Still, the politicians don't want to ruffle the chief of staff's feathers – they're going to get quite enough flak over this as it is – so you'll have to get your recruits from Raptor-qualified folks who just got off active duty or retired. There aren't many retirees, but there are one or two you can talk to. We'll give you a list.'

Cassidy had recovered his composure and got the wheels going again. 'Most of those people will have plans, sir. They're not just leaving active duty – they're going *to* something. They won't be interested in going to Siberia.'

'Your job is to recruit the people you need, out of uniform or in.' Tuck leaned forward and his voice hardened. 'You let me know who you want, and I'll see that he or she is an available civilian pretty damn quick.'

'If I say yes, when would I start, General?'

'The politicians haven't committed to this adventure yet. They're considering it. I won't go along until more details are ironed out.'

'We'll need qualified maintenance people, intel, weather.'

Tuck nodded. 'My aide, Colonel Eatherly, will go over the nuts and bolts with you. Fixing problems is what he does best. He can smooth the road, help straighten it out.'

'Maybe you should give him this job, sir,' Bob Cassidy said, and tried to grin. 'I've never even been to Russia.'

Tuck got to his feet. 'Go get some sleep, Colonel. Come see me in the morning, let me know what you think then. As I said, your name came up. The folks around here tell me you are F-22-qualified, you got us most of the info on the Zero, and you understand the Japanese as well as anyone in uniform. The U.S. ambassador to Japan highly recommends you, as do two of your old fighter bosses I've talked to. They tell me you can pull this off if anyone can. It's your decision.'

'I'll have to think about it, sir.'

As Stanford Tuck shook the colonel's hand, he said, 'You're a professional fighter pilot, Cassidy; this will probably be all the war you'll ever get.'

The general looked Cassidy right in the eye. 'It's going to be a genuine sausage machine. A lot of people are going to die. The process will be damned unpleasant and ugly as hell. The elected leaders of your country refuse to declare war. Do you want to risk your life for Russia, for the Russians? Sleep on it. See me tomorrow.'

'Yes, sir.'

'Everything we have discussed is top secret, Colonel. *Everything.*'

Out in the reception area, one of the enlisted people volunteered to lead Bob Cassidy toward the main entrance and the waiting car.

Combat. People dying.

Lord have mercy.

Kalugin looked like a wolf, an old gray wolf of the taiga from a Russian folk story. He had small black eyes and a fierce, hungry look that hid whatever thoughts were passing behind the features of his face.

Aleksandr Ivanovich Kalugin was a shrewd, calculating paranoid without morals, ethics, or scruples of any kind, a gangster willing to do whatever it took to enrich himself. He had no loyalty to anyone except himself. He was a perfect political animal, ready to strike any pose and make any promise that he thought his listeners wanted to hear.

Like politicians in Western democracies, he paid 'experts' to tell him what it was 'the people' wanted. He was willing, of course, to try to deliver on his promises, if the cost was low and the prospect of personal profit high. The man was a case study for those fools who believed that a politician's character didn't matter as long as he was on their side. The truth was that Kalugin had no side but his own: he was as ready to devour his supporters as he was his enemies.

Today he fixed that wolfish stare on the minister of foreign affairs, Danilov, as the minister expounded on the conversation in the White House between the American national security adviser and the Russian ambassador to the United States.

A vein in Kalugin's forehead throbbed visibly. Finally, he muttered, through clenched teeth, 'The damned Americans are lying.'

'Mr President –'

'They are lying, you doddering fool! They have lied to us ten thousand times and they are lying again. The Japanese are not stupid enough to get trapped in Siberia this winter. That icebox is the most inhospitable hell on this planet in winter, which is what, three, maybe three and a half months away? By October the temperatures will be below freezing and dropping like a stone. Only Russians would be crazy enough to endure that bleak, frozen outhouse that God never visits. The damned Americans are lying. Again!'

'I think that –'

'Get the Japanese ambassador into your office and ask him to his face. Ask him if his country plans to invade Russia. Ask him!'

Kalugin pointed toward the door. Danilov went.

What if the Japanese did invade? The event would ignite a wildfire of patriotism. Business as usual would come to a rapid halt.

Kalugin began to mull the possibilities. It seemed to him that if the Japanese invaded Siberia, an extraordinary window of political opportunity would open for a man fast enough and bold enough to seize the moment. If a man played his cards right . . .

Inadvertently, Kalugin's eyes went to Stalin's portrait, which he kept on the wall even though the dictator was out of fashion in most quarters these days. For a moment, Kalugin fancied that he could see a gleam in the eye of the old assassin.

Bob Cassidy got a room in a hotel in Crystal City, one of those modern buildings with glass walls. By some quirk, his room had a good view of downtown Washington even though the desk clerk assured him he was only being charged the military rate.

He couldn't really get to sleep. The room wasn't dark: light from the city leaked in around the curtains. He dozed at times, and dreamed of being aloft in a cockpit. He was in and out of clouds, the missile warning flashing and sounding in his ears, telling him of invisible missiles racing toward him at twice the speed of sound. He was trying desperately to escape, but he couldn't. The missiles were streaking in . . .

He awoke each time sweating profusely, his mouth dry, his skin itching.

Finally, he fixed himself a drink from the wet bar and drank it quickly. The alcohol didn't help.

He pulled the drapes back and sat looking at the lights. He could just see the capitol dome and the Washington Monument.

A war was coming and all these people were oblivious. Even if they knew, they wouldn't care – as long as the bombs didn't fall here.

General Tuck would want to know his decision in a few hours.

Maybe he should ask about after the war. If he survived, could he get back into the Air Force?

Would he want back in?

F-22s versus Zeros. Jiro Kimura was flying a Zero.

My God, he might end up shooting at Jiro.

He finally dozed off in the chair. The flying dream didn't return. In the new dream, he was young again, just a boy in Kansas, watching clouds adrift on a summer wind in an infinite blue sky.

He awoke for good at 3:00 A.M. It was hopeless. There was no more sleep in him. He took a shower and put on a uniform.

Could the F-22 survive against the Zero? The Raptor was very stealthy, but with Athena, the Zero was invisible, or so Jiro said. How do you fight a supersonic enemy that you cannot locate on radar?

'Taking a squadron of F-22s to Siberia will be a challenge, General,' Bob Cassidy told Stanford Tuck the next morning. The general was sitting behind his desk in his shirtsleeves, drinking coffee. His jacket hung on a hook near the door.

'Logistics will make or break the operation,' Cassidy continued. He sketched out the problems he saw with basing, logistics, early warning, and keeping his people healthy and flying. 'Even the food will have to come from the States.'

'Siberia,' the general muttered, just to hear the sound of the word.

'The logistics problem would be easier if we were taking a squadron to Antarctica.'

The general punched a button on the telephone. In seconds, a door opened and the general's aide appeared.

'This is Colonel Eatherly. I want you to go over everything you've talked about in greater detail with him. He'll take notes and brief me on what he thinks. The president wants to make a powerful political statement against armed aggression. He doesn't want to embroil the United States in World War Three. Yet if we commit a dozen planes to combat in Russia, they must have at least a fighting chance of accomplishing their mission. If the Japanese sweep them from the sky – for whatever reason – we will be worse off than if we did nothing. Offering hors d'oeuvres to a hungry lion is bad policy.'

Tuck loosened his tie and rolled up his sleeves.

Bob Cassidy took a deep breath. He appreciated the stakes involved, but he knew what trained pilots could do with the F-22.

'Subject to the qualifiers we discussed, sir, I think a Raptor squadron could go toe-to-toe with the new Zero. With the right pilots, we can give them a hell of a fight.'

'A dozen planes is all we can give you,' Stanford Tuck said, 'so you are going to be outnumbered by a bunch.' He laid both hands flat on his desk.

'You may as well hear all of it,' the general said. 'We cannot give you the new, long-range missiles. The politicians refused. You can take AMRAAMs and Sidewinders, but nothing that has technology we don't want the Japanese or Russians to see.' AMRAAM stood for advanced medium-range anti-aircraft missile; it was also known as the AIM-120C.

'Sky Eye?'

'No. The thinking is that if foreign powers learn how good Sky Eye is, they will target our satellites in any future conflict.'

'Our satellites are already targets.'

'Low-priority targets.'

'But –'

Tuck raised a hand. 'I'm not here to argue. I didn't make that decision. We have to live with it.'

'Why the hell buy it if we can't use it?' Cassidy asked with some irritation.

'This country's future isn't on the come line just now,' Tuck said with his eyes half-closed. He seemed to be trying to measure Cassidy. 'You and I are on the same side.'

'I'm sorry, sir. I didn't mean –'

'Go talk to Eatherly.'

As Eatherly led Cassidy from the room, he stuck out his hand. 'My friends call me John. Did you get along okay with the old man?'

'I think so.'

In his office, Eatherly pulled a chair around for Cassidy and got out a legal pad.

'Does the general really think an F-22 squadron in Siberia has a chance?'

Eatherly looked surprised. 'What are you saying?'

Cassidy frowned. 'Or does he want me to give him reasons to say no?'

'I believe he was hoping you could show him how this proposal could be made to work,' Eatherly replied thoughtfully. 'If you think it can.'

Cassidy rubbed his face hard. 'I –'

'*You* are going to be leading this parade, Colonel. The tender, quivering ass on the plate this time is yours.'

Bob Cassidy sat lost in thought for a long moment. Then he said, 'My source in Japan says the Zeros are invisible to radar. He says the Japanese acquired – stole – an American project called Athena.'

Eatherly nodded. 'There was a black American project with that name. I checked when I saw your report on the Zero. The American project died years ago.'

'How did it work?'

'It was active ECM. When the signal from an enemy radar was detected, the raw data was put through a superconductive computer, which then used other antennas buried in the aircraft's skin to emit an out-of-sync wave that effectively canceled the enemy radar signal.'

'But what about scatter effect? Radar A transmits a signal, but B receives it?'

'The computer knows the scatter characteristics of the airplane it is protecting, so it emits the proper amount of energy in all directions. That was the heart of it.'

'Why didn't we dvelop it?'

Eatherly shrugged. 'Ran out of money.'

'Terrific.'

'The F-22 is very stealthy,' Eatherly mused. 'With your radar off, you might escape detection until you are into visual range.'

'It isn't that stealthy,' Bob Cassidy replied. 'And the human eyeball isn't that good. What we're going to need is Sky Eye. The satellites are going to have to find these guys and tell us where they are.'

'I'll talk to the National Security people.'

'And we're going to need something to protect our bases. We won't have the planes to stay airborne around the clock. We need an equalizer.'

'Sentinel,' John said, and wrote the word on his legal pad.

'Explain.'

'Sentinel is an automated weapon – highly classified, of course. You deliver it to a site, turn it on, and leave it. When it detects electromagnetic energy on a preset frequency, it launches a small, solid-fuel, antiradiation missile that seeks out the emitter. The missiles have some memory capability, so they can track targets that cease emissions – the capability of these new computer chips is really amazing. Anyway, as I recall, Sentinel has a magazine capacity of forty-eight missiles. The missiles have a range of about sixteen miles.'

'Electrical power will be a big problem in Siberia.'

'Sentinel has rechargable solar cells. All you have to do is reload the magazine occasionally.'

'So Zero pilots are going to be down to their Mark I, Mod Zero eyeballs.'

'Sentinel will definitely encourage them to leave their radars turned off.'

'Nasty.' Cassidy grinned.

'Doesn't the F-22 have the new camouflage skin that changes colors based on the background?' Eatherly asked after they discussed logistics for several minutes.

'The newest ones do,' Cassidy told him. 'Active skin camouflage, or smart skin. The skin has to be installed on the assembly line.'

'How good is it?'

'It really works. Against any kind of neutral background, such as clouds or ocean or haze, the plane is extremely difficult to locate visually when it's more than a couple hundred yards away. Some people can pick it up with their peripheral vision, sometimes. Occasionally you see movement out of the corner of your eye, you know it's there, and yet when you look directly at it, you can't pick it up. It's scary.'

Eatherly made a note. 'Talk to me about maintenance. How many people, how many spares?'

After a morning of this, John Eatherly and Cassidy went back into the chairman's office for lunch. As they ate bean soup and corn bread, Eatherly briefed the general. He ran through proposed solutions to every major problem: personnel, logistics, maintenance, weapons and fuel supply, early warning.

'So what is your recommendation?' the general asked Cassidy when Eatherly was finished.

'Isn't there any way to prevent this war from happening, sir?' Cassidy was staring into the bean soup. He had no appetite.

'The politicos say no.' Stanford Tuck shrugged. 'War happens because a whole society screws itself up to it – it isn't just the fault of the politicians at the top. That society will quit only when the vast majority believes their cause is hopeless.'

'So the F-22 outfit is supposed to help convince them. Show them the error of their ways.'

'I want you to nibble at 'em, worry 'em, shoot down a Zero occasionally, target their air transports, convince the Japanese that they've bitten off more than they can chew.'

'Sir, the Japanese have active ECM that makes their plane invisible. Athena. They will blow us from the sky unless we use the satellites to find the Zeros and point them out to us.'

'The White House says no.'

'I am not taking Americans to Russia to be slaughtered. Without Sky Eye, there is no way. I want no part of it.'

Stanford Tuck helped himself to another spoonful of soup, then put the spoon down beside the bowl. 'You've been in the military for twenty-some years, Cassidy. There's not much I could tell you about this business that you don't already know. I will try to get authorization to use the satellites.'

'I'll be lucky to bring half of them home.'

'I'll do the best I can. That's all I can promise.'

'Those who do come home – can we get back into the Armed Forces?'

'I'll get a letter to that effect from the president. I'm sure he'll sign it.'

'Good.'

Then Tuck added softly, 'Is there anything else you want to tell me, Colonel?'

'I know one of the Zero pilots pretty well, General.'

Stanford Tuck glanced at Eatherly, then cleared his throat. 'After spending a year in Japan, I'd be surprised if you didn't know several,' he said. 'I hate to press you like this, but time is running out. Can you do this job?'

'I can do it, General. My comment about the Zero pilot is personal. The job you are offering is professional, in the best interests of the United States. I know the difference. I just pray to God my friend lives through all this.'

'I understand.' Tuck's head moved a tenth of an inch. It was a tiny bow, Cassidy noted, startled.

'Colonel Eatherly will help you get the ball rolling,' the general said. 'Let's see what we can make happen.'

'Yes, sir,' Cassidy managed to say as Stanford Tuck stuck out his hand to shake.

Tuck held his hand firmly and looked him in the eye. 'Check six, Colonel. And remember what the Good Book says: When you're in the valley, fear no evil.'

6

The first people in Siberia to discover something amiss were the radar operators at the Vladivostok airport, a facility the military shared with the occasional civil transports that had flown the length of Siberia or over the Pole. There weren't many of those anymore. Fuel was expensive, money to maintain aircraft in short supply, and the navigation aids in the middle of the continent were not regularly maintained. Anything or anyone that really had to get to Vladivostok came by rail or sea. Still, the radars that searched the oceans to the east and south were in working order and operators were on duty, even at two o'clock in the morning, near the end of another short summer night.

In Russia change occurred because the government agency responsible ceased paying the bills and, to survive, the people who had lived on that trickle of money wandered on to something else. Money to make the radars work still dribbled in occasionally from Moscow. The task of safeguarding Mother Russia was too sacred for any politician to touch.

The only operator actually watching the screens was also perusing a card game that the other members of the watch section were playing. Occasionally, he remembered to glance at the screens. It was on one of these periscope sweeps that he saw the blip, to the south. Three minutes later, when the blip was still there, and closer, he called the supervisor to look. The supervisor put down his cards reluctantly.

There were no aircraft scheduled to arrive from that direction – there were no aircraft at all scheduled to arrive in Vladivostok until the next afternoon – and repeated queries on the radio went unanswered. As the blip got closer, it separated into many smaller blips, apparently a flight of aircraft.

The radar supervisor called the air defense watch officer on the other side of the base and reported the inbound flight, which would penetrate Russian airspace in about twelve minutes if it maintained the same course and speed.

Two Sukhoi Su-27 fighters were in the usual alert status, which meant each was fully fueled and armed with four AA-10 Alamo missiles and a belt of shells for its 30-mm cannon. The ground crews were asleep in a nearby hut. The pilots, wearing flight suits, were playing chess in another nearby shack. Usually at this time of night, the alert pilots would be asleep, but these two had attended a wedding dinner earlier in the evening and weren't sleepy.

When the duty officer telephoned, ordering a scramble, they dropped everything and ran for their planes as they shouted to awaken the ground crews. One of the pilots opened the door to the ground crew's shack and turned on the light.

At the aircraft, the pilots donned their flight gear as the ground crewmen came stumbling across the mat.

The Sukhois rolled onto the runway eight minutes later, lit their afterburners, and accelerated. The mighty roar washed over the sleepy base like thunder.

After a modest run, the wheels lifted from the concrete and the pilots sucked up gear and flaps. With the afterburners still engaged, the two fighters moved closer together. The pilots then pulled into a steep climb and punched up through the overcast as the leader checked in with the ground control intercept (GCI) controller, who was the same man who had seen the incoming blips, for what was originally one blip had now separated into five, sometimes six, individual targets. The supervisor and most of the watch section were now gathered behind him, watching the scope over his shoulder.

The blips were doing about 250 knots. Probably turboprop aircraft. But whose? Why were so many aircraft coming from the southeast? Why hadn't Moscow transmitted a copy of their flight plans?

The tops of the lower layer of stratus clouds were at fifteen thousand feet tonight. Another cloud layer far above blocked out most of the glow of the high-latitude sky. As they climbed above the lower layer of stratus clouds, the Sukhoi pilots eased their throttles back out of burner and spread out into a loose combat formation. They then killed their wingtip lights, so only the dim formation lights on the sides of the planes enlivened the darkness.

When the fighters were level at twenty thousand feet, the GCI controller turned them to a course to intercept the large formation heading toward Vladivostok.

The leader's attention was inside his cockpit. Although the Su-27 had a HUD, the pilot wasn't using it. Even if he had been, he would probably have died anyway.

He concentrated on flying his aircraft on instruments, and on adjusting the gain and brightness of his radar screen. The task took several seconds. As he examined the scope, he glanced at his electronic countermeasures panel, which was silent. Yes, the switches were on.

A shout on the radio. He automatically raised his gaze, scanned outside.

At eleven o'clock, slightly high, a bright light . . . brilliant!

Missile!

The thought registered on his brain and automatically he slammed the stick sideways to roll left, away from his wingman, and pulled.

The responsive fighter flicked over obediently into 220 degrees of bank. The missile arrived a second and a half after the pilot first spotted the exhaust plume: The fighter's nose had come down no more than ten degrees.

The missile missed the Sukhoi by about six inches. The proximity fuse detonated the warhead immediately under the cockpit area. The shrapnel punched hundreds of holes in the belly of the plane. In less than a second, fuel from punctured fuel lines sprayed into the engine compartment, starting a fire. A half second later, the aircraft exploded, killing the pilot instantly.

The wingman had instinctively rolled right – away from his leader – when he spotted the inbound missile. He also shouted into his radio mike, which was contained within his oxygen mask. It was this warning that the leader heard.

The wingman only rolled about seventy degrees, however, so he could keep the oncoming missile in sight. Still he laid on six G's. He saw the missile streak in out of the corner of his eye and saw the flash as it detonated under the leader's plane.

The flash temporarily blinded him.

Blinking mightily, he slammed the stick back left and pulled while he looked to see if his leader had successfully avoided the missile. He keyed his radio mike, opened his mouth to call.

The wingman never saw the second missile, which impacted his plane in the area of the left wing root and detonated. The explosion severed the wing spar, so the wing collapsed. The hot metal of the warhead ignited fuel spewing under pressure from the ruptured wing tank. Then all the fuel still in the wing exploded. The sequence was over in a few thousandths of a second. The pilot died without even knowing there had been a second missile.

The blossoming fireballs from the two Sukhois were visible for twenty miles in this dark universe.

The pilots of the four Japanese Zeros – White Flight – cruising at max conserve took their thumbs off the fire buttons on their sticks, where they had been hovering in case further missiles were necessary. The leader had been the only plane to fire.

Now White Leader began a gentle left turn to carry the flight back in the direction of Vladivostok. He hoped to orbit in this area to the east of the city in a racetrack pattern, ready to shoot down any other aircraft coming out of Vlad or the bases on Sakhalin Island to harass Japanese aircraft delivering paratroops.

Flying as number three, Jiro Kimura checked the location of the other aircraft in the formation on his computer presentation. The planes used pencil-thin laser beams to keep track of one another. No external lights were illuminated; consequently, the airplanes were invisible in the darkness.

Confident that all four planes were where they were supposed to be, Jiro's thoughts moved on. He banked to keep the leader in position.

Why did he not feel elated? The first two victories of the war had just been won. The Athena devices on the Zeros made them invisible to Russian radar, so the GCI controllers had no clue whatsoever that the Zeros were even airborne. They had launched the Sukhois to investigate the incoming transports. The Sukhoi pilots had been ambushed without warning ... without mercy, without a chance in hell. They were executed.

That was the truth of it.

Jiro felt no pity or remorse, only a tiredness, a lethargy, and a sense of profound sadness.

Flash, flash, two explosions seventeen miles away in the night sky ... and two men were dead. Presumably. Jiro thought the odds of surviving explosions like that must be very slim.

Bang, bang.

Just like that – two men dead.

That was the way he would die, too. The revelation came to him now in his cockpit as he sat there tired, hungry, thirsty, and very much alone. He would die in this cockpit someday just as those two Russians had, without warning, without luck, without a moment to reflect, without an opportunity to make his peace with the universe.

And he had chosen this destiny! Just last evening, his commanding officer had sent for him, showed him a message from the Japanese Intelligence Agency demanding a loyalty investigation. 'You telephoned an American Air Force officer?'

'I attended the American Air Force Academy, sir, as you are aware. I know many Americans. I have kept up my contacts with several of them through the years.'

'Of course,' his CO said. 'These bureaucratic spy fools have not looked at your record. But you see how it is, Kimura. You see how easy it is to compromise yourself. Be more careful in the future.' With that admonition, the CO tossed the message in a pile of paperwork that a clerk was placing in boxes for storage.

'I called this American to –'

His commanding officer didn't want to hear it. He cut him off. 'Kimura, we are going to have a war. You and I will both be in combat within twenty-four hours. I have better things to do just now than write letters to bureaucrats. An investigation, they want. If we are both alive a month from now, I shall write them a letter saying that you are a loyal soldier of Japan. If you are dead, I shall tell them how gloriously you died. Like cherry blossoms falling – isn't that the way the old poems go? If I am dead ...'

The CO had shooed him out.

Now the Russian GCI controller came on the air, calling to his dead pilots. He didn't know they were dead, of course, but they had disappeared from his radar scope, so he was calling, albeit futilely.

Jiro could not understand the words, but he could hear the concern and frustration in the controller's voice.

Jiro kept a wary eye on his electronic warfare (EW) warning indications – they were comfortably silent – monitored the tactical display, and concentrated on staying in proper position in his formation as the controller called and called to men who would never answer.

The ten aircraft approaching Vladivostok were C-130 Hercules, J-models, the most advanced version of the late-twentieth-century military transportation workhorse. Each aircraft was crammed with troops.

The first flight of four aircraft began descending seventy miles from the city. They dropped into a trail formation by alternately dropping gear and flaps. The pilot of the lead plane delayed his dirty-up the longest – he dropped his gear just as he intercepted the instrument landing system (ILS) glide path. He couldn't yet see the runway since the visibility was only three or four miles in this gentle rain.

The ILS was working fine, which was amazing considering how little money the Russians had devoted to their airways system over the last few years. Even if the ILS had been disabled, he would have flown exactly the same approach using the GPS equipment and computers in his cockpit. Still, the flight leader was delighted the ILS was operating. Had it been off, he would have had to worry about how much warning the Russians had had and whether or not the runway was blocked. Since the ILS was functioning, he felt confident the runway would be clear. Just to be on the safe side, however, he compared the ILS indications he was receiving with the computer presentation derived from GPS and the onboard inertial. All the instruments agreed.

The copilot chortled merrily, as did the leader of the paratroops, who stood behind the pilot looking over his shoulder.

The second flight of four C-130s kept their speed up as they dropped toward the city. Level at three thousand feet, in the overcast, the crews opened the rear cargo doors. The paratroopers lined up and connected their static lines.

The planes continued descending toward the city in trail, three miles apart, the paratroopers waiting. Many of the soldiers stood with eyes closed, lips moving as they prayed to their gods and their ancestors. A night parachute jump was hazardous enough, but the Russians had antiaircraft missile batteries and artillery spotted around the city; if they opened fire the C-130s were going to fall like ruptured ducks. And the city was on a peninsula, with water on three sides. Paratroopers hated water. When the chart was unveiled, revealing the location, several gasps were heard as the men saw all that water.

The guns and missile batteries remained silent. The Hercs swept in at 200 knots, slowing to 150 as they dropped lower and lower toward city lights glowing in the cloudy, rainy darkness.

Two of the planes dropped their paratroopers over the old closed Vlad airport, which was being rebuilt.

The other two planes dropped their men north of the wharves along Golden Horn Bay. The first planeload of these troops landed mainly on the streets and small grassy areas, but a gust of wind seemed to catch the last several dozen men of the second stick. The men hanging in their parachutes drifted toward the black water of the bay lying immediately to their right.

Silently, without a cry or shout, the soldiers dropped into the oily waters of the bay and went under. Each man was wearing almost a hundred pounds of gear and weapons, so they had no chance. They were the first Japanese to die invading Siberia.

In the airport tower, the supervisor was unable to establish communications with the approaching aircraft. He spoke into the microphone only in Russian. Trying to communicate with the incoming planes in English, the universal language of international aviation, never once occurred to him.

The thought did occur to him, however, that he had better personally notify the military of the presence of the unknown planes.

He dialed the telephone number of the commanding officer of the army unit that provided airport security. Since it was the middle of the night there was no one in the office to answer the telephone. The army ran a strictly business-hours operation. Consequently, the four ZPU-23 antiaircraft artillery units parked around the airport perimeter that could have shot the incoming Japanese C-130s to bits with just a few bursts of aimed fire were never manned. This was, perhaps, just as well, because near each gun was a Japanese commando in civilian clothes, armed with a sniper rifle equipped with a starlight scope.

The tower supervisor also turned off the airport lights – the runway, taxiway, and approach lights. Vlad airport instantly took on the appearance of the black water that bordered it on three sides.

The lead C-130 broke out of the overcast a mile and a half out on the ILS glide slope. As a precaution, the aircraft was displaying no exterior lights. The pilot looked in vain for the approach and runway lights, then correctly assumed that they had been turned off. He spoke this conclusion aloud to the battalion commander standing behind his seat. The words were just out of his mouth when the ILS needles locked up and the off flag appeared on the face of the instrument. The tower supervisor had ordered the instrument landing system turned off, too.

The copilot was now flying the plane. The ILS failure bothered him not at all. He continued to follow GPS lineup and descent commands on the heads-up display.

At a hundred feet above the runway, the pilot saw lights reflecting off the wet concrete and called it. The copilot saw it, too. The pilot had his hand on the switch to turn on the landing lights, but he decided not to take the risk. There was just enough glare from the city reflecting off the clouds for the copilot to flare the Herc and set it on runway centerline. The pilot pulled the props into reverse thrust and, when the plane had slowed, turned off on the first available taxiway.

The battalion commander slapped the pilot on the shoulder, then turned and went aft to where his men were waiting.

Six minutes after the first Herc was on the ground at Vlad airport, Japanese troops were in the airport control tower and Japanese controllers were running the radar and talking to inbound traffic.

The transition occurred with only the most minor of glitches: The tower guard, a young Russian policeman armed only with a pistol, pulled it from its holster as six soldiers in strange uniforms trotted out of the darkness toward him with their assault rifles at high port. The gesture was futile. No one had told the policeman anything; he had not the least glimmer of an idea that Siberia – the airport – was being invaded. Still, his nervous reaction was, perhaps, understandable.

A pistol was a pistol, so the corporal trotting up with his squad shot the policeman with a burst of three rounds. The soldiers, all wearing body armor, jerked open the door of the building and went thundering through.

The policeman's body lay where it had fallen for the rest of the night. A passing Japanese officer finally noticed the pistol – a seventy-year-old Webley relic from the heady days of World War II Lend-Lease. He picked it up and stuck it in his belt. No one touched the body.

The paratroopers landing at the former closed airport assembled and counted heads. Several of the men had landed in construction ditches and one had fractured a leg by striking a bulldozer that had apparently been employed tearing up concrete. Surprisingly, the Russians were ripping up the crumbling old runways and putting in new. They were also in the process of installing sewers, water, and power lines.

Miraculously, all the paratroopers had somehow missed a construction crane towering a hundred feet in the air. Landing in a major construction site complicated the paratroopers' arrival somewhat, but so far, no one had paid them the least attention.

In accordance with the invasion plan, a company of soldiers assigned to guard the perimeter moved to the fences and took up their positions. The remainder of the soldiers laid out flares and tiny radio transmitters to outline a landing zone in the event the airport runway lights failed for any reason. Some of the larger pieces of construction equipment, including the construction crane, were marked with red warning lights. Then the men waited for the additional paratroopers scheduled to arrive. Within fifteen minutes, more soldiers floated from the misty clouds on white parachutes as the hum of turboprop engines echoed from the surrounding buildings and hills.

When the second wave of troops was on the ground and out of the way, containers carrying machine guns, ammo, and communications gear began to drop from the clouds. The Japanese were dropping most of the men first, then the containers of supplies, just to be on the safe side. Still, they had hoped for only light opposition. So far, there had been none.

Occasionally, a container would drift too far west and fall into Amur Bay amid the fishing and industrial boats moored there, but not too many drifted that far, so no one paid much attention. People were visible on the boats, watching the military operation. No one made any attempt to interfere or even get closer to kibitz better.

Meanwhile, in the heart of the old city of Vladivostok, four unarmed Japanese commandos in civilian clothes watched as a small coaster eased through the gentle swells of the black water inside the Golden Horn, moving toward the public pier. There were no policemen or Russian soldiers anywhere about, the commandos had made sure of that. For the past two days, they had had this area under surveillance. During the hours when they weren't on watch, they played the role of Japanese businessmen at a local hotel and ran up prodigious bills – which they had no intention of paying – for food, vodka, and women.

Two of the commandos walked out to the bollards and caught lines thrown from the coaster's deck. Soon she was against the pier, with two gangways over. Troops in combat dress trotted ashore. They kept right on going across the pier and sidewalk and parking area, stopping at the first major street and forming a perimeter guard.

When the coaster's contingent of fifty men was ashore, the lines were taken in and it backed out into the strait. Another coaster eased out of the darkness up to the pier.

The next day, several major cargo ships would appear in the roadstead, ships carrying tanks, artillery, and all the other supplies and equipment necessary to keep a division fighting for weeks.

Across the bay at the Churkin wharves, a similar scene was being played out. Two of the Japanese cargo ships could get in against this wharf, but the cargo cranes were broken. The Russians had been unloading cargo by hand. The following day, these soldiers would have to have the military situation in Vladivostok well enough in hand that a portable crane could be off-loaded and erected.

The soldiers certainly had encountered no opposition thus far. That would soon change. Telephones were ringing all over Russia; the news from the airport was being discussed in Moscow. Locally, the authorities were hearing of the paratroops' arrival.

At the ferry slip on the west side of the bay, the captain of *Ivan Turgenev*, a ferry loading passengers for Russian Island, across the strait from Vladivostok, saw strange troops in battle dress on the Churkin wharves and called his dispatcher on the radio. The dispatcher was incredulous.

With the diesel engine of his ferry still idling, the captain went ashore. The boozy barflies waiting to be taken home after an evening on the town paid no attention. Some of them were already vomiting over the railing.

At a public telephone in the little terminal, the ferry captain asked the operator for police headquarters. The officer on duty there did believe the captain's story, got the facts as quickly as possible, and even thanked him for calling.

After he hung up, the captain stood watching the troops for a moment from a window in the terminal; then he heard another ferry tooting. *Ivan Turgenev* was late on her departure. He ran back to the boat and headed for the bridge. Invasion or no, the ferries had to keep running.

A half hour after the destruction of the two Su-27s from the Vladivostok airport, the combat air patrol of Zeros known as White Flight was nearing the end of its on-station time. A new flight of four – Yellow Flight – scheduled to enter the area in five minutes was at least fifteen minutes behind schedule. White Leader had listened a few minutes ago to Yellow Leader talking to the tanker on Station Alpha, two hundred miles southeast. Yellow Leader was in a foul mood – the tanker was having equipment problems – but verbal rockets over the radio seemed to have little effect. So that flight was late, and it was not escorting the transports carrying more troops and supplies to Vlad.

There, on the very edge of his tactical screen, something coming west from Sakhalin Island . . . White Leader adjusted the scale of the screen.

Four planes, still climbing. His computer identified them as MiG-29s. Definitely hostile.

He decided to continue to orbit, to let the MiGs come to him. If he flew toward them, he was leaving the back door open for planes coming south from Khabarovsk in the Amur valley.

'White Three, you will fire two missiles at the easternmost targets, upon my command.' This transmission went out over the encrypted radio circuit.

'Roger, White Leader.' That was Jiro Kimura, White Three.

Max range for the missiles under the Zeros' wings was sixty nautical miles. White Leader decided to shoot at fifty, in case one of the missiles had less than a full load of fuel. He studied the tactical display as he orbited.

The MiGs were high, over thirty thousand feet, up where airliners cruise.

Airliners ... Where were the transports? They should be just offshore ... coming north from Hokkaido. Shouldn't they?

White Leader checked the watch on his wrist. He adjusted his tactical screen, pushed buttons. The transports should be identified on this presentation, if they were on time.

Nothing. Drat!

'White Three, White Lead. Do you have any friendly transports on your tac screen?' This transmission was encoded in a discrete, impossible-to-intercept beam of laser light that was aimed only at the other planes in the formation.

'Affirmative. They are –'

Even as Jiro spoke, the MiGs changed course, ninety degrees to their left. Southwest. And the transports appeared on White Leader's tac screen, the very edge of it. The MiGs were on course to intercept.

'White Three, watch the back door. White Two, come with me.' White Leader stroked his afterburners.

The Zeros had been cruising at a very economical .8 Mach. Now the fuel flow increased dramatically, as did the airspeed. The two Zeros slid through the sonic barrier with nary a buffet. Mach 1.2 ... 1.6 ... Mach 2 ... 2.3 ... 2.4. The airspeed stabilized at Mach 2.5.

Below, people asleep in coastal villages and towns awoke to twin thunderclaps, so close together that some people heard only one loud sonic boom. The booms reached the ground miles behind the speeding Zeros, streaking to intercept the MiGs before they got within range of the transports.

Above the clouds, the brilliant glow of the white-hot flames from twin afterburners shot across the sky like missiles. As the planes got away from the land, the stratus clouds thinned to wisps. Here and there, the sky was clear.

The intense heat signature of the two planes appeared as targets on several infrared scanners on coastal antiaircraft missile batteries, batteries recently alerted by telephone calls from frantic men in distant headquarters. One of the missile crews got an IR target lockup and tried to confirm via telephone that the target they were seeing was hostile. While this conversation was taking place, the targets passed out of range and lockup was lost.

The second crew was less professional. The danger of firing a surface-to-air missile at Russian fighters did not occur to them until later. When they got an IR lockup, they pushed the fire button.

Their SAM-3 missile leapt from its launcher as a sheet of dazzling flame poured from the solid fuel rocket motor. The missile accelerated away into the darkness, chasing that hot target.

Unfortunately, the battery crew had committed their missile to a futile stern chase. The missile exhausted its fuel before it closed half the distance to those fleeing Mach 2.5 targets. When the engine fell silent and the missile nosed over, a self-destruction circuit sensed the absence of acceleration and exploded the missile harmlessly.

White Leader got a glimpse of the explosion in his rearview mirror, but he was extremely busy and didn't give it any thought until later, much later, during mission debrief.

He was closing on the MiG-29s at almost a right angle, actually eighty-eight degrees. This would be a full deflection missile shot at nearly maximum range, the worst kind: the missile might not be able to make the corner. Should he wait and turn in behind before shooting? That would increase the chances that a missile would track, but it would let the MiGs get closer to the transports. The MiGs were at seventy-five miles now, closing at a sixty-degree stern angle.

There were two flights of MiGs, two to a flight, and the flights were about three miles apart.

For a second, White Leader wondered if the MiGs knew he was there, knew they, too, were being hunted. He shook the thought off. No time for that now.

Sixty-miles range. He fired one missile, then made a short left turn. This would let the MiGs extend out, put him astern. He still had a ton of closure – they could be doing no more than Mach 1.5. He would get astern and shoot again.

'White Two, shoot on my command.'

'Roger.'

Now, a sixty-degree angle of bank turn to the right. Yes. He was only forty-five degrees off, still closing.

The first missile must have missed, because the MiGs were turning hard, hard right, into the direction that the missile had come from.

'Out of burner, now.'

White Lead and his wingman came off the juice. They slowed as they turned to place the turning MiGs at their twelve o'clock.

Very nice. Range forty miles. Well within the missiles' performance envelope. White Leader triggered his last missile at the leading MiG, the one farthest to his right.

'I've shot at the leader, Two. Blaze away at the rest of them.'

Two said nothing. He answered with missiles. One after the other, two seconds apart, three missiles came off his rails.

Seconds ticked by. The Russian second-element wingman, Tail-end Charlie, lost sight of his lead during all the maneuvering and turned hard left, back toward the transports. He picked the nearest and locked him up with his radar. Just then, White Leader's missile impacted the lead MiG-29 in front of the tail and detonated. The tail was severed from the aircraft, which entered an uncontrollable tumble. The pilot tried to eject, but the tumbling was so violent that he passed out before he could do so. Within seconds, the plane broke up.

From the corner of his eye, Tail-end Charlie saw the fiery streak of the first missile coming in and the flash as it impacted, and he correctly guessed what it was. He had his firing solution on one of the Japanese transports at max range, seventy miles, so he pushed the fire button on his stick and held it down.

The firing circuit had a one-second delay built in before it ignited the missile's rocket engine, a delay designed to prevent inadvertent missile launching. This second was the longest of the young pilot's life. As he waited, he saw in the canopy rail mirror the flash as a Japanese missile exploded just above the cockpit of his element leader. This was the first missile fired by White Two.

Now Charlie's long-range Alamo missile came off the rail and seared the darkness with its cone of white fire.

Instinctively, the MiG pilot rolled upside down and pulled the nose ninety degrees down, straight down, toward the black ocean below.

The second missile from White Two arrived right on time, fatally impacting the other surviving MiG.

The missile aimed at Tail-end Charlie nosed over to track him and increased its speed. Charlie lit his burners, accelerated toward the waiting ocean.

The missile nosed down farther, gravity making it go even faster . . . and it overshot. It exploded harmlessly when its internal computer concluded it had missed.

At the flash of the explosion, Charlie began to pull. He was passing twenty thousand feet, eighty degrees nose-down at Mach 1.6. He came out of burner, pulled until he thought the wings would come off, then pulled some more. The nose was coming up, but not fast enough.

He fought to stay conscious.

Pull, pull, pull, scream into the mask, pull to stay alive.

Nine thousand . . . seven . . . nose thirty degrees down . . .

Nose twenty degrees down . . . ten degrees, passing three thousand feet . . .

At one thousand feet, only three hundred meters above the sea, Tail-end Charlie bottomed out. He was below Mach 1 at this point, but he was alive.

As the nose came above the horizon and he relaxed the G, the Russian pilot glanced at the radar scope on the panel before him. Nothing. It was blank. He laid into a turn in the direction from which the missiles had come. The enemy had to be up there, if only he could point his plane in the proper direction. Unlike the Zero, the MiG-29 lacked computers and passive sensors; the pilot had only radar to enable him to see his enemy.

A streak of fire in the sky caught his eye – another missile!

He was low and slow, trapped against the sea. He did the only thing he could – pulled the nose of the MiG straight up and lit the afterburner.

The missile went through the left wing, snapping it cleanly in two.

With his plane rolling out of control, the pilot of Tail-end Charlie ejected.

His parachute opened normally and he rode it down into the black ocean.

After floating in his life jacket for two hours, he died of hypothermia and exhaustion. During that time his only consolation was the fact that he had fired a missile at a transport before the unseen enemy got him. He never knew that his missile failed to guide.

White Three – Jiro Kimura – watched the spots of flame that were the afterburner exhausts of White One and Two accelerate away into the darkness. They receded more slowly than missile engines, but they did resemble missiles, or wandering stars, points of light growing smaller and smaller as the night swallowed them.

Jiro glanced at his wingman, then turned back toward Vladivostok. He kept his turn shallow, less than a ten-degree angle of bank, so he would not present the belly of the plane to an enemy radar to use as a reflecting surface.

He watched the tactical situation develop on his multifunction tac display. He saw the transports, saw the MiGs go for them, and saw White One and Two dash to cut them off. The missiles that were fired were not displayed, but the disappearance of the MiGs from the screen one by one spoke volumes.

We are winning.

That thought has sustained fighting men for thousands of years. It helped Jiro now, gave him a sense of confidence that no amount of exhortation could.

He was eying his fuel gauges nervously and toying with the idea of breaking radio silence when the tactical display presented a target coming down from the northeast, from the direction of Khabarovsk. A Sukhoi. Now two.

Where is Yellow Flight?

Jiro leveled his wings heading toward Vlad. The Sukhois were about a mile apart, heading southwest. If everyone maintained heading, the Sukhois would pass White Three and Four several miles to the left.

'Three, this is Four. My gadget has overheated. I'm turning it off.'

This unexpected transmission on the plane-to-plane digital laser system shook Jiro. He had just been basking in the glow of Athena's technical excellence, and now his wingman's unit had failed.

It was high time to be out of here. Where is Yellow Flight?

Without Athena to cancel incoming waves of electromagnetic energy from enemy radar, Four was now plainly visible on the screen of every Russian radar looking. Apparently, several of them were looking with interest. Jiro's electronic countermeasures panel lit up – someone was tracking them in high PRF, the firing mode of an antiaircraft missile radar. Actually they were tracking the wingman, but Jiro was close enough to the targeted aircraft to receive the indications on his equipment.

'Break away, Four. RTB.' This meant return to base. 'I'll be right along.'

'My fuel is bingo,' Four said, trying to cushion the embarrassment of his Athena failure.

Jiro's fuel was also getting desperate. But if he didn't cover Four's withdrawal, Four was in for a very bad time.

'RTB,' Jiro repeated. 'Now!'

The other Zero turned away hard. Jiro watched the tactical display and ensured the wingman steadied up as he headed toward Hokkaido.

The Sukhois from Vlad turned fifteen degrees to the left and launched a missile. Two.

Four was too far away for the discrete laser com. Jiro keyed the radio, which was scrambled, of course. Still, he was radiating. 'Two missiles in the air, White Four. Sixty-three miles behind you.' Four should have the missiles on his tactical display, if he had the proper display punched in. Jiro was taking no chances.

The Sukhois were too far away for Jiro to shoot. The Russian missiles had more range than the Japanese.

Perhaps the Sukhois could be diverted with another target. Jiro turned off his Athena device.

The visibility was too poor to see the Russian missiles' exhaust. They were out there, though, thundering along at almost Mach 4, covering two miles every three seconds. The missiles had been fired at nearly maximum range, so White Four was trying to outrun them. He was accelerating too, dumping fuel into his exhaust in exchange for speed. That was not a wise maneuver for a man without fuel to spare, but he was trapped between the devil and the deep blue sea.

Four was accelerating through Mach 2.

Well, he was safe. The missiles would never catch him in a stern chase before they exhausted their fuel.

'Three, this is Four. I'm changing freqs, calling for a tanker. I need fuel to get home.'

'Roger.'

Jiro devoted his attention to the Sukhois, which had turned in his direction. He checked his fuel gauges. He didn't have any to spare on speed dashes, either.

Missile launch. One . . . two from the Sukhois.

Where in hell is Yellow Flight?

'Yellow Leader, White Three. State your position and expected time to arrive on station, please.'

Jiro and the Sukhois were closing head-on at a combined speed of Mach 2.5. The missiles were coming at Mach 4. Closure speed with the missiles, 1.2 miles per second.

He was going to be in range for his missiles in five seconds. They were armed and ready to fire. He had only to punch the fire button on the stick.

Four ... three ... two ... one the in-range symbol appeared on the scope.

If he waited for a few seconds, he would have a better chance of scoring hits. But the fuel!

Jiro pressed the fire button and held it. One potato ... and a missile left in a gout of flame. He released the button, waited for the ready symbol on the HUD, then fired again.

With his left hand, he reached for the Athena switch. He turned it from the standby to the on position. The yellow light stayed illuminated.

Damnation!

He cycled the switch to off, then back to standby. Now to the on position. There was a ten-second warm-up delay built into the circuitry, so that many seconds had to pass before the gear began to radiate, canceling incoming radar waves.

Meanwhile, he dumped the nose and turned hard to the southeast. Nose well down, gravity helping him accelerate.

The incoming missile warning was flashing, showing twenty-one seconds to impact.

He was tempted to engage the afterburners; he eyed the fuel gauge again. No, he didn't have enough. If he did the burner trick, he might end up trying to swim to Japan.

Going down hard. He pushed the stick forward another smidgen, steepening his dive.

Fifteen seconds to impact. He looked outside, tried to see the oncoming missiles.

There!

And he went into the top of the stratus cloud deck.

That was stupid. If he had kept the missiles in sight, he would have had a better chance to outmaneuver them, if Athena refused to work.

Stupid. A stupid mistake.

You are fast running out of options, Jiro, options to save your silly butt.

At twelve seconds to impact, the green light appeared on the Athena panel.

The missiles were still coming. He watched them close on the tactical display. Were they tracking him?

One way to find out. He slapped the stick sideways and turned hard into the missiles. Six G's. Inadvertently, a groan escaped him.

The missiles didn't follow. They passed harmlessly behind and to his left.

Jiro got his nose up, started climbing, and lowered a wing to turn back to the southeast. He needed to get up to at least forty thousand feet for the trip to the tanker at Station Alpha.

He was climbing when he saw his missiles and the Sukhois merge on his tactical display. Target merger, and the Sukhois were gone.

He lived; the Russians died.

Just like that.

Jiro wiped the sweat from his eyes.

7

The Soviet navy was always something of a floating oxymoron, the seagoing service of the world's largest land power. It never received the prestige, money, or priority accorded to the Soviet army. The navy's hour of glory came after the 1962 Cuban missile crisis, when capable blue-water combatants were built in sufficient numbers to form a credible threat to the U.S. Navy and America's global interests. These sleek, heavily armed gray ships sailed the seven seas in packs, proudly waved the red flag, and never fired a shot.

When the bankrupt Soviet Union imploded in 1991, the surviving republics divided up the navy's ships. Russia received the majority, a dubious honor, for she lacked the money to sail or repair them. There wasn't even money to pay the sailors or buy them food. Some of the ships were sold to Third World nations for badly needed foreign exchange, but most were left to rust at their piers.

About half of the Russian far eastern fleet was tied to piers at the three naval bases near Vladivostok when squadrons of four destroyers each steamed into the harbor of each base.

The Japanese navy opened fire from less than a mile away with 127-mm 54-caliber deck guns. Not a single Russian ship fired back.

Most of the Russian ships had no crews, and even the ones that did have sailors aboard were in no condition to get under way, much less fight. At the two bases east of Vlad, all the ships were cold iron, without steam up. In Vlad, only two ships were receiving electrical power from the shore. These were tied to the westernmost pier in Golden Horn Bay. The rest looked, by day anyway, like exactly what they were, rust buckets abandoned to their fate.

It wasn't as if the nation or the navy didn't care about these ships, which had been purchased at an enormous cost, but they could never reach a decision about what to do with them. Every choice had enormous emotional and political implications. So they did nothing. Most of these vessels were now so far gone that they would be useful only if salvaged for scrap.

The Japanese ships steamed slowly in trail, one behind the other, acquired their targets as if this were an exercise, and banged away mercilessly. The explosive shells shredded the upper decks of the Russian ships and punched holes in unarmored hulls. Here and there minor fires broke out, but the ships contained no fuel, no explosive fluids, nothing that would readily burn. All those materials had been stripped off the ships years ago by naval yard workers and sold on the black market.

The two ships that had power and lights received special attention from the Japanese destroyers. Ironically, neither was a combatant. One was a fifty-year-old icebreaker, the other a large oceangoing tug. Both sank at their piers under the Japanese hammering.

Finally, after thirty minutes of shelling, the Japanese were satisfied. Still in trail, keeping to the channel, the four destroyers of each squadron turned smartly and steamed for the entrance of the bay.

The naval base five hundred miles northeast, at Gavan, received a similar treatment, quick, surgical, and vicious. Alas, this base was almost a mirror image of the bases at Vladivostok, a place to moor abandoned ships, but here and there were a few active units, ships that had received some modicum of attention through the years and still had a crew.

One of those craft was a low-freeboard monitor used by the border guard to patrol the Amur River when it was free of ice. The crew, directed by a very junior officer who had the night watch, managed to get one of the vessel's two 115-mm antitank guns unlimbered and loaded.

Their first shot missed, but the second punched a nice hole through the hull of a Japanese destroyer, starting a hot fire.

The Japanese turned the fire of their flotilla upon this one gunboat. The gunners in the armored turret of the 115-mm gun got off two more rounds, both of which missed, before Japanese shells severed all electrical power to the turret.

Later, as the destroyers steamed away, on their way to shell Aleksandrovsk on Sakhalin Island, then Nikolayevsk, at the mouth of the Amur River, the flag officer in charge of the flotilla pondered about that gun crew. Against overwhelming odds, they had fought back bravely. Conquering the Russians, he mused, might not be as easy as wardroom gossip predicted.

Captain Second Rank Pavel Saratov was the skipper of *Admiral Kolchak,* a Russian diesel/electric attack submarine cruising between the southernmost of the Kuril Islands and the Japanese island of Hokkaido. Normally, in accordance with navy doctrine, Saratov would be well out of sight of land while he ran on the surface charging his batteries, but to irritate the Japanese Moscow had ordered him to cruise for the last three days back and forth just outside the Japanese twelve-mile limit, often near the Japanese port of Nemuro.

The boat left its base at Petropavlosk, on the eastern coast of the

Kamchatka Peninsula, two weeks ago. Her first task had been to deliver two navy divers to a shipwreck blocking the channel into Okhotsk, a tiny port on the northern shore of the Sea of Okhotsk that had given the sea its name. Normally, maritime demolition jobs were assigned to the Border Security Forces, but for reasons known only to a bureaucrat buried in Moscow the navy got this one. Saratov couldn't find the wreck. He went ashore and was told by the port manager that the wreck he sought had blocked the channel for ten years, until last winter, when the badly rusted superstructure was destroyed by pack ice, which closed the port annually from December through May. There was nothing left to demolish.

An hour before dawn this rainy, misty morning, Saratov was on the bridge of his boat, the cockpit on top of the sail, or conning tower, pondering his fate. He had once commanded an *Alfa*-class nuclear-powered attack submarine, but the nuke boats were all laid up several years ago when Russia agreed to disable their reactors in return for foreign bank credits. Saratov had not complained – the reactors were sloppily built, old, and dangerous. They had never been properly maintained. Actually, he had been relieved that his days of absorbing unknown quantities of leaking radiation were over.

Many of his fellow submarine officers left the navy then, but Saratov had decided to stay. The entire nation was in economic meltdown; he had no civilian skills or job prospects. He opted to use his seniority to get command of a diesel-powered sub, one that could actually get under way. Not that there was much money for diesel fuel. Twice he had traded torpedo fuel for food and diesel fuel so he could take his boat to sea.

Four and a half years later, here he was, off the coast of Japan, still in command, still eating occasionally. His crew consisted of twenty officers and twenty-five warrants, or *michmen*. Only five of the crew were common enlisted. The Soviet navy's enlisted men had all been draftees, few of whom had the skills or desire to stay past the end of their required service. Those few willing to stay for a career had been promoted to *michmen*. After the collapse of communism the new Russian navy was forced to use the same system since there was no money to attract volunteers. The officers and *michmen* on board, and the five volunteer recruits, were 25 percent of the survivors of the Soviet far eastern submarine fleet. Three other conventional diesel/electric subs were similarly manned – just four boats in all.

It was enough to make a grown man cry.

Admiral Kolchak was a good old boat. She had once been known as *Vladimirskiy Komsomolets*, commemorating a municipal organization of Communist youth, but after the collapse of communism she was renamed – for an anti-Communist hero. She had her problems, of course, but they were repairable problems that came with age and use, not design defects. The crew always managed to get her back to the surface, where her diesel engines could usually be coaxed into life. And none of the sailors had come down with radiation sickness. Two years ago the Libyans almost bought her, then elected to take a boat from the Black Sea fleet instead. That had been a close call.

The communications officer interrupted Saratov's reverie with a radio dispatch from Moscow. It was highly classified and marked with the highest urgency classification, so it had been decoded immediately and brought to him.

He read the paper by the light of the red flashlight he carried. A Japanese attack on Vladivostok?

He went below and read the message again under the good light in the control room.

The message directed him to take his boat to Vladivostok and attack any Japanese ships he encountered. First priority, according to the message, were warships; second, troop transports. Presumably, the troops would be on deck waving Rising Sun flags, which would be visible in the periscope, so he wouldn't waste a torpedo on a ship laden with bags of cement or rubber monster toys.

The navigator was at his station in the control room. Saratov handed the message to him to read as he examined the chart on the navigator's table. The navigator started whispering excitedly with the officer of the deck.

Saratov was measuring distances when he heard the *michman* of the watch say in a normal tone of voice, 'P-3 radar signals.' This would be the fourth P-3 flyover in the last three days.

'Where?' Saratov asked sharply.

'Bearing one one five, estimated range fifteen.'

'Dive, dive, dive! Emergency dive!' Pavel Saratov shouted, and personally pushed the dive alarm.

The P-3 Orion was a large four-engine turboprop airplane with a crew of twelve. Made by Lockheed for the U.S. Navy and periodically updated as electronic technology evolved, P-3s were military versions of the old Electra airframe. They were a much bigger success as antisubmarine patrol planes than they ever were as airliners. The Japanese Self-Defense Force had operated them for decades.

The crew of the P-3 that found *Admiral Kolchak* knew that the submarine had been operating on the surface near the port of Nemuro. Tonight they had been overflying radar contacts and positively identifying them with their 100-million-candlepower searchlight.

Then one of the contacts ahead began to fade.

The radar operator sang out enthusiastically, 'Sinker, sinker, sinker. Thirteen miles, bearing three five zero relative.'

'Estimated course and speed?' That was the TACCO, the tactical coordinator, exasperated that the radar operator had to be asked.

'About zero nine zero magnetic, speed six knots. He's definitely a submarine, going down, down, down.'

The operator was brimming with excitement. *This* was war. After all those years of training, this was the real thing. Ahead was a Russian submarine, diving for the thermal layer; the crew of this airplane, which most certainly included the radar operator, was going to destroy it.

The TACCO, Koki Hirota, was working hard. The submarine had undoubtedly detected the P-3's radar, then dived for safety. Hokkaido was eight miles south; the sub had been cruising eastward on the surface. Once submerged, the submarine would probably turn to complicate the tactical problem. Which direction was it likely that the skipper would pick? Certainly not south, or a course that would take him back into the restricted waters of the strait. But then again . . .

No, no, no. No shortcuts tonight. Let's do it by the book, get this submarine. We'll start a general search, pull the net tighter and tighter, then kill him with a Mk-46 homing torpedo.

The pilot, Masataka Yonai, had finished restarting the number one and four engines. He had been cruising on just two engines as they conducted a general search. With all engines running, he put the plane into a gentle descent. He leveled at two hundred feet above the water and engaged the autopilot. Doctrine called for night searches to be carried out at five hundred feet, day searches at two hundred, but the magnetic anomaly detector, or MAD gear, was slightly more sensitive at the lower altitude. Yonai had his share of the samurai spirit: he wanted this submarine, so the book be damned – he would fly at two hundred feet.

Tension was high in the aircraft as the crew laid a general search pattern of sonobuoys. Some were set to listen above the thermal layer, which should be about 350 feet deep here, and others were set to listen below. It would take several minutes for the deep listeners to get their microphones down.

The northernmost shallow sonobuoy picked up faint screw noises. 'Contact, contact,' the operator sang out. Koki Hirota flipped switches so he, too, could listen. He concentrated very hard. Yes, he could just hear it: a sub.

Thank heavens this is a Russian boat, Koki Hirota thought. If it had been an American submarine – the quietest kind – one plane would have a poor chance of pinning it. In his ten years in patrol planes, Hirota had only found one American boat, and that time, he freely admitted, he had been very lucky. Russian or not, if this skipper down under us is any good, we'll need luck to get him, too.

Hirota ordered a four-thousand-yard barrier pattern to the north of the northernmost sonobuoy.

Yonai complied immediately. He had complete confidence in Hirota, whom he believed to be the best TACCO alive. Yonai now had the airplane thundering along at two hundred knots indicated airspeed, two hundred feet above the water.

He and his copilot concentrated fiercely on the flight instruments. There was no margin for error, not at two hundred feet. The P-3 was a big plane; they were flying it right against the surface of the sea.

The sonobuoys went out of the bay with split-second precision. Hirota selected the ones he wanted from among the sixty-four buoys in the bay and the order in which he wanted them dropped; then the computer spit them out. Forty of the buoys were the cheap LOFAR, or low-frequency, buoys. Eighteen were DIFAR, or directional, buoys used in tight search patterns. And six were the new doppler-ranging buoys that had been developed in secret by Japanese industry. Should the crew need them, more buoys were stowed in the plane and could be dropped manually by the ordnance technician.

The crew had good tools, which they knew how to use. They spent their professional lives practicing.

A murmur went through the plane each time a sonobuoy was dropped. The tension on a contact always racheted to violin-string tautness, which was why most of these men did this for a living. Hunting submarines was the ultimate team sport.

With the string down, the operators pressed their headphones against their ears and listened intently for the slightest stirring in the ocean below, the tiniest hint of screws pushing a man-made leviathan.

'I have it,' shrieked the number-one sensor operator. 'Third and fourth buoys. He's still above the layer.'

Koki Hirota flipped switches and listened intently. He closed his eyes, concentrating with all the power of his being.

The TACCO got just the subtlest of hints, the most exquisite nuance amid the cacophony of the noisy ocean. There was the noise of sea life, rhythmic surf sounds from Hokkaido, and the hum of at least ten ships. Amid all that noise, the submarine was there, definitely there. The sound seemed to be part screw noise, part deck-plate gurgle, maybe a hint of a loose bearing.

The submarine was fading now, perhaps slipping down below the thermal layer, trying to hide.

Hirota switched to the deeper buoys.

Yes, he was quite audible on this buoy.

Hirota checked another. Louder still. Hirota's fingers danced on the computer keys in front of him, and a blip appeared amid the search pattern on the screen.

The submarine skipper was turning, coming back to an easterly heading. Still, he was moving very slowly to minimize his noise signature, maybe three knots. Four at the most.

Should he drop a two-thousand-yard pattern, or a thousand-yard one?

Hirota had only a limited number of sonobuoys, so he couldn't afford to dither.

He was chewing a fingernail on his left hand as he flipped back and forth between the channels, listening alternately on different buoys. He checked the computer, which agreed with his assessment. There was the track, turning back to the east.

They had caught this Ivan in shallow water, and he was trying for deeper.

The TACCO lined the pilot up for another buoy run – keyed the computer for a tight string, a thousand yards between buoys, a bit north of east. He elected to put a DIFAR at each end of the string and a doppler buoy in the middle.

He wanted to wait, to drop the string after the sub steadied out on a new heading, but that was not going to be possible since the sub was fading from buoys already in the water.

Hirota thought the sub skipper's most probable new course would be about 090. The shortest route to deep water was in this direction. Still, Hirota was merely making an educated guess. Or perhaps he sensed the Russian captain's thoughts.

Masataka Yonai turned the P-3 using the autopilot heading selector. Level on the new heading, he corrected his altitude – the autopilot had lost twenty feet in the turn – and reengaged the thing. When he was a new aircraft commander he had insisted on flying all these patterns manually; he had stopped that nonsense only after Hirota convinced him the autopilot could do the job better than any human could.

'Be alert, men. We are tightening the net,' Yonai said over the intercom.

The tension was palpable.

Out went the sonobuoys, like the ticking of a clock.

The last two buoys in the string were still in the airplane when the operator screamed over the intercom, 'I've got him.'

Hirota checked. Yes. The computer was plotting. . . There! Heading 085, speed four knots.

'Yonai, do a slow two-hundred-seventy-degree turn to the left and roll out heading zero eight five degrees for a MAD run. I will direct your turn. We will fly right up his wake.'

Yonai twisted the autopilot heading selector as the flight engineer nudged the throttles forward a smidgen. The extra power would help hold airspeed in the turn. The airplane's altitude was down to 150 feet above the sea. Yonai disconnected the autopilot, concentrated fiercely on the instruments as he coaxed the airplane back to two hundred feet, still in the turn. When the plane rolled level out of the turn, he reengaged the autopilot.

Every man in the plane was concentrating intently on the displays before him. The men listening to the sonobuoys could hear the screws, urgent, insistent.

'He's turning again. We will have to drop a short pattern. Come right ninety degrees and stand by for another heading.'

Hirota stared at the computer display. He was trying to read the mind of the Russian submarine commander.

'He is turning back north,' Hirota declared. 'He knows we're onto him. He may climb back above the layer. Let's put this pattern a thousand yards apart. New heading three six zero, pilot; then I'll call a right turn.'

Silence on the intercom. Everyone was concentrating on doing his job to perfection. Yet even as the new sonobuoy pattern went into the water, the computer lost the track of the submarine. The sub was there, and then it wasn't.

Hirota listened intently on each channel, as did his enlisted specialists. Nothing. The sea was as quiet as the grave.

He must have stopped his engines, Hirota decided, or be moving very slowly, just maintaining steerage.

'He's probably very deep by now,' someone offered.

Hirota triggered an active ping by one of his middle sonobouys in the new pattern, then waited for the others to pick up the echo.

Even before he heard the echo, he heard the thrashing of the submarine's screws. It was a thunder, quite loud.

'He's going to full power,' the number one sensor operator said. 'And I think he's going deeper.'

Yes. Full power. In just a few minutes, the sub would be doing in excess of twenty knots. Maybe twenty-five. If that was a nuclear boat, the speed might be as high as forty-five knots. Hirota's one American sub two years ago had disappeared over the horizon at fifty-two knots.

The computer began a plot.

'I have him,' Hirota told the others, his voice tight with excitement. 'We will do a MAD run. Yonai, come right to zero four five.'

Yonai laid the plane into a forty-degree banking turn. Hirota could feel the increased g.

We are going to nail this sub!

'On around to zero nine zero degrees . . . steady . . . steady . . . We are closing, coming up his wake.'

The damned submarine was still accelerating, making over twenty knots now.

'MAD, MAD, MAD!' shouted the radar operator, who also ran the MAD gear. The needle pegged as the plane flew over the magnetic field of the submarine.

A short, fervent cheer on the ICS. These were disciplined men, but this was a life-or-death game. Yonai positively encouraged enthusiasm in his crew; in the past he had canned people who didn't demonstrate fighting spirit.

Now Yonai laid the big P-3 into another forty-degree-bank right turn. He needed to turn for 270 degrees and come across the submarine again from the beam. If the MAD operator sang out and the TACCO gave his okay, Yonai would drop a Mk-46 homing torpedo.

The torpedo would go out of the bomb bay. When it hit the water, it would turn right and begin a passive sonar search for its target, which, if the P-3 crew had done its work properly, should be within five hundred yards. Once the torpedo detected the sub, the torpedo's seeker would switch to active pinging and home on the submarine. In American movies, submarines outturned and outran torpedoes, but Yonai knew that was pure fiction: the pinging of a Mk-46 torpedo zeroing in was the last thing the submarine crew would ever hear.

Masataka Yonai had the plane over hard, turning tightly. 'Open bomb-bay doors,' he ordered.

'They will not open,' the copilot reported.

Yonai looked at the indicator.

Still closed. Damnation!

'Check the circuit breaker. Quick.'

This was intended for the flight engineer, because the armament panel circuit breakers were aft of him, beside his right elbow.

The autopilot, which had lost altitude in the turns earlier in the search, was doing it again. Just now the plane was passing a hundred feet above the water, descending gently, but no one noticed.

'Sir, the circuit breakers are all in.' All the flight engineer had to do to establish this was run his hand over the panel and ensure none was sticking out.

'Well, cycle it.' Yonai wanted the engineer to pull the bomb-bay breaker out, then push it in again.

'I can't find it,' the engineer confessed, his voice frantic.

Matasaka Yonai was beside himself. They were almost to weapons release, and then this! 'You idiot! It's on the armament panel.'

The copilot turned around, pointed the beam of a flashlight at the panel. 'Right there,' he said. 'It's right there.'

Yonai felt the plane slew as the right wingtip kissed the crest of a wave. He slammed down the autopilot disconnect button and twisted the yoke to the left as he pulled it toward him.

Too late! The right wing buried itself in the next swell.

The drag of the wingtip through the water yawed the nose right, hard, toward the sea. That dug the wingtip deeper into the water. The plane cartwheeled.

The uncontrollable yaw threw the ball in the turn-and-bank indicator as far left as it would go. Yonai felt the yaw and instinctively mashed in full left rudder as his eyes shot to the turn-and-bank indicator. It was the last thing he would ever do.

The cockpit struck the water first. All three of the cockpit crewmen died instantly.

The men in back were flung forward, then crushed as equipment and seats broke free and smashed forward. Then the left wing hit the sea and the fuselage of the airplane came apart.

The splash was stupendous, and almost a minute passed before the roiling waters became calm.

The remains of the P-3 and the men who flew it began the long descent to the seafloor.

In the control room of *Admiral Kolchak*, Captain Pavel Saratov heard the splash. He was wearing headphones so that he could also listen to the sonar as the sonarman called out bearings to sonobuoy splashes. The navigator was plotting the bearings based on range estimates supplied by the captain. Saratov decided where to take his boat based on the picture developing on the chart before him. The chart was crude, the method long abandoned in better-equipped navies, but this was all Saratov had.

The huge splash surprised him, baffled him. It was far too large to be a sonobuoy or torpedo. He closed his eyes and listened intently as rivulets of perspiration coursed down his face and dripped off his chin.

The sonarman spoke first. 'The engine noise is gone.'

He was correct. The background vibration from the four aircraft propellers was no longer audible.

Saratov could hear something grinding. Perhaps the fuselage being crushed?

Could it be? No engine noise, a gigantic splash? Were they miraculously delivered?

Pavel Saratov opened his eyes. Every eye in the control room was on him.

'He crashed,' the captain said.

His listeners couldn't take it in.

'He crashed,' Saratov repeated. 'He hit the water.'

Cheers. Screams. They laughed so hard that tears ran down their cheeks.

Ah, life was sweet.

Jack Innes stood in the doorway of the Oval Office and watched President Hood finish with a group of Eagle Scouts. The photographers snapped away; the president shook hands, smiled, pretended he didn't see Innes. One of his skills was the ability to concentrate totally on the people in front of him, make them feel that during their moment they were his sole concern.

The aide ushered the Scouts and their leader from the office right on the tick of the clock. They had had their five minutes.

As the president seated himself behind his desk, Innes said, 'Japanese forces are invading Siberia. They began around midnight there, which is about an hour ago. The news just came in.'

'I wondered how long Abe would wait.'

'The Russians arrested the leader of the Siberian independence movement eighteen hours ago. Abe went on television at midnight. The native people of Siberia have suffered enough from Russian oppression, he said. The Japanese, their blood brothers, are taking up the standard of their kinsmen.'

Innes continued, telling Hood everything he knew. The president swiveled his chair, looked out the window while he listened. He swiveled back around, glanced at his schedule. When Innes finished, he asked a few questions.

'Okay,' Hood said. 'You know the drill. Get the National Security Council over here, the majority and minority leaders of both houses, all the usual suspects. We'll see what the consensus is.'

'Yes, sir.'

'They'll dither and wring their hands and advise doing nothing.'

'Surely they'll condemn Japanese aggression?'

'Words. Just words. You watch. They won't want to actually *do* anything.'

'You are going to try to make them take action, aren't you?'

'Sooner or later, Jack, we are going to have to screw up the courage to start doing the right thing.'

'The difficulty is knowing what the right thing is.'

'No, sir. It is not. Overeducated quacks and New Age gurus can never see the right thing, but to people with a modicum of common sense the right thing is usually obvious. What everyone wants to avoid is the *cost* of doing the right thing. Take Bosnia, for example, in the early nineties: the Serbs began murdering Muslims, committing genocide, killing every person who might exert an erg of leadership in the new Serbian utopia. They wanted to make the Muslims a slave people. This was a conscious choice, a policy choice of the Serb leadership *because they thought they could get away with it.* For three years, they did. For three years the American leaders wrung their hands, dithered, refused to use force against the Serbs. Genocide! Mass murder! Adolf Hitler's final solution one more time. We condoned it by refusing to lead the effort to stop it, by refusing to pay the price.'

'Bosnia might become another Vietnam, the liberals said.'

Hood took a deep breath, sighed deeply. 'When you refuse to lift a hand to stop evil, you become a part of it. That's as true today as it was two thousand years ago. You watch, Jack. Tonight these people will argue about the dangers – the cost – of standing up to Japan. They will argue that Russia is a corrupt, misruled den of thieves with no one to blame but themselves for the fix they are in. The newspapers lately have been full of it. They will argue that we can't afford to get involved in someone else's fight. They will argue that this mess isn't our problem, that the United States is not the world's policeman. They will refuse to confront evil. Just watch.'

'People don't believe in evil anymore,' Innes reflected. 'It's obsolete.'

'Oh no,' the president said with conviction. 'Evil is alive and well in our time. The problem is that too many people have made their peace with it.'

The first real resistance to the Japanese occupation of Vladivostok came from squad- and platoon-sized groups of young troops led by junior officers. Without orders or coordination, they blocked streets and started shooting. These pockets of resistance were easily surrounded and wiped out. Still, Japanese troops attempting to link up and form a front across the peninsula were delayed. They called for tanks and armored cars to help mop up points of resistance. All of this cost time.

Two hours after dawn, several thousand Russian infantry were actively engaged. The belch of machine guns and the pop of grenades was widespread in the northern parts of the city. Smoke from burning buildings and cars wafted over the city and the bay.

There was no resistance on Russian Island and in the area of the city around Golden Horn Bay because there were no Russian troops there. The police, outnumbered and grossly outgunned, surrendered without a shot. The unarmed civilian population had no choice; they merely watched and tried to stay out of the way.

By 7:00 A.M., a squadron of Zero fighters was on the ground at Vladivostok airport, being refueled and rearmed with missiles and ammunition helicoptered in from a supply ship anchored a half mile out. A dozen helicopter gunships came ashore from another ship, and soon they were attacking Russian positions in the northern areas of the city.

Rain continued to mist down.

The sky was a clean, washed-out blue, with patches of long, thin, streaky clouds down below. On the horizon, the distant Rocky Mountains were blue and purple.

Against this background, Bob Cassidy was looking hard for airplanes. There were two smart-skinned F-22s out there, he knew, and they were joining on him. The damn things are like chameleons, he told himself, marveling that he couldn't see planes less than a mile away.

'Two, do you see me?'

'Got you, Hoppy Leader. I'm at your three o'clock, level. I'm heading three zero five degrees.'

'Lead's three one zero degrees, looking.'

He was looking in vain. The sky appeared empty.

'Three's at your nine o'clock, Hoppy. Level, joining heading three one five.'

Cassidy glanced left, caught something out of the corner of his eye. When he tried to focus on it, it wasn't there. He glanced at his tactical display in the center of his instrument panel. Yep, a wingman on each side, closing the distance, joining up.

He saw the man up-sun at about three hundred yards. He first appeared as a dark place in the sky, then gradually took the shape of an aircraft. He didn't see the down-sun man until he was about two hundred yards away. He was there, then he wasn't, and then he was, almost shimmering.

'This chameleon gear is flat terrific,' he told his wingmen over the scrambled radio channel.

The three fighters entered the break at Nellis Air Force Base in Las Vegas, Nevada, and landed in order, one, two, three. The chameleon gear was off, of course.

They taxied to the ramp and shut down.

The hot, dry summer wind was like a caress on Cassidy's damp head when he removed his helmet. He waited until the ground crew got the ladder in place, then unstrapped and climbed slowly down.

He took a deep breath, removed his flight glove from his right hand. With his bare skin, he touched the skin of the airplane. It felt cool, smooth, hard.

An officer in blues came walking over. He saluted. 'Colonel, we had a call for you from Washington, a Colonel Eatherly. Japan has attacked Vladivostok. They want you back in Washington immediately. They are sending a plane to pick you up. And he wants you to call as soon as possible.'

'Thanks.'

So it was really true. The shooting has started.

Bob Cassidy walked slowly around the F-22, inspecting it with unseeing eyes while he thought of the Japanese officers he knew and the Americans in Japan. He found himself standing in front of the wing root, staring at the little door that hid the mouth of the 20-mm Gatling gun.

He turned and walked quickly toward the maintenance shops. They would have a telephone he could use.

The late-evening meeting at the White House went about as the president expected. The evening had been long, filled with depressing news. The Japanese were overrunning the Russian Far East.

National Security Council staffers used maps and computer presentations to brief the group. When they finished, the mood was gloomy.

The consensus of the group was voiced by the Speaker of the House:

'America must stay neutral: this is not our fight. We must do what we can as a neutral to stop the bloodshed.'

The president didn't say anything. Jack Innes argued the president's position in an impassioned plea.

'This *is* our fight. Every American will be affected by today's events. Every

American has a stake in world peace. Every minute we delay merely increases the cost of the final reckoning. This is our moment. We must seize the initiative now, while we are able.'

Alas, his audience refused to listen.

On the way out of the meeting, the Senate leadership paused for a quiet conversation with the president.

'Mr President, we hear that you are putting very severe pressure on the United Nations to censure Japan, to pass some binding security resolutions.'

'We are talking with other nations at the UN, certainly,' the president said suavely.

The Senate majority leader spoke carefully. 'In my opinion, sir, it would be a major foreign policy mistake to maneuver the UN into the position of advocating the use of armed forces against Japan. My sense of the mood of the Senate is that my colleagues will not support such a policy. You might find yourself dangling from a very thin limb, sir, with no visible means of support. That would be embarrassing, to say the least.'

'Most embarrassing,' the president agreed. There was no smile on his face when he said it.

8

'Any gas, Jack?'

Bob Cassidy had driven from Washington, D.C. He poured himself a cup of coffee and was standing at the cash register in a gas station/convenience store on the outskirts of Baltimore. He could hear the distinctive sounds of a ballpark announcer coming from a radio, apparently one behind the counter.

'Are you Aaron Hudek?'

The man behind the counter looked him over before he nodded affirmatively. The announcer at the ballpark was getting excited. Hudek reached down and turned up the volume slightly. A home run.

Hudek was in his late twenties. His jeans were faded and his blue service shirt had a patch over the breast pocket that bore the name Bud. He was about six feet tall, maybe 180 pounds, with a well-developed upper body. An old blue Air Force belt held up his jeans.

'Your mom said you were working here.'

'Why don't you pay your bill and let the man behind you pay his?'

'Pump three, and coffee.' Cassidy forked over money. 'My name's Cassidy. I need to talk to you.'

'What about?'

'A job.'

'I got one.' Hudek looked at the man behind Cassidy, who held up a quart of oil.

After Hudek pounded the register keys and finished counting the change, Cassidy added, 'It's a flying job.'

Hudek's eyes flicked over Cassidy again. 'I get off in about ten minutes, when the girl working the next shift comes in. We can talk then.'

'Okay.'

It was closer to twenty minutes, but a tree beside the pavement threw some shade on a concrete bench. Cassidy was there when Hudek came walking over. He didn't sit.

'How'd you get my name?'

'From the Air Force files.'

'So you're government?'

'Colonel Bob Cassidy, at least for a few more days.'

'What's the job?' Hudek asked matter-of-factly. He showed no interest in sitting. He didn't seem nervous or in a hurry. He just stood with his arms crossed, looking at Cassidy.

'Have you heard that Japan invaded Siberia?'

'It's been on the radio for a couple days.'

'I'm looking for people with F-22 experience.' Cassidy went on explaining while he watched Hudek's expression. He might as well have been talking in Hindi for all the impression he made. Hudek's expression didn't change an iota. Looking at him one would find it hard to believe he was an honors graduate in electrical engineering from MIT. One of the '10 percenters,' as Cassidy called them. The military flight programs had been so competitive the last twenty years, a person had to be in the top 10 percent of his class at every stage of his life – high school, college, and flight training – if he expected to fly the hot jets. Hudek was brilliant, a superb student, athletic, in perfect health, and he could fly the planes. Yet somewhere, somehow, it had all gone wrong for him.

When Cassidy stopped speaking, Hudek turned his head, checking the vehicles going into and out of the service area, then turned back. 'Russia, huh?'

'Yeah.'

'Well, it's amazing.'

'What is?'

'That you're here. Didn't you read my last evaluation? My last skipper thought I was a stupid son of a bitch, and he said so in just about those words.'

'I read it. I don't give a damn about paperwork or saluting or parking-lot etiquette.'

'You *did* read it.'

'I need fighter pilots.'

'Well, I really ain't interested. All that is behind me now. I haven't flown in three months. Don't miss it. Don't miss the pissy little Caesars in their cute blue uniforms, either.'

'This isn't the peacetime Air Force. This is war, the real thing. I guarantee you, there will be no strutting martinets, no shoe polish, no bullshit.'

'I've heard that song before,' Hudek said with a sneer. 'Now I'm supposed to raise my right hand, then sign on the dotted line. What if you just happen to be wrong? What if your little operation is more of the same fucked-up fire drill I just got out of? Then I'm already in and it's my tough luck, huh?'

'I'll be right there with you. If I'm wrong, we'll be in it together.'

'You're going to be there?' Hudek was incredulous.

'Yep. Are you?'

Hudek put his hands in his pockets and flexed his shoulders. 'Don't believe so,' he drawled finally. 'Even if it's what you say, I've got some other things going. I've done the military thing and it's time to move on, go on down the road. There's this girl . . . She sorta likes me, wants me to settle down, have a kid. Got a deposit down on a little tract house going up in a subdivision near here. Ain't much, but it'll be all mine.'

'Uh-huh.'

'I'm tired of dicking with paper-pushers, tired of always doing what some fathead who happens to be senior to me thinks we oughta do . . . tired of trying to *look good*!'

Cassidy got up and dusted his trousers. Then he passed Hudek his card, on which he had written the telephone number of his hotel in Crystal City. 'Call me. Let me know what you decide.'

'I'm doing that very thing right this minute, Colonel. I'm letting you know. I have definitely decided. Absolutely decided. I don't want to go to a fucking Siberian icebox.'

'Call me.'

'I am *not* going to call you. Listen! *I don't want to go.* I don't even like their food!'

'Tonight. Late. I have another guy to call on. Maybe you know him – Lee Foy?'

'Damnation, can't you hear me? Ain't my mouth working right? I ain't calling you tonight or any other time. I'm telling you right here and now – *I'm not going to Russia.* I don't do Third World shitholes. And I never heard of Foy.'

'He said he knows you. Said he met you a couple years back during the F-22 op eval. Said you were a real good stick but you had a shitty personality. Said you'd give me a ration of crap.'

'Oh! Foy Sauce, the California Chink. Yeah, I know that lying little slant-eyed bastard. Is he going?'

'Maybe.'

'Jesus, taking Foy Sauce – you clowns must be scraping the bottom of the barrel. They're going to shoot all you people down. You'll all be dead in a week.'

'Call me tonight.'

'Where is Foy these days, anyway?'

Cassidy didn't reply. He unlocked his car and got behind the wheel.

Hudek stood watching Cassidy as he piloted the rental car slowly toward the street. He was still standing there when Cassidy went through the light at the corner and glanced back, just before he turned left.

Lee Foy was living in McLean, Virginia. He was an up-and-coming real estate agent. 'I'm making a ton of money,' he told Cassidy. 'I don't speak a solitary word of Chinese, but the company assigns me to every Hong Kong businessman or Chinese official coming to the Washington–Baltimore area.

I always make the sale. Being a hyphenated American has its advantages. I'm getting rich.'

'I've always wondered what a number two in a Stanford graduating class did with his life.'

Lee Foy beamed. 'Couldn't happen to a nicer guy, believe me.'

'Number one in your flight school class, number two in your class at test pilot school. That right?'

'All that is behind me. I'm making serious money now.'

'Uh-huh. Well, I talked to Hudek. You were right about him. He's a jerk of the first water.'

'Good stick, though. Funny thing, but I never met a saint flying a fighter plane.'

'So, are you going to give up all this good living and easy money and come fly for the Russians?'

'Hell no. I told you that yesterday.'

'That was your wallet talking. The shooting has started. Now I appeal to your patriotism, your manhood, your sense of duty.'

'My wallet covers all those things. I'm making good money and I like it a lot.'

'It'll still be here when you get back.'

'When I get back, some other Charlie Chan will be sopping up the gravy, Colonel. The world doesn't stand still for anyone. And we both know that my chances of coming back aren't red-hot.'

'The chances aren't bad, or I wouldn't be going.'

'Don't shit me, Colonel. If you make it, you'll come back a brigadier. *General* Cassidy. You'll retire on a general's pension. You'll spend the rest of your days lying around some 0-club sucking suds, fat and sassy, schmoozing about the good ol' days with old farts in yellow golf slacks and knit shirts decorated with ponies and alligators while you wait for the next retirement check to show up in the mail. Me, if I live through this little adventure, I'll come back a year or two older and a whole lot poorer, with a bout or two of dysentery and a couple cases of clap on my medical record. I'll have to rent apartments to crack addicts to make a buck. Thanks, but no thanks. I'll stay right here in the good ol' US of A and keep the good times rolling.'

'How did you ever become a fighter pilot, Foy, a cynical, moneygrubbing bastard like you? You're a damned civilian.'

'I could make that plane dance, Cassidy. Ask Hudek. But that wasn't a living. Selling real estate to the "Ah so" crowd is a living. Making the sale is my thing.' He pointed downward. 'See these shoes? Damn things are alligator. Cost five hundred bucks a pair on sale for thirty percent off.'

'What's your point?'

'I'm tired of being poor, man. My wall is covered with diplomas I can't spend. I've seen the money and I want some.'

'The Russian government will pay five thousand for every Japanese plane you bag.'

'Five thousand what? Bongo bucks? Yuan, yen, pesos, rubles? Man, that stuff is toilet paper.'

'U.S. dollars.'

'That'll be easy to earn. I'll go up every morning and knock down two bad guys before breakfast. Seriously, Colonel, I make that much selling a condo and I don't have to risk anything to get it. I don't have to bleed, either.'

'Hudek told me not to take you to Siberia. Said you'd be dead in a week. He called you Foy Sauce. Said you can't fly for shit.'

'Fuck Fur Ball. And tell him I said so.' Hudek's nickname was fighter pilot jargon for a dogfight, so named because a computer presentation of two or more three-dimensional flight paths resembled something from a cat's tummy.

Cassidy shrugged.

'Hudek and I weren't butt-hole buddies, but he knew damn well I could fly that plane.'

Cassidy fingered his card. He had written the telephone numbers on it in ink.

'You look at my evals, Colonel. My skippers knew what I could do.'

Cassidy tucked his card in Foy's shirt pocket and turned away.

'You see Fur Ball again,' Foy called, 'you tell him I'll kick his ass on the ground or in the sky. His choice.'

Cassidy rented a car at the airport in Cheyenne and drove. He went through two thunderstorms and passed close to another. By the time he reached Thermopolis he estimated that he had seen four hundred antelope.

He got directions at the biggest filling station in town. 'Which way to Cottonwood Creek?'

The house was at the end of a half mile of dirt road. It had a roof, four walls, and all the windows had glass, but it didn't look like it would be very comfy during a Wyoming winter, when the cold reached twenty below and the snow blew in horizontal sheets. The thought of a Wyoming winter reminded Cassidy of Siberian winters, and he shivered.

A man in bib overhauls came out of the dilapidated little barn next to the house.

'You Paul Scheer?'

'Yeah.'

'Bob Cassidy.'

Scheer came strolling over. 'Somebody called from Washington, said you were coming, but I told them you were wasting your time. Did they give you that message?'

'I got it.'

'Well, it's your time. I got a couple beers in the fridge.'

'Okay.'

There was a redbone hound on the porch. Only his tail moved, a couple of thumps, then it lay still. 'He came with the ranch,' Scheer said, nodding at the dog. Cassidy lowered himself into one of the two porch chairs while Scheer went inside for the beer.

The wind was blowing about ten or twelve knots from the northwest, a mere zephyr. The brush and grass near the house were low, sort of hunkered down, not like the flowers and lush bushes in Japan and Washington, where the winters were milder and the summers twice as long. Cassidy took a deep breath – he could smell the land.

When he and Scheer were drinking beer from cans, Cassidy asked, 'How much ranch you got here?'

'About thirty thousand acres. Fifty-five hundred acres are deeded; the rest is a BLM grazing lease.'

'How many cows?'

'Three hundred and thirty cow–calf units.'

'Sounds military as hell.'

'Doesn't it?'

'As I understand it, Paul, you left the Air Force in 1995 after ten years of active duty, worked for Lockheed-Martin as a test pilot in the F-22 program until last year, then quit and moved to this ranch out here in the middle of Wyoming.'

'That's accurate.'

'If you don't mind my asking, what's a place like this worth?'

Scheer grinned, displaying perfect teeth. The thought crossed Cassidy's mind that some women would consider Scheer handsome.

'What it's worth and what I paid for it are two completely different things. I paid two million. Now, your next question is, "Where did ol' Scheer get two million dollars." The answer is, "Out of my four oh one (k) plan." I'm single, live modestly, don't have any expensive vices. The stock market has been doing fine the last fifteen years, and I have, too. Saw an ad for this ranch one day, got to thinking about it. You know, as I was looking at that ad, it came to me that the time had come. The time had come to cash out and do something stupid. Haven't regretted it one minute since.'

'Have you heard about Siberia?'

'You mean lately? Don't get the paper here and I don't own a TV.'

'Japan invaded Siberia.'

Scheer took a long pull on his beer and crushed the can. 'It's a crazy world,' he said finally.

'Yeah. I'm recruiting fighter pilots. We're giving an F-22 squadron to the Russians, and they are hiring qualified pilots. You were highly recommended.'

'By whom?'

'The head test pilot at Lockheed-Martin.'

Scheer shrugged. 'I miss the flying. The F-22 is a great machine, really great. But . . .' Scheer took a deep breath and sighed. 'This is where I'm going to spend the rest of my life.'

Cassidy looked at his watch. 'I got a few hours. How about a tour.'

'Okay. Let's take the Jeep.'

The road was a washed-out rut with huge mud holes that almost swallowed the Jeep. 'Got to do something about the road,' Scheer muttered.

'What was last winter like?'

'Cold and long.'

Cassidy asked questions to keep him talking, about raising cattle, the weather, the range. Finally, he asked, 'Do you really think this is the place for you?'

Scheer took his time before he replied. 'I'm only the third white man to own this land. Last owner was from Florida, a real estate broker whose wife divorced him after the kids were grown and out of college. He lasted four years. He bought the place from the original homesteader, who was nearly ninety when he sold. He's in a nursing home in Cheyenne now.'

Scheer pointed to some of his cattle, then indicated his boundaries with a pointed finger or a nodded head. After a bit, he remarked, 'Hard to believe, isn't it, that the original white settler is still alive? The country is young.'

Finally Scheer brought the Jeep to a stop on a low ridge. He pointed through the windshield. 'See that low peak? Way out there? My line cabin is just under that peak. It's twenty-five miles from the house to that line cabin.'

'This ranch isn't *that* big!'

'But it is. Most of it lies along this creek, and up there is the head of it. The ranch is the watered grazing land. Everything else belongs to the government. Pretty, isn't it?'

'You could come back to this, after the war.'

'Let's not kid ourselves, Mr. Cassidy. A lot of the guys you recruit are going to get killed.'

Cassidy didn't say anything.

'I'm going to do my living and dying right here, waking up every morning to this.'

'Why don't you level with me?' Cassidy asked. 'You didn't have a wife of twenty years divorce you. You didn't get fired from your job; you aren't hiding from the law. You aren't a hermit, an alcoholic, or a dope addict. Why are you rusticating out here in cow-patty heaven, smack in the middle of goddamn nowhere?'

Scheer looked at Cassidy. He turned off the engine and climbed out. 'You're the first one who asked,' he said. 'Oh, they asked, but not like that.'

Cassidy got out, too, and stretched.

'I'm HIV-positive,' Scheer said. 'Anally injected death serum. Had it for years. Lived longer than I thought I would.'

'So?'

'It's a death sentence.'

'Man, life is a death sentence.'

'We all go sooner or later. I'm one of the sooners.'

'Your "the time has come" speech – that's for the local yokels, right?'

'You're a real smoothy, aren't you, Cassidy?'

'Come to Russia with me. It'll be a hell of a fight. You live through that, you can come back here to wait for the Grim Reaper, watch the cows chew their cuds, listen to the wind, think the big thoughts when the temp drops to twenty below.'

'You're a colonel, right?'

'Right.'

'I didn't get AIDS by licking toilet seats, Colonel.'

'Did you get in any trouble in the Air Force? Or at Lockheed?'

'No.'

'You must have kept your love life and your professional life separate. Keep doing that.'

'So you'd take me to Russia?'

'Of course.'

'You're the first blue suiter I ever told about my sexual orientation.'

'I wouldn't tell any more of 'em, if I were you.'

'But you still want me?'

'You're healthy, right?'

'No symptoms.'

'I don't think we'll do physicals. My branch of the Russian air force won't be very picky. We'll need to fit you for a full-body G suit if they don't still have the one you wore at Lockheed. We will do all the shots. Don't want anyone getting diphtheria or cholera or some other weird disease.'

'I already got my disease.'

'Take me back to my car.'

They got into the Jeep and Scheer started up.

'Here's a card with my telephone number. You know the airplane inside out, and you can teach it. I need you, Scheer, or I wouldn't have made this trip. Think it over and call me.'

They rode the rest of the way back in silence. Scheer didn't drive any faster than he had coming out, but he didn't bother to slow for the mud holes and fords. Cassidy hung on with both hands.

When they pulled into the yard by the house, Scheer killed the engine and said, 'I'll come. Take me a few days or so to find someone to keep an eye on the cattle while I'm gone.'

'Okay.'

'Lockheed oughta still have my G suit. My weight hasn't changed, so it should still fit.'

'I'll call them.'

'I'm assuming that you'll keep this conversation to yourself,' Paul Scheer said.

'I'm making a similar assumption about you,' Cassidy replied, and stuck out his hand to shake.

'What's the Russian air force pay, anyway?'

'I don't know exactly. Washington is still working out the details.'

'I hope the money covers the cost of hiring a hand to look after this place.'

'Well, it will if you get a Zero or two. Probably pay a bonus for every one you knock down.'

'Whose idea was that?'

'Not mine, rest assured. Some Russian experts in the State Department suggested a bonus for every confirmed victory. They say that will impress the Russians with our seriousness.'

'Seriousness.'

'Seriousness is very big in Russia. They didn't just adopt capitalism, they swallowed it.'

Bob Cassidy got into the rental car, headed for the hard road. A mule deer leapt from the brush onto the road in front of him. He checked that his seat belt was fastened.

Cassidy waited in the break area outside the building. The sun felt hot on his arms and face; the breeze coming in off the Pacific felt soothing. He leaned his head back against the wall and closed his eyes. If only he could forget the problems for a little while and just relax, enjoy the heat and the breeze.

'Are you Colonel Cassidy?'

He started to stand, but she motioned for him to stay seated.

The woman before him was of medium height, with short brown hair that framed her face. She cocked her head as she looked at him, and her eyebrows arched slightly.

The thought occurred to him that she was lovely, in a way.

'You're Daphne Elitch?'

'Please! Dixie. Even my mother calls me Dixie.'

'Have a seat, Dixie. Pleased to meet you.'

'So what brings you to Orange County, Colonel?'

'Recruiting.' Cassidy launched into his spiel.

Dixie Elitch listened politely, saying nothing. The breeze played with her hair. Cassidy watched her eyes, which were dark brown and restless. They scanned the other students in the break area, the sky, the grass, and the colonel. Those intelligent eyes didn't stop moving.

Dixie had been a middle-distance runner at the Air Force Academy and had almost made the U.S. Olympic team. She got her degree in astronautical engineering, number two in the class, and turned down an assignment to Cal Tech, where she would have gotten her doctorate. She went to flight school instead, finished first in her class, got F-22s – even though the program was closed at the time – because the commanding general called the chief of staff.

When Cassidy finished, she didn't say anything. After a bit, Cassidy asked if she had questions.

'No. I'm just trying to visualize how it will be. The F-22 is a good plane, but obtaining spare parts, weapons, and fuel will be a horrific nightmare. Everything will be a problem – intel, early warning, basing, everything. What will you do for hard stands? If the enemy catches you on the ground, they'll wipe you out unless the planes are in revetments.'

'We're working on that.'

Dixie examined his face with those restless eyes. 'You aren't going to discuss it because you don't know the answer, I haven't signed on, or you don't want me to bother my pretty little head with men's problems? Which is it?'

'I don't know the answers.'

'You're leading with your chin. What is it you want me to volunteer for?'

'I want you to fly with us.'

'You can't even assure me you're going to fly.'

'I'll solve the problems or live with them, as they arise. That's all I can do.'

'I'm out of the "yessir" crap now,' she said. 'I've got two more weeks of class; then I'm going to be a stockbroker.'

'I see.'

'Cold-call people, explain why they should let me show them the best investments.'

'Uh-huh.'

'How they can get rich in the stock market.'

'Sounds exciting.'

'Why they should pay commissions to my company.'

'Uh-huh.'

'Even though I have no money myself and couldn't take my own advice, even if I were foolish enough to want to.' She laughed, a pleasant, full-throated woman's laugh.

Bob Cassidy felt warm all over. He bit his lip. He wasn't supposed to feel like *that*. This is a professional relationship, he told himself stiffly, and looked away from Dixie Elitch.

'The market is in freefall this afternoon. The Dow industrial average is down to eighteen thousand five hundred, off eighteen percent from its high last week.'

'Sounds like a hell of a time to start selling stocks.'

'Oh, the market will come back. Sooner or later. It always does.'

'So you're not worried?'

'Colonel, we've just been presented with one of the greatest buying opportunities of our age, courtesy of the Japanese government. They will make a lot of people very rich. I hope to be one of them.'

'I see.'

Dixie shivered. 'I'll be glued to a chair in this suburban utopia, wearing my little designer telephone headset, sweet-talking Orange County pluto-crats into buying nursing home stock. Meanwhile, you and your friends will be shooting down those poor innocent Japanese boys in their shiny new airplanes, blowing them out of the sky.'

'Something like that,' Cassidy allowed. He passed her a card with his telephone numbers.

Dixie pressed on the sides of her head. 'Why did I ever think I could do this? I couldn't sell cold beer to a man on his way to hell. I should have my head examined at the funny farm.' She rubbed her face, then glanced at her watch.

'Win the war for us, Colonel. Speaking for myself, I will enjoy the money.'

She stood and held out her hand to shake.

'We could use you in one of those cockpits,' Cassidy said.

'I have committments here.'

'You're not a stockbroker. You're a fighter pilot.'

'Used to be,' Dixie Elitch acknowledged, then joined the other students returning to the classroom.

'Siberia!' Clay Lacy pronounced the word as if it were a benediction. He took a deep breath and said it again.

Bob Cassidy couldn't suppress a smile.

They were sitting in the student union at Cal Tech, where Lacy was working on a masters in electrical engineering. With his military haircut, trim physique, and neat, clean clothing, he looked out of place among the longhaired, sloppily dressed techno-nerds, or so Cassidy thought. But to each his own. Isn't that the mantra of our time?

'Russia.'

'I suppose you've been reading the news, watching the mess on TV?' Cassidy said conversationally. CNN was devoting half of each day to the invasion and half to the falling stock market, which was down to 17,800 now. Just now scenes from Vladivostok were showing on the television at the other end of the room, although the commentary was inaudible. There, a map, showing the Japanese thrusts. Two students were watching. The rest were eating, reading textbooks, holding hands, talking to one another. One was playing a portable video game.

'Oh, a little,' Clay Lacy replied, glancing at the television. 'But I'm so busy. If the world were coming to an end, I wouldn't have time to do more than glance at the headlines.'

'This story is not quite that important,' Cassidy acknowledged. 'Still, we could use you in Russia. You could go back to school when it's over, maybe in a year or so. Do some flying, pocket some change, help out Uncle Sam.'

'It didn't look like we were ever going to have a war,' Clay Lacy explained. 'At least during my career. That's why I got out. That "Peace is our profession" BS is a real crock.'

Cassidy finished his coffee.

'You aren't CIA, by chance?' Lacy asked.

'Just plain old U.S. Air Force.'

'You wouldn't say if you were CIA, would you? You'd say you were in the Air Force.'

'You'll have to trust me, Lacy.'

'No offense, sir.'

'Ask me no secrets and I'll tell you no lies.'

Cassidy's mood was growing more foul by the second. Lacy was a flake. Perhaps he would be better off without him.

After a bit Lacy said, 'The F-22 is one hell of an airplane,' almost talking to himself.

'So is the new Zero, they tell me,' Cassidy muttered.

'If a man missed this fight, he might regret it all his life.'

'I doubt that,' Cassidy snapped. Jiro Kimura flashed into his mind. He bit his lip.

'All his life, he might wonder,' Lacy insisted.

'It won't be easy,' Bob Cassidy remarked, more than a little unhappy with the way this conversation was going.

Lacy looked intense. Too intense. Now Cassidy was almost certain the man was a nut.

'Flying was almost a religion with me,' Lacy said after a moment. 'With me and my friends. We all thought that way. Didn't think I would ever leave it, but . . .' He shrugged. 'That's the way things go. I got tired of the peacetime routine. Got tired of the annual budget slashing in Congress. Tired of the eternal cutbacks and resizing and reductions in force. It's a conspiracy, slashing the defense budget so far that America can't defend itself. It's a conspiracy by foreigners, to throw open our borders. They've always been against everything American.'

Cassidy said nothing.

Lacy went on, 'Of course, I've never been in combat. Can't honestly say how I'll handle it, because I don't know. I *think* everything will be fine. I won't pee my pants. I won't forget to retract the gear or arm the gun. I will manage to do what they trained me to do.'

'Hmm,' Cassidy said.

'I always thought I could kill someone if I really had to. If there were no choice. Then I could do what I had to do. But to go to Siberia to strap on a plane to fight Japanese pilots ... well, the whole thing is slightly unreal. Sitting here, I can feel the doubt. It's tangible. I don't know if I could kill anyone, Colonel.'

'Well, if you have tangible doubts, Clay, you –'

'I think I could, you understand, but I don't know for a fact.'

'Uh-huh.'

'No one could know, until it happened to them.'

'Not everyone is cut out for –'

Lacy mused, 'Maybe that's why I'm here, instead of still in uniform.' He frowned.

Now he looked at Cassidy with a start, as if suddenly realizing he was talking to a colonel. 'I probably shouldn't be saying these things,' he added hastily.

'It's a complicated world we –'

'I'll think about it, sir. Let you know. Do you have a telephone number?'

Cassidy thought for several seconds before he gave the man a card. 'Don't do anything rash,' he told Lacy.

'At night, I miss the flying the worst. I can close my eyes and feel myself blasting through space.'

'Think about it carefully.'

'Maybe I –'

'Kill or be killed. The Japs are pretty damn good, Lacy. The Zero drivers will punch the missiles off the rails and they'll be coming hard. If you don't handle it right you're gonna be toast. Even if you handle it right, you may get zapped.'

'I –'

'You tell me you want to go, Lacy, you better be sure. I don't want your blood on my hands. I'm toting enough of a load through life as it is.'

'I'll think it over and call you, sir,' Clay Lacy promised.

When Lacy had gone to class, Cassidy put a check mark beside his name on the list. Okay, he's a nutcase, but if he can fly the plane and pull the trigger, he'll do.

9

'Svechin has been into the torpedo juice again.'

'Anybody else?'

'Three or four of them have been sipping it, Captain. They do it because Svechin eggs them on.'

Pavel Saratov eyed the chief of the boat, a senior warrant, or *starshi michman,* who averted his gaze.

'They haven't been paid in five months, sir.'

'I know that.'

'They ask why we are here.'

'There is a war. We defend Mother Russia.'

'Ha! There is no money. There is no food. There is no clothing. The electricity is off half the time. There is no medicine, no vodka, no tobacco. The politicians are all thieves, children are sick, people are dying from pollution, industrial poisoning.'

Saratov rubbed his face, then his head.

The chief continued: 'We don't have a country. That is what the men say. We left our families to starve in the dark and sailed away to drown at sea. If the Japanese want Siberia, let them have it. We might be better off under the Japanese. I hear they eat regularly.'

'The men say that?'

'Yes, Captain.'

'What is your opinion?'

'That is what the men say.'

'And you? Answer me.'

The chief's Adam's apple bobbed up and down. 'The men think we are doomed. That we have no chance. The P-3s will find us again. We should surrender while we are still alive.'

'And you?'

'I am a loyal Russian, Captain.'

Saratov said nothing.

'We might sail to Hawaii,' the chief offered tentatively. After a moment of silence, he added, 'Or the Aleutians. Ask for asylum from the Americans. I wish I were an American.'

Saratov played with the chart on the desk. Off to one side lay the messages. The Japanese had taken Nikolayevsk, Petropavlosk, and Korsakov. The Japanese had parachuted into Ostrov and Okha on Sakhalin Island, where Russian troops were resisting fiercely, according to the Kremlin. The Japanese had attacked Magadan and Gavan – no mention by the Kremlin of Russian resistance. Unconventional warfare teams had taken four emergency submarine resupply bases on the northern shore of the Sea of Okhotsk and in the Kurils – probably less than a dozen well-trained men in each team.

Saratov was certain that all these conquests had been ridiculously easy. The four sub resupply bases didn't even have troops assigned anymore, not since the turn of the century.

The officer who decoded these messages, Bogrov, had whispered the news to two friends, who whispered to friends. Every man on the boat had heard the news by now.

'Bring Svechin to the control room in fifteen minutes.'

'Aye aye, sir.'

The cramped space of the captain's cabin held only a bunk, a foldout desk, and a chair. It was on this desk that Saratov had the chart spread. He stared at it without seeing it.

The men were defeated. Without firing a shot, they were ready to surrender.

Every man on the boat had grown up on Communist propaganda, that New Communist Man bullshit, an endless diet of crap about how the Party knows best, the moral imperative to care for everyone according to their needs. All that was over, finally, gone forever. Rampant inflation and an ever-expanding population destroyed the bureaucrats' ability to provide. In an age of ever-increasing scarcity of basic necessities, corruption became endemic, crime rampant. Rusted, rotten, and dilapidated, the social framework shuddered one last time in the rising wind, then slowly collapsed. The Soviet Union died in the wreckage, leaving only starving republics without the resources to cope. Seventeen years later, Russia, the largest republic, was ruled by criminals and incompetents interested primarily in lining their own pockets.

The men on this boat were here solely because they had a better chance of eating in the navy than they did out of it. And it was just a chance. For weeks last winter, everyone at the Petropavlosk Naval Base had survived on a diet of beets. Not even bread. Beets three times a day for four and a half weeks. Meanwhile, old babushkas and abandoned children starved in the streets. There were whispers of cannibalism out in the boondocks, but no one knew anything for certain.

The rest of the world is high-teching its way to wealth and fortune, Saratov reflected bitterly. Even Chinese peasants eat better than poor Russians. The Japanese are rich, rich, rich, not to mention the Americans.

And Pavel Saratov drained the alcohol from a torpedo and sold it on the black market to get money to buy food to feed his crew for this cruise! Of course, the torpedoes were not supposed to have alcohol in them. Their fuel was a devil's brew of chemicals that allowed them to run at up to 55 knots, but the torpedo fuel had deteriorated so much over the years while in storage that it was worthless. The armory people fueled the torpedoes now with alcohol, because they had nothing better.

Perhaps he should take the boat to an American port. He had more than enough diesel fuel to make Adak, in the Aleutians. The P-3s were probably patrolling over the Japanese fleet off Vladivostok and Nikolayevsk, guarding the convoys in the Sea of Japan. The way east was wide open.

He wiped his face with his hands, tried to think.

These thoughts were unworthy. Shameful.

He was a Russian officer. Russian officers had led men valiantly and gloriously for hundreds of years, *hundreds*.

Glory. What crap!

For seventy years a fierce, venal oligarchy had ruled the Russian people. Mass murder, starvation, imprisonment, torture, and terror were routinely used to control the population and prevent unrest. And the Russian people had let it happen.

Russians drank guilt with their mother's milk.

They were beaten. Defeated by life. Defeated by their own stupidities and inadequacies.

His men were typical. Most of them just wanted alcohol – vodka or torpedo juice or fermented fruit, whatever. If you gave them alcohol you owned them, body and soul.

We are animals.

Why was he thinking these thoughts?

No one gave a good goddamn about one little diesel/electric submarine or the fifty men inside her. Fifty men, not the sixty-five the ship was supposed to have. Certainly not the brass in Moscow. Those paper-shuffling tubes of fatty Russian sausage sent this submarine to demolish a wreck that had blocked a channel for *ten* years, and they didn't bother asking if the captain had food to feed the crew. Or fuel. Or charts. Or trained men. Just an order from on high: do this, or we will find someone who can.

His eye fell on the Russian Orthodox liturgy book tucked into a cranny in the angle iron above the bunk. The old book had been given to him long, long ago by his mother. The Communists had never allowed religion in the armed forces, a policy that Saratov failed to understand. Banning religion made sense only to Communists. When the navy got rid of its political officers, Saratov began reading services aloud on Sunday mornings at sea and in port. He didn't ask permission; he just did it. At first some of the men grumbled. They soon stopped. They got that essential alcohol occasionally, now and then food, so what did prayers matter?

He could hear the chief in the control room, six paces aft of his door. Bogrov was talking to the XO, then to Svechin, who was loud and sullen, still drunk.

Saratov opened his desk safe and removed his pistol, a 7.62-mm Tokarev. The magazine was full. He inserted it into the handle, jacked the slide to chamber a round. Then he carefully lowered the hammer. The pistol had no safety. He put it into his pocket.

He took the book with him.

Everyone in the packed control room fell silent when he entered. The extra bodies filled the place, took every square inch not taken by the watch team. Even though he was inured to it, the stench of unwashed bodies took Saratov's breath for a moment. He tossed the old book on the chart table.

Svechin was obviously drunk, not at attention. He eyed the captain insolently.

The boat was submerged. Saratov forced himself to check the gauges as everyone stared at him. The boat was four hundred feet down, making three knots to the southeast.

'Drunk again, eh, Svechin?'

'I don't think –'

'Stand at attention when you speak to me,' Saratov roared. 'All of you. Attention!'

There was a general stiffening all around.

Even Svechin stood a bit straighter. 'I –'

'Alcohol from the torpedoes!'

Svechin looked sullen, half-sick. He refused to look at the captain.

'Russia is at war. The torpedoes are our weapons. You are guilty of sabotage, Svechin. In wartime, sabotage is a capital offense.'

Svechin blanched. The chief's Adam's apple was in constant motion, up and down, up and down.

'Lieutenant Bogrov discusses classified messages as if they were newspaper articles.'

Bogrov was from Moscow, and he believed that gave him some special standing; most of his shipmates came from the provinces, from small squalid villages scattered all over Russia. They had joined the navy to escape all that.

'Captain, I –' Bogrov began.

'Silence, you son of a bitch. I'll deal with you later.'

Svechin was pale now, his lips pinched into a thin line.

Saratov could hear them breathing, all of them, above the little noises of the boat running deep. They breathed in and out like blown horses. And he could still smell their stench, which surprised him. Normally his own stink masked that of the other men.

'You men talk of surrender. Of fleeing to a neutral country.'

Just the breathing.

'Talk, talk, talk. There isn't a man on this boat! God, what miserable creatures you are!'

Better get it over with.

He pulled the pistol from his pocket, gripped it firmly, and cocked the hammer.

'Do you have anything to say, Svechin, before I carry out the penalty prescribed for sabotage in wartime?'

Svechin's tongue came out. He wet his lips. Perspiration made his face shine. He had thick lips and pimples. 'Please, Captain, I didn't mean . . . We are all doomed. We're going to die. I –'

Pavel Saratov leveled the pistol and shot Svechin once, in the center of the forehead. The report was a thunderclap in the small space.

Svechin slumped to the floor. His bowels relaxed. The odor of shit nauseated Saratov.

The captain held the pistol pointed toward the overhead, so everyone could see it, while he waited for his ears to stop ringing. He worked his jaw from side to side.

He had an overpowering urge to urinate, but he fought it back, somehow.

'I should shoot you too, Bogrov.' That came out like a frog croaking.

He moved so that Bogrov was forced to look into his eyes.

'You hear me?'

'Yes, sir.' Bogrov was at rigid attention. He refused to focus his eyes.

Saratov moved to the next man, then the next, staring into the eyes of each in turn.

'Chief, bring the boat to course two three five degrees. One hour after sunset, take the boat to periscope depth and rig the snorkel.'

'Aye aye, captain.'

'Call me then.'

'Aye aye, sir.'

'Put Svechin in a torpedo tube. XO, read the funeral service. Then pop him out.'

'Aye aye, sir,' the XO said.

Saratov used both hands to lower the hammer on the pistol, pocketed it, then went back to his cabin.

He was sitting in his chair with the curtain drawn fifteen minutes later when he heard Bogrov say softly to the chief, 'He shoots a man dead, then orders the XO to pray over him. That's one for the books.'

'Better shut your mouth, sir.' That was one of the steersmen.

'Shut up, both of you,' the chief roared, unable to control himself.

The sun was still above the horizon in Moscow at ten o'clock the evening Kalugin entered the Congress of People's Deputies. He came in through the lobby and walked up the aisle, nodding right and left at deputies he knew, but not pausing to shake hands.

He had been a busy man this past week. During the last seventy-two hours he had had almost no sleep, but it didn't show. As he walked down the aisle toward the raised speaker's platform he looked like an aged lion girding himself for his last great battle.

In fact he had already fought the battle and was the victor. Once he believed that Japan really intended to invade Russia, he had moved swiftly to create a political consensus that the nation's survival was at stake. That was the easy part. Then came the crunch: Kalugin demanded that the elected representatives of the people of Russia grant him dictatorial powers to mobilize the nation and save it.

Of course, he had made many enemies through the years. Those he judged to be his worst enemies, he buried. Seven new corpses were now resting in hastily dug graves in the woods outside Moscow. Several dozen deputies who might be brought around if properly persuaded were locked in Lubyanka. Kalugin bought support where required, appointed ministers, and drafted decrees. Tonight, as he walked into the Congress amid the buzz of crisis, with the television cameras of the world watching, he was ready to declare his victory.

Janos Ilin was one of the people in the gallery, packed shoulder-to-shoulder with his fellow FIS officers. He could see the top of Kalugin's balding head as the president moved through the crowd of sycophant deputies.

A dictator. Another dictator. To solve Russia's problems with brute force and hot blood and endless rules and regulations, administered by powerless little men who lived in terror.

Kalugin, the savior.

Kalugin ascended the dais. Now he approached the podium. Massive applause.

Everyone rose to their feet, still applauding.

Finally, Kalugin motioned for his audience to be seated.

'Tonight is a grave hour in the history of Russia. Japanese forces in the far east have captured Vladivostok; Nikolayevsk; Petropavlosk, on the Kamchatka Peninsula; and Sakhalin Island . . .

'Russia has done nothing to deserve the vicious wounds being inflicted upon her by evil, greedy men, men intent on robbing future Russian generations of their birthright . . .

'Your leaders have today come to me, asking me to wield the power of the presidency *and the Congress* to save holy Mother Russia.'

His voice seemed to grow louder, deeper, to fill the hall, like the thunder of a summer storm on the steppe.

'In the name of the Russian people, I, Aleksandr Ivanovich Kalugin, take up the sword against our enemies.'

When Bob Cassidy walked into the lobby of the McGuire Air Force Base Visiting Officers Quarters to register, the first person he saw was Clay Lacy, sitting in the corner looking forlorn.

'Colonel Cassidy, Colonel Cassidy.' Lacy rushed over. 'I've been waiting for you. I called Washington and they said to come to McGuire, but these people don't have me on their list.'

'Uh-huh.' Cassidy signed his name on a check-in card as the civilian behind the desk watched.

'I need to see your ID card,' the desk clerk said to Cassidy.

'Wearing a colonel's uniform, I look like an illegal immigrant?'

'I just do what I'm told, Colonel.'

Cassidy dug out his wallet, extracted the card, and passed it over.

'Didn't get to talk to you after our interview,' Lacy was saying, 'but I want to go with you. Over there.' He nodded his head to the east. Maybe south. He didn't seem to want to say the word *Russia*. 'I called Washington and they said to come here, to McGuire, so I did. At my own expense. But when I got here, this man said I wasn't on the list, so he couldn't give me a room.'

'Do you really want to go?'

'Oh, yes, sir,' Lacy said, glancing at the clerk behind the desk.

'I'll be frank with you, Lacy. You look like a flake to me.'

Lacy was offended. 'Have you seen my service record?'

'Yeah. You still look like a flake. Think you got the balls for this?'

'Yes, sir.' Lacy set his jaw. He looked as if he might cry.

Well, the folks in Air Force Officer Personnel said this guy was one hell of a pilot. Maybe there was some mix-up on the name.

The colonel shrugged. If Lacy couldn't cut the mustard in the air, he would put him in maintenance, or give him a rifle, make a perimeter guard out of him. Surely there was something useful an overgrown teenager like Lacy could do.

Cassidy turned to the clerk. 'Where's your list for JCS Special Ops?'

The civilian produced a clipboard from beneath the counter. Cassidy looked over the printed list, then added Lacy's name in ink at the bottom. He handed the clipboard back to the clerk.

'Okay, Lacy. You're on the list.'

'Wait a minute, Colonel,' the clerk protested. 'Base Housing sent this list over –'

'Give Lacy a room, mister. Right now, no arguments or I'll have your job.' He said it softly, barely glancing at the desk clerk as he picked up his bags.

The clerk swallowed once, took a deep breath, and watched Cassidy's back as he headed for the elevator. When the elevator door had closed on the colonel, the clerk turned to Lacy. 'ID card, driver's license, or something.'

They gathered that evening in the second-floor television room of the VOQ. Two Air Force policemen sealed the hall.

'For those of you who haven't met me, I'm Colonel Bob Cassidy. My friends call me Hoppy or Butch; you can call me Colonel.'

No one smiled. Cassidy sighed, looked at the list.

'Answer up if you're here. Allen, Cassini . . .'

They answered after each name. He knew about half of them, the ones he had recruited and several he had known from years ago.

He put the list down, looked around to see if he had everyone's attention, then began. 'Thanks for volunteering. You'll probably regret it before long; that's to be expected. About all I can promise you is an adventure. We are going to Germany in the morning on a C-141. There we'll check out the newest version of the F-22. After a week, two at the most, we'll go to Russia. You pilots will be civilians hired by the Russian government. They may even swear us into the Russian army – we'll see how it goes. The aircraft will be loaned to the Russians by the U.S. Air Force. Although the U.S. markings will be removed, the planes will still be U.S. property, so they will be maintained by active-duty Air Force personnel. Any questions?'

There were none.

'Besides me, I think there is only one other pilot in this room who has ever flown in combat. All of you will be veterans very soon. You undoubtedly have some preconceived notions of what combat will be like. What you cannot know now is how it will feel to have another human being trying his absolute damnedest to kill you. Nor can you know what it feels like to kill another person. All that is ahead.'

He looked at their faces, so innocent. Some of them would soon be dead; that was inevitable.

'We all won't be coming back,' he said slowly. 'If anyone wants out, now is the time to say so. You get a handshake and a free ride home from here, no questions asked.'

Nobody said a word. They didn't look at one another, just seemed to focus on places that weren't in the room.

'Okay,' said Bob Cassidy. 'We are all in this together. From now on, you are under my rules. Not Air Force regulations: *my* rules. Disobey my rules here or in Germany, I'll send you home. Disobey in Russia . . .' He left it hanging.

'No telephone calls, no letters, no E-mail, and no one leaves the building. Those of you I haven't met, I will talk to as soon as possible. I want each of you to know what you are in for. That's all.'

Cassidy walked out of the room as someone called the crowd to attention. The people in the room were struggling to snap out of the low lounge chairs as he went through the door. Over his shoulder, he said, 'Preacher, come with me.'

Preacher was Paul Fain, a tallish man with a square face and a ruddy complexion. When he entered the colonel's room, he closed the door behind him and grinned, displaying perfect white teeth. 'Good to see you, Bob.'

Cassidy reached for Fain's outstretched hand. 'What in the dickens are you doing here, Preach? Of all people, I never expected to see your name on that list.'

'Life's an adventure. This sounded like a good one, and when I heard you were in charge, well ... Here I am!'

'What about Isabelle? What did she say when you broke it to her?'

'She wasn't happy, but she knows me, inside and out. We're stuck with each other.'

Fain was the only uniformed ordained minister not in the Chaplain Corps that Cassidy had ever met. He was serving as assistant pastor in his first church when he chucked it all years ago and joined the Air Force. When Cassidy had last seen him, Fain was flying F-22s at Nellis. Isabelle was his long-suffering wife, a woman who thought she married a minister but wound up with a fighter pilot instead.

They chatted for several minutes about old times, and Cassidy made Fain bring him up-to-date on Isabelle and the two children.

Finally, Cassidy said, 'Preacher, I want you to think this Russia thing through. The rest of them' – Cassidy nodded toward the television lounge – 'are adventurers, rolling dice with their lives. Live or die, they don't really care. They want excitement, to try something new, to bet their lives on their skill and courage. A few of them just want to kill somebody. You aren't like them.'

'And you are?'

'Listen to me, Preach. I'm trying to level with you. My wife and kid died years ago. I'm single. I've got nothing in this world. If I get zapped over Russia, no one is going to miss me. No one. The same with that crowd down there. I can order them into combat. When they die I won't lose any sleep over them ... and no one else will either.'

'What makes you think I am different from them?'

Cassidy was embarrassed. 'You're different because I know you. And someone *will* miss you – Isabelle, the kids.'

Fain didn't reply.

Cassidy growled, 'I'll miss you, for Christ's sake. I don't want to take that chance. Go home to Isabelle.'

'No. I volunteered for this fight. Somebody has to be willing to lay his precious neck on the line or the ruthless bastards are always going to keep coming out on top. When God wants me, He can take me. That's always been the case, Bob, and Isabelle can live with it. She has faith in me, and faith in God.'

Cassidy went over to the window and looked out at the summer evening. Clouds were rolling in. Soon the rain should come.

'I guess I don't have faith,' he mused. 'Not that kind, anyway. The ruthless, implacable bastards always seem to come out winners.' He found this whole discussion irritating. Preacher Fain should have stayed at home. 'People live, and then they die. That's the way of the world. I don't want to lose any more friends. I've lost too many people I care about already.'

'I have enough faith for both of us, Colonel.'

Cassidy didn't know what to say. Fain was cool as ice, as usual. 'Okay, Preach. I give up. You want in, you're in. Don't say I didn't warn you. How about sending in Dick Guelich?'

'Thanks, Bob.'

'You're my admin officer. We've got a long night of paperwork ahead of us, so get some pencils and paper and a beer from the fridge, then come on back here.'

'Okay.'

Lee Foy found Aaron Hudek in the entertainment room playing a holographic video game. 'Hey, Fur Ball.'

Hudek didn't look around. He kept squirting energy balls at alien space fighters, who were addicted to head-on attacks. 'Foy Sauce. What are you doing here?'

'Same as you.'

Hudek eventually ran out of energy balls. As he fed more coins into the machine, he said, 'Couldn't resist a chance at those Jap fighter jocks, eh? Gonna pop a few. If they don't get you first.'

'Mr Personality. Gonna be great having you on this expedition.'

'Suck it, Sauce.'

'The road might be rocky, but fortunately we have a world-class diplomat along to impress the locals.'

Hudek was using both hands on the video game's controls, tapping them, massaging them, caressing them while he moaned with pleasure. The suicidal aliens kept ripping in to get fried, almost too fast for the eye to follow.

Foy giggled. 'Still the magic touch with machinery, huh, Fur Ball?'

'Wanta make a bet? A grand to the guy who gets the first kill?' Hudek kept his eyes glued on those incoming alien idiots.

Foy took his time answering. 'The difficulty is collecting from a dead man. When I win, you'll probably be long gone to a better, cleaner world.'

'God, the camaraderie! The male bonding rituals!' Hudek exclaimed ecstatically. 'What a fool I was to think I could live without it.'

Hudek shot down several hundred more aliens; then the game ended abruptly, a few points shy of a free game. He studied the score, then muttered, 'Damn.' He glanced around as he dug in his pocket for more quarters. 'You still here? Stay out of my space, Sauce. I don't have time to wet-nurse you.'

'You're my executive officer,' Bob Cassidy told Dick Guelich. 'You got operations,' he said to Joe Malan. 'We'll land in Germany at the Rhein-Main Air Base. A squadron of F-22s there will transfer all their planes to us and we'll ask for volunteers from the maintenance troops. We should get enough mechanics and specialists to keep the planes flying, at least for a while.

'Our problem is training. I demanded at least a week before we go to Russia. We may get more time, but don't count on it.'

'One week. It's nowhere near enough. We don't have time to train them; they are going into combat knowing just what they know now. What we can do is make them think about combat, shake off the peacetime complacency, key them up, get them sharp.'

'A week isn't enough time,' Guelich said. 'Two months, maybe, but a week?'

'We got seven days.'

'That'll be enough,' Joe Malan said. 'I think everybody has trained to combat ready at one time or another. If we put them in the simulator, concentrate on the systems, refresh on tactics, and talk about what they can expect in the air over Siberia, they'll be at seventy-five or eighty percent. The first Zero they see, they'll get pumped the rest of the way.'

'That's your job, Joe.'

'I have to get transitioned to this plane,' Malan objected. 'I never flew an F-22.'

'Piece of cake,' Guelich told him. 'We'll put you in the magic box first. It's easier than an F-16 or F-18. Very straightforward airframe. You'll pick up the system quickly.'

'What I want to know,' Joe Malan said, 'is how we are going to do all the paperwork. Air Force squadrons have staffs of clerks and ground-pounders doing this stuff, and we don't.'

'What paperwork?'

'A standardization program, evaluations, records; a safety program, lectures, inspections; training records; sexual harassment prevention, counseling, investigations, all of that.'

'Who says we have to do that stuff?'

Malan pulled a message from the Air Force chief of staff from the pile waiting for Cassidy's attention. 'Right here, in black and white.' He began to read from the message.

Bob Cassidy reached for the document, removed it from Malan's hands, and methodically tore it into tiny pieces. He dribbled the pieces into a wastebasket. 'Any questions?'

The others laughed.

An hour later, they had hashed out a plan. Cassidy felt relieved – both Guelich and Malan were professionals. Guelich had given his first impression that the job was impossible, yet when told that they were going to do it anyway, he had jumped in with both feet. Malan immediately started planning how to do it.

Cassidy ran them out finally, so he could get some sleep. He was exhausted. When the door closed, he fell into bed still dressed.

10

When he was maneuvering to consolidate his power, Aleksandr Kalugin dwelled for a dark moment on Marshal Ivan Samsonov, the army chief of staff. The two men were opposites in every way. Kalugin loved money above all things, had no scruples that anyone had ever been able to detect, and never told the truth if a lie would serve, even for a little while. Samsonov, on the other hand, had spent his adult life in uniform and seemed to embody the military virtues. He was honest, courageous, patriotic, and, amazingly, embedded as he was in a bureaucracy that fed on half-truths and innuendo, boldly frank. Ivan Samsonov was universally regarded as a soldier's soldier.

Pondering these things, Kalugin decided he would sleep better at night if Samsonov did not have the armed forces at his beck and call. He had Samsonov quietly arrested, shot, and buried.

With that unpleasantness behind him, Kalugin faced his next problem: whom to put in Samsonov's place. The invasion of Siberia had certainly been a grand political opportunity for Kalugin, but he knew that even a dictator must have military victories in order to survive. He needed an accomplished soldier to win those victories, one who could and would save Russia, yet a man in debt to Kalugin for his place. After the nation was saved, well, if necessary, the hero could go into the ground beside Samsonov. Until then ...

Kalugin pretended to fret the choice for days while the Japanese army marched ever deeper into Siberia. He had already decided to name the man whom Samsonov had replaced, Marshal Oleg Stolypin, but the outpouring of raw patriotism occurring in Russia just then made it seem politic to remain quiet. Since the collapse of communism in 1991, the national scene had too often reflected the public mood: rancor, acrimony, hardball politics, charges and countercharges resulting in political deadlock, which made it impossible for any group to govern. The politicians bickered and postured and clawed at one another while the nation rotted. Until now. At last the Russian people had an enemy they could unite against.

Kalugin thought the moment sublime. He savored it. He was the absolute master of Russia. None opposed him or even dreamed of doing so. All looked to him to save the nation.

Unfortunately, the euphoria would eventually wear off. Sooner or later people would want action. One evening, Kalugin sent a car to Stolypin's dacha in the Lenin Hills to bring the old soldier to the Kremlin.

'I have sent for you,' he told the retired officer when he walked into the president's office, 'because Russia needs you.' Stolypin was escorted by several members of Kalugin's private security force, men he paid personally who did not work for any government agency.

The security people withdrew, reluctantly. They had searched the former soldier from head to toe, looking for weapons, contraband, letters from people in prison, anything. The hallways outside were filled with armed guards, men personally loyal to Kalugin because he had been feeding them and their families for almost twenty years. They were also in the courtyard outside the window, on the roofs across the street. Kalugin was taking no chances.

Now the president offered the old man hot tea. Stolypin had retired from the army before Kalugin won the presidency, so they had never worked together, although they had a nodding acquaintance from parties and official functions.

The marshal was in his early seventies. He had short, white hair and thick peasant's hands. He was stolid, too, like a peasant, and as he sipped his tea, he looked around the president's office vacantly, without interest.

'Tell me frankly,' Kalugin said, 'what we must do to defeat the Japanese in Siberia.'

'I don't know that we can,' the old man replied, then sipped more tea. 'The draft laws have not been enforced for years; the logistics system has collapsed; weapons procurement has stopped . . . Baldly, Mr President, we have no army . . . No army, no navy, no air force.'

'If we spend the summer and fall building an army, can we not win when the Japanese are buried under a Siberian winter?'

'I am not sanguine. Japan is a rich nation. They can supply their forces by air. We will be the ones most hindered by winter.'

'Come, come, Marshal,' Kalugin scoffed. 'The Russian man is tough, able to endure great hardships. Winter is the Russian season.'

'In another age, Mr President, winter was a large battalion. It ruined the French, the Poles, and the Germans. The world has changed since then. Japan is physically closer to the Siberian oil fields than we are. By winter they will be comfortably established, well dug in. Russia will have to mobilize, put the entire economy on a war footing, like we did during World War Two. Even then, we may not win.'

'Enough!' Kalugin roared. 'Enough of this defeatism! I will not hear it. I am the guardian of holy Mother Russia. We will defend her to the very last drop of Russian blood.'

Stolypin shifted uncomfortably in his chair. 'Mr President, everything we do must be based on the hard realities. We must work with the world as it is, not as we wish it to be. The bitter truth is that the armed forces are in the same condition as the rest of Russia. It will take time to change that.'

Kalugin rapped his knuckles on the desk.

'Ask Samsonov,' Stolypin said. 'Get his opinion.'

'What is your advice?' Kalugin said, his knuckle poised above the desk.

'Negotiate the best deal possible with the Japanese – buy time. Rebuild the army. When we are strong enough, drive them into the sea.'

Kalugin made a gesture of dismissal. 'That course is politically impossible. By all appearances, we would be compromising with aggression. The people would never stand for it.'

'Mr President, you asked for a professional opinion and I have given it. Building an army will take time.'

'Nothing can be done in the interim?'

'We can use small units, bleed the Japanese where we can without excessive cost. However, we must ensure that we do not squander assets that we will need to win the victory later.'

'We must do more. More than pinpricks.' Kalugin's face had a hard, unyielding look.

Stolypin shifted his feet. He cleared his throat, sipped tea, and sized up the politician in the tailored gray Italian suit seated behind the desk.

'What does Marshal Samsonov say?' he asked finally. 'Why isn't he here?'

'He's dead. Tragically. A heart attack, two nights ago. We have not announced it yet ... The people put such faith in him.'

Stolypin grimaced. 'A good man, the very best. Ah well, death comes for us all.' He sighed. After a bit, he asked, 'Who is to replace him?'

'You.'

Stolypin was genuinely surprised.

'I'm too old, too tired. You need a young man full of fire. He will need to weld together an army, which will not be a small task.'

'I am giving you the responsibility, Marshal,' Kalugin said crisply. 'Your country needs you.'

'Can we get foreign help? Military help?'

'We are working on that.'

'The military protocol with the United States – will they send troops? Equipment? Fuel? Food? Weapons? God knows, we need everything we can get.'

'They are offering a squadron of planes.'

'A squadron?' Stolypin thundered. He sprang from his chair with a vigor that surprised Kalugin, then paced back and forth. 'A *squadron*! They promised to come to our aid if we destroyed our nuclear weapons. So we did. Fools that we were, we believed their lies.'

He stopped in front of a picture of Stalin hanging over a fireplace and stood staring at it. 'At least some of the politicians believed them.'

'You didn't?'

'Do you have any vodka for this tea?'

'Yes.' Kalugin reached into the lower reaches of his desk for a bottle and poured a shot into Stolypin's tea. Stolypin sipped the mixture.

'I didn't believe any of it, Mr President. The Americans always act in America's best interests, just as we always act in Russia's best interests. They made a promise, just a promise, written on good paper and signed with good ink and worth maybe ten rubles at a curio shop. So I acted in Russia's best interests. I secreted ten warheads, kept them back so they were not destroyed. The last time I saw Samsonov, he said we still have them.'

Kalugin couldn't believe his ears. 'We still have nuclear weapons?'

'Ten.'

'Only ten?'

'Only? We had to lie and cheat to keep ten.'

Kalugin was trying to comprehend the enormity of this revelation. 'Where are the weapons?' he asked after a bit.

'Mr President, they are at Trojan Island.'

'I am not familiar with the place.'

'Trojan Island is an extinct cone-shaped volcano near the Kuril Strait. Although the island is fairly small, the volcano reaches up over two thousand meters, so it is almost always shrouded in clouds, which kept it hidden from satellite photography when we built the base. The nearby waters are deep, ice-free year-round, and there is good access to the Pacific. For these reasons, we built a submarine base there twenty years ago, a base that can only be entered underwater. It is similar to the base at Bolshaya Litsa, on the Kola Peninsula.'

'Do the Japanese know of this place?'

'I would be amazed if they did, sir. The base was officially abandoned when the last of the boomer boats were scrapped. We hid the warheads there for just that reason.'

'Nuclear weapons,' Kalugin mused, his eyelids reducing his eyes to mere slits.

'The use of nuclear weapons involves huge, incalculable risks,' Stolypin said. 'That road is unknown. We devoted much thought to pondering where it might lead years ago, when we had such weapons in quantity.'

'And what were your conclusions?'

'That we would use them only as a last resort, when all else had failed.'

Kalugin merely grunted. He was deep in thought.

Stolypin dropped into a chair, helped himself to more vodka and tea.

Kalugin grinned wolfishly. 'Marshal Stolypin, let us drink to Russia. You have answered my prayers, and saved your country.'

'God saves Russia, Mr President,' Stolypin replied. 'He even saved Russia from the Communists, although He took his time with the Reds. Let us pray that He can save Russia one more time.'

Several minutes later Kalugin asked, 'Are you a believer?'

'I believe in Russia, sir. So does God.'

'You are in charge. Fight them. Give me some victories.'

'I will use what we have,' Stolypin said sourly, 'which is very little. If you expect a furious battle that can be filmed for a television spectacle, you had better get someone else, someone who can make an army from street rabble with a snap of his fingers.'

Kalugin was thinking about nuclear weapons. When he came out of his reverie, he heard Stolypin saying, 'Political posturing is not part of a soldier's job.'

Kalugin handed the old marshal an envelope. 'Your appointment as chief of staff is in here. I signed it before you arrived. Go to headquarters and take charge. Mobilize our resources, fill the ranks, requisition the guns, clothes, food, fuel, all of it. Do whatever you have to do. Any decrees that you need, draft them and send them to me. Together, we are going to save Russia.'

Stolypin reached for the envelope and opened it.

'It is a tragedy that Samsonov is not here,' the old soldier said gravely as he read the papers. 'He was the most brilliant soldier Russia has produced since Georgi Zhukov.'

'I am placing the details in your capable hands, Marshal Stolypin.'

'I have given you the same advice that Samsonov would. I wish to God he were here now.'

'We will feel his loss keenly,' said Kalugin as he walked with Stolypin toward the door.

The sky was growing light in the northeast as Jiro Kimura and three wingmen climbed to 34,000 feet on their way to bomb and strafe the airfield at Khabarovsk, at the great bend of the Amur River. Khabarovsk was a rail, highway, and electrical power nerve center, the strategic key to the far eastern sector. When they held Khabarovsk, the Japanese would own the Russian far east, and not before. The troops were within forty miles now, coming up the railroad and highways from Vladivostok.

For the past two days, Jiro and his squadron mates had flown close air support for the advancing troops, bombing, rocketing, and strafing knots of Russian troops that were preparing positions to delay the Japanese advance. This morning, however, the general had sent this flight to Khabarovsk.

It was going to be a perfect morning. Not a cloud anywhere. To the northeast the rising sun revealed the pure deep blue of the sky and the vastness of the endless green Siberian landscape. From 34,000 feet none of man's engineering projects were visible as the low-angle sunlight flooded the land in starkly contrasting light and shadow. When the sun got a little higher, all one would see from horizon to horizon would be green land under an endless blue sky.

Jiro was flying three or four flights a day, every day. The previous afternoon his plane had needed unexpected maintenance, and he had fallen asleep in the briefing room, after lying down on the floor with his flight gear as a pillow. He was constantly exhausted and always on the verge of sleep.

Some of his comrades were disappointed that the Russians had suddenly withdrawn their airplanes. Jiro had eleven kills when the Russians vanished from the sky, ceding air superiority. One still had to stay alert for possible enemy aircraft, of course, but they just weren't there.

Although the Russians on the ground felt free to shoot like wild men with everything they had, they rarely hit anyone. The Japanese planes stayed out of the light AAA envelope except when actually delivering ordnance. Rear-quarter heat-seekers would also have been a problem if they stayed near the ground for very long, so they didn't.

The Japanese had lost only two Zeros at this stage of the war. One pilot crashed and died while making an approach to Vladivostok as evening fog rolled in. Another had a total electrical failure and lost his wingmen while he busied himself in the cockpit pulling circuit breakers and trying to reset alternators. He and his flight had been on their way to Nikolayevsk, at the mouth of the Amur, when the failure occurred. The luckless pilot never found the city or the base. He crashed in the boondocks a hundred miles northwest of Nikolayevsk when his fuel was exhausted. Fortunately a satellite picked up the plane's battery-powered emergency beeper after the pilot ejected, and a helicopter rescued him the next day.

Jiro retarded his throttles and began his letdown eighty miles from Khabarovsk. The four war planes drifted apart into a combat spread. Jiro and his wingman, Sasai, were ahead and to the right, Ota and Miura behind and to the left. Ota dropped farther back so that he could swing right and follow the first flight if the ground topography required it.

The shadows on the ground were still dark, impenetrable. Jiro looked at his watch. In eight minutes they would arrive at the target, come out of the rising sun. It would be a splendid tactic, if the sun rose on schedule.

He swung farther east to give God another minute or two with the sun.

'Blue Leader, this is Control.' The radio was scrambled, of course, and gave a beep before and after the words.

Jiro pushed his mike button, waited for the beep, then said, 'Control, Blue Leader, go ahead.'

'We believe a plane has just taken off from your target. It is headed three zero zero degrees, ten miles northwest, climbing. Please intercept.'

'Wilco.'

Jiro looked around at Sasai. He pointed toward Ota, then jerked his thumb. Sasai nodded vigorously, then slipped aft and away.

Jiro turned left, advanced his throttles, and pulled his machine into a slight climb. He settled on a course of 275, which should allow him to intercept. Now he pushed buttons on the computer display in front of him. When he was satisfied, he tickled the radar. It swept once.

There was the plane. Thirty-four nautical miles away, interception course

278 degrees. He turned to that heading and reset his armament panel. He had been set up to strafe, then shoot rockets. Now he armed the two heat-seeking Sidewinder missiles that the Zero always carried, one on each wingtip.

He tripped the radar sweep again. Thirty-one miles.

The enemy plane was accelerating nicely, headed almost straight away from Jiro, who was now committed to a stern-quarter approach. He eyed his fuel gauges, then pushed the throttle farther forward. The Zero slid through the sonic barrier without a buffet or bump.

With the throttles all the way forward, but without using his afterburners, the Zero quickly accelerated to Mach 1.3.

Jiro decided to risk another sweep. Twenty-four miles.

He was at ten thousand feet now, so he leveled there. He wanted the other plane above him, against the dark background of the western sky. Far below, out to the left, he could see a faint ribbon of light wandering off to the northwest. That would be the Amur River, flowing southeast to Khabarovsk. On the far side was Manchuria. From Khabarovsk, the river flowed northeast to the Sea of Okhotsk. It was always frozen solid in winter.

He was still fifteen miles from the bogey when he first saw it, a spot of silver reflecting the rising sun, against the dark of the fading night.

It's a big plane, he thought. A transport!

He checked his ECM panel as the implications of that fact sunk in. The panel was dark.

Because you never really trust an electronic device, Jiro turned in his seat and looked carefully about him, concentrating on the rear quadrants.

Empty sky, everywhere.

A transport – defenseless.

He heard Ota tell Control that he was attacking the primary target, and he heard Control acknowledge.

Jiro closed quickly on the transport from dead astern. When it was no more than four miles ahead, Jiro retarded his throttles. The gap between the planes continued to close as he coasted up on it.

The bogey was a four-engine transport, very similar to an old Boeing 707, with the engines in pods on the wings, climbing at full power. Just now it was passing through fifteen thousand feet.

Jiro stabilized a few hundred yards aft, directly behind, well below the transport's wash.

He sat looking at it for what seemed like a long, long time, unsure of what to do. Actually the time was less than a minute, but it seemed longer to Jiro. He slid out to the right, so he could see the side of the plane and the tail, illuminated by the rising sun. Then he dropped back into trail.

Finally he keyed the mike. After the beep, he spoke. The hoarseness of his voice surprised him.

'Control, Blue Leader.'

'Go ahead, Blue Leader.'

'This bogey you wanted investigated. It's an airliner – four-engines, silver. Lots of windows. Aeroflot markings.'

'Wait.'

Silence, broken only by Jiro sucking on his oxygen, with the background hum of the engines. He eased up and under the transport; the roar of the Russian's engines became audible. He could just feel a bit of the rumble of the air disturbed by the big plane's passage, its wash.

He dropped down a bit; the ride smoothed and the Russian's engine noise faded.

'Ah, Blue Leader,' Control said. 'Destroy the bogey and RTB.'

Jiro sat looking at the airliner. They were climbing through twenty thousand feet now.

'Blue Leader, this is Control. Did you copy? Destroy the bogey and return to base.' The mission controller was in Japan, in a basement at the defense ministry probably, staring at his computer screens. The reason his voice sounded so clear and strong on the radio was because the radio signal was directed at a satellite, which rebroadcast it.

Jiro's eyes flicked around the cockpit, taking in the various displays and switches.

He took off his oxygen mask and rubbed his face furiously, then put the mask back on.

'Blue Leader, Control . . .'

Well, there was nothing to be gained by prolonging this. 'Control, Blue Leader.'

'Did you copy, Blue Leader?'

'Understand you want me to destroy this airliner and return to base.'

'Destroy the bogey, Blue Leader. Report bogey destroyed.'

'Control, this thing's an airliner. Tell me that you understand that this bogey is an Aeroflot airliner.'

Silence. He was being grossly insubordinate. He could just imagine the clenched jaws of the senior officers.

Well, hell, if they didn't like it, they could cashier him, send him back to Japan.

'Blue Leader, Control. We understand the bogey has Aeroflot markings. You are hereby ordered to destroy it. Acknowledge.'

'I copy.'

He retarded the throttle, let the airliner pull ahead. The distance began to grow: five hundred yards, a thousand, fifteen hundred.

Jiro flicked a switch on the throttle to select the left Sidewinder. He pulled the nose up, put the dot in the center of the HUD directly on the airliner. The Sidewinder growled: It had locked on one of the big plane's engines.

Jiro squeezed the trigger on the stick. The Sidewinder leapt off the rail and shot forward. Straight as a bullet it flew across the gap toward the four-engined monster.

A puff of smoke. A hit: the inboard left engine.

He sat there watching as the airliner's engine began trailing smoke. Now the big silver plane began to move back toward him, which was an optical illusion. Actually, it was slowing and he was creeping up on it. He retarded his throttles, cracked the speed brakes.

'Fuck.' Jiro said the word in English.

'*Fuck!*' Now he screamed it.

Furious, he selected the right Sidewinder, got the tone, then squeezed it off.

It impacted one of the transport's right engines: another little flash.

The huge silver plane wasn't climbing anymore. Its left wing came down, twenty ... now thirty degrees; the nose dropped. It began a turn back toward Khabarovsk.

'Fall, you Russian bastard,' Jiro whispered. He opened his speed brakes to the stops and dropped his left wing, cutting across the turn, closing the distance. He was out to the left now, in plain view of the pilots if they only took the time to look this way.

The airliner's left engine was visibly on fire. No, the wing was burning. Shrapnel from the missile's warhead must have punctured the wing tank, and jet fuel was burning in the slipstream.

The big silver plane's angle of bank was at least sixty degrees now, its nose down ten degrees.

It was then that Jiro realized that the big plane was out of control.

Perhaps the controls had been damaged by the missile shrapnel or the fire.

He pulled away, got his nose level, and watched the silver plane spiral down into the early-morning gloom.

Down, down, down ... miles to fall ...

Time seemed to stand still. The airliner got smaller and smaller.

The Russian plane was just a tiny silver dot, almost lost from view, when its flight ended in a flash, a tiny smear of fire amid the morning shadows.

That was all. A splash of fire, and they were gone.

Jiro pointed the nose of his plane south, toward Vladivostok. He pushed the throttles forward and let the nose rise into a climb.

'Control, Blue Leader ...'

'Blue Leader, Control, go ahead with your report.'

After an evening of cogitation, Aleksandr Kalugin decided to deliver an ultimatum to Japan threatening nuclear holocaust. Since he had bombs and Japan didn't, he could see no good reason why he should not put the bombs in play. He was not committing himself to any specific course of action, merely threatening one.

He called in Danilov, the foreign minister, and had him draft the ultimatum. Two hours later, he looked the document over carefully as Danilov sat on the edge of his seat, his hands folded in his lap.

Danilov was nearly seventy years old. He had spent his adult life as a professional diplomat. Never had he seen a Soviet or Russian government seriously weigh the use of nuclear weapons. Now, to his horror, Kalugin was threatening their use without even discussing the matter with his ministers. Is this where perestroika and democracy lead? To nuclear war?

'Sir, Japan may not withdraw from Siberia.'

Kalugin finished the paragraph he was reading before he looked at Danilov. 'They might not.'

'They may not believe this ultimatum.'

'What is your point?'

'We have repeatedly assured the world that our nuclear weapons were destroyed. Now, by implication, we are admitting that those statements were not true.'

Kalugin said nothing. He merely stared at the foreign minister, who felt his skin crawl.

'Japan may believe that we do not have any weapons remaining,' the minister observed, 'in which case they will disregard this ultimatum.'

Kalugin went back to the draft document. A sunbeam peeped into the room between the drapes on the high window behind the president, who sat reading, his head lowered.

He might nuke the Japanese, Danilov thought, suddenly sure that the ultimatum was not an idle threat. If they don't pull out of Siberia, Kalugin might really do it.

11

Another clear, hot day. Plumes of diesel exhaust and dust rose into the warm, dry air behind the Japanese army trucks – all forty-seven of them – and gently tailed off to the east. The convoy was on a paved road beside the Amur River – a paved road with a lot of windblown dirt on it – rolling northwest at about twenty miles per hour. They were a day northwest of Khabarovsk, in a wide river valley defined by low hills or mountains to the northeast and southwest. The river, a mile to the left, formed the border with China, but no fences or guard towers marked it.

Most of the trucks carried supplies for Japanese forces a hundred miles ahead. Eight of the vehicles held soldiers, and the fuel, food, water, and cooking supplies necessary to keep the convoy rolling.

The road wasn't much – just a crowned two-laned paved road in a wide, treeless valley. It followed the natural contours of the land in a serpentine way along the path of least resistance. Although there were no signposts to proclaim it, the road was merely an improvement of an ancient trail. There were some culverts, occasionally a bridge, but in many places water routinely washed over the road. Dry now, many of the low places would be impassable in winter.

From the road one could occasionally see sheep or goats cropping the sparse grass, here and there a shack or yurt, once in a great while a rattletrap civilian truck going somewhere or other, trailing its own dust plume. Occasionally, a dirt road led off from the main road. A few of these led to open pit mines in the hills, where manganese or some other ore was extracted from the earth with obsolete, well-worn equipment, sweat, and a lot of hard work.

There were few people in this land. The natives shrank instinctively from the Japanese soldiers, who ignored them. Children in the doors of shacks watched the trucks approach, then retreated to the dark interior as the lead vehicle, a truck with a multibarreled antiaircraft gun mounted on the flatbed, drew near.

The Japanese ate dust and watched the sky. Some of them were wishing the Russian soldiers hadn't destroyed the railroad trestles and bridges as they retreated. If the railroad had remained intact, these soldiers would be riding a train west instead of jolting around in trucks.

The shimmering, brassy sky seemed to reflect the earth's heat back to it. High and far to the west a thin layer of cirrus clouds would diffuse the sun this afternoon, but that was many hours away.

The brilliant sun was hard to look at. When the curves of the road allowed, the older drivers looked anyway, almost against their will, holding up a hand or thumb to block the burning rays and searching the sky while they fought the wheel to keep their trucks on the highly crowned road.

The eagles didn't come from the sun's direction. They came from the northwest, straight down the valley, over this road, swiftly and silently, just a few hundred feet above the ground.

The driver of the lead truck saw them first, less than a mile away, two Sukhoi-27s, streaking in like guided missiles.

He cranked the wheel over and swung the truck on two wheels off the road. The men in back, the gun crew, almost fell out.

He was just quick enough to save their lives.

The cannon shells impacted on the road behind the lead truck and walked straight into the next vehicle, where they lingered for a fraction of a second as the pilot of the lead plane dipped his nose expertly. This truck exploded under the hammering.

As the fireball blossomed, the pilot was already shooting at another truck halfway down the convoy. The truck did not explode; it merely disintegrated as a dozen 30-mm cannon shells impacted in two brief seconds.

The pilot released the trigger and selected a third target, toward the end of the column. Still racing along at five hundred knots, he squirted a burst at that truck but missed.

He glanced left to ensure his wingman was where he should be, then dropped the right wing for a hard turn. After ninety degrees of heading change, he rolled left into a sixty-degree angle of bank. After 270 degrees of turn, he rolled out heading northwest, back toward the column of trucks. His wingman was still with him, out to the left.

Both pilots selected targets as they raced once again toward the trucks, whose drivers were frantically trying to get them off the road on either side. Not that it mattered.

With just the gentlest nudges of their rudders and caresses of their sticks, the pilots pointed their planes at targets chosen at random and squirted bursts from their internal GSh-30-1 guns. Four trucks exploded on that pass. One, which contained artillery ammunition, detonated with an earsplitting crash.

The gun crew in the lead truck was still trying to get the restraining straps off the antiaircraft gun so they could point it when the Su-27s swept overhead and disappeared into the brassy sky in the direction from whence they had come, northwest.

It took the convoy commander an hour to get the undamaged trucks back on the road and rolling. Nine trucks had been destroyed or damaged too badly to continue. One of the nine had not been touched by the strafing aircraft; the panic-stricken driver had tried to drive over several large rocks, which shattered the transmission and tore the rear axle loose from the truck's frame.

Fourteen men were dead, ten wounded. One of the wounded was horribly burned; a sergeant shot him to put him out of his misery.

The soldiers placed the dead men in a row near the road, amid the burned-out trucks. Someone else would have to bury them later. The officer in charge had his orders.

The soldiers got back in the trucks and resumed their journey northwest.

On the third mission of the day, Major Yan Chernov led his wingman, Major Vasily Pervushin, back to the truck convoy on the river road from Khabarovsk. Chernov was the commander of the 556th Fighter Squadron based at Zeya. He and his wingman were flying the only two operational aircraft. The enlisted men had been laboring for days to drain the water from the fuel-storage tanks, then transfer the remaining fuel by hand into the planes. There was no electricity at the base, so the job was herculean, involving hand pumps, fifty-five-gallon drums, and lots of muscle.

Chernov did not think there were any cluster bombs on the base, but while he was airborne on the first strike, his ordnance NCO found some in an ammo bunker that was supposed to be empty. The bombs were at least twenty years old. Still, they were all the Russians had for ground attack, so they were loaded on the planes.

Just now, he and Pervushin, his second in command, raced southeast a hundred feet or so above the ground. Chernov was watching for vehicles off to the left, along the river road.

The two Sukhois were indicating 525 knots, .85 Mach, which was about as fast as it was safe to carry the bombs – they were not supersonic shapes. The treeless plain raced under the Sukhois, almost as if the fighters were motionless in space and the earth was spinning madly beneath them. The illusion was very pleasant.

There, at ten o'clock, on the horizon: a plume of dust.

This morning they had made two passes over the target convoy, the first from the northwest, the second from the southeast. This time Chernov and Pervushin had planned to approach from the southeast and drop the bombs on the first pass. Since they had the ammo in the guns, they wanted to make a second pass, quickly, and the quickest way was a hard turn, then back down the trucks from the northwest to the southeast.

Chernov pointed to the dust, made sure Pervushin nodded his understanding. This convoy was farther northwest than the one they had attacked that morning.

The ECM gear was silent. Not a peep of an enemy radar.

These Japanese, running truck convoys without air cover . . .

There *could* be air cover, of course, running high with their radars off. Chernov glanced up into the afternoon haze, looking for tiny black spots against the high cloud.

Nothing.

Not seeing them didn't mean they weren't there. It simply meant you hadn't seen them.

The dust was passing behind his left wing when he motioned for Pervushin to drift out farther.

Satisfied, he began a shallow turn. He wanted to be wings-level over the road for several miles before he reached the convoy to give himself and Pervushin time to pick out targets.

Turn, watch the ground racing by just beneath the plane, keep the wings at no more than ten degrees of bank, and glance up occasionally, look for enemy fighters. *Watch the nose attitude, Chernov! Don't fly into the ground.*

He reached for the armament panel. Bombs selected. Fusing set. Interval set. Master armament switch on.

Wings level, Pervushin was well out to the right, dropping aft. He would follow Chernov in a loose trail formation.

Five hundred twenty-five knots . . . Chernov let his plane drift up until he was about three hundred feet above the ground. After the clamshell fuselage of the cluster bomb opened, the bomblets needed to fall far enough to disperse properly.

Trucks. A row of them. They appeared to be racing toward him, but he was the one in flight. As Tail-end Charlie disappeared under the nose, Chernov mashed the pickle button on the stick. He could feel the thumps as the bombs were kicked off, all six of them in about a second and a half.

Chernov held the heading for another three seconds, then rolled into an eighty-degree angle of bank with G on and held it for ninety degrees of heading change. Now he rolled the other way and turned for 270 degrees.

He watched the gyro swing, concentrated on keeping the nose above the horizon. With his left hand, he flipped switches on the armament panel, enabling the gun.

Wings level again, the Russian pilot was almost lined up on the trucks, four of which were obviously on fire. He stabbed the rudder and jammed the stick forward, pointing the nose, then eased the stick back ever so slightly.

Squeeze the trigger, squint against the muzzle flashes as the vibration reaches him through the seat and stick, walk the shells through the target truck. Then another.

In four seconds his shooting pass was done, enough time to aim at two trucks; then Chernov was pulling G to get the nose above the horizon and rolling hard right to avoid ricochets. With a positive rate of climb, in a right turn, he raised the nose a smidgen more, twisted in his seat and glanced back over his right shoulder.

Horror swept over him.

A gun, on a truck, shooting, a death ray of tracers . . . Pervushin, on fire, rolling hard left, nose dropping . . .

A tremendous explosion of yellow fire as Pervushin's Sukhoi fighter flew into the ground.

No parachute visible.

Yan Chernov tore his eyes away and checked his nose attitude. He was still climbing.

Damnation!

'Sir, where's Major Pervushin?' the NCO asked Yan Chernov after he raised the canopy and shut down his engines at the Zeya Air Base.

'Dead.'

'Fighters?'

'A gun. One gun. On a truck.'

'Could he have . . .'

'No.'

'His wife is at Dispersal, sir. The trucks carrying the families won't leave for a while, so she came here to wait for him.'

Chernov sat in the cockpit letting the wind dry his face and hair. He was exhausted. Finally he made himself look in the direction of the dispersal shack, a large one-room wooden-frame building on the edge of the concrete. She was standing outside, shading her eyes against the sun, looking this way. The wind was whipping at her dress.

Chernov couldn't do it. It was his duty, but he couldn't.

'Sergeant.'

'Yes, Major.'

'Go tell her.'

'Yes, sir.'

The Zero pulled hard to bring his nose around, setting up a head-on pass. Dixie Elitch horsed her airplane to meet him head-on, trying to minimize the separation and give her opponent as small an angle advantage as possible. Alas, the Japanese pilot's nose lit up; cannon shells reached for her in a stream, as if they were squirted from a garden hose.

'These guys got fangs and will bite you good if you let them,' said the male voice in her earphones. That was Joe Malan, who was back there with the simulator operator, no doubt enjoying himself immensely.

Dixie put on the G to escape the shells. She fully intended to pull right into the vertical, but Malan read her mind. 'If this guy follows you up, you're going to give him another shot. You really don't want to be out in front of one of these people. Are you suicidal?'

By the time he finished speaking, she had unloaded the plane and rolled it 270 degrees. Now she laid the G on. Smoothly back on the stick, right up to nine G's on the HUD. In a real F-22, her full-body G suit would be fully inflated, but the simulator didn't pull G's. It did roll and pitch in a sickeningly realistic manner, however, so the cockpit smelled faintly of stale vomit. So did real cockpits.

She came around hard, turning at thirty-two degrees per second with the help of vectored thrust. No other plane in the world could turn like that, even the Zero.

Unfortunately the Zero had not been standing still or plodding along straight while he waited for her to finish her turn. She craned her head, looking for it.

'No, damn it,' Malan said in her headphones. 'Look at your displays. The infrared sensors are keeping track of this guy. What does your computer tell you?'

'He's high and right. I'm in his left-rear quarter.'

'Pull up and shoot.'

Dixie kept the nose coming. The missile-capability circle came into view on the HUD. As the red dot centered in the circle, she heard a tone, almost a buzz, indicating the heat-seeking Sidewinder missile had locked on. She squeezed off the missile, which roared away from her right wingtip.

A flash.

'Got 'im.'

She relaxed the G.

'Okay, let's go back to base, shoot an instrument approach. Remember, in combat you *must* let the computer help you. The computer is your edge. The computer will keep you alive.'

She wiped the sweat from her face and grunted.

'The computer is the brain of the plane. You're just the loose nut on the stick.'

'Yeah.'

When the session was over and she was standing on the floor under the simulator, Joe Malan replayed her mission on a videotape. He had just started the tape when Bob Cassidy came in, stood behind Dixie, and watched silently.

'He came in so fast from the front I couldn't get a missile shot.'

'He was inside the envelope,' Malan said. 'Did you try to switch to the gun?'

'Never occurred to me,' she admitted.

'I don't think you could have gotten the nose over quickly enough for a shot. You had only about three-quarters of a second, maybe a second. You must ensure you don't cross his nose, give him a shot at you. That is critical.'

'Yes, sir,' Dixie Elitch said.

'Even in a no-radar environment, this guy is making a lot of heat. Your IR sensors will pick him up; the computer will identify him, track him, show you his position at all times. Don't go lollygagging, cranking your head around to try to track him visually. Keep focused on those displays, keep flying, and take a shot when you get one. While you're engaged with this guy, somebody else might be sneaking up to put a knife into you, so kill him as quickly as possible.'

'Okay.'

'Go get some rest. See you back here at eleven tonight. Tonight, we'll do two bogeys at a time.'

'Terrific.'

As Dixie went through the classroom area, Aaron Hudek passed her on his way to the simulator. 'Stick around, babe,' he said, 'and see how it's done.'

'Watching people get zapped in that thing nauseates me,' she shot back.

At the instructor's console of the simulator, Bob Cassidy asked Joe Malan, 'How is she doing?'

'Pretty good. Picks it up quick. All these kids do. The speed with which they absorb this stuff amazes me.'

'Video games. A lifetime of video games.'

'All life is a video game to this generation. Hudek is next, then you.'

Aaron Hudek was standing beside them. 'Make yourself comfortable, Colonel. I'll show you how it's done.' The humble one grinned.

Cassidy snorted.

'I can talk it and walk it, Colonel.'

'I hope.'

'Just watch.' Hudek went up the ladder toward the cockpit, which stood almost ten feet off the floor on massive hydraulically actuated arms.

'I like Fur Ball's brass,' Malan muttered.

'I'll like it too, *if* he can fly.'

Hudek could. Malan started with in-flight emergencies and Hudek handled them expeditiously, by the book. Interceptions were no problem, nor were dogfights where he bounced his opponent. After three of those, he was bounced by a single opponent. He quickly went from defensive to offensive and shot the opponent down. The second opponent was wiser, more wily, but Hudek was patient, working his plane, taking what the opponent gave him, waiting for his enemy to make a mistake.

'He's damned good,' Malan told Bob Cassidy, who was watching Hudek's cockpit displays on the control panel in front of Malan. 'Maybe the best we have.'

A simulator was not a real airplane, nor were the scenarios very realistic. They were merely designed to sharpen the pilots' skills. 'The problem,' Cassidy told Malan, 'is going to be getting close enough to the Zero to have a chance at it. In close, with smart skin and infrared sensors, the F-22 has the edge. Getting there is going to be the trick.'

'I thought you said the F-22's electronic countermeasures would allow us to detect the Zero before it could see us on radar?'

'Theoretically, yes. Say it works – you know the enemy is there, but his Athena protects him from your radar. You can't shoot an AMRAAM – it won't guide. How do you get in to Sidewinder range?'

'I don't know.'

'We'd better figure that out or we'll be ducks in a shooting gallery.'

The following day was even more frustrating for Yan Chernov than the previous one. Everything that could go wrong did. Electricity to the base was off; fueling had to be done by hand; only three airplanes were flyable – three out of thirty-six. The others had mechanical problems that the men were trying to fix, or had been scavenged for parts to keep the other planes flying. One of the three was fueled and armed. Chernov intended to use it to give the Japanese some grief.

The 30-mm cartridges for the cannon were so old that some of them had swelled; these defective cartridges would jam the gun when they were chambered, so all the cartridges had to be checked by hand with a micrometer, the defective ones thrown away, then the good ones loaded by hand into the linkages that made them into a belt. At last, the belt went into Chernov's plane.

After all that, four AA-10 missiles were loaded onto the missile racks. Chernov suited up, strapped in, then tried to start the engines. The left engine wouldn't crank.

Another hour was wasted while mechanics changed the starter drive.

Chernov went back to the dispersal shack and tried once again to call regional military headquarters. At least the telephones worked. But no one answered the ringing phone at regional HQ. The phone just refused to ring at the GCI site in this sector. Maybe the lines were down somewhere . . . or perhaps the Japanese had fired a beam-rider antiradiation missile at the radar to knock it off the air.

Chernov went out onto the concrete ramp and sat down in the shade of a wing so he could watch the mechanics work. He had a lot of things on his mind: antiradiation missiles, telephones that didn't work, Japanese soldiers, and a dead pilot.

To resist a Japanese attack on the base with a few dozen men would be suicidal. He had ordered the base personnel to leave, taking all the military families with them. In the absence of orders from higher authority, the responsibility was his.

Oh well, he would probably be dead in about an hour, so what did it matter what the Moscow bureaucrats thought when they got around to wondering why the antiaircraft guns at the Zeya Air Base were not manned.

He was nervous. Maybe a little scared. He had never been in combat before yesterday. The action then hadn't taken the edge off. His stomach was nervous, his hands sweaty. He was having trouble sitting still.

Today, he knew, there would be Zeros. There should have been Zeros yesterday.

He could do it, though. He told himself that over and over. He was a professional. He had a good airplane; he knew how to use it.

The odds were against him. One plane against ... how many? An air force. Their ECM gear would pick up his radar...

He would leave it off, he decided. Eyeball-to-eyeball would be his best chance.

Maybe his only chance.

'Major, what if the Japanese attack?'

One of the mechanics was standing in front of him, holding a wrench, examining his face with searching eyes. 'You're sitting under the biggest target on the base, the only armed fighter.'

'All these planes look good from the air,' he replied, gesturing toward rows of Sukhois and MiGs parked in revetments.

The mechanic rejoined the others. Chernov stretched out, using his survival vest for a pillow, and watched the sky. The sun was shining through a high cirrus layer. There were scattered clouds at the middle altitudes. The clouds subdued the light, made the sky look soft, gauzy.

Yan Chernov took a deep breath, tried to force himself to relax.

Finally the mechanics came to him. 'We're finished, sir.'

'Good. Very good.'

'It should work.'

'Yes,' he said.

'What do you want to do, Major?' the crew chief asked.

'Help me strap in. Have the men work on getting another plane fueled. Arm it. Check the ammo, load four missiles. If there is time this evening, I will take it up.' If he was alive this evening, that is.

'Some of the other pilots want to fly.'

'No.'

Chernov had no orders to launch strikes on the Japanese. He had already lost one man. Russia might need these men later. No sense wasting them.

This time the left engine started, as did the right.

When the ordnance men and mechanics were satisfied, Chernov gave the signal for the linesmen to pull the chocks. They did so, and he taxied.

He made no radio calls. He didn't turn on the radar or the radio. The ECM panel received careful attention, however, and he tuned the volume so he could hear the sound of any enemy radar the black boxes detected.

He taxied onto the runway, stopped, and quickly ran through his preflight checks. Satisfied, he released the brakes as he smoothly advanced the throttles to the stops, then lit the afterburners.

The heavy Sukhoi accelerated quickly. Just seconds after the plane broke ground, Chernov came out of burner to save fuel.

Airborne, with the gear up and flaps in, Yan Chernov pointed the fighter southeast, down the Amur valley. He leveled at twenty thousand feet and retarded the throttles to cruise at .8 Mach.

The afternoon was getting late. The rolling plain below looked golden in the summer haze, like something from a fairy tale. Here and there were clumps of trees, pioneers from the boreal forest to the north, trying to make it in low places on the prairie. Occasionally a road could be discerned through the haze, but no villages or towns. The haze hid them.

Chernov turned on his handheld GPS, a battery-powered Bendix-King unit made in America and sold there for use in light civilian airplanes. Within seconds, his position came up on the unit. He keyed in the lat-long coordinates of the Svobodny airfield and waited for a direction and distance. There!

One hundred and twenty miles from Svobodny, Chernov's ECM picked up the chirp of a Japanese search radar. He was probably too far out for the operator to receive an echo, which was good. Chernov turned ninety degrees to the left and began flying a circle with a 120-mile radius, with Svobodny at the center. The GPS made it easy.

Yan Chernov concentrated on searching the afternoon sky and listening intently to the ECM.

Not another aircraft in sight.

That was certainly not surprising. Acquiring another aircraft visually was difficult at best beyond a few miles. At the speeds at which modern aircraft flew, when you finally saw it, you might not even have enough time to avoid it. The performance envelope of air-to-air missiles was so large that if you saw the enemy in combat, either you or the other pilot had made a serious mistake, perhaps a fatal one. Still, Chernov kept his eyes moving back and forth, searching the sky in sectors, level with the horizon, above it, and below it. He was alone, which was not the way modern fighters are designed to fight.

The radar that his GCI controller normally used was off the air. Perhaps it had been damaged by a Japanese beam-riding missile. Perhaps the power company had turned off the electricity. Maybe the GCI people had piled into trucks and fled west to escape the Japanese. No one was answering the telephone there, so who knew? Perhaps it didn't matter much one way or the other.

And this was an old plane, an obsolete fighter. Once, not many years ago, the Sukhoi-27 had been the best fighter in the world, bar none. But after the collapse of communism in '91, development of new fighters in the new Russia dried up from lack of money. The nation couldn't even afford to buy fuel for the fighters it had; everything was tired, worn, not properly cared for.

Amazingly, Japan had plenty of planes that performed equal to or better than this one. As Russia rusted, the Japanese built a highly capable aircraft industry.

And here Chernov was, in an obsolete, worn-out plane that hadn't flown – according to the logbook – in nine months and three days, hunting Japanese planes with his naked eyes.

Out here asking for some Japanese fighter pilot to kill him quick.

Begging for it. Kill me, kill me, kill me . . .

According to an intel officer hiding in the city of Svobodny whom he had spoken to on the telephone that morning, the Japanese were flying supplies in from Khabarovsk and bases in Japan.

He thought he saw a plane, and he changed his heading to check.

No. Dirt on the canopy.

He checked his fuel, checked the GPS . . . He wasn't going to be able to stay out here for very long, not if he expected to get back to base flying this airplane.

He was coming up on the Bureya River when he saw it, a speck running high and conning. The guy must be 36,000 or 38,000 feet, headed northwest.

Chernov turned to let the other plane pass off his right wing on a reciprocal heading. If it was a Japanese transport – and all the planes in these skies just now were Japanese – it must be going to Svobodny. Right heading, right altitude . . .

If it was a transport going to Svobodny, there were fighters.

The Russian major glanced at his ECM, listened intently. Not a peep, not a chirp or click.

Well, damnit, there must be fighters, not using their radars. They must be below the transport, below the conning layer, and too small to be visible at this distance.

Thank God he had his radar off, or they would have picked up the emissions and be setting a trap right this minute.

His heart was pounding. Sweat stung his eyes, ran down his neck . . .

He checked his switches – missiles selected, stations armed, master arm on.

The transport was still eight or ten miles away when it went by Chernov's right wingtip. He laid the Sukhoi into a sixty-degree angle of bank and stuffed the nose down while he lit the afterburners, shoved the throttles on through to stage four.

The heavy jet slid through the sonic barrier and accelerated quickly: Mach 1.5, 1.7 . . . 1.9.

Passing Mach 2 he raised the nose into a climb, kept the turn in.

The AA-10 was a fire-and-forget missile with active radar homing. When its radar came on, the Japanese were going to get a heady surprise.

So was Chernov if the Japanese had a couple of fighters fifteen miles in trail behind the transport. He looked left, then right, scanning the sky hurriedly. The sky looked empty. Which meant nothing. They could be there.

The transport was just a dot, a flyspeck in the great vastness, still well above him and conning beautifully. About ten miles, he figured, but he couldn't afford to turn on the radar to verify that. He was closing from fifteen degrees right of dead astern.

He centered the dot in the gunsight, squeezed off a missile. It shot forward off the rail trailing smoke. He lowered the nose, aimed a little left, and fired a second missile. A hard right turn, fifteen degrees of heading change, and a third missile was in the air. Total elapsed time, about six seconds. If there were Japanese fighters there, the missiles would find them.

The third missile had just disappeared into the haze when the ECM squealed in his ears.

The AA light was flashing, and a red light on the instrument panel just below his gunsight: 'Missile!'

Yan Chernov slammed the stick sideways and pulled. The plane flicked over on its side and he laid the G on. A target decoy was automatically kicked out by the countermeasures gear.

Five ... six ... seven G.

A missile flashed over his right wing and detonated. A miss. The Missile warning light went out, but the ECM continued to chirp and flash direction lights. The Japanese were on the air now.

Ten years ago nothing on the planet could turn with a Su-27. It could still out-turn missiles, so Yan Chernov was still alive.

He came out of burner, retarded the throttles as quickly as he dared – he certainly didn't want to flame out just now – and let the G bleed off his airspeed. He got the nose up to the horizon.

A Japanese fighter overshot above him.

There might be two of them ...

His skin felt like ice as he slammed the stick right and rolled hard to reverse his turn. The ECM was singing.

The Japanese pilot was turning left, beginning to roll back upright.

Chernov pulled with all his might to raise the nose.

As the enemy fighter streaked across from right to left, Chernov had his thumb on the 30-mm cannon, which vomited out a river of fire. The finger of God.

The flaming river of shells passed through the wing of the Japanese fighter.

Chernov rolled upside down, pulled as he lit his burners. There had to be someone else out there: the ECM was chirping madly.

The earth filled the windscreen. Going straight down, accelerating ... *Only 23,000 feet, fool.* He rolled the plane and scanned quickly. Nothing. Now the ECM was silent.

He began to pull. Pull pull pull at seven G's, fight to stay conscious. . . The sweat stung his eyes, and his vision began to gray.

He was screaming now, watching the yellow earth rushing up at him, trying to stay conscious.

He was going to make it.

Yes!

Relax the stick, drop to a hundred feet or two, just above the earth, and let the old girl accelerate.

The ECM stayed silent.

He twisted his head, looked behind. Right. Left.

Nothing.

Two planes falling way off the right. On fire – one of them large enough to appear as a black dot against the yellow cirrus layer.

When Yan Chernov taxied into the hard stand at Zeya, his flight suit and gear were soaked. The sweat was still running off him in rivulets, even though he had the canopy open. On the instrument panel, the needle on the G meter that recorded the maximum G pulled that flight rested on 9.

Nine G's with only a stomach-and-legs G suit. The wings might have come off under that much overstress. He would have to have the mechanics carefully inspect the plane.

Chernov waited until the linemen had the chocks in place, then secured the engines.

'Water,' he said. The senior NCO passed up a bottle.

'How did it go, Major?' one of the junior pilots asked after he finished drinking. There were four of them standing there, gazing at the empty missile racks and the gun port with the tape shot away.

'I got two, I think. Maybe three. One of them almost took my scalp.'

'Very good.'

'Luck. Pure luck. They just happened to come along, and I just happened to see them before they saw me.' He shook his head, filled with wonder that he was still alive.

'They are good?'

'Good enough.' He tossed his helmet down, then climbed down from the cockpit. When he was on the ground, he drank more of the water. 'Do you have another plane ready?'

'Yes, Major,' said the senior NCO.

'Two?'

'Just one, sir. We hope to get three more flyable tonight by cannibalizing parts from the down birds. And the fueling takes forever.'

'Any word from Moscow?'

'No, sir. They haven't called.'

'We will fly the planes west in the morning, as many as we have fuel for. As many as we can get started.'

Damn Moscow. With almost no fuel, no spare parts, little food, one-third of the mechanics the squadron was supposed to have, and an inoperative GCI site, he couldn't do much more, even if Kalugin wrote the order in blood. He was being realistic. He had flown a stupid solo mission, almost gotten killed, affected the course of the war not at all, and now it was time to face facts: Russia was defenseless.

'I'll bet Zambia has a better air force than we have,' one of the junior officers muttered.

Chernov took off his flight gear and sat down by a main tire with the water bottle and waved them away.

'Let me rest awhile.'

His mind was still going a thousand miles an hour, replaying the missile shots and the Japanese fighter slashing across in front of his gun. The emotional highs and lows – amazing! He would never have believed that he could feel so much elation, then, five seconds later, so much terror. He was wrung out, like a sponge squeezed to millimeter thickness in a hydraulic press.

Five minutes later one of the NCOs came for him from the dispersal shack.

'Sir, Moscow is on the line. Someone very senior.'

'How senior?'

'He says he's a general, sir. I never heard of him.'

Chernov walked across the ramp and entered the dispersal building, a single room with a naked bulb in the ceiling – not burning, of course; the only light came from the dirty windows. A large potbellied woodstove stood in the center of the room. The four or five enlisted men in the room fell silent when Chernov walked in and reached for the phone.

'Major Chernov, sir.'

'Major, this is General Kokovtsov, aide to Marshal Stolypin.'

'In Moscow?'

'Headquarters.'

'I've been trying to telephone regional headquarters and Moscow since the Japanese invaded. You are the first senior officer I've spoken to.'

The desk soldier had other things on his mind. 'I asked to speak to the commanding officer. Are you in command of the base?'

'Apparently so, General.'

'A fighter base should have a brigadier general in command.'

'Our general retired four years ago and was never replaced. Two of our squadrons were transferred three years ago and took their airplanes with them. The other squadron was decommissioned: The people left, but the airplanes stayed, parked in revetments. My squadron, the Five hundred fifty-sixth, is the last.'

'And you are a major?'

'That is correct, sir. Major Chernov. We used to have a colonel. This spring, he and some of the other officers took several vehicles and left. We haven't seen them since. They said they were going to Irkutsk, near Lake Baikal. To find work. The colonel had relatives in Moscow, I believe. He talked of the city often, so he may have gone there.'

'He had orders?'

'No.'

'He deserted!'

'Call it what you like.'

'Desertion.'

'The colonel drove out of here in broad daylight. The others too. They were owed over eighteen months' pay. They hadn't seen a ruble in six months.'

Silence from Moscow. Finally, the general said, 'Why are you still there?'

'My wife left me five years ago, General. I'm alone. This place is as good as any other.'

'You are loyal.'

'To what? What I am is stupid. The government owes me almost two years' pay. I haven't been paid anything since the colonel was, nine months ago. Neither have these enlisted men. We're selling small arms and ammunition on the black market to get money for food. When we don't have any money, we ask for credit. When we can't get credit, we steal. But enough of this social chitchat – what did you call me to talk about?'

'I'm sorry.'

'Believe me, so am I.'

'Marshal Stolypin wants you to harass the Japanese. Just that. Launch a few sections a day, try to shoot down a transport or two, force them to maximum effort to protect their resources.'

'I thought Stolypin retired years ago. Samsonov is –'

'Samsonov is dead. Stolypin has come out of retirement to lead us against the Japanese.'

'Maybe he can work a miracle.'

'Don't be insubordinate, Major.'

'I'm trying, sir.'

'So what have you done, if anything, to fight the war?'

'I went up a while ago. One plane. They shot at me; I shot at them.'

'One sortie?' he asked, disbelief apparent in his voice.

'Three today. We flew six yesterday.'

'Only nine?'

The jerk! Chernov had dealt with asshole superiors all his adult life. He kept his voice absolutely calm, without even a trace of emotion. 'We can launch one more sortie this evening. We have fuel for perhaps eight more; then we're done.'

'We'll have fuel delivered.'

'The electricity has been off here for a month. No one has paid the power

143

company, so they shut it off. We have to pump the fuel from the tanks to the planes by hand, which takes a lot of time and effort.'

'President Kalugin has signed a decree. The electricity will be turned back on.'

'Terrific. War by decree.' Yan Chernov couldn't help himself. He was losing his composure. Maybe it was adrenaline aftershock.

'We want you to launch some sections to harass the enemy,' the general said from the safety of Moscow. 'Don't be too aggressive, you understand. Inflict just enough pain to annoy them. That is the order of Marshal Stolypin.'

Chernov lost it completely. 'You fool! We worked for four days to get six sorties out yesterday. Two sorties a day on a sustained basis is all we could possibly launch, even if World War Three is declared. My executive officer was killed this morning. We have no food, no fuel, no electricity, no spare parts, no GCI site, no intelligence support, no staff ... *We have nothing!* Have I made it clear? Do you comprehend?'

'I am a general, Major. Watch your tongue.'

'Get your head out of your ass, General. We can't defend this base. We should be flying these planes west to save them. It's just a matter of time before the Japanese attack. It's a miracle they haven't already. I can only assume you and Stolypin *want* the Japanese to attack us, because you are taking no steps to prevent it. When we're dead, you idiots in Moscow won't have to ever feed us or pay us or –'

The headquarters general hung up before the major completed the last sentence. When Chernov realized the line was dead, he quit talking and slammed down the telephone.

Everyone in the room was staring at him.

'Everything that can fly goes west at dawn,' Chernov shouted, spittle flying from his lips. 'Work everyone all night.'

'Yes, sir.'

Chernov turned to face the junior officers who had trickled in while he was on the telephone.

'Get the trucks we have left. Fuel them. Have the men load the tools and all the food we have. They may take their clothes. Nothing else. No furniture or televisions or any of that other crap.'

He was roaring at the top of his lungs, unable to help himself. 'We will drive west, all the way to Moscow. If we get there before the Japanese, we will drag the generals from their comfortable offices and hang them by the balls.'

Yan Chernov stomped out to pee in the grass.

Delivery of the Russian ultimatum to the Japanese was a chore that fell to Ambassador Stanley P. Hanratty. The Russian diplomats had all left Tokyo the day after the invasion, turning out the lights and locking the door of the embassy as they left. The U.S. government offered to assist the Russians diplomatically in the Japanese capital until relations were restored, an offer that Kalugin seized upon. Delivery of the ultimatum was Ambassador Hanratty's first chore for the Russians. Of course, he and the U.S. government were privy to the contents of the note.

Hanratty returned the following morning to the Japanese foreign ministry to receive the Japanese reply. 'We find it difficult to believe, in this day and age,' the Japanese foreign minister said as he handed over the written reply, 'that any government on the planet would threaten another with nuclear war. Still, in anticipation of just such an event, Japan has developed its own nuclear arsenal. Should Russia attempt to launch a first strike upon Japan, the Japanese government will, with profound regret, order a massive retaliatory strike upon Russia.'

It was late in the day in Moscow when Kalugin received the Japanese answer from Danilov. He read the reply carefully, then handed the paper back without a word.

12

By working throughout the long evening and short night, the officers and enlisted men of Major Chernov's squadron at the Zeya Air Base got six planes into flyable condition. The planes were ready a half hour before the true dawn. Chernov had the best one armed with cannon shells and four AA-10 missiles.

Chernov had ordered five of his pilots, the five most senior, to fly to Chita, five hundred nautical miles west, well beyond range of the Zeros. Now he slapped them on the back, watched them strap in, start engines, and taxi. They took off one by one, white-hot exhausts accelerating faster and faster and faster. The roar of their engines filled the night with a deep, rolling thunder.

The fighters kept their exterior lights off and did not bother to rendezvous. They retracted their wheels as they came out of burner and turned west. Still, it was several minutes before the roar of the last plane had faded.

Yan Chernov stood beside the sixth plane and listened until even the background moan was gone and all he could hear were the insects chirping and singing, as they had done on this steppe every summer since the world was young.

The senior warrant officer came over. They shook hands. 'Roll the trucks now,' Chernov said. 'Get the men to Chita, if possible. If not, go as far west as you can. The Japanese may attack at dawn, hoping to catch us sleeping.' He glanced at his watch. The night at these latitudes was only two hours long.

'Do you really think so, Major?'

'There is a chance they'll strike as soon as there is light enough.'

'Why today?'

'I hurt them yesterday. They should have hit us days ago. Now they will.'

'I suppose.'

Chernov shrugged. 'This morning or soon.'

'I've already sent the other trucks on. I'll wait and go with your linesmen.'

Chernov held out his hand. The warrant office took it.

The major smoked the last of his cigarettes as he eyed the northeastern sky, waiting for the first glow of dawn. He had been rationing himself, to make the cigarettes last. When these were gone . . . well, without money . . .

The night was not really dark. At this latitude summer night could accurately be described as a deep twilight. He could see stars, so the sky was clear and visibility good. Chernov had grown up in a village dozens of miles from the nearest town, far from urban light pollution, so stars were old friends.

He had finished his last cigarette and was strolling around the airplane, touching it, caressing it, trying to stay calm and focused, when the stars in the east began to fade.

He climbed to the cockpit and the senior linesman helped him strap in. 'Take care of yourself, sir.'

'Peace and friendship, Sergeant,' the pilot said, repeating the traditional phrase.

He sat alone in the cockpit, watching the sky turn pale. He had no fuel to waste, yet if he delayed his takeoff too long, the Japanese would catch him on the ground. If they came.

He could wait no longer. He gave the signal to the linesman.

Seven minutes later, sitting on the end of the runway, he ran through his takeoff checklist. Everything looked good. The radio didn't work, so he didn't turn it on. The ECM gear did work. He watched the telltale lights intently, listened with the volume turned up to maximum. And he saw and heard nothing.

Maybe the Japanese weren't coming. Maybe he would be shot for cowardice in the face of the enemy. Be shot by that officious desk general who had called yesterday wanting the brigadier. A sick joke, that.

The stars were going fast.

Yan Chernov released the brakes and smoothly shoved the throttles forward to the stops. Pressures good, fuel flow fine, rpm and tailpipe temperatures coming up nicely . . .

Now he lit the burners. The white light of the afterburners split the darkness like newborn stars.

The acceleration pushed him back into the seat. Despite the fact the Sukhoi-27 was a big plane, weighing about 44,000 pounds this morning, it accelerated quickly. Soon the trim lifted the nosewheel off the pavement. He steadied her there, flew her off.

Gear up, then out of burner as soon as possible. When everything was up and in, he turned to the southwest. The most probable direction for an approach by enemy attackers was southeast. If he could make another side attack before they spotted him, he might be able to . . .

He leveled at ten thousand feet and let the speed build to .8 Mach. At this low altitude, fuel flow was high. Nervous, he glanced again at his watch. He had been airborne for six minutes.

After ten minutes of flight, he began a long, slow 180-degree turn. His head was on a swivel, searching the early-morning sky in every direction, especially to the south and east. He was tempted to tap his radar for one sweep, just to see, but he decided it was too dangerous.

The sky to the northeast was a pale blue. Visibility excellent, easily fifty miles. It's just that small airplanes more than a few miles away are exceedingly difficult to see in the great vastness of the sky, he thought. And this early, with the earth below still dark, the task was almost impossible – unless the planes were in that northeast quadrant, silhouetted against the growing light.

He tried to resist the temptation to stare toward the northeast. They would probably approach the base from the southwest, from the darkness!

He searched futilely in all directions.

Nothing.

Maybe the Japanese aren't coming.

What a fucked-up war! *It's every man for himself, comrades. We have fucked up our country so badly that we have nothing to sustain our soldiers with. It's poor, polluted, filled with starving people and radioactive waste.*

Chernov did a 360-degree circle, then another one.

He was sweating.

Well, this idea was stupid. Stupid, stupid, stupid. He should have gone with the others to Chita, talked to the people at headquarters from a telephone there, set up a liaison with a tanker squadron. Su-27s should be operated from a secure, well-defended base, one properly supplied with fuel and ordnance and spare parts, one beyond the range of the Japanese. Then, with the help of airborne tankers, the fighters could be launched on combat missions against the enemy here at Zeya or even at Khabarovsk.

Why dawn? Why did he think they would come at dawn?

He admitted to himself that he didn't know the answer to that question. He just sensed it. A dawn attack seemed to fit.

He glanced at his fuel gauge. Then his watch.

Keep the eyes moving, look at that sky, look for the tiniest speck that isn't supposed to be there.

His ECM chirped. Just a chirp and a flash of light. He eyed the panel, waiting for the light to flash again, waiting for a strobe to indicate direction. Nothing. He looked outside. He couldn't maintain a watch on the damned panel.

Maybe a Japanese pilot had given in to the temptation that Chernov had resisted – maybe he had tickled his radar, let it sweep once, just to verify that . . . to verify . . .

Three tiny specks, way out there, against the blue of the dawn. The sun was just ready to pop over the earth's rim, and above the growing light in the sky he could see moving black specks. Three. No, four. Five. Six. Moving to the west. They would pass well north of Chernov's position.

So.

Six. Damn! Why did there have to be so many?

He turned to the southwest. If he came out of the darkest part of the sky while they were working over the base, he would be difficult to acquire visually.

They would turn their radars on as soon as they suspected he was around. Still, if he got first shot . . .

Yan Chernov eased the throttles forward, right against the stops. He wasn't ready for afterburner yet. Full power without the burners gave him .95 Mach.

Now the ECM panel lit up. The Zeros were looking for planes over Zeya.

He eased the nose into a descent, let the plane accelerate, retrimming constantly. Mach 1, now 1.1, now 1.2. Still at full military power.

He made the turn to go back toward the base, checked the handheld GPS. Master armament switch on.

Four missiles selected, lights red. They were armed and ready. Each squeeze of the trigger on the stick would fire one.

He leveled at five hundred feet, just above the earth. Down to Mach 1.1, decelerating because the engines could not hold him supersonic without the thrust of the afterburners. If only he had a modern plane, like an F-22. Or even a Zero.

Fifteen miles. Fourteen. Thirteen – a nautical mile every six seconds.

He glanced again at the ECM panel. All ahead, nothing behind. *Nothing behind that is radiating*. He took a ragged breath, tried to calm himself. His heart felt like a trip-hammer in his chest.

Ten miles. Nine. Eight . . .

At seven miles he pulled the nose up five degrees and squeezed off an AA-10 missile. Then a second, third, and fourth, as fast as he could pull the trigger. These fire-and-forget missiles had active radar homing. With luck, two or three of them would find targets.

He opened the afterburners full. The acceleration pushed him back into his seat. His fingers flicked the switches to select 'Gun' on the armament panel.

The Japanese must have picked up the radar emissions of the inbound missiles.

Now he flipped the switch that caused his radar to transmit.

The scope blossomed.

He was still looking outside, through the gunsight, when he saw the first flash – a missile hit. Now another. And a third.

The fourth missile must have missed.

Yan Chernov glanced at the radar scope, quickly turned one of the knobs to adjust the gain.

A plane on the left, heading slightly away.

He looked through the gunsight. There! At eleven o'clock.

A *transport*! Parachutes in the air! Paratroops. The Japanese were taking the field. All that registered in Chernov's mind without conscious thought. He was concentrating on the transport.

He was going to get a deflection shot. He was doing Mach 1.4; the other plane, probably two hundred knots max.

He jabbed at the rudder, adjusted the stick with both hands to get the nose where he wanted it. He squeezed the trigger, and the gun erupted, hosing fire.

It was over in two seconds. The stream of white-hot lead was in front of the enemy transport, then, with the gentlest touch on the right rudder, stitched it from nose to tail. The four engine turboprop blew up and Chernov shot just behind the expanding fireball, still accelerating. Mach 1.7 now, all the Sukhoi would give him in this thick air. His eyes registered the sight of more parachutes, but he was busy flying. The enemy radars were emitting in his rear quadrant now. He let the nose sag in order to get down against the earth.

As the seconds ticked by, he felt his shoulder blades tighten. Sure enough, the Missile light under the gunsight began to flash.

Level thirty meters above the ground, Chernov punched out chaff, rolled the plane ninety degrees to the left, and pulled the stick into his gut until the meter read 7 G's. Sweat stung his eyes. The horizon was right there, a line through his gunsight. He fought the temptation to look over his left shoulder, concentrated instead on keeping the horizon below the dot in the gunsight that represented his flight path. If that dot dropped below the horizon, he would be into the ground in seconds, and very, very dead.

A missile went over his right shoulder, exploded harmlessly after it was by.

The next one went off just under the plane, a sickening thud that slammed the plane hard.

He rolled right, through level, into a right turn. Less G now, because the Missile light was off. So was the ECM panel. It shouldn't be. The Japanese were still back there, perhaps trying to catch him. If he could keep his speed up, they never would. He needed to extend out.

For the first time, he glanced at his system gauges, the gauges that told him of his steed's health.

Uh-oh. Hydraulic pressure was dropping; he had three yellow warning lights and a red. The red was a generator.

Oh, God! The ECM panel was silent because it lost power when one of the generators dropped off the line.

Just then another missile exploded above him: a flash, a pop, followed by a rattle of shrapnel against the fuselage.

He leveled the wings. Despite the low altitude, he risked a look aft.

Nothing visible behind. Still Mach 1.6 on the airspeed indicator.

Fuel trailing away behind the right wing. He could just see the fuel boiling off the wing in the rearview mirror. A glance at the gauge for fuel in the right wing. Almost empty.

Another gentle left turn. He consulted the GPS. Fifteen miles from the base, going northeast.

Yan Chernov kept the left wing down about ten degrees, let the nose slowly come toward the north, then the northwest. It seemed as if the wing was almost in the grass of the steppe. The sensation of speed was overpowering, sublime; he was orbiting the planet at a distance of five meters. He watched intently ahead, focused with all his being, tugging the plane over rises and rolling hills. If the wing kissed the earth now, he would never know it: He would be dead before the sensation registered.

He leveled the wings, heading west.

Are the Zeros chasing? They must not have the fuel to chase.

Oil pressure to the right engine was dropping quickly.

Chernov came out of burner. When he did, the right rpm began dropping. He pulled the throttle to idle cutoff, secured the fuel flow.

He still had one engine, one generator.

At fifty miles from the base, he took off his oxygen mask and swabbed the sweat from his eyes and face.

He checked the fuel again. Must be another leak somewhere. He had enough for thirty more minutes of flight, if he didn't have any fuel leaks. With leaks, less. But he was alive.

Pavel Saratov walked the periscope around slowly. The attack scope protruded just inches above the surface of the sea, which fortunately was calm today. Still, a wave occasionally washed over the glass. When it did he paused until he could see again, then continued his sweep. Visibility was about ten miles, he estimated.

There were three ships in view, two going into Tokyo Bay, one leaving. Container ships, one about thirty thousand tons, the other two larger.

Not a warship in sight. Not even a patrol boat.

He flipped the handle so that he could scan the sky. Overcast in all directions. No airplanes.

Back to the ships. Two going northeast, up the channel into the Uraga Strait entrance to Tokyo Bay, one coming out.

The ship nearest the land was too far away and opening the distance, but if he hurried, he could probably get firing solutions on the other two and send them to the bottom. Now.

He had ten torpedoes. He should have had a dozen, which would have been a full load, but there had been only eleven fueled torpedoes in the naval armory, and he had drained the fuel from one to sell for food. These were not new, modern torpedoes – they were the old 53–65 antiship, wake-homing torpedoes, the first of the Soviet wake-homers.

Saratov had loaded the ten torpedoes aboard *Admiral Kolchak* because naval regulations required that the boat be armed whenever it went to sea. Not that anyone gave a damn. Saratov loaded the torpedoes anyway. It seemed to him that if he didn't obey naval regulations, he had no right to demand obedience from the men.

He had always feared the implications if he and the men one day just chose not to obey. Would they then be merely a bunch of bums looking for a meal . . . seagoing bums? Pirates?

He pulled his head back from the scope. The members of the attack team were looking at him expectantly, waiting for him to call ranges and bearings that they could put into the attack computer.

'No warships,' he told Askold, the executive officer.

Askold was from the Ukraine, but he had chosen the Russian navy seventeen years ago, when the union collapsed. The Ukrainian navy looked like a good place to starve. He grinned at Saratov now. 'Let's blast away and get the hell out.'

'There should be warships,' Saratov said, turning his attention back to the periscope. 'The entrance to Tokyo Bay, for God's sake.'

'Are you sure there are no submarines about?' Askold asked the sonar operator, who shook his head no. He looked insulted. If he had heard anything that might be a submarine amid the cacophony of screw noises around the entrance to this bay, he would have said so.

'Give me another few turns on the motors, Chief,' Saratov ordered. The boat was going so slowly that the bow and stern planes were ineffective, which caused the submarine to bob up and down, making the scope rise too far out of the water and then dip under.

'Aye aye, sir.'

After one more complete look around, Saratov ordered the scope lowered. He turned to the chart on the table. 'There should be patrol boats, destroyers, an airplane, something.'

Had he lucked into an interlude when the pickets guarding the entrance to the bay were off watch? If so, he should strike quickly and make his escape.

Askold stood beside him, staring at the chart. 'Ten torpedoes . . . What are we going to do afterward?' He asked the question softly, actually in a whisper.

'I don't know,' Saratov murmured.

'Assuming we survive the afterward.'

'They've left Tokyo Bay unguarded.'

Askold pinched his nose. 'There must be an antisubmarine net across the entrance. That at the very least.'

'There are no picket boats to open and close it. Two freighters are going in now, one coming out. It's wide open.'

'How arrogant are these people?'

'We had four diesel/electric boats at sea in the Pacific when the war started. All the nuke boats are junk. If you were Japanese, wouldn't you put your antisubmarine forces around your invasion fleet?'

'Hmm, the invasion fleet. That *is* the target we were assigned,' Askold said, pretending to be thinking aloud.

'I wonder if headquarters assigned all four of our boats to Vlad?'

'Perhaps,' Askold said slowly. 'Do you think –'

'I only know that there are no antisubmarine forces here,' Saratov interrupted. 'Not even a rowboat.'

Saratov motioned for the periscope. When it was up, he made another complete sweep, then turned so that he was looking at the entrance to Tokyo Bay. The entrance was several miles wide. The bay was huge, over a hundred square miles.

One thing was certain: The Japanese would never expect a Russian sub to go in there. Hell, they weren't even expecting an enemy sub here at the entrance.

There was a huge refinery on the west side of the bay at Yokosuka, near the naval base. North, up the west coast of the bay, was Yokohama, the commercial shipping port. The main anchorage at Yokohama would be full of tankers, bulk freighters, container ships.

Ten torpedoes – six were in the tubes, all of which were in the bow. This class of boat had no stern tubes.

He also had four shoulder-fired RPG-9 antitank rockets that he had obtained in a trade a few years back. The rockets had two-kilo warheads, which would punch a hole in any tank on earth, but they weren't ship killers.

The boat had no deck gun, of course. There hadn't been a deck gun on a Soviet submarine since the last one was removed in the early 1950s. Deck guns made too much noise when the submarine was submerged and were of limited utility when surfaced. Still, in a crowded anchorage, with the sailors taking their time, aiming at big, well-lit, stationary targets at point-blank range, a gun certainly would be nice.

This boat was equipped with tubes to launch four surface-to-air missiles. The tubes were in the sail, and they were empty. Saratov hadn't seen a missile in years.

The two demolition experts and their plastique – he had forgotten about them.

'Down scope.'

The captain surveyed the expectant faces ... so eager, so trusting! The faith of these fools!

Saratov turned back to the chart. After studying it for a moment, he pointed with a finger. 'XO, let's head eastward at slow speed. After dark, we'll surface and recharge the batteries.'

'Yes, sir.' Askold reached for the parallel ruler.

'Sonar, I want you to listen carefully this afternoon. Listen for destroyers, patrol boats, anything that isn't a freighter or fishing smack. Let's see what tonight brings.'

He looked at his watch. Two in the afternoon.

'At three, I want to see all officers in the wardroom.'

The army truck came along the paved highway at a good rate of speed. There wasn't much traffic, only a few trucks, and almost all of them going west to escape the invaders.

Yan Chernov sat on a rock beside the highway, watching the trucks come and go. He had been bleeding from a cut on his arm, but he had torn a strip off his undershirt and bound it up, and now the bleeding seemed to have stopped. Somehow he had also strained his right shoulder in the ejection, although nothing seemed to be broken or ripped. The shoulder ached fiercely; he moved it anyway, trying to work out the soreness.

God, he was tired. He was tempted to stretch out beside the road and sleep.

A bleak landscape. The breeze from the west carried clouds. The clouds obscured the sun now and the air was cool.

He was walking around to keep warm when one of the trucks flying by slammed on its brakes and stopped a hundred meters beyond him.

Yan Chernov picked up his helmet and survival vest and walked toward the truck.

His senior warrant officer got down from the cab, trotted toward Chernov. He stopped, saluted, then pounded Chernov on the back.

13

'Gentlemen, there is no Russian-held territory for us to return to,' Pavel Saratov said to his department heads.

'There may be a few fishing villages too small for the Japanese to bother with,' the youngest one said. He was no more than twenty-three or twenty-four. 'We could abandon the boat and swim ashore.'

'You wish to fish, do you, Krasin?'

The others pretended to chuckle. They were tightly crammed in around the small wardroom table.

Captain Saratov continued: 'Tokyo Bay is the largest port in Asia, perhaps in the world. We have ten torpedoes, four RPG-9s, and a hundred kilos of plastique. I propose to enter the bay, reconnoiter, then hit them where it hurts the most.'

'Captain, why don't we just sink three or four ships out here and be done with it?'

Saratov looked from face to face. Finally he said, 'The question is, What can we do that will hurt them the most?'

'Sir,' the engineer began, 'I don't think it is reasonable to ask the men to risk their lives to kick the Japanese. The fact is, Russia is in no position to oppose Japan. We no longer have the military capability to fight a war in the Moscow suburbs, much less in the western Pacific. The men know all this. What will we gain?'

Pavel Saratov stared at the young officer, stunned. He had never heard such a comment from a junior officer. In the old days when political officers rode the ships, such a comment would have meant the immediate termination of a naval career. He tried to keep his face under control. Finally he said, 'I am not asking the men to do anything. I give orders and they obey.'

They said nothing to that. The execution was too fresh.

'XO?'

'You make the decision, Captain. I am with you wherever you go.' That was an old, old joke. No one laughed. Askold had a weakness for terrible jokes.

'Thank you for that thought, XO. Should we go in? Your candid opinion, please.'

Askold took out a pack of cigarettes, offered them around the table. Even Saratov took one. When they were smoking, the XO said, 'We can hurt them worse inside. Sinking a big tanker in the harbor at Yokohama will have political implications in Japan that we can't begin to calculate. They'll probably get us before too long, no matter what we do. Let's kick them in the balls while we have a leg to swing.'

'What about afterward?' the engineer asked.

Pavel Saratov didn't answer. The young officer reddened.

'I don't know,' the captain said finally.

'There probably won't be an afterward,' one of them said crossly to the offender. 'Do you wanted it written out and signed?'

No one else had anything to say.

'Back to your duties,' the captain said.

'Sir, what should I put into the evening report to Moscow?' the com officer asked.

'Nothing. There will be no evening report. There will be no radio transmissions at all unless I give a direct order.'

'But, sir, we didn't make an evening report last night or the night before. Moscow may think we're dead.'

'The Japanese may think that, too. Let's hope so.'

Bogrov lingered after the others left. He was from Moscow, a naval academy graduate. When he and Saratov were alone, he said, 'You didn't have to shoot Svechin.'

'Oh, you precious little bastard, you think not, do you?'

Bogrov came to attention to deliver the riposte. He must have been thinking about it all day. 'I think that –'

'Shut up! Fool! They *must* understand – all of them. I am master of this vessel. I swore an oath, and *that oath means something to me.* I will fight this boat. Every man will do his duty. I will execute any man who doesn't. No one has a choice – not me, not you, not any of them.'

Bogrov said nothing.

'Everyone whines about conditions at home.' The captain made a gesture of irritation. 'None of that is relevant.'

Pavel Saratov crossed his hands on the table in front of him and lowered his eyes to them. His voice was very low.

'If you say one negative or disrespectful word in front of the men, Bogrov, just one, I will put a bullet into that putrefying mass of gray shit you use for brains. You will obey orders to your last breath, your last drop of blood, or I'll personally stuff your corpse into a torpedo tube.'

Cassidy and his pilots quickly settled into a routine at Rhein-Main Air Force Base in Germany. Every day each pilot spent at least two hours in one of the simulators running intercepts, dogfighting, handling emergencies. Another two hours were spent at the instructor's station watching a comrade fly the box, as the simulator was known. The rest of the working day they studied the manual on the aircraft and took written tests designed to reinforce what they already knew and to find any areas that needed refreshing.

The second evening in Germany, Bob Cassidy got them together as a group in a classroom near the simulator.

'I've been told that some of you want to post mail on the net. Is that right?'

'Yes, sir,' three or four of them muttered.

'Okay, you may do so, but each letter must be censored by another officer. Pick your own censor. Any disputes that can't be resolved amicably by the writer and censor go to Preacher Fain for resolution. All the letters must be encrypted before posting.'

Nods and smiles all around. Four or five of them looked around the room, obviously considering whom they might ask to censor their mail. Bob Cassidy continued:

'Everything we discuss in this room for the rest of the evening is classified. *Everything.*'

All the faces were directed toward him again.

'We are going to Russia this weekend. We're going to be here for four more days, and we'll fly each of those days. We'll go in flights of four, with myself or Dick Guelich leading. We'll keep doing the simulators, but we want to see each of you in the air, see how you handle the plane.

'Sunday, we will fly the planes to Chita Air Base in Siberia. Tankers will escort us there, refuel us en route. We'll go armed, ready to fight our way in.

'The F-22 squadron commanders here in Germany have been more than cooperative. The enlisted technicians that we must have to maintain the planes have volunteered en masse. So have the maintenance and staff officers. I was in the unique position of having more volunteers than we could use, so, after consulting with the squadron COs, I took the very best people available. The Air Force will lift these folks and their equipment to Chita tomorrow.

'As we speak, Sentinel missile batteries are on their way to Russia. The new Russian chief of staff, Marshal Stolypin, has agreed to place these batteries in the positions where the American technicians believe they will be the most effective.

'The Russians view this squadron and the Sentinel missile batteries as tangible proof that America is willing to come to their aid. They are doing everything in their power to help us help them. The burden, quite simply, is on us to perform.

'The time has come to lay the cards on the table, to speak the bald, unvarnished truth. I don't know why you came with me – I have never tried selling before – I doubt if I'll try it again. Regardless of why you are here, you need to know that the odds are excellent that you will die in combat within the next few weeks.

'I want each of you to ask yourself, Is this what I want? Am I willing to kill other human beings? Am I willing to die to help Russia?

'You are volunteers. Tonight is the last night I will send you home with a handshake and a thank-you. There will be no recriminations, no regrets if you come to me tonight and tell me you have reconsidered and want to go home. I understand. Tomorrow is a different deal. Tomorrow you will be in the Russian Air Army. Tomorrow I can promise nothing.'

They looked at each other, trying to see what the people on their right and left thought. Everyone was wearing his poker face and checking to see how well the others wore theirs.

'I can tell you, some of us will die. How many, I don't know. Only God knows. But some of us *will* die. I don't know who. Maybe all. I have no crystal ball. The fighting will be desperate. No quarter will be asked, none given. There are no rules in knife fights or aerial combat.

'We are going to be flying and fighting over some of the most godforsaken real estate on the planet. If you eject, no helicopter will come looking for you. No rescue brigade is going to saddle up to drag your ass out of the bush. The CIA says they will try to help, but I wouldn't hold my breath. If you can't take care of yourself, you are going to die out there a million miles from civilization. I doubt if anyone will ever find your corpse. Siberia is huge beyond comprehension.

'Think about it this evening. I'll be in my room if anyone wants to talk.'

Bob Cassidy left then. Before he went to his room, he went to the base communications office and put in a secure call via the satellite phone to General Tuck's aide in the Pentagon, Colonel John Eatherly. He called each evening, told Eatherly everything. Tonight they discussed the pilots.

'Will any of them quit?'

'Lacy might. I don't know. We'll see.'

'What about Hudek?' Eatherly asked. 'I almost dropped my teeth when I saw his file. I think maybe you're taking a big chance with him.'

'He's a killer, a psychopath.'

'Hmmm...'

'Some of the best aces have been crazy as bed bugs. Guys like Albert Ball, the Red Baron...'

'A dozen or two I could name,' Eatherly agreed.

'So I brought the guy. I hope I don't live to regret it.'

'Well, if he gets too weird, you can shoot him yourself. The Russian regs are a bit more liberal than the UCMJ.' The UCMJ was the Uniform Code of Military Justice, which governed discipline in the U.S. armed forces.

Cassidy laughed at that.

'At least you can laugh,' Eatherly said.

'That's because I don't know how many are going to quit on me. I'd better go find out.'

Bob Cassidy said good night and walked back to the VOQ. In his room he worked on paperwork undisturbed until midnight, then turned out his lights and went to bed. No one even tapped on the door.

After dark, the Russian submarine *Admiral Kolchak* raised its snorkel and started its diesel engines. The boat was twenty miles east of the island of Oshima, outside the entrance of Tokyo Bay. Saratov or the XO kept a constant watch through the periscope. After observing the lights of several freighters, Saratov concluded that visibility was down to about three miles in light rain. Every ship up there was radar-equipped, and the Japanese probably had shore-based radar to help keep track of shipping, so surfacing was out of the question.

He worried about the destroyers that he couldn't see. Was it carelessness, arrogance, hubris that caused the Japanese to leave the door to Tokyo Bay unguarded? Or had they set a trap, a trap to catch a fool?

Saratov had no combat experience, of course. The Soviet/Russian navy had not fired a shot since 1945, before the captain was born. He felt as green as grass, completely out of his element.

Had he assessed this situation correctly, or was there something that he was missing?

Right now a little experience would be a comfort. He consoled himself with the thought that the Japanese didn't have any more experience than he did.

His neck and arms began to ache. He kept his eyes glued to the scope, kept it moving.

Two hours later, he was still at it. He wanted as much of a charge on the batteries as possible before he secured the diesel engines and lowered the snorkel.

If only this were his old nuclear-powered *Alfa* boat! He could stay on the bottom of Tokyo Bay until the food ran out. Not so with this diesel/electric museum artifact; *Admiral Kolchak* could remain submerged for about seven days with the electric motors barely turning over. Even with the engines off, lying on the bottom, seven days was about the limit – the air would be so foul that the men would be in danger of death by asphyxiation.

Every hour he was in the bay the chances of remaining undetected diminished. He had no time to waste. He must either attack the Japanese or sneak away out to sea.

He worked his way toward the entrance, waiting for a ship to come along that was going in. If the Japanese had passive listening devices – hydrophones – at the entrance, the sound of a freighter rumbling through might hide the sound of this boat.

He had to play it like the Japs were listening, because they might be. The damned fools *should be,* anyway.

Midnight passed, then one o'clock. The XO relieved Saratov at the scope for fifteen minutes while he relieved himself, looked at the chart, and drank a hot cup of tea.

It was past two when he saw a big container ship, over fifty thousand tons, steaming along the channel to enter the bay. It was bearing down on the sub, making about ten knots. He was tempted to torpedo it then and there.

No. We can do more damage inside.

He got out of the container ship's way, then muttered to the officer of the deck, 'This one. We go in with this one.'

He kept the snorkel up. Running at ten knots on the battery would quickly drain it, and he couldn't afford that. On the other hand, the boat made a lot more noise with the diesels running than it did on the battery. If the Japs had hydrophones at the entrance to the bay, the odds were good that they would hear the sub.

Even if the Japanese hear it, Pavel Saratov thought, they may not recognize the sound for what it is. Or they may ignore it. He needed a nearly full charge on the battery going in. Tomorrow night he would have little time to put a charge on, and he might need every amp to evade antisubmarine forces. He thought the problem through and made his choice.

He turned the boat and fell in about five hundred meters behind the freighter. It was huge, and lit up like a small city.

With the scope magnification turned up, he could read the words on the stern: LINDA SUE, MONROVIA. There were actually two little spotlights on the stern rail that illuminated the name.

He had spent the evening studying the chart of the bay. He recognized the turn in the channel off Uraga Point and the naval anchorage. He stayed with *Linda Sue* as she steamed slowly and majestically along the channel that would take her to the container piers at Yokohama or Tokyo. There were numerous small craft in the bay, despite the limited visibility and rain – launches, fishing boats, police cruisers.

Several small fishing craft were silhouetted against the city lights on the western shore of the bay, which ran from horizon to horizon. Then he saw a boat anchored just outside the shipping channel. Reluctantly, he ordered the diesel secured and the snorkel lowered. The sound of the diesel exhausting through the snorkel was loud if one was on the surface listening, so Saratov decided to play it safe.

He cruised up to Yokohama and examined the hundred or so ships waiting to get to the piers for loading and unloading. A forest of ships from nations all over the world – all except Russia. Well, they were all fair game as far as he was concerned, discharging and taking on cargo in a belligerent port.

It took five hours to cruise up the bay, then back south, where he picked a spot to settle into the bottom mud a kilometer offshore from a refinery on the northern edge of Yokosuka, north of the naval base. A pier led from the refinery out into the water about a half kilometer. Two conventional tankers were moored to it, but at the very end rested a liquid natural gas – LNG – tanker, with a huge pressure vessel amidships.

He had a splitting headache. He stood in the control room massaging his neck, rubbing his eyes.

No one had much to say. When they did want to communicate, they whispered, as if the Japanese were in the next room with a glass against the wall. Perhaps they sensed they were on the edge of something, something large and fierce and infinitely dangerous.

Saratov smiled to himself, went to his tiny stateroom, and stretched out on the bunk. Although the men didn't know it, the boat was probably safer in the mud of Tokyo Bay than it had been at any time since the start of hostilities.

Tonight. They would roll the dice tonight.

In the meantime, he had to sleep.

The two navy enlisted demolition divers sat across from Pavel Saratov in the wardroom, sipping tea. It was late afternoon. Dirty dishes were stacked to one side of the table.

The demolition men were magnificent physical specimens. Of medium height, they didn't have five pounds of fat between them. With thick necks, bulging biceps, and heavily veined weight lifter's arms, these two certainly didn't look like sailors.

'Where did the navy get you guys?' Saratov asked.

'We were Spetsnaz, Captain,' one of them said. His name was stenciled on his shirt: Martos. The other was named Filimonov. 'They disestablished our unit, discharged everybody. We had a choice – a gang of truck hijackers or the seagoing navy.'

'Hmmm,' the captain said, sipping tea.

Filimonov explained. 'The hijackers were the better deal. Less work, more money. Unfortunately, they liked to brag and throw money around. We thought they would not be with us long. Last we heard only a few are still alive, hiding in the forest.'

'Capitalism is a hard life.'

'Very competitive, sir.'

'I want you to destroy a refinery. Could you do that?'

'A refinery! With the plastique?'

'I thought you might go out through the air lock in the torpedo room, swim ashore – the distance is about a kilometer – plant the explosives, then swim back to us.'

They looked at each other. 'It would be possible, sir. When?'

'Tonight. As soon as it's dark. How long would it take?'

'The longer we have, the better job we can make of it.'

'I want to start fires they can't easily extinguish, do maximum damage.'

'Ahh, maximum damage.' Martos grinned at the captain, then at Filimonov. Half his teeth were gray steel.

Filimonov's face twisted into a grimace. It occurred to Saratov that this was his grin.

'Give us six hours and we will start the biggest fire Tokyo has ever seen.'

'Six hours,' Filimonov agreed. 'Maximum damage.'

'Okay,' Pavel Saratov said. 'Six hours from the moment you exit the air lock.'

'We do not have our usual equipment aboard, Captain. Without some kind of homer, we will have difficulty finding the boat on our return.'

'Any suggestions?'

'We could make a small float, perhaps, anchor it to the air-lock hatch.'

'What if the submarine is on the surface?'

'That would be best for us, sir.'

Saratov made his decision. 'We'll take the risk. We will surface at oh-three-thirty.'

'We'll find the boat, sir.'

'After we surface, we will wait fifteen minutes for you. If you do not return during those fifteen minutes, we will leave without you.'

'If we do not return, Captain, we will be dead.'

Pavel Saratov went to the torpedo room to watch Martos and Filimonov exit through the air lock. Both men had on black wet suits and scuba gear. The plastique, fuses, and detonators were contained in two waterproof bags, one for each man. Two sailors could barely lift each bag.

Both swimmers had knives strapped to their wrists. Saratov wished he had guns to give them, but he didn't. The Spetsnaz had waterproof guns and ammo for their frogmen, but navy divers weren't so equipped.

'Don't fret it, Captain. The knives are quite enough. We are competent, and very careful.'

They went into the air lock one at a time. Martos was first. He climbed the ladder into the lock, donned his flippers, then with one hand pulled the bag of explosives that the sailors held up into the lock. The sailors dogged the hatch behind him.

Five minutes later, it was Filimonov's turn. He, too, had no trouble pulling the bag of explosives the last three feet into the lock. He gave the sailors a thumbs-up as they closed the hatch.

When he heard the outside hatch close for the second time, Pavel Saratov looked at his watch. It was 21:35. At 03:30, he would surface the boat, twenty-four hours after he had secured the snorkel.

Saratov went back to the control room. The XO and the chief were there. 'They are gone. At oh-three-thirty we will rise to periscope depth, take a look around, then surface. I want two men on deck to help get the Spetsnaz swimmers aboard. I want two more men in the forward torpedo room to stand by with the rocket-propelled grenades. If we see a target for the grenades, they can go topside and shoot them. When we get the swimmers aboard and the refinery goes up, we will go to Yokohama and fire our torpedoes into that tea party.'

The faces in the control room were tense, strained.

'We will give a good account of ourselves, men. We will do maximum damage. Then we are going to squirt this boat out through the bay's asshole and run like hell.'

Two or three of them grinned. Most just looked worried. They have too much time on their hands, the captain thought. Too much time to sit idly thinking of Russia's problems, and of girlfriends or wives and children caught in a Japanese invasion. If they are not given something to do soon, they will be unable to do anything.

'I expect every man to do his job precisely the way he has been trained. We will be shooting torpedoes and shoulder-fired rockets. Enemy warships may detect us. Things will be hectic. Just concentrate on doing your job, whatever it is.'

'Aye aye, sir,' the XO, Askold, said.

'Chief, visit every compartment. Tell everyone the plan, repeat what I just said. Every single man must do his job. Go over every man's job with him.'

'Aye aye, Captain.'

'XO, I want another meal served at oh-one hundred. The best we can do. Would you see to it, please?' All this activity would use precious oxygen – the air was already foul – but Saratov felt the morale boost would be worth it. Using oxygen and energy that would be required later if the Japanese found them before they surfaced was a calculated risk. Life is a calculated risk, he told himself. 'Better break out the carbon-dioxide absorbers, too.'

'Yes, sir.'

'Bogrov, send this message to Moscow when we surface.' He passed a sheet of paper to the communications officer. 'I want the navy and the Russian nation to know what these men have done, to know that each and every one of them has done his duty as a Russian sailor.'

'I'll encode it now, sir,' Bogrov said. 'Have it ready.'

'Fine.'

When the Russian sailors aboard *Admiral Kolchak* cleaned up after the postmidnight meal, they had nothing to do but wait. They had had all day and all evening to prepare for action. All loose gear was stowed and the equipment had been checked and rechecked. Every man was properly dressed, red lights were on throughout the boat in preparation for surfacing, each man was at his post.

So they waited, watching the clock, each man sweating, thinking of home or the action to come, wishing for ... well, for it to be over. The uncertainty was unnerving. No one knew how it would go, if the Japanese would find and attack them, if they would make it to the open sea, if a P-3 or destroyer would pin them, if they would live or die.

Many had girls or wives in Petropavlosk, so there was a lot of letter writing. They thought of home, of Russia in the summer, the long, languid days, the insects humming, the steppe covered with grain, girls smiling, kissing in the dark ... It was amazing how dear home and family became when you realized that you might never see them again.

There was a scuffle in the engine room between two young sailors, and the chief handled that. They called for him and whispers went around; Pavel Saratov pretended not to notice.

He lounged on a small pull-out stool, with his head resting against the chart table. He kept his eyes closed. Several of the men thought he was asleep, but he wasn't. He was forcing himself to keep his eyes closed so that he would not look again at his watch or the chronometer on the bulkhead, not be mesmerized by the sweeping of the second hand, not watch the minute hand creep agonizingly along.

The Spetsnaz divers were out there now, planting charges. The refinery was supposed to go up at 03:45. If it didn't, there was nothing he could do about it. Oh, he could squirt a few grenades that way, but the damage they could do was minimal.

It was possible that the Japanese had captured the Spetsnaz divers and were right this minute organizing a search for the submarine that had delivered them. Possible, though improbable. That men capable of taking Martos or Filimonov alive were guarding this particular refinery was highly unlikely.

What if the Japanese spotted the sub from the air?

Someone in a plane, looking down, might have seen the shape of the submarine through the muddy brown water. They might be waiting in the refinery. They might have antisubmarine forces gathered, be waiting for the boat to move before they sprung the trap.

They may have killed Martos and Filimonov. They might be dead now. If they are, I would never know, Saratov thought. They would just not return, and the refinery would not explode.

Someone was fidgeting with a pencil, tapping it.

Saratov frowned. The tapping stopped.

Getting the sub out of the mud of this shallow bay would be a trick. It would probably broach. Well, as long as no one was nearby ... But he would have to be ready to go, keep her on the surface, take her by the

Yokohama anchorage shooting torpedoes ... He and the XO had the headings and times worked out, and the XO would keep constant track of their position, so Saratov wouldn't be distracted by navigation at a critical moment.

He took a deep breath. Soon. Very soon ...

All refineries are essentially alike: industrial facilities designed to heat crude oil under pressure, converting it to usable products. When Martos and Filimonov emerged from the water of Tokyo Bay carrying their bags of explosives, they scurried to cover and paused to look for refinery workers or guards. There were a few workers about, but only a few. Of guards, they saw not one.

Almost invisible in their black wet suits, the two Russian frogmen moved like cats through the facility, pausing in shadows and crouching in corners. Satisfied that they were unobserved and would remain that way for a few moments, they began assessing what they were seeing. Years ago, training for just such a day in the unforeseeable future, they had learned a good deal about refineries.

Now they pointed out various features of this facility to each other. They said nothing, merely pointed.

The absence of guards bothered Martos, who began to suspect a trap. He looked carefully for remote surveillance cameras, or infrared or motion detectors. He removed a small set of binoculars from his bag and stripped away the waterproof cover. With these he scanned the towers and pipelines, the walls and windows. Nothing. Not a single camera. This offended him, somehow. Japan was at war, a refinery was a vital industrial facility, a certain target for a belligerent enemy, and there were no guards! They thought so little of Russia's military ability they didn't bother to post guards. Amazing.

The two frogmen separated.

They took their time selecting the position for the charges and setting them, working carefully, painstakingly, while maintaining a vigilant lookout. Several times, they had to take cover while a worker proceeded through the area in which they happened to be.

Martos had allowed plenty of time for the work that had to be done. Still, with so few people about, it went more quickly than he thought it would.

A little more than an hour after he and Filimonov came ashore, he had his last charge set and the timer ticking away. He went looking for Filimonov, whom he had last seen going toward a huge field of several dozen large white storage tanks that stood beside the refinery.

He was moving carefully, keeping under cover as much as possible and pausing frequently to scan for people, when he first saw the guard.

The guard was wearing some kind of uniform, and a waterproof rain jacket and hat. He had arrived in a small car with a beacon on the roof. When Martos first saw him he was standing beside the car looking idly around, tugging and pulling on his rain gear, adjusting it against the gently falling mist. He reached back inside the car for a clipboard and flashlight.

Now he strolled along the edge of the tank farm, looking at this and that, in no particular hurry.

Did someone mention a war?

Martos scurried across the road into the safety of the shadows of the huge round tanks. He moved as quickly as prudence would allow.

Where was Filimonov?

A large pipeline, maybe a half a meter in diameter, came out of the refinery and ran in among the tanks, with branches off to each tank. Lots of valves.

Filimonov liked pipelines. A ridiculously small explosive charge could ruin a safety shutoff valve and fracture the line.

Martos retraced his steps, looking for his partner. He could just go back to the water's edge and wait, of course, but if he found Filimonov and helped set a charge or two, they would be finished sooner. And it just wasn't good practice to leave a man working on his own without a lookout.

He eased his head around a tank and glimpsed the small beam of light from a flashlight. The guard!

Around the tank, moving carefully in the darkness, feeling his way . . . He waited a few seconds before he looked again. There, now the guard had passed him, walking slowly, looking . . . Had the guard seen something? Or was he just –

A shape blacker than the surrounding darkness materialized behind the guard and merged with him. The flashlight fell and went out.

Now the guard was dragged out of sight between the tanks.

Martos went that way.

He found Filimonov sitting beside the guard, holding his head in his hands. Even in that dim light, Martos could see the unnatural angle of the guard's head, the glistening blood covering the front of the rain jacket. A glance was enough – Filimonov had cut the guard's throat, almost severed his head.

But why was Filimonov sitting here like this?

'Let's go, Viktor.'

Filimonov's shoulders shook.

God, the man was crying! 'Viktor, let's go. What is this?'

'It's a girl!'

'What?'

'The guard is a *woman*! Look for yourself.'

'Well . . .'

'A *woman* guard! Of all the stupid . . .'

'Let's go, Viktor. Let's finish and get out of here.'

'A *woman* . . .' Filimonov stared at the corpse. He didn't move.

A tinny radio voice squawked, jabbering a phrase or two in Japanese, then ended with a high interrogative tone. The guard must be wearing a radio!

Martos found the bag. Checked inside. One charge left. Working quickly, he affixed it to the base of a nearby tank, out of sight of the guard's body. He inserted a detonator into the plastique and wired it to a timer. He checked the timer with his pencil flash. It was ticking nicely, apparently keeping perfect time.

He took Filimonov's arm and pulled him to his feet.

'We have no time for this. She is dead. We cannot bring her back.'

The radio on the guard's belt clicked and jabbered.

'A *woman*. I never killed a . . . Not even in Afghanistan. I didn't know –'

'Viktor Grigorovich –'

'Never!'

Martos hit him then, in the face. That was the only way. Filimonov offered no resistance.

He seized Filimonov's arm and shoved him toward the bay.

'They are going to come looking for her,' said Martos.

'She doesn't weigh forty kilos,' Filimonov muttered softly, still trying to understand.

When Jiro Kimura wrote to his wife, Shizuko, he didn't know when she would get the letter, if ever. All mail to Japan was censored. This letter would certainly not pass the censor, a nonflying lieutenant colonel whose function in life was to write reports for senior officers to sign and to read other people's mail.

Jiro wrote the letter anyway. He began by telling Shizuko that he loved and missed her, then told her about the flight to Khabarovsk, during which he had shot down an airliner.

His commanding officer and the air wing commander had tried to humiliate him when he returned. They were outraged that he had questioned Control.

'The prime minister might have been there. He is personally directing the military effort. He may have given the order for you to shoot down that airplane.'

Jiro hadn't been very contrite. He had just killed an unknown number of defenseless people and he hadn't come to grips with that. He stood with his head bowed slightly. It was a polite bow at best. No doubt that contributed to the colonels' ire. The wing commander thundered:

'You have sworn to obey orders, Kimura. You have no choice, none whatsoever. The Bushido code demands complete, total, unthinking, unquestioning obedience. You dishonor us all when you question the orders of your honorable superiors.'

Kimura said nothing.

His skipper said, loudly, 'An enemy airplane in the war zone is a legitimate target, Kimura. Destruction of enemy airplanes is your job. The nation has provided you with an expensive jet fighter in order that you might do your job. You dishonor your nation and yourself when you fail to obey every order instantly, whether the matter be large or small. You dishonor me! I will not have you dishonoring me and this unit. You will obey! Do you understand?'

Jiro wrote this diatribe in the letter, just as he remembered it. He had felt shame wash over him as the two colonels ranted. His cheeks colored slightly, which infuriated him. His commanding officer misinterpreted his emotions and decided he had had enough of the verbal hiding, so he fell silent. The wing commander also stopped soon after.

Jiro Kimura felt ashamed of himself and his comrades, these Japanese soldiers, with their Bushido code and their delicate sense of honor which required the death of everyone on an airliner *leaving* the battle zone because someone, somewhere gave an order.

They were frightened, little men. Little in every sense of the word, Jiro reflected, and wrote that in his letter to his wife.

He was ashamed of himself because he lacked the moral courage to disobey an order that he thought both illegal and obscene. This also he confessed to Shizuko.

As he paused in his writing and sat thinking, he felt the shame wash over him again. The problem was that he was not a pure Japanese. Those damned Americans and their Air Force Academy! He had absorbed more than just the classroom subjects. The ethics of that foreign place were torturing him here.

The Japanese said he had dishonored his superiors and comrades by his failure to obey. The Americans would say he dishonored himself because he obeyed an illegal, immoral order. The only thing everyone would agree upon was the dishonor.

An American would call a reporter and make a huge stink. Maybe he should do that.

He felt like shit. He wasn't Japanese enough to kill himself or American enough to ruin his superiors. That left him writing a letter to Shizuko.

'Dearest wife . . .'

He loved her desperately. As he wrote, he wondered if he would ever see her again.

14

They sat in the mud near the hole in the chain-link fence that they had cut going in. Martos arranged his scuba gear so that he could slip it on in seconds. Filimonov, on the other hand, sat morosely by his gear, staring out at the blackness of the bay.

Martos checked the fluorescent hands of his watch: 01:12.

They had finished sooner than he thought they would.

The submarine would not rise off the floor of the bay until 03:30. Visibility in the muddy water was limited to a few feet, so their flashlights would be of little use finding the submarine underwater. He knew roughly where it was, a kilometer beyond that liquid natural gas tanker at the end of the tanker pier. Still, he would never find it submerged. They would have to wait for the sub to surface.

Nor was it wise to swim out into the bay now, then spend two hours fighting the currents and tide, drifting God knows where.

Although the refinery was well lit, the two men were nearly invisible on this mud flat between the water and the fence. Black wet suits, a black night, dark mud, rain misting down . . . The tanker pier looked like a bridge to nowhere, with lights every yard or two, stretching out across the black water to the anchored LNG carrier. Now that was a weird-looking ship, with that giant pressure vessel amidships.

Martos eyed his partner.

'Viktor, it wasn't your fault.'

Filimonov had reacted to a perceived threat without thinking. He saw a guard, wearing rain gear, possibly armed, so he had acted automatically.

The other guards would come looking for the woman soon. When she failed to check in on the radio, they would probably assume that the radio had failed, perhaps a dead battery. They would wait a reasonable amount of time, then expect her to check in on her car radio. Finally, they would come looking.

Damn! Things had been going so well.

Even if the security force found some of the demolition charges, they would not find them all. Not before they blew. Yet every one they found was one less to explode, that much less damage to the installation.

'We must expect the unexpected. Everything doesn't always go as planned.'

'I was setting a charge,' Filimonov muttered. 'She surprised me.'

'See, it wasn't your fault. You didn't know the guard was a woman. You are not the Japanese son of a whore who hired this woman, put her in a uniform, and sent her to guard a valuable national asset in wartime.'

Filimonov sighed. He laid down on his back in the mud. He stretched his arms out as if he were on a cross.

'No one in Russia would be so stupid,' Martos said.

Filimonov didn't say anything. This withdrawal bothered Martos.

'You *must* forget this, Viktor. I am your friend. You must *listen*.'

The minutes passed in silence. There was only the lapping of the tiny waves at the water's edge and the faint, distant hooting of a foghorn. Martos could feel the feathery caress of the mist on his face, and the miserable, slithery cold of the wet suit, which he had learned to tolerate years and years ago.

A guard car came down the street, turned the corner, and disappeared in the direction of the tanks. In moments they would find the dead guard's vehicle.

Martos looked at his watch: 01:47.

Ten minutes. Within ten minutes, they would find the body, call for help.

He toyed with the idea of going back to kill these men. Or women. Unfortunately, they would probably call in the alarm to their office, wherever that was, before he could kill them both. Even if he did eliminate them, someone else would come looking.

Martos pulled the top of the wet suit over his head and arranged it around his face. 'Let's get ready, Viktor.'

Filimonov didn't move.

Martos kicked his partner in the side – hard. 'Enough! Get ready. I order you. Put on your gear.'

Filimonov still didn't move.

'You want to stay here? Do you want me to kill you, Viktor Grigorovich? Dead is the only way you can stay on this beach.'

Filimonov turned his head.

'You are my friend, Viktor. My best friend. I know you did not mean to kill a woman – this woman, any woman. I know that God forgives you, Viktor. I know that somewhere in heaven this very minute your mother forgives you. She knows you did not intend to kill a woman. She knows what was in your heart.'

Another guard car came racing down the street, squealed its brakes on the turn, and disappeared, going toward the tanks.

'They have found her, Viktor. They are doing for her what must be done. It is time for us to leave. We have responsibilities, too. The captain will be waiting.'

He tugged at Viktor's arm. 'There are fifty men on that submarine. They will keep the faith. They will be vulnerable there on the surface, waiting for us. We must keep faith with them.'

Nothing.

Martos donned his flippers, put on the scuba tanks, arranged the mask on his face. He tested the regulator, took a breath from the mouthpiece.

'Okay, you bastard. Lie here and get captured. Betray your country. Betray your shipmates. Over a dead guard. You stupid bastard. Your mother was a slut. A whore. She was sucking cocks the night some drunk stuck his –'

Filimonov came for him. Martos dashed for the water.

He moved as fast as he could in the tanks and flippers. Unburdened by gear, Filimonov was quicker. He dragged Martos off his feet in the shallows and went for his throat.

God, he was strong. Fingers like steel bands.

Martos was at a severe disadvantage. He wanted to use just enough force to cause Filimonov to cease and desist; Filimonov wanted to kill.

Martos kneed him in the balls. Filimonov kept coming, got fingers around Martos's throat, began to squeeze.

Martos was under six inches of water, but he didn't have the mouthpiece in. Not that he could have breathed, with Filimonov squeezing his neck. He pounded on Filimonov's head with his fist, tried to get a thumb in his eye.

He was losing strength. The vise around his neck tightened relentlessly.

He pulled his knife and swung at Filimonov's head – once, twice, three times – and felt the pressure on his neck ease. He swung the butt of the knife again with all his strength.

Filimonov lost his grip on Martos's neck.

One last mighty smash of the butt end of the knife into his head caused Filimonov to lose consciousness.

The faceplate of his mask was shattered. Martos discarded it.

Lights. A spotlight! A car, driving along the fence, the driver inspecting the wire with a spotlight.

Martos got a firm grip on the headpiece of Filimonov's wet suit, turned him face up, and dragged him into deeper water. When the water reached his waist he inserted the scuba mouthpiece in his mouth and started swimming, towing Filimonov.

The tide was strong and the night was black. Martos swam with one hand, towing Filimonov with the other, looking over his shoulder at the refinery and trying to swim straight away from it. The salt spray stung his eyes.

Why didn't Filimonov regain consciousness?

He concentrated on swimming, on breathing rhythmically, on maintaining a smooth, sustainable pace. Occasionally he glanced over his shoulder.

Filimonov didn't try to help, didn't move. A concussion?

Two cars were at the fence, near the hole, their headlights pointing over the water. A spotlight played across the water. It went by the swimming men. They were too far out to be seen from the shore.

The Japanese would find Filimonov's flippers and scuba tanks soon, if they hadn't already. They would call in an alarm.

Damn, damn, damn.

If another P-3 caught the submarine in this shallow bay, they were all dead men.

Hell, we're all going to die. We're all condemned. That is the truth that this fool Filimonov doesn't understand.

'Mr Krasin, take the boat up to periscope depth.'

'Aye aye, Captain.'

Krasin was the OOD. He began giving orders.

Everyone was at their post. Everyone was ready. For the last hour no one had said much. They had watched the clock, chewed fingernails, fretted silently. Now the waiting was over. Live or die, it was time to get to it.

The submarine refused to come out of the mud on the floor of the bay. Without way on, the only means of lifting the boat was positive buoyancy. More and more air was forced into the tanks, forcing out the water that held the submarine below the surface.

The keel of the sub was eighty feet down, just below periscope depth. She's going to go up like a cork, the captain thought, resigned.

Seconds later the submarine broke free of the mud's grasp and rose quickly, too quickly.

'All ahead flank,' the captain ordered. 'Full down on the bow planes.'

The submarine broached anyway, broke the surface. Then the water pouring back into the tanks took effect, and the boat got enough way on for the bow and stern planes to get a grip on the water. They helped pull her back under.

'Watch it, Chief,' the captain said sharply, well aware that if they lost control now and drove the sub's bow into the mud, they would probably have to abandon ship.

The chief knew his boat. He got her stabilized and let her sink to periscope depth.

'Up scope,' Pavel Saratov ordered, as if nothing out of the ordinary had happened.

After a quick 360-degree sweep, the captain said, almost as an afterthought, 'Perhaps we should stop engines, Mr Krasin, wait for the Spetsnaz divers. They will not be pleased if we leave without them.'

The XO winked the OOD.

'Stop engines.'

Saratov walked the scope around again, taking his time, looking carefully.

Well, he could see the lights of the refinery, the tankers at the tanker pier, the LNG carrier. Yokohama glowed in the misty darkness. Several dozen anchored ships were in view. The lights of Tokyo farther north were invisible in the misting rain and fog. He saw no ships or boats anchored close by.

Saratov backed off from the scope and gestured with his palm for it to be lowered. 'Gentlemen, I suggest we surface and collect our swimmers.'

The OOD gave the necessary orders, and the submarine rose slowly from the sea.

Martos was very tired. Filimonov had not moved since he knocked him out, and the current was running toward the entrance of the bay, which meant Martos had to swim north constantly in order to remain more or less in one place.

He had not managed to remain in that one place. When the submarine surfaced, he was at least a half mile south of it, swimming toward it while towing Filimonov.

He spit out the mouthpiece. 'It wouldn't hurt' – he took a breath – 'for you to help ... swim a little ... you large piece ... of horse's dung.'

Filimonov remained motionless. Martos knew he had just dinged his friend four or five times with the butt end of his knife, hardly enough to stun a mouse. This hardheaded ox had been hit harder than that in barracks brawls and never even blinked.

He heard the submarine break water. Heard the splash of a large object and heard the sucking sound as it went back under.

He didn't hear it surface the second time, but he heard the metallic clanging of the conning tower hatch being thrown open. He was already swimming in that direction, dragging Filimonov.

'You foolish ... simple ... son of a bitch! Help me.'

Finally he stopped. Ensuring that Filimonov's head didn't go under, he shouted, 'Hey! Over here.'

They would never hear him. He had a flashlight on his belt, so he reached for it. Gone, probably in the fight.

Filimonov's light ... still there.

Something unnatural about the big man. Martos turned the flashlight on and waved it in the general direction of the sub.

'Viktor, speak to me. Say something, my friend.'

He shined the flashlight in Viktor's face. The glare of the light on the white skin took getting used to. It was several seconds before Martos's eyes could focus.

Filimonov's eyes were open, unfocused. They did not track the light. The pupils did not respond. Viktor Filimonov was dead.

What? How ...

'Viktor, you ... you ...'

The sub glided up. The wash pushed him away from it. Two men on deck threw a line. Keeping a firm grip on Filimonov's wet suit, Martos wrapped the line once around his wrist and called, 'Pull us aboard.'

'What's wrong with him?'

'Grab him. Pull him aboard.'

After they pulled Filimonov from the water, they dragged Martos onto the slimy steel deck. He was so tired he could barely summon strength to stand.

'What's wrong with him?'

'He's dead. Get him below.'

The sailors lowered Filimonov's body through the torpedo reloading hatch. Martos was still on deck when one of the large storage tanks at the refinery exploded. At this distance the noise was just a pop, but the rising fireball looked spectacular, even against the background lights of Yokosuka.

'The captain wants to see you, on the bridge,' someone told him.

Filimonov's body lay on the deck walkway, between the racks holding the spare torpedoes. The corpsman was examining it. Martos made his way aft.

From the control room he climbed into the conning tower, then on up the ladder onto the tiny bridge, or cockpit, atop the sail. Pavel Saratov was watching the receding refinery through his binoculars.

'Sir.'

'How did it go?'

'We set the charges. Filimonov killed a guard – a woman. Cut her throat. He became morose. We fought. I thought I knocked him out. Apparently, I killed him.'

Saratov shifted his attention from the fires of the refinery, which was receding behind, to the lights of a ship far ahead, off the port bow. 'Come right ten degrees,' he said to the sailor beside him, who was wearing a sound-powered telephone headset.

The sailor repeated the order into the headset, then confirmed, 'Right ten, sir.'

Martos wanted to get it off his chest. 'When he was a boy, maybe seven or eight, Viktor Filimonov's mother was killed. In Odessa. Some sailor slashed her. She was a whore. The sailor sliced her eighty-nine times. She bled to death.'

'So . . .' the captain said.

'The authorities took Viktor to identify his mother's body. I don't think he ever forgot how she looked, sliced to ribbons, her entrails coming out, blood everywhere . . . Sometimes he talked about it.'

'I want to hear about this, later,' the captain said. 'You did a good job on the refinery. It is burning nicely. I wanted you to know.'

'Yes, sir.'

'Did you mean to kill your partner?'

'No, sir. Absolutely not.'

'We'll talk later. You may go below.'

Martos went.

The captain studied the ship off the port bow. It looked small, about fifteen thousand tons. Not worth a torpedo. They could do much better.

'Not this one,' he said to the talker standing beside him. 'All ahead two-thirds.' The talker repeated the order, and in seconds Pavel Saratov felt the diesels respond.

Too bad about the swimmer.

Several miles behind another fireball rose out of the refinery complex.

The wind in his hair felt good. Saratov inhaled deeply, savoring the musky aroma of tidal flats and salty sea air and the tang of the land.

Martos was in the tiny galley eating bread when the corpsman found him. The diesel engines made the surfaced boat throb. There was just enough swell inside the bay to make it pitch and roll a bit.

'Look at this,' the corpsman said. He opened his hand. 'He had this between his teeth.'

It was a red plastic capsule, waterproof, but ruptured.

'Poison,' Martos whispered.

'Poison?'

'A suicide pill. He must have had it in his mouth.'

'Why would . . .'

'He must have been thinking about it,' Martos said slowly. 'Maybe he accidentally bit it when I whacked him on the head. You bite it, death is nearly instantaneous.'

The corpsman looked at Martos strangely, then turned away.

'An accident,' Martos murmured to himself. 'He must have put it in his mouth as we sat there waiting . . .

'Oh damn!'

The reporter's name was Christine something. She looked like a caricature. Her hair was immaculately coiffed and lacquered so heavily that it reflected the television lights. She wore some kind of horrible safari jacket, something discount stores sell for two-thirds off the day after Christmas.

Her makeup was heavily layered to cover the deep lines that radiated around her eyes. Caked, gaudy lipstick made her mouth look like an open wound. She glanced once at the camera, then stood staring at Bob Cassidy, waiting. She was the pool reporter, chosen by her colleagues to ask the questions because Cassidy had been willing to subject his pilots to only one interview.

The television lights were hot. A trickle of sweat ran down Cassidy's face. He wiped it away.

Someone must have said something to the reporter through her earphone, because she started talking.

'Colonel, I understand you are leading the Americans hired to fly the F-22s?'

He nodded, once.

'If I may ask, why you?'

They were looking for a bastard without a family, and they found me. He didn't say that, of course. 'I volunteered.'

'Why?'

'Why not?'

'How many Americans are with you?'

'About one hundred and fifty.'

'When do you plan to go to Russia?'

'Soon.'

'You aren't very talkative, are you, Colonel?'

'That wasn't one of the qualifications for the job.'

'How much are the Russians paying you?'

'You'll have to ask the State Department that question. Or the Russians.'

'Rumor has it that you get a bonus for every plane you shoot down. Is that true?'

'Ask the Russians. They sign the checks.'

'Isn't that blood money?'

'If they pay it, I assume the money would be for the plane, not the pilot. A plane doesn't bleed, does it?'

'What do you hope to accomplish in Russia?'

'Shoot down Japanese planes.'

She made a sign to the cameraman, and the red light on the camera went out.

'You are being uncooperative, Colonel.'

'This isn't the NFL. I'm here only because the State Department said to make myself available. I am available.'

'I asked to shoot these interviews with an F-22 as background. You refused. Why is that?'

'They aren't my airplanes, ma'am.'

'We asked to talk to the African-American pilot. Which one is he?' She glanced at her list.

' "*The* African-American." That is really grotesque. I'll pretend you didn't say it.'

'You do have a black pilot, don't you?'

'Alas, no.'

'Why not?'

'I don't know. It just happened. I'm politically incorrect. Rip me to shreds.'

'Couldn't you say something about Russia? Perhaps you had a Russian grandparent . . . something about aiding in the fight for freedom, something like that?'

Cassidy looked grim. 'You say it,' he told her, then took off his mike and got out of the hot seat.

Of course, the person the reporters were most interested in interviewing was Lee Foy, but he was having none of it. He was nowhere to be found. Cassidy asked Preacher Fain where Foy was, and was told, 'Foy said something about finding a whorehouse. I'm to say that to this reporter if she asks.'

'Okay.'

Apparently the reporters didn't know he was an ordained minister, so Christine didn't ask all those juicy questions that Fain feared she would. Fain tried to play it straight. He was here to help keep peace in the world, doing his duty, fighting for victims of aggression, defending an American ally, et cetera.

After fifteen minutes, Preacher looked greatly relieved as he got out of the chair.

Most of the pilots gave Christine more of the same, until she got to Clay Lacy. When asked why he was here, he said, 'The fighter-pilot ethos has a compelling purity, a rare strain of selflessness and self-sacrifice that too often we lose sight of in modern life. I find it' – he searched for words – 'almost religious. Don't you agree?'

Christine made a noise.

Lacy continued. 'I want to see how I will face a competent, couragous, dedicated warrior who seeks to kill me. Will I have enough courage? Will I be bold? Will I fight with honor, and die with honor if that is required? These are serious questions that bedevil many people in this perverted age. I'm sure you've thought about these things at length. Haven't you?'

Christine sat staring, her mouth open. Lacy waited politely. 'I see,' she finally managed.

'I'm delighted that you do,' he told her warmly. 'Most of these pilots' – he flipped his hand disdainfully – 'are merely flying assassins, out to kill and be paid for it. They have no ideas, no insight, no intellectual life. I am not like them. I explore the inner man.'

When Lacy went over to the colonel after his interview, he asked, still deadly serious, 'How did I do, sir?'

'Fine, Lacy. Fine. You are now the unit public affairs officer.'

Aaron Hudek gave a performance that was the equal of Lacy's, or perhaps even better. When asked why he had volunteered, he told Christine, 'This is the only war we have.'

'How do you think you will feel, killing a fellow human being?'

'It'll be glorious.' Hudek gave Christine a wolfish grin. 'I can't wait. I'll blow those yellow Jap bastards to kingdom come so goddamn fast they'll never know what hit 'em. Just you watch.'

Stunned, Christine recovered quickly. 'How do you know that you won't be the one who falls?'

'Oh, it ain't gonna be me, lady. I'm too good. I'm the best in the business. The F-22 Raptor is good iron. I can fly that fucking airplane. I'm gonna go through those goddamn Japs like shit through a fan. Can't stand Japs. I guess it's personal with me, something about Pearl Harbor and all that damned so-sorry fake politeness – but I won't let that interfere with what I have to do. I'm going to stay cool and kill those polite little sons of bitches.'

Christine didn't know what to say.

Hudek smiled at the camera, unhooked his vest mike, got up, and walked out, right by Dixie Elitch, who averted her gaze as he passed her.

Dixie sat down in the interview chair and smiled sweetly as one of the technicians hooked up her mike.

'Ms Elitch,' Christine began.

'Captain Elitch, please. That is my rank in the Russian Air Army. I am *very* proud of it.'

She managed to say that with just the faintest hint of a Russian accent. Watching from behind the camera, Bob Cassidy covered his face with his hands.

'*Captain* Elitch,' said Christine, smiling brittlely.

'All my life I have loved Russian things – furs, vodka, Tolstoy, Tchaikovsky, Chekhov, Pavlov . . .' Dixie's recall of things Russian failed her here. She waved airily and motored on:

'I am *so* thrilled to have this opportunity to actually *go* to Russia, to succor her people in their hour of need, to serve this magnificent yet tragic nation in my own small way, and, just perhaps, make a contribution to the betterment of the downtrodden proletariat. And even – dare I say it? – the bourgeoisie.'

'Are all of you people assholes?' Christine snarled.

'Unfortunately, I believe so,' replied Dixie Elitch. She looked straight into the camera and flashed her absolute best 'I'm available tonight' smile.

When he went to bed that night, Bob Cassidy found himself thinking of Dixie. This annoyed him. He had ten thousand things on his mind, and now he was thinking about a woman, one who was off-limits to him. Oh, he knew the engraved-in-stone rule of the modern, sexually integrated armed forces: no fucking the troops. And no flirting, sighing, dating, kissing, marrying, or loving – none of that male–female stuff.

In the brave new Air Force middle-aged colonels who got to thinking night thoughts about sweet young things were usually gone quickly. The 'grab your hat, don't let the door hit you in the ass on your way out' kind of gone.

Bob Cassidy had spent his adult life in uniform, around women now and then, and he had never before gone to bed thinking about one.

Except Sweet Sabrina. He'd thought of her every night when she was alive, and many, many nights since she died. He often dreamed of her, dreamed of touching her again, of kissing her just once more, of somehow reaching across the great gulf that separated them. Robbie was sometimes in those dreams too, sitting on Sabrina's lap, running across a lawn or through the house or laughing while diving into piles of fall leaves.

These dreams used to wake him up, drive the sleep from him. He would walk the empty house, so utterly alone.

Thinking of anyone but Sabrina seemed disloyal somehow.

He tried to conjure up her image to replace the grinning face of Dixie Elitch.

He was thinking of Sabrina – or was it Dixie? – when he finally drifted off.

15

Pavel Saratov knew there were a lot of ships anchored off Yokohama, but he didn't know how many until he was within the anchorage, which extended for miles. Over a hundred, easily, he estimated.

He reduced the boat's speed to six knots. 'The big freighter fifteen degrees right of the bow, about two thousand meters. Containers four deep on her deck. She is our first target.' Saratov was wearing the sound-powered headset. He had sent the talker below. The only other person on the bridge was the second officer, who was scanning behind and to both sides for enemy planes or warships.

'We have her, sir.'

Down below, they were using the radar. All the skipper had to do was designate a target. He had already given orders that they would shoot one torpedo at a time, at targets he picked. He wanted to do all the damage possible.

The torpedoes were huge – twenty-one inches in diameter, twenty-seven feet long – and carried warheads containing 1,250 pounds of high explosive, enough to sink most ships.

Twenty seconds later the first torpedo was on its way. A minute after that they fired another torpedo at a laden bulk carrier. The first one hit the container ship with a dull thud that carried well through the water and was clearly audible aboard the submarine. The bulk carrier and the third target, another container ship, were hit in turn. The fourth torpedo was expended on yet another container ship, a huge one festooned with lights.

Still moving at six knots, the sub was deep inside the anchorage, completely surrounded by ships, when the crew fired the fifth torpedo at a monstrous freighter riding deep in the water. It was close, almost too close, but the torpedo warhead exploded with a boom that sounded quite satisfying to Pavel Saratov. Slowly, almost imperceptibly, the freighter began to sag in the middle. The torpedo broke her back. Yes!

Saratov turned to exit the anchorage to the east. One tube was still loaded. In the torpedo room the crew began the reloading process. It would take about an hour to get one of the huge torpedoes into a tube.

Well, he had given the Japanese something to think about. No doubt they were alerting their antisubmarine forces right now. The sooner he got this boat out of Tokyo Bay, the better.

'Flank speed,' he told the people below. 'Give me every turn you've got.'

Sushi called Toshihiko Ayukawa at home on the scrambled telephone. 'Sir, I thought I should call you immediately. We intercepted a transmission from a Russian submarine. He says he is in Tokyo Bay.'

'What?' Ayukawa sounded wide-awake now.

'It's right off the computer, sir. I thought you should be informed.' The raw, encrypted signal was picked up by a satellite and directed to a dish antenna on top of the building. From there, it went to a computer, which decoded it, translated the Russian into Japanese, and sent it to a printer. The whole sequence took thirty-five seconds – the paper took thirty seconds to go through the printer – if the Russians were using one of the four codes the Japanese had cracked, and if they had encoded their message properly. Sometimes they didn't.

'Read it to me,' Ayukawa said.

Sushi did so. When he had finished Ayukawa spent several seconds digesting it, then asked, 'Have you alerted the Self-Defense Force?'

'Yes, sir,' Sushi said blandly, managing to hide his irritation. Ayukawa's question implied that Sushi was incompetent. Apparently Ayukawa thought he had no time to be polite, to observe the simplest courtesies. In any event he didn't try.

'The explosive charges in the refinery mentioned in the message began exploding twenty minutes ago, sir. The Lotus Blossom refinery at Yokosuka. And a freighter in the Yokohama anchorage has just radioed in, saying it was torpedoed.'

'How long have we had the submarine's message?'

'It came in only minutes ago, sir. I called the Self-Defense Force, alerted harbor security and the Yokosuka Fire District. Then I telephoned you.'

'Very well.' Ten seconds of silence. 'A submarine!'

Ayukawa was appalled. Those military fools told the prime minister that they had sunk all the operational Russian subs that were under way when the war broke out at Vladivostok and Sakhalin Island. They refused to tie up scarce military assets guarding ports in the home islands when every ship was needed to conquer an empire. After all, what could you expect of Russians?

Exploding refineries and sinking ships would prove the military men miscalculated, embarrass everybody, cause the government to lose face. Another disaster caused by overweening pride and shortsightedness. Atsuko Abe, take note.

'I had better call the minister,' Ayukawa said to no one in particular. He hung up the telephone without saying good-bye.

Sushi cradled his instrument and made a face.

The guided-missile destroyer *Hatakaze* was three hundred yards away from a berth at Yokosuka Naval Base pier when the communications officer buzzed the bridge on the squawk box. A flash-priority message from headquarters had just come out of the computer printer: 'Russian submarine attacking ships Yokohama. Intercept.'

Hatakaze's captain was no slouch. He ordered his crew to general quarters, waved away the tug, and steamed out into the bay, working up speed as quickly as the engineering plant would allow.

Hatakaze had been continuously at sea for two weeks. She participated in the destruction of the Russian fleet rusting in Golden Horn Bay and helped shell troops on the Vladivostok neck that were trying to impede advancing Japanese forces. During all that shooting, her forward 127-mm Mk-42 deck gun had overheated, which caused a round to explode prematurely, killing two men and injuring four more. Her aft gun was working just fine. As soon as she could be spared, the force commander sent *Hatakaze* home for repairs. Due to the shortage of ammunition, most of *Hatakaze*'s remaining 127-mm ammo was transferred to other ships, yet she still had a dozen rounds on the trays for the aft gun.

Hatakaze was making twenty knots when the radar operators picked *Admiral Kolchak* from among the clutter of ships, small boats, and surface return. The Russian submarine was making fifteen knots southwestward toward the refinery. That merely made her a suspicious blip; her beaconing S-band radar made the identification certain.

Although the submarine lacked the excellent radar of the Japanese destroyer, the destroyer was a bigger, easier target. The operator of the sub's radar saw the blip of a possible warship – a fairly small high-speed surface target coming out of the Yokosuka Naval Base area – and reported it to Captain Saratov as such.

Pavel Saratov pointed his binoculars to the south, the direction named by the radar operator below.

The rain had stopped; visibility was up, maybe to ten miles.

There was the destroyer, with its masthead and running lights illuminated. After all, these were Japanese home waters.

Saratov pounded the bridge rail in frustration.

The destroyer would soon open fire with its deck gun. If the sub submerged, the destroyer would pin it easily, kill it with antisubmarine rockets – ASROC.

He had known it would end like this. Entering the bay had been a huge gamble right from the start. A suicidal gamble, really.

He looked southwest, at the blazing refinery and the LNG tanker moored at the end of the pier. He had been intending to use the sixth torpedo on that tanker. A maneuverable destroyer, bow-on, would be a difficult target.

Another glance at the destroyer. 'What is the range to the destroyer?' he demanded of the watch below.

'Twelve thousand meters, Captain, and closing. He has turned toward us, speed a little over thirty knots.'

'And the tanker?'

'Two thousand five hundred meters, sir.'

'Give me an attack solution on the destroyer. Set the torpedo for acoustic homing.'

'Aye aye, sir.'

'And keep me informed of the ranges, goddamnit!'

'Yes, captain.'

Submerging in this shallow bay would be suicidal. Saratov dismissed that possibility.

He looked longingly at the LNG tanker, a target of a lifetime. She was low in the water, a fact he had noted as he entered the bay and steamed by her. She was full of the stuff.

'We'll run in against the tanker and cut our motors.' The Japanese destroyer captain wouldn't be fool enough to risk putting a shell into that thing.

With the tanker at our back, Saratov thought, maybe we have a chance. At least he could get his men off the sub and into the water.

'Aye aye, sir.'

'Come thirty degrees right, slow to all ahead two-thirds.'

He heard the order being repeated in the control room, felt the bow of the sub swinging.

'Destroyer at eleven thousand meters, sir.'

Saratov looked back at the oncoming destroyer. *Why doesn't he shoot?*

The refinery was blazing merrily. At the base of the fire, he could just make out the silhouettes of fire trucks. The Spetsnaz divers certainly had done an excellent job.

Saratov swung the glasses to the tanker pier. Several fire trucks with their flashing emergency lights were visible there. He wondered why they were on the pier; then his mind turned to other things. He checked the destroyer again. Why didn't he shoot? They most certainly were in range.

'Twelve hundred meters to the tanker, Captain.'

The captain of the *Hatakaze* could see the burning refinery with his binoculars. He could not see the black sail of the Russian submarine that his radar people assured him was there, but he could see the blip on the radar repeater scope just in front of his chair on the bridge. And he could see the return of the tanker pier and the tankers moored to it. The range to the sub was about nine thousand meters.

ASROC was out of the question, even though the target was well within range. The rocket would carry the Mk-46 torpedo out several kilometers and put it in the water, but the torpedo might home on one of the tankers.

Captain Kama elected to engage the submarine with the stern 127-mm gun. Not that he had a lot of choice. He was already within gun range, but he would have to turn *Hatakaze* about seventy degrees away from the submarine to uncover the gun. Of course, if the gun overshot, one of the shells might hit a tanker. If the LNG tanker went up, the results would be catastrophic.

He decided to wait. Wait a few moments, and pray the submarine didn't shoot a torpedo.

'Prepare to fire the torpedo decoys,' he ordered. 'And watch for small boats. Tell Sonar to listen carefully.' Listen for torpedoes, he meant.

What a place to fight a war!

The refinery fire was as bad as it looked. The conflagration lit up the clouds and illuminated the tanker pier with a ghastly flickering glow. Numerous small explosions sent fireballs puffing into the night sky. These explosions were caused when fire reached free pools or clouds of petroleum products that had leaked from ruptured tanks or pipes.

The firefighters had no chance. There was too much damage in too many places.

As the fires grew hotter and larger, the glow cast even more light on the sea.

The submarine approached the LNG tanker, which was limned by the fire behind it. Saratov could see people moving about on the decks, probably trying desperately to get under way. He imagined the tanker skipper was beside himself.

'All stop,' he told the control room.

The submarine glided toward the tanker, losing way. Two hundred meters separated the two ships.

'Left full rudder.'

The nose began to swing.

'Looks like another destroyer, sir. Coming out of Yokosuka. Bearing one nine five, range thirty-two thousand meters.'

'Keep the boat moving, Chief, at about two knots.'

'Aye aye, sir. Two knots.'

The deck of the submarine was barely out of the water. He had never ordered the tanks completely blown. 'Secure the diesels. Switch to battery power.'

'Battery power, aye.'

Saratov kept his binoculars focused on the Japanese destroyer, which was closing the range at about a kilometer per minute.

The throb of the diesels died away. He could hear the rush of air and the crackling of the refinery fire. Somewhere, over the refinery probably, was a helicopter. He could hear the distinctive whopping of the rotors in the exhaust.

'We have the first destroyer on sonar,' the XO reported.

'Be ready to fire tube six at the destroyer at any time.'

'Aye, Captain. We're doing that now. Destroyer at seven thousand meters.'

'How long until the first reload is ready?'

'Another twenty minutes, Captain.'

Terrific! We have exactly one shot. If we miss . . .

He must have seen us! 'You ready to shoot?'

'Yes, sir.'

Saratov waited, his eyes on the destroyer. He wasn't shooting, which Saratov thought was because the tanker lay just behind. He could hear voices, shouts, in a foreign language that Saratov thought might be English. It certainly didn't sound like Japanese, and it sure as hell wasn't Russian.

'Six thousand meters, and he's slowing.'

Saratov had been waiting for that. The Japanese skipper wouldn't hear much on his sonar at thirty-two knots, yet the high speed was an edge in outmaneuvering the torpedo.

'Tube Six, fire!'

The boat jerked as the torpedo went out, expelled by compressed air.

Aboard *Hatakaze,* the captain was watching the tiny radar blip that was the submarine's sail. If only he would submerge, clear away from that tanker!

The destroyer's speed caused too much turbulence and noise for the bow-mounted sonar, so he had ordered the ship slowed. Way was falling off now.

'Torpedo in the water!'

The call from the sonar operator galvanized everyone. 'Right full rudder, all ahead flank,' Captain Kama ordered. 'Come to a new heading zero nine zero. Deploy the torpedo decoys. Have the after turret open fire when their gun bears.'

The deck tilted steeply as the destroyer answered the helm.

'He's turning eastward, Captain,' the attack team told Saratov, who was still on the bridge, his binoculars glued to his eyes.

'I see that, goddamnit. What's his speed?'

'Fourteen knots. His engines are really thrashing. I think he is accelerating.'

The destroyer was almost beam-on now. Flashes from the gun on the afterdeck! Even with that tanker directly behind the submarine, he is shooting!

'Dive, dive, dive. Let's go down.'

Saratov unplugged his headset. Hanecki was already going through the hatch. The deck was tilting. Saratov clamored through the hatch and pulled it down after him just as the first of the five-inch shells hit the water . . . right beside the sail.

'Periscope depth!'

'Periscope depth, aye.'

They could hear the shells splashing into the water. Damn, the shooting was accurate.

'Running time on the first fish?'

'Thirty more seconds, sir.'

'Give me a ninety-degree right turn. Tell the torpedo officer to get a tube loaded with all possible speed.'

'Aye aye, sir.'

'Thank you, XO.'

They were just flat running out of options. He wasn't ready to tell them yet, but if the last torpedo missed, he was going to surface the boat alongside the tanker and abandon her. He wasn't going to let his men die in this sardine can when they had nothing left to fight with.

He was thinking about this, watching the heading change as the boat turned, waiting for the boat to sink the last five feet to periscope depth, when he heard the explosion. The torpedo! It hit something. But what?

The men cheered. A roar of exultation.

'Quiet!'

'Keep the turn in, Chief, make it a full three hundred and sixty degrees. All ahead one-third. Raise the big scope.'

He glued his eye to the large scope when it came out of the well. The small attack scope was nearly useless at night.

The destroyer was still moving. At least the front half was. The stern . . . Jesus! The torpedo had blown it off.

'The torpedo blew the ass off the destroyer,' Saratov said to the control room crew. 'Pass the word. It is on fire and sinking.'

When the whispers and buzzing died away, Saratov asked, 'Sonar, what do you hear?'

'Not much, Captain. The LNG tanker has started its engines. It will be getting under way soon, I think.'

'Let's get out of here, Captain, while we are still alive.'

The second officer said that. He looked pale as a ghost.

Saratov looked from face to face. Several men averted their gaze; one chewed on his lip. Most met his gaze, however. The second officer couldn't stop swallowing – he was probably going to puke.

Saratov took the microphone for the boat's PA system off its hook, flipped the switch on, adjusted the volume.

'This is the captain. You men have done well. We have hit the enemy hard. We have destroyed a huge refinery, sunk three ships at least and damaged two more. We have just killed a destroyer that was trying to kill us. I am proud of each and every one of you. It is an honor to be your captain.'

He paused, took a deep breath, thought about what he wanted to say.

'We are going to surface in a few moments, see if we can set this LNG tanker on fire; then we are going to get out of this bay, run for the open sea.'

The second officer lost it, vomiting into his hat.

'Do your job. Do what you were trained to do. That is our best chance.'

He put the microphone back into its bracket.

'There's another destroyer up there, Captain.'

'I am aware of that.' Saratov looked at the XO, lowered his voice. 'Let's leave the radar off. Without the radar beaconing, we are just another tiny blip.'

'As long as we keep our speed down,' Askold muttered.

'Sonar, what's the position on that second destroyer?'

'I estimate twenty thousand meters, Captain. It's hard to tell for sure, with all the noise in the water.'

'Keep listening.'

'Do you want to finish reloading one of the bow tubes before we surface, Captain?' Askold asked.

'The Japanese will put the time to better use than we can. Every gray boat they have will be strung across the bay's entrance if we give them time enough.'

He raised his voice. 'Sonar, leave the radar secured. No emissions.'

'Aye aye, sir.'

'Have the forward torpedo room break out the rockets. We will surface, blow the bow tanks. Pop the hatch and put a man on deck with an RPG-9. We might as well try them.'

If the rockets failed – and they probably wouldn't even fire: He'd had them for six, no, seven years – he would just call it a day and run for it. The torpedomen would get a tube reloaded soon, and boy, it would be nice to have a loaded fish when he went down the bay.

'Up scope.'

He walked it around while the XO talked to the forward torpedo room on the squawk box. *Hatakaze*'s bow was on fire, dead in the water. The stern seemed to have sunk. The LNG tanker was still against the pier, the fire in the refinery visible behind it. The second destroyer was not in sight. If that skipper had any sense, he would station himself in the entrance of the bay and wait for the submarine to come to him.

He gave the chief a new heading, to the northeast, so the LNG tanker would be off the port side. *Hatakaze* was three or four kilometers southeast, so that wreck wouldn't be a factor.

In an hour, the sky would be light with the coming dawn, and there would probably be four destroyers waiting.

Pavel Saratov lowered the periscope and gave the order to surface.

Saratov opened the hatch and went up the ladder to the tiny cockpit on top of the sail. The second officer followed, taking up his usual station looking aft and to both sides. The tanker was on the port bow, about eight hundred meters away.

If anything, the refinery fire was more intense, brighter, than it had been fifteen or twenty minutes ago. Several areas that had not been burning before were ablaze now. He could hear the roar of the flames here, almost a kilometer away. The firestorm sounded like rain and wind on a wild night at sea.

Even the clouds seemed to be on fire. They were shot through with sulfurous reds, oranges, and yellows, lighting the surface of the black water with a hellish glare.

The submarine lay inert on the oily sea. Belowdecks, the crew was blowing water from the forward tanks to lift the deck so that it was no longer awash. Saratov and the second officer scanned the surface of the bay for the destroyer they knew was about, somewhere. The bottom of the burning clouds was about a thousand feet above the water and visibility was good, maybe ten miles.

'Who is the shooter?' Saratov asked on the sound-powered headset.

'Senka. He knows all about it.'

'Get him on deck. We haven't got all damned night.'

He shouldn't have said that. Shouldn't have let the men know the tension was getting to him.

Where in hell is that destroyer?

When he put the binoculars down there was a man on deck, reaching down into the hatch. When the man straightened he was holding an ungainly tube in his hands. He put it on his right shoulder.

The batteries in those grenade launchers were probably as dead as Lenin.

Senka didn't waste much time. He braced himself, aimed for the tanker, and fired.

The batteries worked. The rocket-propelled grenade raced away in a gout of fire that split the night open. Straight as a bullet it flew across the water, straight for the giant steel ball that contained liquid natural gas.

A flash. That was it. Two kilos of warhead in a flash, then nothing.

'Try another one. Give him another one.'

At least the rocket reached the target, which Saratov had feared was a bit out of range. The shaped charge must have hit a girder or something, Saratov thought, examining the tanker through his glasses. He could just see the feathery lines of the gridwork of girders that supported the pressure vessel. If the grenade didn't actually reach the pressure vessel, the warhead would never damage it.

Senka didn't waste time. Apparently he knew what he was about. He put the launcher on his shoulder; then he was examining it, then he threw it into the water. He reached down into the hatch for the third one.

Senka fired again. The missile ignited and raced across the black water toward the tanker. Another flash on impact. Then nothing.

'Try the last one; then we are out of here.'

'Five more minutes on the torpedo, Captain.'

Saratov acknowledged.

Where is that second destroyer?

A flash from the right.

Saratov looked. He saw a destroyer, bow-on, headed this way. Another flash from the bow gun.

A shell hit the water just beyond the sub.

Saratov was about to yell 'Dive,' but he saw Senka face the LNG tanker and raise the launcher to his shoulder.

Saratov opened his mouth just as a shell hit the aft top corner of the sail and exploded. A piece of shrapnel caught the captain in the side of the head and knocked him unconscious. The shrapnel disemboweled the second officer, killing him instantly.

The XO reached up through the hatch and grabbed Saratov by the ankles. He had a firm grip on the skipper and was pulling him into the hatch when Senka, on deck, fired the last RPG-9.

This time the rocket went through the gridwork that supported the pressure vessel and vented its shaped explosive charge into the vessel itself, puncturing it.

The intense pressure on the liquefied natural gas inside the vessel caused it to vent out the hole in a supersonic stream that made a high-pitched, earsplitting whistle. Several people on the tanker heard it. That was the last thing they would ever hear. In less than a second, a large cloud of natural gas had formed outside the hole, which was still molten hot from the explosive. The gas ignited.

The fireball from this explosion grew and grew; then the pressure vessel split. A thousandth of a second later, six thousand tons of liquefied natural gas detonated.

The explosion was the worst in Japan since the atomic bombing of Nagasaki, and almost as violent. The LNG tanker was vaporized in the fireball, as was much of the tanker pier. One of the tankers still moored there had been taking on gasoline, and it too detonated, adding to the force of the explosion. The other tanker, off-loading crude oil, was split open by the blast like a watermelon dropped on concrete. Its cargo spontaneously ignited.

The concussion and thermal pulse of the initial blast leveled the remaining structures at the refinery. The petroleum products that had not yet been consumed merely enhanced the force of the expanding fireball. Of course, the people on the tankers and pier and fighting the fires in the refinery were instantly cremated.

When the concussion reached the submarine eight hundred meters away,

Michman Senka, who had fired the final RPG-9, was swept overboard. It didn't matter to Senka, because he was already dead, fried by the thermal pulse of the explosion. The pulse instantly heated the black steel hull of the boat and sent the water droplets and rivulets that had been on the deck wafting away as steam. A tenth of a second later the concussion arrived, denting the submarine's sail, smashing loose dozens of the anechoic tiles that covered the boat's skin and pushing it so hard that the sub went momentarily over on her beam.

Pavel Saratov knew nothing of all this, because he was unconscious. Somehow as the boat went over, the XO managed to pull him through the hatch. A ton or so of water came in before the boat righted itself. Water also poured through the hatch in the forward torpedo room and would have flooded the boat had the sub stayed on its side any longer.

Miraculously, the submarine righted itself, and the men in the forward torpedo room managed to get the hatch closed and secured. In the sail, the men there wrestled with the hatch and dogged it down just as the second concussion and the bay surge from the explosion pushed the boat over on her beam a second time.

When the captain of the destroyer *Shimakaze,* charging for the Russian submarine, saw the fireball growing and expanding, his first thought was that one of the shells from his deck gun had hit the tanker, just exactly the calamity he had warned the gunners against in the event they got a chance to shoot.

The thermal pulse ignited the destroyer's paint. The concussion smashed out the bridge windows and dented the sheet metal as if it had been pounded by Thor's hammer. Since the destroyer was almost bow-on to the blast, it rode through the first concussion with only heavy damage to its superstructure, its radar and antennas and stack. The helmsman was killed by flying glass. He went down with a death grip on the helm. Still making over twenty knots, the destroyer went into a turn. When the second concussion arrived, the ship heeled hard, then righted herself. The bay surge that followed, however, put her over on her beam. Unlike the submarine, she did not come up again.

The fireball from the LNG tank expanded and grew hotter and hotter, brighter and brighter. The temperature inside the submarine rose dramatically – until the men were being parbroiled inside a 150-degree oven. Then the temperature fell, though not as fast as it had risen.

Minutes later, the temperature in the boat almost back to normal, the XO climbed to the bridge to assess the damage. Angry black water roiled over the place where the tanker and pier had been. All the small boats that had dotted the waters of the bay were gone. In three or four places the water appeared to be on fire, but it was gasoline and raw crude burning.

The shore . . . the city was aflame for five miles in both directions. The thermal pulses and concussions had done their work. The surges of air into and away from the fireball had done the rest.

The main periscope was bent, the glass smashed. Whether from the five-inch shell of the destroyer or the blast, Askold couldn't tell. There was no trace of the second officer, whose corpse, like Senka's, had gone to a sailor's grave.

The XO called down a heading change, and ordered more speed. With the main periscope out of action, he kept the boat on the surface.

With her diesels driving her at twenty knots, *Admiral Kolchak* went southward down the bay, charging the batteries as she went. When the first light of dawn appeared in the eastern sky she was rolling in the Pacific swells.

Askold took her under. She was a tiny little boat, swimming through a great vast ocean, so when she disappeared beneath the surface it was as if she had never been.

16

The weeks following the disaster in Tokyo Bay wore heavily on Prime Minister Atsuko Abe. At least 155,000 people died in the explosions and fires that raged out of control for two days in Yokosuka. Emergency workers estimated that 100,000 were injured; at least half the injuries were burns.

Obeying standing orders, when the Yokosuka refinery fire was reported, the duty officer in the war room in the basement of the defense ministry called both Prime Minister Abe and the chief of staff of the Japanese Self-Defense Force at their homes. Both Abe and the general were in the war room when the LNG tanker exploded.

They sat there saying little as the reports came in. A television station quickly launched its helicopter. Soon the stunning visual panorama played endlessly from large-screen televisions mounted in strategic places throughout the room.

Garish, ghastly fires everywhere, a sea of flame and destruction – these were the images burned into the minds of the men watching in the war room, and of the Japanese public, because these scenes were also playing live on nationwide television.

Although Abe did not want the public to witness this calamity, he was powerless to prevent the television stations from showing what they pleased unless he wished to declare martial law, and he didn't. He wasn't about to admit that the situation in metropolitan Tokyo was beyond the control of the civilian government. Not yet, anyway.

The prime minister's first instinct was to blame the catastrophe on an earthquake. A tremor caused fatal damage to the refinery, which finally blew up disastrously. This would have been a good story and certainly plausible, but unfortunately the videotape from the television helicopter proved conclusively that the fire had started in several different places, as many as eight, and spread at least a half hour before the explosion that flattened the refinery and several square miles of nearby city.

Worse, the cameraman in the helicopter managed to get footage of the Russian submarine several minutes before the fatal detonation. She was lying on the surface near the LNG tanker, a recognizable black shape quite prominent against the reflection of the fire in the black water.

When the LNG tanker blew, the helicopter was dashed to earth and shattered as if it were a toy in the hands of some horrible Japanese movie monster. Of course, the television station made a tape of the video feed; they played the footage of the submarine over and over and over. The boat looked evil lying there in the darkness, its decks awash, its silhouette an ominous black shape amid the reflected glare of the holocaust.

The public mood, somber enough after the invasion of Siberia was announced, turned even more gloomy. The racial memory of the B-29 firebombings of World War II was too fresh. Television pictures of burning cities, with the nation again at war, mesmerized the Japanese. The business of the nation ground to a halt as they watched in horror.

Who was responsible?

'Atsuko Abe is responsible for every dead Japanese and every scarred, mutilated survivor.'

A senior member of an opposition party voiced this obvious truth; that sound bite was also carried nationwide by the television stations.

Another senior politician added soberly, 'It appears that our leaders have underestimated the Russians' military capacity.'

Abe's reaction to this criticism was to cast about for ways to end the public's unhealthy fascination with the submarine raid, the burned-out city, and the victims. He demanded legislation to censor the press, to put a stop to the public airing of negative comments. His party had a sufficient majority in the Diet to carry the day. At his insistence, the television went back to baseball and dramas; the newspapers avoided all mention of the war except when running news released by the defense ministry, which they published without comment.

While he got his way, Abe was enough of a politician to realize that he had expended valuable political capital that he might need later, but he saw no alternative. If the public lost faith in the war effort now, before the conquest was assured, he and everything he had tried to achieve would be doomed.

The one bright spot in the censorship fiasco was the removal of the daily list of casualties from Siberia from the nation's front pages. Troops were encountering unexpectedly heavy opposition from ill-equipped Russian units, units that could almost be categorized as guerilla irregulars. Even without the daily butcher's lists, however, the public seemed to sense that all was not going well.

'Where will the Russians strike next?'

All over Japan, people asked that question. There were, of course, no answers. Abe supporters accused the doubters of being unpatriotic. The mood grew even uglier.

Part of the problem was the economy. Japan's stock market was quickly closed by the Abe administration when war broke out. In the real economy, things went rapidly to hell. Demand for Japanese goods in the United

States, Japan's largest foreign market, dropped dramatically. After the submarine disaster, shipowners refused to transport the raw materials and manufactured goods that kept the factories running and people eating. Idled factories laid off workers in huge numbers.

Atsuko Abe wrestled with these problems, too. He and General Yamashita, the military chief of staff, believed that the military should take over the nation's factories and shipping assets. This step was bitterly resisted by key members of Abe's party, who pointed out that the war was supposed to stimulate the economy, not kill it.

'Why is it,' Abe demanded of his party's senior members, 'that everyone is a patriot when patriotism is free, yet when it has a price, it has no friends?'

In western Russia life had become even more severe than it was before the Japanese invasion. Great masses of people were still hungry, factories still idle, and civilian construction projects stalled. Everyone was being squeezed as the military slowly and inexorably took control of every aspect of the nation's life. Every man between the ages of eighteen and twenty-five who could pass a physical was being drafted and sent to recruit depots, there to wait for arms and equipment from obsolete, worn-out factories that were being restarted by decree. Everything – food, fuel, clothing, housing, everything – was being rationed. The censored media printed only propaganda. A people with little hope could see that their country had gone from bad to worse.

The news of the devastation in Tokyo Bay caused by a Russian submarine hit this Russia with a stupendous impact. Pictures of *Admiral Kolchak* and a file photo of Pavel Saratov in his dress uniform were printed in the newspapers, made into posters, and displayed endlessly on television. The meager facts of Saratov's life from his navy personnel file were expanded into a ten-thousand word biography that was printed in every newspaper in Russia west of the Urals. The loss of innocent life in Japan was horrific, frightening, but the image of a few brave men in a small submarine sneaking into the Japanese stronghold to cripple the arrogant, swaggering bully struck a deep chord in Russian hearts starved for good news. The press in Europe, in North and South America, and in Australia picked up the stories and broadcast them worldwide. Within four days of the disaster Pavel Saratov was the best-known Russian alive.

During this orgy of patriotism Marshal Oleg Stolypin was trying to find the wherewithal to defend the nation. As he lay in bed at night trying to sleep, Stolypin had visions of Japanese armored columns following the railroad west all the way to Moscow. He would awaken with the nightmare of Japanese tanks in Red Square fresh in his mind. There weren't enough troops to stop the Japanese if they really made up their minds to do it.

Apparently the Japanese weren't bold enough to risk everything on one wild lunge westward. Or foolish enough. Going blindly where little was known did not appeal to Stolypin's military mind, either. The old gray marshal did not believe in luck. Unlike the late Marshal Ivan Samsonov, Stolypin was not a brilliant man. He was smart enough, but he had to look situations over carefully, weigh all the risks, ponder the possibilities. Once he was sure he was right, however, he was an irresistible force.

Stolypin had quickly assembled and put to work an experienced staff that knew the true state of the Russian army. Armed with presidential decrees and newly printed money, military arms and equipment were broken out of storage and issued to the troops and new recruits, new equipment was rushed into production, and the transportation system was drastically and ruthlessly overhauled.

The marshal concentrated on building his military strength. Any plans he made were going to hinge on the forces at his disposal. Increasing those forces was his first priority.

His second priority was augmenting those forces in Siberia that could hurt the Japanese now. Men, weapons, ammo, and food were sent east by truck, train, and airplane. The marshal well knew that the meager forces in Siberia could not defeat the Japanese, but for the sake of the nation's soul, they had to fight.

One day Stolypin called on Aleksandr Kalugin to discuss the military situation. He found the president sifting through newspaper clippings and watching three televisions simultaneously.

'Saratov has united the Russian people,' Kalugin muttered, waving a fistful of clippings. 'They adore him.'

A few minutes later, apropos of nothing, the president remarked, 'The man who crushes Japan will hold Russia in the palm of his hand.'

He listened distractedly to Stolypin's report.

'We're losing, aren't we?' he demanded at one point.

'Sir, the Japanese are setting up military defenses in depth to protect the oil fields around Yakutsk and Sakhalin Island. They are digging in to stay around Khabarovsk and stockpiling men and equipment for a push up the Amur valley. My staff and I believe they intend to advance as far west as Lake Baikal before winter sets in, set up their first line of defense there.'

During most of this, Kalugin was shaking his head from side to side, slowly, with his eyes closed. 'Questions are being asked in the congress,' he said. 'The deputies want to see progress toward military victory. Our present small-unit actions merely harass the Japanese. Surrendering half of Siberia is not one of our options.'

'Mr President, we do not have the forces to –'

'The people demand action! The deputies *demand* action! *I demand it of you!*'

Stolypin didn't know what to say. He didn't panic – panic wasn't in him.

He repeated the truth to the president. 'We are doing all we can. Every day we grow stronger; every day we are one day closer to victory.'

Kalugin rose from his chair, shouting, 'Lies, lies, lies! Every day the Japanese army advances deeper into Russia. I have listened to your lying promises long enough.'

He spun on the aging marshal, confronted him. 'We must seize the moment. This moment in history is a gift; we must face it with bold resolve. We must not shrink from our duty.' Kalugin lifted his hand before his face and stared at it. 'We must strike with all the might and power we possess. The man who strikes first will conquer.'

He smashed his fist down on a glass table, which shattered into a thousand pieces.

'The prize is Russia, all of Russia. The man who refuses to be reasonable will triumph. That is the way of war. Atsuko Abe knows that. He is also a student of Genghis Khan.'

'Mr President, we are striking the Japanese with all our strength.'

'No! No, Marshal Stolypin, we are not. We have ten nuclear weapons. When these weapons are exploding on Japan, then . . .' Kalugin drew a ragged breath. '*Then* will the victory be ours. We must apply overwhelming military force. Weakness merely tempts them, sir. I have studied these things. I know I am right. We must annihilate our enemies. *Then Russia will be mine.*'

One of the people Stolypin made time for every day was Janos Ilin. Ilin briefed him on the extent of the Japanese penetration of Siberia. Ilin was remarkably well informed. Extraordinarily so. He had the names of the Japanese units, how many men, how much equipment, even the names of the commanders. He used all of this to annotate tactical maps for the marshal, who spent spare moments studying them.

Once the marshal questioned Ilin. 'Where does all this information come from? I never realized the Foreign Intelligence Service was such a font of knowledge. I can't even communicate with my units on a timely basis, yet you seem to be getting these maps from Tokyo every morning.'

'Sir, you know full well I cannot answer that question. If I start telling secrets, I soon won't have any.'

'You are much better informed than the GRU.' The GRU was the army general staff's intelligence arm.

'We work different sides of the street.'

That was the last time the marshal brought up the subject.

When the business of the day was over, Ilin usually lingered a few moments to chat. He was, of course, younger than the marshal and had never worked with him before.

'Are you one of those,' Ilin asked, 'who longs for the old days of glory?'

'Alas, no. The old days were not glorious. Corruption, selfishness,

incompetence, blighted, drunken lives, universal poverty, pollution, wastage
... Believe me, those days are best behind us.'

'But the army? It was huge, capable, the pride of every Russian.'

'The Kremlin gave us plenty of money and we shook our fists in the
world's face. The world trembled, yet the real truth was that the Soviet
Union was never able to do more than defend itself. The nation was always
poor. Our forces were designed for defense, not offense. For example, we
had no ability to mount an invasion of the United States, although the
Americans thought we could. Invading Afghanistan was the limit of our
capability, and we lost there because we couldn't force a quick decision.'

'So what is Russia's destiny?'

'Destiny?' The old man snorted.

'Our future.'

'After we defeat Japan? The great days for Russia all lie ahead. Without
the paranoia of the Cold War, the psychotic babble of the Communists, and
the expense of a huge military establishment, Russia will bloom as she has
never bloomed before. You may live to see it, Ilin.'

A day or so later, as Ilin put away his charts and notes after a briefing, he
said, 'Too bad Samsonov is not here. He was brilliant.'

'That he was,' the marshal agreed. 'He was my prodigy. I know genius
when I see it, and I saw it in him. He was the best we had. Just when we
needed him most, he is gone. Sometimes I wonder if God still loves Russia.'

'God had nothing to do with Samsonov's death,' Ilin said, his eyes
carefully searching the old man's face.

'What are you saying?'

'I want to know if I speak in confidence.'

'Do you think I have a loose tongue?'

'I think you are an honorable man, but if I am wrong we are both
doomed.'

'I have no time for this.'

Ilin's eyes didn't miss a single muscle twitch in Stolypin's face. 'Kalugin
had Samsonov executed. Kalugin's personal bodyguard killed him. They
buried him in the forest thirty miles north of the city.'

The old man's face turned gray. 'How do you know this?'

'My business is to know things. I have spies everywhere. My God, man,
this is still Russia.'

'You have proof?'

From his jacket pocket Ilin produced a small photograph and passed it to
the marshal. Samsonov's head lay on a mound of dirt. There was a large
bullet hole in his forehead. His eyes were open.

'The hole in his forehead was the exit hole. He was shot from behind.'

Stolypin handed over the photo.

Ilin took out a match, struck it, applied it to the corner of the celluloid.
He dropped the flaming picture in an ashtray.

'Why did you tell me this?'

'Kalugin has his men checking out the nuclear weapons at Trojan Island. They took the top experts in Russia with them.'

Marshal Stolypin took a deep breath, then exhaled slowly. He kept his eyes on the residue of the photograph in the ashtray. A wisp of smoke danced delicately in the eddies of air.

Stolypin met Ilin's eyes.

Ilin continued: 'I am told that when Kalugin's men are sent to kill someone, they ask the victim to sit in the front passenger seat. As the car rolls along, they talk of inconsequential things. When the victim is relaxed, off his guard, he is shot in the back of the head. It is quite painless, I believe.'

'So you have warned me.'

Ilin nodded. After a bit, he spoke again, softly. 'Aleksandr Kalugin is another Joseph Stalin. He is paranoid and has no scruples, none whatever.'

'He is insane,' Marshal Stolypin said slowly, remembering his discussion with Kalugin several days before, during which the president smashed a glass table with his fist.

The Russians named the outfit American Squadron and ran stories on television and in newspapers to improve public morale. The capabilities of the F-22 Raptor were extolled to the skies. The Russian reporters called it a 'superplane,' the best in the world. Flown by these ace American pilots, all of whom had volunteered to fly and fight for the Russian Republic, the F-22 would sweep the Japanese criminals from the skies in short order.

Street kiosks sold posters showing the American volunteers standing around an F-22 with the flag of old Russia painted on the fuselage. No one outside the squadron was told that the flag had been painted on with water-based paint. After the photographers left, the linesmen carefully washed the still-damp paint from the aircraft's smart skin.

Col. Bob Cassidy was appalled when the military situation was explained to him at headquarters in Moscow. The Russians were not yet ready to resist the Japanese on the ground with conventional warfare tactics.

When he was taken to meet Marshal Stolypin after the briefing, he kept his opinions to himself. The old man's face revealed nothing. He listened to the translator, nodded, examined Cassidy as if he were looking at a department-store dummy.

Bob Cassidy sat at attention. He felt as if he were back in the Air Force Academy for doolie summer. The old man had that effect.

Now the Russian marshal commented.

'We are doing what we can for Russia, Colonel. I am sure your president would say that he also is doing what he can. I expect you to do likewise.'

'Yes, sir,' Cassidy said, blushing slightly when he had heard the translation.

The marshal continued, absolutely impassive.

'I would like for the American Squadron to attack the Japanese air force. Win air superiority. Once you have it, or while you are winning it, shoot down their transports, prevent them from repairing the railroads. If the Japanese are dependent on ground transportation, we will defeat them this winter.'

'May I ask, Marshal, how much pressure you want us to put on enemy truck convoys?'

'Use your discretion, Colonel. I am of a mind to give the Japanese all of Siberia they wish to take. It is a very big place. On the other hand, if you can create in them a burning desire to return to Japan, you will save many lives.'

The thought occurred to Bob Cassidy that Stolypin must play a hell of a game of poker. 'This winter, your army will attack?'

'This winter,' said Marshal Stolypin, 'we will kill every Japanese soldier in Siberia. Every last one.'

When the aerial wagon train arrived at the air base in Chita, the C-5 transports landed first. The base consisted of two runways, almost parallel, about seven thousand feet long. There wasn't much room for error. The transports landed and taxied off the runway into the parking area while Col. Bob Cassidy kept his flight of six F-22s high overhead. Two other airports, each with two runways, lay a few miles to the southwest. These were old military bases and had not been maintained, so the concrete was crumbling. An emergency landing there would probably ruin jet engines.

Cassidy was keeping a close eye on his tac display. A Washington colonel, Evan Register, had given Cassidy and the pilots accompanying him to Chita a brief last night, before the beer bust.

'The Athena device in the new Zeros will keep them hidden from your radar. And shooting an AMRAAM at a Zero is a waste of a good missile – Athena will never let the darn thing find its target. Leave your radar off. Radiating will make you a beacon for the Zeros – they will come like a moth to light.

'Sky Eye is your edge. The radars in the satellites have doppler capability. While they cannot see the Zeros, they can see the wakes they make in the air, especially when they are supersonic. A supersonic shock wave is quite distinctive.'

'Wait a minute,' one of the junior pilots said, wanting to believe but not quite ready to. 'What's the catch?'

In the back of the room, Cassidy tilted his chair back and grinned. Stanford Tuck had not let him down.

'Well, of course there are some technical limitations,' the Washington wizard admitted. 'This *is* cutting-edge technology. Detecting aircraft wakes with doppler works best in calm air. Summer turbulence, thunderstorms, rain, hail – all such conditions degrade the capability. The computer can sort it out to some extent, but remember the satellites are whizzing along, so the picture is constantly changing, and there is a lot of computing involved. We've been watching the wakes of Zeros for several weeks now. As long as the weather doesn't change, we'll be okay.'

Cassidy looked at his troops and shrugged. What could you do?

At 25,000 feet over Chita, Bob Cassidy wondered how effective Sky Eye was today. The air at this altitude seemed smooth enough. The sun was diffused by a high, thin layer of cirrus, which cut the glare somewhat.

The land below looked uninviting. Chita was a small town on the upper reaches of the Amur River, backed up against a snow-covered mountain range, with another to the south. The arid land reminded Cassidy of Nevada or central Oregon. The runways below looked like bright strips on the yellow-brown earth. From this altitude the aircraft parking mats and a few buildings, probably hangars, were also visible.

Fifteen hundred miles from the sea, the Amur River was a seasonal stream now carrying water from melting snow. Two bridges crossed the river, one for the Trans-Siberian Railroad and one for trucks. Just before the snows came, the river would cease to flow. Any water trapped in it would freeze solid.

Khabarovsk lay a thousand miles downstream. From there, the river flowed northwest another five hundred miles to the Sea of Okhotsk.

The tac display showed empty sky around the F-22 formation. He punched the display to take in all the territory between Chita and Zeya, five hundred nautical miles east. Five hundred nautical miles, the distance between Boston and Detroit. The distances in Siberia were going to take some getting used to. The land was vast beyond imagination. Man had barely made an imprint here.

Cassidy wondered about Jiro Kimura. Was he still alive? And if so, where was he?

Jiro was on his mind a lot lately, just when he should be thinking of something else, concentrating on the job at hand. Cassidy growled at himself and tried to think of other things.

Not a single bogey on the tac display, neither toward Khabarovsk nor Nikolayevsk. That bothered Cassidy. It would be nice if the satellite saw one or two ... but it didn't. Apparently. Subject, of course, to the inevitable high-tech glitches.

Cassidy glanced down at the transports on the airfield. They were quite plain at this altitude. If all was going as planned, the crews were unloading the Sentinel batteries, which were mounted on trailers. The aircraft also brought four Humvees, which would pull the trailers. A Sentinel unit was being spotted on each side of the runway and turned on. The others would be towed away from the base that afternoon and evening, set up in a pattern on local roads in the area. As soon as the units were off-loaded, the two C-

5s would take off and head back over the pole toward Alaska. Tankers were supposed to meet them several hours out.

Tankers had been crucial to the success of this operation, moving airplanes and equipment a third of the way around the globe and arriving ready to fight. Finding a tanker in the vastness of the sky had always been a challenge, a real tightrope act when one was low on fuel. GPS now made the rendezvous phase routine, which was fine by everyone.

Now Cassidy eyed his fuel gauges. The fighters had tanked an hour ago, so they were fat, but Cassidy didn't know how much longer he could remain strapped to this ejection seat. He'd been sitting in this cockpit over six hours. He itched and ached. He squirmed in the seat, trying to give his numb butt some relief.

Another half hour passed. One of the C-5s taxied to the end of the runway, sat there for five minutes, then began to roll. The other was taxiing as the first one lifted off.

Cassidy waited until the C-5s were ten minutes north, then pulled the throttles back and started down.

The first problem the Americans faced was parking their planes. The base was beyond the tactical range of Zeros flying from Khabarovsk, which was cold comfort since the Japanese now had planes at Zeya. And if they used a tanker, they could strike this base anytime they wished from almost anywhere, including Japan.

With that in mind, the F-22s were dispersed all over the field. The revetments were full of obviously abandoned fighters, some of them old MiG-19s and MiG-21s. Some of these antiques had flat tires, oil leaks, sand and bird's nests in the intakes. The Americans pushed and pulled the Russian iron out of the revetments and put the F-22s in. Then they rigged camouflage nets.

Some of the best spots, concrete revetments completely hidden by large trees, were already taken by Sukhoi-27s, which looked ready to fly. The Sukhois were attended by grubby, skinny Russians who smelled bad and didn't speak English. The Americans passed out candy bars and soon made friends. While the candy was eaten eagerly, the Russians really wanted cigarettes, which the Americans didn't have.

Now that he was on the ground, Cassidy thought the Chita area was a bit like Colorado. The base and the small town huddled around the railroad station a few miles away were in a basin, surrounded by snow-covered mountains to the north, west, and south. The air was crystal-clear. From here, it was a long way to anywhere.

At least the communications were first-rate: The Americans had brought their own com gear, portable radios that bounced their signals off a satellite, which meant that the operators could talk to anyone on the planet.

Cassidy got on the horn immediately. He used the cryptological encoder, set it up based on the date and time in Greenwich, then waited until it phased in. When he got a dial tone, he called the Air Force command center in the Cheyenne Mountain bunker in Colorado Springs.

'All quiet, Colonel. They haven't stirred much today.'

Bob Cassidy breathed a sigh of relief. By the following morning, the defenses here would be ready, but not quite yet.

Everything was a problem, from berthing to bathrooms. The pilots got an empty ramshackle barracks and the enlisted got two. The bathrooms were appalling. Each building had one solitary toilet without a seat to serve the needs of the eighty people who would be bunked in that building.

'If my mother saw this, she'd faint dead away. She always wanted me to join the Navy, live like a gentleman,' Bob Cassidy told a little knot of junior officers he found staring into a dark, filthy barracks bathroom.

'Why didn't you?'

'I used to get seasick taking a bath.'

'You've certainly come to the right place, Colonel. You won't have to take baths here.'

'Fur Ball, you and Foy Sauce go dig a hole for an outhouse. Scheer, you take these others and tear down that old shack across the road for wood. Get some tools from the mechanics and watch out for rusty nails. And build one for the enlisted troops, too.'

When Cassidy disappeared, Hudek said disgustedly, 'Outhouses! We've come halfway around the world to build outhouses.'

'Glamour,' Foy Sauce muttered. 'High adventure, fame ... I am so goddamn underwhelmed, I could cry.'

That evening everyone ate in an abandoned mess hall. The stoves used wood from the nearby forest. The doctor who had accompanied the group from Germany refused to allow anyone to drink the water from the taps, so bottled water was served with the MREs – meals, ready to eat. The MREs were opened, warmed somewhat on the stoves, and served.

Later that evening, Maj. Yan Chernov came looking for the commanding officer. He had a translator in tow. After the introductions, he told Cassidy, 'My men need food. We came here from Zeya two weeks ago. The base people have no extra food.'

'How many of you are there?'

'Sixty-five.'

Cassidy didn't hesitate. 'We'll share, Major.' He caught the supply officer's eye and called him over. After a brief conversation, he told the translator, 'Dinner for your people will be in twenty minutes.'

'We have no money. Nothing with which to pay.'

'Zeya is down the valley, isn't it?'

'Yes. East. The Japanese attacked. I shot down a few.'

'With Su-27s?'

'Yes, good plane.'

'My first name is Bob.' Cassidy held out his hand.

'Yan Chernov.'

'Let's have a long talk while you eat. I want to know everything you know about the Japanese.'

The sea was calm, with just the faintest hint of a swell. The boat rocked ever so gently as it ghosted along on its electric engines. Fog limited visibility and clouds blocked out the night sky. A gentle drizzle massaged Pavel Saratov's cheeks as he stood in *Admiral Kolchak*'s tiny cockpit atop the sail. He took a deep breath, savoring the tang of the sea air, a welcome contrast from the stink of the boat.

Alive. Ah, how good it was. Unconsciously he fingered the lumpy new scar on his forehead, a jagged purple thing that came out of his hairline and ran across above his left eye, then disappeared into his hair over his left ear. The fragments of the Japanese shell that struck the bridge had torn off half his scalp.

The corpsman had sewn the huge flap of skin back in place, and fortunately it seemed to have healed. The scar was oozing in several places – an infection, the corpsman said. He smeared ointment on the infected places twice a day. Every morning he used a dull needle to give Saratov an injection of an antibiotic as the crew in the control room watched with open mouths. Saratov always winced as if the needle hurt mightily. He had inspected the bottle of penicillin before the first injection. The stuff was grossly out of date, but since it was all they had, he passed the bottle back to the corpsman without comment and submitted to the jabs.

An hour before midnight. Here under the clouds, amid the fog, it was almost dark, but not quite. A pleasant twilight. At these latitudes at this time of year the night would not get much darker. At least the clouds shielded the boat from American satellites. He wondered if the Americans were passing satellite data to the Japanese. Perhaps, he decided. Saratov didn't trust the Americans.

Behind Saratov, the lookout had the binoculars to his eyes, sweeping the fog. 'Keep an eye peeled,' Saratov told him. 'If the Japanese know we are here, we will have little warning.'

As his wound healed, Saratov had ordered the boat northward, keeping it well out to sea. He lay in his bunk staring at the overhead and eating moldy bread, turning over his options.

He refused to make a radio transmission on any frequency. The danger of being pinpointed by radio direction finders was just too great. One evening the boat copied a message from Moscow. After it was decoded, Askold delivered it to the captain, who read it and passed it back.

'Captain, Moscow says to go to Trojan Island. I have never heard of it.'

'Umm,' Saratov grunted.

'It's not on the charts.'

'It is a submarine base, inside an extinct volcano, near the Kuril Strait. It was a base for boomers. Abandoned years ago.'

'What will we do, Captain?'

'Hold your present course and speed. Let me think for a while.'

Trojan Island. After several days of thought, Saratov decided to try it, because the other options were worse.

Now he spoke into the sound-powered telephone on his chest. 'XO, will you come up, please?'

When the executive officer was standing beside Saratov in the cockpit, he said, 'The island is dead ahead, Captain. Four miles, if our navigation is right.'

'I haven't been here in twelve years,' Saratov muttered. 'I hope I haven't forgotten how to get in.'

'Amazing,' the XO said. 'A sub base so secret that I never heard about it.'

'You weren't in nuclear-powered submarines.'

'What if there is nothing there anymore?'

'I don't know, Askold. I just don't know. It's a miracle the P-3s haven't found us yet. Sooner or later they will. I thought about stopping a freighter, putting all the men aboard and scuttling the boat. We have an obsolete submarine, the periscope is damaged, we're running low on fuel and food, and we have only four torpedos left. We've done about all the damage we can do.'

'Yes, sir.'

The XO concentrated on searching the fog with binoculars.

They heard the slap of breakers on rocks before they saw anything. Probing the fog with a portable searchlight, Saratov closed warily on the rocky coast at two knots. At least the sea was calm here in the lee of this island.

He finally found rocks, rising sheer from the sea.

It took Saratov another hour to find the landmarks he wanted, mere fading gobs of paint smeared on several rocks. He was unsure of one of the marks – there wasn't much paint left – but he kept his doubts to himself. After taking several deep breaths, Saratov turned the boat, got on the heading he wanted, then ordered the boat submerged.

In the control room, he ordered the *michman* to take the boat to a hundred feet, then level off. While this was going on, he studied the chart he had worked on for an hour earlier that day.

'I want you to go forward on this course at three knots for exactly five minutes, then make a ninety-degree right turn. If we go slower, the current will push us out of the channel.'

'Aye aye, Captain.'

'If we hit some rocks at three knots we'll hole the hull,' one of the junior officers said, trying to keep it casual.

'This is a dangerous place to get into,' the captain replied, trying to keep the censure from his voice. Now didn't seem the time to put junior officers in their place. 'Sonar, start pinging. Give me the forward image on the oscilloscope.'

As the submerged boat approached the island, the hole in the rock became visible on the scope. Pinging, afraid of going slower, Saratov aimed for the tunnel.

Around Saratov, everyone in the control room was sweating. 'This is worse than Tokyo Bay,' the XO remarked. No one said a word. All eyes were on the oscilloscope.

As the sub entered the hole, Saratov ordered the speed dropped to a knot. He crept forward for a hundred yards, watching the scope as the sonar pinged regularly. The chamber ended just ahead.

With the screws stopped, the chief began venting air into the tanks. The sub rose very slowly, inching up.

When the boat reached the surface, Saratov cranked open the hatch dogs, flung back the hatch, and climbed into the cockpit.

The boat lay in a black lagoon inside a huge cavern. That much he had expected. What Saratov had not expected were the electric lights that shone brightly from overhead. A pier lay thirty meters or so to port. Standing on the pier were a group of armed men in uniform: Russian naval infantry. Saratov gaped in astonishment.

One of the men on the pier cupped his hands to his mouth and called, 'Welcome, Captain Saratov. We have been waiting for you.'

17

Several of the armed naval infantrymen, Russian marines, on the pier were officers. As the submarine was secured to the pier, Saratov saw that one officer wore the uniform of a general. When the soldiers had pushed over a gangplank, the general skipped lightly across like a highly trained athlete. He didn't bother to return the sailors' salutes.

Saratov didn't salute, either. The general didn't seem to notice. He stood on the deck, looking up at the dents and scars on the sail and the twisted periscope.

'How long will it take to fix this?' he asked, directing his question at Saratov.

'If we had the proper tools, perhaps two days for this damage. The missing tiles will take several weeks to repair, and the new ones may come off again the first time we dive.'

The general climbed the handholds to the small bridge. 'My name is Esenin.'

'Saratov.'

'Shouldn't you be saluting or something?'

'Should I?'

'I think so. We will observe the courtesies. The military hierarchy is the proper framework for our relationship, I believe.'

Saratov saluted. Esenin returned it.

'Now, General, if you will be so kind, I need to see your identity papers.'

'We'll get to that. You received an order directing your boat to this base?'

Saratov nodded.

The general produced a sheet of paper bearing the crest of the Russian Republic. The note was handwritten, an order to General Esenin to proceed to Trojan Island and take command of all forces there. The signature at the bottom was that of President Aleksandr Kalugin.

'And your identity papers. Proving you're General Esenin.'

'Alas, you have only my honest face for a reference.'

'Oh, come on! A letter that may or may not be genuine, a uniform you could acquire anywhere? Do I look like a fool?'

'We also have weapons, Captain. As you see, I am armed and so are my men. If you will be so kind as to observe, they have your sailors under their guns as we speak.'

The soldiers were pointing their weapons at the sailors, who were busy securing the loose ends of the lines. 'All personnel at this base are subject to my authority, including you and your men,' General Esenin concluded.

'I didn't know there were any personnel here.'

'There are now.'

Saratov handed the letter back. He leaned forward, with his elbows on the edge of the combing.

'I congratulate you on your victory in Japan, Captain. You have done very well.'

Saratov nodded.

'By order of President Kalugin, you have been promoted to captain first class.'

'My men are owed five or six months' pay. Can you pay them? Most of them have families to support.'

'Alas, no one will be mailing letters from Trojan Island.'

Saratov turned his head so that the general could not see his disgust.

'How long will it take to ready your boat for sea?'

'The periscope ... if there is another in the stores here, that will take several days. The radar is out of action. We have several cracked batteries. If the people here have the parts and tools and food and fuel and torpedoes, perhaps a week.'

The general nodded abruptly. 'We will repair your boat as speedily as possible, refuel and reprovision it; then you and your crew will take me and a special warfare team back to Tokyo.'

Saratov tried not to smile.

'You look amused, Captain.'

'Let's be honest, "General." This boat will never get into Tokyo Bay a second time.'

'I know it will be difficult.'

Saratov snorted. 'For reasons we can only speculate about, the Japanese left the door open the first time. We grossly embarrassed them. I assume you know the Asian mind? They lost a great deal of face. They will go to extraordinary lengths to ensure that we do not succeed in embarrassing them again. By now they have welded the door shut.'

'No doubt you are correct, but I have my orders from President Kalugin. You have your orders from me.'

'Yes, sir.'

'Just so that we understand each other, Captain, let me state the situation more plainly: this boat is going back to Tokyo Bay. If you do not wish to take it there under my orders, we will give you a quick funeral and your executive officer will have his chance at glory.'

Saratov bit his lip to keep his face under control. Esenin glanced his way and smiled.

'You find me distasteful, Captain. A common reaction. I have an abrasive personality, and I apologize.' His smile widened. 'Then again, perhaps *distasteful* is an understatement. Perhaps, Saratov, like so many others before you, you wish to watch me die. Who knows, you may get lucky.'

Esenin flashed white teeth.

Saratov tried to keep his face deadpan. 'I hope you are a tough man,' he told Esenin. 'When they weren't expecting us, the Japanese almost killed us. Next time, they'll be ready. Dying in one of these steel sewer pipes won't be pleasant. There is just no good way to do it. You can be crushed when the boat goes too deep and implodes, maybe die slowly of asphyxiation when the air goes bad. If we get stuck on the bottom, unable to surface, you'll probably wish to God you had drowned.'

Esenin's smile was gone.

'We might die together, Saratov,' he said. 'Or perhaps I shall watch you die. We will see how the game goes.'

The general climbed down the rungs welded to the sail to the deck. He paused and looked up at Saratov. 'You have five days and nights to get ready for sea. Make the most of them.'

The next day Bob Cassidy took off leading a flight of four. He had slept for exactly two hours. According to the people at Space Command in Colorado Springs, two Zeros had their engines running at Zeya, five hundred miles east. Ready or not, the Americans could wait no longer.

This morning Paul Scheer flew on Cassidy's wing. The second section consisted of Dick Guelich and Foy Sauce.

Cassidy swung into a gentle climbing turn to allow the three fighters following him to catch up. Joined together in a tight formation, the four F-22s kept climbing in a circle over the field. They entered a solid overcast layer at eight thousand feet and didn't leave it until they passed twenty thousand.

In the clear on top, they spread out so that they could safely devote some time to the computer displays in their cockpits. The first order of business was checking out the electronics.

The F-22 acquired its information about distant targets from its own onboard radar, from data link from other airplanes, or via satellite from the computers at Space Command in Colorado Springs. In addition, the planes contained sensors that detected any electronic emissions from the enemy, as well as infrared sensors exquisitely sensitive to heat. The information from all these sources was compiled by the main tactical computer and presented to the pilot on a tactical situation display.

The airplanes shared data among themselves by the use of data-link laser beams, which were automatically aimed based on the relative position of the planes as derived from infrared sensors. Each plane fired a laser beam at the other and updated the derived errors in nanoseconds, allowing the computers to fix the relative position of both planes to within an inch. In clouds or bad weather, the data-link transfer was conducted via a focused, super-high-frequency radio beam.

Each pilot knew exactly where the others were because his computer, the brain of the airplane, presented the tactical situation in a three-dimensional holographic display on the MFD, or multifunction display, in the center of the instrument panel. On his left, another MFD presented information about the engines, fuel state, and weapons. On his right, a third MFD depicted God's view, the planes as they would look from directly overhead while flying over a map of the earth.

The pilot selected the presentations and functions he wanted by manipulating a cursor control on the right or inboard throttle with his left hand. The aircraft's control stick, on the side of the cockpit under his right hand, was also festooned with buttons, so without moving his hands from stick and throttles, the pilot could choose among a wide variety of options that in earlier generations of fighters would have required lifting an arm and mechanically throwing a switch or pushing a button.

The current state of the art in fighter planes, the F-22 Raptor was a computer that flew, capable of a top speed of about Mach 2.5 and maneuvering at over 9 G's. The semi-stealthy design was intended to enable the pilot to detect the enemy before he was himself detected. Alas, the Athena capability of the Zero gave it the edge. In modern war any pretense of airborne chivalry had been completely jettisoned: the pilot who shot first and escaped before the victim's friends could do anything about it would be the victor.

Level at thirty thousand feet, the Raptors accelerated in basic engine to supercruise at Mach 1.3. The pilots flipped a switch to turn on the chameleon skin of their planes. The planes faded from view as their skin color changed electronically to blend them into the summer sky.

As briefed, Scheer turned left five degrees and held the heading until the gap between him and the leader had widened to five miles, then he turned back to parallel Cassidy's course. The second section moved right and spread out in a similar manner. With his four planes spread over twenty miles of sky, Cassidy hoped to optimize his chances of getting one plane into Sidewinder range on any Zero they chanced to meet. If one plane was detected, the others could circle in behind the attacking Zero while it was engaged with its intended victim. That was the plan, anyway, carefully explained and diagramed.

As the cloud deck under them feathered out, the land below became visible under scattered cumulus clouds that were growing as the sun warmed the atmosphere.

The planes flew east. Cassidy began hearing the deep bass beep of a search radar probing the sky on a regular scan. The beep made Cassidy fidgety. Of course, the stealthy shape of the F-22 prevented the operator from getting enough of a return to see the American fighters – he knew that for a fact – but still . . .

The visibility today was excellent. On the left, a huge range of mountains wearing crowns of snow stretched away to the horizon. On the right, another range ran off haphazardly into the great emptiness toward Manchuria. The land was so big, so empty. A pilot who ejected into this trackless wilderness was doomed to die of exposure or starvation. At Cassidy's insistence, the following day the U.S. Air Force would fly in a Cessna 185 on tundra tires, with long-range tanks, to use as a search and rescue plane if the need arose.

To fly the plane and operate the computers – there were actually five of them: three flight-control computers, an air-data/navigation computer, and a tactical computer – the Raptor pilot had to concentrate intently on the torrent of information being presented graphically on his HUD and the three MFDs. There was no time for sight-seeing, for trying to spot the enemy with the human eye. The pilot was merely the F-22's central processing unit.

This thought went through Bob Cassidy's mind as he forced himself to concentrate on the displays in front of him.

The miles rolled by swiftly at Mach 1.3. Not much longer . . .

Clad in a full-body G suit and a helmet that covered his entire head, Cassidy couldn't even scratch his nose. Sweat trickled down his face. Since he couldn't do anything about it, he ignored it.

Cassidy was nervous. He shook his head once to clear the sweat from his eyes, toyed with the idea of raising the Plexiglas face shield on his helmet so he could get his fingers to his face and wipe the sweat away. That would take maybe fifteen seconds, while the plane would traverse almost three and a half miles of sky.

Not yet.

Cassidy took a few seconds to stare at the spot in space where the computer said Scheer had to be. Nothing. The chameleon skin had blended the fighter into the sky so completely it was invisible to the naked eye.

Today, of course, the F-22s had their radars secured, the tac display no longer blank. The Sky Eye had located the enemy and the satellite was beaming down the information. Two Zeros were in the air over Zeya. These must be the two that were on the ground with their engines running an hour ago.

As the range decreased and Cassidy shrank the scale of the display, he realized that the Zeros were on some kind of training mission. They were not in formation. They flew aimlessly back and forth over the base, did some turns, just wandered about. Perhaps the pilots were flying post-maintenance check flights.

At fifty miles, Cassidy and Scheer began their letdown. The transports bringing bombs to Chita would not arrive until tomorrow, so today all the F-22s could do was strafe.

Guelich and Foy stayed high and together. They would go for the airborne Zeros.

Cassidy could hear the baritone beep of a search radar sweeping past his plane. The beeps were quite regular, which made him believe that the operator did not see him. Too little energy was being reflected from the stealthy shape of the F-22 to create a blip on the operator's screen. Finally, as the range closed, the returning energy would be sufficient to create a blip, and the operator would see him. Cassidy wondered how close that would be.

He acquired the airfield at fifteen miles. The afternoon sun was behind him and slightly to his right, so he and Scheer would be essentially invisible as they came over.

Throttling back more, Cassidy let his speed drop to Mach 1. He wanted every second he could to shoot, but he wanted to arrive with minimum warning.

Down to three thousand feet, ten miles, lined up on the ramp, Cassidy pulled the throttles back even farther. Scheer was already separated out to the left, looking for his own targets. The other plane had faded from view. Cassidy had to check the tac display to make sure where Scheer was.

The routine beeps of the enemy radar changed drastically. Now the operator was sweeping the beam back and forth over the two F-22s repeatedly. Nine miles. They had made it in to nine miles before being picked up.

Bob Cassidy was down to five hundred knots when he saw the enemy fighters. There were five of them, parked in a row on the ramp. At least he hoped they were Zeros. They might have been Russian iron, but he didn't have time to make sure. Cassidy turned hard to get lined up, checked to make sure he had the ball in the center, and glanced at the altimeter.

The row of fighters was coming at him fast. And Paul Scheer appeared out of nowhere in his left-frontal quadrant, no more than fifty feet away. Paul was going to strafe these guys, too.

Cassidy throttled back still more. He was down to three hundred knots now.

Scheer opened fire, walked a stream of shells across the parked planes, and broke left. Smoke poured from one of the planes.

Cassidy walked his shells across the planes, too, and broke right.

'Make a pass at the hangars, Paul, and we're out of here. I'll join on you.'

'Yes, sir.'

Cassidy circled to the south as Scheer shot up the hangars. The pilot could see several missile batteries sitting in plain sight. He snapped four fast pictures of the base area with a digital camera. When he got back to Chita, he could plug the camera into a computer and print out the pictures: instant aerial photos.

Paul headed west after his second strafing pass and Cassidy joined on him. They lit burners and climbed away.

No one had fired a shot at the Americans.

Dick Guelich was ten miles behind his intended victim and closing at Mach 1.8 when the bogey dot on the HUD moved left. The guy must be turning, he thought.

He dropped his left wing to compensate and centered the dot.

There, he could see him, just a speck slightly above the horizon, turning left. Five miles, four, now the Sidewinder tone ... and Dick Guelich squeezed off the missile. It leapt off the rail in a fiery streak and disappeared into the blue sky, chasing that turning airplane ahead.

A flash on the enemy airplane! Got him.

Guelich pulled off right and watched the Zero. It rolled upside down, its nose dropped, and then the ejection seat came out.

Lee Foy's Zero was potting along straight and level. Foy's ECM was picking up enemy radar transmissions, but the Zero was pointed in the wrong direction to see the F-22s. Precisely what the Japanese pilot was doing, Foy couldn't imagine. He just prayed that the enemy aviator kept doing it for a few more seconds. At four miles with the enemy in sight, Foy was closing fast, overtaking him with maybe three hundred knots of closure.

Half a world away from the warehouse, Foy decided not to waste a missile. He clicked the cursor on the gun symbol on his main MFD and pulled off a gob of power.

His speed bled down quickly. The enemy pilot kept flying straight and level.

Foy checked his tac display. Nobody around except Guelich, stalking his victim six miles to the west. Because he didn't have religious faith in these gadgets, Foy checked over both shoulders to ensure the sky was clear.

The Zero was still potting along like an airliner going to Newark. One mile away, a hundred knots of closure.

A half mile, seventy knots.

Now, Foy reduced power, put the crosshairs in the bull's-eye made by the horizontal and vertical stabilizers. The center of the bull's-eye was the exhaust pipe.

Foy was coming up from dead astern. *Whump* – he entered his victim's wash and began bouncing around.

Closer still, no more than three hundred yards.

Still closer ...

At a hundred yards, Foy stabilized. Although his plane was bumping along in the Zero's wash, the crosshairs in the heads-up display were skittering around on the enemy plane's tailpipe.

I should have used a Sidewinder! This isn't aerial combat – this is murder.

Unable to pull the trigger, he sat there staring at the Zero. At ninety yards, he could wait no longer.

The Gatling gun hammered at the enemy plane, which seemed to disintegrate under the weight of steel and explosive that was smashing through the fuselage from end to end.

As the Zero faded in a haze of fuel, an alarm went off in Lee Foy's head. He released the trigger as he pulled back hard on the stick. The F-22 responded instantly, climbing away from the gasoline haze just as the Zero caught fire.

The fire ignited the vapor trail, which became a flame a hundred yards long. Then the Zero blew up.

Lee Foy bit his lip, glanced at his tac display to see where Guelich was, then turned that way.

For a moment there, he had flown with his heart, not his head, and he had almost paid the price. He had come very close to dying with the Zero pilot.

'Sorry, pal,' Foy Sauce whispered.

Cassidy, Guelich, and their wingmen were fueling from a bladder on the ground at Chita when four Zeros came hunting late in the summer evening. The Zeros were radiating, searching for airborne bogeys. The F-22 raid on Zeya had caused a seismic shock in the war room in Tokyo.

Two sergeants had just finished setting up a Sentinel battery twenty miles east of Chita on a dirt road that ran through the forest. It had taken every minute of two hours to make that journey over the ruts of a terrible road. They feared the Sentinel would be damaged from all the bumps and jolts.

Finally, the GPS said they were twenty miles east, so they stopped, disconnected the trailer from the Humvee, and activated the unit. First the solar panels had to be turned to the south, then five switches thrown and a key removed, so the unit could not be turned off by anyone wandering by. The whole deal took about a minute, and most of that involved setting the solar panels.

The sergeants had just gotten back into the Humvee and were trying to get it turned around when the first missile leapt upward from the battery, spouting fire. With a soul-shattering roar, the rocket engine accelerated the missile upward too fast for the eye to follow. By the time the sergeants were looking up, all they could see was the fiery plume of the receding missile exhaust.

Even as they craned their necks, too awed to move, the second missile ignited.

As the thunder faded, the sergeant behind the wheel gunned the

Humvee's engine and popped the clutch. He careened past the battery, still on its trailer, and shot off down the rutted road toward Chita.

The pilot of the Zero that took the first missile never even saw the thing coming. He was checking his displays, scanning the sky, and keeping an eye on his flight lead when the missile detonated just a foot away from the nose cone of his aircraft. The shrapnel sliced through the side of the plane, sprayed the nose area where the radar was housed, and shattered the canopy. Shrapnel cut through the pilot's helmet into his skull, killing him instantly. He never even knew he'd been hit.

The second Sentinel missile had been tracking the same radar as the first missile, and when the radar ceased transmitting, the second Sentinel tried to shift targets. It sensed other radars emitting on the proper frequency and selected the strongest signal. The canards went over and the missile began its turn . . . far too late. The flight leader was looking toward his doomed wingman, the flash of the detonating warhead having caught his eye, when the second missile streaked harmlessly between the two planes.

'Missiles coming in!' He said it over the air.

'What kind of missile?' That was Control.

'I don't know. One just struck my wingman, though, and the plane appears to be out of control. He is going down now. Eject, Muto! Eject! Get out while you can!'

Muto was past caring.

The three remaining Zeros were trying to get it sorted out when a Sentinel missile struck another Zero. The pilot lived through the warhead detonation, but his plane was badly crippled. He pulled the throttles to idle to get it slowed while he turned back toward Khabarovsk, where these planes were based.

The flight leader was mighty quick. He turned off his radar and ordered the surviving wingman to do the same. Few pilots would have correctly diagnosed the problem in the few seconds he devoted to it.

Three seconds later, another missile went sailing past a mile away, out of control.

'Beam-riders,' the leader told Control.

He initiated a turn to the east, intending to make a 180-degree turn and head for home.

Halfway through the turn, Dixie Elitch and Fur Ball Hudek came roaring in with their guns blazing. The wingman lost a wing on the first pass.

The leader rolled upside down and pointed his nose at the earth. He had his head swiveling wildly when he caught a brief glimpse of afterburner flame coming from a barely discernible airplane; then the plane was gone.

He had no idea how many planes he faced, and he correctly concluded that the time had come to boogie. He punched out chaff and decoy flares as the Zero rocketed straight toward the center of the home planet.

One of the flares saved his life. Hudek triggered a Sidewinder, which went for a flare.

'Let's not waste fuel,' Dixie said over the air, calling Hudek off.

'Gimme a break, baby. Let me kill this Jap.'

'You heard me, Fur Ball. Break it off.'

Hudek could see the Zero pulling out far below. 'And to think I could be selling used cars in Hoboken.' He flipped on his radar, tried to get a firing solution for an AMRAAM. Ahh ... there it was! The radar was looking right at it. *Should I or shouldn't I?*

'Get off the radio, Fur Ball.'

'You bet, sweet thing. I'll get my CDs going again.'

'Muto and Sugita were hit by missiles. I think they were guiding on our radar beams. When I turned the radar off, several missiles went by, striking nothing. Then we were jumped by fighters. I do not know how many. I think they killed Tashiro then. I ran for my life.'

'Do not be ashamed, Miura. You are still alive to fight again.'

'Colonel, I have not yet told you the most unbelievable part. Do not think I am crazy. Believe that I tell you the truth.'

'Captain Miura, give us your report.'

'I could not see the enemy fighters. They were invisible.'

The colonel looked shocked. Whatever he had been expecting, that was not it.

'Are you sure, Miura? It is often difficult to see other airplanes in a dogfight. Light and shadow, cloud, indistinct backgrounds...'

'I am positive, sir. I got a glimpse of one, saw the afterburner plume. The plane was shimmering against the evening sky, barely visible. It was there and yet it wasn't. Then the angle or the light changed and I lost it. The enemy fighter was there, *but I couldn't see it.*'

In the silence that followed this declaration, Jiro Kimura spoke up. 'That would not be impossible, Colonel. I have read of American research to change the color of metal using electrical charges.'

The colonel was not convinced. 'I have heard of no such research by the Russians.'

'I doubt if the Russians could afford it, sir,' Jiro answered. 'These may be planes from the American Squadron that we have heard about. If so, they are American F-22 Raptors.'

'Write up your report, Miura,' the colonel said. 'I will forward it to Tokyo immediately.'

In the ready room the other pilots had a tape going on the VCR, a tape of a broadcast on an American cable channel. Jiro merely glanced at the television as he walked by ... and found himself looking at Bob Cassidy.

He stopped and stared. Cassidy's voice in English was barely audible, overridden by a male translator.

Cassidy! Oh my God!

'Hey, bitch! You cost me a kill. I could have got that Jap.'

'You call me a bitch again, Fur Ball, and you'd better have a pistol in your hand, because I'm going to pull mine and start shooting.'

Aaron Hudek's face was red. He shouted, 'Don't ever pull another stunt like that on me again. Got it?'

'As long as I'm the flight leader,' Dixie Elitch said heatedly, 'you're going to obey my orders, Hudek. In my professional opinion, we didn't have the fuel to waste chasing that guy. We had another hour of flying to do before we could land to refuel. You knew that as well as I did. At any time during that hour we could have been forced to engage again if more Zeros had come along.'

'All I had to do was squeeze the trigger. I had a radar lockup.'

'Then you should have fired.'

'*You* said not to.' Hudek's voice went up an octave.

'Well, what's done is done. You should have potted him, then joined on me.'

'Aah, sweet thing, I'll bet you didn't want me to shoot the little bastard in the back. Not very sporting.'

'Second-guess me all you like, Hudek, but in the sky, you'd better do what you're told.'

'Or what? You gonna waste some gas shooting me down?'

'No,' Bob Cassidy snapped as he walked over. 'She won't have to do that. Everyone in this outfit is going to obey orders, you included. Disobey an order and your flying days are over. You'll be walking home from here. I guarantee it.'

'Okay, Colonel. You're the boss.'

'You got that right,' Cassidy shot back.

'I was ready to squeeze it off,' Hudek continued. He held up a thumb and forefinger half an inch apart. 'I was that close.' He sighed heavily. 'We're gonna regret letting that last Jap scamper away to tell what he knew. I regret it right now.'

'You had a radar lock-up?' Cassidy asked sharply.

'As the guy was getting out of Dodge.'

'Perhaps the Athena gear wasn't working,' Cassidy mused.

'Maybe. I dunno.'

'You should have pulled the trigger, Hudek. Dixie didn't want you to waste gas. Next time, pull the damned trigger.'

Dixie blew Hudek a kiss.

Fur Ball grimaced, then wandered away looking for something cold to drink. His first combat, and he had let one get away. *Augh!*

Alas, all he would find to drink was water.

There was, he reflected, one tiny spot of light in this purée of incompetence, stupidity, and lost opportunities – Foy Sauce had refused his offer of a bet on the first Zero. Forking over a grand would have really hurt. At least he got half the credit for the guns kill with Dixie. That was something, though, Lord knows, not much.

No doubt the Chink would rag him unmercifully anyway. Double *augh!*

18

Working in shifts around the clock, the men of *Admiral Kolchak* took three days to ship a new periscope and radar antenna. They also took on a full load of torpedoes and diesel fuel, provisioned the ship with canned vegetables and meat, refilled the freshwater tanks, washed their clothes, and took baths. The cracked batteries took more time. There was no way to replace the missing anechoic tiles on the boat's hull, so they didn't try.

It was in the shower that the XO, Askold, approached Pavel Saratov, who was standing in the hot water with his eyes closed, letting it massage his back and head.

'Captain, we've found four missiles for the sail.'

'Are you sure they are the right ones?'

'Twenty years old if they are a day, but I've already loaded one. It fits.'

'Very good, Askold.'

'Sir, where does General Esenin want us to go?'

'Back to Tokyo Bay,' Saratov said after a bit. No doubt Askold picked the shower for his questions because with all this water noise a microphone couldn't overhear their conversation.

'The men are very unhappy.'

'Umm.' Saratov opened his eyes and reached for the soap.

'They'll be ready for us this time.'

'He has written orders, signed by President Kalugin. We don't have any choice.'

Askold concentrated on scrubbing.

'Look at the provisions,' Saratov said. 'Food, torpedoes, diesel fuel – they must have flown this stuff in here over the Pole. Somebody somewhere gave these people a hell of a priority.'

'It's crazy. A diesel/electric boat? A few torpedoes? We can win the war for Russia?'

'Russia's only operational submarine in the Pacific is *Admiral Kolchak*. Our other three were sunk attacking the Japs off Vladivostok.'

'So what are we going to do in Tokyo Bay?'

'Esenin has a mission. He just hasn't bothered to tell us serfs what it is.'

'Captain, the men –'

'XO, the officers and *michmen* and enlisted men of *Admiral Kolchak* are going to obey orders. They are going to do as they are told. They swore an oath to obey, and by all that's holy, they will.'

'Yes, sir.'

'Esenin will shoot anyone who fails to obey orders. If he doesn't, I will. You'd better tell them.'

'Aye aye, sir.'

'This is bigger than all of us, Askold. We have no choice. None at all.'

'I understand, Captain.'

That was the way he put the fear in Askold, who refused to look at him.

When the executive officer left the locker room, still buttoning his shirt, Saratov sat heavily on the bench. He found himself fingering the scar on his forehead.

He should have died in Tokyo Bay. Askold saved his life, and Saratov almost wished he hadn't.

'He intends to nuke Japan,' Janos Ilin told Marshal Stolypin. The old man stared at him stonily, which unnerved Ilin a little. One could never tell what the old bastard was thinking, or if he was. Talking to him was like talking to a portrait.

'He isn't that stupid,' Stolypin said finally.

'He *is* that stupid. Believe me. He thinks if he nukes Tokyo, Japan will collapse and he will be the new czar of Russia. His position will be unassailable.'

Stolypin shook his head from side to side like an old bear. 'We can win without nukes. We are bleeding them with hit-and-run raids. The Americans are in position to fight the Zeros toe-to-toe. This winter, we will unleash an army of half a million men against them. We *can* win, on the battlefield.'

'Kalugin will not wait. He wants to save Russia now.'

'When I saved those weapons, I was thinking of possible conflicts with former Soviet states. Ahh . . . The Japanese have earned their doom.'

'No doubt,' Janos Ilin said crisply, 'but while the Japanese government is collapsing, the military might retaliate with their own nuclear weapons. They have warheads for their satellite-launch missiles, developed in secret. They might launch them at Russia.'

Stolypin goggled. 'Those are the first words I have ever heard about Japanese nuclear weapons. How good is your information?'

'Absolutely reliable. In fact, Kalugin knows the Japanese have nuclear warheads mounted on missiles. He sent them an ultimatum, which they rejected. Prime Minister Abe told him that if he uses nuclear weapons on the Japanese, they will retaliate.'

'I know of no ultimatum.'

'Obviously, Kalugin doesn't believe Prime Minister Abe. And he's willing to bet Russia that Abe is lying.'

'This changes everything,' Stolypin mumbled, and leaned back in his chair.

The old soldier looked out the window, then played with the letter opener on his desk. That and a pen were the only items visible. Stolypin's bureaucratic tidiness bothered Ilin. It was his experience that neatniks were neurotic.

'All these years,' Stolypin muttered, 'the balance of nuclear terror kept anyone from pulling the trigger. Until now ... How do I know you are telling me the truth?'

'I would make this up? For what reason?'

'You come to me with a tale. The president is a madman bent on pulling the nuclear trigger. Perhaps he sent you here to see if I was loyal.'

'Spoken like a true peasant. Your paranoia becomes you, Marshal.'

'If you want to sneer at me, Ilin, do it somewhere else,' the marshal said, his face as calm as a clear summer sky. 'I don't have time for it.'

'I have only the whispered words of men I trust.'

'Whispered words of men I don't know will not move me, Ilin. I want proof. Bring me proof or don't come back.'

Janos Ilin rose from his seat and left the room.

The four F-22s topped the cloud layer in a spread formation. None of the F-22s were transmitting with their radar.

Today Aaron Hudek was Cassidy's wingman, flying five miles out to the leader's left. Dixie Elitch led the second section; she was five miles away to the right, and Clay Lacy was five miles beyond her.

Their heading was slightly north of east. The late afternoon sun shone over their left shoulders. The clouds below were thickening and the gaps looked ragged and gloomy. To the north, east, and south Cassidy could see massive thunderstorms, which were growing out of the turbulent clouds below.

The ECM was silent.

Cassidy still didn't completely trust all this high-tech gadgetry, so he pushed the ECM self-test button. The lights on the ECM panel flashed in a test pattern and the audio beeped and honked. The concert and light show lasted sixty seconds, by which time Cassidy heartily wished he hadn't played with the darn thing. He had tested it on the ground an hour ago.

The autopilot flew the plane nicely. Sitting in the generous cockpit, Cassidy thought the fighter rode like a 747 crossing the Pacific. Not a hint of turbulence. Solid, tight, smooth as silk. Where was the stew with the drinks?

Idly, Cassidy mused about the strange twists of fortune that had brought him here, to a foreign war where the only person on earth who might be considered one of his family was flying a fighter on the other side.

Life is bizarre at times, he decided. Totally unpredictable.

Dixie was a little too far away, but Cassidy didn't want to break radio silence to tell her to tighten up.

Two hundred miles to Zeya. The F-22s would be there in fifteen minutes.

Cassidy twiddled his computer cursor, told the magic box to attack the target he had programmed while still on the ground. The National Security Agency selected the targets by studying satellite reconnaissance photos. They converted latitude and longitude coordinates into code by use of map overlays, then passed the coded coordinates by scrambled satellite data link. The coded coordinates were plotted on maps brought from the States and reconverted to latitude and longitude; the resulting lat/long numbers were handed to the pilots to be programmed into the aircraft's attack computer.

The pilots were given only coordinates: They didn't know what they were bombing. It was a curious disconnect – if you didn't know, you wouldn't feel guilty. *I'm not responsible – the people in Washington told me to push the button and I pushed it.*

Hanging in Cassidy's small internal weapons bay were two one-thousand-pound green bombs. On the nose of each bomb was a GPS receiver, a computer, and a set of four small movable canards, or wings. The target coordinates were fed to the bomb's computer by the aircraft's computer, which also determined where the bomb should be dropped based on the known wind at altitude. As the unpowered bomb fell, the GPS receiver located the bomb in three-dimensional space and fed that data to the computer, which calculated a course to get the bomb where it was supposed to go and positioned the canards to steer it there. The accuracy of the system was phenomenal. Half the bombs dropped from above thirty thousand feet would hit within three meters – about ten feet – of the center of the programmed lat/long bull's-eye.

Today as Cassidy flew toward the Zeya airfield at 34,000 feet at Mach 1.3, the computer figured an attack solution and presented steering commands to the pilot. The plane's autopilot followed the commands with no input from the pilot.

Everything is automated, he thought. The machine does everything for you but die.

Due to the fact that the weapons could steer themselves, at this altitude the window into which they must be dropped was a large oval, or basket. Any bomb put into the basket would have the energy to steer itself to the desired target, if, of course, the computer and GPS receiver in the nose functioned properly. Just in case, the approved procedure was to drop two bombs on each target.

The symbology in the HUD was alive, moving predictably and gracefully as Bob Cassidy threaded his way between thunderstorms to make his supersonic bomb run five miles above the earth. When he was within the basket, he released the first weapon by pushing once on the pickle on the joystick. He felt just the slightest jolt as the first bomb was jettisoned from the weapons bay. Another push sent the second bomb after the first. Behind Cassidy, bombs were falling from the other planes, each of which was running its own attack.

The sonic booms arrived at the Zeya airfield before the bombs did. Four of them in less than a second, like an incoming artillery barrage.

The bombs startled Jiro Kimura, who scanned the cloudy sky. He had been walking toward the headquarters building to report to the base commander, but upon hearing the booms, he spent two seconds looking for enemy airplanes. Then he remembered the Zeros he and his wingman had flown in just an hour ago from Khabarovsk, and he started running back toward the parking mat.

Now he heard the roar of the engines, quite audible five miles under the speeding planes.

Jiro looked up again. He was searching the cloud-studded sky when the first bomb hit the ammunition storage depot on the edge of the base, two miles away. The resulting explosion leveled trees in every direction for a thousand yards. The explosion was so large that the detonation of the second bomb in the middle of the mess went completely unnoticed.

Jiro was facedown in the weed-studded dirt before the concussion of that explosion reached him.

A nearby hangar being used to store rations took two bombs in two seconds, those dropped by Aaron Hudek. After the bombs detonated, the hanger roof rose fifty feet in the air before it began falling. The walls of the building collapsed outward.

The pair of bombs dropped by Dixie Elitch fell on the fuel farm, two miles away from headquarters on the other side of the base. These bombs ignited two fuel fires, which quickly sent enormous columns of black smoke into the darkening evening clouds.

The last set of bombs, those dropped by Clay Lacy, was targeted on the headquarters building behind Jiro. The first bomb hit the northwest corner of the building, causing a fourth of the building to collapse in a pile of rubble. The second missed the building on the east side by ten feet; the explosion fired the brick masonry of the wall like shrapnel through the remaining structure.

The concussion of the two bombs pummeled Jiro Kimura as he lay facedown in the dirt a hundred feet away. Miraculously, the flying debris caused by the two bombs only dusted him with mortar and powdered brick.

When the air cleared, he picked himself up, wiped the dust and dirt from his eyes, and brushed the worst of it from the front of his uniform.

His thoughts began to clear. The people inside the building...

Jiro jerked open the door of the headquarters building and rushed inside. The dust in the air was so thick he could barely see. The electric lights were off. He groped his way down the hall and into the war room. The air was opaque.

Holding a handkerchief in front of his mouth and nose so that he could breathe, Jiro groped his way into the room. Something hit his legs. He bent down, blinking furiously, trying to see. It was a body. Half a body – from the waist down.

The floor was covered with thousands of pieces of bricks.

The air was clearing.

More bodies, and pieces of bodies, arms at odd angles, severed heads . . .

He looked up. As the swirling dust cleared, he could see patches of dark clouds through the gaping hole where the northwest corner of the building had stood. And he could hear the roar of jet engines.

The Americans had just released their bombs when Zero fighters surprised them. Suddenly, the ECM was wailing and the displays showed yellow fighter symbols, Zeros, out to the left and closing rapidly. Then one of the Zeros put a missile into the air and all hell broke loose.

The Americans slammed their throttles into full afterburner and broke hard to avoid the oncoming missile. Cassidy turned into the missile at eight G's, the massive titanium nozzle behind the afterburners tilting the fire cones up to help the jet turn faster. His full-body G suit automatically inflated to keep him from passing out.

The HUD showed targets everywhere. Unfortunately, the computer displayed the targets' positions in real time, not where they would be after Cassidy pointed his plane so that the targets were within the missile's performance envelope when he managed to get a firing solution. Solving that four-dimensional problem by looking at the computer displays while in danger of losing your life was the art of the supersonic dogfight. Some pilots could do it; others flew transports and helicopters.

Cassidy flipped the weapons selector to 'Missiles' while in an eighty-degree bank pulling four G's. A Zero was almost head-on when the aircraft vector dot came rapidly into the missile-capable circle, so he pulled the trigger. An AMRAAM missile roared away in a gout of fire.

The AMRAAM didn't guide! Of course not, stupid! It can't see the Athena-protected Zero.

Cassidy didn't have time to fret his mistake. Another missile streaked across his nose, not a hundred feet away, from left to right.

He had a target down and to his right, so he rolled hard and pulled toward it. The plane was turning away, so if he could outturn it, he could get a high-percentage stern shot. The G's pressed down on him and he felt the G suit squeezing viciously. He fought to inhale against the massive weight on his chest.

Now he had Sidewinders selected on the MFD. The enemy fighter was close, almost too close, but when he got a locked-on tone from the missile,

Cassidy fired. Two seconds later he saw an explosion out of the corner of his eye. *Did I get him?*

He was diving now toward the earth, pulling three G's. He relaxed the G, leveled his wings, reapplied G. Nose coming up, more G, lower the left wing because a Zero was behind and left and high and the missile light on the instrument panel was flashing as the ECM wailed ... Pull, pull, pull!

Another explosion off to the right.

A plane flashed in front, a Zero, and Cassidy slammed the wing down to follow.

Clay Lacy saw the missile that killed him. It was fired by a Zero just two miles away at his four o'clock low, and tracked toward him straight as a laser. Lacy's computer was displaying two possible targets in front of him, recommending the one to the right, when out of the corner of his eye he saw the missile coming. To his surprise, he now realized the Missile warning light was flashing and the aural warning tone wailing at full cry. The missile was less that a second from impact when he saw it, and Clay Lacy knew he had had the stroke.

'Shit,' he said, and pulled into a nine-G grunt.

It wasn't enough. The missile went off just under the belly of the aircraft, blasting shrapnel into the wing fuel tanks and shredding the airplane's belly. Shrapnel coming through the floor of the cockpit killed Clay Lacy less than a second before the aircraft blew up. As the fireball expanded, fed by the aircraft's fuel, two long cylinders – the aircraft's engines – shot out of the explosion and fell in a ballistic trajectory toward the earth five miles below.

The disappearance of one of the three other friendly green fighter symbols from his tac display registered on Bob Cassidy. He was too busy to wonder who had been hit.

He was solidly in the clouds, flying as if he were in the simulator back in Germany.

He rocketed down, doing almost Mach 2, checking the tac display for enemies who might be locking him up for a missile shot. He came out of burner and cracked his speed brakes a few inches to help him slow.

Uh-oh, ten miles off to the right – another Zero, shifting to a high radar PRF (pulse repetition frequency) for a shot. *Now* it was on the display – why hadn't Sky Eye seen the Zeroes when the F-22s were inbound to the base?

He racked the F-22 into a hard right turn, nine G's, over twenty degrees heading change per second at this speed. He saw the streak on the MFD as the enemy fighter launched a missile.

Cassidy flipped his fighter over on its back, pulled the nose thirty degrees down, and lit the afterburners. His plane was automatically pumping out chaff and decoys – they would save him or they wouldn't.

He elected to go under the enemy fighter, too fast for the Zero to get his nose down for another shot.

That was the way it worked out. The enemy's missile didn't guide. Cassidy came out of burner and pulled up to turn in behind the Zero, which was also turning hard to get on his tail, a fatal mistake. Nothing in the sky could turn with a Raptor.

Cassidy selected his gun.

He was going to get a shot, a blind, in-the-cloud shot. He was outturning the Zero. He kept the G on, fought against it as he tried to pull the aircraft vector dot through the target symbol on the HUD so that the two dots would cross at less than a mile.

Now!

He squeezed the trigger and held it down. Fire poured from his Gatling gun.

In the Zero, the Japanese pilot had lost the American on his tactical display. He was turning hard, trying to reacquire the F-22 on radar so that he could fire another missile. He never knew what killed him. The first of the cannon shells from the F-22 passed behind the Zero and he never saw them. Then the river of high explosive swept across his plane.

Several of the shells passed through the left horizontal stabilator; then four shells smashed the left engine to bits. Five shells shredded the main fuel cell behind the cockpit. Three of the shells struck the pilot, killing him instantly. Another two shells went through the nose of the aircraft, smashing the radar. The damage was done in a third of a second; then the stream of shells passed on ahead of the aircraft.

The Zero flew on for three more seconds before fuel hit the hot engine parts and the aircraft exploded.

'Yankees check in.'

'Two's up.' That was Hudek.

'Three.' Dixie.

Four should have sung out here, but he didn't.

'Four, are you there?' Cassidy asked. He was at full throttle, racing west from Zeya.

No answer from Lacy.

'Yankees, stay with me. Lacy, where are you, son?'

'I think he bit the big one, skipper.' That was Hudek.

'Lacy, you flaky bastard, answer me, son. Where are you?'

When they landed back at Chita, night had fallen. The three fighters taxied to their respective revetments and shut down.

In the office they used as a ready room, they put the video discs into the postcombat computer and played the mission again. The computer took the information from all three of the surviving planes, merged it, and presented it as a three-dimensional holograph. They saw the American aircraft and the Zeros, the maneuvering, the missiles flying – all of it was right there for everyone to watch. Every brilliant maneuver and every mistake was there for all to see.

'We fired fifteen missiles and killed six Zeros. One gun kill. We lost a plane and pilot.'

'Too bad about Lacy.'

'God, that's tough.'

'You wasted that AMRAAM when you squirted it at that Zero, Colonel. That Athena gear they have really works.'

'We never picked them up on the ECM. They didn't turn on their radars until we were on top of them.'

'That was their mistake.'

'The satellite never saw these guys until they were on us.'

'Late-afternoon build-ups, lots of thermals . . .'

'Cost us a man.'

'Lacy screwed up, skipper,' Fur Ball Hudek said flatly. 'Look at this sequence.' He pointed at two planes in the holographic display. 'This villain passes behind Flake at a right angle, turns hard into him to get a firing solution. Flake is busy chasing these two over here. See that? Flake had target fixation; he lost the bubble. Clay Lacy's dead because he fucked up.'

That was the nub of it. In this business errors were fatal.

'Okay, let's recap. The Zeros got into us before we knew they were around. Lacy screwed up and got hammered. But the Japs screwed up too. If they had sat fifty miles out squirting missiles at us, we couldn't have touched them. They'll learn from this. Just you watch.'

Cassidy got on the satellite telephone to Washington. He wound up with Colonel Eatherly at home. After Cassidy finished explaining the mission, Eatherly said, 'We have satellites over that area most of the time. Sometimes they can see airplanes. I can't say more than that. I'll talk to General Tuck tomorrow. Maybe he'll eat some ass. But I can tell you right now, Space Command is doing all they can with the technology.'

'I understand.'

'Sorry about your pilot.'

'If the wizards know Zeros are airborne, maybe they could call us on the sat phone. Back up all this techno-crap. Our duty officer could call out traffic over the base radio.'

'We'll do it.'

Cassidy was exhausted. He had no appetite. He wandered off to the lower bunk he called home.

He lay there staring at the ceiling. He had pulled the trigger repeatedly today. What if one of those Japanese pilots had been Jiro? What would Sabrina say?

If he had killed Jiro . . .

A wave of revulsion washed over him. He was too tired to sit up, yet he couldn't sleep.

He lay in the bunk with his eyes open, staring into the darkness.

19

Pavel Saratov was in *Admiral Kolchak*'s control room studying charts of Japanese waters when the XO called down from the sail cockpit.

'Better come up here, Captain, and take a look.'

Saratov put down his pencil and compass and climbed the ladder.

'Look, Captain.' Askold pointed.

On the pier, General Esenin and his troops were milling smartly around a truck carrying four metal containers. A crowd of civilians was unloading welding equipment from another truck.

'What is this, Captain?'

'I don't know.'

'Those look like jet-engine shipping containers. Doesn't make sense.'

'Ummm.'

'Those are the sloppiest naval infantrymen I've ever seen,' Askold grumped. 'They don't wear their uniforms properly. They don't know how to care for their equipment. They have little respect for superior officers . . .' He trailed off when he saw that Saratov had no intention of replying.

After a few minutes, Esenin came across the gangway and called up to the officers on the bridge. 'Come down, Captain, please.'

Saratov descended the ladder. Askold was right behind him.

'I need your technical expertise, Captain Saratov. I wish to weld these four containers to the submarine. Where would you suggest?'

Saratov was dumbfounded. 'Outside the pressure hull? Our speed will be drastically affected.'

'No doubt.'

'Worse, the water swirling around the containers will make noise.'

Esenin frowned.

'What is in the containers, anyway?'

'We will discuss that later. Suffice it to say, I have been ordered to attach these containers to the hull of this ship and I intend to do so. The only question is where.'

'They are going to be in place when we submerge? While we are underwater?'

'Yes.'

'The noise –'

'Explain.' Esenin flicked his eyes across Saratov's face.

'The more noise we make underwater, the easier we are to detect.'

'The easier we are to detect,' Askold added, 'the easier we are to kill.'

Esenin shot Askold a withering look. 'Don't patronize me, little man. My bite is worse than my bark.'

'What is in the containers, General?' Saratov asked again.

'Each contains a nuclear weapon. They have been carefully waterproofed, packed, and so on. The job was cleverly done, believe me. The containers allow water to flow in and out so they will not be crushed when the submarine goes deep. Our job is to deliver these weapons.'

'Deliver?' Saratov murmured, his voice a mere whisper.

'These are old warheads from ICBMs, from the days when our missiles were not very accurate. To ensure the target would be destroyed even if the missile missed by a few miles, the designers heavily enriched the warheads. Each of these weapons yields one hundred megatons.'

'One hundred million tons of TNT equivalent . . .' said Askold, staring at the containers.

Saratov scrutinized the general's face. The man was mad. Or a damned fool.

'You have never been on a diesel/electric submarine, have you?'

'No,' Esenin admitted.

'Any submarine?' Saratov bored in. 'Have you ever been on any submarine?'

'No.'

Saratov tried to collect his thoughts. 'General, I don't know who made this decision, but it was misinformed. A diesel/electric submarine is an anachronism, an artifact from a bygone age. Every decision the captain makes, all of them, revolves around keeping the battery charged.'

Esenin looked unimpressed.

'These boats don't really go anywhere,' Saratov explained. 'They merely occupy a position. They can hide, but they can't run. When discovered, they are so immobile that they can easily be destroyed. Do you understand that?'

'You made it to Tokyo Bay.'

'Indeed. And a heroic feat it was! All the Japanese antisubmarine forces were on the other side of the island, in the Sea of Japan.'

'We will have to be smarter than the Japanese.'

'Smarter? When this boat runs at three knots, it must snorkel one hour out of every twenty-four. At six knots, it must snorkel eight hours out of twenty-four. If we cannot get the snorkel up, we are down to one or two knots, just steerageway.' Saratov felt his voice rise. 'I have been pinned before by American ASW forces. In peacetime. You cannot imagine what it is like, knowing they have you, knowing they can kill you if they wish, anytime they wish. My God, man! I've had dummy depth charges knock tiles off the sub's skin.'

'I think you are a coward.'

Saratov took two deep breaths. 'That may be the case, sir. But coward or not, I think you are a fool.'

'This boat is the only submarine we have in the Pacific,' Esenin said, shrugging. 'It will have to do.'

'We are on a fool's errand, a suicide mission. A competent antisubmarine force will quickly locate and kill us.' Pavel Saratov pointed at the deck. 'Don't you understand? This steel tube will be your coffin.'

'This boat will have to do.'

Saratov couldn't believe it. 'Why don't you go alone, in a rowboat? You will have the same chance of success, and sixty other men won't die with you.'

'Enough of this,' Esenin snarled.

'So if by some miracle we get to Tokyo, we find an empty pier and tie up alongside. Your men steal a truck and you haul the warheads over to the rotunda of the Diet?'

The corner of Esenin's mouth twitched.

'Better weld them to the deck, here in front of the sail,' Saratov said. He walked forward to the open hatch leading into the torpedo room. The men were loading torpedoes this morning. Four were already in. He stood with his back to Esenin, watching the men work the hoist and manhandle the ungainly fish.

The morning was warm, with little wind. Last year's autumn leaves were crunchy underfoot.

Janos Ilin stood on a small hill amid the trees smoking a cigarette. His suit coat was open. Leaning against a tree was a rocket-propelled grenade (RPG) launcher. At the foot of the hill, thirty meters from where Ilin stood, was a paved road.

The road was one of the feeders into the Lenin Hills, north of Moscow. Aleksandr Kalugin had a dacha three kilometers farther north. He would be coming along this road soon, as he did every morning, on his way to the Kremlin with his bodyguards. Kalugin had an apartment in the Kremlin, of course, which he used whenever he did not wish to spend an evening at home with his wife. For reasons unknown to Ilin, last night Kalugin had gone home. He was there now.

Kalugin's armored Mercedes would soon be along. Two other vehicles would accompany it, both large black Mercedes, one in front of Kalugin's vehicle, one behind. Each of the guard cars contained five heavily armed bodyguards who normally wore bulletproof vests. These men were competent, ruthless, and very dangerous. Janos Ilin had but himself and four other men. He intended to kill the bodyguards before they could get out of their cars. If he failed, the bodyguards would kill him.

Ilin had picked this spot with care.

Only a short stretch of road was visible here. The cars would come around a curve fifty meters away. The road was banked and wooded on either side here, so the cars could not leave the road. If the road was blocked, the cars would be trapped.

This whole setup gave Ilin a bad feeling, but he could not afford to spend time finding a better one. Unfortunately, Kalugin was paranoid – with good reason one had to admit – and his security force was top-notch. So far, the president's loyal ones had not caught wind of Ilin's intentions, a situation that could not last forever. Ilin was well aware of the security dynamics: he must strike soon or not at all.

Smoking the cigarette and enjoying the warmth of the morning air, Ilin wished he had more men. He had considered asking Marshal Stolypin for a few, then decided the gain would not be worth the risk. He had spent five years with the men he had now; trust was something that did not grow overnight. And trustworthy or not, every additional person admitted to the conspiracy increased the likelihood that it would be discovered. Janos Ilin, spymaster, well knew about conspiracies, the building blocks of Russian history.

The day before, he had gone to see Marshal Stolypin with a cassette player and a tape. On the tape was a conversation between Kalugin and one of his lieutenants, who at the time was in Gorky.

Stolypin had said nothing as he listened to the two men discussing the nuclear destruction of Tokyo. They debated the American response, discussed the probability that the Japanese might retaliate, and then got down to it.

'Unless we use extraordinary measures, Japan will inevitably win the war,' Kalugin told his confederate. 'Our nation is too poor to finance the effort it will take to win with a conventional army and air force. The gap is too great.'

'You must seize absolute power. Destroy all who oppose you.'

'That would take time, and there is many a pitfall along the way. I have thought long about Russia. No one can take Russia back to where it used to be. No one. And if we try, the deputies will rescind their grants of power. Either the government will fall or Russia will face civil war again.'

'I, too, hear these things.'

'We *must* defeat the Japanese,' Kalugin said. 'Victory or death – those are our alternatives. You understand?'

'I do. Have you seen the genuine affection the people have for Captain Saratov? Crowds chanting his name, resolutions demanding that he be promoted, decorated, his picture plastered all over Moscow . . .'

Stolypin listened to the rest of it, then shoved the cassette recorder back across the table toward Ilin.

'If we want our country, we will have to fight for it,' Ilin said. 'Again.'

The old man rubbed his hair with a hand, looking at nothing.

'He is sending a submarine to Tokyo. Nuclear weapons will be aboard. The plan is to put the weapons in a fault on the seafloor. There is a fanatic aboard, a man named Esenin. He swore an oath to Kalugin. If threatened with destruction, he will detonate the weapons in the mouth of Tokyo Bay.'

'Will he do it?'

'By reputation, he is a patriotic zealot. He was an assassin for the GRU.'

'Yuri Esenin?'

'That's right.'

'I thought he was dead.'

This morning Janos Ilin finished another cigarette without tasting it, then glanced at his watch. It was a few minutes past seven. He stamped his feet impatiently.

The radio came to life. 'Car.'

Fifteen seconds later, a black Mercedes came around the curve and into view. Nope. One of the ministers. Three of them lived near Kalugin along this road. After the car passed the small knoll where Ilin stood, it went by a truck with a high-lift basket and another truck carrying a power pole, then went around the next curve. In the fully extended lift, a man was working on a transformer mounted near the top of a pole. A flagman stood on the road near the lift truck.

'Here they come. Three cars.'

Ilin crushed out his new cigarette on a tree as the second truck, the one with the power pole on it, pulled completely across the road, blocking it. The man in the cab jumped down. He had an assault rifle in his hands.

Janos Ilin knelt. He picked up the rocket-propelled grenade launcher and flicked the safety off.

The first car came around the curve and braked as the flagman waved his red flag. The second and third cars were right behind. Kalugin was in the second car. The first and third cars were full of loyal ones.

Ilin leveled the grenade launcher at the first car, which was now almost stopped, exhaled, and pulled the trigger.

The *whoosh* of the rocket was loud.

The grenade impacted the first car at the passenger's side door. The car jumped forward, a dead foot on the accelerator, the engine roaring. It crashed into the side of the truck blocking the road. Although the car was jammed firmly against the truck, the engine revved higher and higher as the tires squalled and smoked against the pavement.

As Ilin worked feverishly to reload the launcher, the driver of the second car slewed the rear end of his car around in a power slide. Smoke poured from the tires. Over the screeching of the tires, Ilin could hear a machine gun hammering.

Ilin got his grenade loaded as the third car slid to a complete stop. The doors of the car were opening as he pulled the trigger. The rocket struck the engine compartment and the shaped charge exploded inward. Men leaping from the car were cut down by machine-gun bullets, which were being fired from the lift basket above.

Meanwhile, Kalugin's car had completed its turn. At least one of Ilin's men was pouring bullets at it. The bullets made tiny sparks, flashes, where they struck the armor and were deflected.

Kalugin's car shot by the third car on the far side with its tires squalling madly as Ilin slammed another grenade into the launcher. He pointed the weapon at the rapidly accelerating car and pulled the trigger.

The grenade smacked into a tree trunk thirty feet in front of Ilin. The charge severed the trunk and the tree began to topple.

Ilin grabbed his radio. 'He's coming back north.'

'I can't get the goddamn engine started.' The man there was supposed to drive another power-line repair truck across the road.

'Shoot at the tires! Shoot at the tires! Don't let him get away.'

With the grenade launcher in one hand and the radio in the other, Ilin ran down the hill and sprinted for the curve. He heard three short bursts of automatic-weapon fire, then silence. As he rounded the curve, he saw Kalugin's car rounding the far curve, three hundred meters on.

Ilin turned and walked back to the ambush site. One of the men lying on the road by the closest car, the trailer, was still moaning. Ilin drew a pistol and shot him in the head as he went by. The other four men who had been in the car were lying on the pavement in various positions, perforated by machine-gun bullets.

The engine in the car against the truck had stalled. The five men inside were apparently dead.

The flagman was taking no chances. He fired a shot into every head.

'Do the ones in the other car, too,' Ilin told him.

The man who had driven the truck across the road came over to Ilin. As the single shots sounded, he said apologetically, 'We almost pulled it off.'

Ilin shouted at the man in the lift basket, who was on his way down. He had an air-cooled light machine gun cradled in his arms. 'Did you shoot at Kalugin?'

'I got off just one burst. I saw sparks where the bullets were striking the armor. I'm sorry.'

'We blew it,' Ilin said with a grimace.

'Maybe we should get the hell out of here.'

'That is probably a good idea.'

As the limo shot along the two-lane road, Aleksandr Kalugin hung on to the strap in the backseat and shouted at the driver. Still shaken from the assassination attempt, he had already concluded that there was a good chance that his bodyguards, or one of them – perhaps his driver? – had betrayed him. Now he was telling the driver which way to go as they approached each intersection.

It was too dangerous to return to the dacha, so he gave the driver directions for an alternate route into Moscow.

Kalugin pulled the telephone from its storage bracket and dialed an operator. He kept his eyes on the road ahead. He removed his pistol from a pocket and laid it in his lap.

If the driver took a wrong turn, he, Kalugin, would personally put a bullet in the man's brain. He fingered the automatic as if it were a set of worry beads.

An aide in his office answered. Kalugin told him about the ambush in as few words as possible, keeping strictly to the facts. The aide would know what to do with the information.

In odd moments Kalugin made lists of his enemies. The A list included political opponents and rivals in the Congress, bureaucrats who had publicly opposed him in the past, and candidates who had run against him in past elections. The B list included critics, newspaper editors who had printed damaging editorials or news stories, bureaucrats who didn't jump when he growled, businessmen who refused to go along with his suggestions – basically carpers and footdraggers. The C list, the longest, contained everybody else that Kalugin thought less than enthusiastic about his leadership of the nation. Some persons had managed to get on this list by avoiding a handshake at parties or receptions. Several were husbands of women Kalugin thought attractive; some were there simply because he had seen their name in a report or in print and thought that person might someday be dangerous.

He had discussed threats to his power with his top aides on several occasions in the past, developed contingency plans, delegated power to men he trusted, men who owed him for their status, their place, the bread they ate.

Even now, as his car raced along, the aides would be ordering everyone on the A list arrested and interrogated. Perhaps the police would discover the culprits before Kalugin's internal security apparatus did, and if so, fine. Kalugin would proceed on both fronts regardless.

Perhaps something good would come out of this crime against his person. Maybe he could use this event as an excuse to crush some of his most vocal enemies. Their downfall would be a lesson for all the rest.

Three of Kalugin's men were waiting in his office when Janos Ilin arrived for work that morning. The secretary in the outer office gave him the news.

'What do they want?'

'They didn't say, sir. They had a presidential pass, so I put them in your anteroom. They went into the office without my permission.'

When you screw up an assassination, this is what happens, he thought. You walk into rooms wondering if you are about to be arrested and tortured or if they want your help chasing assassins.

Janos Ilin didn't turn a hair. He walked across the anteroom to his office door and opened it. He walked in and stopped. One of them was sitting in his chair, trying to jimmy the locks on the desk drawers. Another was using a pick on the file cabinet's locks.

'What the hell is this?'

'Ah, the man with the keys. Sit down, Comrade Ilin. Sit down. And I'll trouble you for your keys.'

Ilin remained standing.

'Someone tried to assassinate President Kalugin a short time ago. We are investigating.'

'Did they harm the president?'

'No.'

'Why are you investigating here?'

'Sit, Ilin. Sit. The keys, please.'

They worked for over an hour, flipping through files, reading notebooks, looking at every sheet of paper they could find. All the while, Ilin sat and watched, apparently unconcerned. The only things that he didn't want these thugs to see were the files on agents in place in foreign countries. Fortunately, those files were in the agency's central records depository, under continuous armed guard.

'When did this assassination attempt take place?'

'This morning. The president was on his way to the Kremlin.'

'Have you made any arrests?'

'We are trying to decide if we should arrest you.'

Ilin snorted.

'Your sangfroid is quite commendable.'

'I have nothing to hide. I have not lifted a finger against anyone. You can read those files until doomsday and that fact won't change.'

When the leader was finished, he seated himself again behind the desk, in Ilin's chair. From his pocket he produced a list. 'You will arrest these men. Jail them in the cells downstairs, begin their interrogations. Tape every interrogation. These instructions are from the president.'

When they departed, they left one man, who now parked himself beside Ilin's chair. Ilin began making telephone calls as he examined the list. The leaders of opposition political parties, judges, public men ... Marshal Stolypin was not on this list. That meant nothing. He might be on another list.

Kalugin was wasting no time. This list had not been typed this morning.

Ilin called in his deputies, gave instructions.

235

The Japanese air commander in Siberia, Matsuo Handa, spent a tense night huddled with his top subordinates. The American Squadron was costing them planes and pilots. The missiles that sought out the Zero radar, the invisible F-22s – there was a lot on the plate.

One thing that the Japanese commander knew was that he could not sit idly on the defensive waiting for the Americans' next move. Fighting defensively went against all of his samurai instincts. Attack was the policy that best fit the Japanese spirit, he believed. The men wanted to attack and so did he. The only question was how.

Jiro Kimura's squadron commander took his young ace with him to the headquarters conference. He remembered Jiro's comment about the technical feasibility of electronically changing the color of an aircraft's skin, and he wanted the air commander to hear it, too.

'Sir, I do not understand how the American fighters found the Zeros over Zeya,' Jiro Kimura said to Colonel Handa. 'The surviving pilot states that at no time did he receive an ECM warning that American planes were in the area. A postflight check of his electronic countermeasures equipment showed that it was functioning properly. Apparently the Americans were not using radar. How did they find our planes?'

'They must have visually acquired the Zeros,' Colonel Handa said. Most of the senior brass seemed to share this opinion. Jiro didn't believe it.

'Sir, if I may express my opinion,' Jiro said. 'Waiting in ambush with radars off, relying on the ECM to inform us of the enemy's presence, is the wrong way to employ the Zero. This airplane was designed as an offensive weapon. We must search with radar, find the enemy before he can find us, and launch our missiles first. Closing to short range with F-22s is a fatal error.'

'We waited in ambush with our radars off because the F-22 can detect our radar emissions before we can detect the F-22.'

'I understand, sir. Our challenge is to make the Americans fight our fight. We must lure them to a place where we can engage at long range.'

'That's a wonderful proposal, Kimura,' Handa said. 'But it isn't practical. We have not been aggressive enough. That is why we find ourselves in this deplorable situation.'

The conference, Jiro thought, went downhill from that point.

After a discussion of possible options, Colonel Handa decided to lead a daytime strike on Chita. Half the planes would go in low, on the deck, to drop cluster bombs and strafe. The other half would go in high, use their radars for a few seconds out of each minute, and attempt to engage the American fighters while the low planes struck the base. The flight would launch from Khabarovsk, so it would need tankers coming and going.

'Colonel Handa,' Jiro suggested, 'perhaps we should try a night attack first, to further feel out the American capabilities.'

'The planes strafing and dropping cluster weapons need daylight and decent weather to be effective,' the colonel answered. 'We are facing a capable, aggressive enemy who has drawn first blood. We must attack, force him to parry our blows or he will seize the initiative and we will find ourselves on the defensive.'

'We must strike first,' the squadron commanders agreed. Like Colonel Handa, their hearts and minds were geared to the offensive.

When Jiro left the meeting at midnight, he was profoundly discouraged. The colonel was playing right into the Americans' hands, he thought. The enemy expected the Japanese to attack Chita, he argued, so they should not. The colonel's mind was made up. Cassidy already had Handa on the defensive, and Handa didn't want to admit it.

Jiro wandered over to the most dilapidated hangar on the base, where one of his friends, a helicopter pilot, was quartered. 'Tell me, Shoichi, do you people have any of those infrared headsets, the kind you wear when you fly at night?'

'Yes, we have four of them. They are helmets, with earphones, visors, and so on. They will not take an oxygen mask, however.'

'May I borrow one tomorrow?'

'Why?'

'I want to fly with it. I have a theory and wish to test it.'

'For you, Jiro, of course. Here, have a beer.'

When the chief of Asian intelligence at the Japanese Intelligency Agency, Toshihiko Ayukawa, received Agent Ju's message, it had already been decoded and translated. It now rested in a new red file folder. He opened the folder and perused the short, neat columns of Japanese characters. The message read:

> Russia has ten atomic warheads.
> Kalugin has ordered contingency planning for their use against Japan.
> At least four of the warheads will be delivered by submarine, target unknown.

Ayukawa felt the hairs on the back of his neck tingling. Good ol' Agent Ju. He was the one who said Russia had destroyed the last of its nuclear weapons. Only a fool would bet on that as gospel truth, but no doubt that message had been a factor, one of many, in the Abe government's decision to invade Siberia.

Now Ju had changed his tune. Was he lying then or lying now?

Pavel Saratov was the last man to leave the cockpit on top of *Admiral Kolchak*'s sail. He took a final look at the four containers welded to the deck, ensured the boat was stationary in the middle of the small lagoon, pointed at the underwater entrance, then went down the hatch and dogged it after him.

Esenin was in the control room. He seemed a bit less imperious than he usually was, or perhaps it was Saratov's imagination.

'This is the tricky part,' Saratov said to the chief, who nodded. 'We must get steerageway on the boat before it drifts. Let's dive.'

The chief gave the order while Saratov examined the sonar image on the oscilloscope.

Esenin's executive officer was a major, or at least he wore a major's uniform. He looked pale, Saratov thought, as air gurgled from the tanks and seawater rushed in.

Saratov shook his head in annoyance. He should ignore these two and concentrate on the task at hand, which was getting this boat safely out of the mountain.

A half hour later the boat had cleared the tunnel and the shallow water. It was dark up there, and overcast, so Saratov took the boat to snorkel depth and started the diesels.

Two hours later when he went to his tiny cabin, Esenin was already there, sitting in the one chair.

'Ah, Captain, come in. And please close the door.'

The compartment was very small. Saratov squeezed by the chair and sat on the bunk.

'I thought this a good time to discuss our mission, Captain.'

Esenin picked up the rolled-up chart from the desk, removed the string that held it, and spread it out. Saratov looked over his shoulder.

'You know Tokyo Bay? The sound to the south of it?'

'I recognize it.'

'As you can see, marked on this chart in red are a number of major geological faults. You can see where they run.' His finger traced several of the longest. 'The fault in which we are interested is this one.' His finger came to rest. 'It will not be necessary to tie up to a pier and steal a truck.'

Saratov didn't bother to reply.

'I have a recommendation from Revel, a leading geologist in Moscow, who studies these sorts of things with international groups,' Esenin continued. 'He thinks the most unstable fault is this one, at the entrance to Tokyo Bay. It has not moved in at least three hundred years, and it is very ready.

'Our task is to place our four weapons in a row atop this fault, two miles apart. When the weapons detonate, the concussion should break the eastern plate free, causing it to rise significantly.'

'How significantly?' Pavel Saratov couldn't take his eyes from the chart.

'The geologist thinks the potential is there for a movement on the order of ten feet. Of course, explosions of this magnitude will vaporize an extraordinary amount of water, so the sea will rush in to fill the void. Movement of the plate will merely speed the water along.'

'I see.'

'The tidal wave should be quite extraordinary. A tsunami, I believe the Japanese call it. If the professor's calculations are correct, the tidal wave should be two hundred feet high when it washes over Tokyo.'

'Only four warheads?'

'We will explode two simultaneously. The second set will be timed to blow exactly three minutes later. Professor Revel believes the earth should be moving down at that moment, on a long oscillation cycle, so the second set of explosions should reinforce that movement. True, we constructed the scenario hurriedly, but we have great faith in Professor Revel's computer models. It should work. It *will* work.'

'All we have to do,' Saratov said heavily, 'is get over the fault, toss off the weapons, and sail away.'

'I leave it in your capable hands, Captain.'

'I will do all I can, General. Alas, any chance of success lies in the hands of the Japanese. They will be hunting us, and the odds are on their side.'

20

Puffy clouds floating in a calm summer sky greeted the Japanese pilots as they climbed out of Khabarovsk headed for their tanker rendezvous. There were sixteen Zeros divided into two gaggles of eight. Colonel Handa led the eight planes of the high echelon. He had allowed his senior commanders to choose where they wished to fly, and they all wished to fly high, with him. The glory was in shooting down enemy planes in combat, not strafing hangars and barracks.

Still, the commanders put their very best subordinates in the eight airplanes that were going to strike the base.

Colonel Handa had intended to exhort his pilots at the briefing to do their best for the honor of Japan and the Zero pilot corps, but then he thought better of it. I have watched too many American movies, he told himself.

'They're coming,' Lee Foy shouted as he slammed down the telephone. 'Headed this way. Over a dozen. Took off ten minutes ago.'

The American pilots went into the dispersal shack – an old hen coop that they had commandeered, cleaned, and moved to the parking mat – for their final briefing. Everyone was checking his watch. The pilots managed to avoid one another's eyes.

Bob Cassidy was glad the Japanese were on their way. The suspense was over. He had known the Japanese would attack eventually; he just hadn't known it would come so soon.

His people were ready. He had just six planes available, so he divided them into three flights. He would take Paul Scheer north of the base and wait until the Sentinel missiles had forced the Zero pilots to shut off their radars. Then he and Scheer would go in among them.

Dixie and Aaron Hudek were going out to the northwest of the base, Preacher Fain and Lee Foy to the southwest. They would come in when Cassidy called them.

Each plane carried eight Sidewinders and a full load of ammo for the gun. Cassidy had ordered the AMRAAMs left behind. He was betting that the

Sky Eye data link would work. If it didn't, this fight was going to be a disaster.

He was also betting that the Japanese would avoid Chinese airspace and come in from the east, the most direct route from Khabarovsk after avoiding China. If the Zeros circled and came in from another direction, they might find a pair of F-22s with their radar and drop them both.

Every choice involves risks. Life involves risk. Breathing is a risk, Cassidy thought.

He and his pilots needed some luck. If they got a little of the sweet stuff, they could smash the Zeros right here, today, once and for all. And if luck ran the wrong way ... well, you only had to die once.

Cassidy stood in front of the blackboard. He already had all the freqs, altitudes, and call signs written there from the planning session. 'Okay, people. They are on their way. They'll hit the tankers and motor over our way, we hope. Let's go over the whole thing one more time, then suit up. We'll man up an hour and a half before they are expected, and take off an hour prior.'

No one asked a single question. Eyes kept straying to wrist watches. When the brief was over, Cassidy walked outside, went around behind the shack, and peed in the grass. Finally, he suited up, taking his time.

He was standing outside the shack, looking at the airplanes, thinking about Sweet Sabrina and little Robbie and Jiro Kimura when he heard the satellite phone ring. Lee Foy answered. Fifteen seconds went by; then Foy shouted, 'Sixteen Zeros. They've finished tanking and are on their way here. ETA is an hour and twenty-eight minutes from right now.'

'Let's do it!'

'Let's go.'

They grabbed gear and helmets and began jogging for their planes.

When the planes were level at altitude after tanking, Jiro Kimura slid away from the other flight of four Zeros that was assigned to the ground attack mission. He was wearing the night-vision helmet that he had borrowed from the helo pilots, but he didn't have it turned on. He wanted to try that now.

First, he checked his three charges, Ota, Miura, and Sasai. They were precisely in position, as if he had welded them there. They were good pilots, great comrades.

Satisfied, Jiro engaged the autopilot and began fiddling with the helmet. Before takeoff he had turned the gain setting to its lowest reading, as the helo pilot had advised. Now he lowered the hinged goggles down over his eyes. The battery was on, so the goggles were working, or should be.

His eyes slowly adjusted to the reduced light levels. Oh yes, there was the other flight, out there to the right.

He turned his head from side to side, taking in the view. The view to both sides was limited, and he couldn't read the instruments on his panel, but in combat, he wouldn't need to: he could find every dial and switch blindfolded.

The real disadvantage to the helmet was weight. In a helicopter a twelve-pound helmet on a healthy man was no big deal if he didn't have to wear it too long, but in a fighter, pulling G's, the story would be much different. At five G's, the darn thing would weigh sixty pounds, which would be a nice test of Jiro's neck muscles. Ten G's might be enough to snap his neck like a twig.

It just stood to reason that if the Americans had figured out a way to cancel visible light waves, their airplanes still might be visible in the infrared portion of the spectrum.

Jiro's oxygen mask was lying in his lap. The helo helmet had no fittings to accept the mask. The Zero's cockpit was partially pressurized with a maximum three psi differential, so even though the plane was at 25,000 feet, the cockpit was only at 9,000. If the canopy was damaged or lost, Jiro would have to hold the mask to his face with his left hand while he flew with the other.

The F-22s took off in pairs, Cassidy and Scheer first, then Dixie and Hudek, then Fain and Foy. The enlisted troops stood on the ramp watching the planes get airborne, basking in the thunder of the engines. As the wheels came into the wells, the pilots turned on their aircrafts' smart skin. The noise of the engines continued to rumble for minutes after the planes disappeared from view.

After the noise had faded, the senior NCO told the troops to get in the trenches, freshly dug by a backhoe that was sitting near the dispersal shack. They could safely stay out of the trenches for a while but the NCO was too keyed up to wait. Better safe than sorry.

The Zero symbols appeared on Bob Cassidy's tactical display at a range of two hundred miles. He was fifty miles north of the base at twenty thousand feet, cruising at max conserve airspeed, about .72 Mach. Scheer was on his left wing, out about a hundred yards. The symbols were so bunched together, Cassidy couldn't tell exactly how many bogeys were there.

The main problem with Sky Eye was that at long ranges the symbols were grossly compressed, and at short ranges they were unreliable. The gadget seemed to give the best presentation when the bogeys were from five to fifty miles away. Inside five miles, he would be forced to rely upon the F-22s' infrared sensors; the data from all the F-22s was shared, so the computers could arrive at a fairly complete tactical picture.

At least he had dodged the first bullet today: the Zeros were coming in from the east, right up the threat axis.

Cassidy checked the position of the other two flights of F-22s. He thought Preacher Fain was too close to the base.

'Preacher, this is Hoppy. A few more miles south, please.'

Preacher acknowledged.

Cassidy checked everything: the intensity of the HUD displays, master armament switch on, the proper displays on the proper MFDs, cabin altitude, engine gauges . . . He was ready.

Preacher Fain tightened his shoulder harness and ensured the inertial take-up reel was locked, so that he would not be thrown about the cockpit. He adjusted his oxygen mask, wiped a gloved hand across his dark helmet visor, and checked the armament panel.

Fain glanced at his tac display: Lee Foy was right where Fain wanted him, about five hundred feet out and completely behind his leader. With Foy well aft and off to one side, Fain was free to maneuver left, right, whatever, without worrying about a midair collision. And the wingman was free to follow the fight and keep the bad guys off Fain's tail while the leader engaged.

The high Zeros were only forty miles from the base. The low ones were thirty miles out. Eight in each flight. Fain eyeballed the rate of progress of the top group and tightened his turn radius. He wanted to come slicing in behind them just after they got into the Sentinel zone, when they were certain to have their radars off. He wanted to knock as many down as possible in the first pass, then dive to engage the lower ones. The Zeros down low were going to be juicy, pinned against the deck as the invisible F-22s came down on them from above. Oh boy!

The heart of the Sentinel missile system was its computer, which contained a sophisticated program designed to prevent an enemy from causing all the missiles in the battery to be launched by merely sweeping his radar once, shutting down, then repeating the cycle. The program required that the target radar sweep repeatedly and be progressing into the missile's performance envelope at a rate of speed sufficient to enable it to get into range by the time the missile arrived. If these parameters were met, the computer would fire two missiles, one after the other, then sit inactive for a brief period of time before the system would again listen for the proper signals.

The guidance system in the missiles was more sophisticated than the computer in the battery. As the missile flew toward its target, the computer memorized the target's relative position, course, and speed, so in the event the target radar ceased radiating, the computer could still issue guidance signals to the missile. Of course, the probability of a hit decreased dramatically the longer the target radar was off the air. If the target radiated again while the missile was still in flight, the computer would update the target's trajectory and refine its directives to the guidance system.

The system worked best when the missile was fired at an airplane that was flying directly at the Sentinel battery. Due to the geometry of the problem and the speeds of the target and missile, the missile's performance became degraded if it wound up in a tail chase.

As Colonel Handa flew toward the Chita Air Base, he was flipping his radar from standby to transmit, then back again, over and over. He had instructed all the other pilots to leave their radars in the standby position – which meant the radar had power but was not transmitting – but he was scanning with his to see if he could detect any enemy planes aloft, or induce the Americans to fire one of their antiradiation missiles. Handa didn't know that the missiles were fired from automated batteries; indeed, the possibility had never even occurred to him.

The eight strike airplanes had left the upper formation a hundred miles back. They were down on the deck now, five hundred feet above the treetops, flying at a bit over Mach 1.

Handa kept waiting for his ECM warning devices to indicate that he was being looked at by enemy radar, but the devices didn't peep. There seemed to be no enemy radar on the air. Or, thought Handa ominously, no radar that his ECM devices could detect. Perhaps the Americans had taken another technological leap of faith and were using frequencies that this device could not receive. Or perhaps their radars were in a receive-only mode, merely picking up the beacon of his radar when it was on the air. If only he . . .

He dropped that line of thought when the first Sentinel missile shot by his aircraft at a distance of no more than one hundred feet. The brilliant plume of the rocket motor made a streak on the retina of his eye. Handa's heart went into overdrive.

As he scanned the sky for more missiles – the visibility was excellent – he forgot to flip the switch of his radar back to standby. That was when another Sentinel missile, launched automatically almost sixty seconds before, slammed into the nose cone of his fighter.

The thirty-pound missile was traveling at Mach 3 when it pierced the nose cone and target radar in a perfect bull's-eye. Handa's plane was traveling at Mach 1.28 in almost the opposite direction. The combined energy of the impact ripped the Zero fighter into something in excess of two million tiny pieces. The expanding cloud of pieces hit the wall as each individual fragment of metal, plastic, flesh, cloth, and shoe leather tried to penetrate its own shock wave, and failed.

The other Zeros continued on toward the Chita Air Base as the pieces of Handa's fighter began to fall earthward at different rates, depending on their shape. The fuel droplets fell like rain in the cool summer sky, but the motes of metal and flesh behaved more like dust, or heavy snow.

After Colonel Handa's Zero disintegrated, the other seven planes in his flight continued straight ahead. Several seconds elapsed before the remaining pilots realized what had happened. During that time, the planes traversed almost a mile of sky.

Without their radars, the pilots were essentially blind. At these speeds, they couldn't see far enough with their eyes. At that very moment, Bob Cassidy and Paul Scheer were ten miles away, at two o'clock, on a collision course at Mach 2.15. The two American fighters were two hundred yards apart, abreast of each other, with Scheer on the left.

'We'll shoot two each, Paul, then yo-yo high and come down behind them.'

'Gotcha, Hoppy.'

The seekers in Sidewinders had come a long way in the forty years the missile had been in service. The primary advantage of the missile was its passive nature: it didn't radiate, so it didn't advertise its presence. The short range of the weapon was more than compensated for by its head-on capability.

At five miles, Bob Cassidy got a growl and let the first missile go. He still had not acquired the Zeros visually, and of course the Zero pilots had not seen him. He fired the second missile two seconds later, at a range of three miles. With both missiles gone, Bob Cassidy pulled the nose of his fighter into an eighty-degree climb, half-rolled and came out of burner, then pulled the nose down hard as the plane decelerated. He finally saw the Zeros below him, going in the opposite direction, toward the base.

Scheer had fired two Sidewinders almost simultaneously and was also soaring toward heaven and pulling the nose around.

One of the American missiles missed its target due to the rapidly changing aspect angle. It passed the target aircraft too far away to trigger the proximity fuse.

The other three missiles were hits. One went down the left intake of a Zero and detonated in the compressor section of the engine, ripping the plane to bits. Another missed the target aircraft by six inches; its proximity fuse exploded adjacent to the cockpit and killed the pilot instantly.

The warhead of the fourth missile detonated above the left wing of the Zero it was homing on, puncturing the wing with a hundred small holes. Fuel boiled out into the atmosphere.

The pilot felt the strike, saw his flight leader's airplane dissolving into a metal cloud, then saw fuel erupting from his own wing. He had not glimpsed an enemy aircraft and already two Zeros were destroyed, one was falling out of control, and he was badly damaged. He began a hard left turn to clear the area.

Cassidy saw this plane turning and shoved forward on his stick, which, since he was inverted, stopped his nose from coming down. He rolled right ninety degrees onto knife edge and let the nose fall.

The Zero below him continued its turn.

This was going to work out nicely – Cassidy was going to drop right onto the enemy pilot's tail. Cassidy would use the gun.

Dropping in, rolling the wings level, he pushed the thumb button as the enemy plane slid into the gunsight. The plane vibrated, muzzle flashes appearing in front of the windscreen, and the Zero was on fire, with the left horizontal stabilator separating from the aircraft.

Now Cassidy rolled into a ninety-degree bank and pulled smoothly right up to nine G's. He wanted to get around in a hurry to rejoin the fight. For the first time, he took a second to check his tac display for the position of the other five F-22s.

Only he and Scheer were still upstairs. The other two sections were descending in a curving arc.

Dixie Elitch and Aaron Hudek each fired a Sidewinder as they came roaring down on the flight of four Zeros from the northwest. The missiles tracked nicely. Dixie squeezed off another, and a third.

Her first missile converted the target Zero to a fireball, and the second went into the fireball and exploded. Her third missile took out another Zero, just as the pilot flying the third plane, the one struck by Hudek's first missile, ejected.

She was less than two miles from the last Zero and trying to get a missile lock-on tone when Hudek sliced in front, his tailpipes just beyond her windscreen.

Dixie pulled power and popped her boards to prevent a collision.

Hudek didn't bother with a missile. He intended to use his gun. He closed relentlessly on the sole remaining Zero of the flight of four.

Preacher Fain led Lee Foy down on Jiro Kimura's flight. They squeezed off two Sidewinders, one each, and both missiles tracked.

Still wearing the night-vision helmet, Kimura was craning his neck, trying to see what was happening. The Zeros exploding on his right certainly got his attention. He half-turned in his seat, using the handhold on the canopy bow to turn himself around.

And he saw the F-22s, coming down on the Zeros from behind at a thirty-degree angle.

'Break left,' he screamed into his oxygen mask. He was holding the mask with his left hand. Now he dropped the mask and used that hand to hold the helmet steady as he used his right to slam the stick over and pull hard.

Fain's missile couldn't hack the turn. It went streaking into the ground.

Miura wasn't quick enough. Foy Sauce's 'winder went up his right tailpipe and exploded against the turbine section of that engine. Pieces of the engine were flung off as the compressor/turbine, now badly out of balance, continued to rotate at maximum rpm.

Miura felt the explosion, saw the right engine temp gauge swing toward the peg, and knew he was in big trouble. He pulled both engines to idle cutoff as the right engine fire light illuminated and honked on five G's to help slow down. As the plane dropped below five hundred knots, he pulled the ejection handle. Three seconds later the parachute opened, just as his jet exploded.

At this point, the fight was one minute old.

Holding the heavy night-vision helmet and goggles with his left hand, Jiro Kimura turned a square corner. Only he, of all the Japanese pilots, could see the American fighters descending upon them. At one point the G meter recorded eight G's, and Kimura was not wearing a full-body G suit, as the Americans were. He was flexed to the max, screaming against the G to stay conscious, as he honked his mount around.

It was then that Lee Foy made a fatal mistake. Perhaps he didn't see Jiro turning, perhaps he had fixated on his intended next victim, Sasai, or perhaps he was checking the position of his wingman on his tac display. In any event, he didn't react quickly enough to Jiro's turn in his direction, and once Jiro triggered a Sidewinder at point-blank range, he had no more time. The American-designed, Japanese-made missile punctured the F-22's fuselage just behind the cockpit and exploded in the main fuel cell, rupturing it by forcing fuel outward under tremendous pressure. When the fuel met oxygen, it ignited explosively.

Lee Foy had just enough time to inhale deeply and scream into his radio microphone before he was cremated alive.

Aaron Hudek saw the explosion out of the corner of his eye as he was dispatching the last of the Blue Flight Zeros with his cannon. He recognized Foy's voice on the radio.

'Sauce?'

Every F-22 pilot heard Hudek's call.

Jiro Kimura had already fired a second missile. While the first one was in the air, he got a growl on an F-22 four miles away, one turning hard after a Zero. He squeezed it off. Then he turned ten degrees toward an F-22 in burner that was coming at him head-on.

This was Fur Ball Hudek.

The F-22 was shooting. A river of fire, almost like a searchlight, was vomiting from the nose of the American fighter. The finger of God reached for him.

Just how he avoided it, Jiro could never explain. He slammed the stick over and smashed on the rudder and his plane slewed sideways, almost out of control. At that moment, he mashed his thumb down on the gun button.

The shells poured from the cannon in his right wing root.

He wiggled the rudder just as Hudek flashed through the steel stream with his gun still blazing.

Aaron Hudek felt the hammer blows. His left engine fire light went on, the temp went into the red, and the rpm started dropping. He glanced in the rearview mirror and saw fire streaming along the side of the plane.

He started to reach for the ejection handle, but there was another Zero in front of him, this one flown by Jiro's wingman, Ota. At these speeds there was no time to think, but even if there had been, perhaps Aaron Hudek's decision would have been the same. With a flick of his wrist he brought the two fighters together almost head-on.

Jiro's second Sidewinder sprayed the belly of Dixie Elitch's fighter with shrapnel. The plane continued to respond to the controls and the engines seemed okay, but horrible pounding and ripping noises reached Dixie in the cockpit. It sounded as if the slipstream was ripping pieces off.

Automatically, she retarded her throttles, deployed her speed brakes, and pulled the nose skyward to convert airspeed into altitude.

After Cassidy and Scheer fired the last of their Sidewinders, only two of the eight high Zeroes were still under their pilots' control. Still in loose formation, these two nosed down steeply and went to full afterburner. They didn't turn or weave, just kept descending until they were within thirty feet of the valley floor. Their sonic shock waves raised a dust cloud behind them.

Cassidy leveled at ten thousand feet and came out of burner. He didn't want to use all his fuel chasing these two.

'Can you get 'em, Paul?'

'I think so.'

Scheer was gaining on the fleeing pair when Cassidy turned back toward the low fight, which was still being waged near the base.

Preacher Fain was ninety degrees off Jiro's heading and a mile behind him when the Japanese pilot saw him with the infrared goggles. Jiro knew most of his comrades were dead, and if he continued to fight he soon would be, but to ignore this F-22 in his rear quarter would be suicide. Kimura pitched up hard and rolled toward Fain.

Fain was surprised. This was the only Zero that engaged the F-22s.

This guy must see me, he thought. Perhaps the chameleon gear is not working ... He too pitched up, committing himself to a vertical scissors.

Corkscrewing around each other, the two fighters went straight up, each trying for an angular advantage and each failing to get it.

Jiro was beside himself. He was 950 miles from home base, surrounded by enemies, and time was running out. Time was on his opponent's side. He had to end this quickly.

He pulled the throttles to idle, popped the speed brakes. Going straight up, the Zero slowed as if it had hit a wall.

Preacher Fain squirted out in front.

Jiro rammed the throttles forward and thumbed in the boards as he pushed the nose toward Fain.

Sensing his danger, Fain pulled back on the stick with all his strength. The F-22 came over on its back and dipped its nose toward the earth as bursts of cannon shells squirted past.

The shells were going by his belly. Fain continued to pull.

Then he realized the ground was rushing toward him. He was descending inverted, seventy degrees nose-down, in burner, passing eight thousand feet.

Preacher Fain flicked the F-22 upright and pulled until he thought the wings would come off. The G meter read twelve G's when his fighter struck the earth at Mach 1.2.

Dixie Elitch ejected when her airspeed dropped to 250 knots. The airplane was burning by then. She had shut down the left engine when the Left Fire warning light came on, but now the flames were visible in the mirror behind her.

'Dixie's bailing out,' she said over the radio.

She took a deep breath and pulled the handle between her legs with both hands.

The fight had lasted just two minutes.

The maintenance troops at the base saw someone descending in a parachute, but they had no idea it was Dixie. Four of them went after her in a Humvee. The hardest part was finding her, a mile out in the forest from the nearest road. She was hung up in a tree. It took them twenty minutes to get her down, which they accomplished by chopping down the tree. Although shaken, she was none the worse for wear. An hour and a half after her ejection, Dixie and her rescuers walked out of the woods.

Jiro Kimura taxied into the revetment at Khabarovsk, opened the canopy, and shut down. The plane captain installed the ladder while Jiro unstrapped, then scampered up. 'Sir, where are the others?'

'Dead. Or out in the forest. I don't know.'

The plane captain couldn't believe it. He thought Jiro was joking.

As he walked across the ramp with the night-vision helmet and his flight bag, Jiro met his squadron executive officer. 'Where are they, Kimura?'

'They were shot down, sir. All of them. I am the only one left.'

'Including the wing commander?'

'He died first, I think. My flight was well below him then, but I think his aircraft was struck by a missile and disintegrated. Then the Americans jumped us. It was over quickly.'

'F-22s?'

'They never saw them, Colonel. Their airplanes are invisible. Without radar, the others had no chance. I had this.' Jiro held up the helmet. 'I borrowed it from the helicopter squadron. I could see them only in infrared, not regular light.'

'Fifteen aircraft!' The colonel was incredulous.

'Yes, sir.'

'How many enemy aircraft were there?'

'Six or eight. I am not sure. No more than eight, I think.'

The exec reeled. He caught himself. 'Did we get *any* of them?'

'I got one, I think, sir. Another F-22 flew into the ground trying to evade me. If anyone else scored, I do not know about it.'

'I want a complete written report, Kimura, as soon as possible. I will send it to Tokyo.' The colonel turned his back so that Jiro couldn't see his face.

Jiro walked on toward the dispersal shack.

They couldn't all be dead. Surely some of them had ejected safely. Sasai, Ota, Miura . . .

As he walked, Jiro Kimura wiped away tears.

When Cassidy and Elitch got back to the squadron, Paul Scheer was sitting with his feet up on the duty desk, smoking a cigar. He gave them a beatific smile.

'Hear anything from the others?' Cassidy snapped.

'Nope. I watched the discs from your plane and mine. I'm pretty sure they're dead.'

'You look awful damned crushed about it.'

Scheer refused to be flustered. He puffed on the cigar a few times, then took a long drag and exhaled.

'Colonel, it's like this: If I were dead and Fur Ball were sitting here instead of me, I would want him to have a cigar. I would want him to savor this sublime moment. If I could, I would light the cigar for him.'

Scheer stretched out his arms and yawned. 'Best goddamned two minutes of my life. The very best.' He sighed. 'The sad thing is that it's all downhill from here. What could possibly equal that?'

Scheer slowly got to his feet. As cigar smoke swirled around his head, he hitched up his gun belt, reached into his unzipped G suit and scratched, then helped himself to a swallow of water from a small bottle. Opening the desk drawer, he extracted two cigars and held them out.

'One each. This was our stash, Hudek's and mine. When you smoke them, think of Fur Ball and Foy Sauce and the Preacher. Three damned good men.'

Cassidy and Elitch each took the offered cigars.

Paul Scheer strolled out of the room, trailing smoke.

When he was lying in his bunk that evening, Jiro Kimura could not sleep. The morning fight kept swirling through his mind. After a while, he got out his flashlight, pulled the blanket over his head, and wrote a letter to his wife.

Dear Shizuko,

Today we had a big fight with the American fighters, the American Squadron that you have been hearing about. Bob Cassidy is their commanding officer!

Ota, Miura, and Sasai are missing in action and presumed dead. By the time you receive this letter, their families will have been notified.

As you know, I have been very concerned about meeting Cassidy in the sky. Today I must have done so. He was probably there. Beloved wife, you will be proud to know that I did not hesitate to do my duty. I did my very best, which is the only reason I am still alive. Still, I have worried so about the possibility of shooting at Cassidy that I now feel guilty that my comrades are dead. Strange how even secret sins return to haunt you. That is a very un-Japanese thought, but the Americans always assured me it was so. Secret sins are the worst, they said.

I have promised myself to think no more of Bob Cassidy. I will be cold-blooded about this murderous business. I will fight with a tiger's resolve.

I write of these things to you because I may not see you again in this life. It is probable that I shall soon join my friends in death, which is not a prospect I fear, as you know. Still, the thought of my death fills me with despair that you will be left to go on alone, that we will not live long lives together, which was, we always believed, our destiny.

If I die before you, I will be waiting for you in whatever comes after this life. When you are old and full of years, you will rejoin the husband of your youth, who will be waiting with a heart full of love. Know that in the days to come.

Jiro

21

The train was barely an hour north of Vladivostok when it derailed. Isamu Iwakuro felt the engine and cars lurch. He had spent his adult life working as a locomotive repair specialist, and he knew.

The car he was in, the second behind the last locomotive, went over on its side and the lights went out. The car skidded for what seemed to be a long time before it came to rest.

Inside the car, civilians and soldiers and their baggage were hopelessly jumbled. Someone was screaming.

Iwakuro managed to get upright and clamber over several seats toward the door, all the while shouting for everyone to remain quiet and not panic.

Then the explosions began. Steel and smoke ripped through the shattered railroad car.

Antitank grenades!

The explosions popped like firecrackers. All up and down the train, he could hear the hammering of the grenades. And he could hear machine guns, long, ripping bursts.

Something smashed into his shoulder and he went down. Another explosion near his head knocked him unconscious.

When Iwakuro came to, he could see nothing. Night had fallen, although he didn't know it. At first, he thought he was blind. His shoulder was bleeding and hurt horribly, so he knew he was alive. He felt his way over bodies, searching for a way out of the railroad car. He saw a bit of light, finally, just a glimmer from a distant fire.

Somehow, he managed to crawl through a hole in the floor of the railroad car, which was still on its side.

To his right, away from the engine, he saw that one of the freight cars was burning.

Iwakuro crawled directly away from the train. When he had gone at least fifty meters, he sat and tried to bind his coat around his shoulder.

He was sitting in the grass, moaning ever so slightly, when someone shot him in the back.

Rough hands rolled him over. A flashlight shone on his face.

Now someone grabbed him by the hair and rammed a knife into his neck. Isamu Iwakuro filled his lungs to scream, but he was dead before the sound came out.

The man who had shot Iwakuro finished cutting off his head. He dropped it into a bag with six others. His orders were to decapitate every body he found.

Two hundred miles east of Honshu *Admiral Kolchak* was at periscope depth, running at six knots on a course of 195 degrees magnetic. Through the main scope Pavel Saratov could see an empty, wind-whipped sea and sky.

After a careful, 360-degree transit with the scope, Saratov ordered it lowered. The navigator was bent over the chart table when Saratov joined him.

'How fast do you want to go, Captain?' As was usual aboard *Admiral Kolchak*, the navigator asked the question in a low, subdued voice.

'I want to keep a good charge on the batteries at all times,' Saratov answered, automatically making his voice match the navigator's. 'We must be able to go deep and stay there to have any chance against the Jap patrols.'

'We are in the Japanese current, bucking it. We would make better time if we got out of it to the southeast, then headed southwest.'

'Stay in it, right in the middle. We're in no hurry.'

'Do you really think they are looking for us?'

'You can bet your life on it.'

Askold leaned over the table. 'How do you plan to go in, Captain?'

'I have no plans. We must see what develops.'

'Getting out?'

'God knows. We will see.'

'What will you see, Saratov?' The voice boomed in the little room. Esenin was right behind them. As usual, he was wearing the box, a gray metal box about three inches wide, five inches long, and an inch deep. It hung on a strap around his neck. Since the boat had submerged at Trojan Island, he had never been without the box.

'We will see if we can get out of Japanese waters alive,' Saratov said.

'Don't be such a pessimist. This is an opportunity of a lifetime to do something important for your country.'

'For you, General, perhaps. These men have already struck a stupendous blow for Russia.'

'Don't be insubordinate,' Esenin snapped. 'You are in a leadership position.'

'I'm in command of this vessel, and I won't forget it.'

Esenin looked into the faces of the men in the control room. Then he turned to Saratov and whispered, 'Don't push me.'

A P-3 came that night. The sonar operator heard it first. The watch officer called Saratov, who was lying down in his stateroom, trying to sleep.

The plane went by about two miles to the south, flying east.

'He's flying a search pattern,' the navigator said.

'Probably,' Saratov said, 'but the question is, Are we inside the pattern or outside of it?'

The sound of the plane disappeared. After a few minutes the watch team relaxed, smiled at one another, and went back to checking gauges, filling out logs, reading, and scratching themselves. Esenin had stationed one of his armed naval infantrymen in the control room. The man was trying to stay out of the way, but in a compartment that crowded, it was impossible. He had to move whenever anyone else moved.

Saratov eyed the man. He was in his mid-twenties, said almost nothing, obviously understood little of what went on around him. Was he a real naval infantryman? Or was he something else? Apparently, he had never before been to sea, or had he?

The P-3 returned. It went behind the submarine a mile or so to the north, headed west.

'We're in his pattern,' the navigator said.

'Hold this heading. In about ten minutes, we'll cross his original flight path. He'll search behind us.'

That was the way it worked out. Still, the XO and the navigator looked worried.

At midnight, when the captain gave the order to snorkel, the XO wanted to discuss it. 'Sir, the P-3s can pick up the snorkel head on radar.'

'We must charge the batteries, Askold. If we cannot do it here, we will never get into the mouth of the bay and back out.'

Askold bit his lip, then repeated the snorkel order to the chief.

As luck would have it, within thirty minutes the sub entered a line of squalls. Heavy swells and rain in sheets hid the snorkel head. The rocking motion of the boat, just under the surface, made the sailors smile. They knew how rough it was up there.

Saratov drank a cup of tea in the wardroom while Esenin and his number two, the major, silently watched. Then Saratov went to his cabin and stretched out on the bunk.

He couldn't sleep. In his mind's eye he saw airplanes and destroyers hunting, searching, back and forth, back and forth . . .

The sonar operator called the P-3 sixty seconds before it went directly over the submarine. The duty officer immediately ordered snorkeling stopped and the electric motors started. The plane went by, fifteen seconds passed, then it began a turn.

'He's got us,' the watch officer said. 'Call the captain.'

Saratov heard that order as he came along the passageway. 'Take it down to a forty meters,' Pavel Saratov said after the chief reported the diesel engines secured. 'Left full rudder to one zero zero degrees.'

'Left full rudder, aye. New course one zero zero.'

Esenin came to the control room. A moment later the major arrived, just in time to hear the sonar operator call, 'Sonobuoys in the water.' He began calling the bearings and estimated ranges of the splashes as the navigator plotted them.

'Let's get the boat as quiet as we can, Chief.'

'Aye, Captain. Slow speed?'

'Three knots. No more. And go deeper. Seventy meters.'

'Down on the bow planes. Up on the stern planes,' the chief ordered. The *michman* on the planes complied.

Saratov looked at his watch. The time was a bit after 0300.

'P-3 is coming in for another run, Captain. He sounds like he's going to go right over us.'

'Keep me advised.'

'Steady on new course one zero zero.'

'Keep going down, Chief. One hundred meters. Somebody watch the water-temp gauge. Let me know if we hit an inversion.'

'There should be an inversion,' the duty officer muttered, more to himself that anyone else. 'This *is* the Japanese current.'

'P-3's going right over our heads.'

'Come left to new course zero four five.'

Out of the corner of his eye, Saratov noted Esenin's facial expression, which was tense. The major, standing beside Esenin, looked worried.

'One hundred meters, Captain.'

'Make it a hundred and fifty.'

'One fifty, aye.'

'How deep is the water here?' the major asked the navigator, who didn't even check the chart before he answered.

'Six miles. We're over the Japanese trench.'

'So what happens if we can't lose this airplane?'

'He puts a homing torpedo in the water.' The navigator looked at the major and grinned. 'Then we die.'

'Two hundred meters, Chief,' the captain said.

Passing through 170 meters, the temperature of the water began to rise. The duty officer saw it and sang out.

'Just how deep can this boat go?' the major asked the XO.

'Two hundred meters is our design depth.'

The captain missed this exchange. He was wearing a set of sonar headphones, listening with his eyes shut.

At this depth the boat creaked a bit, probably from the temperature change, or the pressure. Saratov heard none of it. He was concentrating with all his being on the hisses and gurgles of the living sea. Ah yes . . . there

255

was the beat of the plane's props. He opened his eyes, glanced at the sonar indicator, which was pointing in the direction of the largest regular, man-made sound. The enemy airplane was almost overhead . . . now passing . . .

Splash! A sonobuoy. Or a torpedo.

'Deeper, Chief. Down another fifty meters.'

'Aye, Captain.'

More sonobuoys. Going away. Well, at least the P-3 didn't have the sub bracketed. The crew was searching for something they had, then lost.

'I think they have lost us, Chief. Now they'll try to find us again. Hold this depth, heading, and speed.'

A wave of visible relief swept through the men in the control room.

Saratov took off one of the sonar earphones and asked Esenin, 'Those shells we welded to the deck – how much pressure are they built to withstand?'

'I don't know.'

'We'll find out, eh,' said Pavel Saratov. 'You can tell them when you get home,' he added, and rearranged the earphones.

Atsuko Abe read the message from Agent Ju and snorted in disbelief. 'How can we believe this?'

'We cannot afford to ignore it,' said Cho, the foreign minister, speaking carefully. 'If there is one chance in a thousand that Ju is correct, that is an unacceptable risk.'

'Don't talk to me of unacceptable risk,' Abe snarled. Cho had been one of the most vocal proponents of taking the Siberian oil fields. Today they were in the prime minister's office off the main floor of the Diet. He normally used this office to confer with members of his party.

Abe shook the paper with the message on it at Cho. 'We lost fifteen Zeros to the American Squadron two days ago. The generals believe we will be able to hold our own from now on, but that is probably just wishful thinking. The essential military precondition to the invasion of Siberia was local air supremacy. It has been taken from us.'

Cho said nothing.

'Last night two hundred civilians and thirty soldiers were killed in a railroad ambush a mere fifty kilometers north of Vladivostok. Guerillas murdered a whole trainload of people in an area that is supposed to be secure, an area that is practically in our backyard.'

Abe straighted his tie and jacket. 'This morning in Vladivostok, the heads were dumped on the street in front of Japanese military headquarters.' Abe looked Cho straight in the eye. 'I can prevent the news being published, but I cannot stop whispers. Corporate executives know their employees are being slaughtered. No Japanese is safe anywhere in Siberia. The executives are demanding that we do *something*, prevent future occurrences.'

Cho gave a perfunctory bow.

'The United Nations is moving by fits and starts to condemn Japanese aggression. When that fails to deter us, someone will suggest an economic boycott. The Russians are very active in the UN – they are shaking hands and smiling and preparing to nuke us. They are willing to do whatever it takes to win. I ask you, Cho, are you willing? Cho?'

'Mr Prime Minister, I advocated invasion. I firmly believe that possession of Siberia's oil fields will allow this people to survive and flourish in the centuries to come. That oil is our lifeblood. It is worth more to us than it is to any other nation.'

Atsuko Abe placed his hands flat on his desk. 'Without air supremacy we will be unable to resupply our people in Siberia this winter. Air supremacy is absolutely critical. Everything flows from that.'

'I see that, Mr Prime Minister.' Cho's head bobbed.

'The American Squadron at Chita must be eliminated. The generals tell me there is only one way to ensure that all the planes, people, equipment, and spare parts are neutralized: we must strike with a nuclear weapon.'

Cho blanched.

'*This* is the crisis,' Abe roared. 'We are committed! We must conquer or die. There is no other way out. We have bet everything – *everything* – our government, our nation, our lives. Do you have the courage to see it through?'

'This course will be completely unacceptable to the Japanese public,' Cho sputtered.

'Damn the public.' Abe slapped his hands on the desk. 'The public wants the benefits of owning Siberia. A prize this rich cannot be had on the cheap. We must pay for it. Nuking Chita is the price. We cannot get Siberia for one yen less.'

'The Japanese people will not pay *that* price.'

Abe waved Ju's message. 'I am not suggesting that we nuke Moscow! Open your eyes, man. The Russians are trying to nuke us!'

'It is the use of nuclear weapons that is the evil, Mr Prime Minister. You know that as well as I. Once we attack Chita, we may be forced to launch missiles at other targets, including Moscow. Once it starts, where will it stop, Mr Prime Minister?'

Abe brushed aside Cho's words, pretended that he hadn't heard. 'Military necessity requires the destruction of the American Squadron. The squadron is Russia's responsibility; Russia must bear the consequences.'

'With respect, the decision is not that easy.' Cho groped for words. 'In 1945 the Americans used the atomic bomb on Japan and blamed Japan for making it necessary. You have just agreed that the Americans were correct all those years ago.'

'I am not going to argue metaphysics, Cho. If Tokyo goes up in a mushroom cloud, will you be willing to use nuclear weapons then?'

'No! Never. The Japanese people will never be willing to use nuclear weapons on anyone. Mr Prime Minister, *you* were the one who demanded that the development of these weapons be kept a state secret, that the public never be informed.'

'Who will tell them that we used them?'

Silence followed this question.

Abe busied himself rearranging items on his desk. Finally, he said:

'A small bomb, eight or ten kilotons, should do the job nicely. We will attack with airplanes, so the rocket people will know nothing. The American Squadron at Chita will be wiped off the face of the earth. The Russians will see that further resistance is hopeless. Siberia will be ours. The United Nations will be forced to recognize a fait accompli. No more Japanese soldiers will die; oil will go to Japanese refineries; natural resources will supply our industries. Our nation, *our people,* will flourish.'

'I tell you now that it will not be so easy.'

'This is the only choice we have,' Abe thundered. 'We must have that oil!'

Cho refused to yield. 'Japan will never forgive us,' he said obstinately.

Atsuko Abe forced himself to relax in his padded armchair.

'Victors write the history books,' he said when he had recovered his composure. 'The Russians are about to have a nuclear accident at Chita. They've had such accidents before, at other places. According to Ju, they have hidden nuclear weapons from international arms-control commissions, thus violating treaties they willingly signed – they are plotting to use these weapons on Japan. These are truths waiting to be discovered by anyone who asks enough questions in the right places.'

Abe pointed at Cho. 'You know that we tried – repeatedly – to settle this matter diplomatically. Kalugin refused to enter discussions. Categorically refused. The Russians are gloating over the Tokyo Bay incident, applauding the catastrophic loss of innocent life, rejoicing at our embarrassment, and the Japanese people are furious.'

He used a finger to nudge the message from Ju lying on the desk in front of him.

'The time has come to give the bastards a taste of their own medicine.'

'What airplane will deliver the weapon?'

'Zeros.'

'The Zeros haven't been doing very well lately. That is the whole problem. What if they fail to get through?'

'Then we will try again with something else. *We will do what must be done.*'

At the morning briefing, Jack Innes told President David Herbert Hood about a note that had been handed to one of the CIA operatives the day before in Moscow by a street sweeper, one of the old women who swept trash and dirt from public places with a long twig broom.

Then he handed Hood a translation of the note.

The Russian government has ordered nuclear attacks on Japan. A submarine is presently attempting to deliver four high-yield nuclear weapons to the sea floor near Tokyo, where they will be detonated to create an earthquake and tidal wave. If for any reason the submarine attack fails, Kalugin is prepared to launch a nuclear attack via air against Tokyo.

'Is this credible?' the president asked.

'We believe so, Mr President. As you will recall, several senior Russian specialists insisted that Russia had not destroyed all their nuclear weapons.'

'I never thought they would, either,' Hood admitted. 'But even if they cheated, every weapon destroyed was one less.'

'The note implies that the submarine is at sea now, so last night we tried to find it with satellite imagery.' Innes flicked off the lights and displayed a large image on the screen behind him. 'This is a computer-generated image of a section of the northern Pacific created from radar and infrared inputs.' Innes used a small flashlight to put a red dot on the screen. 'Here, we believe, is the signature of a snorkeling diesel/electric submarine.'

'Surely the Russians would use a nuclear-powered sub for a mission like that.'

'If they had one, sir, I'm sure they would. The Tokyo Bay attack was carried out with a conventional diesel/electric boat.'

'Where is that sub?' Hood gestured toward the screen.

'When this was put together last night, the boat was about one hundred and eighty miles off Honshu, heading southwest. It's very near the main shipping lanes.'

'Is that the only submarine out there?' the president asked.

'No, sir. The Japanese have two currently at sea. At least we believe they are Japanese.' Innes flipped to a map display and used the pointer. 'One is patrolling in Sagami Bay, the other near the northern entrance to the Inland Sea. All Japan's submarines are diesel/electric boats.'

'Where are our boats?'

Innes projected an overlay on the screen. 'Here, Mr President.'

Hood massaged his forehead for a moment. Finally, he said, 'Normally I'd want some more confirmation before we did anything. This is very tenuous. And yet, Kalugin is capable of this. He would push the button.'

'Remember the report we received last week from the U.S. military attaché in Moscow? He has an interview with Marshal Stolypin. The marshal said the Russians were just trying to get into the fight.'

'A negotiated settlement with the Japanese would not wash in Russia just now,' Hood agreed. 'Still, the evidence for nuclear escalation is damned thin.'

The president smacked the table with his fist. 'That asshole Abe! Nuclear war. Well, we'd better tell the Japanese about all this. Maybe they can sink that sub.'

'Yes, sir.'

'Then get the Japanese and Russian ambassadors over here. Today. At the same time. Demand that they come. I'd better have another chat with those two. And notify the Joint Chiefs – see if they have any ideas.'

'Are you considering military cooperation with the Japanese to thwart any attacks?'

'I am. In the interim, I want to see what the Space Command people can make those satellites do. See if they can come up with some independent verification of that note.'

Hood stood, then took another look at the satellite view of the Russian submarine's snorkel signature, which Innes had returned to the wall screen.

'I have a really bad feeling about helping the Japanese,' Hood said. 'They have sown the wind and now the hurricane is almost upon them. Yet I don't see any other way. If the nuclear genie pops out of the bottle, I don't know what the world will look like afterward. Neither does anyone else. And I don't want to find out.'

At Chita, Yan Chernov, with translator in tow, went looking for Bob Cassidy. He found him in the ready room poring over satellite photos that had been encrypted and transmitted via radio from Colorado.

Chernov glanced at the photos, labeled 'SECRET NOFORN' then turned his attention to the American. 'Colonel Cassidy, I wish to thank you for feeding me and my men.'

'You are leaving?'

'Yes. We have been ordered to shift bases to Irkutsk, on Lake Baikal. We are flying the planes there today. The ground troops will leave tomorrow.'

'We enjoyed having you in the mess.'

'Americans eat better than anyone on earth, except, of course, the French. For years I refused to believe that. Now I am convinced.'

Cassidy laughed. They talked for several minutes of inconsequential things, then bid each other good-bye. With a feeling of genuine regret, Cassidy watched the Russian leave. Major Chernov, he thought, would be a credit to any air force.

As he sat back down to study the satellite photos, he wondered why the Sukhoi squadron was being withdrawn. True, the Zero was more than a match for the Su-27, but with F-22s to keep the Zeros occupied, the Sukhois would be useful in the ground-attack role.

Well, no one had asked his opinion. He should probably tend to his end of the war. His end involved an attack on the Zero base at Khabarovsk this evening, in the twilight hour before dark. He went back to plotting run-in lines.

Janos Ilin took two of his men with him when he visited the gadget room, or, as some called it, 'the James Bond room,' in the old KGB headquarters on Dzerzhinsky Square in Moscow. Here the instruments of espionage were stored, issued, and returned after use. Of course, the man who ran it was known as Q. Unlike the suave British civil servant of the movies, this Q was fat, waddled when he walked, and spent most of his time poring over his records. Dust rested in every corner of the place, undisturbed from year to year.

Q had settled into this sinecure years ago. Like many Russian peasants, a little place to call his own was all Q wanted from life, and this was it. Today he scowled at Ilin and the two men following him as they walked between benches covered with listening devices and tape recorders to the little corner desk where Q did business.

'Good morning, Q,' Janos Ilin said, pleasantly enough.

'Sir.' Q was sullen.

'Some information. You know of the assassination attempt on the president?'

Q looked surprised. 'I had absolutely nothing to do with it, sir. You can't seriously think –'

'We don't think anything. We are here to ask some questions. Where are the records of equipment issues for the last six months?'

'Why, right here. In this book.' Q almost wagged his tail trying to be helpful. He displayed the book, opened it to a random page. 'You see, my method of record keeping is simplicity itself. I put the item in this column –'

'Where are your keys?'

'You can't have the keys. I suppose I could show you anything you want to see, but you can't –'

'The keys.' Ilin held out his hand. He kept his face deadpan. The men behind him moved out to each side, where they could see Q and he could see them.

Q opened a desk drawer. It contained a handful of key rings, each with several dozen keys.

'The inventory, please.'

'What inventory?'

'Don't play the fool with me, man,' Ilin snarled. He could really snarl when aroused. 'I haven't the time or temper for it. I'll ask you again: Where is the inventory of the equipment you have in this department?'

'But ... The inventory is old, sir. It's not completely up-to-date. It's –'

'Surely you have an inventory, Q, because regulations require you to have one. I checked. If you don't, I'm afraid I shall have to place you under arrest.'

Q almost fainted. 'Those black binders on the shelf.' He pointed. 'I don't let people browse through them, you understand. The equipment the service owns is a state secret.'

'I understand completely. Now, if you will go with these gentlemen. They have some questions to ask you.'

Q's panic returned. He was really quite pathetic. 'What if someone comes with a requisition while I am away?'

'This office is closed until you return. Go on.' One of the men reached out and put his hand on Q's arm.

When they were out of the room, Ilin locked the door behind them.

Ilin had, of course, been in this room from time to time over the years, but he had never really looked through the place. He didn't know what Q had here, much less where he kept it. Ilin sat down at the desk with the inventories. As he suspected, they were worthless. They hadn't been updated in twenty years. Still, there was a match between some of the letters and numbers in the inventory list and the numbers in Q's logbook.

Each item in the logbook had a one- or two-word description, a letter and a number, followed by signatures, times, dates, et cetera.

Ilin studied the descriptions. He examined the keys. Ah, the keys were arranged by letter. Here was the A ring, the B ring, and so on.

Ilin began looking around. Q had most of this end of a floor for his collection, eleven rooms filled with cabinets and cases and closets – all locked. The place was almost like a museum's basement, a place to store all the artifacts not on display upstairs.

Ilin inspected the bins and cabinets as he walked from room to room with the logbook in hand. Q had never inventoried this material because he didn't want anyone else to know what was here. He was the indispensable man.

Weapons filled two rooms. So did listening devices. Who would have believed that so many types of bugs existed?

It took Janos Ilin an hour to find what he wanted. There were six of them in a little drawer in an antique highboy from the early Romanov era. The polished wood was three hundred years old if it was a day.

He checked the logbook. None of these items were listed. Ilin examined the half dozen. They had tags on them bearing dates. He selected the one with the latest date. It would have to do.

Back at Q's desk, he put the logbook back on the shelf and returned all the keys to the desk drawer. He stirred them around so that none were in their original position.

Could he safely leave Q alive?

That was a serious question and he regarded it seriously. If the man talked to the wrong people . . .

Perhaps the thing to do was just arrest him. Hundreds of people were in the cells now. One more would make no difference. When this was over Q could go back to his job none the worse for wear, as, one prays, would all the others. There was a risk, of course, but it seemed small, and Ilin would not have any more blood on his hands. The blood was becoming harder and harder to wash off.

How much blood is Kalugin worth?

Ilin left the James Bond department, turning the lights out and locking the door behind him. He rode the elevator up to his floor, then went into a suite of offices adjacent to his. His men were there with Q.

'Put him in the cells. Hold for questioning.'

Q collapsed. One of the agents tossed the last inch of a glass of water into his face.

When Ilin left the room, the man was sobbing.

It was one of those rare summer evenings when the clouds boil higher and higher and yet don't become thunderstorms. Hanging just above the western horizon, the sun fired the cloudy towers and buttes with reds, oranges, pinks, and yellows as the land below grew dark.

Bob Cassidy led his flight of four F-22s south, up the Amur valley, toward the Japanese air base at Khabarovsk. They were low, about a thousand feet above the river, flying at just over the speed of sound. To the east and west, gloomy purple mountains crowned with clouds were just visible in the gathering darkness.

Two F-22s carrying antiradiation missiles to shoot at any radar that came on the air were approaching Khabarovsk from the west. Farther behind were two more F-22s. Joe Malan was leading this flight, which was charged with finding and attacking airborne enemy airplanes.

Earlier that evening Cassidy had vomited so violently he didn't think he could fly. He had started thinking about Jiro and Sweet Sabrina again, and gotten physically ill. The doctor had given him something to settle his stomach. 'I think your problem is psychological,' the doctor had remarked, which brought forth a nasty reply from Cassidy, one he instantly regretted. He apologized, put his clothes on, and went to fly.

The mission had gone like clockwork. Two tankers flying from Adak, in the Aleutians, rendezvoused with the fighters precisely on time a hundred miles north of Zeya. If all went well, they would be at the same rendezvous in sixty-four minutes, when the eight strike airplanes needed fuel to make Chita. If they weren't, well, eight fighter pilots were going to have a long walk home.

As usual, Cassidy was keyed up. He was as ready as a man can be. The wingmen were in position, the data link from the satellite was presenting the tactical picture, and the plane was flying well, smart skin on, master armament switch on, all warning lights extinguished.

And there wasn't a single enemy airplane in the sky. Not one.

The satellite downlink must be screwed up. Again.

'Keep your eyes peeled, people,' Cassidy said over the encrypted radio circuit. Perhaps he shouldn't have, but he needed to.

263

Should he use his radar? Take a peek? If the enemy still didn't know he was coming, they would certainly get the message when his radar energy lit up their countermeasures equipment.

Twenty-five miles. The planes in his flight spread out, angling for their assigned run-in lines. The targets this evening were the enemy aircraft and their fueling facilities: the trucks, bladders, and pumping units.

Where were the Japanese?

Had they caught them on the ground?

His fighter was bumping in mild chop as Bob Cassidy came rocketing toward the air base at 650 knots, almost eleven miles per minute. His targets were a row of Zeros that two days ago had been parked in front of the one large hangar on the base.

There was the hangar! He slammed the stick over, corrected his heading a few degrees. His finger tightened around the trigger, but in vain: the Zeros weren't there.

The ramp was empty when he roared across it five hundred feet in the air, still doing 650 knots.

'There are no Zeros,' somebody said over the air.

Was this an ambush? Were the Zeros lurking nearby to bounce the F-22s? Perhaps the Zeros were on their way to Chita – right now!

'Shoot up the hangars and fueling facilities,' Cassidy told the other members of his flight. 'Watch for flak and SAMs.'

He made a wide looping turn and headed for the city of Khabarovsk. The railroad tracks pointed like arrows toward the railroad station.

Train in the station!

Squeeze the trigger . . . walk the stream of shells the length of it.

God, there are people, soldiers in uniform, running, scattering, the engine vomiting fire and oily black smoke . . .

He made another wide loop, still searching nervously for flak, and came down the river. He found another train, this time heading south toward Vladivostok. He attacked it from the rear, slamming shells into every car.

The entire plane vibrated – in the gloomy evening half-light the beam of fire from the gun flicked out like a searchlight. Flashes twinkled amid a cloud of dust and debris as the shells slammed into the train, fifty a second. Then he was off the trigger and zooming up and around for another pass.

With the throttle back, the airspeed down to less than three hundred, he emptied the gun at the train. He watched with satisfaction as two of the cars exploded and one of the engines derailed.

Climbing over the town, he called on the radio for his wingmen to join for the trip back to Chita.

Where are the Zeros?

22

Admiral Kolchak was running slow, two hundred meters deep, making for the entrance to Sagami Bay, the sound that led to Tokyo Bay. Pavel Saratov sat in the control room with the second set of sonar earphones on his head. About every half hour or so he would hear the faint beat of turboprop engines: P-3s, hunting his boat. Of that, Saratov had no doubt.

Esenin came and went from the control room. Apparently he was wandering through the boat, checking on his people, all of whom wore sidearms and carried a rifle with them. As if they could employ such weapons in this steel coffin. Still, the sailors got the message: the naval infantrymen were there to ensure the navy did Esenin's bidding. Saratov got the message before the sailors did.

Esenin had his little box with him, of course, hanging on the strap around his neck. Now, as he listened for planes and warships, Saratov speculated about what was in the box.

When he had examined that topic from every angle, he began wondering what the sailors were thinking. He could look at their faces and try to overhear their whispers, but that was about it. The crowded condition of the boat did not allow for private conversations, even with his officers. And no doubt Esenin wanted it that way, because he kept his people spread out, with at least one man in every compartment of the boat at all times.

Everyone knew where the boat was going and why. The first day at sea, Saratov had told them on the boat's loudspeaker system.

Now they were chewing their lips and fingernails, picking at their faces, thinking of other places, other things. The absence of laughter, jokes, and good-natured ribbing did not escape Saratov. Nor did he miss the way the sailors glanced at the naval infantrymen out of the corners of their eyes, checking, measuring, wondering . . .

This evening Askold brought Saratov a metal plate containing a chunk of bread, a potato, and some sliced beets cooked in sour cream. As he ate, Askold showed him the chart. 'We are here, Captain, fifty miles from the entrance to the bay.'

Saratov nodded and forked more potato.

'Do you wish to snorkel tonight?'

Saratov nodded yes. When he had swallowed, he said, 'We must snorkel one more time for several hours, before we go in. We are taking a long chance. It's like a harbor up there, ships and planes . . .'

'Can't we go in on the battery charge we have?'

'Not if we expect to come out alive.'

'When?'

'Tonight.'

'We have been lucky. The thermal layer —'

'Lucky, ummm . . .'

'When we leave the Japanese current —'

'The thermal layer will run out.'

'Yes,' Askold murmured, and glanced at his hands. He watched his captain chew a few more bites, then went away.

Jack Innes reported to President Hood in his bedroom at the White House. The president was donning a tux.

'Another disease luncheon,' Hood said gloomily as he adjusted the cummerbund over his belly. 'I'd like to have a dollar for every one of these I've sat through in the last thirty years.'

'The Japanese have sent everything they have after that sub.'

'Where is it now?'

'We don't know.'

Hood looked a question.

'Unless he comes up to periscope depth, we can't see him with the satellite sensors. And there are some storms over the ocean off Japan — he may be under one.'

'How long can an electric boat like that stay under?'

'I asked the experts, Mr President. One hundred and seventy-five hours at a speed of two knots.'

'More than *seven* days?'

'Yes, sir. But the boat must go so slowly that it is essentially immobile. Once the hunters get a general idea where a conventional sub is, it is easily avoided and ceases to be a threat. Speaking of Russians, they deny that the boat in the satellite photo is one of theirs.'

Hood was working on his cuff links. 'Is it?'

'We think so, sir. But it could be Japanese.'

'Or Chinese, Korean, Egyptian, Iranian . . . Seems like everybody has a fleet of those damned things.'

'The Russian response to yesterday's conference is being evaluated at the State Department. The Kremlin denies any intent to use nuclear weapons. On Japan or anyone else. They say there's been some mistake.'

'I hope they don't make one,' Hood said fervently.

'The real question is what the Japanese are up to. They withdrew their

266

Zeros from Khabarovsk to Vladivostok. Space Command doesn't know why.'

'It's a damned good thing the Japs don't have nuclear weapons,' the president said, glancing at Innes.

'The director of the CIA says they don't.'

'Well, Abe told Kalugin that Japan had nukes when he answered Kalugin's ultimatum. Either Abe is the world's finest poker player or the director of the CIA is just flat wrong.'

'Abe doesn't strike me as the bluffing type.'

'Didn't I see an intelligence summary a while back that said the Japanese might have developed a nuclear capability?'

'One of the analysts thought that was a possibility. The CIA brass vehemently disagreed.'

'Have the White House switchboard find the analyst. Have him come to the hotel where they are holding this lunch. When he gets here, come get me.'

'Yes, sir.'

Admiral Kolchak took an hour to rise from two hundred meters to periscope depth. Glancing through the attack scope, Saratov thought, My God, it is raining! Heavily. A squall. Nothing in sight or on the sonar. Who says there is no God?

The crew ran up the snorkel and started the diesel engines, which throbbed sensuously as they drove the boat along at ten knots. The swells overhead gave the submarine a gentle rocking motion. Sitting with his eyes closed, Pavel Saratov savored the sensation.

'They are going to get us this time, Captain,' the sonarman said softly, almost a whisper.

Saratov tried to think of something upbeat to say, but he couldn't. He pretended he didn't hear the *michman*'s comment, which mercifully the man didn't repeat.

'The technological superiority that the Americans have given the Russians must be eliminated, in the air and on the ground. The F-22 squadron base at Chita will be destroyed and the F-22s eliminated as a threat.'

The Japanese officer who made this pronouncement was a two-star general. His short dark hair was flecked with gray. He was impeccably uniformed and looked quite distinguished.

Three of the four Zero pilots sitting around the table nodded their concurrence. The fourth one, Jiro Kimura, did not nod. Despite his fierce resolve, he immediately thought of Bob Cassidy when the general mentioned the F-22 squadron base.

The general didn't seem to notice Jiro's preoccupation, nor did any of the colonels and majors who filled the other seats in the room.

'I have just come from a briefing at the highest levels in the defense ministry in Tokyo. Let me correct that and say the very highest level. As everyone in this room is aware, air supremacy over Siberia is absolutely essential to enable us to supply our military forces and the civilian engineering and construction teams this winter. Without it . . . well, without it, quite simply, we must begin withdrawing our forces or they will starve and freeze in the months ahead. In fact, without air supremacy, it is questionable if we can get the people out that we have there now.

'Frankly, if Japan cannot neutralize the technological edge the Americans gave the Russians, Japan will lose the war. The consequences of such an event on the Japanese people are too terrible to imagine.

'Gentlemen, the survival of our nation is at stake,' the general continued. 'Consequently, the decision has been made at the very highest level to use a nuclear weapon on Chita.'

The room was so deadly quiet that Jiro Kimura could hear his heart beating. He didn't know Japan had nuclear weapons. Never even dreamed it. From the looks of the frozen faces around the room, the fact was news to most of the people here.

'I must caution you that the very existence of these weapons is a state secret,' the general said, albeit quite superfluously.

'The weapons we will use will be of a low yield, about ten kilotons, we believe, although we have never actually been able to verify that yield by testing one of these devices.'

One of the pilots sitting at the table held up his hand. The general recognized him. 'Sir, my father's parents died when the Americans bombed Nagasaki. I cannot and will not drop a nuclear weapon on anyone, for any reason. I took an oath to this effect before I joined the military. My father demanded it of me.'

The general gave a slight bow in the pilot's direction, then said, 'You may be excused from the room.'

The general looked at the colonels. The senior Zero pilot, Colonel Nishimura, rose from his chair against the wall and reseated himself beside Jiro at the table.

Jiro Kimura didn't know what to do. His mouth was dry; he was unable to speak. He was hearing what was said and seeing the people, but he was frozen, overcome by the horror of being here, being a part of this.

The two-star droned on, then used a pointer on the map hanging behind him. Four planes, four bombs, one must get through. The senior man, now Colonel Nishimura, was in charge of tactical and flight planning.

Then it was over and Jiro was walking down the hallway with his fellow pilots, feeling his legs move, seeing the doorway to the building coming toward him, going down the outside stairs, walking across the lawn, and vomiting in the grass.

When he first heard it, Saratov wasn't sure. He pressed the earphones against his head and listened intently. The night had come and gone, he had snatched a couple of hours of sleep, and he was back in the control room, watching the sonarman play with the data on his computer screen and listening to raw sound on his own set of earphones.

A P-3 was up there, somewhere, and the beat of its propellers was insistent. Embedded in that throb . . . Yes. Pinging. Very faint. Far away.

'Captain . . .' said the sonarman, who was in his tiny compartment a few feet away.

'I hear it, too,' Saratov muttered.

He listened for a while, then got off his stool and looked at the chart. 'Where are we, exactly?' he asked the navigator.

'Here, Captain.' The navigator pointed.

'If we stay on this course, we go in the main channel?'

'Yes, sir.'

'General Esenin – ask him to come to the control room.'

Despite the fact that Esenin hadn't had a bath in days, he looked like a Moscow politician, clean-shaven and spotless.

Saratov took off the headphones and handed them to the general. 'Listen.'

After a bit, Esenin said, 'I hear . . . humming.'

'That is a P-3, looking for us. Do you hear a chime?'

After a moment, Esenin said, 'I believe so. Very faintly. Like a bell.'

'That is a destroyer, probably near the entrance to the main channel. He is echo-ranging his sonar. Pinging. Sending out a sound that echoes off solid objects, like submarines.'

'But we hear the noise and can avoid him.'

'If you will, please look at the chart. The destroyer is roughly here, pinging away. Somewhere closer to the mainland will be a Japanese submarine. They will be listening for the sonar ping to echo off our submarine, yet they will be too far away from the emitter for us to hear the echo from their boat. Do you understand?'

'Yes.' Esenin handed the earphones back. 'What do you suggest?'

'I am wondering just how secret your little mission to flood half of Japan really is.'

'Are you suggesting that there has been a security leak?'

'I suggest nothing. I merely observe that the Japanese seem well prepared for our arrival, almost as if someone told them we were coming.'

'I fail to see the relevance of that observation.'

'Perhaps it isn't relevant.'

'We have our orders. We will obey. Now, how do you propose to get us in there?'

'I don't know.'

'Think of something, Captain. Keep us alive to do our duty.'

Saratov put the earphones back on and retreated to his stool. He listened to the pinging and stared at the navigator's chart, which lay on the table a few feet away.

Other people were also talking of duty.

'Colonel Nishimura, I do not think I have the warrior's spirit that will be necessary to complete this mission.'

'Kimura, no sane man *wants* to drop a nuclear weapon. We will do it because it is our duty to our nation.'

'I understand, Colonel. But we all have a similar duty. Someone else can fly this mission and fulfill his duty.'

'I cannot believe you said that, Kimura. The comment is offensive.'

'I do not mean to offend.'

'You are a Japanese officer. You have been chosen for this mission because you have had the most success against F-22s. Your experience cannot be replaced.'

'It is true, I am still alive when others are dead. And it is true, I successfully shot down several F-22s. Both these feats happened because I wore a helicopter night-vision helmet to see the enemy. I was the only pilot to do so. I suggested it to others, including Colonel Handa, who refused because higher authority had not sanctioned it.'

'Ah, yes, good Colonel Handa, a bureaucrat to the backbone. That sounds like him.'

'I survived only because I wore the helmet.'

'Everyone will wear such a device on this mission,' Nishimura replied. 'We have altered them to attach to our regular helmets so that we can also wear our oxygen masks.'

'Then you don't need me,' Jiro rejoined. 'I wish to pass the honor of striking this blow for the nation to one of my colleagues.'

The colonel struggled against his temper. 'You have the experience. Only you. I want to hear no more of this. Honor and duty require this service of you. The future of your country is at stake.'

'Saito was excused. This is also his country. Extend to me the same courtesy that was extended to him.'

'Have you taken an oath, like Saito?'

Kimura lowered his head. 'No, sir,' he admitted.

'All that you are,' the colonel said thoughtfully, 'you owe to Japan, to the Japanese people, who gave you life, nurtured you and educated you and made you the man you are. Your obligation cannot be erased or made smaller.'

'I owe other obligations too,' Kimura murmured.

'I do not wish to discuss this further,' the colonel said. 'We will speak of it no more.'

270

'Gentleman, this is the situation.' Pavel Saratov looked around the packed control room at his officers, and, of course, at General Esenin. 'Above us, P-3s are searching. They cannot find us because we are under an inversion layer, a layer we will probably leave in a few miles. Still, we are deep, traveling slowly, and they would have to go right over us to get a reading on their magnetic gear.'

Saratov certainly had their attention. 'Ahead of us about thirty miles is an enemy warship, pinging regularly. That warship is probably a large destroyer or frigate, carrying one or two helicopters equipped with dipping sonar. We will hear the helicopters as we get closer. Somewhere near that warship is probably one, perhaps even two or more submarines. They are lying deep and quiet, listening for us. I suspect one is on the far side of the destroyer, but it could be anywhere.

'I have considered all our options. If we go in under a freighter, the echo ranging will detect us. No doubt that is why they are doing it.

'We face the classic battery-boat dilemma. If we go in quickly, we will prematurely drain our batteries and need to snorkel in Sagami Bay, which would be suicidal. If we go in slowly, trying to save battery energy, we will expend lots of time and we'll be at the mercy of the tides. Three knots will just hold us in place; then when the tide pushes us, we will get a mere six knots. Alas, that will have to do.

'Our only choice is to be bold. When the tide turns in two hours, we will close the destroyer and shoot two torpedoes set to home on noise. They will probably put decoys in the water. We may get a hit; then again, we may not. Regardless, the confusion factor will be high. That, I hope, will give us an opportunity to slip into Sagami Bay.'

'You really have no plan,' Esenin said, frowning in disapproval.

'You may say that, sir,' Saratov admitted. 'We can only take advantage of opportunities that come our way. The enemy must positively identify every target before they shoot. We have no such handicap. Everyone we hear is the enemy. On the other hand, we can only do what the battery lets us do.'

No one said anything.

'We go so slowly, yet time is critical,' Saratov said. 'We must get into the bay before other antisubmarine forces arrive and join the search. Once inside, we must find our fault and settle onto the bottom.

'Are there any questions?'

They stared at him with drawn, dirty, haggard faces dripping sweat, although the temperature was not warm. Whatever they had been expecting, this wasn't it.

'General Esenin.'

'What if you fail to torpedo the destroyer?'

'Then, sir, we will both get to experience our very first depth charging. I hear that it is a religious experience.'

'You have balls, Saratov. I'll say that for you.'

The *michmen* and naval officers exchanged glances, trying to keep their faces deadpan. Saratov thought he knew what they were thinking, but with Esenin standing there...

'Do you intend to go up and use the periscope, Captain?'

'We must shoot from this depth.'

He bent over the chart table with the XO and navigator beside him. 'Our torpedoes have a range of ten miles. We must get within that range to shoot, but not so close that we are detected. With the destroyer's screw noises and bearing change, we should be able to get an idea of his course and speed, and therefore his relative position and range. Navigator, you and Sonar start a plot. What I think he is doing is circling in a racetrack pattern. I suspect our best maneuver will be to approach that pattern from the seaward side and shoot when the torpedoes have the shortest distance to run.

'XO, let's flood four of the tubes and open the outer doors. The doors make a bit of noise coming open.'

'Aye aye, Captain.'

Saratov donned the sonar earphones and got back on his stool. He checked the clock.

'Mr President, the intel analyst is in the limo outside.'

David Herbert Hood made his excuses, shook hands with the important people at the head table, and headed for the hotel lobby. He shook some more hands there, then got into the limo for the ride to the White House.

The analyst turned out to be a young woman, and she was obviously flustered. She was wearing jeans and tennis shoes. 'Mr President.'

'This is Deborah Buell, Mr President.'

'Glad to meet you. Sorry to call you away from a Saturday at home.'

The analyst assured him there was no problem.

'A while back, you wrote a summary that said that Japan may have nuclear weapons. Do you remember that?'

'Oh, yes, sir. That was several months ago.'

'Why did you think that was a possibility?'

'My section does economic analyses of foreign economies. It seemed to me that a significant percentage of Japan's government spending could not be accounted for in the normal ways. Basically, I thought they were spending a lot of money off-budget. So I began looking at other sectors of the economy where the money could be going. The high-tech engineering firms have been doing very well in Japan for years, and it's hard to see why – the civilian products that they should be producing don't seem to be there. Anyway, to make a long story short, it seemed to me that Japan might have several major black weapons programs. They have the technical wherewithal to make bombs, if they wanted them. So I wrote in the summary that they may have these weapons.' A black program was one so secret the government did not acknowledge its existence.

'What did your superiors think of your reasoning?'

'They thought there was not enough evidence. Still, they reluctantly agreed to let me put it in the summary, labeled as a possibility.'

'Surely you've thought more about this since then?'

'Yes, sir. And I've done more research. I still can't prove it.'

'But you stand by your assertion. It's a possibility.'

'In my opinion, it is.'

'Ms Buell, I appreciate you taking your time to chat about this. After the limo drops me, it can take you back to your car.'

She laughed nervously. 'I'm glad someone reads those summaries, Mr President. The people at the office think they go to the great file cabinet in the sky.'

'No doubt they do, Ms Buell. But I read them first.'

'Mr President, I don't want to talk out of school, but there was an unsubstantiated rumor going around in the intelligence community earlier this summer that the Japanese had operational nukes. It was never more than a rumor and no one could ever verify who started it. Shortly after that, Japan invaded Siberia. It seems possible, to me anyway, that the Japanese started the rumor to discourage any thoughts the Russians might have about using nuclear weapons to defend themselves.'

The president gave the woman a long, hard look as he got out of the car. 'Thank you,' he told her.

As they walked the corridors of the White House, the president asked Innes, 'What are the Japanese doing about that sub?'

'They have at least four airplanes and six surface ships hunting for it between its last known position and the entrance to Tokyo Bay. One of the naval types over there told our people that the Japanese are afraid of a Yokosuka refinery repeat. They don't want another disaster like that on their hands.'

'What if it isn't going to Tokyo Bay?'

'That's what has them worried. They have everything they own in the water east of the Japanese islands looking for this sub. The submarine could be a red herring. The Russians could be about to do something spectacular off Vladivostok.'

'What does Abe say about this development?'

'He remarked to Ambassador Hanratty that if Russia still has nuclear weapons, they have lied to everyone for years.'

'That's news?'

'He wants the United Nations to step in. Pass some sort of resolution promising the use of armed force against anyone who uses nuclear weapons.'

'Uh-huh.'

'And he wants the UN involved in Siberia. Basically, he repeated his demand that the UN give Japan a mandate to act as guardian of the native people, develop the place, and sell Siberian resources for world-market prices.'

'He'll never get that,' the president said as he plopped into his chair behind his desk in the Oval Office.

'He probably knows that. He's just making his position clear.'

'So what do you think?'

'I think both Russia and Japan are up against the wall. The war is out of control. Something is going to happen in the very near future.'

Four hours after the conference in the control room *Admiral Kolchak* was in position. Barely making steerageway, about a knot, just enough to keep the planes effective, she was headed northwest toward the strait that led to Sagami Bay. Five ships had gone overhead, freighters from the sound, going to and from the bay. War or no war, the wheels of commerce continued to turn.

From his stool outside the sonar shack, Pavel Saratov could see the chart. Actually, he was looking almost over the navigator's shoulder, so he could also see the measurements, the lines, the tiny triangles.

The sub was actually approaching the destroyer's racetrack from a forty-five-degree angle. The screw noise would be the loudest when the destroyer was going away from the sub. The torpedo would home on that noise. One hit with these giant ship-killers should be enough. The trick was to get the hit.

Saratov had been sitting on this stool, listening to the sounds, trying to hear another submarine, for the last five hours. Amazingly, he wasn't a bit tired. He was too keyed up.

He had to have a plan for every contingency. Askold had briefed the torpedomen and engineers, ensured everyone knew what was expected and was ready to do it without hesitation.

Sometime during this hustle and bustle, *Michman* Martos eased his head into the control room, looked around, made eye contact with the captain, then left.

Two hours ago, Saratov had conferred with Esenin. 'How accurate is the GPS?' Esenin asked.

'For the best accuracy, we should surface and let the equipment get a position update from the satellites. It is within a few meters now, however.'

'That will have to do,' Esenin said with a frown.

'Yes.'

'When we get to the fault, I will have my men ready.'

'Are they experienced divers?'

'They know what they have to do, believe me. I am going out first.'

'Whatever.'

'You have a Spetsnaz diver aboard.'

'We do. *Michman* Martos.'

'I have had a talk with him. I do not think he is politically reliable.'

'It's been a few years since I heard that phrase.'

'You know what I mean. I need men I can trust.'

'To the best of my knowledge, he didn't volunteer. I do not want any clouds on the man's professional ability, General. He is highly trained, experienced, and up for a medal for his service during the Yokosuka refinery attack. He deserves the honor.'

'No doubt he does,' Esenin said, then went on to another subject.

Now that conversation seemed as if it had taken place in another lifetime. Now there was only the boat, swimming gently forward amid the screw noises and the sounds of the sea. And the pinging: *ping ... ping ... ping ...* Saratov sat with his eyes closed, listening intently to the orchestra.

There were other submarines nearby. Saratov could feel them.

'We shoot in five minutes, Captain,' said the XO.

Esenin was rolling dice with the lives of every man on the boat. He wanted to set off four nuclear devices, to murder tens of millions of people. Even if the four blasts were insufficient to create a tsunami, the fireballs would broach the surface, fry coastal villages, create horrible tides that would inundate vast areas. Detonating these devices near the mouth of Tokyo Bay – perhaps Esenin would get a tidal race going back up the bay after the initial surge out of the bay, toward the blast area.

'Three minutes, Captain.'

He could hear the destroyer, powerful screws, turning ... This was the closest point of approach, four miles. If it didn't detect *Admiral Kolchak* now, the submarine would get its shot.

Esenin didn't seem to understand that if you nuke *them,* you have made it easier for someone to nuke *you.* Probably he thought that aspect of the matter was Kalugin's problem. The people in Moscow. In the Kremlin. Those people.

The destroyer was still turning. The pitch of the screw noises changed as the aspect angle changed.

'Two minutes.'

'Are we ready?'

'Yessir.'

'Sonar, have you heard anything?'

'No, sir.'

'One minute.'

The destroyer was steady on its new course, angling away from *Admiral Kolchak.* It was doing about ten knots, making a mile every six minutes. The submarine was making one nautical mile per hour, so it was essentially dead in the water, screws barely turning over, every nonessential electrical unit off. Even the boat's ventilation fans were off.

'Fire tube one.'

Saratov heard the blast of compressed air that ejected the torpedo from the tube and then heard its screws bite into the sea.

He had taken the precaution of turning down the volume on his earphones, which was a good thing. The torpedo was not quiet.

As the screw noises faded, he slowly twisted the volume knob back to maximum sensitivity.

The running time for this fish was six and a half minutes. Presumably the sonar operator aboard the destroyer would pick up the sound of the inbound torpedo and report it to the captain, who would probably order the launch of acoustic decoys. If the ship's company was competent, the decoys would be in the water in plenty of time. In fact, they might even be launched early.

Saratov took off the sonar headset, eyed the clock as the second hand ticked off a full minute since the first fish went into the water.

'Fire tube two.'

Perhaps the second torpedo would arrive unexpectedly.

After the second fish was launched, he fought the urge to kick the boat to flank speed and go charging past this destroyer, which he hoped would soon be very busy. The risk was too great. Saratov did, however, order up five knots and changed course sixty degrees to the right to clear the area where the torpedoes were launched. A competent antisubmarine commander would have a helicopter in this area dipping a sonar as soon as possible.

Saratov turned sixty degrees to starboard after launching his torpedoes because that course was the most direct one into Sagami Bay. What he didn't know was that this course, chosen for good reason, pointed *Admiral Kolchak* directly at the Japanese submarine *Akashi*.

The sonar operator aboard *Akashi* heard the torpedoes and reported them. 'High-speed screws, two one zero degrees relative.'

'How far?'

'Several miles, sir,' the operator said.

Unfortunately, there was no way he or his captain could instantly determine the target of the torpedoes. Given enough time, any right or left drift in the relative bearing would become apparent. If there was none, the torpedoes were on a collision course.

Time was what was needed, and the captain didn't have any to spare. If torpedoes were aimed at him, he should locate the enemy with active sonar, fire a torpedo in reply, launch decoys, and try to evade the incoming fish. If, on the other hand, the torpedoes were aimed at the beacon destroyer, giving away his submarine's position by the use of active sonar was not immediately necessary. Nor was it advisable.

The captain was well aware of the long-range capabilities of Russian twenty-one-inch torpedoes, and this factor helped tilt the decision. The shooting has started – his ship was in harm's way – he didn't want to waste time waiting for bearing drift that he thought probably was not there. On the other hand, there were two freighters on the surface nearby. The government refused to close this area to civilian shipping. Before he launched a torpedo the captain had to be sure of his target.

'Start pinging,' he told the sonar operator. 'Flood tubes one and two and open the outer doors.' To the officer of the day, he said, 'Come left sixty degrees and give me flank speed.'

The ping of the active sonar raced through the water, and just behind it the noise of the submarine's twin screws thrashing as they bit into the water to accelerate the submarine.

Aboard *Admiral Kolchak*, Saratov and the sonarman both heard the ping and screw noises.

'Quick,' Saratov said to the sonarman. 'A bearing.'

'Zero one zero relative, Captain. A submarine.'

'Set tube three on acoustic homing.'

'Tube three set acoustic.'

'Ten degrees right bearing.'

'Ten degrees right bearing set.'

'Fire tube three.'

'Tube three fired, Captain.'

Both the sonar operators aboard *Harukaze*, the Japanese destroyer manning the picket station between Oshima Island and the Tateyama Peninsula, the eastern entrance of Sagami Bay, heard the unmistakable sound of small high-speed screws when the first of *Admiral Kolchak*'s torpedoes was still four minutes away from the destroyer. Their computers verified what their ears were telling them: torpedoes. They immediately reported the screw noises and the bearing to their superior, the tactical action officer in Combat, who reported it to the bridge on the squawk box. The captain ordered the acoustic decoys deployed. Within sixty seconds, three of the four ready decoys were in the water. One of the decoys, the decoy that should have been ejected the farthest to starboard, was not launched due to a short circuit in the launcher.

While a small knot of sailors and petty officers worked frantically to remedy this glitch, the captain had a decision to make. Should he continue on this course, turn left, or turn right? He elected to turn right, to starboard, for a perfectly logical reason – there was a Japanese submarine to starboard, in the mouth of the bay, and drawing the enemy in that direction seemed like a good idea.

The captain had already turned his ship and was steady on the new course when the OOD reported that one of the acoustic decoys had failed to deploy.

The captain had only seconds to consider this news when Saratov's first torpedo hit an acoustic decoy, destroying it without exploding, and went roaring past the ship about a hundred yards to port.

Harukaze's sonar operators were listening to the decoys and the screw noises. The loss of one decoy changed the pitch of the cacophony. In addition, the sound of the first torpedo dropped in volume and pitch as it receded. The computer displayed a graphic of the torpedo's track. It had missed by only a hundred yards!

The two grinned at each other and shouted congratulations. Tight sphincters relaxed somewhat.

The junior operator was the first to get back to business. He was amazed to hear high-speed screw noises very near, and getting louder. He couldn't believe what he was hearing and stared at his computer screen. Another torpedo!

This is no drill. These are real torpedoes!

'Torpedo,' he shouted as he stared at the bearing presentation on the screen and tried to concentrate so that he could repeat the number to the tactical action officer.

The big Russian ship-killer smashed into the stern of *Harukaze*.

Water being essentially incompressible, most of the force of the explosion was directed into the structure of the ship. The explosion ripped off *Harukaze*'s rudder and both screws, bent the shafts, and smashed a huge hole in the after end of the ship. Water poured into both engine rooms, drowning the engineers who had survived the initial blast concussion.

The ship drifted to a stop and began sinking at the stern.

The echoes from the pings were very faint when they returned to *Asashi*. The Russian submarine was almost bow-on, three miles away, and four hundred feet deeper than *Asashi*. Sounds echoing off the rising seafloor were causing havoc with the computer. In addition, the sonar operator was also trying to determine the bearing drift on the torpedo noises that he was hearing. He was getting a positive drift when the acoustic decoys from *Harukaze* went into the water and complicated the problem. Then the explosion from *Harukaze* reached him, quite loud, water being an excellent conductor of sound. All this input, much of it extraneous, was giving the computer fits.

He reported the explosion and the bearing, relieved and sick at the same time. Relieved because his boat was not the target, and sick because the bearing was to *Harukaze*, which he had been listening to for hours.

He was startled when he heard more screw noises amid the horrifying sounds of ripping metal and bulkheads collapsing. Automatically, he checked the bearing.

'Another torpedo, Captain. Bearing two one zero relative.'

The relative bearing was the same as the first torpedo he heard, but not the magnetic bearing, because *Asashi* had turned sixty degrees.

'Screw noises getting louder, Captain. Little bearing drift apparent.'

'Launch the acoustic decoys,' the captain barked.

'Screw noises on constant bearing, Captain.'

'I asked for decoys, people! Our lives are at stake! *Get them launched!*'

'It will be a few seconds, Captain.'

'Stop all engines.'

'All engines stop.'

'Left full rudder. Come left another sixty degrees.'

'Left full rudder,' the helmsman repeated, just as *Admiral Kolchak*'s torpedo struck the stern of the submarine and exploded.

23

Jack Innes slipped up behind the president as he sipped his after-dinner coffee and whispered the news from Sagami Bay in his ear. President Hood made his excuses to the people around the table and stood up. He followed Innes out of the room.

'A destroyer and a submarine – he torpedoed them both. Only a few dozen men from the destroyer survived. The sub was lost with all hands.'

'What is he trying to do?'

Hood asked the question in such a way that Innes knew the president didn't want an answer. Finally Hood said, 'Better get the Joint Chiefs over here. And the Secretary of State.'

The two men walked to the Oval Office.

After Innes called the duty officer, Hood said, 'Is this the same skipper who blew up Yokosuka?'

'Apparently so. CIA says the Russians have only one boat left, a *Kilo*-class named *Admiral Kolchak*.'

'What was the skipper's name?'

'Pavel Saratov.'

'One obsolete old boat . . .'

'He's a fox, he's in shallow water, and he's been damned lucky.'

'What is he trying to do?'

'I don't know, sir.'

An hour later, Hood asked the Joint Chiefs of Staff that question. 'What is he trying to do?'

Everyone had a guess. Hood waved the guesses away. 'Why haven't the Japanese found this guy? It's an obsolete diesel/electric boat.'

The CNO answered. 'It may be old and have limited capabilities, sir, but battery boats are very quiet. In shallow water they are extremely difficult to detect quickly. The computers have a devil of a time with the bottom echoes.'

'Quickly?'

'They have to snorkel every day or two, Mr President. Given a couple days, trained hunters will find them every time.'

'Gentlemen, to get back to it, the question we must answer is this: What trouble can Pavel Saratov cause with his little submarine?'

'Obviously, he can sink a lot of ships,' someone said.

'He could have done that without going into the lion's den.'

With the help of computer graphics, they reviewed the military situation. 'Whatever Captain Saratov hopes to accomplish, sir,' the CNO said, summing up, 'he had better hurry. He sank that destroyer three hours ago right there.' He used a laser pointer. 'Even if he dashed away at fifteen knots – and that is a real juice-draining dash – he's within forty-five miles of that position. The Japanese have four destroyers closing that area and they are flying in sonar-dipping helicopters from other naval bases. Regardless of what Pavel Saratov intends, he and his crew are rapidly running out of time.'

'Gentlemen,' the president of the United States said, 'I think Captain Saratov intends to deliver a nuclear weapon. How he will do it, I don't know. My concern is that Japan may be tempted to retaliate if they have nuclear weapons.'

They sat in absolute silence as the president looked from face to face. 'We have given Japan all the information we possess on Captain Saratov's submarine. I wish we could do more.'

'Perhaps, Mr President,' General Tuck said, 'we should threaten both Russia and Japan with nuclear retaliation by the United States if they use nukes on each other.'

Dead silence greeted that suggestion. President Hood rubbed his temple. 'I don't have what it takes to push the button,' he said finally. 'I couldn't do it. Kalugin and Abe might have the stuff, but I don't. They would know we were bluffing. My daddy always told me, Never point a gun at a man unless you're willing to shoot.'

Saratov was bent over the chart of Sagami Bay, measuring distances to Esenin's fault, when the sonarman said, 'Helicopter, Captain. He's hovering, I think.'

A hovering helo could only mean one thing: a sonar-dipping ASW chopper.

'Pass the word – back to silent routine. Tell the torpedo room to stop reloading the tubes. Absolutely no unnecessary noise.'

Saratov glanced at the depth indicator, which registered twenty-five meters. Here in the shallow water of the bay, that was as deep as he could go.

At least the water was noisy. There were fishing boats, ships, pleasure craft, high-speed ferries, all roaring back and forth here in Japan's inland waters. Pavel Saratov donned the headphones and closed his eyes so he could concentrate better. A cacophony of screw noises smote his ears, some of them quite loud.

On the other hand, he had those four damned bomb containers welded to the deck topside. Even at two knots, those things had to gurgle. Not to mention the missing anechoic tiles.

The chopper was there all right, barely audible. The sonarman had good ears.

'Start a plot,' he told the *michman,* slapping him on the back.

'I already have, Captain.'

'It will take us about an hour to get over the fault. Once we are on the bottom, we will be tougher to find.'

The *michman* didn't answer. He knew a great deal about this business and wasn't buying happy propaganda.

'Helo has moved to another location. A little closer.'

'Say the bearing.'

'Two six five relative.'

'Two six five relative,' Saratov repeated to the navigator, who drew a line on the chart.

'One rotor or two?' Saratov asked the sonar *michman.*

'One, I think.'

That meant the helo was relatively small. Perhaps it didn't carry any weapons.

Five minutes went by. No one in the control room said anything. They stared at a gauge, a control wheel, a lever, something, but not at one another. Saratov thought it strange, but in tense moments, they seemed to avoid eye contact with one another. And they listened. What they wanted to hear, of course, was nothing at all.

'He's breaking hover, fading. Sound is being masked by a speedboat. There is also a freighter going into the bay. He's about a mile from us.'

'Turn the sensitivity down,' Saratov suggested.

'It is down, sir. It's just damned noisy out there.'

'Okay, okay.'

Esenin was looking at his watch, now looking at nothing, obviously thinking big thoughts.

The air in the boat was foul. Saratov could smell himself, and he smelled bad.

'Uh-oh. He's right on top of us. He put his sonar pod in the water right over us.'

'One knot,' Saratov told the chief of the boat. He said it so quietly that he had to hold up one finger to ensure the chief understood.

Several of the sailors were holding their breath.

The beating of the rotors, a mechanical rhythm, pounded against Saratov's ears. The helicopter was very near.

Now he broke hover and moved a bit, not very far.

'He's got us, I think,' the sonarman said, biting his lip.

'Listen for a destroyer. He'll be coming at flank speed.'

After a few minutes, the helo moved again, to the other side of the boat.

'He's got us,' the sonarman said disgustedly, his face contorting. 'He really does, Captain.'

'Listen for the destroyer.'

The sonarman nodded morosely.

'XO, how old were those missiles you loaded in the sail launchers?'

'Twenty years, Captain.'

'Much deterioration?'

'Some corrosion on the bodies of the missiles, but all the electrical contacts were good.'

Another five minutes passed. The helo moved again. The tension was excruciating.

'Where is he now?'

'Starboard rear. He's dunked his thing in all four quadrants.'

'Take us up, Chief. Periscope depth. Sonar, get the radar ready. We'll stick the sail up, shoot at this guy and put him in the water, then dash over to the general's fault.'

'How quiet do you want to go up?' the chief asked.

'I agree with Sonar – the jig is up. Let's do it fast, before this guy gets out of range.'

As the boat hit periscope depth, Saratov brought up the periscope for a quick sweep. He wasn't interested in the chopper – he knew where it was – but other ships in the vicinity. He walked the periscope in a complete circle, pausing only once for a second or two, then ordered the scope down.

'Okay, gang. He's up there. And we have a destroyer or frigate on the way. He's bow-on to us. We stick the sail out and kill the chopper, then go back to periscope depth and shoot at the destroyer.'

'Why are you engaging this ship?' Esenin demanded.

'I'm trying to buy you some time, you goddamned fool. Now shut up!'

To the chief, he said, 'Surface. Let's go up fast, hold her with the planes, shoot, and pull the plug.'

'You heard the captain. Surface.'

As the sail cleared the water, the sonar *michman* fired off the tiny radar on its own mast. He knew the quadrant where the chopper was, and that is where he looked first.

'He's running dead away from us.'

'Radar lock!' the sonarman called.

'Fire a missile!'

The antiaircraft missile went out with a roar, straight up, then made the turn to chase the chopper. Being a man of little faith, Saratov fired two more missiles before the sub slid back under the waves.

'I think we got a hit, Captain,' the sonarman said, pressing his headphones against his ears.

'Level at periscope depth, Chief. Flood tubes five and six and open outer doors. New course zero four five. Lift the attack scope and stand by for a bearing.'

'Helo just went in the water. I can hear the destroyer.'

'We'll wait until the destroyer is closer.'

'Down the throat?' Askold asked, his brow furrowed deeply.

'We have two fish loaded. We hit with one of them or we die.'

'Destroyer is echo-ranging, Captain.'

Everything happens slowly in antisubmarine warfare. In this life-or-death duel, the charging destroyer seemed to take forever to close the distance. The men in the control room wiped their faces on their sleeves, checked their dials and gauges, eyed the captain, wiped the palms of their hands on their filthy trousers . . . and prayed.

'Up scope.'

Saratov snapped off a bearing, focused the scope, and then dropped it into the well. The scope had been out just five seconds. As it was going down, the XO read the range off the scope's focus ring.

'Five thousand one hundred meters.'

'He's going to start shooting, Captain,' said one of the junior officers.

'Quiet. Control yourself. Sonar, does he have us?'

'It's hard to tell. He's hasn't focused his pings yet. I think the shallow water is bothering him. Or all the civilian traffic. And he is going too fast.'

'Let's pray he doesn't slow down. He won't hear the fish until they are right on him.'

'He should be about three thousand meters, Captain.'

'Up scope.'

'Bearing and range, mark. Down scope.' Five seconds.

'He's coming off the power, Captain.'

'Two thousand meters.'

'Fire tube five!'

'Tube five fired.'

One mile. The torpedo was doing forty-five knots, the destroyer slowing . . . maybe twenty. Fifty-five knots of closure. The torpedo would be there in a few seconds more than a minute.

Twenty seconds, thirty . . .

'Up scope.'

Saratov grabbed the handles as the scope came out of the well. 'He's turning to our left. Bearing fifteen left on tube six.'

'Fifteen left, aye.'

'Tube six, fire. Down scope.'

Aboard ASW frigate *Mount Fuji,* the combat control center crew was well aware that the submarine in front of them was armed and dangerous. They had received a data link from the helicopter before it was shot down and knew the location, even though they hadn't yet located the sub on sonar.

The decision not to focus the echo-ranging signals was a conscious attempt to make the submarine skipper think he was still undetected. *Mt Fuji*'s captain ordered the ship slowed to enable the sonar to hear better. As Saratov surmised, the sonar operators were having great difficulty picking the submarine out of the background noise.

When the sonar chief petty officer called, 'Torpedo in the water,' the tactical action officer ordered the antisubmarine rockets fired.

They rippled off the launcher as the frigate turned right, to Saratov's left, to avoid the oncoming torpedo. The ship turned quicker than the torpedo, which missed.

When he was firing his last fish, Saratov saw the rockets' muzzle blast and knew the moment was at hand.

As the scope went into the well, he ordered, 'All ahead flank; come right ninety degrees.'

He looked at the faces staring at him. 'Antisubmarine rockets,' he said as the sonarman called the splashes.

The second torpedo went off under the frigate's keel, tearing the bow off. The noises of the sea rushing in and bulkheads collapsing were audible in the sub even without a headset. The men just started to cheer when the submarine shook under a hammer blow.

'Starboard side, Captain. It hit the outer hull. Yes, and holed it.'

The chief started giving rapid-fire orders. The holed tank was quickly identified and air pumped into its mates in an attempt to preserve buoyancy and keep the sub from impacting the bottom of the bay.

While all this was going on, Saratov consulted the chart. He used a ruler to plot the course he wanted to the fault, then ordered the rudder over.

The odor of feces was quite noticeable. Someone had lost control of his bowels. Maybe several people had.

Hanging on to the bulkhead, General Esenin never took his eyes off Pavel Saratov.

'It could have been worse,' Askold said philosophically.

Amid the confusion, the sonarman said to no one in particular, 'We're going to die.'

A squalid, shoddy monument to bureaucratic stupidity and inefficiency, the city of Irkutsk in central Asia nevertheless stunned first-time visitors by the spectacle of its setting. The extraordinary waters of Lake Baikal, on whose shores the town sat, were a dark blue, almost black under the shadows of drifting clouds. The lake was so deep that it was once thought to be bottomless. In truth it was a huge inland sea 375 miles long, containing one-fifth of the planet's fresh water. The surface stretched away until it merged with the horizon.

Towering along the western shore of the lake was a range of high mountains, still snowcapped from the previous winter. More rugged, craggy blue mountains lay to the south and east.

Since arriving in Irkutsk, Yan Chernov had not taken the time to admire the view. He spent every minute in meetings with generals and colonels who had flown in from Moscow.

'You will escort a strike on Tokyo,' he was told. Amid the transports with Aeroflot markings at the base sat a half-dozen MiG-25s, elderly Mach-3 single-seat interceptors. These planes, Chernov was told, would actually carry the bombs. Of all the planes the Soviets had built through the years, which the Russians had inherited, only MiG-25s had a chance against Zeros. MiG-25s could use their blazing speed to outrun the Japanese interceptors – dash in, drop their weapons, and dash away before the Zeros could shoot them all down.

A Moscow general with an amazing display of chest cabbage held up one finger. 'Only one,' he said. 'Only one has to get through.'

Another strike launched at the same time would target the Japanese missile-launch facilities on the Tateyama Peninsula. Chernov knew the colonel leading that strike, although not well.

The problem with the MiG-25s, which was the reason for these meetings and conferences, was their limited range. The bombers would have to be fueled from airborne tankers several times to make this flight, one far longer that anything the Mikoyan designers had ever in their wildest fantasies envisioned for their superfast fighter. Like all Soviet fighters, the MiG-25 had been designed to defend the homeland.

Getting the tankers into position to refuel the MiGs prior to and after their dash was Chernov's job. He was to escort them and defend them from Zeros.

Just listening to the Moscow generals and their staffs explain the mission, annotate charts, assign frequencies and call signs, and talk about the whole thing as if it were possible – indeed, as if it were a routine military operation – Chernov didn't know whether to laugh or cry. The whole thing was ludicrous. At the very start of this exercise in military stupidity, Chernov tried to explain to the staff weenies that the Sukhois didn't have much of a chance against semi-stealthy Zeros: 'Zeros are a technological generation beyond our plane. Two generations ahead of the MiG-25,' he said.

None of the brass was interested. He would do as he was told – it had all been decided in Moscow.

Now Chernov sat and listened and made notes. He looked out the window and watched the second hand of the clock on the wall sweep around and around, counting off the minutes. Dawn was still several hours away.

An hour before man-up time, the briefers were finished. The pilots were told to relax, make a head stop.

Chernov wandered over toward the barracks and found an empty bunk.

Stretched out, trying to relax, trying to put it all in perspective, he felt the insanity sweep over him. He felt as if he were drowning. Nuclear weapons. Nuke Tokyo. Mushroom clouds. Millions dead.

If any of the MiGs got through, that is.

And afterward, meeting the tankers, trying to get enough fuel to make it back to a Russian-occupied base . . .

'What if the Japanese retaliate?' someone had asked the Moscow brass, only to be told, 'The Japanese don't have nuclear weapons.'

'We hope,' Yan Chernov said loudly.

'President Kalugin is absolutely certain.'

'Bet he said that in a telephone call from his dacha on the Black Sea,' one of the junior pilots said, and his comrades laughed. The Moscow brass frowned, then pretended that they had heard nothing.

The men weren't happy, but they had never heard anyone in uniform suggest Japan might be a nuclear power, so the possibility of thermonuclear retaliation seemed remote. Getting to Japan was the worrisome part.

Well, if the Zeros didn't get them, the usual Russian leadership and efficiency problems would ensure this complex plan ground to a halt well before the planes landed safely back at Irkutsk.

Chernov lay in the darkness, trying to relax. Sleep was impossible. Man-up time in less than an hour.

His thoughts began to drift. Scenes from his youth growing up on a collective farm flashed through his mind. He had wanted something more, and so had applied himself faithfully and diligently to gain top honors in school. The work paid off. He had been noticed.

So what had he gained?

His life had been a great adventure. Truly. The flying, the new and different places, the exhilaration of combat, the thrill of victory – a man would never have gotten any of that back on the collective farm, with that eternal wind always blowing, howling across the plain, scouring away seed, soil, hopes, dreams, everything.

If his father and mother could only see how far he had traveled along this road.

He was seized with the most powerful longing. Oh, if only he could spend another day with his parents, sitting in their tiny cottage, looking out the door at the plowed fields as his father talked about the earth.

All that was over. Gone.

In a few hours, he would be dead and none of it would matter.

The submarine bumped once, scraped along the seafloor for a few feet, then settled into the muddy bottom of Sagami Bay and began tilting ever so slowly to port.

'Captain,' Esenin said sharply as the list passed five degrees. Even he was holding on.

Six degrees . . .

'At twelve degrees, we lift her and try another spot.'

Eight . . .

'We are so close,' Esenin muttered.

Ten degrees . . . barely moving . . . Then all movement stopped.

A sigh of relief swept the control room.

'Fifty-two meters,' someone said, reading the depth gauge.

Suddenly Saratov realized how tired he was. He had to hang on to the chart table to remain erect.

'Here we are, General. Wounded, running out of air, with exhausted batteries, and the entire Japanese navy searching for us. I don't know how much time we have.'

The tense hours had taken their toll on Esenin. He had to summon the energy to speak. 'You have gotten us here, Saratov. That is the critical factor. At this place, we can save Russia.'

'Right.' The sourness in Saratov's tone narrowed Esenin's eyes.

'We leave this spot when and only when I say.' Esenin looked into every man's face. 'I am taking two divers with me. We will exit through the air lock. We will open a container and put one of the weapons onto the sea floor. Then we will come back inside and you will move the boat one mile west along the fault, where we will do it again. When the last weapon is on the bottom, you will take us out of here.'

Esenin glanced at his watch.

'When will the weapons detonate?' Saratov asked.

'In twelve hours. Planting each weapon will take an hour, plus an hour to move the boat – seven hours total. That will give us five hours to exit the area.'

'We don't have seven hours,' Saratov told him. 'You might have one or two. Three at most.'

'You think they'll be on us by then?'

'I guarantee it.'

Esenin's lips compressed into a thin line.

'The warheads are armed now, aren't they?' Pavel Saratov asked.

'Do you know that, or are you guessing?'

'The box.' He nodded at the box on Esenin's chest. 'It could only be a trigger.'

'We decided that detonation of the weapons at sea would be preferable to letting them fall into enemy hands. Fortunately for us, that necessity did not arise. Still, it might. If it does, I have faith that Major Polyakov will do what has to be done. He will have custody of the box while I am outside the boat.'

Esenin took off the box and placed it on the chart table. He opened it.

'As you can see, there is a keyboard for typing in a code.' He punched in a four-digit number with a forefinger. 'There,' he said. 'The code is entered. Now the circuitry is armed.'

Saratov stepped forward for a look. 'You armed that goddamned thing?'

'It was too dangerous to sail around with the bombs armed. They are armed now.'

Esenin's hand came up. He had a pistol in it. He jabbed the barrel against Saratov's chest. 'No closer, Captain. You have had your fun at my expense. From here on, this is my show.'

Polyakov and the naval infantry *michmen* also had their pistols out and pointing.

The major grinned at Saratov. 'I will guard the box, Captain.'

'You have brought us far, Pavel Saratov,' Esenin said, flashing his Trojan Island grin, 'yet we still have far to go. You will let us down if you let anything happen to you.'

'You don't really give a damn if you live or die, do you, Esenin?'

'Sometimes it is easier that way.'

Saratov got back onto the stool where he had spent the last twelve hours. 'You people better get at it. It is just a matter of time before the Japs arrive.'

The dinner hour had passed when Janos Ilin made an evening call on Marshal Stolypin at military headquarters in Moscow. He found the old man in a sour mood. When the door closed and they were alone, the soldier said, 'Fool! Incompetent! Bungler!'

'What can I say?'

'This morning he gave the order to launch nuclear strikes against Japan. He sent three planes to bomb Tokyo and three to bomb the Japanese missile facility at Tateyama. And, of course, there is the submarine with four weapons aboard trying to put bombs on the ocean floor outside Tokyo Bay. I argued against it, told him no, no, a thousand times no, and he almost sacked me. Ran me out.'

'Oh, too bad. *Too bad!* Have we heard anything from *Admiral Kolchak?*'

'Not a word. From all the intercepts of Japanese traffic, it appears Captain Saratov has gotten into Sagami Bay. Against all odds. It's an amazing feat.'

'What does Kalugin say?'

'He doesn't believe the Japanese have warheads on missiles that they can use as ICBMs. Refuses to admit the possibility.'

'I was hoping you had an appointment with him in the near future.'

'Umph.'

The old man sat looking out the window. He looked ten years older than he had a month ago.

'You have done what you could, Marshal.'

'I should be home in my garden.' Stolypin sighed. 'My legacy to Russia –

I argued futilely against a suicidal course already decided upon by a dictator. Fifty years of soldiering I did, and he wouldn't listen.'

'Perhaps it *is* time for the garden.'

'I just sent an aide over with a letter of resignation effective at midnight tonight. I should go home now and be done with all of this.' Stolypin looked at his watch. 'I have my last staff meeting in a few minutes. Perhaps I should sit in on it, say farewell.'

'How goes it? Truly.'

'The situation is not as bleak as Kalugin believes. We are building an army; we are equipping it, finding food and fuel and transportation ... We could whip the Japanese this winter. We will have half a million men to put against them. With air superiority, we will crush them.'

'Kalugin refuses to wait?'

'He says the UN will give the oil fields away before spring. Maybe he is right. The world has changed so.'

'I must see Kalugin tonight.'

'I tried to explain ... Time is on our side. Every day that passes, we get stronger. Six months from now, they will be losing troops wholesale; we'll be bleeding them mercilessly; the Diet will be arguing about how much money the army costs ... *Then we could have them!*'

The telephone rang. Stolypin sat looking at it, listening to the rings, before he finally extended a hand and picked up the instrument. 'Yes.'

He listened a bit, then said, 'Janos Ilin of the FIS is also here. He would like an audience, too. May I bring him along?'

He listened a bit more, grunted, then hung up.

'One of Kalugin's flunkies. The president wants to see me about the letter.'

'Of resignation?'

'Yes.' Stolypin ran his fingers over the desk, put the telephone exactly where it was supposed to be, and flipped off an invisible mote of dust.

'They said you could come, if you wished.'

'Thank you.'

'Don't thank me. He'll probably have me shot for treason and you for being in the same room.'

As they walked into the courtyard, Ilin put a hand lightly on the marshal's arm and brought him to a stop. 'Have you any indication that Kalugin suspects you or me of trying to kill him?'

'None. So far.'

'Kalugin will purge the bureaucracy, the military, and the Chamber of Deputies as soon as the military situation is looking up.'

'I am an old man. I am resigned to my fate. Rest assured, I will say nothing.'

'I wasn't thinking of you or me. I was thinking of one hundred and fifty million Russians who deserve better than Aleksandr Kalugin.'

With that, Ilin walked on toward the car.

The soldier holding the car door saluted the marshal, and he returned it. Stolypin and Ilin seated themselves in the limo and the soldier closed the door behind them.

There was a glass between the passengers and the driver of the car. 'Can he hear us?' Ilin asked.

'No.'

'I want to tell Kalugin personally of some critical intelligence reports that I have just received.'

'With me there?'

'You might as well hear it now. Both Japan and the United States know of Kalugin's determination to use nuclear weapons. The missions he has ordered may well fail.'

'How do they know? A spy? A traitor?'

'The Japanese call him Agent Ju.'

'You know this person's identity?'

'It is someone in Kalugin's circle, I think. Someone very close to him.' This was a lie, of course, but Stolypin didn't know that.

Stolypin goggled. 'Why, for Christ's sake?'

'Money, I think,' Janos Ilin told him. 'Originally. Now, I do not know. Power? Insanity? I intend to tell Kalugin about this agent, tell him what I know. And tell him, again, that Japan has nuclear weapons.'

'A traitor! In times like these!'

'Especially in times like these,' Janos Ilin replied.

The foul, stale air inside the boat was dead, unmoving. All the circulation fans were off to save the batteries and minimize noise. Each man was trapped in a cloud of his own stink.

The boat had been lying on the bottom for an hour. Esenin and his two divers had gone out through the air lock twenty minutes ago.

During the past hour, several ships had passed near enough to be heard without sonar. Only Saratov and the sonar operator knew more than that, because only those two wore headsets. Saratov had just concluded that there were six ships within audible range when the sonar operator whispered that there were seven. They were going back and forth near the location where the frigate had gone under, probably pulling sailors from the water.

Right now *Admiral Kolchak* lay on the bottom six miles from that position.

The number of planes was a more difficult problem because the beat of their props came and went. There had to be several, perhaps as many as four.

The ships and airplanes would find the submarine before too long. Although the sub was sitting on the bottom, a MAD would go off the scale if a hunter came close enough.

Pavel Saratov sat looking at Major Polyakov, who was seated on the navigator's stool, facing the captain's right.

Without Esenin around, Polyakov had become lethargic. Saratov thought he had little imagination. He was not stupid, just unimaginative, without ambition or ideas. There are a lot of people in the world like that, Saratov reminded himself, and they seem to do all right. It is certainly not a crime to leave the thinking to others.

Given all of that, the question remained: Why would Polyakov push the button, killing himself and every man on the boat?

'You would kill yourself, would you, Polyakov?'

'I will do what has to be done for my country, Captain. I believe in Russia.'

'And you are the only one who does?'

Polyakov eyed Saratov suspiciously. Apparently he thought this some kind of loyalty test. 'Of course not,' he said. 'Aleksandr Kalugin loves Russia too.'

'I see.'

'I don't want to talk about these things.'

'These subjects are uncomfortable.'

'I am a soldier. I obey my superior officers. All of them.'

'Is Esenin a soldier? A real soldier?'

'What else would he be?' Polyakov's brows knitted.

'You've met him before in your career, have you?'

'No. The naval infantry is a big outfit. Of course there are officers I do not know.'

'And *michmen*?'

'Plenty of *michmen* I don't know.'

'Where are you from, Polyakov?'

'St Petersburg, Captain. My father was a shipyard worker.'

It went on like this for several minutes. The major answered the captain's questions because he was the captain, but his answers revealed no inner doubts. The faces of the sailors standing and sitting in the small room reflected the ordeal they had been through, and the horror of the abyss at which they found themselves. They looked at Polyakov as if he were a monster, which seemed to bother the major not at all. Esenin had chosen well.

Just then, the screw noises of a ship became audible. Saratov glanced up at the overhead, as did most of the people in the compartment, including Polyakov. The noise became louder and louder.

As the ship thundered directly over the sub, Pavel Saratov removed the Tokarev from his pocket and shot Major Polyakov in the head.

The major toppled sideways off the stool and fell onto the deck. The box remained on the chart table. Saratov reached for it with his left hand as he pointed his pistol at the naval infantry *michman* standing openmouthed facing him, his rifle in his hand. The chief of the boat reached for the *michman*'s rifle and pistol, took them from him.

'This is where the road forks, Chief. Are you with me or not?'

'We're with you, Captain. All the men.'

'Go disarm the infantrymen forward. Collect all the weapons and bring them in here. And send *Michman* Martos to me. Hurry. We don't have much time.'

The navigator swabbed the sweat from his face with his sleeve. He was near tears. 'Oh, thank you, Captain. I'd rather die than start World War Three.'

'If we don't have some luck, son, we may do both. Now take the major's pistol and disarm the infantrymen in the engine room and battery compartment.'

'And if they won't give me their guns?'

'Shoot them, and be damned quick about it. Now go.'

Saratov hefted the box. It was very light. He used a pocketknife to pry off the back, which was held on with just three screws.

The box contained only a battery. No transmitter. It was a dummy.

'Captain,' said the sonar *michman*. 'A helo just went into a hover off our port side. He is very close. He must have dipped a sonar pod.'

24

The Tokyo bombers took off first, three MiG-25s, one after another. The four Sukhoi escorts, with Yan Chernov in the lead, took the runway as the last MiG lifted off. Chernov and his wingman made a section takeoff, Chernov on the left. Safely airborne, Chernov turned slightly left so that he could look back over his shoulder. Yes, the other two Sukhois were lifting off.

In less than a minute, the four fighters were together and climbing to catch the three MiGs, which were climbing on course as a flight of three aircraft, spread over a quarter of a mile of sky.

The Tateyama strike was scheduled to follow ten minutes behind. Alas, this whole evolution hinged on successfully rendezvousing with tankers at three places along this route. The tankers had been launched from bases farther to the east hours ago.

Or so a Moscow general said, after much shouting into a telephone.

A coordinated strike, precision rendezvous, over a dozen aircraft moving in planned ways over thousands of miles of sky – the Russians hadn't even attempted exercises this complicated in years. If the tankers weren't at the rendezvous points, if the equipment in the tankers didn't work, if the tankers or strike planes had mechanical problems, if a tanker pilot screwed up, if the Japanese attacked with Zeros – any of these likely eventualities would prevent the bombers from reaching Japan.

The Moscow general with the chest cabbage didn't want to talk of these things.

The morning was cool, but the day was going to be hot. Already clouds were forming over mountain peaks and ridges and drifting over the valleys, portending rain. Here and there a cumulonimbus was growing in the thermals, threatening to develop into an afternoon thunderstorm. All these clouds were below the fighters, which were cruising at forty thousand feet.

The oxygen tasted rubbery this morning. Yan Chernov sucked on it, glanced at his cockpit altitude gauge, and tried to rearrange his bottom on the ejection seat to get more comfortable.

As briefed, Chernov split his flight of four planes into two sections. He stationed himself and his wingman three miles ahead and to the right of the strike formation, and the other section in a similar position on the left side.

He looked at his watch. An hour and a half to the first tanker rendezvous.

The major sat listening to the electronic countermeasures equipment and watching the clouds in the lower atmosphere. There were dust storms down there, opaque areas that hid the land. Amazing how good the view was from this altitude. God must see the earth like this, he thought.

After a careful scrutiny of their credentials, the car bearing Stolypin and Ilin was allowed to cross the small bridge at the main entrance of the Kremlin and discharge its passengers. The two men then entered a nearby room to be strip-searched.

First, each man emptied the contents of his pockets into a plastic bin: watch, money, keys, credentials, everything. Other security officers began examining the attaché cases they carried.

They disrobed in separate cubicles in full view of two of Kalugin's loyal ones, who then scrutinized their naked bodies. They stood naked in the cubicles while their clothes were examined under a fluoroscope, a device much like the machines used in airports to examine hand baggage.

The security men fluoroscoped every item of clothing, including shoes, belts, and ties.

When they brought his clothes back, Ilin put them on. Then he left the cubicle and went to a table where an officer was playing with his keys and glasses. The officer, who was about forty and fat, examined the comb, looked at the pictures in the wallet, then turned the wallet inside out and ran it through the fluoroscope again.

The examination was as thorough as Ilin had ever witnessed.

Another officer handed back his money, keys, and watch, then sat looking at the FIS identity card and pass. He ran the ID cards through a black light, ensured they were genuine, then scrutinized both cards under a magnifying glass before passing them back.

Ilin had brought two pens with him that evening, one a ballpoint and the other an American fountain pen. The fat officer sat there pushing on the button of the ballpoint, running the point in and out, *click, click, click,* as he passed each of Ilin's cigarettes through the fluoroscope. When he finished with the cigarettes, he put them back in a tin cigarette case bearing the KGB insignia and laid it on the table. He made a few marks on a scratch pad with the ballpoint, then laid it down and picked up the fountain pen. He uncapped it and scrawled a bit, looked at it under a magnifying glass, then put the cap back on and placed it beside the ballpoint.

Ilin had been wearing two rings, one with the old KGB insignia engraved on an opal, the other a plain gold wedding ring that had belonged to his grandfather. He normally wore the wedding ring on his right hand since he wasn't married.

The KGB ring fascinated the security guard. Of course he studied it under the fluoroscope. Then he began picking at the stone with a penknife, trying to get it out of the setting.

'You are going to destroy my ring?' Ilin asked, his temper showing a little. He motioned to the supervisor. 'This officer is trying to destroy my ring.'

'He is just doing his job.'

'You pay him to pry stones out of settings?'

'Let me see the ring.' The supervisor pulled out a magnifying glass and studied the stone under it.

'If you want, I can leave it with you and pick it up when I leave,' Ilin suggested.

The supervisor passed the ring to him and put the glass away.

Meanwhile, the security officer at the table tackled Ilin's cigarette lighter, a crude souvenir bearing a Nazi swastika. He ran a fingertip over the swastika and looked at Ilin with an eyebrow raised.

'My father's,' Ilin said. 'He killed the German officer who owned it.'

The guard flipped the lighter several times: A flame appeared. He then took it completely apart. He removed the cotton packing, examined the wick and the wheel, then put the thing back together.

Finally he shoved the pile across the table for Ilin to pick up. He didn't say anything, just sat there staring at Ilin as he pocketed his items and adjusted his tie.

The marshal took a bit more time getting dressed. When he came out of his cubicle, the officer in there followed along and watched him pocket his personal items and put his watch back on his wrist.

None of the security officers said a word.

When the marshal was dressed, he picked up his attaché case and looked at Ilin.

'This way,' one of the guards said.

They had a long hike – across several courtyards and up two flights of stairs, then down several long, long hallways filled with paintings of long-forgotten eighteenth- and nineteenth-century noblemen.

Finally, they entered Kalugin's reception area. Two plainclothesmen frisked them again while a male secretary watched.

Only then were they shown into Kalugin's office. One of the security men closed the door behind them and stood inside, his back against the door.

Aleksandr Kalugin raised his gaze from the paperwork lying on his desk. 'Ah, Marshal Stolypin. Janos Ilin. I have been waiting for you.'

The first Russian tanker rendezvous went off like clockwork, which shocked Chernov a little. One by one, the MiGs queued up on the tanker and got a full load of fuel, then made room for the Sukhois. Even though the MiG pilots hadn't flown two flights in the previous six months, they hung in proper position as if they practiced every day.

There were three tankers: one for the Tokyo strike, one for the Tateyama strike ten minutes behind, and one spare.

The Tateyama strike team showed up as the Tokyo strike team departed the rendezvous racetrack on course.

The strike teams were passing a hundred miles north of the American base at Chita. From here to the next rendezvous, they were within range of the Zeros at Khabarovsk. Chernov turned up the sensitivity of his ECM.

When they had walked out to their planes two hours before, one of the pilots asked another, 'How is it going to feel to bomb Tokyo?'

Chernov overheard the question, but he didn't hear the reply.

The real question, Chernov mused now, was how each of them was going to live with the knowledge that he had helped slaughter millions of people. Ten million? Twenty? Thirty?

Thirty million human beings was certainly within the realm of possibility, he decided. Perhaps more.

What in hell were those fools in Moscow thinking?

Was Siberia worth that much blood?

He shook his head wearily. He was a soldier. It was shameful to think these thoughts, treasonous thoughts.

He adjusted his oxygen mask and checked his engine instruments and the fuel remaining and the position of his wingman, Malokov, or something like that. Chernov had never flown with him before. He was a new man, from a squadron near Moscow. The whisper was that the idiot had volunteered for this mission.

Maybe he wanted a medal, a promotion, recognition, his picture in the newspapers as a hero of the Russian Republic. Or was he filled with hatred for the treacherous archenemy, Japan? One of the civilians from Moscow had addressed the pilots, and that is the way he'd referred to the Japanese.

Chernov craned his head and searched the high sky until he had located all three of the MiG-25s, lying out there like fish in an invisible sea. Sharks.

His mother – what would she have said about all this?

Maybe Malokov felt like Chernov. Maybe he was just tired of living and wanted to die.

'Come in, gentlemen, come in.' Aleksandr Kalugin gestured toward the seats in front of the desk. He picked up a sheet of paper. 'What is this, Marshal? A resignation?'

'Mr President, I think it is time for someone else to serve as chief of staff.'

Kalugin sat back in his chair, hitched up his trousers. 'Stolypin, you have served your country well. You are building us an army, one we need. There is a war on. You cannot be spared.'

He said all of this as the guard watched from his post at the door. The man stood with his arms folded across his chest.

'I disagree completely with your decision to escalate this conflict. The

Japanese may have nuclear weapons and they might use them on Russia. That is a risk we cannot take.'

'Your objections have been noted. Yet *I* decide what risks we shall run. *I* am the man responsible.'

'This is no small matter, Mr President. I feel that I must resign. You need soldiers who, even if they disagree, can support your government's policies. I can't.'

'Marshal Stolypin, the Japanese do not have nuclear weapons. I do not know who whispered this false information to you' – he held up his hand – 'and it is no matter. Nuclear weapons are my concern.'

'Sir, I disagree most vehemently.'

'Your resignation letter says you have been in the army since you were seventeen years old. Fifty-four years.'

Stolypin nodded.

'Everyone in uniform obeys the orders of their superiors, including the chief of staff. You know that. I don't care about your support. You have expressed your opinion, I have decided the issue, and now you will obey and soldier on. You will serve on until I release you from your obligation.'

Kalugin seized a pen and wrote across the letter, 'Denied. Kalugin.' Then he passed it across to the marshal.

'National policy is mine,' Kalugin said, his face devoid of expression. 'We cannot wait six months to fight the Japanese on even terms. Nor can we give up a piece of our country. The Japanese must be violently expelled. They must shed their blood. *Now!*

'The Russian people are united as they haven't been since World War Two. This is our opportunity to weld these desperate, hopeless people into a nation. If we fail to seize this opportunity, we may never get another. One powerful, united nation, with the dissenters silenced at last – we owe this duty to Mother Russia.'

Kalugin sneered. 'On the telephone minutes ago, the American president threatened an economic and political boycott, "total political isolation," he said, if Russia uses nuclear weapons on the Japanese aggressors.' Kalugin shook his head balefully. 'The man doesn't understand that the very life of Russia is at stake. *This is our moment.*'

Stolypin took a deep breath, then exhaled. He glanced at Ilin, who had been paying strict attention to Kalugin.

Ilin half-turned to see what the door guard thought of all this. The man was still standing with his arms crossed. His eyes met Ilin's.

Stolypin muttered something inaudible. He drew a handkerchief from his pocket and wiped at his hands and face.

'What did you say?' Kalugin asked.

'I think you are wrong, Mr President,' Stolypin said flatly. 'However, I took an oath many years ago. I will obey.'

Kalugin decided to be satisfied with that. His gaze shifted to Ilin. 'Why are you here?'

'Mr President, I came with Marshal Stolypin,' Janos Ilin said, 'to share some critical intelligence with you. As you know, the Americans are aware of your plans to use nuclear weapons. The Japanese also. A spy told them.'

Kalugin blinked several times, like an owl. Or a lizard.

Ilin drew his chair closer and leaned forward. 'I believe this traitor is on your staff.'

'Who is it?'

'The Japanese call him Agent Ju, or Agent Ten. He has been giving the Japanese information for years. Now he is passing secrets to the Americans.'

Kalugin almost snarled. 'Can you find this man?'

'We are looking, Mr President. I came today to warn you.'

'I suspected it,' Kalugin shot back. 'But we will root him out. You are to cooperate with my loyal ones. Give them everything they ask for.'

'Yes, sir.'

'We must reinstitute political background checks. Find out what people believe, what they are saying privately. We must know who is reliable and who isn't. I see no other way. Your agency will be tasked with much of this new mission, just as it was in the old days. The modern reforms didn't work.' Kalugin crossed his hands on the desk. 'A lot of people did not believe in the new ways. This will be a popular move.'

'Yes, sir.'

'Have your director arrange an appointment with me for tomorrow. We will not waste time on this.'

Kalugin leaned back in his chair and levered himself erect. 'Gentlemen, I wish to thank you for your devotion to your nation, and to me.' He came around the table and stood before them. 'I embody our country now. *I* am Russia, its spirit and its soul. I shall guard her well. That is my sacred trust.'

Ilin was on the president's right side, and as Kalugin stepped for the door, he kept pace. The moment came as the guard turned and reached for the knob. For just a few seconds, his back was turned.

Janos Ilin had the fountain pen in his hand. He thrust it a few inches from Kalugin's mouth and pushed in hard on the refill lever. A cool, clear spray shot from a pinhole just under the nib of the pen.

Startled, Kalugin inhaled audibly. 'What —' he demanded loudly.

Then his heart stopped. As he fell forward, Ilin caught him, lowered him to the floor.

Ilin dropped to his knees beside the president. He felt his carotid artery. 'My God, his heart has stopped! He's had a heart attack!'

To the guard, he said, 'Quick, call the medics! The president has had a heart attack!'

As the guard rushed from the room, Ilin squirted another charge from the pen into Kalugin's mouth just to be sure. The pen then went into his pocket. He pulled off Kalugin's tie, ripped open his coat and shirt, and began cardiopulmonary resuscitation.

He was pumping hard on the dead man's heart when the medical team rushed in thirty seconds later. Ilin had already cracked some ribs; he felt them go.

The white-coated professionals quickly checked the president's vital signs as five loyal ones gathered around. A medic jabbed a needle straight through Kalugin's chest into his heart and pushed the plunger in. Then they zapped him with the paddles.

The body twitched.

Again with the paddles.

Nothing.

Janos Ilin blotted the perspiration from his brow with the sleeve of his suit jacket. Marshal Stolypin stood watching the medics with a thoughtful expression.

Three of Kalugin's lieutenants were hovering. One asked the guard, 'What did you see?'

'He had a heart attack. That man caught him as he collapsed. It *was* a heart attack. I never took my eyes off him.'

At length, the medics decided the case was hopeless. They packed their gear and left the room. Kalugin was still lying on the floor, his shirt and coat wadded up on the floor beside him. The guard was nowhere in sight. The loyal ones followed the medics. The last one glanced at Ilin and Stolypin, shrugged, then hurried after the others.

Stolypin picked up the telephone and placed a call. It took several minutes to get through to the person he wanted. Meanwhile, Ilin closed Kalugin's eyes and draped the dead man's suit jacket over him.

'This is Marshal Stolypin. I am calling to rescind the order given by President Kalugin to attack Japan with nuclear weapons . . . He is dead . . . Yes, the president is dead. A heart attack just a few minutes ago . . . There is no mistake; I swear it . . . Don't give me that! I've known you for twenty years, Vasily. I order you not to launch those planes.'

Stolypin listened a moment, then covered the mouthpiece with his hand. 'He can't stop them. They took off two hours ago. Five loyal ones are still in his headquarters, armed to the teeth. The pilots were specifically ordered not to turn back for any reason.'

Stolypin listened for several more seconds, then grunted a good-bye.

Ilin wandered out of the room into the reception area. Marshal Stolypin followed him.

The reception area was empty.

The men walked along the corridor the way they had come in. They met no one. At the head of the grand staircase there was a window. Through it they could see the lighted grounds of the Kremlin and the main gate. The loyal ones were walking quickly toward the gate. Even as Ilin and Stolypin watched, the grounds emptied. Not a single person remained in view.

'The pilots were ordered to bomb Japan, then return to Irkutsk.'

'Will they do it?'

'If they have wives and children, I imagine it will not occur to them that they have a choice.'

'Perhaps, Marshal,' Ilin said, 'we should use the hot line to call Washington. The American president may be able to help.'

Side by side, they walked the empty corridor back to the president's office.

'He was mad, you know,' Stolypin said.

'Yes.'

Pavel Saratov stood under the air lock in the forward torpedo room, watching *Michman* Martos check his scuba tanks and strap them on.

'Three against one,' Saratov said. 'I wish we had someone to send with you.'

'It will be all right.' Martos was trying to concentrate on checking out his gear, getting it on correctly. The captain obviously had other things on his mind, which was okay. That was why he was the captain.

'Try to figure out how the timers work and turn them off.'

'It may take a few minutes.'

'Nuclear war, the end of the world ... I won't be a part of it.'

'I understand, Captain.' Martos glanced at Saratov, who looked years older than he had a month ago. These last few weeks had aged them all, Martos reflected.

'You're all traitors,' one of the naval infantrymen put in. He had been disarmed and was sitting on a nearby bunk, watching Martos get ready. 'General Esenin will –'

Saratov glanced at the senior torpedo *michman*, who backhanded the infantryman across the mouth.

'Any more noise, tape his mouth shut.'

'Aye aye, sir.'

The *michman* wearing a sound-powered telephone headset spoke up: 'Captain, Sonar reports two destroyers at ten thousand meters, closing quickly.'

Saratov smacked Martos on the arm. 'Hurry.'

'Aye, Captain.'

Martos pulled his mask over his face and scurried up the ladder into the lock. As the torpedomen sealed the hatch closed, Saratov headed for the control room. White faces watched him every step of the way. He tried to keep his gait under control, but the sailors must have thought he was galloping.

'Two destroyers,' the sonarman reported. 'About ninety-five hundred meters. And two more helicopters.'

'Are they echo-ranging?'

'Yes, sir.'

Askold had been wearing the extra sonar headset, and now he passed it to the captain without a word. He looked very tired.

As he waited inside the dark lock while the cold water rushed in, Martos felt the dogged-down hatch above his head. Esenin had closed the hatch once he was outside the ship. Had he left the hatch open, no one else could have used the air lock. Was closing the hatch a tactical error, or was Esenin waiting for someone to come out through the lock?

Locked in this steel cylinder as the water rose past his shoulders, Martos recalled that Esenin and one of his men had gone out first, then the third man. That third man must have closed the hatch behind him.

The cold water shot into the lock under pressure. This small, totally dark steel chamber with cold seawater flooding in was no place for a person suffering from claustrophobia. Martos had conquered his fear of the lock long ago.

The water was over his head now. Breathing compressed air from the tank on his shoulders, Martos waited until the sound of water coming in had stopped completely. He could just hear the pinging of the Japanese sonars probing the dark waters.

Saratov was right: they were running out of time.

Martos reached above his head and grasped the wheel on the outer hatch. He applied pressure. The wheel resisted. Martos braced himself and grunted into his mask as he twisted with all his strength.

The wheel turned ninety degrees, and he pushed on the hatch. It opened outward.

Martos flippered up and out.

The light was dim, visibility in the murky, dark water was very restricted. He could see, at the most, ten feet.

He had his knife out now, in his right hand, ready. He cast a quick glance in all directions, including upward.

Keeping his chest just inches off the steel deck plating, Martos swam aft.

The first two containers loomed into view. They appeared to be closed, with the metal bands that encircled them still attached.

As he got closer, he could see someone between the containers, someone in a semi-erect position, facing aft. The other two men must be beyond this guy.

Martos's adrenaline level went off the chart. He was ready.

He flippered up and over the left container, which was about four feet high, so that he came at the man he could see from behind his left shoulder. As he closed he saw the other two, their heads bent. They had the container behind this one open and were bent over, working on whatever it contained. A light source near what they were working on silhouetted them in the murky water.

Martos took in the scene at a glance as he closed swiftly on the nearest man, still motionless. The head of the man across from him jerked up just as he stabbed with the knife, burying it to the hilt in the side of the nearest man's neck.

With a ripping, twisting motion, he jerked the knife free as dark blood spouted like ink. Martos used his left hand to slam the victim away. His momentum carried him toward the man who had jerked his head up.

He slashed with the knife, but the man kicked backward, so the knife missed its target.

As he went by the third man, Martos slammed an elbow into his mouthpiece, causing it to spill out.

Scissoring hard with his legs, the Spetsnaz fighter shot toward the second man and slashed again with the blade. This time, the knife clanked into a wrench the man had in his hand.

The man dropped the wrench. The human shark that had attacked him bored in relentlessly. Another slash with the blade at his air line bit deep into his shoulder.

The panicked man got a hand on Martos's goggles and snatched them away.

This time, Martos drove the blade deep into the man's abdomen and ripped it free with one continuous motion, then pushed the dying man away and spun to face his last opponent.

'Eight thousand meters, Captain. They were making at least thirty knots. Now one of them is slowing. The other is charging toward us.'

Ping! That damned noise.

'The helos? Where are they?'

'One is overhead, sir. I think he has dipped a sonar pod.'

Saratov could hear the steady *whop-whopping* beat of a helicopter in his earphones. It *did* sound as if the chopper was in a hover.

Ping!

'How long has Martos been out?'

'About a minute, sir.'

Everyone in the control room was looking at him, waiting for him to hatch a miracle, pull a rabbit from the hat. Pavel Saratov made a show of reaching into Askold's shirt pocket for a cigarette, lighting it, and taking a deep, slow drag.

Esenin was no amateur. He fought like a trained professional, without wasted effort, making every move count. He kept his eyes on Martos's abdomen, not his face. He had his knife in his right hand. And the bastard was grinning! Martos saw the flash of white teeth just before Esenin placed the scuba mouthpiece back in his mouth.

For the first time, Martos felt fear.

Was the general grinning because he was going to kill Martos with a knife, or was he grinning because this damned bomb he had been working on was now set to explode?

Esenin slashed with the knife and Martos countered, but in slow motion, because all their movements were slowed by the water. At first blush, avoiding a slow-motion attack seemed easy, until you realized that your movements were inhibited to the same degree. Then underwater hand-to-hand combat became a horrible, twisted nightmare.

Martos got his left hand on Esenin's right wrist and gripped it fiercely. Before Martos could deliver a killing thrust with his right, Esenin seized his wrist.

Locked together, they struggled.

Martos was the stronger of the two. He could feel Esenin yielding, and at that moment, Esenin got his feet up and kicked. The two men flew apart.

Martos had to look at the bomb. There was a panel with glowing numbers.

Esenin launched himself off the front of the submarine's sail. Martos flippered hard to avoid him and slashed with his knife as Esenin went under him. He felt the blade bite flesh.

Esenin whirled to face him. The shoulder of his wet suit was leaking dark black blood, or perhaps Martos only imagined it. In the dim murk it was hard to tell.

This time as Esenin came forward, he held the knife low, ready to slash upward.

Martos used his hands to move himself backward, waiting for his moment.

Something rammed itself into his left shoulder. Stunned by pain and shock, Martos looked down at his shoulder. Protruding from the wet suit was the tip of a knife blade, gleaming in the watery twilight.

25

They were waiting when Atsuko Abe entered the war room in the basement of the defense ministry. The foreign minister, Cho, was there with four other ministers and half a dozen senior politicians from the Diet. The chief of staff of the Japanese Self-Defense Force, General Yamashita, stood in their midst.

'What are you doing here?' Abe demanded of the group as they bowed. Without waiting for an answer, he walked around them. He went to the prime minister's raised chair and climbed into it.

'A Russian submarine is in Sagami Bay, just outside the mouth of Tokyo Bay,' Abe said. 'I suppose you've heard. Come, let us see about it.'

They turned to face him. The raised chair resembled a throne, Cho thought, annoyed that such a thought should intrude at a time like this.

'The submarine can wait, Mr Prime Minister,' Cho replied. 'We have come about a more serious matter.'

Abe looked from face to face, scrutinizing each.

'My conscience forced me to violate the security laws,' Cho continued. 'I told these gentlemen of your plans to use nuclear weapons to destroy the American air base at Chita. My colleagues decided that verification must be obtained before any decision was possible on a matter this serious. General Yamashita agreed to meet with us. He confirmed that you ordered this attack.'

Abe's eyes flashed angrily. 'Without air superiority, gentlemen, our position in Siberia is untenable. We cannot resupply our forces through the winter. Does anyone dispute that?'

No one spoke.

Abe bored in. 'General Yamashita? Do you concur with my assessment?'

Yamashita gave a tiny affirmative bow.

'We must eliminate the American F-22s or lose the war. If we lose the war, this government will fall. If this government falls, Japan will lose its last, best hope for greatness. Surely you see our dilemma. Desperate situations call for extreme remedies – I have the courage to do what must be done.'

'Mr Prime Minister,' Cho said, 'sometimes defeat is impossible to avoid. The wise man submits to the inevitable with grace.'

'Defeat is never inevitable. Our resolve must be as great as the crisis.'

'To struggle against the inevitable is to dishonor oneself.'

Abe flared at that shot. 'How dare you speak to me of honor!' he roared.

Cho gave not an inch, which surprised Abe. He didn't think the old man had it in him. 'I speak of our honor, ours collectively, yours and mine, the honor of the people in this room, and the honor of Japan. We must choose a course worthy of ourselves and our nation.'

'And that is?' Abe whispered.

'We must withdraw from Siberia. Nuclear weapons are abhorrent to the Japanese people. To have them as a deterrent is one thing, but to use them on a foe when the life of the nation is not at stake is quite another.'

'The life of Japan *is* at stake.' Abe looked again at every face, trying to read what was written there. 'We are a small, poor island in a vast ocean bordered by great nations. We are caught between China and the United States. With Siberia, Japan can also be great. Without it . . .' His voice trailed off.

'Your failing, Mr Prime Minister,' Cho said slowly, 'is that you have never been able to admit the possibility of visions other than your own. But the time for discussion is past. The decision has been made. The Japanese government will not betray the ideals of the Japanese people.'

Abe seemed to shrink in his large chair.

General Yamashita stepped forward and presented a piece of paper. 'Please sign this, Mr Prime Minister, canceling preparations for the nuclear strike.'

Abe made the smallest of gestures, motioning the paper away. 'I cannot,' he said in a hoarse whisper. 'The strike was launched a half hour ago.'

'Call it back,' one of the senior politicians said harshly.

Atsuko Abe smiled grimly. 'The possibility always existed that weak men might lose their resolve. The pilots were ordered to ignore any recall orders.'

The politicians stood in stunned silence, trying to comprehend the enormity of the step taken by Abe.

Cho was one of the first to find his tongue. 'Come with me,' he said to General Yamashita. 'We will call the American president.'

David Herbert Hood was still on the telephone with Marshal Stolypin when the call from the Japanese defense ministry came in. Hood listened in silence to the translation of the words of Foreign Minister Cho. When he realized that Cho was saying the nuclear strike against Chita had been airborne from Vladivostok for forty-two minutes, Hood pushed the button on the telephone that allowed everyone in the room to hear the translator, and in the background, the voice of Cho talking rapidly in Japanese.

Hood was horrified. The news that a nuclear strike couldn't be recalled struck him as complete insanity. The Russians had done the very same thing.

'Mr Cho,' Hood replied, trying to keep control of his voice. 'I just got off the telephone with the Russian chief of staff. Are you aware that Russia launched a nuclear strike via aerial bombers against Tokyo and the missile-launch facilities on the Tateyama Peninsula two hours ago?'

The translator fired ten seconds of Japanese at Cho, who asked in horror, 'Tokyo?'

'Tokyo,' thundered David Hood. 'And the crazy sons of bitches sent planes without any way to recall them.'

Cho said something to try to get the message straight.

In a moment, Hood continued: 'Yes, sir. The Russians did do that. They are doing it now. Six MiG-25 bombers, three for each target, with Sukhoi-27s for escort.'

He handed the telephone to Jack Innes. 'Tell them where the Russian strike is. They may be able to intercept it.'

While Innes talked, Hood scanned the giant display that covered most of the wall in front of him. It was a presentation of raw data from the satellites, massaged by the best computer programs yet devised. What Hood focused upon were the symbols marking unknown airborne targets in eastern Siberia. There were several. One of the formations the Americans were watching was undoubtedly the nuclear strike, probably that one a hundred miles north of Khabarovsk.

The chairman of the Joint Chiefs, General Stanford Tuck, was standing beside him. 'Nukes,' Hood told him. 'The bastards are trying to nuke each other.'

'What are the targets?'

'The Russians are sending two strikes, one against Tokyo, one against the missile-launch facilities on the Tateyama Peninsula. Meanwhile, the Japanese are trying to nuke the F-22 base at Chita.'

Tuck was horrified. 'Tokyo . . .'

'The F-22 squadron,' Hood said, pursing his lips. 'There are hotheads in Congress who will want Japanese blood if they use a nuke to kill Americans.'

'How did we get to the edge of the abyss?' Stanford Tuck asked.

'How do we keep from falling in?' Hood countered. He pointed to the computer presentation on the wall. 'The Russians are too far east to be intercepted by the F-22s. It would be a futile tail chase. The Japanese are going to have to take care of themselves. Our only option is to scramble the F-22s to intercept the Japanese strike headed their way.'

'The planes near Khabarovsk must be the Japanese,' Tuck said. He grabbed a satellite telephone.

Stunned by the agony of the knife that had been rammed through his left shoulder from behind, *michman* Martos almost lost his scuba mouthpiece. His instinct and years of training saved him. Without conscious thought, he turned and grabbed his assailant's throat with his left hand and buried his knife in the man's stomach again. Continuing the same movement, he then spun the man toward Esenin and flippered as hard as he could.

The agony in his shoulder was extraordinary, so bad that he could barely stay focused.

Esenin tried to push the dying naval infantryman out of the way so that he could get at Martos, but while he was using his hands for this, Martos pulled his knife from the human shield and stabbed Esenin under his left armpit.

Esenin twisted away before Martos could withdraw his weapon. He floated away, looking down at his left side, reaching with his right hand.

Martos turned back toward the bomb.

Lights ... numbers ... Where was the on-off switch?

As he looked for it, the sheer volume of the pinging noises got his attention. And a noise like a train. Martos looked up, toward the surface a hundred feet above.

He saw the destroyer speeding over, and splashes. Out to either side of the racing ship's hull, splashes.

Depth charges! The Japanese destroyer was dropping depth charges!

'Depth charges in the water, Captain.'

'All hands into life jackets. Let's pray these charges are set too shallow. If we survive them, we'll blow the tanks, surface the boat, and abandon it. Pass the word.'

Every man in the boat was talking to someone, reaching for something, bracing himself.

'Close all watertight fittings.'

Saratov heard the hatches clanging shut. He reached for a life jacket and pulled it on, fumbling with the straps.

He was still at it when the first depth charge exploded.

The detonation rocked the sub, causing circuit breakers to pop and emergency lighting to come on.

Another blast, like Thor pounding on the boat with his mighty hammer.

Then the worst of all, three stupendous concussions in close succession.

Silence. 'Damage reports?' Saratov shouted the question into the blackness. Even the emergency lights were out.

The reports came back over the sound-powered telephone. The boat was still intact.

'Emergency surface. Blow the tanks. All hands stand by to abandon ship.'

Martos had only a few seconds, so he looked again at the panel on the bomb still sitting in its cradle on the transport container. Esenin and his helpers had merely opened the container by releasing the two steel bands that held it together. Surely these damned fools weren't arming the thing before they got it off the submarine?

But it *was* armed.

Martos tried to remember – as he knifed the first man, Esenin had been on his left, and doing something to this panel. What?

Which is the power switch?

Running out of time . . . Which one is it?

He heard a powerful click, and instinctively he slammed his knees into the fetal position and hugged them.

The concussion smashed into his left side like a speeding truck. For a second or two, he lost consciousness.

Another blast, and another. These blasts were above him and to his right, farther away than the first, which had almost opened him up like a ripe tomato.

Martos concentrated on staying conscious and keeping his mouthpiece in place as the shock waves from the explosions hammered at him.

The knife buried in his shoulder helped. The pain was a fire that burned and burned, and his mind couldn't shut it out.

Then the explosions were over.

Amazingly, he was still alive. And deaf. He could hear nothing. His eardrums must have burst.

He tried to find the warheads, the containers, but couldn't. The water was opaque.

The rising submarine hit him, carried him upward on an expanding tower of bubbles, a universe of rising bubbles.

Instinctively, Martos used both hands to grasp the slippery tiles of the deck, which was pushing him up, up, toward the light.

He was going upward too fast. He was going to get the bends. He could feel his abdomen swelling. Oh, sweet Christ!

More and more light, coming closer and closer . . .

When the submarine surfaced, Pavel Saratov used the public address system. The emergency power was back on, so the loudspeakers worked.

'Abandon ship. All hands into the water.'

Already the control room crew had the hatch open to the sail cockpit.

'Let's go. Everybody out,' Saratov roared. Amazingly, the sonar *michman* held back. 'I'm sorry, Captain. What I said –'

'Forget it, son. Out. Up the ladder.'

He waited until the last man was out of the control room and conning tower area, then Pavel Saratov climbed the ladder to the cockpit. The daylight shocked him. The men that preceded him were in the water, wearing their life vests, paddling away from the sub. Men were still coming out of the torpedo room forward and the engine room aft. The swells – they weren't so large, but they were lapping at the open engine room hatch.

The destroyers were circling. One was coming back with a bone in its teeth. The choppers were out there circling . . .

Saratov's attention turned to the bomb containers welded to the deck forward of the sail. Three of them were still sealed. One, however, was open. The top of the container was missing, but the steel straps were there, loose. Entangled in one was a body in a wet suit, wearing a scuba tank. Saratov climbed down the handholds on the port side of the sail to the deck and carefully walked forward on the wet tiles.

The man entangled in the strap moved. Esenin.

The hilt of a knife protruded from under his left arm.

Saratov lifted Esenin's head. 'Where is Martos?'

'Captain, over here.'

The cry was from beside the sail, on the starboard side.

Saratov went aft. Martos was trying to get erect. He had found a handhold on the sail to hold on to as the sub came up from the depths; otherwise, the water would have washed him away.

The point of a knife was sticking out of Martos's shoulder. 'Don't pull it out,' Martos said. 'I'll bleed to death.'

'Can you get in the water and swim? The Japanese may start shooting.'

'I can barely hear you. I think my eardrums are ruptured.'

Saratov raised his voice, 'I said –'

'We must check the bomb. I think Esenin armed one, started a timer. Help me.'

The two men went over to look, Saratov half-carrying the Spetsnaz fighter.

'See the numbers, ticking down.'

'We need something to break into this, to cut the circuits.'

'The knife in Esenin,' Martos said. 'Get it.'

Saratov moved the three steps and pulled the knife from the tangled man. He handed it to Martos, who raised it in the air with his right hand and jabbed it into the electronic box with all his strength. The knife went in about three inches. Martos pried with the blade.

'Captain!'

The call came from the water. Saratov looked in that direction. Askold was calling. Now he pointed. 'Water . . . the engine-room hatch. The boat is flooding.'

Now he could feel the deck shifting. The bow was rising.

'Quickly,' he said to Martos.

'I –' Martos passed him the knife and ripped at the top of the control box that he had pried loose. It gave. He bent it, trying to enlarge the opening. The deck was shifting, rising from the sea and tilting.

'Help me,' Martos gasped.

Saratov grabbed the Spetsnaz fighter with his left hand and used his right to slash the exposed wires.

'Keep me from falling and give me the knife,' Martos gasped. Saratov handed over the knife and grabbed Martos with both hands.

Martos sawed with the blade against the wires. Several parted. He sawed some more.

The bow was completely out of the water. Nearby, sailors in lifejackets were shouting.

Saratov looked up. A Japanese destroyer was coasting to a stop less than fifty meters away. Faces lined the rail. Someone on the bridge was using a bullhorn, shouting and waving an arm. Beside him were men with rifles.

'The boat is going to go under, Captain,' Martos said.

'Cut the last of the wires.'

'The suction will take us down.'

'Perhaps. Cut the damned wires.'

'I am trying.'

The bow rose higher and higher into the air. Saratov heard a bulkhead inside the submarine tear loose with a bang.

When the angle of the deck got to about sixty degrees, Saratov lost his grip on Martos, who was still holding the clock part of the mechanism. He dropped the knife and grabbed the clock with both hands.

Then the wires holding the clock mechanism tore away and Martos slid down the deck into the sea.

Holding on precariously, Saratov checked the mechanism. The clock was gone, all the lights off.

Then he could hold on no longer. He started to slide down the deck, then kicked away with his feet and fell into the water.

As the boat loomed above him, he stroked for Martos.

Towing the diver by his air hose, Saratov turned his back on the boat and paddled away as hard as he could.

He hadn't gone far when he heard shouting. He looked. *Admiral Kolchak* was going under.

As the boat went into the depths for the last time, Esenin was conscious, trying to free himself from the steel cable that held him trapped.

With a huge sigh as the last of the air rushed from the boat's interior, the bow of *Admiral Kolchak* disappeared into the sea.

The swirling undertow dragged Saratov under. He held on to Martos's air hose with a death grip.

When he thought his lungs would burst, he opened his eyes.

He was still underwater, rising toward the surface.

Gagging, he sucked the air, then pulled Martos up and got his head above water. 'Breathe, damn it! Breathe.'

Martos coughed, gagged, spit water, then sucked in air.

'Don't die on me, Martos.'

'Yes, Captain,' Martos said, and passed out, still in Saratov's grasp.

The Sukhois and MiGs were thirty minutes away from the second tanker rendezvous when Major Yan Chernov flipped his radar switch to the transmit position. He and the other Sukhoi pilots had been listening passively for radar transmissions by Japanese Zeros and not radiating themselves. So far, they had heard nothing.

Now he adjusted the sensitivity and gain on the scope, ran the range out to maximum, and watched the sweep go back and forth, back and forth.

The scope was empty, of course, just like the dusty sky. The dust in the atmosphere diffused the sunlight and limited visibility. Maybe six miles visibility here, he decided, but worse to the south.

Perhaps the damned tankers would not show up. Screwups of this order were an everyday occurrence in Russian life. That the first set of tankers had showed up in the proper place, on time, was a minor military miracle, worthy of comment wherever uniformed professionals gathered. A similar miracle two hours later was too much to expect.

So Chernov's thoughts went. He turned his head and looked for all his charges, the bombers and the escorts. When he squinted against the glare, he could just see the second section of Sukhois, about four miles away to the south, at this altitude.

And of course his eyes dropped to his fuel gauges. He had enough to get to the tanker rendezvous and fly for another fifteen minutes. That was it.

No doubt the other fighters and bombers were in a similar condition.

Without fuel from the tankers, the three MiG-25 bombers and their Sukhoi escorts would flat run out of gas. The Tateyama strike would suffer a similar fate.

Chernov looked at the chart of this area that he had folded on his lap. The rendezvous position was plainly marked. Unfortunately, there were no runways within range if Chernov and his charges didn't get fuel.

Watching the radar sweep was mesmerizing. With the plane on autopilot, Chernov had time to study the scope, twiddle the knobs, search the vast sky visually, look at his chart.

Finally he saw it, a dot on the scope, well left of course, 140 miles away. It was moving slowly across the scope toward the extended centerline of Chernov's airplane.

This blip was the tanker formation, of course. Right on time. Right where they should be. And not a Zero in sight.

At a hundred miles, the tankers turned toward the oncoming fighters. They were now in their racetrack pattern. They would spend five minutes on their present heading, then do a 180-degree turn to their right to the reciprocal heading, where they would do another five-minute leg. The fighters would rendezvous on them.

The distance to the tankers was only twenty miles when they began their

180-degree right turn. What had been one blip on Chernov's radar was now three separate, distinct targets.

Jiro Kimura had been awake for thirty hours. The night before, he had lain down but sleep was impossible. He thought of his wife, Shizuko, of Bob Cassidy, of duty, honor, and country and tried to decide what all of it meant, if anything.

He was trapped, like a fly in amber. He had too many loyalties to too many things. There was no way to resolve the conflicts.

The sun fell softly from the dust-filled lemon sky. Windstorms in Manchuria had lifted dust high into the atmosphere, limiting visibility. Here between Vlad and Khabarovsk, the dust was particularly thick. The forecasters said that the dust would thin when the flight rounded the corner of Chinese airspace at Khabarovsk and headed west for Chita.

Three miles ahead and a mile to the right, cruising several thousand feet below, was the converted Boeing 747 tanker that would pass fuel to the four Chita-bound fighters after Khabarovsk was passed. Jiro could just make it out in the yellowish haze. He and his wingman were stationed in the tanker's left-rear quadrant to guard against American or Russian fighters lining up for a gun or Sidewinder shot. The flight leader, Colonel Nishimura, had also stationed himself and his wingman behind the tanker, on the right side, in the quadrant that he felt it most likely the F-22s would attack from. That the F-22s would attack the four bomb-carrying Zeros before they began their bombing run on Chita, the colonel regarded as a fact barely worth discussion. Of course the Americans would attack!

Jiro also thought an attack highly probable. At the brief the colonel had made the classic Japanese warrior's mistake – he underestimated his Western opponent. He seemed to think that Bob Cassidy and company were going to be easy kills, even made a half-joking, disparaging reference to them.

Jiro hoped that somewhere his old friends killed by F-22s were having a good laugh at Nishimura's naïveté. Or stupidity. Whichever.

When Cassidy came slashing in, Nishimura was going to get a quick education. He would probably die before he realized his folly.

Jiro had recommended that the Zeros use their radars until they were fifty miles from Chita. 'Only at Chita have we encountered anti-radiation missiles, which must be ground-based. We must use our radars to find the F-22s before they find us.'

Nishimura refused. 'Athena will prevent them from seeing us. If we leave our radars off there is no way they can detect us.'

'Sir, I respectfully disagree. We must rely on Athena for our protection, and use our radar to detect and kill the F-22s before they get within Sidewinder range.'

Nishimura refused to listen. He knew better.

Jiro looked down and left, at the tip of the bomb just visible under his left wing. The weapon was a white, supersonic shape.

At seven miles, Yan Chernov located the Russian tankers visually. They were in a trail formation, each plane a mile behind the others and stepped up a thousand feet. The lead tanker was the designated donor for the Tokyo strike.

Instead of swinging in behind the lead tanker, Chernov climbed several thousand feet and lined up a mile or so astern of the third tanker in line, Tail-end Charlie, the spare.

His wingman, Malakov, was on his right wing, of course, but much closer than he should be. Now less than a hundred feet separated them. When Chernov looked over, Malakov was signaling madly with his hands. No doubt in the next few seconds Malakov would break radio silence.

Chernov patted his head, then pointed at Malakov, the hand signal for passing the lead. Malakov patted his own head, confirming the lead change.

Now Malakov added throttle and his plane moved out in front of Chernov, who flipped his armament selector switch to 'Gun.' He didn't waste time. With Malakov moving away, Chernov eased the stick ever so gently to the right to turn in behind him. As the crosshair in the heads-up display approached the cockpit area of Malakov's fighter, Chernov squeezed the trigger on the stick. A river of fire vomited from the cannon at the rate of fifty 30-mm shells a second. Chernov didn't waste shells — at this point-blank range, a quarter-second burst was quite enough.

He released the trigger and pulled up abruptly.

Malakov's Sukhoi nosed over in a gentle parabola toward the earth 42,000 feet below.

A wave of fear and horror and self-loathing swept over Yan Chernov.

By an exercise of iron will, he forced himself back to the business at hand.

Armament selector switch to 'Missile,' green lights on all four missiles, radar lock on Tail-end Charlie, squeeze the trigger on the stick and wait one second.

Whoosh – the missile on the outboard station was away. It shot across the mile of sky separating the tanker from Chernov's fighter, then exploded in the area of the tail. The left wing of the tanker dropped precipitously; then the nose went down.

Chernov didn't have time to watch it fall. He had already locked up the middle tanker with the radar, and now he launched a missile at it. Four seconds later, the third missile left the rail, aimed at the lead tanker.

That missile, the third one, struck the first of the MiG-25s joining on the lead tanker to get fuel. The fighter exploded.

'Zeros,' Chernov shouted into the radio. 'Six Zeros.'

The Russian fighters scattered like flushed quail.

314

Chernov took his time. He doubled-checked the radar lock-on, ensured the last missile was slaved to it, then carefully squeezed the thing off.

It left with a flash, trailing a wisp of smoke, then turned toward Mother Earth seven miles below and disappeared into the haze at Mach 3.

Chernov switched back to 'Gun.' He was out of missiles.

Throttles forward, burners lit to close the distance quickly ... at a half mile, he had the HUD crosshairs on the tail of the large, defenseless four-engine tanker.

At a quarter of a mile he pulled the trigger. Like a laser beam, the streak of flame from the gun reached out and touched the tanker's fuselage. Chernov held the trigger down for a long burst.

Fire! A lick of fire from the fuselage, still absorbing fifty cannon shells a second.

The tanker's right wing dropped. Chernov was out of burner now, still closing, only a hundred meters aft. He pulled the crosshairs out to a wing, touched the trigger, then watched as the cannon shells cut it in half.

He released the trigger and slammed the stick left, trying to roll out of the doomed tanker's slipstream.

As he did a stream of tracers went over his head, just a few feet above the cockpit.

Yan Chernov didn't want to kill any more Russians. He rolled onto his back and pulled the nose straight down.

Several miles below, he saw a tanker – this must be the second one – descending in a circle and trailing a stream of fuel that stretched for a mile or so behind. He yanked his nose over and pulled the power back, deployed the speed brakes. He had to be sure. If one of the tankers survived to give fuel to a MiG-25, all this pain and blood would be for naught.

Even as he pulled the nose toward the tanker, the stream of fuel pouring from the injured tanker caught fire. Two seconds later the big four-engined airplane exploded with a dazzling flash.

Yan Chernov plummeted earthward. Somewhere above him, one of the members of the second section might be coming down behind, angling for a shot.

Chernov didn't look back.

When the call came from the White House on the satellite telephone, the duty officer took it. He handed it to Paul Scheer, who listened carefully, jotted some info on the duty officer's desk tablet, then said, 'Yes, sir' three times before he put the instrument back in its cradle.

'Four Zeros are on the way, all of them carrying nuclear weapons. They plan to nuke this base.'

'Where?' Cassidy asked.

'Right now they're just south of Khabarovsk. The White House wants us to intercept them and shoot them down.'

'The White House?' Cassidy asked when the shock of hearing the word *nuke* wore off a bit.

'You won't believe this, Skipper, but the voice sounded like President Hood's to me.'

That had been an hour ago. Now, Cassidy, Scheer, Dixie Elitch, and one other pilot, a man named Smith, were on their way eastward.

Before Cassidy manned up, he vomited on the concrete. Jiro was out there – Cassidy knew it. He *knew* it for a certainty.

He was living a nightmare.

'Are you okay, sir?' the crew chief asked.

'Must be something I ate,' Cassidy mumbled.

When Yan Chernov leveled off a few hundred feet above the ground, doing Mach 2, he looked over his shoulder. He was only human.

Nothing to the right, nothing to the left, nothing behind. The sky appeared empty. Where the other Russian fighters might be, he didn't know.

He scanned the terrain ahead, then the sky behind.

Nothing. ECM silent.

Fuel? The warning light on the instrument panel was lit. A thousand pounds remaining, perhaps.

He was in a valley headed north, with mountains to the east and west. The land below was covered with pines. There were no roads in sight, just an endless sea of green trees with the mountains in the distance.

He pulled the power to idle and pulled the nose up, zoom-climbing.

At five thousand feet, he saw the wandering scar of a dirt road through the forest.

He advanced the throttle to a cruise setting and picked the nose up to a level-flight attitude. He was doing less than five hundred knots now.

He should just jump out and be done with it. Wander in the forest until he starved or broke a leg.

He had his left hand on the ejection handle on the left side of the seat pan, but he didn't pull it.

Four hundred pounds of gas.

The road was beneath him now, running northwest toward the distant mountains. He turned to follow it.

A road would lead somewhere – to a place where there were people.

He didn't think consciously about any of this, but it was in the back of his mind.

The gauge for the main fuel cell still read a few hundred pounds above empty when the engines died.

Chernov let the plane slow to its best glide speed.

He straightened himself in the seat, put his head back in the rest, and pulled the ejection handle.

26

The flight of four F-22s leveled off at 38,000 feet, conning in the dust-laden sky. Bob Cassidy wasn't worried about the white ice crystals streaming behind the engines – visibility was so bad the Japanese wouldn't see the contrails.

He played with the satellite data down-link and adjusted his tac display. The screen was blank. That worried him. With the dust and the thermals, maybe the satellites weren't picking up the Zeros.

He looked longingly at the on-off switch for the radar. He badly wanted to turn it on, sweep the sky.

If the Americans missed the Zeros in this crud, everyone at Chita was going to be cremated alive. Assuming the brass in the White House war room knew what they were talking about.

This whole thing was insane. Nuclear weapons? In this day and age?

He was fretting, examining miserable options, when he realized he wasn't strapped to his ejection seat. Oh, he had armed the seat all right, just before takeoff. Unfortunately, he had forgotten to strap himself to it, so if he ejected he was going to be flying without wings or parachute. Even an angel needs wings, he thought.

He engaged the autopilot and began snapping Koch fittings, pulling straps tight. There.

Amazing how a man could forget that. Or maybe not. He had too much on his mind.

'Hey, Taco! Any word from Washington?'

Taco Rodriguez was the duty officer, sitting by the satellite telephone in Chita. The encrypted radio buzzed, then Cassidy heard Taco's voice.

'They rounded the corner at Khabarovsk, Hoppy, and left the tanker. Four of them, they say. About five hundred miles ahead of you. Call you back in a bit.'

'Thanks, Taco.'

The F-22s were making Mach 1.4, better than a thousand knots over the ground. Presumably, the Zeros were also supercruising. Five hundred miles – the flights would meet in about fifteen minutes.

A quarter of an hour. Not much. Just a whole lifetime.

He had just four F-22s to intercept the Zeros. Cassidy would have brought more along if he had had them. His only other planes, exactly two, were being swarmed over by mechanics. Several more planes were inbound from Germany, but this morning he had just four flyable fighters.

The ground crewmen had been pretty blasé about the whole gig when the pilots manned up, Cassidy thought. The word went around the base like wildfire: *The Japs are on their way to nuke us!* Still, the men did their jobs, slapped the pilots on the backs, grinned at them, and sent them on their way.

Just before the canopy closed, the crew chief had said to Cassidy, 'Go get 'em, sir.' Like it was a ball game or something. Like his ass wasn't also on the line.

Good-looking kid, the crew chief. Not Asian, of course, but he did look a bit like Jiro. About the same age and height, with jet black hair cut short.

Jiro wouldn't be out here in this dirty sky with a nuclear weapon strapped to his plane. Naw. He was probably back in Japan someplace, maybe even home with Shizuko. Sure.

Bob Cassidy wiped his eyes with a gloved hand and tried to concentrate. The tac display was still blank.

How good was that info the brass in Washington passed to Taco Rodriguez? Could Cassidy rely on it? There were two hundred Americans and several thousand Russian lives on the pass line at Chita. Just how many souls should you bet on that Washington techno-shit, Colonel Cassidy, sir?

Bob Cassidy lifted his left wrist and peeled back the Nomex flap to get a squint at his watch.

Fourteen minutes. He had fourteen minutes left in this life.

Dixie Elitch lifted the visor on her helmet and swabbed her face with her glove.

The dirty sky irritated her. Dirt at these altitudes was obscene, a crime against nature.

The Japs infuriated her. Nukes.

She checked her master armament switch, frowned at the blank tac display, and flicked her eyes around the empty yellow sky.

Maybe I should have stayed in California, found a decent man, she thought. God, there must be at least one in California.

'If I live through this experience, I am going back to California, going to find that man.' She told herself this aloud, talking into her oxygen mask over the drone of the engines reaching her through the airframe.

Well, Dixie, baby, that's a goddamn big if.

Paul Scheer was the calmest of the F-22 pilots. When he'd been diagnosed with a fatal disease three years ago, he had worked his way through the gamut of emotions one by one: denial, rage, lethargy, acceptance.

The comment that had struck him with the most impact during those days of shock and pain was a quote he had seen in a magazine in a waiting room: 'We are all voyagers between two eternities.'

Out of one eternity and into another. That's right. That's the truth of it.

Scheer sat relaxed, his eyes roaming the instrument panel.

Layton Robert Smith III, riding Scheer's wing, was an unhappy man. He shouldn't be here. He had been in the *United States* Air Force for nine years, nine peaceful, delightful years, cruising without sweat or strain toward the magic twenty. Eleven years from now he planned to retire from the blue suits and get a job flying corporate moguls in biz jets. Weekends in Aspen, nights in New York and San Fran, occasional hops to the Bahamas, he could handle it. Fly the plane when the paycheck man wanted to go, then kick back.

His mistake had been volunteering to fly an F-22 from Germany to these idiots at Chita. Praise God, if he lived through this he was going to get NEVER VOLUNTEER tattooed on his ass. In Chita, that damned Cassidy had shanghaied him, called Germany, said he needed Smith III 'on his team.'

And Colonel Blimp in Germany had said yes!

Layton Robert Smith III was scared, angry, and very much a fish out of water. He stared at his master armament switch, which was on.

Holy shit!

The Japanese were going to try to kill Smith III. The prospect made his blood feel like ice water pulsing through his temples.

He should have told Cassidy to stick it up his ass sideways. *Now* he knew that. What would Cassidy have done? Court-martial him for refusing to join the *Russian* air force? Hell, there was nothing Cassidy could do, Smith told himself now as he lawyered the case, then wondered why he hadn't thought of that two hours ago.

Maybe he should just turn around, boogie on back to Chita.

Look at this dust, would you! You don't see shit like this floating over the good ol' US of A. Or even in Germany. What the hell kind of country is this where you fly through dirt?

Smith III told himself he should quit worrying about the injustice of it all and concentrate on staying alive.

Jiro Kimura adjusted his infrared goggles. They were attached to his helmet above his oxygen mask, and they were too heavy. He would have to hold the helmet in place with his left hand while he pulled G's, or helmet, goggles and all, would pull his head down to his chest.

Maybe he wouldn't have to pull any G's. Perhaps the colonel was right about the radar. At least he had a plan.

Jiro looked at his watch. Shizuko was teaching at the kindergarten this morning. She was there now, telling stories to the children, singing songs, comforting the ones who needed a hug.

He had been so very lucky in his marriage. Shizuko was the perfect woman, without fault. She was the female half of him.

He loved her and missed her terribly.

With the goggles on, Jiro Kimura scanned the dusty sky. He suspected he would have only seconds to see the Americans and react – and not many seconds at that.

The forecasters had been wrong about this dust. There seemed to be no end to it.

He checked his watch again. Yes, it was time. Jiro gave a hand signal to his wingman, then pulled the power back and began a descent.

'Call the Japanese and Russian ambassadors,' President David Herbert Hood told the national security adviser, Jack Innes. 'Ask them to come to the White House again as soon as possible.' It was one o'clock in the morning in Washington.

Innes didn't ask questions. He got up from the table and went to a telephone in the back of the White House war room.

Hood turned to General Tuck, the chairman of the Joint Chiefs. 'It's time for us to get in the middle. Congress has been loath to get involved. Things have changed. We've got to step between these people before they trigger something no one can stop.'

'Yes, sir.'

'I want to get on television later this morning, when the sun comes up, talk to the nation and to the Japanese and Russian leadership.'

The secretary of state asked, 'Sir, shouldn't we get the congressional leadership over here first, get their input?'

'They can stand behind me when I talk to the nation. Putting out fires is my job, not theirs. And let's raise U.S. forces to Defense Condition One.'

'Whom are we going to fight?' General Tuck asked.

'Anybody who doesn't like the gospel I'm going to read to them.'

Bob Cassidy was breathing faster now, although he didn't notice it. As the minutes ticked by, he was sorely tempted to use the radar. What if the satellites couldn't pick the Zeros out of this goo? Maybe the Zeros' Athena gear wouldn't work.

'Taco, talk to me.'

'Hoppy, Washington says they are at your twelve-thirty, three hundred miles. Space Command is having some difficulty, they say ... but they won't say precisely what.'

Cassidy growled into his mask, shook his head to keep the sweat from his eyes.

He checked his watch again. If the Zeros were transmitting with their

320

radars, he should pick up the emissions. Maybe the Sentinel batteries had educated them. Perhaps the Zeros were running silent, as were the F-22s. In that case, the advantage would go to the side with outside help. The satellites were Cassidy's outside help, and just now they didn't seem all that reliable.

He played with the tac display, trying to coax a blip to appear on its screen. Nothing.

'Two-fifty miles, Hoppy.'

'Can the satellites see us?'

'Wait one.'

If the satellites could see the F-22s, Cassidy could safely divide his flight into sections, secure in the knowledge that the other three F-22s would remain on his tac display even though the dust blocked out the laser data link between planes. Of course, the question remained: If the satellites could see the Zeros, why weren't they appearing on the tactical displays?

And if the satellites were blind, the F-22s had to stay together to ensure they didn't shoot down one another.

Was it or wasn't it?

A minute passed, then another.

The tension was excruciating. Unable to stand it any longer, Cassidy was about to fire a verbal rocket at Taco when he got a bogey symbol on his scope, way out there, 260 miles away. He put the icon on the symbol and clicked with the mouse.

Zero. Quantity one plus. One thousand seventy-nine knots over the ground. Heading 244 degrees magnetic. Altitude four hundred, which meant forty thousand feet. Distance 257 miles 256 . . . 255 . . . The numbers flipped over every 1.8 seconds.

'Stick with me, gang,' he said into the radio, and turned left thirty degrees. He would go out to the north, then turn and come in from the side, shooting at optimum range as the F-22s flew into the Zeros' right-stern quarter.

When he was ten miles or so to the north of the Zeros' track, Cassidy turned back to his original course. The two formations rocketed toward each other.

Please, God. We need to kill these guys. It's a hell of a thing to ask you for other men's deaths, but these guys are carrying nukes. If even one gets through, they could kill everyone at Chita.

His formation was where it should be, spread out but not too much so — everyone in sight in the little six-mile visibility bowl.

Cassidy wondered what his wingmen were thinking. Perhaps it was better that he didn't know.

Still only one plus on the quantity of Zeros. *Damn the wizards and techno-fools!*

Fifty miles . . . forty . . . thirty . . . At twenty, Cassidy spoke into the radio:

'Okay, gang, get ready for a right turn-in behind these guys. Try for a Sidewinder lock. On my word, we will each fire one missile. Then we will continue to close and kill survivors.'

'Two, roger,' replied Dixie.

'Three's got it,' said Scheer.

'Four,' Smith answered.

Cassidy would not have brought Smith if Taco hadn't been trying to get over a case of diarrhea; the idiot drank some water from the shower spigot. Joe Malan was fighting a sinus infection, the others were exhausted: Cassidy had kept planes in the air over the base every minute he could these past few weeks.

Smith had no combat experience, none whatever. Still, he was the only person Cassidy had to put in a cockpit, so he had to fly. Life isn't fair.

'Turn . . . now!'

Cassidy laid his fighter into the turn. The Zeros continued on their 244-degree heading. After ninety degrees of turn, the Zeros were dead on his nose, ninety degrees off, five miles ahead, and two thousand feet above him, according to the tac display. Cassidy looked through the heads-up display and got a glimpse of one, then lost it.

Damn this dust!

He got a rattle from his Sidewinder. It had locked on a heat source. Cassidy kept the turn in. His flight was sweeping in behind the Zeros.

Through his HUD, he saw specks. Zeros. Two.

Two?

Were there other Zeros? Where were they?

'Let 'em have it, gang.' Cassidy touched off a 'winder. 'There's only two Japs in front of us. They've mousetrapped us.'

'Red Three, the Americans are behind us. I have them in sight.' Colonel Nishimura made this broadcast over his encrypted radio, and fifteen miles behind him, twenty thousand feet below, Jiro Kimura heard his words.

Jiro and his wingman turned their radars to transmit.

Yes. The four F-22s appeared as if by magic.

'Five miles at your four-thirty position, Red One,' Jiro said into the radio as he locked up the closest F-22 and pushed the red button on his stick. The first missile roared away.

As he was locking up his second target, his wingman fired a missile.

They alternated, putting six missiles in the air.

Meanwhile, Colonel Nishimura turned hard right and his wingman turned hard left, pulling six G's each, trying to evade the missiles the Americans had just put into the air.

Bob Cassidy knew for certain he had been ambushed when his ECM indicators lit up. The strobe pointed back over his left shoulder; the aural warning began deedling; the warning light on the HUD labeled 'Missile' lit up, then seconds later began flashing. The Japanese planes behind him had just launched missiles.

Cassidy already had fired his first missile. As the targets in front of him separated, he squeezed off a second at the target turning right, Colonel Nishimura, although he didn't know who was in the plane.

Cassidy's chaff dispensers kicked out chaff bundles and the ECM tried electronically to fool the radars in the missiles aimed at him. All this was done automatically, without Cassidy's input.

Bob Cassidy was busily trying to turn a square corner to force any missiles chasing him to overshoot. He lit his afterburners and pulled smoothly back to eleven G's, two more than his airplane was designed to take. His vision narrowed, he screamed to stay conscious, and the two missiles behind him overshot.

Nishimura's wingman signed his own death warrant when he turned left, a flight path that carried him out in front of the Americans. Two Sidewinders were aimed at him, and they had no trouble zeroing in. The first went up his tailpipe and exploded; the second went off twelve inches above the main fuel tank, puncturing the tank with hundreds of bits of shrapnel and shredding it. The plane caught fire in a fraction of a second.

Without thinking, the pilot pulled the ejection handle. He died instantly when the ejection seat fired him from the protection of the cockpit. A sonic shock wave built up on his body and disemboweled him before he and his ejection seat could slow to subsonic speed.

Nishimura was lucky. Two of the missiles fired at him went for decoy flares that he had punched off. The other failed to hack his turn. Unfortunately, his flight path was taking him into the area directly downrange of the Americans.

Jiro Kimura's first missile smashed into Paul Scheer's airplane several feet forward of the tail. Scheer knew something was wrong when he lost control of the plane – it simply stopped responding to control inputs. Instinctively, he glanced at the annunciator panel, which told him of problems with the plane's health; he saw that every light there was lit.

What the lights and engine gauges could not tell him was that the plane had broken into two pieces. The tail was no longer attached to the main fuselage.

He glanced at the airspeed indicator. Still supersonic.

The nose was falling and the stick position had no effect. It was then that Scheer glanced in the rearview mirror and realized the tail was gone.

The attitude indicators showed the plane in a steepening dive. He retarded the throttle to idle and popped the speed brakes open. They came completely out and would probably have slowed the plane below Mach 1 had it not been going straight down.

Then the plane began to spin like a Frisbee.

Paul Scheer fought to stay conscious. He wanted to experience every second of life left to him.

Layton Robert Smith III never realized Japanese planes were behind the Americans, so the explosion that blew off half his left wing was a complete surprise.

He had managed to get one Sidewinder in the air and was preparing to launch another at Colonel Nishimura when the explosion occurred under his wing. He had his ECM gear on and the audio warnings properly adjusted, but in the adrenaline-drenched excitement of shooting missiles to kill people, he never heard the warnings or saw the flashing lights.

Shooting to kill *was* exciting. He had never felt so alive. He had never even *suspected* that the joy of killing another human being could be this sublime.

Then the Japanese warhead went off under his wing and his plane rolled uncontrollably, faster and faster and faster. He blacked out from the G, despite the best efforts of his full-body G suit. When the G meter indicated sixteen times the force of gravity, Layton Robert Smith III's heart stopped. He was dead.

The coffin of steel, titanium, and exotic metals containing his corpse smashed into the earth forty-two seconds later.

One of the missiles missed Bob Cassidy by such a wide distance that its proximity fuse failed to detonate the warhead. There was another radar target beyond Cassidy, one slowing to subsonic speed in a very hard turn. The missile might have missed it – the angle-off and speeds involved were beyond the missile's guidance capability – had not the target turned toward the oncoming missile – turned just enough.

The proximity fuse in the missile detonated this time. The shrapnel penetrated the cockpit canopy and decapitated Colonel Nishimura. The hit was a one-in-a-million fluke, a tragic accident.

Dixie Elitch somehow avoided the shower of missiles that killed Scheer and Smith. She had also turned a square corner, and now she found that she had a head-on shot developing with one of the Japanese planes far below, one of the two that had fired the missiles. Both these planes were now on her tac display. She locked up a Sidewinder and fired it, then another.

One of the missiles guided; the other went stupid.

Dixie didn't have time to watch. Her ECM was wailing, so she pulled straight back on the stick and lit her burners. She wanted to get well above this fur ball and pick her moment to come down.

Jiro Kimura knew that if he remained in this dogfight, the odds of being the last man left alive were slim. The Zeros had come to bomb Chita, not to shoot down American fighters. Kimura rolled over on his back and pulled his nose straight down. Going downhill, he came out of burner in case one of the Americans was squirting off Sidewinders.

He rotated his plane onto the course he wanted, 260 degrees, and began his pullout. He would get down on the deck and race for Chita while the Americans milled about with Nishimura and the others.

The last Japanese pilot in the fight was Hideo Nakagawa, who had the reputation as the best fledgling pilot in the Japanese Self-Defense Force. He came by it honestly. He was very, very good.

And he was lucky. The first Sidewinder Dixie Elitch triggered in his direction went stupid off the rail; the second lost its lock on his tailpipe and zagged away randomly after six seconds of flight.

The instant Nakagawa realized the second missile was not tracking, he pulled his plane around to target Bob Cassidy, who had come to the conclusion that both the Zeros in front of him were fatally damaged and so was completing his turn toward the threat in his rear quadrant.

Both pilots were in burner – Nakagawa in a slight climb, Cassidy in a gentle descent. And both were almost at Mach 2.

Nakagawa managed to get a lock on Cassidy, whom he saw only as a radar target. He squeezed off the radar-guided missile, then pulled his infrared goggles down over his eyes to see if he could locate the American visually. There he was! At about five miles. Nakagawa switched to 'Gun.'

Cassidy saw the flash of the missile's engine igniting under Nakagawa's wing or he would never have been able to avoid it. He pulled the stick aft into another square corner while he punched off decoy chaff and flares.

The missile maintained its radar lock on Cassidy's plane, but it couldn't hack the ten-G turn. It went under Cassidy and exploded harmlessly.

Nakagawa pulled with all his might to get a lead on Cassidy's rising plane. As the two fighters rocketed toward each other, he squeezed off a burst of cannon fire, then overshot into a vertical scissors.

Canopy-to-canopy, Bob Cassidy and Hideo Nakagawa went straight up, corkscrewing, each trying to fly slower than the other plane and fall in behind. The winner of this contest would get a shot; the loser would die.

Nakagawa dropped his landing gear.

When he saw Nakagawa's nosewheel come out of the well, Cassidy thought he had the stroke. Nakagawa drifted aft with authority.

Cassidy shot out in front. He jammed both throttles to the stops, lit the burners, and pulled until he felt the stall buffet, bringing the plane over on its back, all the while waiting for cannon shells to hit him between the shoulder blades.

Nakagawa had a problem. The designers of the Zero had placed a safety circuit in the gun system to prevent it from being accidentally fired with the airplane sitting on the ground. Only by manually shifting a switch in the nosewheel well could the cannon be fired with the gear extended. Another peculiarity of the Zero was the fact that the pilot must wait for the gear to extend completely before he reversed the cycle and raised them again. Nakagawa sat in his Zero, indicating 240 knots, waiting for the gear to come up while watching Bob Cassidy dive cleanly away. Furious, he screamed into his mask.

He stopped screaming when a Sidewinder missile went blazing by his aircraft, headed for Mother Earth. He looked up, keeping his left hand under the infrared goggles, just in time to see an F-22 turning in behind him.

Fortunately the gear-in-transit light was out, so he turned hard into his attacker.

The slow speed of Nakagawa's Zero caused Dixie Elitch to misjudge the lead necessary. Her first cannon burst smote air and nothing else.

She was going too fast. She overshot the accelerating, turning Zero. With engines at idle and speed brakes out, she pulled G to slow and stay with her corkscrewing opponent.

This guy was damned good! Amazingly, his nose was rising and he was somehow gaining an angular advantage.

The G's were awesome, smashing viciously at her. She fought to stay conscious, to keep the enemy fighter in sight.

He was canopy-to-canopy with her, descending through twenty thousand feet. He was close . . . too close. Somehow she had to get some maneuvering room.

She slammed the stick sideways, fed in forward stick. The other plane kept his position on her as she rolled. She stopped the roll and brought the stick back a little. Instantly, the enemy plane was closing, canopy-to-canopy . . . fifty feet between the planes. She looked straight into his cockpit, looked at his helmet tilted back, at him looking at her as they rolled around each other with engines at idle and speed brakes out. She saw the infrared goggles and in a flash realized what they were. So that is how he kept track of the invisible F-22!

What she failed to realize was that Nakagawa was trying to hold his helmet and goggles in position with his left hand while he flew with his right. What he needed was a third hand to operate the throttle.

Then he was above her, on his back . . . and too slow, out of control. He released the stick with his right hand and reached across his body to slam the throttle forward.

Dixie realized Nakagawa had stalled as his plane fell toward her. Before she could react, the two planes collided, canopy-to-canopy.

Bob Cassidy had pulled out far below and relit his burners to climb back

into the fight. He was rocketing up toward the two corkscrewing fighters –
two on his HUD, but he could only see the Zero. They were too close
together to risk a shot.

Just as he caught a glimpse of the F-22 alongside the Zero, the two
fighters embraced.

The planes bounced apart, then exploded.

Jesus!

Cassidy rolled and went under the fireball.

Jiro Kimura was on the deck, streaking toward Chita with both burners lit.
His radar was off. His GPS gave him the bearing and distance: 266 degrees
at 208 miles.

Using nuclear weapons was insanity, but Japan's lawful government
made the decision and gave the order. Jiro Kimura had sworn to obey. He
was going to do just that, even if it cost him his life.

Right now imminent death seemed a certainty: he was hurtling toward it
at 1.6 times the speed of sound. The odds were excellent that more F-22s
would intercept him very soon. They were probably maneuvering to
intercept at this very second.

Even if he dropped the weapon successfully, he would not have the gas to
get back to the tanker waiting over Khabarovsk. He was using that gas now
to maximize his chances of getting to his drop point. He was going to be
shot down or eject. If he ejected, the Siberian wilderness would kill him
slowly. If by some miracle he lived, the nuclear burden would probably ruin
him.

All this was in the back of his mind, but he wasn't really thinking about
it; he was thinking how to get to the weapon-release point. He had F-22s
behind and F-22s ahead, he believed. And at Chita, the Americans had those
missiles that rode up his radar beam.

Jiro Kimura didn't think he was going to get much older.

Where, he wondered, was Bob Cassidy? Was he in one of the F-22s that
had been shot down, or was he in one of the planes waiting ahead?

A warning light caught his eye. Athena! The super-cooled computer was
overheating. He turned it off.

At that moment, Cassidy was fifty miles behind.

The last Zero was not on his tac display. The dust in the air must have
screwed up the satellite's ability to see planes in the atmosphere, he
reflected.

According to the White House, there had been four Zeros, each carrying
a bomb. Three had gone down; the last had escaped. If the pilot abandoned
his mission and returned to base, there was no problem. Knowing the
professionalism and dedication of the Japanese pilots, Cassidy discounted
that possibility.

If the pilot had gone on alone to bomb Chita, there was no one there to stop him. So Cassidy zoomed to forty thousand feet and lit his afterburners. Just now he was making Mach 2.2, maximum speed, toward Chita.

The blank tac display was a silent witness to the fact that the three F-22s he had taken off with were no longer in the air.

The radio was silent.

He had to find that enemy plane. Dixie Elitch was certainly dead, killed in the explosion of those two planes just a moment ago. Smith III and Paul Scheer . . . who knew? Maybe they managed to eject. Then again, maybe not.

He had to catch that Zero. He checked his fuel. If that plane reached Chita . . .

Cassidy reached for the radar switch, turned it on. It might not help, but it couldn't hurt.

He wondered which plane Jiro had been in.

Jiro was one of the best they had, so he was undoubtedly one of them. Even as Cassidy thought about it, the question answered itself. The best pilots always find a way to survive. One Zero was still in the air. With a growing sense of horror, the possibility that Jiro Kimura was in the cockpit of that plane congealed into a certainty.

Yes. *It must be Jiro!*

The ECM indicated that an F-22 was behind him. Jiro watched the strobe of the direction indicator. Yep!

The American probably hadn't seen him yet, which gave him a few options. He could turn right or left, try to sneak out to the side. Or he could turn and engage. If he kept on this heading, the American would get within detection range before Jiro got to the drop point; then he would launch a missile.

Jiro turned hard left ninety degrees, as quickly as he could to minimize the time that the planform of his airplane was pointed toward the enemy reflecting radar energy.

Cassidy saw the blip appear. Forty-three miles. It was there for a few seconds; then it wasn't.

The enemy pilot turned.

Right or left? At least he had a 50 percent chance of getting this right.

Right. He turned twenty degrees right and stared at the radar. In a minute or so, he would know. Luckily, he was faster than the Zero, but only because he was high. The thinner air allowed him to go faster.

The seconds ticked by. He couldn't afford to wait too long for this guy to appear, or he would never catch him if he went the other way. But he had to wait long enough to be sure.

Cassidy swabbed the sweat from his eyes.

The enemy pilot must be Jiro.

If he turned left too soon, before he was certain that Jiro wasn't ahead of him, he was giving Jiro a free pass to kill everyone at Chita – all of them.

Dixie was already dead. Scheer. Foy Sauce. Hudek.

When the sixty seconds expired, Cassidy turned forty degrees left. He had made up his mind – one minute. Not a second less or a second more.

Steady on the new course, he wondered if he should have stayed on the other course longer.

Dear God, where is this Zero?

By the time Jiro realized the American had turned back toward him, it was too late. The American fighter was too close. If he turned now, the American pilot would pick him up for sure. Yet if he stayed on this heading – once again he was pointed straight for Chita – the American would see him before many miles passed.

Perhaps . . .

He applied left rudder and moved the stick right, cross-controlling. Perhaps he could make a flat turn.

Cassidy was beside himself. He couldn't think, couldn't decide on the best course of action. The Japanese fighter had escaped him.

Every decision he had made had turned out badly. His comrades were dead, a Zero had escaped . . . and a boy he loved like his own son was either dead or was flying that plane and going to kill everyone at Chita – with one bomb.

He swung the nose of the plane from side to side, S-turning, watching the tactical display intently. If the radar picked up anything, it would appear there.

Nothing. Bob Cassidy came out of burner to save some gas and laid the F-22 over into a turn. He would do a 360-degree turn, see if he could see anything. If not, he would go to Chita and sit overhead, waiting for the Zero to show up. Of course, the Zero pilot would probably announce his presence by popping a large mushroom cloud.

There it is! *There!* A coded symbol appeared on the radar screen and on the tac display.

Cassidy slammed the throttles into maximum afterburner. The fighter seemed to leap forward.

Although Jiro Kimura didn't know it, the F-22 Raptor was so high, looking down, that its radar had picked up a return from the junction between his left vertical stabilizer and the fuselage.

He realized the enemy pilot had him when he saw the ECM strobe getting longer and broader. The F-22 was closing the distance between them, and that could only mean that he was tracking the Zero.

Jiro had no choice. He dropped a wing and turned to engage.

Since he had the nuclear weapon taking up a weapons station on his left wing, Jiro had had only two radar-guided missiles, and he had shot them both. He had also fired a Sidewinder, leaving him one.

As the two fighters raced for each other, he got a heat lock-on tone and squeezed it off.

Cassidy was already out of burner and popping flares. He didn't have the Zero visually, but this guy wouldn't wait. He would shoot as soon as possible, and Cassidy was betting that since he wasn't using his radar, he would shoot a Sidewinder.

When the missile came popping out of the yellow haze from almost dead ahead, Cassidy rolled hard right, then pulled the stick into the pit of his stomach.

Pull, pull, fight the unconsciousness trying to tug you under while the chaff dispenser pops out decoy flares . . . And the missile went off behind the F-22.

The Zero was turning back toward Chita. Cassidy had him again on the tac display.

How far is Chita?

Holy . . . it's only thirty miles.

This guy is almost there!

With his nose stuffed down, Cassidy came down on the fleeing Zero like a hawk after a sparrow.

At six miles, he visually acquired the Zero, which appeared as a small dot against the pale, yellowish sky.

The speed he gained in the descent was the only edge Cassidy had or he would never have caught Jiro Kimura.

Perhaps he should have launched his last missiles at him, or closed to gun range and torn his plane apart with the cannon. He did neither.

Cassidy came down, down, down, closing the range relentlessly.

He knew Jiro was flying the Zero. He had to be.

He wanted it to be Jiro.

Looking over his shoulder, holding his helmet and infrared goggles, Kimura saw the F-22 at about three miles. The pilot kept the closure rate high.

There is time, Jiro thought. *If I yank this thing around, I can take a head-on shot with the cannon.*

But he didn't turn.

He was flying at four hundred feet above the ground. He put his plane in a gentle left turn, about a ten-degree angle of bank. He glanced over his shoulder repeatedly, waiting for the approaching pilot to pull lead for a gun shot.

And he waited.

It's Cassidy! He's going to kill me because I couldn't kill him.

330

The distance was now about three hundred meters.

Two hundred . . .

One hundred meters, and the F-22 was making no attempt to pull lead. It was still closing, maybe thirty or forty knots.

Jiro realized with a jolt what was going to happen.

He grabbed a handful of stick, jerked it hard aft.

The damned helmet . . . He couldn't hold it up, so he lost sight of the incoming F-22.

Bob Cassidy's left wingtip sliced into the right vertical stabilizer of the Zero.

The planes were climbing at about fifty degrees nose-up when they came together.

Jiro felt the jolt and instinctively rolled left, away from the shadowy presence above and behind him. This roll cost him the right horizontal stabilator, which was snapped off like a dead twig by the left wing of the F-22.

Two feet of the left wingtip broke off the F-22, which was in an uncontrolled roll to the right.

Bob Cassidy's eyes went straight to the airspeed indicator. He'd had enough time in fighters to have learned the lesson well – never eject supersonic.

Fortunately, the climb, the lack of burner, and the retarded throttles – he had pulled them to idle just as his wing sliced into the Zero – combined to slow the F-22. In seconds, it was slowing through five hundred knots.

Amazingly, Cassidy regained control. He automatically slammed the stick left to stop the roll, and the plane obeyed. He dipped the wing farther, looking for the Zero.

There! The enemy fighter was slowing and streaming fuel.

Get out, Jiro! Get out before it explodes!

Jiro Kimura fought against the aerodynamic forces tearing at the crippled fighter. He had no idea how much damage his plane had sustained in the collision, but at least it wasn't rolling or tumbling violently.

He glanced in the rearview mirror, then looked again. The right vertical stab was gone!

And the right horizontal stab!

Even as the damage registered on his mind, the plane began rolling. He saw the plume of fuel in his rearview mirror.

Jiro tried to stop the roll with the stick.

The roll continued, wrapping up.

Sky and earth changed places rapidly.

The airspeed read three hundred knots, so Jiro pulled the ejection handle.

When he saw the Japanese pilot riding his ejection seat from his rolling fighter, Bob Cassidy devoted his whole attention to flying his own plane.

With full left rudder and right stick, the thing was still going through the air.

Chita was fifteen miles northwest.

Bob Cassidy gently banked in that direction. He looked below, in time to see Jiro Kimura's parachute open.

He pulled the power back, let the badly wounded fighter slow toward 250 knots. As the speed dropped he fed in more and more rudder and stick.

He sensed that the airplane would not fly slowly enough for him to land it. Forget the gear and flaps – he would run out of control throw before he slowed to gear speed. He was going to have to eject. And he didn't care. A deep lethargy held Bob Cassidy in its grip.

Ten miles to Chita.

After all, in the grand scheme of things, the fate of individuals means very little. Nothing breaks the natural stride of the universe.

But he was still a man with responsibilities. 'Taco, this is Hoppy.'

'Yo, Hoppy.'

'All four of the enemy strike planes are down. I am the last one of ours still airborne.'

'Copy that.'

'Relay it, please, on to Washington.'

'Roger that.'

'And tell the crash guys to look for me. I'm about to eject over the base.'

'Copy. Good luck, Hoppy.'

'Yeah.'

He kept the speed up around three hundred. The plane flew slightly sideways and warning lights flashed all over the instrument panel as the base runways came closer and closer.

When he was past the hangar area, with the plane pointed toward Moscow, Bob Cassidy pulled the ejection handle.

27

Two mechanics driving a Ford pickup found Jiro Kimura in an area of scrub trees on the side of a hill ten miles from the air base. Jiro had broken his right leg during the ejection. When found, he was still attached to his parachute, which was draped over a small tree.

After the mechanics got the Japanese pilot to the makeshift dispensary, Bob Cassidy went to see him. He just stood looking at him, trying to think of something to say.

'I figured it was you flying that plane, Jiro.'

'And I knew it was you behind me.'

Cassidy didn't know what to add.

'The doc is going to set your leg. They'll give you a sedative. We'll talk tomorrow.'

'You should have killed me, Bob.'

'Shizuko would have never forgiven me.'

Jiro didn't say anything.

'I would have never forgiven myself,' Bob Cassidy said to Jiro Kimura. Then he walked away.

Cassidy sat down on a rock outside the building and ran his fingers through his hair. He could hear a television that someone had turned up loud. The satellite dish was in the lawn in front of Cassidy.

President Hood was speaking. Cassidy could hear his voice.

The sun was warm on his skin.

He was sitting like that, half-listening to the television, imagining the faces of his dead pilots, when he realized Dick Guelich was squatting beside him.

'Hoppy, I was thinking perhaps we should send the Cessna to look for survivors. The others who went with you this morning? Did anyone . . .'

'They're dead.' His mouth was so dry, the words were almost impossible to understand. He cleared his throat and repeated them. 'They're dead.'

'Dixie?'

'Midair with a Zero,' Cassidy whispered. 'In a dogfight. Didn't see a chute.'

'Scheer and Smith?'

'Hit by missiles, I think. At those speeds . . .' He gestured to the east. 'Send the Cessna. Let 'em look.'

'I'm sorry, Colonel.'

'Get those other two airplanes up. Have the pilots go out at least a hundred miles. Make sure they are no more than twenty miles apart, so one can help the other if he's jumped.'

'I've briefed them, sir.'

'When those planes from Germany land, fuel them and get them armed. Send the pilots to me for a brief. I don't think the Japs will try it again but they might.'

'Yes, sir,' Guelich said, and he was gone.

It felt good to sit. He had neither the energy nor desire to move.

Poor Dixie. Now, there was a woman.

The sun seemed to melt him, make him so tired that he couldn't sit up. He slid down to the grass, put his back against the rock.

'I did my best, Sabrina . . . Honestly . . .'

When the tears came, there was no way to stop them. Bob Cassidy didn't try.

The bayonet was in excellent condition even though it was old. The army issued it to Atsuko Abe's father when he was inducted in 1944 at the age of sixteen. Of course, the elder Abe never saw combat. If he had, presumably the bayonet would now decorate the home of some American veteran's son. The boy soldier spent his military career guarding antiaircraft ammunition dumps in northern Japan. The army disintegrated after the war. Abandoning his Arisaka rifle, young Abe hitchhiked back to his home village. For reasons that he never explained, he kept the bayonet and the scabbard that housed it.

Almost a small sword, the bayonet was about eighteen inches long, with a straight, narrow blade. It had a wooden handle, which suited it admirably for military tasks like slashing brush and opening cans. Originally the blade was not very sharp, but as a youngster Atsuko had ground a keen edge on the steel, including the tip. In a nation with strict laws on the ownership of handguns, the old bayonet made a formidable weapon.

Abe always displayed it on a small wooden stand designed to hold a samurai sword, across the room from his shrine.

This evening Atsuko Abe sent the servants away. He ensured the doors to the prime minister's residence were locked, then retreated to his chamber, where he bathed and donned a silk kimono that his wife had given him years ago, before she died.

He spent some time sitting on a mat in front of his shrine writing letters. He wrote one to his sister, his only living relative, and one to the emperor, Hirohito, son of the late Emperor Naruhito. He apologized to them both.

He asked his sister's forgiveness for shaming the family. He begged forgiveness of the young emperor for failing Japan. The Japan of which Abe spoke was not the workaday nation of crowded cities, apartments, factories, and tiny farms where he had lived most of his life; it was an idealized Japan that probably only existed in his dreams.

The brush strokes on the white rice paper had a haunting beauty. Oh, what might have been! Abe finished the letter to the emperor and signed his name. He put each letter in an envelope, sealed it, wrote the name of the recipient, and placed the envelopes on the shrine.

The final letter was to his father, who had been dead for twenty years. He explained his dreams for Japan, his belief in her greatness, and bitterly told of the shipwreck of those dreams. He had misjudged the Japanese people, he said. They had betrayed him. And themselves. It was shameful, yet it was the truth, and future generations would have to face it.

That letter also went into an envelope, but after putting it on the shrine and praying, he dropped it into the incense burner, where it was consumed. Abe lit a stick of incense and watched the smoke rise toward heaven. He wafted some of the smoke toward him so he could get a sniff.

Finally Atsuko Abe realized he just wanted to get it over with. He was ready for the pain, ready for whatever comes after life.

He bared his belly, then drew the bayonet from its scabbard. The ancient and honorable way to commit the act of *seppuku*, or *hara-kiri*, is to stab deep into the belly, pull the blade across the stomach, severing the aorta, then turn the blade in the wound and pull it upward. The cuts lead to massive internal hemorrhaging, and death soon follows. The disadvantage is that few men have what it takes to inflict this kind of injury upon themselves. To preserve their honor, condemned samurai in olden days equipped themselves with an assistant, the *kaishaku-nin*, usually a close friend, who would decapitate the warrior after he had made the ritual cut, or before, if the assistant glimpsed the slightest indication of pain or irresolution.

Of course, Abe had no *kaishaku*, for his honor demanded that he suffer.

Atsuko Abe reached forward and grasped the handle of the bayonet with both hands. He took several deep breaths, readying himself. To fail here would dishonor him still further.

Sweat popped out on his brow. He said one last prayer and, using both hands, rammed the bayonet deep into his gut.

The pain about felled him.

With steadfast courage, he pulled the sharp blade across his belly. He got it about halfway when his strength failed him. The pain robbed him of his resolve. He summoned all his will and courage and twisted the blade.

The agony was astounding.

The final cut and it would be all over.

Moaning, gnashing his teeth, and trying to stifle a scream he felt welling up, he pulled the handle upward.

His hands slipped.

There was only a little blood seeping out of the wound. If he didn't get the blade out, he would suffer here for a week.

With one last mighty heave, he pulled the bayonet free of his flesh. The little sword got away from him, flew halfway across the room and landed with a clatter.

The blood came better now, although the pain was only a little less than with the blade in.

Try as he might, he could not remain sitting upright. He toppled slowly onto his side.

He bit his lip, then his tongue. Blood flowed from his mouth, mixed with the perspiration that covered his face.

He should have drunk more wine. That would have dulled the pain.

At least honor was satisfied. He had failed Japan, but not his honorable ancestors, whom he soon would join.

Time passed. How much, he didn't know. His mind wandered as he slipped in and out of consciousness.

Then he heard a man's voice. Doors opening. A questioning voice. His senses sharpened; the pain in his stomach threatened to overwhelm him.

The door to his room slid open. He tried to turn to see.

Abe caught a glimpse of the face. It was the chief of the domestic staff. A civil servant in his fifties, the man had risen through the ranks of the domestic staff since joining it as a young man. Now the staff chief stood wordlessly, taking it all in, then left, closing the door behind him.

Atsuko Abe moved, trying to ease the agony. Nothing seemed to work.

When he realized he was groaning, he began actively chewing on his lips and tongue. Anything to keep from shaming himself further.

Episodes of the past few months played over and over in his mind: the meetings with his ministers; General Yamashita; Emperor Naruhito; speaking before the Diet. The jumbled, mixed scenes ran through his mind over and over again.

Oh, if only he had it to do one more time.

A door opened below. The sound was unmistakable. What was the time? The small hours of the morning. The staff chief had been here – what? Two hours ago, at least.

Who could this be?

The door opened.

A woman was standing there. Abe tried to focus.

She came across the room, stood in front of him.

Masako. Empress Masako.

Shame flushed Atsuko Abe, then turned to outrage. That a woman should see him like this! The staff chief had dishonored him, the prime minister.

'Your Majesty,' he managed. Summoning every ounce of strength he possessed, he managed to lever himself into a sitting position. 'Please leave me. You shame me with your presence.'

She stood before him, looking around, taking in the blood-soaked white mat, the bayonet, the shrine, saying nothing. She was wearing a simple Western two-piece wool suit, white gloves, sensible shoes, and a stylish matching hat. In her left hand she held a small white purse embroidered with pearls.

She looked down at the purse and opened it. Using her right hand, she extracted a pistol.

'Your Majesty, no. I beg –'

'This,' she said evenly, 'is for my husband. And my son.'

With that, she leveled the pistol and shot Atsuko Abe in the center of his forehead. His corpse toppled forward.

Empress Masako put the pistol back in the purse, snapped the catch, and walked out of the room without a backward glance.

The two weeks after the untimely death of Aleksandr Kalugin were busy ones for Janos Ilin. He helped with the security at Marshal Stolypin's inauguration, and he assisted police in rounding up and disarming Kalugin's loyal ones. He whispered long and loudly to prosecutors about which loyal ones should be brought to trial. He argued that Kalugin's key lieutenants had to answer for their crimes. Private armies, he thought, were bad for democracy and bad for business. President Stolypin helped carry the day. He didn't think much of private armies, either.

One evening Janos Ilin sat in his office, trying to assess the pluses and minuses of the late Russo-Japanese War. Tomorrow Captain First Rank Pavel Saratov and the surviving crewmen of the submarine *Admiral Kolchak* were flying in from Tokyo. President Stolypin would meet them at the airport and decorate every man. Saratov would be declared a hero of the Russian Republic and be promoted to rear admiral. From the reports Ilin had seen, Saratov richly deserved the honor.

Today the American president had announced a new foreign-aid bill for Russia, the largest in American history, one that for the first time gave substantial tax credits to American firms that invested in Russia. And soon American firms would have money to invest. The last two weeks had been the biggest in the history of the American stock market. Everyone, it seemed, had suddenly decided that peace was wonderful.

Atsuko Abe's death led to a new government in Japan, one that Ilin thought might be more attuned to the future than the past. The inescapable fact was that Russia was rich in natural resources and Japan had capital and technical know-how. Put together in the right kind of partnerships, there should be something there for everyone.

Something for everyone was the way the world worked best, Janos Ilin thought. Soon it would be time for Agent Ju to send another message to

Toshihiko Ayukawa. This time Ju would point out the best people in Russia to approach for Siberian joint ventures, people who could make things happen.

For a while there, Ilin thought Ju's message reporting the destruction of all of Russia's nuclear weapons had backfired. For months the outcome of that gambit had looked grim indeed. Still, looking back, he thought – as he had when he drafted the message – that enormous risks were justified. Russia had little to lose and everything to gain if a foreign enemy forced her to fight.

The nuclear raids on Japan had been a close squeak. He had never suspected Kalugin would go over the edge, order the use of nuclear weapons. Fortunately, nothing had come of it, but Kalugin certainly had tried.

Yuri Esenin and the bombs on board a *Kilo*-class sub – that was an effort doomed from the beginning. Only the skill and courage of Pavel Saratov had allowed the sub to get as far as it did.

The air raids on Japan were another matter. When they were launched, the spymaster thought his worst nightmare had come true. Then the planes just disappeared.

Ilin, of course, set out to discover what had happened.

After reading the reports of the interrogations of the survivors of the Tokyo/Tateyama Peninsula raids, Ilin thought it likely that Yan Chernov had shot down the Russian tankers, dooming all the planes to crash landings. It was his voice, two survivors believed, that warned of airborne Zeros, yet not a single enemy fighter had been seen.

One of Ilin's agents in an American seismic exploration unit working in Siberia said that a man answering Chernov's description had shown up two days after the raid attempt with only a flight suit on his back, nothing else. The Americans fed him and gave him a job. He was still there, the informant said.

Either Chernov or the Japanese had shot down the Russian tankers, dooming the strike planes. Whichever, Ilin thought the nuclear strike on Japan was a matter best forgotten.

Poor Russia, a land without hope. Now it had some. With Kalugin gone, with the government rejuvenated and foreign nations willing to make investments, hope was peeping through the rubble.

Perhaps hope would continue to grow. With all this hope and billions in foreign capital, Russia might even grow into a country worthy of its patriots, men like Yan Chernov and Pavel Saratov.

Time would tell.

Cuba

To Tyler

Acknowledgements

In theory a speculative work of adventure fiction has the same requirement for technical accuracy as a story about space aliens set in the thirtieth century, yet as a practical matter many readers demand that this author at least stay in reality's neighborhood while spinning his tales. For their aid in contributing to technical accuracy the author wishes to thank Michael R. Gaul, Captain Sam Sayers USN Ret., Mary Sayers, Captain Andrew Salkeld USMC, and Colonel Emmett Willard USA Ret., as well as V-22 experts Colonel Nolan Schmidt USMC, Lieutenant Colonel Doug Isleib USMC, and Donald L. Byrne Jr. As usual, the author has taken liberties in some technical areas in the interest of readability and pacing.

Ernestina Archilla Pabon de Pascal devoted many hours to helping the author capture the flavor of Cuba and earned the author's heartfelt thanks.

A very special thank-you goes to the author's wife, Deborah Buell Coonts, whose wise counsel, plot suggestions, and endless hours of editing added immeasurably to the quality of this tale.

Cultivo una rosa blanca,
*   En julio como en enero,*
*   Para el amigo sincero*
*   Que me da su mano franca.*
Y para el cruel que me arranca
*   El corazón con que vivo,*
*   Cardo ni oruga cultivo;*
*   Cultivo la rosa blanca.*

José Martí

I grow a white rose
    In July the same as January,
    For the sincere friend
    Who gives me his open hand.
And for the cruel one who pulls me
    away
    from the dreams for which I live,
    I grow neither weeds nor thistles,
    I grow the white rose.

Prologue

His hair was white, close-cropped, and his skin deeply tanned. He wore only sandals, shorts, and a paper-thin rag of a shirt with three missing buttons that flapped loosely on his spare, bony frame. A piece of twine around his waist held up his shorts, which were also several sizes too large. His dark eyes were restless and bright behind his steel-framed glasses, which rested on a large, fleshy nose.

The walk between the house and barn winded him, so he sat on a large stone in a bit of shade cast by a cluster of palm trees and contemplated the gauzy blue mountains on the horizon and the puffy clouds floating along on the trade wind.

A man couldn't have found a better place to live out his life, he thought. He loved this view, this serenity, this peace. When he had come here as a young man in his twenties he had known then that he had found paradise. Nothing in the first twenty-six years of his life had prepared him for the pastel colors, the warmth and brilliance of the sun, the kiss of the eternal breeze, the aroma of tropical flowers that filled his head and caressed his soul.

Cuba was everything that Russia wasn't. After a lifetime in Siberia, he had wanted to get down and kiss the earth when he first saw this land. He had actually done that, several times in fact, when he had had too much to drink. He drank a lot in those days, years and years ago, when he was very young.

When the chance to stay came he had leaped at it, begged for it.

'After a time you will regret your choice,' the colonel said. 'You will miss Mother Russia, the sound of Russian voices, the young wife you left behind. . . .'

'She is young, intelligent, ambitious. . . .' he had replied, thinking of Olga's cold anger when informed she could not accompany him to Cuba. She was angry at *him* for having the good fortune to go, not angry at the state for sending him. She had never in her life been angry at the state for anything whatsoever, no matter how bleak her life or prospects – she didn't have it in her. Olga was a good communist woman, communist to the core.

'She will be told that you have died in an accident. You will be proclaimed a socialist hero. Of course, you may never write to her, to your parents, to your brother, to anyone in the Soviet Union. All will believe you dead. For them, you will be dead.'

'I will have another life here.'

'These are not your people,' the colonel observed pointedly a bit later in the discussion, but he didn't listen.

'Olga is a patriot,' he remembered telling the colonel. 'She loves the state with all her soul. She will enjoy being a widow of a socialist hero. She will find another man and life will go on.'

So he stayed, and they told her that he was dead. Whether she remarried or stayed single, got that transfer to Moscow that she dreamed about, had the children she didn't want, he didn't know.

Looking at the blue mountains, smelling the wind, he tried to conjure up the picture of her in his mind that he had carried all these years. Olga had been young then so he always remembered her that way. She wouldn't be young now, of course, if she still lived; she would be hefty, with iron gray hair which she would wear pulled back in a bun.

His mind was blank. Try as he might, he couldn't remember what Olga looked like.

Perhaps that was just as well.

He had found a woman here, a chocolate brown woman who cooked and washed for him, lived with him, slept with him and bore him two children. Their son died years ago before he reached manhood, and their daughter was married and had children of her own. His daughter cooked for him now, checked to make sure he was all right.

Her face he could remember. Her smile, her touch, the warmth of her skin, her whisper in the night . . .

She had been dead two years next month.

He would join her soon. He knew that. He had lost seventy pounds in the last twelve months and knew that something was wrong with him, but he didn't know just what.

The village doctor examined him and shook her head. 'Your body is wearing out, my friend,' the doctor said. 'There is nothing I can do.'

He had had a wonderful life here, in this place in the sun in paradise.

He coughed, spat in the dirt, waited for the spasms to pass.

After a while he slowly levered himself erect and resumed his journey toward the barn.

He opened the board door and stepped into the cool darkness within. Little puffs of dust arose from every footfall. The dirt on the floor had long ago turned to powder.

The only light came from sunbeams shining through the cracks in the barn's siding. The siding was merely boards placed on the wooden frame of the building to keep out the wind and rain . . . and prying eyes.

In truth the building wasn't really a barn at all, though the corners were routinely used to store farm machinery and fodder for the animals and occasionally to get a sensitive animal in out of the sun. Primarily the building existed to hide the large, round concrete slab in the center of the floor. The building was constructed in such a way that there were no beams or wooden supports of any kind above the slab. The roof above the slab was merely boards cantilevered upward until they touched at the apex of the building.

The white-haired old man paused now to look upward at the pencil-thin shafts of sunlight which illuminated the dusty air like so many laser beams. The old man, however, knew nothing about lasers, had never even seen one: lasers came after he had completed his schooling and training.

One corner of the building contained an enclosed room. The door to the room was locked. Now the old man fished in his pocket for a key, unlocked the door, and stepped inside. On the other side of the door he used the key to engage the lock, then thoughtfully placed the key in his pocket.

He was the only living person with a key to that lock. If he collapsed in here, no one could get in to him. The door and the walls of this room were made of very hard steel, steel sheathed in rough, unfinished gray wood.

Well, that was a risk he had agreed to run all those years ago.

Thirty-five . . . no, thirty-eight years ago.

A long time.

There was a light switch by the door, and the old man reached for it automatically. He snapped it on. Before him were stairs leading down.

With one hand on the rail, he went down the stairs, now worn from the tread of his feet.

This door, these stairs . . . his whole life. Every day . . . checking, greasing, testing, repairing . . .

Once rats got in down here. He had never found a hole that would grant them entrance, though he had looked carefully. Still, they had gotten in and eaten insulation off wiring, chewed holes in boards, gnawed at pipes and fittings. He managed to kill three with poison and carried the bodies out. Several others died in places he couldn't get to and stank up the place while their carcasses decomposed.

God, when had that been? Years and years ago . . .

He checked the poison trays, made sure they were full.

He checked consoles, visually inspected the conduits, turned on the electrical power and checked the warning lights, the circuits.

Every week he ran a complete set of electrical checks on the circuitry, checking every wire in the place, all the connections and tubes, resistors and capacitors. Occasionally a tube would be burned out, and he would have to replace it. The irony of burning up difficult-to-obtain electrical parts testing them had ceased to amuse him years ago. Now he only worried that the parts would not be available, somewhere, when he needed them.

He wondered what they were going to do when he became unable to do this work. When he died. Someone was going to have to take care of this installation or it would go to rack and ruin. He had told the Cuban major that the last time he came around, which was last month, when the technicians came to install the new warhead.

Lord, what a job that had been. He was the only one who knew how to remove the old nuclear warhead, and he had had to figure out how to install the new one. No one would tell him anything about it, but he had to figure out how it had to be installed.

'You must let me train somebody,' he said to the major, 'show someone how to take care of this thing. If you leave it sit without maintenance for just a few months in this climate, it will be junk.'

Yes, yes. The major knew that. So did the people in Havana.

'And I am a sick man. Cancer, the doctor says.'

The major understood. He had been told about the disease. He was sorry to hear it.

'This thing should be in a museum now,' he told the major, who as usual acted very military, looked at this, tapped on that, told him to change a lightbulb that had just burned out – he always changed dead bulbs immediately if he had good bulbs to put in – then went away looking thoughtful.

The major always looked thoughtful. He hadn't an idea about how the thing worked, about the labor and cunning required to keep it operational, and he never asked questions. Just nosed around pretending he knew what he was looking at, occasionally delivered spare parts, listened to what the old man had to say, then went away, not to reappear for another three months.

Before the major there had been a colonel. Before the colonel another major . . . In truth, he didn't get to know these occasional visitors very well and soon forgot about them.

Every now and then he would get a visitor that he could not forget. Fidel Castro had come three times. His first visit occurred while the Russians were still here, during construction. He looked at everything, asked many questions, didn't pretend to know anything.

Castro returned when the site was operational. Several generals had accompanied him. The old man could still remember Castro's green uniform, the beard, the ever-present cigar.

The last time he came was eight or ten years ago, after the Soviet Union collapsed, when spare parts were so difficult to obtain. That time he had asked questions, listened carefully to the answers, and the necessary parts and supplies had somehow been delivered.

But official visits were rare events, even by the thoughtful major. Most of the time the old man was left in peace and solitude to do his job as he saw fit. Truly, the work was pleasant – he had had a good life, much better than anything he could have aspired to as a technician in the Soviet Rocket

Forces, doomed to some lonely, godforsaken, windswept frozen patch of Central Asia.

The old man left the power on to the console – he would begin the tests in just a bit, but first he opened the fireproof steel door to reveal a set of stairs leading downward. Thirty-two steps down to the bottom of the silo.

The sight of the missile resting erect on its launcher always took his breath for a moment. There it sat, ready to be fired.

He climbed the ladder to the platform adjacent to the guidance compartment. Took out the six screws that sealed the access plate, pried it off, and used a flashlight to inspect the wiring inside. Well, the internal wiring inside the guidance unit was getting old, no question about it. It would have to be replaced soon.

Should he replace the guidance wiring – which would take two weeks of intense, concentrated effort – or should he leave it for his successor?

He would think about the work involved for a few more weeks. If he didn't feel up to it then, it would have to wait. His health was deteriorating at a more or less steady pace, and he could only do so much.

If they didn't send a replacement for him soon, he wouldn't have enough time to teach the new man what he needed to know. To expect them to find someone who already knew the nuts and bolts of a Scud I missile was ridiculous. These missiles hadn't been manufactured in thirty years, were inaccurate, obsolete artifacts of a bygone age.

It was equally ridiculous to expect someone to remove this missile from the silo and install a new, modern one. Cuba was poor, even poorer than Russia had been when he was growing up. Cuba could not afford modern missiles and the new, postcommunist Russia certainly could not afford to give them away.

Not even to aim at Atlanta.

Those were the targeting coordinates.

He wasn't supposed to know the target, of course, but that rule was another example of military stupidity. He took care of the missile, maintained it, tested it, and if necessary would someday fire it at the enemy. Yet the powers that be didn't want him to know where the missile was aimed.

So when he was working on the guidance module he had checked the coordinates that were programmed in, compared them to a map in the village school.

Atlanta!

The gyros in the guidance module were 1950s technology, and Soviet to boot, with the usual large, forgiving military tolerances. No one ever claimed the guidance system in a Scud I was a precision instrument, but it was adequate. The guidance system would get the missile into the proper neighborhood, more or less, then the warhead would do the rest.

The old warhead had an explosive force equal to one hundred thousand tons equivalent of TNT. It wouldn't flatten all of Atlanta – Atlanta was a mighty big place and getting bigger – but it would make a hell of a dent in Georgia. Somewhere in Georgia. With luck, the chances were pretty good that the missile would hit Georgia.

The new warhead . . . well, he knew nothing about it. It was a completely different design than the old one, although it weighed exactly the same and also seemed to be rigged for an airburst, but of course there was no way for him to determine the altitude.

Not that it mattered. The missile had never been fired and probably never would be. Its capabilities were mere speculation.

The old man took a last look at the interior of the control module, replaced the inspection plate and inserted the screws, then carefully tightened each one. Then he inspected the cables that led to the missile and their connectors. From the platform he could also see the hydraulic pistons and arms that would lift the cap on the silo, if and when. No leaks today.

Carefully, holding on with both hands, he climbed down the ladder to the floor of the silo, which was just a grate over a large hole, the fire tube, designed so the fiery rocket exhaust would not cook the missile before it rose from the silo.

The rats may have got into the silo when he had the cap open, he thought. Yes, that was probably it. They got inside, found nothing to eat, began chewing on wire insulation to stay alive.

But the rats were dead.

His woman was dead, and he soon would be.

The missile . . .

He patted the side of the missile, then began climbing the stairs to the control room to do his electrical checks.

Nobody gave a damn about the missile, except him and maybe the major. The major didn't really care all that much – the missile was just a job for him.

The missile had been the old man's life. He had traded life in Russia as a slave in the Strategic Rocket Forces for a life in paradise as a slave to a missile that would never be fired.

He thought about Russia as he climbed the stairs.

You make your choices going through life, he told himself, *or the state makes the choices for you. Or God does. Whichever, a man must accept life as it comes.*

He sat down at the console in the control room, ran his fingers over the buttons and switches.

At least he had never had to fire the missile. After all these years taking care of it, that would be somewhat like committing suicide.

Could he do it? Could he fire the missile if ordered to do so?

When he first came to Cuba he had thought deeply about that question.

Of course he had taken an oath to obey and all that, but he never knew if he really could.

Still didn't.

And was going to die not knowing.

The old man laughed aloud. He liked the sound so much he laughed again, louder.

After all, the joke was really on the communists, who sent him here. Amazingly, after all the pain and suffering they caused tens of millions of people all over the planet, they had given him a good life.

He laughed again because the joke was a good one.

1

Guantánamo Bay, on the southeast coast of the island of Cuba, is the prettiest spot on the planet, thought Rear Admiral Jake Grafton, USN.

He was leaning on the railing on top of the carrier *United States*'s superstructure, her island, a place the sailors called Steel Beach. Here off-duty crew members gathered to soak up some rays and do a few calisthenics. Jake Grafton was not normally a sun worshiper; at sea he rarely visited Steel Beach, preferring to arrange his day so that he could spend at least a half hour running on the flight deck. Today he was dressed in gym shorts, T-shirt, and tennis shoes, but he had yet to make it to the flight deck.

Grafton was a trim, fit fifty-three years old, a trifle over six feet tall, with short hair turning gray, gray eyes, and a nose slightly too large for his face. On one temple was a scar, an old, faded white slash where a bullet had gouged him years ago.

People who knew him regarded him as the epitome of a competent naval officer. Grafton always put his brain in gear before he opened his mouth, never lost his cool, and he never lost sight of the goals he wanted to accomplish. In short, he was one fine naval officer and his superiors knew it, which was why he was in charge of this carrier group lying in Guantánamo Bay.

The carrier and her escorts had been running exercises in the Caribbean for the last week. Today the carrier was anchored in the mouth of the bay, with two of her larger consorts anchored nearby. To seaward three destroyers steamed back and forth, their radars probing the skies.

A set of top-secret orders had brought the carrier group here.

Jake Grafton thought about those orders as he studied the two cargo ships lying against the pier through a set of navy binoculars. The ships were small, less than eight thousand tons each; larger ships drew too much water to get against the pier in this harbor. They were *Nuestra Señora de Colón* and *Astarte*.

The order bringing those ships here had not come from some windowless Pentagon cubbyhole; it was no memo drafted by an anonymous civil servant or faceless staff weenie. Oh, no. The order that had brought those ships to this pier on the southern coast of Cuba had come from the White House, the top of the food chain.

Jake Grafton looked past the cargo ships at the warehouses and barracks and administration buildings baking in the warm Cuban sun.

A paradise, that was the word that described Cuba. A paradise inhabited by communists. And Guantánamo Bay was a lonely little American outpost adhering to the underside of this communist island, the asshole of Cuba some called it.

Rear Admiral Grafton could see the cranes moving, the white containers being swung down to the pier from *Astarte*, which had arrived several hours ago. Forklifts took the steel boxes to a hurricane-proof warehouse, where no doubt the harbormaster was stacking them three or four deep in neat, tidy military rows.

The containers were packages designed to hold chemical and biological weapons, artillery shells and bombs. A trained crew was here to load the weapons stored inside the hurricane-proof warehouse into the containers, which would then be loaded aboard the ship at the pier and transported to the United States, where the warheads would be destroyed.

Loading the weapons into the containers and getting the containers stowed aboard the second ship was going to take at least a week, probably longer. The first ship, *Nuestra Señora de Colón*, Our Lady of Colón, had been a week loading, and would be ready to sail this evening. Jake Grafton's job was to provide military cover for the loading operation with this carrier battle group.

His orders raised more questions than they answered. The weapons had been stored in that warehouse for years – why remove them now? Why did the removal operation require military cover? What was the threat?

Admiral Grafton put down his binoculars and did fifty push-ups on the steel deck while he thought about chemical and biological weapons. Cheaper and even more lethal than atomic weapons, they were the weapons of choice for Third World nations seeking to acquire a credible military presence. Chemical weapons were easier to control than biological weapons, yet more expensive to deliver. Hands down, the cheapest and deadliest weapon known to man was the biological one.

Almost any nation, indeed, almost anyone with a credit card and two thousand square feet of laboratory space, could construct a biological weapon in a matter of weeks from inexpensive, off-the-shelf technology. Years ago Saddam Hussein got into the biological warfare business with anthrax cultures purchased from an American mail-order supply house and delivered via overnight mail. Ten grams of anthrax properly dispersed can kill as many people as a ton of the nerve gas Sarin. What was that estimate Jake saw recently? – one hundred kilograms of anthrax delivered by an efficient aerosol generator on a large urban target would kill from two to six times as many people as a one-megaton nuclear device.

355

Of course, Jake Grafton reflected, anthrax was merely one of over one hundred and sixty known biological warfare agents. There were others far deadlier but equally cheap to manufacture and disperse. Still, obtaining a culture was merely a first step; the journey from culture dishes to a reliable weapon that could be safely stored and accurately employed – anything other than a spray tank – was long, expensive, and fraught with engineering challenges.

Jake Grafton had had a few classified briefings about CBW – which stood for chemical and biological warfare – but he knew little more than was available in the public press. These weren't the kinds of secrets that rank-and-file naval officers had a need to know. Since the Kennedy administration insisted on developing other military response capabilities besides nuclear warfare, the United States had researched, developed, and manufactured large stores of nerve gas, mustard gas, incapacitants, and defoliants. Research on biological agents went forward in tandem at Fort Detrick, Maryland, and ultimately led to the manufacture of weapons at Pine Bluff Arsenal in Arkansas. These highly classified programs were undertaken with little debate and almost no publicity. Of course the Soviets had their own classified programs. Only when accidents occurred – like the accidental slaughter of 6,000 sheep thirty miles from the Dugway Proving Ground in Utah during the late 1960s, or the deaths of sixty-six people at Sverdlovsk in 1979 – did the public get a glimpse into this secret world.

Nerve gases were loaded into missile and rocket warheads, bombs, land mines, and artillery shells. Biological agents were loaded into missile warheads, cluster bombs, and spray tanks and dispensers mounted on aircraft.

Historically nations used chemical or biological weapons against an enemy only when the enemy lacked the means to retaliate in kind. The threat of massive American retaliation had deterred Saddam Hussein from the use of chemical and biological weapons in the 1991 Gulf War, yet these days deterrence was politically incorrect.

In 1993 the United States signed the Chemical Weapons Convention, thereby agreeing to remove chemical and biological weapons from its stockpiles.

The US military had been in no hurry to comply with the treaty, of course, because without the threat of retaliation there was no way to prevent these weapons being used against American troops and civilians. The waiting was over, apparently. The politicians in Washington were getting their way: the United States would not retaliate against an enemy with chemical or biological weapons even if similar weapons were used to slaughter Americans.

When Jake Grafton finished his push-ups and stood, the staff operations officer, Commander Toad Tarkington, was there with a towel. Toad was slightly above medium height, deeply tanned, and had a mouthful of perfect white teeth that were visible when he smiled or laughed, which he often did. The admiral wiped his face on the towel, then picked up the binoculars and once again focused them on the cargo ships.

'Glad the decision to destroy those things wasn't one I had to make,' Toad Tarkington said.

'There are a lot of things in this world that I'm glad I'm not responsible for,' Jake replied.

'Why now, Admiral? And why does the ordnance crowd need a battle group to guard them?'

'What I'd like to know,' Jake Grafton mused, 'is why those damned things were stored here in the first place. If we knew that, then maybe we would know why the brass sent us here to stand guard.'

'Think Castro has chemical or biological weapons, sir?'

'I suspect he does, or someone with a lot of stars once thought he might. If so, our weapons were probably put here to discourage friend Castro from waving his about. But what is the threat to removing them?'

'Got to be terrorists, sir,' Toad said. 'Castro would be delighted to see them go. An attack from the Cuban Army is the last thing on earth I would expect. But terrorists – maybe they plan to do a raid into here, steal some of the darn things.'

'Maybe,' Jake said, sighing.

'I guess I don't understand why we are taking them home for destruction,' Toad added. 'The administration got the political credit for signing the Chemical Weapons Treaty. If we keep our weapons, we can still credibly threaten massive retaliation if someone threatens us.'

'Pretty hard to agree to destroy the things, not do it, and then fulminate against other countries who don't destroy theirs.'

'Hypocrisy never slowed down a politician,' Toad said sourly. 'I guess I just never liked the idea of getting naked when everyone else at the party is fully dressed.'

'Who in Washington would ever authorize the use of CBW weapons?' Jake muttered. 'Can you see a buttoned-down, blow-dried, politically correct American politician ever signing such an order?'

Both men stood with their elbows on the railing looking at the cargo ships. After a bit the admiral passed Toad the binoculars.

'Wonder if the National Security Agency is keeping this area under surveillance with satellites?' Toad mused.

'No one in Washington is going to tell *us*,' the admiral said matter-of-factly. He pointed to one of the two Aegis cruisers anchored nearby. 'Leave that cruiser anchored here for the next few days. She can cover the base perimeter with her guns if push comes to shove. Have the cruiser keep her gun crews on five-minute alert, ammo on the trays, no liberty. After three days she can pull the hook and join us, and another cruiser can come anchor here.'

'Yes, sir.'

'There's a marine battalion landing team aboard *Kearsarge*, which is supposed to rendezvous with us tomorrow. I want *Kearsarge* to stay with *United States*. We'll put both ships in a race-track pattern about fifty miles south of here, outside Cuban territorial waters, and get on with our exercises. But we'll keep a weather eye peeled on this base.'

'What about the base commander, sir? He may know more about this than we do.'

'Get on the ship-to-shore net and invite him to have dinner with me tonight. Send a helo in to pick him up.'

'Sir, your instructions specifically directed that you maintain a business-as-usual security posture.'

'I remember,' Jake said dryly.

'Of course, "business as usual" is an ambiguous phrase,' Toad mused. 'If anything goes wrong you can be blamed for not doing enough or doing too much, whichever way the wind blows.'

Jake Grafton snorted. 'If a bunch of wild-eyed terrorists lay hands on those warheads, Tarkington, you and I will be fried, screwed, and tattooed regardless of what we did or didn't do. We'll have to will our bodies to science.'

'What about the CO of the cruiser, Admiral? What do we tell him?'

'Draft a top-secret message directing him to keep his people ready to shoot.'

'Aye, aye, sir.'

'*Nuestra Señora de Colón* is sailing this evening for Norfolk. Have a destroyer accompany her until she is well out of Cuban waters.'

'Yo.' Toad was making notes on a small memo pad he kept in his hip pocket.

'And have the weather people give me a cloud-cover prediction for the next five days, or as far out as they can. I want to try to figure out what, if anything, the satellites might be seeing.'

'You mean, are they keeping an eye on the Cuban military?'

'Or terrorists. Whoever.'

'I'll take care of it, sir.'

'I'm going to run a couple laps around the deck,' Jake Grafton added.

'May I suggest putting a company of marines ashore to do a security survey of the base perimeter? Strictly routine.'

'That sounds feasible,' Jake Grafton said. 'Tonight let's ask the base commander what he thinks.'

'Yessir.'

'Terrorists or the Cuban Army – wanna bet ten bucks? Take your pick.'

'I only bet on sure things, sir, like prizefights and Super Bowls, occasionally a cockroach race.'

'You're wise beyond your years, Toad,' the admiral tossed over his shoulder as he headed for the hatch.

'That's what I tell Rita,' Toad shot back. Rita Moravia was his wife.

Jake Grafton didn't hear the rest of Toad's comment. 'And wisdom is a heavy burden, let me tell you. Real heavy. Sorta like biological warheads.' He put the binoculars to his eyes and carefully studied the naval base.

2

The night was hot and sultry, with lightning playing on the horizon. From his seat on the top row of the stadium bleachers Hector Juan de Dios Sedano kept an eye on the lightning, but the storms seemed to be moving north.

Everyone else in the stadium was watching the game. Hector's younger brother, Juan Manuel 'Ocho' Sedano, was the local team's star pitcher. The eighth child of his parents, the Cuban fans had long ago dubbed him El Ocho. The family reduced the name to 'Ocho.'

Tonight his fastball seemed on fire and his curve exceptional. The crowd cheered with every pitch. Twice the umpire called for the ball to examine it. Each time he handed it back to the catcher, who tossed it back to the mound as the fans hooted delightedly.

At the middle of the seventh inning Ocho had faced just twenty-two batters. Only one man had gotten to first base, and that on a bloop single just beyond the fingertips of the second baseman. The local team had scored four runs.

Hector Sedano leaned against the board fence behind him and applauded his brother as he walked from the mound. Ocho looked happy, relaxed – the confident, honest gaze of a star athlete who knows what he can do.

As Hector clapped, he spotted a woman coming through the crowd toward him. She smiled as she met his eyes, then took a seat beside him.

Here on the back bench Hector was about ten feet from the nearest fans. The board fence behind him was the wall of the stadium, fifteen feet above the ground.

'Did your friends come with you?' he asked, scanning the crowd.

'Oh, yes, the usual two,' she said, but didn't bother to point to them.

Sedano found one of the men settling into a seat five rows down and over about thirty feet. A few seconds later he saw the other standing near the entrance where the woman had entered the stadium. These two were her bodyguards.

Her name was Mercedes. She was the widow of one of Hector's brothers and the current mistress of Fidel Castro.

'How is *Mima?*'

Tomorrow was Hector's mother's birthday, and the clan was gathering.

'Fine. Looking forward to seeing everyone.'

'I used the birthday as an excuse. They don't want me to leave the residence these days.'

'How bad is he?'

'*Está to jodío*. He's done in. One doctor said two weeks, one three. The cancer is spreading rapidly.'

'What do you think?'

'I think he will live a while longer, but every night is more difficult. I sit with him. When he is sleeping he stops breathing for as much as half a minute before he resumes. I watch the clock, counting the seconds, wondering if he will breathe again.'

The home team's center fielder stepped up to the plate. Ocho was the second batter. Standing in the warm-up circle with a bat in his hands, he scanned the faces in the crowd. Finally he made eye contact with Hector, nodded his head just enough to be seen, then concentrated on his warm-up swings.

'Who knows about this?' Hector asked Mercedes.

'Only a few people. Alejo is holding the lid on. The doctors are with him around the clock.' Alejo Vargas was the minister of interior. His ministry's Department of State Security – the secret police – investigated and suppressed opposition and dissent.

'We have waited a long time,' Hector mused.

'*Ese cabrón*, we should have killed Vargas years ago,' Mercedes said, and smiled at a woman who turned around to look at her.

'We cannot win with his blood on our hands.'

'Alejo suspects you, I think.'

'I am just a Jesuit priest, a teacher.'

Mercedes snorted.

'He suspects everyone,' Hector added.

'Don't be a fool.'

El Ocho stepped into the batter's box to the roar of the crowd. He waggled the bat, cocked it, waited expectantly. His stance was perfect, his weight balanced, he was tense and ready – when he batted Hector could see Ocho's magnificent talent. He looked so . . . perfect.

Ocho let the first ball go by . . . outside.

The second pitch was low.

The opposing pitcher walked around the mound, examined the ball, toed the rubber.

The fact was Ocho was a better batter than he was a pitcher. Oh, he was a great pitcher, but when he had a bat in his hands all his gifts were on display; the reflexes, the eyesight, the physique, the ability to wait for his pitch. . . .

The third pitch was a strike, belt-high, and Ocho got around on it and connected solidly. The ball rose into the warm, humid air and flew as if it had wings until it cleared the center field fence by a good margin.

'He caught it perfectly,' Mercedes said, admiration in her voice.

Ocho trotted the bases while everyone in the bleachers applauded. The opposing pitcher stood on the mound shaking his head in disgust.

Ocho's manager was the first to greet him as he trotted toward the dugout. He pounded his star on the back, pumped his hand, beamed proudly, almost like a father.

'What else is happening?' Hector asked.

'The government has signed the casino agreement. Miramar, Havana, Varadero and Santiago. The consortium will provide fifty percent of the cost of an airport in Santiago.'

'They have been negotiating for what – three years?'

'Almost that.'

'Any sense of urgency on the part of the Cubans?'

'I sense none. The Americans were happy with the deal, so they signed.'

'Who are these Americans?'

'I thought they were Nevada casino people, but there were people in the background pulling strings, criminals, I think. They wanted assurances on prostitution and narcotics.'

The Cuban government had been negotiating agreements for foreign investment and development for years, mainly with Canadian and European companies. Tourism was now the largest industry in Cuba, bringing 1.5 million tourists a year to the island and keeping the economy afloat with hard currency. Now the Cuban government was openly negotiating with American companies, with all deals contingent upon the ending of the American economic embargo. Fidel Castro believed that he could put political pressure upon the American government to end the embargo by dangling development rights in front of American capitalists. Hector Sedano thought Fidel understood the Americans.

'The tobacco negotiator, Chance – how is he progressing?'

'He is talking to your brother Maximo. Then he is supposed to see Vargas. Tobacco will replace sugarcane as Cuba's big crop, he says. The cigarettes will be manufactured here and marketed worldwide under American brands. The Americans will finance everything; Cuba will get a fifty-percent share of the business, across the board.'

'Is this Chance serious?'

'Apparently. The tobacco companies think their days are numbered in the United States. They want to move offshore, escape the regulation that will eventually put them out of business.'

Hector sat silently, taking it all in as the uniformed players on the field played a game with rules. What a contrast with politics!

Mercedes was a treasure, a person with access to the highest levels of the Cuban government. She brought Hector Sedano information that even

Castro probably didn't have. The big question, of course, was how she learned it. Hector told himself repeatedly that he didn't want to know, but of course he did.

He glanced at the woman sitting beside him. She was wearing a simple dress that did nothing to call attention to her figure, nor did it do anything to hide it.

She was a beautiful woman who needed no makeup and never wore any. Every man she met was attracted to her, an unremarkable fact, like the summer heat, which she didn't seem to notice. Extraordinarily smart, with a near-photographic memory, she had almost no opportunities to use her talent in Cuban society.

Except as a spy.

'Will Maximo be at *Mima*'s party tomorrow?'

'He said he would.'

'Should I be shocked if he acts possessive?'

Mercedes glanced at him, raised an eyebrow. 'He would not be so foolish.'

Well, just who was she sleeping with? Hector glanced at her repeatedly, wondering. She appeared to be concentrating on the ball game.

The only thing he knew for sure was that she wasn't sleeping with him, and God knows he had thought about *that* far more than any priest ever should. Of course, priests were human and had to fight their urges, but still . . .

Castro . . . Of course she slept with him – she was his mistress – that was how she got access. But did she love him?

Or was she a cool, calculating tramp ready to change horses now that Castro was dying?

No. He shook his head, refusing to believe that of her.

Where did Maximo fit in? As he sat there contemplating that angle, he wondered how Maximo saw her?

Mercedes left after watching Ocho pitch an inning. He faced three batters and struck them all out.

When the game was over, Hector Sedano stayed in his seat and watched the crowd file out. He was still sitting there when someone shouted at him, 'Hey, I turn out the lights now.'

The darkness that followed certainly wasn't total. Small lights were illuminated over the exits, the lights of Havana lit up the sky, and lightning continued to flash on the horizon.

Sedano lit another cigar and smoked it slowly.

After a few minutes he saw the shape of a man making his way along the aisle toward him. The man sagged down on the bench several feet away.

'Good game tonight.' The man was the stadium keeper, Alfredo Garcia.

'Yes.'

'Your brother, El Ocho, was magnificent. Such talent, such presence.'

'We are very proud of him.'

'To have such talent ... if I had had his talent, my life would have been so different.'

'You would have found another way to get to where you are.'

'I saw that she was here, with her security guards circling.... What did she say?'

'What makes you think she tells me anything?'

'Come, my friend. Someone whispers in your ear.'

'And someone is whispering to Alejo Vargas.'

'You suspect me?'

'I think you are just stupid enough to take money from the Americans and money from Alejo Vargas and think neither of them will find out about the other.'

'My God, man! Think of what you are saying!' Alfredo moved closer. Sedano could see his face, which was almost as white as his shirt.

'I am thinking.'

'You have my life in your hands. I had to trust you with my life when I first approached you. Nothing has changed.'

Sedano puffed on the cigar in silence, studying Garcia's features. Born in America of Cuban parents, Garcia had been a priest. He couldn't leave the women alone, however, and ultimately got mixed up with some topless dancers running an 'escort' service in East St Louis. After a few months the feds busted him for violation of the Mann Act, moving women across state lines for immoral purposes, i.e., prostitution. After the church canned him, he jumped bail and fled to Cuba. Garcia had been in Cuba several years when he was recruited by the CIA, which asked him to approach Sedano.

Hector Sedano had no doubt that Garcia had the ear of the American government – in the past four years he had supplied Sedano with almost a million dollars in cash and enough weapons to supply a small army. The money and weapons always arrived when and where Garcia said they would. Still, the question remained, who else did the man talk to?

Who did his control talk to?

Hector had stockpiled the weapons, hidden them praying they would never be needed. He used the money for travel expenses and bribes. Without money to bribe the little fish he would have landed in prison years ago.

Hector Sedano shook his head to clear his thoughts. He was living on the naked edge, had been there for years. And life wasn't getting any easier.

'Castro is dying,' he said. 'It is a matter of weeks, or so the doctors say.'

Alfredo Garcia took a deep breath and exhaled audibly.

'I tell you now man-to-man, Alfredo. The records of Alejo Vargas will soon be placed in my hands. If you have betrayed me or the people of Cuba, you had better find a way to get off this planet, because there is no place on it you can hide, not from me, not from the CIA, not from the men and women you betrayed.'

'I have betrayed no one,' Alfredo Garcia said. 'God? Yes. But no man.'

He went away then, leaving Sedano to smoke in solitude.

Fidel Castro dying! Hector Sedano could hear his heart beat as he tried to comprehend the reality of that fact.

Millions of people were waiting for his death, some patiently, most impatiently, many with a feeling of impending doom. Castro had ruled Cuba as an absolute dictator since 1959: the revolution that he led did nothing more than topple the old dictator and put a new one in his place. Castro jettisoned fledgling democracy, embraced communism and used raw demagoguery to consolidate his total, absolute power. He prosecuted and executed his enemies and confiscated the property of anyone who might be against him. Hundreds of thousands of Cubans fled, many to America.

Castro's embrace of communism and seizure of the assets of the foreign corporations that had invested in Cuba, assets worth several billions of dollars, were almost preordained, inevitable. Predictably, most of those corporations were American. Also predictably, the United States government retaliated with a diplomatic and economic blockade that continued to this day.

After seizing the assets of the American corporations who owned most of Cuba, Castro had little choice: he had to have the assistance of a major power, so he substituted the Soviet Union for the United States as Cuba's patron. The only good thing about the substitution was that the Soviet Union was a lot farther away than Florida. Theirs was never a partnership of equals: the Soviets humiliated Fidel at almost every turn in the road. When communism collapsed in the Soviet Union in the early 1990s, Cuba was cut adrift as an expensive luxury that the newly democratic Russia could ill afford. That twist of fate was a cruel blow to Cuba, which despite Castro's best efforts still was a slave to sugarcane.

Through it all, Castro survived. Never as popular as his supporters believed, he was never as unpopular as the exiles claimed. The truth of the matter was that Castro was Cuban to the core and fiercely independent, and he had kept Cuba that way. His demagoguery played well to poor peasants who had nothing but their pride. The trickle of refugees across the Florida Straits acted as a safety valve to rid the regime of its worst enemies, the vociferous critics with the will and tenacity to cause serious problems. In the Latin tradition, the Cubans who remained submitted to Castro, even respected him for thumbing his nose at the world. A dictator he might be, but he was 'our' dictator.

A new day was about to dawn in Cuba, a day without Castro and the baggage of communism, ballistic missiles, and invasion, a new day without bitter enmity with the United States. Just what that day would bring remained to be seen, but it was coming.

The exiles wanted justice, and revenge; the peons who lived in the exiles' houses, now many families to a building, feared being dispossessed. The foreign corporations that Castro so cavalierly robbed wanted compensation. Everyone wanted food, and jobs, and a future. It seemed as if the bills for all the past mistakes were about to come due and payable at once.

Hector Sedano would have a voice in that future, if he survived. He sat smoking, contemplating the coming storm.

Mercedes was of course correct about the danger posed by Alejo Vargas. Mix Latin machismo and a willingness to do violence to gain one's own ends, add generous dollops of vainglory, egotism, and paranoia, stir well, and you have the makings of a truly fine Latin American dictator, self-righteous, suspicious, trigger-happy, and absolutely ruthless. Fidel Alejandro Castro Ruz came out of that mold: Alejo Vargas, Hector knew, was merely another. He could not make this observation to Mercedes, whom Hector suspected of loving Fidel – he needed her cooperation.

Alfredo Garcia found a seat near the ticket-taker's booth from where he could see the shadowy figure on the top row of the bleachers. He was so nervous he twitched.

Like Hector Sedano, he too was in awe of the news he had just learned: Fidel Castro was dying.

Alfredo Garcia trembled as he thought about it. That priest in the top row of the bleachers was one of the contenders for power in post-Castro Cuba. There were others of course, Alejo Vargas, the Minister of Interior and head of the secret police, prominently among them.

Yes, Garcia talked to the secret police of Alejo Vargas – he had to. No one could refuse the Department of State Security, least of all a fugitive from American justice seeking sanctuary.

And of course he cooperated on an ongoing basis. Vargas's spies were everywhere, witnessed every conversation, every meal, every waking moment . . . or so it seemed. One could never be certain what the secret police knew from other sources, what they were just guessing at, what he was their only source for. Garcia had handled this reality the only way he could: he answered direct questions with a bit of the truth – if he knew it – and volunteered nothing.

If the secret police knew Alfredo had a CIA contact they had never let on. They did know Hector Sedano was a power in the underground although they seemed to think he was a small fish.

Garcia thought otherwise. He thought Hector Sedano was the most powerful man in Cuba after Fidel Castro, even more powerful than Alejo Vargas.

Why didn't Hector understand the excruciating predicament that Alfredo Garcia found himself in? Certainly Hector knew what it was like to have few options, or none at all.

Alfredo was a weak man. He had never been able to resist the temptations of the flesh. God had forgiven him, of that he was sure, but would Hector Sedano?

As he sat in the darkness watching Hector, Alfredo Garcia smiled grimly. One of the contenders for power in post-Castro Cuba would be Hector's own brother, Maximo Luís Sedano, the finance minister. Maximo was Fidel's most trusted lieutenant, one of his inner circle. Three years older than Hector, he had lived and breathed Castro's revolution all his life, willingly standing in the great man's shadow. Those days were about over, and Maximo's friends whispered that he was ready – he wanted *more*. That was the general street gossip that Garcia heard, and like most gossip, he thought it probably had a kernel of truth inside.

For his part, Maximo probably thought his only serious rival was Alejo Vargas. He was going to get a bad shock in the near future.

And then there were the exiles. God only knew what those fools would do when Fidel breathed his last.

Yes, indeed, when Fidel died the fireworks would begin.

Hector Sedano was taking the last few puffs on his cigar when his youngest brother, El Ocho, climbed the bleachers. Ocho settled onto a bench in front of Hector and leaned back so that he could rest his feet on the bench in front of him.

'You played well tonight. The home run was a thing of beauty.'

'It's just a game.'

'And you play it well.'

Ocho snorted. 'Just a game,' he repeated.

'All of life is a game,' his older brother told him, and ground out his cigar.

'Was that Mercedes I saw talking to you earlier?'

'She is here for *Mima*'s birthday.'

Ocho nodded. He seemed to gather himself before he spoke again.

'My manager, Diego Coca, wants me to go to the United States.'

Hector let that statement lie there. Sometimes Ocho said outrageous things to get a reaction. Hector had quit playing that game years ago.

'Diego says I could play in the major leagues.'

'Do you believe him?'

Ocho turned toward his older brother and closest friend. 'Diego is a dreamer. I look good playing this game because the other players are not so good. The pitch I hit out tonight was a belt-high fastball right down the middle. American major league pitchers don't throw stuff like that because all those guys can hit it.'

'Could you pitch there?'

'In Cuba my fastball is a little faster than everyone else's. My curve breaks a little more. In America all the pitchers have a good fastball and breaking ball. Everyone is better.'

Hector laughed. 'So you aren't interested in going to America and getting rich, like your uncle Tomas?' Tomas had defected ten years ago while a team of baseball stars was on a trip to Mexico City. He now owned five dry-cleaning plants in metropolitan Miami. Oh, yes, Tomas was getting rich!

'I'm not good enough to play in the big leagues. Diego tells me I am. I think he believes it. He wants me to go, take him with me, sign a big contract. I'm his chance.'

'He wants to go with you?'

'That's right.'

'On a boat?'

'He says he knows a man who has a boat. He can take us to Florida, where people will be waiting.'

'You believe that?'

'Diego does. That is what is important.'

'You owe Diego a few hours of sweat on the baseball field, nothing else.'

Ocho didn't reply. He lay back on his elbows and wiggled his feet.

'Why don't you tell me all of it,' Hector suggested gently.

Ocho didn't look at him. After a bit he said, 'I got Diego's daughter pregnant. Dora, the second one.'

'He knows this?'

Ocho nodded affirmatively.

'So marry the girl. This is an embarrassment, not dishonor. My God, *Mima* was pregnant when Papa married her! Welcome to the world, Ocho. And congratulations.'

'Diego is the girl's *father*.'

'I will talk to him,' Hector said. 'You are both young, with hot blood in your veins. Surely he will understand. I will promise him that you will do the right thing by this girl. You will stand up with her in church, love her, cherish her. . . .'

'Diego wants the best for her, for the baby, for me.'

'For himself.'

'And for himself, yes. He wants us to go on his friend's boat to America. I will play baseball and earn much money and we will live the good life in America. That is his dream.'

'I see,' said Hector Sedano, and leaned back against the fence. 'Is it yours?'

'I haven't told anyone else,' Ocho said, meaning the family.

'Are you going to tell *Mima*?'

'Not on her birthday. I thought maybe you could tell her, after we get to America.'

'*Está loco*, Ocho. This boat . . . you could all drown. Hundreds –

368

thousands of people have drowned out there. The sea swallows them. They leave here and are never heard from again.'

Ocho studied his toes.

'If they catch you, the Americans will send you back. They don't want boat people.'

'Diego Coca says that –'

'Damn Diego Coca! The Cuban Navy will probably catch you before you get out of sight of *Mima*'s house. Pray that they do, that you don't die out there in the Gulf Stream. And if you are lucky enough to survive the trip to Florida, the Americans will arrest you, put you in a camp at Guantánamo Bay. Even if you get back to Cuba, the government won't let you play baseball again. You'll spend your life in the fields chopping cane. Think about *that*!'

Ocho sat silently, listening to the insects.

'Did you give Diego Coca money?' Hector asked.

'Yes.'

'Want to tell me how much?'

'No.'

'You're financing his dream, Ocho.'

'At least he's got one.'

'What's that mean?'

'It means what I said. At least Diego Coca has a dream. He doesn't want to sit rotting on this goddamned island while life passes him by. He doesn't want that for his daughter or her kid.'

'He doesn't want that for himself.'

Ocho threw up his hands.

Hector pressed on, relentlessly. 'Diego Coca should get on that boat and follow his dream, if that is his dream. You and Dora should get married. Announce the wedding tomorrow at *Mima*'s party – these people are your flesh and blood. Cuba is your country, your heritage. You owe these people and this country all that you are, all that you will ever be.'

'Cuba is *your* dream, Hector.'

'And what is yours? I ask you a second time.'

Ocho shook his head like a mighty bull. 'I do not wish to spend my life plotting against the government, making speeches, waiting to be arrested, dreaming of a utopia that will never be. That is life wasted.'

Hector thought before he answered. 'What you say is true. Yet until things change in Cuba it is impossible to dream other dreams.'

Ocho Sedano got to his feet. He was a tall, lanky young man with long, ropy muscles.

'Just wanted you to know,' he said.

'A man must have a dream that is larger than he is or life has little meaning.'

'Didn't figure you would think it was a good idea.'

'I don't.'

'Or else you would have gone yourself.'

'Ocho, I ask you a personal favor. Wait two weeks. Don't go for two weeks. See how the world looks in two weeks before you get on that boat.'

Hector could see the pain etched on Ocho's face. The younger man looked him straight in the eye.

'The boat won't wait.'

'I ask this as your brother, who has never asked you for anything. I ask you for *Mima*, who cherishes you, and for Papa, who watches you from heaven. Have the grace to say yes to my request. Two weeks.'

'The boat won't wait, Hector. Diego wants this. Dora wants this. I have no choice.'

With that Ocho turned and leaped lightly from bench to bench until he got to the field. He walked across the dark, deserted diamond and disappeared into the home team's dugout.

Although he was born in Cuba, El Gato's parents took him to Miami when he was a toddler, before the Cuban revolution. He had absolutely no memory of Cuba. In fact, he thought of himself as an American. English was the language he knew best, the language he thought in. He had learned Spanish at home as a youngster, understood it well, and spoke it with a flavored accent. Still, hearing nothing but Cuban Spanish spoken around him for days gave him a bit of cultural shock.

He and two of his bodyguards had flown to Mexico City, then to Havana. He had always kept his contacts with the Cuban government a deep, dark, jealously guarded secret, but rumors had reached him, rumors that Castro was sick, that important changes in Cuba were in the wind. The rumors had the feel of truth; his instincts told him.

El Gato, the Cat, didn't get rich by ignoring his instincts. He decided to go to Cuba and take the risk of explaining it away later. If the exiles in Florida ever got the idea that he had double-crossed them, money or no money, they would take their revenge.

Courage was one of El Gato's long suits. He didn't accumulate a fortune worth almost a half billion dollars by being timid. So he and his bodyguards boarded the plane. That was almost a week ago. He had been steadily losing money in the casinos every day since while waiting. Now the waiting was over.

Tonight he was to see the man he came to meet, Alejo Vargas. In five minutes.

He checked his watch, then pocketed his chips and walked for the door of the club, the Tropicana, the jewel of Havana. His bodyguards joined him, like shadows.

El Gato left the casino via the back entrance. The three men walked a block to a large black limousine sitting by the curb and climbed into the rear seats.

Two men were sitting on the front-facing seats.

'El Gato, welcome to Havana. I confess, I didn't think we would ever meet on Cuban soil.'

'Miracles never cease, Señor Vargas. The world turns, the sun rises and sets and we all get older day by day. Wise men change with the times.'

'Quite so. This is Colonel Santana, head of the Department of State Security.'

El Gato nodded politely at Santana, then introduced his bodyguards, men Santana didn't even bother to look at.

'I was hoping, Señor Vargas, that you and I might have a private conversation, perhaps while these gentlemen watched from a small distance?'

Vargas nodded his assent, pushed a button, and spoke into an intercom to the driver. After about fifteen minutes of travel, during which nothing was said, the limo pulled up to a curb and all the men got out. The car was sitting on a breakwater near Morro Castle, with the dark battlements looming above them in the glare of Havana reflecting off the clouds.

Vargas and El Gato began strolling.

'The cargo is aboard,' El Gato said, 'and the ship has sailed. I presume you kept me waiting to see if that event would occur.'

'When you proposed this operation, I had my doubts. I still do.'

'I cannot guarantee success,' El Gato said. 'I do everything within my power to make success possible, but sometimes the world does not turn my way. I understand that, and I keep trying anyway.'

'The waiting will soon be over,' Vargas said.

'Indeed. In many ways. I hear rumors that Fidel will not be with us much longer.'

Vargas didn't reply to that remark.

'Change is rapidly coming to Cuba,' El Gato began, 'and the thought occurred to me that a man with friends in Cuba under the new order would be in an enviable position.'

'You have such friends?'

'I am here to test the water, so to speak, to learn if I do.'

'After your years of opposition to Castro, any friends you have will not be very vocal about it.'

'Noisy friends I have aplenty in Florida. No, the kind of friends I need are the kind who keep their friendship to themselves and help when help is needed, who give approvals when asked, who nod yes at the appropriate time.'

'How much money have you given the exiles' political movements over the years?'

'You wish to know the figure?'

'Yes. I wish to learn if you will be honest with me. Obviously I have sources and some idea of the amount. Come now, impress me with your frankness and your honesty.'

'Over five million American,' El Gato said.

This was twice the figure Vargas expected, and he looked at the American sharply. If El Gato was lying, exaggerating the number to impress Vargas, it didn't show in his face.

'Some of that money, a small amount it is true, came directly from the Cuban government,' El Gato said. 'I believe you authorized those payments.'

'You have a sense of the sardonic, I see,' Vargas said without humor. One got the impression he had not smiled in his lifetime, nor would he.

El Gato nodded.

'You had a commodity to sell, we wished to buy. We paid a fair price.'

'Come, come, Señor Vargas. Let's not pretend with each other. I arranged for you to acquire the equipment and chemicals necessary to create a biological warfare program. What you have done with those chemicals and equipment I don't know, nor do I want to know. But you know as well as I that if the American government found out about the sale I would be ruined. And you know that I made no profit in the transaction.'

Vargas nodded, a dip of the head.

'Nor have I asked for money for arranging to steal *Nuestra Señora*.'

'That is true, but if the operation succeeds, we would have paid a fair amount.'

'I do not want your money.'

'You want something. What?'

El Gato walked a few paces with his hands in his pockets before he spoke. 'After Castro I envision a Cuba much more friendly to American interests, more open to a free flow of capital in and out. A great many people in the United States have a great deal of money accumulated that they want to invest in Cuba, which they will do as soon as the United States government allows them to do so, and as soon as the Cuban government guarantees these investors that their investment will not be confiscated or stolen with hidden taxes or demands for graft. A man who could guarantee that his friends would be fairly treated in Cuba could make a lot of money. He would be a patron, if you will. And if he carefully screened his friends, Cuba would get a vetted flow of capable investors who would perform as promised.'

'Something for everyone,' Vargas said.

'Precisely.'

'Just so that I understand – are you suggesting that you want to be that man, *el jefecito*?'

'I could do it, I believe.'

'The exiles expect to come to Cuba at Castro's death and take over the country. They want billions in repatriations. I tell you now, you have helped fuel their expectations with your five million dollars.'

What he failed to mention was the fact that the Cuban government had played to the fears of the peons who stayed, telling them they would be thrown from their homes if the exiles ever returned.

El Gato smiled. 'Like the exiles, you fail to clearly see the situation. They are Americans. They make more money in America than they ever could in Cuba. They will never return in significant numbers. In fact, if the borders are thrown open, the net human flow will be toward the United States, not back to Cuba. If the American government would allow it, a million Cubans a year would leave this island. You would be wise to let people go where they wish to go.'

'You are saying the exile problem will just disappear?'

'Except for a few bitter old men, yes, I believe it will. The young ones have gotten on with their lives. They have no old scores to settle.'

'So you betray these old ones for your own profit?'

'Señor Vargas, if they wish to nurse old grudges and dream of a time which is long past and will never come again, who am I to tell them no? Most of these people are quite harmless. Those who aren't can be dealt with when they cause problems. A public apology to dispossessed old people, a plea for healing, a few pesos, and the exiles could be appeased.'

'Assassination plots against Castro and the like?'

'Plots that never get off the ground are harmless. Let them have their meetings and their thunderous denunciations. These people will pass from the scene soon enough.'

Vargas made a gesture of irritation. He had his own opinions and didn't really wish to hear other people's. 'Colonel Santana will take you and your men to your hotel.'

'Thank you.'

'I can promise you very little, El Gato. I understand that you cannot guarantee the future, but the North Koreans must fulfill their part of our bargain. If they do, there is a chance, just a chance, that I may rule after Castro.'

El Gato waited.

Vargas continued: 'I will not forget what you did for me, for Cuba. If the day ever comes when I am in a position to help you, feel free to ask. What I can do then will have to be decided upon that day.'

'That is more than I hoped for,' El Gato said, genuine warmth obvious in his voice. 'I thank you for that promise.'

3

The F-14 Tomcat hung suspended in an infinite blue sky, over an infinite blue sea. Or so it seemed to Jake Grafton, who sat in the front cockpit taking it all in. Behind him Toad Tarkington was working the radar, searching the sky ahead. The air was dead calm today, so without a visual reference there was no sensation of motion. The puffy clouds on the surface of the sea seemed to be marching uniformly toward the rear of the aircraft, almost as if the sky were spinning under the airplane.

The fighter was cruising at 31,000 feet, heading northwestward parallel with the southern coast of Cuba, about a hundred and fifty miles offshore.

'I sure am glad you got us off the ship, sir,' Tarkington said cheerfully. 'A little flying helps clean out the pipes, keeps everything in perspective.'

'That it does,' Jake agreed, and stretched.

He had the best job in the navy, he thought. As a battle group commander he could still fly – indeed, an occasional flight was part of the job description. Yet his flying days would soon be over: in just two months he was scheduled to turn over the command to another admiral and be on his way somewhere.

He searched the empty sky automatically as he thought again about where the next set of orders might send him. If the people in the flag detailing office in the Pentagon had a clue, they certainly weren't talking.

Ah, it would all work out. The powers that be would send him another set of orders or retire him, and it really didn't matter much which way it went. Everyone has to move on sooner or later, so why not now?

Maybe he should just submit his retirement papers, get on with the rest of his life.

With his right hand he hit the emergency disconnect for the autopilot, which worked as it should.

Without touching the throttles, Jake Grafton smoothly lifted the nose and began feeding in left stick. Nose climbing, wing dropping ... rolling smoothly through the inverted position, though with only seventy degrees of heading change. The nose continued down – keep the roll in! – and the G increased as the fighter came out of the dive and back to the original heading, only 1,400 below the entry altitude. Ta-ta! There you have it – a sloppy barrel roll!

Jake kept the stick back and started a barrel roll to the right.

'Are you okay up there, sir?' Toad Tarkington asked anxiously.

'You ask that of me? The world's finest aerobatic pilot? Have you no respect?'

'These whifferdills are not quite up to your usual world-class standards, so one wonders. Could it be illness, decrepitude, senility?'

They were passing the inverted positon when Jake said, 'Just for that, Tarkington, you can put us on the flight schedule every day so we can practice. An hour and a half of high-G maneuvers seven times a week will teach you to respect your elders.'

'You got that right,' Toad replied, and moaned as if he were in pain as Jake lifted the Tomcat into a loop.

'War Ace One Oh Four, this is Sea Hawk. You have traffic to the northwest, one hundred miles, heading south at about 30,000.'

'Roger, Sea Hawk.'

Coming down the back side of the loop, Jake turned to the northwest.

'Admiral, I know you think I was loafing back here,' Toad said obsequiously, 'but I had that guy on the scope. Honest! I was just gonna say something when that E-2 guy beat me to the switch.'

'Sure, Toad. These things happen. If you're going to nap, next time bring a pillow.'

'This guy is coming south, like he's out of some base in central Cuba, about our altitude. Heck of a coincidence, huh?'

The F-14 had an optical camera mounted in the nose that was slaved to the radar cross-hairs.

'Tell me when you see him,' Jake murmured.

'Be a couple miles yet. Let's come right ten degrees just for grins and see what happens.'

Jake again had the fighter on autopilot. He pushed the stick right, then leveled on the new course.

At fifty miles Toad had the other airplane on the screen of his monitor. A silver airplane, fighter size, with the sun glinting off its skin. The electronic countermeasures (ECM) panel lit up as the F-14's sensors picked up the emissions of the other plane's radar.

'A MiG-29,' Jake said.

'What's he doing out here?' Toad wondered.

'Same thing as we are. Out flying around seeing what is what.'

'I thought the Cubans had retired their MiG-29s. Couldn't keep paying the bills on 'em.'

'Well, at least one is still operational.'

Even as they watched, the MiG altered course to the left so that he would have a chance to turn in behind the F-14 when their flight paths converged.

Jake Grafton was suddenly sure he didn't want the MiG behind him. The Soviets specifically designed the MiG-29 to be able to defeat the F-14, F-15, F-16 and F/A-18 in close combat; it was, probably, the second-best fighter in the world (the best being the Sukhoi Su-27 Flanker). Jake altered course so the two planes would converge head-on.

What would the MiG pilot do?

If the Cuban pilot opened fire over the ocean, over a hundred miles from land, who would ever know?

'Sea Hawk, One Oh Four, are you getting this on tape?'

'Yes, sir. We're recording.'

'This bogey is a MiG-29.'

'Roger that. We've been tracking him for twenty-five minutes now.'

The range was closing rapidly, but still Jake didn't see the MiG. He looked at the target dot in the heads-up display, but the sky was huge and the Cuban fighter too far away, although it was almost as large as the F-14.

The MiG was about four miles away when Jake finally saw it, a winged silver glint that shot by just under his right wing. Jake Grafton disconnected the autopilot and slammed the stick over.

He pulled carefully, cleanly, craned his head and braced himself with his left hand as he kept the turning MiG in sight.

The Cuban fighter rolled out of his turn heading north. Jake leveled out on a parallel course. Careful not to point his nose at the Cuban, Jake let the Tomcat drift closer on a converging course.

When the planes were less than a hundred yards apart, he slowed the closure rate but kept moving in.

Finally the two planes were in formation with their wingtips about twenty yards apart.

'Look at that thing, would you?' Toad enthused. 'Have you ever seen a more gorgeous airplane?'

'I hear it's a real dream machine,' Jake agreed.

'Oh, baby, the lines, the curves . . . The Russians sure know how to design flying machines.'

'If this guy has to jump out of that thing,' Jake asked Toad, 'do you think Cuban Air-Sea Rescue is going to come pick him up?'

'I doubt it,' Toad replied. 'And I suspect he knows that.'

'He's got a set of cojones on him,' Jake said. 'Bet he can fly the hell out of that thing, too.'

In the Cuban fighter, Major Carlos Corrado took his time looking over the American plane. This was the first time he had ever seen an F-14. Amazing how big they were, with the two men and the missiles under the wings.

Carlos was lucky he had this hunk of hot Russian iron to fly, technical generations ahead of the MiG-19s and 21s that equipped the bulk of Cuba's tactical squadrons, and he damn well knew it. Cuba owned three dozen

MiG-29s and had precisely one operational – this one – which Corrado kept flying by the simple expedient of cannibalizing parts from the others.

He checked his fuel. He had enough, just enough, to get home. Sure, he had no business being out here over the ocean, but he wanted to fly today and the Cuban ground control intercept (GCI) controller said the American was here. One thing led to another and here he was.

Now Carlos Corrado was on course to return to his base near the city of Cienfuegos, on Cuba's southern coast. He checked the compass, the engine instruments, then turned back to studying the American plane, which hung there on the end of his wing as if it were painted on the sky.

A minute went by, then the man in the front seat of the American plane raised his hand and waved. Carlos returned the gesture as the big American fighter turned away to the right and immediately began falling behind. Carlos twisted his body in his seat to keep the F-14 in sight for as long as possible. Big as it was, the F-14 disappeared into the eastern sky with startling rapidity.

Carlos Corrado turned in his seat and eased the position of his butt.

The Americans were two or three technical generations beyond the Cubans, so far ahead that most Cuban military men regarded American capabilities as almost superhuman. They had read of the Gulf War, of the satellites and computers and smart weapons. Unlike his colleagues, Corrado was not frightened by the Americans. Impressed by their military capability, but not frightened.

If I were smarter, he thought now, *I would be frightened.*

But the Americans and Cubans would never fight. They had not fought since the Bay of Pigs and doubtless never would. Castro would soon be gone and a new government would take over and Cuba would become a new American suburb, another little beach island baking in the sun south of Miami, Key Cuba. When that happy day came, Carlos Corrado told himself, he was going to America and get a decent flying job that paid real money.

Doña Maria Vieuda de Sedano's daughters arrived first, in the early afternoon, to tidy up and do the cooking for the guests. They had married local men who worked the sugarcane and saw her every day. In truth, they looked after her, helped her dress, prepared her meals, cleaned and washed the clothes.

It was infuriating to be disabled, to be unable to *do*! The arthritis that crippled her hands and feet made even simple tasks difficult and complex tasks out of the question.

Doña Maria managed to shuffle to her favorite chair on the tiny porch without help. Her small house sat on the western edge of the village. From the porch she could see several of her neighbors' houses and a wide sweep of the road. Across the road was a huge field of cane. A cane-cooking factory stood about a half mile farther west. When the harvest began, the stacks belched smoke and the fumes of cooking sugar drifted for miles on the wind.

Beyond all this, almost lost in the distance, was the blue of the ocean, a thin line just below the horizon, bluer than the distant sky. The wind coming in off the sea kept the temperature down and prevented insects from becoming a major nuisance.

The porch was the only thing Doña Maria really liked about the house, though after fifty-two years in residence God knows she had some memories. Small, just four rooms, with a palm-leaf roof, this house had been the center of her adult life. Here she moved as a young bride with her husband, bore her children, raised them, cried and laughed with them, buried two of the ten, watched the others grow up and marry and move away. And here she watched her husband die of cancer.

He had died . . . sixteen years ago, sixteen years in November.

You never think about outliving your spouse when you are young. Never think about what comes afterward, after happiness, after love. Then, too soon, the never-thought-about future arrives.

She sat on the porch and looked at the clouds floating above the distant ocean, almost like ships, sailing someplace. . . .

She had lived her whole life upon this island, every day of it, had never been farther from this house than Havana, and that on just two occasions: once when she was a teenage girl, on a marvelous expedition with her older sister, and once when her son Maximo was sworn in as the minister of finance.

She had met Fidel Castro on that visit to the capital, felt the power of his personality, like a fire that warmed everyone within range. Oh, what a man he was, tall, virile, full of life.

No wonder Maximo orbited Fidel's star. His brother Jorge, her eldest, had been one of Castro's most dedicated disciples, espousing Marxism and Cuban nationalism, refusing to listen to the slightest criticism of his hero. Jorge, dead of heart failure at the age of forty-two, another dreamer.

All the Sedanos were dreamers, she thought, poverty-stricken dreamers trapped on this sun-washed island in a sun-washed sea, isolated from the rest of humankind, the rest of the species. . . .

She thought of Jorge when she saw Mercedes, his widow, climb from the car. The men in the car glanced at her seated on the porch, didn't wave, merely drove on, leaving Mercedes standing in the road.

'*Hola, Mima.*'

Jorge, cheated of life with this woman, whom he loved more than anything, more than Castro, more than his parents, more than *anything*, for the Sedanos were also great lovers.

'*Hola,* my pretty one. Come sit beside me.'

As she stepped on the porch, Doña Maria said, 'Thank you for coming.'

'It is nothing. We both loved Jorge. . . .'

'Jorge . . .'

Mercedes looked at Maria's hands, took them in her own, as if they weren't twisted and crippled. She kissed the older woman, then sat on a bench beside her and looked at the sea.

'It is still there. It never changes.'

'Not like we do.'

The emotions twisted Mercedes's insides, made her eyes tear. Here in this place she had had so much, then with no warning it was gone, as if a mighty tide had swept away all that she valued, leaving only sand and rock.

Jorge – oh, what a man he was, a dreamer and lover and believer in social justice. A true believer, without a selfish bone in his body . . . and of course he had died young, before he realized how much reality differed from his dreams.

He lived and died a crusader for justice and Cuba and all of that . . . and left her to grow old alone . . . lonely in the night, looking for someone who cared about something besides himself.

She bit her lip and looked down at Doña Maria's hands, twisted and misshapen. On impulse leaned across and kissed the older woman on the cheek.

'God bless you, dear child,' Doña Maria said.

Ocho came walking along the road, trailed by four of the neighborhood children who were skipping and laughing and trying to make him smile. When he turned in at his mother's gate, the children scampered away.

Everyone on the porch turned and looked at him, called a greeting as he quickly covered the three or four paces of the path. Ocho was the Greek god, with the dark hair atop a perfect head, a perfect face, a perfect body . . . tall, with broad shoulders and impossibly narrow hips, he moved like a cat. He dominated a room, radiating masculinity like a beacon, drawing the eyes of every woman there. Even his mother couldn't take her eyes from him, Mercedes noted, and grinned wryly. This last child – she bore Ocho when she was forty-four – even Doña Maria must wonder about the combination of genes that produced him.

Normally an affable soul, Ocho had little to say this evening. He grunted monosyllables to everyone, kissed his mother and Mercedes and his sisters perfunctorily, then found a corner of the porch in which to sit.

Women threw themselves at Ocho, and he never seemed to notice. It was almost as if he didn't want the women who wanted him. He was sufficiently different from most of the men Mercedes knew that she found him intriguing. And perhaps, she reflected, that was the essence of his charm.

Maximo Luís Sedano's sedan braked to a stop in a swirl of dust. He bounded from the car, strode toward the porch, shouting names, a wide grin on his face. He gently gathered his mother in his arms, kissed her on both her cheeks and forehead, kissed each hand, knelt to look into her face.

Mercedes didn't hear what he said; he spoke only for his mother's ears.

When she looked away from Maximo and his mother she was surprised to see Maximo's wife climbing the steps to the porch. Maximo's wife – just what *was* her name? – condemned forever to be invisible in the glare of the great man's spotlight.

Another dominant personality – the Sedanos certainly produced their share of those – Maximo was a prisoner of his birth. Cuba was far too small for him. Amazingly, because life rarely works out just right, he had found one of the few occupations in Castro's Cuba that allowed him to travel, to play on a wider field. As finance minister he routinely visited the major capitals of Europe, Central and South America.

Just now he gave his mother a gift, which he opened for her as his sisters leaned forward expectantly, trying to see.

French chocolates! He opened the box and let his mother select one, then passed the rare delicacy around to all.

The sisters stared at the box, rubbed their fingers across the metallic paper, sniffed the delicious scent, then finally, reluctantly, selected one candy and passed the box on.

One of the sister's husbands whispered to the other, just loud enough for Mercedes to overhear: 'Would you look at that? We ate potatoes and plantains last month, all month, and were lucky to get them.'

The other brother-in-law whispered back, 'For three days last week we had absolutely nothing. My brother brought us a fish.'

'Well, the dons in government are doing all right. That's the main thing.'

Mercedes sat listening to the babble of voices, idly comparing Maximo's clean, white hands to those of the sisters' husbands, rough, callused, work-hardened. If the men were different, the women weren't. Maximo's wife wore a chic, fashionable French dress as she sat now with Doña Maria's daughters, whispering with them, but inside the clothes she was still one of them in a way that Maximo would never be again. He had traveled too far, grown too big. . . .

Mercedes was thinking these thoughts when Hector arrived, walking along the road. Even Maximo stopped talking to one of his brothers, the doctor, when he saw Hector coming up the path to the porch.

'Happy birthday, *Mima.*'

Hector, Jesuit priest, politician, revolutionary . . . he spoke softly to his mother, kissed her cheek, shook Maximo's hand, looked him in the eye as he ate a chocolate, kissed each of his sisters and touched the arms and hands of their husbands and his brothers, the doctor and the automobile mechanic.

Ocho was watching Hector, waiting for him to reach for his hand, his lips quivering.

Mercedes couldn't quite believe what she was seeing, Hector hugging Ocho, holding him and rocking back and forth, the young man near tears.

Then the moment passed.

Hector refused to release his grip on his brother, led him to Doña Maria, gently made him sit at her feet and placed her hands in his.

Ah, yes, Hector Sedano. If anyone could, it would be you.

'They do not appreciate you,' Maximo's wife told him as they rode back to Havana in his car.

'They are so ignorant,' she added, slightly embarrassed that she and her husband should have to spend an evening with peasants in such squalid surroundings.

Of course, they were his family and one had duties, but still . . . He had worked so hard to earn his standing and position, it was appalling that he should have to make a pilgrimage back to such squalor.

And his relatives! The old woman, the sisters . . . crippled, ignorant, dirty, uncouth . . . it was all a bit much.

And Hector, the priest who was a secret politician! A man who used the Church for counterrevolutionary treason.

'Surely he must know that you are aware of his political activities,' she remarked now to her husband, who frowned at the shacks and sugarcane fields they were driving past.

'He knows,' Maximo murmured.

'Europe was so nice,' his wife said softly. 'I don't mean to be uncharitable, but truly it is a shame that we must return to *this*!'

Maximo wasn't paying much attention.

'I keep hoping that someday we shall go to Europe and never return,' she whispered. 'I do love Madrid so.'

Maximo didn't hear that comment. He was wondering about Hector and Alejo Vargas. He couldn't imagine the two of them talking, but what if they had been? What if those two combined to plot against him? What could he do to guard against that possibility, to protect himself?

Later that evening Hector and his sister-in-law, Mercedes, rode a bus into Havana. 'It was good of you to stay for *Mima*'s party,' Hector said.

'I wanted to see her. She makes me think of Jorge.'

'Do you still miss him?'

'I will miss him every day of my life.'

'Me too,' Hector murmured.

'Vargas knows about you,' she said, after glancing around to make sure no one else could hear her words.

'What does he know?'

'That you organize and attend political meetings, that you write to friends, that you speak to students, that most of the priests in Cuba are loyal to you, that many people all over this island look to you for leadership. . . . He knows that much and probably more.'

'It would be a miracle if none of that had reached the ears of the secret police.'

'He may arrest you.'

'He will do nothing without Fidel's approval. He is Fidel's dog.'

'And you think Fidel approves of your activities?'

'I think he tolerates them. The man isn't immortal. Even he must wonder what will come after him.'

'You are playing with fire. Castro's hold on Vargas is weakening. Castro's death will give him a free hand. Do not underestimate him.'

'I do not. Believe me. But Cuba is more important than me, than Vargas, than Castro. If this country is ever going to be anything other than the barnyard of a tyrant, someone must plant seeds that have a chance of growing. Every person I talk to is a seed, an investment in the future.'

' "Barnyard of a tyrant." What a pretty phrase!' Mercedes said acidly. The last few years, living with Fidel, she had developed a thick skin: people said the most vicious things about him and she had learned to ignore most of it. Still, she deeply admired Hector, so his words wounded her.

'I'm sorry if I –'

She made sure her voice was under control, then said, 'Dear Hector, Cuba is also the graveyard of a great many martyrs. There is room here for Vargas to bury us both.'

He was remembering the good days, the days when he had been young, under a bright sun, surrounded by happy, laughing comrades.

All things had been possible back then. Bullets couldn't touch them, no one would betray them to Batista's men, they would save Cuba, save her people, make them prosperous and healthy and strong and happy. Oh, yes, *when we were young* . . .

As he tossed and turned, fighting the pain, snatches of scenes ran through his mind; student politics at the University of Havana, the assault on the Moncada Barracks in Santiago, guns banging and bullets spanging off steel, off masonry, singing as they whirled away. . . . He remembered the firefights on the roads, riding the trucks through the countryside, evenings making plans with Che and the others, how they would set things right, kick out the capitalists who had enslaved Cuba for centuries.

Che, he had been a true believer.

And there were plenty more. True believers all. Ignorant as virgins, penniless and hungry, they thought they could fix the world.

In his semiconscious state he could hear his own voice making speeches, explaining, promising to fix things, to heal the people, put them to work, give them jobs and houses and medical care and a future for their children.

Words. All words.

Wind.

He coughed, and the coughing brought him fully awake. The nurse was there in the chair watching him.

'Leave me, woman.'

She left the room.

He pulled himself higher in the bed, used a corner of the sheet to wipe the sweat from his face.

The sheets were thin, worn out. Even *el presidente*'s sheets were worn out! A sick joke, that.

Everything in the whole damned country was broken or worn out, including Castro's sheets. You didn't have to be a high government official to be aware of that hard fact.

On the dresser just out of reach was a box of cigars. He hitched himself around in bed, reached for one, then leaned far over and got his hand on the lighter.

The pain made him gasp.

Madre mia!

When the pain subsided somewhat he lay back in the bed, wiped his face again on the sheet.

He fumbled with the cigar, bit off the end and spat it on the floor. Got the lighter going, sucked on the cigar . . . the raw smoke was like a knife in his throat. He hacked and hacked.

The doctors made him give up cigars ten years ago. He demanded this box two days ago, when they told him he was dying. 'If I am dying, I can smoke. The cancer will kill me before the cigars, so why not?'

When the coughing subsided, he took a tiny puff on the cigar, careful not to inhale.

God, the smoke was delicious.

Another puff.

He lay back on the pillow, sniffed the aroma of the smoke wafting through the air, inhaled the tobacco essence and let it out slowly as the cigar smoldered in his hand.

The truth was that he had made a hash of it. Cuba's problems had defeated him. Oh, he had done the best he could, but by any measure, his best hadn't been good enough. The average Cuban was worse off today than he had been those last few years under Batista. Food was in short supply, the economy was in tatters, the bureaucrats were openly corrupt, the social welfare system was falling apart, and the nation reeled under massive short-term foreign debt, for it had defaulted on its long-term international debt in the late 1980s. The short-term debt could not be repudiated, not if the nation ever expected to borrow another peso abroad.

He puffed on the cigar, savoring the smoke. Then he shifted, trying to make the ache in his bowels ease up.

Of course he knew what had gone wrong. When he took over the nation he had played the cards he had . . . evicted the hated Yanqui *imperialistas* and seized their property, and accepted the cheers and adulation of the people for delivering them from the oppressor. Unfortunately Cuba was a tiny, poor country, so he had had to replace the evicted *patrón* with another, and the only one in sight had been the Soviet Union. He embraced communism, got down on his knees and swore fealty to the Soviet state. With that act he earned the undying hatred of the politicians who ruled the United States – after several assassination attempts and the ill-fated Bay of Pigs invasion débâcle, they declared economic warfare on Cuba. Then the cruelest twist of the knife – the Soviet Union collapsed in 1990–91 and Cuba was cut adrift.

Ah, he should have been wiser, should have realized that the United States would be the winning horse. The Spanish grandees had bled Cuba for centuries, worked the people as slaves, then as peons. After the Americans ran the Spanish off, American corporations put their men in the manor houses and life continued as before. The people were still slaves to the cane crop, living in abject poverty, unable to escape the company towns and the company stores.

A few things did change under the Americans. The island became America's red light district, the home of the vice that was illegal on the American mainland: gambling, prostitution, drugs, and, during Prohibition, alcohol. Poor Catholic families sent their daughters to the cities to whore for the Yanquis.

The capitalists bled Cuba until there was no blood left – they would keep exploiting people the world over until there were no more people. Or no more capitalists. Until then, the capitalists would have all the money. He should have realized that fundamental truth.

He had grown up hating the United States, hating Yanquis who drank and gambled and whored the nights away in Havana. He hated their diplomats, their base at Guantánamo Bay, their smugness, their money ... he despised them and all their works, which was unfortunate, because America was a fact of life, like shit. A man could not escape it because it smelled bad.

God had never given him the opportunity to destroy the Yanquis, because if He had ...

Fidel Castro was intensely, totally Cuban. He personified the resentment the Cuban people felt because they had spent their lives begging for the scraps that fell from the rich men's table. Resentment was a vile emotion, like hatred and envy.

Well, he was dying. Weeks, they said. A few weeks, more or less. The cancer was eating him alive.

The painkillers were doing their job – at least he could sit up, think rationally, smoke the forbidden cigars, plan for Cuba's future.

Cuba had a future, even if he didn't.

Of course, the United States would play a prominent role in that future.

With the great devil Fidel dead, all things were possible. The economic embargo would probably perish with him, a new *presidente* could bring . . . what?

He thought about that question as he puffed gingerly on the cigar, letting the smoke trickle out between his lips.

For years Americans had paraded through the government offices in Havana talking about what might be after the economic embargo was lifted by their government. Always they had an angle, wanted a special dispensation from the Cuban government . . . and were willing to pay for it, of course. Pay handsomely. Now. Paper promises . . . He had enjoyed taking their money.

He had made no plans for a successor, had anointed no one. Some people thought his brother, Raúl, might take over after him, but Raúl was *impotente*, a lightweight.

He would have to have his say now, while he was very much alive.

But what should the future of Cuba be?

The pain in his bowels doubled him up. He curled up in the bed, groaning, holding tightly to the cigar.

After a minute or so the pain eased somewhat and he puffed at the cigar, which was still smoldering.

Whoever came after him was going to have to make his peace with the United States. They were going to have to be selective about America's gifts, rejecting the bad while learning to profit from the good things, the gifts America had to give to the world.

That had been his worse failing – he himself had never learned how to safely handle the American elephant, make the beast do his bidding. His successors would have to for the sake of the Cuban people. Cuba would never be anything if it remained a long, narrow sugarcane field and way point for cocaine smugglers. If that was all there was, everyone on the island might as well set sail for Miami.

Maybe he should have left, said good-bye, thrown up his hands and retired to the Costa del Sol.

Next time. Next time he would retire young, let the Cubans make it on their own.

Like every man who ever walked the earth, Castro had been trapped by his own mistakes. The choices he made early in the game were irreversible. He and the Cuban people had been forced to live with the consequences. Life is like that, he reflected. Everyone must make his choices, wise or foolish, good or bad, and live with them; there is no going back.

There is always the possibility of redemption, of course, but one cannot unmake the past. We have only the present. Only this moment.

When the pain came this time, the cigar dropped from his fingers.

He lay in the bed groaning, trying not to scream for the nurse. If he did, she would give him an injection, which would put him to sleep. The needle was going to give him peace during his final days, but he wasn't ready for it yet.

The pain had eased somewhat when he felt a hand on his forehead. He opened his eyes. Mercedes.

'You dropped your cigar on the floor,' she whispered.

'I know.'

'Shall I call the nurse?'

'Not for a while.'

She used a damp cloth to wipe the perspiration from his face. The cloth felt good.

'Light the cigar.'

She did so, put it in his hand. He managed one tiny puff.

'You talked to Hector?'

'Yes.'

'What did he say?'

'He was surprised. He didn't know it would be so soon.'

'That was your impression?'

'Yes.'

'And the tobacco deal with the Americans? What did Hector say when you told him about it?'

'Just listened.'

'The birthday party, Maximo came?'

'Yes. Brought a box of French chocolates and his wife, who wore a Paris frock.'

Fidel's lips twisted. He could imagine what the other people at the party thought of that. Maximo could charm foreign bankers and squeeze a peso until it squealed, but he was no politician.

'Did you warn Hector about Alejo?'

'Yes.'

'What did he say?'

'He made light of it.'

Fidel thought about that. Remembered the cigar and took another puff.

'He thinks the threat will be the generals,' he said finally, 'but it won't. The generals don't know it, but the troops will follow Hector. Alejo Vargas is his most dangerous opponent, and if Hector Sedano doesn't understand that, they will bury him a few days after they bury me.'

'Admiral, next weekend when we're in the Virgin Islands, what say we put the barge in the water and go water-skiing?'

The person asking the question was the admiral's aide, a young lieutenant who flew an F/A-18 on her last cruise. Her boyfriend was still in one of the Hornet squadrons; the last time Jake Grafton approved the barge adventure, the boyfriend was invited to go along.

Now Jake sighed. 'I'm not sure where we're going to be next weekend,

Beth.' He had no intention of getting very far from Guantánamo Bay while those warheads were still in that warehouse, but of course he couldn't say that. 'Check with ops, Commander Tarkington.'

'Yes, sir,' Beth said, trying to hide her disappointment.

The new Chief of Staff, Captain Gil Pascal, Toad Tarkington, and the admiral had put their heads together, carefully listed the forces available should an emergency arise, and drafted a contingency plan. 'Nothing's happened in all these years,' Jake told them, 'but Washington must have had a reason for telling us to keep an eye on the place. They must know something we don't.'

Gil Pascal met the admiral's gaze. He had reported to the staff just a week ago. 'Sir, as I recall, the orders said to "monitor" the loading of the weapons onto the containership.'

' "Monitor"?' muttered Jake Grafton. 'What the hell does that mean? Is that some kind of New Age bureaucrat word? It doesn't mean anything.'

'I guess my question really is, how much force are you willing to use without authorization from Washington?'

A faint smile crossed the lips of Toad Tarkington. Only a man who didn't know the admiral would ask that question. Anyone who started shooting in Jake Grafton's bailiwick had better be ready for a war, Toad thought. He had managed to wipe off the smile by the time the admiral answered:

'Whatever it takes to keep those warheads in American hands.'

Pascal took his time ordering his thoughts. 'Shouldn't we be talking contingencies with Washington, Admiral?'

Jake Grafton opened a top-secret message folder that lay on his desk in front of him. 'I already sent a query to CNO. This is the answer.'

He passed the message to Pascal. 'Monitor weapons on-load diligently, using your best judgment,' the message read, 'but do not deviate from normal routine. Revealing presence of chemical and biological weapons in Cuba not in the national interest. Risks of transfer have been carefully considered at the highest level. Should risk assessment change you will be informed.' The final sentence referred to the original message.

'Five sentences?' Toad Tarkington asked when he had had his chance to read the message. 'Only five sentences?'

Reading naval messages was an art, of course. One had to consider the identity and personality of the sender, the receiver, the situation, any correspondence that had passed before.... The situation in Washington was the unknown here, Jake concluded. If the CNO had been at liberty to say more, he would have: Jake knew the CNO. The lack of guidance or illumination told Jake that the chief of naval operations wanted him to be ready for anything.

'We'll have to do the best we can with what we have,' the admiral said now to Pascal and Tarkington. 'I want a plan: we need someone watching at all times, a quick reaction force that can meet any initial incursion with

387

force, a reserve force to throw into the fray to absolutely deny access, and flash messages ready to go informing Washington of what we have done.'

Toad and Gil Pascal nodded. A plan like this with the forces that the admiral had at his disposal would be simple to construct. No surprises there.

'There is always the possibility that we may not be able to prevent hostiles from getting to the warheads, if they choose to try. We also need a plan addressing that contingency.'

'Surely this nightmare won't come to pass,' Gil Pascal said. 'Your assessment of the risk differs markedly from that of the National Security Council.'

'I'm sure the powers that be think it quite unlikely anybody will try to prevent us from removing the weapons from Cuba, and I agree. On the other hand, they must know something they can't share with us. If the risk were zero, they wouldn't have sent us here with orders to monitor, whatever the hell that is. Gentlemen, I just want to be ready if indeed we win the lottery and our number comes up.'

Toad thoughtfully put the message from Washington back into its red folder. He pursed his lips, then said thoughtfully, 'One thing is for sure – something is up.'

4

Alejo Vargas thought he had the finest office in Havana, indeed, in all of Cuba, and perhaps he did. He had the whole corner of the top floor, with lots of glass. Through the large windows one got a fine view across the rooftops of Morro Castle and the channel leading into Havana Harbor from the sea. The desk was mahogany, the chairs leather, the carpet Persian.

William Henry Chance paused to take in the view, then nodded appreciatively. He turned, saw the old United Fruit Company safe in the corner, now standing open, and the display of gold and silver coins from the Spanish Main under glass. He paused again, ran his eye over the coins just long enough to compliment his host.

'Very nice,' Chance said, and took the chair indicated by Alejo Vargas. At a nearby desk sat Vargas's Chief of Staff, Colonel Pablo Santana, who nodded at Chance when he looked his way, but said nothing.

Colonel Santana was dark, with coal black eyes and black hair combed straight back; he had some slave and Indian somewhere in his bloodline. He slit the throats and pulled the trigger for Alejo Vargas whenever those chores needed to be done.

Chance forced himself to ignore Santana and look at his host. 'I appreciate you taking the time from your busy day to see me, General,' the American said, and gave Vargas a frank, winning smile.

Chance was tall and angular, with craggy good looks, and dressed in a light gray suit of a quality one could not obtain in Cuba for love or money. He appeared perfectly at ease, as if he owned the building and were calling on a tenant.

No wonder the Russians lost the race to the Americans, Vargas thought ruefully. A true Latin male, he was acutely aware of his own physical and social shortcomings, his lack of grace and self-assurance, so he was quick to appreciate the desired qualities in others.

'I understand you have been discussing a business arrangement for the future with officials of several departments,' Vargas began.

'That is correct, General. As you probably know, I represent a consortium of stockholders in several of the major American tobacco companies. My errand is discreet, not for public discussion.'

Vargas certainly did know. He had a complete dossier on William Henry Chance in the upper right-hand drawer of his desk, a dossier decorated with a half dozen photos, photocopies of all the pages of Chance's passport, and one of his entry in *Who's Who*. A senior partner in a major New York law firm, Chance had represented tobacco companies for twenty-five years. That Chance was the man in Havana talking to the Cuban government was a sure signal that major money was behind him.

Indeed, Chance was in Vargas's office today because Fidel Castro had asked Vargas to see him.

'Alejo,' Fidel had said, 'our future depends on Cuba getting a piece of the world economy. The Americans have kept us isolated too long. If we can make it profitable for the Americans to lift the embargo, sooner or later they will. The Yanquis can smell money for miles.'

If William Henry Chance knew that Castro had personally asked Vargas to see him, he gave no sign.

The less he understands about our government, the better, Vargas thought. He cleared his throat, and said, 'I am sure you understand our concern, Señor Chance. Cuba is a poor nation, dependent on sugarcane as the mainstay of the economy, a crop that is, as usual, a glut on the world market. Your client's proposal, as I understand it, is to cultivate tobacco in Cuba instead of sugarcane.'

Chance gave the tiniest nod. A trace of a grin showed on his lips. He glanced at Santana, who was scrutinizing him with professional interest, the way a cat examines a mouse.

'Your comprehension is perfect, General.'

'Through the years, señor, the price of tobacco on the world market has been even lower than that of sugar.'

'This meeting shall be a great help to my clients,' Chance declared. 'Here today I will show you the many benefits that will accrue in the future to the nation that keeps an open mind about tobacco. I am not talking about cigar leaf, you understand, which is a tiny percentage of the world market. I am talking about cigarette tobacco.'

'The price of which will collapse in America when the American government ends its subsidy to American tobacco farmers.'

'Indeed,' said William Henry Chance. 'The United States government *will* soon cease supporting the price. But of greater interest to our clients, the government will increasingly regulate and tax the cigarette business. Plainly stated, the government is hostile to our industry. The current administration has stated that their eventual goal is to put the industry out of business.'

Chance moved his shoulders up and down a millimeter, settled deeper into his chair. 'The American public is gradually giving up the cigarette habit. In a few years the only Americans smoking will be rebellious youth and addicted geriatrics.'

Chance leaned forward slightly in his chair and looked Alejo Vargas straight in the eye. 'The future of the cigarette industry is to sell American brands to non-Americans. All over the world people in developing countries want the image American cigarettes present: prosperity, sex appeal, luxury, a rising status in the world. These images are no accident. They have been carefully created and nurtured at great expense by the American cigarette companies.'

Chance paused here to see if his host had anything to say. He didn't. Alejo Vargas sat silently with a blank, expressionless face. Not a single muscle revealed a clue about its owner's thoughts. Through the years Alejo had had a lot of experience listening to Castro's long-winded expositions.

William Henry Chance summed up: 'Minister, under the benevolent eye of a government that wants the industry to succeed, the prospects for profit are enormous. In the future the cigarette companies will grow the tobacco, process it, advertise, and sell the cigarettes. Cubans could own part of the companies, which would pay taxes and employ Cubans at a living wage. Here is a product that could be produced locally and sold worldwide. Cigarettes could be gold for Cuba in the twenty-first century.'

Now Alejo Vargas smiled. 'I like you, Señor Chance. I like your style.'

'You can't fool me,' Chance shot back. 'You like my message.'

'Cuba needs industries in addition to sugar.'

'The key, General, is a stable government that will protect the industry. Let me be frank: my clients have a great deal of money to invest, but they will not do so without the clear, unequivocal prospect of a stable government that will guarantee their right to do business and earn a fair profit.'

'Any promises or guarantees must come from the proper ministries of our government, with the consent of our president, Señor Castro,' Alejo Vargas said from the depths of his padded leather chair.

'It is the future of Cuba I wish to discuss with you, General. I state unequivocally that my clients will not invest a dime in Cuba until such time as the American government lifts the economic embargo. Candidly, the embargo will not be lifted as long as Castro remains in office.'

'Your candor deserves equal honesty on my part,' General Vargas said. 'Castro will remain in office until he chooses to leave of his own free will or until he dies. Do not be mistaken – regardless of what drivel you hear from the exiles, Fidel Castro is universally admired, loved, revered as a great patriot by virtually everyone in Cuba. There is no opposition, no movement to remove him . . . none of that.'

'It is the distant future I wish to discuss with you.'

'Very distant,' the general said.

'After Castro.'

'I do not have a crystal ball, Señor Chance. I may not live so long.'

'Nor I, sir. But very likely the cigarette industry will still be in business and looking for new opportunities to grow.'

'Perhaps,' Alejo Vargas admitted, and cocked his head slightly. He had seen transcripts of Chance's telephone calls to the United States and a transcript of the conversations that had taken place in his room. The man hadn't said one word about Castro's health nor had anyone mentioned it to him.

Still, it was a remarkable coincidence that he was here in Havana talking about post-Castro Cuba, and Castro was dying.

Alejo Vargas didn't believe in coincidences. His instincts told him that William Henry Chance was not who he appeared to be. As he listened to Chance talk about cigarette marketing and demographics in the Third World, he removed the file on Chance from his desk drawer. Holding the file in his lap where Chance could not see it, he carefully reviewed the information it contained. The photographs he could not scrutinize closely but he was willing to accept them as genuine. Mr William Henry Chance of New York City was probably a senior partner in a large law firm – after looking once more at the file Vargas would have been shocked if he weren't. All the right things were in the file. At least the file collectors were thorough, if nothing else, Vargas thought. Still, Chance's position and profession might be an elaborate cover.

When he finished with the file Vargas returned it to the desk drawer just as Chance was summing up. The lawyer had charts and graphs. Vargas didn't even glance at them. He studied Chance's eyes, the way they focused, how they moved, how the muscles tensed and relaxed as he talked.

It was possible, Vargas decided. William Henry Chance might be CIA.

Thirty minutes later when Chance was packing his charts and graphs to leave he pulled a small package from his briefcase and offered it to Vargas. 'Here's something you might enjoy, General. Sort of an executive pacifier. These things are hot right now in the States so I picked up a few at the airport.'

Vargas unwrapped the tissue paper. He was looking at a small plastic frame from which three odd-shaped crystals dangled, suspended by strings.

'These crystals are man-made and react to differential heating,' Chance explained. 'You put this on the windowsill and the crystals dance around, refracting the sunlight. Very colorful.'

'Thank you,' Vargas said mechanically, and sat the toy on his desk.

When Chance was gone Colonel Santana called an aide, who examined the device visually, then took it away to be examined electronically.

An hour later the aide returned with the toy in hand. 'It is what it appears to be, sir, merely three lumps of oddly shaped crystal on strings. The crystals and frame are entirely solid; they contain nothing.'

'Americans! Executive pacifier!' Vargas said contemptuously.

Colonel Santana put the toy on a south-facing windowsill, watched the crystals dance in the sun for a moment, then forgot about it.

William Henry Chance took his time walking to his hotel, the Nacional, a classic 1930s masterpiece near Havana harbor. He left his locked briefcase in his room, then went downstairs to the hotel restaurant, which charged truly stupendous amounts of American dollars for very modest food. In fact, the only currency the hotel staff would accept was American dollars. Colorful wooden panels with ceramic borders, and peacocks wandering around like refugees from an aviary, gave the place an over-the-top Caribbean look, Chance thought, sort of South Miami Beach racheted one notch too tight.

Chance ordered a sea bass, blackened and grilled, black beans and rice, avocados, and a *mojito*, a delicious concoction of lime juice, sugar, mint leaves, and rum – just what the doctor ordered to prevent scurvy. He savored the fish, sipped a second *mojito*, contemplated the state of the universe and his fellow diners.

The hotel staff, he knew, were employees of the Cuban secret police. When they weren't rushing here and there with daiquiris and fruit drinks they worked for Vargas, spied on the guests, listened to their conversations, searched their luggage, filled out written reports.

Chance knew the routine. He also knew that the Cubans would learn nothing by watching him because there was nothing to learn.

As he drank his second *mojito* he carefully reviewed everything Vargas had said during his interview. He thought about the general's face, the total lack of expression when the demise of Fidel Castro was discussed.

Of course Alejo Vargas knew that Castro was dying. He must know. What Vargas didn't know was that the CIA was equally aware of Castro's medical condition.

When Chance finished dinner he went out on the street for a walk. First he had to work his way through the crowd of Cubans loafing around the entrance to the hotel. Knots of poor, bored Cubans with nothing to do and nowhere to go thronged the sidewalks in front of every nightclub and casino listening to the music that floated out through open doors and windows. Occasionally people danced or sang, but mostly they just passed the time chatting and watching the tourists, and beggars and prostitutes trying to extract dollars from them.

Several blocks away Chance stopped to buy bread. The man who sold him the bread gave him a peso in change.

One peso meant yes, two meant no.

Chance smiled, nodded his thanks, and walked on.

The crystal device was working. The vibrations of human voices in the room changed the motion of the crystals in predictable, minute amounts. When a powerful optical device was focused on the crystals, the refracted

393

light was processed through a computer into human speech. The crystals were a totally passive listening device.

So far so good, Chance reflected, and walked on aimlessly, for the exercise, drinking in the sights, sounds, and smells of Havana. She was like a painted old whore, he thought, trying to keep up appearances. The tourist attractions were gay and lively, temples of hedonism set in a gray communist wasteland.

Outside the tourist area the city reeked of destitution and decay. The crumbling, rotting buildings were choked to the rafters with people, often four families to every apartment. The people fought daily battles to get enough food and basics to sustain life. Away from the clubs and hotels, the faces of the people were gloomy, drawn, without hope.

The poison of communism had done its work here, as it had in every nation that had ever embraced it. After the revolution the government expropriated almost all private property, from the vast estates of the rich to the corner grocery. Hopeless, grinding poverty became nearly universal. Forty years after the revolution the average wage was ten dollars a month, girls from all over Cuba flocked to Havana to prostitute themselves on the streets, everything necessary for a decent life was outrageously expensive or unavailable at any price. The social justice that the communists had promised was as far away as ever: the pain and misery that blighted and made wretched millions of lives had not brought that goal one step closer.

The tourist attractions were the supreme irony, of course. These monuments to greed and sins of the flesh were owned and operated by the socialist state to attract hard currency. The dollars were brought in and spent here by decadent capitalists who earned the money exploiting the workers of the world somewhere else.

If Karl Marx only knew. With the banners of social justice flying in the blue tropic sky, the Cubans had joined the Pied Piper of the Sierra Maestra as he marched bravely down the road to hell. The crumbling buildings, decrepit old cars, hookers on every corner, universal hopelessness – it looked as if the whole parade had almost arrived.

Very curious, William Henry Chance thought. Curious as hell.

From this vantage point he could see all of it, his whole life, as if it were a play being performed before him. The memories came back vivid and clear, the scenes scrolling before his eyes. The mistakes and lost opportunities and petty vendettas played endlessly, inevitably, and he lived it all again, powerless to change a word or gesture.

He was in pain these days, a lot of it, and the doctor this morning had given him a strong narcotic. Now he floated, half asleep, the pain that had doubled him into the fetal position now a tolerable dull ache. Even as his mind raced, his body relaxed.

Mercedes Sedano sat in a chair in the darkened room beside the bed, looking into the gloomy darkness and lost in her own thoughts.

She reached for Fidel when he moaned and put her hand on his forehead. He had always liked the sensual coolness of her fingers. Her touch now seemed to quiet him. He relaxed again, then tossed restlessly as the ghosts of the past paraded through the recesses of his mind.

An hour later, his eyes opened, though they didn't focus. Finally the head moved and the eyes sought her out.

Fidel Castro said nothing, merely looked.

He could feel the narcotic wearing off. The pain was coming back. He opened his mouth to ask for the doctor, then thought better of it.

He licked his lips. 'I want to make a videotape,' he whispered, barely audible.

'Are you strong enough?'

'For a little while, I could be, I think. It must be done.'

'What will you say?'

'I don't know exactly. I need to think about it.'

'When do you wish to do this tape?'

'Soon, I think, or never.'

'Tomorrow?'

'Yes, tomorrow. Tell the doctor. I must be alert tomorrow, if only for a little while.'

'Why?'

'I want to dictate my political will.'

She leaned forward and put her face next to his. 'Can you visit a moment with me?'

'*Te quiero, mujer.*'

'*Y yo te adoro, me viejo.*'

'We will talk for a little bit, then the doctor and the needle.' He was perspiring now, his body becoming tense.

'I am being selfish. I will call the doctor now.'

'In a moment. I want to tell you . . . I love you. You have been the rock I have held on to the last few years.'

She wiped away her tears and kissed him.

Then he said, 'I have made many mistakes in my life, but I have always tried to do what I thought best for Cuba. Always. Without fail.'

'Why do you think I love you so?'

'I want the Cuban people to remember me well. They are my children.'

'They will never forget.'

'I must help them march into the future.'

He drew his knees to his chest. His eyes were bright, perspiration coursed from his forehead and soaked into the pillow.

'Tomorrow,' he whispered. 'I will think. Get the doctor now.'

She squeezed his hand, then left the room.

Maximo Sedano spent the evening on his yacht cruising in sight of Morro Castle. The breeze blew the tops off occasional waves under a deep blue sky. Maximo's two guests looked decidedly pale as they huddled with him around the small table near the galley.

'If Castro dies, will the drug smugglers continue to do business with us?' asked Admiral Delgado, head of the Cuban Navy. For the last fifteen years he had limited his nautical activities to visiting patrol boats tied to piers.

'If we can guarantee the continued safety of their products and their people, of course,' Maximo said.

'We can't guarantee anything,' General Alba, Chief of Staff of the Cuban Army, said bitterly. 'The whole thing is going to fall apart; we are going to lose something very sweet.'

It was typical of Delgado and Alba, Maximo thought, that their very first thought of the future was of their pocketbooks. Money. These small, petty men lived for the bribes. Truly, they were unable to see what lay outside of the tiny circle where they lived their miserable, corrupt lives.

Alas, the best military man in Cuba under the age of eighty, the air force chief, died last month. Castro had yet to name a replacement, and probably would not.

Maximo sighed. 'Nothing lasts forever,' he said. 'But change always presents opportunity, if one knows where to look for it. Gentlemen, it all boils down to this: Who will rule Cuba when the dust settles after the funeral?'

'It won't be you,' General Alba said curtly. 'Five of my regional commanders are in Hector Sedano's pocket, and there is little I can do about it unless I relieve them and put someone else in their place.' He gave a tiny shrug. 'Castro must endorse the order. If I make a major move like that without his consent, he will sack me.'

'He is sick.'

'His aides will sack me, using his authority. I cannot disobey Fidel while he draws breath. You know that as well as I.'

'Perhaps you should shoot these disloyal subordinates,' the admiral said slowly, eyeing his colleague.

'If you have some loyal men who will wait until the right moment,' Maximo added.

'When Castro dies?'

'No. When I give the word. Not until then.'

'I have some loyal men, certainly,' the general said. 'I have spread the money around, made sure it got all the way down the chain. Only a fool plays the pig or hands great wads of money to someone else to distribute. My men get their share. The devil of it is that the disloyal ones think Alejo Vargas puts it in their pockets. They think he is the good fairy.'

'Will they obey you without question?'

'The loyal men will obey *me*, yes.'

'And will *you* obey *me?*' Maximo Sedano demanded.

General Alba stared at Maximo impudently. 'I will not lift a finger to put you on the throne as the new Fidel unless . . .' he said roughly, still looking Maximo straight in the eye, 'unless you represent my interests, which are also the interests of my men, and you have a chance to win. I don't think that you have such a chance.'

'I hear you, Alba. We have worked together for years; there is enough sugar here for all of us.' Maximo glanced at the admiral. 'Do you agree?'

'Oh, there's enough. But money isn't everything. The fact is that Alejo Vargas is a blackmailer and has been gathering his filth for twenty years. His spies are everywhere; he sees and hears everything.'

The admiral picked up the thought. 'Vargas has corrupted people you would not suspect, and those he can't corrupt, he blackmails. I give you my honest opinion: You have no chance against this man.'

'Without friends, I do not, that is true.'

'I tell you now, Maximo, you have no friends who wish to die with you. Few men do.'

'What I cannot understand,' the soldier said, 'is why Fidel tolerated your brother's antics. He has been told repeatedly of Hector's activities, of the meetings, the speeches, the subtle criticism of Fidel and the choices he made. Why does Fidel tolerate this?'

'I asked him that question once,' Maximo said, 'a year or so ago. Believe me, he has been carefully briefed on Hector Sedano.'

'What did he say?'

'He said Hector was a barometer. The people's reactions to his message told Fidel how unhappy they were with him, with the government. People routinely lie to government clerks, but if they go out of their way to listen to Hector Sedano make a speech, that means something. For my part, I think Fidel wisely considers what the Church might think. Like it or not, Hector is a priest. Fidel has carefully reached out to the Vatican the last few years – he cannot afford to antagonize the pope.'

'Are you saying he doesn't care what Hector says?'

'Three or four years ago when Hector first came to his attention, I think Fidel found him extremely irritating. Believe me, I warned Hector repeatedly, tried to get him to use reason, to control his tongue. He ignored me. Flouted me.

'I think Fidel intended to imprison Hector when he had said enough to convict himself with his own mouth. I told Hector he was playing with fire. But as Fidel got sicker, I think he lost interest. He just listens to the reports now, asks a few questions about the size of the crowds, who was there, and goes on to another subject.'

'Surely Fidel doesn't intend that Hector Sedano rule after him?' Admiral Delgado asked, his disapproval of Castro's attitude quite plain.

'If we are to have a chance at the prize, we must strike when Fidel breathes his last,' Maximo said. 'And quickly. Alejo Vargas must be assassinated within hours of Castro's death. Within minutes.'

'We would have to kill Santana too,' the general said. 'I have trouble sleeping nights knowing he is out there listening to everything, planning, scheming at Alejo's side.'

'Who is going to do this killing?' the admiral asked.

No one spoke.

'Our problem is going to be staying alive,' the general said, 'because Alejo Vargas and Santana will eliminate us at the slightest hint that we might be a threat.'

'What about Hector?'

'Hector will have to dodge his own bullets.'

'You are sheep,' Maximo muttered, loud enough for them to hear, 'without the courage to take your fate in your own hands. The wolves will rip out your throats.'

Toad Tarkington and his wife, Lieutenant Commander Rita Moravia, were seated in the back corner of the main wardroom aboard *United States*, drinking after-dinner coffee and conversing in low tones. A naval test pilot, Rita was on an exchange tour with the Marine squadron aboard *Kearsarge* so that she could gain operational experience on the tiltrotor Osprey prior to its introduction into navy squadrons.

As usual when he was around Rita, Toad Tarkington had a smile on his face. He felt good. *Life is good*, he thought as he watched her tell him what their son, Tyler, now four years old, had said in his most recent letter. She had received the missive earlier today. Of course Tyler wrote it with the help of Rita's parents, who looked after him when Rita and Toad were both at sea.

Yes, *life is good!* It flows along, and if you surround yourself with interesting people and interesting problems, it's worth living. Toad grinned broadly, vastly content.

'May I join you?' Toad and Rita looked up, and saw the new chief of staff standing there with a cup of coffee in his hands.

'Please do, Captain. Have you met my wife, Rita Moravia?'

Gil Pascal hadn't. He and Rita shook hands, said all the usual getting-acquainted things.

After they discussed the command that the captain had just left, Pascal said, 'I understand that you two have known Admiral Grafton for some years.'

'Oh, yes,' Toad agreed. 'I was just a lieutenant in an F-14 outfit when I first met him. He was the air wing commander, aboard this very ship in fact. We went to the Med that time, had a run-in with El Hakim.'

'I remember the incident,' Pascal said. 'The ship went to the yard for a year and a half when she got back to the States. And Admiral Grafton was awarded the Medal of Honor.'

Toad just nodded. 'Rita met the admiral a few months later in Washington,' Toad said, trying to move the conversation along. Conversations about El Hakim made him uncomfortable. That was long ago and far away, when he was single. Now, he realized with a jolt, things were much different – he had Rita and Tyler.

He was thinking about how being a family man changed his outlook when he heard Rita say, 'Toad has served with Admiral Grafton ever since then. Somehow he's always found a billet that allowed him to do that.'

'You know Admiral Grafton pretty well then,' Pascal said to Toad.

'He's the second best friend I have in this life,' Toad replied lightly. He was smiling, and deadly serious. 'Rita is *numero uno*, Jake Grafton is number two.'

From there the conversation turned to Rita's current assignment, evaluation of the new V-22 Osprey. After a few minutes Toad asked Rita, 'May I get you more coffee?'

At her nod, Toad excused himself, took both cups and went toward the coffee urn on a side table. Normally a steward served the coffee, but just now they were cleaning up after the evening meal.

Captain Pascal asked, 'Have your husband's assignments hurt his career?'

Rita knew what he meant. Toad had not followed the classic career path that was supposed to lead to major command, then flag rank. 'Perhaps.' She gave a minute shrug. 'He made his choice. Jake Grafton appeals to a different side of Toad's personality than I do.'

'Oh, of course,' said the captain, feeling his way. 'Spouses and friends, very different, quite understandable . . .'

'Jake Grafton can trade nuances with the best bureaucrats in the business, and he can attack a problem in a brutally direct manner.' Rita searched for words, then added, 'He always tries to do the right thing, regardless of the personal consequences. I think that is the quality Toad admires the most.'

'I see,' said the chief of staff, but it was obvious that he didn't.

As Toad walked toward the table with a coffee cup in each hand, Rita Moravia took a last stab at explanation: 'Jake Grafton and Toad Tarkington are not uniformed technocrats or clerks or button pushers. They are warriors: I think they sense that in one another.'

The shadows were dissipating to dusky twilight as Ocho Sedano walked the streets toward the dock area. Over each shoulder he carried a bag which he had stitched together from bedsheets. One contained a few changes of clothes, a baseball glove, several photos of his family – all that he wished to take with him into his new life in America. Truly, when you inventory the stuff that fills your life, you can do without most of it. Diego Coca said to travel light and Ocho took him literally.

The other bag contained bottles of water. He had searched the trash for bottles, had washed them carefully, filled them with water, and corked them. Diego hadn't mentioned water or food, but Ocho remembered his conversation with his brother, Hector, and thought bringing water would be a wise precaution.

He also had two baked potatoes in the bag.

Diego would laugh at him – they were not going to be at sea long enough to get really hungry, or so he said.

Please, God, let Diego be right. Let us be in America when the sun rises tomorrow.

There would be a man waiting in the Keys, waiting on a certain beach. Diego showed Ocho a map with the beach clearly marked in ink. 'He was a close friend of my wife's brother,' Diego said. 'A man who can be trusted.'

The boat was fast enough, Diego said, to be in American waters at dawn. They would make their approach to the beach as the sun rose, when obstructions to navigation were visible, when they could check landmarks and buoys.

Diego was confident. Dora believed her father, looked at him with shining eyes when he talked of America, of how it would be to live in an American house, go to the huge stadiums and watch Ocho play baseball while everyone cheered . . . to have a television, plenty to eat, nice clothes, a *car*!

Dios mio, America did sound like a paradise! To hear Diego tell it America was heaven, lacking only the angel choir . . . and it was just a boat ride away across the Florida Straits.

Of course, Diego said they would probably get seasick, would probably vomit. That was inevitable, to be expected, a price to be paid.

And they could get caught by the Cubans or Americans, get sent back here. 'We'll be no worse off than we are now if that happens,' Diego argued. 'We can always try again to get to America. God knows, we can't get any poorer.'

Dora with the shining eyes . . . she looked so expectant.

She was the first, the very first woman he had ever made love to. And she got pregnant after that one time!

When she first told him, he had doubted her. Didn't want to believe. She became angry, threw a tantrum. Then he had believed.

He thought about her now as he walked the dark streets, past people sitting in doorways, couples holding hands, past bars with music coming through the doorways. He had spent his whole life here and now he was leaving, an event of the first order of magnitude. Surely they could see the transformation in his face, in the way he walked.

Several people called to him, 'El Ocho!' Several fans wanted to shake his hand, but no more than usual. This was the way they always acted as he walked by – this was the way people had treated him since he was fifteen.

He left the people behind and walked past the closed fish markets and warehouses. His footsteps echoed off the buildings.

The boat was in a slip, Diego said, behind a certain boatyard.

He rounded the corner, saw people. Men, women, and children standing in little knots. Hmm, they were right near the slip.

They were standing around the slip.

He saw Diego standing on the dock, and Dora.

People stepped out of the way to let him by.

'All these people,' he said to Diego, 'Did you announce our departure at the ballpark? I thought we were going to sneak out of here.'

Diego had a sick look on his face. 'They're going with us,' he said.

'*What?*'

'The captain brought his relatives, my brother heard we were leaving, talked to some of his friends. . . .'

Ocho stared at the boat. The boat's name on the stern was written in black paint, which was chipping and peeling off. *Angel del Mar*, Angel of the Sea. The boat was maybe forty feet long, with a little pilothouse. Fishing nets still hung from the aft mast. The crowd – he estimated there were close to fifty people standing here.

'How many people, Diego? How many?'

'Over eighty.'

'On that boat? In the Gulf Stream? *Está loco?*'

Diego was beside himself. 'This is our chance, Ocho. We can make it. God is with us.'

'God? If the boat swamps, will He keep us from drowning?'

'Ocho, listen to me. My friends are waiting in Florida. This is our chance to make it to America, to be something, to live decent. . . . This is *our* chance.'

People were staring at him, listening to Diego.

Ocho looked into the faces looking at him. He tore his eyes away, finally, looked back at Diego, who had his hand on Ocho's arm.

'No. I am *not* going.' He pulled his arm from Diego's grasp. 'Go with one less, you will all have a little better chance.'

'You *have* to go,' Diego pleaded, and grabbed his arm.

'Ocho,' Dora wailed.

'You have to go,' Diego snarled. 'You got her pregnant! Be a man!'

5

Eighty-four people were packed aboard *Angel del Mar* as she headed for the mouth of the small bay under a velvet black sky strewn with stars. A sliver of moon cast just enough light to see the sand on the bars at the entrance of the bay.

The boat rode low in the water and seemed to react sluggishly to the small swells that swept down the channel.

'This is insane,' Ocho said to Diego Coca, who was leaning against the wall of the small wheelhouse.

'We'll make it. We'll reach the rendezvous in the Florida Keys an hour or two before dawn. *Vamos con Dios.*'

'God had better be with us,' Ocho muttered, and reached for Dora. The baby didn't show yet. She was of medium height, with a trim, athletic frame. How well he knew her body.

As far as he knew, he was the only one on the boat who had brought water or food. Oh, the other passengers had things, all right, sacks and boxes of things too precious to leave behind: clothes, pictures, silver, Bibles, rosaries, crucifixes that had decorated the walls of their homes and their parents' and grandparents' homes.

Boxes and sacks were stacked around each person, who sat on the deck or on his pile. Men, women, children, some merely babies in arms... It appeared to Ocho as if the Saturday night crowd from an entire section of ballpark bleachers had been miraculously transported to the deck of this small boat.

The breeze smelled of the sea, clean, tangy, crisp. He took a deep breath, wondered if this were his last night of life.

He pulled Dora closer to him, felt the warmth and promise of her body.

Well, this boatload of people would make it to Florida or they wouldn't, as God willed it. He had never thought much about religion, merely accepted it as part of life, but through the years he had learned about God's will. He was not one of those athletes who crossed himself every time he went to the plate or prepared to make a crucial pitch, vainly asking God for assistance in trivial matters, but he knew to a certainty that most of the major events of life – be you ballplayer, manager, father, husband, cane

402

worker, whatever – are beyond your control. Events take their own course and humans are swept along with them. Call it God's will or chance or fate or what have you, all a man could do was throw the ball as well as he could, with all the guile and skill he could muster. What happened after the ball left your fingers was beyond your control. In God's hands, or so they said. If God cared.

For the first time in his life Ocho wondered if God cared.

He was still thinking along these lines when the boat buried its bow in the first big swell at the harbor entrance. Spray came flying back clear to the wheelhouse. People shrieked, some laughed, all tried to find some bit of shelter.

People were moving, holding up clothing or pieces of cardboard when the next cloud of spray came flying back.

The boat rose somewhat as she met each swell, but she was too heavily loaded.

'We're not even out of the harbor,' muttered the man beside Ocho. His voice sounded infinitely weary.

Dora hugged Ocho, clung to him as she stared into the night.

She barely came to his armpit. He braced himself against the wall of the wheelhouse, held her close.

The boat labored into the swells, flinging heavy sheets of spray back over the people huddled on the deck.

The door to the wheelhouse opened. A bare head came out, shouted at Diego Coca: 'The boat is overloaded, man! It is too dangerous to go on. We must turn back.'

Diego pulled a pistol from his pocket and placed the muzzle against the man's forehead. He pushed the man back through the door, followed him into the tiny shack and pulled the door shut behind him.

The man next to Ocho said, 'We may make it ... if the sea gets no rougher. I was a fisherman once, I know of these things.'

The man was in his late sixties perhaps, with a deeply lined face and hair bleached by the sun. Ocho had studied his face in the twilight, before the light completely disappeared. Now the fisherman was merely a shape in the darkness, a remembered face.

'Your father is crazy,' Ocho told Dora, speaking in her ear over the noise of the wind and sea. She said nothing, merely held him tighter.

It was then he realized she was as frightened as he.

Angel del Mar smashed its way northward under a clear, starry sky. The wind seemed steady from the west at twelve or fifteen knots. Already drenched by spray, with no place to shelter themselves, the people on deck huddled where they were. From his position near the wheelhouse Ocho could just see the people between the showers of spray, dark shapes crowding the deck in the faint moonlight, for there were no other lights so that the boat might go unnoticed by Cuban naval patrols.

'When we get to the Gulf Stream,' the fisherman beside Ocho shouted in his ear above the noise of the wind and laboring diesel engine, '... swells ... open the seams ... founder in this sea.'

In addition to heaving and pitching, the boat was also rolling heavily since there was so much weight on deck. The roll to starboard seemed most pronounced when the boat crested a swell, when it was naked to the wind.

Ocho Sedano buried his face in Dora's hair and held her tightly as the boat plunged and reared, turned his body to shield her somewhat from the clouds of spray that swept over them.

He could hear people retching; the vomit smell was swept away on the wind and he caught none of it.

On the boat went into the darkness, bucking and writhing as it fought the sea.

Late in the evening William Henry Chance met his associate at the mahogany bar in El Floridita, one of the flashiest old nightclubs in Old Havana. This monstrosity was the dazzling heart of prerevolutionary Havana in the bad old days; black-and-white photos of Ernest Hemingway, Cary Grant, and Ava Gardner still adorned the walls. The place was full of Americans who had traveled here in defiance of their government's ban on travel to Cuba. As bands belted out salsa and rhumba, the Americans drank, ate, and scrutinized voluptuous prostitutes clad in tight dresses and high heels.

Chance's associate was Tommy Carmellini, a Stanford law school graduate in his late twenties. The baggy sportscoat and pleated trousers did nothing to show off Carmellini's wide shoulders and washboard stomach. Still, a thoughtful observer would conclude he was remarkably fit for a man who spent twelve hours a day at a desk.

'Looks like the Cubans have come full circle,' Chance said when Carmellini joined him at the bar. He had to speak up to be heard above the music coming through the open windows.

'Goes around and comes around,' Tommy Carmellini agreed. 'I wonder just how many different social diseases are circulating in this building tonight.'

When they were outside on the sidewalk strolling along, William Henry Chance pulled a cigar from the pocket of his sports jacket, which was folded over his left arm. He bit off the end of the thing, then cupped his hands against the breeze and lit it with a paper match. The wind blew out the first two matches, but he got the cigar going with the third one. After a couple puffs, he sighed.

'Smells delicious,' Carmellini said.

'Cuban cigars are the real deal. Gonna be the new in thing. You should try one.'

'Naw. I just might like cigars. I've made it this far without smoking, I'm going to try to go all the way.'

They paused outside a nightclub and listened to the music pouring out. 'That's a good band.'

'If you close your eyes, this sorta feels like Miami Beach.'

'Miami del Sud.'

They walked on. 'So what do you hear?'

'The pacifiers are working. All three of them. This afternoon Vargas talked to his subordinates about this and that, the minister of finance had phone sex with a girlfriend, and Castro's top aide talked to the doctors for an hour.'

'How is the old goat doing?'

'Not good, the man said. The doctors talked about how much narcotics to administer to ensure he didn't suffer.'

'Any guesses when?'

'No.'

'The Cuban exile, El Gato, where does he fit in?'

'Don't know yet.'

'He's in the casino now with three Russian gangsters, people he knows apparently, playing for high stakes.'

'El Gato is supposed to be an influential and powerful enemy of the Castro regime,' Chance muttered. 'Sure does make you wonder.'

'Yeah,' said Carmellini. He and Chance both knew that the FBI had an agent and three informers in El Gato's chemical supply business looking for evidence that it was the source of supply for some of the makings of Fidel Castro's biological warfare program. So far, nothing. Then El Gato unexpectedly swanned off to Havana. Chance and Carmellini were coming anyway, but now they had a new item added to their agenda.

And Castro was dying.

'I'd like to know what the Cat is going to tell all his exile friends when he gets back to Florida,' Tommy Carmellini said. 'Maybe if he winds up in the right offices we'll find out, eh?'

That reference to the executive pacifiers made Chance grin. He puffed the cigar a few times while holding it carefully between thumb and forefinger.

'You don't really know much about smoking cigars, do you?'

'Is it that obvious?'

'Yes, sir.'

Chance put the cigar between his teeth at a jaunty angle and puffed fearlessly three or four times. Then he took the thing from his mouth and held it so he could see it. 'Wish I could get the hang of it,' he said. 'Cuba seemed like a good place to learn about cigars.'

He tossed the stogie into a gutter on the street.

'Makes me a little light-headed.' Chance grinned sheepishly and wiped a sheen of perspiration from his brow.

He stood listening to the sounds of the crowd and the snatches of music floating from the bars and casinos, thinking about biological weapons.

Angel del Mar was only a half hour past the mouth of the harbor when the fisherman beside Ocho Sedano pulled at his arm to attract his attention. Then he shouted, 'We will reach the Gulf Stream soon. The swells will be larger. We are too deeply loaded. We must get rid of what weight we can.'

The boat was corkscrewing viciously. Ocho nodded, passed Dora to the fisherman, pulled open the wheelhouse door and carefully stepped inside.

The captain worked the wheel with an eye on the compass. The faint glow from the binnacle and the engine RPM indicator were the only lights – they cast a faint glow on the captain's face and that of Diego Coca, who was wedged in beside him, the gun still in his hand. Both men were facing forward, looking through the window at the sheets of spray being flung up when the bow smacked into a swell with an audible thud. The shock of those collisions could be felt through the deck and walls of the wheelhouse.

'You are suicidal,' the captain shouted at Diego. 'The sea will get worse when we reach the Gulf Stream. We are only a mile or two from it!'

Diego backed up, braced himself against the aft wall of the tiny compartment, pointed the pistol in the center of the captain's back. He held up his hand to hold off Ocho.

'You took the money,' Diego said accusingly to the captain.

'Don't be a fool, man.'

'*America!* Or I shoot you, as God is my witness.'

'You want to drown out here, in this watery hell?'

'You took the money!' Diego shouted.

Ocho stepped forward and Diego pointed the pistol at him. 'Back,' he said. 'Get back. I don't want to shoot you, but I will.'

Ocho Sedano leaned forward. 'I think they are right, what they say. You *are* crazy. You will kill every man and woman on this boat. Even the babies.'

'The boat is overloaded,' the captain said without looking at Ocho. 'We have to get some weight off. Throw the fishing gear over, the baggage, everything.'

Ocho pulled the door open and stepped out onto the pitching deck. He took Dora from the fisherman, pushed her into the wheelhouse, and pulled the door until it latched.

'We must get rid of some weight. Everything goes overboard but the people.'

The fisherman nodded, took the bags near his feet and threw them into the white foam being thrown out by the bow. Then he grabbed Ocho's bag and tossed it before the young man could stop him.

Madre mia!

Walking on that bucking deck was difficult. Ocho made his way forward, picking up every sack and box in reach and throwing it into the sea. Some people protested, grabbed their belongings and tried to prevent their loss, but he was too strong. He tore the bags from the women's grasp and heaved heavy boxes as if they were empty.

Up the deck he went toward the bow, drenched every time the bow went in, throwing everything he could get his hands on into the foam created by the bow's passage.

Other people were throwing things too. Soon the deck contained only the people, who huddled in small groups, their backs to the spray. The nets hanging on the mast were lowered to the deck, then put into the sea and cut loose.

Near the bow the motion was vicious. The salt sea spray slamming back almost took him off his feet. He caught himself on a line that stabilized the mast, then worked his way aft holding on to the rail.

He thought the boat was riding easier, but maybe it was only his imagination.

Then they got into the Gulf Stream. The swells grew progressively larger, the motion of the boat even more vicious.

How much of this could the boat take?

People cried out, praying aloud, lifted their hands to heaven. He could hear the women wailing over the rumbling of the engine, the pounding of the sea.

He tried the door to the wheelhouse.

Locked!

He rattled the knob, twisted it fiercely, pulled with all his strength.

'Open up, Diego.'

He pounded futilely on the door.

Six people were huddled in the lee of the tiny wheelhouse, blocking the door. One of them was Dora. He leaned over her, pounded futilely on the door with his fist.

He looked down at Dora, who had her head down.

Frustrated, drained, sick of himself and Diego and Dora, he found a spot against the aft wall of the wheelhouse and buried his head in his arms to keep the spray from his face.

He was drifting, thinking of his mother, reviewing scenes from his childhood when Mercedes shook him awake. Still under the influence of the painkilling drugs, Fidel Castro opened his eyes to slits and blinked mightily against the dim light.

'Maximo is here, Fidel, as you asked.'

He tried to chase away the past, to come back to the present. His mouth was dry, his tongue like cotton. 'Time?'

'Almost midnight.'

He nodded, looked around the room at the walls, the ceiling, the dark shapes of people and furniture. He couldn't see faces.

'A light.'

She reached for the switch.

When his eyes adjusted, he saw Maximo standing in the shadows. He motioned with a finger. Yes, it was Maximo: now he could see his features.

'Mi amigo.'

'Señor Presidente,' Maximo said.

'Closer, in the light.'

Maximo Sedano knelt near the bed.

'I don't have much time left to me,' Castro explained. His mouth was so numb that he was having trouble enunciating his words.

'I want the money brought back.'

'To Cuba?'

'Yes. All of it.'

'You will have to sign and put your thumbprints on the transfer cards.'

'The money was never mine, you understand.'

'I had faith in you, Señor Presidente. We all had faith.'

'Faith . . .'

'I will go to my office now, then return.'

'Mercedes will admit you.'

Ocho Sedano was soaked to the skin, covered with vomit from the woman beside him, when he heard the cry. Holding onto the wheelhouse wall with one hand and the net boom mast with the other, he levered himself erect, braced himself against the motion of the boat.

Waves were washing over the bow, which seemed to be lower in the water. The bow wasn't rising to the sea the way it did when he sat down an hour ago, or maybe the waves were just higher.

Someone was against the rail, pointing aft.

'Man overboard!'

'Madre mia, have mercy!'

Another swell came aboard and two people braced against the lee rail were swept into the sea as the boat rolled.

Ocho turned to the wheelhouse, pulled people from against the door and savagely twisted the latch handle. He pounded on the door with his left fist.

'Let me in, Diego! So help me, I will kill you if you don't turn the boat around.'

The bow began turning to put the wind and swells more astern.

A muffled report came from inside the wheelhouse.

Ocho braced himself, then rammed his left fist against the upper panel of the door. The wood splintered, his fist went through almost to his elbow. He reached down, unlatched the door, jerked it open.

The captain lay on the floor. Diego Coca stood braced against the back wall, his hands covering his face. The pistol was nowhere in sight. The wheel snapped back and forth as the seas slammed at the rudder.

Ocho bent down to check the captain.

He had a wet place in the middle of his back, right between his shoulder blades. No pulse.

At least the boat seemed more stable with the swells behind it.

For how long? How long would the engine keep running?

The fisherman opened the door, saw Ocho at the wheel, the dark shape lying on the floor.

'Is he dead?' the man shouted.

'Yes.'

'We must put out a sea anchor in case the engine stops. If the boat turns broadside to the sea, it will be swamped.'

'Can you do it?'

'I will get men to help,' the fisherman said, and closed what was left of the door.

A great lassitude swept over Ocho Sedano. His sin with the girl had brought all of these people here to die, had brought them to this foundering boat in a rough, windswept night sea with a million cold stars looking down without pity.

Then he realized that the forward deck was empty.

Empty!

The people were gone. Into the sea . . . that must be it! They were swept overboard.

'Ocho.'

Diego put his hand on the young man's shoulder, gripped hard.

'I didn't mean to shoot him. As God is my witness, I did not mean for this to happen. It was an accident.'

Ocho swept the hand away.

He pointed through the glass at the forward deck. 'They are gone! Look. *The people are gone!*'

'I did not mean for this to happen,' Diego repeated mechanically.

'What?' Ocho demanded. 'What did you not intend? For the captain to die? For your daughter to drown at sea? For all of those people on that deck to die? What did you not intend, Diego?'

Oh, my God, that this should happen!

'*Answer me!*' he roared at Diego Coca, who refused to look forward through the wheelhouse windshield.

'Look, you bastard,' Ocho ordered through clenched teeth, and grabbed the smaller man by the neck. He rammed his head forward against the glass.

'See what your greed and stupidity have cost.'

Then he threw Diego Coca to the floor.

The impact of the disaster bowed Ocho's head, bent his back, emptied his heart. Diego's guilt did not lessen his, and oh, he knew that well. He, Ocho Sedano, was *guilty*. His lust had set this chain of events in motion. He felt as if he were trying to support the weight of the earth.

Maximo Sedano's office in the finance ministry reflected his personal taste. The furniture was simple, deceptively so. The woods were hardwoods from the Amazon rain forest, crafted in Brazil by masters. Little souvenirs from his travels across Europe and Latin America sat on the desk and credenza and hung on the walls, small things of little value because expensive trinkets would be impolitic.

He turned on the light, then walked to the huge floor safe, which he unlocked and opened. He found the drawer he wanted, removed a stiff document envelope, took it to his desk and adjusted the light.

With the contents of the envelope spread out on the highly polished mahogany, Maximo Sedano paused and looked around the room with unseeing eyes. He blinked several times, then leaned back in his chair and stretched.

There were four bank accounts in Switzerland, all controlled by Fidel Castro. The last time Maximo computed the interest, the amount in the accounts totaled $53 million. Castro had been very specific when the accounts were opened years ago; the accounts were to be denominated in United States dollars. This choice had worked out extraordinarily well through the years as the currencies of every other major trading nation underwent major inflation or devaluation. The United States dollar was the modern-day equivalent of gold, although it would certainly be poor politics for any member of the Castro regime to say so publicly.

Fifty-three million dollars.

Quite a sum.

Enough to live extraordinarily well for a millennium or two.

Fidel kept that little nest egg in Switzerland just in case things went wrong here in this communist paradise and he had to skedaddle. No sense living on government charity in some other squalid communist paradise, like Poland or Russia or the Ukraine, when a little prior planning could solve the whole problem. So Fidel rat-holed a fortune where only he could get at it and slept soundly at night.

Now he wanted the money back in Cuba.

Not that the money ever really belonged to the Cuban government. The money came from drug dealers, fees for using Cuban harbors for sanctuary, fees for being able to send shipments directly to Cuba, stockpile the drugs, then ship them on when the time was right.

The money was really just Castro's personal share of the drug fees. An even larger chunk of the profits had gone to army, navy and law enforcement personnel, all of them, every man in the country who wore a uniform had been paid; another chunk went to Castro's lieutenants and political allies. Maximo had received almost a half million dollars himself. All in all, the deals with the drug syndicates had been good public policy – the drug business was highly profitable, giving Castro money to buy loyalty and so remain in power, and the business corrupted America, which he hated. Ah, yes, the money came from the United States despite the best efforts of the American government to prevent it. Fidel had savored that irony too.

Fifty-three million.

Maximo pursed his lips as he thought about the life of luxury and privilege that a fortune that size would buy. The money could be invested, some hotels, bank stock, invested to earn a nice income without touching the principal.

He could stay in the George V in Paris, ski in St Moritz, shop in London and Rome and yacht all over the Mediterranean.

God, it was tempting!

Fifty-three million.

All he had to do was get Castro's thumbprint on the transfer order. Without that thumbprint, the banks would not move a solitary dollar.

Really, those Swiss banks . . . Maximo had urged Castro to transfer the money to Spanish and Cuban banks for months, ever since the dictator was diagnosed with cancer. If he died with the money still in Switzerland, prying money out of those banks was going to be like peeling fresh paint from a wall with fingernails. And the drug dealers thought their racket was profitable!

But why be a piker? Why settle for $53 million when there was a lot more, somewhere?

From his pocket he removed a coin, a gold five-peso coin dated 1915. There was a portrait of José Martí on one side and the crest of Cuba on the other.

Gold circulated in Cuba until the revolution, until Fidel and the communists declared it was no longer legal tender and called it in, allowing the peso to float on the world market.

Maximo rubbed the gold coin with his fingers. By his calculations, based upon Ministry of Finance records, almost 1.2 million ounces of gold were surrendered to the government in return for paper money.

One million, two hundred thousand ounces . . . about thirty-seven *tons* of gold. On the world market, that thirty-seven tons of gold should be worth about $360 million.

A man who could get his hands on that hoard would be on easy street for the rest of his life. Yes, indeed.

The only problem was finding it. It wasn't in the Finance Ministry vaults, it wasn't in the vaults of the Bank of Cuba, on account at banks in Switzerland or London or New York or Mexico City . . . it was gone!

Thirty-seven tons of gold, vanished into thin air.

If a man could lay hands on that gold . . . well, Alejo Vargas and Hector Sedano could fight over the presidency of Cuba, and may the better man win. Maximo would take the gold. If he could find it.

He had a few ideas about where it might be. In fact, he had been quietly researching the problem since he took over the Finance Ministry. Eight years of ransacking files, talking to old employees, looking at clues, thinking about the problem – the gold had to be in Cuba, in Havana. Thirty-seven tons of gold.

A life of ease and luxury in the spas of Europe, mingling with the rich and famous, surrounded by beautiful women and the best of everything . . .

But first the $53 million.

He would type the account numbers on the transfer orders and the accounts the money was to be transferred to. He would use the secretary's typewriter. He had the account numbers written in the notebook he removed from the safe. He flipped through the notebook now, found the page, stared at the numbers.

How closely would Fidel check the order?

The man is sick, drugged, dying. He is barely conscious. Unless he has the numbers of the accounts in the Bank of Cuba by his bedside, he'll be none the wiser.

But what if he does? What if he has the numbers written down in a book or diary and hands the transfer order to Mercedes to check? What then?

Fifty-three million. More money than God has.

He remembered the old days when he was young, when Castro walked the earth like Jesus Christ with a Cuban accent. Ah, the fire of the revolution, how the true believers were going to change the world!

Instead, time changed them, America bled them, and life defeated them.

Maximo had been loyal to Fidel and the revolution. No one could ever say he was not. He had been with Fidel since he was twenty-four years old, just back from the university in Spain. He had endured the good times and the bad, never uttered a single word of criticism. He had faith in Fidel, proclaimed it publicly and demanded it of others.

Now Castro was dying. In just a few days he would be beyond regrets.

Fifty-three million.

The pounding the overloaded boat had taken bucking the heavy Gulf Stream swells opened the seams somewhat, and now the fisherman was pumping out the water with the bilge pump, which received its power from the engine-driven generator.

'As long as we can keep the engine running, as long as the seams don't open any more than they are, we'll be all right.'

'How much fuel do we have on board?'

The fisherman went to check.

Ocho was at the helm, steering almost due east. With the wind and sea behind her, the *Angel del Mar* rode better. Now the motion was a rocking as the swells swept under the stern. Very little roll from side to side.

Of the eighty-four people who had been aboard when the boat left the harbor in Cuba, twenty-six remained alive. The captain's body lay against the wheelhouse wall.

Ocho found Diego's pistol and put it in his belt. He physically carried Diego from the wheelhouse and tossed him on the deck.

Fifty-seven living human beings, men, women, and babies, had gone into the sea. There was no way in the world to go back to try to rescue them. Even if he and the fisherman could find those people in the water, in the darkness, in this sea, the pounding of heading back into the swells would probably cause the boat to take on more water, endangering the lives of those who remained aboard.

No, the people swept overboard were lost to their fate, whatever that might be.

The living twenty-six would soon join them, Ocho told himself. The boat was heading east, away from Florida.

Perhaps if the sea calmed somewhat, they should bring the boat to a more southerly heading and return to Cuba.

That, he decided, was their only chance.

Cuba. They would have to return.

Why wait? Every sea mile increased the likelihood of the engine quitting or the boat sinking.

He turned the helm a bit, worked the boat's bow to a more southerly heading. The roll became more pronounced. The wind came more over the right stern quarter.

How long until dawn? An hour or two?

The door to the wheelhouse opened. Diego was standing there, the whites of his eyes glistening in the dim light. 'Turn back toward Florida! No one wants to go back to Cuba.'

'It's the only way. We'll all die trying to make it to Florida in this sea.'

'I was dead in Cuba all those years,' Diego Coca shouted. 'I refuse to go go back! I refuse.'

Ocho hit him in the mouth. One mighty jab with his left hand as he twisted his body, so all his weight was behind the punch. Diego went down backward, hit his head on the deck coaming, and lay still.

Dora wailed, crawled toward her unconscious father.

Ocho closed the door to the wheelhouse, brought the boat back to its southeast heading.

Soon the door opened again and the fisherman stepped inside. 'We have fuel for another ten or twelve hours. No more than that.'

'We'll be back in Cuba then.'

'That's our only chance.'

The stars in the east were fading when the engine quit. After trying for a minute to start the engine, the fisherman dashed below.

Ocho abandoned the helm. The boat rolled sickeningly in the swells.

At least the swells were smaller than they were earlier in the night, in the middle of the Gulf Stream.

The fisherman came up on deck after fifteen minutes, his clothes soaked in diesel fuel. 'It's no use,' he said. 'The engine has had it.'

'What about the water in the bilges? Is it still coming in?'

'We'll have to take turns on the hand pump.'

'What are we going to do about the engine?' Ocho asked.

The fisherman didn't reply, merely stood looking at the swells as the sky grew light in the east.

6

The van drove up to the massive, 250-feet-tall extra-high-voltage tower beside the drainage canal on the southern outskirts of Havana and backed up toward it. The base of the tower was surrounded by a ten-foot-high chain link fence with barbed wire on top. The access door in the fence was, of course, padlocked.

The driver of the van and his passenger were both wearing one-piece overalls. They stretched, looked at the wires far above, and scratched their heads while they surveyed the ramshackle four-story apartment buildings that backed up to the canal. One of the men extracted a pack of cigarettes from his overalls and lit one. The nearest apartments were at least sixty meters away, although for safety reasons the distance should have been much more. Each of the extra-high-voltage (EHV) lines overhead carried 500,000 volts.

The driver of the van was Enrique Poveda. His passenger was Arquimidez Cabrera. Both men were citizens of the United States, sons of Cuban exiles, and bitter enemies of the Castro regime.

Poveda had parked the van so that the rear doors, when open, almost touched the gate in the chain link fence. Now he reached into the van, seized a set of bolt cutters, and applied the jaws to the padlock on the gate. One tremendous squeeze and the bar of the padlock snapped.

Cabrera threw the remnants of the padlock into the back of the van. He opened the gate in the fence, set a new, open padlock on the hasp, and stood looking up at the tower.

The best way to cut the power lines the tower carried would be to climb the tower and set shaped charges around the insulators. Unfortunately, the lines carried so much juice that the hot zones around the wires were eleven feet in diameter, more in humid weather. No, the only practical way to cut the lines was to drop the towers, which would not be difficult. A shaped charge on each leg should do the job nicely. Cabrera looked at the angle of the wires leading into the tower, and the angle away. Yes, once the legs were severed, the weight and tension of the line should pull the tower down to the side away from the canal, into this open area, where the lines would either short out on the ground or break from the strain of carrying their own weight.

Timing the explosions would be a problem. This close to all that energy, a radio-controlled electrical detonator was out of the question. Chemical timers would be best, ones that ignited the detonators after a preset time, although chemical timers were not as precise as mechanical ones.

All that was for a later day, however. The decision on when the tower must come down had yet to be made, so today Cabrera and Poveda would merely set the charges. They would return later to set the timers and detonators.

Poveda finished his cigarette and strapped on his tool belt. This was the fourth tower today. Only this one and one more to go.

'You ready?' he asked Cabrera.

'Let's do it.'

Ocho Sedano lived with his older brother Julio, Julio's wife, and their two children in a tiny apartment atop a garage just a few hundred yards from Doña Maria's house. Julio worked in the garage repairing American cars. The cars were antiques from the 1950s and there were no spare parts, so Julio made parts or cannibalized them from the carcasses behind the garage, cars too far gone for any mechanic to save. When he wasn't playing baseball, Ocho helped.

Hector found his brother Julio working in the shop by the light of several naked bulbs. 'Where is Ocho?'

'Gone.'

'Gone where?'

Julio was replacing the valves of an ancient straight eight under the hood of an Oldsmobile. The light was terrible, but he was working by feel so it didn't really matter. He straightened now, scowled at his older brother.

'He has gone to try his luck in America.'

'You didn't try to stop him?'

Julio looked about at the dimly lit shop, the dirt floor, the shabby old cars. He wiped his hands on a dirty rag that hung from his belt. 'No, I didn't.'

'What if he drowns out there in the Gulf Stream?'

'I have prayed for him.'

'That's it? Your little brother? A prayer?'

'What do you think I should have done, Hector? Tell the boy that he was living smack in the middle of a communist paradise, that he should be happy here, happy with his labor and his crust? Bah! He wants something more from life, something for himself, for his children.'

'If he dies –'

'Look around you, Hector. Look at this squalid, filthy hovel. Look at the way we live! Most of Cuba lives this way, except for a precious few like dear

Maximo, who eats the bread that other men earn. You saw him yesterday at *Mima*'s – nothing's too good for our dedicated revolutionary, Maximo Sedano, Fidel's right-hand ass-wipe man.'

Julio snorted scornfully, then leaned back under the hood of the Olds. 'I told Ocho to go with God. I prayed for him.'

'What if he dies out there?'

'Everybody has to die – you, me, Fidel, Ocho, all of us – that's just the way it is. They ought to teach you that in church. At least if Ocho dies he won't have to listen to any more of Fidel's bullshit. He won't have to listen to yours, either. God knows, bullshit is the only thing on this island we have a lot of.'

'Have you told *Mima* that he left?'

'I was going to keep my mouth shut until I had something to tell her.' Julio turned his head to look at Hector around the edge of the car's hood. 'Ocho is a grown man. He has taken his life in his own two hands, which is his right. He'll live or die. He'll get to America or he won't.'

'He should have waited. I asked him to wait.'

'For what?' Julio demanded.

Hector turned to leave the garage.

'What are we waiting for, Hector? The second coming?'

Julio came to the door and called after Hector as he walked away down the street: 'How long do I have to wait to feed my sons? Tell me! I have waited all my life. I am sick and tired of waiting. I want to know now – *how much longer?*'

Hector turned in the road and walked back toward Julio. 'Enough! *Enough!*' he roared, his voice carrying. 'You squat here in this hovel waiting for life to get better, waiting for someone else to make it better! You have no courage – you are not a man! If the future depends on rabbits like you Cuba will always be a sewer!'

Then Hector turned and stalked away, his head down, his shoulders bent forward, as if he were walking into a great wind.

The Officers' Club at Guantánamo Bay Naval Station was sited on a small hill overlooking the harbor. From the patio Toad Tarkington and Rita Moravia could see the carrier swinging on her anchor near the mouth of the bay.

These days the O Club was usually sparsely populated. The base was now a military backwater, no longer a vital part of the US military establishment. For the last few years the primary function of the base was to house Cuban refugees picked up at sea.

Still, the deep blue Caribbean water and low yellow hills under a periwinkle sky packed picture-postcard charm. With cactus and palm trees and magnificent sunny days, the place reminded Toad of southern California. If the Cubans ever got their act together politically, he thought, this place would boom like southern California, with condos and high-tech industries sprouting like weeds. Hordes of people waving money would come here from Philly and New Jersey to retire. This place had Florida beat all to hell.

He voiced this opinion to Rita, the only other person on the patio. It was early in the afternoon; the two of them had ridden the first liberty boat in after the ship anchored. Jake Grafton sent them packing because today was their anniversary.

They had a room reserved at the BOQ for tonight. They intended to eat a relaxed dinner at the club, just the two of them, then retire for a private celebration.

'The Cubans may not want hordes from Philly and Hoboken and Ashtabula moving in,' Rita objected.

'I wouldn't mind having a little place in one of these villages around here my own self,' Toad said, gesturing vaguely to the west or north. 'Do some fishing, lay around getting old and fat and tan, let life flow by. Maybe build a golf course, spend my old age selling balls and watering greens. This looks like world-class golf country to me. Aaah, someday.'

'Someday, buster,' Rita said, grinning. Toad liked to entertain her with talk about retirement, about loafing away the days reading novels and newspapers and playing golf, yet by ten o'clock on a lazy Sunday morning in the States he was bored stiff. He played golf once every other year, if it didn't rain.

Now he sipped his beer and inhaled a few mighty lungfuls of this clean, clear, perfect air. 'Feel that sun! Ain't life delicious, woman?'

They had a nice dinner of Cuban cuisine, a fresh fish, beans and rice. By that time the club was filling up with junior officers from the squadrons aboard ship, in for liberty. The noise from the bars was becoming raucous when Toad and Rita finished their dinner and headed back to the patio with cups of coffee.

'Maybe I better check on my chicks,' Rita said, and detoured for the bar.

Toad paused in the doorway, staring into the dark room, which was made darker by the brilliant sunlight shining outside the windows.

'Commander Tarkington!' Two of the young pilots came over to where Toad stood with his coffee cup. 'Join us for a few minutes, won't you? We're drinking shooters. Have one with us.'

Rita was already standing by the table. Toad allowed himself to be persuaded.

A trayful of brimming shot glasses sat on the small round table. As Toad watched, one of these fools set the liquor in the glasses on fire with a butane cigarette lighter.

'Okay, Commander, show us how it's done!'

Toad looked at Rita, who was studying him with a noncommittal raised eyebrow.

418

He sat down, one of the youngsters placed a glass in front of him. The blue flame was burning nicely.

It had been years since he did this. Was it Rota, that time he got so blind drunk he passed out while waiting for the taxi? Ah, but the navy was politically correct now. Nobody got drunk anymore.

Toad steadied himself, took a deep breath, exhaled, and poured the burning brandy down his throat. It seemed to burn all the way down. Some of the liquid trickled from his lips, still on fire, but he licked it up with his tongue. Was he burning? He didn't think so. He wiped his mouth with the back of his hand just to make sure.

The members of his audience were gazing at him with openmouthed astonishment. 'Jesus, sir! We always blow the fire out before we drink it.'

Toad didn't know whether to laugh or cry. 'You goddamn pussies,' he said, and tossed off another one.

'Our anniversary, and you're drunk!'

Toad Tarkington felt like he had been hit by a large truck, an eighteen wheeler, at least. He turned in the bathroom door and looked carefully at his spouse. He squinted to make his eyes focus better.

'I am *not* drunk! A bit tipsy, I will grant you that. But not drunk.' He swelled his chest and tried to look sober. 'Those puppies, thinking they could drink an old dog like me under the table.' He snorted his derision. ' "We blow the fire out before we drink." Ha, ha, and ha!'

Rita was sooo mad! 'Oh, you –'

'Excuse me.' Toad held up a finger. 'Just a minute or two, and we will continue this discussion until you have said everything that needs to be said. There is undoubtedly a lot of it and I am sure it will take a while. Just one little minute.' He closed the bathroom door and retched into the commode. Then he swabbed his forehead with a wet washcloth.

He felt better. He stared at himself in the mirror.

You look like hell, you damned fool.

He took a long drink of water, swabbed his face with a towel, then opened the door, and said, 'Okay, you were saying?'

She wasn't there. The room was empty.

Even her bag was gone.

He lay down in the bed. Oh, that felt gooood. Maybe he should just lie here for a few minutes until she cooled off and he sobered up completely, then he would find her and apologize.

The room was whirling around, but when he rolled on his side it steadied out somewhat and he drifted right off.

Jake Grafton was alone at a table in the corner of the O Club dining room when Rita Moravia saw him and came over. He stood while she seated herself.

'You're by yourself? Where's Toad?'

'Sleeping it off. He was in the bar with your young studs and had four drinks. Four! He's whacked.'

Jake Grafton chuckled. 'I don't think I've seen him drink more than an occasional beer or glass of wine with dinner in years.'

'He doesn't,' she said. 'Poor guy can't handle it anymore.'

'Heck of an anniversary celebration,' Jake said, eyeing her.

'I've been lucky,' Rita said simply. 'Toad Tarkington and I were made for each other. I don't know how the powers that rule the universe figure out who marries whom, but I sure got lucky.'

'I know what you mean,' Jake said. Then he smiled, and Rita knew he was thinking of his wife, Callie. Jake Grafton always smiled when he thought of her.

'So, maybe you should join me for dinner,' Jake said, 'since Toad is temporarily indisposed and Callie is temporarily not here.'

'I've already eaten, and tongues might wag, Admiral,' she said with mock seriousness.

'And probably will. Won't do me or thee any good.'

'I'm not going to live my life to please pinheads,' Rita replied. 'I'll join you for a drink.'

After they gave their orders to the waiter, Jake said, 'Tell me about the V-22. I've been wondering about that plane but haven't had the chance to talk to you.'

Away Rita went, talking about airplanes and flying, two subjects they both enjoyed immensely. The breeze coming through the open doors of the dining room stirred the curtains and made the candles on the tables flicker in the evening twilight.

They were drinking after-dinner coffee when Rita remarked, 'Toad says that you still haven't heard from Washington about your next set of orders.'

'That's right.'

'I don't want to talk about something you would rather not discuss, but he says they may ask you to retire.'

'They might. I've thrown my weight around a few times in the past and made some enemies, in uniform and out.' He shrugged. 'Every flag officer gets passed over for a promotion at some point and asked to retire. My turn will come sooner or later. Maybe sooner.'

'Are you looking forward to retirement?'

'Haven't thought about it that much,' he said. 'To be honest, the prospect of spending more time with Callie has great appeal.' He rubbed his forehead, then grinned ruefully. 'It'll hurt if they don't find me another job, give me another star next year. Yet even a CNO gets told it's time to go. When it happens to me, Callie and I will get on with the rest of our lives. The truth is, when I decided to stay in the navy after Vietnam I never expected to get this far: thought it'd be terrific if I made commander or captain. Here I am with two stars in charge of a carrier battle group.' He snorted derisively. 'Guess it all goes to prove I'm an ungrateful bastard, huh?'

'It goes to prove you're human.'

'You are very kind, Rita.'

'You've really enjoyed the navy, haven't you?'

'Every tour has been a challenge, an adventure. Every set of orders I've had, I've thought, Oh, wow, this will be fun. I can't say I've enjoyed every day of it, because I haven't, but it's been a good career. Like most people who have worn the uniform, I did the best I could wherever they needed me. I've worked with great people all along the way. I have no regrets.'

One of Jake's aides came over to the table, smiled at Rita, then whispered in the admiral's ear. 'The ship that left here four days ago carrying biological warheads to Norfolk never arrived. It is overdue.'

'Civilization begins when the strong finally realize they have a duty to protect the weak. That duty is the foundation of civilization, the bedrock on which everything else rests.'

Hector Sedano stood in the pulpit and looked at the sea of sweating, glistening faces that packed the church to overflowing. He could feel the heat from their bodies. There must be close to two hundred people jammed in here.

Hector continued: 'For centuries we, the people, have abdicated our duty to a few strong men. Rule us, we said, and do not steal too much. Do not be too corrupt, do not betray us too much, do not shame us beyond endurance. Protect the weak, the elderly, the helpless, the sick, the very young, protect them from those who would prey upon them. And protect us. If you grant us protection you may steal a little, enough to become filthy rich, as long as you do not rub our faces in it.

'We give unto you, the strong one, a great trust because the faith to face the evil in the world is not in us.

'O strong one, protect us because we lack the courage to protect ourselves.'

The crowd was rapt, wanting more.

Hector Sedano had given this very same speech more than a hundred times. Only the faces in the audience were different. He leaned forward, reached out as if to grab the people. They had to understand, to feel his passion, or Cuba would never change. Perspiration ran down his face, soaked his shirt.

'I say to you here tonight that our duty can be ignored no longer. The hands that made the universe are delivering our destiny into our very own human hands. We must seize the day when it comes. We must acknowledge before God and before each other that the future of this nation is *ours* to write, *ours* to invent, *ours* to live, and *ours* to answer for before the throne of heaven on Judgment Day.'

A thunderous applause shook the tiny church.

When it died, Hector continued, 'I say to you that the future of *our* families is on *our* heads, that the fate of this people is *our* responsibility and *our* destiny.

'We shall drink every drop that God pours for us, be it sweet or bitter, be it thin or full, be it a tiny trickle or a great river. We shall not turn aside from that righteous cup.'

The applause swelled and swelled and filled the room to overflowing; it spilled through the open doors and windows and rushed bravely away to do battle with the silence and darkness of the night.

'We pulled it off,' Admiral Delgado told Alejo Vargas. '*Nuestra Señora de Colón* is stranded on a rocky reef near the entrance to Bahia de Nipe. Santana is ready and waiting.'

'What took so long?'

'When she left Guantánamo the Americans sent a destroyer to accompany her. The captain was beside himself – he thought the destroyer would accompany them all the way to Norfolk. He faked an engineering casualty in the Windward Passage, crawled along at three knots. Of course, then the destroyer refused to leave. He finally had to announce that he had fixed the problem and steam off at twelve knots before the destroyer turned back.'

Vargas smiled. 'If this works, I will be very grateful to you, Delgado.'

'There are real problems, which we have discussed. I give this operation no more than a fifty percent chance of success.'

'Fifty percent is optimistic,' Alejo Vargas replied. 'I suspect the odds are a lot worse than that. Yet they are good enough to take a chance, and if we don't do that, we have only ourselves to blame, eh?'

'Doing business with the North Koreans is an invitation to be double-crossed. How do you know they will perform?'

'We need long-range ballistic missiles, the North Koreans want well-designed, well-made biological warheads. The exchange is fair.'

'I still do not trust them,' Delgado countered. 'This is a once-in-a-lifetime deal.'

Vargas changed the subject: Delgado was not a partner, he was the hired help. 'Tell me about your evening cruise with Maximo Sedano.'

'He wants political backing when Castro dies.'

'What did you promise him?'

'I told him you buy people or blackmail them, that he has no chance.'

'And Alba?'

'He agreed with my assessment.'

Vargas smiled. 'Let us hope Maximo stifles his ambitions. For his sake.

You told the man the honest truth; if he chooses to disregard it the consequences are on his head.'

Delgado said nothing. He suspected Vargas had already talked to Alba: the admiral hoped the general didn't try to dress up the tale. Telling Vargas the truth was the only way to stay alive.

Toad Tarkington was sitting by the window in the BOQ room thinking about biological weapons and marines dug in around a warehouse when Rita unlocked the door and came in. She was still in uniform. His head was thumping like a toothache and he felt like hell.

'Some anniversary,' he said. 'I feel like an ass.'

She came over to the chair, knelt and put her arms around him.

'This wasn't the way the evening was supposed to go. I'm sorry, Rita.'

'Our life together has been terrific, Toad-man. You're still the guy I want.'

He hugged her back.

'Let's go to bed,' she said.

7

The emotional impact of what he had done didn't hit Maximo Sedano until the jet to Madrid leveled off after the climbout from Havana airport.

He took the transfer cards bearing Castro's thumbprint from his inside left breast pocket, and holding them so no one else in first class could read them, studied them carefully.

He was holding $53 million in his hands and he could feel the heat. Hoo, man! He had done it!

He took a chance, a long chance. When he walked into Castro's bedroom he had had the real transfer cards in his left jacket pocket and the ones bearing his bank account numbers in his right. Mercedes wasn't there that second time he was admitted, which was a blessing. His former sister-in-law was too sharp, saw too much. She might have decided something was wrong merely from looking at his face.

So it was just Fidel and a male nurse, a nobody who handled bedpans and urinals. There wasn't a notebook or ledger anywhere in sight, and Fidel certainly was in no condition to closely scrutinize the cards. He signed the cards, transferring the money to Maximo, then let Maximo put his thumb in an ink pad and press it on each of them.

Fidel said little. He had obviously been given an injection for pain and was paying minimal attention to what went on around him. He merely grunted when Maximo said good-bye.

The Maximo Sedano who walked into that bedroom was the soon-to-be unemployed Cuban finance minister with a cloudy future. The Maximo Sedano who walked out was the richest Cuban south of Miami.

Just like *that*!

The icing on the cake was that the Swiss accounts should have perhaps a million more of those beautiful Yanqui dollars as unpaid interest. Every penny was going to be transferred to Maximo's accounts at another bank in Zurich. It wouldn't be there long, however. Tomorrow morning after he turned in these transfer cards to Fidel's banks, he would walk across the street and send the money from his accounts to those he had opened in Spain, Mexico, Germany, and Argentina. These were commercial accounts held by various shell corporations that Maximo had established years ago to launder money for Fidel and the drug syndicates, accounts over which he had sole signature authority. The shell corporations would quickly write a variety of very large checks to a half dozen other companies Maximo owned. After a long, tortuous trail around the globe and back again, the money would eventually wind up in Maximo's personal accounts all over Europe.

The scheme hinged on the bank secrecy laws in various nations, not the least of which was Switzerland, and the fact that anyone trying to trace the money would see only disorganized pieces of the puzzle, not the big picture.

Maximo smiled to himself and sighed in contentment.

'Would you care for a drink, sir?' the flight attendant asked. She was a beautiful slender woman, with dark eyes and clear white skin.

'A glass of white wine, please, something from Cataluña.'

'I'll see what we have aboard, sir.' She smiled gently and left him.

Maximo told himself that he would find a woman like that one of these days, a beautiful woman who appreciated the finer things in life and appreciated him for providing them.

His wife was expecting him to return to Cuba in three days: 'I must go to Europe in the morning,' he had told her. 'An urgent matter has arisen.'

She wanted to go with him on this trip of course – anything to get off the island, even for a little while.

'Darling, I wish you could, but there wasn't time to make reservations. I got the only empty seat on the airliner.'

She was not happy. Still, what could she say? He promised to bring her something expensive from a jeweler, and that promise pacified her.

The flight attendant brought the glass of wine and he sipped it, then put his head back in the seat and closed his eyes. Ah, yes.

He had a new identity in his wallet: an Argentine passport, driver's license and identity papers, a birth certificate, several valid credit cards, a bank account and a real address in Buenos Aires, all in the name of Eduardo José López, a nice common surname. This identity had been constructed years before and serviced regularly so that he might move money around the globe when drug smugglers sought to pay Fidel Castro. Becoming the good Señor López would be as easy as presenting the passport when checking into a hotel.

He had the papers for two other identities in a safe deposit box in Lausanne, across the lake from Geneva.

Maximo Sedano fingered the bank transfer cards one more time, then reclined his seat.

How does it feel to be rich? Damned good, thank you very much.

Lord, it was tempting. Just walk away with the money as Señor López, and poof! disappear into thin air.

And yet, the gold was there for the taking. His plans were made, his allies ready ... all he had to do was find the gold and get it out of the country.

He reclined his seat, closed his eyes, and savored the feeling of being rich.

Doña Sedano was sitting on her porch, inhaling the gentle aroma of the tropical flowers that grew around her porch in profusion and watching the breeze stir the petals, when she saw Hector walking down the road. He turned in at her gate and came up to the porch.

After he kissed her he sat on the top step, leaned back so he could see her face.

'Why aren't you in school, teaching?' she asked.

He made a gesture, looked away to the north, toward the sea.

There was nothing out that way but a few treetops waving in the wind, with puffy clouds floating overhead.

He turned back to look into her face, reached for her hand. 'Ocho went on a boat two nights ago. They were trying to reach the Florida Keys.'

'Did they make it?'

'I don't know. If they make it we won't hear for days. Weeks perhaps. If they don't reach Florida we may never hear.'

Doña Maria leaned forward and touched her son's hair. Then she put her twisted hands back in her lap.

'Thank you for telling me.'

'Ocho should have told you.'

'Good-byes can be difficult.'

'I suppose.'

'You are the brightest of my sons, the one with the most promise. Why didn't you go to America, Hector? You had plenty of chances. Why did you stay in this hopeless place?'

'Cuba is my home.' He gestured helplessly. 'This is the work God has given me to do.'

Doña Maria gently massaged her hands. Rubbing them seemed to ease the pain sometimes.

'I might as well tell you the rest of it,' Hector said. 'Ocho got a girl pregnant. He went on the boat with the girl and her father. The father wants Ocho to play baseball in America.'

'Pregnant?'

'Ocho told me, made me promise not to tell. He did not confess to me as a priest but as a brother, so I am exercising an older brother's prerogative – I am breaking that promise.'

She sighed, closed her eyes for a moment.

'If God is with them, they may make it across the Straits,' Hector said. 'There is always that hope.'

Tears ran down her cheeks.

It was at that moment that Doña Maria saw the human condition more clearly than she ever had before. She and Hector were two very mortal people trapped by circumstance, by fate, between two vast eternities. The past was gone, lost to them. The people they loved who were dead were gone like smoke, and they had only memories of them. The future was . . . well, the future was unknowable, hidden in the haze. Here there was only the present, this moment, these two mortal people with their memories of all that had been.

Hector stroked his mother's hair, kissed her tears, then went down the walk to the road. When he looked back his mother was still sitting where he had left her, looking north toward the sea.

Ocho was probably dead, Hector realized, another victim of the Cuban condition.

When, O Lord, when will it stop? How many more people must drown in the sea? How many more lives must be blighted and ruined by the lack of opportunity here? How many more lives must be sacrificed on the altar of political ambition?

As he walked toward the village bus stop, he lifted his hands and roared his rage, an angry shout that was lost in the cathedral of the sky.

The pain was there, definitely there, but it wasn't cutting at him, doubling him over. Fidel Castro made them get him up, had them put him in a chair behind his desk. He wanted the flag to his right.

Mercedes and the nurse helped him into his green fatigue shirt.

He was perspiring then, gritting his teeth to get through this.

'Do you know what you want to say?' Mercedes asked.

'I think so.'

The camera crew was fiddling with the lights, arranging power cords.

'I want to say something to you, right now,' she whispered, 'while you are sharp and not heavily sedated.'

His eyes went to her.

'I love you, Fidel. With all my heart.'

'And I you, woman. Would that we had more time.'

'Ah, time, what a whore she is. We had each other, and that was enough.'

He bit his lip, reached for her hand. 'If only we had met years ago, before –'

He winced again. 'Better start the tape,' he said. 'I haven't much time.' He straightened, gripped the arms of the chair so hard his knuckles turned white.

With the lights on, Fidel Castro looked straight into the camera, and spoke: 'Citizens of Cuba, I speak to you today for the last time. I am fatally ill and my days on this earth will soon be over. Before I leave you, however, I wish to spend a few minutes telling you of my dream for Cuba, my dream of what our nation can become in the years ahead. . . .'

The door opened and Alejo Vargas walked in. Behind him was Colonel Pablo Santana.

'Well, well, *Señor Presidente.* I heard you were making a speech to the video cameras this afternoon. Do not mind us; please continue. We will remain silent spectators, out of the sight of the camera, two loyal Cubans representing millions of others.'

'I did not invite you here, Vargas.'

'True, you did not, *Señor Presidente*. But things seem to be slipping away from you these days – important things. The world will not stop turning on its axis while you lie in bed taking drugs.'

'Get out! This is my office.'

Alejo Vargas settled into a chair. He turned to the camera crew. 'Turn that thing off. The lights too. Then you may take a short break. We will call you when we want you to return.'

The extinguishment of the television lights made the room seem very dark.

Colonel Santana escorted the technicians from the room and closed the door behind them. He stood with his back against the door, his arms crossed.

'If you are pushing the button near your knee to summon the security staff, you are wasting your time,' Vargas said. 'Members of my staff have replaced them.'

'Say what you want, then get out,' Castro said.

Vargas got out a cigarette, lit it, taking his time. 'I am wondering about Maximo Sedano. The night before last he was here, you signed something for him, he left this morning on a plane to Madrid, with a continuation on to Zurich. What was that all about?'

Fidel said nothing. Mercedes noticed that he was perspiring again.

'I am in no rush,' Vargas said. 'I have all the time in the world.'

Fidel ground his teeth. 'He went to move funds. On a matter of interest to the Finance Ministry.'

'The question is, where will the funds end up when their electronic journey is over? Tell me that, please.'

'In the government's accounts in the Bank of Cuba, in Havana.'

'I ask this question because the man who was here last night did not see you check the account numbers in any book or ledger. You have the account numbers memorized?'

'No.'

'So in reality you don't know where Maximo Sedano will wire the money?'

'He is a trustworthy man. Loyal. I cannot be everywhere, see everything, and must trust people. I have trusted people all my life.'

'How much money are we talking about, *Señor Presidente*?'

'I don't know.'

'Millions?'

'Yes.'

'Tens of millions?'

428

'Yes.'

'*Dios mio*, our Maximo must be a saint! I wouldn't trust my own mother with that kind of money.'

'I wouldn't trust your mother with a drunken sailor,' Mercedes said. 'Not if he had two centavos in his pocket.' She handed some pills to Castro, who glanced down at them.

'Water, please,' he whispered. He put the pills on the desk in front of him.

Vargas continued: 'If we ever see the face of Maximo Sedano again, *Señor Presidente*, you have me to thank. I am having one of my men meet the finance minister in Zurich. We will try to convince Maximo to do his duty to his country.'

Mercedes handed Fidel a glass of water. He picked up several of the pills, put them in his mouth, then swallowed some water. Then he put the last pill in his mouth and took another swig.

Vargas was a moral nihilist, Castro thought, a man who believed in nothing. There were certainly plenty of those. He had known what Vargas was for many years and had used him anyway because he was good at his job, which was a miserable one. *We entrusted it to a swine so that we need not dirty our hands.*

Another mistake.

'I need rest,' he said, and tried to rise.

'No,' Vargas said fiercely. He leaned on the desk with both hands, lowered his face near Fidel. 'You still have a statement to make before the cameras.'

'Nothing for you.'

'You think you have nothing to lose, do you not? You think, Alejo could kill me, but what is that? He merely speeds up the inevitable.'

Fidel looked Vargas square in the eye. 'I should have killed you years and years ago,' he said. He took his hands from the arms of his chair and wrapped them around his stomach.

'There is no regret as bitter as the murder you didn't commit. How true that is! But you didn't kill me because you needed me, Fidel, needed me to ferret out your enemies, find who was whispering against you and bring you their names. Help you shut their mouths, cut out the rot without killing the tree.

'Kill me? Without me how would you have kept your wretched subjects loyal? Who would have kept these miserable *guajiros* starving on this sandy rock in the sea's middle from cutting the flesh from your bones? Who would have provided the muscle to keep you in office when the Russians abandoned you and nothing went right? When everything you touched backfired?

'Kill me? *Ha!* That would have been like killing yourself.

'Now I have come for mine. Not centavos, like in the past. I want what is mine for keeping you in power all these years, for keeping the peasants from slicing your throat when in truth that was precisely what you deserved. You are a miserable failure, Fidel, as a man and as a servant of Cuba. And you are going to die a revered old man – God, what a joke! Hailed as the Cuban Washington for the next ten centuries. . . .'

Vargas sneered.

'Now *I* have the power of life or death, Fidel. I think you will make your statement in front of the camera. You will name me, Alejo Vargas, your loyal, trusted minister of interior as your successor; you will plead with all loyal Cubans everywhere to recognize the wisdom of your choice.'

Sweat ran in rivulets from Fidel's face, dripped from his beard. His voice came out a hoarse whisper. 'Forty years service to my country, and you expect me to hand Cuba over to you? To rape for your profit? Not on your life.'

'Don't be a fool. You have nothing to bargain with.'

'Kill me. See what you gain,' Fidel said, his voice barely audible.

'You'll die soon enough, never fear. But before you do Colonel Santana will butcher Mercedes on this table while you watch.'

'Have you no honor?'

'Don't talk to me of honor. You have told so many lies you can't remember ever telling the truth. You have profaned the Church, denied God, sent loyal Cuban soldiers to die in Angola, demanded that generation after generation give their blood to fulfill your destiny as Cuba's savior. You have impoverished a nation, reduced them to beggary to salve your ego. I spit on you and all that you would have us become.'

And he did.

Fidel brought a hand up to wipe away the spittle. 'Fuck you!' he whispered.

'And you too, *Líder Máximo!*' Vargas shot back. 'I do not pretend to be God's other son, strutting in green fatigues and spouting platitudes while the people worship me. But enough of this. Before we get to the camera, tell me where the gold is.'

'The gold?'

'The gold, Fidel. The gold from the peso coins that the Ministry of Finance melted down into ingots, the gold ingots that you and Che and Edis López and José Otero carried away. How much gold was there? Forty or fifty tons? You certainly didn't spend it on the people of Cuba. Where is it?'

A grimace twisted Castro's lips. 'You'll never find it, that's for certain. Edis and José died within weeks of Che. I am the only living person who knows where that gold is; I am taking the secret to my grave.'

'The gold isn't yours.'

'Nor is it yours, you son of a pig.'

'We will let you watch us cut up Mercedes. We will make a tiny incision on her abdomen, pull out a loop of small intestine. I will ask you questions, and every time you refuse to answer Colonel Santana will pull out more intestine. You will tell us everything we want to know or we will see what her insides look like. Colonel?'

Santana grabbed Mercedes by the arms. With one hand he grabbed the front of her dress and ripped it from her body.

Fidel Castro's jaw moved. Then he went limp, slumping in his chair.

'*Fidel!*' Mercedes screamed.

Vargas leaped for Castro, pried open his jaw and raked a piece of celluloid from his mouth with his finger.

'Poison,' he said disgustedly. He felt Castro's wrist for a pulse.

'Stone cold dead.' He tossed down the wrist and turned toward Mercedes.

'*You* gave him the poison! He had the capsule in his mouth.'

Alejo Vargas slapped her as hard as he could.

'And this is for insulting my mother, *puta!*' He slapped her again so hard she went to her knees, the side of her face numb. 'If you do it again I will cut your tongue out,' he added, his voice almost a hiss.

Then Vargas took a deep breath and steadied himself. The sight of Fidel Castro's corpse drained the rage from him and filled him with adrenaline, ready for the race to his destiny. He had waited all his life for this moment and now it was here.

'Listen to this,' the technician said, and handed the earphones to William Henry Chance. They were crammed into a tiny van with the logo of the Communications Ministry on the side. The van was parked on a side street near Chance's hotel, but with an excellent view of the Interior Ministry.

Chance put on the headphones.

'We recorded this stuff early this morning,' the technician told Chance's associate, Tommy Carmellini. 'Getting to you without stirring up the Cubans was the trick. Wait until you hear this stuff.'

'What is it?' Carmellini asked.

'Vargas and his thug, Santana, in the minister's office. They're talking about a speech they want Castro to make in front of cameras. A political will, Vargas called it. They are writing it, debating the wording.'

'What do they want it to say?'

'They want Castro to name Vargas as his successor, his heir.'

'Will he do that?'

'They seem to think he will.'

'Have we heard anything back from Washington about that ship reference – the *Colón*? . . . *Nuestra Señora de Colón*?'

'No. Something like that will take days to percolate through the bureaucracy.'

'I was hoping the reference to North Koreans and biological warheads would light a fire under somebody.'

'It always takes a while before we smell the smoke of burning trousers.'

Carmellini watched Chance's face as he listened to the tape. William Henry Chance, attorney and CIA agent, certainly didn't look like a man who would be at home in the shadow world of spies and espionage. But then appearances were often deceiving.

Carmellini had been a burglar – more or less semi-retired – attending the Stanford University Law School when he was visited one day by a CIA recruiter, a woman who took him to lunch in the student union cafeteria and asked him about his plans for the future. He still remembered the conversation. He was going into business, he said. Maybe politics. He thought that someday he might run for public office.

'A prosecution for stealing the Peabody diamond from the Museum of Natural History in Washington would probably crimp your plans, wouldn't it?' she said sweetly.

He gaped. Sat there like a fool with his mouth hanging open, the brain completely stalled.

He had seen her credentials, which certainly looked official enough. Central Intelligence Agency. The Government with a capital G. But there had never been the slightest hint that anyone was on his trail. Not even a sniff.

'It would do that,' he managed.

After a bit, the question of how she knew formed in his mind, and he began trying to figure out how to ask it in a nonincriminating way.

'You're wondering, I suppose,' she said matter-of-factly between sips of her coffee, 'how we learned of your involvement.'

Unable to help himself, he nodded yes.

'Your pal talked. The Miami PD got him on another burglary, so he threw you to the wolves to get a lighter sentence.'

Well, there it was. His very best friend in the whole world and the only guy who knew everything had sold him out.

'You need some better friends,' she said. 'Your friend is a pretty small-caliber guy. A real loser. He got eight years on the state charge. Moving stolen property across state lines is a federal crime of course, and Justice hasn't decided if they will prosecute.'

It quickly became plain that at that moment in his life, the CIA was his best career choice.

After finishing law school, Carmellini spent a year in the covert operations section of the agency. Now he was an associate of William Henry Chance, who had been with the CIA ever since he left the army after the Vietnam War. The cover was impeccable – both men were really practicing attorneys and CIA operatives on the side.

Carmellini remembered the first time he met William Henry Chance. He was running a ten-kilometer race in Virginia one weekend when Chance came galloping up beside him, barely sweating, and suggested they have lunch afterward.

Chance mentioned a name, Carmellini's boss at the agency. 'He said you were a pretty good runner,' Chance said, then began lengthening his stride.

Tommy Carmellini managed to stay with Chance all the way to the tape but it was a hell of a workout. Chance didn't work at running; he loped along, all lean meat, bone, and sinew, a natural long-distance runner. Carmellini, on the other hand, was built more like a running back or middle linebacker.

About half of Carmellini's time was spent on agency matters, half on the firm's business. He was a better covert warrior than he was a lawyer, so he had to work hard to keep up with the bright young associates who had not the slightest idea that Carmellini or Chance were also employed by the CIA.

Sitting in a telephone company van in the middle of Havana listening to intercepted conversations, Tommy Carmellini wondered if he should have told the CIA to stick it. He would probably be getting out of prison about now, free and clear.

And broke, of course. His friend had fenced the diamond and spent all the money, never intending to give Carmellini his share.

On the table was a set of photos the technicians had taken of the University of Havana science building. They had had the place under surveillance for the last two days.

Carmellini looked at the photos critically, as if he were going to burgle the joint. There were guards at every entrance, some electronic alarms: getting in would take some doing.

After a while Chance handed the headphones to a technician. He sat looking at Carmellini with a frown on his face.

'I think Vargas plans to kill Fidel,' Chance said finally.

'When?'

'Soon. Very soon. Today or tomorrow, I would imagine.'

'And then?'

'Your guess is as good as mine.'

The men left alive aboard *Angel del Mar* were unable to get the engine restarted, so it drifted helplessly with the wind and swell. Ocho took his turn in the tiny, cramped engine compartment. Something down inside the engine was broken, perhaps the crankshaft. Rotating the propeller shaft by hand made a clunky noise; at a certain point in the shaft's rotation it became extremely difficult to turn. Admitting finally that repairing the motor was hopeless, Ocho backed out of the small compartment. His place was taken by someone else who wanted to satisfy himself personally that the engine was indeed beyond repair.

After a while they all gave up and shut the door.

Without the engine they had to work the bilge pump manually. Fifteen minutes of intense effort cleared the bilges of water. With daylight coming through the hatch one could just see the water seeping in between the planks where the sea had pounded the caulking loose. It took about fifteen minutes for the bilges to fill, then they had to be pumped again. A quarter hour of work, a quarter hour of rest.

'If we can just keep pumping,' the old fisherman said, 'we stay afloat.'

'If the water doesn't come in any faster,' Ocho added. He was young and strong, so he spent hours sitting here in the bilge working the pump, watching the water come in.

Twenty-six people remained alive. The captain's body was still in the wheelhouse, where he had fallen. No one wanted to take responsibility for moving him.

After a morning working the bilge pump, Ocho Sedano stood braced against the wheelhouse and, shading his eyes, looked carefully in all directions. The view was the same as it was yesterday, swells that ran off to the horizon, and above it all a sky crowded with puffy little clouds.

At least the sea had subsided somewhat. The wind no longer tore whitecaps off the waves. The breeze seemed steady, maybe eight or ten knots out of the southwest.

One suspected the boat was drifting northeast, riding the Gulf Stream. The nearest land in that direction was the Bahamas.

The United States was north, or perhaps northwest now. A whole continent was just over the horizon, with people, cities, restaurants, farms, mountains, rivers ... if only they could get there.

Well, someone would see this boat drifting before too long. Someone in a plane or fishing boat, perhaps an American coast guard cutter or navy ship looking for drug smugglers. They would see the *Angel del Mar* drifting helplessly, give the people stranded on her water and food, then take them to Guantánamo Bay and make them walk through the gate back to Cuba. Or maybe they would be taken to hospitals in America.

Already some of these people needed hospitals. They had vomited too much, been without water for too long. They had become dehydrated, their electrolytes dangerously out of balance, and if left unattended would die. Just like the people swept over the side last night.

Of course, knowing all this, there was absolutely nothing Ocho Sedano could do. He too felt the ravages of thirst, felt the aching of the empty knot in his stomach. Fortunately he had not been seasick, had not retched his guts out until he had only the dry heaves like so many of these others lying helpless in the sun.

The wheelhouse cast a little shade, so he dragged several people in out of the sun. Maybe that would help a little.

The sea seemed to keep the boat broadside to it, so the shade didn't move around too much, which was a blessing.

There wasn't room in the shade for everyone.

'The sail,' said the fisherman. 'There is an old piece of canvas around the boom. Let's see if we can get it up.'

They worked with the canvas in the afternoon sun for over an hour, trying to rig it as a sail. It wasn't really a sail, but an awning. Finally the fisherman said maybe it was best used to catch rain and protect people from the sun, so they rigged it across the boom and tied it there.

Ocho dragged as many people under it as he could, then lay exhausted on the board deck in the shade, his tongue a swollen, heavy, rough thing in his dry mouth.

Sweating. He was going to have to stop sweating like this, stop wasting his bodily fluids. Stop this exertion.

Nearby a child cried. She would stop soon, he thought, too thirsty to waste energy crying.

He sat up, looked for Dora. She was sitting in the shade with her back against the wheelhouse. Her father, Diego Coca, lay on the deck beside her, his head in her lap. She looked at Ocho, then averted her gaze.

'What should I have done?' he asked.

She couldn't have heard him.

He got up, went over to where she was. 'What should I have done?'

She said nothing, merely lowered her head. She was stroking her father's hair. His eyes were closed, he seemed oblivious to his surroundings and the corkscrewing motion of the drifting boat. His body moved slackly as the boat rose and fell.

Ocho Sedano went into the wheelhouse. Above the captain's swollen corpse the helm wheel kicked back and forth in rhythm to the pounding of the sea.

Ocho held his breath, turned the body over, went through the pockets. A few pesos, a letter, a home-made pocketknife, a worn, rusty bolt, a stub of a pencil, a button . . . not much to show for a lifetime of work.

Already the body was swelling in the heat. The face was dark and mottled.

He dragged the captain's stiff body from the wheelhouse, got it to the rail and hooked one of the arms across the railing. Then he lifted the feet.

The dead man was very heavy.

Grunting, working alone since none of his audience lifted a hand to help, Ocho heaved the weight up onto the rail and balanced it there as the boat rolled. Timing the roll, he released the body and it fell into the sea.

The corpse floated beside the boat face up. The lifeless eyes seemed to follow Ocho.

He tore himself away, finally, and watched the top of the mast make circles against the gray-white clouds and patchy blue.

When he looked again at the water the captain's corpse was still there, still face up. The sea water made a fan of his long hair, swirled it back and forth as if it were waving in a breeze. Water flowed into and out of his open mouth as the corpse bobbed up and down.

The long nights, the sun, heat, and exhaustion caught up with Ocho

Sedano and he could no longer remain upright. He lowered himself to the deck, wedged his body against the railing, and slept.

'That freighter that left Gitmo last week, the one carrying the warheads?'

'I remember,' Toad Tarkington said. 'The *Colón*, or something like that.'

'*Nuestra Señora de Colón*. She never made it to Norfolk.'

'What?' Toad stared at the admiral, who was holding the classified message.

'She never arrived. Atlantic Fleet HQ is looking for her right now.'

Toad took the message, scanned it, then handed it back.

'We sent a destroyer with that ship,' the admiral said. 'Call the captain, find out everything you can. I want to know when he last saw that ship and where she was.'

In minutes Toad had the CO on the secure voice circuit. 'We went up through the Windward and Mayaguanan passages,' Toad was told. 'They were creeping along at three knots, but they got their engineering plant rolling again and worked up to twelve knots, so we left her a hundred miles north of San Salvador, heading north.' The captain gave the date and time.

'The *Colón* never arrived in Norfolk,' Toad said.

'I'll be damned! Lost with all hands?'

'I doubt that very much,' Toad replied.

Toad got on the encrypted voice circuit, telling the computer technicians in Maryland what he wanted. Soon the computers began chattering. Rivers of digital, encrypted data from the National Security Agency's mainframe computers at Fort Meade, Maryland, were bounced off a satellite and routed into the computers aboard *United States*.

On the screens before him he began seeing pictures, radar images from satellites in space looking down onto the earth. The blips that were the *Colón* and her escorting destroyer were easily picked out as they left Guantánamo Bay and made their way through the Windward Passage.

The screens advanced hour by hour. The three-knot speed of advance made the blips look almost stationary, so Toad flipped quickly through the screens, then had to wait while the data feed caught up.

Jake Grafton joined him, and they looked at the screens together.

The two blips crawled north, past Mayaguana, past San Salvador, then they sped up. The destroyer turning back was obvious.

As Jake and Toad watched, the blip that was the *Colón* turned southeast, back toward the Bahamas archipelago. Then the blip merged into a sea of white return.

'Now what?'

'It's rain,' Jake said. 'There was a storm. The blip is buried somewhere in that rain return. Call NSA. See if they can screen out the rain effect.'

He was right; the rain did obscure the blip. But NSA could not separate the ship's return from that caused by rain.

'See if they can do a probability study, show us the most probable location of the *Colón* in the middle of that mess.'

The computing the admiral requested took hours, and the results were inconclusive. As the intensity of the showers increased and decreased, the probable location of the ship expanded and contracted like a living circle. Jake and Toad drank coffee and ate sandwiches as they waited and watched the computer presentations.

Jake wandered around the compartment looking at maps between glances at the computer screen and conversations over another encrypted circuit with the brass in the Pentagon. The White House was in the loop now – the president wanted to know how in hell a shipload of chemical and biological warheads could disappear.

'What do you think happened, Admiral?' Toad asked.

'Too many possibilities.'

'Do the people in Washington blame you for not having the *Colón* escorted all the way to Norfolk?'

'Of course. The national security adviser wants to know why the destroyer left the *Colón*.'

Toad bristled. 'You weren't told to escort that ship, you were told to guard the base. Escorting that ship out of the area wasn't your responsibility.'

'Somebody is going to second-guess every decision I make,' Jake Grafton said, 'all of them. They're doing that right now. That comes with the stars and the job.'

'Hindsight is a wonderful thing.'

'I'll be out on the golf course soon enough, and the only person who will second-guess me then will be my wife.'

Despite the best efforts of the wizards in Maryland and aboard ship, the location of the *Colón* under the rain of the cold front could not be established. Jake gave up, finally.

'Tell them to move forward in time. Let's see where the ship was after the storm.'

But when the rain ceased, the computer could not identify the *Colón* from the other ship returns. There were thirty-two medium-to-large sized vessels in the vicinity of the Bahamas alone.

Toad stayed on the encrypted circuit to the NSA wizards. Finally he hung up the handset and turned to the admiral.

'They can assign track numbers to each blip, watch where they go, and by process of elimination come up with the most likely blips. There is a lot of computing involved. The process will take hours, maybe a day or two.'

Jake Grafton picked up the flight schedule, took a look, then handed it to Toad. 'Put the air wing up in a surface search pattern. Let's see what we can find out there now.'

Toad turned to the chart on the bulkhead. 'Where do you want them to look?'

'From the north coast of Cuba north into the Bahamas. Look along the coast of Hispaniola, all the way to Puerto Rico. Do the Turks and Caicos. Have the crews photograph every ship they see. Have NSA establish current ship tracks, then match up what the air crews see with what the satellite sees. Then let's run the current plot backward.'

'Someone got a lucky break with the rain storm,' Toad commented. 'Maybe they were playing for the break, maybe it just happened.'

'Send a top secret message to the Gitmo base commander. Find out everything they know about the crew of that ship.'

Jake Grafton tapped the chart. 'The president gave everyone in uniform their marching orders. Find that ship.'

8

Maximo Sedano flashed his diplomatic passport at the immigration officer in the Madrid airport and was waved through after a perfunctory glance. His suitcase was checked through to Zurich, and of course customs passed his attaché case without inspection. Traveling as a diplomat certainly had its advantages – airport security did not even x-ray a diplomat's carry-on bags.

The Cuban minister of finance wandered the airport terminal luxuriating in the ambiance of Europe. The shops were full of delicacies, books, tobacco, clothes, liquor, the women were well turned out, the sights and smells were of civilization and prosperity and good living.

In spite of himself, Maximo Sedano sighed deeply. Ah, yes . . .

Spain or one of the Spanish islands would be his choice for retirement. With Europe at his feet, what more could a man want? And retirement seemed to Maximo to be almost within reach.

What was the phrase? 'Fire in the belly'? Some Yanqui politician said to win office one must have fire in the belly.

After a morning of thinking about it, Maximo concluded he didn't have the fire. After Fidel died, Fidel's brother, Raúl or Maximo's brother Hector, or Alejo Vargas, or anyone else who could kill his rivals could rule Cuba – Maximo had given up trying for that prize. He'd take the money.

And all the things money can buy: villas, beautiful women, yachts, gourmet food, fine wine, beautiful women . . . Someone else could stand in the Plaza de la Revolucion in Havana and revel in the cheers of the crowd.

He filed aboard the plane to Zurich and settled cheerfully into his seat. He smiled at the flight attendant and beamed at the man across the aisle.

Life is good, Maximo told himself, and unconsciously fingered his breast pocket, where the cards were that contained Fidel's signature and thumbprints.

Why go back?

Fifty-three or -four million American dollars was more than enough. To hell with the gold!

As the jet accelerated down the runway, Maximo told himself that the only smart thing was to take the money and retire. Now was the hour. Reel in the fish on the line – don't let it off the hook to cast for another.

439

He could transfer the money, spend three or four days shuffling it around, then leave Zurich on the Argentine passport as Eduardo José López. Maximo Sedano would cease to exist.

Off to Ibiza, buy a small cottage overlooking the sea, find a willing woman, not too young, not too old . . .

Yes.

He would do it.

The sudden death of Fidel Castro caught Alejo Vargas off guard. The dictator's death was supposed to be days, even weeks, away. Unfortunately Vargas's political position was precarious, to say the least. He really could have used Fidel's endorsement, however obtained. At least now no one would get it.

Although he had lived his whole life in his brother's shadow, Raúl Castro nominally held the reins of government. Alejo Vargas thought that without Fidel, Raúl was completely out on a limb, without a political constituency of his own.

While he tried to analyze the moves on the board, Vargas had Colonel Santana lock Mercedes in a bedroom, seal the presidential palace, and put a security man on the telephone switchboard. He didn't want the news of Fidel's death to get out before he was ready.

Vargas left Santana in charge of the palace and took his limo back to the ministry. Of course he refrained from using the telephone in his limo to issue orders. The Americans listened to every radio transmission on telephone frequencies and would soon know as much about his business as he did. He sat silently as the limo carried him through the afternoon traffic to the ministry.

There he called his most trusted lieutenants to his office and issued orders. Bring Admiral Delgado and General Alba to this office immediately. Find and arrest Hector Sedano.

Alejo Vargas stood at the window looking at Morro Castle and the sea beyond. Far out from shore he could just make out the deep blue of the Gulf Stream, which appeared as a thin blue line just under the horizon. An overcast layer was moving in from the southeast and a breeze was picking up.

A historic day . . . Fidel Castro, the towering giant of Cuban history was dead. The end of an era, Vargas thought, and the beginning of a new one, one he would dominate.

Despite the timing surprise, Vargas really had no choice: he was going to have to go forward with his plan. He had concluded a month or so ago that the only course open to him upon the death of Castro was to create a situation that would induce the Cuban people to rally around him. He would need boldness and a fierce resolve if he were to have a chance of success, but he was just the man to risk everything on one roll of the dice. After he personally loaded them.

Colonel Santana brought an American artillery shell to Havana yesterday, one removed from *Nuestra Señora de Colón*. The thing was in the basement of the ministry now, under armed guard. The Cuban leadership had known for years that the Americans had CBW weapons stored at Guantánamo. Now the Americans were removing the things, but too late! Thanks to El Gato, Vargas had one he could show the world. Soon he hoped to have a great many more.

Alejo Vargas took a deep breath, stretched mightily, helped himself to a cigar. He lit it, inhaled the smoke, and blew it out through his nose. Then he laughed.

'I want a little house with a garden. Every day food to eat. Children. A doctor to make them well when they get sick. A man who loves me. Is that so much?'

Dora's mouth was so dry she didn't enunciate her words clearly, but Ocho knew what she meant. They lay head to head under the awning in the shade as the *Angel del Mar* pitched and rolled endlessly in the long sea swells.

Surrounded by a universe of water they couldn't drink, the twenty-six humans aboard the boat were tortured by thirst and baked by the sun. Many had bad sunburns now, raw places where the skin had blistered and peeled off, leaving oozing sores. The old fisherman dipped buckets of water from the sea and poured salt water over the burns. He gently poured sea water on the small children, who had long ago ceased crying. Perhaps the water would be absorbed by their dehydrated tissues. If not, it would at least help keep them cool, ease their suffering somewhat.

Near Dora a woman was repeating the Rosary, over and over, mumbling it. Now and then another woman joined in for a few minutes, then fell silent until the spirit moved her again.

It seemed as if everyone left alive had lost someone to the sea that first night. The cries and grief were almost more than people could bear when they realized who had been lost, and that they were gone forever. Mothers cried, daughters were so distraught they shook, the hopelessness hit everyone like a hammer. The mother of the captain, who saw him dead, shot in the back, could neither move nor speak. As Dora talked, Ocho watched the woman, who sat now at the foot of the mainmast, holding on to it with one hand and a daughter or daughter-in-law with the other.

Every now and then Ocho sat or stood and searched the horizon. Nothing. Not a boat, not land, not a ship. Nothing.

Oh, three airplanes had gone over, two jets way up high making contrails and a twin-engine plane perhaps two miles up that had crossed the sky straight as a string, without the slightest waver as it passed within a half mile of *Angel del Mar*, rolling her guts out in the swells.

To see the airplanes, with their people riding inside, safe, full of food and drink, on their way from someplace to somewhere else, while we poor creatures are trapped here on this miserable boat, condemned to die slowly of thirst and exposure . . .

Surely the boat would be found soon . . . by somebody! Anybody! How can the Americans not see us? How?

Do they see us and not care?

Ocho was standing, watching for other ships and listening to Dora talk of the house she wanted, with the flowers by the door, when he realized that the dark place he could see to the west was a rain squall.

'Rain,' he whispered.

'*Rain.*' He shouted the word, pointed.

The squall was upon them before anyone could muster the energy to do anything. The people stood with their mouths open as raindrops pounded them and soaked their clothes and ran off the awning and along the deck, to disappear into the scuppers.

'The awning! Quickly. Make a container from the awning to trap the water!'

Ocho untied one corner with fingers that were all thumbs, the old fisherman did another corner, and they held the corners up, trapping water.

They had a few gallons when the rain ceased falling.

Several of the men tried to lean over, drink from the awning.

'No. Children first.'

Ocho managed to catch one man by the back of the neck and throw him to the deck.

'Children first.'

One by one the children were allowed to drink all they could hold. Then the women.

Several of the men got a swallow or two each, then the water was gone.

Ocho sat down, wiped the sweat and water from his hair and sucked it from his fingers. The only water he had gotten had been from holding his mouth open.

Dora had drunk her fill. Now she lay on the deck with her eyes closed.

Diego Coca had even gotten a swallow. He looked about with venomous eyes, then lay down beside his daughter.

'We must rig the awning so that it will catch water if the rain comes again,' Ocho said to the old fisherman.

They worked at it, cut a hole in the low place in the canvas and put a five-gallon bucket under the hole.

If it will just rain again, Ocho thought, studying the clouds. *Please God, hear our prayer.*

'Why are you here, on this boat?' the old fisherman asked Ocho, who stared at him in surprise.

'Why are you here?' the fisherman repeated. 'You aren't like us.'

Ocho looked around at his fellow sufferers, unable to fathom the old man's meaning.

'These people are all losers,' the old man said, 'including me. We came looking for something we will never find. Why are you with us?'

'It's time for someone to relieve López on the pump. I will do it for a while, then you relieve me, old man.'

'We are going to die soon, I think,' the old man said.

Ocho hissed, 'There are children listening. Watch your mouth.'

'When we can pump no more we will swim. Then we will die. One by one people will drown, or sharks will come.'

'Look for a ship,' Ocho said harshly, and went below.

Sharks! The old windbag, scaring the children like that.

Of course sharks were a possibility. Blood or people thrashing about in the water would attract them, or so he had always heard. Sharks would rip people apart, pull them under.

He pumped for a bit over twenty minutes, then took a break. The water came in fast. After five minutes he began pumping again. Another twenty-one minutes of vigorous effort was required to empty the bilge.

The water was coming in faster than it did yesterday. Pumping the handle manually seemed to require more effort too, though he knew he just had less energy. Pump, pump, pump, take a brief rest in the stinky bilge, then pump again. . . .

The more tired he grew the more hopeless he felt. All of them were doomed. Dora, the baby growing within her, the baby that he had put in her womb . . .

It was his fault. If he had been man enough to say no, to not surrender to lust, all these people would still be in Cuba, they would have a future to look forward to, not watery death. All the people who had been swept to their death would still be alive.

Alive! He had no idea of the horrible things he was setting in motion when he opened her dress, felt the ripeness of her body, felt the heat of her.

The guilt weighed on him, made it hard to breathe. He must do what he could to save them all. That was the only honorable choice open to him. Save as many as possible and maybe God would forgive him.

Maybe then he could forgive himself. . . .

And he shouldn't give up hope yet. As he worked the pump handle he scolded himself for being so negative, for not having faith in God, in His plan for the twenty-six human beings still alive on *Angel del Mar.*

Soon a ship would come. The sailors would see the boat and rescue them. Give them cool, clean water, all they could drink; and food. Let each of them eat their fill. Soon it would come. Any minute now.

He pumped and pumped, sweat burned his eyes and dripped from his nose, though not so much as he sweated yesterday. He was very dehydrated. The salt had built up in his armpits, his groin, and it cut him. With his free hand he scratched, which only made the burning worse.

Any minute now a ship will come over the horizon. Soon . . .

Maximo Sedano took a taxi from the Zurich airport to an excellent hotel in the heart of the financial district where he had stayed on six or eight previous visits. The hotel was old, solid, substantial, almost banklike, yet it was not the primo hotel. This was the last time he stayed here, he told himself. Eduardo José López would stay at the best hotel in town because by God he could afford it. And because the staff over there had never seen him as Maximo Sedano.

He would have to make many adjustments, avoid photographs, avoid places where prominent Cubans might see him, like the heart of Madrid or London or Paris. Of course, if Vargas was assassinated in the turmoil following Fidel's death, he could relax his vigilance somewhat. Vargas was a bloodhound, a humorless man with a profound capacity for revenge. Still, if Vargas came out on top after the succession struggle in Havana, he would have many things on his mind, and a missing ex-finance minister would of necessity be far down on the list.

Maximo would take his chances. He was in Europe, the money was in the banks just down the street, the loud and clear call of destiny was ringing in his ears.

He was sipping a drink and thinking about where he might go for dinner when he heard a knock on the door.

'Yes?'

'Delivery.'

'I ordered nothing. There has been a mistake.'

'For the Honorable Maximo Sedano.'

Curious, he opened the door.

The man standing in the hallway was European, with thinning hair and bulging muscles and a chiseled chin. And he was holding a pistol in his right hand, one pointed precisely at Maximo's solar plexus.

The man backed Maximo into the room and closed the door.

'Your passport, please?' A German accent.

'I have little money. Take it and go.'

'Sit.' He gestured toward a chair by the bed with his pistol. Maximo obeyed, thankfully. His knees were turning to jelly and he had a powerful urge to urinate.

'Now the passport.'

Maximo took the diplomatic passport from his inside pocket and passed it across. Taking care to keep the pistol well away from Maximo and still pointed at his middle, the man reached for the passport with his left hand.

He glanced at the photo and name, grinned, and tossed the passport on the bed. The man took a seat.

'You look white as a sheet, man. Are you going to pass out?'

He felt dizzy, light-headed. He put his hand to his forehead, which felt clammy.

'Loosen your tie,' the German ordered, 'unbutton your collar button, then put your head between your knees.'

Maximo obeyed.

'Don't breathe so fast. Get a grip on yourself. If you aren't careful you'll hyperventilate and pass out.'

Maximo concentrated on breathing slowly. After a few seconds he felt better. Finally he straightened up. The pistol was nowhere in sight.

'Vargas said you were a jellyfish.' The German shook his head sadly.

'Do you work for him?' He was shocked at the sound of his own voice, the pitch of which was surprisingly high.

'I do errands from time to time,' the German replied. 'He pays well and the work is congenial.'

'What do you want?'

'Vargas wanted me to remind you that you were sent to do an errand. You are to transfer the money to the proper accounts tomorrow and return to Cuba. If you do not, I am to kill you.'

The German smiled warmly. 'I will do it too. There is a side of my personality that I am not proud of, that I do not like to admit, but it is only fair that I should tell you the truth: I like to kill people. I enjoy it. I don't just shoot them, bang, bang, bang. I see how long I can keep them alive, how much I can make them suffer. I own a quiet little place, out of the way, isolated. It is perfect for my needs.'

The German's eyes narrowed speculatively. 'You seem a miserable specimen, but I like a challenge. I think with a little prior planning I could probably make you scream for at least forty-eight hours before you died.'

Maximo's heart was hammering in his ears, thudding along like a race horse's hooves.

The German picked up the telephone, told the operator he wished to place a call to Havana. He gave her the number.

One minute passed, then another.

'Rall here. For Vargas.'

After a few seconds, Rall spoke again. '*Buenos días, señor*. I have given him your message.'

The German listened for a few more seconds, then passed the telephone to Maximo.

The Cuban minister of finance managed to make a noise, and heard the voice of Alejo Vargas:

'The money must arrive tomorrow, Maximo. You understand?'

'Your thug has threatened me.'

'I hope Señor Rall has made the situation clear. It would be a tragedy for you to die because you did not understand your duty.'

The line went dead before Maximo could answer. He sat with the instrument in his hand, trying to keep control of his stomach. Rall gestured, so he handed the phone to him.

The German listened to make sure the connection had been severed, then placed the instrument back in its cradle. He stood.

'I don't know what else to say. You understand the situation. Your destiny is in your hands.'

With that the German went to the door, opened it and passed through, then pulled the door shut behind him until it latched.

Maximo ran to the bathroom and vomited in the commode.

William Henry Chance was lying on the bed in his hotel room reading a magazine when he heard the knock on the door. He opened it to find Tommy Carmellini standing there.

'Hey, boss,' Carmellini said. 'Let's take a walk.'

'Give me a moment to put on my shoes.'

Chance did so, pulled on a light sportscoat, and locked the door behind him on the way out.

Neither man spoke as they rode the elevator downstairs. Out on the sidewalk they automatically checked for a tail. No one obviously following, but that meant little. If the Cubans had burned them as CIA, they could have watchers in every building, be filming every move, every gesture, every movement of the lips.

So neither man said anything.

Carmellini directed their steps toward one of the larger casinos on the Malecon. Latin music engulfed them as they walked into the building. The place reminded Chance of Atlantic City, complete with crowds of gray-haired retirees buying a good time, mostly Americans, Germans, English, and Spaniards. No Cubans were gambling, of course, just foreigners who had hard currency to wager.

The only Cubans not behind the tables were prostitutes, young, gorgeous, and dressed in the latest European fashions. At this hour of the evening the cigar smoke was thick, the liquor flowing, and the laughter and music loud.

The two men drifted around the casino, taking their time, checking to see who was watching them, then finally sifted out of the building through a side door. At the basement loading dock a man was inventorying supplies in a telephone repair van. Chance and Carmellini climbed in, the man closed the door, and the van rolled.

'Vargas is having a powwow in his office,' Carmellini reported. 'It sounds as if Castro is dead.'

'Nobody lives forever,' Chance said lightly. 'Not even dictators.'

'That isn't the half of it. They're talking about biological weapons again.'

'Bingo,' Chance said, a touch of satisfaction creeping into his voice.

'Yeah. Vargas says there is a warehouse full of biological warheads at Gitmo.'

It took a whole lot to surprise William Henry Chance. He gaped.

'Not only that,' Carmellini continued, 'he has one of the things. He's going to show it to the Cuban people, prove to the world what perfidious bastards the Americans are.'

'He's got an American CBW warhead?'

'You'll have to listen to the tape. Sounded to the technician like the thing was stolen from a ship.'

'Biological warheads at Guantánamo Bay? That's gotta be wrong! Have these guys been smoking something?'

'I think Vargas and his pals have gone off the deep end. Either that or they plan to plant some biological agents in Guantánamo after they crash through the fence.'

'Maybe they know we're listening to them,' Chance said. 'Maybe this whole thing is a hoax.'

'Could be,' Tommy Carmellini agreed, but to judge by his tone of voice, he didn't think so.

Maximo Sedano was committed. He couldn't transfer the money to Cuban government accounts in Havana because the transfer cards contained the wrong account numbers. Changing the numbers was out of the question: any alteration to the cards would be instantly spotted and cause the Swiss bankers to suspect forgery.

Maximo carefully arranged the combination locks on his attaché case and opened it. At the bottom was a pistol, a very nice little Walther in 7.35 mm. The magazine was full, but there was no round in the chamber. Maximo chambered a round and engaged the safety.

He put the pistol in his right-hand trouser pocket and looked at himself in the mirror.

He put his hand in his pocket and wrapped his fingers around the butt of the weapon.

He had to go to the banks tomorrow, act like a bureaucrat shuffling money for his government while they shoveled $53 million plus interest into his personal accounts. Well, if he could kill the German and get away with it, he sure as hell could keep his cool while the Swiss bankers made him rich.

Could he kill Rall?

How badly did he want to be rich?

He stood at the window looking at the Limmat River a block from the hotel, and beyond it, the vast expanse of Lake Zurich. Beyond the lake half-hidden in the haze were the peaks of the Alps, still white with last winter's snow.

He certainly didn't want to go back to Cuba.

A drink of scotch whiskey from the minibar helped settle his nerves.

An hour later he left the hotel. He turned left, crossed the Limmat River on the nearest bridge, and headed for the main thoroughfare. Perhaps an hour of daylight left, but not more. He didn't look around him, sure that Rall was somewhere near. He took his time strolling along, pretending to enjoy the early summer day and the ebb and flow of the crowd, many of whom were young people on school holiday.

Finally he turned into an old cobblestoned street too narrow for vehicles and walked up it toward the hill which loomed above the downtown area. Medieval buildings rose up on either side and seemed to lean in, making the street seem even narrower and more confining than it really was as the daylight faded from the sky.

He found the restaurant he remembered and went inside. Yes, it was as he recalled, with the tables and chairs just so, the kitchen beyond, and past the kitchen, the rest room. One with an old tank mounted high in the wall with a pull chain.

How long had it been?

Two years, at least.

The waiter was new, didn't seem to recognize him. Not that he should, but it might be inconvenient if he should later recall seeing Sedano here this evening.

Maximo sat with his back against the wall, so that he could see both the front doorway and the door to the kitchen.

He ordered an Italian red wine, something robust, while he studied the menu.

The truth was Maximo was so nervous that he didn't think he could eat anything. The automatic felt heavy on his thigh, its weight an ominous presence that he couldn't ignore.

He tried to slow his breathing, make his pulse stop racing.

He used his handkerchief to wipe his hands, his face. He was used to the heat of Cuba; he should not be perspiring like this! *Get a grip, Maximo – if you cannot control yourself you will soon be dead. Or a subject for that pervert's experiments.*

He wondered if Rall had told the truth about torturing people.

Just thinking about that subject and the way the bastard told him about it – with obvious relish – made his forehead break out in a sweat. He swabbed with the handkerchief again.

There were two couples and another single man in the restaurant. Only one waiter shuttled back and forth through the kitchen door.

Maximo moved to a different seat at the same table so that he could see through the kitchen door. Yes, now when the waiter came through the door he could see most of the length of the narrow kitchen. The chef was moving back and forth, working on something in a pot, checking the oven, taking things from a refrigerator. . . .

'More wine?'

The waiter was there, holding the bottle.

'If you please.'

As the waiter poured, Maximo murmured, 'Have you a rest room?'

'Yes, of course. Through the kitchen, on the left in back.'

'I do not wish to disturb the chef.'

'Do not stand on ceremony, sir.'

He waited, sipping the wine, trying not to stare through the kitchen door. When the waiter returned he ordered, something, the first thing he saw on the menu.

One of the two couples left, the second finished their dinner and ordered coffee, the other man's meal came at about the same time as Maximo's.

He was just starting on the main course when the chef came to the door, wiped his hands on a towel, and said something to the waiter. Then he stepped outside into the narrow street and lit a cigarette. Night had fallen.

Maximo got up and headed for the rest room.

As the kitchen door closed behind him, he looked for the drawer or shelf that held the tools.

Quickly now . . .

He opened one drawer . . . the wrong one.

Next drawer, forks, knives and spoons.

Next drawer . . . *yes!*

He saw what he wanted, and quick as a thought reached, palmed it, and strode for the rest room.

Ten minutes passed before he was ready for the dining room again. The chef was back at his pots and pans. He nodded as Maximo walked by.

Maximo resumed his seat, took his time, stirred the food around on his plate but could eat nothing more. He took a few more sips of wine, then ordered coffee.

He was just reaching for the bill at the end of the meal when Rall dropped into a seat at his table.

'I should have come in earlier, let you buy me a meal.'

'Get out.'

'Oh, don't be impolite. I wish to talk to you awhile, to learn what you do for the Cuban government.'

'If you wish to know can I pay more than Vargas, the answer is probably no. I am just a civil servant. I suggest you take up the question with Vargas.'

Maximo took enough money from his wallet to pay for the meal and a tip and dropped it into the tray on top of the tab.

'I have a diplomatic passport. If you do not leave I will have the waiter call the police.'

'And have me arrested?'

'Something like that.'

Rall stared into Maximo's eyes. 'I don't think you appreciate your position.'

'Perhaps. Have you properly evaluated yours?'

'A roaring mouse.' Rall pushed himself away from the table, rose, and walked out the front door.

Maximo lingered, considering.

He left the restaurant a half hour later, his right hand in his pocket around the butt of the pistol. He looked neither right nor left, walked purposely along the thoroughfares. He crossed the Limmat River and walked toward the main train station, which was well lit and still crowded with vacationing students laden with backpacks. The students sat around in circles, sharing cigarettes and talking animatedly as they waited for their trains.

Maximo Sedano had no doubt that Rall was a killer. He didn't know anything about the man except what he had said, but he knew Alejo Vargas. Vargas was just the man to order a killing, or to do it himself. The list of Castro's enemies who had disappeared through the years was long enough to convince anyone that Vargas's enmity was not good for one's health.

Maximo could hear footsteps behind him as he walked through the train station.

A few students looked up at him, glanced behind him at whoever was following. . . .

That had to be Rall.

What if it were someone else? What if Rall were not alone?

If there were two men, he was doomed. He was betting everything that there was only one man, one man who thought him an incompetent coward.

Well, he was a coward. He had never had to live by his wits, face physical danger. He was frightened and no doubt it showed. He was perspiring freely, his temples pounding, his breath coming in short, quick gasps.

He entered a long, dingy hallway, following the signs toward the men's room. The hall was empty.

He could hear the footsteps coming behind, a steady pace, not rushed. The man behind was making no attempt to walk softly. He was confident, in complete control, the exact opposite of the way Maximo Sedano felt.

He fought the urge to run, to look over his shoulder to see precisely who was back there following him.

Time seemed to move ever so slowly. He was aware of everything, the noise, the people, the dirty floor and faded paint, and the smell of stale urine and feces wafting through the door of the men's room as he entered.

No one in the room. The stalls, empty.

Maximo walked to the back wall, turned, and faced the door. He kept his hand in his pocket. He grasped the butt of the pistol tightly, his finger wrapped around the trigger.

Rall walked into the room, stopped facing him.

'Well, well. We meet again.'

Maximo said nothing. He swallowed three or four times.

'Are you going somewhere on the train? Am I delaying your departure?'

Maximo bit his tongue.

'What do you have in your pocket, little man?'

He tilted the barrel of the pistol up, so that it made a bulge in his trousers.

Rall grinned. The naked bulb on the ceiling put the lower half of his face in shadow and made his grin look like a death's-head grimace.

The German reached into his jacket and pulled out his pistol. He leveled it at Maximo.

'If you are going to shoot me, little man, go ahead and do it.'

Sweat stung Maximo's eyes. He shook his head to clear the sweat.

Rall advanced several paces, moving slowly.

'Take your hand out of your pocket.'

Now the German leveled his pistol. Pointed it right at Maximo's face. 'I will shoot you with great pleasure unless you do as I say.'

'Everyone will hear,' Maximo squeaked, and withdrew his hand from his pocket. Automatically he raised both hands to shoulder height.

Rall kept advancing. When he passed under the lightbulb his eye sockets became dark shadows and Maximo couldn't see where he was looking.

Rall came up to him, slapped him with his left hand, then felt Maximo's right trouser pocket. At this distance Maximo could see Rall's eyes. His hands were together above his head.

'A gun!' the German said with a hint of surprise in his voice.

He reached for it, put his left hand into Maximo's pocket to draw it out. As he did so he glanced downward.

With his right hand Maximo pulled the handle of the ice pick loose from the strap of his wristwatch and drew it out of his sleeve. With one smooth, quick, savage swinging motion he jabbed the pick into the side of Rall's head clear up to the handle.

Rall collapsed on the floor. Maximo kept his grip on the handle of the ice pick, so the shiny round blade slipped out of the tiny wound, which was about an inch above Rall's left ear.

Maximo bent down, retrieved his pistol. Rall's pistol was still in his hand, held loosely by his flaccid fingers.

There was almost no blood on the side of Rall's head.

Rall tried to focus his eyes. His body straightened somewhat; one hand tightened on the pistol in an uncontrolled reflex, then relaxed.

The German groaned. Muscle spasms racked his body.

Maximo took a deep breath and exhaled explosively. He wiped at the perspiration dripping from his face. His shirt was a sodden mess. Squaring his shoulders, he walked out of the men's room without another glance at the man sprawled on the floor. As he walked down the hallway toward the main waiting room he passed two male students carrying backpacks, but he purposefully avoided eye contact and they didn't seem to pay him any attention.

He walked at a steady, sedate pace through the terminal and out into the night.

9

William Henry Chance sat in the back of the van listening to the tape of Vargas's conversation with his generals. Normally the fidelity of this system was acceptable. Every now and then a word or phrase was garbled or inaudible, the same drawback that affected every listening technology. People mumbled or talked at the same time or turned their heads the wrong way or talked while smoking. Still, this evening he was only catching occasional words.

Chance strained his ears. Phrases, occasionally a plain word, lots of garbled noise . . .

'Is this the best we can do?'

'The sky was overcast, the window was in shadow with the evening coming on.'

'What about the laser?'

If the crystals were illuminated with a laser beam in the nonvisible portion of the spectrum, the vibrations could be read with the large magnification spotting scope at the usual distance. The problem was getting the laser close enough to the crystals. Maximum range for the laser was less than one hundred meters, so the van with the laser had to be parked literally in front of the building.

'We didn't want to take the risk without your permission.'

Ah, yes, risk. This equipment had been brought into Cuba by boat. The four technicians – of Mexican or Cuban descent – had arrived the same way.

Miguelito was from south Texas, the son of migrant laborers. He didn't learn English until he was in his late teens. He had recorded the conversations, listened to the audio as the computer processed it. 'What did you think, Miguelito?' Chance asked. Chance's Spanish was excellent, the result of months of intense training, but he would never have a native speaker's ear for the language.

Miguelito took his time answering. 'It is difficult to say. I hear phrases, pieces of sentences, stray words . . . and my mind puts it all together into something that may not have been there when they said it. You understand?'

Chance nodded.

'What I hear is a conversation about biological weapons in Guantánamo Bay.'

'You mean using biological weapons against Guantánamo Bay?'

'That is possible. But my impression was that the weapons were already there.'

'Castro. Did they talk about Castro?'

'His name was mentioned. It is distinctive. I think I heard it.'

'Is he still alive?'

'I do not know.' Miguelito looked apologetic.

'Biological weapons inside the US facility is impossible. They must be intending to use them against the people there.'

Miguelito said nothing.

'I'd better listen,' Chance said.

'I will play for you the best part,' Miguelito said. 'Give me a few moments.' He played with the equipment. After about a minute he announced he was ready with a nod of his head. Chance and Carmellini donned headsets.

Noise. They heard noise, occasionally garbled voices, but mostly computer-generated noise as the machine tried without success to make sense of the flickering light coming through the high-magnification spotting scope. Every now and then a word or two in Spanish. 'Guantánamo . . . attack . . .' Once Chance was sure he heard the word 'biological,' but even then, he wasn't certain.

Finally he removed his headset.

Miguelito did likewise.

'Perhaps they are talking about possible targets when and if,' Carmellini suggested. 'After all, they can spray this stuff into the air from a truck upwind and kill everyone on the base.'

Chance grimaced. What he had here was absolutely nothing. He was going to need something more definite before he started talking to Washington via the satellite.

'They did a lot of talking about political matters, people and districts, whom they supported and so on,' Miguelito said. 'It is not much better than what you have just heard – they talked of this before the sun went down – but I got the impression that Vargas wanted Delgado and Alba to abandon any commitments they had to Raúl Castro or the Sedanos and throw in with him.'

'Hmmm,' said William Henry Chance. He tried to focus on Miguelito's comments and couldn't. Biological weapons were on his mind.

He recalled Vargas's face, remembered how he had looked as Chance had sat there discussing a Cuban-American cigarette company. The strong, fleshy face had been a mask, revealing nothing of its owner's thoughts. That poker face . . . that was his dominant impression of Vargas.

The man certainly had a reputation: he was ruthless efficiency incarnate, a thug who smashed heads and sliced throats and got answers from people who didn't want to talk. Every dictatorship needed a few sociopaths in high places. He was also subtle and smooth when that was required. Nor had he yet surrendered to his appetites, surrendered to the absolute corruption that absolute power inevitably causes. Not yet, anyway.

Yes, Alejo Vargas was a damned dangerous man, one who apparently possessed the brains and managerial skills necessary to produce biological weapons and the brutality to use them.

El Gato may have shipped the Cubans material that they could use to culture bacteria or viruses, but as yet there was no hard evidence that the Cubans had done so.

That tantalizing word, 'biological.' Why would the interior minister and the head of the Cuban Army and Navy use that word if they weren't talking about weapons? Sure as hell they weren't talking about barracks sanitation or the condition of the mess halls.

If there was a biological weapons program, Chance told himself, the evidence would be inside the ministry, the headquarters of the secret police. There must be paper, records, orders, letters – something! No one could run a serious project like that without paper, not even Vargas.

The evidence is *inside that building,* he told himself.

After Fidel died of the poison she had handed him, Mercedes was locked in her bedroom by Vargas and Santana. Which was just as well.

She pulled a blanket over herself and curled up on the bed in the fetal position. The silence and afternoon gloom were comforting.

Amazingly, no tears came. Fidel had been dying for months; she was relieved that he had finally come to the end of the journey, the end of the pain.

In the stillness she listened to the sound of her breathing, the sound of her heart pumping blood through her ears, listened to an insect buzzing somewhere, listened to the distant muted thump of footfalls and doors closing, people engaged in the endless business of living.

She saw a gecko, high on the wall, quite motionless except for his sides, which moved in and out, just enough to be seen in the dim light coming in through the window drapes. He seemed to be watching her. More likely he was waiting for a fly, as he did somewhere every day, as his ancestors had done since the dawn of time, as his progeny would do until the sun flamed up and burned the earth to a cinder. Then, they say, the sun would burn out altogether and the earth, if it still existed, would wander the universe forever, a cold, lifeless rock, spinning aimlessly. Until then geckos clung to walls and God provided flies. Amazing how that worked.

She wondered about Hector, wondered if he would be found and arrested, or murdered and shoveled into an anonymous grave. God knows she had done everything possible to warn him. Perhaps the man didn't want to be warned: perhaps he knew the task before him was impossible. Perhaps he really believed all that Jesuit bullshit and in truth didn't care if he lived or died. Most likely that was it.

The truth was that the more you knew of life, of the compromises one must make to get from day to day, the more you realized the futility of it all. None of it meant anything.

Man lived, man died, governments rose and fell, justice was done or denied, venality was crushed or triumphant; in the long run none of it mattered a damn. The world spun on around the sun, life continued to be lived. . . .

When we perish from human memories we are no more. We are well and truly gone, as if we had never been.

She threw aside the cover and sat up in bed, hugging her knees. She thought again of Fidel, and finally let him go. She then had only the twilight, the room falling into darkness.

Toad Tarkington was waiting for Jake Grafton beside the V-22 Osprey on the flight deck of *United States*.

The Osprey was a unique airplane, with a turbo-prop engine mounted on the end of each wing. Just now the pilot had the engines tilted straight up so that the 38-foot props on each engine would function as helicopter rotor blades. The machine could lift off vertically like a helicopter or make a short, running takeoff. Once airborne the pilot would gradually transition to forward flight by tilting the engines down into a horizontal position. Then the giant props would function as conventional propellers, though very large ones. The machine could also land vertically or run on to a short landing area. A cross between a large twin-rotor helicopter and a turbo-prop transport, the extraordinarily versatile Osprey had enormous lifting ability and 250-knot cruise speed, capabilities exceeding those of any conventional helicopter.

Jake Grafton stood looking at the plane for a few seconds as it sat on the flight deck. With its engines mounted on the very ends of its wings – a position dictated by the size of the rotor blades – the machine could not stay airborne if one of the rotor transmissions failed. It could fly on one engine, however, if the drive shaft linking the good engine to the transmission of the distant rotor blade remained intact.

The Osprey's extremely complicated systems were made even more so by the requirement that the wings and rotors fold into a tight package so that the plane could be stored aboard ship. The transitions between hovering and wing-borne flight were only possible because computers assisted the pilots in flying the plane. Complex controls, complex systems – Jake thought the machine a flying tribute to the ingenuity of the human species.

The evening looked gorgeous. The sky was clearing, visibility decent. The late afternoon sun shone on a breezy, tumbling sea. Jake took a deep breath and climbed into the plane.

He put on a regular headset so that he could talk to the flight crew. ''Lo, Admiral.'

'Hello, Rita. How are you?'

'Ready to rock and roll, sir. Let me know when you're strapped in.'

'I'm ready.' Jake settled back and watched Toad and the crewman strap in.

Lightly loaded, the Osprey almost leaped from the flight deck into the stiff sea wind, which was coming straight down the deck. Rita wasted no time rotating the engines forward to a horizontal position; the craft accelerated quickly as the giant rotors became propellers and the wings took the craft's weight.

An hour later Rita Moravia landed the Osprey vertically on a pier at Guantánamo between two light poles. The sun was down by then and the area was lit by flood lights.

A marine lieutenant colonel stood waiting. He had the usual close-cropped hair, a deep tan, the requisite square jaw, and he looked as if he spent several hours a day lifting weights.

As they walked toward him Toad muttered, just loud enough for Jake to hear, 'Another refugee from the Mr Universe contest. If you can't make it in bodybuilding, there's always the marines.'

'Can it, Toad.'

The lieutenant colonel saluted smartly. 'I am deploying a company around the warehouse, Admiral. We're taking up positions now.'

'Excellent,' Jake Grafton said. 'I brought an aerial photo that was taken this afternoon' – Toad took it from a folder and passed it over – 'if you would show me where you are placing your people?'

'Yes, sir.' Lieutenant Colonel Eckhardt, the landing team commander, used the photo and a finger to show where he would put his company. He finished with the comment, 'My plan is to channel any intruders into these two open areas formed by these streets, then kill them there.'

'What are your alternatives?'

They discussed them, and the fact that Eckhardt planned to divide one platoon between several empty warehouses and use them as reserves. 'I think this will be a very realistic exercise, sir,' the colonel finished. 'I have even had ammunition issued to the men, although of course they have been instructed to keep their weapons empty.'

'Colonel Eckhardt, this is not an exercise.'

'Sir?'

'That warehouse, warehouse nine, contains CBW warheads. They are being loaded aboard this freighter and the one that left the other day for transport back to the states, where they are supposed to be destroyed. The first ship that left carrying the damned things has disappeared. We're hunting for it now. I don't know just what in hell is going on, so I'm putting your outfit here just in case.'

'What is the threat, sir?'

'I don't know.'

Jake could see Eckhardt was working hard to keep his face under control.

'If the Cubans or anybody else comes over, under, around, or through the perimeter fence, start shooting.'

'Yes, sir,' Eckhardt said.

'Have your people load their weapons, Colonel. They will defend themselves and this building. No warning shots – shoot to kill.'

'If we are assaulted, sir, how much warning would you expect us to have?'

'I don't know. Maybe days, maybe hours, maybe no warning at all.'

'The more warning I have, sir, the fewer lives I am likely to lose.'

'I will pass that on to Washington, Colonel. When I know something is up, you'll hear about it seconds later. That's the best I can do.'

'Yes, sir.'

'Just so we're on the same sheet of music, Colonel, I want that warehouse defended until you are relieved or the very last marine is dead.'

Eckhardt said nothing this time. Toad Tarkington's grim expression softened. Eckhardt could have said something like, 'Marines don't surrender,' or some other bullshit, but he didn't. Toad was taking a liking to the lieutenant colonel.

'Anything you need from me,' Jake Grafton continued, 'just ask. The battle group and the base commander will supply you to the extent of our resources. The cruiser will provide artillery support – I want you to interface with the cruiser people in the next hour or two, make sure you're ready to communicate and shoot.'

'Yes, sir.'

'Which brings up a point: I see that your people are building bunkers from sandbags.'

'Yes, sir. We're trying to fortify some positions, create some strong-points.'

'Get a couple of backhoes from the base people, get someone to locate the utilities, and dig fortifications. Jackhammer the concrete. By dawn I want your people dug in to the eyes.' This order might be stretching the phrase 'business as usual,' but Jake wasn't worried. Freighters carrying weapons don't normally turn up missing.

'Yessir.'

'What are you going to do if the Cubans send tanks through the fence?'

'Their tanks are old Soviet T-54s, I believe,' Lieutenant Colonel Eckhardt said. 'We'll channel them into these two avenues,' he pointed at the aerial photo, 'then kill them – cremate the crews inside the tanks.'

'Okay. When your people are dug in, dig any tank traps that you want. You have carte blanche, Colonel.'

458

'Nobody is going into that warehouse, sir.'

'Fine. We'll keep the Cuban Navy off your back and give you air support. The cruisers will provide artillery. Call us if you see or hear anything suspicious.'

Toad passed the colonel a list of radio frequencies and they discussed communications for several minutes.

Jake took that opportunity to wander off, to look at the warehouse from all angles.

He was standing beside six large forklifts that were parked near the main loading dock when Toad and Eckhardt walked over to him. 'Don't isolate these forklifts from the pier when you're digging up concrete,' Jake advised.

'Of course not.'

'One other thing,' Jake said. 'You'd better break out the MOPP suits and have them beside every man.' MOPP stood for mission-oriented protective posture, a term designed by career bureaucrats to obfuscate the true nature of chemical and biological warfare protection suits.

The colonel was going to say something about the suits, then he decided to pass on it.

They talked for several minutes about the battalion's problems, how the colonel was deploying it. The colonel told Jake he was putting people on the roofs of all the warehouses.

As Jake and Toad walked back to the Osprey, Lieutenant Colonel Eckhardt turned toward warehouse nine and scratched his head. He didn't for a minute believe that building contained chemical and biological weapons.

He frowned. A hijacked freighter? He had been in the Corps long enough to know how the navy operated: this was just another readiness exercise but the admiral didn't have the courtesy or decency to say so. 'Let's keep the grunts' assholes twanging tight.' MOPP suits, in the heat of the Cuban summer!

Yeah.

'Cuba must learn to live with the elephant,' Hector Sedano told the crowd of schoolteachers and administrators. 'Our relations with the United States have been the determining factor in our history and will be the key to our future. Any Cuban government that hopes to make life better for the people of Cuba must come to grips with the reality of the colossus ninety miles north.'

That was the nub of his message, pure and simple. He was careful never to criticize Fidel Castro or the government, knowing full well that to do so would be the height of folly, an invitation to a prison cell. Most of the people in this room were teachers, a few were agents for the secret police. Cuba was a dictatorship, a fact as unremarkable as the island status of the nation.

Still, he was talking about the future, about a day still to come when all things might change, a day that Cuba would have to face someday, sometime. Everyone in the room understood that too, including the secret police, so no one objected to his remarks. Hector Sedano talked on, talking about education, jobs, investment, opportunities, the building blocks of the life sagas of human beings.

When he finished he sat down as the thunder of applause rolled over him. He thought that his audience's reaction was not to his message, which in truth was not that new or fresh or interesting, but to the fact that he was a private citizen speaking aloud on sensitive political subjects. This his audience found most remarkable. They stood on their feet, applauded, pressed forward to touch him, to give him a greeting or blessing, reached between people to touch his clothes, his hands, his hair.

Afterward he sat and spoke privately to a knot of people who wanted to be with him when that someday came. He was more open, spoke about specifics but still spoke guardedly, careful not to speak openly against the government or to criticize Fidel.

In his heart of hearts Hector Sedano knew that Fidel Castro must know what he had to say, must know his message almost as well as he himself did. Everything that the government knew, Fidel knew, for he was the government.

And still Fidel let him speak. That was the remarkable thing, and Hector had a theory about why this might be so. When he was a young revolutionary in jail, Fidel had written a political tract in defense of the Cuban revolution that became its manifesto. He entitled it, 'History Will Absolve Me.' In it he defined 'the people' as 'the vast unredeemed masses, those to whom everyone makes promises and who are deceived by all.'

Maybe, Hector thought, Fidel Castro was still looking for absolution from those who would come after. Maybe he was thinking about 'the people' even now, thinking of the promises he had made and the reality that had come to pass.

When he was leaving the school, on the way to the borrowed car with two friends who accompanied him, Hector found himself surrounded by well-dressed men, obviously not local laborers.

'Hector Sedano,' said one, 'you are under arrest. You must come with us.'

He was stunned. 'What am I charged with?' he demanded.

'That is not for us to discuss,' the man said, and took his elbow. He pushed him toward a government van.

'They are arresting Sedano,' someone shouted. The shout was taken up by others. As a crowd gathered, shoved closer, shouting threats and obscenities, the men around the van pushed Hector into it and jumped in themselves. In seconds it was in motion.

Hector protested. He had done nothing wrong, he was not wanted for any crime.

The man showed him a badge. 'You are under arrest,' he said. 'We have our orders. Now be silent.'

The van raced through the streets of the city, then took the highway toward Havana.

Maximo Sedano was too excited to sleep. The adrenaline aftershock of stabbing an ice pick into Vargas's thug should have floored him, but the thought of $53 million, plus interest, kept him wide awake. That and the possibility of sirens.

He lay in the darkness listening. Every now and then he heard a siren moaning, faint and faraway. He waited in dread suspense for that moan to join others and become a wailing convoy of police vehicles converging on his hotel, followed by the stamping of a horde of policemen charging upstairs to arrest him. He twitched with every howl in the night, though they were few and faint and never seemed to grow louder. In the silence between moans he amused himself by trying to calculate the amount of interest that might be due on Castro's hoard.

He hadn't seen a statement in about six months . . . call it six months exactly, half a year. Interest at 2.45 percent, on $53 million . . . almost 650,000 American dollars.

Ha! The interest alone would buy a nice small villa on Ibiza. Of course he should not rule out Majorca, nor Minorca for that matter, until he had traveled over each of the islands and seen local conditions for himself, and checked the real estate market. No, indeed. He would visit all the Balearic Islands in turn, including Formentera and Cabrera, stay at local inns, drink local wine, eat lamb and beef and fish prepared as the islanders preferred . . .

Ahh, his dream was within his grasp. Tomorrow. In just a few short hours. When the banks opened he would go immediately to the one with the largest account, submit the transfer card, then to the next one, and finally, the one with the smallest amount on deposit, a mere $11 million.

Maximo paced the room, stared out the window at the lights of the city that housed his fortune, paced some more.

He was full almost to bursting, too excited too sleep.

He had almost run back to the hotel from the railroad station. He had taken his time though, walked slowly and unhurriedly, paused to feed the ducks under one of the Limmat bridges, slipped the ice pick into the river when no one was watching, then walked on to the hotel so full of joy and happiness he could barely contain himself.

At about four in the morning he began to wind down somewhat, so he lay down on the bed. In minutes he was asleep.

When Maximo awoke the sun was up, he could hear a maid running a vacuum sweeper in the next room.

He checked his watch. Almost eight-thirty.

He showered, shaved, put on clean clothes from the skin out, then

461

packed his bags. He would come back to the hotel this afternoon when he had finished his banking and check out. He wanted to be long gone if Santana showed up looking for Rall and the money.

There was a continental breakfast laid out in the hotel dining room, so Maximo paused there for coffee and a French roll.

Suitably fortified, with his attaché case in his left hand and the transfer cards signed by Fidel in his inside breast pocket, Maximo Sedano set off afoot for the bank that was to be his first stop. It was a mere two blocks away, a huge old building of thick stone walls and small windows, a building hundreds of years old with the treasure of the ages in its vaults.

He spoke to a clerk, was ushered into a small windowless office to see a middle-aged man who wore a green eyeshade and spoke tolerably good Spanish. Maximo surrendered the appropriate transfer card and settled down to wait after the clerk left the room.

The bank was quiet. Footsteps were lost on the vast wood and stone floors. Humans seemed to be the intruders here, temporary visitors who came and went while the bank endured the storms of the centuries, a monument to the power of capital.

Five pleasant minutes passed, then five more.

Maximo was in no hurry. He was prepared to wait quite a while for $53 million, even if it took all day. Or several days. After all, he had waited a lifetime so far. But he wouldn't have to wait long. The clerk would be back momentarily.

And he was.

He came in, looked at Maximo with an odd expression, handed him back the transfer card with just the slightest hint of a bow.

'I am sorry, señor, but the balance of this account is so low that the transfer is impossible to honor.'

Maximo gaped uncomprehendingly. He swallowed, then said, 'What did you say?'

'I am sorry, señor, but there has been some mistake.'

'Not on my part,' Maximo replied heatedly.

The clerk gave a tight little professional smile. 'The bank's records are perfectly clear.' He held out the transfer card. 'This account contains just a few dollars over one thousand.'

Maximo couldn't believe his ears. 'Where did the money go?'

'Obviously, due to the bank secrecy laws I have limited discretion about what I can say.'

Maximo Sedano leaped across the table at the man, grabbed him by his lapels.

'Where did the money go, fool?' he roared.

'*Someone with the proper authorization ordered the money transferred, señor. That much is obvious. I can say no more.*' And the clerk wriggled from his grasp.

462

The story was the same at the next two banks Maximo Sedano visited. Each account contained just a few dollars above the minimum amount necessary to maintain the account.

The horror of his position hit Maximo like a hammer. Not only was there no money here for him, Alejo Vargas would kill him when he got back to Cuba.

He told the bank officer at the last bank he visited that he wanted to make a telephone call, and he wanted the bank officer there to talk to the person at the other end.

He called Vargas at home, caught him before he went to his office.

After he had explained about the accounts, he asked the bank officer to verify what he had said. The officer refused to touch the telephone. 'The bank secrecy laws are very strict,' he said self-righteously. Maximo wanted to strangle him.

Vargas had of course listened to this little exchange. 'There is no money,' Maximo told the secret-police chief. 'Someone has stolen it.'

'You ass,' Vargas hissed. '*You* have stolen the money. *You* are the finance minister.'

'Call the other banks, Alejo,' he urged. 'They are here in Zurich. I will give you their names and the account numbers. Listen to what the bank officers have to say.'

'You are a capital ass, Sedano. The Swiss bankers will not talk to me. The money was deposited in Switzerland precisely *because* those bastards will talk to no one.'

'I will call you from their office and have them speak to you.'

'Have you lost your mind? What are you playing at?'

This was a scene from a nightmare.

'If I had the money I would not set foot in Cuba again, Vargas. We both know that. Use your head! I don't have the money: I'm coming home.'

He tried to slam the instrument into its cradle and missed, sent it skittering off the table. Fumbling, he picked it up by the cord, hung the thing properly on the cradle.

The account officer looked at him with professional solicitude, much like an undertaker smiling at the next of kin.

Perhaps the banks have stolen Fidel's money, Maximo thought. *These Swiss bastards pocketed the Jews' money; maybe they are keeping Fidel's.*

He opened his mouth to say that very thing to the account officer sitting across the table, then thought better of it. He picked up his attaché case with the pistol in it and walked slowly out of the bank.

The van took Hector Sedano to La Cabana fortress in Havana. It stopped in a dark courtyard where other men were waiting. They took him into the prison, down long corridors, through iron doors that opened before him and closed after him, until finally they stood before an empty cell in the isolation area of the prison. Here they demanded his clothes, his shoes, his watch, the things in his pockets. When he stood naked someone gave him a one-piece jumpsuit. Wearing only that, he was thrust into the cell and the door was locked behind him.

The journey from the everyday world of people and voices and cares and concerns to the stark, vile reality of a prison cell is one of the most violent transitions in this life. The present and the future had been ripped from Hector Sedano, leaving only his memories of the past.

Hector was well aware of the fact that he could be physically abused, beaten, even executed, at the whim of whoever had ordered him jailed. People disappeared in Cuban prisons, never to be heard from again.

The parallels between his situation and that of Christ while awaiting his crucifixion immediately leaped to Hector's Jesuit mind. Not far behind was the realization that Fidel Castro had also been imprisoned before the revolution.

Perhaps prison is a natural stage in the life of a revolutionary. Imprisonment by the old regime for one's beliefs was de facto recognition that the beliefs were dangerous and the person who held them a worthy enemy. The person imprisoned was automatically elevated in stature and respect.

These thoughts swirled through Hector's mind as he sat on a hard wooden bunk without blankets and gave in to his emotions. He found himself shaking with anger. He paced, he pounded on the walls with his fists until they were raw.

Finally he threw himself on the bunk and lay staring into the gloom.

Angel del Mar pitched and rolled viciously as she wallowed helplessly in the swells. In every direction nothing could be seen but sea and cloudy sky. The sky was completely covered now with cloud, the wind was picking up, and the swells were getting bigger, with a shorter period between them. Aboard the boat, many people lay on their stomach and hugged the heaving deck.

Everyone on board suffered from the lack of water, some to a greater degree than others. Ocho Sedano, who had had only a few mouthfuls since the boat left Cuba and had pushed himself relentlessly, without mercy, was desperate. His eyes felt like burning coals, his skin seemed on fire, his tongue a thick, lifeless lump of dead flesh in a cracked, dry mouth.

He wasn't perspiring much now. Of all his symptoms, that one worried him the most. As an athlete he knew the importance of regulating body temperature.

Dora lay in the shade cast by the wheelhouse and said nothing. She had been sick a time or two; vomit stained her dress. She seemed to be resting easier now.

Beside her lay her father, Diego Coca. He was conscious, his eyes fierce

464

and bright, his jaw swollen and misshapen. He hadn't moved in hours, unwilling to let anyone else have his spot in the shade.

Ocho sat heavily near Dora, scanned the sea slowly and carefully.

My God, there must be a ship! A ship or boat – something to give us food and water . . .

In all this sea there must be hundreds of fishing boats and yachts, dozens of freighters, smugglers, American Coast Guard cutters hunting smugglers, warships . . . Where the hell are they? Where are all these goddamn boats and ships?

From time to time he heard jets flying over, occasionally saw one below the clouds, but they stayed high, disappeared into the sea haze.

Under the mast an old woman sat weeping. She was the one who grieved for the captain, for some of the people who were washed overboard that first night. She wept silently, her shoulders shaking, her breath coming in gasps.

He wanted to hug her, to comfort her, but there was nothing he could say. His brother Hector would have known what to say, but Ocho did not.

He looked longingly at Dora, Dora who was once beautiful, and he could think of nothing to say to her. Nothing.

All the promise that life held, and they had thrown it away on a wild, stupid, doomed chance. Diego had led them, prodded them, demanded they go, and still he could think of nothing to say to Diego.

He was so tired, so lethargic. He had pumped for hours, just keeping up with the water. If the water came in any faster . . . well, he didn't want to think about it. They would all die then. They would have little chance swimming in the open sea.

Ocho slumped over onto the moving deck. He was so tired, if he could just sleep, sleep. . . .

The old fisherman shook him awake. The sun was setting, the boat still rolling her guts out in the swell.

'A fish . . .' He held it up, about eighteen or twenty inches long. 'No way to cook it, have to eat it raw. Keep up your strength.'

With two quick swipes of his knife, the fisherman produced two bleeding fillets. He offered one to Ocho, who closed his eyes and bit into the raw fish. He chewed.

Someone was clawing at him, tearing at the fish.

He opened his eyes. Diego Coca was stuffing a piece of the fish in his swollen mouth.

The old man kicked Diego in the stomach, doubled him over, then pried his jaws apart and extracted the unchewed fish.

'He's manning the pump that keeps you afloat, you son of a bitch. He has to eat or every one of us will die.'

Diego got a grip on the fisherman's knife and lunged for him.

He grabbed for the slippery flesh, swung wildly with the knife.

This time the old man kicked him in the arm. The knife bounced once on the deck, then landed at an angle with the blade sticking into the wood, quivering.

The fisherman waited for the boat to roll, then kicked Diego in the head. He went over backward and his head made a hollow thunk as it hit the wooden deck. He went limp and lay unmoving.

Retrieving his knife, the fisherman ate his chunk of raw fish in silence. Ocho chewed ravenously, letting the moisture bathe his mouth and throat. He held each piece in his mouth for several seconds, sucking at the juices, then reluctantly swallowing it down.

Dora watched him with feverish eyes. He passed her a chunk of the fish and she rammed it into her mouth, all of it at once, chewed greedily while eyeing the old man, almost as if she were afraid he would take it from her.

After she swallowed it, she tried to grin.

Ocho averted his eyes.

'Your turn on the pump,' the old man said.

Diego lay right where he had fallen.

Ocho got up, went into the wheelhouse and down into the engine room. The water in the bilge was sloshing around over his shoes as he began working the pump handle, up and down, up and down, endlessly.

Hours later someone came to relieve him, one of the men in the captain's family. Ocho staggered up the stairs, so exhausted he had trouble making his hands do what he wanted.

The people on deck had more fish. Ocho sat heavily by the wheelhouse. In the dim light from the stars and moon, he could see people ripping fish apart with their bare hands, stuffing flesh into their mouths, wrestling to get to fish that jumped over the rail when the boat rolled.

He collapsed into a dreamless sleep.

10

One of the butlers unlocked the bedroom door and took Mercedes to see Colonel Santana, who was standing behind Fidel's desk sorting papers. He didn't look up when she first came in. She found a chair and sat.

'The government has not yet decided when or how to announce the death of *el presidente*. No doubt it will happen in a few days, but until it does you are to remain here, in the residence, and talk to no one. Security Department people are on the switchboards and will monitor all telephone calls. The telephone lines that do not go through the switchboard have been disconnected.'

He eyed her askance, then went back to sorting papers. 'After the official version of Fidel's death is written and announced, you will be free to go. I remind you now that disputing the official version of events is a crime.'

'Everyone swears to your history before you write it?' she snapped.

Santana looked at her and smiled. 'I was searching for the proper words to explain the nub of it and they just came to you' – he snapped his fingers – 'like that. It is a gift, I think. When you say it so precisely, I know you understand. Ignorance will not be a defense if there is ever a problem.'

Mercedes got up from the chair and left the room.

She wandered the hallways and reception rooms, the private areas, the offices, all now deserted. Every square foot was full of memories. She could see him talking to people, bending down slightly to hear, for he had been a tall man. She could not remember when he had not been the president of Cuba. When she was a girl, he was there. As a young woman, he was there. When she married, was widowed, when he took her to be his woman . . . always, all her life there was Fidel.

Such a man he had been! She was a Latin woman, and Fidel had been the epitome of the Latin man, a brilliant, athletic man, a commanding speaker, a perfect patriot, a man who defined machismo. The facets of Fidel's personality that the non-Latin world found most irritating were those Cubans accepted as hallmarks of a man. He was self-righteous, proud, sure of his own importance and place in history, never admitted error, and refused to yield when humiliated by the outside world. He had struggled, endured, won much and lost even more, and in a way that non-Latins would never understand, had become the personification of Cuba.

And she had loved him.

In the room where he died the television cameras and lights were still in place, the wires still strung. Only Fidel's body was missing.

She stood looking at the scene, remembering it, seeing him again as he was when she had known him best.

Still magnificent.

Now the tears came, a clouding of the eyes that she was powerless to stop. She found a chair and wept silently.

Her mind wandered off on a journey of its own, recalling scenes of her life, moments with her mother, her first husband, Fidel. . . .

The tears had been dry for quite a while when she realized with a start that she was still sitting in this room. The cameras were there in front of her, mounted on heavy, wheeled tripods.

These cameras must have some kind of film in them, videotape. She went to the nearest camera and examined it. Tentatively she pushed and tugged at buttons, levers, knobs. Finally a plate popped open and there was the videocassette. She removed it from the camera and closed the plate. There was also a cassette in the second camera.

With both cassettes concealed in the folds of her dress, Mercedes strode from the room.

A wave breaking over the deck doused Ocho Sedano with lukewarm water and woke him from a troubled, exhausted sleep. *Angel del Mar* was riding very low in the water. Even as he realized that the bilges must be full, another wave washed over the deck.

Ocho dashed below. The old fisherman slumped over the pump, water sloshed nearly waist-deep in the bilge. Ocho eased him aside, began pumping. He could feel the resistance, feel the water moving through the pump. He laid into it with a will.

'Sorry,' the old man said weakly. 'Worn out. Just worn out.'

'Go up on deck. Dry out some, drink some water.'

The old man nodded, crawled slowly up the steep ladder. He slipped once, almost smashed his face on one of the steps. Finally his feet disappeared into the wheelhouse.

Three rain showers during the night had allowed everyone on board to drink their fill, to replenish dehydrated tissue, and when Ocho last looked, there were several gallons of water in the bucket under the tarp that no one could drink.

Ocho was no longer thirsty, but he was hungry as hell. There had been no more fish. Without line, hooks, bait, or nets they were unable to catch fish from the sea. Unless the creatures leaped onto the deck of the boat they were out of reach. So far, there had been no more of those.

The tarp they caught the water in gave the liquid a brackish taste, which everyone ignored. Still, water on an empty stomach made one aware of just how hungry he was.

Ocho pumped, felt his muscles loosen up, enjoyed the resistance that meant the pump was moving water. After fifteen minutes of maximum effort he could see that the water level was down about six inches. He settled in to work at a steady, sustainable pace.

The horizon remained empty. Empty! Not a boat or sail. Endless swells and sky in every direction.

It was almost as if the Lord had abandoned them, left them to die on this leaky little boat in the midst of this great vast ocean, while planes went overhead and boats and ships passed by on every side, just over the horizon.

We won't have to wait long, Ocho thought. *Our fate is very near. If the chain on this pump breaks, if we run out of energy to pump, if the swells get larger and waves start coming aboard, the boat will break up and the people will go into the sea. That would be our fate, to drown like all those people who went overboard that first night.*

They are dead now, surely. Past all caring.

Amazing how that works. Everyone has to die, but you only have to do it once. You fight like hell to get there, though, and when you arrive the world continues as if you had never been.

As he pumped he wondered about his mother, how she was doing, wondered if he should have told her he was going to America.

An hour later Ocho was still pumping, the water was down several feet and the boat was riding better in the sea. And he was wearing out. He heard someone coming down the ladder, then saw feet. It was Dora.

She clung to the ladder, watched him standing in water to his knees working the pump handle up and down, up and down, up and down.

'It's Papa,' she said.

He said nothing, waited for her to go on.

'I think he has given up.'

Ocho kept pumping.

'Speak to me, Ocho. Don't insult me with your silence.'

Ocho switched arms without missing a stroke. 'What is there to say? If he has given up, he has given up.'

'Will we be rescued?'

'Am I God? How would I know?'

'I am *sick* of this boat, this ocean!' she snarled. 'Sick of it, you understand?'

'I understand.'

She sobbed, sniffed loudly.

Ocho kept pumping.

'I don't think you love me,' she said, finally.

'I don't know that I do.'

She watched him pump, up and down, rhythmically, endlessly.

'Doesn't that make you tired?'

'Yes.'

'We're going to die, aren't we?'

He wiped the sweat from his face with his free hand. 'All of us, sooner or later, yes.'

'I mean now. This boat is going to sink. We're going to drown.'

He looked at her for the first time. Her skin was stretched tightly over her face, her teeth were bared, her eyes were narrowed with an intensity he had never seen before.

'I don't know,' he said gently.

'I don't want to die now.'

He lowered his face so that he wouldn't have to look at her, kept the handle going up and down.

She went back up the ladder, disappeared from view.

Ocho paused, straightened as best he could under the low overhead and looked critically at the water remaining in the boat. He was gaining. He stretched, crossed himself on the off chance God might be watching, then went back to pumping.

The CIA's man in Cuba was an American, Dr Henri Bouchard, a former college professor who lived and worked inside the American Interest Section of the Swiss embassy, a complex of buildings that in former days housed the American embassy and presumably someday would again. The Cubans watched the American diplomats very closely, so this officer had no contact with the agency's covert intelligence apparatus on the island. He kept himself busy watching television, listening to radio, collecting Cuban newspapers and publications and writing reports based on what he saw, heard, and read. His diplomatic colleagues were congenial and the life was semi-monastic, which he found agreeable.

The man who ran the covert side of the business was a Cuban who had never set foot inside the US Interest Section and probably never would. He owned a wholesale seafood operation on the waterfront in Havana Harbor. Every day the fishing boats brought their catch to his pier and every day he purchased what he thought he could sell. Both the price he paid and the price he charged were set by the government: had there not been a black market for fish he would have starved.

The cover was decent. A Cuban fishing boat could meet an American boat or submarine at sea, passing messages or material in either direction. The spymaster's delivery trucks visited every restaurant, casino, and embassy in the capital. With people and things coming and going, the old man could keep his pulse on Cuba. He was called el Tiburón, the Shark.

William Henry Chance had no intention of ever meeting el Tiburón unless disaster was staring him in the face. The CIA man in the American Interest Section was another matter.

'Ah, yes, Mr Chance. Delighted to meet you, of course.'

Dr Bouchard shook hands with Chance and Carmellini as he peered at them over the top of his glasses. He led them down several narrow hallways to a tiny, windowless cubicle in the bowels of the building.

'Sorry to say, this is the office. Security, you know. They used to store food in here. Damp but quiet.' He took a stack of newspapers off the only guest chair and moved them to his desk, extracted a folding metal chair from behind his desk and unfolded it for Carmellini, then settled into his chair.

The knees of all three men almost touched. 'So how are you enjoying Cuba?'

'Fascinating,' Chance muttered.

'Yes, isn't it?' Professor Bouchard beamed complacently. 'Six years I've been here, and I don't ever want to leave. I don't miss the snow, I'll tell you, or the faculty politics, feuds, dog-eat-dog jealousy over department budgets – thank God I'm out of all that.'

Chance nodded, unwilling to get to the point.

'We met once or twice before, I think,' Chance reminded Bouchard.

'Oh, yes, I do seem to recall. . . .'

They discussed it.

'My associate, Mr Carmellini. I don't think you've met him.'

The pleasantries over at last, Chance edged around to business. 'You have a few items in your storeroom that we need to borrow, I believe.'

'Certainly. The inventory is in the safe. If you gentlemen will step into the hall for a moment . . .'

They did so and he fiddled with the dial of the safe. When he had the file he wanted and the safe was closed and locked, he seated himself again at his desk. Chance sat back down. Carmellini remained standing.

'This is the inventory, I'm sure. Yes. What is it you want?'

'Two Rugers with silencers, ammunition, two garroting wires, two fighting knives, a dozen disposable latex gloves, two self-contained gas masks –'

'Let's see . . .' The professor ran his finger down the list. 'Guns, check. Ammo, okay. Knives . . . knives . . . oh, here they are. Wires, garroting, check . . . gloves . . . masks. Yes, I think we have what you need. Do you want to take this stuff with you?'

'I think so. In a suitcase of some kind, if you can manage that.'

'I'll have to give you one of mine. You can return it or pay me for it, as you prefer.'

'We'll try to return it.'

'That's best, I think. The accounting department is so difficult about expense accounts. You gentlemen wait here; I'll see what I can do. While you're waiting would you like a cup of coffee, a soft drink?'

'I'm fine,' Chance said.

'Don't worry about me,' Carmellini said.

'This will take a few minutes,' the professor advised. 'Would you like to wait in the courtyard? The flora there is my hobby, and the eagle from the Maine Memorial is a rare work of art.'

'That's the big eagle over the doorway?'

'Yes. After the revolution Castro demanded it be removed from the Maine Memorial. That was about the time he announced he was a communist, before the Bay of Pigs. Difficult era for everyone.'

'Ah, yes. We'll find our way.'

'I'll look for you in the courtyard when I have your items,' the professor said, and scurried off.

The eagle was huge. 'Quite a work of art,' Carmellini muttered.

'Too big for you,' Chance said.

'I don't know about that,' Carmellini replied, and glanced around to see if there was any way to get the thing out of the mission ground with a crane. 'Run a mobile construction crane up to the wall, send a man down on the hook, haul it out. I could snatch it and be gone in six or seven minutes.'

Chance didn't even bother to frown. Carmellini had a habit of chaffing him in an unoffensive way; protest would be futile.

'The professor is the most incurious man I've ever met,' Tommy Carmellini said conversationally a few minutes later.

'He doesn't want to know too much.'

'He doesn't want to know anything,' Carmellini protested. 'People who don't ask obvious questions worry me.'

'Hmmm,' said William Henry Chance, who didn't seem at all worried.

The professor came looking for them a half hour later. After he had scrawled an illegible signature on a detailed custody card, Chance offered the professor a photo of a man that his surveillance team had taken outside the University of Havana science building. The man was in his sixties, slightly overweight, balding, and looking at the camera almost full face. He didn't see the camera that took the picture, of course, since it was in the van.

'If you could, Professor, I would like you to send this to Washington. I want to know who this man is.'

'American?' Dr Bouchard asked, accepting the photo and glancing at it.

'I have no idea, sir. We've seen him around here and there and wondered who he might be. Would you have the folks in Langley try to find out?'

'Of course,' the professor said, and put the photo in his pocket.

Toad Tarkington was in a rare foul mood. He snapped at the yeomen, snarled at the flag lieutenant, fumed over the message board, and generally glowered at anyone who looked his way.

This state of affairs could not go on, of course, so he went to his stateroom, put on his running togs, and went on deck for a jog. The tropical sea air, the long foaming rollers, the puffy clouds running on the breeze, the deep blue of the Caribbean – all of it made his mood more foul.

None of the leads to find the *Colón* had borne fruit. The ship was still missing, the captain and crew had stayed aboard her all the time she was tied to the pier in Guantánamo, the gloom seemed impenetrable. The air wing was still searching, but as yet, nothing! And of course the temperature of the rhetoric coming from the White House and Pentagon was rising by the hour.

Toad was jogging aft from the bow when a petty officer from the admiral's staff flagged him down. 'The AIs have a photo of the *Colón*!'

'Where is she?'

'Aground on a reef off the north shore of Cuba.'

Toad bolted for the hatchway that led down into the ship, the petty officer right behind.

The photo was of the *Colón*, all right. The ship looked as if it were wedged on some rocks, almost as if it grounded during a high tide. Now the tide was out and the *Colón* was marooned.

'When was this picture taken?' Toad demanded of the air intelligence officers.

'Yesterday.'

'And no one recognized it?'

'Not until today.'

Toad growled. 'Have you passed this to the admiral?'

'Yes, sir.'

'Show me the location.'

The AI pinpointed the location on a sectional chart.

Toad called Jake Grafton. 'I want to see that ship,' Jake said. 'As soon as possible. We'll take an F-14 with a TARPS package.' TARPS stood for tactical air reconnaissance pods. Each pod contained two cameras and an infrared line scanner.

Cuba is an island surrounded by islands, over sixteen hundred of them. Most of the islands on Cuba's north shore are small, uninhabited, rocky bits of tropical paradise, or so they looked to Jake Grafton, who saw them through binoculars from the front seat of an F-14.

The ship was about three miles offshore, stranded on rocks that just pierced the surface of the sea. The breaking surf looked white through the binoculars.

The freighter was plainly visible, listing slightly. Some of the weapons containers were visible on the main deck. Jake checked the photo in his lap, which was taken yesterday by an F/A-18 Hornet pilot with a handheld 35-mm camera. Yep, the containers visible in the photo were still in place aboard the ship.

Although the Cubans claimed a twelve-mile territorial limit, the United States recognized but three. *Nuestra Señora de Colón* was stranded on a reef in international waters, the AIs assured Jake. They had checked with the State Department, they said.

South of the ship was the entrance to Bahia de Nipe, a decent-sized shallow-water bay.

Was the ship on her way into the bay when she went on the rocks?

Jake was making his initial photo passes a mile to seaward of the *Colón*. In the event the Cubans chose to send interceptors to chase him away, he had a flight of F-14s ten miles farther north providing cover. Above them was an EA-6B Prowler electronic warfare airplane, listening for and ready to jam any Cuban fire-control radar that came on the air. According to the electronic warfare detection gear in Jake's cockpit, he was being painted only by search radars. That, as he well knew, could change any second.

He had just completed a photo pass from west to east and was turning to seaward when the E-2 came on the air. 'Battlestar One, we have company. Bogey twenty miles west of your posit, heading your way. Looks like a Fulcrum.' A Fulcrum was a MiG-29.

Jake keyed his radio mike. 'Roger that. I'll make one more photo pass before he gets here, then exit the area to the north.'

He tucked the nose down and let the Tomcat accelerate. The plane was alive in his hand – the descending jet bumped and bounced in the swirling, roiling tropical air under the puffy cumulus clouds drifting along on the trade wind.

'Cameras are on and running,' Toad Tarkington said from the back seat.

Staying just outside the three-mile limit, Jake flew past the stern of the stranded freighter one more time, which meant he was probably getting fine views of her stern and oblique views of her flanks.

'Since we're here . . .' he muttered, and dropped a wing as he eased the stick and throttles forward.

In the back seat, Toad Tarkington was monitoring the recon package. 'I sure am glad we're staying out of Cuban airspace,' he told Jake. 'I'd feel a lot more comfortable outside the twelve-mile limit, but that's asking too much of this technology. A ship sitting on the rocks like this, looks like a setup to me. They're looking to mousetrap some dude flying by snapping pictures and perforate his heinie.'

'Yeah,' said Jake Grafton, and leveled off at a hundred feet above the water. He had the F-14 flying parallel with the axis of the ship, offset with the ship to his right since the recon package was mounted under his right engine.

'Got the cameras and IR scanner going?'

'Oh, yeah, looking real good,' Toad said, just as he picked up the seascape passing by the canopy with his peripheral vision. He looked right just in time to see the freighter flash by, then Jake Grafton pulled back on the stick and lit the afterburners. The Tomcat's nose rose to sixty degrees above the horizon and it went up like a rocket, corkscrewing back toward the ocean, as the E-2 Hawkeye radar operator called the bogey for the Showtime F-14 crews who were Jake's armed guard. Both RIOs said they had the bogey on radar.

'Like I said,' Toad told Jake, 'sure is great we're staying outside Cuban airspace.'

'Great,' his pilot agreed.

'Don't want to piss anybody off.'

'Oh, no.'

'Wonder why that ship ended up where it did?'

'Maybe the photos will tell us.'

'Bogey is six miles aft, Battlestar One,' the E-2 Hawkeye radar operator said, 'four hundred knots, closing from your eight o'clock.'

'You wanna turn toward him, Admiral, let me pick him up on the radar?' Toad asked this question.

'No, let's clear to seaward.'

'I got him visual,' Toad said as the Tomcat climbed past fifteen thousand feet. 'He's a little above us, pulling lead.'

'Pulling lead?' Jake looked over his left shoulder, found the MiG-29.

'He could take a gunshot anytime,' Toad said.

'He's rendezvousing,' Jake said, 'Gonna join on our left wing, looks like.'

And that is what the MiG did. He closed gently, his nose well out in front, his axis almost parallel, a classic rendezvous. The MiG stabilized in a parade position, about four feet between wingtips, stepped down perhaps three feet. Despite the bumpy air the MiG held position effortlessly.

Jake Grafton and Toad Tarkington sat staring at the helmeted figure of Carlos Corrado in the other cockpit. Toad lifted his 35-mm camera, snapped off a dozen photos of the Cuban fighter and the two air-to-air missiles hanging on the racks.

'Think he knows we were inside the three-mile limit?' Toad asked Jake.

'His GCI controller told him, probably.'

Corrado stayed glued to the F-14. He paid no attention to the other Tomcats that came swooping in to join the formation, didn't even bother to glance at them.

Jake Grafton slowly advanced his throttles to 95 percent RPM. The MiG was right with him. Leaving the power set, he got the nose coming up, began to roll away from the MiG, up and over to the inverted and right on through, coming on with the G to keep the nose from scooping out ... a medium-sloppy barrel roll.

Now a barrel roll to the left. The two F-14s behind Carlos Corrado moved into trail position, behind and stepped down slightly, to more easily stay with the maneuvering airplanes, but Corrado held his position in left parade as if he were welded there.

Now a loop. Up, up, up and over the top, G increasing down the backside, the sea and sky changing position very nicely, the sun dancing across the cockpit.

'This guy's pretty good,' Toad remarked grudgingly.

'Pretty good?'

'Okay, he's a solid stick.'

Now a half loop and half roll at the top, fly along straight and level for a count of five, roll again and half turn into a lopsided split S, one offset from the vertical by forty-five degrees. Coming out of the dive Jake let the nose climb until it was pointed straight up; he slowly rolled around his axis, then pulled the plane on over onto its back and waited until the nose was forty-five degrees below the horizon before rolling wings level and beginning his pullout. Through it all Carlos Corrado stayed glued in position on Jake's wing.

Coming out of the last maneuver, Jake Grafton turned eastward. The MiG-29 stayed with the American fighters for fifteen more minutes, until the flight was near the eastern tip of Cuba, Cape Maisi, and turning south. Only then did Carlos Corrado wave at Jake and Toad and lower his nose to cross under the F-14.

Out of the corner of his eye Jake saw Toad salute the MiG pilot as he turned away to the west.

'Wonder why that ship ended up on those rocks?' Toad Tarkington mused aloud. Jake Grafton, Gil Pascal, Lieutenant Colonel Eckhardt, Toad, and several of the photo interpretation specialists were bent over a table in the Air Intelligence spaces studying the photographs from the F-14's reconnaissance pod.

'Maybe the person at the con was lost,' the senior AI speculated.

'Or didn't know the waters,' the marine suggested.

'Maybe the Cubans wanted it there,' Gil said.

Jake Grafton used a magnifying glass to study photos of the island closest to the stranded freighter.

'Here's a crew setting up an artillery piece,' he said, and straightened so everyone could see. 'If they planned to strand the ship on those rocks, one would think they would have set up guns and a few SAM batteries in advance.'

'Maybe that's what they want us to think.'

'How far is the ship from the nearest dry land?'

'Three point two nautical miles, sir.' That was one of the photo interpretation specialists, a first class petty officer. 'If you look at this satellite photo of the main island, Admiral, you will see that there are two

SAM batteries near this small port ten miles south of where the *Colón* went on the rocks.'

'That's probably where the ship was going when it hit the rocks,' Jake said. 'Or where it had been. So how many artillery and missile sites are in the area?'

'Four.'

'We'll have EA-6B Prowlers and F/A-18 Hornets overhead, HARM missiles on the rails, F-14s as cover. The instant one of those fire-control radars comes on the air, I want it taken out.'

'When do you want to land aboard the ship?' Eckhardt asked.

Jake Grafton looked at his watch. 'One in the morning.'

'Five hours from now?'

'Can we do it?'

'If we push.'

'Let's push. I talked to General Totten in the Pentagon. He agrees – we should inspect that ship as soon as possible. For me, that's five hours from now. We will go in three Ospreys. The lead Osprey will put Commander Tarkington and me on the ship; Lieutenant Colonel Eckhardt will be in the second bird leading a rescue team to pull us out if anything goes wrong. The third Osprey will contain another ten-man team, led by your executive officer.'

Captain Pascal zeroed in immediately. 'Do the people in Washington know that you intend to board that ship, Admiral?'

'No, and I'm not going to ask.'

'Sir, if you get caught – a two-star admiral on a ship stranded in Cuban waters?'

'The ship is in international waters. We must find out what happened aboard the *Colón* after it left Guantánamo. The stakes are very high. I am going to take a personal look. While I'm gone, Gil, you have the con.'

'Admiral, with all due respect, sir, I think you should take more than just one person with you. Why not a half dozen well-armed marines?'

'I don't know what's on that ship,' Jake explained. 'There may be people aboard, there may be a biological hazard, it may be booby-trapped. It just makes sense to have a point man explore the unknown before we risk very many lives. I am going to be the point man because I want to personally see what is there, and I make the rules. Understand?'

The news about the loss of a ship loaded with biological weapons arrived in Washington with the impact of a high-explosive warhead on a cruise missile.

When the National Security Council met to be briefed about the ship the president was there, and he was in an ugly mood.

'Let me get this straight,' he said, interrupting the national security adviser, who was briefing the group. 'We decided to remove our stockpile of

477

biological and chemical warheads from Guantánamo Bay when we heard Castro might be developing biological weapons of his own. Is that correct?'

'The timing was incidental, sir. They were scheduled to be moved.'

'Scheduled to be moved next year,' the president said acidly. 'We hurried things along when the CIA got wind that El Gato might be shipping lab equipment to Cuba. Will you grant me that?'

'Yes, sir.'

'Just for the record, why in hell were those damned things in Gitmo in the first place?'

'A computer error, sir, back when the Pentagon was prepositioning war supplies at Guantánamo. Somehow the CBW material got on the list, and by the time the error was discovered, the stuff was on its way.'

The president's lip curled in a sneer. 'Did this circle jerk happen under my administration?'

'No, sir. The previous one.'

The president glanced at the ceiling. 'Thank you, God.'

He took a deep breath, exhaled, then said, 'So we decided to clean up old mistakes. We didn't want to take the chance Castro knew of our CBW stockpiles at Gitmo when we started fulminating about his.' The president was addressing the national security adviser. 'But to cover our asses, you wanted a carrier battle group that just happened to be in the Caribbean to keep an eye on things while you got the weapons out. Just having the navy hanging around would keep the Cubans honest, you said.'

'Yes, sir.'

'And now a ship full of weapons from the Gitmo warehouse is on the rocks off the Cuban coast.'

'The ship is on the rocks, but we don't know if any weapons are still aboard.'

'Are you going to court-martial the admiral in charge of the battle group?' the president asked the chairman of the joint chiefs, General Howard D. 'Tater' Totten, a small, gray-haired man who looked like he was hiding inside the green, badged, bemedaled uniform of a four-star army general.

'No, sir. He was told to quote monitor unquote the situation in Guantánamo, not escort cargo ships. He actually had the cargo ship that was hijacked escorted out of Cuban waters, but he didn't direct that it be escorted all the way to Norfolk. No one did, because apparently no one thought an escort necessary.'

'Was the ship hijacked?'

'We don't know, sir. We've been unable to contact it by radio.'

'How are we going to find out if the weapons are still aboard?'

'Send marines aboard tonight to look.'

'I don't think that ship is stranded in international waters,' the secretary of state said.

'Your department told us it was,' Totten shot back.

'That was a first impression by junior staffers. Our senior people demanded a closer look. We are just not sure. The determination depends on where one draws the line that defines the mouth of the bay. Reasonable people can disagree.'

Totten took a deep breath. 'Mr President, we don't know what happened aboard that ship. We don't know if the weapons are aboard. If they have been removed, we need to learn where they went. Now is not the time to split hairs over the nuances of international law. Let's board the ship and get some answers, then the lawyers can argue to their hearts' content.'

'That's the problem with you uniformed testosterone types,' the secretary of state snarled. 'You think you can violate the law anytime it suits your purposes.'

The president of the United States was a cautious man by nature, a blow-dried politician who had maneuvered with the wind at his back all his life. His national security adviser knew him well, General Totten thought, when he said, 'Preliminary indications are that the stranded ship is in international waters, Mr President. The naval commander on the scene has the authority to examine a wreck in international waters if he feels it prudent to do so. Let him make the decision and report back what he finds.'

'That's right,' the president said. 'I think that is the proper way for us to approach this.'

'Will you pass that on to the battle group commander?' the national security adviser asked General Totten.

The general reached for an encrypted telephone.

Jake Grafton and Toad Tarkington went aboard the V-22 parked at the head of the line on the flight deck of USS *United States*. Marines filed aboard the second and third airplane. Tonight the carrier was thirty miles northeast of Cape Maisi – the distance to the stranded freighter was a bit over a hundred miles.

Jake was more nervous than he had been in a long, long time. Before he left the mission planning spaces this evening, he looked again at the chart that depicted the threat envelope of the two surface-to-air missile sites on the Cuban mainland just a few miles from the stranded freighter, *Nuestra Señora de Colón*. The freighter was well inside those envelopes, and the Ospreys would be also.

Jake had had a long talk with the EA-6B electronic warfare crews and the four F/A-18 Hornets that would be over the Ospreys carrying HARMs. HARM stood for high-speed antiradiation missile. Enemy radars were the targets of HARMs, which rode the beams right into the dishes. HARMs even had memories, so if an enemy operator turned off his radar after a HARM was launched, the missile would still fly to the memorized location.

'If the Cubans turn on the SAM radars, open fire,' Jake told his guardian angels. 'Don't wait until their missiles are in the air.'

'Yes, sir.'

Jake had heard nothing from Washington waffling on the assertion that the *Colón* was in international waters, so as far as he was concerned, that fact was a given. The Cubans had no right to fire on ships or planes in international waters. If they did, Jake Grafton would shoot back. Of course, if the Cubans shot first, they would probably kill a planeload or two of Americans, Jake Grafton included. The crews of the EA-6B Prowlers and Hornets were well aware of that reality.

As he sat in the Osprey Jake Grafton wondered if the enlisted marines in the other two planes understood the risks involved in this mission. He suspected they didn't know, and in truth probably didn't want to. Their job was to obey their officers; if the officers led them into action, fretting about the odds wasn't going to do any good at all.

That thought led straight to another: Did he understand the risks?

'You okay, Admiral?'

That was Toad.

Jake Grafton nodded, smiled. A friend like Tarkington was a rare thing indeed. He hadn't asked Toad if he wanted to risk his life on this mission; the commander would have been insulted if he had.

The warm noisy darkness inside the plane seemed comforting, somehow, as if the plane were a loud, safe womb. After takeoff Jake sat for five minutes with his eyes closed, savoring the flying sensations, recharging his batteries. Then he made his way toward the cockpit and squatted behind the pilots, both of whom were wearing night-vision goggles. From this vantage point Jake could see the computer displays on the instrument panel. The flight engineer handed him a helmet, already plugged in, so that he could talk to the pilots and listen to the radio.

He heard the Prowler and Hornets checking in, the F-14s, the S-3 tankers.

He heard Rita call twenty miles to go to the mission coordinator in the E-2 Hawkeye. She had the Osprey flying at a thousand feet above the water, inbound at 250 knots.

'Visibility is five or six miles,' she told Jake over the intercom. 'Some rain showers around. Wind out of the west northwest.'

'Okay.'

'We'll do it like we planned,' she continued, making sure Jake, the copilot, and her crew chief all understood what was to happen. 'I'll hover into the wind, then back down toward the ship, put the ramp over the fantail.'

'Ten miles,' the copilot sang out.

Jake took off the aircraft helmet and donned a marine tactical helmet, which contained a small radio that broadcast on one of four tactical frequencies. Repeaters in the Ospreys picked up the low-powered helmet transmissions and rebroadcast them so that everyone on the tactical net could hear, including the mission coordinator in the E-2, the people aboard the carrier, and the pilots of the airborne planes.

Jake pulled on a set of night-vision goggles and looked forward, through the Osprey windscreen. The night was gone, banished. He could see the stranded freighter, still several miles away, see the surf breaking on the rocks, the containers stacked on deck, the empty sea in all directions. He looked toward the nearest land, an island just over three miles away; he could just make out the line of breaking surf.

The Osprey was slowing: Rita rotated the engine nacelles toward the vertical position as she transitioned from wing-borne cruising flight to pure helicopter operation. Computers monitored her control inputs and gradually increased the effectiveness of the rotor swashplates as flaperons, elevators and rudders lost their effectiveness due to the decreasing airspeed. The transition from wing-borne to rotor-borne flight was smooth, seamless, a technological miracle, and Jake Grafton appreciated it as such.

Jake Grafton kept his eyes on the ship. No people in sight. The bow of the ship was on the rocks. The ship had a small forecastle superstructure, with the main superstructure and bridge on the stern of the ship. The ship's cargo was in holds amidships, with extra containers stacked between the bridge and forecastle. The ship had two large cranes, one forward, one aft. She had a single stack, and probably – given her size – only one screw.

Jake could see that the containers on the deck were jumbled about, several obviously open and empty. Others, a whole bunch, seemed to be missing.

Now Rita swung into the wind, away from the *Colón*.

The ramp at the back of the aircraft was open, with Toad and the crew chief waiting there. Jake Grafton walked aft to join them.

The crew chief gave Rita directions on the ICS, back fifty feet, down ten, as she watched her progress on a small television screen that had been rigged in the cockpit for this mission.

Lower, closer to the ship ... and the ramp touched the deck.

'Go, go, go,' the crew chief shouted.

Jake spoke into his voice-activated boom mike: 'Let's go!'

The fixed deck of the stranded freighter felt strange after a half hour in the moving Osprey. The wash from the mighty, 38-foot rotors was a mini-hurricane here on the fantail, a mixture of charged air and sea spray, dirt, and trash from the deck and containers.

Jake and Toad crouched on the deck as the Osprey moved away. The ramp had been against the deck for no more than fifteen seconds.

Jake spoke into his lip mike, made sure the mission coordinator could hear him. Gripping an M-16 in the ready position, Toad led them forward along the main deck. Jake Grafton carried a video camera, which was running, and two 35-mm cameras. The video and one of the still cameras

481

were loaded with infrared film, the other 35-mm contained regular film and was equipped with a flash attachment.

First stop was the main deck, where he inspected the containers there. Many had doors hanging open, some still had the doors closed, but all the containers were empty. Although he wasn't sure how many containers were supposed to be there, the area around the main hatches was remarkably clear. The hatches themselves were not properly installed. One hatch was ajar.

No people about. None. The ship seemed totally deserted and firmly aground. Jake could feel no motion.

He used a flashlight to look into the hold. This section of the hold didn't seem to be full. Many of the containers were open.

Filming with the video camera, pausing now and then to shoot still photos, the two men searched until they found a ladder that led down into the hold. Toad waited by the hatchway, his M-16 at the ready.

Jake went down the ladder into the dark bay.

He had his night-vision goggles off now; in total darkness they were useless. He snapped on the flashlight, looked around, fingered the pistol in the holster on his hip.

This hold was half-empty, with the packing material that had been wrapped around the warheads strewn everywhere. The place was knee-deep in trash. The containers that were there were obviously empty.

Jake didn't stay but a minute or so, then he climbed back up the ladder.

'Let's check the bridge,' he said to Toad over the tactical radio.

They went aft along the main deck and climbed an outside ladder to the bridge, which stretched from one side of the ship to the other.

'They've cleaned her out,' Toad remarked over the tac net.

'Yeah,' Jake replied, and kept climbing.

On the bridge Jake again removed the night-vision goggles and used a flashlight. He wanted to see whatever was there in natural light.

What he found were bloodstains. A lot of blood had been spilled here on the bridge; pools of congealed, sticky black blood lay on the deck. People had walked in it, tracking the stuff all over.

'Not everyone was on the payroll,' Jake muttered, and quickly completed his search. He aimed the video camera at the stains, then snapped a couple photos with the regular camera using the flash.

Toad used a flashlight to search for the log book and ship's documents. 'The safe is open and empty,' he told Jake Grafton. He came over to watch the admiral work the cameras.

'Where in hell are the warheads?' Toad asked aloud.

'The Americans are aboard the *Colón*, Colonel.'

The man shook Santana awake. He held a candle, which flickered in the tropical breeze coming through the screen.

Santana sat up and tossed the sheet aside. He consulted his watch.

He got out of bed, walked out onto the porch of the small house and searched the night sea with binoculars. Nothing.

He lowered the binoculars, stood listening.

Yes, he could hear engine sounds, very faint . . . jet engines, the whopping of rotors. . . .

'How long have they been aboard?'

'I don't know, sir. With this wind it is hard to hear helicopter noises. When I heard the voices on the radio, I came to wake you.'

'Admiral, look at this.' Toad came over to where Jake was standing, showed him the screen of a small battery-operated computer. 'I'm picking up radio transmissions, even when we are not using the tactical net. Something on the ship is broadcasting.'

Jake Grafton pulled his mike down to his lips. 'Hawkeye, this is Cool Hand. Has anyone been picking up radio transmissions from the target?'

'Cool Hand, Hawkeye. They started about a minute ago, sir, when you went up on the bridge. We have them now.'

'What kind of transmissions?'

'Amazingly, sir, I'm receiving clear channel radio. I'm actually hearing you talk on this other frequency.'

'What the hell? . . .'

Oh, sweet Jesus!

'This damned ship is wired to blow. The bastards are listening to us right now. We gotta get off!' With that he gave Toad a push toward the door of the bridge. Toad ran. Jake Grafton was right behind him.

Colonel Santana couldn't see anything through the binoculars, but he heard those American voices coming through the radio speaker. The microphones were on the bridge.

'Anytime, Tomas,' he said.

Tomas keyed the radio transmit button three times. A flower of red and yellow fire blossomed in the darkness.

Santana aimed the binoculars and focused them as the last of the explosions faded. He could see the flicker of flames as they spread aboard *Nuestra Señora de Colón*. These Americans! So predictable! Santana chuckled as he watched.

'Into the ocean,' Jake shouted.

Toad vaulted over the rail into the blackness. As he fell he wondered if there were rocks or salt water below.

Toad Tarkington and Jake Grafton were in midair when the bridge exploded behind them. Jake felt the thermal pulse and the first concussion.

Then the dark, cool water closed over his head and he went completely under.

As he began to rise toward the surface, he felt more explosions from inside the ship. The concussions reached him through the water like spent punches from a prizefighter.

When he got his head above water, flames illuminated the night.

Above the noise of the explosions and flames, he could hear Tarkington cursing.

11

After Rita pulled them out of the ocean and flew them back to the carrier, Toad Tarkington and Jake Grafton were checked in sick bay, then they showered and tried to snatch a few hours sleep.

Toad gave up on sleep – too much adrenaline. He lay in his bunk thinking about leaping over the bridge rail without knowing whether rocks or water lay beneath, and he shivered. The shock of the impact with the water had been almost a deliverance.

He turned on the light and looked at the photos of Rita and Tyler he had taped to the bulkhead. *Really stupid, Toad-man, really stupid. Grafton must have checked the location of the rocks, knew where he could jump and where he couldn't, and you never once thought to look.*

He got up, dressed, and headed for the computers, where he typed out a classified E-mail for the people at the National Security Agency. After breakfast he was ready to brief Jake Grafton and Gil Pascal.

'Before she was stranded, *Nuestra Señora de Colón* went into this little Cuban port at the west end of Bahia de Nipe. She was there for six hours, then she steamed out and went on the rocks where we found her. If you look at this satellite photo you can see a boat nearby, probably taking the crew off after she piled up. The folks at NSA in Fort Meade say they can see ropes from the ship to this boat that the crewmen could slide down.'

Toad Tarkington stood back so Jake Grafton and Gil Pascal could study the satellite photos that he had pinned to a bulletin board in the mission planning spaces.

'Where are the weapons now?' Gil Pascal asked.

'In this fish warehouse.' Toad pointed at the photo with the tip of a pencil. 'Right here.'

'It's an easy SEAL target,' the Chief of Staff commented.

'Too easy,' Jake Grafton said, then regretted it.

'When did the freighter reach this port?'

'Noon, three days ago.'

'And they spent the afternoon off-loading it?'

'Yes. It went onto the rocks that night.'

'Too easy.' Now he was sure.

'What do you mean?'

'These people aren't stupid. They know about satellite reconnaissance; they knew we would see them off-loading the ship in this port; they wanted us to see that. The question is, Why did they go to all the trouble of putting on a show for us? What are they hiding?'

Toad flipped through the satellite photos, looking at date-time groups. 'Here is the ship coming into the bay, there it is against the pier at Antilla, here it is being off-loaded, here is an IR photo of it going out to the rocks after dark, here is an IR shot of the freighter and the boat that probably took the crew off.'

'Radar images?'

Toad had a handful of those too.

'I want to know where this ship was between the time the destroyer left it and the time it showed up in this Cuban port.'

'NSA is still working on that stuff. Perhaps in a few hours, sir,' Toad said.

'Call me.'

'The weapons weren't on the ship,' the national security adviser told the president in the Oval Office. 'The ship was empty when it went on the rocks. Apparently the Cubans booby-trapped it – the thing exploded a few minutes after the admiral went aboard to inspect it.'

'Casualties?'

'None, sir. We were lucky. If the admiral had taken more people with him, I can't say the results would have been the same.'

'So where are the weapons?'

'NSA thinks they are in a warehouse on the waterfront in the center of the town of Antilla. They are studying the satellite sensor data now.'

'Shit!' said the president.

William Henry Chance and Tommy Carmellini ate dinner in the main restaurant of the largest casino on the Malecon. The fact that 99 percent of the Cubans on the island didn't eat this well was on Chance's mind as he watched the waiters come and go amid the tables filled with European diners. Plenty amid poverty, an old Cuban story so common as to be unremarkable.

Carmellini merely played with his food; he was too tense to enjoy eating, had too much on his mind. Chance tried to concentrate on a superb string quartet playing classical music in the corner of the room.

To the best of his knowledge, he and Carmellini had not been followed on their expeditions around the capital, although he knew very well that a really first-class surveillance would be impossible to detect. With enough men, enough radios and automobiles, the subjects could be kept in sight at all times yet no one would be directly behind them, following where they could be seen or noticed. The subjects would seem to be alone, moving of their own will through the urban environment, yet their isolation would be an illusion.

He knew all that, yet he could detect no tails or signs of people that might be watching, taking an interest in him or Carmellini. Chance was no neophyte – he had a great deal of experience in this line of work, he knew what was possible and he knew what was likely.

He thought about all these things as the flawlessly decked-out Cuban waiter served coffee. The music formed a backdrop to the babble of conversation from his fellow diners, who were gabbing in at least five languages, perhaps six.

Chance sipped the coffee, let his eyes wander the room. No one was paying the slightest attention. Not a single furtive glance, no hastily broken eye contact, no one studiously ignoring him.

Well, if he and Carmellini were going to do it, tonight was the night. The longer they stayed in Havana, the more likely it was that they would attract the interest of the Department of State Security, the secret police. The interest of Santana and Alejo Vargas.

The truth was that Vargas might have burned them, might have devoted the resources necessary to learn everything about them. Vargas or his minions might be waiting tonight in the science hall, waiting to catch them red-handed, to embarrass the United States, perhaps even to execute Chance and Carmellini as spies.

In this line of work the imponderables were always huge, risks impossible to quantify. Still, he and Carmellini were going to have to look inside that building, see what was there.

If there was a biological weapons program in Cuba, it had to be in that building, which housed the largest, best-equipped laboratory known to be on the island. And the most knowledgeable people were nearby, the microbiologists and chemists and skilled lab technicians that would be needed to produce large quantities of microorganisms.

Chance was well aware that the most serious technical problem a researcher faced when constructing a biological weapon was how to keep the microorganisms alive inside a warhead or aerosol bomb for long periods of time. Some biological agents were easier to store than others, which was why they were most often selected for weapons research. For example, the spores of anthrax were very stable, as were the spores of the fungal disease coccidioidomycosis, which incapacitated but rarely killed its victims. Of course, the naturally occurring strains of an infectious disease could have been altered to make the microorganisms more stable, more virulent, or to overcome widespread immunity: years ago researchers produced a highly infective strain of poliomyelitis virus for just these reasons.

Idly he wondered about the microbiologist who ran the program. Who was he? What were his motivations? Perhaps that question answered itself in a totalitarian society, but it was worth researching, when he had some time. If he ever had some time.

'Ready?' Chance muttered to Carmellini, who drained the last of his coffee.

The two men paid their bill in cash and left the casino. They got into a car parked at the curb, one driven by one of their associates, and sped off into the night.

In a dark, deserted lane on the outskirts of the city the car in which Chance and Carmellini rode met the former telephone van they had used before, but now it bore the logo of a wholesale food supplier.

Inside the van Carmellini and Chance changed into black trousers, a black pullover shirt with a high collar, black socks, and black rubber-soled shoes. When they were dressed, they sat listening to the insects, drinking water, monitoring a radio frequency. One of their colleagues was observing the science building at the university. He checked in every fifteen minutes. So far he had seen nothing out of the ordinary.

'Why did you get into this line of work?' Chance asked Carmellini as they sat listening to the chirp of crickets.

'The challenge of it, I guess. I had an uncle who cracked a few safes . . . he was a legendary figure. The only time he ever went to the pen was for tax evasion: he did a couple years that time. I was always asking him questions. He told me if I wanted to be a safecracker, go to work for a firm that manufactured and installed the things. That was good advice. I installed safes for several summers while I was in college, got too cocky for my own good. Thought I had this stuff figured out, you know? One thing led to another, and before you know it I was cracking the things.'

Chance nodded.

'Here I am still at it. Only this time I won't go to the pen if they catch me.'

'Yeah. The Cubans will probably execute us as soon as Vargas gets through with us, if there's anything left to execute.'

'The way I figure it, I finally made the big leagues.'

'You optimists, always looking on the bright side.'

'Which brings up a point. You got us garroting wires and knives and pistols. I never carry weapons. I'm a safecracker, not a killer.'

'You'll probably become a dead safecracker if they catch you in there.'

'I've never carried weapons. Ever.'

'A wise precaution if you are burgling gentlemen's safes. You're in the major leagues now.'

'Listen, Chance —'

'This isn't a game, Tommy. Speaking for myself, I want to keep breathing. You'll do as I say.'

The driver parked the van in an alley near the science building. He sat hunched over the wheel watching people on the sidewalks as Chance and Carmellini examined the building through binoculars. They were behind him, in the body of the van, looking forward through the windshield.

The way in, they decided, was through the roof. To get there, they would need to go into the building beside the science building, a lecture hall, ascend to the top floor, then get access to the roof. From here they would need to cross to the roof of the science hall, then find a way in.

The lecture hall was locked at night, though it was not guarded.

It was one in the morning when the van stopped in the empty alley behind the lecture hall. The two men in back pulled on latex gloves, swung on backpacks, then went out the van's side door.

The door was not wired with an alarm. Carmellini picked the lock in thirty seconds, and they were in.

The van drove away as the door closed behind them.

They stood in the darkness letting their eyes adjust to the gloom.

Carmellini led off. Behind him Chance took out his pistol and thumbed off the safety, keeping the pistol pointed downward at the floor.

The weak light filtering through windows in classrooms and thence through open doors to the hallway did little to alleviate the darkness. The floors were uncarpeted concrete, the walls massive masonry, the ceilings at least twelve feet high. The building was devoid of decoration or even a trace of architectural imagination.

Carmellini moved like a shadow, making no detectable noise. Chance seemed to be making enough noise for both of them. He could hear himself breathing and his heart pounding, could hear the echoes of his footfalls in the cavernous hallways.

Keeping near the wall, they climbed the stairs to the second floor. Carmellini moved slowly, steadily, listened carefully before turning every corner, then lowered his head, keeping it well below the place one would naturally look for it, and peeped around the corner. Then he slithered around the corner out of sight; Chance followed as silently as he could.

The top of the staircase put them out on the fourth floor of the building. There had to be another staircase, probably very narrow, leading to the roof. Where might it be?

Carmellini was ready to go explore when he suddenly held up his hand. He held a finger to his lips.

Chance listened with all the concentration he could muster.

He *could* hear something! Voices?

Carmellini slowly inched along the hallway toward an open door, then froze there.

He came back down the hallway to Chance, put his lips against Chance's ear. 'A couple of kids making love.'

The silenced Ruger felt heavy in Chance's hand.

'Gonna kill 'em?'

Not shooting them was a risk, sure.

Chance listened carefully. The lovers were whispering. No other sounds. 'Find the stairs up.'

The stairs were at the end of a hall, behind a locked door. Carmellini worked on the lock in the darkness for almost a minute before he pulled the door open.

They closed the door behind them and climbed the totally dark staircase, feeling their way. They ended up in a stuffy, black attic. Chance used the flashlight. Furniture, desks, chairs, stacked everywhere. In the middle of the attic was another stairway up.

The door to the roof was also locked, this time with a padlock, which was on the interior side of the door.

'What if there is a padlock on the other side?' Chance asked.

'Then we're screwed. Unless you want to kick this thing down.'

'No.'

'Let's try to get this lock open, then the door.'

'Okay.'

The lock was rusty, corroded. After several minutes' effort Carmellini admitted his defeat and used a wire saw to cut through the metal loop of the lock. That took two minutes of intense effort but didn't make much noise, considering.

With the lock off and hasp pulled back, they pushed at the door. It refused to open. With both men heaving, the door slowly opened with great resistance, and groaned terribly.

'That'll wake the dead,' Chance muttered, and wiped the sweat from his face as Carmellini slipped out onto the roof.

Chance followed along.

The metal roof sloped away steeply in several different planes. Moving on hands and knees they worked themselves over toward the edge that faced the science building.

'Let me do this,' Carmellini whispered, and extracted the rope from his backpack. 'Get out of the way, up by the door.'

Chance went.

The glare of the city and the streetlights below illuminated the roof quite well, too well in fact. While it was easy to see where to walk, anyone below who bothered to look could probably see the black shapes silhouetted against the glare of the sky.

Chance huddled against the dormer that formed the staircase up from the attic. He watched Carmellini on the edge of the roof, shaking out the rope, checking the grappling hook. Now he began to twirl the hook above his head, letting out more and more line to make the hook swing an ever-larger circle. Just as it seemed the circle was impossibly wide, he cast the line and hook across the chasm separating the buildings at a metal vent sticking up out of the roof.

The hook made an audible metallic sound as it hit the far roof, then it began sliding off.

Carmellini quickly pulled in line in huge coils, but too late to stop the grappling hook from sliding off the roof.

He kept pulling on the line. In seconds he had the hook in his hand and bent down against the roof.

Someone was down below. Even back here Chance could hear voices. He scanned the surrounding roofs, the streets that he could see, the blank windows looking at him from other buildings.

Minutes ticked by, the voices below faded.

Now Carmellini was standing, swinging the rope and hook, now casting it . . . and it caught! He tugged at it, worked his way back up the roof to where Chance was kneeling.

Carmellini put the end of the rope around the dormer, pulled it as taut as possible, then tied it off.

'Well, there is our way across,' the younger man said. 'You want to go first, or should I?'

'Anchored solid, is it?'

'You bet.'

'Age before beauty,' Chance said, and tugged on leather gloves, wrapped his hands around the rope. He worked out hand over hand, then draped his lower legs over the rope. His backpack dangled from his shoulders.

Hanging from the rope like this took a surprising amount of physical strength. The rope sagged dangerously with his weight, becoming a vee with him at the bottom, which made it more difficult to move along it.

Gritting his teeth, trying to keep his breathing even, William Henry Chance worked his way along the rope, taking care not to look down. At one point he knew he was over the chasm but it didn't matter: if he slipped off the rope the fall would kill him, whether he hit the roof and slid off or missed it clean.

He kept going, doggedly, straining every muscle, until he felt the bag dragging along the roof of the science building. Only then did he unhook his legs from the rope and let them down to the roof. Still pulling on the rope, he heaved himself up by the vent and grabbed it.

The grappling hook was holding by one tong. He wrapped the rope around the vent and set the hook, then tugged several times to make sure it would hold.

Wiping his forehead, he breathed heavily three or four times. He had one hand on the rope, so he felt the tension increase with Carmellini's weight. He peered at the other building. Carmellini came scurrying along the rope like a goddamn chimpanzee.

The younger man was over the gap between the buildings when the rope broke, apparently where it was anchored atop the lecture hall. Carmellini's body fell downward in an arc and disappeared from view. An audible thud

491

reached Chance as Carmellini's body smacked against the side of the science building.

'*Our Lady of Colón* was under this storm system, out of sight of the satellites passing over, for six hours,' Toad Tarkington explained to Jake Grafton. They were bent over a table in Mission Planning, studying satellite radar images. 'When next it reappeared, it was steaming for Bahia de Nipe at twelve knots, yet its average speed of advance while it was out of sight was two knots.'

'Two?'

'Two.' Toad showed him the positions and measurements.

'So it was stopped somewhere.'

'Or made a detour.'

'What if the ship rendezvoused with another ship and the warheads were transferred?'

'Possible, but if you look at these other ship tracks, it doesn't seem very likely. All these other tracks were going somewhere, with speed-of-advance averages that seem plausible.'

'Okay. What if the ship stopped and the crew dumped some of the weapons in the water? Maybe all of them. Dumped them in shallow water for someone to pick up later. How deep is the water in that area?'

'That area is the Bahamas, Admiral. Pretty shallow in a lot of places in there.'

'Have NSA put that area under intense surveillance. Have them study every satellite image since that storm passed. If those warheads were dumped overboard from the *Colón*, someone is going to come along to pick them up. We have to get there before that somebody gets them aboard.'

'Yes, sir.'

'Ask Atlantic Fleet to get a P-3 out to that area as soon as possible, have the crew search for anchored or stationary ships. Any ships not actually under way. Understand?'

'Yes, sir.'

Jake Grafton rubbed his forehead, trying to decide if there was anything else he should be doing.

'Uh, Admiral . . .' Toad began, his voice low. 'I want to thank you for saving my assets last night. I about had a heart attack after we jumped over that rail, everything behind us blowing up, wondering if we were going to go into the water or splatter ourselves on a rock pile. That was truly a religious experience.'

A wry grin crossed Jake Grafton's face. 'Wish I had paid more attention to where those rocks were before crunch time arrived. Talk about jumping out of the frying pan into the fire! For a few seconds there I thought we had had the stroke.'

'You didn't know?' Toad was aghast.

'What say we don't mention this to Rita or Callie,' Jake said, and walked away. He had another meeting to attend.

William Henry Chance grabbed the rope, which extended over the side on the science building roof into the darkness. The rope was still taut. Tommy Carmellini must be hanging on the end of it!

Chance braced himself and began pulling, hand over hand, and almost ruptured himself.

He got no more than six feet of rope up when he realized he wasn't in the right position. Moving carefully, he braced himself against the vent pipe and got the rope over his shoulders. Now he used his whole body to help raise it.

Two more feet.

Four.

A dark spot, a head, coming above the eave, struggling to climb.

Chance held the rope steady as Carmellini heaved himself over the edge of the roof and began crawling up the slope, still holding onto the rope.

'Man, I thought I had bit the big one,' Carmellini said between gasps. Leaning against the chimney, Chance blew equally hard.

'I'm getting too old for this shit,' Carmellini muttered.

'Next time get a desk job.'

'Why in hell do you think I went to law school?'

Chance coiled the rope and inspected it. It had frayed through where it was wrapped around the dormer on the other building. He showed the place to Carmellini, then put the rope in his knapsack.

'Let's go.'

Carmellini used a glass cutter on a pane of a dormer window, then they went in.

Chance took a chance and used the flashlight. This attic was stacked with laboratory equipment: dishes, warmers, mixing units, microscopes, a spectrometer, a bunch of equipment large and small that he couldn't identify.

'Let's put on our masks,' Chance said, 'just in case.'

They donned the gas masks, made sure the filter elements were on tight. The mask could provide only filtered air: it had an inhalation and exhalation valve and a black faceplate with two large clear lenses to see through. The mask was attached to a hood that went over the head and shoulders of the user. Pull strings sealed the hood so air could not get in around the user's neck. When they had the mask on, both men removed the leather gloves they had been wearing and donned a pair of latex gloves. They stuffed their trousers inside their socks.

With Carmellini in the lead, the two men stealthily descended the stairs.

The laboratory was in the basement, so Chance and Carmellini had to pass through the main floor to get there.

The elevator would be the best way from the top of the building to the bottom, but it might be monitored from the guards' station at the main entrance. Certainly it should be: nothing could be simpler than to have a warning light come on when the electric motor that ran the elevator engaged. Chance and Carmellini took the stairs.

Carmellini was leading the way now. Using the flashlight, he examined the door to the staircase for alarms, then opened the door a crack and examined the stairwell. Fortunately the stairwell was lit. If this building were in the States it would be festooned with infrared sensors, motion detectors, microphones, and remote cameras controlled from a central station. However, this was Cuba.

At each landing, Carmellini extended a small periscope and looked around the corner.

On the second floor his inspection of the stairs leading down revealed a camera mounted on a wall above the landing, focused on the door in from the main floor. There was probably a camera mounted above the door to the main floor, a camera that looked back toward this camera.

Carmellini studied the camera through the periscope, twisted the magnification to the maximum and refocused. He kept the instrument steady by bracing himself against the wall.

The security camera was fifteen or twenty years old if it was a day. No doubt there were ten or twelve cameras on a sequential switch, so the video from each one was shown in turn on a monitor at the guards' station. The guard was probably reading something, eating, talking to another guard, if he was paying any attention at all.

From his backpack Carmellini removed a strobe unit and battery. He plugged the thing together, switched on the battery, and waited for the capacitor to charge. The bulb had a set of silver metal feathers around it so that the light could be focused. Carmellini tightened the feathers around the bulb as much as they would go. When the capacitor's green light came on, he eased the light around the corner, exposing his head for the first time. One quick squint to line up the light, then holding the thing tightly against the wall to steady it, he retracted his head, closed his eyes and buried his head in the crook of his arm. William Henry Chance did likewise. The short, intense burst of light should burn out the camera's light-level sensor, rendering it inoperative.

The flash was so bright Carmellini saw it through his closed eyelids.

The two men slipped down the stairs. Standing just under the camera that had just been disabled, Carmellini used the periscope again. Yes. Another camera, just over the door to the main floor.

He waited ten more seconds for the capacitor to fully charge, then stuck it around the corner and flashed the light.

'Let's *go!*'

With Chance behind him, Tommy Carmellini went down the stairs to the main floor and used his periscope to examine the landing on the stairs leading down. Nothing.

On down to the landing, peeking around the corner.

'Motion detector,' he whispered to Chance.

Chance was breathing heavily inside the mask. It wasn't the exertion, he decided, but the tension. He must be audible at fifty paces. He tried to ignore the sound of his own rasping and listen.

Were the guards coming? Two cameras were down – had they noticed? Would they come to inspect the things?

Or were the guards congregating right now, calling in troops?

'Microwave or infrared?' Chance asked, referring to the motion detector.

'One of each.'

'Beautiful.'

'Probably two independent systems.'

'Oh, Christ!'

'That's a poor way to install them, actually. This is old technology, *Mission Impossible* stuff. We'll just walk by the infrared detectors – all this clothing will help shield our body heat. If we move right along we should be okay.'

'And the microwave system?'

Carmellini had already removed a device the size of a portable CD player from his backpack. 'Jammer,' he said, and examined the controls.

He turned it on and, holding it in front of him, walked down to the motion detectors. The one on the left was the microwave one, with a coaxial cable leading away from it. Carmellini pulled the cable an inch or so away from the wall and wedged the jammer into that space.

'Come on,' he whispered, and opened the door into the basement.

The two men found themselves in a hallway. Directly over their head was a camera that pointed the length of the hall, covering the door halfway down that must lead into the lab.

Carmellini took a small battery-powered camcorder from Chance's backpack. He held it under the security camera for about a minute, filming the view down the hallway, then pushed the play button. The device now replayed the same scene on a continuous loop, and would do so until the batteries were exhausted. He slid a collar around the coaxial cable leading from the camera, tightened it, then used a pair of wire cutters to slice the coax away from the security camera.

The door into the lab had an alarm on it, one mounted high.

'The alarm rings if the circuit is broken,' Carmellini whispered. 'It's designed to prevent unauthorized exit from the lab, not entry. Won't take a minute.'

He worked swiftly with a penknife and length of wire. By wiring around the contact on the door and jam, he made the contact impossible to break.

Sixty seconds later he gingerly tried the door. Reached for the handle and –

Locked!

Now to work with the picks.

'They locked an emergency exit?' Chance demanded.

'Yeah. Real bastards, huh?'

Tommy Carmellini knew his business. When the lock clicked, he put his picks back in his knapsack, pulled the knapsack into position, and palmed his pistol.

'You ready?'

'Yeah.'

Carmellini eased the door open, looked quickly each way with just one eye around the jam.

The door opened into a well-lit foyer. The entire opposite wall of the room was made of thick glass, which formed a wall of a large, well-equipped laboratory. No people in sight. And no security cameras or motion detectors.

Both men came in, pistols in their hands and pointed at the floor. Chance pulled the door shut behind them.

They knelt by the long window and with just their heads sticking up, surveyed the scene.

Row after row of culture trays, units for mixing chemicals, deep sinks, storage cabinets, big sterilizing units, stainless steel containers by the dozen, analysis equipment, retorts, microscopes . . .

'Holy damn,' Carmellini said softly. 'They are sure as hell growing something in there.'

'Something,' Chance agreed.

On the end of the room to their left was a large air lock.

'That's the way in.'

'Do we have to go in?'

'We need samples from those culture trays.'

Chance led the way. He walked, holding the pistol down by his right thigh.

Around the corner slowly, looking first.

There were actually two air locks. After they went through the first one, they found themselves in a dressing room with a variety of white one-piece coveralls hanging on nails. Each man donned one, pulling it on over his clothes, then zipping it tightly, fastening the cuffs with Velcro strips. Gas masks were there too, but they were already wearing masks.

The second lock was equipped with a large vacuum machine which suctioned dust and microorganisms from the white coveralls.

They opened the door to the lab and stepped inside.

'The culture trays,' Chance said, and led the way. From his backpack he took syringes, quickly screwed on needles.

The glass trays sat on mobile racks, three dozen to a rack. They were readily transparent, so he could look inside, see the bacteria growing on the food mix at the bottom of the tray.

He selected a rack of trays, pulled one tray from the rack and laid it on the marble-topped counter nearby. He opened it. Used a syringe. With the syringe about half-full, he unscrewed the needle, deposited the syringe in a plastic freezer bag and sealed it.

Meanwhile Carmellini had been exploring. As Chance sealed up his second sample from this rack of trays, Carmellini came back, motioning with his hand. 'Better come look. Looks like they are growing several kinds of cultures.'

The second kind looked similar to the first, but the organisms were of a slightly different color. Chance selected a tray, took a sample, then replaced the tray on the rack, as he had the first one.

He was finishing his second sample from this batch when, out of the corner of his eye, he saw Carmellini motion for him to get down.

He dropped to a sitting position, finished sealing the syringe bag.

He put the samples into his knapsack, reached up on the countertop for his pistol.

Carmellini was creeping along below the counter with his pistol in his hand.

Someone was in the air lock. By looking down the aisle between the counters Chance could just see the top of his head as he pulled on the gas mask in the dressing room.

Whoever it was was coming in.

Carmellini looked at Chance, lifted his hands in a query: Now what?

Chance made a downward motion. Maybe this person would just come in, get something, then leave.

It would be impossible, he decided, to sneak out while the person was in the lab. Although the lab was large, at least a hundred feet long, anyone in the air locks could be seen from anywhere in the lab unless the viewer was behind a piece of large equipment.

Shit!

Well, the Cubans were about to discover that their lab was no longer a secret. That was not a disaster; unfortunate, perhaps. Perhaps not.

The person coming in wore a complete protection suit and mask. Not a square inch of skin was exposed.

Large for a woman. A man, probably. Almost six feet. Hard to tell body weight under a bag suit like that, but at least 180 pounds.

He checked the safety on the pistol. On. With his thumb he moved it to the off position, checked it visually.

Now the person was coming out of the air lock, walking purposefully down the aisle between the counters and trays of cultures.

William Henry Chance stood up, pointed the pistol straight in the face of the masked person walking toward him.

The man froze. If it was a man. Stopped dead and slowly raised his hands.

Out of the corner of his eye Chance saw Tommy Carmellini moving toward the Cuban.

'Find something to tie him with,' he said loudly, hoping Carmellini would understand his muffled voice.

Carmellini seemed to. He held up a roll of duct tape. He moved toward the man, who turned his head so that he could get a good look at Carmellini.

Carmellini had his pistol in his hand. His holster was under the white coverall, as was Chance's, so both men had carried their pistols with them in their hands.

Now Carmellini placed the pistol on a counter, well out of the man's reach. He walked behind him.

The man pushed backward, slamming Carmellini against a counter.

Damnation! Chance couldn't shoot for fear of hitting Carmellini. As if the .22-caliber bullets in the Ruger would drop a big man at this distance.

Chance walked around the counter, up the aisle, intending to shoot the Cuban in the head from as close as he could get.

Carmellini kicked violently and the Cuban went flying back into a rack of culture trays. Three or four of the trays fell from the rack and shattered on the floor.

The man launched himself at Carmellini, who ducked under a right cross. The man kept right on going, heading for the pistol lying on the counter.

Carmellini caught him by the back of his coverall and swung him bodily around. With a mighty punch he sent the man reeling backward, straight into the rack of culture trays he had already hit. The man slipped, fell amid the broken glass.

Without sights, wearing the silencer, the Ruger was hard to aim. Chance squeezed off a round anyway. Where the bullet went he never knew.

Before he could fire again the man screamed in agony. All his muscles went rigid. He bent over backward, screaming in a high-pitched wail.

'Let's go!' Carmellini yelled.

The man got control of an arm. He tore at his mask, trying to get it off, all the while screaming and thrashing around on the floor amid the broken glass.

'Holy shit.'

The stricken man finally just ran out of air. All motion stopped. He was bent over backward, almost double, his head within a few inches of his heels.

Careful not to step on the broken glass, Chance bent over the man. He carefully took off the gas mask.

Eyes rolled back in his head, every muscle taut in a fierce rigor, the man seemed almost frozen.

'He must have torn his suit,' Chance muttered to himself. *The Cubans must have vaccinated everyone with access. Why didn't the vaccination protect him?*

'Let's get our asses through the air lock and get the fuck outta here,' Carmellini said loudly.

They stood in the vacuum room for the longest time, neither man willing to be the first to leave.

'We must go,' Carmellini said at last, after almost ten minutes of suction, after using a high-pressure jet of air from a hose to blast every nook and fold of the coverall.

They hung the coveralls on the nails. Stood in the next air lock, were vacuumed again, then they were out, still wearing their gas masks.

'We might kill everyone in Havana,' Chance said.

'We'll never know it,' Carmellini shot back. 'We'll be in hell before they are.'

'Can't figure out why the vaccination didn't protect him.'

'Later. How the hell are we going to get out of here?'

'The easiest way is to just walk out the front door, shoot both the guards, and walk around the corner to the van.'

'They'll see us going up the stairs.'

'The elevator. We'll use the elevator. Keep the pistols where they can't see them.'

'You are fucking A crazy, man. One crazy motherfucker.'

The elevator was right there with the door open. Chance walked in. When Carmellini was aboard, he pushed the button to take it up.

With their pistols down by their legs, they walked out of the elevator, straight for the guard shack at the front door.

Only one man was there, reading something. He looked up as they approached. Now he stood.

'*Qué pasa –?*' he began, and Chance shot him in the forehead from six feet away.

The guard toppled over backward.

Chance and Carmellini kept going, out the door at a walking pace, down the sidewalk under the streetlights looking like two refugees from a flying saucer, and around the corner. They jerked open the rear door of the van and jumped in.

Chance ripped off the mask.

'Let's get the hell outta here,' he roared at the driver, who was as surprised at their sudden appearance as the guard had been. 'Drive, damn it, drive!'

As the van jostled and swayed through the city streets, they sat in the back staring at each other, waiting for the disease to hammer them.

Waited, and waited, and waited . . .

12

Six hours after William Henry Chance and Tommy Carmellini walked out of the University of Havana science building, Dr Bouchard was on his way to Washington via Mexico City with two of the culture samples in his diplomatic pouch. Three hours later one of the lowest-ranking mission employees with diplomatic status left on a plane to Freeport, there to transfer to a flight to Miami, and then on to Washington. This employee carried the other two samples in her diplomatic pouch.

Chance and Carmellini were dropped at their hotel after changing clothes in the van. 'Burn those clothes immediately, and don't touch them with your bare hands,' Chance told the driver.

At the hotel both men went straight to their rooms, stripped, and stood in the shower for as long as they could stand it.

Standing under the shower head Chance waited for the first symptom to announce its arrival. Every now and then he shuddered, despite the hot water, as cold chills ran up and down his spine. He had a raging headache. When he got out of the shower he toweled himself dry, got in bed and arranged a wet, cool washcloth across his forehead.

The lab worker writhing on the floor, the startled face of the guard the instant before he died – these scenes played over and over in his mind. The death throes of the lab worker were bad enough, but the face of the guard, when he saw the pistol rising, saw the silencer, knew Chance was going to shoot: *that* face Chance would carry to his grave.

He shouldn't have had to kill the guard. The truth of the matter was that he panicked when the lab worker died horribly; he stood in the air locks thinking he or Carmellini would be next, any second. He had wanted out of that building so badly he had thrown caution to the wind and bolted blindly for the front door. It was a miracle that there weren't two or three guards standing by the main entrance, that they didn't have guns out as the two figures from biological hell stepped out of the elevator.

Ah, the stink of Lady Luck.

Lying there in the darkness he thought about microorganisms, wondered what was in the sample vials, wondered why the lab worker, who must have been immunized, died such a painful, horrible death.

One thing was certain: The Cubans were well on their way to having biological weapons. And the only conceivable target was the United States.

With his head pounding, unable to sleep, he turned on his small computer and typed an E-mail reporting the intrusion and his findings. After he encrypted the message, he used the telephone on the desk to get on the Web and fire the message into cyberspace.

Then he went back to bed, and finally to sleep.

The American stood amid the shards of glass looking at the body of the lab worker. He wore a protective garment that covered him head to toe and a mask that filtered the air he breathed. He looked at everything, taking his time, then exited the laboratory through the air lock.

Alejo Vargas was waiting for him. He said nothing, merely waited for the American to talk.

'The virus has apparently mutated,' the American said finally. 'I thought the strain was stable, but . . .' He gave the tiniest shrug.

'Mutated?'

'Possibly.'

'Come now, Professor. I have not asked for scientific proof. Tell me what you think.'

'A mutation. A few days with the electron microscope would give us some clues. We need to do more cultures to be sure. It would help if I could dissect the dead man, see how the disease affected him.'

'Like you did the others?'

'You told me they were killers, condemned men. We had to *know*!'

'What if the disease gets away from you at the morgue? What if it spreads to the general population?'

'With the proper precautions the danger is minuscule. Man, the advancement of human knowledge requires –'

'No,' Vargas said. He gestured to the lab. 'If that gets away from us, for whatever reason, there won't be a human left alive on this island.'

'Then don't ask me for opinions,' the professor snapped. 'You can guess as well as I.'

Alejo Vargas's eyes narrowed to slits. His voice was cold with fury. 'I wanted to use an anthrax agent, but no, you insisted on poliomyelitis. Now you tell me it mutated, as I feared it might.'

The damned fool, the American thought. Of course he had insisted on a virus – for Christ's sake, his life work was studying viruses, not bacteria.

Vargas continued, pronouncing the sentence: 'We spent all this money, built the warheads, installed them, and we took huge risks to do it. Don't talk to me of acceptable *risks*.'

The professor was not the type to calmly submit to lectures from his intellectual inferiors. 'Don't get wrathy with me, Vargas. You're a stupid, ignorant thug. I didn't design the universe and I can't take responsibility for it. I merely try to understand, to learn, to increase the store of man's knowledge.'

The American lost his temper at that point and spluttered, 'Biology isn't engineering, goddammit! Sometimes two plus two equals five.'

Vargas turned his back on the professor. He stared into the lab, which appeared cold and stark under the lights yet was full of poisonous life.

'I don't understand what happened in there,' the American said. 'He didn't just fall. It looks like there was a struggle.'

'Someone broke in,' Vargas said.

The professor was horrified. 'Broke in? Past the guards? Who would be so foolish?'

'Someone who wanted to see what was in there,' Vargas said, and turned to look at the other man's face. A note of satisfaction crept into his voice as he added, 'Probably Americans. Perhaps CIA.'

The professor looked startled, as if the possibility had not crossed his mind.

'Come, come, Professor, don't tell me you thought your work here in Cuba would remain a secret forever.'

'I am a scientist,' the American said. 'Science is my life.'

Vargas snorted derisively. 'Your life!' he said softly, contemptuously.

The professor lost it. 'Fool!' he shouted. 'Idiot! You sit in this Third World cesspool and think this crap matters – *fool!*'

'Perhaps,' Vargas said coldly. He was used to Professor Svenson, an unrepentant intellectual snob, the very worst kind, and American to boot. 'I would like to stay and trade curses with you today but there is no time. The workers are waiting outside. You are going to show them how to clean up the lab, then you will determine exactly what happened to the viruses. You will write down all that must be done to check the warheads. You will have the report hand-delivered to me. If you fail to do exactly what I say, you will go into the crematorium with the lab worker. Do you understand me, Professor?'

'You can't threaten me. I'm –'

Alejo Vargas flicked his fingers across the professor's cheek, merely a sting. He stared into his eyes. 'You suffer from a regrettable delusion that you are irreplaceable – *I* can cure that. If you wish, you can go to the crematorium right now. Two body bags are not much more trouble than one.'

When Vargas left, Olaf Svenson sat and hid his face in his hands.

He had never thought past the scientific problems to the ones he now faced. Oh, he should have, of course: he knew that Vargas intended to put the virus into warheads. He shut his mind to the horror – he wanted to see if the mutation could be controlled. No, he wanted to see if *he* could control the mutation of the viruses. The scientific challenges consumed him. Vargas had the money and the facilities – Olaf Svenson wanted to do the research.

He was going to have to get out of Cuba, and as soon as possible. The university thought he was in Europe – that was where he would go. The CIA probably had no evidence, or not enough to prosecute him in an American court. If he went to the airport and took a plane now they probably would never get enough – Vargas certainly wasn't going to be a willing witness.

He waited a few minutes, long enough for Vargas to clear off upstairs, then stood and took a last fleeting look at the lab. With a sigh he turned his back on what might have been and walked to the elevator. In the lobby he took the time to give detailed instructions to the workers who would clean up the lab, answered the foreman's questions, then watched as they boarded the elevator. When the elevator door closed behind the workers, Professor Svenson nodded to the guards at the entrance of the building, set off down the street and never looked back.

The P-3 Orion antisubmarine patrol plane flew over a sparkling sea. The morning cumulus clouds would form in the trade winds in a few hours, but right now the sky was empty except for wisps of high stratus.

The glory of the morning held no interest for the P-3's crew, which was examining an old freighter anchored in the lee of an L-shaped cay. A few palm trees and some thick brush covered the backbone of the little island, which had wide, white, empty beaches on all sides.

'Whaddya think?' the pilot asked his copilot and the TACCO, the tactical coordinator, who was standing behind the center console.

'Go lower and we'll get pictures,' the TACCO suggested. He passed a video camera to the copilot.

The pilot retarded the throttles and brought the plane around in a wide, sweeping turn to pass down the side of the freighter at an altitude of about two hundred feet. The copilot kept the video camera on the freighter, which was fairly small, about ten thousand tons, with peeling paint and a rusty waterline. A few sailors could be seen on deck, but no flags were visible.

'I'll get on the horn,' the TACCO told the pilot, 'see if the folks in Norfolk can identify that ship. But first let's fly over the ship, get the planform from directly overhead.'

The TACCO knew that the computer sorted ship images by silhouettes and planforms, so having both views would speed up the identification process.

Professor Olaf Svenson was standing in line at Havana airport to buy a ticket to Mexico City when he saw Colonel Santana arrive out front in a chauffeur-driven limousine. Through the giant windows he could clearly see Santana get out of the car, see the uniformed security guards salute, see the plainclothes security men with Santana move tourists out of the way.

Svenson turned and rushed away in the other direction. He dove into the first men's room he saw and took refuge in an empty stall.

Was Santana after him?

The acrid smell of a public rest room filled his nostrils, permeated his clothing, made him feel unclean. He sat listening to the sounds: the door opening and closing as men came and went, feet scraping, water running, piss tinkling into urinals, muttered comments. Sweat trickled down his neck, soaking his shirt.

Slam! Someone aggressively pushed the rest room door open until it smashed against the wall.

The minutes crawled.

Santana was an animal, Svenson thought, a sadist, a foul, filthy creature who loved to see fellow human beings in pain. Svenson had seen it in his eyes. Even the smallest of bad tidings was delivered with a malicious gleam. Svenson suspected that as a boy Santana had enjoyed torturing pets.

What would Santana do to an overweight, middle-aged scientist from Colorado who tried to escape the country?

The door slammed into the wall again, and Svenson jumped.

Torture? Of course. Santana would want to inflict pain. Svenson felt his bowels get watery as he thought about the pain that Santana could dish out.

Every sound caused him to move, to jump.

He consulted his watch again. Just a few minutes had passed.

O God, if you really exist, have mercy on me! Don't let Santana find me. Please!

Home. He wanted to go home so badly. To his apartment and cats and flowers in planters. To his neat, safe little haven, where he could shut out the evil of the world.

Someone slapped the side of the stall, said something unintelligible in Spanish. Probably wanted him to hurry up, to get out and let the next man in.

Svenson made a retching sound. And almost lost his breakfast.

He tried retching audibly again, less forcefully.

The person standing beside the stall walked away, the door to the rest room opened and closed.

Where was Santana?

Maybe he wasn't coming. Surely by now if he were searching the terminal he would have looked into this restroom.

Could it be?

Or perhaps Santana was standing outside, waiting for him to come out, for the sheer joy of dashing his hopes when he thought the coast was clear. Santana would do a thing like that, Svenson told himself now.

He felt so dirty, so wretched. He wiped at the sheen of sweat on his face, wiped his hands on his trousers.

He watched the minute hand of his watch, watched it slowly circle the dial, counted the seconds as it moved along so effortlessly.

With every passing minute that Santana didn't come he felt better. Yes. Perhaps he wasn't looking. He must not be. If he were looking he would have been in this restroom, would have opened the door, would have jerked him from the stall and arrested him and put the cuffs on him and dragged him across the terminal and thrown him into a police car.

But Santana didn't come.

After an hour of waiting, Olaf Svenson began thinking about how he was going to get out of the country. He needed another passport. If he used his own, the security people might not let him through the immigration checkpoint.

He pulled up his pants, washed his hands thoroughly, and went out into the main hall of the terminal. Keeping an eye out for Santana, he went to the ticket desk for Mexicana Airlines and stood where he could watch the agent. When handed a passport, the man glanced up, comparing the face to the photo. Just a glance, but a glance would be enough. Using a stolen passport with a photo that didn't match his face was too much of a risk. Svenson knew he would have to use his own, dangerous though it would be.

Screwing up his courage, Olaf Svenson got in line. 'Ciudad Mejico, por favor.' He handed the passport to the agent, who glanced into his face, then handed the passport back.

An hour later Svenson went through the immigration line. The uniformed official didn't look up, merely compared the passport to a typed list that lay on his desk, then passed it back. He did not stamp the document.

Olaf Svenson took a seat in the waiting area and used a filthy handkerchief to wipe perspiration from his forehead.

A reprieve. The powers that rule the universe had granted him a reprieve.

He would have liked to have had the opportunity to study the latest viral mutation, but the risk was just too great. A lost opportunity, he concluded. Oh, too bad, too bad.

When the plane from Madrid touched down at Havana airport with Maximo Sedano aboard, Colonel Santana and two plainclothes secret police officers were there to meet him. They stood beside Maximo while he waited for his luggage, then the two junior men carried it to the car while Maximo walked beside Santana.

Colonel Santana said nothing to the finance minister, other than to say Alejo Vargas wanted to see him, then he let the bastard stew. He had learned years ago that silence was a very effective weapon, one that cost nothing and caused grievous wounds in a guilty soul. All men are guilty, Santana believed, of secret sins if nothing else, and if left to suffer in silence will usually convince themselves that the authorities know everything. After

506

a long enough silence, often all that remains to do is take down the confession and obtain a signature.

One of his troops drove while Santana rode in the back of the car with his charge. Not a word was uttered the whole trip.

Maximo seemed to be holding up fairly well, Santana thought, not sweating too much, retaining most of his color, breathing under control. The colonel smiled broadly, a smile that grew even wider when he saw from the corner of his eye that Maximo Sedano had noticed it.

Ah, yes. Silence. And terror.

The car drove straight into the basement of the Ministry of Interior, where Maximo Sedano was hustled to a subterranean interrogation room.

'I demand to see Vargas,' Maximo said hotly when they shoved him into a chair and slammed the door shut.

'You demand?' asked Santana softly, leaning forward until his face was only inches from Maximo. 'You are in no position to demand. You may ask humbly, request, you may even pray, but you don't demand. You have no right to demand anything.'

Santana seated himself behind the desk, across from Maximo. He took out the interrogation form, filled out the blanks on the top of the sheet, then laid it on the scarred wood in front of him.

'Where,' Santana asked, 'is the money?'

Maximo Sedano inhaled through his nose. He smelled dampness, urine, something rotting, meat or vegetable perhaps ... and something cold and slimy and evil. It was here, all around him, in this room – the very stones reeked of it. Before Castro the secret police belonged to Fulgencio Batista, and before him Geraldo Machado, and so on, back for hundreds of years. This was a secret room that never saw the light, where justice did not exist, where force and venality and self-interest ruled. Here shadow men without conscience or scruple wrestled with the enemies of the dictator. The room reeked of fear and blood, torture and maiming, pain and death.

Maximo pushed the images aside. With a tenuous composure, carefully, completely, honestly, he explained about the accounts and the German and the people at the bank. He related what they said to the best of his memory. He told about the ice pick and the men's room, everything, withholding only his intention of transferring the money to his own accounts.

Santana had questions, of course, made him repeat most of it two or three times. When the colonel had it all written down, Maximo signed the statement.

'Where are the transfer cards?' Santana asked.

'In Switzerland. I left them at the bank.'

'Why?'

'If there has been some mistake, if the money was stolen by someone at the bank, then the banks have valid, legal transfer orders they must honor. They must send the money to the Bank of Cuba.'

'So where is the money?'

'It is not in those accounts, obviously. I think the money has been stolen.'

For the first time, Santana was openly skeptical. 'By whom?'

'By someone who had access to the account numbers. *El Presidente* insisted on keeping a record of them in his office. I would look there first.'

'Why not your office? Is it not possible one of your aides learned the numbers, passed them to someone who – ?'

'All the numbers of the government's foreign accounts, including the accounts controlled exclusively by *el Presidente,* are kept in a safe in my office under my exclusive control. None of my staff has access – only me.'

Again Santana smiled. 'You realize, of course, that you are convicting yourself with your own mouth?'

Maximo threw up his hands. 'I tell you this, Santana. I do not have the money. If I had fifty-four million dollars I would not have taken the plane back to Cuba. I would not be sitting in this shithole talking to a shithead like you.'

Santana ignored the insult and jotted a few more lines on his report. Personally he believed Maximo – if the man had the money he would have run like a rabbit – but to say so would give Maximo too much leverage. And Maximo said that he killed a man with an ice pick, which certainly seemed out of character. Santana raised an eyebrow as he thought about Rall. Maximo Sedano killing Rall – well, the world is full of unexpected things.

He left Maximo Sedano sitting in the chair in the interrogation room while he went to find Vargas. The minister was in his office listening to a report of the laboratory burglary from one of the senior colonels, who had just returned from the university.

Santana knew nothing of the burglary, had not been informed before he went to the airport. He stood listening, asked no questions, waited for Alejo Vargas.

An hour passed before Vargas was ready to talk about Maximo. 'He is downstairs in an interrogation room,' Santana said. 'Here is his statement.' He passed it across. Vargas read it in silence.

'The money is not in the accounts,' Vargas said finally.

'So he says.'

'And you think he is telling the truth?'

'Sir, I don't think Maximo Sedano has what it takes to steal that kind of money and come back here to face you. He knew he would be met at the airport. He was expecting it.'

Vargas said nothing, merely blinked.

'Actually, his suggestion about the account numbers at the president's residence is a good one. If there was a leak, it was probably there. Fidel probably left the book lying around – he had no organizational sense.'

'And?'

'I know of no one in Cuba with the computer expertise to get into the

Swiss banks electronically and steal that money, but there are plenty of people in America who could. A lot of them work for the American government.'

'People were stealing money from banks long before computers were invented,' Vargas objected. 'Anybody could have bribed a bank officer and stolen that money. The Yanquis are the most likely suspects, however.'

Vargas well knew that everything that went wrong south of Key West was not the fault of the United States government, but he was too old a dog to think that the people who ran the CIA were incompetent dullards too busy to give Cuba a thought.

'The Americans say that shit happens.'

'They often make it happen,' Vargas agreed, and stood up. 'Let us talk to Maximo. Perhaps we can save a soul from hell.'

Going down the stairs Vargas said to Santana, 'Maximo has been plotting to get himself elected president when Castro passes. Today would be a good time to let him know that such a course is futile.'

'Yes, sir.'

'Some pain, I think. Nothing permanent, nothing life threatening. We will need his expertise in finance later on.'

'Yes, sir.'

A petty officer came to find Jake Grafton. The sailor led the admiral to the Air Intelligence spaces, where he found Toad and the AIs gathered around a television monitor.

'A P-3 took this sequence a few hours ago,' Toad told the admiral, 'in the Bahamas. It's an anchored North Korean freighter. The P-3 is going to fly directly overhead here in a minute and get a shot looking straight down. We'll freeze the video there.'

The perspective changed as the plane came across the top of the ship. The clear blue water seemed to disappear, leaving the ship suspended above the yellow sandy bottom. Just before the P-3 crossed above the ship, Toad froze the picture.

He stepped forward, pointing to dark shapes resting on the sand under the freighter. 'I think we've found the rest of the stolen warheads,' he said. 'The people on the *Colón* dumped them here in the ocean for the North Koreans to pick up later.'

Jake stepped forward, studied the picture on the television screen. 'Can this picture be computer enhanced?'

'They are working on that in Norfolk right now.'

'How certain are they about the identification of the ship?'

'Very sure. Undoubtedly North Korean.'

When the National Security Council met to be briefed about developments in Cuba, the president's mood was even uglier than it had been a few days before. He listened with a frozen frown as the briefer described the biological warfare research laboratory in the science building at the University of Havana. He covered his face with a hand as the briefer explained that some of the warheads from *Nuestra Señora de Colón* appeared to be resting on a sandy ocean floor in the Bahamas, with a North Korean freighter anchored nearby.

'The good news,' the briefer said brightly, 'is that the freighter seems to be in Bahamian territorial waters.'

'Do you have a plan?' the president asked General Totten.

'Yes, sir. At our request, the Bahamians have formally requested that a United States ship board and search the North Korean freighter, which has violated their territorial waters. The nearest US ship will be there in three hours.'

'And if the North Koreans raise the anchor and sail away?'

'We'll stop the ship anyway, remove any United States government property that we find.'

'Another international incident!' the president grumped. 'The North Koreans will shout bloody murder, then the Cubans will join the chorus.'

The national security adviser jumped right in. 'Sir, the Cubans can't prove we had CBW warheads in Gitmo.'

'Can't prove? If Fidel Castro doesn't have a stolen artillery shell on his desk right now I'll kiss your ass at high noon on the Capitol steps while CNN –'

'Sir, we think –'

'*Let me finish!* Don't interrupt! I'm the guy the congressmen are going to fry when they hear about this fiasco. Let me finish.'

Silence.

The president swallowed once, adjusted his tie. 'And now,' he said, trying to keep the acid out of his voice, 'we learn the Cubans have a biological weapons lab in a building in the heart of Havana, at the university there. Is that correct?'

'Yes, sir.'

'What I would like to know is this: Have the Cubans got any way of using biological weapons on the United States right now? Today? Have they got a delivery system?'

'Sir, we don't know.'

'Well, by God, in my nonmilitary opinion we ought to find out just as fast as we can. Does anybody in this room agree with that proposition?'

'Yes, sir.'

'Another thing I want to know: Somebody explain again how the goddamned Chemical Weapons Treaty will make countries like Cuba decide not to build biological and chemical weapons.'

The silence that followed that question was broken by the chairman of the joint chiefs, General Tater Totten:

'The Chemical Weapons Convention Agreement won't dissuade anyone who wants these weapons from building them. All it will do is force us to rid ourselves of the weapons that deter others from using these things. Chemical and biological weapons are only employed when a user believes his enemy cannot or will not retaliate in kind. Your staff knew that and wanted the treaty anyway so that you could brag about it on the stump and win votes from soccer moms who don't know shit from peanut butter.'

The president eyed General Totten sourly, then surveyed the rest of them. 'At least somebody around here has the guts to tell it like it is,' he muttered.

The chairman continued: 'Doing the right thing isn't the same as getting the right result. We could use more of the latter and less of the former, if you ask me.'

'Don't push it, General,' the president snarled.

The gray-haired general motored on as if the president hadn't said a word. 'To get back to your question, of course the Cubans have a delivery system, or several. Biological weapons are the easiest of all weapons to employ. The delivery system could be as simple as planes rigged to spray microorganisms into the atmosphere: after all, Cuba is just ninety miles south of Key West; jets could be over Florida in minutes. Or a few teams of Cuban saboteurs could induce the toxins into the water supply systems of major cities – tens of millions of people could be infected before anyone figured out there was even a problem.'

Here was the classic dilemma: The US was prepared to fight a nuclear war to the finish and lick anyone on the planet in a conventional war. Hundreds of billions of dollars had been spent on networks and communications, on precision weapons and missile systems, on an army, navy and air force that were the best equipped, trained, and led armed forces on earth. So if there were an armed conflict, no sane enemy would confront the United States on a conventional or nuclear battlefield: guerrilla warfare and terror weapons were the alternatives.

'What the Cubans probably don't have,' General Totten continued, 'is the engineering and industrial capacity to turn tankfuls of toxins into true weapons, weapons that are safe to handle, can be stored indefinitely, and aimed precisely. That's why they want to get their hands on that shipload of biological warheads.'

'So how do we prevent the use of CBW weapons?' the president asked.

'You have to deter the bad guys,' Tater Totten explained. 'You have to be willing to do it to them worse than they can do it to you. And they have to know that you will.'

'You're saying that if the Cubans murder ten million Americans, we have to kill every human in Cuba?'

'That's right. Mutually assured destruction.'

'M-A-D.'

'Insane. But there is no other way. If these people think you lack the resolve to retaliate in kind, you just lost the war.'

'If anyone kills Americans we will retaliate,' the president said. 'That's been US policy since George Washington took the oath of office.'

The general concentrated on straightening a paper clip, then bending it into a new shape.

Finally, when the president had had his say, when the national security adviser had summed up the situation, the chairman spoke again: 'The agent in Havana who found the lab had a request. It was in the last paragraph of his message this morning. Mr Adviser, do you wish to discuss it?'

The adviser obviously didn't wish to discuss it; he could have raised the point at any time during the meeting and hadn't. A flash of irritation crossed his face, then he said, 'I've gone over that request with the staff, and with State, ah, and both staff and State feel it is completely out of bounds.'

'What request?' the president asked curtly.

'Sir, staff and State feel the request is absolutely out of the question; I struck it from the agenda.'

'What request?' the president repeated with some heat.

'The agent wants Operation Flashlight to happen at one-thirty A.M. tomorrow,' Tater Totten said.

'And that is?' the president said, frowning.

'He wants the power grid in central Havana knocked out.'

'Oh. Now I remember. You want to blow some high-voltage towers.'

'That's correct, sir. This operation was discussed and approved three weeks ago.'

'Oh, no. Three weeks ago I gave a tentative approval, tentative only. Sabotage of a power network of a foreign nation is a damn serious matter. Back when I was in school we called that an act of war.'

'It still is,' the national security adviser said. He was something of a suck-up, General Totten thought.

'I think this matter deserves more discussion,' the president said.

'Yes, sir.'

'What happens if the people setting these charges are arrested?'

The director of the CIA reluctantly stepped in. 'Sir, that is one of the inherent risks of clandestine operations. The men who set the charges know the risks. We know the risks. The fact is that the possible gains here make the risks worth running. That's the same cost-benefit analysis we make before we authorize any clandestine operation.'

'What if one of these people is arrested? Can the Cubans prove they work for the CIA?'

'No, sir. They will appear to be Cuban exiles, in Cuba creating mischief on their own hook.'

'This operation gives me a bad feeling in the pit of my stomach,' the president said. 'There are too many things going wrong all at once.'

General Totten could hold his tongue no longer. 'There is no time to be lost,' he said. 'Four vials of microorganisms taken from a biological warfare laboratory located just ninety miles south of Key West in the capital of a communist country hostile to the United States are this very minute being examined in laboratories in the Washington area. Cuba could become another Iraq, armed to the teeth with chemical and biological weapons. This nation cannot afford to let that happen. Cuba is only *ninety* miles away. The risk is simply too great.'

The president glared around the room. Looking for someone to blame, General Totten thought.

'Mr President, Flashlight will take hours to pull off,' the CIA director said. 'I've already given the order for it to proceed.'

'You've already given the order?' The president repeated the words incredulously.

'There was no time to be lost,' the director shot back. 'These things take hours to set in motion. The execution time is one-thirty A.M., less than six hours away.'

The chairman of the joint chiefs leaned forward in his chair, rested both elbows on the mahogany table. 'Mr President, we have no choice in this matter. None at all. If this administration fails to move aggressively to learn exactly what the Cuban threat is and take steps to meet it, you will almost certainly be impeached and removed from office by Congress for dereliction of duty.'

The president looked as if he were going to explode. This was a side of him the voters never saw. A control freak, like most politicians, he hated just being along for the ride. Watching the president seethe, Tater Totten knew his days on active duty were numbered. The CIA director had better start thinking about retirement, too.

'Who is our agent in Cuba?' the president demanded.

The director looked startled. Names of agents were closely held, never discussed in meetings like this. Yet he couldn't refuse to answer a direct question from the president of the United States. 'Sir, if you need that information, I could write it on a sheet of paper.' The director grabbed a notepad and did so. He tore off the sheet, folded it once, and passed it down the table. The president put the folded paper in front of him but didn't open it.

'I want to know who authorized this man' – the president tapped on the folded paper with a finger – 'to go to Cuba to see what cesspools he could uncover.'

'Sir, this mission was authorized by this council two months ago.'

'Then why in hell didn't someone mention it when we were discussing getting our warheads home from Guantánamo Bay? Why wasn't that cargo ship escorted from pier to pier? Why in hell didn't we get those warheads

513

out of there two months ago, two years ago? *Why in hell can't you people get a goddamn grip?*

Silence followed that outburst. It was broken when the chairman said, 'Instead of fretting over the timing, let's pat ourselves on the back for being smart enough to have an agent in Havana. It's the Cubans' weapons lab, not ours.'

When Tater Totten walked out of the room, he still had his letter of resignation from the joint chiefs in his pocket. He had prepared it when the national security adviser struck Operation Lightbulb from the agenda. Maybe he should have laid the letter on the president and retired to the golf course before these fools drove this truck off the cliff. He had no doubt the mess in Cuba was about to blow up in their faces, and soon.

The American warship nearest the unnamed cay where the North Korean freighter was anchored was a destroyer out of Charleston, South Carolina, manned by naval reservists on their annual two-week tour of active duty. The destroyer had been on its way to Nassau for a weekend port call when the flash message rolled off the printer.

The destroyer's flank speed was 34 knots, and she was making every knot of it now as she thundered down the Exuma Channel with a bone in her teeth.

From five thousand feet Jake Grafton could see the destroyer plainly even though it was twenty miles away. And he could see the wake lengthening behind the North Korean freighter, *Wonsan*.

'Damn scow is getting under way,' Rita said disgustedly. She was flying the V-22. 'It'll be in international waters long before the destroyer gets there.'

'Wonder how many warheads they pulled out of the water?'

'We're going to find out pretty soon,' Jake muttered. 'If this guy stops and lets us board him, he won't have a warhead aboard. If he refuses to heave to, he's got a bunch.'

'What are you going to do, Admiral, if he refuses to stop?'

Jake Grafton didn't have an answer to that contingency, nor did he want to make the decision. If that eventuality came to pass he would ask for guidance from Washington, pass the buck along to people who would probably refer it to the politicians.

'The *Wonsan* is turning northeast,' Rita observed. 'She'll probably go between Cat Island and San Salvador.'

'Let's go down,' Jake Grafton said, 'hover in front of this guy, see if he'll stop.' He was sitting on the flight engineer's seat just aft of the pilots.

Five minutes later the Osprey was in helicopter flight with the rotors tilted up, descending gently in front of the *Wonsan*, which was up to five or six knots now. Jake Grafton could see four people on the bridge, standing close together and gesturing at the Osprey. The copilot was watching the clearance, telling Rita how much maneuvering room she had.

'Closer,' Jake said.

Rita Moravia kept the Osprey moving in. Luckily the wind was from the west, so she could keep the twin-rotor machine on the starboard side of the freighter, yet pointed right at the bridge. This kept the wind on her starboard quarter.

She stopped when the distance between her cockpit and the bridge glass was about fifty yards. The right rotor was still well above the top of the freighter's crane, which was mounted amidships.

'Closer,' Jake said again, 'but watch your clearance.'

The copilot glanced nervously at Jake. 'Give me clearance,' Rita snapped at him, which brought him back to the job at hand.

She maneuvered the Osprey until it was completely on the starboard side of the *Wonsan*, then she dropped it until she could see the length of the bridge.

The captain – he might have been the captain, wearing a dirty, white bridge cap – stepped through the door of the bridge onto the wing and stood looking into the cockpit, fifteen feet away. He had his hands pressed against his ears, trying to deaden the mighty roar of the two big engines. The downwash from the rotors raised a storm of sea spray, which was soaking him, and now it carried away his hat.

'Closer,' Jake said one more time.

'The air is sorta bumpy coming around this superstructure.'

'Yeah,' the admiral said.

Ten feet separated the nose of the V-22 from the rail of the bridge wing. Rita eased the Osprey forward a foot at a time, until the refueling probe and three barrels of the turreted fifty-caliber machine gun that protruded from the nose were no more than eighteen inches from the rail.

'Aim the gun at the captain,' Jake said.

The copilot flipped a switch, then looked at the captain's head, and the machine gun faithfully tracked, following the aiming commands sent to it from the gunsight mounted on the copilot's helmet.

The captain's face was now less than ten feet from Jake Grafton's. He was balding, a bit overweight, in his late fifties. The rotor wash lashed at him and tore at his sodden clothes, making it difficult for him to keep his footing. Groping for a rail to steady himself against the fierce wind, he looked at the three-barreled machine gun, which tracked him like a living thing, then at Jake Grafton on the seat behind the Osprey pilots.

The captain turned and shouted something over his left shoulder; he held on with both hands as he went through the door onto the enclosed bridge.

'Watch it,' Jake muttered into his lip mike. 'This guy may be fool enough to turn into you.'

Rita was the first to realize what was happening. She felt the need to turn left to hold position. 'The ship is slowing,' she said. 'I think he's stopped his engines.'

In a few seconds it became obvious that she was correct. Rita backed away until the distance between the cockpit and ship was about fifty feet.

'I think he lost his nerve, Admiral.'

'Look at the stuff on his deck,' the copilot said, pointing. 'Looks like he pulled up a bunch of warheads.'

The freighter was drifting when the destroyer arrived a half hour later and coasted to a stop several hundred yards away. In minutes the destroyer had a boat in the water.

When armed Americans were standing on the *Wonsan*'s deck, Jake tapped Rita on the shoulder.

'Let's go home.'

'I listened to the tape from Alejo Vargas's office this afternoon,' Carmellini said to Chance. They were walking the Prado looking for a place to eat dinner. To have a decent selection and palatable food, the restaurant would have to be a hard-currency place. Although the best restaurants were in ramshackle houses in Old Havana, tonight Chance wanted music, laughter, people.

'Someone told Vargas all about the break-in at the university lab, the contamination, the dead lab worker. They spent most of the day running the fans at the lab, trying to lower the count of the stuff in the air before they went in.'

'What did they say about the dead man, why he died?'

'That had them stumped. He was vaccinated. They called in a Professor Svenson.'

'Olaf Svenson?'

'No one used a first name.'

'It must be him. I've heard of him. Damned potty old fool. He was at Cal Tech for years. Thought he was at Colorado now. A genius, almost won a Nobel Prize.' He snapped his fingers. 'That photo we gave Bouchard – that must have been Svenson.'

'Well, he is their main man down at the lab, to hear the conversation at Vargas's office.'

'So why did the lab worker die? Wasn't he vaccinated?'

'The stuff mutated, according to the professor. Mutated again, he said.'

'Well, what the hell is it? Did they say that?'

'Some kind of polio.'

'Polio doesn't kill that quickly,' Chance objected.

'This kind does. The lab worker wasn't the first, apparently. The professor wanted to dissect him like the others but Vargas ordered the body burned immediately.'

They paused on a corner, watched the people who filled the sidewalks under the crumbling buildings. Just down the walk to the left a Cuban was trying to sell trinkets to a pair of Germans and having no luck. To the right a tall young white guy, American or Canadian probably, was locked in a passionate embrace with a local girl.

'Sun, sex, and socialism,' Carmellini muttered. 'Makes you wonder why there aren't more Cubans.'

Chance closed his eyes, enjoyed the caress of the breeze on his face and hair. He could hear snatches of music amid the honk of car horns and traffic sounds. Havana was very much alive this evening, as it was every evening.

Finally he opened his eyes, looked again at the Cubans and tourists swirling about him. And Carmellini standing there, quite nonchalant, looking bored.

'Do they have any ideas about who broke in?'

'Americans. CIA scum. No evidence, but they're sure.'

Chance nodded.

'There was talk,' Carmellini continued, 'of rounding up likely suspects, doing some thorough interrogations, just to see what might turn up. That was Colonel Santana's suggestion: apparently he is a rare piece of work. Vargas overruled him. Said they couldn't torture tourists every time the CIA did something they didn't like or soon they wouldn't have any tourists.'

'Sensible.'

'Anything else?'

Carmellini shrugged, scratched his chin. 'I listened to almost three hours' worth of that stuff, and you know, they didn't mention Fidel Castro even once.'

'Didn't say his name?'

'Nope. And the technician said he hadn't heard them mention Castro all day.'

'Curious.'

'It's odd. I would have thought –'

After a bit Chance said, 'The lab is just the tip of the iceberg. There must be machinery for drying out the cultures, for packing the microorganisms into warheads or mixing them into some sort of chemical stew to be sprayed from planes. There must be trucks that transport this stuff from place to place. And then there are the weapons: where the hell are they?'

They went into one of the nightclubs and found an empty table. Six whores were sitting around the table beside them. The girls were drinking daiquiris and having a fine, loud time. One of the girls looked the two men over while the band tuned up just a few feet away.

'Washington wants more information,' Carmellini said, ignoring the whores.

'They would.' Chance chewed on his lip for a bit, then picked up the wine list. 'Tonight's the night we go into Vargas's safe. Are you comfortable with that?'

Carmellini took his time answering. Chance was about to repeat the question when he said, 'If the alarms are off.'

'They'll be off.'

'Sure.'

'Trust me.'

When the waiter came they ordered dinner.

'So tell me again about the Ministry of Interior,' Carmellini said. 'Everything you can recall. Everything.'

Chance leaned back, closed his eyes, tried to visualize how the building looked when he had stepped from the taxi out front on his way to his meeting with Alejo Vargas.

'There is a guard kiosk out front on the sidewalk. You then walk through the front entrance to the guard station inside. They check your credentials again, call whoever you say you want to see. This person comes to get you, leads you through the halls to the office you are to visit.'

'Cameras?'

'Security cameras mounted high in corners, monitored by the main guard station. There are two separate systems, at least, with pictures playing on separate monitors.'

'Infrared sensors?'

'I think so. . . .' The fact is he should have paid more attention. Looked more carefully, consciously noted what he was seeing. 'Yes, I remember seeing one.'

'Motion detectors?'

'No.'

'Laser alarms?'

'Yes, mounted at ankle height.' Presumably these were only on when the building was not occupied.

'Alarms on the windows?'

'Yes.'

'Vibrators on the glass?'

'No.' If there had been vibrators, the computer would have had a much more difficult job sorting out the voices from the electronic noise of the vibrators when it tried to read the light refracted by the crystals.

'Were there internal security doors, doors that might be closed when the building is not occupied?'

'Yes. Every hall had them, but I doubt they were ever used.'

'And internal security stations?'

'I saw none.'

Carmellini thought about it. Closed security doors made a burglar's access more difficult, but they provided a peaceful, quiet place for a burglar to work once he had gained entry.

'Do they have backup power when the power goes off?' Carmellini mused.

'They must,' Chance replied thoughtfully. 'A backup generator of some type. I'm going to walk in assuming that they do, but I'll be improvising as I go.'

'We'll sure as hell find out soon enough, won't we,' Carmellini said, and grinned. That was the first grin he had managed all afternoon. The death of the lab worker had hit him hard, but the cool execution of the guard at the front door by William Henry Chance had hit him like a punch to the solar plexus. Chance just gunned the man down and kept on trucking, as if killing another human being were something he did every morning before lunch.

All evening Carmellini had studied the older man, watched him for a sign that the murder of the guard was anything more than absolutely routine. And he had seen nothing. Nothing at all. Chance looked as if he might be having dinner in a restaurant in the Bronx with a Yankees game from a kitchen radio as background noise.

Carmellini stared at the food on the plate that the waiter put in front of him. He didn't want a mouthful. But what he wouldn't give for a stiff drink! He sipped at a glass of water, felt his stomach knot up.

'Order a drink,' Chance said as he used his knife and fork. 'One. Something on the rocks. You need it. We have a long night ahead.'

Carmellini looked around for the waiter, and found himself staring at one of the whores at the next table, who gave him a big grin. He grinned back. A man just has to keep things in perspective.

13

The sun had been down for several hours when Enrique Poveda and Arquimidez Cabrera drove up to the fourth EHV tower they hoped to blow. After a quick look around, they unlocked the padlock on the gate and put on their tool belts. Each of the men picked a tower leg and started up. About ten feet above the ground they found the shaped charges of C-4 plastique still firmly taped to the steel legs. Working in the darkness by feel, each man took a chemical timer from his belt, a device about the size and shape of a fountain pen, and inserted it into the plastique. The timer was already set to explode as near to 1:30 A.M. as possible.

After setting the timers, they climbed down to the ground, then ascended the other two legs. In minutes they were back on the ground.

They locked the padlock, closed up the back of the van, and drove away.

'One more,' Poveda said. He wished he had a map or diagram, but all that had been left behind in Florida. There he and Cabrera and the US Army power grid expert had labored for days over satellite reconnaissance photos, photographs taken from the ground by not-so-innocent tourists, and computer-generated diagrams. They selected the target towers and committed their locations to memory. Not a single sheet of paper left the room with them.

So now Cabrera pointed down one street and Poveda motioned toward another. The men chuckled. 'I am very sure,' Poveda said. 'Two blocks down, right turn, then on for a half mile.'

'Okay.'

'I am glad it was tonight,' Cabrera said. 'The charges had been in place too long, the new padlocks were there too long, I was getting nervous – you know what I mean, my friend?'

Poveda grunted. He knew. His stomach felt as if it were tied in a knot. He hadn't felt this uptight about an operation since his first one, fifteen years ago, when he was very young. He had been to Cuba many times since, eight as he recalled, and none of them were as tense as that first time, until now.

The Cubans had almost caught him and his partner that time. The partner was eventually caught six years later and died under interrogation, or so they heard months after that. Poveda had promised himself then and there that he would never be taken alive, that he would not die in a Cuban prison.

Communists! He made a spitting motion out the open window. The communists took everything from the people in Cuba who had worked and saved and built for the future, and gave it to the people who had not. Now look at the place! Everyone poor, everyone on the edge of starvation, the cities and towns and factories rotting from lack of investment. The communists ran off the people who could make Cuba grow, the people the nation needed to feed everyone else. Ah, these bastards deserved their misery, and by God they had had some. Universal destitution was Castro's legacy, his gift to generations yet unborn.

Poveda was a pessimist. He knew that soon Castro would be dead and things would change in Cuba. 'They'll forget Fidel's faults, remember just the good,' he told Cabrera, for the hundredth time. 'You wait and see. In a hundred years the church will make him a saint.'

'Saint Fidel.' Cabrera laughed.

'I shit you not. That is the way of the world. The people he pissed on the most will call him blessed.'

'Saint or devil, we'll fuck the son of a bitch a little tonight,' Cabrera said as the van pulled up to the last tower.

Poveda killed the van's engine and lights and the two men got out. Silence.

'Awful quiet, don't you think?' Poveda asked.

Cabrera stood by the van's rear doors, listening, looking around. Poveda dug in his pocket for the key to the padlock, inserted it.

It wouldn't fit. He tried another.

'What's wrong?'

'Key doesn't seem to want to go in this lock.'

'Let's get the fuck outta here, man,' Cabrera said, and started for the van's passenger door.

A spotlight hit them.

'Put up your hands,' boomed a voice on a loudspeaker.

Poveda dropped to his knees, pulled a 9-mm pistol from his pocket. He didn't hesitate – he aimed at the spotlight and started shooting.

Something hit him in the back. He was down beside the rear tire trying to rise when he realized he had been shot. People shooting from two directions, muzzle flashes, thuds of bullets smacking into the van like hailstones. A groan from Cabrera.

'I'm hit, Enrique.'

'Bad?'

'I think . . . I think so.' He grunted as another bullet audibly smacked into his body.

The bullet that hit Poveda had come out his stomach. He could feel the wetness, the spreading warmth as blood poured from the exit wound. Not a lot of pain yet, but a huge gaping hole in his belly.

He lifted the pistol, pointed it at Arquimidez Cabrera, his best friend. There, he could see the back of his head. He fired once; Cabrera's head slammed forward into the dirt. Then he put the barrel flush against the side of his own head and pulled the trigger.

Sitting in the back of a van just down the street from the Ministry of Interior, William Henry Chance watched the second hand of his watch sweep toward the twelve. It passed 1:30 A.M. and swept on.

The lights stayed on. Carmellini was looking at his own watch.

'What the hell is wrong now?' Carmellini asked.

'I don't know.'

'Oh, Lord.'

They sat there in the van looking at the lights of the city.

'It went bad,' Tommy Carmellini said. 'Time for us to boogie.'

'We'll give them a few minutes.'

'Jesus, when it doesn't go down as planned, something is wrong. What are you waiting for, a phone call from Fidel? Let's bail out while our asses are still firmly attached.'

'If I had any brains I wouldn't be in this business,' Chance replied tartly.

His watch read exactly ten seconds after 1:32 A.M. when the lights of downtown Havana flickered. 'All right,' Carmellini said, and whacked his leg with his hand.

The lights flickered, dimmed, came back on, then went completely out. All the lights. Only automobile headlights broke the total darkness.

'That's it. Let's go,' Chance said to Tommy Carmellini. They opened the back of the van and climbed out while the driver of the van started the engine. Chance walked the few steps back to an old Russian Lada parked at the curb behind the van and got into the passenger seat. Carmellini started the car and turned on the headlights while the van pulled away from the curb.

The two agents drove down the street toward the Ministry of Interior, a hulking immensity even darker than the night.

The three guards at the main entrance of the Ministry were illuminated by the headlights when Tommy Carmellini drove up. He killed the engine and pocketed the key as William Henry Chance got out on the passenger side.

Of course the guards had seen Chance's uniform from the car's interior light while the door was open – now they flashed the beam of a flashlight upon him. Then they saluted.

Chance was dressed in the uniform of a Security Department colonel. He had been to the building several days ago in the daytime wearing civilian clothes: he thought it highly unlikely that anyone who had seen him then would recognize him now. It was a risk he was willing to take. Still, his stomach felt as if he had swallowed a rock as he returned the guards' salute, and spoke:

'We were just a block away when the power failed all over this district.'

'Yes, Colonel. Just a minute or two ago.'

'And you are?'

'Lieutenant Gómez, sir, the duty officer.'

'Have you taken steps to start the emergency generator, Gómez?'

'Ahh ... I was about to do so, Colonel. It is in the basement. I was waiting to see if the power would come back on immediately. Often these outages last but moments and —'

'The darkness seems widespread, Gómez. Let us start the generator.'

'Of course, Colonel.' The lieutenant began giving directions to his two enlisted men, who obviously knew nothing about the emergency generator. The lieutenant began by telling them which room the generator was in.

Chance interrupted again. 'Perhaps you would like to take them there, supervise the start-up, Lieutenant. My driver and I will guard the front entrance until you return.'

'Of course, Colonel.' With his flashlight beam leading the way, the lieutenant and the two enlisted men made for the stairs.

Carmellini opened the trunk of the car, extracted a duffel bag, which he swung over one shoulder. Without a word to Chance he disappeared into the dark interior of the building.

Carmellini took the main staircase to the top floor of the building, then strode quickly down the hall to Alejo Vargas's private office. The door was locked, of course.

Working in total darkness, Carmellini ran his hands over the door. One lock, near the handle. From the bag he extracted a small light driven by a battery unit that hooked on his belt. He donned a headband, then stuck the light to the headband with a piece of Velcro.

He checked his watch. It was 1:36 A.M.

He examined the lock, felt in the bag for his picks.

Hmmm. This one, perhaps. He inserted it into the lock.

No.

This one? Yes.

The latex gloves didn't seem to affect his feel for the lock.

Carmellini had always enjoyed pick work. The exquisite feel necessary, the patience required, the pressure of time usually, the treasure waiting to be discovered on the other side of the door ... the CIA had been a damned lucky break. Without that break he would have certainly wound up in prison sooner or later when his luck ran out, because no one's luck lasts forever.

He inserted a smaller pick, felt for the contacts ...

And twisted, using the strength of his fingers.

The bolt opened.

He stowed the picks, picked up the duffel bag, and opened the door.

Dark office, with the only light coming through the windows, the glow of headlights on the street below, somewhere the flicker of a fire.

The safe sat in the corner away from the windows. It was old, and huge, at least six feet tall, three feet wide and three feet deep. Painted on the door of the safe was a pastoral scene; above the landscape arranged in a semicircle were the words 'United Fruit Company.'

After a quick glance at the safe, Carmellini turned his attention to the rest of the room. He searched quickly and methodically. First the drawers of the desk. One of them held a pistol, one a bottle of expensive scotch whiskey and several glasses, one pens and pencils and a blank pad of paper. Several lists of names, phone numbers, addresses . . .

The lower right drawer of the desk was locked. A small, cheap furniture lock. He opened it with a knife, began examining files. The files seemed to be on senior people in the government, girlfriends, vices, lies told, bribes offered and accepted, that kind of thing.

He flipped through the files quickly, stacked them on the desk, and moved on.

The crystals were on the windowsill. A rack of books was below the window. A cursory check revealed no files peeking out between the books.

The displays of old coins didn't even rate a glance. Back before he worked for the government the coins would have made his juices flow, but not now.

On to the credenza. Many files in there. Carmellini sampled them, looking for anything on biology, weapons, strange code names. When he saw something he didn't understand he opened the file and glanced at the papers inside. People – most of these files were on people. Unfortunately Tommy didn't recognize the names. He added the files to the stack on the desk.

Now he came to the safe. They must have lifted it to this floor with a crane before the windows were installed, he thought. He checked every square inch of the exterior to see if the safe was wired. No wires.

Tommy Carmellini tried the handle.

No.

Turned the circular combination dial ever so carefully to the right, maintaining pressure on the handle. If the safe had been closed hastily, all the tumblers might not have gone home. He took his time.

No. The safe was locked.

He checked his watch. Now 1:47.

The lights would come on soon, powered by the emergency generator.

He opened the duffel bag and began extracting items. The first item he removed was a telescoping rod which he extended and positioned over the safe's combination dial; he secured it there with clamps placed on each side of the safe. Working quickly, with no lost motion, he clamped a small electric motor to the rod, then adjusted the jaws protruding from the motor so that they grasped the dial of the safe.

Other sensors were placed on the top, bottom, left, and right sides of the safe door. These sensors were held in place by magnets.

Wires led from the sensors and electric motor to a small computer, which he now took from the bag and turned on. There was one lead remaining, which he connected to a twelve-volt battery which was also in the bag.

As he waited for the computer to boot up he checked all the leads one more time. Everything okay.

Tommy Carmellini pursed his lips, as if he were whistling.

This contraption was of his own design, and with it he could open any of the older-style mechanical safes, if he were given enough time. An electrical current introduced into the door of the safe created a measurable magnetic field. The rotation of the tumblers inside the lock caused fluctuations in the field, fluctuations that were displayed on the computer screen. Finally, the computer measured the amount of electric current necessary to turn the dial of the lock; an exquisitely sensitive measurement. Using both these factors, the computer could determine the combination that would open the safe.

Sitting cross-legged in front of the safe with the computer on his lap, Carmellini tugged the latex gloves he was wearing tighter onto his hands, then manually zeroed the dial of the lock. Now he started the computer program.

The dial rotated slowly, silently, driven by the electric motor clamped to the rod. After a complete turn the dial stopped at 32. The number appeared in the upper right-hand corner of the screen. After a short pause, the dial turned to the left, counterclockwise, as Carmellini grinned happily.

In his mind's eye he could visualize the lock plates rotating, the tumblers moving. . . .

The line on the screen that tracked the magnetic field twitched unexpectedly. Carmellini frowned. He hadn't moved, the building was quiet.

Another squiggle, so insignificant he almost missed it. And another.

Someone was coming. Someone was walking softly down the hall; the sensors were picking up the shock waves of their footfalls as the waves spread out through the structure of the building.

Careful to make no noise at all, Tommy Carmellini sat the computer on the duffel bag, stood up and moved over behind the door. As he did he drew the Ruger from its holster under his shirt and thumbed off the safety, then turned off the light attached to his headband. Now he transferred the pistol to his left hand. With his right he reached into a hip pocket and extracted a sap, a flexible length of rubber with the business end weighted with lead.

The darkness appeared total as his eyes adjusted. Gradually a bit of glare from headlights faintly illuminated the room.

Carmellini had good ears, and he couldn't hear the footfalls. He could hear the tiniest whine, however, that the electric motor made as it turned the dial of the lock, the distant honking of some vehicle blocks away, and faintly, ever so faintly, the wail of a fire or police siren.

Tommy Carmellini stopped breathing, stopped thinking, stood absolutely frozen as the knob on the door slowly turned, then the door began to open.

William Henry Chance walked slowly back and forth in front of the glass doors that marked the main entrance to the Ministry. The duty officer and his two men were in the basement, doing God knows what to the emergency generator. Chance wondered how long it had been since the generator had been fueled, oiled, checked carefully, and started.

The second hand on his watch seemed frozen. He checked his watch, walked, watched cars and trucks pass by, adjusted his duty belt and pistol, reset the cap on his head, strolled some more, promised himself he wouldn't look at the luminous hands on his watch, finally peeked anyway. A minute. One lousy minute had passed.

Someone was coming along the sidewalk . . . a uniformed guard carrying an AK-47 at high port. He must be stationed at one of the side or rear entrances. The man stopped, slightly startled, when he saw Chance's figure standing in the door. Now he peered closer. And saluted.

'Sir, I am looking for the duty officer.'

'He is in the basement, starting the emergency generator. Is there someone else at your post?'

'Uh, yessir. I was coming around to check if –'

'I think you should stay at your post. The emergency power for the building will come on in a few minutes, then you can make your request of the duty officer.'

'Yes, sir. But the last time we started that thing, all the alarms went off, every one of them. The duty officer always wanted the alarms off before he turned the power back on.'

'I am sure he will take care of that. He knows the system.'

'Yessir.'

'And when was the emergency generator last used, anyway?'

'The big storm last year, sir. Eight or nine months ago, I think.'

'Go back to your post.'

'Yes, sir.' The man saluted, turned, and marched down the sidewalk. Chance could hear his footsteps for several seconds after he disappeared into the gloom.

The guy accepted him as Cuban, as had Lieutenant Gómez and his men. If they only knew the hundreds of hours of language classes that Chance had endured to learn the accent, to get it exactly right!

All in anticipation of a moment that might never come. Yet the orders did arrive, and here he was, walking around in the foyer of secret police headquarters in Havana spouting Cuban Spanish like José Martí.

He went to the guards' station, used his flashlight to examine the equipment there. The video monitors were of course blank, everything off, but where was the tape? If the power came on while he was there he didn't want to give Alejo Vargas a souvenir videotape of the men who cracked his safe.

Ah, here was the videotape machine, in this cabinet. He pushed the eject button, futilely. Without power the machine would not eject the tape that it contained. He used the Ruger – four shots into the heads of the machine.

The brass kicked out on the floor. He picked them up, pocketed them.

More pacing. Each minute was an agony of waiting.

When the power was restored to the building, he had expected the alarms to go off in Vargas's office, and to have to cover Carmellini as he made his exit. By whatever means necessary, he intended to be the only man at the main entrance when Carmellini emerged. Yet if alarms were a normal occurrence, perhaps violence would not be necessary.

The silenced Ruger rode inside his shirt under his left armpit. The pistol was an assassin's weapon, shot a .22 Long Rifle hollow-point bullet that would do minimal damage unless fired into someone's brain at point-blank range. Wounds in the limbs or body would be painful but not immediately incapacitating. The Ruger's only virtue was the silencer that dramatically muffled the report, reduced it from an ear-splitting crack to a soft, wet pop that was inaudible beyond a few feet.

He wondered how Carmellini was coming on getting the safe open. *Come on, Tommy!*

Footsteps from within the building.

Here came a flashlight.

'Ah, Colonel, the lieutenant sent me to tell you that it will not be much longer, that the generator will start very soon.'

'Yes.'

'He is having difficulty, the mechanical condition is not as it should be.'

'I understand. I have faith in your lieutenant.'

The man went back down the hallway in the direction from whence he came.

More pacing.

At least three more minutes had passed when the lieutenant came down the hallway. The occasional flicker of passing headlights revealed him to be a large, rotund man.

'I am sorry, Colonel, but we cannot make the cursed thing run.'

'No harm done, if your guards stay alert. And I can always come back tomorrow for my errand, I suppose.'

'We will stay alert, sir. Our duty is our trust.'

'You and your men have done what you can, have you not?'

'We could awaken Colonel Santana, I suppose. Perhaps he knows more about the generator than any of us.'

Chance tried to keep his voice under control. 'Colonel Santana is in the building, then?'

'Yes, sir. He came in about an hour ago. He went to his apartment on the top floor. I think he was investigating the incident of the two saboteurs that were killed near a high-voltage tower south of town.'

'A high-voltage tower? That sounds like attempted sabotage.'

'Oh, yes, sir.'

'I hadn't heard of that incident.'

'Enemies of the regime, sir. Apparently some of them were successful.'

'Santana is the very man I came to see,' Chance declared. 'Still, I did not expect to find him asleep. I suggest you give the generator one last mighty heroic effort, and if you are unsuccessful, I shall awaken Colonel Santana.'

When the doorknob had turned as far as it would go, the door to Alejo Vargas's office slowly opened. Tommy Carmellini was behind the door, still as a statue in the park, with a sap in his right hand and the silenced Ruger in his left.

Now a flashlight beam shot out, swung quickly around the room, hit the safe and swung away for an instant, then returned to the door of the safe. The apparatus Carmellini had attached to the door was quite plain in the small beam, as was the tangle of wires that ran to the computer.

Faster than he would have ever believed possible, the door smashed Tommy Carmellini in the face. The impact stunned him, threw him backward against the wall.

The man sprang into the room, swung something that smacked Carmellini in the skull and made him see stars.

He was falling, off-balance, the other man coming for him in a brutal, ferocious way, when he got the Ruger more or less pointed and began pulling the trigger as fast as he could. He could barely hear the pops.

He fell to the floor and his assailant leaped on him, began smashing him in the face with his fist, repeatedly.

Swinging his right hand with all his might, Carmellini hit the other man in the side of the head with the sap. And again.

The man was slumping, falling to the left.

Carmellini gathered his strength and smashed the man again, one more time, square in the head.

The man rolled onto the floor, slumped on his back.

Carmellini sat up, his breath coming in ragged gasps. Part of his face was numb, he was drooling from a mighty punch to the mouth.

He forced himself to his knees. He pocketed the sap, reached for the flashlight, which was lying on the floor still lit. He played the light on the face of his assailant.

Santana.

Oooh, damn!

He checked the pistol. He had fired at least five shots. A couple of the spent brass were lying near Santana, who had a bloody place on his chest, one on his neck. Hit twice, at least.

Maybe one of the little .22 bullets would kill him.

Maybe not.

Tommy Carmellini found to his surprise that he didn't care one way or the other.

He put the pistol back in its holster, wiped his face with his shirt, and went back to the computer.

The combination was right there on the screen, all three numbers. The dial wasn't moving.

He tried the handle, put some weight on it. It moved.

The safe was open!

He wiped his face on his sleeve, willed himself back to his task. First he stowed the computer and sensors and telescoping rod in his duffel bag. Then he opened the safe, examined its contents with Santana's flashlight, then turned on his headband light.

Lots of papers, files, two shelves of them. The top shelf consisted of files on people, each file had a person's name. These were the files he had come to find. He raked these into his duffel bag.

Ah, on the second shelf . . . files labeled with numbers. He looked inside one. Engineering drawings, possibly of a warhead . . .

He dumped everything that looked interesting into his duffel bag, including the stack of files on Vargas's desk.

Oh, here was a file about supplies from a Miami laboratory supply house . . . one about susceptibility studies, lethality, vaccines . . . he stuffed all these in the bag, began checking another handful.

The hell with it! He would take everything. The files on the bottom shelf might prove as interesting as those on the top. The bag would be heavy, but he could lift it. He transferred the files to the bag as quickly as he could.

When he had all the files, he hoisted the bag experimentally. Eighty pounds, at least. Room for a few more things . . .

What else did Vargas keep in his safe? A small laptop computer. Well, he certainly didn't need that anymore. Into the bag with it.

He was pawing through one of the side drawers when he sensed movement behind him.

As he turned Santana's fist grazed his jaw – his turn had been just enough to save his life. The headband and light flew away, somewhere, the little beam flashing around crazily.

He groped for his sap, swung it in a roundhouse right and connected with bone.

Santana went sideways to the floor.

No time for this! The man is too dangerous!

He pulled out the Ruger, thumbed off the safety and was ready when Santana came off the floor again. The pistol coughed.

Santana's momentum drove his body forward and he collapsed against Carmellini's feet.

The American stepped around the body. He put the pistol away, stowed the headband light, zipped the duffel bag closed.

After a quick last look around, Tommy Carmellini went to the door, made sure it would lock behind him. He came back for the duffel bag, hoisted it to his left shoulder.

Out in the dark hall, he pulled the door shut, made sure it was locked, then walked quickly down the dark hallway for the stairs.

Tommy Carmellini held the Ruger down by his leg as he descended the stair and walked across the lobby toward the shadowy figure standing in the doorway.

As he walked the lights came on. Instantly an alarm sounded, loud enough to wake the dead.

He squinted against the light. That was Chance standing in the doorway.

'Into the car, quickly now,' Chance said. The alarms were wailing and every light in the building was on, with not a soul in sight. If they could be gone before the lieutenant and his men got back up here, he wouldn't have to kill them – they couldn't have seen his face very well in the darkness.

His watch read 2:04 A.M.

Chance stood in the doorway with euphoria flooding over him while Carmellini stowed the bag in the backseat of the car, got into the driver's seat, and started the engine. Three long strides, he jerked open the passenger's door and jumped inside, and Carmellini fed gas.

The lights in the rest of the city were still off, however, so when the car pulled away from the building the night swallowed it.

'What did you get?'

'I got the safe open – took two drawers full of files, everything made of paper that was in there, some files from a desk. Got a laptop, too.'

'Well done.'

'Someone came in while I was there. Santana, I think. Left him for dead.'

'Was he dead?'

'I didn't take the time to check, and to be honest, I really don't care one way or the other. I put six bullets into the son of a bitch and whaled on him a while with the sap. If he isn't dead he ought to be.'

Chance flipped on the interior light of the car, just long enough to check Carmellini's face. 'Looks like he got a piece or two of you.'

'Oh, yeah. He was damned quick.'

'Did he get a look at your face?'

'I don't think so. Pretty dark. And he's probably dead. Don't sweat it.'

Chance grunted and stared out the window at the dark, decaying city.

The voyagers on the *Angel del Mar* saw a ship during the night. It came out of one dark corner of the universe and passed within a half mile of the derelict as the people aboard shouted and waved the single working flashlight.

The ship was a freighter of some type, huge, with lights strung all over the topside and superstructure. It raced through their world and disappeared into the void as quickly as it came, leaving the people gasping on deck, exhausted, starved, devoid of hope.

A child had died earlier in the evening, just at sunset, and some of the people aboard had wanted to eat it. 'She is beyond caring, and her body can give us life,' one man said, a sentiment several agreed with.

The old fisherman went below to tell Ocho, who was taking his turn on the pump, which meant he had to pump out the water that had accumulated because the man before him could not keep abreast of it, as well as the water that came in on his watch. He was on the ragged edge of total exhaustion, but he listened to the old fisherman as he struggled with the pump handle.

'Maybe . . .' Ocho began, but the old man would not listen.

'To eat her would be sacrilege, the moral death of every one who tastes her flesh or watches others eat it. All flesh must die, but to face God with that on our souls would be unforgivable. Come with me! *Come!*'

He half dragged Ocho up the ladder. Together they swung hard fists left and right, reached the corpse, and tossed it into the sea.

In the fading light the old fisherman stood with his back to the wheelhouse and shouted at the others, some too weak to move. He damned them, dared them, kicked at those who came too close, punched one man so hard he nearly went overboard.

The child's body floated, supported by the great vast moving ocean, just out of reach, moving with the rise and fall of the swells. Some of the people looked at it, others refused to. When the last of the light faded the body disappeared into the total darkness.

Ocho went back down the ladder to the hold, which reeked of vomit and filth. He worked the pump handle like an automaton.

Finally the fisherman relieved him, helped him up the ladder.

He was lying by a scupper when the ship went by. He roused himself, stood with a hand on the rail, tried to shout and found he had no voice left.

Then someone tried to push him overboard.

There was no mistake. The hard shove in the back, the continuing pressure.

Only his raw strength saved him. Ocho turned and swung blindly, felt his fist connect with cartilage and bone, swung several more times before the man went down.

Ocho collapsed from the exertion. He crawled forward, intent on beating the man as long as he had strength to swing his fists, but Dora was there, sobbing, and stopped him.

'No, no, no, my God!' she howled. 'You are killing him!'

'He tried to shove me over.'

'Oh, damn you, Ocho. If it weren't for you, we would be safe in Cuba.'

'Me?'

'You were his ticket out. You! This is your fault.'

'And you are blameless. With the baby in your body you risked your life.'

'I am not pregnant! I have never been pregnant! He made me tell you I was so you would come.' And she dissolved in sobbing.

Ocho lay in the darkness trying to think, trying to see the boat and the people as God must see them, looking down from above.

Fortunately rain fell occasionally, enough to fill the bucket and let people drink. Maybe God was sending the showers.

He was starving, though, and oh so tired.

His whole life had dissolved into nothing and was soon to end, and he didn't care. He tried to tell Dora that it didn't matter but he couldn't and she was sobbing hysterically, and in truth he really didn't care.

After another turn at the pump, Ocho came back on deck and looked for Diego and Dora, to say something – he didn't know what – but something that would make their burdens easier to carry.

But Diego wasn't there. He wasn't in the hold and he wasn't in the wheelhouse and he wasn't on deck. Ocho scanned the sea, checking in all directions, looking for a head bobbing amid the heaving swells.

Dora was curled in a ball near the bow. He shook her.

'Where's Diego?'

She had a dazed look on her face, as if she didn't understand the words. He repeated the question several times.

She looked around, trying to understand.

'I do not see him,' Ocho said, trying to explain. 'Did he fall overboard?'

She stared at him with eyes that refused to focus. Her face was vacant, blank. Finally her eyes focused.

'He climbed the rail last night. Jumped in the ocean.'

Ocho looked again on both sides of the boat, staggered to the port side so he could look aft past the wheelhouse. Then he returned.

She was lying down again, curled up, her chin against a knee.

He left her there, laid down and tried to rest.

14

'Who did this to you?'

Alejo Vargas asked the question of Colonel Santana while he lay on a gurney in the hospital emergency room being prepped for surgery. He had four bullets in him and a wicked wound on his forehead where a bullet had ricochetted off his skull. His jaw and one cheekbone were severely swollen, his nose smashed, he had lost two teeth, and he obviously had a concussion. The pupil in his right eye was dilated and refused to focus.

'I don't know,' Santana managed. He tried to swallow, almost choked on his tongue. After gagging several times, he seemed to relax.

'American?'

'I do not know. Nothing was said, it was dark. He was waiting behind the door when I went in.'

'One of the bullets penetrated the wall of his chest, Minister,' the doctor said. 'We must get it out and stop the hemorrhaging. He needs a transfusion and rest.'

Vargas left the emergency room. The car drove him back to the ministry and he took the elevator to his office.

The workers had the worst of the damage cleaned up. Still, the door to the safe was standing open and the drawers within were empty.

The priceless files on the generals and top government people that had taken twenty years to compile, gone – like a storm in the night. Every sin known to man was somewhere in one of those files: marital infidelity, theft, rape, incest, sodomy, even murder. Those files were the key to his power, to his ability to make things happen anywhere in Cuba. And now they were gone.

Hector Sedano was his first suspect. Of course Hector himself was in La Cabana, but someone could have robbed the safe on his behalf.

And it could be one of the generals, or Admiral Delgado. Any one of those ambitious fools.

Raúl Castro? A possibility, but he discounted it. Then the fact that he thought Raúl Castro an unlikely suspect made him suspicious. He would have Raúl checked, followed day and night, everyone he spoke to would be scrutinized.

Truly there was much to do. Much to do.

The electrical outage made the burglary possible. Four towers down, two dead saboteurs.

There was a trail out there, and some diligent investigating would eventually lead him to the man or men who did this crime.

Not that it would do any good. Whoever had those files would undoubtedly destroy them immediately.

All his plans, all that work ... up in smoke.

Alejo Vargas didn't believe in coincidences. Whoever robbed that safe made extensive preparations. This was no spur-of-the-moment thing – the robbery was carefully, meticulously planned.

He looked again at the safe. Not a mark on it. Someone had dialed the combination. He had heard that such things were possible, but he had never seen it done. Nor heard of it being done in Cuba. Yesterday he would have said there was not a man in Cuba with that kind of talent.

And the files on the biological program were gone.

The day after the break-in at the lab.

The lab break-in wasn't Hector's style – he would have no reason to burgle the place, nor would anyone else – there was nothing there to steal.

Except poliomyelitis viruses. Would Hector gain political advantage by publicizing the biological weapons program, proving its existence?

The Americans ...

Alejo Vargas stood looking at his empty safe, thinking about Americans. The Americans were a possibility, he reluctantly concluded.

He got a magnifying glass from the top drawer of his desk, examined the door of the safe as carefully as he could.

There were marks, scratches, several together. He could see them. But how long had they been there? What were they made by?

There was no one to tell him, and he decided finally that perhaps it didn't matter. The people who opened this safe and stole the keys to Cuba had brought down the power grid in central Havana. That was where the trail began.

He spent a few seconds in contemplation of his revenge when he caught these men.

'Minister, here is Lieutenant Gómez, who had the duty last night.'

'You saw these men, Gómez?'

'Two men arrived just seconds after the lights went out, sir. I saw the colonel for a few seconds in a flashlight beam. The driver, no.'

'What did this man look like?'

'He was tall, not fat.'

'His accent?'

'None that I noticed, sir.'

'Come, come, Lieutenant. Was he from Cuba, from Havana or Oriente, or did he speak Castilian Spanish?'

'From Havana, I thought, sir. He sounded like you and me.'

'What did he say?'

'That we should start the emergency generator.'

'So you did?'

'Yes, sir. Without power the alarms were disabled, we could not talk to each other on the telephone, the security of the building was compromised. My men and I went to the basement and worked on the generator. I came back upstairs once and reported to the colonel, told him we were having difficulties; he said he had faith. When we got the generator going and went back upstairs, the colonel and his driver and vehicle were gone.'

'You had never seen this colonel before?'

'Not to my knowledge, sir.'

'Would you recognize him if you saw him again?'

'Oh, yes, sir.'

No, he wouldn't, Vargas decided. If this colonel thought there was a glimmer of a chance Lieutenant Gómez would recognize him then or later, he would have killed him. Gómez was alive because he posed no threat.

Vargas dismissed Gómez and called in his department heads to give them orders.

With no ceremony and no conversation, Mercedes Sedano was released from the presidential palace. A butler came to the door, suggested she pack.

The electrical power was still off. It had been off when she awoke this morning, and she was given stale bread and water for breakfast.

She put the clothes she wished to keep in two shopping bags that were on the floor of the closet, sandwiched the cassettes in between them, and took a last look around the apartment. The butler returned five minutes later and led her out. Without electricity the palace looked dark and grim. She wanted desperately to be gone, to bring an end to this phase of her life. She bit her lip to keep herself under control.

The butler paused in an empty hallway, looked around to ensure that there were no maids about, then whispered, 'They've arrested your brother-in-law Hector Sedano. He is in La Cabana.'

Then he took her to the door of the palace, said a barely audible good-bye, and closed the door behind her.

She walked past the guards and continued down the street to the bus stop. The electrical power seemed off everywhere, yet the streets of Havana hustled and bustled as usual. Didn't they know Fidel was dead?

She dared not ask.

On the bus she saw a newspaper lying on a nearby seat and scanned the front page. The usual stuff, nothing about Fidel.

So they had not announced his death.

She transferred to another bus, left her clothes with a friend in a shop on the Malecon. The shop was closed because of the lack of electricity, but Mercedes tapped on the window until her friend came to open the door.

Her friend was very agitated. She drew Mercedes into the tiny dark storeroom. 'I have heard they arrested Hector. What does it mean?'

'I do not know,' Mercedes told her, shaking her head.

'Hector's friends are on fire,' said the shopkeeper, 'and he has many, many friends. I heard there was a riot in Mariel after he was arrested. The newspapers have nothing on it, yet the story is on everyone's lips. People are coming in, asking me about it, because they know I know you.'

Mercedes assured the woman she knew nothing, that she was as mystified as everyone on the street.

She rode buses through the city to La Cabana.

The guard at the gate recognized her name and sent a man to fetch the duty officer, a Captain Franqui. He treated her with respect, took her to his office, a dark cubicle near the gate, and sent a note to the commandante. While the note was being delivered he apologized for the lack of electricity. 'It has not been off this long in years.'

In five minutes she and Franqui were in the commandante's office. He was a heavy-set, balding officer who looked as if he were frightened of his own shadow.

'I have my orders,' he said. 'I cannot admit you. He is to see no one.'

'Fidel sent me,' she said simply, without inflection. 'Hector is my brother-in-law.'

The commandante looked as if wild horses were trying to tear him in half. Obviously he knew of the relationship between Mercedes and Fidel. The blood drained from his florid face as he weighed his fear of Fidel against his fear of Vargas.

Captain Franqui understood the commandante's dilemma. 'Perhaps, if I may be so bold, sir, it might be best if you were indisposed, at lunch perhaps, and I acted on my own initiative in light of the lady's impeccable credentials.'

The commandante grasped at this straw. 'I cannot be everywhere or make every decision, can I?'

'No, sir. If you will excuse us?' Captain Franqui took Mercedes's elbow and steered her expertly from the office into the hallway.

'I myself am an admirer of Hector Sedano,' Captain Franqui confided as they walked. 'He is a great patriot and a man of God. Surely he will serve Cuba well in the years ahead.'

After several minutes of platitudes, she found herself standing in front of Hector's cell in the isolation wing. None of the other cells contained people. Captain Franqui disappeared, leaving the two of them alone.

'Are they listening?' she whispered.

'Probably not,' he said. 'The electricity is off, and they would need it to listen.'

'How long have you been here?'

'Two days. For two days I've been sitting alone in this hole. No one comes to see me.'

'They will admit no one. I told them Fidel had sent me, and the commandante was afraid to refuse.'

'Ah, yes, Fidel.'

'He is dead.'

'I am sorry, Mercedes,' he said softly, so softly she almost missed his words.

'It had to happen. He and I both knew it, accepted it.'

Hector sighed. 'That explains my arrest, then.'

'Two days ago.'

'The cancer finally, eh?'

'Poison! He poisoned himself rather than make a tape naming Vargas as his successor.'

Hector crossed himself.

'It was not a sin,' she said, desperate to explain. 'He merely speeded things up a few days.'

Hector leaned forward, let his forehead touch the cool steel bars.

'I heard there was a riot in Mariel after you were arrested.' Her voice was very soft, a whisper in church.

'I did not know that.'

'A friend told me.'

'Have you heard from Ocho?'

'Nothing. Is he not at home?'

'He went on a boat with some others. They were going to America.'

'I have heard nothing.'

Hector sagged, fought to stay erect. He looked so ... so different than Fidel, Mercedes thought. He was not tall, vigorous, oozing machismo. And yet Fidel thought Hector could lead Cuba!

She got as close to the bars as she could, and whispered, 'I need to talk to the Americans as soon as possible. Should I see the little man you gave the Swiss bank account numbers to? The stadium keeper?'

'He might betray you. He talks to Vargas too. I tried to frighten him, and may have succeeded too well.'

'Who, then?'

'Go to the American mission. Ask for the cultural aide, I think his name is Bouchard. He is CIA, I believe.'

'Fidel signed bank transfer orders for Maximo, who went flying off to Switzerland, just as we thought he would. I have not heard if he got the money.'

'He will not come back if he gets it,' Hector said.

'Maximo would steal it,' she agreed. 'But do you think the Americans will ever give the money back?'

'I have heard their courts are fair. I would rather try to get the money back from them than from Maximo.'

She nodded at that.

'Why do you want to talk to the Americans now?' Hector asked.

She told him.

The secret police had the bodies of the two saboteurs laid out in the basement of police headquarters when Vargas saw them. Two Latin-looking males who had spent many years in the United States, from the look of their dental work. Exiles, probably.

Vargas examined their clothes, which were in a pile, and stirred through the contents of the van. He examined the chemical timers and C-4 shaped charges, the guns and electrical tape, and tossed everything back on the table.

CIA.

No doubt in his mind.

Four extra-high-voltage towers had collapsed, killing power to the two substations that fed central Havana and the government office buildings located there.

A neat and tidy operation.

And as soon as the power went off, a team of burglars entered the Interior Ministry and robbed the safe in his office, carrying away files that he had spent twenty years collecting.

The Americans.

And he had not an iota of proof, nor would he ever get any.

The burglars also stole his laptop computer, and the thought of its loss gave him pause. Certainly not as valuable as the files, the laptop had many things on it he wished the Americans did not have.

He had used the computer to derive the trajectories for the missiles' guidance systems, which had to be reprogrammed when the war-heads were changed, the new biological warheads being significantly lighter than the old nuclear ones. Still, if the Americans didn't know about the missiles, perhaps they wouldn't pay much attention to that file.

What the burglary showed, Alejo Vargas concluded, was that time was short. The Americans could move fast and decisively – to win the game he was going to have to move faster.

I'm ready, he told himself. *Now is the hour.*

'I am Bouchard, the cultural attaché.'

Mercedes Sedano smiled, shook the offered hand.

'Please sit down.' Bouchard looked embarrassed, as if he rarely entertained visitors in this small office, which was packed with Cuban magazines and newspapers. Four candles sat atop the piles. 'The power is still out,' he said by way of explanation. 'And the emergency generator ran out of fuel an hour ago.'

'I don't know how to begin, Doctor,' she said.

'I am not a real doctor,' he said apologetically. 'I am a scholar.'

'My brother-in-law is Hector Sedano,' she explained. 'He said I should come to you.'

'My work is strictly cultural, señora. I work for the American state department studying the culture of Cuba. I cannot imagine how I could be of service to you, or anybody else. I write studies of Cuban music, literature, drama. . . .'

'I know nothing about the branches of the American government,' she said.

Bouchard smiled. 'I know very little myself,' he confided.

'You still haven't asked why I am here.'

'I ask now, señora. What may I do for you?'

'My brother-in-law, Hector Sedano, says you work for the CIA. He –'

Bouchard was horrified. His hands came up, palms out. 'Señora, you have been severely misinformed. As I have just explained, I am a scholar who –'

'Yes, yes. I understand. But I have a problem that –'

He clapped his hands over his ears. 'No, no, no. You have made a great mistake,' he said.

She sat calmly, waiting for him to lower his hands. When he saw that she was not going to speak, he did so. 'I must show you my work,' Bouchard said, and dug into a drawer. He came up with a handful of paper, which he thrust at her. 'I recently completed a major study of –'

She refused to touch the paper. 'Fidel Castro is dead,' she said.

Bouchard froze. After a few seconds he remembered the paper in his hand and laid it on top of the nearest pile.

'I was there when he died. We were filming a statement to the Cuban people, a political will, if you please.' She produced two videotapes from her large purse and laid them on the nearest pile.

'He died before he finished his speech,' she explained. 'Which is inconvenient and, in a larger sense, tragic.'

'I *assure* you, Señora Sedano, that I am a poor scholar, mediocre in every sense, employed here in Cuba because I tired of the publish-or-perish imperative of the academic world. My work is of little import to the United States government or anyone else. *I do not work for the CIA.* There has been some mistake.'

Mercedes maintained a polite silence until he ran out of words, then she said, 'Fidel and I watched an American movie a few months ago, about dinosaurs in a park – an extraordinary story and an extraordinary film. We marveled at the magic that could make dinosaurs so lifelike upon the screen. It was almost as if the moviemakers had some dinosaurs to film.

Perhaps the magic had something to do with computers. However they did it, they made something that had been dead a very long time come back to life.'

Bouchard didn't know what to say. Agency regulations did not permit him to tell anyone outside the agency who his employer was. He twisted his hands as he tried to decide how he should handle this woman who refused to listen to his denials.

'Did you say something?' she asked.

'I don't like movies,' Bouchard muttered. 'There are no good actors these days.'

'Perhaps not living,' said Mercedes Sedano. 'But you must admit the magicians have given new life to some dead ones. You and your friends could perform a great service for Cuba if you would take these videotapes to the moviemakers and let them bring Fidel back to life. For just a little while.'

Bouchard picked up the cassettes, held them in his hands as he examined them.

'I suppose the cultural attaché might be able to pass these things along,' Bouchard admitted. 'What is it you wish Fidel had lived to say?'

Mercedes nodded. She looked Bouchard straight in the eyes and told him.

Maximo Sedano huddled in his great padded leather chair at the Finance Ministry staring out at the Havana skyline. He took another sip of rum, eased the position of his injured hand. He was holding it pointed straight up. The doctor who set the broken bones in his fingers assured him elevating the hand would help keep the swelling down.

That pig Santana! He whipped out his pistol and smashed it down on the fingers of Maximo's left hand so quickly Maximo didn't even think of jerking it away. Three broken fingers.

Then the son of a bitch laughed! And Vargas laughed.

Vargas had whispered in his ear: 'You aren't going to be the next president of Cuba, Maximo. You have no allies. Delgado and Alba will obey me to their dying day, as you will. You have a wife and daughter and your health. Be content with that.'

He said nothing.

'Your brother Hector is in prison charged with sedition. I suggest you meditate upon that fact.'

Maximo sipped some more rum.

His fingers hurt like hell. The doctor gave him a local anesthetic and a half dozen pills when he set the fingers, but now the anesthetic was wearing off and the pills weren't doing much good.

He probably shouldn't be drinking rum while taking these pills, but what the hell. A man has to die only once.

Where was the $53 million?

Somewhere on the other side of the black hole that was the Swiss banking system.

Face facts, Maximo. You can kiss those bucks good-bye. Those dollars might as well be on the backside of the moon.

He spent some time dwelling on what might have been – he was only human – but after a while those dreams faded. The reality was the pain in his hand, and the fact that he was stuck in this Third World hellhole and would soon be out of a job. Whatever government followed Fidel would appoint a new finance minister.

He had no chance of succeeding Castro, and he let go of that fantasy too. He didn't have the allies in high places, he wasn't well enough known, and if he had been he would be in a cell beside Hector this very minute.

Hector's plight didn't cause him much concern. He and Hector had never been close, had never had much in common. Well, to be frank, they loathed each other.

A pigeon landed on the ledge outside his window. He watched it idly. It searched the ledge for food, found none, then took off.

Maximo watched it. The pigeon circled the square in front of the ministry and landed on a statue that stood near the front door. Maximo had never liked the statue, some Greek goddess with a sword. Still, it gave the building a certain tone, so he had never ordered it moved.

Statues. At least he got the goddess instead of that larger-than-life bust of Fidel that the Ministry of Agriculture –

He stared at the goddess. She was made of bronze. Some kind of metal that had turned green as the rain and sun and salt from the sea worked on it.

The bust of Fidel in front of the Ministry of Agriculture was of course manufactured and erected after the revolution.

So were the statues in the Plaza de Revolucion. And some of the statues in Old Havana, at the Museo de Arte Colonial, at the Catedral de San Cristobal de la Havana, on some of the minor squares.

After the revolution! After the government collected all the gold pesos, or before?

The Museum of the Revolution! The old presidential palace was converted to a propaganda temple that would prove to all generations the venality of Batista, the dictator Fidel had overthrown. Maximo recalled reading somewhere that Fidel had personally supervised the renovation and conversion of the old building.

Thirty-seven tons of gold. Fidel had squirreled it away somewhere.

What he needed to do was go to the Museum of the Revolution, lock himself in a room with the collection of Havana newspapers. After the revolution, after the gold was collected, what was Fidel doing?

Thirty-seven tons of gold.

'One sample vial from the Cuban lab contained a new, super-infectious strain of poliomyelitis. The viruses are so hot they kill in seconds.'

The members of the National Security Council didn't say anything.

'The scientists said they never saw anything like it,' the national security adviser continued. 'The four sample vials contained three different strains of the polio virus. Two of the vials contained the same type of virus.'

'Is the vaccination we were all given as children effective against these strains?' The chairman of the joint chiefs asked this question.

'Apparently not. The scientists will need more time to verify that, but apparently . . . no.'

The president looked glum. 'Talk about a choice. We can wait until the Cubans use that stuff on us or we can bomb the lab right now.'

'No, sir,' the chairman said. 'There is no guarantee a bomb would kill that virus. Bombing the lab would probably just release the viruses to the atmosphere and kill everyone in Cuba who happened to be downwind.'

The silence that followed that remark was broken by the secretary of state, who asked, 'Do the scientists have an estimate on how long those viruses can live outside the lab?'

'Not yet,' the national security adviser replied. He took a deep breath and referred back to his notes. 'Here is the situation in Cuba as we believe it to be: We received a report two hours ago from our man in Havana who says he was told earlier today that Fidel Castro is dead. He is sending some videotapes in the diplomatic pouch.'

'Dead, huh?' said the president. 'I'll believe it when they put his corpse on display in a tomb on the Plaza de Revolucion.'

Someone tittered.

The national security adviser continued to read from his notes. 'Review of the documents from the safe of the secret police chief, Alejo Vargas, indicates that the Cubans have installed biological warheads on intermediate-range ballistic missiles.'

'*What?*' the president demanded. He pounded on the table with the flat of his hand to silence everyone else. In the silence that followed, he roared, 'Where in hell did those people get ballistic missiles?'

The national security adviser looked like he was in severe pain. 'From the Russians, sir. In 1962. Apparently the Russians left some behind after the Cuban missile crisis. You may recall that Castro refused to let the UN inspection team into the country to verify that all the missiles had been removed.'

'How good is this information?'

'The man who sent it is absolutely reliable.'

The president mouthed a profane oath, which the chairman of the joint chiefs thought a succinct summation of the whole situation.

15

In a country as poor as Cuba safe houses were hard to come by. The one that William Henry Chance and Tommy Carmellini found themselves in was an abandoned monastery on a promontory of land on the south coast of the island. Surrounded by tidal flats and dense vegetation, the sprawling one-story building was an occasional refuge for drug smugglers and young lovers, who had left their trash strewn about. The rotten thatched roof remained intact over just one room, the kitchen. A roaring fire burned in the fireplace, which apparently the monks had used primarily for cooking.

From the window three fishing boats were visible, wooden boats with a single mast, manned by one or two men. The crew of two of the boats were rigging trot lines, the other was hauling in a net. Chance examined each through binoculars. They looked harmless enough – he doubted if any of the boats had an engine or radio.

'What do you think?' Carmellini asked.

'We have a little time, but I don't know how much.'

'Guess it depends on how efficient the secret police and the military are.'

'Umm,' Chance grunted, and after one more sweep of everything in sight, put down the binoculars.

Tommy Carmellini sat feeding sheets of paper from the secret police files into the fire as fast as they would burn. He merely scanned the pages as he ripped them from the files and tossed them into the flames.

'Vargas and his guys were certainly thorough,' Carmellini commented. 'They looked under every rock.'

'And found every slimy thing that walks or crawls,' Chance agreed. Vargas's laptop was on, so Chance resumed his examination of the files.

'Sort of like J. Edgar Hoover.'

'Secret police are pretty much alike the world over,' Chance muttered. He moved the cursor to the next file on the list and called it up.

'How many missiles are there on this island?' Carmellini asked as he tore paper.

'I have found six missile files, so far. There may be more – I see some references to material that doesn't seem to be on this computer.'

'Six? With locations?'

'Names only. Every missile has a name: Miami, Atlanta, Jacksonville, Charleston, New Orleans, and Tampa.'

'What about Mobile?'

'Don't see it on here.'

'Birmingham, Orlando, the army bases in Alabama?'

'Nothing.'

'I find it hard to believe that in the decades since 1962, the Cubans have managed to keep the secret of their ballistic missiles.'

Chance didn't reply. He had never agreed with the agency's spending priorities, which were heavily slanted toward reconnaissance satellites. The people in Washington were sold on high-tech computer and sensor networks for the collection of intelligence. Hardware and software didn't turn traitor and were easy to justify to the bean counters. The spymasters seemed to have lost sight of a basic truth: networks could only collect the information their sensors were designed to obtain. And they could be fooled. If garbage goes in, garbage comes out.

Ah, well. The world keeps turning.

'How long is that going to take?' Chance asked, referring to the files and the fire.

'Couple hours at this rate.'

Chance glanced at his watch. A few minutes after one o'clock in the afternoon. The rendezvous with the submarine was set for ten o'clock tonight, almost nine hours away. 'If we have to run for it, we'll take everything we haven't burned.'

He and Carmellini and the four US Navy SEALs on guard in the grasses and bushes out front would try to escape if the Cubans attacked the place. Two speedboats were fueled and ready inside the old boathouse, and a submarine would meet them fifty miles south.

Unfortunately he had no way of knowing if the submarine was already lying submerged at the rendezvous position or if the skipper planned to arrive punctually. If he was already there, Chance, Carmellini, and the SEALs could leave now. If the sub wasn't at the rendezvous, the two boats would have to spend the afternoon and evening rolling in the swell, hoping and praying the Cuban Navy didn't come over the horizon.

We'll wait, Chance decided, glancing at his watch again, though Lord knows the waiting was difficult.

It would be a serious mistake to underestimate Alejo Vargas. The Cuban secret police had over forty years of practice finding and arresting people who sneaked onto the island – one had to assume they were reasonably good at it.

Chance didn't want to get into a firefight with the Cuban military or secret police. Leaving a body behind would be bad, and leaving a live person to be captured and tortured would be absolute disaster.

If the Cubans came riding over the hill, Chance and his entourage were leaving as quickly as possible. They could take their chances on the open sea. That decision made, Chance turned his attention back to the computer screen in front of him.

Two months ago when he and Carmellini were handed this mission, William Henry Chance would not have bet a plugged nickel they could pull it off. Polish the Spanish in over a hundred hours of classes, be in the right place at the right time when the power went off, break into Alejo Vargas's safe in secret-police headquarters, carry out the files that Vargas had spent twenty years accumulating, the files he could trade for political support after Castro's death.

Amazingly, they had pulled it off. Every file that went into the flames was one Vargas would never use.

Chance glanced at Carmellini, who was using a stick to stir the fire, keep the paper burning.

Yep, they had pulled it off. And stumbled upon a biological weapons program and Fidel's collection of old Soviet ballistic missiles.

Six missiles. No locations.

The locations must be well camouflaged or the satellite reconnaissance people would have seen them long ago. On the other hand, if they knew what they were looking for . . .

Chance went to the door, called softly to the SEAL lieutenant. 'Mr Fitzgerald, would you set up the satellite telephone again?'

'Of course. Take about five minutes.'

'Thank you.'

While the lieutenant was getting the set turned on and acquiring the com satellite, Chance continued to check the computer. When he hit a file labeled 'Trajectories' he sensed he was onto something important.

The file was a series of mathematical calculations, complex formulas. Hmmm . . . *Let's see, if one could figure out where the warheads were aimed, then one could use the known trajectory to work back to the launch site. That's right, isn't it?*

'Mr Chance, they're on.' The lieutenant handed him the satellite phone.

In Washington, DC, the director of the CIA and the national security adviser listened without comment as the voice of the agent in Cuba came over the speaker phone. He gave them the news as quickly and succinctly as he could. They had the secret-police files, were burning them now though the task would take several more hours, they had a computer containing a file of what appeared to be missile-trajectory calculations, and there were at least six ballistic missiles in Cuba, maybe more. Chance gave the men in Washington the names of the missiles.

'Well done,' the director said, high praise from that taciturn public servant.

When the connection was broken, the national security adviser and the

CIA director sat silently, lost in thought. The spymaster was thinking about Alejo Vargas and the possibility he might seize control of the government in Cuba upon the death of Castro. The other man was thinking about ballistic missiles and microscopic viruses of poliomyelitis.

'Another Cuban missile crisis,' muttered the adviser disgustedly.

The CIA director grinned. 'Why don't you look at the silver lining of this cloud for a change? Fate has just presented us with a rare opportunity to clean out a local cesspool. We ought to be down on our knees giving thanks.'

The adviser didn't see it that way. He knew the president regarded the upcoming death of Castro as a political opportunity, a chance to change the relationship between Cuba and the United States and escape the bitter past. Perhaps the president would decide to just ignore the weapons, pretend they didn't exist. Then he could hold out the olive branch to the Cubans, get what he wanted from them, get credit for progressive leadership from the American electorate, and negotiate about the weapons later.

Tommy Carmellini was burning the last of the files when William Henry Chance noticed that two of the fishing boats were no longer in sight. 'When did they leave?' he asked the naval officer, Lieutenant Fitzgerald.

'Several hours ago, sir. I noticed one of them going west under sail then, but I confess I haven't been paying much attention to the others.'

Carmellini checked his watch – 5:30 P.M. Still three or four hours of daylight left.

'Anything stirring out here?' Chance asked.

'No, sir. Pretty quiet. An old man and a girl walked along the road toward the monastery about three P.M., then turned and went back the way they had come.'

'Did they see your men?'

'No, sir.'

'Well . . .' In truth, Chance was nervous. He felt trapped, completely at the mercy of forces beyond his control. He took a deep breath, tried to relax as Carmellini stirred the ashes of the fire to ensure that all the paper he had thrown in was totally consumed.

'Would you like some MREs, sir?' the navy officer asked. 'My men and I are getting hungry.'

Surprised at himself for not noticing his hunger sooner, Chance said, 'Why not?' He hadn't had a bite since last night.

They were munching at the rations when a helicopter came roaring down the coast from the west. The craft was doing about eighty knots, Chance guessed, when it went over the old monastery. It continued west for a half mile or so, then laid into a turn.

'Shit,' said Tommy Carmellini.

'Lieutenant, I think he's onto us,' Chance told the SEAL officer.

'If he is, his friends can't be far away,' the SEAL said. Standing in the center of the room so he was hidden in shadow, he used the binoculars to look at the chopper.

'Two men, one looking at us with binoculars.'

'Maybe it's time we set sail,' Chance said as he folded the laptop and zipped it into its soft carrying bag. Then he put the whole thing in a waterproof plastic bag, which he carefully sealed.

'Stay down, stay clear of the windows,' the lieutenant said, and darted out the door away from the chopper.

Chance and Carmellini sat on the floor with their backs to the window. The chopper noise came closer and closer, then seemed to stop. It sounded as if the craft were hovering about a hundred feet to the east of the crumbling building. The rotor wash was stirring the remnants of the roof thatch that Chance could see.

Then he heard the sharp crack of a rifle. Two more reports in quick succession. The tone of the chopper's engine changed, then he heard the sound of the crash.

He risked a peek out the window. The wreckage of the helicopter lay on the rocks by the water's edge. Amazingly, one of the rotor blades was still attached to the head and turning slowly. A wisp of smoke rose from the twisted metal and Plexiglas. Chance could see the bodies of the two men slumped motionless in what remained of the cockpit. As he watched the wreckage broke into flames.

'Sorry about that,' the lieutenant said as he burst into the room, 'but the copilot was holding a radio mike in his hand. I think it's time we bid Cuba a fond farewell.'

'Let's go,' Chance agreed.

The boats were fast, at least thirty knots. In the swell of the open sea beyond the peninsula they bucked viciously. Salt spray came back over the men huddled behind the tiny windscreen every time the boat buried its bow.

Chance settled back, wedged himself into place with the computer on his lap.

They were well out to sea, heading due south, when a Cuban gunboat rounded the eastern promontory and gave chase. A puff of smoke came from the forward deck gun and was swept away by the wind.

The splash was several hundred yards short.

The lieutenant at the helm altered course to put the gunboat dead astern. The Cuban captain fired twice more; both rounds fell short. Then he apparently decided to save his ammunition.

The boats ran on to the southwest.

Tommy Carmellini caught Chance's eye and gave him a huge grin.

Yeah, baby!

The distance between the speedboats and the gunboat slowly widened over the next hour. After a while the gunboat was only visible as a black spot on the horizon when the boat topped a swell. As the rim of the sun touched the sea, the Americans realized the crew of the gunboat had given up and turned back toward the north.

Then they heard the jets. Two swept-wing fighters dropping down astern, spreading out as they came racing in, one after each boat.

'MiG-19s,' the lieutenant shouted. 'Hang on tight.'

The shells hit the sea behind the boat and marched toward it as quick as thought. Lieutenant Fitzgerald spun the helm, the boat tilted crazily, and the impact splashes from the strafing run missed to starboard.

The jet that strafed Chance's boat pulled out right over the boat, no more than fifty feet up. The thunder of the engines was deafening.

The jet made a climbing turn to the left, a long, lazy loop that took it back for another strafing run. His wingman stayed in trail behind him.

'Turn west, into the sun,' Chance shouted to Fitzgerald, who complied. The other boat did the same. The boats came out of their turns with the sun's orb dead ahead, a ball of fire touching the ocean.

The jets behind overshot the run-in line, so they made a turn away from the boats, letting the distance lengthen, as they worked back to the dead astern position.

Fitzgerald handed Chance his M-16. 'As he pulls out overhead, give him the whole magazine full automatic.'

Chance nodded and lay down in the boat.

As the jets thundered down, Fitzgerald turned the boat ninety degrees left, then straightened. The MiG's left wing dropped as he swung the nose out to lead the crossing boat. He steepened his dive. As the muzzle flashes appeared on his wing root, Fitzgerald spun the helm like a man possessed to bring the boat back hard east, into the attacker.

The shell splashes missed left this time: Chance let go with the M-16 pointing straight up, in the hope the MiG would fly through the barrage.

Whether any of his bullets hit the jet as it slashed overhead, he couldn't tell. The plane pulled out with its left wing down about thirty degrees, but its nose never came above the horizon. Perhaps the sun dead ahead on the horizon disoriented the pilot. The left roll continued as the plane descended toward the sea, then it hit with a surprisingly small splash. Just like that, it was gone.

The other jet was climbing nicely. The pilot had found his target: the other speedboat was upside down in the sea.

Fitzgerald turned toward the upset boat, kept his speed up.

The wingman took his time – he must realize this would be the last strafing run because the light was failing, and perhaps he was running low on fuel.

He came off the juice, kept the power back, so on this pass he was doing no more than 250 knots, a pleasant maneuvering speed.

Fitzgerald turned his boat so that he was heading straight for the jet. He had the throttle wide open. The jet steepened his dive.

The pilot held his fire and fed in forward stick.

Fitzgerald spun the helm as far as it would go and the boat laid over on its beam in a turn.

The jet didn't shoot, but began pulling out. William Henry Chance let go with a whole magazine.

Closer and closer the plane dropped toward the sea, the nose still coming up, contrails swirling off the wingtips from the G-loads. The belly of the MiG almost kissed the water, came within a hair's breath, and then the jet was climbing into the sky trailing a wisp of smoke.

'Maybe you hit him,' Fitzgerald shouted.

'He sure came close enough.'

Now the jet was turning toward the north, still climbing and trailing smoke. Soon it was out of sight amid the alto-cumulus clouds.

The overturned boat had been hit by cannon fire, which punched at least six holes in the bottom. One man in the water had a broken arm, the other two were dead. A cannon shell had hit one of the men in the torso.

Chance and Carmellini managed to get the injured man aboard.

'The bodies too,' Fitzgerald demanded. 'They're my men.'

'What about the Cuban pilot?' Carmellini asked Fitzgerald.

'He's probably dead,' the SEAL lieutenant said. 'If he isn't, I hope he's a good swimmer.'

The naval officer used a handheld GPS to set his course to the submarine rendezvous.

Jake Grafton walked down the hill from the Officers' Club and along the pier between the warehouses. He walked past foxholes and strongpoints made from piles of torn-up concrete, each of which contained a handful of marines, wide-eyed young men in camouflage clothing and helmets, armed to the teeth. Someone in every strongpoint watched every step he took. He walked by the muzzles of a dozen machine guns and a few light artillery pieces.

The whole area was well lit by floodlights mounted on the eaves of every warehouse. Some marines were gathered around a mobile kitchen, eating hot MREs, and some were gathered around a headquarters tent near the hurricane-proof warehouse. They all carried gas masks on their belts.

Jake stopped at the tent and said hello to the landing force commander, Lieutenant Colonel Eckhardt, who was still awake and keeping an eye on things at this hour. The colonel poured Jake a cup of coffee.

'Your chief of staff, Captain Pascal, was here about an hour ago, Admiral,' the colonel said. 'He tells me that cleaning out that warehouse will take three more days. The ordnance crew from Nevada is working around the clock.'

Jake nodded. Gil Pascal was briefing him four times a day.

'The men have been told that this whole operation is classified, not to be discussed with unauthorized personnel,' Eckhardt replied.

'Fine. Is there anything I can do for you, anything you need?'

They discussed logistics for a few minutes, then the colonel said, 'I assume you're keeping up with the news out of Havana, Admiral.'

'I was briefed before I came ashore,' Jake replied.

'I got a message from Central Command advising me that there are large riots going on in three or four major Cuban cities.'

'I have heard that too.'

'Does that have any bearing on our posture here, sir?' the marine officer asked.

'If I knew what the hell was going on, Colonel, you're the first man I'd tell. Washington isn't telling me diddly-squat. I don't think they know diddly-squat to tell. Yes, the intel summary says people are rioting in the streets in several Cuban towns, everyone in Washington is waiting for Castro to tell his people to shut up, for the troops to wade in. So far it hasn't happened.'

'Maybe Castro is dead,' Lieutenant Colonel Eckhardt speculated.

'God only knows. Just keep your people alert and ready. Three more days. Just three more.'

16

Try as they might, Ocho Sedano and the old fisherman could not get the water out of *Angel del Mar.* With both of them pushing and pulling on the pump handle they could just keep up with the water coming into the boat. If either of them stopped, and the other lacked the strength to work the pump quickly enough, the water level rose.

They struggled all night against the rising water. At dawn they knew they were beaten. No one else on the boat was willing to come below and pump. Some said they were afraid of being trapped below deck if the boat should go under, and others plainly lacked the strength. The passengers of the *Angel del Mar* lay about the deck horribly sunburned, semiconscious, severely dehydrated and starving.

On the evening of the previous day one woman drank sea water. The old fisherman didn't see her do it, but he knew she had when she began retching and couldn't stop. She retched herself into unconsciousness and died sometime during the night. When he went up on deck in the middle of the night, she was dead, lying in a pool of her own vomit.

The other children were also dead. Three little corpses, now still forever.

No one protested when he threw their bodies overboard.

Then he went below to help Ocho.

The losing battle was fought in total darkness against an inanimate pump handle and their own failing strength in a tossing, heaving boat as water swirled around their legs. Ocho prayed aloud, sobbed, babbled of his mother, of his deceased father, of the days he remembered from his youth.

The old fisherman remained silent, not really listening to Ocho – who never stopped pumping – but thinking of his own life, of the women he had loved, of the hard things life had taught him. He would die soon, he knew, and somehow that was all right, a fitting thing, the proper end to the great voyage he had had through life. Life pounds you, he thought, knocks out the pride and piss of youth. Live long enough and you begin to see the big picture, see yourself as God must see you, as a flawed mortal speck of protoplasm whose fate is of little concern to anyone but you. You work, eat, sleep, defecate, reproduce, and die, precisely like all the others, no different really, and the planet turns and the star burns on, both quite indifferent to your fate.

He understood the grand scheme now, and thought the knowledge worth very little. Certainly not worth the effort of telling what he knew to the boy, who would also die soon and lacked the fisherman's years and experience. No, the boy would not appreciate the wisdom that age had acquired.

When the gray light from the coming day managed to find its way down the hatch and showed him the level of the water sloshing about, the old fisherman said 'Enough. Out. Up the ladder before she goes under.' He pulled Ocho away from the handle, shoved him up the ladder.

'Up, up, damn you. I want out of here too.' The words made Ocho scramble out of the way.

The sea was empty in every direction. The old fisherman looked carefully, then shook his head sadly. Where were the ships and boats that were usually here? Why had no one seen the drifting wreck of the *Angel del Mar*?

'Into the ocean with you. The boat is sinking. You must get into the water, swim away, so the mast and lines will not trap you and pull you under when she sinks.'

They stared at him uncomprehendingly.

'Into the water, or not,' he said softly, 'as you choose. May God be with you.'

And he walked aft and stepped off the stern of the ship into the sea. The salt water felt refreshing, welcomed him.

Ocho Sedano stood on the rail a moment, then stumbled and fell in. He paddled toward the old man.

'Ocho!' Dora stood there on deck, calling to him.

'You must swim,' Ocho said. 'The boat is sinking.' There was little freeboard remaining, the deck was almost awash. Indeed, even as he spoke a wave broke over the deck.

Dora looked wildly about, unwilling to abandon the dubious safety of the boat. Other people joined her, some on hands and knees, unable to stand. They looked at the two men in the water, at the horizon, at the swells, at the sky.

One woman rocked back and forth on her heels, moaning softly, her eyes open.

'Swim,' the old man told Ocho. 'Get away before it goes.'

He turned his back on the boat and began swimming. Ocho followed. After a minute or so Ocho ceased paddling and looked back. The boat was going under, people were trying to swim away. He heard a woman screaming – Dora, perhaps.

The mast toppled slowly as the swells capsized *Angel del Mar*. Then, with an audible sigh as the last of the air escaped, the boat went under.

Heads bobbed in the swells – just how many Ocho couldn't tell.

He ceased swimming. There was no place to go, no reason to expend the energy.

He was so tired, so exhausted. He closed his eyes, felt the sun burning on his eyelids.

He opened them when salt water choked him. He couldn't sleep in the sea.

So that was how it would be. He would struggle to stay afloat until exhaustion and dehydration overcame him and he went to sleep, then he would drown.

The screaming woman would not be quiet. She paused only to fill her lungs, then screamed on.

A line in the sky caught his attention. A contrail. A jet conning against the blue. Oh, to be there, and not here.

He was listening to the screaming woman, trying not to go to sleep, when he felt something bump against his foot. Something solid.

He lowered his face into the water, opened his eyes.

Sharks!

The president of the United States sat listening to the national security adviser with a scowl on his face. The president usually scowled when he didn't like what he was hearing, the chairman of the joint chiefs, General Tater Totten, thought sourly.

The adviser was laying it out, card by card: The Cubans had at least six intermediate-range ballistic missiles, which the staff thought were probably sited in hidden silos, away from the cameras of reconnaissance planes and satellites. According to the documents obtained from the safe of Alejo Vargas, the missiles now carried biological warheads, apparently a super-virulent strain of polio. Some of the warheads stolen from *Nuestra Señora de Colón* were now stacked in a warehouse on the waterfront in a Cuban provincial town, Antilla.

Complicating everything were the riots and demonstrations going on in the large cities of Cuba. No one was moving aggressively to quell the unrest; the army was not patrolling the cities; in fact, people in Cuba were openly speculating that Fidel Castro was dead.

CIA believed that Castro was indeed dead; the director said so at the start of the meeting.

'If Castro has bit the big one, who is running the show down there? Who is the successor?' The secretary of state asked that question.

'Hector Sedano, we hope,' the adviser said, glancing at the president, who was examining his fingernails. 'Operation Flashlight was designed to whittle Alejo Vargas down to size.'

'Stealing a safeful of blackmail files will hurt Vargas, but it won't do much to help Hector Sedano,' General Totten muttered. 'I seem to recall a CIA summary that says Hector might be in prison just now.'

'That's right,' the director agreed, nodding. 'We think the rioting is directly due to the fact Sedano is in prison. The lid is coming off down there.'

'We've had our finger in a lot of Cuban pies,' the president said disgustedly, folding his hands on the table in front of him. 'Probably too many. I seem to recall that the CIA did some fast work with a computer, emptied Fidel's Swiss bank accounts.'

'The money is still in those banks,' the director said quickly. 'We just created a few new accounts and moved the money to them. Don't want anyone to think we are into bank robbery these days.'

'Why not? This administration has been accused of everything else,' the president said lightly. Poking fun at himself was his talent, the reason he had made it to the very top of the heap in American politics. He laced his fingers together, leaned back in his chair. 'If we had any sense we would let the Cubans sort out their own problems. Lord knows we have enough of our own.'

A murmur of assent went around the table.

Tater Totten sighed, took his letter of resignation from an inside jacket pocket and unfolded it, placed it on the table in front of him. Then he took out another letter, a request for immediate retirement, and placed it beside the first. He smoothed out both documents, put on his glasses, looked them over.

The secretary of state was sitting beside him. She looked over to see what Totten was reading. When she realized she was looking at a letter of resignation, she leaned closer.

'What is today?' Tater whispered. 'The date?'

'The seventh.'

General Totten got out his ink pen, wrote the date in ink on the top of the letter of resignation and the letter requesting retirement. Then he signed both letters and put his pen back in his pocket.

'. . . our willingness to work with the new government. In fact, I think this would be an excellent time to end the American embargo of Cuba. . . .' The national security adviser was talking, apparently reciting a speech he had rehearsed with the president earlier today. As the adviser talked, the president had been looking around the room, watching faces for reactions. Just now he was looking at Tater Totten with narrowed eyes.

He knows, the general thought.

When the adviser wound down, the president spoke before anyone else could. 'General Totten, you look like a man with something to say.'

'We can't ignore six ICBMs armed with biological warheads. We can't ignore a lab for manufacturing toxins. We can't ignore a warehouse full of stolen CBW warheads.' He leaned forward in his chair, looked straight at the president, whose brow was furrowing into a scowl. 'Fifty million Americans are within range of those missiles. We must move *right now* to disarm those missiles, put the Cubans out of the biological warfare business, and recover those stolen warheads. We have absolutely no choice. When they find out what the threat is, the American people are not going to be in the mood to listen to excuses.'

Tater Totten looked around the table at the pale, drawn faces. Every eye in the room was on him. 'If one of those missiles gets launched at America, everyone in this room will be responsible. That is the hard, cold reality. All this happy talk about lifting embargoes and a new era of peace in the Caribbean is beside the point. We can't ignore weapons of mass destruction aimed at innocent Americans.'

The silence that followed lasted for several seconds, until the president broke it. 'General, no one is suggesting we ignore those missiles. The question is how we can best deal with the reality of their presence. My initial reaction is to wait until a new government takes over in Cuba, then to talk with them about disarmament and return of the stolen warheads in return for lifting the embargo. Reasonable people will see the advantages for each side.'

'Your mistake,' General Totten replied, 'is thinking that reasonable people will be involved in the negotiations. Reasonable people don't build CBW weapons of mass destruction – unreasonable people do. Unreasonable people use them to commit murder for ends they could achieve in no other way, ends they think are worth other peoples' blood to attain. Now, *that*, by God, is reality.'

The secretary of state had snaked the chairman's letter of resignation over in front of her while he was speaking. Now she showed it to the director of the CIA, who was on her left.

'What is that document?' the president asked.

'My letter of resignation,' Tater Totten said blandly. 'I haven't decided whether to submit it now or later.'

As the president's upper lip curled in a sneer, the secretary of state put the letter back on the table in front of the general.

'Totten, you son of a bitch! *I'm* the man responsible.'

'I have to sleep nights,' Tater shot back.

'You reveal classified information to the press, I'll have you prosecuted.' The president knew damn well that Totten would hold a press conference and tell all. 'You'll spend your goddamn retirement in a federal pen,' the president snarled.

'Bullshit! When the public finds out about polio warheads on ICBMs aimed at Florida, the tidal wave is going to wash you away.' General Totten pointed a finger at the president. 'Don't fuck this up, cowboy: there are too many American lives at stake. Now isn't the time for a friendly game of Russian roulette.'

'Okay,' the president said, lifting his hands and showing the palms. 'Okay! What's the date on that letter?'

'Today.'

'Make it a week from today. We'll do this your way, and a week from today you're permanently off to the golf course with your mouth welded shut.'

Totten got out his pen, changed the date on both the letters, and passed them across the table to the president, who didn't even glance at them.

'Better get cracking, General,' the president snarled.

'Yes, sir,' said Tater Totten. He rose from his chair and walked out of the room.

At the same time the president and National Security Council were meeting in Washington, the Council of State of the communist government of Cuba was meeting in Havana.

'Where is Fidel?' someone roared at Alejo Vargas as he walked into the room, flanked by Colonel Santana on one side and a plainclothes secret policeman on the other. Santana limped as he walked. He was heavily bandaged about the head and left arm, and moved like a man who was very sore.

Vice President Raúl Castro watched Alejo Vargas take his seat at the table beside the other ministers. His face was mottled, his anger palpable. He motioned for silence, smacked a wooden gavel against the table until he got it, then looked Vargas straight in the face.

'Where is my brother?'

'Dead.'

'And you have hidden the body.'

'The body is being prepared for a state funeral. I didn't think anyone would object.'

'Liar!' Raúl Castro spit out the word. He stood, leaned on the table, and shouted at Vargas. '*Liar!* I think you murdered Fidel. I think you murdered him so that you could take over the country.' He waved at the window. 'The people out there think so too. You have murdered my brother and arrested the man that he hoped would eventually succeed him, Hector Sedano. Jesus, man, the whole country is coming apart at the seams; they are rioting in the streets!'

Alejo Vargas examined the faces around the table while Raúl shouted. Maximo Sedano was there, his face impassive. Many of the faces could not be read. Most of them merely wanted food to eat and a place to live, something better than the people in the cane fields had. They went to their offices every day, obeyed Fidel's orders, took the blame when things went wrong – as they usually did – watched Fidel take the credit if things went right, and soldiered on. That had been a way of life for these people for two generations – forty years – and now it was over.

'. . . the people loved Fidel,' Raúl was saying, 'honored and respected him as the greatest patriot in the history of Cuba, and I think you, Alejo Vargas, had a hand in his death. I accuse you of his murder.'

'Watch your mouth,' Santana told him, but Raúl turned on him like an enraged bear.

'I am vice president of the republic, first in line of succession upon the death of the president,' Raúl thundered at the colonel. 'Maintain your silence or be evicted.'

Alejo Vargas had already removed his pistol from his pocket while he sat at the table listening to Raúl. Now he raised it, extended it to arm's length, and squeezed the trigger. Before anyone could move he pumped three bullets into Raúl Castro, who fell sideways, knocking over his chair. The reports were like thunderclaps in the room, leaving the audience stunned and slightly deafened.

Alejo Vargas got to his feet, holding the pistol casually in front of him in his right hand.

'Does anyone else wish to accuse me of murder?'

Total, complete silence. Vargas looked from face to face, trying to make eye contact with everyone willing. Most averted their eyes when he looked into their face.

'Colonel Santana, please remove Señor Castro from the room. He is ill.'

As a bandaged Santana and the plainclothesman were carrying out the body, Alejo Vargas again seated himself. He placed the pistol on the table in front of him.

'I will chair this meeting,' he said. 'We are here today to decide what must be done in light of the recent death of our beloved president, Fidel Castro. He fought a long, valiant fight against the disease of cancer, which claimed him four days ago. Of course the news could not be publicly announced until the Council of State had been informed and decisions reached on the question of succession.

'I do hereby officially inform you of the tragedy of Fidel Castro's passing, and declare this meeting open to discuss the question of naming a successor to the office of president.'

With that Vargas reached across the table and seized the gavel that Raúl Castro had used. He tapped it several times on the table, sharp little raps that made several people flinch.

'This meeting is officially open,' he declared. 'Who would like to speak first?'

No one said a word.

'The news of our beloved president's death has hit everyone hard,' Vargas said. 'I understand. Yet the business of our nation cannot wait. I hereby nominate myself for the office of president. Do I hear a second?'

'I second the nomination,' said General Alba, his voice carrying in the silence.

'Let the record show that I move to make the nomination unanimous,' Admiral Delgado said, his voice quavering a little.

'I second that motion,' General Alba replied, 'and move that the nominations be closed.'

One would almost think they rehearsed that, Alejo Vargas thought, and gave the two general officers a nod of gratitude.

Sharks!

The silent predators came gliding in even as Ocho Sedano watched with his face in the water, gray, streamlined torpedoes swimming effortlessly through the half-light under the surface. They seemed to be swimming toward the place where the *Angel del Mar* had just gone under. No doubt the turbulence and noise from the sinking boat attracted them.

The people thrashing about on the surface were also making noise. Nature had equipped the sharks to sense the death struggles of other creatures, and to come to feed.

He raised his head from the water, shouted, 'Sharks. Sharks.' His voice was very hoarse, his throat terribly dry. He sucked up a mouthful of salty seawater, then spat it out.

'*Sharks!* Do not struggle. Swim away from the wreck, from each other.'

He didn't know if anyone heard him or not.

A scream split the air, then was cut off abruptly, probably as the person screaming was pulled under.

Another scream. Shouts of 'Sharks!' and calls to God.

He felt something rub against his leg, and kicked back viciously. With his face in the water he could see the shark, a big one, maybe eight feet, swimming toward the concentration of people in the water.

He turned the other way, began swimming slowly away.

The old fisherman was nearby, doing the same.

'Do not panic,' the old man said. 'Swim slowly, steadily.'

'The others . . .'

'There is nothing we can do. God is with them.'

He heard several more screams, a curse or two, then nothing. He didn't want to hear. And he was swimming into the wind, so the sound would not carry so well.

Dora was back there. If she got off the boat. He couldn't remember if she leaped from the boat before it sank. Perhaps she drowned when the boat went down. If so, that was God's mercy. Better that than being eaten by a shark, having a leg ripped half off, or an arm, then bleeding in agony until the sharks tore you to pieces or pulled you under to drown.

That there were still things on this earth that ate people was an evil more foul than anything he had ever imagined.

He tired of swimming and stopped once, but the old fisherman encouraged him.

'Don't die here, son. Swim farther, get away from the sharks.'

'They're everywhere,' Ocho replied, with impeccable logic.

'Swim farther,' the old man said, and so he did.

Finally they stopped. How far they had come they had no way of knowing. The sea rose and fell in a timeless, eternal rhythm, the wind occasionally ripped spume from a crest and sent it flying, puffy clouds scudded along, the sun beat down.

'We will die out here,' he told the old man, who was only about ten feet away.

The fisherman didn't reply. What was there to say?

Even the tragedy of Dora couldn't keep him awake. He kept dozing off, then awakening when water went into his nose and mouth.

In the afternoon he thought he saw a ship, a sailing ship with three masts and square sails set to catch the trade winds. Maybe he only imagined it. He also thought he saw more contrails high in the sky, but he might have imagined those too.

He would swim until he died, he decided. That was all a man could do. He would do that and God would know he tried and forgive him his sins and take him into heaven.

Somehow that thought gave him peace.

'Gentlemen, your backing this morning touched me deeply.'

Alejo Vargas was sitting with General Alba and Admiral Delgado in his office at the Ministry of Interior. Colonel Santana was parked in a chair near the window with his leg on a stool and a bandage around his head.

'What happened to you, Colonel?' General Alba asked.

'I was in an accident.'

'Traffic gets worse and worse.'

'Yes.'

'Gentlemen, let's get right down to it,' Alejo Vargas began. 'Right now I don't have the support of the people. The mobs are out of control. We must restore order and confidence in the government; that is absolutely critical.'

Delgado and Alba nodded. Even a dictator needs some level of popular support. Or at least acceptance by a significant percentage of the population.

'I propose to move on two fronts. I will send a delegate to Hector Sedano, see if he can be enlisted to endorse me. Getting out of prison will be an inducement, of course, but one can't rely on anything that flimsy. I thought of naming him as ambassador to the Vatican.'

'That would be a popular move,' Alba thought, and Delgado agreed.

'All my adult life I have been a student of Fidel Castro's political wiles,' Vargas continued. 'I learned many things from watching the master. This may seem to you gentlemen to be heresy, but without the United States, Castro would have lasted only a few years in power – had the world turned in the usual way he would have been overthrown by a coup or mass uprising when it became obvious that he could not deliver on his promises. Fidel Castro survived because he had a scapegoat: he had the United States to blame for all our difficulties.'

'One should not say things like that publicly, but there is much truth in that observation.'

'The Yanquis never failed to play their part in Fidel's little dramas,' Delgado agreed, and everyone in the room laughed, even Santana.

When his audience was again attentive, Alejo Vargas continued: 'I propose to unite the Cuban people against the United States one more time, and this time I shall be out in front leading them.'

Jake Grafton had dinner that evening with the commanding officers of the units in the battle group. In addition to the skippers of the ships, the marine landing force commander, Lieutenant Colonel Eckhardt, and the air wing commander aboard *United States* were also there. Held in the carrier's flag wardroom, the dinner was one of those rare official functions when everyone relaxed enough to enjoy themselves. Surrounded by fellow career officers, Admiral Grafton once again felt that sense of belonging to something bigger than the people who comprised it that had charmed him about the service thirty years ago. The tradition, the camaraderie, the sense of engaging in an activity whose worth could not be measured in dollars or years of service made the brutally long hours, the family separations, and the demands of service life somehow easier to endure.

He was basking in that glow when one of his aides slipped in a side door and handed him a top-secret flash message from Washington. Jake put on his glasses before he took the message from the folder.

He scanned the message, then read it again slowly. Ballistic missiles in Cuba, biological warheads, Castro dead – he thanked the aide, who left the room.

Jake read the message again very carefully as the after-dinner conversation buzzed around him. The message ordered him to stage commando raids on the suspected ballistic missile sites, 'as soon as humanly possible, before the missiles can be launched at the United States.'

'Gentlemen, let us adjourn to the flag spaces,' Jake Grafton said, and led the commanders from the wardroom.

When the group was together in the flag spaces, with the door closed behind them, Jake said, 'The course of human events has catapulted us straight into another mess. I just received this message from Washington.' He read it to them. When he finished, no one said anything. Jake folded the message and returned it to the red folder.

He turned to the captains of the two Aegis-class guided-missile cruisers that were assigned to his battle group:

'I want you to get under way as soon as you get back to your ships. Take your ships through the Windward Passage, then proceed at flank speed to a position between the island of Cuba and the Florida Keys that allows you to engage and destroy any missiles fired from Cuba toward the United States. Make every knot you can squeeze out of your ships. Every minute counts. When you come up with an estimated time of arrival, send it to me. We won't lift a finger against the Cubans until both your ships are in position.'

He shook hands with the captains, and they strode out of the room.

'The rest of us might as well get comfortable. Looks like we are in for a long evening.'

Ocho Sedano looked at it for fifteen minutes before the thought occurred to him that he should find out what it was. Something white, floating perhaps fifteen feet away, slightly off to his right.

Now that the existence of the white thing had registered on his consciousness, he made the effort to turn, to stroke toward it.

He had been in the water all day. The sun would soon be down and he would be alone on the sea. After the sharks this morning there had been only Ocho and the old man; now the fisherman no longer answered his calls. Hadn't for several hours, in fact. Maybe he just drifted out of hailing range, Ocho thought. That must be it.

The sharks killed all the others, sparing only the two men who had gone off the sinking boat first and swam away from the group. At least he thought the others were dead – he had no way of knowing the truth of it.

He had thought about the decision to swim away from the sinking *Angel del Mar* all day, off and on, trying to decide just what instinct had told him and the old man to get away from the others. Drowning people often drag under anyone they can reach – no doubt that knowledge was a factor in the old man's thinking, in his thinking, for he did not want to put the responsibility for his life on anyone but himself.

Perhaps those who were attacked by the sharks were the lucky ones. Their ordeal was over.

Dora – had she been one of them?

Diego Coca was already dead, of course. He died . . . a day or two ago . . . didn't he? Jumped into the sea and swam away from the *Angel del Mar*.

Ah, Diego, you ass. I hope you are burning in hell.

He reached for the white thing, which of course skittered out of reach. He paddled some more, reached up under it.

A milk jug. A one-gallon plastic milk jug without a cap, floating upside down. Apparently intact. He lifted the milky white plastic jug from the sea, let the water drain out, then lowered it into the water. The thing made a powerful float.

He pulled it toward him.

Hard to hold on to, but very buoyant.

How could he hold it, use the power of its buoyancy to keep himself afloat through the night?

Inside his shirt? He worked the jug down, tried to get it under his shirt. The thing escaped once, shot out of the water. He snagged it, tried it again.

The second time he got it under his shirt. The thing tried to push him over backward, but if he leaned into it, he could keep his weight pretty much balanced over it. Then he could just float, ride without effort.

As long as he could keep the open neck facing downward, the jug would keep him up.

Ocho was celebrating his good fortune when a swell tipped him over. He fought back upright, adjusted the jug in the evening light.

Maybe he should just forget the jug – he seemed to be working as hard staying over it as he did treading water.

With the last rays of the sun in his face, he decided to keep the jug, learn to ride it.

'I'm going to be rescued,' he said silently to himself, 'going to be rescued. I must just have patience.'

After a bit he added, 'And faith in the Lord.'

Ocho was a Catholic, of course, but he had never been one to pray much. He wondered if he should pray now. Surely God knew about the mess he was in – what could he conceivably tell Him that He didn't already know?

In the twilight the water became dark. Still restless, still rising and falling, but dark and black as the grave.

He would probably die this night. Sometime during the night he would go to sleep and drown or a shark would rip at him or he would just run out of will. He was oh so very tired, a lethargy that weighed on every muscle.

Tonight, he thought.

But I don't want to die. I want to live!

Please, God, let me live one more day. If I am not rescued tomorrow, then let me die tomorrow night.

That was a reasonable request. His strength would give out by tomorrow night anyway.

The last of the light faded from the sky, and he was alone on the face of the sea.

La Cabana Prison was an old pile of masonry. In the hot, humid climate of Cuba the interior was cool, a welcome respite from the heat. Yet in the dark corridors filled with stagnant air the odor of mold and decay seemed almost overpowering. The iron bars and grates and cell doors were wet with condensation and covered with layers of rust.

During the day small windows with nearly opaque, dirty glass admitted what light there was. At night naked bulbs hanging where two corridors met or an iron gate barred the way lit the interior; and for whole stretches of corridors and cells there was no light at all.

Hector Sedano saw the flashlight even before he heard people coming along the corridor. One flashlight and two or three, maybe even four people – it was difficult to tell.

The flashlight led the visitors to this cell, and it turned to pin him on the cot.

'There he is.'

'I will talk to him alone.'

'Yes, *Señor Presidente*.'

One man remained standing in the semidarkness outside the cell after the others left. After the flashlight Hector's eyes adjusted slowly. Now he could see him – Alejo Vargas.

Vargas lit a short cigarillo. As he struck the match Hector closed his eyes, and kept them closed until he smelled tobacco smoke and heard Vargas's voice.

'Father Sedano, we meet again.'

Hector thought that remark didn't deserve a reply.

'I seem to recall a conversation we had, what – two or three years ago?' Vargas said thoughtfully. 'I told you that religion and politics don't mix.'

'You even had a biblical quote ready to fire at me, Mark twelve-seventeen. Most unexpected.'

'You didn't take my advice.'

'No.'

'You don't often follow advice, do you?'

'No.'

'I came here tonight to see if you wish to make your peace with Caesar and join my cabinet, perhaps as our ambassador to the church.'

'You're the president now?'

'Temporarily. Until the election.'

'Then the title will become permanent.'

'I don't think anyone will want to run against me.'

'Perhaps not.'

'But let's take it a day at a time. Temporary acting president Vargas asks you to serve your country in this capacity.'

'And if I say no?'

'I want to sleep with a clean conscience, which is why I came here tonight to make the offer.'

'Your conscience is easily cleansed if that is all it takes.'

'It does not trouble me too much.'

'A man who lives as you do, a lively conscience would hurt worse than a bad tooth.'

'So your answer is no.'

'That it is.'

'But at least you considered my offer, so I can sleep knowing you chose your own fate.'

'My fate is in God's hands.'

'Ah, if only I had the time to discuss religion with you, an intelligent, learned man. Time does not allow me that luxury. Still, I have one other little thing to discuss with you, and I caution you, this is not the time for a yes or no answer. This thing you must think about very carefully and give me your answer later.'

Sedano scratched his head. Vargas probably couldn't see past the glow of his cigarillo tip, so it didn't matter much what he did.

'I want to know what Fidel did with the gold from the pesos. I want you to tell me.'

'Me? I was six years old when he melted the gold, if he did.'

'I think you know. I think Fidel told Mercedes, and Mercedes told you. So I have come to ask you where it is. Will you tell me?'

'She didn't tell me about gold.'

'I should not have asked so quickly. I told myself I would not do that, then I did. I apologize. I will ask you later, when you have had time to think about the question and all the implications.'

'I can't tell you what I don't know.'

'Well, think about it; that is all I ask. Of course I will talk to Mercedes. I think she also told you or the CIA about Fidel's Swiss bank accounts. When Maximo went to get the money it was not there. I would like to have been there to see the look on Maximo's face – ah, yes, *that* was a moment, my friend!'

He chuckled, then drew on the cigarillo, made the tip glow.

'Maximo thinks the Swiss stole it; he is very gullible. I smell the CIA. The CIA could reach into Swiss banks as easily as you and I breathe.'

'The world is quite complex.'

'Isn't it?' Vargas sighed. 'All the strings lead to Mercedes. She knew too much for her own good. I think she will do the right thing. She is a loyal patriot. With Colonel Santana asking the questions, I have faith that she will do what is best for Cuba.'

Hector could feel the sweat beading up on his forehead. He made sure his voice was under his complete control before he spoke. 'For Cuba?'

'For Cuba, yes. Cuba and me, our interests are identical. I want the gold, Father, and I intend to get it. As you sit here rotting, you think about that.'

Alejo Vargas turned and walked away, still puffing on the cigarillo.

The smell of the tobacco smoke lingered in the cell for hours. Hector fancied that he could still smell it when daylight began shining through the window high in the wall at the end of the corridor.

564

17

The submariners put the computer in a plastic garbage bag to keep it dry, then put bag and computer into a backpack that one of the sailors had for his liberty gear. William Henry Chance put on the backpack and the sailors adjusted the straps.

'You should be okay, sir,' they said. At a nod from the sound-powered telephone talker, Chance started up the ladder with Tommy Carmellini right behind him. They came out of the hatch on the submarine's deck forward of the island. The deck wasn't much, merely wet steel that curved away right and left into the black ocean.

Hovering in the darkness overhead was a helicopter – the downwash from the rotor blades made it hard to breathe. Amid the flashing lights and spotlights, his eyes had a hard time adjusting – Chance felt almost blind. One of the sailors on the deck put a horse collar over his head and he went up into the chopper first. Then Carmellini.

A strong set of hands pulled him into the chopper. After a wave at the officers in the sail cockpit, Carmellini used hands and feet to get over to the canvas bench opposite the open door where Chance had found a seat.

Forty-five minutes later the helicopter landed on the flight deck of USS *United States*. As the rotors wound down, an officer in khakis came to the chopper's door, and shouted, 'Mr Chance? Mr Carmellini?'

'Right here.'

'My name is Toad Tarkington. Will you gentlemen come with me, please. The admiral is waiting.'

Tommy Carmellini felt completely out of place, completely lost. After the submarine and the helicopter, the strange sounds, smells, and sensations of the huge ship under way in a night sea seemed to max out his ability to adjust.

The compartment where Toad took the two agents was packed with people, all talking among themselves. Still, compared to the flight deck and the sensations of the helicopter, it was a oasis of calm. Toad led them to a corner of the room and introduced them to Rear Admiral Jake Grafton.

Grafton was a trim officer about six feet tall. The admiral's gray eyes captured Tommy's attention. The eyes seemed to measure you from head to toe, see all there was to see, then move on. Only when the eyes looked elsewhere did you see that Grafton's nose was a trifle too large, and one side of his forehead bore an old scar that was slightly less tan than the skin surrounding it.

Toad Tarkington was several inches shorter than the admiral and heavier through the shoulders. He was a tireless whirlwind who dazzled a person meeting him for the first time with quick wit and boundless energy, which seemed to radiate from him like the aura of the sun. He smiled easily and often, revealing a set of perfect white teeth that would have made any dentist proud.

Jake Grafton and William Henry Chance stood behind Toad watching him work Alejo Vargas's computer. Toad stared at the screen intently while his fingers flew over the keys.

Soon they were plotting positions on a chart. 'Those missiles have to be at these locations, Admiral,' Toad said, pointing at the places he had marked on the chart, 'or the data in the computer is worthless.' He looked over his shoulder at Chance. 'Could this computer be a plant?'

Chance glanced at Carmellini, who was sitting in a chair against the wall studying the layout and furnishings of the planning space and the knots of people engaged in a variety of tasks. The roar of conversation made the place seem greatly disorganized, which Tommy realized was an illusion. Charts on the wall decorated with classified information, planning tables, file cabinets sporting serious padlocks, battle lanterns on the overhead, copy machines, burn bags – the place reminded him of the inner sanctums of the CIA's headquarters at Langley.

'Very doubtful,' Chance answered, and bent over to study the chart Toad was marking.

'I make it six sites,' Toad said.

'Could there be more missiles?' Jake Grafton asked. He too glanced at Carmellini, then turned to Chance. 'You see the pitfalls if there are missiles we don't know about?'

'Yes, sir. I can only say we have seen evidence for at least six.'

'Six silos,' Toad mused, studying the locations.

'There is a warhead manufacturing facility someplace on that island,' Chance said. 'The viruses would have to be dried out, put in whatever medium the Cubans believe will keep them alive and virulent and dormant until the warhead explodes, then the medium sealed inside the warheads. The facility will not be large, but it will have clean rooms, air scrubbers, remote handling equipment, and I would think a fairly well equipped lab on site.'

'Any ideas?' Jake Grafton.

'I was hoping that the satellite reconnaissance people might be able to find the site if we tell them what to look for.'

'We'll have them look, certainly, but you have no independent information about where this facility might be?'

'No.'

Jake motioned to Carmellini, who leaned in so that he could hear better. 'Here is the situation,' the admiral said. 'The White House has ordered us to go get those missile silos as soon as possible. Bombing the silos is out – we are to remove the warheads and destroy the missiles. What my staff and these other folks here tonight are trying to decide is how best to go about doing what the president wants us to do. Obviously, if we had enough time we could bring in forces from the States and assault the silo locations with forces tailored for the job. If we had enough time we could even do a dress rehearsal, make sure everyone is on the same sheet of music. Unfortunately, the White House wants the silos taken out as soon as possible.'

'How soon is possible?' Chance asked.

Jake Grafton took a deep breath, then let it out slowly. 'That's the sixty-four dollar question. We must find out what's there before we go charging in.'

He stood, walked over to a chart of Cuba that was posted on the bulkhead. He was looking at a penciled line on the chart that went through the Windward Passage and along the northern coast of Cuba, all the way to the narrowest portion of the Florida Straits. The cruisers should be in position by six o'clock this evening.

Jake turned from the chart and gestured at the people at the planning tables. 'These folks are just looking at possibilities. We must assemble sufficient forces to do the job, yet we run huge risks if we take the time to assemble overwhelming force. There is a balance there. When we see the latest satellite stuff we'll have a better idea.'

'I would be amazed if there are any troops around these silos,' William Henry Chance said. 'Their existence has been overlooked by two generations of photo interpretation specialists. The Cubans know that the whole island is painstakingly photographed on a regular basis – we've been looking at those damned silos for forty years and didn't know what they were. They must be underground and well camouflaged.'

'I'm not sending anybody after those things until I know what the opposition is,' Jake said bluntly. 'I don't launch suicide missions.'

'Are the silos your only target?' Chance asked.

Jake Grafton examined the tall agent with narrowed eyes. 'What do you mean?'

'The Cubans grew the viruses for their warheads in a lab in the science building of the University of Havana. If we walk off with the warheads in the missiles, there is nothing to prevent the Cubans from cooking up another batch and putting it in planes to spray all over Florida and Georgia and wherever.'

'You are suggesting that we target their lab?'

'I highly recommend it. Chances to step on cockroaches are few and far between: we better put Alejo Vargas out of business while we have the chance.'

'All I can do is make a recommendation to Washington,' the admiral said.

'And the processing facility. If we are going to take Cuba out of the biological warfare business, we should do it right.'

'Can we bomb any of these places?' Toad Tarkington asked.

'Oh, no,' Chance said. 'A bomb exploding in a lab full of poliomyelitis virus would be the equivalent of a biological warhead detonating. The virus would be explosively liberated. Everyone downwind for a couple hundred miles, maybe even farther, would probably die. No, the only way to destroy the virus is with fire.'

Jake Grafton scratched his head.

'The temperature would have to come up really quickly to kill the viruses before the place started venting to the atmosphere,' Chance added. 'A regular old house fire wouldn't do it. We need something a lot hotter.'

'The fires of hell,' Toad said, and his listeners nodded.

The first batches of satellite imagery began coming off the printers within an hour after the suspected silo locations were encrypted and transmitted. The air intelligence specialists were soon bent over the images, studying them with magnifying glasses. Before long Jake Grafton was shoulder to shoulder with the experts.

'This first location looks like it's smack in the middle of a sugarcane field,' the senior Air Intelligence officer groused.

Jake Grafton didn't have to think that over very long. 'Let's assume that our global positioning is more accurate than the Cubans'.'

'You mean they don't know the silos' exact lat/long locations?'

'Precisely.'

'Well, the nearest building to this sugarcane field is this large barn, which is about three-quarters of a kilometer away.' The specialist pointed. Jake used the magnifying glass.

'That could be it,' he muttered. 'Let's see what we can dig out of the archives. How long has this barn been here, have there ever been any large trucks around – let's look in all seasons of the year – and are Cuban Army units nearby? I'm really interested in army units.'

'Power lines,' the senior AI officer mused. 'Strikes me that there ought to be a large power feed nearby.'

'It sort of fits,' Toad Tarkington said to Jake. 'If they built the barn first, then they could dig the silo inside the barn and truck the dirt out at night, pour concrete, do all the work at night.'

'Install the missile at night when the thing is finished,' the AI officer said, continuing the thought, 'and if they had no unusual activity near the barn, no one would ever be the wiser.'

'Prove to me that that is what they did,' Jake said. 'And prove that we won't be sending troops into an ambush.'

The admiral stood amid the banks of computers and watched the operators trade data via satellite with the computers at the National Security Agency in Maryland.

The CIA agents were fed and given bunks to sleep in. They went without protest. Someone brought Jake Grafton a cup of coffee, which he sipped as he walked around the intel and planning spaces thinking about intermediate-range ballistic missiles with biological warheads.

Dawn found Ocho Sedano still afloat, still hanging grimly on to the milk jug and treading water. He had stopped thinking hours ago. Hunger and exhaustion had sapped his strength and thirst had thickened his blood. He was not asleep, nor was he awake, but in some semiconscious state in between.

He found himself looking into the glare of the rising sun as it rose from the sea. The realization that he had made it through the night crossed his mind, as did the certainty that today was the last day.

Today, someone must find me today . . .

The television lights were on and the cameras running when Alejo Vargas walked to the podium in the main reception room of the presidential palace in Havana. For forty years Fidel Castro had used this forum to speak to the Cuban people and the world – now it was Alejo's turn.

'We are here,' he began, 'at a desperate hour in our nation's life. The greatest Cuban patriot of them all, Fidel Castro, died here five days ago. Everyone listening to my voice knows the details of his career and the greatness of the leadership he provided for Cuba. I was with him when he died' – here Vargas wiped tears from his eyes – 'and I can tell you, it was the most profound moment of my life.

'Yesterday the Council of State elected me interim president, to hold office until the next meeting of the National Assembly, which as you know elects members of the Council of State and selects its president. I swore to the ministers and the Council of State that I would uphold the Constitution and defend Cuba with all my strength. Now I swear it to you.'

He paused again and gathered himself. 'Today there are people on the streets who accuse me of murdering Fidel. May God strike me dead if I am guilty of that crime.'

He paused, took several deep breaths, and since God didn't terminate him then and there, continued:

'Fidel Castro died of cancer. His body shall lie in state for the next three days. If you love Cuba, I invite you to pay your respects to this great man, and to look at his corpse. See if there is a single mark of violence on the body. My enemies have accused me of many things, but the murder of Cuba's greatest patriot is the most vicious cut of all. I too worshiped Fidel. Look at the body carefully – let the evidence of your own eyes prove the falsity of these accusations against me.'

Here again he had to pause to wipe his eyes, to steady himself before the podium.

'I have been accused of other crimes, so I take this opportunity to bare my soul before you, to tell you the truth as God Almighty knows it, so you will know the lies of my enemies when you hear them. My enemies are also whispering that I killed Raúl Castro at a meeting of the Council of State yesterday, when the facts of his brother's death were first announced. The truth is Raúl was murdered as he stood at the table discussing the hopes and dreams of his dead brother, by Hector Sedano. Raúl Castro was shot down before a dozen eyewitnesses, myself included. I swear to you this day that Hector Sedano will pay the price the law requires for his crime.'

He paused again here, referred to his notes. Someone had to take the fall for shooting Raúl, so why not Hector?

'The story of our country is a story of struggle, a struggle between the socialist people of Cuba and the evil forces of capitalism, forces controlled and dominated by the United States, the colossus to the north. The struggle was not won by Fidel, although he fought the great fight – it continues even today. For example, while they are representing to the world that they are destroying their inventory of chemical and biological weapons, the United States has introduced these weapons to Cuban soil.'

The camera panned to the artillery shell resting on its base on a table beside the podium.

'Here is an American artillery shell loaded with the bacteria that causes anthrax, one of the deadliest diseases known to man. This shell was stored in a warehouse at the American naval base at Guantánamo Bay, which is sacred Cuban soil. The Americans were unwilling to keep their poisonous filth in their own country, so they exported it to ours.

'I have this day asked the ambassadors of five of the nations who keep embassies in Havana to send their military attachés to inspect this warhead. Here is a sworn document these officers executed that states the shell is as I have represented, a biological warhead.' He fluttered the paper, then held it up so the camera could zoom in.

'The revelation here today of the United States's perfidy will undoubtedly provoke a reaction from the bandits to our north. Fidel always knew that the day might come when we would have to defend ourselves again from American aggression, so he installed a battery of intercontinental ballistic missiles in Cuba for defensive purposes. These missiles are operational and ready now to defend our sacred soil. Rest assured, my fellow Cubans, that we shall resist American aggression, that we shall fight to defend Cuba from those who would destroy her, and we shall make her great for the generations to come.

'Thank you.'

As a speech to a Cuban audience accustomed to Fidel's six-hour harangues full of baroque phrases and soaring rhetoric, Alejo's little effort seemed underdone. He had actually made a conscious effort not to sound like Fidel. Watching the tape of the speech, he thought it went well.

'Air it immediately,' he said to the television producer, and walked back toward Fidel's old office.

Alba and Delgado were there to meet him. They had known that Vargas intended to blame Raúl's murder on Hector Sedano when he made this speech: indeed, they had already signed eyewitness affidavits swearing that they saw Hector shoot the man. That Alejo Vargas had the cojones to make the big lie stick meant a lot to these men who had spent their lives in an absolute dictatorship and knew that the man at the top had to be completely ruthless, without scruple of any kind, to survive. Fidel had been willing to crush his enemies any way he could; Vargas seemed to have the same talent, so perhaps he had a chance.

The two military men shook Vargas's hand. 'Tell us, *Señor Presidente,* what the Americans will do.'

'I have thrown the ballistic missiles in their face,' Vargas said. 'I expect the Americans to go to the United Nations Security Council and ask for sanctions, perhaps a world trade embargo sanctioned by the UN. Now that the missiles have been discussed in public, the American government cannot ignore them, even if they want to.'

'Do you anticipate an attack?'

'I do not, but we must take precautions. The missiles sit in hardened silos impervious to air attack, or nearly so. It is possible that the Americans might attempt commando raids. I suggest you move troops to the sites, have them dig in around the silos.'

'And if the Americans attack and we cannot repulse them?'

'This dog will bite. Fire the missiles.'

Alba grinned. His hatred of the Yanquis was common knowledge. 'If the Americans do attack, when would you expect it?'

'They will try diplomacy first. Only if that fails will they try military action.'

'Still, I would like to move the troops immediately.'

'By all means,' said Alejo Vargas. 'We will have television cameras film your men digging in to defend Cuba.'

'And the missiles? Are you going to film them?'

'Of course. Cuba is a sovereign nation. The world has changed since the 1962 missile crisis. We have an absolute right to defend ourselves, and if necessary we shall. Any noise the Americans make will rally the Cuban people to us.'

Even as Vargas talked to his military men, the president of the United States's advisers were arguing for diplomatic initiatives before military options were weighed. 'We must go to the United Nations first,' the secretary of state stated forcefully.

'What if the UN turns us down?' the president asked in reply.

'We need political cover,' the secretary shot back. 'A significant percentage of Americans think Castro was a hero, a champion of the downtrodden, and we unfairly bullied him. The fact that he was an absolute dictator with zero regard for human rights means very little to the political left. Then there is the casualty problem – the American people won't tolerate seeing their soldiers killed while fighting for oil or corporate profits in foreign wars.'

'What bullshit!' snapped Tater Totten. 'I'm really sick of listening to Vietnam draft evaders tell us that Americans don't have the guts to fight for civilization.'

'I am *not* a draft evader,' shouted the secretary of state, her face red, her cheeks quivering. 'I demand an immediate apology!'

'Shut up, both of you,' the president growled.

'I apologize,' Tater Totten muttered, almost as if he meant it.

The president had done some hard thinking since Tater Totten demanded that the presence of the Cuban missiles be addressed before any other matter with Cuba was put on the table. Six missiles with biological warheads aimed at the southeastern United States – Cuban missiles today were every bit as serious as when John F. Kennedy had to deal with them, he decided. If the administration asked for the blessing of the UN Security Council and didn't get it, he would be worse off than if he ordered military action immediately.

The lab and processing facility worried him too. If Cuba could manufacture polio virus and put it in an aerosol solution, any plane that could fly across the Straits of Florida could attack the United States.

By the time Alejo Vargas's broadcast was translated and replayed for the National Security Council, the president strongly believed that the American people would react angrily to the presence of missiles in Cuba. The outrage of the congressmen and senators who heard the speech convinced him.

He called on Tater Totten again. 'I'm getting the cold sweats just thinking about this crap. Tell me what we are going to do to make sure the Cubans don't shoot those missiles.'

'Sir, the best insurance is to go after the missiles, the lab, and the processing facility as soon as humanly possible, before the Cubans get troops in there to defend them.'

'When is humanly possible?'

'Tomorrow night would be the earliest possible date. Every day we wait allows us to assemble more forces. Conversely, every day we wait the risk increases: Tomorrow Vargas can move more troops to guard those silos; he could get wind of what's coming and threaten to release polio virus by airplane, by missile, or have somebody with a aerosol bomb in a suitcase turn it loose God knows where.'

'So why not go tomorrow night?'

'We must put enough people and firepower in there to get the job done. It's a nice calculation.'

'Do you want me to make that decision?'

'I recommend that you leave the decision to the military professional who is there, Rear Admiral Grafton. He's spent thirty years in uniform training for this moment, for this decision.'

The president grunted.

The Chairman continued, 'By tonight we will have two Aegis cruisers in the Florida Straits between Cuba and Florida. Jake Grafton ordered them there on his own initiative. He's a good man. The cruisers have the capability of shooting down ballistic missiles coming out of Cuba.'

'Do the Cubans know that?'

'Someone in Cuba might – the information is in the public domain – but I doubt that Alejo Vargas knows much about US naval capability.'

'You hope he doesn't, because if he does, they might launch before the cruisers get in range.'

Tater Totten nodded affirmatively.

'This Grafton, I've heard that he goes off half-cocked, doesn't obey orders, isn't a team player.'

'I don't know who said that, but Jake Grafton is the best we have. War is his profession. Alejo Vargas is an amateur playing at war – there is a vast difference.'

'Grafton has enemies.'

'Who doesn't?'

'What if the Cubans launch their missiles and the cruisers miss?'

'Then the shit will really be in the fan, Mr President. Americans will die, a lot of them. You'll have to decide how much of Cuba you want to wipe off the face of the earth.'

'We're going to hold a news conference to reply to Vargas this afternoon.'

'I wouldn't mention biological weapons, if I were you,' Tater Totten advised. 'Let your audience assume the Cuban missiles still have nuclear warheads. Germs scare people more than bombs, perhaps because they are invisible. And we've lived with the bomb for fifty years.'

The president pursed his lips thoughtfully.

Autrey James, Petty Officer Third Class, USN, always watched the ocean from his station in the door of the helicopter. It was a point of pride with him. He once spotted two fishermen whose boat had sunk off Long Island and was given a medal and had his name and photograph in the newspapers, but the part of that adventure that he remembered best was his grandmother's reaction when she read of his exploits. 'You *save* people, Autrey, what a marvelous profession!' Grandmom's comment somehow said it all for Autrey James; whenever his helo was airborne, he watched the ocean. Maybe someday he would save another life.

So that was the reason Autrey James spotted the tiny object on the surface of the immense ocean and called it out to the pilots on the ICS.

'Yo, Mr P., looks like a man in the water at ten o'clock, two miles,' Autrey James said.

'Are you kidding me, James? You got eyes that good?'

'Looks like a man to me, sir, but I could be wrong.'

'Well, we'll motor over that way just to find out if you are.'

The helicopter was an SH-60B Seahawk from USS *Hue City*, one of the two Aegis-class cruisers that Jake Grafton had sent charging northwest. The cruisers were doing just that right now, running abreast of each other a mile apart, making 32 knots, twenty-five miles east of the helicopter's position.

Hue City's commanding officer had launched his helo so the crew could get some flight time and he could find out what was over the horizon, beyond the range of his surface-search radar.

'Dog my dingies, James, danged if that ain't a survivor. Is he alive, do you think?'

'His head's still up, sir. Give me a hover and I'll put the basket in the water.'

The basket was just that, a basket on the end of a winch cable. All the survivor had to do was crawl in, then James could winch the basket up to the chopper and help the survivor out.

Unfortunately, with the basket in the water just in front of him, the survivor made no attempt to get in.

'He ain't gettin' in, Mr P.' Autrey James told the pilot. He was leaning out the door of the helicopter so that he could see the survivor and the basket.

'Maybe he's dead.'

'I don't think so. Looks like his head is out of the water. Dead men don't float like that.'

'You wanna jump in and help?'

'On my way,' said Autrey James. The pilot lowered the chopper to just a few feet above the water and James jumped into the sea.

One look at the survivor's face told him the man was near death, too weak to help himself. With some pushing and pulling, James got the survivor into the basket. The other enlisted man in the chopper winched him up, then dropped the basket for James.

When James had his helmet on again, he informed the pilot, 'We'd better head back quick, Mr P. This guy is in real bad shape. His eyes don't focus.'

'Try to give him some water.'

'I'll try, but we need to get him to a doc.'

Autrey James leaned over the survivor, who was deathly cold, and shouted to make himself heard above the loud background noise, 'Hey, man, you're one lucky dude. You're gonna be okay. Just hang on for a few more minutes.'

'Blankets,' James said to the other crewman. Both of them wrapped the survivor in wool blankets.

'*Gracias*,' said Ocho Sedano, and tried to smile. Then exhaustion overcame him and he passed out.

The carrier and her battle group got under way at dawn. *Kearsarge* stayed in Guantánamo Bay and began loading the marines that had been guarding warehouse number nine. The last of the warheads were going aboard the cargo ship this afternoon, then it would sail. When it left, *Kearsarge* would also get under way with the marines, all nineteen hundred of them.

The battle group steamed south from Guantánamo Bay. For about an hour the southern hills of Cuba were visible from the decks of the ships, but they soon dropped over the horizon and all that could be seen in any direction was the eternal ocean, always changing, always the same. It was then that the carrier launched an E-2 Hawkeye, which carried its radar up to 20,000 feet. Everything the Hawkeye's early warning radar saw was datalinked to the carrier's computers, where specialists kept track of the tactical picture.

Toad Tarkington took Jake aside and showed him the latest message from the National Security Council. He was directed to destroy the viruses in the laboratory in the University of Havana's science building, find and destroy the warhead-manufacturing facility, and to remove the warheads from the six missiles and destroy them in their silos.

As Jake read the message, Toad said, 'They don't want much, do they?'

'Where in hell is the warhead-manufacturing facility?' Jake groused. He went to find William Henry Chance to ask him that question. He found Chance in the wardroom drinking coffee with Tommy Carmellini. They were the only two people there at ten in the morning.

'Do you have any idea where we might find this factory for making biological warheads?'

'Sit down, Admiral. Let me buy you a cup of navy coffee.'

Jake sat. Carmellini went for the coffee while Jake repeated the question.

'It has to be someplace between the science building and the missile silos,' Chance said. 'No one in their right mind would want to haul that stuff very far. A traffic accident of some type . . .'

Jake Grafton's brows knitted. He tapped on the table. 'If you were going to haul polio viruses around, what kind of truck would you use?'

Chance shrugged. 'I don't know,' he said.

'I've been thinking about it for five hours now, and I've got an idea. We'll

575

run it though the recon computers and see what pops out.' He got up from his chair.

'Mind sharing your epiphany?'

'I'd haul the stuff in milk trucks. Clean, sterile, and sealed. A dairy should have a sterile environment and the equipment to mix the viruses with some sort of a base, then load them into warheads.'

Jake turned and marched from the room just as Carmellini approached with the extra coffee cup and saucer.

'He didn't stay long, did he?'

'No,' Chance grunted, and sipped at the coffee Carmellini had brought from the urn in the corner of the room.

'Think Grafton's big enough for this job?' Carmellini asked.

'Yeah. I think he is.'

Three dairies met Jake's specifications – they were located between Havana and the first of the missile silos, which were arranged in a line beginning forty miles east of Havana and going east from there. The silos were about fifteen miles apart.

'Cows. See if they have cows around them.'

'When?'

'The latest satellite photography. Whenever that was.'

Two of the dairies no longer had cattle in the adjacent fields. The one that did was scratched off the list. The other two were examined minutely by the carrier's intelligence center experts and the National Security Agency photo interpreters in Maryland, who conferred back and forth via encrypted satellite telephones. The experts decided that neither dairy could be eliminated as a possible site for the warhead factory.

'We'll do 'em both,' Jake Grafton said.

By three that afternoon the staff and air wing planners had come up with a draft plan. Actually the task, destruction of eight targets, was a relatively simple military one. Tomahawk missiles could take out the lab and the dairies without muss or fuss. They could probably also destroy the missiles in their silos, as the silos were hardened in a simpler age, when the threat was unguided air-dropped bombs. With their ability to power-dive straight down on a hardened target and penetrate ten or twelve feet of reinforced concrete, Tomahawks were the weapon of choice.

And they were out of the question. The president absolutely refused to take the chance that polio viruses might escape from a bombed lab or silo and kill tens of thousands of Cubans in their beds. An event like that would be political dynamite, with repercussions beyond calculation. No, the politicians said, American troops were going to have to lay their lives on the line to prevent just such an occurrence. And, Jake Grafton well knew, some of them would die.

He had already put the wheels in motion. Preliminary messages had been sent to other commands, asking them for the assistance Jake thought he would require. A thousand details remained to be worked out by the various staffs involved, but the machine was in motion. The primary task Jake still had to address was setting the day and hour for the attack.

As he stood looking at the charts of Cuba that covered the wall in the planning space, Jake and his staff wrestled with the timing question. Captain Gil Pascal, the chief of staff, argued that the operation should be delayed until such time as U-2s could fly a photo recon mission and get the very latest enemy troop positions.

'Vargas made a speech today,' Jake replied. The speech and a translation had played several times on television. Jake had even stopped once to watch it.

'*Hue City* and *Guilford Courthouse* are racing for the Florida Straits,' Toad Tarkington argued. 'This battle group is under way. The Cubans may find out about these ship movements and put two and two together and get their wind up. They may be able to put twenty-four hours of delay to better use than we can.'

'That's the nub of it, isn't it?' Jake mused, and stood looking at the charts, trying to imagine how it would be.

Sure, things would go wrong. People were going to have the wrong frequencies, go to the wrong places, everything that could go wrong would. Still, the missions were simple.

The real issue, Jake concluded, was the follow-up. What were you going to do if the troops ran into more trouble than they could handle? How would you extract them? How would you destroy the target?

Jake called the Pentagon on the satellite telephone. He was patched through via land line to General Totten at the White House.

After the usual greetings, Jake said, 'Sir, two points. First, I would like to address the proposal to delay the operation until Patriot SAM batteries can be moved into southern Florida. If we pop a Cuban missile over southern Florida the cloud of viruses may drift over to Miami or Tampa. I don't think we gain anything by waiting for Patriot batteries.'

'We've about reached the same conclusion here, but there has been vigorous debate. What is your second point?'

'In my view, the key to getting this done is our willingness to do whatever is required to accomplish the mission.'

'The president is listening, Admiral. Explain yourself.'

'As I see it, General, our choice is to either wait until we are convinced we can pull it off, or go now before the Cubans have a chance to garrison these sites with troops. The lab in Havana presents problems that the other sites do not. We will have to tackle the lab after the missiles are destroyed.'

'Okay.'

'If the troops assaulting the silos run into more Cubans than they can handle, we must either add more forces or extract our men. If we elect to extract our people, we still have the problem of the missile in the silo and we will have handed the Cubans a victory in a fight we cannot afford to lose.'

'What do you propose?'

'We won't be able to go back later with more people. We get one bite of the apple, sir. I propose that you authorize me to use whatever force is required to accomplish the mission, short of nuclear weapons.'

Jake Grafton heard the president loudly say, 'I'm not giving him or anybody else the authority to risk a catastrophic release of toxins. No.'

'We'll call you back,' General Totten said, and hung up.

Mercedes went to stay with Doña Maria Vieuda de Sedano, to cook for her and clean and do whatever needed to be done. She had stayed with her mother-in-law in the past, after her husband, Jorge, died – fortunately the two women genuinely liked each other.

She and Doña Maria ate lunch on the little porch of the bungalow so they could enjoy the breeze blowing in from the sea. It was strong today, whipping the palm fronds and rippling the sugarcane. Little puffy clouds threw severe shadows that raced over the ground.

Doña Maria had gone back inside for a nap and Mercedes was sewing a blouse together when a limo drove up and Maximo got out. He came up the short walk, paused at the steps, and looked at her. 'I thought I would find you here,' he said.

'*Mima*'s sleeping.'

'I came to see you.'

She nodded, continued working on the blouse. He stayed on the dirt and scraggly grass, walked around so the porch railing was between them.

'Vargas made a speech this morning. It was on television.'

'Hmm,' she said. Doña Maria did not have a television, and Maximo knew that.

'He is the president now.'

'I have heard.'

'Did he really kill Fidel?'

'No.'

Her thread broke. She got out the spool of thread and rethreaded the needle.

'Would you tell me if he had?'

'What did you come for, Maximo?'

'I need your help.'

She knotted the thread and began a new seam.

'You don't think much of me, do you?'

'I don't think of you at all.'

He leaned on the porch railing, crossing his arms. 'Where did Fidel hide the gold?'

'I didn't know he had any,' she said, not looking up from her work. 'He didn't even have gold in his teeth.'

'The gold pesos the government called in after the revolution – that gold.'

'I have no idea,' she said.

'I think you do. I think Fidel told you.'

'Think what you like.'

'He wouldn't let the secret die with him.'

'Maximo, look at me. If I had a pocketful of gold, would I be sitting here on the porch of a tiny, ninety-five-year-old bungalow with a thatched roof beside the road to Varadero, sewing myself a shirt?'

'I don't think you have it – I think you know where it is.'

She snorted and went back to the needle and the seam.

'You don't want the gold for yourself, I know. But I need it. Not all of it, just a little. I must get out of Cuba.'

A strand of hair fell across her face. She brushed it back.

'We could leave together, Mercedes, if we had some of that gold. You could go anywhere on earth you wanted, live the rest of your life without worry, without fear, without need. Think of it! A new life, a new beginning. How much of this heat and dirt and hopeless poverty do you want, anyway?'

'Forget the gold, Maximo. If there is any, it is not for you.'

He backed away from the railing, stood in the sun with the sea wind playing at his hair. 'Think about it,' he said. 'Vargas is no fool; he wants the gold too. One of these days he will send Santana around to see you. Think about what you are going to say to him when he comes.'

He walked to the waiting limo. The driver turned the car in the road and headed back toward Havana.

Toad Tarkington was the only person in the room with Jake as they waited for the chairman of the joint chiefs to call from the White House.

'What do you want from them, Admiral?'

'I want the authority to do whatever I have to do to destroy those viruses,' Jake Grafton explained. 'Once the shooting starts, *we have to win.*'

'What if the president won't give you that authority?'

'He has a right to say that. We'll go do our best, and if we can't cut it without using Tomahawks or laser-guided weapons, then we'll call him up and say so.'

'What is the problem here?' Toad demanded. 'If there is a toxin release he won't be the guy responsible. Fidel Castro and Alejo Vargas are the guilty parties. This is *their* country.'

Jake shook his head. 'If there is a toxin release in America, the president must be able to prove that he did everything humanly possible to prevent it. If there is a release in Cuba . . . well, he will need to show people around the world that he did what he could to prevent it while still eliminating the threat to the US. Elimination of the threat is the key here, and I hope they understand that in Washington.' He smacked the wall with his hand. 'Dammit, we only get one shot at those viruses.'

'I wonder if anyone in Washington is thinking about the Bay of Pigs,' Toad mused. 'That turned into a débâcle because Kennedy wasn't willing to commit enough resources.'

'*I've* been thinking about it,' Jake Grafton said.

When the telephone rang, General Totten was on the line. 'Admiral, we shall word it like this: "Your mission is to eliminate the threat to the United States. In completing your mission you are instructed to do everything within your power to minimize the possibility of a toxin release in Cuba. You may use any forces and weapons in your command except nuclear or CBW weapons, and you may request assistance from any command in the US armed forces." '

'Yes, sir.'

'I'll have that on the wire as soon as possible.'

'Yes, sir. I want to thank you and the president. We'll do our best.'

'I know you will, sailor. When are you going?'

'Tomorrow night, sir. In view of all the factors involved, that is my choice.'

18

Over Cuba the next morning the cloud cover was typical for that time of year: as the sun rose the prevailing westerly winds spawned cumulus clouds over the warming land. The longer the clouds remained over land, the higher they grew. In the area east of Havana where the Americans believed the missile silos and processing lab were located the cloud cover averaged forty or fifty percent by ten in the morning, enough to inhibit satellite and U-2 photography of the area. Infrared photography was not affected by the clouds, nor were the synthetic-aperture radar studies done by air force E-3 Sentry AWACS aircraft.

Oblivious to the intense scrutiny that the island was now getting from the Americans, General Alba conferred that morning with Alejo Vargas, then ordered troops and tanks moved into position around the silos. There were actually eight silos, but only six held operational missiles. The other two missiles had been used as sources of spare parts through the years. Had Alba and Vargas realized what was coming, they might have elected to dissipate the American military effort by garrisoning all eight silos: as it was, they didn't think of it.

The sun had been up just two hours when two C-130 Hercules landed at the naval air station at Key West, Florida. On the civilian side of the field people stood and watched as the Hercs parked on the other side of the runway. Soon navy personnel began unloading the transports. The civilian kibitzers did not know what the pallets and canisters contained, and after a while they went on about their business. Four armed marines in combat gear took up locations where they could guard the transports.

Among other things, the transports had delivered belted 20-mm ammunition for miniguns, Hellfire missiles, flares, and 2.75-inch rockets. They also delivered tools and spare parts to work on Marine Corps AH-1W SuperCobras.

Two hours after the Hercs landed, the first two SuperCobras settled onto the military mat. By noon sixteen of the mottled green helicopters were parked in the sun.

The two-man crews didn't leave the base, but went into an old, decrepit navy hangar nearby for briefings.

Two more C-130s wearing marine markings landed an hour or so later. They parked near the first two. As navy trucks began refueling the planes, marines disembarked and spread their gear on the ramp. They lounged around, a few walked a safe distance away and lit cigarettes, and after a while a navy truck brought hot food.

Troops, tanks, and trucks were moving in Cuba by noon, blocking roads and creating traffic jams. By midafternoon the E-3 Sentry crews had alerted the National Security Agency, which passed the information on to USS *United States*. Jake Grafton went to the ship's intelligence center to see what the computers could tell him.

After listening to the briefer, Jake Grafton muttered, 'Damn.'

He went over the data, then asked, 'How much combat power are they moving, and when will it be in place?'

In New York City the US ambassador to the United Nations paid a call on the Cuban ambassador. After exchanging civilities, the American said bluntly, 'My government has asked me to inform you that if the Cuban government releases biological toxins of any kind in the United States, for any reason, the American government will massively retaliate.'

' "Massively retaliate"?' The Cuban's eyes widened. 'What does that mean?'

'Sir, I was instructed to deliver the message, not to interpret it. Here is the statement in writing.' The American handed over a sheet of paper and took her leave.

Aboard USS *Hue City*, now under way precisely halfway between Cuba and Key West at ten knots, Ocho Sedano awoke in midafternoon from a deep sleep. He found that he was in a hospital bed on a small ward, with two intravenous solutions dripping into his veins. His vision was blurred, he could not focus his eyes.

The doctor on the ward noticed that he was awake and came over to check him. In a few minutes an American sailor who spoke Spanish came to interpret.

'Your eyes are sore from the salt of the water. They will get better. Can you tell us your name, señor?'

'Juan Sedano,' he whispered, because he could not talk above a whisper. 'They call me El Ocho.'

'And where are you from?'

'Cuba.'

'How long were you in the sea?'

'Two days and nights, I think. I am not sure. Maybe more than that.'

The doctor put a solution into Ocho's eyes while the questions and answers were flying back and forth. After blinking mightily Ocho thought he could see a little better. The doctor was examining Ocho's fingertips and the calluses on his hands. Now he held up Ocho's hand and peeled off a callus. Then he smiled. 'You were very lucky.'

The translator interpreted.

'Where am I?' Ocho asked.

'Aboard *Hue City*, a United States Navy ship. You were rescued by a helicopter. The man who saw you in the water wants to shake your hand when you awaken. He saved your life. May I call him?'

'I would like to meet him.'

It felt very comfortable lying there, looking at the fuzzy beds and blurred people bustling about, checking him over, so different from *Angel del Mar.* Or floating on the sea.

Maybe he was dead. He examined that possibility but concluded it was not so. This was not a bit like the heaven he envisioned, and he was hungry. He told the interpreter of his hunger, and the man went to talk to the doctor, who had wandered off.

They brought food about the same time that Autrey James came breezing in with one of his pals, who had a camera. James was a happy fellow with a wide smile – the white teeth in a dark face were the only details that Ocho could see. James got down beside the bed and posed while the man with the camera took many pictures. Another man with a camera came, some kind of television camera, and he and James shook hands again. Several men in khaki stood behind the camera watching.

The interpreter relayed the questions from Autrey James and the television cameraman. When did you leave Cuba, What was the name of the boat, How many people were there?

'Eighty-four people.'

'Eighty-four?' asked the interpreter in disbelief.

'Eighty-four,' whispered Ocho Sedano.

'What happened to the boat?'

'It sank.'

'And the people?'

'They went into the water . . . sharks.'

'Sharks?'

'Some people were swept over the side during a storm our first night at sea. Diego Coca shot the captain, some people died of thirst . . . Diego jumped into the sea. The children died of exhaustion and hunger, I think – it is really impossible to say. There was no food or water, only rain to drink. When the boat sank those who were left were eaten by sharks. If they didn't drown. I hope Dora drowned.

'The old fisherman and I were spared. . . . Did you find him? The old fisherman? Did you see him in the ocean?' He clawed at Autrey James, who drew back out of reach.

'No,' the interpreter said. 'You were the only one.'

They went away then, all of them, left him to eat the food and stare at the ceiling and think about the fact that he was alive and all the others were dead.

The others were dead. He was alive. What did that mean?

Was God crazy?

Why me?

He was thinking about that when someone came to put solution in his eyes again. This time the solution made him cry.

He sobbed for a minute or two, then his body gave out and he slept.

'Why did you not put the gold in a bank vault?'

Mercedes had asked this question of Fidel several years ago, when he first told her of the gold pesos. As she sat on her mother-in-law's small porch completing her blouse, she remembered the question, and Fidel's answer:

'If we kept the gold in a bank, the international bankers would have learned of it eventually, would have demanded that we post it as security for a loan. Then a hurricane would come or the bottom would drop out of the sugar market one year, and the gold would be gone.'

'But the gold does not help Cuba. Why own it?'

'The gold is ours,' he said obstinately. 'When it is gone it is gone for all Cubans forever.'

'But you hid it, so it is gone now.'

'Oh, no. You and I know where it is. As long as it is hidden, it belongs to Cuba.'

She couldn't shake him – he had the peasant's love of the secret hoard, the instinctual drive to bury a can of money or hide it in a mattress, just in case. No matter how bad things got in the house, the money was always there, hidden, an asset that could be tapped to stave off starvation or disaster.

He said as much when he admitted, 'In the middle of the night, when I am alone and the world is heavy on my shoulders, I remember we still have the gold.'

Fidel and Che Guevara hid it together, for Cuba. Guevara was killed in Bolivia and apparently took the secret to his grave. Fidel didn't want to – he told the one person on this earth he trusted.

She wished she didn't know this thing. As she worked on the last seam of the blouse, she thought about this great secret, about what she should do.

Mercedes Sedano had confided in no one, had written nothing down. With Fidel dead the gold was only one heartbeat away from being lost forever. She must do something, but what?

Fidel had been a knot of contradictions. She had argued with him –

challenged the macho man himself – and he had admitted some of his failures, which was a rare moment for him. Not all of his errors, but some.

'I am the only communist in Cuba,' he said, laughing. 'Becoming a communist was a mistake – of course I can never say that in public. We had to declare our independence from the American financiers and corporations. In the fullness of time it turned out that the Russian horse couldn't run the race, which was unfortunate, but that didn't mean we were wrong in the first place.' He shrugged.

He had the Latin's ability to accept life's vicissitudes as they came with courage and grace.

'The best thing about communism was the dictatorship. The economic twaddle meant nothing. Someone had to show the Cuban people they could stand on their own feet, that they didn't need to sell their souls to the Americans or the Catholic Church.' He smiled again, made a gesture toward heaven. 'The truth is we were too poor to afford the Church or the Americans.'

If Santana or Vargas tortured her, she would tell them about the gold. To suffer horribly and die for a secret that you thought illogical was worse than stupid – it would be a sin.

Did he ever wonder what she would do if she found herself in this situation?

She finished the last seam, shook out the blouse, and held it up so she could view it.

Had Fidel really trusted her to make the decision that was best for Cuba, or did he just think that she would keep her mouth shut?

For Maximo Sedano the question was simple and stark: Where was the gold?

Rumors had circulated for forty years, and not a flake had ever surfaced. Several men swore they had helped melt the coins into ingots in a smelter in the basement of the Ministry of Finance, but they never knew what happened to the ingots. Alejo Vargas had been running the secret police for twenty years and the Ministry of Interior for the last ten and probably hunting for the gold for at least nineteen, and he hadn't found it. At least Maximo didn't believe he had. In forty years no loose ends had unraveled ... so there must have been no loose ends.

The conclusion Maximo drew from these facts was that only a very few people – Fidel, perhaps his brother Raúl, maybe Che – had known the secret in the first place. Today the secret might be known by a few people who had been close to them. In any event, there were no elderly workmen about who liked to run their mouth when they drank their rum – Vargas would have found anyone like that years ago.

So the gold wasn't made into statues, poured like concrete into a floor or foundation, made into bricks and used to construct a state building, or transported to some flyspecked hovel and buried under the floor. No. If the gold had been hidden this way, someone involved in the labor would have talked during the last forty years.

If there were secret records waiting to be discovered or letters in bank vaults, Maximo would never discover them. All he had were his wits.

With Fidel dead and Alejo Vargas ascendant, Maximo was using his wits now, applying them as never before.

In search of inspiration, he walked the streets of Havana to the Museum of the Revolution.

Like so many revolutionaries who swashbuckled through the pages of human history, after his victory Fidel found it expedient to enshrine himself as the savior of the nation so that he might remain at the helm permanently. Of course, to properly do the job it was also necessary to build a monument to the venality and depravity of his enemies, because great heroes need worthy opponents. Amazingly, all this good, evil, and greatness fit neatly under one roof: the presidential palace that had been the residence of Fulgencio Batista.

Maximo walked quickly through the exhibits that detailed Batista's corruption – what he sought would not be there.

He quickly found what he was looking for. Fidel the savior, '*El Líder Maximo*,' portraits, busts, memorabilia, candid and posed photographs, heroic paintings – all of this was enough to turn the stomach of anyone who had actually known the man, Maximo thought. Alas, Fidel had been very flawed clay: megalomaniacal, filled with a sense of his own magnificent destiny, boorish, opinionated, pigheaded, insufferable, prejudiced, loquacious to a fault, and, all too often, just plain wrong. What a tragedy that this self-anointed messiah was stranded in this third world backwater and never had the opportunity to save the species, which he could have done if only God had sent him to Moscow or Washington.

Maximo tried to stifle his disgust and concentrate upon the displays before him.

Fidel and Che Guevara, Camilo Cienfuegos, the other immortals . . . The university, the Moncada Barracks, the trial, prison, handwritten letters, exile, guerrilla days . . .

He carefully looked at everything, then wandered on. He came to a room devoted to the fall of Havana; Fidel riding into the city on a tank, ecstatic children. Then Fidel the ruler; Fidel the baseball player; Fidel and Che fishing in the Gulf Stream; Fidel with Hemingway, Richard Nixon, Khrushchev, Kosygin, the famous and the infamous, always togged out in those abysmal green fatigues; dozens of shots of Fidel with his mouth open in front of crowds . . . God, how the man could talk to a captive audience!

Maximo was in the next room looking at photos of Fidel eating rice and beans with schoolchildren when the incongruity of the photo of Fidel and Che fishing struck him. Odd, that.

He went back to it. The two were on some kind of fishing boat, with fighting chairs and big rods, fishing for marlin probably.

Wait a minute . . . The marina where Maximo kept his boat . . . When he first moved it there the harbormaster had once told him that Fidel used to leave from that marina to fish.

Now he remembered. Yes. The old man said Fidel and Che fished often, every few days, went out by themselves, often spent the night at anchor in the harbor. After a year or so they tired of it, the old man said wistfully, never came back. The boat belonged to the Cuban Navy – seized from an American – and was eventually converted to a gunboat.

He could remember the old man talking, could see the wind playing with his white hair as he stood on the dock in the sun talking about his hero, Fidel, about that moment one day long ago when their lives came close together.

The harbormaster had been dead for years. The new man was far too young to remember anything.

What if the gold were on the floor of Havana Harbor?

Each night Fidel and Che could have lowered hundreds of pounds of it over the side of the boat free from observation. Given enough nights . . .

Over time the gold could have gradually disappeared from the Finance Ministry. If no one but Fidel and Che handled the gold, there was no one to talk.

Maximo could see logistical problems with this possibility, of course, but not insurmountable ones.

He left the museum deep in thought.

'The air force's AWACS reports that the Cuban military is moving toward the silo sites, Admiral.'

The briefer was a commander, the senior Air Intelligence officer on the carrier battle group's staff.

'The troops are being moved from barracks in the Havana area. We can see tanks and trucks, which presumably contain supplies and troops. The columns are moving slowly, eight to ten miles per hour. Cuban troops have already arrived at missile site number one. Just arriving on sites two and three. We estimate that there will be no Cuban military presence on sites four through six until tomorrow morning after dawn.'

'Why so slow?' Jake Grafton asked.

'These are old tanks, Soviet T-54s. We think they see no reason to risk breakdowns by driving faster. The consensus seems to be that the Cubans aren't on full alert.'

'Okay,' Jake Grafton said, because there was nothing else to say. The god of battles was dealing the cards.

The briefer continued, pointing out bridges and crossroad choke points, and Jake tried to concentrate, which was difficult. When the briefer finished, Jake dismissed his staff and sat staring at the map on the bulkhead.

The plan was good: the weather would be typical, the forces he had should be adequate, they knew their jobs ... but if the Cubans fired those missiles at the United States, two Aegis cruisers were all he had to prevent the missiles from reaching their targets.

Should this whole operation be delayed until antimissile batteries could be moved to south Florida?

Every hour of delay meant more American troops would die taking those missile sites. Yet if the missiles successfully delivered their warheads, the results would be catastrophic.

He looked again at the plan – at the timing, at the units assigned.

Biological weapons. Poliomyelitis.

He could always use more people, of course. One of the primary goals of warfighting – some people argued, the *only* goal – was to direct overwhelming force at the point where the enemy was most vulnerable. Or as Bedford Forrest put it, 'Get there firstest with the mostest.'

Already the Cubans were digging in around silos one and two. What if the forces he had committed couldn't crack those nuts?

The urge to wait for a bigger hammer had Jake Grafton in its grip now. He felt like David with his slingshot. Maybe he needed more Aegis cruisers, some Patriot missile batteries, more cruise missiles, troops, Ospreys, airplanes.

If one of those missiles got through ...

He found a handkerchief in his hip pocket and mopped his face.

His stomach tried to turn over.

He hadn't felt like this since Vietnam. Way back in those happy days he had been responsible only for his bombardier's life and his own miserable existence. All things considered, that load had been relatively light.

This load ...

Well, Jake Grafton, Uncle Sugar's been paying you good money all these years while you've been getting fat and sassy on the long grass. It's payback time.

In midafternoon Toad Tarkington went to the communication spaces to call his wife, Rita Moravia, on one of the ship-to-ship voice circuits. He had done this a time or two before and the chief petty officer was accommodating when the circuits were not in use for official business. This afternoon he asked the chief for an encrypted circuit but they were all busy – the chief handed him a clear-voice handset. Toad called *Kearsarge* and left a message for his wife. Ten minutes later she called him back.

'Hey, Toad-man.'

'Hey, Hot Woman.'

Tonight, he knew, she would be flying a V-22 Osprey, hauling troops to missile silo two.

'Just wanted to hear your voice,' Toad said, as matter-of-factly as he could. He could envision this conversation coming over radios in ships throughout the battle group and in Cuban monitoring stations. He had no intention of giving away secrets nor of entertaining kibitzers.

Rita was equally circumspect. 'Got a letter from Tyler. He wrote it with Na-Na's help, of course.'

'How's Ty-Guy doing?'

'He has a girlfriend, the Goldman girl across the street.'

'That's my boy,' Toad said. 'A lover already. A chip off the old brick.'

Aboard *Kearsarge* Rita was holding the handset in a death grip. She loved life: her son, her husband, her job, the people she worked with – every jot and comma of her life. Oh, of course there were days when the stress and problems threatened to overwhelm her ability to cope, but somehow she managed. In the wee hours of the night when she paused to evaluate, she knew that she wouldn't change a thing. Not one single thing.

Now she realized that Toad hadn't spoken in several seconds.

'I wouldn't change a thing,' Rita said.

'I was thinking the same thing,' he said.

'From day one.'

'I remember the first day I saw you. Wow.'

'When we were at Whidbey, I thought you hated me.'

'And I thought you didn't like me.'

'Thank God you finally screwed up the courage to kiss me.'

'Wish I could now,' he shot back.

Tears ran down her cheeks. She wanted to tell him how much he had meant all these years, how grateful she was that they shared life, and nothing came out. She put her hand over the mouthpiece so he wouldn't hear her cry.

'Next time we're together, better not wear lipstick,' he said.

'I never wear lipstick,' she managed, her voice barely under control.

'It's a good thing, too,' he said, his voice cracking.

The silence grew and grew.

'Well, I gotta go,' Toad finally said. 'They wanna use this circuit to trade movies or something.'

'Yeah.'

'*Vaya con Dios*, baby.'

'You too, Toad-man.'

Toad found Jake Grafton in Combat huddled with Gil Pascal, the chief of staff. He listened to the conversation for a moment, then realized that the admiral was trying to assure himself that he had adequate forces to win. Tonight!

After a bit Jake turned toward Toad. 'Let's have your two cents,' he said.

'If we need anything, sir, it's a bigger reserve. We have three V-22s with twenty-four marines each to go wherever they are needed. A while ago the CO of the carrier's marine det asked if he and some of his people could get in on the fun. He called *Kearsarge* and found there is one extra Osprey. It's being used as a backup to the first wave, but if it isn't needed, then it'll be an extra.'

Gil Pascal frowned. 'The carrier's marines haven't been briefed,' he pointed out.

Jake glanced at Toad and raised one eyebrow.

'Sir, I was hoping you would let me go with them,' Tarkington replied cheerfully. 'I'm as briefed as it's possible to get.' Actually, as Ops, Tarkington wrote the plan.

'You've been planning to spring this on me all day, haven't you?'

'I could take a satellite phone, give you a worm's-eye view of the action, let you know if there is really a problem.'

'Did the marine det CO approach you with this marvelous idea, or did you approach him?'

Toad turned his eyes to the ceiling. 'An officer I know well used to say, "You know me." '

'I think I know that guy too,' Jake said, and chuckled. 'Oh, all right, damn it – you can go. Gil and I will try to hold the fort without you. If the backup Osprey isn't needed, you'll be part of the cavalry. Tell the grunts to saddle up.'

The Spanish-speaking sailor who acted as an interpreter shook Ocho Sedano awake. 'Ocho,' he said. 'Ocho, a question has arisen. We wish to know if you are related to Hector Sedano.'

Ocho opened his eyes and focused on the interpreter, who appeared reasonably clear. His eyes were better, much better. He rolled over, then sat up in bed. He was still in sick bay aboard *Hue City*.

'Welcome back to the land of the living,' said the American sailor.

'It is good to be alive,' Ocho whispered.

'Did you ever give up hope?'

'I suppose. I thought I would die, and was waiting for it. But I always wanted to live.'

The sailor grinned. This was the first American he had ever gotten to know, and he had a good grin, Ocho thought.

'The officers want to know,' the sailor said, 'if you are related to Hector Sedano.'

'He is my brother.'

'I will tell them.'

Ocho nodded, then rubbed his head and stretched. He was hungry and thirsty. A glass of water was sitting on a rolling table beside the bed, so he drained it.

'May I have some food?'

'I will bring some.'

Ocho looked the sailor in the eyes. 'I want to go back to Cuba. I should never have left.'

'I will tell them,' the sailor said, and left him there.

William Henry Chance and Tommy Carmellini argued with Toad about how many marines wearing CBW suits should go into the warhead factory with them. 'Just Tommy and I,' Chance said. 'The more people that are in there the greater the chance of an accident.'

'How are you going to get your gear in there?'

'An armload at a time. It will take a little longer, but with only two guys going in and out, this whole evolution will be safer.'

'What if the Cuban Army shows up while you're working?'

'The marines can defend us until the place goes up.'

They were in a ready room under the flight deck dressing in a corner under the television set, which was showing a continuous briefing by the Air Intelligence types. Radio frequencies, threat envelopes, timing, call signs, weather, everything was on the tube.

Carmellini was paying close attention to the briefers, Chance was arguing with Toad. 'And I'm not taking a rifle or hand grenades or rations or any of that combat crap.'

'A pistol, then.'

'Got my own. Don't want two.'

'Why are you being so obstinate, Mr Chance?'

Chance sat down heavily in one of the ready-room chairs.

'I guess I've got a bad feeling about this commando stuff,' he said. 'Charging in decked out like Captain America with rifle in hand scares me silly. Everybody and his brother will start shooting, and with cultures above-ground in vulnerable containers . . .' He shivered. 'If we sneak in in civilian clothes . . . well, that's what I'm used to. This military stuff frightens me.'

'You're going to look funny walking into a dairy in civilian clothes with flares on your shoulders if there are Cuban troops sitting around the place guarding the cows.'

'You're right, I know.' Chance shrugged.

'Gonna be an adventure,' Tommy Carmellini tossed in.

'You guys are big boys,' Toad Tarkington said. 'I'm not going to nursemaid you. But this isn't a game – a lot of lives are at stake. If you screw this up and we gotta go back in there later and fix it, you guys better be dead. Don't bother coming back.'

Toad said it matter-of-factly, as if he were discussing a payroll deduction. Chance suddenly felt small.

591

'Okay,' he said. 'Two other guys in CBW suits. But I'm in charge. If I go down, Tommy is.'

'Fine,' said Toad Tarkington, and went to find an encrypted telephone.

Terror wasn't going to be enough to keep Alejo Vargas in office. He knew that. He could put the fear of God in the little sons of bitches and keep it there, but to sleep nights in Fidel's house he was going to have to govern the country, to give a little here, a little there, and so on. He was prepared to do that – he had watched Fidel manipulate these people all of his adult life.

Today he sat in his office at the Ministry of the Interior – he had had no time to move to the presidential palace – receiving the members of the Council of State, of which he was the president.

'Señor Ferrara, it is a pleasure to see you again.'

Ferrara was short, fat, and wheezed when he moved. He was a member of the Council of State and the minister of electric power. He dropped into a chair across the desk from Vargas and wiped his forehead with a handkerchief.

'Good day, Señor President.'

Colonel Santana handed Vargas Ferrara's affidavit. Vargas merely glanced at the signature, then laid it in his top right-hand drawer with the others. He didn't read it because he knew exactly what the affidavit contained – an emotional eyewitness account of the murder of Raúl Castro by Hector Sedano. Vargas and Santana had drafted the document this morning.

Before each member of the Council of State met with Vargas, Santana presented them with an affidavit for signature. Most intuitively understood that signatures were mandatory, and those that didn't had the facts of life explained to them. So far, all had signed.

'I appreciate your support in this matter, Ferrara.'

'I will be frank with you, Vargas. That document means nothing.' He gestured toward the desk drawer. 'You may be able to crack the whip in Havana, but the people do not support you. They want Hector Sedano in the presidential palace.'

'They will find a place in their heart for me.'

'Fidel Castro lasted for over forty years because he had the support of the people. The members of the National Assembly, the Council of State, the ministers, could not oppose him because they had no base of support. The Department of State Security didn't control the population – Fidel did.'

'He did not tolerate opposition, nor will I.'

Ferrara said nothing.

What was it about Ferrara? Something was in the files, but he hadn't looked at that file in years, and now it was gone. 'Was it your daughter?'

Ferrara's face became a mask.

'Your daughter ... something about your daughter ...'

He stared into Ferrara's eyes.

'Help me a little.'

Even Ferrara's wheezing had stopped.

'Maybe it will come to me.' Alejo Vargas leaned back in his chair. 'Or maybe I will forget completely.'

Santana came in just then, handed him a sheet of paper, and said, 'The ambassador to the United Nations received this note from the American UN ambassador.'

'Thank you for stopping by, Señor Ferrara. I appreciate you executing this affidavit. I look forward to working with you in the future. Good day.' Ferrara went.

Vargas read the note. 'Any other American reaction to my speech or their president's?'

'Yes, sir. As we expected, the American pundits generally support their president, but there are many who feel the United States has goaded Cuba into military adventurism with their political shunning of Castro. This feeling is widespread in Europe. Around the world there are many who feel that Cuba has endured much oppression at America's hands.'

Vargas nodded. All the world roots for the underdog.

'The American carrier battle group that was in Guantánamo is now south of the Isle of Pines. They have only a few planes aloft.'

'And General Alba? Is he getting troops into position around the silos?'

'Yes, sir.'

'Make sure the air force is on full alert, the army, the navy, the antiaircraft missile batteries, everyone. If the Americans come we will bloody their nose, perhaps even launch a missile. One missile will teach them a bitter lesson. They have never seen anything like that virus: they will have no stomach for it. The error of their ways is about to become quite apparent.'

'You do not believe this "massive retaliation" threat?'

'It is laughable,' he scoffed. 'No American president will ever order the use of weapons of mass destruction, even in retaliation. The Americans stopped making war years ago – they use force to send messages to "bad" governments, never to kill the civilians who support that government. Guilt is the new American ethic: they would be horrified at the murder of the hungry.' He waved his hand dismissively, then became deadly serious:

'The Yanquis may, however, screw up the courage to use force against our armed forces. If so, the Cuban people will rally to the flag and we shall heroically defend our national honor. And use the missiles to show them the error of their ways.'

'Cubans are patriots,' Santana agreed. 'After the Bay of Pigs, Castro was president for life.'

'A man with the right enemies can do anything,' Vargas declared, and smiled.

19

While Alejo Vargas and Colonel Santana were conferring in Havana, the Americans opened fire. Three Spruance-class destroyers that had sailed from Mayport soon after sunrise were now fifty miles off the Florida coast headed south, well away from the coastal shipping lanes. They began launching Tomahawk cruise missiles from the vertical launchers buried in the deck in front of their bridges. Although each ship carried forty-eight Tomahawks in their vertical launch tubes, they only launched twenty missiles each.

On the bridge of USS *Comte de Grasse* the captain watched with binoculars as his missiles leveled out from their launch climb and disappeared into the sea haze. One of the missiles dove into the ocean, making a tiny splash.

'There went three million bucks,' he muttered.

After the launch was complete, he called down to Combat on the squawk box. 'How many successfully launched?'

'Nineteen, sir.'

'And the other ships?'

'Twenty and eighteen, Captain.'

'What is the time of flight?'

'An hour and twenty minutes, sir.'

'Very well. Report the launch.'

Not bad, the captain thought, and gave orders to secure from General Quarters.

God help the Cubans, he thought, then turned to the navigator to discuss the voyage to the Florida Straits, where *Comte de Grasse* and her sister ships would join the Aegis cruisers already there.

Aboard USS *United States*, Jake Grafton seated himself in the admiral's raised chair in Combat and surveyed the computer displays. Gil Pascal, the chief of staff, was also there along with the ship's air wing commander, the Combat Control Center officer and the members of his staff.

Jake leaned over and whispered to Pascal. 'See if you can find me some aspirin, please.'

'Yes, sir.'

He was looking over the plan and watching the display of commercial traffic going in and out of José Martí International Airport in Havana when a chief petty officer handed him the encrypted satellite phone.

'Admiral Grafton, sir.'

'This is the president, Admiral. How goes the war?'

'We already have Tomahawks in the air, sir, but the Cubans won't know what's coming for an hour or so.'

'We're sweating the program here in Washington,' the president continued. 'Our feet are getting frosty. If we chicken out, could the airborne Tomahawks be intentionally crashed?'

Jake Grafton took a deep breath and exhaled before he answered. 'Yes, sir. That is possible.'

'Let's hold on to that option. I'm sitting here with General Totten and the senior leadership of the Congress. I want your opinion on this question: Should we postpone this show for a day or two? Or indefinitely? What are your thoughts?'

Jake Grafton licked his lips. In his mind's eye he could see ballistic missiles rising from their silos on pillars of fire, and sailors, just like the ones manning the computers here in Combat aboard *United States*, sitting in front of radar scopes and computer keyboards aboard the Aegis cruisers.

'Mr President, I have also been thinking about the risks. The only thing I can promise is that we will do our best. No one can guarantee results. Still, in my opinion, considering just the military risks, we should go now, without delay.'

'Thank you, Admiral,' the president said.

'Jake, this is Tater Totten.'

'Good evening, sir.'

'Just wanted to say good luck,' the general said, then the connection broke.

Jake Grafton handed the handset to the chief.

'Here is your aspirin, Admiral,' Gil Pascal said, holding out water and three white pills.

Four EA-6B Prowlers sat on the ramp at NAS Key West. Their crews stood lounging around the aircraft. They had flown in just an hour ago, and now the fuel trucks were pulling away. The crews had huddled with the crew of the two C-130 Hercs parked on the ramp, studying charts and checking frequencies. Now it was time to man up.

As the marines in full combat gear filed aboard the Hercs, the crews of the Prowlers strapped in and started engines. Two of the Prowlers carried three electronic jamming pods on external stations and two HARM missiles. HARM stood for high-speed anti-radiation missile. The other two Prowlers carried four HARMS and one jamming pod on the center-line station.

With the engines running, the pilots closed the Prowlers' canopies and taxied behind the Hercs toward the duty runway. No one said anything on the radio.

The flight deck of USS *United States* came alive. A small army of people in brightly colored shirts swarmed around the airplanes that packed the deck as the flight crews manned up and started engines.

Light from the setting sun came in at a low angle like a bright spotlight, illuminating the towering cumulus which dotted the surface of the sea, and made everyone facing west squint or shade their eyes.

Soon the plane guard rescue helicopter engaged its rotors and lifted off the deck as the first airplanes began taxiing toward the bow and waist catapults.

Aboard USS *Hue City* and USS *Guilford Courthouse*, the two Aegis cruisers on station in the Florida Straits, the afternoon had been a busy one. Twenty-five miles of ocean separated the two ships, but they were linked together electronically as tightly as if they were wired together at a pier.

As the Hercs and EA-6Bs taxied at Key West, and *United States* prepared to launch her air wing, the weapons officers aboard the cruisers checked the ships' inertial systems one more time, compared the GPS locations yet again, then gave the fire order.

The first of the Tomahawk missiles rose vertically from their launchers on fountains of fire. The wings of the missiles popped out, then the missiles began tilting to the south as they accelerated away into the evening sky.

The first missiles from each ship were still in sight when the second ones came roaring from the launchers. Each ship launched sixteen missiles, then turned to stay in the race-track pattern they had been using to hold station.

Sitting in the Combat Control Center aboard *United States,* Jake Grafton felt the thump as the first bow catapult fired. A second later he felt the number-three cat on the waist slam a plane into the air. His eyes went to the monitor, which was showing a video feed from a camera mounted high in the ship's island superstructure. Each catapult stroke was felt throughout the ship as the planes were thrown into the sky, one by one.

A half dozen planes were still on deck awaiting their turn on the catapults when the destroyers in the carrier's screen began launching Tomahawk cruise missiles.

The television cameraman in the ship's island swung his camera to catch the fireworks. The picture captured the attention of the people in Combat, who paused to watch the missiles roar from their launchers on fountains of reddish yellow fire, almost too brilliant to look at.

When the last of the missiles was gone, the camera returned to the launching planes.

Gil Pascal said to Jake, 'It'll go well, Admiral.'

Jake nodded and took another sip of water.

The sun seemed to be taking its good ol' time going down, Lieutenant Commander Marcus Gillispie thought.

He was at the controls of an EA-6B Prowler that had just launched from *United States.* He had worked his way around towering buildups reaching up to 10,000 feet and was now above them, looking at the evening sky. The last of the red sunlight played on the tops of the clouds, but the canyons between them were purple and gray shading to black. As Gillispie climbed he delayed the sun's apparent setting for a few more minutes. Soon the last of the red and gold faded from the cloud tops below.

A very high cirrus layer stayed yellow and red for the longest time as Marcus circled the carrier at 30,000 feet. Two F/A-18 Hornets came swimming up from the deepening gloom to join on him.

'You guys all set?' Marcus asked his three crewmen.

His crewmen counted off in order.

The Prowler was the electronic-warfare version of the old A-6 Intruder airframe. While the Prowler bore a superficial resemblance to its older brother, the electronic suite in the aircraft could not have been more different: the Prowler was designed to fight the electronic battle in today's skies, not drop bombs.

The airframe was also longer than the old A-6, lengthened to accommodate four people and a massive array of computerized cockpit displays. The people sat in ejection seats, two in the front, two in the back. Only one of the crewmen was a pilot, who sat in the left front seat: the other three were electronic-warfare specialists. And they were not all men. One of the guys in back tonight was a woman, a lieutenant (junior grade) on her first cruise.

Marcus looked at his watch, then keyed his mike. He waited while his encryption gear timed in with the ship's gear, then said, 'Strike, this is Nighthawk One. I have my chicks and am ready to leave orbit. Request permission to strangle the parrot.'

'Roger, Nighthawk One. Call feet dry.'

'Wilco.'

Marcus Gillispie rolled the Prowler wings level heading northwest for the city of Havana. Then he engaged the autopilot. When he was satisfied that the autopilot was going to keep the plane straight and level, he flashed his exterior lights, then turned them off, leaving only a set of tiny formation lights illuminated on the sides of the aircraft above the wing root. Finally he reached down and turned his radar transponder, his parrot, off. The Prowler and the two Hornets on her wing were no longer radiating on any electromagnetic frequency.

The pilot looked back past his wingtips at the Hornets. One was on each wing now. Like the Prowler, their missile racks were loaded with HARMs. The Hornets also carried two Sidewinders, heat-seeking air-to-air missiles, one on each wingtip, just in case.

Already the displays in the Prowler were alive with information. The electronic countermeasures officer, ECMO, in the seat beside the pilot, was really the tactical commander of the plane. His gear, and that of the two electronic-warfare officers in the back cockpit, provided a complete display of the tactical electronic picture. The information the computers used was derived from sensors embedded all over the aircraft in its skin, and from the sensors of one of the HARM missiles, which was already on line.

The ECMO with Marcus Gillispie was Commander Schuyler Coleridge, the squadron commanding officer, who wound up in the right seat of Prowlers because his eyes were not quite 20/20 uncorrected when he graduated from the Naval Academy. The truth of it was, he thought he had the better job. Pilots, he liked to say, just drove the bus – ECMOs fought the war.

He had one to fight tonight. The Cubans were going to get really riled when those Tomahawks started popping, he thought, and then the fireworks would start.

Just now Coleridge was busy running his equipment through its built-in tests. Everything was working, as usual. That routine fact was the greatest advance of the technological age, in Coleridge's opinion. In his younger days he had had a bellyful of fancy equipment that couldn't be maintained.

He was sweating just now, even though the cockpit temperature was positively balmy. And he knew his fellow crewmen were sweating – this was the first time in combat for all of them.

It will go all right, he thought. After the tension he had suffered through this afternoon and evening, Schuyler Coleridge actually welcomed the catapult shot. *Let's do it and get it over with.*

All four of the squadron's EA-6Bs were aloft just now, and the other three also had pairs of Hornets attached.

As Coleridge looked at the search radars sweeping the Cuban skies, he wondered if there were going to be MiGs.

'Okay, people,' Coleridge told his crew, 'let's go to work.'

A search radar on the southern coast of Cuba drew his attention. The signal was being received by the HARM sensors, which routed the electronic signal through the plane's computer and displayed it on the tactical screen.

Coleridge checked his watch. 'Any second now,' he muttered to his crewmen.

The Cubans had their search radars wired into sector facilities, which performed the functions of air traffic control (ATC) for civilian aircraft and early warning and ground control interception (GCI) for military aircraft. ATC radars in developed countries rarely searched for non-transponder-equipped targets, but due to the dual usage of these radars, such sweeps were routine. Consequently one of the controllers in the Havana sector was the first to notice a cloud of skin-paint targets closing on the Cuban coast from the south.

His call to the supervisor was echoed by a call from a controller looking at targets headed south toward the north coast of the island.

The shift supervisor stood frozen, staring over the operator's shoulder at the radar screen. He had wondered if something like this might not happen after Alejo Vargas's television speech, but when he asked the site manager about the possibility of Cuba being attacked by the United States, the man had laughed. 'The world has changed since the Bay of Pigs, Pedro. You are safe – have courage.' The response humiliated the shift supervisor.

Now the supervisor picked up his telephone, called the manager in his office. 'You'd better come see this,' he said with an edge on his voice. 'Come quickly.'

The manager was looking over the supervisor's shoulder when the first Tomahawk crashed into the antenna of the main search radar on the southern coast. In seconds three more radars went off the air.

The stunned men turned their attention to the radars on the north coast, and were just in time to watch the blip of a Tomahawk from *Hue City* fly right down the throat of the radar and knock it out.

The supervisor turned to the manager and calmly said, 'Apparently the war you didn't believe would happen is happening now.'

The stunned manager watched in horror as screen after screen went blank.

'The Americans rarely leave things half-done, or so I've heard,' the supervisor continued. 'I would bet fifty pesos that this building is also a target of a cruise missile. If you gentlemen will excuse me, I think I will go home for the evening.'

With that, he turned and walked briskly from the room.

'Everyone out,' the facilities manager shouted. 'Outside, everyone outside.'

The men at the consoles needed no urging. They bolted for the doors.

The shift supervisor was outside, walking quickly for the bus stop, when he heard a Tomahawk. He fell to the ground and covered his head with his hands as the missile dove into the roof of the sector control building and its 750-pound warhead exploded with a thundering boom. Within the next fifteen seconds, two more missiles crashed into the building.

After waiting another minute just to be sure, the supervisor stood and surveyed the damage. Clouds of tiny dust particles formed an artificial fog, one illuminated by flame licking at the gutted building. The stench of explosives residue and smoke lay heavy in the night air.

One hundred fifty missiles swept across central Cuba, some coming from the north, some from the south. The targeting had been done quickly, but the information that made it possible had been mined from databases painstakingly constructed from satellite and aircraft photo and electronic reconnaissance over a period of years.

Four dozen Tomahawks were targeted against every known radar dish within a hundred miles of the missile silos – search, air traffic, antiaircraft missile, and artillery radars – all of them, two missiles for each antenna.

Another fifty Tomahawks attacked every Cuban Air Force base along the five-hundred-mile length of the island. Some of the Tomahawks carried bomblets instead of high-explosive warheads: these swept across aircraft ramps, scattering bomblets over the parked MiGs, damaging them and setting some on fire. Other cruise missiles dove headfirst into the Cuban Air Force's hangars, weapons storage facilities, and fuel farms. Fixed antiaircraft surface-to-air missile (SAM) sites received two or three missiles each.

Alejo Vargas learned of the American attack when the telephone he was using went dead in his hand. He frowned, jiggled the hook, then replaced the handset on its base. Only then did the dull boom of the explosion in the central Havana telephone exchange reach him. A Tomahawk had dived through the roof.

More explosions followed in quick succession as two more cruise missiles hurled themselves into the telephone exchange. One of the problems the Americans faced with the employment of cruise missiles was assessing damage after the attack. The solution was to fire multiple missiles at the same target to ensure an acceptable level of damage.

The thought that the presidential palace might be a target never occurred to Alejo Vargas. He went to the nearest window and stood listening to the roar of Tomahawks overflying the city on their way to radar and antiaircraft gun and missile installations sited around José Martí International Airport. The five-hundred-knot missiles were invisible in the darkness, but they weren't quiet.

The missiles had passed when someone near the harbor opened up with an antiaircraft gun firing tracers. The bursts of tracers went up like fireworks and randomly probed the darkness as the hammering reports echoed over the city.

Colonel Santana came into the room and joined Vargas at the window. 'The telephone system in the city is out.'

'It's probably out all over Cuba,' Vargas replied.

'They are attacking much sooner than you thought they would.'

'No matter. The results will be the same. Get a car to take us to Radio Havana. I will make an address to the nation.'

'The Americans may use missiles on the radio stations or power plants.'

'It is possible, but I doubt it. Get the car.'

Santana went after a car as Vargas thought about what he would say to fan the fires of patriotism in every Cuban heart.

The two C-130s Hercs and four EA-6B Prowlers that had left Key West were level at ten thousand feet when they crossed the northern shoreline of Cuba. The C-130s actually were flying with their wingtip lights on so that the Prowlers could easily stay in formation with them. Inside the Hercs the pilots were using global positioning system (GPS) units to navigate to the missile silo sites.

The Prowler crews watched their computer displays and listened to their emission-detection gear, waiting for the Cubans to turn on a radar, any radar. The night was deathly quiet. The Tomahawks had done their work well.

As the Hercs crossed over the first of the dairy farms, two men leaped from each plane. Forty seconds later two more went as they crossed over the second possible lab site. Then the Hercs made a gentle, lazy 270-degree turn to get lined up for the run-in to the missile silos.

José Martí Airport and the surface-to-air missile sites that surrounded it were only thirty miles west. Not a peep from them. If the Tomahawks missed any of the mobile radars, the operators had not yet screwed up the courage to turn them on, for which the Hercules crews were thankful. The Prowler crews, however, with HARM missiles ready on the rails, were feeling a bit disappointed. After all the sweating, there should be more *action*.

Aboard USS *United States*, the datalink from the E-3 Sentry AWACS over Key West revealed the aerial fire drill going on over Havana as commercial flights tried to find their way into José Martí Airport without the aid of air traffic controllers with radar. Some of the flights announced they were diverting, and headed for the United States or Jamaica or the Cayman Islands. The others queued up and landed VFR as Jake Grafton watched the computer displays with his fingers crossed. While he didn't want to be responsible for the crash of a civilian airliner, he couldn't delay this operation until there was a temporary lull in civilian air activity.

As the first Herc approached silo one, two men leaped from the open rear door. Seconds later, two more leaped from the second transport.

The jumpers fell away from the airplanes like stones.

Over silo two, marines leaped in pairs from each of the Hercs, and so on, until the transports had overflown and dropped recon teams at all six silo sites. Then they turned northward, toward the sea.

The Prowlers followed faithfully.

At that moment a SAM control radar near silo two came on the air, probing for a target.

The Prowlers with the Hercs picked up the signal, of course, and two of them dropped their wings to turn back toward the threat.

Forty miles south of silo two, Schuyler Coleridge also picked up the SAM radar, an old Soviet Fansong. As he slaved the HARM to the signal, his pilot, Marcus Gillispie, turned the plane ten degrees to point at the offending radar. Although the new missiles could be fired at very large angles, a quick turn by the launching aircraft shortened the missile's flight time by a few seconds.

'Fire,' Coleridge ordered, and Gillispie punched off the HARM, which shot forward off the rail in a blaze of fire.

Coleridge keyed the radio. 'Fox Three,' he said, letting everyone on the freq know that a beam rider was in the air.

The HARM zeroed in on the side lobes of the radiating Fansong, whose operator was trying to lock up a Herc for an SA-2 launch. The operator never realized the beam rider was in the air.

The missile actually flew into the back of the antenna dish at almost Mach 3 and went several feet through it before the warhead exploded.

The warhead contained thousands of 3/16th-inch tungsten-alloy cubes, which were three times denser than steel. The warhead blasted these cubes in all directions, obliterating the radar antenna and wave guides, shredding the trailer on which the antenna was mounted, and knocking out the equipment in the trailer. The flying cubes also killed the radar operator and severely wounded the three other occupants of the trailer.

Another HARM launched by one of the F/A-18 Hornets on the Prowler's wing arrived six seconds later and impacted a tree just a few feet from the smoking, gutted trailer. Although the target radar had been off the air for six seconds, the missile's strap-down inertial allowed it to fly to the place where the computer memory believed the radar to be. The shrapnel from the warhead severed the tree and sprayed the shell of the trailer yet again, killing one of the already wounded men.

Major Carlos Corrado was sleeping off a hangover when the roar of a Tomahawk going over woke him. His eyes came open. He heard the staccato popping of bomblets from the Tomahawk, but had no idea what caused the sound. He thought the Tomahawk was a low-flying airplane.

Groggy, aching, sick to his stomach, he was hugging a commode when another Tomahawk went over. In ten seconds the sound of the bomblets detonating on the planes parked on the flight line reached him through his alcoholic haze. Then one of the planes exploded with a rolling crash that shook the barracks.

Corrado staggered outside and looked toward the flight line, where at least three planes were burning brightly.

'Holy Mother!'

Suddenly sober, Corrado went back inside and hastily donned his flight suit and boots.

He was jogging toward the flight line when another Tomahawk went over scattering bomblets. The missile flew on, out of sight.

As Corrado rounded the corner and the flight line came into view, the first cruise missile that had scattered bomblets dove into one of the hangers.

There wasn't much of an explosion, but in seconds a hot fire was burning in the wooden structure.

Corrado's personal fighter was parked between the burning hangar and another, which would probably be struck within seconds. The maintenance men had been working on the plane today, which was why it was not on its usual parking place at the head of the flight line.

Running men helped Corrado push the plane away from the burning hangar, the wall of which was perilously close to collapse.

'There is no fuel in the plane,' someone shouted.

'Get a truck,' Corrado roared in reply. 'And ammunition for the guns.'

The words were no more out of his mouth when the second missile crashed into the untouched hangar.

Corrado seethed as linemen fueled his plane and serviced the guns. He was still on the phone in the dispersal shack talking to someone at the base armory when the truck carrying missiles braked to a squealing halt near the fighter, a silver MiG-29 Fulcrum. Now he called the sector GCI site. The telephone rang and rang, but no one answered.

Corrado stuck an unlit cigar in his mouth and stomped out to the plane. 'Careful there, fools. Do it right. Do not embarrass me.'

He was watching the last of the 30-mm cannon shells going into the feed trays when one of the Havana colonels showed up.

'You aren't going up in this thing, are you, Corrado?'

'We are servicing it as a joke, dear Colonel. Every Saturday night when the Americans attack we put the cannon shells in, then take them out on Sunday morning.'

'Don't trifle with me, Major. I won't stand for it.'

'You pompous limp-dick! Go find a whore and let the real men fight.'

'Do not insult me, you sot. You stink of rum and vomit! Show some respect!'

'Why should I? Your putrid face insults you every day.'

The colonel was so angry he spluttered. 'I absolutely forbid you to fly this airplane without written orders from Havana.'

'Court-martial me tomorrow.'

'The Americans will destroy this airplane if you take it off the ground. To fly it is sabotage, a crime against the state. If you attempt to fly it, I will shoot you.' The colonel pulled out his pistol and showed Corrado the business end.

Corrado ignored the gun. 'You are a traitor,' he roared, 'who wants the Americans to win. Defeatist! Coward!'

'I will shoot anyone who helps you defect in this airplane,' the colonel screamed. He pointed the pistol at the troops closing the servicing doors on the MiG-29. 'Counterrevolutionaries! Saboteurs!'

Corrado used his fist on the colonel. The second punch, in the ear, did the trick. The man went to his knees, then onto his face. He didn't get up.

One of the linemen picked up the pistol while the major massaged his knuckles. His hand hurt like hell but didn't seem to be broken.

In truth Corrado wasn't much of a man. He had abandoned a wife and child years ago and hadn't heard from them since – didn't want to hear from them, because they would probably want money. What money he got his hands on he drank up; he even sold military equipment on the black market to pay for alcohol. His ability to fly a fighter plane was his sole skill, his only worthwhile accomplishment in thirty-six years of life. Now, unexpectedly, miraculously, he had a chance to use that skill to defend something larger than himself, to make his miserable life mean something – and no strutting Havana rooster was going to cheat him out of it.

Carlos Corrado gestured at the men. 'Get the missiles loaded, you lazy bastards,' he shouted. 'There's a war on.'

Richard Merriweather rode his parachute into a cornfield. At least, he thought it was corn – long, stiff stalks, head-high. He checked himself over; he was sore, but nothing broken. He stood and wrestled the chute toward him, then began scooping out a hole to bury it. He was finishing the job when he heard someone coming toward him.

'Sergeant?'

'Yo. You okay?'

'Yeah,' said Kirb Handy.

'Set up the GPS. Figure out where we are.'

With the parachute disposed of, Merriweather put on his night-vision goggles and took a careful look around. He was well out in the center of this field, near as he could tell.

Merriweather sat down in the dirt beside Handy, who was also wearing night-vision goggles. Handy punched buttons on the GPS.

'This thing says we are a mile and a half southwest.'

'I'll buy that.'

'Missed the landing zone by a half mile.'

'Not bad at all.' Merriweather unslung his weapon and checked it over. Then he got to his feet.

'The other two guys should be around,' Handy muttered.

'They'd better be. We don't have much time.'

After a careful check of the GPS unit, the two men started walking northeast toward missile silo number six. They had gone only about a hundred meters when they came to the bank of a stream, a fairly wide stream.

'What the hell is this?' Merriweather demanded, and got out his map. He and Handy huddled behind a tree studying the thing.

'Holy shit,' Handy said. 'We're in the wrong place. We're at least four miles from the damned silo. Look here.' He pointed to the stream. 'That has gotta be this thing in front of us.'

'So where's the other half of our team?'

'Gotta be over there, near the silo.'

'Let's get on the phone, give 'em the bad news.'

'Oh, man,' Handy moaned softly. 'This ain't good.'

The four-man recon team for silo number two approached the barn via a large seasonal drainage ditch that ran more or less in the right direction. Fortunately the sides were relatively dry, though the ditch contained a few inches of water and the bottom felt soft.

They stopped moving when they were about fifty meters from the barn where they believed the silo to be. They were completely surrounded by Cuban Army troops. Two tanks stood outside the barn, trucks were parked in a nearby grove of trees, and troops were setting up a cooking tent near the farmhouse's well. Other soldiers were down in the woods to the left, presumably digging latrines.

'Must be a couple hundred of 'em,' Asel Tyvek whispered to Jamail Ali, who was lying in the ditch beside him.

'Sure as hell we can't stay here,' Ali whispered. 'It's just a matter of time before somebody inspects this damn ditch with a flashlight.'

'The silo must be in that barn. Gotta be. If we crawl down this ditch, we should get within thirty yards of the thing. When the shit hits the fan, maybe we can get in there.'

'Let's spread out, man, fifty yards apart,' Jamail Ali suggested. 'If they find one of us, the others will have a chance.' Tyvek nodded and Ali whispered to the other two men, and pointed. They disappeared into the darkness.

Tyvek keyed the mike on his helmet-mounted radio. In seconds he was talking to a controller aboard USS *United States*, telling her what he saw around the missile silo.

'Twelve minutes,' the female voice from *United States* said in his ear. 'Twelve minutes.'

'Roger that, Battlestar. Twelve minutes.'

Norman Tillman and the three men of his recon team were up to their knees in cow shit. They waded through the barnyard and shoved the mooing dairy cattle out of the way so that they could get to the door of the barn, a possible biological weapons manufacturing site.

'I thought there weren't any damn cows around here,' Tillman's number two muttered unpleasantly.

Tillman took off his night-vision goggles, got his flashlight in hand, and took a firm grip on his rifle. He nodded at his number two, who carefully opened the barn door, which creaked on its rusty hinges anyway. Tillman launched himself through the door opening. He slipped on something, fell, and slid for several feet on his chest. Much to his disgust, he could identify the substance he was lying in by its smell.

Tillman stood, used the flashlight. He was standing in a conventional wooden barn that had not been mucked out in several weeks. Two cows turned and stared at the light. They looked nervous, as if they wanted to run, then began bawling. Cursing under his breath, Norman Tillman went on through the building, checking it out.

Five minutes later he stepped outside and keyed his helmet radio. 'Battlestar, this is Team One. Negative results. Nothing here but cows.'

'Roger, Team One. Stand by for a pickup.'

'Team One standing by. Out.'

'I thought there weren't any cows at these sites,' one of the men said.

'Yeah, but the cows didn't know they were supposed to be on vacation.'

'Maybe we landed at the wrong dairy farm.'

Tillman thought that over. Naw. That would be quite a screwup. More likely, the cows were being held in a nearby field when the recon photos were taken.

'Sarge, somebody coming.'

The men dove facedown into the dirt-and-manure mix at their feet. The person coming turned out to be a farmhand in civilian clothes. The marines made him sit with his back against the barn wall where they could watch him, but they didn't tie his hands.

At first the man was frightened. He got over it when one of the troops offered him a cigarette and lit it for him.

Tillman crawled over a fence out of the muck and sat down under a tree to wait for the helicopter. One man watched the farmer while the other two posted themselves as sentinels.

20

'There are several hundred troops and three or four tanks around silos one and two, Admiral, and at least two tanks and a squad of soldiers around three. Four and five appear to be unguarded. The recon team checking out silo six seems to have been dropped in the wrong place – only two of the four have reported in; they estimate they are three miles from the silo. We haven't been able to contact the other two men.'

The briefer was an Air Intelligence officer who zapped the map with a laser flashlight pointer whenever he mentioned a silo.

Jake Grafton wasn't paying much attention to the map, which he had memorized. He glanced at his watch, compared it with a clock on the bulkhead.

'Lab site Alpha is a dairy farm. The recon team checking out Bravo reports jackpot, but not many troops – no more than a dozen. The Osprey will be there in less than ten minutes.'

The admiral got up from his chair, stretched, rubbed the back of his neck. So far it was going better than he expected it would. So far. Nobody shot down yet, only one recon team lost . . .

'Is someone monitoring Cuban radio and television?'

'Yes, sir. The National Security Agency. They will keep us advised.'

'Ummm.'

'What are we going to do about silo six, Admiral?' Gil Pascal asked.

'Nothing we can do. The assault team will have to go into the landing zone blind.'

'The Cuban Army may be waiting.'

'They might,' Jake Grafton agreed.

He put on his headset and switched between radio channels. By simply flipping switches he could monitor the aircraft tactical channels. In addition, with the new tactical com units, he and his staff could hear everything that was said on the helmet radios worn by marine officers and NCOs.

Since the signals were rebroadcast and ultimately picked up by the satellite, they were also being monitored in the war room of the White House. One of Jake's concerns was that the politicians or senior officers would be tempted to step into the middle of the operation. Although the Washington kibitzers could not communicate on the nets, they could quickly get in touch with someone who could, and an order was an order, even if ill-considered.

He would worry about the politicians when the meddling started, he decided, not before.

Doll Hanna was the recon team leader at dairy Bravo. He was sitting on a biological warhead assembly plant and he knew it. There wasn't a cow in sight, two clean, modern dairy trucks sat near the entrance to the barn, and Hanna could hear air conditioners running. And the Cuban Army was guarding the place.

From where he lay he could see two soldiers in cloth hats with rifles in their arms standing in front of the main entrance. He knew that there were men on the door in the rear of the building and in the old thatch-roofed farmhouse nearby.

Doll Hanna touched the transmit button on his radio. 'Willie, you take the two guys on the north side. Fred, you got the farmhouse. Goose, these two on the main entrance.'

All three men acknowledged.

Doll was wearing his night-vision goggles so he could see Goose crawling behind the milk trucks, then under them, working his way toward the entrance. It was eerie watching Goose sneak along, knowing the guards couldn't see him.

Taking out two men was a challenge. Either one could raise the alarm.

Goose moved like he had all night.

He didn't, Doll Hanna well knew. The Osprey was out there now circling, but it wouldn't come in until he called the area clear. Still, the plane only had so much fuel and the Cubans wouldn't stay quiet forever.

In fact, a truckload of soldiers could come rolling in here any minute. The troops in the Osprey, when they arrived, would set up a perimeter to keep the Cuban military away.

'Doll, this is Fred. I'm going to make some noise over here.'

'Okay.'

No doubt Goose and Willie heard that transmission. Noise would cause the guards to do something. If necessary, Goose and Willie could just shoot them down.

Hanna heard the faint sound of a slamming door come from the direction of the farmhouse.

The guards near the main door to the dairy got to their feet, looked at each other, then started toward the house. One stopped, told the other to stay, then went on with his weapon at the ready. As he went around the truck out of sight of the guard at the door, Goose got him with a knife.

Then Goose waited.

The man at the door called out to his friend.

Nothing.

The guard looked worried. He called again, got no answer, then walked forward twenty feet or so. He stopped, cocked his head, stood looking into the darkness and trying to hear over the hum of the big air conditioners.

He was standing like that when Goose stepped out from behind the truck and threw a knife. The guard dropped his rifle and pitched forward on his face.

Hanna got up, trotted for the door of the barn. He passed Goose, who was bending over the second guard checking to make sure he was dead. Carefully Doll eased the door open and looked inside.

There were people inside, all right, behind transparent plastic curtains that formed biological seals. They were wearing full body-and-head CBW suits, so they looked like spacemen walking around in there between trays of cultures and rows of worktables.

They had apparently heard nothing above the noise of the air-ventilation system, which was a loud, steady hum.

Doll eased his head back. The people in there would have to wait until the experts arrived.

Major Carlos Corrado walked onto the runway of the Cienfuegos Air Base. The runway lights were off and the night was fairly dark considering that two hangars and at least five aircraft were ablaze. He could hear people shouting, about fire, about water, about missiles, about staying under cover. Straining hard he could hear several cruise missiles – and airplanes – up there in the darkness – American airplanes, because in order to save money, the Cuban Air Force, the *Fuerza Aerea Revolucionaria,* did not fly at night.

What was happening? Where was the war?

Carlos Corrado had no illusions about the difficulties involved in engaging the American military. His MiG-29, a stripped Soviet export version, had only the most rudimentary of electronic detection equipment and lacked any active countermeasures. And his GCI site was probably in the same condition as the burning hangars behind him.

If he left his radar off he would not beacon on the Americans' detection equipment. And he would be electronically blind.

Perhaps if he stayed low . . .

Another cruise missile roared overhead and dove into the last undamaged hangar. The 750-pound warhead rocked the base, then the hangar collapsed outward, its walls silhouetted black against the yellowish white fireball caused by the warhead.

Well, if the Americans were pounding Cienfuegos, they must be pulverizing José Martí International in Havana.

Havana. The war would be in Havana, so that was where he would go.

The V-22 Osprey twin-engine tiltrotor assault transport was the ultimate flying machine, or so Rita Moravia liked to tell her husband, Toad Tarkington. It hovered like a helicopter and flew like an airplane, operated from the deck of an airborne assault ship, and was at its best after the sun went down.

So here she was, in the pilot's seat of a V-22 on her way to a ballistic-missile silo in the Matanzas Province of central Cuba with 24 combat-ready marines, loaded for bear. She had made a vertical takeoff from *Kearsarge* and was now thundering along at two thousand feet over the Cuban countryside at 250 knots, navigating by GPS and monitoring the forward-looking infrared display (FLIR), which revealed the countryside ahead as if the sun were shining down from a cloudless sky.

Rita's copilot was Captain Crash Wade, USMC, who earned his nickname in an unfortunate series of ski adventures, not flying accidents. Wade paid careful attention to the multi-function displays (MFDs), computer presentations of everything the pilots needed to know, on the instrument panel in front of him.

Rita was paying careful attention to the voice on the radio, which was that of Asel Tyvek, NCO in charge of the marine recon team at silo number two. Rita didn't know his real name, just his call sign, Blue One.

'Old Rover, this is Blue One. I want you to hold four minutes out while we get some ordnance on this LZ. It's sizzling hot.'

'Old Rover, Roger.' Rita keyed the intercom. 'Okay, Crash, do a holding pattern.'

'How come we got the hot LZ?' Crash wanted to know.

'Just lucky, I guess,' Rita replied, and selected an intercom button that would allow her to talk to the lieutenant in the cargo bay with his troops.

Asel Tyvek and Jamail Ali were side by side in the ditch, just thirty yards or so from the barn. The other two members of the team were also in the ditch, but well left and right.

'We ought to get in the barn,' Ali whispered, 'in case the Cubans want to get in there too.'

'Man, those little boards ain't gonna protect anybody from anything. You just be ready in case the Cubans start diving into this damned ditch with us.'

'Listen, I can hear our guys coming.'

Tyvek strained his ears. Yep, he could just detect the distinctive beat of chopper rotors. 'Snake One, Blue One,' he whispered into his radio. 'Cuban troops all around the barn. At least two tanks, eight or nine trucks, a couple hundred men. We're in a ditch near the barn.'

'Got your head down?'

'Yeah.'

Tyvek could hear the choppers distinctly now. He eased his weapon up, put his finger on the safety. The Cubans were going to be looking for cover very shortly, and he didn't want to share the ditch.

The SuperCobras eased up over the tree line, barely moving. Tyvek knew what was going to happen next, and it did. He heard the roar as Hellfire antiarmor missiles screamed toward the tanks, and he heard the explosions as they hit.

He lifted his head above the ditch line for a quick peek. The tanks were smoking hulks. Even as he watched, more missiles tore into the trucks.

Not a standing figure could be seen. Everyone was on the ground, crawling or lying still.

The two SuperCobras came closer. The noise of their engines was quite plain now. The flex three-barreled 20-mm cannons opened up and rockets shot forward from the pylons under the stubby wings.

The men in the yard realized they couldn't stay where they were – the area was a killing zone. Some jumped up and ran for the ditch. Fortunately few of them seemed to have weapons in their hands – the attack had caught them by surprise.

'Here they come,' Tyvek shouted, and opened up on the men closest to the ditch. He couldn't shoot them fast enough. Men dashed for the cover of the ditch as he and Ali and the other two poured fire into them and the SuperCobras lashed the area with ordnance.

Tyvek spoke into the voice-activated mike on his helmet-mounted radio. 'We're gonna need some help, Old Rover. Whenever you can get here.'

Something heavy fell across Tyvek's legs. He spun and fired at the same time, but the man was already dead: Ali had shot him.

'They're going into the barn!' Ali shouted. He fired a whole magazine at three men trying to get through the front door. One of the men disappeared inside.

Jamail Ali scrambled over the edge of the ditch and ran for the barn while Tyvek screamed at the SuperCobra gunners not to shoot him.

'Snake One Four, this is Orange One.' Richard Merriweather let go of the mike and waited for an answer from the SuperCobra inbound to silo six.

'Orange One, Snake One Four.'

'Man, we're on the wrong side of this river or creek five or six clicks south of the LZ. How about seeing if you can find us.'

'Are you standing up?'

'In plain sight.'

Merriweather and his partner, Kirb Handy, stepped away from the trees. With their night-vision goggles, the SuperCobra crewmen should have no trouble seeing two men standing in an open field, and they didn't.

Both the helicopters settled to earth and the marines on the ground ran to them.

The pilot of the lead chopper opened his canopy as Merriweather ran over. 'Where are the other guys?'

'Haven't seen them or talked to them. Don't know.'

'Seen any bad guys?'

'Nope. How about a ride over toward the barn?'

'Sit on the wheel and grab hold. We run into trouble, you gotta get off if we drop down low.'

Merriweather gave the pilot a thumbs-up and arranged himself on the wheel. Handy was clinging to the wheel on the other side.

The chopper came slowly into a hover, then dipped its nose and began moving forward. Merriweather held on for dear life as the rotor downwash and slipstream tore at his clothing, helmet, and gear, and threatened to rip the night vision goggles from his head.

What a stupid idea this was! How in hell had they ended up four miles south of the goddamned landing zone? If he ever again laid eyes on that son of a bitch who flew the Herc, he was going to stomp his ass.

Bryne and McCormick – those two were missing. If they were okay surely they would have checked in on the radio. Maybe their parachutes didn't open. Maybe they fell into that river. Maybe the Cubans captured them as soon as they hit the ground. Maybe, maybe, maybe . . .

He could see the barn now. The chopper was just a few feet above the trees, making an approach to the area right in front of the damn thing. The other chopper was flying over the trees, three or four hundred yards away – close, but not too close.

Nobody in sight around the barn. Not a soul.

Merriweather jumped when the chopper was three feet off the ground, and fell on his face. He got up, staggered out from under the rotor blast.

Handy appeared at his elbow.

The glow of a cigarette tip showed in the door. Someone sitting there!

Merriweather froze, his M-16 at the ready.

A marine sat in the open door smoking a cigarette. His face and neck were coated with green and brown camo grease. His helmet and night-vision goggles lay in the dirt beside him.

Merriweather walked over to the man, who said, 'No one around.'

'Where's Bryne?'

McCormick nodded toward the east. 'Over there about a hundred yards. Parachute streamed, backup didn't open.'

'Your radio?'

'Broke. Bryne's got smashed.' McCormick stood, took a last drag on the cigarette, and tossed it away. 'Been sitting here waiting for you. The place is deserted, quiet as a graveyard.'

'Too bad about Bryne.'

'Left two little kids. Too fucking bad.'

The interior of the barn was large, empty, and dark. Merriweather used a flashlight, looked in every corner, inspected the ceiling, the floor, the nooks and crannys.

Then he spoke into his boom microphone. 'Let's get the Osprey into the LZ, set up a perimeter.'

Through her night-vision goggles, Rita Moravia could see the silo two landing zone and the hovering SuperCobras plain as day as she made her approach in the Osprey. She saw bodies lying everywhere, still-warm bodies radiating heat, and she saw living men. She transitioned to hovering flight and lowered the Osprey toward the ground between the choppers. A cloud of dirt and dust rose up, obscuring everything. She went on instruments.

On the intercom she told the lieutenant to get ready.

As soon as the wheels hit, the marines in back charged out the door of the Osprey and kept right on going for fifty yards, when they went down on their stomachs with their rifles at the ready.

Rita didn't wait to see what was going to happen next. As soon as her crew chief said the last marine was out, she lifted the Osprey into the air, climbed straight up out of the dust cloud and only then began the transition to winged flight.

The lieutenant was named Charlie Herron, and he had his orders. His primary responsibility was to ensure that the missile in that silo never left the ground. As his feet hit the ground, he flopped on his belly and waited while the roaring Osprey climbed away. When the dust began to clear, he spotted the barn and went for it on a run.

Bodies and body parts lay scattered everywhere. The living men he passed sat in the dirt with empty hands reaching for the sky. Herron shouted over the radio, 'Cease-fire, cease-fire. They are surrendering.'

Inside the barn he found Asel Tyvek standing over a dead Cuban.

'Over here, Lieutenant. I think this wooden thing is a door.'

Tyvek and Herron opened the wooden door, which revealed a steel door with built-in combination lock. 'Think there's anybody in there?' Herron asked. After all, Tyvek had been here longer than he had.

'I don't know, sir.'

'Well, we gotta get in there. Let's blow the door.'

A charge of C-4 took less than a minute to rig. The two men took cover behind a wooden stall.

The explosion was sharp, a metallic wham that rang their ears.

The demolition charge cut the lock clean out of the door and warped it. The two men pried the door open. A stairway lit by naked light bulbs led away downward. Herron and Tyvek took off their night-vision goggles and let them dangle around their necks. With Herron in the lead with his pistol in his hand, the two of them descended the stairway.

Aboard *United States* Jake Grafton was getting the blow-by-blow update.

Air Intelligence officers annotated the maps and briefers told him of every report from the silos.

'Heavy firefight around silos one and two.'

'No opposition at sites four, five and six.'

'Ospreys on the ground at sites two, three, and four.'

'SuperCobra hit and in trouble at site one.'

'Team leader into silo two.'

'Recon leader into silo six.'

Each report was entered on a checklist: there were eight of them, one for each silo and dairy site.

First Lieutenant Charlie Herron and Asel Tyvek found the control room of silo two empty. A series of stairs and more steel doors led downward to the bottom of the concrete structure. The doors weren't locked. When he opened the last door, there was the missile towering upward. The shiny, painted fuselage reflected pinpoints of light from the naked bulbs arranged around the top and sides of the concrete silo.

Under the missile was a steel grate over a black hole. That was the flame pit, to exhaust the flame and gases when the missile was launched.

A circular steel stairway led up to a catwalk. From the catwalk it appeared a person could reach over and gain access to the missile's warhead and control panel.

Herron holstered his pistol and turned to Sergeant Tyvek. 'See if you can figure out a way to safety this bottle rocket so they can't fire it from Havana while I'm working on it.'

'Lieutenant, I've got bad news for you. I don't know shit about guided missiles.'

'Well, you sure as hell don't want to be standing here with your thumb up your butt if they light this thing off. Now go look for a switch or something.'

'Yes, *sir*,' Tyvek said, and disappeared back up the stairway.

Herron took the steps two at a time. He hoped he would find what he expected when he got to the catwalk, although he thought a lot of the old Russian engineer's explanation had been pure bullshit. Somebody had found an engineer in Russia who said he helped design these missiles – the guy was in his eighties. They had him on television for an hour explaining how the business end of the missile was put together. The engineer spoke not a word of English so a translator did the talking. The man had a hell of a memory or was lying through his teeth. Herron was about to find out which was the case.

'If it's typical Russian stuff,' the American briefer said, 'you'll be able to work on it with pliers and screwdrivers. American designers could learn a lot from Russian engineers, who design for ease of maintenance.' They gave each officer and NCO who might get near a missile a small tool pouch.

Herron examined the access panel, which was only about six inches long by six inches high, and curved, a part of the missile's skin. The screws holding it in place looked like Dzus fasteners. They weren't, though: they were plain old screws. Careful not to drop them, he unscrewed them one by one and put the screws in a shirt pocket. There were a dozen screws, just like the Russian engineer said. Okay! So far so good.

Sweat dripped down his nose, ran into his eyes. He wiped the palms of his hands on his camo pants and used his sleeve to swab his face, then went back to twisting the screwdriver. He worked as quickly as he could. Finally he took out the last screw.

Carefully, ever so carefully, Herron pulled off the access panel and laid it on the catwalk by his feet. He dug a small flashlight from his pocket. Looking through the access panel, he could see lots of wires. And a stainless-steel sphere about the size of a basketball. That, he concluded, must be the biological warhead. The missile had been designed for a nuclear warhead, which would have been round, so the biological warhead had to go into the same space. Yet the warhead was too large to come out this little six-inch access hole.

Charlie Herron reached through the hole to his elbow, felt upward with his ear against the skin of the missile. Yes, he could feel the latch. He opened it. Now down . . . one there too. Right, then left.

With the last latch open, he pulled at the panel he had his arm in. It came out in his hand, making a hole at least twenty inches across. So the engineer had been telling the truth.

Herron turned to put the panel on the catwalk . . . and dropped it.

It fell, striking the side of the missile, finally landing on the grate at the bottom with a tinny sound, much like the lid of a garbage can.

Charlie Herron grabbed the rails of the catwalk and held on to keep from falling.

He wiped his face on his sleeves, the palms of his hands on his trousers.

Using a pair of wire snips, the lieutenant began clipping wires, then pulling the ends out of the way so he could see how the warhead was held in place.

William Henry Chance and Tommy Carmellini stepped from their Osprey transport wearing their CBW suits. Two marines similarly clad followed them. Each marine carried a cylinder about six feet long and five inches in diameter balanced on his shoulder.

Doll Hanna was waiting for them as they approached the main entrance. 'I count five people in the clean area,' he said. 'They don't know we're here yet. The air-circulation system is pretty loud.'

Chance went to the partially open door and eased his head around for a peek. He counted the people inside. Five.

He had been thinking about this moment ever since Jake Grafton asked him to take out this facility. If the integrity of the sealed area was broken before the fire got hot enough to destroy the virus, some of the virus might escape. If there were any free viruses in the air inside there, or if one of the culture trays was broken, intentionally or unintentionally . . .

How much was some? Who could say?

He pulled his head back, looked at Doll Hanna, looked at the marines carrying the cylinders on their shoulders.

Well, it was a hell of a risk. A *hell* of a risk.

Just then William Henry Chance wished he were back in New York City, eating dinner at a nice restaurant or preparing a case for trial or sitting at home with the woman who had shared his life for the past ten years. Anywhere but here.

'Give me your rifle,' he said to Hanna, who handed him his M-16.

'Is it loaded?'

'Full. Selector is on single shot. This is the safety.' Hanna touched it.

'Okay,' said William Henry Chance.

He turned to Carmellini. 'If worse comes to worst, you know what to do.'

Carmellini didn't say anything. *The dumb shit is probably wishing he was safe and snug in a federal pen,* Chance thought.

He pointed the rifle at the ground and held it close to his leg, then eased the door open and stepped inside. No Cuban saw him. They were looking intently at something in a sealed unit with remote-control arms. A radio was playing somewhere, playing loudly.

Chance stepped into the air lock, stood there looking at the people while he waited for the interior door to unlock automatically.

He recognized the voice on the radio: Alejo Vargas. The gravelly flat delivery was unmistakable.

'My fellow Cubans, now is the hour to rally to the defense of our holy mother country. Tonight even as I speak the nation is under attack from American military forces, who have leveled the awesome might of their armed forces against the eleven million peaceful people of Cuba.'

Ten seconds passed, fifteen, twenty. After a half minute, the interior door clicked. Chance pushed it open and stepped into the lab.

Racks holding eight or ten culture trays each stood beside the benches. He lifted the rifle, thumbed off the safety, walked forward toward the working figures, who still had their backs to him. The tables on both sides of the aisles contained tools, parts, glassware, specialized instruments.

'Join with me in fighting the forces of the devil, the forces of capitalism and exploitation that seek to enslave the Cuban people so that the Yanquis can manufacture more dollars for themselves. . . .'

One of the workers spotted Chance when he was ten feet away, and turned in his direction.

Chance gestured with the rifle, motioned for them to raise their hands. They did so.

I should just shoot them, he thought, acutely aware of the culture trays just beside his elbow, and theirs.

Maybe I won't have to.

Backing up between two tables, he jerked his head back the way he had come, toward the air lock, gestured with the barrel of the rifle.

'Our hour of glory is now,' Alejo Vargas thundered, 'an hour that will live in all of Cuban history as the supreme triumphant moment of our people, that moment in the history of the world when we humble people struck back against the enslaver and oppressor and became forever free. . . .'

Slowly, watching Chance, the closest man began moving, passed him, kept walking with his hands up.

The second man passed.

The third . . .

He was turning to look at the fourth man when the man grabbed the barrel of the rifle with one hand and stabbed Chance in the solar plexus with the other.

William Henry Chance looked down at the handle sticking out of his abdomen. A screwdriver! The man had stabbed him with a screwdriver.

The man was fighting him for the rifle!

A shot. He heard a shot over the noise of the air-circulation fans. The man who stabbed him collapsed.

More shots.

Chance fell. His legs didn't work anymore and he was having trouble breathing.

'Kill the American enslavers wherever you find them, wherever they choose to shovel their odious filth onto a committed socialist people,' Vargas shouted over the radio. 'Beloved Cuba, the mother of us all, needs our strong right arms.'

On the floor, his vision narrowing to tiny points of light, fighting for air he couldn't get, William Henry Chance felt someone roll him over. Through the face plate on the mask of the man who held him, he could just make out Carmellini's features.

'You should have shot 'em,' Carmellini shouted. 'You stupid bastard, you should have shot 'em.'

Chance was trying to suck in enough air to reply when his heart stopped.

Carmellini and the two marines in CBW suits carried the aluminum cylinders they had brought from the Osprey into the lab and set them down. There was not a moment to be lost. Bullets had gone through several of the men lying dead on the floor and punctured the transparent plastic walls of the facility.

The two marines went back after more cylinders while Carmellini brought plastic cans of gasoline through the air lock. He didn't have time to wait for the lock to work, so he jammed the door so it would not close.

Please God, don't let the viruses out.

With six cylinders on the floor near the cultures and ten gallons of gasoline sitting nearby, Carmellini was ready. The five Cubans who were working in the lab lay where they had fallen. Chance's body lay where he died. Carmellini ignored the bodies as he worked.

He gestured to the marines to leave, then turned to the nearest cylinder, which was a five-inch-diameter magnesium flare designed to be dropped from an airplane. A small steel ring was taped to the side of the thing – he tore that off and pulled it out as far as it would go, which was about a foot. Then he gave it a mighty tug, which tore it loose in his hand.

He laid the cylinder on the wooden floor and walked for the air lock. As he went through he released the door, allowing it to close.

He still had a few seconds, so he stood in the lock as the suction tore at his CBW suit, trying to cleanse it of dust and stray viruses.

But he was running out of time.

He pushed the emergency button and let himself out of the lock through the exterior door. Walking swiftly, he exited the barn and strode for the waiting Osprey.

Doll Hanna was standing there with a rifle in his arms.

'Let's get the men –' Carmellini began, but the ignition of the flare stopped him. The glare of a hundred-million-candlepower magnesium fire leaked out of the barn through the door and cracks in the siding.

'Let's get the hell out of here before it goes up like a rocket,' Carmellini shouted, and trotted for the Osprey.

Three minutes later, with all the people aboard and the plane airborne, he went to the cockpit and looked back. The fire was as bright as a welder's torch, so brilliant it hurt his eyes to look. The heat of the first flare had set off the second, and so on. The heat from the first few flares probably caused the gasoline cans to explode, raising the temperature dramatically and helping ignite the other flares.

'Think the fire will kill all the viruses?' the pilot asked.

'I don't know,' Carmellini said grimly, and went back to his seat. He didn't have any juice to waste on the merely worried.

21

There were just too many Cuban troops at silo one. The two SuperCobras assigned there expended their Hellfire missiles on the tanks and trucks, then scourged the area with 20-mm cannon shells. Between them the assault choppers fired fifteen hundred rounds of 20-mm. As the first two assault choppers left the arena to refuel and rearm, Battlestar Control aboard *United States* routed other SuperCobras to the site. They began flaying the area with a vengeance.

The problem was that the troops were fairly well dug in. Almost a thousand men had arrived in the area early that morning under an energetic young commander who had ordered trenches dug and machine guns emplaced in earth and log fortifications. Two small bulldozers helped with the digging.

The machine-gun nests were gone now, victims of Hellfire missiles, but the troops in trenches were harder to kill. Fortunately for the Cubans, the trenches were not straight, but zigged and zagged around trees and stones and natural obstacles.

The young commander was dead now, killed by a single cannon shell that tore his head off when he tried to look over the lip of a trench to find the SuperCobras. Most of his officers were also dead. One of the SuperCobras had been shot down by machine-gun fire. A Cuban trooper with an AK-47 killed the pilot of another with a lucky shot in the neck. The first chopper managed to autorotate down, and the crew jumped from their machine into a empty trench. The copilot of the second machine flew it out of the battle and headed for the refueling and rearming site the marines had established in a sugarcane field between silos three and four.

The SuperCobras on site were almost out of ammo, and they too went to the refueling site, where they were fueled from bladders and rearmed with ammo brought in by Ospreys from *Kearsarge*. Then they rejoined the fray.

The noise of eight assault choppers hovering around the battlefield that centered on the barn did the trick. One by one, the Cubans threw down their weapons and climbed out of their trenches with their hands over their heads.

Several of the SuperCobras turned on their landing lights and hovered over the barn, turning this way and that so that their lights shone over the men living and dead that littered the ground.

Minutes later an Osprey landed just a hundred feet from the entrance to the barn. Toad Tarkington was the last man out. He was ten feet from the V-22 and running like hell when it lifted off and another settled onto the same spot. Marines with rifles at the ready came pouring out.

With his engines running and the canopy closed, Major Carlos Corrado taxied his MiG-29 toward the runway at Cienfuegos. Two men walked ahead of the fighter with brooms, sweeping shrapnel and rocks off the concrete so the fighter's tires would not be cut. They weren't worried about this stuff going in the intakes: on the ground the MiG-29's engines breathed through blow-down panels on top of the fuselage while the main intakes remained closed.

Inside the fighter Corrado was watching his electronic warning equipment. As he suspected, the Americans had a bunch of radars aloft tonight, everything from large search radars to fighter radars. He immediately recognized the radar signature of the F-14 Tomcat, which he had seen just a week or so ago out over the Caribbean.

Yep, they were up there, and as soon as his wheels came up, they would be trying to kill him.

Carlos Corrado taxied his MiG-29 onto the runway and shoved the twin throttles forward to the stop, then into afterburner. The MiG-29 rocketed forward. Safely airborne, Corrado raised the landing gear and came out of afterburner. Passing 400 knots, he lowered the nose and retarded the throttles, then swung into a turn that would point the sleek Russian fighter at Havana.

Inside the barn at silo one, Toad Tarkington took in the carnage at a glance. He was the first American through the door.

Cannon shells and shrapnel from Hellfire warheads had played hob with the wooden barn structure. Holes and splintered boards and timbers were everywhere — standing inside Toad could see the landing lights of the helicopters and hear Americans shouting.

Apparently several dozen men had taken refuge in the barn; their bloody bodies lay where the bullets or shrapnel or splinters from the timbers cut them down. The floor and walls were splattered with blood.

Toad found the wooden door, got it open, used his flashlight to examine the steel inner door. He set three C-4 charges around the combination lock and took cover.

The charges tore the lock out of the door and warped the thing so badly it wouldn't open. Toad struggled with it, only got it open because two marines came in to check out the interior and gave him a hand.

The stairway on the other side of the door was in total darkness. Not a glimmer of light.

With his flashlight in his left hand and his pistol in his right, Toad slowly worked his way down.

He saw lightbulbs in sockets over his head, but they were not on. Once he came to a switch. He flipped it on and off several times. No electrical power.

At the bottom of the stairs he came to a larger room. The beam of the flashlight caught an instrument panel, a control console. A bit of a face . . .

Toad brought the light back to the face.

A white face, eyes scrunched against the flashlight glare. An old man, skinny, with short white hair, frozen in the flashlight beam, holding his hands above his head.

The radar operator in the E-3 Sentry AWACS plane over Key West was the first to see the MiG-29 get airborne from Cienfuegos. He keyed the intercom and reported the sighting to the supervisor, who used the computer to verify the track, then reported it to Battlestar Control.

The AWACS crew reported the MiG as a bogey and assigned it a track number. They would be able to classify it as to type as soon as the pilot turned on his radar.

Unfortunately, Carlos Corrado failed to cooperate. He left his radar switch in the off position. He also stayed low, just a few hundred meters above the treetops.

There are few places more lonely than the cockpit of a single-piloted airplane at night when surrounded by the enemy. Corrado felt that loneliness now, felt as if he were the only person still alive on Spaceship Earth.

The red glow of the cockpit lights comforted him somewhat: this was really the only home he had ever had.

The lights of Havana were prominent tonight – he saw the glow at fifty miles even though he was barely a thousand feet above sea level. He climbed a little higher, looking, and saw a huge fire, quite brilliant.

Carlos Corrado turned toward the fire. Perhaps he would find some airborne targets. He turned on his gun switch and armed the infrared missiles.

The E-2 controller datalinked the bogey information to the F-14 crew patrolling over central Cuba at 30,000 feet. There should have been two F-14s, a section, but one plane had mechanical problems prior to launch, so there was only one fighter on this station.

The bogey appeared on the scope of the radar intercept officer, the RIO, in the rear seat of the Tomcat. He narrowed the scan of his radar and tried to acquire a lock on the target, which was merely a blip that faded in and out against the ground clutter.

'What the hell is it?' the pilot demanded, referring to the bogey.

'I don't know,' was the reply, and therein was the problem. Without a positive identification, visual or electronic, of the bogey, the rules of engagement prohibited the American pilot from firing his weapons. There were simply too many American planes and helicopters flying around in the darkness over Cuba to allow people to blaze away at unknown targets.

The darkness below was alive with lights, the lights of cities and small towns, villages, vehicles, and here and there, antiaircraft artillery – flak – which was probing the darkness with random bursts. Fortunately the gunners could not use radar to acquire a target – the instant they turned a radar on, they drew a HARM missile from the EA-6Bs and F/A-18s that circled on their assigned stations, listening.

The F-14 pilot, whose name was Wallace P. 'Stiff' Hardwick, got on the radio to Battlestar Control. 'Battlestar, Showtime One Oh Nine, request permission to investigate this bogey.'

'Wait.'

Stiff expected that. Being a fighter pilot in this day and age wasn't like the good old days, when you went cruising for a fight. Not that he was there for the good old days, but Stiff had sure heard about them.

'That goddamn Cuban is gonna zap somebody while the people on the boat are scratching their ass,' Stiff told his RIO, Boots VonRauenzahn.

'Yeah,' said Boots, who never paid much attention to Stiff's grousing.

Carlos Corrado saw that a building was on fire, burning with extraordinary intensity. Never had he seen such a hot fire. He assumed that the building had been bombed by a cruise missile or American plane and began visually searching the sky nearby for some hint of another aircraft.

He flew right over the V-22 Osprey carrying Tommy Carmellini and Doll Hanna back to the ship and never saw it.

A lot of flak was rising from the outskirts of Havana, so Carlos turned east, away from it.

In the black velvet ahead he saw lights, and steered toward them. At 500 knots he closed quickly, and saw helicopters' landing lights! They were flying back and forth over a large barn!

They must be Americans – they sure as hell weren't Cuban. As far as he knew, he was the only Cuban in the air tonight.

Corrado flew past the area – now down to 400 knots – and did a 90-degree left turn, then a 270-degree right turn. Level, inbound, he retarded the throttles of the two big engines. Three hundred knots . . . he picked the landing lights on some kind of strange-looking twin rotor helicopter and pushed the nose over just a tad, bringing the strange chopper into the gunsight. Then he pulled the trigger on the stick.

The 30-mm cannon shells smashed into Rita Moravia's Osprey with devastating effect. She was in the midst of a transition from wing-borne to rotor-borne flight and had the engines pointed up at a seventy-degree angle. The rotors were carrying most of the weight of the twenty-ton ship, so when the cannon shells ripped into the right engine and it ceased developing power, the V-22 began sinking rapidly.

The good engine automatically went to emergency torque and transferred some of its power to the rotor of the bad engine through a driveshaft that connected the two rotor transmissions.

With shells thumping into the plane and warning lights flashing, Rita felt the right wing sag. Some of the shells must have damaged the right transmission!

The ground rushed at her, even as cannon shells continued to strike the plane.

She pulled the stick back and left, trying to make the right rotor take a bigger bite.

Then the machine struck the earth and the instrument panel smashed into her night vision goggles.

In the missile control room, Toad Tarkington held his flashlight on the old man as he produced a candle from his pocket and a kitchen match. He lit the match and applied it to the candle's wick.

One candle wasn't much, but it did light the room. Toad turned off the flashlight and stood there looking at the old man.

Muffled crashing sounds reached him, echoed down the stairwell, but no one came. Toad's headset was quiet too, probably since he was underground.

'Do you speak English?' Toad asked the white-haired man in front of him.

The old man shook his head.

'*Español?*'

'*Sí, señor.*'

'Well, I don't.'

Toad walked over and checked the man, who had no visible weapons on him.

He had a handful of plastic ties in his pocket. These ties were issued to every marine for the sole purpose of securing prisoners' hands, and feet if necessary. Toad put a tie around the old man's hands. The man didn't resist; merely sat at the control console with his face a mask, showing no emotion.

'Cuban?' Toad asked.

'*Nyet.*'

'Russki?'

The white head bobbed once, then was still.

Toad used the flashlight to inspect the console, to examine the instruments. This stuff was old, he could see that. Everything was mechanical, no digital gauges or readouts, no computer displays ... the console reminded Toad of the dashboard of a 1950s automobile, with round gauges and bezels and ...

Well, without power, all this was academic.

His job was to get that damned warhead out of the missile, then set demolition charges to destroy all this stuff, missile, control room, and all. He left the Russian at the console and opened the blast-proof door across the room from the stair where he had entered.

Another stairway led downward.

Toad went as quickly as he dared, still holding the flashlight in one hand and his pistol in the other.

He went through one more steel door ... and there the missile stood, white and massive and surreal in the weak beam of the flashlight.

The aviation radio frequencies exploded when Rita's plane was shot down as everyone tried to talk at once.

Battlestar Control finally managed to get a word in over the babble, a call to Stiff Hardwick. 'Go down for a look. Possible hostile may have shot down an Osprey.'

Stiff didn't need any urging. He rolled the Tomcat onto its back, popped the speed brakes, and started down.

'Silo one,' Boots said. 'This bogey is flitting around down there like a goddamn bat or something, mixing it up with the SuperCobras and Ospreys. Let's not shoot down any of the good guys.'

'No shit,' said Stiff, who was sure he could handle any Cuban fighter pilot alive. This guy was meat on the table: he just didn't know it yet.

Carlos Corrado pulled out of his strafing run and soared up to three thousand feet. He extended out for eight or nine miles before he laid the fighter over in a hard turn.

He had seen helicopters down there, at least two. It was time to use the radar.

As he stabilized inbound he flipped the radar switch to 'transmit.' He pushed the button for moving targets and sure enough, within seconds the pulse-doppler radar in the nose of the MiG-29 had found three. The rest of the drill was simplicity itself – he selected an Aphid missile, locked it on a target, and fired. Working quickly, he selected a second missile, locked on a second target, and fired.

He had to keep the targets illuminated while the Aphids were in flight, so he continued inbound toward the silo.

One of the SuperCobras exploded when an Aphid drilled it dead center. The second missile tore the tail rotor off its target, which spun violently into the ground and caught fire.

Carlos Corrado flew across the barn, holding his heading, extending out before he turned to make another shooting pass.

Toad Tarkington found the circular steel ladder leading upward in the missile silo and began climbing.

When he reached the catwalk he walked around the missile, examining the skin. There was the little access port, six inches by six inches, with the dozen screws! That had to be it.

Toad Tarkington put the flashlight under his left armpit and got out a screwdriver.

He had three screws out when the flashlight slipped out of his armpit and fell. It bounced off the catwalk and went on down beside the missile, breaking when it hit the grate at the bottom.

The darkness in the silo was total.

Toad Tarkington cursed softly, and went back to taking out screws. He worked by feel. Someone would come along in a minute, he thought, bringing another flashlight. If someone didn't, he would take the time to go find another.

The trick, he knew, would be to hold on to the screwdriver. He only had one, and if he dropped it, it would go down the grate.

He heard muffled noises from above, but he couldn't tell what they were. It didn't really matter, he decided. Getting this warhead out of this missile was priority one.

Carefully, working by feel, he removed the screws from the access panel one by one. When he had the last one out, he pried at the panel. It came off easily enough and he laid it on the catwalk near his feet.

So far so good. He carefully stowed the screwdriver in his tool bag and wiped the sweat from his face and hands.

Okay.

Toad reached up to find the latch that the ancient Russian engineer on television had said should be here. God knows where the CIA found that guy!

Yep. He found the latch.

He rotated it. Now the latch on the left. He was having his troubles getting that latch to turn when the lights came on in the silo.

From instant darkness to glaring light from twenty or more bulbs.

Toad Tarkington pulled his arm from the missile, clapped his hands over his eyes and squinted, waiting for his eyes to adjust.

He could hear a hum. Must be a fan or blower moving air.

No. The hum was in the missile, just a foot or two from his head.

Something winding up. The pitch was rising rapidly.

A gyro?

What was going on?

Toad started down the ladder, moving as fast as he could go, intending to go to the control room to see what in hell was happening.

He heard a grinding noise, loud, low-pitched, and looked up. The cap on the silo was opening.

Holy...

He still had his tools. If he could get that access panel off and cut the guidance wires, the wires to control the warhead...

Toad Tarkington scrambled back up the ladder.

The little six-by-six access hole gaped at him. He ran his arm in, trying to reach the other latches that would allow the large panel to come off.

He got one open. The gyro had ceased to accelerate – it was running steadily now, a high-pitched steady whine.

Holy shit!

He was out of time: the fire from the missile's engines would fry him to a cinder.

He heard the igniters firing, popping like jet engine igniters.

The rocket motors lit with a mighty whoosh.

Toad grabbed for the access hole with both hands, held on desperately as the missile began to rise on a column of fire.

The noise was beyond deafening – it was the loudest thing Toad Tarkington had ever heard, a soul-numbing roar that made his flesh quiver and vibrated his teeth.

Rising ... the missile was rising, dragging him off the catwalk.

He clung to the access hole with all his strength,

The missile came out of the silo, past the floor of the barn, accelerating, going up, up, up....

The tip of the missile burst through the rotten, shattered roof and threw wood in every direction.

As it did Toad curled his feet up against the fuselage of the missile, released his hold on the access hole, and kicked off.

He flew through the darkness, bounced on the collapsing roof, felt the blast of furnace heat as the rocket motors singed him, then he was falling, falling....

Stiff Hardwick couldn't believe his eyes. He had his F-14 Tomcat down at 4,000 feet, fifteen miles from silo one, and was impatiently waiting for Boots to sort out the villain from the other airborne targets in the area when he saw the ballistic missile rising into the night sky on a cone of white-hot fire.

'Jesus Christ!' he swore over the radio, 'the bastards have launched one.'

'Lock it up, Boots,' Stiff screamed, still on the radio, although he thought he was on the intercom. 'Lock it up and we'll shoot an AMRAAM.' The acronym stood for advanced medium-range air-to-air missile.

Boots was trying. The problem was that the ballistic missile was essentially stationary in relation to the earth. It was accelerating upward, of course, but its velocity over the ground was close to zero just now. The designers of the F-14 weapons system did not envision that the crew would want to shoot missiles at stationary targets, so Boots was having his troubles.

Frustrated, he snarled at Stiff, 'Go to heat, goddamnit. Shoot a 'winder at that exhaust.'

'A 'winder ain't gonna dent that fucking thing,' Stiff replied, his logic impeccable. He was on the ICS now. 'We'll come up under it and shoot as it accelerates upward.'

'Okay! Okay!'

And that is what he did. As the missile accelerated upward, Stiff Hardwick kept his nose down, punched the burners full on and accelerated in toward the launch site, then pulled up to put the climbing, accelerating ballistic missile in front of him.

Now Boots got a radar lock.

The symbology on the HUD was alive, showing the target, the boresight angle, the drift angle. . . .

Stiff Hardwick lifted his thumb to fire the first AMRAAM. As he did an infrared missile from Carlos Corrado's MiG-29 went up his right tailpipe and blew a stabilator off the F-14.

Jake Grafton heard all of it. 'A missile is in the air! Just came out of silo one!' was the shout over the radio.

He picked up the red telephone, the direct satellite connection with the White House.

'Mr President, I don't know what happened, but apparently the Cubans have launched one.'

The president must have heard the shouts over the net the same as Jake did. His question was, 'What is the target?'

Jake had the targets memorized. 'It came out of silo one, sir. The target is Atlanta.'

'Thank you, Admiral,' the president said mechanically, and hung up.

When Toad Tarkington came to the night was quiet. He was lying on cool earth, the sky above was dark . . . and there was a marine standing over him with his mouth moving.

He was deaf. He had lost his hearing.

Toad sat up, fell over, forced himself into a sitting position again. He ached all over, every muscle and tendon screamed in protest. But he was alive.

He got to his feet, swaying. The marine helped steady him.

The barn was right there beside him.

He pulled his pistol, staggered for the entrance.

The interior was a shambles, the stench nearly unbearable from bodies fried and seared by the exhaust of the missile.

Toad pulled boards out of the way to get to the open door that led down to the control room.

The lights were still on. Using a palm on one wall to steady himself, he descended the stair.

The old man was still sitting at the console, still wearing the tie around his wrists.

He looked at Toad dispassionately.

'You bastard,' Toad said. He said the words but he could barely hear them. 'You foul, evil old man.'

A young marine who had followed Toad down the stairs grabbed the whitehaired old man, shoved him toward the stairs. 'Get going, you old fart! Upstairs, upstairs.'

Tarkington sagged to his knees on the floor, then stretched out. He was so tired. . . .

Boots VonRauenzahn pulled the ejection handle, and both he and Stiff Hardwick were launched from Showtime One Oh Nine a fraction of a second apart.

Stiff got his wits about him as he hung in his parachute harness in the night sky. He could see the ballistic missile accelerating into the sky – it was now a bright spot of light amid the stars – and he could see the burning wreckage of his Tomcat as it fluttered toward the ground.

He couldn't see the MiG-29 that had shot him down. He could hear him though, a rumble that muffled the fading roar of the ballistic missile heading for space.

What he didn't know was that Carlos Corrado had decided that his fuel state didn't allow him to jab the Americans anymore this night. He was on his way back to Cienfuegos. With his radar off.

The SPY-1B radar aboard *Hue City* acquired the rising ballistic missile as it rose over the rim of the earth and transmitted the information by datalink to *Guilford Courthouse,* which picked up the missile on its own radar seconds later.

Hue City's tactical action officer (TAO) in the Combat Control Center reached out and pushed the squawk-box button for the bridge, notifying her captain. 'Sir, we have a possible ATBM threat, bearing one hundred seventy-five degrees true.' An ATBM was an antitactical ballistic missile threat.

The information from the SPY-1B radar was fed into the Aegis weapons system, which used the radar to control SM-2 missiles. The TAO waited for the computer to present the specifics of the target's trajectory.

Her orders were to shoot down any missiles launched from Cuba over the Florida Straits. To do that, she would use the latest version of the SM-2 missile, of which her ship carried eight. *Guilford Courthouse* also carried eight of these weapons, which had an extraordinary envelope. They could fly as far as 300 nautical miles and as high as 400,000 feet, about 66 nautical miles.

The ballistic missile that was flying now was still climbing and accelerating. The trick was to shoot it over the Florida Straits before it got out of the SM-2 envelope.

The captain was on the squawk box. 'You may fire anytime,' the old man said.

The TAO was Lieutenant (junior grade) Melinda Robinson. Her mother had wanted her to be a dancer and her father wanted her to take up law, his profession, but she chose the navy, confounding them both.

Just now she concentrated on the computer presentations on the large, 42-inch by 42-inch console in front of her.

'Two missiles,' Robinson ordered. She was tempted to fire four, but the Cubans might launch more ballistic missiles, so she couldn't afford to run out of ammo.

'Fire one,' she said.

The SM-2 Tactical Aegis LEAP (lightweight exoatmospheric projectile) missile roared from the vertical launcher in front of the ship's bridge in a blaze of fire.

Two seconds later a second missile roared after the first.

Guilford Courthouse also fired two missiles.

The solid fuel third-stage boosters of the SM-2 missiles lifted them through the bulk of the atmosphere, and finally separated at an altitude of 187,000 feet. The second stages ignited now, lifting the interceptor missiles higher and higher.

At 300,000 feet the second stage of the missile pitched over and ejected the nose cone of the missile, exposing the infrared sensor of the kinetic-energy kill vehicle. The motor continued to burn for another sixteen seconds, carrying the kill vehicle higher and still faster. At 370,000 feet the kill vehicle was aligned by its GPS-aided inertial unit and was ejected from the missile.

Tracking the target now at 375,000 feet of altitude, the kill vehicle homed in on the ballistic missile's final stage at 6,000 miles per hour.

And hit it.

The second missile missed by a hundred feet, the third struck a piece of the target missile, and the fourth missed by seven feet.

'Admiral Grafton, *Hue City* reports the ballistic missile was destroyed over the Straits.'

Jake picked up the telephone to the White House and waited for someone to answer.

'*Hue City*, an Aegis cruiser, reports the Cuban missile was destroyed over the Straits.'

The president didn't say anything, but Jake could feel his relief. When he did speak, he sounded tired. 'How many warheads are still in those missiles?'

'Only one left, sir. Number four. There are no Cubans there but the marines are having trouble getting the warhead out of the missile.'

'Are you destroying the missiles when they are sanitized?'

'Yes, sir. A magnesium flare ignited near the nose cone. The heat melts it, then finally ignites the solid fuel and causes an explosion in the silo.'

'You destroyed the warhead manufacturing facility?'

'Yes, sir.'

'All that's left is the lab at the university?'

'That's correct.'

'I want it destroyed, Admiral.'

'There will be casualties, sir, American and Cuban. That thing is smack in the middle of downtown Havana.'

'I understand that. Destroy it.'

'We'll do it tomorrow night,' Jake Grafton said.

Toad Tarkington found Rita putting a bandage on her copilot, Crash Wade, who had smashed his face into the instrument panel when their Osprey crashed. Half the marines aboard had been injured, but by some miracle only two were killed. The Osprey was a total loss.

Toad put his hands on Rita's shoulders. She turned and he saw a large goose-egg bump on her forehead, one already turning purple. One of her eyes was also black and slightly swollen.

He knelt beside her. 'How's your head?'

'I'm okay. Didn't even knock me out.'

'And Crash?'

'The wound that's bleeding is pulpy – I think his skull is smashed. He doesn't seem to recognize me or anybody.'

When she had Wade's wounds bandaged, she and Toad walked over to a tree and sat down. 'Somebody said a MiG shot us down, Toad. Cannon holes all over the right engine nacelle. I couldn't save it.'

She was so tired. When he leaned back against the tree she put her head down in his lap.

22

By dawn Jake Grafton had five biological warheads locked up aboard *United States*; five intermediate-range ballistic missiles had been melted and burned in their silos; and every uniformed American and flyable military aircraft was out of Cuba. It had been a tight squeeze.

Over half the SuperCobra helicopters lacked the fuel to return across the Florida Straits to Key West, nor was there room for them on the decks of US ships off the Cuban coast. More fuel in flexible bladders was flown in from *Kearsarge*. The choppers were refueled, then launched for Key West. Four of the SuperCobras had been shot down, and one had suffered so much battle damage it was unsafe to fly and had to be destroyed.

Prowlers and Hornets armed with HARM missiles continued to patrol over central Cuba all night, ready to attack any radar that came on the air. Above them F-14s cruised back and forth, ready to engage any bogey brave enough to take to the sky.

Several Cuban Army units probed gently at the marines guarding the silo sites while they prepared to withdraw, but a few bursts of machine-gun fire and mortar shells from the marines were enough to discourage further attention. The marines eventually disengaged and pulled out unmolested.

When he landed his MiG-29 at Cienfuegos, Major Carlos Corrado found that he couldn't get fuel. Two cruise missiles had destroyed the fuel trucks and electrical pumping unit; all fueling would have to be done by hand, a slow, labor-intensive process. Disgusted, Corrado walked to the nearest bar in town, where he was a regular, and proceeded to get drunk, his usual evening routine. By dawn he was passed out in his bunk in the barracks, sleeping it off.

In Havana the next morning, Alejo Vargas summoned the senior officers of the Cuban Army, Navy, and Air Force to the presidential palace for a verbal hiding.

'Cowards, fools, traitors,' he raged, so infuriated he quivered. 'We had them in the palm of our hand, and all we had to do was make a *fist*. A red-handed apprehension of the American pirates would have brought the applause and respect of the Cuban people. A haul of American prisoners in uniform would have given us instant credibility. *This* was our chance.'

'*Señor Presidente,* the troops would not obey. They refused to attack. When the troops refuse to obey direct orders, what would you have us do?'

'Shoot some generals,' Vargas snapped. 'Shoot some colonels. Scared men fight best.'

'If we shot the generals and colonels the men would shoot us,' General Alba explained, and he meant it. 'The Americans are too well equipped, too well trained, too well armed. Their firepower is overwhelming. To fight them toe-to-toe would be suicidal, and the men know that.'

Alba's logic was unassailable. To complain now that the Cuban Army, Navy, and Air Force did not do what he, Vargas, knew they could not do was illogical and self-defeating. No military force on the planet could whip the Americans in a stand-up fight, which was precisely why he had spent the last three years developing a biological-warfare capability.

Temper tantrums will get me no place, Vargas reminded himself, and willed himself back under control. He sat down at his desk, made a gesture to the others to seat themselves.

'Gentlemen, we must move forward. I have trust and confidence in you, and I hope you have the same in me. You are of course correct – we cannot overcome the Americans militarily. We must outwit them to prevail. With your help, it still can be done.'

They sat looking at him expectantly.

'The laboratory where the biological agent for the warheads was created is in the science building of the University of Havana. Last night the Americans destroyed the warhead-manufacturing facility and our six operational ballistic missiles. All the American cruise missiles, the airplanes, the assault troops were employed to that end. Tonight the Americans will try to destroy the laboratory.'

'Why did they not attack the lab last night?' Alba asked.

'You are the military man – you tell me. Perhaps they lacked sufficient assets, perhaps they did not have political support to create massive amounts of Cuban casualties or sustain significant American casualties – I do not know. The most likely explanation is that they were afraid of inadvertently releasing biological agents. Whatever, the lab is still intact and capable of producing polio viruses in sufficient quantity to supply a weapons program. The minds directing the American military effort will not ignore that laboratory.'

'*Señor Presidente,* what would you have us do?'

Alejo Vargas smiled. He leaned forward in his chair and began explaining.

'Tell me what happened,' Jake Grafton said to Toad Tarkington when Toad got back aboard the carrier. The sky was gray in the east by then, and Toad was filthy and bone tired.

A stretcher team from the ship's hospital met the Osprey on the flight deck and took Rita and Crash Wade below for examination.

Toad told his boss everything he thought he would want to know about the battle around silo one, about the missile rising, holding on to the tiny open access port, kicking off as the missile went through the barn roof, falling. . . .

He didn't tell Jake that he was so scared he thought he was going to die, and he left out how he felt when they told him Rita had been shot down just in front of the barn. He didn't mention how he felt when he realized she was alive, bruised up but alive. He didn't have to tell him, because Jake Grafton could read all that in his face.

The admiral listened, looking very tired and sad, and said nothing. Just nodded. Then patted him on the shoulder and sent him to take a shower and get a few hours' sleep.

The young CIA officer, Tommy Carmellini, sat in the dirty-shirt wardroom with a stony face, his jaw set. Chance was dead and he didn't want to talk about it.

He talked about the mission when Jake Grafton asked, however, told the admiral how it had gone, assured him that all the cultures in the building had been destroyed.

'The problem is that the bastards may have cultures stashed anyplace. Vargas may have a potful under his bed, just in case.'

'Yes,' Jake Grafton said, 'I understand.'

He did understand. To be absolutely certain of eradicating all the poliomyelitis virus in Cuba, he would need to burn the whole island to a cinder.

Jake went to his stateroom and tried to get a few hours' sleep himself.

Tired as he was, sleep wouldn't come. He tossed and turned as he thought about the battle just ended and the one still to come. What had he learned from last night's battle?

What could go wrong tonight?

After an hour of frustration, he took a long, hot shower. This time when he lay down he dozed off.

Two hours later he was wide awake. He put on a clean uniform and headed for his office.

Toad was already there huddled with Gil Pascal. 'Rita's okay,' he told Jake. 'Crash Wade didn't make it. Amazing, isn't it? One dead, one just bruised.'

'Can Rita fly tonight?' Jake asked.

Tarkington swallowed hard, nodded once.

'She's the best Osprey pilot we've got,' Jake said. 'She's got the flight if she wants it.'

'She'd kill me if I asked you to leave her behind.'

'She probably would, and you such a handsome young stud. What a loss to the world that would be.'

'The Osprey that is bringing the survivor from *Hue City* will be here in twenty minutes. I'll bring him to your cabin.'

'Hector Sedano's brother?'

'That's correct, sir. And the message said he wants to go back to Cuba.'

Maximo Sedano parked his car on the pier so he wouldn't have to carry his gear very far. Scuba tanks, wet suit, flippers, weight belt, mask, he had the whole wardrobe.

He got all that stuff aboard the boat, checked the fuel, then cast off.

The gold was in Havana Harbor; he was sure of it. He had a chart that he had laid off in grids, and he had labeled each grid with a number that reflected a probability that he thought reasonable. The area off the main shipping piers didn't seem promising, nor did the busy areas by the fishing piers. The area off the private docks where Fidel had kept his boat seemed to Maximo to be the most likely, so that was where he would look first.

He took the boat to the center of the most promising area and anchored it.

It was inevitable that people would see him, so he had told everyone who asked that he was studying old shipwrecks in Havana Harbor. He knew enough about that subject to make it sound plausible – he could talk about the American battleship *Maine* and three treasure galleons that went on the rocks here in the harbor during a hurricane.

If he found it, he would not let on. If he found the gold, he would leave it where it was until he could come back for it with paid men and the proper equipment.

If.

Well, every man needs a dream, he reflected, and this was his. Better this than dying defending a ballistic-missile silo. Those fools.

The gold was near. He knew it. Sitting here on the boat he could feel its power.

God damn you, Fidel.

Juan Sedano, El Ocho, got out of the Osprey with a look of wonder on his face. The airplane, the aircraft carrier, the jets and noise and hundreds of foreigners, few of whom spoke his language – it was quite a lot for a young man who had never before been out of Cuba.

He got out of the Osprey wearing a set of navy dungarees, a white T-shirt, and a *Hue City* baseball cap, and carrying a pillowcase containing clothes, underwear, toilet items, and souvenirs given him by the men and women of *Hue City*, everything from photographs of the ship to CDs and *Playboy* magazines.

Toad Tarkington met Ocho on the flight deck and led the tall, broad-shouldered young man into the island and up the ladder to the flag bridge, where Jake Grafton and an interpreter, a lieutenant fighter pilot of Latin descent, were waiting. Jake took Ocho and the lieutenant into his at-sea cabin, where the three of them found chairs.

'When did you leave Cuba?' Jake Grafton asked Ocho after the introductions.

'Six or seven days ago,' the lieutenant said, 'he isn't sure. He lost track of the days at sea.'

'Tell him that Fidel Castro is dead, that his brother Hector is in prison.'

The Spanish-speaking junior officer did so.

Ocho's reaction was unexpected. Tears streamed down his face. 'He asked me not to leave Cuba. He must have known that Fidel was dying, that something was happening. I left anyway.'

He wiped at the tears, embarrassed. 'I love my brother. He is my idol, a true man who believes in something larger than himself. I cry because I am ashamed of myself, of what I have done. He asked me not to go and I refused to listen.'

'Tell me about Hector,' Jake Grafton asked gently.

The admiral had expected to spend five minutes with the boy, but the five minutes became fifteen, then a half hour, then an hour. Ocho told of going to meetings with Hector, of the speeches he made, of his many friends, of antagonizing the regular priests and the bureaucrats while he spread the message of a coming new day to anyone who would listen, and many did.

Jake gave Ocho part of his attention while he thought about the lab in the science building in the University of Havana.

When Ocho finally began to run dry, Jake picked up the telephone and called Toad. 'I'm in my at-sea cabin,' he said. 'Have the guys in the television studio play that tape we downloaded from the satellite this morning on the television in this stateroom. No place else.'

'Yessir.'

Toad called back in three minutes. 'Channel two, Admiral.'

Jake turned on the television.

In a few seconds Fidel Castro came on the screen. He was obviously a sick man. He was sitting behind a desk, wearing a green fatigue shirt.

'Citizens of Cuba, I speak to you today for the last time. I am fatally ill. . . .'

The young lieutenant translated.

'I wish to spend a few minutes telling you of my dream for Cuba, my dream of what our nation can become in the years ahead. It is imperative that we end our political isolation, that we join the family of nations as a full-fledged member. To make this transition a reality will require major changes on our part, and a new political vision. . . .'

Jake Grafton moved closer to the television set, adjusted his glasses, and studied the image of Fidel Castro. The man was perspiring heavily, obviously in pain, and every so often he would move slightly, as if seeking a more comfortable position.

'For years I have watched with admiration and respect,' Fidel continued, 'as Hector Sedano moved among our people, making friends, telling them of his vision for Cuba, preparing them for the changes and sacrifices that will be necessary in the days to come.'

Fidel winced, paused, and took a sip of water from a glass setting nearby. Then he continued:

'We as a nation do not have to give up our revolutionary commitment to social justice to participate as full-fledged members of the world economy. We would be traitors to the heroes of the revolution and ourselves were we to do so. In the past few years the Church, in which so many Cubans believe, has come to understand that one cannot be a true Christian without an active commitment to social justice, the commitment that every loyal Cuban carries in his breast as his birthright. The Church has changed to join us. Now we also must change.

'The time has come for this government to renounce communism, to embrace private enterprise, to act as a referee to ensure that every Cuban has a decent job that pays a living wage and every enterprise pays its fair share of taxes . . .'

In less than a minute Fidel reached his peroration:

'Hector Sedano is the man I believe best able to lead our nation into this future.'

The tape ended anticlimactically a few seconds later. A tired, haggard Fidel spoke to someone off-camera, said, 'That's enough.'

Jake Grafton reached out, turned off the television.

Ocho was stunned. 'I thought Fidel was dead!'

'He is dead. He made this tape before he died.'

'That was not a live performance?'

'No. A film, a videotape.'

'And you have it!' Ocho's eyes were wide in amazement. 'They must have played the videotape on television, and you copied it. But if it has been on television in Havana, why is Hector in prison?'

'The tape has never been on television,' Jake said. 'As far as I know, you are the very first Cuban to see it since it was made.'

Ocho stared, trying to understand. Finally he asked, 'What are you going to do with it?'

'I was wondering,' Jake Grafton said, 'if you would take it back to the lady who gave it to us. I believe she is your aunt by marriage, Mercedes Sedano?'

'Mercedes!' Ocho gaped. 'She was Fidel's mistress. Why did she give you the tape?'

'You will have to ask her. Will you return the tape to her?'

'Of course. When do you want me to do this?'

'This evening, I think. By the way, are you hungry?'

'Oh, yes. I like the hamburger. *Muy bueno.*'

Jake and the lieutenant took Ocho to the flag wardroom for lunch. Ocho talked of baseball, of Cuba, of his brother Hector, and Hector's dreams for a free Cuba. He talked even with his mouth full, so the lieutenant who was translating didn't get much to eat. Jake let the young Cuban talk.

After lunch the admiral asked for Tommy Carmellini, so Toad Tarkington went looking for him. Carmellini was asleep. He smelled of liquor, which Toad ignored – after all, the man was a civilian.

When Toad got Carmellini into the admiral's office, he asked the chief petty officer to bring coffee, which Carmellini accepted gratefully.

'I've been thinking about your comment,' Jake Grafton said.

'What comment?' Carmellini asked between sips of hot black coffee.

'About Vargas having jugs of cultures under his bed.'

'Umm.' Carmellini drank more coffee. When he saw that the admiral was expecting him to say more, he shrugged. 'That was a flippant comment. I'm sorry.'

Jake Grafton scratched his chin. 'I thought it was . . . profound, in a way.'

'How's that?'

'We can't burn the island down.'

'That would be impractical,' Carmellini agreed. 'We'd have eleven million Cubans to house and feed afterwards.'

'So where does that leave us?'

Tommy Carmellini searched the faces of the naval officers.

'There's a presidential directive against assassinating heads of state,' the CIA man said cautiously.

'I have seen references to such a directive,' Jake Grafton said, 'though I haven't read the thing.'

'Trust me. It exists.'

'Friend, I believe you. That's sound public policy and I don't have anything like that in mind. Our objective is the lab and the cultures: that's more than enough to keep us busy. You've been there before and know the layout. Will you go back with us tonight?'

Tommy Carmellini nodded slowly. 'I appreciate your asking, Admiral. I'd be delighted.'

'We are planning a military assault. It is going to be a holy mess, I think. Vargas will probably ambush us on the way in or booby-trap the lab to blow up after we've fought our way in there. Maybe both.'

'He's that kind of guy,' Carmellini agreed.

'Hector Sedano's brother is aboard ship. He was picked up floating in the ocean north of Cuba two days ago after the boat he was on sank. Everyone else aboard drowned or was a victim of shark attack. This kid is either

Hector's brother or a liar of Clintonian dimensions. They call him El Ocho. I want you to talk to him, feel him out. He impressed me as an extremely competent, capable young man. Talk to him, then come back and tell me what you think.'

Toad Tarkington was in the Air Intelligence Center studying satellite images and radar images from an E-3 Sentry AWACS plane circling, flying a race track pattern over the Florida Straits. The University of Havana science building was at the center of all the images.

'What's happening in Havana?' Jake asked.

'The streets are full of people,' Toad said. 'Especially around La Cabana Prison. Do you think they are there to break Hector out?'

'They're there because he is,' Jake muttered, and used a magnifying glass to study the infrared images of the science building.

Toad pointed at the picture with the tip of a pen. 'Tank,' he said. 'Vargas is going to be waiting with his guns loaded.'

'Is he taking cultures out of the building? Do any of the specialists in Maryland have any opinions on that?'

'No one has seen any milk trucks. He'd be a fool to haul that stuff through Havana in a regular truck.'

'Desperate men do foolish things,' Jake Grafton said, and laid the magnifying glass back on the table.

As the sun was setting, Jake received a call from the White House. 'I just watched that tape of Fidel,' the president said over the encrypted circuit.

'It's impressive. We are going to deliver it to the woman who gave it to us, see if she can get it on television tonight.'

'Maybe that will pan out,' the president said. 'The American Interest Section in Havana says that the crowd outside the prison is restless. Local police are nowhere in sight.'

A wave of relief swept over Jake Grafton. 'That's the best news I've heard today, sir.'

'I'm really worried about those viruses.'

'Sir, we'll do what we can.'

'Just what are you going to do, Admiral?'

'Improvise as I go along. Do you really want to know?'

'I guess not,' the president said heavily.

Alejo Vargas was in the office area across the hallway from the lab in the University of Havana science building when General Alba came in with old General Rafael Zerquera, the titular head of the Cuban armed forces, the chief of staff. The old man was at least eighty-five, probably a bit more, and he walked with a cane. With the two military men were several ministers, including Ferrara and the mayor of Havana. Behind them were six young officers, all wearing sidearms.

'*Señor Presidente*,' General Zerquera began, and looked around the room for a chair. He found one and his aide helped him to it, though Vargas had not invited anyone to sit.

The general looked around slowly, taking everything in. Through the window one could see the air lock across the hallway that led to the sealed laboratory.

'I called your office, called the Ministry of Interior – they could not tell me where you were. The army knew, however.'

Vargas said nothing.

'I saw a missile launched last night – everyone in central Cuba saw or heard it.' The old man shook his head, remembering. 'Weapons to destroy cities, kill millions – Fidel knew that if the Yanquis ever found out about the missiles, they would seek to destroy them. He was right. And he knew that if the missiles were ever used on the United States . . .'

Zerquera cocked his head, looked at Vargas. 'So you launched at least one, and it never reached its target.'

'What's done is done,' Vargas snapped. 'How do you know the missile did not reach its target?'

'Because we are still alive,' Zerquera said. 'If you think the Yanquis will not retaliate, you are a dangerous fool.'

Vargas had to restrain himself. Zerquera had many friends; it would be impossible to stop tongues from wagging if he were shot here, in front of these junior officers.

'And then there is this lab,' Zerquera continued blandly, gesturing at the window glass and the laboratory beyond. 'Here you grow the poison to murder Cuba. If you use this on the Americans, they will retaliate. If it escapes, Cubans will die horribly.'

Vargas took a deep breath before he answered. 'We are moving the cultures.'

'Moving them where?'

'To a place where they will be safe.'

'Excuse me, *Señor Presidente*, for my failure to understand. What other place in Cuba has the sealed ventilation system and biological alarms and other safeguards that exist here?'

'There are none.'

'So there is no place safer than this building.'

'Tonight the Americans will probably attack this building in order to destroy the cultures. They burned several facilities last night that contained cultures, and they will probably burn this one. I am not a prophet, yet I make that prediction with a great degree of confidence.'

'The president of the United States can destroy this building and everything it contains with a telephone call,' General Zerquera said softly, 'and there is nothing on earth we can do about it. In my opinion the viruses should be destroyed, if it can be safely done. An escape of the polio viruses

639

from whatever containers they are in will kill vast numbers of our people unless the containers are housed in a specially prepared place, like this laboratory.'

Vargas looked exasperated. 'You exceed your authority, General, when you –'

Zerquera stopped him with a hand. 'No, no, no! *You* exceed *your* authority when you endanger the Cuban people in order to gratify your ambition.'

'Do not cross me, old man,' Vargas snarled.

'I am not going to interfere in politics, Alejo. I never have. The Cuban people will decide who they want to lead them – neither you nor the exiles nor Fidel nor the president of the United States can dictate who the Cuban people will choose. For forty years they wanted Fidel, a loquacious eccentric with much personal charm and too little wisdom, in my opinion. Yet a new day has come.'

Vargas gestured angrily. 'These others have brought you here with lies about me.'

General Rafael Zerquera got to his feet. He leaned on his cane, examined every face, and ended with his eyes on Vargas. 'A nation matures much like a man does. Youth makes mistakes: with age and experience comes wisdom.'

'You waste our time,' Vargas said through his teeth.

'You will not remove the cultures from this building. The risk to the population is too great.'

Vargas stepped forward to slap the old fool, but one of the aides stopped him with the barrel of a pistol pointed right at his face.

'Another step, *Señor Presidente*,' the young man said, 'and you are dead.'

Zerquera turned and headed for the door. He went through it, then took the elevator up to street level. The civilians followed him. Alba and the young officers stayed.

'You, Alba? You have betrayed me?'

'I obey my conscience,' Alba said, and posted his men in front of the lab.

'Kill anyone who tries to remove anything from that room,' the general told them.

As the last of the daylight faded, a helicopter from USS *United States* crossed the southern shore of the island of Cuba flying northwest. The helicopter stayed low, just above the treetops. In the cockpit both the pilot and copilot were wearing night-vision goggles. Behind them in the bay sat Tommy Carmellini and Ocho Sedano. A .50-caliber machine gun was mounted in the open door. The gunner wearing night-vision goggles sat on the jump seat, looking out.

Overhead EA-6B Prowlers and F/A-18 Hornets with their HARM missiles ready crossed the coast at the same time. These airplanes were there to attack any Cuban radars that came on the air tonight. So far, all was quiet. Above the Prowlers and Hornets, F-14 Tomcats patrolled back and forth.

One of the F-14 pilots was Stiff Hardwick. He and his RIO had ejected last night almost on top of silo one, so they had ridden home in an Osprey. The RIO, Boots VonRauenzahn, sustained a green-twig fracture to the left arm; he was sporting a cast tonight and couldn't fly. The junior RIO in the squadron, Sailor George, drew the short straw and was sitting behind Stiff tonight.

Stiff had had a hell of a bad day. First the shoot-down by a Cuban fighter pilot, then he endured a day of razzing from his peers, all of whom had a great laugh at his tale of woe, then tonight he had to fly with Sailor, a quiet woman who never had much to say around the testosterone-charged ready room.

On the way out to the plane this evening, Boots had put his good arm around the shoulders of his pal, Stiff. 'Sailor will take good care of you. Don't fret the program, shipmate.'

Stiff snarled something crude in reply and stomped off.

He was the sole victim of the entire Cuban Air Force – fighter pilots generally ignored helicopters, so the Osprey and choppers destroyed by the MiG pilot didn't register on Stiff's radar screen. He was never, ever going to be able to live down the ignominy of last night. His squadron mates would probably tattoo a ribald memorial of his disgrace on his ass some night when he was drunk or chisel it on his tombstone. His skipper had almost put somebody else in his place on the flight schedule tonight – Stiff begged shamelessly: 'You gotta let me fly,' he sobbed, 'give me a chance to redeem myself.'

'You aren't going to do anything stupid out there, are you?' the skipper asked, his voice tinged with suspicion.

'Oh, no, sir,' Stiff assured the man.

So here he was, off to slay the dragon if he came out of his lair. And that goddamn Cuban fighter jock was probably still swilling free beer on the tale of the damned Yanqui who pulled up in front of him and lit his afterburners.

Actually Carlos Corrado hadn't thought much about his aerial victory. He awoke in the early afternoon with a blinding headache and treated himself to his usual hangover regimen – a cup of coffee, a cigar, and a puke.

He felt a little better this evening but thought he should forgo food. He would eat after he flew, he decided.

The powers that be didn't call the base today, of course, because the telephone system was hors de combat. Alas, a desk-flying colonel drove down from Havana.

'Please stay on the ground, Corrado. I would make that an order, but knowing you, you would disobey it. So I ask you, please do not fly tonight. Please do not allow yourself to be shot down. Please do not shame us.'

Carlos Corrado told the colonel where he could go and what he could do to himself when he got there.

Tonight he sat on the concrete leaning up against a nose tire of his steed, which was parked between two gutted hangars. The troops had worked all day getting the MiG-29 fueled, serviced, and armed. It was ready. Now all Corrado needed to know was where the Americans were and what they were up to. Of course there was no one to tell him.

The walls of the hangars were still standing and magnified the sounds of the sky. As he chewed on his cigar butt, Corrado could hear jets running high. The growl was deep and faint.

The planes were American, certainly, and they had fangs. If he went heedlessly blasting into the sky, his life was going to come to an abrupt, violent end.

Where were they going?

Havana? He thought they would go there last night and they never got near the place.

Of course, the headquarters colonel knew nothing. At least, he had nothing to say. Except that Corrado was a fool. Only a fool would attack the American war machine head-on, he said.

Corrado got out a match and lit the butt. He puffed, coughed, chewed on the soggy mess.

Well, hell, we're all fools, really. Does any of this matter? And if so, to whom?

Rita Moravia settled the V-22 onto the flight deck of the *United States* and watched as Jake Grafton came trotting out from the island. Toad and a dozen marines carrying aircraft flares followed him. The marines had their rifles slung over their shoulders and wore their Kevlar helmets. Under the red lights shining down from the ship's island superstructure, the shadowy procession looked like something from a dream, a vision without substance.

She felt the substance as the men trooped up the ramp in the back of the plane and the vibrations reached her through the fuselage. Soon Jake Grafton was looking over her shoulder.

'Toad says you're okay. Now tell me the truth.'

'I'm okay, Admiral.' She turned and flashed him a grin. The bruise on her forehead was yellow and blue now.

'Whenever you're ready,' Jake said, and strapped himself into the crew chief's seat.

23

It was a rare summer night, with a clean, clear sky, visibility exceeding twenty miles. A series of rain showers had swept the Florida Straits earlier in the evening, cleaning out the haze and crud.

Major Jack O'Brian sat in the cockpit of his F-117 looking at the cities below as he flew down the west coast of Florida, out to sea a little so as to avoid airplanes on the airway. O'Brian had one radio tuned to his squadron's tactical frequency, which he was merely monitoring in case the mission was scrubbed at the last minute, and on the other he listened to Miami Center. He wasn't talking to the air traffic controller either. His transponder was off. He was cruising at 36,500 feet, 500 feet above the flight level, so he should miss any airliner that he failed to see. Of course, an airliner going under him would not see him because his plane was midnight black and the exterior position lights were off.

The stealth fighter was also invisible to the controller at Miami Center, who had his radar configured to receive coded replies from transponders. Even if the controller chose to look at actual radar returns, the skin paints, he would not have seen the F-117, which had been designed to be invisible to radars at long distances.

This feature also hid the stealth fighter from the American early-warning radars that were sweeping these skies looking for outlaw aircraft that might be aloft in the night, such as drug smugglers. And in just a few minutes it would hide it from Cuban radars probing the sky over the Florida Straits. If there were any.

Completely unseen, a black ghost flitting through the night, Jack O'Brian's F-117 passed Tampa Bay and continued south toward Key West. It was flying at Mach .72 to conserve fuel. The fighter had tanked over Tallahassee and would tank again in just a few minutes over two hours near Tampa. But first, a little jaunt to Havana.

Navigation was by global positioning system, GPS. The pilot had entered the coordinates of his destination into the computer before he even started the engines of his airplane, and now the computer and autopilot were taking him there. All he had to do was monitor the system, make sure everything functioned as it was designed to.

O'Brian sucked on his oxygen mask, reached under it to scratch his nose, readjusted his flight gloves, and generally fidgeted around in his seat. He was nervous – who wouldn't be? – but quite confident. After all, there was very little danger as long as the aircraft's systems continued to work properly. The craft truly was invisible at night. Of course it did have a small infrared signature and could be seen by an enemy searching the skies with infrared detectors, but there was no reason to suspect the Cubans were doing any such thing.

Barring a freak accident, like getting hit by a random unaimed artillery shell or having a midair with a civilian plane, the Cubans would never know the F-117 had even been around. Certainly they would never see it on radar or with the naked eye.

The Cubans might get wise when and if he dropped some bombs, but even so, there was nothing they could do about an invisible bomber.

The biggest risk, Jack O'Brian decided, was having a midair with one of the other three F-117s that were out here prowling around.

The second plane was running twenty miles back in trail, a thousand feet above this one, and the others an equal distance up and back, all with their own hard altitudes. Jack glanced again at his altimeter, just to be sure.

Key West came into view on schedule, a bit off to his left. The lights of the other Keys looked like a handful of pearls flung into the blackness of the night.

Then Key West lay behind and the lights of Havana appeared ahead. Jack O'Brian reduced power and set up a descent.

Angel One, the helicopter from *United States*, landed in the cane across the road from Doña Maria Sedano's house. Ocho got out of the chopper and walked across the road toward the house. Tommy Carmellini trailed along behind him.

Mercedes was standing on the porch as Ocho walked up. They launched themselves at each other, hugged fiercely. Mercedes didn't even glance at Carmellini, who was dressed in a civilian shirt and trousers but had a pistol strapped to his waist.

Mercedes kept her arm around Ocho, took him into the house where his mother was sitting in a chair.

Carmellini sat on the porch, watched the occasional car and truck go by. The vehicles slowed, their passengers gawking at the idling helo, but they didn't stop.

Soon Ocho came outside with Mercedes. She had the videotape in her hand. Ocho introduced Carmellini.

'If the videotape is to have maximum effect, it should be aired immediately,' Carmellini told Mercedes, who held the tape tightly with both hands.

'We are going to get Hector out of prison,' Ocho said, anxious to explain. 'We could take you to Havana television and leave you, if you wish.'

Mercedes nodded, so Ocho put his arm around her and led her to the helicopter. Doña Maria was visible in the door of her cottage; Ocho waved at her before he climbed into the helo.

Jake Grafton used an infrared viewing scope to examine the streets of Havana. He was sitting in the copilot's seat of the V-22 Osprey, which Rita had racked over in a right bank, orbiting the downtown. The city was well lit – not as well lit as an American city, but almost. The central core of the city was dark – the electrical power had yet to be restored.

The area around the University of Havana seemed deserted. No tanks, no armored personnel carriers, no barricades, apparently no troops. The streets looked empty.

Strange.

Or maybe not so strange. Maybe the lab was empty, the viruses moved to God knows where.

Everyone in Cuba seemed to be in the streets around La Cabana Prison; at least a hundred thousand people, Jake estimated. Bonfires burned in the streets near the prison, huge fires that appeared as bright spots of light on the infrared viewing scope.

He looked for the antiaircraft guns which he knew were there. He found them, but at this altitude he couldn't see people around them. 'Go lower,' he told Rita. 'Two thousand feet.'

Still circling to the right, she eased the power and let the Osprey descend.

Jake turned his attention to the prison, an island of darkness on the edge of the stricken city center. The main gate was an opening in a high masonry wall that surrounded the huge old stone fortress. The gate seemed to be closed, but at this altitude and angle, it was difficult to be sure. Immediately behind the gate sat a tank – Jake had seen enough of those planforms to be absolutely certain. Two more tanks sat in the courtyard ... and some automobiles. Jake adjusted the magnification on the infrared viewer. Now he could see individuals, walking, standing in knots, talking through the fence – yes, the main gate was closed.

Two antiaircraft batteries sat beside the prison, old Soviet four-barreled ZPUs with optical sights. They were useless against fast movers but would be hell on helicopters.

The roof of the prison was flat, and apparently empty. No. Correct that. Snipers on the corners. Damn!

Jake checked the radio to ensure he was on the proper frequency, then keyed the mike. 'Angel One, this is Battlestar One, where are you?'

'Angel One's on its way to the television station to deliver a passenger.'

'Let me know when you lift off from there.'

'Roger that, Battlestar.'

'Night Owl Four Two, call your posit.'

Jack O'Brian in the F-117 replied, 'Night Owl Four Two is overhead at ten.'

'La Cabana Prison is our object of interest tonight, Four Two. I want single bombs, all to stay within the walls. Can you do that?'

'We can try, sir. You know the limitations on my equipment as well as I do.'

'Your best efforts. Lots of friendlies outside the wall. First target is the antiaircraft battery inside the prison walls on the north side. Do you see it?'

'Wait.' Seconds ticked by.

'Got it.'

'The second target is the antiaircraft battery on the south side.'

'Night Owl Four Four is on station at eleven thousand, Battlestar. Why don't we each run one of those targets? I'll take the north one.'

The two F-117 pilots discussed it and Jake approved.

Jack O'Brian had several possible ways to drop the bombs he carried in the internal bomb bay. If he were bombing through a cloud deck or in rain or snow, he would release the unpowered weapon over the target and let it steer itself to the GPS bull's-eye through use of a GPS receiver, a computer, and a set of canards mounted on the nose of the weapon. Tonight, since the sky was reasonably clear, he would illumine the target with a laser beam while overflying it, and let the unpowered bomb fly itself to the laser-designated bull's-eye. If O'Brian could keep the laser beam directly on the spot he wished the bomb to hit, he should be able to achieve pinpoint, bomb-in-a-barrel accuracy.

Once again O'Brian carefully checked his electronic countermeasures panel, which was dark. The Cubans were off the air, which was comforting.

Now he adjusted the focus of the infrared camera in the nose. The display blossomed slowly, continued to change as he got closer and the grazing angle increased.

He could see the gun plainly owing to the camera's magnification. He sweetened the crosshairs just a touch as the airplane motored sedately toward the target, still cruising at ten thousand feet, and turned on the laser designator, which was slaved to the crosshairs.

Jack O'Brian checked his watch. 'Night Owl Four Two is thirty seconds from drop.'

'Four Four is a minute out.'

'Don't turn on your laser until you see my thing pop.'

'Roger.'

Armament panel set for one bomb, laser mode selected, laser designator on, master armament switch on, steady on the run-in heading, autopilot engaged, crosshairs steady on the target – no drift – system into Attack. A tone sounded in his ears and was broadcast over the radio on the tactical frequency. O'Brian knew that several people were listening for that tone, including the pilot of the other F-117 Night Owl Four Four, Judy Kwiatkowski.

He watched for unexpected wind drift. Not much tonight – what little wind there was was well within the capability of the bomb to handle.

Counting down, the second hand on the clock on the instrument panel ticking . . . The release marker marched down and he felt the thump as the bomb bay doors snapped open. Immediately thereafter the bomb was released, the tone stopped, then the doors closed again.

With the bomb in the air, it was essential that the crosshairs on the laser designator stay precisely on the target because the bomb was guiding itself toward this spot of invisible light.

He took manual control of the crosshairs, kept them right on the artillery piece beside the old fortress.

The aspect angle of the target was changing, of course, as the airplane flew over it and beyond. Now it was behind the plane, the crosshairs right on the target.

Then, suddenly, the antiaircraft artillery piece disappeared in a flash as the five-hundred-pound bomb struck it dead center.

Thirty seconds later the gun on the south side of the building was hit by Judy Kwiatkowski's weapon.

'Very good, Night Owls,' Battlestar said. 'The next target is the tank nearest to the main gate. I think one bomb will discourage the tankers. Four Four, I want you to bomb the main gate. Tell me if you see it.'

'Four Four has the target.'

'How long until the weapons hit?'

'Give us ten minutes to go out and make another run.'

'Ten minutes will do fine,' Jake Grafton said, then turned to Rita.

'After the bombs hit the tanks and main gate, I want you to land on the roof. The guys in back will go out shooting and take care of the snipers. Let me go talk to Eckhardt and Toad.' Both officers were riding in the back of the Osprey with the grunts.

Jake unstrapped and got out of the copilot's seat. In a moment Lieutenant Colonel Eckhardt climbed into the seat and used the infrared scope. 'See the snipers?' the admiral asked. 'I want you and your people to shoot them or capture them, whatever.'

'Yes, sir.' The colonel got out of the seat.

'Ten minutes, Rita. Start your clock.'

'Aye, aye, sir,' Rita said, and began figuring the best way to approach the prison.

A man from the control tower ran to find Carlos Corrado and tell him that American aircraft were over Havana. The people in the tower heard the news on short-wave radio from headquarters.

'Havana.'

Corrado threw away his cigar butt and got into his flying gear.

Five minutes later he was taxiing. He didn't stop at the end of the runway to check the systems or controls, but added power and stroked the burners. The big fighter responded like a thoroughbred race horse and lifted off after a short run.

Of course he left his radar off.

Still, the crew of the US Air Force E-3 Sentry over the Isle of Pines picked up a skin-paint return of the MiG almost immediately.

'Showtime One Oh Two, we got a bogey lifting off Cienfuegos, looks like he's on his way to Havana on the deck. Try to intercept. Over.'

Stiff Hardwick had been airborne for an hour and ten minutes. The recovery aboard *United States* would begin in exactly thirty-five minutes. This bogey was on the deck using fuel at a prodigious rate, and when Stiff came swooping down from 30,000 feet his fuel consumption would also go through the roof. Fuel would be tight. Very tight. If he had to stroke the throttles to drop this turkey, he was going to need a tanker.

'One Oh Two will probably need a tanker.'

'Roger that. Showtime One Oh Seven –' this was Stiff's wingman, who was orbiting a thousand feet above Stiff '– remain on station.'

'One Oh Seven aye.'

'Showtime One Oh Two is on the way,' Stiff told the E-3 controller.

'That's the spirit,' Sailor Karnow said from the rear cockpit.

'Shut up, babe. Just do your thing and keep the crap to yourself.'

'You got it, dickwick. I'm behind you all the way.'

The helicopter landed in the street in front of the television station and Mercedes stepped out. Ocho waved as it lifted off, leaving her standing there with her hair and skirt blowing wildly, clutching the videotape.

El Ocho, alive and well! It seemed like a miracle. Truly, she had thought he was dead, lost at sea.

'I have seen the tape,' Ocho had shouted over the noise of the helicopter as they rode above the lights of Havana. 'Fidel wanted Hector to lead Cuba. His opinion will sway many people.'

Yes, she nodded, fighting back tears.

'Why did you give the tape to the Americans?'

'Vargas would have taken it from me,' she replied.

Ocho accepted that because he knew it was true. That tape would destroy Alejo Vargas.

'Make them show it on television,' Ocho had shouted. 'We will get Hector out of prison.' He grinned broadly, showing all his teeth. The future was arriving all at once.

She watched the helicopter disappear into the night sky, then turned and walked into the television station.

One of the most horrifying threats any soldier can face is being in the bull's eye of a modern guided weapon. The stealth fighters were out tonight, dropping their weapons with extraordinary precision. The bombs came in too fast for the human eye to follow, especially in the light conditions prevailing in Havana this night. For the Cuban troops surrounding the old prison, it was as if a giant invisible sharpshooter were somewhere in the clouds hurling bombs.

The two bombs on the antiaircraft guns frightened the soldiers and made the crowd nervous. Watching from the Osprey, Jake Grafton thought for a moment the crowd might stampede: with this many people jamming the streets that would be a human disaster. Still, he could not take the risk the guns or tanks would open fire on the inbound helicopter or the Osprey, both of which he wanted to land on the prison's roof.

Through the infrared viewer Jake could see the soldiers instinctively moving away from the tanks. He could see men getting out of the hatch, jumping to the ground, walking away.

On the street the crowd was also pushing back, crowding away from the old fortress.

Minutes passed and nothing happened. The packed rows of humanity on the street seemed to relax, to thin as the people instinctively sought their own space.

Jake heard the first bomb tone come on. An officer – Jake assumed he was an officer – climbed up on one of the tanks, waved his arms at his men.

The bomb tone ceased: the weapon was in the air.

Now the officer standing on the tank put his hands on his hips – Rita had the Osprey down to a thousand feet, only a mile from the building, set up to begin her transition to helicopter flight, so the activity in the prison courtyard was as clear to Jake as if he had been watching it on television.

'Angel One, this is Battlestar One. Come on in.'

'Roger that, Battlestar.'

The Cuban officer was still standing on the tank when it disappeared in a flash as the bomb hit it.

When the cloud of smoke and debris cleared, no one was moving within a hundred feet of the blasted tank, of which only tiny pieces remained. The bomb must have penetrated the armor in front of or behind the turret, Jake thought.

Now the second bomb tone ended. Cuban troops were running out of the prison complex through the main gate, which Jake belatedly realized was open. The men were dropping their weapons, throwing away their helmets and running as fast as their legs could carry them.

The five-hundred-pound bomb from Night Owl Four Four exploded in the gate and the running men disappeared in a flash.

'Put it on the roof,' Jake Grafton told Rita Moravia.

'Okay, I got this guy,' Sailor Karnow told Stiff Hardwick. 'He's bogey one.'

The symbol was right there in front of Stiff on the heads-up display.

'About thirty miles or so,' Sailor said matter-of-factly. She would sound bored if they were giving her an Academy Award. That was another thing about her Stiff didn't like. Well, the truth was, he hated her guts, but he knew better than to say so in the new modern politically correct gender-neutral navy to which they both belonged. A few off-the-cuff remarks like that to the boys could torpedo a promising career.

'Lock the son of a bitch up,' Stiff told his RIO.

'You can't shoot this dude,' Sailor said, still bored as hell. 'There are four stealth fighters flapping around down there, three Ospreys and a helicopter, or did you sleep through the brief? You can't shoot without the blessing of Battlestar Strike, which you ain't likely to get.'

Twenty-five miles now. Stiff had the F-14 coming down like a lawyer on his way to hell, showing Mach 1.7 on the meter. He was fast crawling up this MiG's ass.

'Don't just sit there with your thumb up your heinie, honey. Get on the goddamn horn.'

'Battlestar Strike,' Sailor drawled on the radio. 'This is Showtime One Oh Two. We got us a situation developing out here.'

Rita didn't use her landing light until the last possible moment, snapping it on just in time to judge the final few seconds of her approach. As it was, only one of the demoralized snipers on the roof took a shot at the plane, a wild, unaimed shot that punched a hole in the fuselage near the port gear and spent itself against a structural member. Then the marines charging out of the back of the beast fired a shot over his head and the sniper threw down his rifle. The other snipers had already done so.

In seconds the chopper from *United States* came out of the darkness and set down alongside the V-22. Tommy Carmellini and Ocho Sedano came scrambling out.

All this was new to Ocho. With wide eyes he looked at the Osprey, at the marines, at the skyline of Havana, at the bonfires in the street and the tens of thousands of people.

Toad Tarkington appeared at Jake's elbow. 'I think I know how to get off this roof,' Toad said.

'Lead on,' Jake told him.

'Uh, Showtime One Oh Two, negative on the permission to shoot. That's negatory, weapons red, over.'

'Strike, goddamn it,' Stiff Hardwick roared, 'We're sitting right on the tail of a goddamn MiG on his way to Havana to kill some of our people. I got the son of a bitch boresighted.'

'Showtime, there are too many friendlies over Havana. Weapons red, weapons red, over.'

'How about I pop this guy with my gun? Request weapons free for a gunshot. Over.'

'Wait.'

Stiff was off the power, idling along at about 400 knots, five miles behind the bogey. Of course, the bogey didn't know he was there. The Cuban MiG-29s had very primitive electronic detection equipment, which consisted of a light and an auditory signal in the pilot's ear. These devices told Carlos Corrado he was being looked at by an American fighter radar but failed to tell him where or how close the thing was, the two pieces of information that he needed the most.

As he closed on Havana and listened to the tone and watched the light, which didn't even flicker, Carlos Corrado pondered on the irony of knowing American fighters were out there somewhere and not being able to do anything about it. If he turned on his radar, he would beacon to the Americans, who would then come at him like moths to a flame. His only chance was to keep the radar off.

If the Americans launched a weapon at him, he had a few flares he could punch off, of course, and some chaff. It was not much, but it might be enough. If it wasn't, well, he had had a good life.

Carlos began looking right and left as he crossed the suburbs of the city. Amid all the lights he spotted some fires, and the center of the city was dark, without power, but all in all, Havana looked pretty normal. Amazing, that!

'Battlestar Strike, this is Showtime. Still waiting on that permission. This MiG is posing right here in front of me, begging for it. Do I zap it or what?'

'We are still checking with the air force,' Battlestar told Stiff, 'trying to find out exactly where everyone is. Don't want any accidents out there, do we?'

Stiff keyed the intercom. 'Assholes,' he roared at Sailor Karnow. 'They are all stupid fucking assholes.'

'I hear that,' said Sailor, sighing. 'I've known it for years. I should have joined the WNBA.'

Toad Tarkington led the procession along the dark corridor of La Cabana prison. Apparently the power had not yet been restored after the high-voltage towers fell. Everyone following Toad had a flashlight.

The corridors were alive with echoing sound, shouts, curses, doors clanging, screams, shots.

'Hurry,' Grafton shouted, and ran toward the shouts.

As he suspected, the mob was in the building. As he and Toad rounded a corner, their flashlights fell on a solid wall of humanity dragging two uniformed officers. Carmellini shouted. The human wall halted.

'This is Ocho Sedano,' Carmellini shouted, 'Hector's brother. He is here to free Hector.'

The man dragging a fat officer by the collar of his uniform demanded, 'Who are you?' Obviously drunk, this man had the commandante's pistol in his hand, but he didn't raise it or point it. The flashlights were partially blinding him, but he could still see the front end of Toad's M-16.

'We are here at El Ocho's request.' Carmellini proclaimed loudly. 'He has asked for our help to free his brother Hector.'

The mob moved forward, probably in response to a surging push from the people behind.

'Give us the officers,' Jake said to Carmellini, 'and we will bring Hector from his cell.' Carmellini shouted the message in Spanish.

The members of the mob didn't like it, but they were facing six rifles in a narrow stone corridor. The people at the head of the mob released the officers and turned to shout at those behind them.

The marines grabbed the two officers and pushed them away along the corridor.

Carmellini talked earnestly to the officers. 'They will lead us there,' he told Jake. 'Colonel Santana arrived an hour ago. He was with the commandante until just a few minutes ago.'

'Hurry,' Jake Grafton urged. 'The mob is out of control.' He had drawn the .357 Magnum he wore in a holster around his waist and now had it in his right hand.

'Showtime One Oh Two, Strike, the air force is having trouble confirming the location of all their machines.'

'Strike, this guy is hanging it out, begging for it, trolling right over the damn city looking for some white hats to zap. Are you gonna cry at the funeral after he kills some of our people?'

This comment was of course grossly out of line: Stiff Hardwick was a mere lieutenant – an O-3 – and the decisions in Strike were being made by an officer with the rank of commander – O-5 – or even captain – O-6. He was going to be in big trouble when he got back to the ship, but he didn't care. The primary object of war was to kill the enemy, and by God, the son of a bitch was right there. He'd deal with the peckerheads later.

Another minute passed. They were over the heart of Havana now. The oily black slash of Havana Harbor was quite prominent, as were the dozens of fires that now surrounded the walls of the old La Cabana fortress.

'This guy is starting a turn,' Sailor told Stiff, referring of course to the bogey.

Carlos Corrado should have been searching the night sky over Havana for the planes he knew were here, but he wasn't. He was only human. He was looking at the red warning light and listening to the buzz that told him that a hostile fighter's radar was illuminating his aircraft.

The light and tone had been on for five minutes now. The miracle was that Carlos Corrado was still alive. Five minutes in front of an aggressive American fighter pilot was about six lifetimes ... and *still* the American hadn't pulled the trigger!

Carlos didn't know why, but he suspected the reason had something to do with the fact they were tooling over the rooftops of Havana.

Ocho Sedano and the Americans ran through the corridors of La Cabana Prison until they came to a massive steel gate. It was closed but unlocked; they used the commandante's keys to lock it behind them. Then they entered a cellblock full of men screaming to be freed. Hundreds of arms reached through the bars, trying to reach the Americans.

The guards led them to Hector, who was in a cell in a corridor off the main cellblock. 'They have no key to the cell,' Carmellini told Jake.

'Use C-4. Blow it,' the admiral said.

Hector reached through the bars and got his hands on Ocho. They hugged while Jake Grafton held the flashlight and Tommy Carmellini set the explosive.

'Have you seen Santana?' Carmellini asked Hector.

'Yes. He was here.'

'Where is he now?'

'He heard you coming and ran.'

When the plastic explosive blew the lock apart on Hector's cell, Ocho jerked the door open and hugged him fiercely. 'I apologize, Hector,' he said. 'Please forgive me.'

Jake Grafton dragged them apart. 'There is no time,' he shouted, and pushed them toward the corridor.

The sounds of the mob tearing at the steel bars that barred the way into the cell block could be heard above the shouts of the men in the cells.

Toad led his party the other way. Another door, precious seconds wasted while the officers fumbled for a key, then they were through and going up a stairway. More stairs, then along a long, dark corridor lit only by flashlights.

As they rounded a turn someone ahead fired a shot at them. The bullet spanged off a wall, and miraculously failed to connect with human flesh.

Suddenly sure, Tommy Carmellini told Jake, 'It's Santana. You go on. I'll get the bastard.'

'We don't have time for personal vendettas,' Jake Grafton snapped.

'I'm a civilian, Grafton. I can take care of myself. Go on!'

Jake led his party onward.

When they came out onto the roof the Osprey's position lights and flashing anticollision light revealed a crowd of at least three hundred people. They completely surrounded the Osprey and helo and the marines with rifles who held them off. The pilots must have shut down the engines due to the large number of people nearby. Lieutenant Colonel Eckhardt walked back and forth behind the marines, an imposing martial figure if ever there was one. Fortunately no one in the crowd seemed to be armed.

Jake and Toad forced their way through the crowd.

It was Ocho who stepped in front of the crowd and began to speak. 'This is my brother Hector, the next president of Cuba.'

The crowd cheered lustily.

'I am El Ocho. I wish to know if you love Cuba?'

'*Sí!*' they roared.

'Do you believe in Cuba?'

'*Sí!*'

'Will you fight for Cuba?'

'*Sí!*'

'Will you follow me and put Hector Sedano in the presidential palace?'

'*Sí! Sí! Sí!*' The crowd breathed the word over and over and swarmed around Ocho.

'Come,' said Jake Grafton, and pulled Hector toward the Osprey.

24

As Jake Grafton and the others climbed the stairs toward the roof of La Cabana Prison, Tommy Carmellini doused his flashlight and held it in his left hand. He stood in the darkness waiting for his eyes to adjust to the dim light.

He had a pistol that the marines aboard ship had given him, a 9-mm, that felt cold and comforting in his grip. He closed his eyes, listened to the cheers and shouts from the roof, waited until he heard the chopper and Osprey get airborne.

Finally the corridors of the old fortress grew quiet.

Santana was in here someplace.

Jake Grafton had his thing and he was hard at it. William Henry Chance had his thing, trying to control biological and chemical weapons in Third World countries, and he had died doing it. Tommy Carmellini's thing was cracking safes. Sure, he was doing it for the CIA now instead of stealing diamonds from rich matrons, but somehow that wasn't enough. There comes a time in a man's life when he begins to tally up the score. When Carmellini realized Grafton wasn't going to take the time to step on the cockroach Santana, he knew he had to.

He stepped forward now, walking the way Hector had indicated that Santana had gone.

Taking his time in the near-total darkness – there was just enough light to see the outline of the corridor – walking, listening, walking, listening again, Tommy Carmellini moved to the end of the corridor and stopped.

He could hear metal on metal, as if someone was trying to open a lock. The sound came from the corridor on the right.

Tommy Carmellini bent as low as he could get, eased his head around the corner.

Yes, the sound was clearer now.

Ever so slowly he edged around the corner, crossed the corridor to the other side, began moving forward into the blackness, toward the sound.

The noise stopped.

Carmellini froze. Closed his eyes to concentrate on the sound.

The pistol was heavy in his hand.

The sound began again.

Forward, ever so stealthily, moving like a glacier, just flowing slowly, silently, effortlessly. . . .

The man was just ahead. Working on a lock. Probably on one of those steel gates.

Again the sound stopped.

Carmellini froze, not trusting himself to breathe.

The other man was here, he could feel him. But where?

Time seemed to stop. Tommy Carmellini held his breath, stood crouched but frozen, knowing that the slightest sound would give away his position. Santana was . . .

Suddenly Carmellini knew. He was right . . .

There! He pointed the pistol and pulled the trigger.

The muzzle flash strobed the darkness, and revealed Santana swinging the butt of his rifle, swinging it at Carmellini's head.

He tried to duck but the rifle struck his shoulder and sent him sprawling. He held on to the pistol, triggered two more shots, which came like giant thunderclaps, deafening him with their roar.

The flashlight was gone, lost when he fell. His left shoulder was on fire where the rifle butt struck him, his arm numb. He could hear Santana running, shuffling along, the sound fading.

He felt for the flashlight with his right hand, couldn't find it, paused and listened and searched some more. There! He picked it up without releasing the pistol. Now he put the pistol between his legs, tried to work the flashlight with his right hand. It was broken. He set it on the floor out of the way.

He listened, heard the faintest of sounds, then nothing.

Tommy Carmellini slowly got to his feet and began moving back the way he had come, after Santana.

'Showtime One Oh Two, Battlestar Strike. You are cleared to engage the bogey with a gun. Weapons free gun only, acknowledge.'

'Weapons free gun only, aye,' sung out Stiff Hardwick, and jammed his throttles forward to the mechanical stop. The engines wound up quickly; Stiff eased the throttles to the left, stroked the afterburners. The big fighter leaped forward and began closing the five-mile gap between the two planes.

Carlos Corrado glanced over his left shoulder, for the hundreth time, expecting to see nothing, but this time he saw the plume of flame that was Hardwick's burners. *The Yanqui must be right behind me.*

Enough!

He slammed the throttles to the hilt, dropped the left wing and pulled right up to six Gs. The MiG-29 then showed why it was one of the most maneuverable fighters in the world – it turned on a dime.

As it did, Carlos Corrado fought the G and flipped his radar switch to the transmit position.

Leveling up after a 180-degree turn, the radar scope came alive ... and there was the American – close. Too close! Jesus Christ!

Without time to even consider the problem, Carlos Corrado punched off an Aphid missile, which roared off the rail in a blaze of fire straight for the F-14.

Sailor Karnow saw the bogey wind into a left turn, and called it to Stiff, who instinctively lowered his right wing to stay in the MiG's rear quadrant.

What Stiff wasn't prepared for was the unbelievable quickness with which the MiG-29 whipped around and pumped off a missile.

The sight of the fiery exhaust of the Aphid missile coming at him from eleven o'clock and the wailing of the ECM in his ears, telling him that he was being painted by a MiG-29 pulse-doppler radar, reached Stiff Hardwick's brain at the very same instant. Before Stiff could react in any way, the missile shot over his canopy inches above his head. Fortunately for Stiff and Sailor and their progeny yet unborn, the Aphid had not flown far enough to arm, so the missile passed harmlessly.

'*Holy shit!*' Sailor shouted into her oxygen mask.

Stiff Hardwick hadn't spent the last four years flying fighters for nothing – his instincts were finely honed too. As the Aphid went over his head, he jerked the nose of his fighter toward the closing MiG, visible only as a bogey symbol on the HUD, and pulled the trigger on the stick. The 20-mm M-61 six-barreled cannon in the nose lit up like a searchlight as a river of fire streaked into the darkness.

Carlos Corrado saw the finger of God reaching for him and slammed his stick back, then sideways. The MiG's nose came up steeply and the right wing dropped in a violent whifferdill that carried it up and out of the way of the fiery stream of cannon shells.

Completing the roll, Carlos Corrado pushed the nose of his MiG downward, toward the city, and let the plane accelerate without afterburners, the light of which would beacon to the American. Or Americans, if there were more than one, which was probable.

Carlos pulled out just above the rooftops and thundered across the city. He had lost track of the enemy's location because he could not see him visually or with his radar. He desperately needed his GCI site just now to call the enemy's position, but of course the GCI people had been knocked off the air and were either dead or drunk.

Still, the contest appealed to his sporting instincts. He decided to try for one in-parameters missile shot before he called it a night and went looking for a bar.

His radar was still on, still looking at nothing.

Without further ado, Carlos pulled the stick back and let the MiG's nose climb. Up past the vertical, G on hard, the MiG used its fabulous turning rate to fly half of a very tight loop. Upside down with its nose on the horizon, Carlos slammed the stick sideways and rolled upright. The F-14 was out to his left, turning toward him. Corrado flipped his switches to select an infrared missile, turned toward the American until he got a tone in his headset, and squeezed it off.

Then he killed his radar and turned hard ninety degrees right to exit the fight.

'Oh, no,' Stiff Hardwick swore as he saw the missile coming at him from ten o'clock.

He lit his afterburners and dropped the right wing slightly and willed the Tomcat to accelerate, trying to force the missile into an overshoot, while he punched off chaff and flares with a button on his right throttle.

The missile tried to make the turn but couldn't. Perhaps the IR seeker in the nose locked onto a flare. In any event, as it flew past the tail of the Tomcat its proximity fuse caused the warhead to detonate, spraying shrapnel into empty air.

The MiG-29 was gone. It had disappeared.

'You know, dickwick,' Sailor Karnow told her pilot, 'I think God is really trying to tell us something.'

Carlos Corrado knew that he had had more than his share of luck this night. Although he was flying a tremendously maneuverable airplane, the electronic detection and countermeasures systems were generations behind the F-14 that had followed him around. Why the F-14 had not shot him down he couldn't guess, but he was wise enough to know that luck sorely tried is bound to turn.

He decided to put his MiG on the ground while it was still in one piece. Fortunately there was an airport nearby, Havana's José Martí International, right over there in the middle of that vast dark area. Since there was a war on, someone had turned off the runway lights.

Corrado pulled off the power, let the fighter slow to gear speed, then snapped the landing gear down. Flaps out, retrim, and swing out for an approach to where the runway ought to be. On final he turned on his landing light and searched the darkness below.

There! Concrete.

He squeaked the MiG on and got on the brakes.

He left the landing light on to taxi.

'Showtime One Oh Two, the MiG is landing at José Martí.' That was the air force controller in the Sentry AWACS plane.

Stiff Hardwick was climbing through five thousand feet at full power when he heard that transmission. Fortunately he had committed a map of the Havana area to memory, so he knew precisely where José Martí International lay. He cut the power and lowered the nose.

'What in hell do you think you're doing, Stiff?' Sailor demanded.

'Shut up.'

'We barely got enough fuel to make the tanker as it is, pea brain. You go swanning around down here for a few more minutes begging that Cuban to give you the shaft and we'll be swimming home.'

'I'm gonna get that Cuban son of a bitch. Gonna strafe him on the ground. Gonna kill that bastard deader than last week's beer.'

Sailor Karnow knew the pilot was serious. Here was a frustrated man if ever she had met one. As the plane dove for the black hole that was José Martí International, she tried to reason with Stiff:

'You can't shoot the guy on the ground at a civilian airport. There's no lights down there, you might kill a bunch of civilians!'

'There he is! I can see the fucking guy taxiing – he's still got his landing light on! *There he is!*'

Sailor Karnow was losing her patience. '*You pull that trigger, Jake Grafton will cut your balls off, you silly son of a bitch!*'

Stiff Hardwick knew the jig was up. Sailor was right – he hated women who were always right. He reached up and safetied the master arm switch. And kept the Tomcat coming down.

Edged the throttles forward as he dropped lower and lower, boresighting that barely moving plane down there with the single landing light shining forward. The needle on the airspeed indicator crept past Mach 1.

The radio altimeter deedled, he kept going lower. . . .

'Don't fly into the ground, you idiot!' Sailor pleaded from the rear cockpit.

The fear in her voice probably saved both their lives. Stiff eased back on the stick just a smidgen, an almost microscopic amount, so the F-14 rose another ten feet above the ground as it roared over Carlos Corrado's taxiing MiG-29 like a giant supersonic missile. The American fighter passed a mere four feet over the MiG's tail; the shock wave shattered the MiG's canopy.

Then Stiff pulled the stick back in his lap and lit the burners and went rocketing upward like a bat out of hell.

'Better get on the horn and get us a tanker, baby, or you're gonna be my date in a life raft tonight.'

Sailor had the last word. 'Honest to God, dickwick, you oughta think about taking up another line of work.'

Tommy Carmellini wondered if he had managed to put a bullet into Santana. That was a lot to hope for, but still . . . three shots, and the man no more than five, six feet away?

With luck.

A man needs luck as he goes through life. Life is timing, and timing is experience plus luck.

Carmellini wondered just how much experience sneaking along dark corridors Santana had had through the years. He hadn't impressed Carmellini as the sneaking type. One never knew, though.

He found himself moving slower and slower, listening with his eyes closed, concentrating. He could hear . . .

Breathing. Coming from somewhere ahead. Definitely breathing.

Jake Grafton had Rita circle out over the harbor while he talked to other airplanes he had inbound. After a few minutes, he told her to fly toward the university.

Looking through the infrared viewer, he could see that the streets around the university were deserted. Not a car or truck moving, none parked, no people.

Alejo Vargas was down there, all right.

Jake got out of the copilot's seat and went aft to talk to Hector Sedano, who was sitting beside Lieutenant Colonel Eckhardt. Jake pulled one of the Spanish-speaking marines along to translate.

'Do you know of the biological-warfare laboratory in the science building of the university?'

No, Hector didn't. Jake took a minute to explain.

'My government has sent me to destroy the polio viruses that are in that lab, and the equipment that was used to grow them. Do you have any objection to me doing that?'

Hector did not, as long as innocent lives were not lost unnecessarily.

Talking loudly over the aircraft's high internal noise, Jake continued while the young marine, a buck sergeant, translated: 'I promise you, we will proceed with all due care. The stakes are very high, those viruses must be destroyed. If you will join me in this humanitarian effort representing the new Cuban government, I believe the job can be done with a minimum loss of life.'

'Tell me of this laboratory,' Hector Sedano demanded. 'What you know of it, and how it came to be.'

The feeling was coming back in Tommy Carmellini's left arm. It hurt like hell now, like someone had tried to carve on his shoulder with a dull knife.

Ignore the arm. Listen!

He froze. He hadn't realized it, but there were cells on both sides of the corridor, cells with open doors.

Santana must be in one of them. Which one?

A sound like a sigh.

He heard it! From the left, maybe ten feet.

Frozen like a chunk of solid ice, Carmellini didn't move. He continued to breathe, but very shallowly, taking all the time in the world.

Minutes passed. How many he couldn't say.

He could hear the murmur of the mob somewhere below. No doubt they had turned all the prisoners loose.

The other man was being extremely quiet. Extraordinarily so.

Carmellini finally began moving, reluctantly, ever so slowly, like the shadow of the sun as it marches across a stone floor. And he made about the same amount of noise.

He was in the cell, feeling his way ... when his left foot touched something that shouldn't be there.

Like a cat he reacted, the pistol booming faster than thought.

In the muzzle flash he saw that Santana lay stretched on his back on the floor, his eyes open to the ceiling.

The bastard was dead.

From the cockpit Jake Grafton could see the crowds below on the streets. Rita had the Osprey flying at 2,000 feet, and Jake could see the swarms of people with his naked eye, without using the infrared viewer, though he used it occasionally to check on the progress of the crowd.

Rita swung the Osprey over the university district, and he picked out the science building.

He watched the mass of humanity flow into the district, surge along toward the science building.

He used the viewer, steadied it carefully and cranked up the magnification. Yes, the knot of humanity at the front of the crowd, that had to be around Ocho. El Ocho, as the Cubans called him.

The boy was fearless. This afternoon when Jake explained to Ocho that there was a strong probability that the soldiers would refuse to fire on the civilians, might even disobey their officers if ordered to fire, Ocho merely nodded.

Perhaps the ordeal in the ocean had toughened Ocho, or perhaps he had always been impervious to fear. That emotion affected people in an extraordinary variety of ways, Jake knew.

Looking through the viewer it was difficult to be sure, but apparently soldiers were joining the crowd with Ocho as he walked along.

He wanted to let Hector accompany Ocho, but his better judgment told him no. A single sniper, one frightened soldier, and the last best hope of Cuba might be dead in the street. With the viruses still in that lab, that was a risk Jake Grafton was not yet prepared to take.

As he watched, he wished he were with Ocho. That walk must be sublime, he thought.

Ocho Sedano knew a great many people because he had spent years accompanying his brother to speeches, sitting in planning sessions, helped him dig holes to hide weapons.

Many more people, however, knew Ocho. Every Cuban between eight and eighty knew of the star pitcher who threw the sizzling fastballs and hit home runs when his turn came to bat. Many people recognized him, shouted to him as he walked along, then decided to shake his hand and join the throng behind him.

As the human river turned the corner onto the avenue that led to the university, a knot of soldiers left the shelter of a doorway and came toward Ocho. He didn't stop, kept striding along the center of the street.

'Halt!' the senior officer shouted. He was a major. 'You are entering a military area! You can go no farther!'

Ocho didn't even slow his pace. The soldiers had to join the crowd to keep from being trampled.

'You! Stop these people! This is a secure area, by order of Alejo Vargas.'

'We will not stop.' Ocho laughed. 'Do you think you can stop the sun from rising?'

The soldiers hurried along, trying to talk to Ocho, who refused to slow his pace.

'You are El Ocho?' one of the younger soldiers asked.

'The days of Vargas are over, my friend,' Ocho explained. 'Give away your gun and come along with us.'

The sheer numbers and weight of the people pushing along frightened the major, who had a pistol in his hand. Even as his subordinates handed their weapons to the nearest people in civilian clothes, he placed himself in front of Ocho, who didn't stop walking.

'I order you to stop, Sedano!' he shouted, and pointed the pistol at Ocho's head.

'You would make me a martyr, would you?' Ocho asked the major, who was trying to match Ocho's stride. 'Look around you, man. No one can stop them.'

The major fired the pistol into the air. His face was drawn and pale, almost bloodless. 'Stop or I shoot you down, as God is my witness.'

'*Mi amigo*,' said Ocho Sedano, 'For days at sea I was ready to die; all the fear drained from me. There is none in my heart now. My death will not stop these people: nothing can stop the turning of the earth. Still, if you feel you must kill me, make your peace with God and pull the trigger.'

Then he smiled.

El Ocho was a madman, the major realized. Or a saint. The major wiped at the perspiration on his forehead, and handed Ocho the pistol.

Ocho passed the weapon on. He put his arm around the major's shoulders. 'Come,' he said. 'We will walk to the promised land together.'

Like a wall of water rushing along a dry arroyo, the human river flowed along the avenue toward the university as airplanes droned through the darkness overhead.

In the foyer of the science building, Alejo Vargas heard the airplanes. He looked at the politicians and young soldiers who waited silently behind him, blocking the doors to the stairs and the elevator, and he looked at his aides, who were nervously looking out windows, trying not to fidget.

Where was Santana?

The man should be here: he was Alejo Vargas's one loyal friend on this earth.

Vargas paced back and forth, stood in the doorway and listened to the airplanes, wondered if the troops he had hidden in the surrounding buildings were loyal, would still fight. Over two thousand heavily armed men were waiting for the Americans. This time the Yanquis would not escape: this time there would be prisoners to parade before the cameras, vanquished foes to kneel at his feet as Cuba cheered. This time . . .

A car rocketed up to the front of the building and a man leaped out, a uniformed colonel with the Department of State Security. He ran up the stairs, came running through the door, saw Vargas and ran toward him.

'The television,' he said breathlessly. 'On the television, they are showing a tape of Fidel.'

'Yes?' said Vargas, his brows knitting.

'Fidel made the tape before he died. He wants Hector Sedano to be the president after him.'

'What?' Vargas didn't believe a word of it.

'They run the tape, which takes about six minutes, then run it again, over and over and over.'

'That's impossible,' Vargas said, turning toward the politicians, who had moved closer. 'Fidel made no such tape before he died. He wanted to make a tape naming me as his successor, but his illness prevented it.'

'They are showing a tape on television,' the colonel insisted. 'Fidel says the nation must change, and Hector Sedano is the man to lead that change.'

'It's a trick!' Vargas roared. 'The Yanqui CIA is playing a trick on us.'

Every face was openly skeptical.

'Fidel is dead! Don't you people understand that?'

A rising symphony of babbling voices and helicopter noises came through the open door.

'What is happening?' Vargas demanded, turning in that direction. 'Where are the soldiers?'

He saw heads climbing the stairs, many heads, then a mob of people in civilian clothes and army uniforms poured through the doorway, forcing their way in. The room filled rapidly.

People in the doorway stood aside for two men who walked through together, one a tall, rangy young man and the other of medium height, wearing a one-piece faded prison jumpsuit.

They stopped in front of Vargas.

Hector's voice was plainly audible to every person in the room when he said, 'Alejo Vargas, I arrest you in the name of the Cuban people for the murder of Raúl Castro.'

Vargas's hand darted inside his jacket for a pistol, but before he could get it out a dozen hands reached for him, pulled him to the floor, and took the weapon from him.

25

Maximo Sedano spent the night aboard his yacht in Havana Harbor. He heard the planes and the explosions of bombs falling around La Cabana Prison, but he didn't go ashore. He had worked until night fell, hunting for the gold that he was sure lay on the floor of Havana Harbor.

He found a great deal of junk and trash, but no gold.

As the bombs were falling he drank some rum, idly studied the skyline, thought about gold.

Thirty-seven tons of gold. My God, what a man could do with a fortune like that! Cars, yachts, women, all the good things in life.

He was filthy from the muck and pollution of the harbor. The water tank on the boat was not large, so he sponged off as best he could and resolved to take a shower ashore at the first opportunity.

The next morning he began diving as soon as the sun came up. Boats came and went and Maximo worked steadily. He changed tanks once.

The work was maddening. The most probable location for the gold was the marina anchorage, where Fidel and Che must have spent the nights they were anchored. Here is where they must have dumped the gold overboard!

Yet it wasn't on the floor of the harbor. He thought mud and sediment might have covered the ingots, but even when he dug, he could find nothing.

He wasn't being systematic enough, he decided as he lay exhausted on the deck of his boat, his broken fingers aching like bad teeth.

He knew he couldn't go on today, so he took the dinghy and motored ashore. He had his empty tanks along for the harbormaster to fill.

Tired, working one-handed, Maximo took several minutes to get the small boat tied up and the empty air tanks onto the dock. He picked them up and carried them toward the harbormaster's shack.

The man was sitting inside reading a newspaper.

'Can you fill these?' Maximo asked.

The harbormaster looked up to see who was asking, then brightened. 'Señor Sedano, of course. I am so delighted to hear about your brother. Congratulations.'

'What?'

The look of surprise on his face must have shocked the harbormaster, who held out the newspaper. 'Surely you know,' he said. 'Your brother Hector is the new president of Cuba.'

Maximo took the paper, sank down into the only empty chair, stared at the headlines.

'What a night!' said the harbormaster, beaming like the sun. 'History in the making. Hector and El Ocho, what a team!'

'Amazing.'

'And look! The newspaper published a letter from your sister-in-law, Mercedes. Forty years ago Fidel hid the peso gold under the floor of the presidential palace. It's still there, every ounce of it. *Sixty tons of gold* the nation owns, eh! Isn't that amazing?'

The gray US Navy ammo ship anchored in the bay and put a launch into the water. The coxswain brought the small boat around to a gangway. In a few minutes the trill of a bosun's pipe could be heard, then a series of bells over the ship's loudspeaker.

A group of officers and sailors in white uniforms came down the gangway and climbed aboard the launch.

The town of Antilla, Cuba, lay baking in the sun. The waterfront was lined with fishing craft. The only ships at the pier were two small coasters, about a thousand tons each. The launch maneuvered against the pier and Rear Admiral Jake Grafton stepped ashore. Gil Pascal and Toad Tarkington followed him onto the pier.

'That's the warehouse over there,' Toad said, and pointed.

Jake just nodded. He waited as a knot of Cubans came walking out on the pier toward him.

'Where's the translator?'

'Right here, sir,' said an enlisted man, who stepped forward beside Jake. He too was togged out in his best white uniform.

After the usual diplomatic greetings, Jake, Captain Pascal, and the translator went with the Cubans toward the warehouse, leaving Toad alone on the pier.

Tarkington strolled along, looking here and there, his arms held behind his back.

He was standing near the head of the pier when he heard a noise. He stepped to the edge, leaned over.

A man in a black diving suit covered with muck and slime was dragging his gear out from under the pier into the sun.

'I was wondering where you guys were,' Toad said conversationally.

'Some days you're the pigeon, some days you're the statue,' the navy SEAL said. 'Three days we've been living under here like harbor rats, watching that warehouse. We searched it the first night, Commander – the

666

warheads were in there. And they're still there; the Cubans haven't taken anything out.'

'Where's your partner in crime?'

'Over on the other side of those coasters. He'll be along in a bit. Think we could get a ride out to the ship? I've been dreaming of a hot shower, a hot meal, and a clean bunk.'

'I think that can be arranged.' Toad reached down, helped lift the diving gear onto the pier.

When the SEAL was standing on the pier beside him, dripping onto the splintered boards, Toad said, 'How'd you like your Cuban vacation?'

'I want better accommodation for my next visit.'

As the president of the United States feared, the aftermath of the second Cuban missile crisis, as the press called it, was a political disaster in Washington, with howls of outrage from the press and demands from frightened senators and congressmen for investigations and the resignations of everyone in the executive branch.

The president watched General Tater Totten retire from a distance, didn't go to the small Pentagon ceremony, let the White House spinmeisters whisper that Totten was somehow partially responsible for the journey to the brink of the abyss. Sensing that he couldn't win a whisper war, Totten kept his mouth shut and departed with dignity.

Amid the impassioned breast-beating and public denunciations, the director of the CIA decided that he too had had enough of Washington. He had a final conversation with the president in the Oval Office after he submitted his resignation but before the White House announced his departure.

'Sorry to see you go,' the president muttered politely, not meaning a word of it. The director nodded knowingly.

'Don't know if this congressional investigation can be derailed or not,' the president said, not willing to look the director in the eye. 'A lot of what happened will be classified forever, so I don't really see what they stand to gain by stirring through the ashes.'

'They'll investigate anyway,' the director predicted gloomily. 'That's what I want to talk to you about. At one of those meetings during the crisis you asked for the name of our top man in Cuba, and I wrote it down for you. I don't know if you ever looked at that name, but it would be absolute disaster if that person's name were revealed to a congressional investigator.'

'After you wrote it down, I looked at the name,' the president said, speaking slowly. 'Not at the meeting, but later. Didn't expect to recognize it, but then was amazed that the last name was the same as the priest who was thrown in prison.'

'Mercedes Sedano was Castro's mistress and an intelligence treasure. She told us of drug deals, Vargas's blackmail files, Fidel's secret bank accounts. . . . When she wanted the tape made of Fidel naming Hector as his successor, there wasn't time to go through the usual drops and cutouts, so she went directly to the American Interest Section of the Swiss embassy. None of this must come out, Mr President. If the Cubans find out she was whispering to us, Hector Sedano's government might fall. And she might lose her life.'

'That sheet of paper no longer exists,' the president said. 'I suggest you destroy the files.'

A few minutes later as the director was preparing to leave, the president said, 'I have never understood spies. Why did that woman betray her country?'

The director blinked like an owl. 'I don't know that she did,' he replied, and walked out of the Oval Office for the last time.

On a Wednesday morning in November Tommy Carmellini parked his car in a large parking garage in downtown Denver and got his backpack from the trunk.

The weather was gorgeous, a sunny, mild day with air so clear the peaks of the Rockies looked close enough to touch. Autumn leaves lay packed in gutters and windrows waiting for tomorrow's wind to blow them around.

Carmellini walked two blocks to the Sixteenth Street mall. While he was waiting for a free shuttle bus he bought a copy of the *Denver Post* from a vending machine. Like so many of the young people, he was dressed in tennis shoes, faded jeans, and a threadbare pullover sweater. An unzipped windbreaker was tied around his waist. A backpack hung over one shoulder. The shuttle bus stopped at the end of every block to let people on and off. Hanging from a strap, Carmellini kept his backpack pressed against the rear window of the bus.

At the western end of the mall Carmellini let himself be swept along with the flow of people into the regional bus depot. He found a bus to Boulder, climbed aboard, and dropped the fare into the change box, then eased into a window seat five rows behind the driver. He kept his backpack on his lap.

The bus filled quickly. In minutes the driver closed the door and pulled out of the station.

Tommy Carmellini opened the newspaper and examined the front page. All US sanctions against travel and commerce with Cuba were lifted, and the US was opening an embassy in Havana. There was a photo of the president of the United States shaking hands with Hector Sedano at a news conference in Washington.

Tommy flipped through the paper. On page four he found a short item reporting a Florida grand jury indictment of El Gato, a Cuban exile living in Miami, charging him with selling unnamed equipment to the Cuban government in violation of the laws existing at the time. According to the newspaper, El Gato was the only person indicted.

Carmellini folded the paper and tucked it in the seat pocket in front of him.

Cuba was long ago and far away. Of course he still read the news and classified summaries, and heard people talking about Cuba and the people he met there. Microsoft and Intel were building big factories in Havana, and Phillip Morris was buying one of the oldest cigar companies for beaucoup bucks. Rear Admiral Jake Grafton was now an assistant to some bigwig in the Pentagon, Commander Toad Tarkington went with him as an aide, and Toad's wife, the newly promoted Commander Rita Moravia, was the executive officer of a fighter squadron. Hector Sedano was doing an enviable job running Cuba, and some fighter pilot nobody ever heard of named Carlos Corrado had been promoted to general and put in charge of the Cuban Air Force.

Life goes on.

Most of the seats on the bus to Boulder were occupied. The sun coming through the windows and the motion of the bus were very pleasant, and many people dozed. The seat beside Carmellini was empty, so he relaxed his grip on the backpack and closed his eyes.

He was awake when the bus crossed Davidson Mesa into Boulder, roaring down the turnpike at seventy-five. He marveled at the upthrust granite slabs of the Flatirons which formed a spectacular backdrop behind the town.

As the bus cruised by the university on its way downtown, Tommy Carmellini walked to the door by the driver and waited. He got off at the next stop and stood looking at the red stone buildings of the university as the bus accelerated away in a cloud of diesel exhaust.

He had a map in his hip pocket, but he had studied it so much he didn't need to refer to it today. He strolled along, readily recognized the student union, and went from there.

The buildings were built all of a pattern, and with throngs of students coming and going, seemed to proclaim the glory of man's quest for knowledge in the bright November sunshine.

Carmellini glanced at his watch a time or two, then strolled along with his hands in his pockets. He found the building he wanted, opened the door, and went in. He took the stairs up to the top floor.

The hallway was lined with doors, lots of doors. He walked along, examining them. Each door bore the name of a faculty member, and most had a small card advertising the faculty member's office hours taped to the frosted glass.

He found the one he wanted, checked the hours. He was early, by ten minutes.

He knocked.

No answer.

Should he wait here in the hallway, or ... perhaps the library? The hallway was empty, but someone could come along at any moment.

Of course the professor might not come at all. Carmellini recalled his own college days: a student could spend weeks trying to waylay a tenured assistant professor in his office.

Well, if this didn't work he would try something else. Just what, he didn't know.

He decided on the library. He turned and started down the hall. He had taken three or four steps when the door opened behind him and a man in his sixties stuck his head out.

'Did you knock?'

'Yes.'

'Got a watch? Can you read? Office hours don't start for ten minutes.'

'Yes, but –'

'Oh, come on in.'

Carmellini carefully closed the door behind him. The office was tiny, merely a cubbyhole with a desk and computer for the professor and one extra chair. Bookshelves filled with books lined both side walls. A shelf under the window behind the professor was piled willy-nilly with papers, manuscripts, files. The glass in the window didn't look as if it had been cleaned in years.

'If this is about your thesis, we're going to need more time than I have available today, so –'

'You're Professor Svenson, right?'

'That's right.' The professor had seated himself behind his desk. He looked up into Carmellini's face and adjusted his glasses. His features twisted into a frown.

'Your face doesn't . . . You're? . . .'

'Your name is Olaf Svenson?'

'What do you want?'

Tommy Carmellini unzipped the backpack, pulled out the pistol with the silencer. He thumbed off the safety.

A look of terror crossed Svenson's face. 'The government has no evidence,' he said. 'They decided not to prosecute. They –'

Tommy Carmellini shot Olaf Svenson in the center of the forehead from a distance of four feet. Svenson collapsed in his chair, his head tilted back.

Carmellini stepped around the desk, put the muzzle of the silencer against the side of the professor's head and pulled the trigger twice more. Two little pops.

He bent down, retrieved the spent cartridges that had been ejected from the pistol, pocketed them, then safetied the weapon and returned it to his backpack.

He had touched only the doorknob. He extracted a handkerchief from his pocket and wiped the interior knob carefully, then pulled the door open. He pushed the little button to lock the door, then stepped into the hallway and pulled it shut. One hard twist of the cotton handkerchief on the outside

670

knob, then he was walking away down the hallway and no one could ever prove he had been there.

Surrounded by young adults strolling, laughing, and visiting with each other on the sun-dappled grass, Tommy Carmellini walked across the campus with his head down, the backpack over his shoulder, thinking of Cuba.

Hong Kong

To John and Nancy Coonts

Acknowledgements

Doing background research for a novel like this is always an adventure. Friend and neighbor Gilbert Pascal, engineer and physicist, read and offered valuable suggestions on draft chapters as the tale developed. Paul K. Chan read and commented upon the manuscript.

The plot of this tale was a collaboration between the author and his wife, Deborah, who delights in dreaming up literary tangles.

Revolutions and revolutionary wars are inevitable in class society, and without them it is impossible to accomplish any leap in social development and to overthrow the reactionary ruling classes and therefore impossible for the people to win political power ...

The seizure of power by armed force, the settlement of the issue by war, is the central task and the highest form of revolution. This Marxist-Leninist principle of revolution holds good universally, for China and for all other countries.

– Mao Tse Tung

1

One tiny, red, liquid drop of blood was visible in the center of the small, neat hole in China Bob Chan's forehead an inch or so above his right eye. Chan's eyes were wide open. Tommy Carmellini thought his features registered a look of surprise.

Carmellini pulled off his right latex glove, bent down, and touched the cheek of the corpse – which was still warm.

Death must have been instantaneous, and not many minutes ago, Carmellini thought as he pulled the glove back onto his hand.

The diminutive corpse of China Bob Chan lay sprawled behind his Philippine mahogany desk in the library of his mansion on the south side of Hong Kong Island.

When Carmellini had eased the library door open a few seconds ago, he had seen the shod foot protruding from behind the desk. He scanned the room, then entered the library.

The side of the room opposite the door consisted of a series of large plate-glass windows accented with heavy burgundy drapes. Through the windows was a magnificent view of the harbor at Aberdeen. Beyond the harbor was the channel between Hong Kong Island and Lamma Island. A few lights could be seen on sparsely populated Lamma, and beyond that island, the total darkness of the South China Sea. Tonight the lights of the great city of Hong Kong, out of sight on the north side of the island's spine, illuminated a low deck of stratus clouds with a dull glow.

The band at the party on the floor below this one was playing an old American pop hit; the tune was recognizable even though the amplified lyrics were muffled by overstuffed furniture and shelves of books that reached from floor to ceiling.

Tommy Carmellini looked around, trying to find the spent cartridge. There, a gleam of brass near the leg of that chair. In the subdued light of the library he almost missed it.

He stepped over, bent down, looked.

7.65 millimeter.

That cartridge was designed for small, easy-to-conceal pocket pistols.

Difficult to shoot accurately, they were serious weapons only at point-blank range.

Standing in front of the desk, he put his hands on his hips and carefully scanned the room. Somewhere in this room Harold Barnes hid a tape recorder eleven days ago when he installed the wiring for a satellite dish system.

Presumably Chan had ordered the system so that he could watch American television. Perhaps he was a fan of C-Span, which was broadcasting the congressional hearings concerning foreign – i.e., Chinese – donations to the American political parties in the last election; in the past ten days his name had certainly been mentioned numerous times in those hearings.

Alas, Barnes had left no record of where he hid the recorder. He had been shot in the head the night after he completed the installation.

Carmellini was certain Barnes would have used a recorder, not a remote transmitter, which would have been too easy to detect and find. One reason he was certain was that he had known Barnes, a quiet, careful, colorless technician who had gone through the CIA tradecraft course with Carmellini. Who would have suspected that Barnes would be the first of that class to die in the line of duty?

The mikes ... Harold ostensibly spent four hours on the television satellite dish system, a system he should have been able to install in two. If he followed normal practice, he would have hardwired at least two tiny microphones, one for each track of the recorder.

The chandelier over the mahogany desk caught Tommy's eye. Ornate, with several dozen small bulbs, it would attract Harold Barnes like sugar attracts a fly.

Carmellini studied the chain that held the chandelier. There was a wire running down it ... no, two wires – one black wire and the other smaller, carefully wound around the chain.

Barnes could have put a mike in the chandelier, another anywhere in the room – maybe the desk or over by the reading area – and hidden the recorder behind some books, perhaps on the top shelf. Surely there were tomes that didn't get removed from the shelves once a decade.

Carmellini stepped to the nearest bookcase, studied the spines of the books that filled the thing. Not a flake of dust.

A diligent maid would not be good.

So ...

He pulled a chair over under the chandelier, then stood on it.

Aha! There it was, taped in the junction of the main arms of the chandelier. With the bulbs of the chandelier burning brightly, the tiny recorder would have been almost impossible to see from the floor.

Carmellini reached. In seconds he had the two reels out. Maybe three-quarters of the tape had been used, about six hours' worth.

Back on the floor, he was tempted to put the reels into his pocket, then thought better of it. He pulled up a trouser leg and carefully shoved them down into one sock.

He had a new tape in his other sock, but with China Bob dead, the recorder seemed superfluous. Should he cut the wires and remove the device?

How much time did he have?

If China Bob Chan killed Harold Barnes, why was the recorder still there? Was he waiting for someone to come for the tape?

Suddenly aware that time was fleeing, Tommy Carmellini pushed the chair back to its former position. He vigorously rubbed the upholstered seat of the chair to remove any marks his shoes had made.

As he straightened, he heard a noise. It seemed to come from the secretary's office. When he stepped in that direction the light in the smaller office came on.

Carmellini moved swiftly and flattened against the wall. The door to the secretary's office was to his right. He listened intently for footsteps.

Carmellini desperately wanted to avoid being caught in this room with a dead man on the floor and a tape in his sock. True, he had diplomatic immunity as the assistant agricultural officer at the consulate, but the publicity and hullabaloo of an arrest and interrogation, not to mention expulsion from the country, would not be career-enhancing.

He heard the scrape of a chair being moved.

Coiled, ready to lash out if anyone came through the door, he approached it, staying back far enough that he remained away from the glare of the light.

Someone was sitting behind the secretary's desk, someone small. My God, it was a kid! A boy, perhaps ten or twelve.

Carmellini stepped back so he would be out of sight if the youngster glanced this way.

Now he heard a computer boot up.

There was one other exit from this room, at the far end. Carmellini didn't know if the door was locked, but it led to another suite of offices which opened into the hallway near the elevator.

He walked toward the door, moving quietly and decisively.

The knob refused to turn. Locked. There was a keyhole, but he could not see the brand name or type of lock.

He removed a leather packet from his pocket and unfolded it, revealing a carefully chosen selection of picks. He took one, inserted it in the lock.

As he bent down to work on the lock, he saw for the first time the heads of the bolts in the door. They had been painted the same dark color as the door to make them less noticeable.

Even if he got the lock open, the door was bolted shut.

He put the pick away and stowed the packet in an inside jacket pocket as he walked back toward the secretary's open door.

Standing at least six feet from the door, he moved so he could see inside.

The kid was at the computer, typing.

Now he sat back in the chair, waiting ...

In seconds a naked woman appeared on the screen, a woman holding what appeared to be a giant penis in her hand. Now she –

Jesus, the kid is into porno!

Just what the woman was going to do with the penis, Tommy Carmellini never discovered, for at that instant the door from the hallway opened and a woman walked in. The boy took one look at the intruder and closed the screen, but not before the woman got a good look at it.

She cuffed him once, said something in Chinese.

The boy ran through the icons, closed the Internet connection as the woman spouted Chinese as quickly as her lips would move.

Carmellini stepped back against the wall and waited.

He heard the computer go off, heard the scrape of the chair and footsteps, then the door to the hallway close firmly.

He peered into the office.

Empty.

He opened the hallway door a crack, just enough to see the woman and boy disappear into the elevator at the end of the hallway.

He paused for a second, then went back into the library and scooted the chair under the chandelier. Installing the new tape in the recorder took about thirty seconds; then he found the on-off switch and turned off the recorder. He put the chair back where it belonged and rubbed the seat again.

At the door in the secretary's office, Carmellini checked to ensure no one was coming, then stepped into the hallway and pulled the door shut until it latched. Strains of Gershwin's 'An American in Paris' were audible here.

As he walked toward the staircase that led to the rooms below where the party was being held, Carmellini stripped off his latex gloves and put them in his pocket.

Downstairs he found Kerry Kent sipping champagne and talking animatedly with a long-haired intellectual type who was gazing hopefully at her. Kerry was a tall English woman with a spectacular mass of reddish brown hair who spoke both Cantonese and Mandarin fluently. On most working days she labored as a translator at the Greater China Mutual Aid Society, an insurance firm, but in reality she was an officer in the British Secret Intelligence Service, the SIS. Tonight she was wearing an elegant dark blue dress that just brushed her ankles and a modest borrowed diamond necklace.

'Oh, there you are, darling,' she said lightly, laying a hand on Tommy's arm. 'I have been talking to this brilliant playwright – ' She said his name.

'His new play is opening next week in the West End. My sister told me quite a lot about it, actually. What a coincidence! When we get back to London we must see it.'

Carmellini shook hands with the scribbler and gently led Kerry away. 'Did anyone watch me come in?' he asked, just loud enough for her to hear over the hubbub of cocktail party chatter and music.

'I don't think anyone was paying much attention. What were you doing up there?'

'Watching porno on the Internet. Fascinating stuff! I'll tell you all about it later. Who is this sicko stalking you?'

He was referring to a Chinese man who was standing six feet away and openly staring at Kerry. When she moved, he moved.

'An admirer from the provinces, obviously, hopelessly smitten. All my life I've had this devastating effect on men. It's such a bore. I'm thinking of having chest reduction surgery to end these unwanted attentions.'

That comment was intended as a joke, for Kerry had a slim, athletic figure.

Carmellini snarled at the staring man and guided Kent away by the elbow.

'Did you get it?' She meant the tape.

'It wasn't there. China Bob is stretched out behind his desk with a hole in his head.'

'Dead?' A furrow appeared between her eyebrows.

'Very.'

'You found the recorder?'

'In the chandelier. But the tape was missing.'

Kerry Kent sipped champagne as she digested Carmellini's lie. Just why lying to her was a good idea he couldn't say, but his instinct told him not to trust anyone. Someone shot Harold Barnes, and another someone, perhaps the same one, put a bullet in China Bob Chan's head – and Carmellini had known Ms. Kent for precisely three days, not exactly a long-term relationship.

There were at least three ways to get from this floor of the mansion to the floor above: two staircases and an elevator. Carmellini had slipped up one set of stairs after he went to the men's room, which was out of sight of the ballroom, just down the hall toward the back stairs. Anyone in this room could have done precisely the same thing in the last few hours, and probably several of them had.

Perhaps the tape held the answer.

Carmellini scanned the crowd one more time, trying to fix the guests in his mind. The cream of Hong Kong society was here tonight.

'Tell me again,' he said to Kerry Kent, 'who these folks are.'

She scanned the crowd, nodded toward a man in his sixties in the center of a small crowd. 'That's Governor Sun Siu Ki, surrounded by his usual entourage – officials and bureaucrats and private industry suck-ups. The gentleman of distinction talking to him is Sir Robert MacDonald, the British consul general. The tall, blond Aussie semi-eavesdropping on those two is Rip Buckingham, managing editor of the *China Post*, the largest English-language daily in Hong Kong. Beside him is his wife, Sue Lin. Over in the far corner is the American consul general, Virgil Cole, talking to China Bob's sister, Amy Chan. Let's see, who else?'

'The fellow in the uniform with the highball, standing by the band.'

'General Tang, commanding the division of People's Liberation Army troops stationed in Hong Kong. He's been in Hong Kong only a few weeks. The papers ran articles about him when he arrived.'

'The man talking to him?'

'Albert Cheung. Educated at Oxford, the foremost attorney in Hong Kong. Smooth and silky and in the know, or so I've heard.'

She continued, pointing out six industrialists, three shipping magnates, and two bank presidents. 'These people are the scions of the merchant and shipping clans that grew filthy rich in Hong Kong,' she said, and named names. 'If ever a group mourned the departure of the British, there they are,' she added. 'Never saw so much of the upper crust chatting it up together.'

Any person in the room could have gone upstairs and popped China Bob, Carmellini reflected. All of them had probably excused themselves and gone in search of the facilities once or twice during the evening. Or someone could have ridden the elevator from the basement or walked to the library from another area of the house. The field was wide open. Still, Tommy Carmellini took one more careful look at each of the people Kerry had pointed out, then said, 'Perhaps we should leave now before the excitement begins.'

'A marvelous suggestion. Let me say a few good-byes as we drift toward the door.'

Five minutes later, as they stood waiting for the consulate's pool car to be brought around, Carmellini asked Kerry, 'So what's on the agenda for the rest of the evening?'

'I don't know,' she said lightly and turned toward him. He accepted the invitation and kissed her. She put her arms around him and kissed back.

'You are such a romantic,' she said when her lips were free.

'And single, too.'

'I haven't forgotten.'

'I don't recall mentioning my marital status before.'

'You didn't. Your reputation preceded you. Tommy Carmellini, unmarried burglar, thief, second-story man ...'

'And all-around good egg.'

'James Bond without the dash and panache.'

'Don't knock the recipe until you've tried it.'

'You'll have to sell me.'

'I'm willing to give it a go, as you Brits say.'

'Tell me about the Internet pornography. Little details like that spice up action reports, make them interesting.'

The consulate pool car pulled to a stop in front of them, and the valet got out. 'I was saving that morsel for later,' Carmellini said as he tipped the man and accepted the keys. 'After all, the night is young.'

2

The morning sun shone full on the balcony of the fifth-floor hotel room when Jake Grafton opened the sliding glass door. The bustle and roar from the streets below assailed him, but he grinned and seated himself at the small, round glass table. As he sipped at a cup of coffee he sampled the smells, sights, and sounds of Hong Kong.

His wife, Callie, stepped out on the balcony. She was dressed to the nines, wearing only a subtle hint of makeup, with her purse over her shoulder and her attaché case in her left hand.

As she bent to kiss Jake he got a faint whiff of scent. 'You smell delicious this morning, Mrs. Grafton.'

She paused at the door. A furrow appeared between her eyebrows. 'What are you going to do today?' she asked.

'Loaf, read the morning paper, cash some traveler's checks, and meet you for lunch.'

'When are you going to start on your assignment?'

'I'm working on it this very minute. I know it doesn't look like it, but the wheels are turning.'

Today was the third day of the conference, an intense seven-day immersion in Western culture for Chinese college students. Callie was one of the faculty.

'I'm soaking up atmosphere,' Jake added. 'This trip was billed as my vacation, as you will recall.'

Perhaps it was the rare sight of her husband in pajamas at eight on a weekday morning that bothered her. She smiled, nodded, and said good-bye.

As Jake worked on the coffee he surveyed the old police barracks immediately across the road from the hotel. The barracks was surrounded by a ten-foot-high brick wall, which hid it from people on the street. Three stories high, it was constructed of whitewashed brick or masonry in the shape of a T. The windows in the base of the T, which was parallel to Jake, revealed rooms with bunks, lockers, showers, laundry rooms, and a kitchen and dining hall, all set in from outside balconies that ran the length of each floor, much like an American motel. The top of the T was an administration building, apparently full of offices. Police cars filled the parking spaces around the building.

The lawn, however, was a military encampment, covered with troops, tents, fires, and cooking pots. Here at least five hundred People's Liberation Army, or PLA, troops were bivouacked, covering almost every square yard of greenery. Pencil-thin columns of smoke from the fires rose into the still morning air.

In colonial days the Royal Hong Kong police force must have been a nice life for single British men who wanted to do something exotic with their lives, or at least live their mundane lives in an exotic locale and make a very nice living in the process. Like most colonial police forces, the Royal Hong Kong force was famously corrupt, had been since the first Brit donned a uniform and strolled the streets.

Today Chinese policemen and soldiers scurried to and fro like so many ants. Jake wondered if there were any British policemen still wearing the Hong Kong uniform.

Jake Grafton drained his coffee cup and turned his attention to the English-language newspaper, the *China Post,* which had been slid under the door of the room early this morning.

The financial crisis in Japan was the lead article on the front page, which contained lengthy pronouncements from the Chinese government in Beijing. The article also contained a quote from the American consul general, Virgil Cole.

Jake read the name with interest and shook his head. He had flown with Cole on his last cruise during the Vietnam War, and the two of them had survived a shootdown. And he hadn't seen the man since. Oh, they corresponded routinely for years after Cole left the navy, but finally in one move or other the Graftons lost Cole's address, and the Christmas cards stopped. That was ten or so years ago.

Tiger Cole. After his broken back healed, he had gotten out of the navy and gone to grad school, then got into the high-tech business world in Silicon Valley. When he was named consul general to Hong Kong two years ago, *Fortune* magazine said he was worth more than a billion dollars. Of course, he was also a generous donor to political causes.

Maybe he should call Tiger, ask him out to dinner. Then again ... He decided to wait another day. If Tiger didn't call, he would call him.

On the second page of the paper was a column devoted to a murder that apparently happened last night. The body was discovered just before press time. Jake recognized the victim's name – China Bob Chan – and read the article with a sinking feeling. As the key figure in a campaign finance scandal in Washington, China Bob had been getting a lot of press in the United States of late, most of it the kind of coverage that an honest man could do without. Chan's untimely demise due to lead poisoning was going to go over like a lead brick on Capitol Hill.

On the first page of the second section of the newspaper Jake was pleasantly surprised to find a photo of Callie with two of the other Americans on the seminar faculty, along with a three-paragraph write-up. Amazingly, the reporter even spelled Callie's name correctly. He carefully folded that page to keep.

All in all, Jake thought, the newspaper looked exactly like what it was, a news sheet published under the watchful eye of a totalitarian government intolerant of criticism or dissent. Not a word about why the PLA troops were choking the streets, standing at every street corner, every shop entrance, every public facility, nothing but the bare facts about China Bob's murder, not even an op-ed piece about the implications of his death vis-á-vis Chinese-U.S. relations.

Jake's attention was captured by several columns of foreign sports scores on the next-to-the-last page. Australian football received more column inches than the American professional teams did, Jake noted, grinning.

He tossed the paper down and stretched. Ahhhhh . . .

Someone was knocking on the door to the room.

'Just a minute!'

Jake checked his reflection in the mirror over the dresser – no need to scandalize the maid – then opened the door a crack.

A man in a business suit stood there, a westerner . . . Tommy Carmellini.

'Come in.' Jake held the door open. 'I'm not going very fast this morning, I'm afraid.'

'Have you seen the morning paper?'

'China Bob?'

'Yes.'

'I saw the story.'

'It's true. Chan's as dead as a man can get.'

'Let me take a shower, then we'll go downstairs for some breakfast.'

'Okay.' Tommy Carmellini sat down in the only chair and opened his attaché case.

When Jake came out of the bathroom fifteen minutes later, Carmellini was repacking his sweep gear in the attaché case. 'No bugs,' he told Jake.

'The phone?'

'Impossible to say. I have no idea how much impedance and resistance on the line are normal.'

'Okay.'

'How did you know the story was true?'

'Alas, I met China Bob last night a minute or two after he had joined the ranks of the recently departed. He was warm as toast and the hole in his head was brand-new. There was a spent 7.65-millimeter cartridge under a table a few feet away.'

'Who shot him?'

'I didn't. That's all I know for sure.'

'Do you have the tape on you?'

Carmellini sat and removed it from his sock. He passed it to Jake Grafton, who examined it cursorily and put it in a trouser pocket.

After they had ordered breakfast in the hotel restaurant, the two men talked in general terms about the city in which they found themselves. Jake told Carmellini that he and Callie had met in Hong Kong, in 1972. 'Haven't been back since,' Jake said, 'which was a mistake, I guess. It's a great city, and we should have come every now and then to watch it evolve and grow.'

Carmellini was only politely interested. 'How come,' he asked the admiral, 'they sent me over here to help you out? You're not CIA.'

'You sure about that?' Jake Grafton asked. Carmellini noticed that Grafton's gray eyes smiled before he did. His face was tan and lean, although the nose was a trifle large. The admiral had a jagged, faded old scar on one temple.

'Few things these days are exactly what they appear to be,' Carmellini agreed. 'As I recall, when I met you last year you were wearing a navy uniform and running a carrier battle group. Of course, the agency is going all out on cover stories these days.'

Jake chuckled. 'I was pushing paper in the Pentagon when they were looking for someone to send over here to snoop around. Apparently my connection to Cole from way back when got someone thinking, so . . . Anyway, when they asked me about it, I said okay, if my wife could come along. So here I am.'

Carmellini frowned. 'How did I get dragged into this mess? I had a pair of season tickets to see the Orioles and a delightful young woman to fill the other seat.'

'I asked for you by name,' Jake replied. 'The new CIA director tried to dissuade me. Carmellini is a thief, he said, a crook, and last year when someone murdered Professor Olaf Svenson, Carmellini's whereabouts couldn't be accounted for. Seems that you were on vacation at the time, which is not a felony, but it made them do some digging; of course nothing turned up. No one could prove anything. Still, your record got another little smirch.'

'He said that?'

'He did. Apparently your personnel file is interesting reading.'

'You know how football players talk about adversity?' Tommy Carmellini remarked. 'I've had some of that, too. And smirches. Lots of smirches.'

'Uh-huh.'

'So if you know I'm smirched, how come you asked for me?'

'My aide, Toad Tarkington, suggested you. For some reason you impressed him.'

'I see.'

Their breakfast came. After the waiter left, Jake said, 'Tell me about last night. Everything you can remember.'

Carmellini talked as he ate. 'They have me working with this woman from SIS, a Brit named Kerry Kent. She's a knockout and speaks Chinese like a native. I've known her exactly three days and an evening.'

'Uh-huh.'

Carmellini explained about the party, about how Kent got two invitations and took him along as her date. Two hours into the evening, he explained, he saw his chance and sneaked upstairs.

'I was pretty spooked when I found China Bob all sprawled out. I got the tape out of the recorder and installed a new one, so anyone checking the machine would think the original tape didn't work. That was my thinking, which wasn't very bright on my part. I did have the presence of mind to turn the recorder off, so maybe anyone finding it will buy that hypothesis. Then again ...

'By the time I got downstairs the thought occurred to me that I didn't know beans from apple butter. Anybody in Hong Kong could have killed China Bob, for any conceivable reason. Including, of course, my companion for the evening, Kerry Kent. She spent fifteen minutes in the ladies' just before I went upstairs, or so she said. Just to be on the safe side, when I got downstairs after retrieving the tape I told her it wasn't in the recorder.'

Jake Grafton looked up from his coffee. 'And ...'

'And damn if she didn't frisk me when we were outside waiting for the valet to bring the car around. Gave me a smooch and a hug and rubbed her hands over my pockets.'

'You sure she was looking for the tape?'

'She patted me down.'

'Maybe she was trying to let you know she was romantically interested,' Jake suggested with a raised eyebrow.

'I had hopes,' Carmellini confessed. 'She's a nice hunk of female, tuned up and ready to rumble. But she had me take her straight home. She didn't even invite me up for a good-night beer.'

'I thought secret agents were always getting tossed in the sack.'

'I thought so, too,' Carmellini said warmly. 'That's why I signed on with the agency. Reality has been a disappointment.' Another lie, a little one. Carmellini joined the CIA to avoid prosecution for burglary and a handful of other felonies. However, he saw no reason to share the sordid details with his colleagues in the ordinary course of business, so to speak.

'Did she find the tape on you?'

'No. I had it in my sock.'

'Did she have a pistol on her?'

'She didn't have a pistol in her sock, and believe me, there wasn't room for one in her bra.'

'Her purse?'

'A little clutch thing – I gave it a squeeze. Wasn't there. Of course, whoever shot China Bob probably ditched the pistol immediately.'

'So who are your suspects for the killing?'

'It could have been anybody in Hong Kong. Anybody at the party or anybody who came in off the street and went straight upstairs. Still, Kent or the consul general are high on my list. As I mentioned, she camped out in the ladies' just before I went upstairs. I saw Cole coming down the stairs five minutes before I went up.'

Virgil Cole, the perfect warrior. Jake was the one who had hung the nickname 'Tiger' on him, back in the fall of 1972 when Cole became his bombardier-navigator after Morgan McPherson was killed. This morning Grafton took a deep breath, remembering those days, remembering Cole as he had known him then. Those days seemed so long ago, and yet . . .

The Chinese employees of the Bank of the Orient had known the truth for days, and they had told their friends, who withdrew money from their accounts. As the news spread, the queues in the lobby had grown longer and longer.

This fine June morning a crowd of at least two thousand gathered on the sidewalks and in the manicured square in front of the bank, waiting for it to open. The bank was housed in a massive, soaring tower of stone and glass set in the heart of the Victoria business district, between the slope of Victoria Peak and the ferry piers. Its name in English and Chinese was of course splashed prominently across the front of the building in huge characters. In still larger characters lit day and night mounted on the side of the building at the twenty-story level so they would be visible from all over the island, from Kowloon, indeed, on a clear day from mainland China itself, was the name of the bank in Japanese, for the Bank of the Orient was a Japanese bank and proud of it.

After urgent consultations and many glances out the window at the crowd, which was growing by the minute, bank officials refused to open the doors. Instead, they called the Finance Ministry in Tokyo. While the president of the bank waited by the telephone for the assistant finance minister for overseas operations to return his urgent call, someone outside the bank threw a rock through a window.

One of the cashiers called the police. The police took a look at the crowd and called the governor, Sun Siu Ki. Sun didn't go look; he merely called General Tang Tso Ming, the new commander of the division of the People's Liberation Army that was stationed in Hong Kong.

A half hour later several hundred armed soldiers arrived. They spread themselves two deep across the street on each end of the crowd. They also surrounded a park across the street from the bank where many people were waiting. There really weren't enough soldiers to physically prevent the crowd from moving, so the soldiers did nothing but stand in position, waiting for orders. Then four tanks clanked up, ripping up asphalt, and stopped with their big guns pointed at the crowd.

General Tang arrived with the tanks. He looked over the crowd and the soldiers, had his officers adjust the placement of the troops, then went to the door of the bank and pounded on it with his fist. When it didn't open, he pulled his pistol and rapped on the door sharply with the butt.

Now the door opened.

General Tang and two of his colonels marched into the Bank of the Orient and demanded to see the president.

As they walked along the sidewalk toward the Star Ferry, Tommy Carmellini said, 'Admiral, I'm really flying blind. The people at Langley sent me over here with orders to help you out, but they didn't tell me what this is all about.'

'They sent me over here,' Jake Grafton told the CIA officer, 'because I knew Tiger Cole in Vietnam. Apparently I'm one of the few people in government who know him personally. Washington wants to know what in hell is going on in Hong Kong.'

'What do they think is going on?'

They each bought first-class tickets on the ferry and went up on the top deck. As the ferry pulled out, Jake Grafton said, 'China is coming to a crisis. The whole country is tinder ready to burn. One spark might set it off. The Communists want to stay in power by delivering economic prosperity, which can come only if the economic system changes. They are trapped in this giant oxymoron; they want economic change without social and political change. On the other hand, the United States wants a big piece of the China pie. So the American establishment has traded technology and capital for access to Chinese markets and low-cost labor. In other words, they have invested in the political status quo, which is the dictatorial Communist system.'

Tommy Carmellini nodded his understanding.

Jake continued. 'The Communist system distorts and corrupts everything. The only way a Chinese importer can get goods into the country is to obtain a government import license. These licenses are restricted to prevent private entrepreneurs from competing against state-owned enterprises. Enter China Bob Chan and a thousand like him. If you are an enterprising Chinese businessman, for a fee Chan will obtain for you an import license from a government official – in effect, he splits the bribe. This system ensures that the bureaucracy is corrupted from top to bottom. Every single person in government is on the take, party members, officials of every caliber and stripe, army generals, everybody. This system generates enormous profits that go into their pockets, and the industrialized West gets to sell high tech to China.'

'Only the public loses,' Carmellini murmured.

'Precisely. Anyway, to get specific, the Chinese government used China Bob Chan to make political contributions in America and grease the wheels to get American export licenses for restricted technology, some of it military. As a general rule, government licenses always create opportunities for graft of one sort or another, in China and America. In this case the PLA, the People's Liberation Army, wanted the American military technology. Unfortunately, China Bob pocketed about half the money the PLA paid him to do all this American greasing. The guy who dealt with China Bob on behalf of the army was General Tang, now the PLA commander here.'

'Uh-huh.'

'The story is that Tang was sent here to find and apprehend a political criminal, Wu Tai Kwong. Remember the man who stood in front of the tank in Tiananmen Square in 1989?'

'I thought he was dead.'

'He may be. But dead or alive, he's public enemy number one; he gave the Commies the finger. These people are paranoid.'

'That's an occupational hazard with absolute dictators,' Tommy Carmellini said lightly.

'Anyway, that is what the army says it's doing here. In reality, Tang and the army are here to prevent a political uprising in Hong Kong. The CIA thinks China Bob Chan washed the money to finance the revolution.'

'He was working both sides of the street?'

'The CIA thinks so. The politicians in Congress wanted someone to come over here and root around and give an independent assessment of how deep the consul general is in all this. The White House picked me, for lack of someone better.'

'Virgil Cole?'

'That's right.'

'Why you?'

'Well, basically, I got the impression that I'm supposed to worm my way into Cole's confidence and get him to say things to me that he wouldn't say to anyone else. That was the thinking in Washington, anyway. It stinks, but that's the sordid truth.'

'Maybe it's all bullshit,' Carmellini suggested. 'Rumors go round and round. I'm an expert on rumors.'

Grafton had his arms on the railing of the boat. 'Cole is apparently having a relationship of some type with Amy Chan. Her father was a British soldier and her mother was a Chinese girl who came to Hong Kong when the Nationalist cause collapsed and Mao took over on the mainland. The mother got in just before the door slammed shut, took up prostitution to feed herself. She was supposedly really good-looking, became a high-class hooker, ended up falling for this Brit soldier and having Amy by him. Of course the soldier was a shit and went tooling off to Britain when his tour was up – seems he had a wife there, too.

'Anyway, Amy's mother saved her money and sent her daughter to America for an education. She had a degree from UCLA and was working at the American consulate processing visa applications when Cole arrived. They hit it off right from the start.'

'Uh-huh.'

'Her half-brother was China Bob Chan. He used Cole as his poster boy to advertise his influence with the Americans. Amy had him over to the mansion every other night. China Bob paraded him in front of government toads, General Tang, everybody and anybody who came down here from Beijing. This has been going on about a year. Cole has been talking to congressional investigators, so he is aware of the intricacies of all this. Still, the Tiger Cole I remember from way back when wouldn't give a good goddamn what anybody thought about his love life.'

'That's my impression of him, too,' Carmellini mused. 'I've seen his dossier and spent an hour or so with him, and I'd say you are pretty close to the mark.'

'We're here to find out what Cole and China Bob have been up to,' Jake said. 'I want to listen to that tape you brought over. Callie will help me with the Chinese.' He had the thing in *his* sock just now.

'I'll have to get a player out of the communications room at the consulate,' Tommy Carmellini told Jake as they joined the throng waiting to get off the boat when it slid into its dock in the Central District. 'It takes a special machine to play the thing.'

'Let's get bugs in Cole's office in the consulate. Search his desk, see what you can learn. As soon as you can, open the safes and start going through the files. I want to see anything that implicates Tiger Cole in a conspiracy to overthrow the Chinese government. If there is not a shred of physical evidence, I want to know that, too.'

'Jesus! Where'd you learn how to do investigations?'

'We don't have time for subtleties. I want to know what in hell is going on in Hong Kong, and I want to know *now*. If representatives of the American government are members of a conspiracy to overthrow the lawful government of China, that could be construed as an act of war.'

As they walked out of the Star Ferry terminal, Tommy Carmellini nodded at the admiral and set off for the consulate on Garden Road.

The president of the Bank of the Orient was Saburo Genda. When General Tang and his officers were escorted into his office, he was on the telephone with Governor Sun, trying to explain the situation.

'We do not have money on hand to pay all the depositors waiting outside,' Genda explained as patiently as he could.

He listened to a burst of Chinese, which he spoke reasonably well, then answered, 'Of course the bank is solvent. Yes, we have reserves. Unfortunately, we just do not have sufficient cash in the vaults to pay all the people waiting outside. ... Yes, we will open in a few hours. You have my assurances, sir.'

He hung up the telephone and wiped his forehead.

Tang wanted to know why the bank wasn't open.

Genda ran through it all again.

'Get some money,' General Tang said.

'We are trying, General, but since we don't have printing presses in the basement, we must obtain currency from other banks. We are in the process of doing that now.'

Tang disliked being patronized, which he thought a slight on his dignity and his position, and he told Genda that in no uncertain terms.

He was just winding up when the telephone rang. Genda answered.

'Sir, the Finance Ministry in Tokyo is on the line.'

Genda switched to Japanese and began talking into the telephone, leaving the general to stew. Tang felt out of place in this huge, opulent office decorated with tropical hardwoods and designer furniture, four stories high in a grand temple dedicated to the gods of money.

Tang Ming was a peasant's son, born during World War II, whose earliest memories were of his family fleeing before advancing Japanese troops.

He had spent his adult life in the army. From skin to backbone he was a soldier. A firm believer in the social goals of communism, he was, like a majority of his fellow countrymen, a cultural and racial xenophobe. Before his assignment to Hong Kong he had actually seen foreigners on only two occasions in his life, both official visits to Beijing. He had seen the foreigners at a distance, not talked with them.

Sitting in this huge office and watching an impeccably attired senior Japanese executive babble in a foreign tongue about matters he didn't understand made General Tang Ming restless and irritable.

Someone with a cellular telephone called the editor of the *China Post*, Hong Kong's leading English-language newspaper, and informed him about the restless crowd in front of the Bank of the Orient. The editor, Rip Buckingham, had heard rumors for the past two days about the possible collapse of the bank, so as he listened to the caller describe the crowd and the troops, his gut told him, *This is it.*

Rip called the newsroom and ordered four reporters and two photographers dispatched to the scene immediately. Then he extracted an eyewitness account from the caller while he jotted notes.

When he finally let the caller go, Rip automatically glanced out the window of his corner office at the giant Coca-Cola sign on top of the Bank of the Orient building, an imposing seventy-story skyscraper in Hong Kong's Central District. In a typical Hong Kong deal, the developer of the building played off competing consumer giants, one against the other, for the honor of having their logo prominently displayed on the masthead of the new bank building, the biggest one in the colony. Reportedly the local Coke bottler had paid a fee in excess of ten million dollars U.S. to the developer just for the privilege of putting a sign up there. That was in 1995, two years before the British turned over the colony to the Chinese Communists.

No one is building buildings like that in Hong Kong now, Rip thought bitterly.

Rip was an Australian who had enjoyed a wonderful, vagrant youth. He repaired slot machines in Las Vegas, worked as a motorman on San Francisco trolleys, sailed the Pacific and Indian oceans in the forecastles of rusty Liberian tramps, and bicycled across most of China, including the entire route of the ancient Silk Road, from Tyre on the eastern edge of the Mediterranean to Sian in central China. Finally, in his late twenties, Rip Buckingham came to rest in Hong Kong, where he got a haircut and traded his sandals for leather shoes. He even married a local girl.

Rip turned to the computer sitting on a stand beside his desk and began writing. He wanted to get the eyewitness account down while it was fresh and immediate. He was still working on it when his reporters began calling in on their cellular telephones. He folded the facts they had gleaned into the story he was writing and asked questions.

Unlike a reporter operating in a Western nation, Rip did not telephone the governor's officer or the police or the PLA to elicit comments or give those officials a chance to dispute the accounts his reporters were getting. He had done that years ago when he first took over the managing editor's position, and before long was told by some government functionary, 'You can't print that.' The police then came to the newspaper office to ensure that he didn't.

So far he had managed to avoid the wrath of the Communist officials who ruled Hong Kong. It hadn't been easy. He was, he often thought wryly, becoming a master at damning with faint praise. I'm the king of innuendo, he once grumped to his wife. Actually, as he well knew, he had escaped censorship only because his paper was published in English, a language that few government officials spoke with any fluency. All the Chinese-language newspapers had a squad of resident apparatchiks from the New China News Agency who had to approve everything.

As Rip worked on the story, a sense of impending doom came over him. There were several hundred banks in Hong Kong, most of them privately owned, yet China had no Federal Deposit Insurance Corporation. Chinese banks outside of Hong Kong were owned by the state and theoretically could not fail. Of course, if those state-owned banks were examined using Western accounting standards, all were insolvent.

The problem was the desperate financial straits of the Chinese government, which saw the privately owned banks in Hong Kong as a source of low-interest loans for noncompetitive state-owned industries that would collapse without cash infusions, industries that employed tens of millions of mainland workers.

The Japanese who owned the Bank of the Orient had refused to make those loans to the Chinese government. Now the bank was failing, and thousands of people were going to be flat-ass broke after a lifetime of work and saving.

What was the Chinese government doing to prevent that outcome, if anything?

As luck would have it, after he left the Star Ferry terminal Jake Grafton wandered along with the crowd, lost in thought. When he at last began paying attention to his surroundings he found himself in the square outside the Bank of the Orient, shoulder-to-shoulder with several thousand other people. The doors of the bank were apparently locked. From time to time people came out of the crowd to try the doors, which refused to open.

Armed soldiers in uniform were visible here and there, but they were well back, away from the crowd, and seemed to be making no attempt to disperse it or prevent people from approaching the door of the bank to rattle it, pound on it, or press their foreheads against the glass and look in.

Here and there knots of people argued loudly among themselves, waved passbooks, and stared openly and defiantly at the soldiers.

For a moment, Jake thought of wandering on, finding another bank to cash his traveler's checks. Surely they all weren't closed today.

Yet something made him linger. He found a few empty inches on a flower bed retainer wall and parked his bottom.

Meanwhile, in the executive suite of the bank, President Saburo Genda was getting bad news from the assistant finance minister in Tokyo.

'We will not loan the bank additional funds. I'm sorry, but the prime minister and the finance minister are agreed.'

President Genda's forte was commercial loans to large companies. He had spent much of his adult life dealing with wealthy businessmen with a firm grasp of economic reality. He fought now to keep his temper with this obtuse government clerk.

'You don't understand,' he said, his voice tightly under control. 'We are experiencing a run on the bank. There is a crowd of several thousand depositors outside demanding their money. Without additional cash, the bank cannot pay them. Without more money, the bank will collapse.'

'I am sorry, Mr. Genda,' said the bureaucrat. 'It is you who do not understand. The government has decided to let the bank fail. It would simply cost too much to save it.'

'But – '

'The Bank of the Orient made far too many real estate loans in Hong Kong at astronomical evaluations. As you know, the market collapsed after the Communists took over. It may be twenty years before the market recovers. Indeed, it may never recover.'

'Mr. Assistant Minister, your ministry has known about the bad loans for years. Your colleagues were working with us. We have the assets to pay our depositors, but the assets are in accounts in Japan and you have frozen them. Those funds belong to this bank! Make them available for us to pledge and we will borrow the cash we need locally.'

'I am sorry, Mr. Genda. The government has decided to offset the bank's assets against the amounts the bank owes the government.'

'You can't do this,' Genda protested. 'This isn't the way things are done. You are violating the banking regulations!'

'The decision has been made.'

'Have you discussed the failure of the bank with the governor of Hong Kong or the Chinese government in Beijing?'

'We have. Since the bank is not Chinese, they did not choose to guarantee its debts.'

Genda continued, almost pleading, trying to make the bureaucrat see reason. 'This is a Japanese bank! Many of our senior people are former Finance Ministry officials. We have close ties with the government, extremely close ties.'

'I am sorry, Mr. Genda,' the civil servant said politely. 'As I said, the decision has been made. We here in the Ministry expect you to take personal responsibility for the condition of your institution. Good-bye.'

The assistant minister hung up, leaving Saburo Genda standing with the telephone in his hand, too stunned to hang it up, too stunned to speak to his subordinates standing around the room waiting for a report. He felt as if his head had just been separated from his body. In two minutes of conversation, the civil servant at the Finance Ministry had ruined him: He could never work in a bank again; his whole life had just been reduced to rubble.

'Open the bank,' General Tang said in Chinese. 'I order you to open the doors of the bank.'

'The bank is ruined,' Saburo Genda told the soldier, his lips barely able to form the words. 'Tokyo refuses to guarantee our borrowings of cash to pay the depositors.'

Tang Ming tried to understand. Foreigners! 'But this is a bank. You have much money in the vault. Give it to the people who want it, and when you run out, tell them they will have to come back another day.'

'Then the riot will occur in our lobby.'

'You must have money!' Tang gestured to the crowd. 'What have you done with all of their money?'

Genda had had it with this fool. 'We loaned it out,' he said through clenched teeth. 'That is the function of banks, to accept deposits and make loans.'

Tang Ming stretched to his full height. He looked at Genda behind his great, polished desk, a whipped dog, and his two colonels and Genda's secretary and the crowd beyond the window.

'Come,' he murmured at the colonels and strode out.

The tangible anger of the crowd made Jake Grafton uneasy. He sensed it was high time for him to be on his way, time to be out of this group of angry Asians who were working themselves up for a riot.

Still he lingered. Curiosity kept him rooted.

Although he spoke not a word of Chinese, he didn't really need the language to read the emotions on people's faces. A few people were openly crying, weeping silently as they rocked back and forth in sitting positions. Others were on cellular phones, presumably sharing their misfortune with family and friends.

The number of wireless telephones in use by the crowd surprised Jake – China was definitely third or fourth world. There was money in Hong Kong, a lot of which had been invested in state-of-the-art technology. Still, most of the people in this square existed on a small fraction of the money that the average American family earned.

As Jake sat there with two thousand American dollars' worth of traveler's checks in his pocket that he could get cashed at any bank in town, the vast gulf between the comfortable, middle-class circumstances in which he had lived his life and the hand-to-mouth existence that so many hundreds of millions – billions – of people around the world accepted as their lot in life spread before him like the Grand Canyon.

He was no bleeding heart, but he cared about people. Always had. He found people interesting, could imagine himself in their circumstances; this was one of the qualities that made him a leader, a good naval officer, and a decent human being.

General Tang Ming climbed into a small van with public address system speakers mounted on the roof. Sitting in the passenger seat of the van holding a microphone, the general explained the facts as he understood them: The bank had loaned all the money it had and had no more to pay to the people in the crowd. It would not open its doors.

Since waiting for an event that would not happen was futile, Tang ordered the crowd to disperse. The language he used was Mandarin Chinese, the dialect of northern China, of Beijing, and of most of the soldiers under his command. Unfortunately, it was not the language of the people in the crowd, most of whom spoke Cantonese or English.

As General Tang harangued the crowd in the street outside the Bank of the Orient over a loud, tinny PA system in a language few understood, the crowd became more boisterous. Some people began shouting, others produced stones and bits of concrete from construction sites that they threw toward the bank windows. Several men nearest the main entrance to the bank pounded on the door with their fists, shouting, 'Open up and pay us!'

Others in the crowd, sensing approaching disaster, tried to leave the area by passing through the cordon of soldiers. Almost by reflex, the greatly outnumbered soldiers tried to hold the crowd back. They struck out with billy clubs and rifle butts. Inevitably the conflict panicked onlookers, many of whom gave in to their urge to flee all at the same time. Those in the center of the crowd began pushing those on the fringes toward the soldiers.

A shot was fired. Then several shots.

General Tang was still holding forth on the PA system from the passenger seat of the van when the first fully automatic burst was triggered into the crowd by a frightened soldier.

People screamed. More shots were fired into the crowd, random insanity, then the soldiers were either trampled or ran before the fear-soaked mob trying to escape.

A sergeant in one of the tanks on the edge of the park tried to aid the escape of his fellow soldiers, who ran past the tank in front of a wall of running civilians who were also desperate to escape. The sergeant opened fire at the civilians with a machine gun mounted on top of the main turret. The bullets cut down several dozen people before the gun jammed.

In three minutes the sidewalk and street in front of the bank contained only dead, dying, and wounded people, many of them trampled. More than a hundred people lay on the pavement and grass and in the flowerbeds, some obviously dead, some bleeding and in shock.

General Tang climbed out of the public address van and stood staring uncomprehendingly at the human wreckage. He hadn't recognized the muffled pops as shots since the public address system was so loud, and he was initially pleased when the people he could see from the van began to move. Alas, by then the situation was out of control. Surprised by the panic evident among the civilians he could see through the van's windshield, Tang stopped speaking and heard, for the first time, the shooting, the shouting, and the screaming.

Staring now at the people lying in the otherwise empty street, he became aware that several officers were beside him, shouting questions.

The thought that ran through the general's head was that the crowd should not have run. It was their fault, really. He certainly hadn't given orders for the soldiers to shoot.

'Pick them up,' he said and gestured toward the dead and wounded. The officers beside him looked puzzled.

'Pick them up,' General Tang repeated. 'Take them to the hospital. Clear the street.'

When the first shot was fired, a nervous Jake Grafton raked two old ladies from their perch on the retaining wall and shoved them onto the ground. Then he threw himself on top of them.

He didn't move until the shooting was completely over and most of the people on their feet had fled. Only then did he stand and look about him at the bodies, at people bleeding, at people like himself who had taken what cover they could find.

He helped the two old women to their feet. Neither was hurt. They looked about them with wide, fearful eyes. Without a word they walked away, away from the bank and the soldiers and the gunshot victims.

Jake Grafton lingered a moment, watching the soldiers check the people lying on the concrete. Then, with his hands in his pockets, he walked through the troops and along the street away from the square.

The soldier who fired the first shot was from a fishing village on the northern Chinese coast. Eighteen years old, he had been in the army for nearly two years. He had been in Hong Kong for two weeks and two days – he was counting the days so he could accurately report to his family when he next sat down with a scribe to dictate a letter. His name was Ng Choy, and now he was crying.

Sitting on the hard, clean, bloody pavement of the bank square, he couldn't stop the tears. The body of the man he had shot was lying beside him. In his panic Ng had triggered a burst of seven shots, all of which hit this middle-aged man in the chest. By some fluke, after the man was shot his heart continued beating for almost half a minute, pumping a prodigious quantity of blood out the bullet holes. The sticky mess was congealing now and turning dark.

Ng Choy didn't understand any of it. He didn't understand why he was here, what everyone had been shouting about, what the sergeant had wanted him to do, why this man had tried to wrestle him out of the way, and he didn't understand why he had shot him.

So he sat there, crying uncontrollably, while his fellow soldiers walked around him, carrying away the wounded and the dead.

Finally two soldiers picked up the corpse beside Ng, leaving him on the cold pavement with his rifle and the pool of sticky blood.

Rip Buckingham cradled the telephone automatically between his cheek and shoulder. 'How many dead?' he asked the reporter on the line.

'Fifteen, the soldiers say. One woman died as they loaded her into the ambulance. At least forty more were injured by bullets. I estimate a dozen or two were trampled – it will be impossible to get an accurate count of the injured.'

'Get to the bank officials. Find out why they wouldn't open the doors of the bank.'

The story would be front-page news around the world, with a big, bold headline: 15 KILLED IN HONG KONG BY PLA TROOPS. The teaser under the main headline would read, *Crowd at Japanese Bank Fired Upon.*

Ten minutes later Rip was told, 'I talked to a cashier. The officers of the bank are in a meeting and unavailable. The bank is insolvent. Tokyo refused to loan it any more money.'

'*What?*'

'Yes. The Japanese are letting the bank fail. The word is Tokyo already poured twenty billion yen into it. Apparently that's the limit.'

This story is growing by leaps and bounds, Rip thought.

He called a man he knew on a Japanese newspaper and asked for help. In twenty minutes the Tokyo newsman called back with confirmation from the Finance Ministry. The government of Japan had decided not to save the Bank of the Orient, a Japanese-owned bank headquartered in Hong Kong. After consultations with Finance Ministry officials, the Chinese authorities had elected not to intervene.

Rip looked at his watch. There was still time. He grabbed a notebook and his sports coat and headed for the door.

The army was cleaning up the mess in front of the Bank of the Orient, loading bodies in ambulances and the backs of army trucks. Rip stood watching for several minutes. There were few onlookers; the soldiers standing around didn't seem in the mood for gawkers. Yet because he wasn't Chinese, it was several minutes before the nearest soldier gestured for him to move on.

Rip went to the office tower entrance of the bank building and showed his press pass to the security guard. It took some talking and several hundred Hong Kong dollars, but eventually he managed to get into the executive suite on the fourth floor.

He explained to the receptionist that he wanted to talk to the president of the bank. He gave her his card: 'Rip Buckingham, Managing Editor, *China Post*,' with the *China Post* lettering in the company's trademarked style.

The receptionist told him to take a seat.

He looked at the art on the walls and at the magazines on the table. He really didn't expect to see any bank officer. He thought it would be helpful to see the street in front of the bank again, see it knowing it was an important place, so he could visualize the scene the reporters were describing to him. And he had the time before deadline. So he was surprised when the receptionist appeared in the doorway and said, 'Mr. Genda has a few minutes. Come this way, please.'

Saburo Genda had a corner office. Through the window Rip caught a glimpse of the last army truck leaving. Except for a few police guards, the square was empty.

Genda was slumped in a large stuffed chair beside the desk with his back to the square. He didn't look up as Rip entered, didn't pay any attention to him until the Australian was seated across from him. He had Rip's card in his hand. He glanced at it.

'So, Mr. Buckingham,' Genda said in accented English, 'ask your questions.'

The Japanese executive looked, Rip thought, like he had slept in his clothes. He had the fashionably gray hair, the dark power suit and tie, the trim waistline ... and he looked exhausted, worn out.

'What happened, Mr. Genda?'

'They killed the bank.'

'They? Who is *they*?' Rip asked as he wrote down the previous reply in shorthand.

'The Finance Ministry. They seized our assets in Japan. They refused to let us draw on those assets for the cash we need to operate on a daily basis. The news leaked out, there was a run on the bank ... We are out of business, insolvent. The bank has,' Genda took a deep breath and exhaled, 'collapsed.' He raised his arms and let them fall to the arms of the chair. He looked at his hands as if he had never seen them before.

'You are saying the Finance Ministry chose to put you out of business?'

'Yes.'

'Do you know why?'

'They said it was the bad real estate loans.'

'But I thought they have known about those loans for years.'

'They have.'

'Then ...'

'Someone in Japan made a decision, Mr. Buckingham. I don't know who or why. The decision was to make the bank fail.'

'Make it fail? You mean allow it to fail.'

'No, sir. When the Finance Ministry seized our Japanese assets, the Ministry forced the bank to close its doors. There was no way it could stay open. They took a course of action that made the failure of the bank inevitable.'

Rip made a careful note of Genda's exact words.

'Mr. Genda, I have heard that the Bank of the Orient refused the Chinese government's demands for low-interest loans. If the bank had made those loans, would it have failed today?'

Genda tried mightily to keep a straight face. He started to answer the question, then thought better of it. He lowered his head. He seemed to be focused inward, no longer aware of Rip's presence.

Rip tried one more question, then rose and left the office. He pulled the door shut behind him.

3

'Tell me again about Tiger Cole,' Callie Grafton said to her husband. They were eating lunch on the balcony of their hotel room. Jake had related his adventure at the bank square this morning and the fact that Tommy Carmellini had dropped by for breakfast.

'I remember you and Tiger flew a plane from the carrier into Cubi Point during the final months of the Vietnam War,' Callie said, 'and I went to the Philippines to meet you. I remember meeting him at the airport when you showed me the plane before you left.'

Jake nodded. He, too, remembered. 'A few weeks after that we were shot down,' he said.

'As I recall,' Callie said, 'he was tall, silent, intense.'

'That was Tiger. He never had much to say, but when he did, people listened.'

She had been a junior translator at the U.S. consulate in Hong Kong in those days. And now Tiger Cole was the consul general. Who would have guessed?

'Tiger broke his back in the ejection,' Jake continued, recalling days he hadn't thought about in years. 'After we were rescued he spent a long time in the hospital, then they sent him to Pensacola for rehabilitation. He finally said to hell with it and pulled the plug. I think he went back to college in California, got a master's in something or other, then got involved in the computer industry.'

'I lost his address about ten years ago,' Callie explained. 'He sent us Christmas cards, then we moved or he moved or whatever.'

Jake Grafton chuckled. 'Sometimes life deals you an ace. Last month *Fortune* magazine said he was in on the ground floor of three big high-tech start-ups.'

'And now he's the consul general,' Callie said distractedly. 'Why do you want me to translate this tape?'

Jake summarized his morning conversation with Carmellini while Callie finished her salad. 'The tape may contain something worth knowing. China Bob was a rainmaker, a wheeler-dealer who played every angle he could find. Something on that tape might shed some light on what is happening in this town.'

'You mean on what the Americans are doing to help make it happen?'

'If they are.'

'This CIA officer, Carmellini? Do you trust him?'

'I met him last year in Cuba,' Jake explained. 'He was working with a CIA officer who was subsequently killed. The dead officer told me Carmellini was a safecracker before the CIA recruited him.'

'That doesn't sound like anything I'd want on my résumé,' Callie shot back.

'It may not take all kinds, but we sure as hell got all kinds.'

'Are we going to do this tonight?'

'I don't know. Whenever Carmellini shows up with a tape player.'

'I certainly don't want to sit around this hotel room all evening waiting for him.'

'I didn't say we should.'

'Why don't you call Tiger Cole, invite him to go to dinner with us?'

'You think he'd go?' Jake asked dubiously.

'For heaven's sake, of course he'd go! Unless he has another commitment, then he'd probably want to set something up for tomorrow. Call him. Tell him you're in town and want to have dinner. I always thought you saved his life after you two were shot down.'

'That's true,' Jake admitted. 'But he's the consul general and pretty busy and – '

'You're a two-star admiral in Uncle Sam's navy, Jake Grafton. You can buy a drink anywhere on this planet.'

Rip Buckingham was about ready to send the bank story to the makeup room when he received a telephone call from the governor's office.

'This is Governor Sun's assistant, Mr. Buckingham. Your newspaper is running story about tragedy in front of Bank of Orient? This morning?'

'Yes.'

'Governor Sun Siu Ki has issued statement. Statement go in story.'

The aide's English was almost impossible to follow, so Rip replied in Cantonese. 'Read it to me,' he said, trying to keep the dejection out of his voice.

'A crowd of justly outraged citizens gathered this morning at the Bank of the Orient to withdraw their money panicked when bank officials shamefully failed to open their doors,' said the aide, reading slowly. 'In the rioting that followed, several people were killed by the gallant soldiers of the People's Liberation Army while they were restoring order. The officials of the Bank of the Orient will be held responsible for this tragedy . . .'

There were several paragraphs more, and as the governor's assistant dictated in Cantonese, Rip wrote it down in English, in his own private shorthand. He read it back to ensure he had it, then quickly typed out the statement on his computer. He put a note above the statement for the front-page editor, directing him to put the governor's statement in a box in the center of the page. However, he didn't change a word of his story, which gave the facts, without comment, as they had been gathered by his reporters.

When he had sent the story for the *China Post* on its electronic way, he called it up again and made some changes. His fingers flew over the keyboard, changing the slant of the story, trying to capture the despair of Saburo Genda and the hopelessness of the crowd waiting for money that rightfully belonged to them and would never be paid. He also tried to capture the callousness of the soldiers who used deadly weapons on defenseless people.

When he had finished this story, he E-mailed it and the governor's statement to the Buckingham newspapers worldwide. The *China Post* was owned by Buckingham Newspapers, Ltd., of which Rip's father, Richard, was chairman and CEO. Richard Buckingham started with one newspaper in Adelaide at the end of World War II, and as he liked to tell it, with hard work, grit, determination, perseverance, and a generous helping of OPM – other people's money – built a newsprint empire that covered the globe. Richard still held a bit under sixty percent of the stock, which was not publicly traded. A series of romantic misadventures had spread the rest of the shares far and wide; even Rip had a smidgen under five percent.

Thirty minutes after Rip E-mailed the story to Sydney, the telephone rang. It was his father.

'Sounds like Hong Kong is heating up,' Richard growled.

'It is.'

'When are you going to pack it in?'

'We've had this conversation before, Dad.'

'We have. And we are going to keep having it. Sometimes in the middle of the night I wake up in a sweat, thinking of you rotting in some Communist prison because you went off your nut and told the truth in print about those sewer rats.'

'All politicians are sewer rats, not just ours.'

'I'm going to quote you on that.'

'Go right ahead.'

'So when?'

'I don't know that my wife or mother-in-law will ever leave, Dad. This is their place. These are their people.'

'No, Rip. *You* are their people. You are the husband and son-in-law, and in China that counts for just about everything. You make the decision and they will go along with it. You *know* that.'

'What about the *Post*?'

'I'll send someone else to run it. Maybe put it up for sale.'

'Nobody is going to pay you serious money for a newspaper in Communist China, Dad. Not here, not now.'

'We'll see. You never had a head for business, Rip. You are a damned good newspaperman, though, a rare talent. You come to Sydney, I'll give you any editorial job in the company except mine, which you'll get anyway in a few years.'

'I'll think it over.'

'The thought of you in one of those prisons, eating rats ... Oh, well.' Without waiting for a response, his father hung up.

The massacre in front of the Bank of the Orient was the hot topic of conversation among the American Culture conference attendees during the afternoon break. One of Callie Grafton's fellow faculty members told her about it as she watched the attendees whispering furiously and gesturing angrily. Three or four of them were trying to whisper into cell phones. Callie didn't tell her informant that Jake had been in the crowd in front of the bank and had given her an eyewitness account at lunch.

At least twenty people were killed, the faculty member said, a figure that stunned Callie. Jake hadn't mentioned that people were killed, only that there had been some shooting. Obviously he didn't want her to worry. 'Ridiculous to worry, after the fact,' he would say, and grin that grin he always grinned when the danger was past.

Through the years Jake had wound up in more than his share of dangerous situations. She had thought those days behind her when he was promoted to flag rank. An admiral might go down with his ship, it was true, in a really big war, but who was having really big wars these days? In today's world admirals sat in offices and pushed paper. And yet ... somehow this morning Jake wound up in the middle of a shooting riot!

Perhaps we should go home, Callie mused, and then remembered with a jolt that Jake was here for a reason and couldn't leave.

She tried to forget riots and bodies and her husband's nose for trouble and concentrate on the conference.

Unfortunately, one of the attendees was a government official, a political officer sent to take notes of the questions and answers and jot down the names of any Chinese who might be 'undermining the implementation of the laws,' in the phrase the official used to explain his presence to the faculty.

This official was a bald, middle-aged party apparatchik, a generation removed from most of the attendees, who were students in their early to mid-twenties. The first day Callie Grafton found herself fixating on the man's facial expressions when any student stood to ask a question.

Angry at herself for feeling intimidated, she still had to carefully phrase her comments. While she could not be prosecuted for political deviancy, her participation in the conference could be terminated by this official on the spot. That sanction was used the very first day against a political science professor from Cornell. Callie was ready to pick up her notebook and follow him out the door, then decided a precipitous leave-taking would not be fair to the students, who came to hear her comments on American culture.

That first evening Callie remarked to Jake, 'Maybe taking part in this conference was a mistake.'

'Maybe,' he agreed, 'but neither of us thought so when the State Department came up with the invitation.' State had procured a conference faculty invitation for Callie as a cover for the Graftons' presence in Hong Kong. 'Don't be intimidated,' Jake continued. 'Answer the students' questions as best you can, and if the organizers give you the boot we'll see the sights for the rest of our stay. No big deal.'

Today after the break, the questions concerned the American banking system. Hu Chiang had asked questions often during the last three days, and he was ready when the room fell silent.

'Mrs. Grafton,' he asked in Chinese, the only language in use during the conference, 'who decides to whom an American bank will lend its money?'

Hu was tall, more muscular than the average Chinese youth, Callie thought, which made him a fairly typical Hong Kong young adult, most of whom had enjoyed better nutrition while growing up than their mainland Chinese peers.

'The bank lending committee,' Callie answered.

'The government gives the committee guidance?'

'No. Government sets the financial standards the banks must adhere to, but with only minor exceptions, the banks loan money to people and enterprises that are most capable of paying back the loan with interest, thereby earning profits for the owners of the bank.'

This colloquy continued for several minutes as the party boss grew more and more uncomfortable. Finally, without even glancing at the listening official, Hu asked, 'In your opinion, Mrs. Grafton, can capitalism exist in a society that lacks political freedom?'

The official sprang from his seat, turned to face Hu, and pointed his finger. 'I can sit silently no longer. That question is a provocation, an insult to the state. You attempt to destroy that which you do not understand. We have the weapons to smash those who plot evil.' He turned toward Callie. 'Ignore the provocations of the criminal elements,' he ordered peremptorily, closing the discussion. Then he sat heavily and used a cloth to wipe his face.

Callie was trembling. Although she could speak the language, she felt the strangeness of the culture acutely. She was also worried that she might somehow say something to jeopardize the conference or the people who had invited her.

'Mr. Hu merely asked my opinion,' Callie said, trying to hold her voice steady. 'I will answer the question.'

The official's face reddened and his jowls quivered. 'Go,' he roared at her, half rising from his seat and pointing toward the door. 'You insult China with your disrespectful attitude.'

Callie gathered her purse and headed for the door. As she walked she addressed her questioner, Hu Chiang, who was still standing in the audience. 'The answer to your question, Mr. Hu, is no. Political freedom and economic freedom are sides of the same coin; they cannot exist independently of each other.'

'I got thrown out,' she told Jake when she unlocked the hotel room door and found him on the balcony reading.

'I thought you would, sooner or later,' he said and grinned broadly. 'Still glad we came?'

She slumped on the side of the bed and held her head in her hands.

Jake put his arms around her. 'Hey, I called the consulate. Tiger Cole wants us to come to dinner tomorrow night.'

'I told you so,' Callie Grafton said through her tears, then tried to smile.

Removing the tape player that would play the miniature tape he had taken from China Bob's library from the tech shop in the basement of the consulate presented Tommy Carmellini with several problems, the most intractable of which was that the device could not be in two places at once. Kerry Kent had access to the office. Carmellini thought that if she chose to look for the player while it was missing, she would realize that Carmellini had lied to her, that he didn't trust her. She might even conclude that she was a possible suspect in China Bob's murder.

The problem was that the tape player was a unique device that played a nonstandard small tape that held up to eight hours of recording, so Carmellini couldn't hope to buy one over the counter at a gadget shop.

Tommy Carmellini thought about all of this as he stood in the small shop staring at the one serviceable tape player. Or was there only one? The room was chock-full of electronic components and gizmos, perhaps he just didn't know what was there. He began searching under the workbench, then worked his way to the large steel filing cabinets that stood against the back wall.

Aha! On the top of the cabinet behind an obsolete commercial Sanyo reel-to-reel tape player was another small player that looked as if it could handle the tape from China Bob's. He got it down, blew the dust off it, sat it beside the first one. Yes. The same model, controls, etc. He plugged the thing in and found a tape in one of the drawers that looked like it would fit. When he had the tape properly installed on the reels, he pushed the Play button.

Nothing. The thing was broken.

Without a qualm, he put the working machine in his attaché case and left the broken one in its place. There were several headsets lying around, so he selected one and tossed it into the case, too.

He found Kerry writing a report in the office the CIA officers used. The senior man was there, Bubba Lee, schmoozing with two of the other permanent men, George Wang and Carson Eisenberg. All three were Chinese-Americans; Lee and Wang had two Chinese parents, Eisenberg had a Chinese mother. All could speak perfect Cantonese and pass for natives, which they often did. This morning they wanted to shoot the breeze about Harold Barnes, who had been in Hong Kong for only a couple of months before he was killed.

'I went to the police department this morning,' Eisenberg told Tommy, 'to see if they have developed any leads on Barnes. They were all atwitter over China Bob's murder last night. You and Kerry got out of there just in time. They kept everyone else until dawn, including Mr. Cole.'

'Did they ever find the murder weapon?'

'Little automatic, nickel-plated?'

'Could have been.'

'Found it in the secretary's office just outside the library, in the trash can.'

'That makes sense,' Kerry Kent said. 'If I had just shot someone, I would want to get rid of the weapon as soon as possible.'

Tommy Carmellini stared at her in amazement. She was either ditsy or had more brass than any broad he had ever run across.

Lee and the others spent a very pleasant half hour going over the Chan layout with Tommy, speculating about motives, generally rehashing everything, and reaching no conclusions.

Then, finally, the men returned to their offices, closed their doors, unlocked their private safes, and got on with the business of covert and overt espionage, leaving Carmellini to the gentle company of the British transplant, Kerry Kent.

'I wonder who has the tape,' she said. 'Barnes was always such a careful workman. One must assume the device worked and someone swiped the tape.'

Carmellini shrugged.

'One has to assume,' she continued, 'that the tape is the key to the mystery.'

'If you think I have it, you're barking at the wrong dog,' he said.

She came over to the desk where he was sitting, squatted so her face was level with his. No more than twelve inches separated them. 'You can trust me, you know.'

'So you think I have it.'

'I don't think you trust me.'

'Whatever would give you that impression? I've known you three whole days ... no, four now. Four delightful days of humdrum work and one evening of romance lite. You kissed me what? Twice? I trust you as much as you trust me.'

'I never mix business and pleasure.'

'So there's no hope for us? Wait until my mother hears the news; she had such high hopes. Now get up off the floor and go sit in a chair. A woman kneeling before me will give people the wrong impression and create a tragic precedent.'

Kerry did as he asked.

'What I'd like to know,' he said, 'is how many people paraded through that library before and after me, looked over China Bob's corpse, then went back to the party and didn't say a word to anyone.'

'This morning a request came in from the chairman of the congressional committee,' she informed him. 'Congress invited China Bob to Washington to testify.'

'All expenses paid, no doubt.'

'The poor man is probably better off dead,' Kerry said firmly. 'His position between the Chinese and the Americans was going to get scorching hot.'

'Whoever shot him did him a real favor,' Carmellini agreed. He picked up his attaché case and walked out of the office.

'I had just graduated from college when I first came to Hong Kong,' Callie Grafton told her husband as they walked the streets of Kowloon, taking in the sights, sounds, and smells. 'I felt like I had finally come to the center of the earth's civilization, the place where all the currents and tides came together.

'I remember my first ride on the Star Ferry as if it were yesterday. The white-and-green boat was *Morning Star*, very propitious, you must agree, for a girl making her way in the world for the very first time. All of the thirty-nine-ton double-ended diesel boats are named for stars, and between them made four hundred and twenty crossings a day between Kowloon and Central. Each crossing took about ten minutes, regardless of the weather or sea conditions. The boats began running at six-thirty in the morning and stopped at eleven-thirty at night. There were two classes of passengers – first class, which rode on the upper deck, and second, which rode on the main deck.

'Everyone who lived or worked or visited Hong Kong rode on these ferries. On days off I would ride the ferries a dozen times a day, looking at the people and listening to them talk, laugh, cry, giggle ... Chinese laborers and wealthy merchants and sons and daughters and wives and mistresses and teenage toughs, English civil servants and nannies, Australian adventurers, tourists from everywhere on earth, Europeans, Russians, American sailors, Malays, Filipino maids, Japanese businessmen, Hindus, Sikhs –

everyone came to Hong Kong, to make money and a new life for themselves or just to see it, to learn the truth of it. All the roads of the earth lead to this place.

'I loved the city. It was British, colonial, civilized, grand and trivial, yet it wasn't. It was Chinese, but not quite. It was timeless, yet everyone was in a hurry and the city was being transformed before my eyes.

'From this city I could feel the power of China, the thousand million people, the ancient and the new, the way of the seeded earth. I came to think of China as a giant oak, deeply rooted and enduring through the centuries while the lives of men changed like the seasons.

'In this city I can still feel the pulse of the earth. I can stand in the crowded places and listen to the hundreds of voices, all babbling about the things that fill human lives. I can hear the generations talking of the things that never change, the dreams, ambitions, and concerns that make us human.'

Jake Grafton squeezed his wife's hand, and they walked on.

Rip Buckingham's brother-in-law, Wu Tai Kwong, was a delivery driver for the Double Happy Fortune Cookie Company. Rip was happily married and living in Hong Kong when he learned that his wife's younger brother was involved in the anti-Communist movement in Beijing. The whole thing seemed innocent enough . . . until that same brother-in-law stood in front of the tank in Tiananmen Square in 1989 and had his photo plastered on every front page in the world. That incident made him a criminal. And a dedicated revolutionary.

Now, of course, he was a fugitive . . . and living in Rip's basement. Although he was a notorious political criminal and the object of the greatest manhunt in Chinese history, the government had no idea what Wu looked like now, where he was from, who his family was, or what name or names he might be using. Perhaps this was to be expected in a nation where public records were spotty at best, a nation where a significant portion of the population was illiterate and without identity papers of any kind, a nation with more than a hundred million migrants who roamed at will, looking for work.

Still, the Chinese authorities knew with an absolute certainty that sooner or later they would get their man. They had offered a large reward for Wu Tai Kwong. Human nature being what it is, they had merely to wait until someone betrayed him.

Wu Tai Kwong, being who he was, was not hiding. True, he wasn't broadcasting his whereabouts and he was using a false name and false identity papers, but he had no intention of stopping his political activities. He hated the Communists and intended to destroy them or be destroyed by them, whichever way fate spun out the story.

The tale could go either way, he realized. Someone who knew or suspected who he might be would tell someone, and so on, and the rumors would spread like ripples in a pond. Still, Wu had to talk to his friends, had to plan, to plot, to conspire against those he hated. He did so knowing that any day could be his very last, for he knew that once the Communists caught him they would execute him quickly, then broadcast the news of their triumph.

This afternoon he stopped his delivery van at various corners on Nathan Road and picked up the solitary people standing there waiting. He picked up four men and a woman in this manner, then found a quiet place to park near the old Kai Tak airport. These people knew him, knew his real name, knew the risks he took, and he trusted them with his life. Since they literally held his life in their hands, they also trusted him.

Today this 'gang of six' discussed the current situation, the public anger at the failure of the Bank of the Orient, the predictable resentment against the PLA for shooting into an unsuspecting crowd.

'Is this the spark? Is now the hour?'

They debated the question hotly.

To overthrow the Communists, Wu Tai Kwong had argued for years, two things must come to pass. The great mass of people must be aroused against the government, and the army must refuse to fight the people.

'There are things still to be done,' Hu Chiang argued. 'We are almost ready, but not quite.'

'The police know far too much,' the woman replied. Alas, keeping the existence of a large subversive organization a total secret was impossible. People whispered, some tried to sell information to the authorities, others wanted to betray their colleagues and the movement for reasons that ran the gamut of human emotions. 'There are too many leaks, too many people talking. We must wait no longer. Every day we wait the danger grows, yet we grow only marginally stronger.'

'We are bribing the police,' one man pointed out when his turn to talk came. 'Every day the number of people who want money grows. It is inevitable that someone will take a bribe and turn us in ... if they haven't called Beijing already. We must act now!'

Wu waved them into silence. 'There is another factor. The Americans suspect that the American consul, Cole, has moved money into Hong Kong. They are trying to trace the money, find out where it went. China Bob Chan is dead, but the trail is not cold. If we wait too long, the Americans may decide to tell Beijing what they know ... or suspect.'

'So that is the decision?' Hu Chiang demanded.

'I will not make the decision,' Wu told them. 'We will vote. Now.'

Only Hu Chiang voted to wait.

'Then it is decided,' Wu told them. Even Hu looked relieved that the waiting was over, he thought.

'The longest journey begins with the first step. Let us begin.'

As he started the van to drive away, Wu remarked, 'We must win or die.'
'Win or die,' they murmured.

The house where the Buckinghams lived perched precariously on the side of the mountainous spine of Hong Kong Island, just below the Victoria Peak tram station. From it one had a magnificent view of the central business district, Kowloon, and the harbor.

The roof of the building was flat. Paved with tile and equipped with lawn chairs and sun umbrellas, it made a wonderful patio on almost any day clouds did not obscure the sun. At the head of the staircase was a small room with large windows that Lin Pe, Rip's mother-in-law, used as a greenhouse.

When he got home, Rip found his wife, Sue Lin Buckingham, on the roof sitting under an umbrella, reading. He removed a cold beer from the refrigerator in the greenhouse and sagged into a lawn chair beside her. As he summed up the events of the day, his wife put down her book and listened in silence.

Sue Lin was a rarity, a highly educated Chinese woman. She had never known her father, who died before she was born. Her mother made a small fortune in fortune cookies and insisted that her daughter get an education. Sue Lin spent her teenage years at a private school in California, then got bachelor's and master's degrees from the University of California at Berkeley.

Rip Buckingham, Australian bum and Chinese aficionado, fell for her the very first time he saw her. She had not been similarly smitten, but he persisted. Eventually he won her heart, a triumph that he still regarded as the great accomplishment of his life. She was, he thought, the most gracious lady he had ever met.

This evening she listened in silence to Rip's narrative of the Bank of the Orient debacle and his summary of Governor Sun's statement.

'The statement was really an order telling you how to write the story, wasn't it?'

'Yes, I suppose.' Rip took a big swallow of beer, then stared glumly at his toes.

'The government may shut down the newspaper. You've been expecting it.'

'I know. I just kept hoping it wouldn't happen.' He swept his hand at the city before them. 'This is our city, our place. We have done nothing wrong. The paper merely prints the news in a fair, unbiased manner. What's wrong with that?'

Sue Lin didn't reply. 'Perhaps they won't shut you down.'

Rip sipped some more beer. 'It's time we thought about leaving.'

'We can go anytime,' his wife responded without enthusiasm. They both held Australian passports. 'But I don't want to go without Mother. You know that. And Mother won't leave Hong Kong.'

'She always said she wouldn't leave, sure, but this place is going to explode,' Rip argued. It was hell trying to use logic on women who didn't want to hear it. 'This isn't the city that it used to be. She *must* see that! And she had money in the Bank of the Orient. In the middle of listening to the reporters and writing the story, that thought ran through my head.'

'Money or no money, she won't leave without my brother. Absolutely not.'

'I guarantee you he won't leave alive. Not a chance in hell.'

'He's all she has from her early life.'

'Bull! She has both of you! I know there were three other children, but that was thirty-some years ago. They are adults with children of their own or they're dead.'

'Rip, you don't understand.'

'I *do* understand. And I think it's time your mother listened to reason. When this place explodes, your brother is going to be leading the revolution. The government is going to figure out who he is – who his mother is, who his sister is, who his brother-in-law is. While Wu is busy answering destiny's call, the Communists are going to put you, me, and your mother against the wall and shoot us dead. *We're running out of time!* If we don't leave we'll die here. We've *got* to get the hell out of China!'

'Don't be ugly.'

'Why don't you listen to reason?'

Sue Lin held out her hand. He took it.

'Our world is coming apart,' Rip told her. 'Everything is cracking, breaking, shattering into thousands of pieces. I feel helpless, doomed. At any second the great quake will come and this little world where you and I have been so happy is going to cease to exist.'

Tears ran down her cheeks. She turned her back on him and wiped them away.

They were sitting side by side, holding hands and looking at the city, when the cook called from the greenhouse and told them dinner was ready.

4

Tommy Carmellini was waiting in their hotel room when the Graftons returned after dinner. He was sitting in the darkness well back from the window.

'Did the maid let you in?' Jake asked sharply.

'No, sir. I let myself in. I didn't want the staff to know I was here.'

'Next time wait in the lobby.'

'Right.'

'Callie, this is Tommy Carmellini.'

'Mrs. Grafton, you can call me Jack Carrigan. That's the name I travel under.'

'So you have two names, Mr. Carmellini?'

'Sometimes more,' he admitted, grinning.

'Most people are stuck with only one,' Callie said, 'the one their parents picked for them. It must be nice to have a name that you pick yourself and can toss when you tire of it.'

'That *is* one of the advantages,' Carmellini agreed cheerfully.

'I brought the tape player.' He gestured toward the bed, where the device rested. 'I don't speak Chinese. To me it just sounds like a bunch of birds twittering.'

Jake flipped on the rest of the lights as Callie seated herself on the bed across from Carmellini. She eyed the tape player distastefully. 'What's on the tape?' she asked.

Carmellini leaned forward and looked into her eyes. 'A CIA officer was murdered just hours after he planted two bugs and a recorder in the library of a man named China Bob Chan. Two nights ago China Bob was shot and killed in that library by a party unknown. I got there before the body cooled and took the tape from the recorder. That tape is probably the best evidence of the identity of the person who killed Chan. In fact, it may be the only evidence we'll ever get. It also might shed some light on who killed the CIA officer.'

'You told Jake that Tiger Cole, the consul general, might have killed Chan.'

'Mrs. Grafton, anyone in Hong Kong could have gone into that library and shot China Bob.'

Callie glanced at Jake, who said nothing.

'The recorder was voice-activated,' Carmellini explained, 'so that valuable space on the tape wouldn't be wasted recording the street noises that penetrated an empty room. When the sound level dropped below the electronic threshold, the tape would play on for a few seconds, then stop. Places on the tape where the recorder stopped were marked as audible clicks.'

'We'll play it later,' Jake Grafton said in a tone that settled the issue.

'Sure.' Carmellini rose to go. 'Nice to meet you, Mrs. Grafton.'

Callie merely nodded.

Buckingham Lin Su, or as she wrote it in the Western style, Sue Lin Buckingham, found her mother, Lin Pe, in her study consulting her fortune book. Lin Pe lived in her own three-room apartment in the Buckinghams' house. Just now she was smoking a cigarette which she had fixed in a short black plastic holder. The smoke rising from the cigarette made her squint behind the thick lenses of her glasses.

Sue Lin broke the news. The Bank of the Orient had collapsed, failing to open its doors today. Depositors trying to withdraw their money had been fired upon by soldiers.

Lin Pe took the news pretty well, Sue Lin thought, considering that her company kept all its accounts at the Japanese bank because it paid the highest interest rates in Hong Kong.

Lin Pe listened, nodded, and when Sue Lin left, got the accountant's latest summary from her desk and studied it.

The Double Happy Fortune Cookie Company, Ltd., was a profitable international concern because of one person – Lin Pe. Thirty years ago when she came to Hong Kong from a village north of Canton, she found a job in a factory that baked fortune cookies for export to America. Before she went to work there she had never even heard of a fortune cookie. The little fortunes printed on rice paper inside the cookies charmed her. She wrote some in Chinese and one day showed her creations to the owner, an alcoholic old Dutchman from Indonesia who also mixed the cookie batter and cleaned up the place at night, if he was sober enough. He translated a few, they went into the cookies, and Lin Pe had found a home.

When the Dutchman died five years later of cirrhosis of the liver, she bought the company from his heirs. It thrived, because Lin Pe was a very astute businesswoman and because the fortunes she put into her cookies were the best in the business.

About three dozen fortunes were in use at the cookie factory at any one time. Writing good fortunes was a difficult business. She was hard put to come up with three or four good new ones per month, which meant some of the old ones had to be used again. Lin Pe kept a book, her 'book of fortunes,' in which was recorded every fortune she had ever written and notations on what months it had been used. She changed the fortunes going into the cookies on a monthly basis.

Just now she put down the accountant's summary and consulted the fortune list she had constructed for use next month.

'Happiness will find you soon.' She had used this fortune before and thought it one of her best. Other cookie people wrote 'You will find happiness,' but that was bland, without wit or snap. Lin Pe sent the happiness searching for you.

'Your true love is closer than you think.' Love, Americans seem enamored with it. Many of the letters she received from restaurant owners in America pleaded with her to use more love fortunes in her cookies. Lin Pe had never been in love herself, so to write these fortunes she had to imagine what it might be like. This was becoming more and more difficult as the years passed.

'Beware . . . use great care in the days ahead.' When she saw this fortune in her book, she inhaled sharply.

It was her fortune.

One cookie in three thousand contained that fortune. Yesterday she plucked a cookie off the conveyor belt as it was about to go into the packing machine, and that was the fortune inside.

She closed the book, unable to continue. She shivered involuntarily, then sat staring out the window.

Rip Buckingham disliked the Communists, and her son Wu hated them. Neither knew them like Lin Pe did, for she had lived through the Great Cultural Revolution. Occasionally she still awoke in the middle of the night with the stench of burning houses and flesh in her nostrils, listening for the shouts, the sobs, the screams. She had fled to Hong Kong to escape that madness; now the storm seemed to be gathering again out there in the darkness. She could feel its presence.

The money. Its loss was a disaster, of course, but perhaps the Japanese could be shamed into paying it back. The neat little men with their perfect haircuts and creased trousers must know the importance of keeping faith with their customers, even if the law didn't require it.

The cookie company could run a few days without writing checks. Lin Pe began considering whom she might borrow money from to meet the payroll. Rip and Sue Lin had plenty of money and would have loaned her all she wanted without giving it a thought, but Lin Pe was too proud even to consider that course of action. Amazingly, the possibility never crossed her mind. From her desk drawer she removed a private list of her fellow businesspeople and studied that.

Rip Buckingham's idea of the perfect way to spend an evening was to loaf in a lawn chair on his roof reading newspapers from all over the world as he sipped beer and listened to music. Occasionally he would pause to watch a ship slip through the harbor on its way to or from the open sea.

Hong Kong didn't have enough dock facilities, so many of the freighters had their cargo on- and off-loaded onto lighters, which were towed back and forth between their anchorages and the ships by tugboats. Flotillas of ferryboats were in constant motion crossing and recrossing the strait, fuel boats cruised for customers, tour and party boats dashed about, here and there someone sculled a sampan through the heaving ridges of waves and wakes.

Rip was not enjoying the view tonight.

He finished with a Beijing newspaper and threw it onto the pile with the Hong Kong dailies. He grabbed a Sydney paper and started flipping though it.

The problem was that he liked being a newspaperman. He liked going to the office, saying hello to everyone, reading the wire service stories, tapping away on his computer as the cursor danced along, then seeing it all in print. He liked holding the paper in his hand, liked the heft of it, liked the way that it felt cool to the touch. He liked the smell of newsprint and ink, liked the idea of trying to catch the world every day on a pound of paper. A newspaper was worth doing, and Rip Buckingham didn't want to do anything else.

And he wanted to keep doing it here. In Hong Kong.

He was still stewing, and trying to get into last Sunday's *Washington Post*, when his wife came through the greenhouse leading two men. Rip recognized them immediately – Sonny Wong and Yuri Daniel.

Wong Ma Chow, 'Sonny,' was a gangster, the leader of the last of the tongs. He made a huge fortune in Hong Kong real estate, then lost it in the collapse that followed the British departure. Since then he had returned to the service business. Whatever service you wanted, Sonny could provide . . . for a price.

Rip had seen Yuri Daniel, Sonny's associate, around town for four or five years. Rip had never before had any dealings with him, nor had he wanted to. Yuri was a Russian or Ukrainian or something like that, reportedly from one of those hopelessly poor, squalid villages in the middle of the vast Eastern European plain. Rumor had it that he left the mother country in a large hurry with a suitcase full of money taken at gunpoint from a Russian mobster. How much truth was in the rumor was impossible to say, but it was a nice rumor.

Yuri's expressionless face, with its cold, blank eyes and pallid features, certainly didn't inspire trust. Inspecting it at close range, Rip idly wondered why Sonny chose to be in the same room with Yuri Daniel.

'Hey, Sonny.'

'Hey, mate. What do you hear on the Bank of the Orient thing?'

'At least fifteen dead.'

'The lid is gonna blow off this place. People aren't going to take this lying down. Even I had money in that goddamn thing.'

'Tea? Beer?'

'Beer would be great.'

Sue Lin was still there, and now she nodded at Rip and went for the refrigerator.

'First time I've been up here,' Sonny said, surveying the view from a chair beside Rip. 'Hell of a view you got here, yessir. Hell of a view. You're right up here with the upper crust, looking down on the world.'

Yuri sat on Sonny's other side, turned slightly away from the two of them. He hadn't yet said a word.

Sue Lin brought the beer, then left them. She paused at the door of the greenhouse and looked back, catching Rip's eye. She raked her windblown hair from her eyes, then went in, closing the door behind her.

'... owned a building just below here some years back,' Sonny was saying. He pointed. 'That one right there, with the little garden on the roof. The value of that building went up to four times what I paid for it. I was collecting fabulous rents every month, then it all just ... just melted away, like ice cream in the noonday sun.'

'Yeah.'

'One day, the whole thing ...' He sighed.

Rip sipped a beer. Sue Lin had brought one for each of them. Yuri was looking at the ships in the harbor to the west.

'I always liked this view,' Sonny said. 'Always.'

'Yeah.'

'These are the last days of Hong Kong, Rip. It's coming to an end.'

Rip didn't say anything to that. What was there to say?

'Got your message that you wanted me to drop by. So what can Wong and Associates do for the scion of the Buckingham clan?'

'China Bob Chan.'

'Too bad, huh?'

'Got any ideas on who might have done it?'

'It wasn't me, Rip.'

'Hey, Sonny. If I thought there was the slightest possibility, I would have respected your privacy. What I'm after is any background or insight you might be able to provide, not for attribution, of course. What was China Bob into?'

'You've been following the American thing ... ?' Sonny began. 'The PLA was giving him money to contribute to American political campaigns. Don't ask me why. The generals think the American politicos are as crooked as Chinese politicians. And they may be right – there was a guy in the American embassy in Beijing who was handing out visas to the United

States to anyone who said he would go over there and contribute to the president's reelection campaign.'

'Uh-huh.'

'Chan was into the usual stuff here. And he was big into smuggling people, which I won't touch. It's too dirty for me, Rip, but not for China Bob.'

'Where to?'

'Anywhere. Malaysia, Australia, America, anywhere people wanted to go, China Bob would do the deal. Course he didn't always deliver – it's a smelly business.'

'Did he do passports?'

'S.A.R. passports, but no one wanted those,' Wong said. Hong Kong became a Special Administrative Region of China in 1997 when the British turned over the colony. 'I heard that for the right price – and the right price was very high – China Bob could produce genuine passports. That's not generally known around, I believe.'

'Was he doing that a lot, do you think?'

'No country I know about is granting visas to people holding S.A.R. passports, so there isn't a lot of demand for those. The refugee problem has these other countries scared silly. The old British colonial passports are a dreg on the market – you can't get into America or Australia or Singapore or Indonesia or anyplace I know with one of those. Even Britain is worried about tens of thousands of Chinese refugees flooding in. No one is granting entry visas.'

Rip sipped some more of his beer and waited.

'Guy like China Bob had a lot of deals going,' Sonny said, thinking aloud. 'The guy who sold China Bob blank American passports will deal with me, if you want. Faking an Australian visa on an American passport shouldn't be a problem.'

'You and China Bob were sorta competitors, weren't you?'

Sonny bristled slightly at that remark. 'Our businesses paralleled each other at times,' he admitted. 'There was room for both of us.'

'You're talking a forged passport?'

'Genuine. The real thing, right out of the lock box at the consulate. The source is very reliable.'

'Uh-huh.'

'He's not honest, you understand, but he is reliable. That's a critical difference in business, one so few people appreciate.'

'I think I see it,' Rip told Sonny, who nodded as if he were pleased.

'I put the passport with Australian entry visa in your hands,' Sonny explained. 'You take your Chinese relative to the airport, put her on Qantas to Sydney. She breezes through immigration at both ends. Guaranteed.'

'How much?'

723

'Twenty grand American. Cash. Half in advance, half on delivery of the documents.'

Rip whistled. 'Is that what China Bob was into?'

'He did a little of that. And he brought stuff in. He could get import permits for darn near anything; anything he couldn't get a permit for he could smuggle in. Money, import, smuggling – those were his main businesses, but he did some people, too. For fifty grand he could put your cousin on a freighter going to the United States. The Philippines were a real bargain, though, only about four thousand. Your cousin would be in a locked container with some other passengers. He'd have to take his own food and water with him, but he wouldn't get a sunburn. About eight days at sea, five hundred a day. Hell, Rip, it would cost more money than that to send him on a cruise ship.'

'The passengers didn't always get there, though,' Rip pointed out.

'Rip, I just couldn't say. Dumping the cargo at sea – something like that the people involved don't talk about. Oh, you hear whispers, but people like to whisper. Gives them something to do.'

Rip waved away that possibility. He knew those kinds of things were happening, but he really didn't believe China Bob had gotten his hands that filthy for the paltry dollars involved.

Rip glanced at the Russian. On the other hand, Yuri looked like he would cheerfully cut your throat for cigarette money.

'Was Bob into Chinese politics, do you think?'

'Hey, Rip, I don't think the guy intentionally set out to die young.'

'Well, he figured wrong somewhere, that's for sure.'

'Everyone makes mistakes occasionally. Even China Bob.'

'Think someone double-crossed him, one of his associates maybe?'

'I doubt if somebody shot him to get his wife. Wives being what they are, not too many people kill to get one. To get rid of one, yes.' Wong snorted at his own wit. When the noises stopped, he said, 'A double cross is likely. Though if I were a betting man, I would put my money on the PLA. Rumor had it Bob might go to America, embarrass a lot of important people.' He shrugged.

'Thanks for coming by tonight, Sonny.'

'Okay. Now tell me the real reason you called.'

'I enjoy seeing your smiling face.'

'I didn't shoot him, Rip. Bob and I did a lot of business together. His death leaves me scrambling, trying to salvage some things we had going. I'm not saying his death will be a net loss to me – I figure over time everything will balance out. You gotta be philosophical. These things happen.'

'Uh-huh.'

Sonny Wong gave up. 'Great view you got here, Rip.'

'Yeah.'

'You ever want a passport for your mother-in-law, call me.'

'I'll keep that in mind.'

'Come on, Yuri. Let's go find some beds.'

With her husband's help, Callie Grafton got the small tape reels properly installed on the player and pushed the play button. She was wearing the headset Carmellini had brought. Before her was a legal pad and pen on which she made notes and summarized the conversations as she listened. She made no attempt at a word-by-word translation. Occasionally she had to rewind the tape and listen to portions of conversations several times to make sure she had the meaning right.

Midnight came and went as she listened intently, occasionally jotting notes.

Finally she took a break, stopped the tape, and took off the headset. After she had helped herself to water, she muttered to her husband, who was out on the balcony watching the lights of the city; 'What are you going to do with the tape after I finish with it?'

'I don't know. Depends on what's on it.'

'I'm about halfway, I think. I don't understand everything I've heard, but Chan was apparently laundering money.'

'For whom?'

'For the PLA. The money was going to America.'

'Okay.'

'The congressional investigators might be able to put voices and facts together to make something of all this.'

'Perhaps.'

She stood silently, stretching. Finally she lowered her arms and massaged his neck muscles. 'Do you think Tiger killed him?'

'Hon, I don't know. I'm waiting for you to tell me what you think.'

'What are you going to do if he did?'

'I don't know that either.'

She went back inside and put on the headset.

It was three in the morning when Callie Grafton removed the headset and turned off the tape player. Jake was curled up on the bed, asleep.

She went out on the balcony and saw that rain had fallen during the night. Just now the air was almost a sea mist, which made the lights of the city glow wondrously.

She had listened to the ten minutes prior to the gunshot, which the tape captured, three times.

China Bob Chan had been a human, and presumably somewhere there was someone who cared for him, perhaps even loved him. Try as she might, Callie could work up no sympathy for the murdered man. He was gone and that was that.

She turned off the lights and lay down on the bed. She was so exhausted she wondered if she could relax enough to sleep. Then her eyes closed and she was out.

The sound of morning traffic coming through the open sliding-glass door woke Jake. Callie was asleep on the bed beside him.

Being as quiet as possible, he got up and put on running shorts, shirt, and shoes, made sure he had a key to the room, then slipped out and made sure the door locked behind him.

Down on the street the day was in full swing. People filled the sidewalk, all in a hurry, all rushing somewhere. Jake tried to stay out of their way until he got to Kowloon Park, with its semi-empty sidewalks. As he jogged through the park he passed morning exercise classes engaged in slow, stylized calisthenics that reminded him of ballet.

He ran the entire length of the park and out onto the sidewalks of Austin Road, where he headed for the docks on the western side of the peninsula.

He had gone only a few dozen yards along Austin Road when he realized that he was being followed. Someone was jogging behind him, huffing loudly. And there was a car on the street, creeping along.

Jake Grafton glanced back over his shoulder, taking in the car and the man in casual pants who was running behind. He was a couple hundred feet back, and running was obviously not a sport with him. The guy was wearing the wrong shoes and carrying too much weight, for starters.

The thought of Callie asleep in a hotel room with the tape of China Bob's last hours on the bed beside her flashed through Jake's mind.

When he reached the street that ran beside the dock area, Canton Road, he turned left, south, to head back toward Tsim Sha Tsui on the southern tip of the peninsula. He kept his pace steady and tried not to look over his shoulder, though he did glance back once to make sure his tail had not collapsed on the sidewalk.

He veered left onto Kowloon Park Drive, just loping along.

Ahead was a ramp up to an overpass that went across the street and into the lobby of a major hotel. Looking neither right nor left, Jake took the ramp, made the turn at the top, and slowed just enough to go through the glass doors, which reflected the early morning glare.

His tail came thudding up the ramp, made the turn, charged for the door with his head down, inhaling deeply as he tried to get enough air to ease the pain in his chest. On the street below the car that had been keeping pace with the runner accelerated away.

Jake Grafton caught the tail by the throat as he came through the door and slammed him into a marble pillar, where the man collapsed, too stunned to move.

Glancing around to be sure no one was paying too much attention, Jake picked the man up by his pants and shirt and shoved him back out the door onto the ramp. There he slammed the man's head into the ramp railing, and the man passed out.

After he eased the heavy man to the concrete, Jake patted him down. He had a small automatic in a holster in his sock, so Jake relieved him of that and pushed it down inside his own athletic sock. A wallet . . . he didn't need that anymore, either. A few keys, matches, an open pack of Marlboros . . .

Grafton spent no more than ten seconds searching the man, then he straightened and went on into the hotel, leaving one middle-aged Western woman staring open-mouthed at him. No one else seemed interested.

Callie was still asleep when Jake let himself into the hotel room. The tape was still in the player.

Jake examined the pistol, a Chinese-made automatic, loaded. He put it in his luggage.

The wallet he had taken from the tail contained Hong Kong dollars and a variety of cards, all displaying Chinese characters.

He was toweling off after his shower when Callie awoke.

'Hey, beautiful woman, did you sleep okay?'

She sat up in bed, looked around at the bright room and the daylight streaming through the gauzy drapes.

'I don't know who killed that man, Jake.'

'Couldn't tell from the tape?'

'Impossible to say. But China Bob was into everything. Everything! He smuggled people, money, dope . . . he was even bringing in computers and guns.'

'Computers?'

'I couldn't make much sense of it.'

'Was Cole on the tape?'

'I don't know. I don't know his voice.'

'You'll meet him again tonight.'

'I don't know that I want to.'

'Hey, kiddo. We're the first team, okay? What say we have breakfast and see some sights?'

5

The governor of Hong Kong, Sun Siu Ki, sat at his desk in City Hall puffing a cigarette as he listened to an interpreter translate Rip's story of the fatal riot in front of the Bank of the Orient from the *China Post*. A copy of the offending paper lay on the corner of the desk in front of him, out of his way. Spread out where he could read them were the front pages of three Chinese-language newspapers.

Sun couldn't believe his eyes or ears: Every editor in Hong Kong had apparently decided today was the day to tell the most outrageous lies about the government.

The copy of the leading Chinese-language paper had been hand-delivered to the governor's office by one of the newspaper's censors, who was horrified when he saw the paper rolling off the press. The lead headline and story on the Bank of the Orient failure was certainly not the one he had approved, and he wrote a note to the governor stating that fact.

The headline and story reported that Beijing had ordered the Bank of the Orient to close its doors since it had refused to lend money at superlow rates to customers designated by Beijing. The unspoken inference was that bribes in Beijing were the price of access to easy credit.

The censor had the presses stopped, but not before a truckload of the libelous papers had already left to be installed in vending machines in the northern area of Kowloon.

The other two papers carried slightly different versions of the same story. According to them the bank failure was the direct result of lending to unnamed politically connected entities who were unable to repay the loans, which had been made at ridiculously low rates. The morning editions of these papers had been distributed. The governor's aide bought these copies from vendors at the Star Ferry terminal on his way to work.

Everyone in Hong Kong was reading these lies.

The aide was in the next room, talking to the censors involved. Apparently both of them swore the stories were not the ones they approved for publication.

If the newspapers weren't enough, already this morning the governor had received a call from army headquarters: Several thousand people were sitting in the plaza outside the closed Bank of the Orient. They were peaceful enough, but they were there, a visible, tangible, unspoken challenge to the Communist government. As he listened to the interpreter, Sun Siu Ki was thinking about those people.

Behind his desk was a large window. Through that window, when he bothered to look, the governor could see a breathtaking assortment of huge glass-and-steel skyscrapers – one of which was the Bank of the Orient – designed by some of the world's premier architects. These buildings were the heart of one of the most vibrant, energetic cities on earth, a city as different from the old, decaying Chinese cities of the interior as one could possibly imagine. This difference had never impressed Sun Siu Ki.

A career bureaucrat, he was governor of Hong Kong because of his family's political connections in Beijing. He knew little about capitalism, banking, or the way Western manufacturing, shipping, and airline companies operated, and nothing at all about stock markets or the international monetary system. The wealth and dynamic energy of Hong Kong struck him as foreign ... and dangerous.

A wise person once observed that Hong Kong was China the way it would be without the Communists. Nothing resembling that thought had ever crossed Sun Siu Ki's mind or caused him a moment's angst.

Baldly, he was in over his head. He didn't see it that way, however.

Sun believed that he knew what he needed to know, which was how to surf the political riptides of the Communist upper echelons in Canton Province and Beijing.

The problem du jour was the defiance of the government's authority by the people in the streets ... and the newspapers. As bad as the uncensored stories were in the Chinese press, the headline in the *China Post* was the most outrageous: 15 MASSACRED AT BANK OF ORIENT.

Sun Siu Ki had replaced a governor who didn't attack pernicious foreign ideas with sufficient vigor. If people saw that the Communists were too soft to defend themselves, they were doomed: They would be swept away, eradicated as thoroughly as the Manchus. Being human, the party cadres were doing their damnedest to prevent just such a disaster.

Many of the readers of the *China Post* were not Chinese. The newspaper's reactionary stories inflamed the foreign devils, and they wrote outrageous, incendiary letters to the editor, which that fool published. All this caused faraway officials of the foreign banks to fear the loss of their money. Foreigners thought only of money. The culpability of the *China Post* was plain as day to Sun Siu Ki.

He gestured the interpreter into silence and seized a sheet of fine, cream-colored paper with the crest of Hong Kong on the top. There were still many boxes of paper bearing this logo in the attic of Government House. Thrifty Sun saw no incongruity in using paper bearing the likeness of the British lion. He wrote out an order for the offending newspaper to cease publication and signed it with a flourish. After further thought, he wrote out an order for the arrest of the editor. A few weeks in jail would teach him to mind his tongue.

While he was at it, he wrote out arrest orders for all of the editors involved. The time had come, Sun told himself, to whip these people back into line and show them who was in charge.

With the newspaper editors dealt with, Sun began to ponder the best way to handle the protesters in front of the bank.

The CIA contingent was summoned to the consul general's office just minutes after they arrived at work.

'What's going on?' Tommy Carmellini asked Kerry Kent, because she was more fun to talk to than the three men. Prettier, too.

'Didn't you see the crowd in front of the Bank of the Orient when you came in this morning? The ferry from Kowloon was packed; the only topic of conversation was the demonstration they were on their way to join.'

The consul general's office was large and sparsely furnished, apparently reflecting the taste of the current occupant. Virgil Cole was several inches over six feet, with wide shoulders and short blond hair that was suspiciously thin on top. Ice-cold blue eyes swept the people who trooped in and stood in front of his desk.

Carmellini had spent a few moments with the consul general when he checked in last week. Cole had said little, merely welcomed him to Hong Kong, shook hands, muttered a pleasantry or two, and sent him off. He had also attended a meeting that Cole had chaired.

Cole stood behind the desk now, looked into each face. 'There's a crowd gathering in front of the Bank of the Orient this morning,' he said without preliminaries. 'Tang and the army will probably run them off before long.'

No one disputed that assessment.

'I want to know what's going on in City Hall.'

'We have some excellent sources there, sir,' Bubba Lee began, but Cole waved him into silence.

'They are marvelously corrupt – I know that. The problem is our whisperers are too low on the totem pole. I want to know what Beijing is telling Governor Sun and General Tang and what those two are telling Beijing, and I want to know it now, in real time.'

Lee took a deep breath and said, 'The only way we can get that information, sir, is to tap the telephones.'

'While you are at it, bug Sun's office. Do it today.' Cole nodded curtly at Lee, then seated himself in the chair behind his desk and picked up the top document in his in-basket.

Apparently the spooks had been dismissed. Lee turned without a word and led his colleagues from the room.

Out in the hallway with the doorway closed, Lee faced them. 'You heard him. He's the most garrulous man I ever met.'

'A dangerous blabbermouth,' Carson Eisenberg agreed.

'Nevertheless, he's given us our marching orders, so let's dive in. Carmellini, your star is rising.'

As they walked toward the CIA office, Carmellini said, 'Can anyone get us a couple of telephone company trucks and some uniforms?'

'Tommy, you are in a city where money doesn't just talk, it sings like Pavarotti. You can get anything in Hong Kong; the only question is the price.'

'We need a floor plan of City Hall. Blueprints would be better.'

'Blueprints, yes,' said George Wang. 'We bought them from a butler when the British were still in residence.' He waggled his eyebrows at Kerry Kent, who stayed deadpan.

'Okay,' said Tommy Carmellini, 'this is how we're going to do it . . .'

Rip Buckingham was in his office on the second floor of the newspaper, closeted with the newspaper's headline writer, when he heard a commotion on the stairs. By the time he got to the door the policemen were up the stairs and shouting fiercely at two reporters who were trying to keep them from coming in. One of the policemen, a sergeant, tired of a zealous reporter's interference and threatened to chop him in the side of the neck.

'Ng Yuan Lee, what are you doing?' Rip shouted in Cantonese, which froze the sergeant. He snarled at the reporter, who drew back.

'Rip Buckingham, I have a warrant.'

'You're kidding, right?'

'No,' the sergeant said, extracting a piece of paper from his pocket. 'They have issued a warrant for your arrest, signed by the chief judge. The governor demanded it.'

Rip Buckingham threw up his hands in resignation. He didn't, however, argue with the sergeant and his colleague, who were merely doing their jobs.

'I'm sorry, Rip,' Marcus Hallaby, the headline writer, told him from the office door. 'God, I'm sorry! I just didn't think the headline was that big a deal, and . . .' Marcus was crying. He was also half soused, precisely the same condition he had been in yesterday afternoon when he wrote the massacre headline, precisely the same condition he had been in for the last ten years. He covered his face with his hands and sagged against the wall.

'Hey, Marcus, it wasn't your fault,' Rip said, trying to sound like he meant it. After all, he had been the one who always refused to fire Marcus when headlines irritated people he couldn't afford to irritate. These little storms blew in several times a year. For a day or two there was lightning and thunder, then the sky would clear and Marcus would still be there, contrite, apologetic, slightly drunk. . . . The damn guy just couldn't handle life sober and Rip had never been able to condemn him for that.

'It was the story,' he told Marcus. 'And the governor . . .'

'We must shut down the newspaper, Buckingham,' the sergeant said gently. 'We have our orders. Everyone must leave the building. We will put a guard on the doors.'

'Who gave these orders?'

'Governor Sun Siu Ki.'

'May I see the paper, please?'

The order was in Chinese. Buckingham read it while the sergeant wiped his hatband and ran his hand through his hair. He ignored the curious staffers standing nearby and turned his back on Marcus, who was sobbing audibly. Rip folded the document and handed it back to the officer.

'Perhaps it will help if I tell all the staff in English what they must do.' He said it easily, without even a hint of temper, and the sergeant agreed again. As a very young man touring China, Buckingham had learned the fine art of self-control.

Some of the staffers wanted to argue with the officers, but Buckingham wouldn't permit it. With sour looks, muttered oaths, and tears, the staffers – two-thirds of whom were Chinese – turned off the computers and office equipment and vacated the building. Buckingham remained the epitome of gracious affability, so he was given permission to have a private conversation with an assistant before the policemen took him away. Most of the staff milled helplessly on the sidewalk as the police car disappeared into traffic.

Jail held no terrors for Rip Buckingham. He had been incarcerated on several occasions in his footloose past when local policemen didn't know quite what to make of a six-foot-three Australian bicycling through forbidden areas, that is, areas in China off the beaten track, in which tourists were not permitted. He usually talked his way out of their clutches, but now and then he spent a few nights in the local can.

Fortunately his gastrointestinal tract was as impervious to bacteria as PVC pipe. Had his GI tract been more normal, one suspects he would not have strayed so far from tap water. He would probably be in Sydney now, married to one of the local sheilas, with one and a half blond kids, holding down some make-work position in his father's worldwide newspaper empire while the old man groomed him to follow in his footsteps, et cetera, et cetera.

As he rode through the streets of Hong Kong in the police car, wedged in the backseat between Sergeant Ng and his colleague, Rip Buckingham thought about the et ceteras. He also thought about his father, Richard Buckingham, and what he would say when he heard the news. Not the news his son had been arrested, but that the paper had been shut down.

Amazingly, for a man who owned fifty-two newspapers located in six countries, his father never really understood the romance of the printed word. Richard Buckingham saw newspapers as very profitable businesses with enviable cash flows. 'Newspapers,' he liked to say, 'are machines for turning ink and paper into money.'

Measured on Richard's criteria, the *China Post* had once been one of his best. B.C. Before the Communists.

Strange, Rip thought. He was thinking about the paper as if it would never publish again. Well, perhaps its day was over. For that matter, perhaps Hong Kong's day was over.

The Brits just turned over the keys and walked away. They went home to their unimpressive little island on the other side of the world and pretended Hong Kong never happened.

Maybe that was the wise thing to do.

Rip Buckingham shook his head, angry at himself. He was becoming demoralized. This was his city, his and Sue Lin's. She was born in Hong Kong, grew up here; he had adopted it.

Sue Lin loved Hong Kong.

Well, he thought defensively, he did, too. The city belonged to everyone who loved her. God knows, there were millions of people who did.

Despite his best efforts at keeping his spirits up, he was glum when the police car rolled through the gate of the city prison.

Damn Communists!

Sue Lin Buckingham told her mother that Rip was in jail, on a warrant demanded by Governor Sun Siu Ki. Policemen had arrested him, closed the newspaper. And this morning another riot was developing in front of the Bank of the Orient.

'Rip was foolish,' Lin Pe told her daughter in Cantonese, the only language in which she was fluent. She spoke a little English, but only when she had to. She acquired most of her English from American movies which she watched on a VCR, running scenes over and over until she understood the dialogue.

The news about Rip annoyed her. He had no respect for authority! 'He has been baiting the tiger with his news stories and editorials, and now the jaws have snapped shut. Only a fool spits in the eye of a tiger.'

'The paper was losing circulation, Mother, and advertising.' Sue Lin was tense, unhappy over the news of her husband's jailing, and her mother's simplistic reaction angered her. As if this lifelong capitalist didn't understand the dynamics of the marketplace! 'The *Post* used to make money because it was *the* newspaper for Hong Kong bankers and businesspeople to read. Rip knew that he had to address the concerns of the people he wanted as readers or he would lose them. And when he lost them, he would lose the advertisers who wanted to reach them. It's that simple.'

'Apparently Sun Siu Ki isn't concerned about Rip's advertisers,' the mother snapped.

'Sun Siu Ki is an extraordinarily stupid bastard.' Rip Buckingham's Chinese wife was no shrinking violet.

'That may be,' her mother agreed evenly. These young people! 'But he represents the government in Beijing, in precisely the same way that the old governor represented the queen in her palace in London. The difference, which dear Rip chooses to ignore, is that the English queen never laid eyes on a copy of the *China Post*. She didn't give a' – she snapped her fingers – 'what Rip Buckingham said in his silly little newspaper in Hong Kong, on the other side of the planet. The people in Beijing don't share Queen Elizabeth's indifference. They apparently do read Rip's scribblings. They're a lot closer, their skin is a lot thinner, and Sun is their long right arm.'

Sue Lin sank into a chair. 'Oh, Mother, what are we going to do? Rip is in jail. No one knows how long they intend to keep him. They may even send him to a prison on the mainland.'

Her mother's expression softened. 'The first thing to do,' she said, 'is to call Albert Cheung, the lawyer. He knows everything. He will know what to do.'

Lin Pe made the call. After talking to three people who pretended they never heard her name before in their lives, she got through to Albert Cheung, an illegal refugee from mainland China who was so smart that he won a scholarship to study law at Oxford. When he returned to Hong Kong, with a trace of a British accent and a fondness for tweeds, he managed to elbow his way to the top of the legal heap and into the inner sanctums even though he had no family in the colony. He had had a finger in every big deal in Hong Kong for the past twenty years. He was filthy rich and slowing down, yet he was too smart to pretend that he didn't remember Lin Pe.

'It has been years since I've heard from the chairman of the Double Happy Fortune Cookie Company, Limited,' Albert Cheung said.

'You've been getting your dividends every quarter,' Lin Pe told him. Albert took stock instead of a fee when she floated the initial public offering for her company on the Hong Kong exchange.

'Yes, indeed,' he said. 'I was wondering, have you ever thought of selling the company? Retiring to a life of leisure? Travel the world, see the Great Pyramids, the Acropolis – ?'

'I've had some other things on my mind, Albert. Like getting my son-in-law out of jail.'

'Rip Buckingham? See, I keep up. But I didn't know he was in jail. What has he done?'

'Sun Siu Ki closed the *Post* today and arrested him. Could you find out how long they intend to keep him?'

'So the tiger has him in his jaws?'

'Yes.'

Cheung sighed. After a few seconds he said, 'Many things are possible if you are willing to pay a fine. Would you – ?'

'Within reason, Albert. I will not be robbed by anyone.'

'I saw the headline in the morning *Post*: '15 Massacred at Bank of Orient.' And the PLA did the shooting. That headline was not wise, Lin Pe.'

'I think Sun Siu Ki was just fed up.'

'Perhaps the bank closing had – '

'Rip Buckingham's world is collapsing. He's been fighting back the only way he can.'

'I'll see what I can do, Lin Pe. Give me your telephone number.'

She did so, asked about his wife and children, then hung up.

'He'll see what he can do,' Lin Pe told her daughter. 'It will cost money.'

'The newspaper will pay.'

'The newspaper is finished,' said Lin Pe. 'It will never publish again.'

'Richard Buckingham is a powerful man.'

'Sun Siu Ki and the people in Beijing probably never heard of Richard Buckingham, and if they have heard, they don't care,' Lin Pe said, which was, of course, true. To see beyond the boundaries of China had always been difficult. Even the queen of England, she reflected, knew more about the outside world than the oligarchy in Beijing.

'The next thing to do,' Lin Pe said, 'is to call your father-in-law. Someone from the newspaper has probably called him already, but you should do so now.'

As her daughter walked from the room, Lin Pe added, 'Don't forget, all calls out are monitored.' She went back to writing fortunes.

Well, there it was. A way to get some money and get out before Wu Tai Kwong set China on fire. Sell the fortune cookie company to Albert Cheung!

The traders at the Hong Kong stock exchange had expected a wild ride in the aftermath of the collapse of the Bank of the Orient, but the ride was worse than anyone imagined it might be.

At the opening bell the traders were faced with massive sell orders, while the buy orders were minuscule. Prices went into freefall. Ten minutes went by before exchange officials finally learned that the computer system was at fault. Most – but not all – of the sell orders had an extra zero added just before the decimal, increasing the size of the orders by a factor of ten. On the other hand, some – not all – buy orders had their final digit dropped somewhere in cyberspace, shrinking them to a tenth of their original size.

The result was chaos. Since not every order was affected, the orders had to be checked by hand, which drastically limited the number of orders that could be processed. Unable to cope, officials closed the market.

Exchange officials quickly determined that they had a software problem, but finding the cure took most of the day. While they were working on it, one of the exchange officials was called to the telephone. The governor's aide was on the line demanding an explanation. For the first time, the exchange official mentioned the possibility of sabotage.

'Sabotage?' the governor's aide asked incredulously. 'How could anyone do that?'

'Probably a computer virus of some type,' he was told.

'Are you certain that is the case?'

'Of course not,' the exchange official snapped.

Sun Siu Ki was on the telephone to Beijing when the phones went dead. He tried another line, couldn't even get a dial tone, so he motioned to an aide that there was a problem and handed the instrument to him.

Sun turned to General Tang, explained that Beijing wanted the bank demonstrators dispersed and, if possible, wanted to avoid a bloody incident that the press would publicize around the world, inflaming foreign public opinion. 'Remove the press from the area,' Sun advised, 'before you remove the hooligans. That way the foreign press will be unable to use provocations as propaganda. Still, first and foremost, these hooligans must not be permitted to flout the authority of the state. That is paramount.'

Tang understood his instructions and the priorities they contained. Both men firmly believed that the state could ill afford to give an inch to anyone challenging its authority or resolve. Perhaps they were right, because both men knew Chinese history and their countrymen.

In any event, they were determined men who believed that the party and the government could and should use every weapon in the arsenal, indeed, every resource of the state, to fight for the survival of the revolution. And if pushed, they were fully capable of doing just that.

The telephones had been off for ten minutes when Tang left the governor huddled with his aide, who tried to explain that the computers at the stock exchange had been sabotaged. As Tang rode out of the City Hall parking area in his chauffeur-driven car, two telephone repair vans passed him on their way in.

Three men wearing one-piece telephone company jumpers and billed caps climbed from the vans. Tommy Carmellini removed an armload of tools and equipment from the van he came in while Bubba Lee talked to the security guard in Chinese. Carson Eisenberg unloaded the equipment they needed from the other van. The men strapped on tool belts. When Lee motioned to them to follow, they picked up their equipment and trooped along in single file into City Hall.

Tommy Carmellini was worried. He was an obviously non-Chinese worker who didn't speak a word of the language. The other two spoke Chinese, of course, and they had assured Tommy that there would be no problem, but still . . .

When he walked into City Hall, Carmellini took the bull by the horns.

The very first Chinese he saw, he brayed, as Australian as he could, 'G'day, mate. Where's your switchbox?'

Carson Eisenberg repeated the question in Chinese, the official pointed and said a few words, and they were in!

The CIA officers went to work on the telephones. Since the system was an ancient government one, this involved picking up each handset and using a noisemaker that allowed a colleague in a manhole just up the street to identify the line and tap it. After each line was identified, there was much shouting in Chinese into the instruments for the benefit of the watching civil servants.

As the crew worked their way from office to office, Carmellini inspected the building and its security system. He did this as one of the uniformed guards stood beside him quietly observing his every move. Carmellini smiled at the guard, nodded, then ignored him.

The building looked modern enough. The hallways and rooms were spacious, with hardwood floors, but, like government offices the world over, looked crowded and cramped.

Carmellini was in the foyer of the governor's office examining the door locks and alarms when one of the staff began staring at him. Carmellini glanced at the man . . . and recognized him: It was the guy who had stared at Kerry Kent at China Bob Chan's party the other night!

The man's brows knitted; he knew he had seen Carmellini before but couldn't quite remember when or where. His puzzlement was obvious.

Carmellini headed for the hallway with his escort right behind.

The staffer followed.

Uh-oh!

He had seen a men's room a moment ago and he headed for it now, his entourage in tow. Inside he went into a stall and shut the door.

He listened as the staffer and the security escort chattered away, their remarks totally unintelligible.

Carmellini unzipped his overalls, shrugged them off his shoulders, and sat.

He sat listening for almost fifteen minutes, then flushed noisily and rearranged his clothing.

When he opened the stall door, the room was empty.

Carmellini was listening at the door of the men's room when he heard footsteps. He got away from the door just in time. It swung open, and the man, wearing a PLA officer's uniform, looked startled. Tommy nodded pleasantly and walked out.

The hallway was empty. He went down a flight of stairs, walked toward the service entrance, passed the table with the two security guards, and went out into the parking area. The other three men were still inside. Carmellini got behind the wheel of one of the vans and sat staring at the side of City Hall, waiting.

Everybody in Hong Kong seemed to be on their way to the Central District this morning. Public transportation facilities were packed, with long lines of people waiting to board subway trains, buses, taxis, and the Star Ferry at Tsim Sha Tsui. PLA soldiers at the Central District subway station, the MTR, tried to prevent people leaving the trains at that stop, but there were too many people and the soldiers were overwhelmed. Taxis and buses were directed not to discharge passengers when they stopped at the usual stops, so they stopped in the middle of city blocks and opened their doors. By ten in the morning at least ten thousand people were in the square in front of the Bank of the Orient and on the surrounding sidewalks.

That was the situation when General Tang arrived direct from the governor's office in City Hall. He became angry with his officers, whom he felt should have made greater efforts to prevent the crowd from gathering.

'Since we failed to prevent the crowd from gathering, now we must make it disperse,' he instructed the staff, only to be told that the officers doubted they had enough soldiers present to make much of a show. Ordering the crowd to leave without sufficient soldiers to enforce the order would make the PLA appear ridiculous, an object of scorn.

'In accordance with your instructions, sir, we have used our men to prevent news media from congregating here.'

'Why not prevent everyone from congregating?'

'We tried, sir, but we simply did not have enough men.'

Tang lost his temper. 'Why did you wait for me to tell you to get more men? This demonstration is a direct affront to the government. It is a crime against the state and will not be tolerated! Order the police to send all available men here. They should have been here already, preventing this crowd from gathering in an unlawful assembly.'

'Sir, we have discussed this matter with the police, who say they have no spare men to send. All are engaged in law enforcement and traffic control duties elsewhere.'

'Get more soldiers, as many as you need. Have them brought here by truck as soon as possible.'

'Yes, sir.'

Tang found a vantage point in a third-floor office of a nearby building. The civilians who worked for a shipping company were ejected and the soldiers moved in. From here Tang could see that the crowd below consisted of men, women, and children, all well behaved. People sat visiting with each other and, as the noon hour approached, ate snacks brought from home. Water and food vendors worked the crowd.

'Why have you allowed these vendors to congregate here?' Tang demanded of his staff. 'Run them off.'

The soldiers tried. The vendors promptly gave away everything on their carts and obeyed the soldiers, who laughed along with the crowd. Watching from above, Tang was coldly furious.

738

'Two hours, sir. We will have another two hundred men here within two hours.'

'By truck?'

'Yes, sir. The trucks must go through the Cross-Harbor Tunnel, which is crowded at this hour.'

Tang could contain his fury no longer. He stormed at the staff, berated them at the top of his lungs. When he had vented his ire, he retired to a private office and slammed the door.

Jake and Callie Grafton spent the morning cooped up with a flock of middle-aged British and American tourists riding a small tour bus around the coast of Hong Kong Island. They visited the mandatory jewelry factory – they looked but didn't buy – and rode a sampan to a fish restaurant in the harbor at Aberdeen.

A barefoot old woman in a loose cotton shirt and trousers, brown as a nut, with a lined, seamed face, sculled the tourists over. The restaurant was one of a half dozen in the harbor, all built on barges. Permanently anchored, covered with Victorian gingerbread painted in bright, gaudy primary colors, the restaurants somehow still managed to bear a faint resemblance to a pagoda.

These much-photographed temples of capitalism made Jake smile. Callie's mood, however, was somber; she hadn't smiled all morning.

After they had given the waiter their order – the waiter seemed to know an extraordinary amount of English, although Callie chatted with him in Chinese – Jake and Callie Grafton were left in semiprivacy with glasses of wine. They were seated in a booth by a window that looked across acres of fishing boats and the residential sampans of the boat people. Beyond the harbor were rooftops and high-rises, all the way up the mountain.

'You don't seem too happy about your glimpse into China Bob's affairs,' Jake said tentatively.

'I'm sorry. I've got no right to be such a stick in the mud.'

'Not your fault. The guy was a probably a shit.'

'Sssh! People might be listening.'

'I hope not.'

'Let's just say he was a foul, evil man who made his living on the misfortunes of others.'

'That would be fair.'

'The tape was really hard to figure out,' Callie explained, 'and I don't think I've got it yet. I would say that at least half of the tape is made up of his side of telephone conversations. When he was silent too long, the tape stopped and one hears that infuriating beep, and the first few words of his next sentence are missing.

'Of course, he also had conversations with people in his office, and sometimes during those conversation he would take telephone calls.

'The tape is full of beeps, missing words, mumbled words, incomprehensible garble, and Chinese spoken too fast for me. Sometimes Chan and a visitor would both speak at the same time . . . sometimes they both shouted at the same time. Everyone around here smokes, have you noticed that?'

'Yes.'

'They talk with cigarettes dangling from their mouth. . . .' She sighed. 'The tape needs to be gone over by experts. All I got were snatches of conversation, words and phrases, sometimes a bit of give and take, usually just bits and pieces.'

'And you don't know who killed Chan?'

'No. There is a beep – which means the tape was stopped – then a bit of a phrase, incomprehensible, and the shot. Nothing after that. The tape stops.'

'Before that, what was on the tape?'

'Someone talking about an import permit for computers.'

'Okay.'

'And before that, an argument about money. It seems someone gave Chan money to give to people – I think in America – and he pocketed at least half of it, according to the man who shouted at him.'

'You said Chan was into human smuggling?'

'That was the subject of several conversations, I think. Hard to be sure. I got the impression that it would be better for everyone if the cargo didn't survive the voyage.'

'You aren't crying for China Bob?'

'I wouldn't mind throwing a shovelful of dirt in his face.'

'Hmm.' Jake took a sip of wine.

'Where's the tape now?' Callie asked. 'Did you leave it in the room?'

'It's in my pocket.'

'Oh. Okay.'

'Along with a pistol I took off a guy who was following me this morning when I went jogging.'

'You're kidding me.'

'Nope. A little automatic. Loaded.' Jake removed the man's wallet from another pocket and passed it to Callie. 'See if you can figure out who this guy is.'

She ignored the money, Hong Kong dollars equivalent to about forty dollars American, and examined each of the cards. 'I don't know many Chinese characters,' she said tentatively, 'but none of this stuff looks like an official ID card. I would think that in Hong Kong everything is in English and Chinese.'

She returned the documents to the wallet and passed it back. Jake took out the money and put it in his shirt pocket, so he could leave it on the table after lunch as a tip.

As they were eating lunch he realized that two people were watching him and Callie from the kitchen door and whispering together. One was a man who didn't look like he was kitchen help.

After a few minutes the man took a seat at an empty table by the door and devoted himself to studious contemplation of the menu.

'When we get back to the hotel,' Jake said to his wife, 'I want to see if I can get you a flight back to the States.'

'I don't want to go back alone.'

'And I don't want you in the middle of a civil war. I'm going to have a heart-to-heart talk with Cole, and then I think I'll go back, too. Sending me over here to root around was a bad idea from the get-go.'

'You're worried about the man who followed you this morning, aren't you?'

'I'm getting worried about everything. We're in way over our heads.'

As they rode the sampan back to the tour bus, he slipped the wallet into the water. When no one was looking, he did the same with the pistol.

Callie reached for Jake's hand. 'Come on, Romeo, hold my hand. We're smack in the middle of an exotic city and I could use a little romance.'

Lin Pe rode the tram down Victoria Peak. It was but a short walk from Rip and Sue Lin's house to the tramway, and the motorman always stopped on the way down when he saw her standing there. She stepped aboard and wedged herself in among a carful of plump, rosy-pink Germans. With barely a lurch the car continued its descent of the steep grade.

At the bottom she set off on foot, walking quickly, her small purse clutched tightly in her left hand.

Huge buildings rose on all sides, towering palaces of glass and steel. Around them traffic swirled on multilane streets that could be crossed only at over- or underpasses. Hiking the concrete canyons was strenuous, but Lin Pe could remember dawn-to-dark days in the rice paddies from her youth. Nothing could be as strenuous as those lean times, with too much work and not enough to eat.

The human sea thickened as she approached the bank square. Acres of people crowded the sidewalks and spilled into the streets. Most seemed content to stand right where they were since the bank square wasn't all that big. Still, Lin Pe pressed forward, worming her way through.

There were some soldiers about, but they were standing back, well out of the way. Lin Pe walked right by them and edged her way carefully into the middle of the square, where she finally found a tiny area of unoccupied concrete and sat.

The bank loomed before her like a dark, black cliff, blocking out the sun. When she looked straight up she could see a patch of blue sky.

She folded her hands in her lap and spoke to the woman beside her. They chatted politely for a moment – both had money in the closed bank – then fell silent, each lost in her own thoughts.

When Lin Pe had been very young there had been a man. He had worked hard and given her six children. One died in infancy; the three eldest she left behind with his parents after he died. The two youngest, Sue Lin and Wu, she carried away, one in each arm, when she decided she must go. Without her man, burdened with the children and his parents, both of whom were vigorous enough then but growing older, she would never be able to make it. She had too many children ever to attract another man. So she left.

She sat in the square thinking about the children she left behind, as she did for a few minutes every day. Finally her mind turned to fortunes. Thinking up fortunes had been the most important thing in her life for many years now, and she returned to it whenever the world pressed in.

'Go always toward the light' had been one of her favorites. The words seemed to mean more than they said, which was why the fortune appealed to her. She thought about it now, about what inner meaning might be hiding in the words.

By midafternoon Tang's officers believed they had enough soldiers to force the crowd to leave, so they sent a staff officer to man the loudspeaker mounted on a van.

Like a thick, viscous liquid, the thousands of people began slowly flowing outward from the bank square. The crowd was orderly and well behaved and obeyed the soldiers with alacrity.

Thirty minutes after the order was given, only a few hundred civilians were still in sight from Tang's third-story window.

He turned to his officers. 'Wait for more soldiers, you said, so we waited. And when told to go, the people went like sheep. For hours they sat here illegally, in open and notorious defiance of the government. They have made fools of us again.'

One of the senior colonels tried to argue that the reason the crowd dispersed in an orderly fashion was because there were so many troops in sight, but Tang was having none of it. The government had been defied; he could feel it.

'Another crowd may return tomorrow,' Tang said, 'so I want enough troops stationed on the streets to deny access to this square. And put tanks in the square. We will advertise our strength.'

One of the people who did not leave the square was Lin Pe. She was sitting against a curb with a flower bed behind her, and she was very small. The soldiers ignored her.

When she was almost the last civilian left in the square, Lin Pe slowly levered herself erect and turned her back on the bank.

Eighteen-year-old Ng Choy watched her leave. He didn't know her, of course. She was just a small, old woman, one of thousands he had seen in and around the square that day.

Ng Choy turned his attention back to the stain on the concrete where the man he had shot yesterday had fallen.

His rifle was heavy in his hands.

There were three of them, and they would probably have killed Tommy Carmellini if he hadn't been scanning the faces in the crowd. He was walking from the consulate toward the Star Ferry, trying to go with the ebb and flow of packed humanity. He was renting a room by the week in a cheap hotel in Kowloon until he found an apartment, and he was on his way there after work. Hordes of people jammed the sidewalks and spilled into the streets this afternoon, even more than usual for Hong Kong, a notoriously crowded city.

The eyes tipped him off. The man was fifteen feet or so away, standing by a power pole, when he saw Carmellini. His eyes locked on the American, who happened to glance straight at him. The man was several inches shorter than Carmellini and powerfully built. He left the spot where he had been standing on an interception course.

Instinctively, Carmellini turned and started the other way. And saw another set of brown eyes staring into his as a man closed in from the direction of a street vendor's cart.

Carmellini didn't hesitate. He leaped for this second man, so quickly that he took his assailant by surprise. Carmellini knocked the man down as he went over and through him and kept on going.

As he turned a corner he looked back, and that was when he realized there were three of them pushing and shoving people out of the way as they chased him.

Oooh boy!

Tommy Carmellini stepped off the jammed sidewalk and began running along the gutter, between the sidewalk and the traffic coming toward him. Behind him the three thugs did the same.

Of course he was unarmed.

Carmellini was carrying a thin attaché case that contained a Hong Kong guidebook, a Chinese-English phrasebook for tourists, and a Tom Clancy paperback. After he got through the first intersection he glanced behind him. His pursuers were successfully dodging traffic, still coming, so he tossed the case into the street and settled down to some serious running.

He loosened his tie and the top button of his shirt.

After three blocks the street became limited access and separated from the sidewalk. Carmellini stayed in the street.

The three thugs following had lost some ground.

As he went under an underpass a speeding truck grazed Carmellini and bounced him off the concrete abutment. He kept his feet but he lost a step or two. When he topped the underpass his pursuers were closer.

Oh, man! That damned tape. He didn't have it and he didn't know what was on it! Of course the guys behind him wouldn't believe *that*! No doubt they were out to get the tape and permanently shut his mouth.

A few more blocks and he was into the Wanchai District, today as tame and touristy as North Beach in San Francisco, but in its day home to some of the raunchiest whorehouses east of Port Said.

But how did they know about the tape?

As he ran he worked on that problem in a corner of his mind.

The crowd here was only a bit thinner than the throng in the Central District, but the night was young.

Running down the street in his suit and tie pursued by three thugs, looking futilely for a cop, Tommy Carmellini was a victim looking for a crime site. Twice he ran by knots of armed soldiers standing on street corners, and the soldiers made no move to stop him or the three men following.

Insane! Like something from a pee-your-pants anxiety nightmare.

He considered possible courses of action and rejected them one by one. Dashing through a nightclub, darting into a building, jumping on a moving truck . . .

When he saw the entrance to the MTR, the subway, he didn't hesitate. He charged down the stairs and hurtled the turnstile.

He went around two sharp turns . . . and there was his opportunity. About nine feet or so over his head was a scaffolding on the side of a wall, for repairing light fixtures or something.

Without even pausing, Carmellini launched himself. He caught the bottom pole – the scaffolding was of bamboo poles – and swung himself upward. He hooked a leg and was up, flat on the walkway, when the three men chasing him rounded the corner and shot underneath.

This wasn't the time or place for a breather.

Quick as a cat, Tommy Carmellini swung down and charged back up the stairs, fighting the stream of people coming down. Out on the street he slowed to a walk and joined the crowd flowing along Hennessey Road.

Kerry Kent. As he walked he remembered how she hugged him at the party as they waited for the car, subtly ran her hands over him. Could she be the rotten apple?

And if she wasn't, who was?

6

Jake and Callie Grafton had dinner in Tiger Cole's private apartment at the consulate. Jake wondered if he would have recognized the consul general if he had seen him on the street. Cole was several inches over six feet, with wide shoulders and thinning, sun-bleached hair. No doubt the hair was graying ... His eyes were as blue as ever and still seemed to look right through you, or perhaps it was only Jake's imagination, a trick of memory from years ago.

Small talk wasn't Cole's forte. He listened politely to Callie, who tried to fill the silence with the story of the conference fiasco, impressions of Hong Kong, and a running commentary on Jake's career through the years. She told him about Amy and about Jake's current assignment at the Pentagon, and wondered about Cole's life. His answers were short, almost cryptic, but he looked so interested in what she was saying that she kept talking. Finally, over the main course, she fell silent.

'You two are very lucky,' Cole said, 'to have found each other. You seem very happy together.'

'We are,' Jake Grafton said and grinned at his wife.

'I was married three times,' Cole continued, speaking softly. 'Had a girl by my first wife and a boy by my second. The boy died two years ago of a drug overdose. His heart just gave out. He'd been in and out of rehab facilities for years, could never kick the craving.' Cole stirred his dinner around on the plate with his fork, then gave up and put the fork down. He sipped at the wine, which was from California.

'I wasn't a good father. I never understood the kid or the demons he fought. I thought he was stupid and I guess he figured that out.'

'Jesus, Tiger!' Jake Grafton said, 'That's a hell of a thing to say!'

Cole looked at Callie. 'Now *that* is the Jake Grafton I remember. Was never afraid to say what was on his mind.'

Grafton finished the last of his fish and put his silverware on his plate.

'I wondered about you,' Cole continued. 'Wondered if you were still the way I remembered, or if you had turned into a paper-pushing bureaucrat as you went up the ladder.'

'I see you're still the silver-tongued smoothie who charmed your way through the fleet way way back when,' Jake shot back.

'Yep, still an asshole.' Cole flashed a rare grin. 'My presence in the diplomatic game is a stirring testament to the power of political contributions. I knew you were wondering – that's the explanation in a nutshell.'

'You owe Callie an apology for sitting there like a bump on a log letting her carry the conversation.'

Cole bowed his head toward Callie. 'He's right, as usual. I apologize.' She nodded.

'When I saw the newspaper article a couple years ago announcing your appointment, I had a chuckle,' Jake said. 'You're so perfectly suited for the diplomatic corps, why'd you take this appointment?'

'After the kid died I needed to get the hell out. I was wasting my life with people with too much money and not enough humanity. I didn't like them and I didn't like the man I had become. When this opportunity came I grabbed for it like a drowning man going after a rope.'

'You certainly had some interesting experiences in Silicon Valley,' Jake commented. 'You helped design key networking software, you started a company that got one of the biggest contracts to make the Chinese telephone and air traffic control systems Y2K compliant ... Certainly sounds as if you had your plate full.'

'You did some checking on me before you came to Hong Kong.'

Jake Grafton chuckled. 'I did. I made some inquiries when I got the chance to come to the conference here with Callie.'

'The company did the bulk of the Y2K China stuff after I left.'

'You were over here then, weren't you?'

'That's right. I had to put my shares in a blind trust.'

'So just how advanced are the Chinese computer systems?'

Cole made a face. 'They've bought some state-of-the-art stuff. Hong Kong is as wired as any American city. On the mainland it's a different story; only the most obvious public applications have been computerized. The reason their growth rate is so high is that they are leapfrogging tech levels. For example, the first telephone system some cities are getting is wireless.'

Cole fell silent. It was obvious he didn't want to talk about computers or high tech, so Callie changed the subject. 'Tell us about Hong Kong,' she said.

A glimmer of a smile appeared on Cole's face, then quickly vanished. This was a subject that interested him. 'The rich are getting richer and the poor are getting left farther behind. That happens throughout the industrial world, but in China there is no social mobility mechanism. If you are born a poor peasant you can never hope to be anything else. In an era of rapid change, that hopelessness becomes social dynamite. The reality is that the forces of social, economic, and political change are out of everyone's control, and the dynasty of Mao Tse Tung is numbered. Every day the tensions are ratcheted tighter, every day the pressure builds.'

'These demonstrations in the Central District that the government is dispersing with troops – what is that all about?'

'A Japanese bank failed and the depositors lost their money. The Chinese government doesn't want to attempt to overhaul the banking system, which is state-owned and insolvent. The government has used the banks to fund bad loans to state-owned heavy industry. They can't fix the system, so they ignore the problem.'

'Isn't that dangerous?'

Cole shrugged. 'The state-owned industries and the banks are insolvent. To wipe out all the debts is to admit that socialism is a failure and fifty years of policy has been one massive error. To make that admission is to forfeit their mandate to rule.'

'So there's no way out?'

'The crunch is inevitable.'

'Since Callie got thrown off the platform at her conference and these demonstrations keep getting bigger and bigger, we thought we might go home early,' Jake said, stretching the truth only a little. 'I called the airlines this afternoon with no luck. There are no seats at any price. Everyone and their brother is trying to get out of Hong Kong.'

'A lot of people are worried. They certainly ought to be.'

'Someone said the troops are after a political criminal.'

'The troops are hunting a man named Wu Tai Kwong, public enemy number one, which is a measure of how paranoid the government has become. The man who stood up to them in Tiananmen Square in 1989 has become a symbol of resistance and must be ruthlessly crushed.'

'One brave man,' Jake commented.

'Ah, yes. Courage. Courage, daring, the wisdom to wait for the moment, and the wit to know it when it arrives. That's Wu Tai Kwong.'

'You speak as if you know him,' Callie observed.

'In some ways, I think I do,' Tiger Cole replied thoughtfully.

'So you think communism will collapse in China?'

'Communism is an anachronism, like monarchy. It's died just about everywhere else. It'll die here one of these days. The only question is when.'

'What does Washington say about all of this?' Jake wondered.

Tiger Cole chuckled, a dry, humorless noise. 'Wall Street doesn't like revolutions, and the market is the god Americans worship these days.' He talked for several minutes of the politics driving Washington diplomacy.

Later, as they stood at the window staring up the unblinking commercial signs on the tops of the neighboring skyscrapers, Cole said, 'The industrial West is operating on the same fallacy that brought the British to Hong Kong a century and a half ago. They think China is a vast market, and if they can just get access, they will get rich selling Western industrial products to people so poor they can barely feed themselves. "It will work now," the dreamers say, "because the Chinese are going to become the world's premier low-cost labor market, earning real money manufacturing goods to be sold in the industrial West."' Cole threw up his hands.

Callie asked, 'Do China's Wu Tai Kwongs have a chance?'

'I think so,' Tiger Cole said. 'The little people have everything to gain and nothing to lose. The king has everything to lose and nothing to gain. There is only one way that contest can end.'

'It's going to cost a lot of blood,' murmured Jake Grafton.

'Lots of blood,' Tiger agreed. 'That too is inevitable. In China anything worth having must be purchased with blood.'

Tommy Carmellini didn't go to his hotel in the evening; he went back to the consulate. He found the equipment he wanted on the shelves in the basement storage room, signed it out, then went upstairs to steal an attaché case. He found a leather one he liked in the CIA spaces under one of the desks. It was a bit feminine for his tastes, yet Kerry Kent would never miss it. Her desk was locked, of course, but the simple locks the furniture manufacturers put on the drawers could be opened with a paper clip. Carmellini settled down to read everything Kent had in her desk.

Letters from England – he gave those only a cursory glance. Lots of travel brochures, letters from girlfriends, two from men – lovers, apparently – a checkbook. He went through the checks, used her pocket calculator to verify that she was indeed living within her income, examined the backs and margins of the check register to see if by chance she had jotted down a personal identification number. Indeed, one four-digit number on the back of the register was probably just that. Tucked under the checks was a bank debit card.

Well, it was tempting. She had caused him a bad moment this evening. Either she sent the thugs or someone she reported to made the call, he felt certain.

Her desk took an hour. He checked his watch, then began on the desks of his CIA colleagues. All the classified documents were supposed to be locked in the fireproof filing cabinets or the safe. Tonight didn't seem like the evening to open those, but perhaps tomorrow night or the night after.

He was working on the boss's desk when he heard someone coming. He closed the drawers, went to his own desk, and selected a report from the in-basket. He had it open in front of him when one of the marines from the security detail stuck his head in.

'How's it going, sir?' the lance corporal asked.

'Just fine. Everything quiet?'

'As usual.'

'Terrific.'

'Gonna be much longer?'

'Couple hours, I think.'

Twenty minutes per desk was sufficient for each of the three men. Other than personal items of little significance, Carmellini found nothing that aroused his curiosity.

Since he was doing desks tonight, he decided he might as well do Cole's. The consul general's office was locked, of course, but Carmellini had the door open in about eighty seconds.

A reasonable search of the bookcases, desk, and credenza would take a couple of hours. He checked his watch. The night was young.

Tommy Carmellini picked the locks on Cole's desk, opened the drawers, and began reading.

Tiger Cole had just said good-bye to the Graftons when his telephone rang. 'Tiger?'

He recognized the voice. Sue Lin Buckingham. She didn't waste time on preliminaries. 'I know Rip would want you to know, so I called. He's in jail. The authorities shut down the *Post* today and arrested him.'

'Have you called a lawyer?'

'Lin Pe called Albert Cheung. I think Albert will get him out of jail tomorrow.'

'Tell Rip to come see me.'

'I'll tell him.'

Cole hung up the phone and poured himself another glass of California Chardonnay.

He snorted, thinking about Jake Grafton and the innocent grin that had danced across his face when he admitted he had 'made some inquiries.' Yeah. Right. Grafton had probably read his dossier cover to cover.

So he already knew that Cole's company did all the Y2K testing and fixing on some of China's largest networks . . .

Hoo boy. Talk about irony! He had thought the U.S. government would take months to figure out what happened in Hong Kong. It turned out some dim bulb in Washington who didn't have one original thought per decade decided to send Jake Grafton to look around.

Cole took another sip of white wine and contemplated the glass. He had spent most of his professional life around very bright people, some of them technical geniuses. Jake Grafton was a history major, bright enough but no genius, the kind of guy many techno-nerds held in not-so-secret contempt.

Grafton's strengths were common sense and a willingness to do what he thought was right regardless of the consequences. Cole remembered him from Vietnam with startling clarity: No matter what the danger or how frightened he was, Jake Grafton never lost his ability to think clearly and perform flawlessly, which was why he was the best combat pilot Cole ever met.

Yes, Cole thought, recalling the young man he had flown with all those years ago, Jake Grafton was a ferocious, formidable warrior of extraordinary capability, a precious friend and a deadly enemy.

Perhaps it was Cole's good fortune that fate had brought Grafton here. His talents might be desperately needed in the days ahead.

Cole checked his watch, then walked out of the apartment, locking the door behind him.

The sign on the door said, 'Third Planet Communications.' Cole used his key.

The office suite was on the third floor of a building directly across the street from the consulate. As luck would have it, Cole could look out his office window directly into the Third Planet suite.

With several hundred of the brightest minds in Hong Kong on its payroll, Third Planet was an acknowledged leader in cutting-edge wireless communications technology. In the eighteen months it had been in business it had become one of the leading wireless network designers and installers in Southeast Asia. Although Cole had put up the capital to start Third Planet, he didn't own any of the stock. In fact, the stock was tied up in so many shell corporations that the ownership would be almost impossible to establish. Cole was, however, listed on the company disclosure documents as an unpaid consultant, just in case any civil servant got too curious about his occasional presence on the premises.

Tonight Tiger Cole walked through the dark offices to a door that led to a windowless interior room. A man sitting in front of the door greeted him in Chinese and opened the door for him.

The lights were full on inside the heavily air-conditioned room, which was stuffed with computers, monitors, servers, routers – all the magic boxes of the high-tech age.

Five people were gathered around one of the terminals, Kerry Kent, Wu Tai Kwong, Hu Chiang, and two of Third Planet's brightest engineers, both women. Cole joined them.

'We're ready,' Wu said and slapped Cole on the back.

Another warrior, Cole thought, shaking his head, a Chinese Jake Grafton.

'Is the generator in the basement on?' Cole asked. Through the years he had noticed that these kinds of petty technical details often escaped the geniuses who made the magic.

Yes, he was informed, the generator was indeed running.

'Let's do it,' Cole said carelessly, trying not to let his tension show.

One of the female engineers began typing. In seconds a complex diagram appeared on the screen. Everyone watching knew what it was: the Hong Kong power grid. The engineer used a mouse to enlarge one section of the diagram, then did the same again.

Finally she sat looking at a variety of switches.

The other engineer pointed with a finger.

The mouse moved.

'Now we see if the people of China will be slaves or free men,' Wu said.

Months of preparation had gone into this moment. If the revolutionaries could control China's electrical power grids, they had the key to the country. Hong Kong was the test case.

The engineer at the computer used one finger to click the mouse.

The lights in the room went off, then came back on as the emergency generator picked up the load in the office suite. The computers, protected from power surges and outages by batteries, didn't flicker.

Cole and the other witnesses rushed from the room, charged across the dark office to the windows that faced the street.

The lights of Hong Kong were *off*!

Tears ran down Cole's face. He was crying and laughing at the same time. He was trying to wipe his face when he realized Wu was pounding him on the back and Kerry Kent was kissing his cheeks.

When Cole got his eyes swabbed out, he looked across the street at the consulate. The emergency generator there had come on automatically, so the lights were back on.

Tiger Cole wondered how long it would be before it occurred to Jake Grafton to ask if Cole's California company had worked on the computers that controlled the Hong Kong power grid.

As they rode the ferry back to Kowloon, Jake asked Callie, 'Did you recognize his voice?'

'Yes. He talked to Chan about computers. Chan was trying to cheat him.'

'But you don't know if he killed Chan?'

'The identity of the killer is impossible to determine by listening to the tape.'

'May I send it off to Washington?'

'Jake, do whatever you think is right.'

'Well ...'

'You didn't tell Tiger why you are here.'

'I thought I'd call him tomorrow. Before we got down to business I wanted a social evening.'

'I'm not going with you for that.'

'I should see him alone,' Jake agreed.

They had just gotten off the ferry on the Kowloon side and were walking toward their hotel when the lights went off. One second the city was there, then it wasn't. The effect was eerie, and a bit frightening.

Callie gripped Jake's arm tightly.

When the electricity went off all over the city of Hong Kong, it also failed at the new airport on Lantau Island. And in the air-traffic-control rooms at the base of the tower complex. Fortunately there were only a few airplanes under the control of the Hong Kong sector, and those were mostly freighters on night flights.

The air-traffic-control personnel worked quickly to get the emergency generators on so that the radars could be operated and the computers rebooted. The computers were protected by batteries that should have picked up the load but for some reason didn't. The emergency generators were on-line in three minutes and the radars sweeping the skies in three and a half.

The computers, however, were another matter. When the controllers finally got one of the computers on-line, the hard drive refused to accept new data via modem. Manually inputted data was changed in random ways – flight numbers were transposed, altitude data were incorrect, way points were dropped or added, and the data kept changing. It was almost as if the computer had had a lobotomy.

The second computer had the same problem as the first, and so did the third. The controllers worked the incoming flights manually, but without the computers they were in a severely degraded mode.

Inside the new, modern, state-of-the-art terminal, conditions were worse than they were in the tower. The restoration of power via emergency generators brought the lights back on, but the escalators wouldn't work, the automated baggage system was kaput, none of the flight display screens worked, the people-mover train refused to budge – its doors were frozen in place – and the jetways that allowed access to and from the planes could not be moved. Fortunately there were few passengers in the terminals and concourses, but those who were there were trapped until service personnel could get to them.

When power was finally restored from the main feeds, the computers still refused to work. The airline companies' reservations computers, fax machines, and Internet terminals seemed to be working fine, but the airport had ceased to function.

The technicians in the Hong Kong harbormaster's office were also having problems. The radars that kept track of the myriad of ships, barges, tugs, and boats of every kind and description in Victoria Harbor and the strait were working, but the computer that processed the information and presented it to the harbor controller was no longer able to identify or track targets. When the technicians tried the backup computer, they found it had a similar disease.

The people who had caused these problems sat and stood in front of the computer monitors at Third Planet Communications in a merry mood. Someone opened a bottle of Chinese wine, which they drank from paper cups.

The virus programs they had written and loaded on the affected computers seemed to be working perfectly. As Cole explained to Wu and

Kent all those months ago, 'Remember the chaos that was supposed to happen when Y2K rolled around, and didn't? We must make it happen now. Revolutions are about control, which is the essence of power: We must take control away from the Communists. When the Communists lose their power they lose their leadership mandate. It's as simple as one, two, three.'

Tonight Cole told Wu, 'The revolution has begun.'

He shook hands all around and headed for the door with a light step. Tomorrow would be a hell of a day and he needed some sleep.

Tommy Carmellini hailed a taxi in front of the consulate. The driver took him back to his hotel via the Cross-Harbor Tunnel, creeping along through the blacked-out city with a solid stream of cars and trucks.

The rear door of the hotel was locked. To discourage thieves, no doubt, Carmellini thought as he opened it with a pick. The job took less than a minute. With the electricity off, of course there was no alarm when the door opened. There wouldn't have been an alarm even if the power had been on – the door wasn't wired, a fact Carmellini had ascertained fifteen minutes after he checked into the place.

He went up the back stairs and carefully unlocked his room. An old-fashioned metal key, thank God, because the card scanners in use at the new hotels would not be working, leaving all the patrons locked out of their rooms.

No one was in the room waiting for him.

Carmellini changed into black trousers, a long-sleeved dark shirt, and tennis shoes. The equipment from the consulate went into a knapsack, as did a roll of duct tape, a small flashlight, a glass cutter, a few small hand tools, and an extensive assortment of lock picks: everything necessary for a quiet night of burglary.

Kerry Kent lived in an apartment house on a side street off Nathan Road, a mile or so north of the Star Ferry landing at Tsim Sha Tsui. The building was about ten stories high, filled the block, and was ten or fifteen years old, Tommy Carmellini thought.

The street was unnaturally quiet. A few people were up and about at two in the morning, but without electrical power to drive the gadgets, the night was very still. Carmellini could hear traffic on Nathan Road and, from somewhere, the rumble of a train.

He checked the scrap of paper where he had written the apartment number.

Kent's pad should be on the seventh floor, he decided, and went into the building to examine the apartment layout. The elevators weren't working so he climbed the dark staircase. Okay, the first floor was the one above the ground floor, so she would be on the eighth floor.

He walked along the hall until he found the apartment that corresponded to hers, which was twenty-seven.

Back outside on the sidewalk he examined the windows and balconies, counted upward. Okay, Kent's was the balcony with the two orange flowerpots and the bicycle chained to the rail.

He stood on the sidewalk just a moment, adjusting his backpack, listening, looking. . . .

When he was sure no one was observing him, Tommy Carmellini leaped from the sidewalk and grasped the bottom of the wrought-iron slats in the railing on the first-floor balcony. He could tell by the feel that the iron was rusty. Would it hold his weight?

Using upper-body strength alone, he drew himself up to the edge of the balcony floor and looked. And listened.

When he was convinced it was safe, he pulled himself up hand over hand until he could hook a heel over the rail, which squealed slightly in protest.

In seconds he was balanced on the rail, still listening . . .

He straightened, examined the underside of the floor of the balcony above him. He reached up for the rails, grasped them, and gradually gave them his weight, making sure the slats and railings were not too rusty or broken.

Up the side of the building he went, floor by floor, silently and quickly. Two minutes after he left the street, he was crouched on Kerry Kent's balcony examining the door, which was ajar. For ventilation, probably, since the night was warm and pleasant. As he listened for sounds from inside the apartment, he examined the windows of the apartments across the street, looking for anyone who might have watched him climb the side of the building.

Only when he felt certain that he was unobserved did he remove two tiny remote microphones, bugs, from his backpack, and a roll of duct tape. Using a knife, he trimmed two pieces of tape about two inches long from the roll and stuck them on the front of his shirt, where they were accessible. Then he returned the knife and tape roll to the backpack.

Due to the low probability that Kent routinely swept for bugs, these would transmit to a recorder as long as their batteries lasted, a time frame that depended on how many hours a day noise was generated in the apartment. They should last a couple of weeks if she didn't watch too much television or leave the radio on continuously. Months if electric power wasn't restored to the building.

The recorder had to be nearby, outside if possible, where Carmellini could get at it without too much effort. He planned to find a place to install it after he got the microphones in place.

Just to be on the safe side, he removed the backpack, which contained the burglary tools he wouldn't need since she left the sliding glass door ajar, and placed it on the floor out of his way.

Now he got to his feet, crouched to present as small a silhouette as possible to any casual observer, and inched the door open with his latex-clad fingertips. Applying steady pressure, he got the door moving and kept it moving, as slowly as possible.

When he had it open enough, about fourteen inches, Carmellini stood, turned sideways, and stepped in.

Moonlight was the only illumination. As his eyes adjusted to the gloom Carmellini could see that the apartment consisted of just one room and a bath. The kitchen area, a sink and stove, was located in the inside corner of the room to the right of the door. The area to the left of the door was the bathroom. The rest of the apartment, which was about the size of a standard American motel room, contained a Western-style bed, a few chairs, and a dresser. A television sat atop the dresser. Posters of famous paintings adorned the walls.

And in the bed, asleep apparently, were Kerry Kent . . . and a man. From this angle Carmellini could see only his hair – the man appeared to be Chinese. Kent's bare leg stuck out from under the sheet and light blanket that covered them.

Carmellini stood in the darkness listening. Heavy, deep, rhythmical breathing.

From where he was standing he examined the apartment, looking for a place for the bugs.

The head of the bed certainly looked inviting. It was some kind of wooden latticework; he could reach in and stick a bug on the back of the top of the headboard. It should be out of sight there and safe enough, unless someone moved the bed and examined the headboard.

The other one . . . perhaps under the bedside nightstand that held the telephone.

The decisions made, Tommy Carmellini stepped forward with bugs and tape ready.

Like a silent shadow he moved to the edge of the bed and bent down. He reached up under the nightstand and was affixing the first bug when Kerry Kent's deep breathing stopped.

She was facing away from him, thank God, but she might turn over.

He froze.

Yes, she was turning toward him. He waited until she had completed her move and was breathing regularly again, then he felt to make sure the tiny transmitter's antenna was hanging down freely. It was. Now he slowly stood, staying perfectly balanced, moving at the speed of a glacier, making no noise at all.

To get the other bug behind the headboard meant that he had to reach across her, above her face, and put it in place without jiggling the headboard in any way, for the movement of the headboard would be transferred to the bed.

He didn't let his limbs come to a stop but stayed fluidly in motion, each move thought out and planned so that he stayed balanced on both feet.

He got the tape, with the bug in the center of it, in the proper position and pressed firmly so that it would stick to the wood. The antenna seemed to be hanging in place behind one of the lattices.

He had pulled his arm back and was ready to turn when her breathing changed abruptly and she awoke. One second she was asleep, the next she was awake. Just like that.

Carmellini stood frozen. He was about eighteen inches from her head. If she decided to get up to go to the bathroom, this was going to get very interesting.

Can a person feel the presence of another human being, one absolutely silent and motionless?

There are those who swear they can. Tommy Carmellini believed that some people could, and he stood now willing his heart to beat slowly lest she hear it.

For the first time he was also aware of the faint voices and traffic rumble that could be heard through the open balcony door, which had of course been almost closed before he arrived. Would she notice the noise? Or the coolness of the night air?

She turned in bed again, rubbed against the sleeping man.

Oh, great! She'll wake him!

She mumbled something in Chinese ... and the man stirred.

He turned, put his arm around her.

Seconds passed, his breathing deepened.

Tommy Carmellini realized he was sweating. Perspiration was trickling down his nose, down his cheeks. He dared not move ...

If I don't relax, she's going to smell me!

The seconds dragged. She adjusted her position in the bed ... and finally, little by little, her breathing slowed and grew deeper.

Carmellini began moving toward the open door. He didn't walk, he flowed, gently, steadily, smoothly....

On the balcony he debated if he should close the door. If it made a noise now ... no! The risk was too great.

After scanning the other balconies and the apartment buildings across the street to ensure he didn't have an audience, Carmellini went over the rail. He leaned back, checked the balcony below as best he could, then lowered himself onto the railing. Balancing carefully, he released his grip on the wrought-iron slats above and coiled himself to go down another floor.

In half a minute he was standing on the street. He was wiping his hands on his trousers when the electrical power was restored to the neighborhood, bringing the lights on. Televisions and radios that had been on when the power failed blared into life.

What is it his mother used to say? 'You're going to get caught, Tommy, one of these days. Sneaking around like you do ain't Christian. People'll get mean when they catch you sneaking, one of these days.'

One of these days, he thought. *But not today.*

He began looking for a place where he could hide the recorder.

As Tommy Carmellini walked south on Nathan Road toward his hotel, a van whipped to the curb and a man jumped out with a bundle of paper in his arms. He put the stack on top of a newspaper dispenser, cut the plastic tie that bound it together, then got back in the van, which rocketed off down the street.

Carmellini paused by the stack and took a sheet off the top. A flyer of some type. In Chinese, of course.

He folded it and put it in his pocket.

Wonder what that is all about?

7

Governor Sun Siu Ki didn't have newspapers to worry about this morning; he had shut down the politically incorrect rags and jailed the editors. No, the rag du jour was a flyer that had been distributed by the tens of thousands throughout the Special Administrative Region, the old colony, of Hong Kong.

The flyer, titled *The Truth,* was a single sheet of paper printed on both sides with Chinese characters. It contained a highly critical account of the Bank of the Orient debacle and shooting, blaming the entire incident on the Chinese government's attempted looting of the bank and on the overaggressiveness of the People's Liberation Army. The sheet called for mass demonstrations to demand that the authorities cease requiring bribes from banks, release the jailed newspaper editors, and allow the publication of uncensored news. The sheet was signed by a group calling itself the Scarlet Team.

'This is outrageous, inflammatory, antirevolutionary criminal propaganda,' the governor told his assistant, who agreed completely with that assessment. 'Have the police find the people who did this and arrest them.' Sun hammered on the desk with his fist as he added, 'I will not tolerate these criminal provocations! Find these people!'

'Yes, sir,' said the aide.

The governor wadded up the offending flyer and threw it into the wastebasket beside his desk.

He took a deep breath, then tackled the next item on the morning's agenda. 'Has electrical power been restored throughout the city?'

'Yes, sir. Apparently so. The engineers are still trying to determine why the load was lost in the first place. Unfortunately, power fluctuations apparently caused extensive damage to the computer systems at Lantau Airport and Harbor Control.'

'When will the systems be operational again?'

The aide didn't know the answer to that one. He would find out and report back, he said, which didn't please the governor.

Everything seemed to be going wrong all at once. As if to emphasize that fact, the secretary came in to announce that the ministry in Beijing was on the telephone.

The minister was worried. Questions were being asked at the highest levels. Did Sun need more help handling the situation in Hong Kong?

'No, certainly not,' Sun replied. 'Criminal elements are taking advantage of events that are out of anyone's control, but the government is firmly in charge.'

Because Albert Cheung was somebody important, the warden of the prison had Rip Buckingham brought to his office. There was a room in the prison for lawyers and clients to meet, but it consisted of a long table with chicken wire down the middle and a guard at each end. There was no privacy.

Albert had known the Chinese warden a long time – he slipped him a handful of currency when they shook hands. After the guards brought Rip, the warden and guards left together, leaving Rip and Albert alone.

'I thought Lin Pe might call you,' Rip said, sinking into a stuffed chair. 'You'll have to excuse my odor. They're having trouble with the showers and soap.'

'Lin Pe called me yesterday. Then I went to see Governor Sun. We negotiated. I went back this morning and we negotiated some more. To make a long story short, he wants a hundred thousand Hong Kong.' Actually Sun Siu Ki had wanted two hundred thousand, but Albert had beaten him down. This he didn't mention. He didn't like to discuss money with his clients, except when absolutely necessary. Discussing money offended his sense of dignity.

Rip grunted noncommittally. He was thinking how clean and comfortable Albert Cheung looked. Wearing an impeccable gray suit and conservative silk tie, he looked as if he had just stepped out of the Pall Mall Club in London. Rip was wearing filthy khaki chinos, a nondescript blue shirt, and penny loafers without socks. His clothes looked like he had worn them day and night for a month, although it had been only two days.

'Your wife wants you home,' Albert said tentatively.

Rip Buckingham didn't want to talk about his wife. She had come to visit him yesterday and the prison staff had refused to let her in unless she paid a bribe. That, Rip knew, was pretty much standard procedure these days. Sue Lin refused to pay. Or so one of the guards told him last night. That certainly sounded like her, Rip reflected. She was tough, and Rip liked that a lot.

He picked up a pencil from the warden's desk and stroked it with his fingers as he asked, 'What do I have to do to reopen the paper?'

'Sun and I did discuss that matter,' Albert acknowledged.

'How much?'

'Well, it's not that simple. Apparently people in Beijing have been talking to the governor.'

'Uh-huh.'

'You'll need to sign a contract with Xinhua for editorial services. That will cost you so much a month.' Xinhua, the New China News Agency, was the Communist government's propaganda organ.

'How much?' Rip asked idly.

'I don't know. It probably won't be nominal.'

'We sometimes run Communist government press releases as news,' Rip told the lawyer, 'but only if they're newsworthy. My staff decides. You'd be amazed at the reams of trash bureaucrats generate. My readers aren't interested.'

'You don't have to print anything you don't wish to print. However, the agency will assign an editor, who must approve anything that you do want to print.'

'Censorship.'

'Call it that if you like.'

'For Christ's sake, Albert!'

'Rip, be reasonable. This isn't a comfortable little chunk of England anymore, with British judges and British law. *This is China!* You have to go along to get along.'

Buckingham said a dirty word.

'Give me the authorization to pay Sun and I'll get you out of here. You think about the paper. We'll talk later.'

Rip broke the pencil in half and tossed the pieces on the warden's desk. 'I won't publish the paper under those conditions,' he said. 'I can tell you that right now. But it isn't my paper. It belongs to Buckingham News, Limited, which may soon be looking for a new managing editor.'

'Buckingham News, that's your father, right?'

'Rich owns about sixty percent of it, I think. My sisters and I own small pieces, some of the stock is in executive compensation plans, and the rest is owned by some hot dollies Dad took a fancy to. He gave them stock certificates instead of diamonds.'

'Does that work?' Albert asked curiously.

'Dad says it depends on how many shares you give them,' Rip said, his face deadpan. He shrugged. 'Buckingham News pays no dividends, there's no market for the stock, and Dad has absolute control. About all a shareholder can hope for is that the certificates will be worth real money someday. One might think of it as a sort of pension plan for the women.'

'What does Mr. Buckingham do with the profits if he doesn't pay dividends?' asked the Hong Kong attorney. 'I assume there are profits.'

'He buys more newspapers, cable television networks. He got into satellite distribution of television signals years ago. He said that technology would ultimately have a greater impact on the human race than the invention of movable type. Certainly it's going to have a greater impact on the third world.'

Rich may be a noxious old fossil, his son reflected, but he had vision. Rip told the lawyer, 'As a matter of fact, I think Buckingham News owns the company with about fifty percent of the satellite dish business in Hong Kong.'

'Very progressive,' said Albert Cheung.

'In any event, the women seem happy and Dad appears to be doing all right.'

'Wonderful, wonderful.'

'Quite. But I don't know what Dad will do about the *Post*. The only principle to which he is irrevocably and totally committed is making money.'

'Yes.'

'A lot of money.'

Albert Cheung looked interested. 'I like money myself,' he remarked blandly.

'Go pay the man and get me the hell out of here,' Rip Buckingham told the lawyer. 'The company in this place is fascinating but the food isn't anything to brag about.'

'Mr. Cole, there's a Rear Admiral Grafton on line one.'

'Thank you,' Cole said to his secretary and picked up the phone.

'Hello, Jake.'

'I just called to thank you for last night. It was good seeing you again.'

'And you.'

'I was wondering if I could drop by today and have a chat about government business? Could you give me an hour or so?'

'Come at lunch and I'll buy.'

'About twelve?'

'See you then.'

When Sue Lin heard her brother, Wu, come in, she went downstairs to his room and knocked. He immediately opened the door. He was here to change clothes, which was about all he ever did at this house.

'We need to talk,' she said softly in English, worried as always that the domestics would overhear.

Only two years older than Sue Lin, Wu had always awed her, ever since she could remember. Never had she met a man with his inner calm, a man whose strength radiated like heat from a fire. He was, she thought, the most masculine of men, a man so strong emotionally and spiritually that nothing on this earth could shake him.

Of course he attracted people, men and women, like a magnet attracts iron filings. In a reflective moment Rip had compared Wu to Christ. 'If he was preaching a new religion he could convert the world,' Rip said, and Sue Lin thought Rip was probably right.

As Wu looked at her his face softened. 'Of course,' he said, nodding gently. 'May I continue to change, or would you like to go upstairs?'

'Go on,' she said, motioning toward the closet, and told him about Rip being arrested and the newspaper closed.

'I have heard,' Wu said. 'I am sorry for Rip.'

'Albert Cheung will get him out, but the paper . . . the governor will probably keep it closed.'

She sat in the only chair in the small room. 'The day has almost arrived, hasn't it?'

'Its coming was inevitable,' Wu replied calmly. Sue Lin had never seen him excited – she didn't think anything could disturb his inner peace.

'Rip is worried. If the authorities finally learn that you are my brother, Lin Pe's son, Rip thinks they will take their frustrations out on us.'

'Rip is probably correct,' Wu said softly. He rarely raised his voice. 'His understanding of the scope of the official mind seems quite complete.'

'He wants us to leave Hong Kong now.'

'Sister of mine, I advise you to obey your husband.'

'Mother will not leave.'

'Her destiny is not yours.'

'Wu, for God's sake, you must tell Mother to leave! She will listen to you! She ignores my pleas.'

Wu sat on the bed and took his sister's hand. 'Leaving China would cost Lin Pe her life. *This* is who she is. On the other hand, you have your husband, your life together, which you can live anyplace on the planet. Lin Pe does not have that.'

'Are you saying that Rip and I should leave you two here?'

'This country, these people, they are my life also.'

Sue Lin Buckingham jerked her hand from his grasp. 'I think the new maid is suspicious of you. She watches you from the window, pretends she knows no English when it is obvious she understands some of it. She may be a police spy.'

'What would you have me do?'

At that Sue Lin threw up her hands and left the room.

Albert Cheung drove Rip to the building that housed the newspaper. It was raining again, a steady drizzle. Albert wanted to take him home but Rip insisted on going to the office.

There were two policemen with shotguns standing under an overhang outside the building.

Albert pulled his Mercedes into the alley that led to the parking area in back. 'Thanks, Albert,' Rip said and released his seat belt.

As Rip reached for the door handle, Albert put a hand on his arm and said, 'Wait a minute, Rip. I want to give you some advice, if you'll listen.'

'I'll listen. I won't pay for your advice, but I'll listen.'

'It's time for you to go. Take your wife, go back to Australia. That is your place. That is where you belong.'

Rip growled and reached for the door handle.

'Listen to me,' Albert said sharply. 'The British are gone. For one hundred and fifty years this city was a part of Britain. It was as English as tea and toast. No more. Those days are *over*. And everyone has to adjust to the new reality.'

'I've adjusted. I just don't like it.'

'Like it or not, Hong Kong is now part of China, and China is an absolute dictatorship. The British ways – free speech, democracy, open, honest government, a tolerant, pluralist society, the rule of law, open debate about the public's business, fair play – all that is dying or dead. People here must jettison the old ways and adopt the new. They have no choice – *they have to do it!* I've been reading your paper: You rail against the incoming tide.'

Rip tried to rebut Albert Cheung. 'I have tried to fairly – '

'"Fairly"? Don't be ridiculous. *Fair* is a British concept, not Chinese. There is nothing you can do.'

'This is my home, too,' Rip said savagely.

'Stop playing the fool. Get on a plane.'

Rip sat for a moment listening to the slap of the windshield wipers. 'Why don't you leave?' he asked the lawyer.

'I happen to be Chinese, you may have noticed. And there is money to be made here.'

'There are six million people in Hong Kong without anyplace else to go.'

'You're wasting your breath trying to save the world, Rip. You won't get a halo. You won't even get a thank-you.'

'Don't charge me for this advice, Albert.' Rip got out of the car, shut the door firmly behind him.

Albert Cheung sped away without another look at Rip.

Maybe the cops would have let him in the building, maybe not; Rip didn't try. He went around back and unlocked his motorcycle, an old Harley-Davidson he had imported from Australia.

Motorcycles were popular in Hong Kong – mainly Japanese bikes, fast and fuel-efficient – but not as ubiquitous as they were in Singapore or Bangkok. The British always discouraged motor vehicles for private use by making it expensive to register one or get a driver's license. The Communists continued that policy. Still, a lot of people today had the money or political connections, so there were more and more motorcycles. Those who couldn't afford to go first-class rode Chinese iron. With no demand for forty-year-old Harleys, thieves weren't interested, or so the theory went. Rip always locked his anyway.

He turned on the fuel cock, adjusted the choke, and started kicking. The engine caught on the third kick.

763

He was warming the engine when the woman who ran a small newsstand across the street came looking for him.

'Rip, why have the police closed the building?' Originally from Hunan Province, she had lived in Hong Kong at least twenty years. Rip had deduced that one time by questioning her closely about Hong Kong news stories she could remember.

'The governor has ordered the paper closed, Mrs. Guo,' Rip told her. 'He didn't like what he read.'

'You did not go to jail? I heard they arrested you.'

'I went to jail.' He gave her a brief summary, then said good-bye. 'My wife is waiting for me. She worries.'

'Yes, yes. Go home to her.' Mrs. Guo went back along the alley with her head down, as if she were walking against a storm. Hard times ...

The Chinese are used to hard times, Rip reflected. They've never known anything else.

He put the motorcycle in motion.

The streets were still crowded. Traffic sprayed water on Rip, who had to concentrate to keep his motorcycle under control.

Rip had first seen Hong Kong as a teenager in the mid-eighties, when there were still vestigial traces of the nineteenth-century city, and large swatches remained unchanged from the days of World War II. Back then many people could talk for hours about the Japanese occupation from their personal experience. Not many of those old people were left, of course, and few people now asked about the old days. Nobody cared anymore.

That was the way of the world, Rip knew. Certainly the way of China. The past – good or bad – was soon forgotten. There was always today to be lived through and tomorrow to prepare for. Venerable ancestors were, of course, worthy and honorable and all that, but, alas, they were quite dead.

It was that Chinese focus on the now that intrigued Rip Buckingham. For the Chinese, he thought, all things were possible. Coolies and peasants from the rice paddies had built this modern city, were constantly transforming it, and in turn were transformed by it. It was an extraordinary metamorphosis.

Today not a single building remained from the nineteenth century. The commercial buildings were fifty-story-plus avant-garde statements in steel and glass. Mile after mile of high-rise apartment buildings housed more than six million people. The thought of living in one was a daunting prospect for Westerners, but the fact remains, six million people were decently housed.

As he rode the Harley through traffic and tried to ignore the drizzle and road spray, Rip Buckingham marveled again at the raw power of this great city. Chinese signs were freely intermingled with the logos of international corporations and brand names. Rip thought this mixture symbolic of Hong Kong, where East and West met, transforming both.

Hong Kong was a vast human stew, and by choice Rip was right in the middle of it.

He inched his way up the narrow, twisty roads that grooved the northern face of Victoria Peak, then guided the motorcycle into a driveway and triggered a radio-controlled garage-door opener in a house glued to the side of the peak. Buckingham News actually owned the place, which was a good thing since Rip could never have paid for it on his salary.

As he was getting off the machine inside the garage his wife came through the door.

'You're soaked,' she said.

'Doesn't matter. I stunk from jail.'

She kissed him.

He hit the button to close the outside door, then led her up the stairs to the living room. A large window looked out on the Central District and Kowloon across the strait. As Rip told his wife about jail and the governor, he automatically glanced outside. Kowloon was almost hidden in the rain and mist.

'I called your father.'

'What did he say?'

'Just that you should call when you could. I asked him if I should hire Albert Cheung, and he said yes.'

Rip stretched and nodded. 'I need to take a shower, put on some dry clothes. I'll call him later.'

'What are we going to do, Rip?'

'I don't know,' he said, meaning it. 'This place is our life. Sun Siu Ki just took it from us.'

'They won't let you keep publishing the *Post*.'

'I know.'

'Things are changing.'

'I know. *I know!* You told me. The police told me. Albert Cheung told me. I know, I know, and *goddamn*, I resent it.'

'Mother won't leave without my brother.'

Rip took his wife's hand. 'I know that, too,' he said gently and kissed her.

An hour later, after he had a long, hot shower and put on fresh clothes, Rip called his father's office in Sydney. Soon Rich's voice boomed through the instrument.

Rip told him about the cease publication order and the demands of Sun Siu Ki.

'Dad, I don't think we should run the paper under these conditions. It's censorship. Knuckling under to the Communists will cost Buckingham News its standing in the international community, and that ultimately will mean loss of ad revenue all over the globe.'

'That paper is worth a hundred million,' Richard Buckingham thundered into the telephone.

Rip had to hold the instrument away from his ear. The old man sounded like he was in the next room.

'Bloody Chinks! A hundred million!' Rich ripped off a couple oaths, but the volume was going down. 'All the bloody lies they've told the last fifteen or twenty years, about how great it was going to be in Hong Kong when they took over ... Makes me want to puke!'

'Yessir,' Rip agreed.

'And the bloody Brits.' Richard added them to his list. 'Believing those lies ...'

'Maybe it's time to pack it in,' Rip said reluctantly, trying to get back to the business at hand. 'Maybe in a few years the government here will see the benefits of a free press.'

'They don't really have a choice,' Richard rumbled. 'The world has outgrown censorship. But you're right – we can't buck the bastards head-on. Pay off the *Post* employees. Send me the names and qualifications of everyone who wants to work for another Buckingham paper and is willing to move. We'll see what we can do.' There was a second of dead sound, then he added, 'Move at their own expense, of course.'

'Yes, sir.'

'I'd like to see you and Sue Lin. Come on home.'

'In a few weeks. We have to wrap up some things here.'

'Righto, mate.'

'And Dad? Thanks.'

'For what?'

'For seeing this my way.'

'See you in a few weeks.'

Richard Buckingham hung up the telephone and sat staring out the window at the artsy-fartsy roof of the Sydney Opera House. He called in Billy Kidd, who had been his number two since Richard was the publisher, editor, and sports writer of the *Wangeroo Gazette*.

'The Commies have shut down the *Post* in Hong Kong,' he began. After Richard told Billy what he knew, he added, 'I want a story about the shutdown and I want it on the front page of every paper I own. Call Rip at home and have him write it. Use a file photo of him.'

'Righto.'

'Top of the front page, Billy.' Richard picked up a legal pad and pencil from his desk and handed it to Billy, who could take a hint. He began taking notes.

'Billy, someday those Commie bastards are going to regret screwing with me. Bad press is the only lever I have, and by God, I'm going to use it.'

Richard Buckingham got out of his chair and paced the office. 'Put the one-baby story on the telly chat shows again. More Falun Gong persecution stories. Bang the drum every day. And I mean every day, Billy. A new, different, bad slant each and every day.'

'Whatever you want, Richard. But I don't think that – '

'And I want something about those hundred million migrants roaming around China that the Commies are cracking down on. I'm tired of reading about these lawless vagrants threatening the economic prosperity of the new China. The corrupt, venal Communist regime is threatening the economic prosperity of the new China. They are prosecuting the harmless kooks in the Falun Gong movement, jailing people whose only crime is to want a little bit of life's sweetness. Massive pollution, sweatshops, child labor – China's the last big sewer left on earth, and that's the way we'll write it from now on. Fax it to the managing editor of every paper.'

Billy finished taking notes and asked sourly, 'Anything else?' He had been with Richard Buckingham too long to cower.

'Communism is as dead as Lenin. The Buckingham newspapers and television networks are going to trumpet that news loud and clear. Find a politico to write it, somebody important or somebody who wants to be important.'

'You – '

'And why does the free world tolerate the crimes against humanity that the Chinese government perpetrates on those who can't defend themselves? Maybe an article, "TIANANMEN SQUARE REVISITED."'

Billy scribbled furiously. 'You're the boss,' he said.

'You're damn right I am,' Richard roared. 'Those bloody Chinks didn't like the coverage they got from the *China Post* – they're going to shit when they see the press they're getting from now on. When anybody anywhere says anything bad about Red China, I want to read it in the papers and hear about it on the telly news shows. From this day forward Buckingham News is the world's foremost voice urging the overthrow of the Communists in Beijing.'

Rich punched the air and sat down. 'You and I are going to do at least one good thing before we go, Billy-boy,' he said conversationally.

Billy Kidd launched himself from Richard's office. Billy knew that when Richard was on a tear you didn't get many openings, so he bolted at the first one he saw.

An hour later Richard called Billy on the intercom. 'Don't we own a big piece of a direct TV company in Hong Kong?'

'That's right. China Television, Limited. Very profitable.'

'Sell it as fast as you can. Maybe a competitor will buy it. Get what you can and let's move on.'

'Richard, I know you're angry, but China Television is worth serious money. Satellite television is here now; China is on its way to becoming the largest market on earth. Those little dishes are selling like Viagra.'

Richard Buckingham's answer was matter-of-fact. 'I'm going to piss on a lot of Commies, Billy. I don't want something of mine hanging out where they can cut it off, throw it in the dirt, and stomp on it. Get rid of China Television – we'll take the loss out of their hides.'

Billy refused to quit. 'No one will pay what it's worth,' he insisted.

Richard was patient. 'Billy, with the Communists in power, nothing in China is worth real money. That's the lesson the Americans and British and Japanese are going to learn the hard way.'

A man was waiting on the street when Jake stepped out of the hotel. He was standing under an overhang to stay out of the rain. As Jake walked along the sidewalk with Callie's umbrella, the man got into a car that had been parked in the taxi space in front of the building.

Jake ignored the tail. He was acutely aware of the Chan tape in his pocket. For some reason he was relieved that he had ditched the wallet and pistol he had taken from the man who had followed him yesterday.

As he entered the ferry terminal, the car outside pulled to the curb, and two men got out of the rear seat.

Jake saw them board the *Star of the West* just before the gangplank came over. The second man aboard had a bandage on his head; this was the fellow whom Jake had relieved of wallet and pistol. He boarded on the lower deck. The other man came to the upper deck, where Jake was, but he stayed well away from the American.

Exiting the Central District ferry terminal, Jake hailed the only taxi he saw. He didn't bother checking to see what the men following him did.

When Jake entered Cole's office, Cole came around his desk and shook hands. 'We have a choice,' he said. 'We can have lunch served here, go to the cafeteria, or slip down the street to a restaurant with wine and all the trimmings. What will it be?'

'Here, if that's okay with you?'

'Here it is. Have a seat and let me talk to the secretary.'

In a few minutes Cole was back. He sat in one of the black leather guest chairs beside Jake.

'I guess I should have leveled with you last night,' Jake said. 'I'm here on official business. A lot of Washington bigwigs are getting nervous about the situation in Hong Kong. More to the point, they are getting nervous about China Bob Chan and your relationship to him. They managed to talk the White House into sending me over here to talk to you, see what I can find out, and report back.'

A look of puzzlement crossed Cole's face. 'Why you?'

'Someone found out that we flew together way back when, the politicians are embarrassed about China Bob, I was getting on a four-star's nerves at the Pentagon, someone with some stroke at the National Security Council thinks I can work miracles. It all happened at once, so here I am.'

768

'Uh-huh.'

'When this trip got suggested, I initially said no. Then Callie was asked to do the culture conference, sort of as a cover ...' He shrugged.

'Ask your questions.'

'Are you or your friends having me followed around town?'

'You're being followed?'

'Two men followed me here this morning. Presumably they're outside somewhere, waiting for me to come out.'

Cole looked genuinely surprised. 'Jake, I have no idea.'

'I guess it all boils down to this: Are you or are you not a member of a conspiracy to overthrow the government of China?'

Cole whistled. 'Jesus! You flew all the way over here from Washington to ask me that question?'

Jake Grafton scratched his head. 'Well, I think the folks in Washington expected me to be a bit more circumspect, but, essentially, yeah. If the answer to that question is no, the next question is, Have you ever given advice or anything of value to anyone whose goal is the overthrow of the government of China?'

Cole pinched his nose, looked at Grafton, and grinned. The grin started slowly and spread. Jake knew he didn't grin often.

Finally Cole broke into a laugh. He was still chuckling when the secretary came in with a tray. On the tray were two bowls of soup, several sandwiches, and a couple cans of Coke. Tiger Cole's face returned to its normal detached expression. As the man left the room the consul general muttered, 'I always serve American drinks to guests. Today is Coke day. Tomorrow is Pepsi.'

Cole tasted the soup. 'You are a rare piece of work, Grafton. When they taught you to go straight for a target way back when, you learned the lesson well.'

Jake tried the soup himself. It was something Chinese, a watery vegetable, okay but nothing to write home about. No crackers in sight. He popped the can of Coke and took a sip. At least the drink was cold.

Cole pointed his spoon at Jake, then decided to use the spoon on the soup. Once a chuckle escaped him.

They ate in silence. Finally Cole finished soup and sandwich and leaned back in his chair to sip on the soft drink.

'Do you know how ironic this is, that of all the people on this planet, you, Jake Grafton, are the one who comes flying out of my past to ask about my future.'

'I haven't asked about the future,' Jake shot back. 'It's the present the weenies in Washington are worried about.'

'Ah, yes. The present.'

Cole walked around the desk and stood at the window looking out. He couldn't see much, merely a gloomy forest of skyscrapers with glass sides on a dreary, rainy day.

'This warm front is supposed to get out of here tonight,' he said. 'The next three or four days will be bright and sunny.'

'Uh-huh.' Grafton finished his Coke and set the empty can on the tray along with the dirty dishes.

Cole returned to the desk, sat in his regular chair, folded his arms on the desk, and looked Jake Grafton in the eye. 'Some ground rules. We'll play this game my way or not at all.'

Grafton adjusted his position in his chair. 'What are the rules?'

'I'll answer your questions completely, frankly, truthfully, but you can't tell a living soul for one week.'

Jake thought about that. 'The problem,' he said after a bit, 'is that you are in the diplomatic service of the United States. If a private citizen wants to saddle up and ride off to a revolution, that's between him and whoever is running the universe this week. If a diplomat does it, that's a different case altogether.'

'A point well taken,' Cole said. 'I gave this some thought while we ate. Let's do this: If you will agree to the conditions I stated, complete silence for a week, I'll write out a letter of resignation, leave the date blank, and give it to you. You fill in the date anytime you wish and see that the people in Washington get it – no sooner than a week from today.'

Now it was Jake Grafton's turn to go to the window and look out. 'Why don't you just tell me some lie to get me out of your hair?'

'Ooh boy, that's rich! Coming from you. When they asked you way back when whether or not you had ever bombed an unauthorized target, what did you say?'

'I said yes.'

'Indeed you did. You were the rarest of rarities, a truly honest man. Sorry, but I don't have it in me to lie to Jake Grafton.'

'Listen, Tiger. I can't stay silent for a week. Not if you tell me you're up to something you shouldn't be up to.'

Cole cocked his head and looked at Jake with an odd expression. 'What should I be up to?'

'Don't give me that!'

'Do you know what these Communists are? Do you know what they represent?'

Jake Grafton leaned across the desk toward Tiger Cole. 'If the government of the United States told me to pull the trigger,' he whispered hoarsely, 'I'd be willing to personally send every Communist in the world straight to hell. But as long as I'm in the United States Navy I don't have the luxury of choosing that course of action without orders. Neither do you when you're representing the United States of America. Write out that resignation and date it today. I'll send it in for you.'

Cole leaned back in his chair and rubbed his eyes.

After a bit he asked, 'When are you going to send it in?'

Grafton threw up his hands. 'I don't know!'

Cole spun around to the PC that sat on a stand near the desk, turned it on, put stationery in the printer tray, and started typing. Three minutes later a letter rolled off the printer. Cole read it through, signed it, then handed it to Grafton.

Jake took his time reading the letter, then folded it carefully. 'Got an envelope?'

Cole got one from a drawer and handed it across the desk.

Jake put the letter in the envelope, then stowed it in an inside breast pocket of his sports coat.

'Any more questions?' Cole said.

'Want to tell me why?'

Cole leaned back in his chair and stretched. He looked out the window at the slabs of skyscraper glass while he collected his thoughts, then turned his attention back to Grafton.

'I should have died that December day in 1972 when I was lying in the jungle muck in Laos with a broken back. Would have died, too, if I had been flying with an average mortal man. But no! As fate would have it I was flying with Jake Grafton, the warrior incarnate. Jake Grafton wasn't leaving that jungle without me – it was both of us or neither of us. So he fought and we both lived. I can close my eyes and remember it like it was yesterday. That moment was the most important of my life.'

Cole turned toward the window and the gloomy, rainy day. 'And I remember the day I became a millionaire,' he continued, speaking softly. 'We did an initial public offering. I went from owing thirty-three thousand dollars in student loans and two thousand on an old Chevy to a net worth of twenty-three million bucks just like *that*!' He snapped his fingers, turned back toward Jake, and snapped them again.

'One day in September three years ago I became a billionaire. The tech stocks were going up like a rocket, the valuations were . . . but you know all that. You see, we designed software for complex data networks and wireless telephone systems and burglar alarms and car security systems and toys that talk . . . magic technoshit. Stuff. In a world full of stuff, we were the kings of the new magic stuff. The world beat a path to our door.

'So there I was, filthy rich, able to buy anything on the planet . . . and none of it meant pee-squat. My boy died of dope, and I got the hell out. That was where I was when I was asked to help overthrow the Communists.'

Tiger Cole leaned forward in the chair. 'I've been in Hong Kong two years and gave a hundred million or so to the revolution, and the value of my stock holdings has just kept climbing. I'm worth *two* billion dollars,

Jake. *Two billion!* I've squandered my life on bad marriages to stupid women. Wasted it, and the system gave me *two ... billion ... dollars.*'

Cole spread his hands, as if that explained everything. Obviously he thought it did.

'Who asked you to help overthrow the Communists?' Jake Grafton said.

'Ahh ...' A trace of a smile appeared on Cole's face. 'You already know or you wouldn't have asked.'

Jake Grafton stood, went to the door of the office, and pulled it open several inches. He looked back at Cole, still sitting behind the desk. 'Some dreams are bigger than others,' he said.

Cole nodded.

'The sandwich was okay. The soup's terrible.'

Jake Grafton pulled the door completely open and walked out of the office.

8

Rip Buckingham was on a squash court batting balls against the wall when Tiger Cole arrived at the athletic club. 'I heard the governor shut down the paper,' Cole said after he closed the door to the court.

'Yep. I spent a couple of nights in the can.'

'You've been begging for it for years.'

'Already I feel cleaner, closer to God. I'm going to try to get arrested more often, work up to once or twice a month.'

They played hard for twenty minutes, then returned to the dressing room. They were the only men in the shower. As the water ran, Rip told Cole, 'The rain is supposed to stop tonight. Wu says tomorrow is our day.'

'Okay.'

'Kerry is counting on your help with the computers.'

'I can't guarantee anything. We need another week to verify our methodology.'

'We don't have a week.'

'I didn't think he'd wait.'

'Hard to believe the time has come.'

Cole just nodded. He thought, life's transitions always come at the worst possible time.

'How about the governor? What is he saying to Beijing?' Rip knew that Cole had had the CIA bug City Hall.

'He doesn't have a clue,' Cole said. 'If the Chinese government knows what's going down, they haven't told him or Tang.'

'I'd like to bring Sue Lin and her mom to the consulate,' Rip muttered, barely loud enough for Cole to hear above the sound of running water.

'Rip, we've been all through that three or four times. Take them to the Australian consulate.'

'If it goes bad the PLA will overrun the Australians. The Americans are the only people they don't have the balls to take on.'

'Take the women to the airport tonight and put them on a plane to Sydney.'

'The old woman won't go, can't go – doesn't have a passport – and the daughter won't go without the old woman.'

'For Christ's sake! Have your father send a private jet; land them somewhere in the damned outback. There has to be at least one immigration official in Australia who can be bought.'

'There are probably dozens, but the women don't *want* to leave.'

'Rip, it's time to stop sweating the program. If we lose we'll all be dead. The women know that.'

'Jesus, another philosopher!' Rip glowered at the older man.

Cole was right, of course. Still, Rip thought he would feel better if he had somehow managed to get Sue Lin and Lin Pe out of the line of fire. If that made him an unrepentant chauvinist, so be it.

'Had a talk with Sonny Wong a few nights ago,' he told Cole. 'The bastard says someone in your consulate is selling him genuine American passports.'

'Think he was lying?'

'No.'

Tiger Cole finished washing and went into the dressing area. When Rip joined him, he said in a low voice, 'That explains a lot.'

'A lot of what?'

'China Bob Chan knew far too much. He and Sonny did dozens of deals together through the years.'

'So who's leaking?'

'Only two people have access to the passports. One of them has to be in on it, maybe both. One of them is a woman who sleeps with one of the CIA dudes.'

'Didn't one of consulate staffers just in from the states get killed a week or so ago?'

'A CIA officer. Shot to death on the street after he planted bugs in China Bob's library.'

They finished dressing in silence and left separately.

The bakery for the Double Happy Fortune Cookie Company was housed in a warehouse near the Chinese University in the New Territories. After the Dutchman died, Lin Pe moved the bakery here for a reason: Even though wages for cooks and laborers were low, wages for students were even lower. By paying students more than the going wage, Lin Pe managed to staff her business with some of the brightest, most talented workers in Hong Kong.

The cookie packaging and storage facilities for bulk bakery supplies were located on the first floor. The actual baking of the cookies and printing of Lin Pe's fortunes occurred on the second floor. In the company offices on the third floor where Lin Pe had kept the books by hand for many years, banks of computers manned by students studying computer and electrical engineering were operating around the clock. Behind the warehouse several delivery vans were parked, as well as a half dozen full-sized trucks that were used to transport overseas cookie shipments to the airport.

Wu Tai Kwong had taken the situation as he found it. The bakery employees were now one of the key cells of the revolutionary committee; threads ran from the bakery to dozens of cells in the university and in factories and offices all over town. From there, the threads ran all over China. Wu Tai Kwong well knew that a local uprising in Hong Kong was doomed; he was playing for much bigger stakes.

This afternoon he lingered on the loading dock with several of his key lieutenants smoking, watching the rain fall, and making last-minute plans.

The time for waiting was over. The spontaneous protests in front of the failed Bank of the Orient had deeply impressed Wu and his friends. The willingness of unarmed citizens to defy the PLA was, Wu thought, a direct measure of the depth of their antigovernment feelings. The Communists also understood that fact, which was the reason they reacted so violently to peaceful protests.

The conspiracy dynamic was also pressing mercilessly. As the organized circle of government enemies expanded, secrecy became nebulous. The enforcers who had ruthlessly punished security lapses when there were relatively few conspirators – and even executed government spies – became powerless as the group expanded exponentially. Whispers at the rank-and-file level became impossible to prevent. Absolute secrecy could be enforced only in a few key cells. Fortunately Virgil Cole, the American, had signed on a year ago and contributed vast sums of money, money that was used to bribe the regular and secret police and anyone else whose silence was deemed necessary.

The government in Beijing knew it had sworn blood enemies, of course, but Beijing was far away, with dozens of layers of corrupt officialdom between here and there. Still, even an absolutely corrupt government could bestir itself if the threat was perceived as grave enough.

Time, Wu told his friends, was running out. Now or never. Fight or submit. Fight or die.

Today his friends watched his facial features as he talked, listened intently to every word. Wu recruited them to his vision and held them enthralled with the power of his personality, nothing else. Energy radiated from him, life, *power* . . .

Some of the women who came within his personal orbit thought of him as a semireligious figure, a modern-day Buddha or Confucius. He wasn't: Wu Tai Kwong was a fierce, driven man of extraordinary personal courage who had ordered executions of traitors and occasionally pulled the trigger himself. He believed in himself and his convictions with a righteous fervor that ordinary people would label irrational. What the people who knew him well saw was a man with the wisdom, courage, determination, and titanic ego necessary to lead a nation as large as China into a new day.

Wu removed a cell phone from his pocket. 'Do we go?' he asked them one last time.

Positive nods all around.

Wu dialed the number.

One ring, two.

'Hello.' Cole's voice. How well Wu knew it.

'Go,' he said and flipped the mouthpiece shut, severing the connection.

'The new day is almost here,' Wu said now to his friends and laughed heartily. He would have laughed on Judgment Day. His laughter seemed to calm the taut nerves of those around him, some of whom forced themselves to smile.

Wu Tai Kwong took a last drag on his cigarette, tossed the butt into a rain puddle, got into the delivery van he normally used, and drove out of the Double Happy Fortune Cookie Company parking lot.

He joined the flow of traffic in the crowded street and crept along toward the first light. The windshield wipers fought a losing battle with the rain, which was coming down harder now than it had all day. Perhaps it was only his imagination.

Another van pulled out in front of him, inched its bumper out into the space between Wu and the vehicle ahead, and of course he had to let it in.

The driver got the van into the traffic stream ahead of Wu, and of course didn't make it through the first light.

Sitting behind the van, thinking of rain and soldiers and millions of angry people, Wu failed to take alarm when the back door of the van ahead opened and two men hopped out. They slammed the door closed, then one stepped to the passenger door of Wu's van and one to the driver's door. They jerked the doors open.

The man on Wu's side had a pistol in his hand, one that he seemed to produce from thin air. Wu looked left – the man climbing into the passenger seat also had a pistol, one pointed at Wu's midsection.

'Put the van in park,' the man said standing beside him, 'and move over. I'll drive.'

Wu floored the accelerator. The van jumped forward, smashing into the back of the vehicle ahead. The man standing on the driver's side fell to the street while the man on the passenger's side who was half in and half out hung on to the door for dear life.

Wu slammed the vehicle into reverse and cranked the wheel over as he jammed the accelerator back down.

A bullet smashed the driver's window. Wu felt the thump of the wheel rolling over the fallen man just before the van impacted the vehicle behind. Wu kept the accelerator mashed down, the rear wheels squalled . . .

The man on Wu's left was inside the vehicle now, swinging at his head with a pistol. Wu drove his right hand into the man's teeth, then slammed on the brake and tried to get the transmission in reverse.

The engine stalled.

In the silence that followed Wu could hear the gasping oaths of the man in the passenger seat. He was grinding on the starter when the man hit him a glancing blow in the head with the pistol.

Wu tried to elbow the man, punch him in the face, but he passed out when the man hit him in the head with the gun a second time.

Jake Grafton unlocked the door to his hotel room and couldn't believe his eyes. The room was trashed. The bed had been stripped, the mattress stuffing strewn everywhere, the furniture broken, the television smashed . . . every item of clothing he and Callie had brought to Hong Kong lay somewhere in the middle of that mess. Even the carpet had been peeled back around the walls.

'Callie?'

He walked into the room, checked to make sure she wasn't in the bathroom or closet or lying under the mess or behind the dresser.

'*Callie?*'

He knew what they had been searching for – the tape. They didn't find it because it was in his pocket.

Where was Callie? She could be downstairs, or shopping, or getting her hair done. . . .

'*Callie!*' He roared her name.

A woman peered through the open doorway from the hall. A Chinese woman, the maid. She asked something in Chinese.

'The lady who was here?' he replied. 'Where did she go?'

The maid shook her head uncomprehendingly, stared in amazement at the sea of trash.

Jake Grafton brushed by her and hurried along the hallway. Unwilling to wait for an elevator, he charged down the stairs, trying to think.

He raced for the manager's office and blew by the secretary. The manager was a Brit. 'Someone trashed my room' – he gave the man the number – 'and my wife is missing! Call the police!'

The man stood gaping at Jake, so Jake repeated it, then went charging out of the office.

He had to find a phone.

Fumbling with the telephone book, barking at the operator, he finally got through to the American consulate. 'Tommy Carmellini, please.'

In less than a minute Carmellini was on the line.

'Grafton. This morning someone did a real messy search of my hotel room. My wife is missing.'

Several seconds of silence followed as Carmellini digested the news. 'The tape,' he said. 'Did they get it?'

'No. Who was it?'

'God knows.'

'*I* want to know.'

'Well, I sure as hell don't know what to tell you, Admiral. If they snatched your wife, you'll probably be hearing from them.'

'Unless they have plans for making her talk.'

Carmellini didn't respond.

'Is the consul general there this afternoon?' Grafton asked.

'I don't know.'

'I'm coming over there. See you in about a half hour. Find me a weapon.'

Jake Grafton slammed the telephone down and marched through the lobby to the street. He passed two uniformed police on their way into the building and didn't stop.

Tiger Cole was in his office. With Carmellini in tow, Jake stormed past the secretary and barged in. Cole was on the telephone. '... The trade agreements can be interpreted as – ' One look at Grafton's face stopped the words.

'May I call you back, Mr. Secretary? A crisis has arisen here that I must deal with.' He listened for a second or two, muttered something, then hung up.

'What in the world – ?'

'Someone trashed my hotel room searching it and my wife is missing.' Jake came around the desk and seized Cole's lapels. 'If you know who has her or where she is, now is the moment to come clean.'

'Hey!' Cole tried to pull Grafton's hands off.

The admiral held on fiercely and lowered his face toward Cole. 'If anything happens to Callie I'll kill you,' he snarled. 'Anything! Do you understand me, Cole?'

The consul general became very still. 'I understand, Jake.'

Grafton released Cole and straightened.

'Who has her?'

'I don't know. Tell me about it.'

Jake sat on the desk. He described the room. 'When I left her to come here for lunch, she was fine. Going to go downstairs for lunch, but she said she would be waiting for me when I got back from the consulate. She wasn't, and the place had been violently trashed. Whoever did it was looking for this!' He pulled the tape from his pocket and showed it to Cole. 'This is the tape from China Bob Chan's library, removed from the recorder within minutes after his death.'

Cole's brow knitted. 'How'd you get it?'

'Mr. Carmellini gave it to me. He was sent over here to help with my investigation. The death of Harold Barnes seemed a good place to start.'

Jake turned to Carmellini. 'Anything of interest on your searches or bugs?'

'No, sir. Not yet.'

'What's he searching?' Tiger asked.

'Everything in this building,' Grafton barked. 'Safes, filing cabinets, desks, hard drives, databases, trash cans, everything. I want to know what the fuck is going on in Hong Kong and I want to know *now*!'

Cole took a deep breath. 'Did you bug this office, Carmellini?'

'Yes, sir.'

'Disable the bugs and leave us alone. Admiral Grafton asked a question and he deserves an unrecorded answer.'

Carmellini took less than a minute to remove the hidden wireless microphones. One was stuck to the eraser of a pencil, one of a dozen pens and pencils protruding from a coffee cup on Cole's desk; another was pinned to the window curtain behind his chair.

When the door closed behind Carmellini, Cole said, 'I don't know who kidnapped your wife.'

'Did you know it was going to happen?'

'No. I'm amazed that it did.'

'Let's take it by the numbers. What in hell are you mixed up in?'

'As you surmised at lunch, a group of revolutionaries is about to kick over the lantern. I'm one of them.'

'Uh-huh.'

Cole raised his hands questioningly.

'Did your group kill Harold Barnes, or have him killed?'

'To the best of my knowledge, no.'

'Don't start that quibble shit with me, Cole! You are ten seconds away from a phone call to Washington. Did anyone in your group kill Harold Barnes? Tell me what you think.'

'No.'

'Who killed him?'

'I don't know. I thought at the time it might be someone in the CIA who was in bed with China Bob.'

'Where did China Bob fit in all this?'

Cole took a deep breath and leaned back in his chair. 'I wish I knew the correct answer to that. I was using him as a conduit to get untraceable money into Hong Kong to fund the revolution. About a hundred million American dollars went through his hands.'

'Your money?'

'Yes.'

'*Jesus*, Tiger! What in the hell are you doing, man?'

'Violently overthrowing the Communist government of China. I thought it was a great investment.'

'Did the thought ever cross your mind that perhaps the best thing you could do for your fellow Americans was let the Chinese solve their own problems?'

'I'm not going to justify my actions to you or anybody else,' Cole said coldly. 'I've done what I believed was the right thing for my fellow man – all of them. You and the people in Washington can put that on my tombstone or stick it up your ass, I don't care which.'

'Okay, okay.' Jake held up his hands. 'What else was Chan into?'

'He smuggled some computers into the country for me.'

'Was he making campaign contributions to American politicians?'

'I believe so.'

'Who supplied the money?'

'The PLA.'

'What else was he up to?'

'Anything that would turn a dollar. Chan liked money and had a finger in every pie in town. That's probably what got him killed.'

'Someone thought he knew too much about too many things?'

'I suspect that's the gospel truth.'

'Did he know your money was going to fund a revolution?'

'I believe he thought I was in the drug business, but he may have guessed the truth at some point.'

Jake Grafton held both hands to his head. 'I can't believe this shit!'

Cole smacked the desk with the flat of his hand. 'Don't give me any sanctimonious crap! I won't listen to it! Thirty years ago America's liberals refused to fight for freedom in Asia – now they're partners with the propaganda ministry of the Communist government as investors in China.com. Anything for a goddamn buck! Yeah, I'm funding a revolution. If the warm, well-fed, comfortable, educated establishment bastards in America lose some money or bleed a little, it'll break my slimy heart.'

Jake Grafton took his time answering. 'You can't give freedom to people, Tiger. It's something they have to earn for themselves. If they don't want freedom enough to fight for it, they won't value it.'

'The Chinese are going to fight, all right,' Cole shot back. 'They're going to do their share of bleeding.'

'Okay,' Jake Grafton said.

When Cole calmed down, he asked, 'Did Callie listen to the tape that Carmellini brought her?'

'Yes.'

'All of it.'

'She said she did.'

'Who knew about the tape?'

'Carmellini, and whoever he told. He brought us a special player and earphones to listen to the thing. I presume he got them out of the closet here at the consulate.'

Tiger Cole took a deep breath. 'Let's make some assumptions, see where they take us. Let's assume that whoever grabbed Callie is interested in the contents of that tape.'

Jake Grafton nodded.

'We know China Bob was taking money from the PLA to give to

American politicians,' Cole continued. 'And we know he wasn't passing all of it along. The PLA has figured this out, too, but I fail to see why they would care what was on that tape. If a PLA officer killed China Bob, he wouldn't care if the American government knew it. The Chinese government doesn't care. Oh, Beijing might be embarrassed about the congressional revelations, but the government really doesn't *care*. Do you understand me?'

'I guess.'

'For these people, Beijing is the center of the universe. What the Americans think or don't think is as important as the shape of the craters on the back side of the moon.'

'Okay.'

'The only reason the PLA would want the tape is because there's something on it that threatens them. If they knew about the revolutionaries, they wouldn't need the tape. Do you agree?'

'I'm listening.'

'That leaves someone else Chan dealt with. Not me, because it's too late for you or anyone else to stop the train. The danger to the revolution is past.'

'I accept that for now,' Grafton said. 'If the shit hits the fan tomorrow. If it doesn't . . .'

'The tape would be of value only to someone who doesn't know the timetable, someone who thinks that he can sell the information that's on it or use it for blackmail. He's assuming that the world he knows is still going to be there, otherwise the tape has no value.'

Jake took the tape from his pocket and placed it on Cole's desk. 'Do you have anybody who could translate this for me?'

'Yes. Kerry Kent.'

'Is she in the building?'

'Yes.' He pushed the button on the intercom and said his secretary's name. 'Is Mr. Carmellini waiting out there?'

'Yes, sir.'

'Please have him go to the CIA office and ask Ms. Kent to come see me.'

When he released the intercom button, Cole told Grafton, 'She's a British SIS agent on a foreign assignment. She works here.'

'Do you want the Brits to hear this?'

'I don't think she'll pass it along to London.'

'Think or know?'

'She's Wu Tai Kwong's girlfriend.'

'I'm not going to sit here for six hours while she listens to the tape. Gimme your best guess. Who snatched Callie?'

'The first possibility that pops into my head is a local gangster named Sonny Wong. I have reason to believe that people in this building are feeding him information, maybe even selling him passports.'

'Do you know who these people are?'

'Suspicion only.'

'What else is Wong into?'

'His primary occupation is smuggling: refugees, dope, diamonds, guns, whatever will earn a buck.'

'Where do I find this star of the social register?'

'You need to see a man named Rip Buckingham. He's a friend of mine. I'll give you his address. We won't call because the telephones might be tapped, but I'll write a note for you to take with you. Go over to his house.'

'Does he know about the plan for revolution?'

'Yes.'

'He's one of the inner circle?'

'Yes.'

'What does he know?'

'As few of the specifics of my business as possible. Like all good conspirators, we compartmentalize all we can, just in case. Obviously he knows details that I don't. He's as familiar with the big picture as I am, of course.'

Jake Grafton could sit still no longer. He walked to the window and back, rubbing his hands. 'I need a weapon, a pistol. Got one you could loan me?'

Cole hiked a foot up on his lower desk drawer, pulled up a trouser leg, and pulled down his sock. He was wearing an ankle holster. 'It's a five-shot Smith and Wesson thirty-eight with a two-inch barrel,' he said as he unstrapped the holster. 'The police will get real pissy if they catch you toting it around. About all it's good for is shooting yourself.'

'Would you have done that if they arrested you?' Jake murmured.

'Hell no. I've got diplomatic immunity,' Cole said.

'Is immunity bulletproof?'

'Nope. Which is why I carried the pistol.'

Cole was writing down Rip Buckingham's address on a Post-it when the intercom buzzed. The secretary's voice came through the box. 'Sir, Mr. Carmellini is back with Ms. Kent. And there is a call from a Mr. Wong. He says he has something that might be of interest to you.'

Cole looked up and met the unblinking gray eyes of Jake Grafton.

'Send Carmellini and Kent in,' he told the box, 'and I'll take the call.' When Carmellini and Kent were seated beside Jake Grafton, Cole pushed the speaker button on the telephone.

'Cole.'

'Mr. Cole, my name is Sonny Wong. I don't think we have ever formally met, but you may have heard someone mention my name.' Wong spoke decent English, but the accent was unmistakable.

'I have indeed heard your name.'

'I have come into the possession of several items you may wish to redeem, Mr. Cole. One is an American lady named Grafton.'

9

The color drained from Jake Grafton's face as Tiger Cole said, 'I'm listening.'

'You may remember our mutual friend, China Bob Chan? It seems that a tape recording was made in his library the evening he died.'

Wong paused. Cole said nothing. Kerry Kent looked at Tommy Carmellini, who kept his gaze fixed on the telephone.

'Still there, Mr. Cole?'

'Yes.'

'This lady has listened to the tape. I don't have the tape, mind you, just the woman. She heard you shoot China Bob, Mr. Cole.'

'So?'

'You have diplomatic immunity in China, but the American State Department might take a dim view of murder. Conceivably, the American government could waive your immunity and turn you over to the Chinese for trial. A federal indictment in the United States is more probable. This woman could put you in prison for the rest of your life.'

'I'm still listening.'

'The other item I have is even more marketable. Amazingly, with the entire resources of the Chinese government devoted to the search for public enemy Wu Tai Kwong, I have managed to apprehend the criminal.'

'Why are you telling me all this?'

'I think the authorities would be very interested in both of my prizes, Mr. Cole. As you know, they have offered a very tempting reward for Wu. I propose to sell both these people to you or to the Chinese government. Think it over.'

'You son of a bitch! Who are you trying to bullshit? Sun will throw you in the same hole he's got waiting for Wu. If Wu won't talk, I will.'

Sonny chuckled. 'You underestimate the gratitude that will overflow Sun's hard little heart if I produce Wu Tai Kwong. Waving Wu's head in Beijing will make Sun's fortune – the bastard may wind up as our next premier.'

'You're the biggest liar west of Little Rock.'

'Everybody has a price.'

'What's yours?'

'Fifty million American dollars.'

'I think you're trying to hijack the revolution.'

'Hijack it? I'm trying desperately to profit from it.'

'Without Wu, there won't be a revolution.'

'Crap,' shot back Sonny Wong. 'No one can stop it now. You'll lead it yourself. Or I will.'

'I'd be a fool to pay.'

'You'd be a fool not to. Your choice.'

'Fifty million?'

'Yep. Transferred by you into a Swiss bank account. You have three days to make the transfer or I make a delivery to the People's Liberation Army.'

Cole took a deep breath. 'What account?'

'One of my colleagues will call you with the information, a Mr. Daniel. Should you decide to redeem one person and not the other, discuss that with Mr. Daniel.'

'I'll want to talk with both parties right now to make sure they are alive and well cared for.'

'Discuss the details with Mr. Daniel.'

'If anything happens to them I – ' Cole began but he was talking to a dead telephone.

He pushed the button to cut the connection.

They all sat staring at the telephone.

After a moment, Grafton said, 'Callie said the tape is inconclusive. She said anyone listening to it couldn't determine who fired the shot that killed Chan.' He picked up the tape from the desk, fingered the reels, then laid it down again.

'It's money Wong's after,' Cole muttered. 'If he doesn't get money, he'll probably kill her.'

'But he wants the tape,' Jake objected. 'Wants to know what's on it.'

'Yeah. He and China Bob did a lot of business together. God only knows what the two of them talked about. He wants the tape, too.'

'Wu Tai Kwong?'

'The political criminal.'

'Why would you care about him?' Tommy Carmellini asked.

'Who do you think is leading the revolution?'

'I guess I hadn't put two and two together.'

'Wu isn't his real name. As fate would have it, he's Rip Buckingham's brother-in-law. If we can overthrow the Communists and Wu lives long enough, he's going to be the first elected president of the new Republic of China.'

'And Wong wants you to pay a ransom for him?'

'If I don't pay for Wu, Sonny Wong will indeed turn Wu over to the

People's Liberation Army, which will pay Sonny the posted reward and execute Wu.'

'Fifty million dollars is a lot of kale,' Tommy Carmellini remarked, rubbing his chin.

'Callie and I have been pretty diligent savers and investors,' Jake said, 'and we have about one-fifth of one percent of that amount.'

Cole waved a hand dismissively. 'I'll pay it,' he said.

'They may kill them anyway.'

'We'll set up a trade. They produce Wu and Callie, I make the call authorizing a wire transfer of the money. When the money is in his bank, we leave.'

Jake Grafton shook his head slowly. 'He'll have to kill you and Wu after you make the call. Wong can't afford to let Wu live to send an army to hunt him down. Hell, he'll have to kill us all so nothing leaks out.'

Cole's face wore a blank expression. His mind was obviously going at a mile a minute.

'How come this Wong knows so much about the revolution?'

'He's involved, obviously.'

'Obviously. How is he involved? What's his role in all this?'

'Not now,' Tiger Cole said, frowning. 'I can't tell you now.'

'*Goddamn you!*' Jake Grafton roared. 'That asshole kidnapped my wife!'

'I'm sorry, Jake,' Tiger Cole said.

The admiral struggled to get himself under control. He played with the pistol, checked it, then pulled up his trouser leg. When he spoke again it was in a normal tone. 'If you had nothing to do with Callie's kidnapping, you have nothing to apologize for,' he said as he strapped the ankle holster to his right leg. 'If you did, I'll kill you, Cole. It's that goddamn simple.'

'How did Sonny Wong capture Wu Tai Kwong?' Carmellini asked.

'Everyone in Hong Kong knows Wu is somewhere in the city,' the consul general replied. 'The revolutionary movement has more leaks than the *Titanic*.'

'So why hasn't Wu been arrested before?'

'Because we've paid off the police.' Cole shrugged. 'Everyone in the Chinese government is corrupt, all of them. This is the third world!'

'Can we get help from the police to get Callie back? Wu?'

'Beijing has posted a huge reward for Wu. The cops are corrupt, but you are fooling yourself if you think no one will call the PLA to turn him in. They will!'

'Okay,' said Jake Grafton. 'Let's talk about Callie. Only a few people knew she was going to listen to that tape. Carmellini, you're one of them. Who'd you tell?'

'No one, Admiral.'

'Somebody figured it out.'

'Kerry Kent,' Tommy said bitterly.

'You ass,' she hissed and went for him with her fingernails.

Carmellini grabbed her wrists. He was far too strong for her. 'Don't play the injured lover with me,' he sneered with all the contempt of a man who had never been in love. 'I've heard that song before. You're the number-one suspect on my list.'

'I trust her,' Cole said, in a tone that ended the argument.

Carmellini pushed Kent away. If looks could kill, he would have received a fatal wound just then.

'The postmortem can wait,' Jake Grafton said. 'We've got other fish to fry.' He picked up the tape from Cole's desk and put it in his pocket.

The maid brought Rip the cell phone. He was sitting on his roof under a dripping umbrella. The air was now a fine sea mist; occasionally a whisper of breeze tossed a handful of droplets on his face, almost like a kiss.

The maid didn't look at him, merely handed him the phone and left.

Rip pushed the button and answered.

'Rip, this is Sonny Wong.'

'Hey, Sonny.'

'Got some bad news for you, Rip. Hate having to deliver it like this, but the world is pressing in, if you know what I mean.'

'Like what?'

'Like I have your brother-in-law as an unwilling guest.'

'My brother-in-law?'

'Yeah. Wu. Remember him? Drives for the Double Happy Fortune Cookie Company? Is wanted by the government for political crimes? The million Hong Kong dollars reward? That brother-in-law.'

'Jesus, Sonny, I thought we were friends.'

'We are, Rip, but this is business. Hong Kong is about to blow up in our faces, no thanks to your brother-in-law, who has done everything within his power to light the fuse. It's been a grand party, but it's over. A guy has to look out for number one. You and I are not friends ten million American dollars' worth. That's what it will cost you to see Wu in one piece again.'

'I don't have that kind of money, Sonny. You know that.'

'Ah, but your father does. Call him! Tell Richard Buckingham that if I don't get the money, your brother-in-law Wu Tai Kwong will be turned over to General Tang Ming of the PLA, who will probably shoot him before he writes the reward check. Or strangle him. For some reason, those guys still like to strangle people. So old-fashioned and messy. Uncivilized too, but probably very satisfying on some level. Almost orgasmic.'

'You're a perfect bastard, Sonny.'

'Not quite perfect but I'm working on it. If I were Richard Buckingham's heir, like a certain person I know, I wouldn't have to be. You know what I'm saying? It's an accident of birth, really, that I was born in a sewer, poor

786

as a flea on a starving rat, and I've been digging and scratching every minute since then to get out of it.'

'Let me talk to Wu.'

'You're going to have to take my word on this, Rip. Wu is sleeping right now; I don't want to wake him.'

'How do I know you've got him?'

'If you're really worried about that point, I'll have someone drop by with a finger. What the hell, he's got ten. He'll never miss a few.'

'Okay, okay.'

'You talk to Richard. I'll call you back in a few hours, give you the particulars on a Swiss bank account that I'm trying to fatten up. You can plan on transferring the money there.'

With that Sonny hung up.

Rip went inside looking for Sue Lin. He found her in the kitchen. 'Where's the maid?'

'The new one?'

Rip nodded.

'After she gave you the phone, she went downstairs, got her umbrella, and left. Didn't say a word to me. I happened to look out the window and saw her walking toward the tram.'

'Wu's been kidnapped.'

'*What?*'

'Sonny Wong has him. He wants ten million American dollars or he'll turn him over to the government and collect the reward.'

She sat and put her face in her hands. Rip put his arms around her shoulders and found she was shaking.

'Hey.' He knelt in front of her, opened her hands. Tears streamed along her cheeks. 'Hey.'

'I've seen this Sonny Wong,' she whispered. 'He is evil.'

'Sue Lin, I've known him for years. Yeah, he's a crook, but he's always been straight with me. He's just wants money. Unfortunately we looked like an easy mark.'

'He'll kill Wu.'

'We'll pay the money. I'll bet he'll let him go.'

'With the city full of people who worship Wu?' she protested, shaking her head. 'Sonny Wong will kill him and take the first plane out before anyone finds out the truth.'

The sound of a man groaning woke Callie Grafton. She opened her eyes and looked around. It took several seconds before she realized what she was looking at. She was in a small stateroom, perhaps on a ship, lying on a narrow bed, a lower bunk. Across the aisle, almost within reach, lay a man with his back to her. He was the one groaning.

Blood stained his shirt and the sheet on which he lay.

She extended her arm . . . and felt a sharp pain roar through her skull. Slowly she put her hands to her head and pressed. She had the mother of all headaches.

Her head throbbed with every heartbeat. Gradually the pain seemed to ease somewhat, and once again she extended her hand to the groaning man.

His back was warm.

Callie moved, painfully, until she could touch the man.

She swung her feet over the edge of the bunk and sat up, which almost split her head with pain. In a minute or so the pain lessened and she could see and function.

Ever so slowly, she stood, turned the man over, and examined him.

His left hand was bloody. She looked. His little finger was missing, leaving only an oozing, partially scabbed wound.

She tore at the sheet, finally got a strip off it, and wrapped the strip around the man's hand as a crude bandage.

He had stopped groaning. When she finished she realized his eyes were open and he was looking at her with intelligent brown eyes. He was Chinese, in his mid-thirties perhaps.

'You've lost a finger,' she said in Chinese.

'They cut it off.'

She sat back down on her own bunk, put her aching head in her hands. It was coming back: the knock on the hotel room door, the voice – she thought it was the maid or bellman. When she opened the door, several men rushed in. They grabbed her mouth to keep her from screaming and threw her on the bed and one of them produced a hypodermic.

That was all she remembered. That and the fear.

Now she was sitting in a stateroom . . . she could feel the boat rocking in the waves. It must be a small ship to rock like this. There was a round porthole with the glass painted over; a bit of light leaked through the scratches in the paint. That light was all that illuminated the tiny room.

When she turned her head she could see that the man on the bunk had rolled over. Now he was looking at her.

'Does your hand hurt?'

'Not too much,' he said.

'Who are you?'

'You wouldn't know me.'

'Do you have a name?'

'Wu.'

'I'm Callie.'

'Callie.' He said it experimentally.

'Where are we?'

'I think we have been kidnapped. They knocked me out, so I don't know.'

'Me, too.'

She still had her watch, which was unexpected. Almost three o'clock. The men had burst into the hotel room about ten a.m.

She wondered if it were the same day.

She lay down and thought about her husband.

'Commander Tarkington?'

'That's right.' Tommy Carmellini pressed the telephone to his ear to help himself concentrate. The voice that sounded in his ear from the other side of the Pacific was certainly clear enough.

'My name is Tommy Carmellini. We met last year in Cuba. Do you remember?'

'Yes.' Tarkington sounded sleepy. The telephone call had awakened him.

'Admiral Grafton asked me to call you. He needs your help.' Tarkington was Jake Grafton's aide.

'I got a pencil. Shoot.' Now Toad was alert.

'His wife has been kidnapped,' Carmellini said.

'Callie Grafton? *Gawd damn!*' The Toad-man whistled through his teeth.

Carmellini glanced around the office. Kerry Kent and the three CIA dudes were all staring at him, listening to his every word.

'We believe the man behind it is a Hong Kong citizen named Sonny Wong,' Carmellini continued. 'I don't know his real name. He is associated with a Russian national named Yuri Daniel. The admiral asked me to call you. He wants the CIA to run those two through the computers and see what they can come up with. Wong may have some bank accounts in Switzerland or some other bank haven. Look for passports, visas, travel records, wire transfers, anything.'

'Okay.' Toad's voice was crisp and businesslike.

'Have the National Security Agency set up a study of telecommunications traffic in the Hong Kong area. Obviously we are interested in the Graftons, Sonny Wong, Yuri Daniel, kidnapping, ransom, anything along those lines.'

'I'll talk to them in a few hours. Tell the admiral I'll go through the agency director's office. Shouldn't be a problem. Anything else?'

'That will do it for now.'

'Heard anything about Callie? Is she okay?'

'We don't know.'

'Does this Wong dude want money or what?'

'Money.'

'Wow!' said Toad Tarkington. 'That Wong must have really bad karma – I can smell it from here. Jake Grafton is the last man on the planet I'd want blood-crazy mad at me. You tell the admiral I'm on my way to the office as soon as I get my pants on.'

Jake Grafton sat at the conference table in Cole's office and tried to clear his thoughts. There was stationery in the trays under the computer printer, so he helped himself to a couple of sheets. He took a U.S. government black ballpoint from his shirt pocket and clicked the point in and out while he collected his thoughts.

The National Security Adviser had sent Jake to Hong Kong to find out what was going on; the man was entitled to know.

Jake wrote quickly in a clear, legible longhand detailing what he had learned. The consul general was involved in a conspiracy to overthrow the Chinese government and had resigned. Cole had been in the building when China Bob Chan was killed, may have talked to him, and may have been somehow involved in his death. The enclosed tape was made in Chan's library by the recorder planted by Harold Barnes and should be listened to by Chinese-language experts.

He wrote two pages total, then put the handwritten sheets and the audiotape in a large padded envelope, which he sealed. He wrote the National Security Adviser's name on it and handed it to Cole.

'I want you to send this to Washington in the next diplomatic pouch. The Chan tape is in there.'

'Okay.'

'I'm relying on your honor, Cole.'

'I am well aware of that fact, Jacob Lee, and will try not to take offense at the fact you felt the need to point it out.'

'I'm all out of apologies,' Grafton replied coolly.

'I'll put the envelope in the pouch,' Cole said. 'The problem is the airlines – nothing is coming in or going out of Lantau since the air traffic control computers crapped out.'

'Did you have anything to do with that?'

'I certainly hope so.'

Jake scratched his head, trying to make up his mind. 'I want the tape in the bag and on its way,' Jake said finally, 'so I won't be tempted to trade the damned thing to this Wong asshole for Callie.'

'Okay.'

'And the time has come for you to resign.' Jake took Cole's letter of resignation from his pocket and tossed it on the desk. 'Fax that thing to Washington.'

'Now?'

'Right now.'

Cole took a deep breath. 'Okay,' he said.

The intercom buzzed. 'Mr. Cole. There's a small package here for you. The sergeant at the gate brought it up. He says you should see it.'

'Is he still there?'

'Yes, sir.'

'Have him bring it in.'

The marine was square as a fire plug and togged out in a khaki shirt and blue trousers with a red stripe up each seam. He looked pale.

'Did you X-ray the package, Sergeant?' Cole asked.

'Yes, sir. There's no bomb. Looked like a bone.'

'A bone?'

'Well, three little bones. Jesus, sir, it looks like a finger.'

Cole cut the brown wrapping paper away from the box with a letter opener, then cut the tape that held the top on.

Jake Grafton was looking over Cole's shoulder when he opened the box. It was a finger, all right, freshly severed, if the still-soft blood was any indication.

'Thank you, Sergeant,' Cole said softly and sent the marine on his way.

Jake Grafton stood still as a statue, staring at the finger.

'It isn't Callie's,' he said.

'Probably Wu's,' Cole muttered and used the intercom to ask the secretary to have Kerry Kent come up to the office.

While they were waiting Jake walked around the office looking at Cole's memorabilia. He was thinking of Callie, wondering how he was going to get her back, when he realized he was looking at an old photo of himself and Tiger Cole. The thing was in black and white, framed, sitting on an out-of-the-way shelf behind the conference table. He and Cole were standing in front of a bomb-laden A-6 in their flight gear, obviously on a flight deck. Neither man was grinning.

Those were simpler days.

Kerry Kent knocked, then came charging into the office. She looked into the box, and clapped her hand over her mouth.

'Those bastards,' she said between clenched teeth. 'Those fucking bastards.'

Victoria Peak and the tops of the buildings were wreathed in fog when Jake Grafton walked out the front entrance of the American consulate. The rain had stopped, leaving the air tangibly wet, thick, warm, and heavy.

He walked slowly, taking his time, watching for people who might be paying attention to him.

He had to will himself to walk slowly, to analyze and think logically about the situation and what he could do to affect it.

The tension in everyone he met was visible – all the pedestrians were on edge, regardless of age, sex, race, or how they were dressed. Without smiles or nods, the people walked briskly with their heads down, avoiding eye contact, avoiding each other, hurrying toward the great unknown.

He stood in line and bought a ticket on the tram, then waited a minute or two with the crowd for the tram to descend the mountain. He let other people board the car in front of him, arranging it so he was one of the very last aboard, and told the motorman where he wanted off.

The car got underway almost noiselessly as the cable pulled it up the tracks. The only sound Jake could hear was the faintest rumble from the wheels, or perhaps he was only feeling the vibration of the steel wheels on the steel rails. The grade was about thirty percent, he estimated. A series of stairs ran alongside the cable car's track for those in the mood for a serious climb.

No one in the car spoke. All studiously avoided looking at each other as the car silently climbed the steep grade. The buildings slid past and the fog thickened.

The car stopped at a tiny platform about three-quarters of the way up the side of the mountain. Jake got off, then the car resumed its journey and disappeared into the fog.

He walked along the street, found the right house, rang the bell.

A man opened the door, a man in his late thirties, perhaps even forty. 'Rip Buckingham?'

'Come in, please.'

When the door closed behind him, Jake said, 'I suppose Wong called you.'

'Yes. My wife is upstairs. Wu is her brother.'

They sat at a table in the kitchen, with a window beside them that gave a view of some nearby housetops amid the gloom.

'Cole said they took your wife.'

'Yes.'

'Sonny won't be able to stay in Hong Kong after this.'

'If he gets fifty million from Cole, he won't want to.'

'He also wants ten million from me. From my dad, actually, Richard Buckingham.'

'Buckingham News?'

'Yeah.'

Jake considered the situation in silence as he sized up Rip Buckingham and tried to figure out how much steel was in him. Finally he said, 'Wong won't be able to live comfortably anywhere if he releases Callie and Wu alive to testify against him. Switzerland isn't an extradition haven.'

'After Wong gets his money, he'll kill everybody who might cause him trouble,' Rip said heavily. 'A man once told me that four hundred Chinese each paid Sonny fifty grand American to go to America. The ship sailed away and was never seen again.'

'Twenty million dollars,' Jake muttered after doing the math in his head.

'I don't know if the story is true,' Rip continued, 'but I know Sonny. He doesn't take unnecessary chances.'

Tommy Carmellini had his equipment set up in the attic of the consulate. He had worked for three nights bugging and wiring selected offices, one of which was the CIA office. Another was the consul general's. Grafton wanted to know what was going on – Carmellini intended to find out.

Just now he settled into the folding chair he had stolen from the immigration office and donned a headset, which was plugged into the amplifier. The tape recorder was recording all the microphone inputs simultaneously for later study. Without interfering with the recording, he flipped through the channels, listening to various bugs in turn, sampling the audio.

The CIA office was his main concern. He listened to them chat, matched up voices with the faces in his memory. They were still squeezing the juice from the kidnapping. Well, an admiral's wife doesn't get snatched every day.

Kent also knew that Sonny Wong claimed he had Wu. She wasn't sharing that tidbit with the others, Carmellini noticed. In fact, she was sharing very little.

A remark of Bubba Lee's set the tone. 'Man, calling Washington and telling NSA to get on the case – that Grafton *is* somebody.'

'Yeah, but who?' That was Eisenberg.

'An admiral in the navy. Don't they sometimes get posted to the intel community?'

'Sometimes.'

'Well, that sailor has some stroke, or thinks he has.'

'Thinks he has, yeah.'

'Do you buy it about Sonny Wong? Does a snatch sound like something he would do?'

'Never can tell, man. Things are getting twangy tight around this town. Riots, people shot in the streets, power off half the night . . .'

'Did you hear about the airport?' Was that Bubba Lee? 'The computers out there rolled over and died. People trapped on the concourses, no water in the fountains or toilets, flights canceled. I heard someone went crazy and threw a chair through a plate-glass window.'

'Whole goddamn town is falling apart.'

'Hey, the whole goddamn *country* is falling apart, if you ask me.'

There was more of it, thirty minutes or so. At some point Carmellini realized that there were only two men talking. Eisenberg had been silent a long time, as had Kerry Kent. Maybe they were no longer in the room.

Didn't Cole say Eisenberg knew the woman in the passport office?

Carmellini flipped to that microphone. A loud conversation in Chinese drowned out everything else in the room.

Disgusted, Tommy Carmellini turned the selector to listen to the mike in the consul general's office.

Yep, there was Kent.

' – might kill him. I've been saying for months that he should have an armed bodyguard around the clock. Does anyone pay any attention to the fears of a woman? What does *she* know? What could *she* possibly contribute to this – '

'He didn't want a bodyguard! You know that. Stop this goddamn whining.'

'Whining? They may *kill* him!'

'Indeed. He's been a fugitive for a dozen years, with his life hanging by a thread. The revolution continues regardless. The world keeps turning, the tide is coming in . . . at last!'

'What are you doing to get him back alive?'

'I'm paying the damned ransom.'

'What else?'

'What else do you think I should do?'

'I don't know!' she moaned. 'I only know that I want him *alive*! I need him, China needs him — *everything* depends on him. *Everything!*'

'Tell me some more about Sonny Wong,' Jake Grafton said to Rip Buckingham, 'everything you can remember.' They were still in Rip's kitchen, seated in front of the window. The rain had stopped and the fog was lifting, revealing the skyscrapers of the Central District.

'Sonny's the head of the last of the old-line Hong Kong criminal gangs, or tongs,' Rip told the American. 'He's sort of an anachronism, a fossil from the wilder days.'

'Kidnapping isn't anything new,' Jake said sourly.

'No,' Rip admitted. 'I thought Sonny was above poopy little capers like this, but apparently not.'

'I want to know everything, who his associates are, what he does for money, where he lives, what he eats, his habits — vices, women, kids, everything.'

'What's on your mind?'

'I want my wife back.'

'That may be impossible.'

Jake Grafton gripped the edge of the table and squeezed as hard as he could. All these years, ups and downs and ins and outs, good times and hard times, the tiny triumphs and disasters and little victories that fill our days . . . to have her life end here, now, snuffed out by a criminal psychopath who wants money?

When his muscles began quivering from the exertion, Jake Grafton released the table. He rubbed his hands together, thought about Callie, about their adopted daughter, Amy. 'Let's hope not,' he said to Rip, so softly that the Australian almost missed the response.

10

British consul general Sir Robert MacDonald spent a long afternoon with his staff writing a situation report for the Foreign Office. While so engaged he received a telephone call from the foreign minister in London, who was worried.

'The PM wants to know what in the world is going on out there,' the foreign minister said after the usual pleasantries.

'The authorities are having some public relations difficulties,' replied Sir Robert, never one to overlook the obvious. He had gone to school with the PM, who loathed him. Forced to accept Sir Robert into the government, the PM had sent him as far from London as he possibly could. 'A few technical problems too, I'm afraid,' the consul general continued. 'Rather inconvenient when the power goes off at odd hours.'

'The Buckingham newspapers published a provocative piece in today's U.K. and American editions,' the foreign minister informed Her Majesty's Hong Kong representative. 'I wonder if you've seen it?'

'Afraid not. The locals shut down the *China Post*, which was Buckingham's little rag hereabouts. Of course, they shut down all the newspapers – I'm sure my staff sent you that information in the morning report.'

'Richard Buckingham signed this piece himself. He says that a revolution is about to sweep China, one that will overthrow the Communists.'

'His son was the editor of the *China Post*,' Sir Robert replied. Rip had been a thorn in MacDonald's side since the day the man arrived from London. 'Governor Sun tossed him in jail,' he said, unable to keep the satisfaction completely out of his voice. 'He's out now, of course. Perhaps he had something to do with the article.'

'I see,' the FM said slowly.

'It's always a mistake to quarrel with a man who buys ink by the barrel,' Sir Robert continued, repeating a comment his wife had made to him on several occasions when he took offense at *China Post* editorials. 'Richard Buckingham can say anything he wants in his newspapers and there's jolly little the Chinks can do about it. But talk of revolution is rot, pure rot. The Communists are firmly in control. They have a division of troops in the colony.'

Sir Robert still referred to Hong Kong as a colony, which it had ceased to be in 1997, even though his staff and the Foreign Office had repeatedly requested him not to.

'The Orient Bank fiasco was very poorly handled,' the consul general told the foreign minister now. 'I expressed our dismay at the senseless loss of life. Appalling. I told Sun that myself. Still, the Chinese brook no nonsense from dissenters.' That was a serious understatement. The authorities were positively paranoid about dissenters, which caused them diplomatic problems throughout the Western world, including the U.K.

The FM was not so sure about the Communists' control of the political situation. 'The world turns,' he said. 'I seem to recall that a few years ago everyone thought that the Communists in Russia had a firm grip – '

'China is not Russia,' Sir Robert shot back, quite sure he was on solid ground. 'The conditions are completely different.'

'I'll convey your views to the PM,' the foreign minister said wearily.

'Do that,' Sir Robert said. 'Good-bye.'

He was amazed at the credulity of the people in London. Of course, they were eight thousand miles from the scene of the crime, but still ... a revolution? Here? Because Richard Buckingham said so in his newspapers?

Governor Sun also had a busy afternoon. Between calls from Beijing demanding detailed facts he didn't have and issuing directives that made little sense, Sun huddled with key members of his staff, who were trying desperately to establish why the electrical power had failed last night throughout the S.A.R. and why so many of the computers that controlled critical government functions were on the blink.

'Could it be sabotage?' Sun demanded. Like so many of the bureaucrats in Beijing, he had a healthy respect for the unvoiced anger of the people. Baldly, he feared the people he ruled. Repeatedly throughout Chinese history rioting mobs had overthrown dynasties and warlords. Anger and frustration could transform peasants into fierce giants capable of slaying dragons, and Sun well knew it.

Like so many Chinese officials who had held office as the dynasties rose and fell through the millennia, Sun instinctively wanted to control the people he ruled, ensure they stayed in their place, obedient and quiet. For that to happen in this day and age living conditions in China had to improve, which inevitably caused expectations to rise faster than they could be met. It was a vicious cycle with a bad ending; Sun didn't want to be the man on the spot when the music stopped and the whole thing exploded.

Then there were the reactionary capitalist forces that the Communists had struggled against since the first day of the Long March. Always the reactionaries were there, waiting for a misstep, a mistake. Waiting.

Sun's aides knew his fears, and they thought they knew the seething maelstrom that was Hong Kong. They soothed him now, told him that there was no evidence of sabotage, when in fact they had no knowledge of why the computers had failed. 'A voltage spike, the engineers think,' the aides told the governor, who wanted to believe.

'A voltage spike' was the message he gave to Beijing.

American consul general Virgil Cole was not telling his government the truth either. Unlike Governor Sun and Sir Robert MacDonald, who thought they were reporting the truth to their superiors, Cole was lying and knew it. He knew precisely why the power went out last night in Hong Kong and he knew why the airport and harbor computers had failed. He knew what had happened and he knew the plan for going forward.

Of this, he told the United States government precisely nothing.

The Chinese desk at the State Department wanted reports and updates and answers to specific questions, all of which Cole farmed out to his staff. He told the staff more or less what he wanted them to tell Washington, which was the truth as far as it went, but not the complete truth, not by a long shot.

Cole blamed the crisis on the Chinese government's demand for loans at nominal interest rates, loans the government had no intention of ever paying back. The nongovernment stockholders in Hong Kong banks were taking their money and clearing out, which was the root cause of the Bank of the Orient failure. The shootings of unarmed civilians were directly due to the incompetence of the officers of the People's Liberation Army and a government that was paranoid of any dissent whatsoever.

Subsequent problems – power and equipment failures – Cole cavalierly blamed on technical incompetence. When the CIA resident, Bubba Lee, told him of Sun's 'voltage spike' explanation to Beijing, Cole tossed that into his latest report to Washington.

During his tenure in Hong Kong, Virgil Cole had repeatedly told the American government that the Chinese government was a corrupt tyranny, with a gross disregard for human rights. The ruling oligarchy was paranoid, cowardly, greedy, technically incompetent, and devoid of personal honor. Cole had said all this so many times the people in Washington laughed about it, yet in the past he had made sure he didn't make himself so obnoxious that the powers that be would fire him. Oh no.

He referred his staff now to some of his past missives on governmental incompetence. When they returned with drafts of the reports Washington demanded, Cole read them with interest, made a few corrections, signed the things, and sent them off.

Lying to the government was a bad business, of course, and he had fretted over it for a year. When you put garbage in, you got garbage out. His conscience used to trouble him more than it did now, although it still twinged him a little.

This evening his lies didn't even make the long list. He was thinking of

Wu Tai Kwong, Callie Grafton, and all the things that had to be done. The letter of resignation was also on his mind. It had been faxed off hours ago, and he was now awaiting an explosion from Washington.

It was time to go. He didn't need the consulate anymore.

If the Chinese arrested him, they knew far too much and the revolution was doomed. But they didn't know. So there was a chance, a good chance, he believed.

Time was running out. Lives were at stake, millions of lives. Tens of millions. *Hundreds of millions!*

He looked out the window. The frontal clouds had dissipated; blue sky was visible up there between the towering glass skyscrapers. Across the way was the Third Planet office. With the sky the way it was, the windows there were opaque.

Although Cole didn't know it, inside those offices Kerry Kent and Wu Tai Kwong's top lieutenants were holding a council of war. There were seven of them, each in charge of a specialized group of fighters. They were Wu's friends ... although perhaps disciples might be a better description.

They took the news of Wu's kidnapping badly. Three of them were for finding Sonny Wong and demanding Wu's immediate return as the price of Wong's life.

Kerry Kent tried to dissuade them. 'Sonny Wong has thought of that move,' she argued. 'Virgil Cole will pay the ransom. If he doesn't, we'll get Wu back in pieces. Do you want Wu alive or Wong dead?'

'That's Wong's choice,' Hu Chiang said tartly.

'No, it's ours,' Kerry shot back. 'We've a revolution to fight. I want Wu back more than anyone in this room, but first and foremost, we must continue the fight that is his life. And ours. That is our first priority.'

Hu was not persuaded, but two of Wu's other friends took up Kerry's argument. 'The hour is *now*,' Wei Luk argued. 'Wu Tai Kwong is a general in our army, it is true, but even generals are soldiers. Our cause is more important than any one person. We must not jeopardize it by taking sides in an internal squabble.'

'Internal squabble?' Kent said incredulously. 'Sonny Wong wants fifty million American dollars from Virgil Cole. That's ransom.'

'Cole should have donated his money to the cause,' Wei Luk replied stoutly. 'If he had, he would not now need us to stop the revolution to save his pocketbook.'

'His pocketbook? You fool! Wu Tai Kwong's life is at stake. Sonny Wong is threatening to murder him!'

'Perhaps he merely threatens. I think Cole is too worried about his money.'

Hu Chiang managed to stop this fruitless argument. 'Enough!' he shouted. '*Enough!* Kerry Kent said the revolution must be our first priority, and I agree. We cannot stop the revolution to search Hong Kong for one man. We must strike now. If we do not, for any reason, we endanger the lives of every member of the Scarlet Team. Let Cole pay the money. There will be time later to deal with Sonny Wong. There is nowhere on this earth he can go to escape us.'

Wei Luk agreed with that, and so did the others.

Around sunset two men came to the door of the stateroom – it *was* a stateroom, Callie had decided, in a yacht or small ship. She and Wu had tossed and turned on their bunks all afternoon. Worried as she was, she still fell asleep for an hour or two, which she attributed to the drug they had injected her with. She still felt groggy, unable to focus properly.

One of them stood in the door and motioned to Callie. 'Come with us,' he said in Cantonese. She went. Pretending she didn't know Chinese would require some serious acting. She didn't feel up to the effort, so she didn't try.

One in front, one behind, they led her along a narrow passageway lined with doors. She got a glimpse out a porthole, saw that this deck was six or eight feet above the waterline and that the yacht was tied to a pier. It was some kind of yacht, she decided, an old one, though still maintained in excellent shape.

The man in front opened a door off the passageway, held it and motioned her through.

A man sat behind a small desk. He was not Chinese; European, perhaps, of medium height and weight, perhaps a hundred and fifty pounds. With a bony head and thin face and pinched nostrils.

'Sit,' he said in English, and she took the only empty chair.

The two men who had brought her came into the small room – which was no bigger than the stateroom where she had spent the day – and stood with their backs to the door.

'Mrs. Grafton,' the man said and pushed a sheet of paper and ballpoint pen an inch or two toward her. 'We wish you to write a statement.'

Russian. With that accent, he was a Russian.

She made no effort to pick up the pen.

The Russian waited a few seconds, then said, 'Pick up the pen. You will write with it.'

When Callie failed to obey he reached across the desk and slapped her, a stinging slap. He was remarkably quick with his hands.

Tears came to her eyes, which infuriated her. She sat there staring into his face through her tears.

'Perhaps I should explain. Pick up the pen or we will break your left arm.'

She reached for the thing, got it in her right hand, put both hands back in her lap.

'Very good,' the Russian said. 'A first step. We make progress.'

He leaned back in his chair and made a steeple with his fingers. 'Before you begin writing, I will explain what we want. You listened to a tape that was recorded in the library of China Bob Chan the evening that he died. There were various conversations on the tape. Who were the people talking and what did they say?'

She looked at the pen in her right hand, so she didn't see the slap coming. God, the man was quick as a cat.

'Look at me, Mrs. Grafton. I am not nice. Nice is not a thing I have. I want something from you and I will hurt you to get it. I will cut your face, break your bones, break your head, cut out your eyes, watch men rape you ... whatever it takes. I do not care if you live or die. Do you understand me?'

She nodded.

'Good. Very good!' the Russian said. He folded his hands on the table in front of him. 'Did you listen to the tape?'

She decided not to talk. If you don't resist evil you become a part of it, she told herself. She saw the slap coming and went with it, but still the blow numbed her face. And another. And yet again.

She felt herself starting to go out, slipping away. Her eyes refused to focus.

Hands grabbed her roughly, held her in the chair. When she could focus again Wu was there, with a man on each side holding him. Wu's hands were bound by plastic ties and the ties were secured to his belt.

'Mrs. Grafton,' the Russian said carefully. 'Listen to me. I want to know what you know. If you do not talk, I will kill this man who spent the afternoon with you.' That said, he drew a knife and inserted the point into Wu's arm. The color drained out of Wu's face, but he said nothing.

'He is very tough,' the Russian said, grinning at Callie. 'But he bleeds.' He made a lengthwise cut in the man's arm about four inches long and wiped the knife on her blouse. 'If you do not answer my questions I am going to cut him into little pieces and feed him to the fish.'

He was as good as his word. He slowly inserted the knife into Wu's bicep, at least an inch deep, and slowly drew it down toward his elbow as the blood welled from the cut.

'I'll talk,' Callie said, unable to watch.

'Where is the tape now?'

'My husband has it.'

'Who brought you the tape?'

'Tommy Carmellini.'

'Is Carmel – is he CIA?'

'Yes.'

'Does your husband work for CIA?'

'Navy. He is in the navy.'

'Why did Carmel bring him the tape?'

'Because I speak Chinese and Carmellini doesn't.'

The Russian thought about that for a moment, then went on. 'Did you hear China Bob Chan on the tape?'

'I think so.'

'Virgil Cole?'

'Yes.'

'Who else?'

'I don't know.'

He lunged for her, his hand swinging, and she jerked back. One of the men behind her grabbed her hair.

The Russian slapped her, then said again, 'Who else?'

'I didn't recognize the other voices.'

The Russian glanced at the man behind her, and he released her hair.

She had cut her tongue on the inside of her mouth. The blood tasted coppery and felt slimy, and she had to swallow it.

'I am going to ask a question, Mrs. Grafton. I want the truthful answer. No lies, please. Lies will be very bad for you. Do you understand?'

'Yes.' This time it came out a whisper. Blood was still streaming from Wu's wounds and dripping on the deck.

'Who killed China Bob Chan?'

'I don't know.'

'Oh, Mrs. Grafton, I hoped I would not need to hurt you, and now you lie to me. Too bad, too bad.'

The Russian came around the desk and reached for her. Callie spit blood in his face. When he blinked and drew back to avoid it, she slashed at his face with the ballpoint.

One of the men behind her jerked her half out of the chair, turned her, and hit her so hard she passed out.

When she came to she was in a cold, cold place, in absolute darkness. She felt around her . . . and felt something cold, like cold, dead flesh.

She was in a meat locker.

And she was freezing. Sore, not completely conscious, she curled up in a fetal position to try to conserve her body heat.

Rip Buckingham wanted to talk. He had been carrying this great burden in his breast for months and months and finally here was someone he could tell, someone who also had a huge stake in how the tale would end, someone with whom he could share his fears.

He started by telling Jake everything he knew about Sonny Wong, and then he couldn't stop. He told him about Lin Pe and Sue Lin and Wu Tai Kwong, about Wu's romance with the British SIS agent Kerry Kent, told him how Kerry approached Virgil Cole and asked for his help, how Cole agreed to help fund the revolution and teach key cell members the fundamentals of cyberwarfare.

'Soon,' Rip said. 'Very soon. The revolution will start and the world as we know it will come to an end.'

Jake Grafton listened without saying a word. He knew some of it, surmised more, but Rip filled in the gaps and made the story whole.

'They are going to find out who Wu really is and come for Lin Pe and Sue Lin. They are going to drag them off to prison, strangle them. The Chinese think like that. If I can't shoot you I'll piss in your well and strangle your mother.'

'And the women refused to leave,' Jake suggested.

'How did you know?'

'If they had agreed you wouldn't still be here, would you?'

'I suppose not.'

'How soon is soon?'

'Tonight maybe. Tomorrow. Tomorrow night. I don't know, but it's got to happen quickly.'

'Does this Sonny Wong know the timetable?'

'Only if he has a spy at the very top levels of the Scarlet Team. Each cell has a name. The top one is the Scarlet Team.'

'How do you start a revolution, anyway?'

'Wu never told me. He didn't want me to know too much.'

'Well, let's you and me go see if we can find Mr. Wong.'

Rip didn't think much of that idea. 'He won't have Callie or Wu with him,' he objected.

'I want to see him.'

'Why?'

'I want to talk to the man,' Jake explained. 'Give him a reason not to harm Callie.'

'Sonny isn't the kind of man who is easily convinced of anything,' Rip explained. 'Especially where money is involved. Talking won't do any good.'

'That depends on what we say,' Jake said patiently. 'And how we say it. You'll see. I'm fairly good at delivering messages.'

'I can't see how this will help,' Rip protested, but Jake's mind was made up.

They rode the tram up the mountain – because the first cable car was going up – and got a taxi at the visitors' center on top. 'Wong has a floating restaurant in Aberdeen,' Rip told the admiral, who wondered if it was the same one that he and Callie had eaten at yesterday. He hoped not. The thought that Wong might have made a dollar off him rankled.

'Whenever I want to talk to the guy I leave a message there,' Rip continued. 'For all I know, Sonny sleeps there sometimes. One other thing I forgot to mention: He has an associate, not a partner, but a chief lieutenant. The man is Russian, Yuri Daniel. Avoid him if you can. Just being around him makes my skin crawl.'

To Jake's relief, Wong's was not the restaurant where he and Callie had eaten. It was the next one down, gaudy as a painted whore, sporting enough lights to decorate the White House Christmas tree.

Jake and Rip lined up at the same little wharf and took a sampan across the choppy black water to the restaurant. The main dining area was almost empty.

'With air traffic screwed up and all the electrical problems, the tourists are staying in their hotels,' Rip opined.

The maître d' let them have their pick of window seats, then left them.

'I'm not hungry,' Jake said. 'Let's go see if Wong is around. Where are the offices?'

'The second floor, or deck, I think.' Rip pointed to a small black door near the kitchen entrance.

'Lead on.'

The door was unlocked. Rip pushed it open. There was a man sitting inside. Rip spoke to him in Chinese, asked if Wong were around.

The man looked Rip over, asked his name, then went upstairs.

In about a minute a medium-sized Chinese man in his fifties came down the narrow stairs. He broke into a grin, which revealed crooked teeth. 'Rip Buckingham, as I live and breathe,' the man said in English. 'This is a surprise. Who is your friend?'

'Jake Grafton.'

'I'm Sonny Wong,' the Chinese man said but didn't offer a hand. 'Come upstairs. We'll talk there.' He turned and led the way back up the narrow staircase. Rip and Jake followed. The man who had been sitting in the foyer also came along.

Wong's office was roomy enough, furnished with a practical desk and some overstuffed chairs, and decorated with the stuff curio stores sold to tourists, stuff that looked valuable but probably wasn't – carved elephants, ivory pagodas, here and there a hand-carved chess set.

Sonny Wong turned to face his guests. 'So, Mr. Grafton, did you come to buy your wife back?'

'I came to explain why you should release her unharmed.'

'Oh, no harm come to her if Virgil Cole pay the money I asked. If not . . .'

'Cole will pay,' Jake said, looking around, then focusing on Sonny. 'You got a nice life here in Hong Kong. Rip tells me you've got a lot of stuff, a restaurant, houses, apartments, boats, money, women . . . Virgil Cole is going to pay you. If you send my wife back alive and in the pink, you can continue to live your good life here in Hong Kong. We'll chalk this little episode up as an adventure and go on down the road.'

Sonny smiled. He looked at Rip. 'Do you think Cole would pay more to get you and Mr. Grafton back alive?' He turned toward the telephone on his desk. 'Why don't we ask him?'

Jake Grafton drew Cole's .38 snub nose from his right trouser pocket, turned, and shot the guard at the door square in the heart. The shot was like a thunderclap in that small space.

Wong turned, quick as a cat, but too late.

Jake Grafton rammed the barrel of the snub nose against his lips.

'If you even twitch, I'm going to blow your brains all over that desk.' He stared into Wong's eyes, trying to see if the man would do something stupid. Then he felt his pockets.

Rip Buckingham was standing frozen, staring at the dead man by the door, his jaw slack.

Jake marched Wong backward around the desk, opened and closed drawers. Sure enough, in one he found a pistol, a small automatic. It felt heavy enough.

'Rip.'

Buckingham turned toward him. Jake tossed him the automatic with his left hand.

'See if this is loaded.'

'I don't know ...'

'Pull the slide back, see if there is a shell in the chamber.'

Rip bent over slightly, his long hair falling across his face. He used both hands on the pistol. 'It's loaded,' he reported.

'Find the safety, put it to the off position.'

After several seconds, Rip said, 'Okay.'

'Fire a shot into that chair.'

Rip extended the pistol to arm's length, aimed, and pulled the trigger. The shot wasn't as loud as the boom from the snub nose, but it was loud enough.

'You're armed,' Jake told him. 'Go search all the rooms on this deck. Make sure Callie and Wu aren't here. Shoot anyone who looks at you cross-eyed. No conversation, just shoot them. Go!'

To his credit, Rip Buckingham went.

Keeping the snubbie against Wong's teeth, Jake began searching his desk. The papers were written in Chinese, which was no help to Jake. He tossed the stuff all over as he scanned it, looking for ... well, anything. Anything at all.

'You want to call the police?' Jake asked Wong.

Wong didn't reply.

'We can tell them about the kidnapping, have them call the American consul general, who will verify that the wife of an American flag officer was kidnapped by you and you personally demanded a ransom. American trade being what it is with China, I think the authorities might take a damn dim view of your activities, Mr. Wong.'

Jake didn't call the police because Callie would probably be dead by the time the police got to her. He didn't say that, of course, but that was the nub of it.

He marched Wong back around the desk and made him sit in a chair while he searched the dead man. This man was also armed, another small automatic. Jake pocketed it.

He sat across from Wong, kept the .38 in close to his body, and pointed right at Wong's solar plexus.

'I misjudged you, Mr. Grafton.'

'If I knew where she was, Wong, I'd kill you here and now and go get her.'

'I believe you.'

Jake sat silently, staring at the Chinese. For his part, Sonny Wong kept his mouth shut and didn't move.

The minutes crawled by. The telephone rang. Jake didn't answer it. After four rings the noise stopped.

Jake heard no shots, no shouts, no loud noises. Which was a good thing for Sonny Wong, because he would have been the first to die. Jake thought the man knew that, for he sat silently and still.

Eight minutes later, Rip returned. He had put the automatic in his pocket. 'There were some living apartments,' he told Jake, 'some men who looked at me curiously, but your wife and Wu aren't here.'

'Let's go,' Jake said, rising from his chair. 'Wong, you'll lead the parade. The thing you'll feel in your back is the barrel of this pistol. Honest to God, if there is any trouble from anyone, I'm going to empty this thing into your back. Now let's go.'

Down the stairs they went. They went out into the dining room, then into the kitchen. Five people were there, four men and a woman, preparing dishes for the patrons. Jake stood so they couldn't see the pistol he had on Wong and had Rip get everyone out of the kitchen.

When all five had left, Jake told Rip, 'Go out into the main dining room. Announce that there is a small fire in the kitchen and everyone should leave in an orderly way. Customers and employees, everyone. Don't let them panic. Just herd them off this barge.'

'A fire?'

'A small fire.'

Rip looked around the kitchen, looked at Sonny standing there with a blank face, looked at Jake. 'What about the people upstairs?' he asked.

'Working for Sonny Wong, they take their chances. If they have time to get out, good for them. If they don't, too bad. Now do as I say.'

'What about Wong?'

'He can leave with me or die here. His choice.'

Rip Buckingham took a deep breath. 'When you deliver a message, you really deliver, Grafton.'

Jake walked Wong over to the stove, a large gas burner with blue flames

805

from several of the jets. Nearby was a deep-fat fryer full of hot grease. Jake turned the flames under it up as far as they would go.

He traced out the gas lines, which were routed along the junction of the deck and bulkhead. Through a door, into a storage room. There it was, a tank of bottled gas or propane, Jake couldn't tell which.

Jake led Wong to the door to the dining area. He pushed it open a crack, watched Rip getting the small crowd off the floating restaurant onto sampans. Some of the employees kept looking toward the kitchen, but Rip insisted that Sonny himself wanted everyone to leave.

'Give me your shirt,' Jake said to Wong.

The Chinese unbuttoned the short-sleeve shirt and handed it over. With the pistol right against Wong's neck, Jake marched him to the deep fat fryer and dipped the shirt in. When it had absorbed a fair amount of grease, he tossed it onto the stove. The grease flared up.

Taking a step sideways to get a good view, Jake thumbed back the hammer of the revolver and aimed at the gas line. He missed with the first shot, but his second was rewarded with a loud hissing of escaping gas.

Jake eared back the hammer one more time, put the pistol against Wong's lips.

'There is no place on this planet you can hide, Mr. Wong. If any harm comes to my wife, I'm declaring war on you.'

Then Jake ran. Out the kitchen door, across the dining room as fast as he could scramble toward the sampan dock at the main entrance. He heard Sonny Wong running behind him.

The kitchen exploded with a dull boom.

Rip Buckingham was standing alone on the dock. There were no boats.

The fire came out the kitchen door; the dining room quickly filled with smoke.

Jake said, 'Shall we?' to Rip, took a last look at Wong, then dove into the black water. Rip was right behind him.

11

When the van brought Eaton Steinbaugh home after his radiation treatment, his wife, Babs, was waiting by the curb. He felt like hell. Babs helped him inside. He wanted to go to the study and lie down on the couch, and today she let him. Usually she insisted he go to the bedroom and get in bed, but not today.

'You got an E-mail,' she told him.

'Did you print it out?' he whispered.

'Don't I always?'

She handed him the sheet of paper. The message was from Hong Kong, somebody in Hong Kong – he had never before seen that E-mail address. The body of the message was a series of letters, arranged as if they were a word. He counted the letters. Twelve of them.

The letters appeared to be a code. And they were, but the code wasn't in the message. The twelve letters *was* the message.

He handed the sheet of paper back to Babs.

'Want to tell me what that means?' she said sharply.

'Within four hours.'

'Cole?'

'Yes.'

'Really, Steinbaugh, I don't know about you. Sick as you are and you're messing in other people's business. All away around the world, in China, no less.'

'Umpf.'

'They could prosecute you.'

'For what?'

'How would I know? Something, that's for sure.'

'They already did that,' her husband replied. 'Years and years ago.' When he was twenty he spent two years in a federal penitentiary for hacking into top-secret Pentagon computer files. Of course he was thrown out of the university and ended up never going back. That was over ten years ago.

'Prison didn't teach you a damned thing, obviously,' she snapped, and walked out with her head down.

A husband dying of cancer was a heavy load, and he appreciated that. Not much left for Babs to smile about.

Virgil Cole!

It was really happening.

Cole promised him it would. 'Have faith,' he said. 'The time will come.'

'I might be dead by then,' Eaton Steinbaugh told Cole. He hadn't been diagnosed with cancer then. Maybe it was a premonition.

'Hey, man, the Lord might call us all home before then. Just do your best to make it work when the hour comes.'

'They might change the codes. They might change the system.'

'If they do, they do. That's life. I don't want you to guarantee anything. Just do the best you can and we'll all live with it, however it turns out.'

Babs was sure as hell wrong, he reflected wryly, about what he learned in prison. While doing his time he taught a computer course for the inmates. Every day he had hours alone on the machine, hours in which he was supposed to be preparing lesson plans. He spent most of those hours hacking into networks and databases all over the globe. What he didn't do was tamper with the data that were there, so no one came looking for him. Locked up with nothing to occupy his mind, the hacking kept him sane.

That was then. Today just getting into a network was tougher, and a lot of the security programs had alarms that would reveal the presence of an unauthorized intruder. System designers finally were waking up to the threat.

But Eaton Steinbaugh had also learned a few things through the years. One was that getting in was a lot easier if you had access to the software and constructed a back door that you could use anytime you wanted.

He became a back door specialist. As soon as he was released from prison he was heavily recruited by software companies. Through the years he took jobs that interested him, and the demand for his skills forced the companies to pay excellent wages. For his own amusement, when he designed or worked on networks, he put in a trapdoor for his own use.

He was working for Virgil Cole's company when Cole called him in one day. Cole found one of the back doors, which was the first time anyone ever managed that trick.

That Cole! He was one smart cookie, shrewd and tougher than cold-rolled steel. Steinbaugh had never met a man like him.

Cole didn't fire him. Just told him to do a better job on the back doors or take them out.

He was working for Microsoft when Cole telephoned him eighteen months ago, wanted him to accept a job with Cole's company, which Cole was no longer with, go to China to do some Y2K remediation.

Steinbaugh had always refused Y2K remediations, which he regarded as mind-numbing grunt work, but he did it because Cole asked.

On his way to Beijing he went through Hong Kong and dropped in to see

Virgil Cole at the consulate. Cole took him to the best restaurant in town, which was French of course, where they ate a five-star gourmet dinner on white linen in a private alcove and sipped on a two-thousand-dollar bottle of wine.

'You didn't have to do this for me, you know,' Eaton Steinbaugh told Virgil Cole.

'I needed an evening out, and you're a good excuse.'

They were sipping cognac and sucking on Cuban cigars after dinner when Steinbaugh remarked, 'When you stop and reflect, life's contrasts are pretty amazing, aren't they?'

'What do you mean?'

'Well, I grew up in blue-collar Oakland, Dad worked on road-paving crews, we never had a whole lot. Then I wound up in prison, which was a bummer. Since then I've been all over the world, married, had a kid, and here I am in Hong Kong having a five-star dinner with a billionaire, just like I was somebody. You know?'

Cole laughed. Later Steinbaugh realized that Cole had hoped for this reaction, indeed, had played for it.

'I spent a lifetime working to get here, too,' he said. 'The low point in my life was a night in Vietnam. I was a bombardier-navigator on A-6 Intruder aircraft. One night near the end of the war the gomers shot us down.'

'I didn't know that,' Steinbaugh said.

Cole continued: 'I remember lying in the jungle with a broken back waiting for the North Vietnamese to find and kill me. I was absolutely certain I had come to the end of the road. And I was wrong.' He lifted his glass in a silent toast to Steinbaugh, and drank. Steinbaugh did likewise.

When he had his glass back on the table, Cole said, 'If the Chinese people can get rid of the Communists, who knows, perhaps in the fullness of time they too will have some of the same opportunities that have enriched our lives.'

'Yeah,' Steinbaugh agreed, for the comment seemed innocuous enough.

'I want your help to make it happen.'

Steinbaugh wasn't sure how to answer that.

'I want you to install some of your back doors,' Cole said, looking him straight in the eyes.

'Where?'

'On some systems in Beijing. You're going to be working on some systems in the Forbidden City, the Chinese Kremlin. I want you to install back doors so that when the time comes, you can get into those systems and control them, screw them up, or disable them.'

'When will the time come?'

'When the revolution starts.'

'Jesus Christ!' Steinbaugh's eyes got big in surprise. He had sort of suspected that Cole had something on his mind when he asked him to

809

come to see him in Hong Kong on his way to Beijing, but in his wildest imaginings he hadn't envisioned anything like this. 'A revolution! Me screwing with government computers to help a revolution – wouldn't that be an act of war or something?'

'I'm no lawyer,' Cole said, 'but I suspect you're right.'

The consul general's cigar had gone out, so he fussed over it, scraped off the ash, and got the thing smoldering again. When he saw that Eaton Steinbaugh was still listening, he went into specifics, some of which were very technical.

Steinbaugh was even more amazed, then he wasn't. Cole didn't do anything by guess or by God. He had thought about this, about what he wanted.

'Cyberwarfare,' Steinbaugh said.

'That's right. We must divert the government's attention, confuse them all to hell, make it as difficult as possible for them to figure out what the threat is. That's the first goal. Second, we want to make it difficult for the Communists to respond militarily to the real threat when they figure out what it is. Third, we must deprive them of control over the people, the economy, the course of events. If we can deprive them of the power to make things happen, we will win.'

'We?'

'You and me.'

'Oh, come on.'

'The revolutionaries.'

'You're one of them?'

'Yep.'

'Goddamn,' Steinbaugh said.

Of course he agreed to do it.

Eaton Steinbaugh had pretty well finished the Beijing assignment when he got sick and had to go home to California. He was just thirty-five years old, and the doctors said he had terminal cancer. He mailed Cole a note, told him he'd better hustle the future right along, make it happen soon. Cole knew what he meant.

Now, today, this message arrived.

Within four hours.

One more message to go.

Steinbaugh got up from the couch and turned on the computer. He had set up the E-mail system so it would notify him immediately of any incoming mail.

Babs heard the computer noises and came to the door.

'You're really going to do it, aren't you?'

'Yes.'

'You're a damned fool, Eaton. As if you don't have troubles enough, a

810

dying man about to face the Lord and answer for all you've done, bad and good. I don't know how many felonies you're going to commit now.'

'Neither do I. This is sort of fun, huh?'

She shook her head and went back to the kitchen.

Well, Babs was Babs. She was a good woman, although she knew absolutely nothing about computers, which were his passion. Truthfully, she didn't know much about men, either, or at least Eaton Steinbaugh – didn't know why he did what he did, made the choices he made. She thought him a fool for hacking as a young man and for his back doors, which he had made the mistake of mentioning a few years ago when they were talking about how fascinating his work was. Practical and unimaginative as always, she thought him a complete flaming idiot for helping Cole. He knew that, and somehow it didn't matter. She had never had any romance in her soul. Still, he loved her and she loved him, each in their own way, and that was good enough for this life.

When Jake Grafton got back to the consulate with Rip Buckingham, Tiger Cole's office was in an uproar. Even though it was almost midnight the lights were on, the secretary and two hovering aides looked white as ghosts, and Cole was on the phone. Since it was midnight here, it was noon in Washington.

Cole was standing beside the desk holding the telephone to his ear, looking out the window.

Although Jake didn't realize it, Cole was looking straight at the windows of the office of Third Planet Communications. There was a man at the window looking this way, but with the lights behind him, Cole didn't recognize him. Cole hoped the man was Hu Chiang on a break – Third Planet was going to be a busy place a bit later tonight.

On the telephone an undersecretary of state was demanding to know what the hell Cole had been up to in Hong Kong. The fax of Grafton's letter to the National Security Adviser had apparently found its way to his desk, and the undersecretary was shouting.

'A gross breach of trust, Cole. Outrageous! I have called the Justice Department. The lawyers there are recommending that the FBI investigate you for a possible treason prosecution. Do you hear me? *Treason!*'

'I don't know what to say, Mr. Podgorski. I suppose this incident will be an embarrassment to the administration.'

'An embarrassment? You suppose? It'll be a nightmare, Cole. How could you? You know the president is on a tightrope over China, and now *this!*'

'Darn. What was I thinking? A public discussion of the administration's willingness to deal with tyrants won't win you any friends, I fear.'

'Public discussion? Is that a threat?'

'You don't think I'm going to plead guilty to some trumped-up political charge or refuse to talk to the press, do you?' Cole asked dryly.

'Prosecutions are political acts. I promise you that you will be reading my repeated requests that the administration stand up for the human rights of China's enslaved citizens in *The New York Times*. This whole issue is going to get a full, complete, open airing. Perhaps my friends in Congress will decide to hold hearings.'

'Asshole! You asshole! I'm sending the FBI to arrest you. They'll be on the next plane.'

'I'll pack my toothbrush,' Cole told Podgorski and hung up the telephone.

'Sounds like it hit the fan in Washington,' Jake Grafton said.

'They are agitated. My resignation was sudden, unexpected. After mature reflection, I suspect they will claim executive privilege covers my resignation and the reasons for it. They may even refuse to acknowledge I was an appointee of the administration.'

Cole grinned. He did it so rarely that the effect was startling, as if a powerful light had been turned on. And as suddenly as it appeared, it was gone.

'Why are you dripping on my carpet?' Cole asked. His gaze went to Buckingham. 'Both of you?'

'Little fracas at Sonny Wong's restaurant in Aberdeen,' Jake said.

Rip added, 'Grafton started a fire. We had to swim for it.'

'Did you kill him?' Tiger Cole asked, referring to Sonny.

'No.' Jake sighed. 'I was sorely tempted. I almost wish I had. Wanted to put the fear in the bastard. Maybe he'll send her back. Even if he doesn't, maybe he'll keep his hands off her.'

The secretary looked at the admiral like he was insane. Both the aides were trying to keep control of their faces, with little success.

Rip Buckingham was beside himself. He shooed the secretary and aides from the room. When they were gone, he whispered hoarsely at Cole, 'This man's crazy. He shot a man dead in Wong's office. Pulled a gun from his pocket and shot him right in the bloody ticker. Didn't say a bloody word, just ... bang.'

Cole shook his head. 'That sure sounds like Jake Grafton.'

Jake pulled the pistol from his pocket, opened the cylinder, and picked out the empties. 'Need some more shells. Some gun oil too, if you have any. Salt water isn't good for these things.'

Buckingham sank into a chair and put his head in his hands.

'I called my attorneys in California,' Cole said. 'They need a day to sell some stock, raise some cash. They will be ready to wire-transfer the money to that Swiss account the day after tomorrow.'

'The day after tomorrow,' Grafton echoed. 'When Wong calls, why don't you tell him that he has to take them to a neutral place? I'll meet him there. When I see them safe and sound, I'll call you and you can wire the money. That way killing us won't solve his problem.'

'It'll be a start.'

'To be safe,' Jake explained, 'he has to kill Wu and you and everyone in the revolutionary movement who might oppose him or seek revenge. If all of you are in one place, after he gets the money he can just blow up the building and solve his problem.'

'Okay. But how are you going to get Wu and Callie out of harm's way after he gets his money?'

'I don't know yet. I'll have to think about it.'

'I don't think it can be done,' Tiger Cole said softly.

'Sonny can't afford to be known as the man who killed Wu,' Rip said. 'Sure, a lot of people know that he kidnapped Wu. But if he kills him . . .'

Cole opened a desk drawer, extracted a small box, and walked to the chair where Buckingham sat. 'This is your brother-in-law's finger,' he told Rip. 'Sonny Wong had it delivered this afternoon.'

Buckingham looked in the box and turned pale.

'We need Wu alive. China needs him.'

'Don't patronize me,' Rip said crossly. 'I'm a big boy.'

'How about doing another story for your dad? The last one was very good – got 'em in an uproar in Europe and Washington.'

'Okay,' Rip said, brushing the hair back out of his eyes. He handed the box back to Cole.

'You can use a computer in the office across the street. More on the coming revolution, about the goings-on in Hong Kong. E-mail it to Richard for tomorrow's papers. We want to make damn sure the world knows who the guys are in the white hats.'

Rip took a deep breath, his eyes still on the box.

'What do I say about Wu?'

'Don't mention him by name. 'Unnamed patriots' is the phrase. Nothing about Sonny Wong.'

After Rip left, Cole used the intercom to ask the secretary to get Jake some clean clothes from his apartment. Then he asked the admiral, 'Want a drink? I got some bourbon.'

'Yeah.'

'What did you tell Wong?'

'Not to harm Callie.'

'I'm sorry, Jake. Sorry you and Callie got mixed up in this.'

'Yeah.'

Jake was buttoning one of Cole's shirts when there was a knock on the door. Tommy Carmellini stuck his head in.

'I thought I'd find you here, Admiral. You left a note on my desk asking for a report?'

'I did. Come in.'

Carmellini dropped into an overstuffed chair and watched Jake put on his wet shoes over dry socks. 'You want it here, where Mr. Cole can hear?'

'Yep. What have you found out?'

The CIA officer removed a small notebook from an inside jacket pocket and flipped it open. 'The clerk selling the passports to Sonny Wong is a woman named Elizabeth Yeager.' He spelled the last name. 'She delivers the passports to her bedroom buddy, Carson Eisenberg, a CIA guy who is on Wong's payroll. She's been making false computer entries and writing up files to cover the thefts, so all the numbers will match when the department is audited.'

'How did you find out this information?'

'I opened the safes down there, checked the logbooks, then went into the secured cabinets.'

'Jesus!' Cole said. 'And I thought this place was reasonably secure.'

'Not even close,' Carmellini shot back.

'Do you have Eisenberg's contact?' Jake asked.

'Name, phone number, and address. And I got his banking information, where he's been depositing the cash he got from Wong.'

'What else?'

'Kerry Kent has been talking to some people in her apartment in Chinese. Don't know what it means without a translator, and don't know which translator around here I can trust. I sent the tape off to Washington.'

'Uh-huh.'

'The consul general uses English in his office, fortunately. He had a conversation earlier today with Kerry Kent about a plane that was supposed to arrive at seven this evening at Lantau Island. She was worried that with the airport closed, the plane couldn't land. Cole didn't think that would be a problem.'

Carmellini looked at Cole. 'Was it a problem, sir?'

'You're still taping conversations in this office?'

'Yes, sir. After you and the admiral had your little talk, I wired you up again.'

'Goddamn you, Carmellini! I told you – '

'Can't fire me,' Carmellini said smugly and grinned. 'I work for him.' He jerked his thumb at Grafton.

'Don't be a prick.'

'It's genetic. Folks often remark upon that fact. You'd think I worked for the IRS or – '

'Can it,' Jake Grafton snapped. 'Anything else?'

'Yeah. Cole's been lying to you.'

Grafton's eyes narrowed. He glanced at Cole, then concentrated on Carmellini. 'Explain.'

Carmellini extracted a sheaf of folded paper from another pocket. 'The National Security Agency has been doing some intercepts on certain E-mail addresses, and they passed along some dillies that Cole had been sending and receiving.'

Cole sat down behind his desk. He didn't look too upset.

'Seems that Mr. Cole has been E-mailing people in the states about something called York units. They are supposed to be on that plane.'

'York?'

'York units. Don't know what those are, but it is obvious to me from reading this correspondence that Mr. Cole is not a traitor, that certain people in the United States government are cooperating with him and providing him with technical and logistical support. Six York units, tech manuals, computers, WB cell phones, the list goes on and on.'

'I know what York units are,' Jake muttered and glanced again at Cole. As usual the consul general's face revealed nothing of its owner's thoughts.

'Anything else?' Jake said to Carmellini.

'That about covers the waterfront, I think.'

Jake looked at Cole. 'What do you want to do about Eisenberg and the Yeager woman?'

'Can't prosecute them with illegally obtained evidence.'

'They don't know how we got the evidence,' Carmellini pointed out.

'Have the personnel officer call them in and fire them,' Cole said to Carmellini. 'Then give them a choice: They can go home and be prosecuted for theft and espionage, or they can stay in Hong Kong. If they want to stay, run them out of the consulate. Tell them if they ever show up in the states again they *will* be prosecuted.'

'Yes, sir.'

Jake frowned at Carmellini. 'We're going to need some weapons that have a little more oomphf than this thirty-eight. Send the head marine up here and let me talk to him.'

Carmellini nodded and headed for the door.

'Take the bugs with you,' Jake added.

There were three of them, tiny things, cleverly hidden. Carmellini pocketed them, then left the room and closed the door behind him.

'Want to tell me about it?' Jake said.

'The administration wants the Communist era in China to end, and they are willing to help the rebels make it happen. But they don't want anyone to know they helped.'

'You're the fall guy?'

'I suppose. They had to have someone to blame and I volunteered. I thought you had figured that out. Life in California was getting to be a burden that I couldn't carry, and . . .' Cole shrugged.

Jake just nodded. He finished off his whiskey in one gulp and set the glass on the table by the couch.

'I guess the left hand and the right hand are still strangers in Washington,' Cole added.

'Yeah,' Jake Grafton replied. 'They never tell all of it.'

'Do you know these people who kidnapped us?' Callie Grafton asked Wu Tai Kwong between chattering teeth. He had used a piece of sheet to wash her wounds after she was brought back to the stateroom around midnight. He thought she had had a mild concussion, but she was shivering uncontrollably from her hours in the meat locker.

'I know them,' he replied. He had ripped a sheet into strips and wrapped them around the cuts in his arm. The bleeding seemed to have stopped.

'They wanted to know what was on the tape. The CIA had a bug hidden in China Bob Chan's library and taped the conversations there the night he died. I listened to the tape.'

'Sonny Wong is worried about what you heard.'

'You think?'

'He might be on the tape.'

'So who is Sonny Wong?'

'A gangster. Maybe the last big one in Hong Kong. There are many little gangsters, people who want to be big, but Sonny *is* big. Makes lots of money.'

Callie wrapped herself tighter in the blankets. She couldn't stop shivering. Her face hurt like hell and she was bruised and ached all over, but the deep cold she felt was worse.

'Is this about money?' she asked. 'Is that why we were kidnapped?'

'I think so.' Wu sat down on his bunk. His hand and arm were hurting. He rested his elbow on his knee with the hand elevated. 'Cole has so much. The temptation was too much for Sonny.'

Callie waited for Wu to say more. She saw a broad-shouldered, medium-sized Chinese man of about thirty years, not handsome, not ugly, the kind of man who could melt into any crowd bigger than three. Or could he? There *was* something . . .

'Sonny Wong is the security chief,' Wu said. 'Every revolution needs someone to enforce secrecy or the whole thing will collapse of its own weight. That is his job.'

Callie began to see it. 'So if someone talked to the police . . .'

'Sonny heard of it. He had people in every cell who reported to him. He plugged the leaks.'

'He killed people who talked?'

Wu lowered his head. 'Sometimes,' he admitted. 'Sometimes people saw the error of their ways and agreed to talk no more.'

'He's a thug.'

'An enforcer. It takes more than dreamers with stars in their eyes to make a revolution.'

'He's the dirty end of the stick.'

The metaphor threw Wu. Callie didn't feel like explaining.

'You trusted him that much?' Callie pressed.

'No one else wanted the job. No one wanted blood on his hands.'

'How did you know this loyal murderer wouldn't betray you?'

'I didn't know. Anyone could have betrayed me, any hour of any day.'

'Who is your thug in Beijing, Shanghai, et cetera?' Callie asked.

'Sonny has friends throughout most of China. Really, there was no one else who could do the job.'

Callie was unwilling to leave the subject. 'So you must have known that someday Wong might turn on you, take over the entire organization, put himself at the head? There is plenty of precedent, I believe. Saddam Hussein and Joe Stalin leap immediately to mind.'

'That was a possibility,' Wu Tai Kwong reluctantly admitted.

'So what did you plan to prevent that move from succeeding?'

'I planned to kill him before he killed me.'

'Looks like you may have miscalculated,' Callie snapped.

Thoroughly disgusted, she carried the blankets into the tiny bathroom and shut the door. The door had no lock.

12

Virgil Cole's daughter, Elaine, was an associate professor of mathematics at Stanford University. She was attending a women's political caucus in Washington, D.C., when she received a coded E-mail from her father. Like the message received by Eaton Steinbaugh, the E-mail consisted of a nonsense word, a dozen random letters, from an address in Hong Kong.

She received the message at noon when she checked her E-mail on her laptop in her hotel room. She got off-line, left the computer running, and gazed about her distractedly, the political meeting forgotten.

She opened the drapes on the window. Georgetown was visible but none of monumental Washington, which was out of sight to the right.

She had a small notebook in her computer case. She got it out now, opened it, and examined the notes she had written there. The handwriting was neat, almost compulsively so. She had made the notes the last time she was in Hong Kong visiting her father, over spring break.

Being Virgil Cole's daughter had always been a mixed blessing. He was quiet and unassuming, brilliant and rich. Somehow her mother's second husband never measured up. He was very nice, and yet ... When she was young she had thought her mother was crazy for not staying with her father, but as an adult, she could see how difficult Cole was, especially for her mother, who was neither brilliant nor quiet and unassuming.

Perhaps it had all worked out for the best.

Except for her half-brother, of course, who had never come to grips with the fire in his father's soul.

A Chinese revolution. Yes, that was Virgil Cole. A great impossible crusade to which he could give all of his brains and energy and determination would attract him like a candle attracts a moth.

She had never seen him so full of life as he was in April during her visit. A crusade! A holy war!

She had seen the fire in his eyes, so of course she said yes when he asked her to help. He didn't come right out and baldly ask. He explained what was needed, how the worm programs were already in place and at the right time needed to be triggered from a location outside of Hong Kong, triggered in such a way that the identity of the person doing it could never be established . . . beyond a reasonable doubt.

He explained the worms, how they were designed, and she carefully wrote down the instructions she needed to make them dance.

She played with her computer keyboard, checked the E-mail again.

So the revolution was *now*.

And she was going to help.

And she might never see her father again.

She was mulling that hard fact when the execute message came. She turned off the computer and stored it carefully in its carrying case. She left the case on the bed and took only the notebook with her.

She caught a taxi in front of the hotel and told the driver she wanted to go to the main public library.

Sure enough, the library had a bank of computers that allowed Internet access. The librarian at the desk near the computers was a plump, middle-aged woman. 'The fee is a dollar,' the lady told Elaine, who dug in her purse for a bill. 'Such a terrible irony – the computers are here for people who can't afford their own, but the users must help defray the cost.'

'I understand.'

'Everything costs, these days,' the librarian said. 'We're fighting the battle with the library board to get the fee eliminated, but so far they won't yield.'

'Yes.'

'Our only rule is no pornography. If people keep calling up pornographic sites, I'm afraid the computers will have to be removed.'

'Do you check to see what people are viewing on the Net?' Elaine asked, pretending to be horrified at this privacy intrusion.

'Oh, no,' the librarian assured her. 'But people do walk behind the cubicles, and they talk, you know!'

'Indeed they do. I'm here today to do some research for my thesis.'

'Let me know if you need any help,' the librarian said and turned to help the next person, a pimpled teen with unkempt long hair who looked as if he might be very interested in porno.coms. As Elaine walked away, the library lady began briefing this intent young man on the evils of cybersex.

With the notebook of passwords and computer codes on the table beside her, it took Elaine less than fifteen minutes to get through the security layers into the main computer of the central bank clearinghouse in Hong Kong. Once there, she began searching for the code that her father assured her would be there.

Virgil Cole answered the ringing cell phone on his office desk with his usual 'Hello.' He listened a moment, then broke the connection.

'The York units are in,' he told Jake Grafton, who was stretched out on Cole's couch thinking about his wife. 'Want to see them?'

'I thought Sergeant York was a paper program.'

'It's hardware now.'

'You got six?'

'That's right.'

'Steal 'em?'

'No.'

'Buy 'em?'

'Not quite. Let's say the American government retains legal title and I have custody.'

'Let's go look.' Jake reached for his shoes. 'I was wondering how you red-hot revolutionaries were going to avoid being massacred by the division of troops the PLA has stationed in Hong Kong. This is it, huh?'

There was not much traffic on the streets at this hour, but Jake Grafton paused in the entrance way of the consulate. Half hidden in the shadows, he restrained Cole with a touch on the arm while he scanned the street in both directions.

Only when he was sure there was no one waiting did he mutter at Cole and step through the entrance.

Cole led the way across the street and along the sidewalk for fifty yards. They went down the first alley they came to, then down a ramp to a loading dock under the skyscraper. A tractor-trailer rig was flush against the loading dock.

Cole climbed the stairs, nodded at two men sitting on the dock, and knocked on the door. A man carrying an assault rifle opened the door. Cole and Grafton went in.

The Sergeant York units were two-legged robots about six and a half feet tall. The legs had three knees – back, front, back – with three-pronged feet. They had articulated arms and, where human hands would be, three flexible grasping appendages, almost like jointed claws, which ended in sharp points. Two were hinged to close inward and one outward, almost like an opposed thumb.

Mounted on the right side of the torso on a flexible mount was a four-barreled Gatling gun that fired standard 5.56 millimeter rounds from a flexible belt feed. Capacity was two hundred rounds.

And the York units had heads mounted on flexible stalks that could turn right or left, be raised or lowered. Two Yorks were standing on the concrete floor back-to-back, turning their heads and looking about with an ominous curiosity.

'The best part,' Cole said with more enthusiasm than Grafton thought he had in him, 'is the tail. What do you think of the tail?' The prehensile tail was only about eighteen inches long, thick where it came out of the body and tapering quickly.

'It's cool.' Jake could think of no other reply.

'The engineers wanted three legs, and the army absolutely refused to buy the thing if it had more than two – they were worried about their image.

The tail was my compromise. It helps with stability, balance, agility, shock absorption. . . . With the tail the York is quicker and faster, and can leap higher. And it gives us room for more batteries, which are heavy.'

'What were those soldiers thinking?'

'Yeah.'

Three Chinese men were watching Kerry Kent walk a York out of the semitrailer. She used a small computer unit, much like a laptop. There were no wires. Like Grafton the Chinese men watched the Sergeant York robots and whispered to each other.

Jake Grafton felt mesmerized by the spectral stare of the robots that were outside the trailer. Their heads never stopped moving. They had no mouth or nose, but in the eye-socket position – the widest part of the head – were two cameras. The one on the right side had a lens turret on the face. As Jake inspected the nearest one, the turret rotated another lens in front of the left camera, if it was a camera.

'What the hell are these things looking at?' he asked Cole.

'Us, the room we're in, everything. They are learning their surroundings.'

'Smart machines?'

'These things use a combination of digital and analog technology in their central processors so they can learn their surroundings without having to carry around computers the size of grand pianos. It's a neural network, modeled on the human brain. That breakthrough in computer design was one of the advances that took robot technology to another level.'

'I see,' Jake said as the third robot walked to a spot beside the other two and came to a stop. It tilted its head a minute amount, almost quizzically, as it scrutinized the two men.

'One of the fascinating things about neural networks,' Cole continued, 'is that the network needs rest periods or the error rate increases. Nap times.'

'What is that thing looking for?' Jake asked, indicating the curious York.

'Just checking for weapons. When they're in a combat mode, they fire on unidentified persons carrying weapons.'

'They can't shoot at everyone with a weapon. How do the Yorks separate the good guys from the bad guys?'

'It's a complex program, based on physical characteristics – such as size, clothing, sex, possession of a weapon – and aggressive behavior. Some behavioral scientists worked with our programmers to write it.'

'Sex?'

'Most soldiers are men. That's a fact.'

'I see.'

'My main contributions to the Sergeant York project were some breakthroughs in ultrawide bandwidth radio technology. They communicate with their controller and with each other via UWB, which as you probably know has some unusual characteristics, unlike UHF or VHF.

'So these things talk to each other?'

'They are a true network – what one knows, they all know. Information is exchanged via UWB on a continuous basis, which means that these six are soon working from a very detailed three-dimensional database. Each unit also contains a UWB radar, so it can see through walls and solid objects. Very short-range, of course. The radars are off-the-shelf units, stuff being used to inspect bridge abutments for cracks and look for lost kids in storm sewers.'

'What about the stalk on top of the head?'

'There is a flexible lens there for looking around corners. The sensor on the right side of the head works with visible light, the left with infrared. At night the sensitivity on the right sensor automatically increases so it can handle starlight.'

The fourth York walked out of the truck and took a position beside the others but facing off at a ninety-degree angle.

'These units are prototypes,' Cole explained, 'not the refined designs the U.S. army will get as production units. These lack sensors in the rear quadrant, so they usually want to face in different directions so they will get the three-hundred-and-sixty-degree panorama.'

'They "want"?'

'Sergeant York has artificial intelligence. The operator can position the units, monitor their performance, override automatic features, approve target selection and the like, but these things can be turned loose on full automatic mode – then they fight like an army. They *are* an army. We developed them to fight and win on the conventional battlefield, the tactical nuke battlefield, and urban battlefields like Mogadishu. The Somali experience was the catalyst for their development.'

Jake whistled, and two of the York units turned their heads to look at him.

'I guess I forgot to mention audio. They have excellent hearing in a much wider frequency spectrum than the human ear can handle.'

'How much battle damage can they sustain?'

'A lot. They are constructed of titanium, the internal works are shielded with Kevlar, and Kevlar forms the outer skin. Still, mobility is their main defense.'

'Two legs and a tail ... how mobile are they?' the admiral asked.

Cole pointed to the Kevlar-coated areas on the nearest York's leg, the shapes of which were just visible under the skin. 'The major muscles are hydraulic pistons; the minor ones are electromechanical servos – which means gears, motors, and magnets. A couple of ring-laser gyros provide the balance information for the computer, which knows the machine's position in relation to the earth and where the extremities are; it uses the pistons and servos to keep the thing balanced. York is extremely agile, amazingly so considering it weighs four hundred and nine pounds without ammunition.'

'Power?'

'Alas, batteries. But these are top-of-the-line batteries and can be recharged quickly or just replaced in the field, a slip-out/slip-in deal. In addition, since the outer layer of each unit's Kevlar skin is photoelectric, outdoors on a sunny day the batteries will stay pretty much charged up as long as excessive exertion is not required of the unit.'

Jake Grafton shook his head, slightly awed. 'How much does one of these damned things cost?'

'Twice the price of a main battle tank, and worth every penny. They can use every portable weapon in the NATO inventory. Hell, they can even drive a hummer or a tank if you take out the seat and make room for the tail.'

'Uh-huh.'

All six were out of the semitrailer now. They arranged themselves in a circle, each facing outward. They made a small whining sound when they moved, a sound that would probably be inaudible with a typical urban ambient noise level.

'Preproduction prototypes,' Cole said when Jake mentioned the noise. 'The production units won't make those noises.'

Kerry Kent came over, her wireless computer in her hand. 'Let me introduce you to Alvin, Bob, Charlie, Dog, Easy, and Fred.'

She was referring to the small letter on the back of each unit's head and on both shoulders. The nicknames were slight twists on the military phonetic alphabet system.

'The New York Net,' Jake Grafton said. He wasn't trying to be funny because he wasn't in the mood: The thought merely whizzed through his cranium and popped out about as fast. Kent and Cole looked at him oddly without smiling.

She showed Jake the computer presentation. 'Each unit can be controlled by its own computer, or one computer can control as many as ten units. When I'm in network mode, I can see what each unit is seeing or look at the composite picture.' She moved an icon with a finger and tapped it. Jake leaned forward. The picture did have a remarkable depth of field, although it was presented on a flat screen.

She tapped the screen again. 'As you can see, I can designate targets, tell specific units to engage it, or let the computer pick a unit. I can assign each unit a task, tell it to go to a certain position, assign targets, basically run the fight with this computer. Or I can go to an automatic mode and let the system identify targets in a predetermined order of priority and engage them.'

'What if your computer fails or someone shoots you?'

'The system defaults to full automatic mode, which happens to be the preferred mode of operations anyway.'

Jake shook his head. 'The bad guys are going to figure out what they are up against pretty quickly. Maybe rifle bullets will bounce off these guys, but grenades, rockets, mortars, artillery?'

'Mobility is the key to the York's survival,' Kerry rejoined. She tapped the screen.

Charlie York stirred. It tilted its head back to give itself a better view of the overhead, which was about twelve feet up. It crouched, swung its arms, and leaped with arms extended.

It caught the edge of an exposed steel beam and hung there, its tail moving to counteract the swaying of its body. Everyone in the room exhaled at once.

Jake stood there for several seconds with his mouth agape before he remembered to close it. The dozen Chinese men in the room were equally mesmerized. After a moment they cheered.

'The units can leap about six feet high from a standing position,' Kerry Kent explained. 'On the run they can clear a ten-foot fence. They normally stand six feet six inches high; at full leg extension they are eight feet tall.'

'Very athletic,' Cole said, nodding his head. He didn't grin at Jake, but almost.

'How long are you going to let Charlie hang from the overhead?' the admiral asked Kent.

Her finger moved, and Charlie dropped to the floor. The unit seemed to catch itself perfectly, balancing with its hands, arms, and tail. Now Charlie looked at Jake, tilted its head a few inches.

In spite of himself, Jake Grafton smiled. 'Wow,' he said.

A half dozen men began checking the Yorks, inspecting every visible inch. They had been trained at Cole's company in California as part of a highly classified program. One man began plugging extension cords into the back of each unit to recharge the batteries. The other men busied themselves carrying crates of ammunition out of the back of the semitrailer and stacking them against a wall.

'So tomorrow is the day?' Jake muttered to his former bombardier-navigator.

'Yep,' said Tiger Cole.

'Another big demonstration in the Central District?'

'Yep. The army will be there. We'll strap them on with the Yorks.'

'Jesus Christ! A lot of civilians are going to get caught in the cross fire.'

Cole nodded once, curtly.

'Do it at night, Tiger. Maximize the advantage that high tech gives you. These Yorks probably see in the dark as well as they do in the daytime.'

'This isn't my show.' Tiger's voice was bitter. 'I argued all that and lost. Revolution is a political act, I was told, the first objective of which is to radicalize the population and turn them against the government. Daytime was the choice.'

'Explain to me the difference between your set of high-minded bloodletters and the high-minded bloodletters you are trying to overthrow.'

'That's unfair and you know it. You know who and what the Communists are.'

Grafton let it drop. This wasn't the time or place to argue politics, he decided. After a bit he asked, 'Why only six of these things? Why not a dozen?'

'It will be a couple years before the first production models come off the assembly line,' Cole told him. 'We got all there are.'

'I hope they're enough.'

'By God, so do I,' Tiger Cole said fervently.

'Here's a sandwich and some water, Don Quixote,' Babs Steinbaugh said. She scrutinized the computer monitor. The E-mail program was still there, waiting.

Eaton Steinbaugh sipped on the water. The sandwich looked like tuna salad. Babs read his mind: 'You have to eat.'

He took the duty bite, then laid the sandwich down. Yep, tuna salad!

'China is so far away,' she mused. 'What can you do from here?' Here was their snug little home in Sunnyvale.

'Everything. The Net is everywhere.' His answer was an oversimplification, of course. Steinbaugh didn't speak a word of Chinese, yet he knew enough symbols to work with their computers. He wasn't about to get into a discussion of the fine points with Babs, however, not if he could help it.

'This Cole . . . is he paying you anything?'

'No.'

'Did you even ask for money?'

'We never discussed it, all right? He didn't mention it and neither did I.'

'Seems like if you're going to do the crime, you oughta get enough out of it to pay the lawyers. For Christ's sake, the man's filthy rich.'

'Next time.'

She grunted and stalked away.

Babs just didn't appreciate his keen wit. Next time, indeed!

As he waited he thought about the trapdoors – sometimes he referred to them as back doors, because he had installed them – which were secret passages into inner sanctums where he wasn't supposed to go. While in Beijing he had worked on the main government computer networks in the Forbidden City. The powers that be didn't want to let him touch the computers, but Cole's company had the contract and the Chinese didn't know how to find the problems and solve them, so they were between a rock and a hard place. After much bureaucratic posturing and grandstanding, they let him put his hands on their stuff.

The network security system was essentially nonexistent. That was deplorable, certainly, but understandable in a country where few people had access to computers. Constructing and installing a back door was child's play once he figured out the Chinese symbols and Pinyin commands. A Pinyin dictionary helped enormously.

Installing back doors in other key government computer systems was not terribly difficult either, for these computers all were linked to the mainframes in the Forbidden City.

Like all top-down systems, the Communist bureaucracy with its uniform security guidelines and procedures was extremely vulnerable to cybersabotage. The best ways to screw with each computer system tended to be similar from system to system, but what worked best with railroad timetables and schedules usually didn't work at all for financial systems. Putting it all together was a sublime challenge, the culmination of his lifelong interest in logical problems. Eaton Steinbaugh enjoyed himself immensely and was bitterly disappointed when the reality of his cancer symptoms could no longer be ignored.

His illness did create another problem, however, one that he took keen interest in solving. The whole point of triggering the inserted code programs from outside Hong Kong was to prevent compromising the computer facility there – Third Planet Communications. But the person doing the triggering was going to leave a trail through the Internet, a trail that government investigators could later follow back to the guilty party.

Unless the guilty party disguised his tracks, made the trail impossible to follow. One way to do that was to use a generic computer, one dedicated to public use, so the identity of the user could never be established beyond a reasonable doubt. Due to his illness, Steinbaugh thought he might be unable to leave his home. He spent a delightful week working up a way to cover his trail through cyberspace and thought he had the problem solved. He wrote a program that randomly changed the ID codes buried throughout his computer's innards – called 'cookies' – every time the codes were queried by another computer. He liked the program so much that when the China adventure was over he intended to post it on the Internet for the use of anyone seeking to screw with the commercial Web sites that were constructing profiles of visitors to sell to advertisers and each other, a practice that formed the slimy foundation of E-commerce. Of course, if he wasn't as clever as he thought he was, the FBI was going to be knocking on his door one of these days.

Not that it mattered. In or out of jail, Eaton Steinbaugh only had a few months to live, at the most.

Today, when the computer on his desk began signaling that he had an incoming E-mail, he began pecking at the keys in feverish anticipation.

Yes, there it was. From Virgil Cole. A series of numerals. He counted them.

Eleven.

That was right. Eleven random numbers. The guys at NSA would undoubtedly rack their brains for days trying to crack the code that wasn't there.

As soon as possible.

That was the message.

Start as soon as possible.

Too excited to sit, Steinbaugh got up, stretched, stared at the screen. Start with a bang, he decided.

He sat back down and began.

In less than a minute he was at the door of the main government computer in Beijing looking for his back door.

He typed. Pushed the Enter button.

Nothing.

Don't tell me those bastards have changed the access codes.

Not to worry. He had anticipated that possibility.

There! He found it.

He typed some more, inputting a code that no one else on earth knew.

And voilà!

In, in, in!

Ha ha ha ha ha!

Eaton Steinbaugh consulted his notebook, the one in which he had painstakingly written everything, just in case. A copy of the book was in his lawyer's hands, with instructions to send it to Cole when Steinbaugh died.

He found the menu he wanted, typed some more.

In three minutes he was face-to-face with a critical operational menu, one that gave him a variety of choices. He stared at the Pinyin, consulted his notebook, carefully scrolled the page . . . yes. Here it was.

He moved the mouse. Positioned the cursor over the icon just so. Clicked once.

Sure enough, the system now gave him access to yet another system, with another menu.

This menu had five choices: safe, arm, fire, self-destruct, exit.

He positioned the icon over the one he wanted, then clicked the button on the mouse.

Just like that. That was all it took.

Sue Lin Buckingham was waiting for Rip when he got home. He had written another story for the Buckingham newspapers predicting imminent revolution in Hong Kong and sent it to Sydney via E-mail. It would be published under his father's byline, of course, as the first one was.

'Your father sent an E-mail,' Sue Lin said. 'He will wire the money to Switzerland tomorrow.'

Rip just nodded. All the members of the Scarlet Team had been in the Third Planet office except Wu and Sonny Wong. Amazingly, the team was going on with the plan despite the fact that one of their members had kidnapped the leader.

Wu had put it together, pushed the entire population of Hong Kong – and China, for the revolutionary movement was nationwide – toward this day with the force of his personality and leadership ability. Now he was a prisoner, held for ransom to enrich Sonny Wong, and nothing could be done!

Rip Buckingham stared at his wife's drawn features. 'I don't know what to say,' he told her. 'I saw Wong earlier this evening at his restaurant. He has Wu, all right. Perhaps Wong will release your brother, perhaps he will kill him. Regardless, we march on.'

'Can't the senior leadership force Wong to release Wu?'

'There isn't time for that distraction, they say.' Rip's upper lip curled. 'Some of them seem to think Sonny will share the money with them.'

'You think?'

'I don't know what to think.'

Rip threw himself in a chair. 'I once saw an avalanche in the Andes,' he mused. 'It started slowly enough, but once it began to move no power on earth could stop it. The moving snow carried everything with it – trees, rocks, dirt, more snow. It got bigger and bigger and moved faster and faster . . .'

He looked at his wife. 'Perhaps they are right. Perhaps going forward is our only choice.'

She poured him a glass of wine.

'Have you told your mother?' he asked.

'Not yet.'

The military base in the arid lands of western China was not a garden spot. Too far from the ocean to receive much moisture, its weather was dominated by the Asian continental high. In the summer the area was too hot, in the winter far too cold, and too dry all the time. High peaks with year-round caps of snow were visible to the north and southwest. And always there was the wind, blowing constantly in a vast, clear, clean, open, empty sky.

The high desert was as physically different from the humid coastal lands of China as one could possibly imagine. Still, for the Chinese, the reality of the place was determined by a far different factor, one that had nothing to do with terrain or weather: The high desert was very sparsely populated.

For people who spent their lives in densely populated urban or rural environments, surrounded by relatives and cousins and lifelong friends, life in the empty desert was cultural shock of the worst sort. The isolation marked each and every one of the soldiers. Some it broke, some it made stronger, all it changed.

The primitive living conditions at the base didn't help. True, China had developed the high-tech industries that created the nuclear weapons and intercontinental ballistic missiles that were the reason the base existed, but the troop barracks were uninsulated and the men used latrines. The water was not purified, so minerals stained the teeth of the men who had been here for years.

Lieutenant Chen Fah Kwei hated the place. Tonight he was the duty officer in the underground bunker that housed the missile launch controls. There were six missiles in this complex, new ones outfitted with the latest fiber-optic ring-laser gyros and high-speed guidance systems. Truly it was an honor to be the soldier in charge of this arsenal of national power, but Lieutenant Chen wished his transfer to Shanghai would come through soon. He had honor enough to last a lifetime, and he wanted to live someplace with eligible women, laughter, music, books, films . . .

Tonight he thought longingly about these things while he inspected his teeth. He was using his knife blade for a mirror. As he studied the reflection of his open mouth in the highly polished blade, he decided that, indeed, the minerals were turning his teeth yellow. He tried to consume the minimum amount of water, swallowed it as quickly as he could, but still the minerals were ruining his teeth.

Glumly, he glanced at the monitors of the main computer, which displayed the status of the six missiles in their silos. Bored, sleepy, and homesick, he was playing with his knife when he felt the first thump, a physical concussion that actually rocked his chair.

At first he thought it was an earthquake, but nothing else happened.

He glanced at the monitor.

Missile One. The status had gone red. Silo temperature was off the scale, hot. Now the fire light began flashing.

Stunned, he stared at the monitor for several seconds while he tried to comprehend the information displayed there.

A fire! There was a fire in Silo One.

He flipped a switch on the panel before him, and instantly a black-and-white television picture of the inside of the silo appeared on a monitor mounted high in the corner of the control room.

He stared at the picture. He couldn't see anything. The missile wasn't there. All he could see was . . . was . . .

Flames.

Flames!

He pushed the red alarm button on his console. He could hear the distant klaxon, which was ringing here, in the barracks, and in the fire station. Men to fight the fire, that was what he needed.

He looked back at the television . . . and the set was blank. The fire had burned up the camera or the leads.

The computer monitor . . . Still getting readouts, but they were cycling. The temperature was going through thirteen hundred degrees Fahrenheit.

Missile fuel and liquid oxygen must be feeding the fire. At those temperatures the concrete of the silo would burn, the cap would rupture, and nuclear material from the warhead might be ejected into the atmosphere, to be spread far and wide by the wind.

Lieutenant Chen Fah Kwei pushed another alarm button on his panel. The wail of the siren warning of a possible nuclear accident joined the blare of the klaxon.

What had happened?

The missile must have ruptured, spilling fuel all over the interior of the silo, where it caught fire.

That must be –

Even as those thoughts raced through Chen's mind, he felt another thump in the seat of his pants.

The monitor. *Silo Two!*

His fingers danced across the controls, bringing up the camera.

A sea of fire.

Sabotage?

The telephone rang. Chen snagged it.

The colonel. 'Report,' he demanded.

'Sir, the missiles are blowing up in the silos. Two have gone.'

Even as he spoke the third missile exploded.

'Impossible,' the colonel told him.

'The silos are on fire!' Chen screamed. 'I can see the fire on the television monitors. The temperatures are unbelievable. The concrete will burn.'

'Activate the automatic firefighting system.'

'Which silos?'

'All of them,' the colonel roared.

Chen did as he was told. The firefighting system would spray tons of water into the silos as fast as the huge pumps could supply it.

The system was on and pumping as the missiles in Silos Four, Five, and Six exploded in order.

The control room was crammed with people shouting into telephones and talking to each other at the top of their lungs when Chen realized that one explanation of the tragedy was that the self-destruct circuits in the missiles had been triggered.

Of course, he had not triggered anything. The safety caps on the self-destruct switches were still safety-wired down. To destroy a missile in flight, the appropriate cap had to be forcibly lifted and the switch thrown before a self-destruct order was sent to the computer.

But what if the computer received or generated a self-destruct order without the button being pushed? Was that possible? It seemed to have happened six times!

Perhaps, Lieutenant Chen thought, *the thing I should have done after the first explosion was turn off the main computer.*

13

Ma Chao was a fighter pilot in the air force of the People's Liberation Army. Based at Hong Kong's new international airport at Chek Lap Kok on Lantau Island, across the runway from the main passenger terminal, his squadron was equipped with Shengyang J-11 fighters, a Chinese license-built version of the Russian-designed Sukhoi Su-27 Flanker, one of the world's premier fighters.

Major Ma's squadron came to Hong Kong in 1997 upon the departure of the British. For Ma Chao and his fellow pilots, the move to Hong Kong had been a cultural shock of the first magnitude. They had been stationed at a typical base several hundred miles up the coast, across the strait from Taiwan. Ma Chao had grown up in Beijing and attended the military academy, where he was selected for flight training.

His first operational posting was to the squadron where he still served, almost twenty years later. When he first reported the squadron was equipped with the Chinese-made version of the Russian MiG-19, called the F-6.

The F-6 was the perfect plane for the Chinese air force. It was a simple, robust, swept-wing day fighter, easy to maintain and operate, adequately armed with three 30-millimeter cannon and two air-to-air heat-seeking missiles. Although the fuel capacity was relatively limited, as it was in all 1950s-era Soviet designs, the plane's single engine was powerful enough to give it supersonic speed.

Ma had loved the plane, which was a delight to fly. Unfortunately he didn't get to fly it often. The fuel and maintenance budget allowed each pilot to fly no more than two or three times a month, and then only in excellent weather. Fearful that the undertrained pilots might crash if they tried to fly aggressively, the generals insisted that the planes be flown as near to the center of their performance envelopes as possible. These doctrine limitations were universal throughout the air force.

Although the Chinese licensed the Su-27 design from the Russians for manufacture in order to upgrade the capabilites of their air force, the set-in-stone training limitations did not change. Ma and his fellow fighter pilots were strictly forbidden to perform aerobatic maneuvers or stress the airplanes in any way that might increase the risk of losing the plane. Consequently, their fortnightly training flights consisted of a straightforward climb to altitude, followed by a straight and level intercept under the control of a ground-based radar operator – a ground-controlled intercept, or GCI – then a return to base.

Ma Chao had spent his adult life with this system, never questioning it. The revelation occurred in Hong Kong a month after he arrived. One evening a woman he had come to know showed him a videotape of an Su-27 aerobatic performance at a Paris air show years before. Ma was astounded by the airplane's capabilities, which had been there all the time, waiting for the pilot with the courage to utilize them.

It seemed that all the assumptions upon which Ma Chao's life was based were equally suspect. Ma Chao soon discovered that Hong Kong, with its high-tech, high-rise, high-rent hustle and bustle and diversity, was as close to paradise as he would ever get. Every trip away from the squadron spaces was sensory overload, a cultural adventure that Ma and his friends found extraordinarily fascinating.

When he was finally approached by members of Wu Tai Kwong's Scarlet Team, he was an easy recruit. From the cockpit of an Su-27 he could see the future. Wu Tai Kwong was absolutely right: The great city of Hong Kong that Ma Chao flew over every two weeks was the future of the Chinese people; the rice paddies and poverty of the mainland were the past.

This June night Ma Chao was in the barracks preparing for bed when his cell phone rang. The cell phone was one of the wonders of the new age – Ma hadn't even known such things existed until he came to Hong Kong. This one was very special and could not be purchased commercially. This phone handled normal cellular telephonic communications well enough, but it also received covert wide bandwidth messages that were broadcast over commercial television signals. Since the WB signals degraded normal television reception slightly, this technology was never going to be approved for commercial use.

Tonight the message was a single line of traditional Chinese poetry. Ma Chao knew precisely what the code meant: Tomorrow!

Sonny Wong also knew what the message meant when he heard it. The senior leadership of the Scarlet Team had decided that the cause was more important than Wu Tai Kwong.

Sonny was certain that would be the decision, but it was nice to see events work out as he had predicted they would.

The government had provided the opening; the Scarlet Team would lead the revolution of the Chinese people. Sonny Wong would collect fifty million dollars from Virgil Cole and ten million from Rip Buckingham, a nice comfortable fortune that he would keep in Switzerland. This pile would be his safety net, his rainy day money, to be used if the Communists proved too tough to crack.

Once he had the money, he would eliminate Wu, Virgil Cole, and Hu Chiang. With these three out of the way, he would be in position to take over the Scarlet Team.

Yes, indeed, thought Sonny Wong, if he played his cards correctly, he could conceivably wind up as the next ruler of China. Emperor Wong. President Wong. Premier Wong. Whatever.

Or he could sell the Scarlet Team to the Communists and retire rich, rich, rich ... live on the French Riviera, play baccarat at Monte Carlo....

The loss of the restaurant this evening was an irritant, but only that.

He had dealt with brashness and disrespect before – and those fools were long gone. Jake Grafton was as good as dead: Sonny had already given the order.

Many of the students at the University of Hong Kong were not asleep this night. They were huddled together in apartments and bars all over the city. When the WB cell phones rang and they heard the coded message, a cheer went up.

Then they dispersed, went home to try to sleep a few hours and prepare for the day to come.

One of the people with a WB cell phone – made in California and smuggled in by China Bob Chan for Third Planet Communications – was Lieutenant Hubert Hawksley of the Hong Kong police. Hawksley had come to Hong Kong as a soldier in the British army way back when and liked it so much he wangled a police job when his army enlistment was up.

Other British policemen left when Hong Kong was turned over to the Communists, but Hawksley stayed. Through the years he had enjoyed a fine income, very little of which came to him in his pay envelope. He found the oriental way of life congenial and thought he understood the Chinese. Try as he might, he could not imagine that the Communists would be less corrupt than the colonial British. That opinion proved to be prophetic.

One of Hubert Hawksley's many professional acquaintances was Sonny Wong. Sonny had paid Hawksley quite a pile of money over the years. The thing about Sonny was that he was regular. Every month as regular as the post the money arrived. Cash.

One day a year or so ago Sonny had approached Hawksley at the floating restaurant, one of Hawksley's hangouts. He had joined the policeman at the bar, torn up Hawksley's tab, and ordered a beer himself.

'Are you hearing any rumors these days?' Sonny wanted to know when he finally got around to business.

'About what?'

'Sedition. Treason. Antirevolutionary goings-on.'

'All the time,' the policeman said genially. 'The regime is vigilant. The secret police are on the job.'

'They pass intelligence to you?'

'Of course. We keep them informed, they keep us informed.'

'I was wondering if you might make me a copy of any information you receive along those lines. My friends and I would be willing to pay.'

'How much?' Hawksley asked sharply.

'Five thousand Hong Kong a month.'

'My risk is large,' Hawksley replied.

'Six, then.'

'Seven.'

Sonny paused to think that over. 'Of course,' he said, 'our long-standing arrangements would be unaffected.'

'Of course.'

'In addition to knowing what the state security people tell you, we would like to . . . shall we say . . . edit . . . any reports along these lines that the force passes to state security.'

'Ahhh . . .'

Hawksley ordered another glass of stout while he thought about whom he would have to bribe to make that happen. He explained the organizational reality to Wong, then tried to estimate what the responsible people would need in the way of money to help Wong out.

'They mustn't know my name, of course,' Sonny muttered. 'Some of them might take my money and whisper my name. That would be bad.'

'Not cricket,' Hawksley agreed.

They settled on a figure of twenty thousand Hong Kong, which had to be adjusted up a couple of thousand when one of the captains on the force proved to be greedier than Hawksley had estimated.

Since then Hawksley had learned a great deal about the Scarlet Team, and he had passed much of what he learned right back to Sonny. Various people had tried to betray Wu Tai Kwong, of course, and they had disappeared from Hong Kong, never to be seen again. A few people thought they could become police informants, one or two wanted to explain about sabotage plans.

At one point Hawksley knew so much he began to fear for his life. He wrote down what he knew, made a copy, then gave the copy to Sonny with a remark or two about the original.

Sonny had merely smiled, raised the money to twenty-five thousand a month.

Still, Hubert Hawksley began to think seriously about early retirement and a return to England. He mentioned these plans to Sonny one day, and Sonny tried to dissuade him.

'I know too much,' Hawksley told the gangster.

'Not at all. Anyone in your position is going to learn a great deal, and you are a reliable man. The next man might not be. Stay awhile, see this through. Earn all the money you can. Leave Hong Kong a wealthy man.'

He stayed, of course.

And now, in the wee hours of the morning, the WB cell phone given to him by a woman trying to avoid prosecution for theft squawked into life, waking Hawksley from a sound sleep. He knew the significance of the message. Afterward he lay awake in the darkness thinking about what was to come.

Today, he decided, was going to be an excellent day to call in sick.

All over China the special cell phones rang, stimulated by a WB signal piggybacking on the signals of every television station in the country, and all over China the owners of the cell phones listened with mixed emotions.

For some, the message was a signal for a mission that had to be accomplished on an agreed timetable. For others, the signal meant to wait a little while longer. For all, it was a message heralding the coming of a new day.

The single-sheet flyers were piled willy-nilly on street corners, in subway, store, and office building entrances, and in the entrances to the endless blocks of government-owned apartment buildings. The headline on the front page trumpeted: BANK RECORDS WIPED OUT IN MASSIVE COMPUTER FAILURE.

The story began:

A massive computer failure last night at the Hong Kong bank clearinghouse wiped out the computerized records of member banks, which are all the banks in Hong Kong. Sources say that the computerized account records of the borrowers and depositors of the affected banks have been destroyed and will have to be reconstructed from backup tapes where they exist, and by hand from written records, which all banks maintain, before the banks can again open for business. The task will take weeks.

It is common knowledge that various high government officials have demanded and received personal loans at ridiculously low interest rates from Hong Kong banks, which were the only banks affected by the clearinghouse computer failure.

The story continued, citing no sources but implying that the government had willfully destroyed the bank records to hide official corruption.

Very little of the story was true, a fact Rip Buckingham had pointed out to Wu weeks ago when he was asked to write it. 'The government,' Wu said, 'has told so many lies that people are ready to believe the worst. The goal is to put government officials on the defensive. The story in the flyer must create doubt in people's minds.'

The story did more than that, though. It called for a general strike and a mass demonstration in the Central District today to protest the malfeasance of the government.

Lin Pe was up at first light. She had been rising at that hour ever since she could remember and saw no reason to change at this stage of her life. She used the early morning hours to work on her fortunes or the books of the Double Happy Fortune Cookie Company, occasionally to correspond with friends. Every few weeks she had to sign all the company checks that her accountant had prepared, payroll and suppliers and utilities and the like. The checks were there on the table, but since the bank collapsed, it was ridiculous to sign them.

This morning she got out the fortune book and sat reading while she waited for a good idea to arrive. When inspiration was hard to find, as it often was, she would wait patiently. If she didn't think about too many other things a good idea would show up eventually.

She had a lot on her mind these days: Wu, the frozen accounts at the Bank of the Orient, her daughter Sue Lin, Rip, whether she should sell the cookie company to Albert Cheung . . .

Sue Lin knocked, then came into the room carrying a flyer.

'Mother,' she said, 'all the banks will be closed.'

Lin Pe read the story, then laid the flyer aside and sat looking out the window at the great city. 'I can't meet my payroll,' she said softly.

'Oh, no one will expect to be paid,' Sue Lin said dismissively. 'Too much is happening.' She sat down facing her mother and told her about Wu's kidnapping.

Old Lin Pe listened to everything her daughter had to say and asked no questions. When Sue Lin ran out of steam she sat silently looking at her mother, who rubbed her hands together, then smoothed her hair.

'Wong will kill him after he gets the money,' Lin Pe said finally.

'Maybe not,' Sue Lin said, unwilling to cross that bridge. She felt so helpless. 'What can we do?'

Her mother sat staring at the wall, saying nothing.

As Jake Grafton walked the streets to the ferry landing in the hour after dawn, he had to thread his way around the citizens of Hong Kong, who were engrossed in the flyers that littered the streets and sidewalks.

Jake had tried to get some sleep on the couch in Tiger Cole's office, but he had tossed and turned, unable to stop thinking about his wife. He had dropped off for a few minutes, only to have a nightmare about her, which woke him and left him unable to get back to sleep.

At one point Tommy Carmellini came in, wanting to tell him what he had heard on his listening devices. About the only thing worth reporting,

836

according to Carmellini, was a call Kerry Kent got earlier in the evening. 'She said yes, paused, yes again, paused, no, then another yes and hung up.'

'So?'

'I don't know who called her, but it wasn't a social friend.'

'Doesn't sound like it,' Grafton agreed.

As the sun rose he had stood at Cole's window watching the traffic on the street below and the people on the sidewalk reading the flyers.

Cole wasn't there. He had gone out at some point. No doubt he is off leading the charge, Jake thought gloomily.

He couldn't shake the thought that this mess was Cole's fault.

If the bastard had minded his own business, stayed in California getting rich making magic technoshit for robots and the like, Callie would be safe and sound, not in danger of being murdered by a goddamn Asian gangster.

That thought made him angry. There would be plenty of time later for recriminations, but now was the time to figure out how to rescue Callie.

That's the mission, Jake, and it's high time you put the brain in high gear and got cracking.

He decided that he should go back to the hotel. If by chance Callie had been released, perhaps she would go there. The chances were small, but still . . .

'Goddamn it!' He had said the words aloud, then stood there grinding his teeth.

He needed a bath, a shave, and a change of clothes.

If Sonny Wong has any sense, someone will be waiting to ambush me as I walk out the front door of the consulate.

With that thought in mind, Grafton went out the back of the compound in a truck that had just delivered a load of fresh vegetables. When the truck stopped for a light two blocks down the street, Grafton raised the rear door and jumped down, then lowered the door and slapped it twice.

Now, walking through the streets, he was struck by the number of youngsters and the elderly out and about on a weekday morning. They weren't the dressed-for-success business types who filled the Central District office towers during weekdays. These folks wore jeans and cotton pants and T-shirts. They carried backpacks and sacks of food.

The damn fools are going to the big demonstration!

Governor Sun Siu Ki read the news of the clearinghouse computer disaster in the flyer labeled *The Truth* as he dressed for the day. An aide had brought him one of the sheets.

'Is this true?' he demanded, waving the offending paper at the aide.

'Yes, sir. The director of the clearinghouse called us with the news at three this morning. The entire clearinghouse staff is working now to determine the extent of the damage.'

Sun was not the swiftest civil servant in Hong Kong, but he wasn't stupid.

'How did the writers of this flyer get the news so quickly, get it printed and onto the streets?'

'Sir, we do not know. These flyers were thrown out of trucks all over the S.A.R. as early as five a.m.'

'This computer failure the story speaks of, could it have been sabotage?'

'We do not know.'

'Find out,' Sun snapped. 'Immediately,' he added and shooed the aide out.

The story was libel, of course. Well, probably libel.

Sure, there were grotesquely greedy men in government – there had been misfits and rogues in every government in every age since the world began. And of course some of these misfits might have twisted arms in the Hong Kong banking community. But to suppose that these people, if they did owe money to the local banks, would destroy the banks so they wouldn't have to pay it back? The whole thing was preposterous, pure poppycock.

And even if the story were true, this rag should never have printed it. The sole purpose of such a story was to lower the people's respect for the government and the men who made it function.

Mao would never have tolerated such disrespectful diatribes from anyone, Sun told himself primly, and certainly he should not.

Regardless of what the bureaucrats in Beijing thought, the time had come to take off the gloves with these people. Show them the government's steel backbone and this type of libelous misbehavior will stop.

Sun was capable of applying the pressure, of crushing enemies of the state. He didn't have many skills, but at least he had that one. He picked up the telephone on his desk and told his secretary to call General Tang.

Tang came to City Hall by car to confer with Sun. The two of them ate a hurried breakfast of rice and fish at Sun's desk while they waited for a call to Beijing to be returned. An aide came in and told them that the subway trains refused to operate this morning. 'It is the doors,' the aide said. 'The administrator of the system says the doors will not open on the trains.'

'Can't they be opened manually?'

'Yes, but then they cannot be closed. The chief engineer blames the fluctuations in the power grid.'

When the minister in Beijing called, he was obviously distraught. 'First Hong Kong, now the nation is under attack. We do not even know who the enemy is, and he is wounding us seriously.'

Sun didn't have a clue what the minister was talking about. He made noises anyway.

The minister explained: 'Several hours ago our ballistic missiles exploded in their silos, starting horrible fires that threaten to contaminate large areas. Last night the Hong Kong and Shanghai banking systems collapsed, the stock exchanges cannot open, the railroad dispatch computer refuses to come on-line, refineries all over the country have had to shut down to prevent dangerous conditions progressing to explosions and fires ... and every air traffic control and GCI radar in the country is mysteriously broken. The nation is wide open to an aerial invasion, and we won't know it is coming until enemy troops arrive at the gates.' His voice rose an octave here.

The minister paused to get himself under control. 'Obviously the nation is under cyberattack. The telephone network has been used to sabotage critical computers. The premier has decreed that the telephone system be shut off on the hour, in ten minutes, until such time as the critical systems can be brought back on-line, our enemies identified and rendered harmless, and future attacks of this sort guarded against.'

Sun couldn't believe his ears. He pushed the mute button on the speaker phone and asked General Tang, 'What is a cyberattack?'

'Computers,' Tang replied.

The minister was still going on, about how Sun should notify Beijing immediately of any change in the situation in Hong Kong, and then he hung up, leaving Sun staring at the little telephone speaker on his desk, quite unable to grasp the importance of what he had just heard.

'They are turning off the telephone system?' he asked General Tang.

'So he said.'

'The Taiwanese,' Sun said bitterly. 'I have argued for years that China must bring those rascals to heel. Events will prove me right.'

'I suspect the Japanese,' General Tang shot back. 'They are our natural enemies.'

They finished eating in silence, each man deep in his own thoughts.

When they pushed the plates back, they discussed the situation. They were on dangerous ground and they knew it. The nation under cyberattack from unknown enemies, the power of the government being tested here in Hong Kong ...

The right course of action was unclear. Still, they were the men who would have to answer to Beijing for inaction as well as action.

When he had heard Tang out, Sun issued his orders. 'Today many unhappy people will congregate in the Central District. They will once again attempt to embarrass the government.' The British legacy was still causing problems, Sun thought sourly. 'That challenge to the government's mandate to rule is, in my judgment, our most important problem. Put your troops in the downtown and refuse to let the demonstrators in.'

'The subway problems will keep people from coming into the Central District,' Tang remarked. He assumed that most of the city's citizens would want to demonstrate against the government, an assumption that Sun didn't challenge.

'The time has come to be firm,' Sun declared. 'We must show the people the steel of our resolve. Show them the might of the state they hold in such contempt.'

Lest there be a misunderstanding, Sun added darkly, 'I abhor the useless effusion of blood, but if we do not hold our ground now, that failure will cost more blood.'

'We will give the order to disperse, then enforce it.'

'We must tell the people,' Sun told the general. 'Go from here to the television studio. Stand in front of the camera and tell the people to stay home. Tell them the nation is under attack, but we shall prevail because we have the resolve of a tiger.'

'Only one television station is still operating,' the senior aide informed them. 'The others have had power outages or equipment failures.'

'All?' Sun demanded.

'Yes, sir. During the night they went off the air, one by one.'

'Sabotage,' said Tang. 'Could this be related to the nuclear weapons disaster?'

'Impossible,' the governor opined. 'Here in Hong Kong we are dealing with criminal hooligans.'

Had the brain trust in City Hall asked about the situation with the radio stations, they would have been more alarmed. Of Hong Kong's dozens of stations, only one was still on the air. The morning DJ at this station atop Victoria Peak was a Hong Kong personality named Jimmy Lee, easily the most popular man on the south China coast.

Lee was funny, irreverent, crazy, with it, and cool, a combination that delighted the young people and brought smiles to the faces of everyone else. Listening to Jimmy Lee was always a breath of fresh air.

Jimmy Lee wasn't himself this morning, though. The man was constitutionally unable to keep a secret – it wasn't in him. Everything he knew eventually slipped out, usually when he least wanted it to. Normally this trait didn't do him any harm since his off-kilter personality was his stock-in-trade. For the past two weeks, though, Jimmy Lee had been the possessor of a huge secret, one that had grown heavier with each passing day.

He had joked so much about Wu Tai Kwong, the phantom political criminal, that Wu had concluded Lee could be an ally. So one morning one of Wu's lieutenants was waiting when Lee finished his morning show.

At first Lee didn't believe the man knew Wu Tai Kwong, as he said he did, but the man's serious demeanor and his anti-Communist sentiments assuaged his doubts. The man returned to the station for private conversations week after week for months. Lee finally realized that the man wasn't a government agent and that he indeed knew Wu Tai Kwong.

Eventually the man enlisted Lee to become a spokesman of the revolution. Two weeks ago he was told about the upcoming battle of Hong Kong, presented with a cell phone, and told about the message that he would receive on the designated day.

Jimmy Lee had not told a soul this fantastic secret, which was a remarkable testament to the supreme effort he was making to control himself. He had thought deeply about it for two weeks, brooded upon it, had nightmares about it. The reality was that the revolutionaries wanted him to commit treason ... when the telephone rang.

Treason! If the revolution failed, Jimmy Lee's life would be forfeit. The government would hunt him down and execute him publicly.

This morning Lee was almost incoherent on the air. He played songs but babbled nonsense when he had to speak. He had never been able to resist food, was almost a hundred pounds overweight, yet this morning he was unable to eat. Sweating profusely, nauseated, able to talk only in monosyllables, he was questioned by his producer ... and he told everything.

The producer refused to believe Lee. He was unaware that this was the last radio station on the air in Hong Kong. He knew nothing about the disasters in the stock market, the airport, the subways ... none of that had been published by the government, which like all Communist governments was loathe to admit or discuss problems.

Lee talked on. He produced the cell phone. He told about meeting a friend of Wu Tai Kwong's, told about how the army would be confronted today, about the explanations he was to make over the radio ... and then he produced the cassette.

The producer put the cassette into a player and listened to a minute or two of it while Jimmy Lee hyperventilated.

The male voice on the cassette was as calm and confident as a human can be, calling for people to rally behind the freedom fighters, obey the revolutionary leaders, and kill PLA soldiers who refused to surrender.

The producer turned off the cassette player and sat chewing his fingernails while he considered what he should do. The first thing, he decided, was to let the New China News Agency censor listen to this tape. The man worked for the government, knew how things worked. He would know what to do about the tape.

Lin Pe was not thinking of resolve, although she had as much as the governor and then some. She was thinking of the strange ways human lives are twisted by chance, or fate, call it what you will.

She dressed in her newest clothes, brushed her hair, made herself look as nice as she could. In her purse she put her notebook – so she could write down any fortunes that crossed her mind in the course of the day – two rice cakes, and a bottle of water. She ensured the house key was already in the purse, then went to find her daughter, who was giving the maids their daily instructions. The television was on – General Tang was telling people to stay home.

When Sue Lin finished with the maids, she told her mother, 'Rip wanted us both to stay home today. He said the streets will be dangerous, there may be shooting.' Her mother would respect Rip's opinion, Sue Lin knew, more than she would her daughter's, for her mother had not lost her lifetime habit of deference to men.

'I think the rebellion will begin today,' the old lady said calmly. 'Today is the beginning of the end for the Communists.'

'Richard Buckingham is paying the money today, Mother. Wu Tai Kwong will probably be home this evening.'

Lin Pe merely nodded. Then she went out the door and along the street toward the tram, which would take her down the mountain to the Central District.

The matter was quite simple, really. Her son thought this struggle was worth his life. That being the case, it was worth hers, too.

14

At the Victoria ferry landing, people were streaming off the overloaded ferries from Kowloon and patronizing a small army of food vendors, who were selling fish and shark and rice cakes as fast as they could fry it. Not many children, considering. Here and there Jake Grafton saw people reading sheets of *The Truth,* sometimes three and four people huddled together looking at the same piece of paper. The people looked somber, grim, though perhaps it was just his imagination.

Not many people were interested in going to Kowloon, so there was no line. Jake went right aboard the ferry *Star of the East.*

As the boat approached Kowloon he could see the sea of humanity waiting to board the ferries to Victoria. With the subways out of service, this crowd was to be expected. The terminal was packed, with a large group of people outside on the street, waiting to get inside.

As soon as the boat tied up, Jake was off and walking at a brisk pace. Outside the terminal the crowd swallowed him. He thought about getting something to eat in McDonald's, which was about fifty yards away, but it too was packed full, with people waiting to get into the place.

For the first time since he had arrived in Hong Kong the sheer mass of China threatened to overwhelm him. People everywhere, densely packed, all talking, breathing, shouting, pushing ...

He made his way along Nathan Road and turned into the street that led by his hotel. Fewer people here, thank God.

The manager was in the lobby trying to calm a crowd of tourists from Germany. The common language was a heavily accented pidgin English.

So sorry, the manager explained, but the airlines had canceled all flights; daily bus tours of Hong Kong were canceled; trains to Canton, Shanghai, and Beijing were not running; telephone calls to Europe were not going through; credit cards could not be accepted for payment of bills; money-changing services at front desk temporarily suspended. So sorry. All problems temporary. Not to worry, all fixed soon. So sorry.

Behind Jake he heard an elderly British male voice say with more than a trace of satisfaction, 'Bloody place is falling apart. *Knew* it would! Wasn't like this in the old days, I can tell you.'

In the corner an American college student was trying to comfort his girlfriend. In the snippet he heard, Jake gathered that the girl was worried that her parents would be worried.

Jake waited until the manager made his escape from the unhappy Germans, then waylaid him. He told him his name, reminded him of the trashed room, wanted to know where his luggage was.

The manager signaled for a bellhop, then spoke to the uniformed man in Chinese.

Jake was escorted to the elevator and taken to the top floor of the building. They had laid out his and Callie's luggage in a three-room suite, the best in the house, probably. The sitting room and bedroom both had balconies.

The crowd was so dense it intimidated Lin Pe, and she had lived in dense Chinese cities much of her life. There was an intensity, an anticipation, that seemed to energize the people.

She fought against the flow of people and managed to get aboard a ferry to Kowloon, as it turned out the last one, because the authorities demanded that the Star line stop carrying demonstrators to Victoria and forced the crews off the boats.

In Kowloon Lin Pe began walking. On Nathan Road she caught a bus and rode it north for several miles, then transferred to a bus going to Kam Shan, near Tolo Harbor. She got off the bus at Shatin and walked a quarter of a mile through town. Shatin was huge, with more than a half million people living there now. Lin Pe remembered when it was just a small town, not many years ago.

She stopped at a small corner grocery where she knew the proprietor. After the usual polite greetings, she found a seat on an empty orange crate under a sign advertising scribe services. The letter writer would not be here for hours, but people with little to do often passed the time by sitting here, so no one would say anything.

From her perch on the orange crate she could see the entrance to the main PLA base in the New Territories. Nothing much seemed to be happening on the base, which was good.

From her bag Lin Pe extracted her WB telephone. She turned it on, then called in and reported that she was in position. Then she turned the phone off to save the battery.

Jake Grafton took a shower, shaved, and put on clean clothes that fit; Cole's were too large. He strapped the Smith & Wesson to his right ankle and put on the shoulder holster containing the Model 1911 Colt .45 automatic he had requisitioned from the marines at the consulate. Over this he donned a clean sports jacket. He put a hand grenade in each pocket. Just another happy tourist ready for a day of fun and games in good ol' Hong Kong.

He checked with the hotel operator to see if he had any messages. Yes, a voice mail. He listened as the senior military adviser on the National Security staff told him that his mission was canceled, he could come home anytime.

He tried to return the call and got as far as the hotel operator. All lines overseas were out of service. So sorry.

So Tiger Cole and the Scarlet Team had isolated the place.

He turned on the television. Only one channel was still on the air – the others were showing test patterns or blank screens.

Oooh boy!

Jake Grafton went out on the bedroom balcony, which also overlooked the police station. Not many troops on the lawn. He could hear a helicopter circling overhead, though he couldn't see it.

There was a division of troops in Hong Kong, Tiger said, China's best . . . with tanks, artillery, and twelve thousand combat-ready soldiers.

Jake's attention was drawn to the street in front of the hotel, eight stories below him. A convoy of trucks had pulled up alongside the hill and wall of the police station, and people were streaming from every truck.

In thirty seconds the street was a sea of people. A van-type truck was sitting at the main gate, the driver talking to the guard.

On the street the people were removing ladders from the trucks. My God! They were armed. Assault rifles, it looked like.

The ladders went against the wall, people swarmed up them.

As they reached the top of the wall, they got off the ladders, walked along the wall. There must be interior ladders or stairs, Jake thought.

The driver was out of the truck at the gate, holding a pistol on the guard. People ran by the truck into the compound.

Jake had a grandstand seat. In less than a minute, several hundred armed civilians were running through the compound.

Shots! He could hear shots! Some of the soldiers were shooting! And being shot at!

The reports rose into a ragged fusillade, then slowed to sporadic popping.

A dozen or so soldiers wearing green uniforms lay where they had fallen.

Now a convoy of trucks came streaming through the main gate.

In two minutes all the shooting stopped, even the occasional shot from inside the administration building. Several of the trucks were backed up to a loading dock, and a small human chain began passing weapons out of the building. As fast as one truck was loaded, it pulled out and another took its place.

Jake Grafton looked at his watch. The time was 8:33 a.m.

Welcome to the revolution!

He had to get to Victoria while he still could. Cole had said the Scarlet Team intended to confront the People's Liberation Army with Sergeant

Yorks. That would be the acid test. Either the Yorks could stand up to trained troops or the revolution would be over before lunch.

But all those people heading for the Central District – Grafton wondered if he had what it takes to sacrifice innocent people for the greater good. He thought of Callie and concluded that he didn't.

The New China News Agency censor assigned to Jimmy Lee's radio station listened to the Wu Tai Kwong cassette tape with a growing sense of horror. Jimmy Lee was sitting on a nearby stool near collapse – the producer had taken his place at the microphone. The tape sounded authentic. Any doubts the censor had were wiped away by the conviction in that taped voice ... and the call for people to kill PLA soldiers who refused to surrender their arms.

The censor called his superior officer on the telephone, but no one answered. Too early. His superior wouldn't come to work for another hour yet, and with the subway out, maybe not then. The man lived way up north in the New Territories.

The censor swallowed hard and telephoned City Hall.

He ended up with an aide to Governor Sun and began telling him of the tape and the upcoming battle in the streets.

Callie Grafton awoke stiff and sore from her beating the previous evening. Places on her face were blue and yellow, and one side of her face was severely swollen. Sometime during the night she stopped shivering ... thankfully, but her ordeal had drained her.

Still, she was in better shape than she thought she would be. When those thugs were pounding on her she thought she might die.

She had awakened on and off during the night, waited fearfully for the men to return, to drag her off for another interrogation or session in the meat locker, but it didn't happen.

Perhaps this morning.

She tried to recall everything she could remember about the Vietnam prisoners of war she had met or read about. The men she had known were ordinary men who had endured torture, starvation, and beatings for years and somehow survived. One looked at them expecting them to be different somehow – and no doubt they were on the inside – but the difference didn't show in the facade they presented to the world. They looked ordinary in every respect.

Perhaps the lesson was that they were ordinary yet had somehow found extraordinary courage. Or maybe that courage is in all of us and we just don't know it. Or need it.

I am as tough as those guys, she told herself, thinking of the POWs. She wanted to believe that even though she didn't.

'He wants me to implicate Cole in murder,' she told Wu Tai Kwong.

He nodded.

'What does he want from you?'

'A confession that he can give to the Communists, one that he can use to justify a fat reward for my capture.'

'He will turn you over to the government?'

'I'll be dead by then. He'll give them my corpse and demand a huge reward. The confession will be the ... how do you say it? The sauce upon the cake?'

'Icing on the cake.'

'Knowing Sonny,' Wu continued, 'he has demanded money from everyone, Cole, the government, everyone. He keeps me alive so he can prove that I am alive, should that become necessary. Then he will kill me and sell my corpse.'

'Do you really believe that?'

'He cannot set me free. I have many friends. I will find him and kill him, no matter where on earth he goes to hide. He knows that. He will kill me.'

'Are you frightened?'

'Of what? Death?'

'Dying.'

'Yes.'

'But not of death?'

'I have achieved my dream. The revolution has begun. The regime is crumbling and the revolution will speed its collapse. Sonny Wong can do nothing to stop it. The government can fight, delaying the day of its doom, but it cannot prevent the inevitable.'

A terrible smile spread across the face of Wu Tai Kwong. 'I have won,' he whispered. 'I have undermined the levee – the sea *will* come in.'

Despite the fact that she was no longer cold, Callie Grafton shivered. 'When the regime collapses, what will happen then?' she asked.

'The people will execute the Communists. That is inevitable. And fitting. That is the fate of all dynasties when they fall. The Communists will go like the others.'

Jake Grafton went out the main door of the hotel and turned right, headed for Nathan Road and the ferry landing. Two men who had been lounging against the wall followed him.

He glanced back just before he turned the corner – they were keeping their distance.

Rounding the corner, another man stepped away from the wall with a pistol in his hand. It must have been in his pocket.

Jake didn't think, he merely reacted. He dove for the pistol, seizing it and wrenching it away from the man.

No doubt Grafton's sudden appearance had startled the man, who must have thought that the sight of the weapon would freeze Grafton, make him stand still in the hope of not being shot. In any event, the American's move was so unexpected that it succeeded.

Jake Grafton's adrenaline was flowing nicely. With his assailant's pistol in his left hand, he hit him with all his might in the throat and dropped the man to the sidewalk, gagging.

Now he ran, fighting the crowd, toward the waterfront.

Soldiers were spread across the pier in front of the ferry landing.

They've stopped the ferries!

Jake veered right, toward the small basin beside the huge shopping mall for cruise ship passengers. In this basin small boats normally took on and discharged passengers for harbor tours.

There were a handful of tour boats tied to the pier, all of them sporting little blue-and-white awnings to keep off the sun and rain. Jake ran along the pier until he saw a man working on one. The engine was running, although the boat was still securely moored.

By now Jake had the pistol in his pocket that he had taken off the man in the street. He was going to have a nice collection of these things if he lived long enough.

He looked behind him. The people who had been following were apparently lost in the crowd, which filled most of the street.

He pulled out his wallet, took out a handful of bills, replaced the wallet in his hip pocket. He jumped down into the boat and waved the bills at the boatman, who was in his early thirties, with long hair that hung across his face.

The boatman said something in Chinese. Jake gestured toward Victoria. 'Over there,' he said and offered the money again.

The boatman ignored the money. He pointed back toward the soldiers and shook his head.

Okay.

Jake looked at the boat's controls as the boatman showered him with Chinese. The throttle was there, a wheel, a stick shift for a forward-reverse transmission . . . the boat was idling.

'Out. Get out!' Jake pulled the pistol just far enough from his pocket for the boatman to see it, then pointed toward the pier.

Frightened, the boatman went. As he did, Jake Grafton jammed the money he had offered into the man's shirt pocket. Must be my genial expression, Jake thought as he ran forward to untie the rope on the pier bollard.

With it free, he made his way aft as quickly as he could.

Where are the men who were following me? Did they lose me in the crowd?

That must be it. They're probably searching frantically right this minute.

With the bow and stern lines loose, Jake scrambled back to the tiny cockpit and spun the wheel while he jammed the throttle forward. The boat surged ahead, caroming off the boat moored in front of it.

He didn't waste time but headed for the entrance to the basin.

There, on the pier! The men who followed him from the hotel! They stood watching. Now one of them removed a cell phone from his pocket and made a call.

There was a nice breeze and a decent sea running in the strait, so the little tour boat began pitching the moment it cleared the mouth of the basin.

Some soldiers around the ferry terminal were shouting and gesturing at him, so Jake turned his boat to the northeast, away from Hong Kong Island. *Those guys are itching to shoot someone,* he thought and decided to get well out of rifle range before he turned south to cross the strait.

In the helicopter circling over the police station, Hu Chiang also looked at his watch. The assault on the police barracks had gone like clockwork, for which he was supremely grateful. Wu Tai Kwong was supposed to be in the left seat of this chopper running the show; the others had insisted that Hu Chiang take Wu's place.

As he watched the trucks loading small arms at the police barracks, Hu Chiang wondered just where Wu was ... and Sonny Wong. No one had seen Sonny in days.

He had almost refused to take Wu's place as the tactical leader. Generalissimo Hu Chiang – the thing was ridiculous. If the choice had been his he would have declined. Yet he remembered what Wu had said, so long ago when the revolution was just a dream: 'The cause must be bigger than we are, worth more than we are, or we are wasting our lives pursuing it.'

'We cannot make a utopia, fix all that is wrong with human society,' he had told Wu.

'True, but we can build a civilization better than the one we have. To build for future generations is our duty, our obligation as thinking creatures.'

Duty. That was Wu's take on life. He was doing his duty.

So Hu Chiang was in the chopper this morning, half queasy, trying to keep his wits about him as the faithful stormed the police barracks on the southern tip of the Kowloon peninsula.

From this seat a few hundred feet up he could see much of Hong Kong harbor, which was dotted with dozens of moored ships from all over the earth and squadrons of lighters and fishing boats. He could see the airport at Lantau, the Kowloon docks and warehouses, the endless high-rises full of people with hopes and dreams of a better life, the office towers of Victoria's Central District, and the spine of Hong Kong Island beyond.

The most interesting portion of the view was to the north, toward mainland China, hidden this morning in the June haze. Hong Kong was but a first step, then the revolution must go north, with or without Wu Tai Kwong or Hu Chiang. ...

The radio sputtered again. The leader of the barracks assault was checking in. 'Mission completed,' he said, so proud he almost couldn't get the words out.

'Roger,' Hu Chiang replied and directed the chopper pilot to circle over the entrance to the highway tunnel under the strait.

The army had it blocked off this morning, of course. Forty or so troops were visible, a truck, and ... a tank!

Yep. There it sat, right in front of the harbor tunnel entrance, squat and massive and ominous.

Hu Chiang picked up the mike and began talking.

Another helicopter, this one belonging to the PLA, was circling over Victoria's Central District and the southern tip of Kowloon. General Tang was in the passenger seat. He had had the chopper pick him up at City Hall and was now looking the situation over.

He had certainly not expected the crowds that he saw coming toward Victoria's Central District from the west and east. Connaught Road was crammed with people, as were Harcourt Road and Queensway, an endless stream of people coming from the Western District, Wanchai, and Happy Valley, all headed toward Central.

He had his troops deployed in the heart of the Central District and around City Hall, with his headquarters in the square in front of the Bank of the Orient.

The troops there seemed to be properly positioned, but the size of the crowds stunned Tang. This massive outpouring of people in defiance of the government he had not expected. It was almost as if ... as if the people *expected* to swallow the troops.

For the first time, General Tang wondered if Sun Siu Ki or the party leaders in Beijing understood what was happening in Hong Kong.

A cry for help from the Kowloon police barracks snapped General Tang back to unpleasant reality. He motioned to the pilot of the helicopter, who swung out over the strait and flew toward the southern tip of Kowloon.

The pilot pointed out another chopper to General Tang, who had trouble seeing it at first.

'A television station helicopter,' the pilot said over the intercom. 'I have seen it many times before. They must be taking pictures for the television.'

That, of course, was the last thing that General Tang wanted. Television pictures of this mass outpouring of antigovernment sentiment would shake the regime to its foundations. The people in Beijing had no idea, none at all!

Tang waved angrily at the television helicopter. The pilot looked directly at him, then looked away.

'Can you talk to that pilot?' Tang demanded.

'Yes.' The army pilot changed the channels on the radio and called the helicopter.

Hu Chiang didn't hear the army pilot's call because he was talking on a different frequency to the squad leader in charge of the trucks carrying the weapons from the police barracks. These trucks had to get through the tunnel to Victoria, so the tank and army troops were going to have to be neutralized. Hu's pilot heard the call, though, and told Hu about it on the intercom.

'Trouble,' the television station pilot said. 'If we ignore him too long, he will have everyone in the world shooting at us.'

'Let's do it to him first,' Hu said and pointed west toward the harbor as he spoke into the microphone on his headset. The pilot took the TV chopper in the indicated direction.

Tang forgot about the civilian helicopter when he got a glimpse of the police barracks and the uniformed bodies still sprawled upon the lawn, which had been used as a campground. Tang knew corpses when he saw them, and those men looked real dead.

He saw the trucks, which must be loading the weapons Tang knew were stored in the barracks.

He directed his pilot eastward.

The streets of Kowloon were packed with cars. With the tunnel to Victoria closed, there was no place for the Hong Kong Island traffic to go, so a massive traffic jam was the result. Traffic in the city was always bad, yet today it was impossible. People had abandoned the cars in gridlocked intersections. The weapons thieves were fools to assault the police barracks with the streets impassable.

They certainly weren't going to make a fast getaway in all this traffic. His order to close the tunnel, he thought with a bit of pride, may have proved their undoing.

He again spoke to the pilot, who took him east a half mile until the machine was over the entrance to the harbor tunnel.

The troops were where they were supposed to be, the tank was there ... They just needed to be told that there were armed criminals in the vicinity ... to be ready!

He consulted the printed frequency list his staff had given him this morning, then dialed the radio to the proper channel. He keyed the mike and began speaking. When he did so he naturally looked down at the people he was talking to, the soldiers surrounding the tank.

He was three words into his message when the tank exploded.

The explosion was not a massive fireball: but a cloud of smoke that jetted from the side of the thing, then seemed to envelop it.

As if it were hit by a wire-guided antitank weapon, General Tang thought, then realized that was exactly what had happened.

Out of the corner of his eye he saw a streak of fire in the air, not large. Before he could react a loud, metallic bang shook the chopper, followed by a severe vibration, then a slew to the right.

'We've been hit,' the pilot shouted over the intercom. He wrestled with the cyclic and collective, trying to gain control, even as the helicopter spun faster and faster to the right and began falling.

Michael Gao was a thirty-six-year-old security analyst with a finance degree from Harvard. He worked for one of the large American mutual funds that regularly invested in the Hong Kong market . . . when he was working. Just now he was engaged in high treason against the government of a sovereign nation. Dress it up any way you like, he thought wryly, shooting down an army helicopter with a Strella missile is going to be difficult to explain away in court. Ditto popping a tank.

He had wrestled with these issues a thousand times in the past year and always came back to the fact that he personally wanted the Communists out of power in China. He believed it would be better for everyone, including himself, if some form of democratic government were installed in Beijing. And he believed the conversion worth a major national convulsion. That being the case, it logically followed that he should personally commit himself to making it happen. So he had.

No going back now, he told himself as the helo competed the last few revolutions of its out-of-control spiral and smashed onto the top of a gravel dike around the tunnel entrance.

The chopper didn't explode or burn. After the dust from the impact settled, just a wisp of smoke rose from the crumpled wreckage. No one emerged from the cockpit – no doubt the crew was dead or dying.

No one rushed to their aid.

Michael Gao realized with a start that he was hearing the popping of small arms. He looked down from the top of the building where he stood and watched his friends snipe at the troops around the smoking hulk of the tank.

With a gut-wrenching certainty, Michael Gao knew that if there had been any men in the tank, they too were now dead. The armor-piercing sabot he had fired raised the temperature of the metals it penetrated so high that the materials forming the tank's interior would spontaneously ignite and cook the crew, if by some miracle they survived the initial concussion and thermal shock.

The soldiers near the tunnel entrance were lying in the street or trying to find cover. Bursts of automatic rifle fire created sparks where the bullets ricocheted off concrete and little puffs where they impacted. This was ridiculous! The rebels didn't have time for this.

Gao leaned over the edge of the roof, shouted to the man who was on the roof of the lower building across the street, the one facing the tunnel entrance. 'Use the loudspeaker!'

The man picked up the microphone. 'PLA soldiers! Lay down your arms. You are surrounded. We will kill you all unless you lay down your arms and surrender.'

One by one, the demoralized soldiers threw their assault rifles on the street and raised their arms in the air.

When the general's helicopter went down, Hu Chiang told his pilot to circle back over the tunnel entrance. He arrived in time to see the last of the soldiers guarding the tunnel throw down their arms.

The problem was the cars and trucks that filled the streets from curb to curb ... and the tank that smoldered in the tunnel entrance. In their planning sessions the rebels had anticipated both problems. They had two solutions, both painted yellow and made by Caterpillar. They were on flatbed trucks parked in the rubble of a building being demolished. Now they came clanking onto the street with their blades down.

Vehicles that couldn't move were bulldozed out of the way. Trucks were pushed up onto sidewalks, cars were stacked one atop the other. All this was accomplished in a bedlam of people running, screaming, protesting, begging the armed rebels not to ruin their cars ... all to no avail. The bulldozers pushed and shoved and made a way, and soon the first truck carrying weapons taken from the police barracks armory was waiting near the tunnel entrance. The truck was covered with armed rebels hanging on every available protuberance.

One of the bulldozers backed up to the tank, and a cable was hooked to the thing. Then the dozer began pulling, dragging the tank out of the way.

When it was clear, the other bulldozer raised its blade and led the trucks into the tunnel.

Governor Sun's secretary thought the New China News Agency weenie on the telephone was some kind of flake. This story of Jimmy Lee falling apart, worried about committing treason ... Jimmy Lee? The top one percent of the top one percent of cool?

He put the radio censor on hold and told his colleague at the next desk, 'Another nut case. This one wants to talk to the governor.'

'The governor will refuse.'

'I know.'

'He will be angry you asked.'

'What should I do? Perhaps the man is telling the truth.'

The man at the next desk surrendered. 'Tell the governor. Let him make the decision.'

At Lantau Airport Ma Chao and his fellow fighter pilots were directed to don their flight gear and wait in the ready room, which they did. Apparently during the wee hours of the night Beijing had ordered a full alert.

Unfortunately, no amplifying orders had been received over the military radio communications net. The telephone system was down, silencing the faxes and computers. An old Bruce Lee movie was playing on the television.

The ready room was abuzz with speculation. Everyone seemed to have an opinion – the more outlandish, the louder the proud possessor proclaimed it. They argued, wondered, gestured, and guessed. The Americans and Taiwanese were invading. The Japanese had declared war. There had been a coup in Beijing.

Ma Chao and his friends sat silently, taking it in, saying little. They thought they knew what was happening, but without explanations or verification from headquarters, they couldn't be certain. Nor was there a need for immediate action.

Patience was needed, and Ma Chao had plenty. Like all the pilots, he was wearing a sidearm. He had the flap unbuttoned so he could get it out and into action quickly.

As he listened to the fantastic scenarios that were being paraded before the group as quickly as they were concocted, he thought about the commanding officer and his department heads, all Communists, all loyal to the regime, as far as Ma Chao knew.

When the crunch came Ma Chao and his three fellow conspirators were going to have to take charge, and that probably meant they would have to shoot some of the senior men. Ma Chao sat in the ready room wondering if he could do it.

He had assured Wu Tai Kwong that he could. 'I am a soldier,' he said. 'I have the personal courage to do what must be done.'

'You could shoot men you have served with for many years?'

'I do not know,' he finally replied, truthfully.

'Ah, my friend, on men like you the revolution will succeed or fail. You must use your best judgment, but you must not surrender. You must face unpleasant reality and do what the situation requires of you.'

He had nodded, knowing the truth of Wu's words.

Wu always told the truth. All of it, never just a piece, and he never sugarcoated it. You got bald reality from him.

'Chinese pilots are poorly trained,' Wu told him and explained how Western air forces trained their pilots. 'You Chinese pilots fly straight and level, relying on the ground controller to find the enemy and steer you to him. What if the ground controller is off the air, or the enemy refuses to fly straight and level, waiting for you to assassinate him? What then? Could you improvise?'

Ma Chao did not answer. He thought about the question but refused to state a mere opinion.

'When the revolution begins,' Wu said, 'you will have to weigh the situation and make the best decision you can, then go forward confidently, aggressively, believing in yourself. There will be no one to give you orders. You must decide for yourself what needs to be done, then do it. What we require of you is the courage to believe in yourself.'

Ma Chao thought about that courage now as he sat in the ready room waiting for the earth to turn.

Governor Sun's secretary found that his boss was tied up with an engineer who was trying to explain the difficulty with the subway doors. 'The problem is in the computer,' the engineer explained.

'The computer opens and closes train doors?'

'Yes,' the engineer said, pleased that Sun was with him so far. 'Something has gone wrong with the software. We must find the problem before we can fix it.'

'I thought you said the problem was power fluctuations?'

'Power fluxes caused the problem with the software.'

The secretary went back to the New China News Agency man he had on hold. 'The governor is busy. Why don't you tell me the message? I'll write it down and give it to him when he has a moment.'

'This is very important,' the censor said. 'The message is too important and too long to be written down.'

The secretary rolled his eyes. 'I'll have the governor call you. How is that?'

'I will await his call.' The censor dictated the telephone number at the radio station, then hung up.

The secretary threw the call-back slip into the governor's in-basket.

The soldiers on duty at the Victoria end of the Cross-Harbor Tunnel heard echoes through the tunnel of the small battle in Kowloon. They also saw General Tang's helicopter crash and assumed, correctly, that it had been shot down.

They waited in nervous dread for what might come next. There were only a dozen of them, a small squad, manning a police barricade in front of the tunnel entrance. They were young, the oldest a mere twenty-four, from rural villages far to the north. They had joined the army to escape the drudgery of the rice fields. Only four of them could read the most basic of the Chinese ideographs.

They were armed with old Kalashnikov assault rifles and one machine gun. When they heard the clanking of the bulldozer coming through the tunnel, they assumed it was the tank that they knew had been positioned at the Kowloon end.

Relieved, they relaxed and the sergeant in charge walked down the tunnel to meet the tank coming the other way. He went about fifty yards and waited.

When he realized he was looking at a bulldozer, and behind it trucks, the sergeant knew something was happening that no one had told him about. He turned and scampered back up the tunnel, shouting to his men.

Unsure of what to do, the men waited for direction.

The uncertainty ended as the bulldozer emerged from the tunnel. Two men atop the dozer opened fire on the soldiers standing about.

The other soldiers might have killed these two men and some of the men following the dozer on foot if they had been given a chance, but they weren't. A machine gun atop a nearby building swept the tunnel entranceway with a long burst, sending the bullets back and forth, knocking the standing soldiers down like bowling pins.

The three-second burst was enough. Men emerging from the tunnel shot the survivors as the bulldozer rolled over two bodies. The trucks turned into the crowded streets and stopped. Men inside the truck beds began passing out assault rifles and ammunition to the crowd of young men and women who had been lounging there.

At the biggest television station in Hong Kong the atmosphere was strictly business as usual when Wei Luk and three other rebels walked in. There were no guards in the lobby, armed or unarmed, and no guards in the reception area; just two potted palms and large photos of the station's news stars. One of the stars was a man named Peter Po, who, like Wei Luk and his friends, had bet his life that communism could be successfully overthrown.

Wei Luk glanced at the smiling picture of Peter Po and then stepped over to the receptionist, a beautifully made-up young woman with an expensive coiffure and long, painted nails. She gave Wei and his friends a dazzlingly professional smile.

Their pistols were in their pockets, so they looked presentable enough. Wei Luk smiled, told the girl that he had an appointment with Peter Po.

'And these other gentlemen?'

'Them too.'

She picked up the phone, pushed a button, waited a bit, then asked his name. He gave it.

'At the end of the hallway take a right,' she told him after she had talked to Mr. Po, 'then it's the third door on the left.'

The girl pointed toward a green steel door with a small window. She unlocked it with a hidden button as Wei Luk pushed.

Po welcomed them into his office. He was wearing the television uniform, a suit and tie.

'I thought there was a guard,' Wei Luk said.

Peter Po nodded. 'I told him today would be a good day to stay home sick, and he agreed.'

'Okay.'

Peter Po looked at his watch. 'When do you think?'

'I don't know. When the truck delivers weapons and more men, then and only then.'

Fortunately Governor Sun had not yet realized that the rebellion had begun, so no one at City Hall had sent police or troops to secure the one operating television station or shut it down. A rebel broadcast would cause them to cure this error as quickly as possible, however. Until an armed force could be resisted, the rebels thought it wise to hold their tongue.

Yet the rebels were now inside and the police and army were out. Peter Po had a script and knew how to run the equipment in the building so that the rebel leadership could talk to the people of Hong Kong.

Wei Luk's orders were to ensure that the police and soldiers stayed out of the building, to the last man. 'Fight until there are no bricks left stuck together,' Wu Tai Kwong had told him.

'Take your places,' Wei told his men now. He directed one of the men to go back to the lobby and sit with the receptionist.

'Let no one else through the door. Call when the truck arrives.'

The crowd in the Central District of Victoria chanted antigovernment slogans, sang snatches of songs, surged along the streets carrying everyone with them, a giant human river.

The crowd came to a stop against the ring of PLA troops that surrounded the Bank of the Orient square. There were five hundred soldiers in the streets around the plaza, all armed with assault rifles and wearing riot-control shields and face masks. The trucks that had delivered them there were parked on the streets inside the military perimeter.

At the four corners of the plaza the officer in charge, Tang's number two, Brigadier General Moon Hok, had ordered machine guns placed in nests built of sandbags. In the center of the plaza he had placed two tanks. Between them sat a command car bristling with radio aerials.

General Moon was in the command car when he learned that General Tang might have crashed. While the PLA was attempting to verify why their helicopter had ceased all transmissions, Moon got out of the vehicle and stood looking at the sea of soldiers in the square and the huge buildings that surrounded it.

From a military point of view, the position was not a good one. The buildings were man-made high points that would afford an enemy excellent positions from which to shoot down into the square, creating a killing zone.

He called a colonel over, told him to assign squads to search each of the buildings adjoining the square. The colonel walked away to make it happen.

As Moon Hok listened to the noise of the boisterous crowd echoing through the urban canyons and the radio noise emanating from the command car, he decided to use his troops to push the crowd back one block in all directions, thereby putting the buildings that faced the square within his perimeter. Tang had told him to bring no more than five hundred men this morning because the square wouldn't physically hold any more; now he was contemplating holding nine blocks with the same five hundred men. They would be thin, very thin.

What if the crowd rioted, got completely out of control?

Could Tang be dead?

The noise of the crowd made the hair on the back of Moon Hok's neck rise.

He got on the radio and called for another five hundred men to join him. It would be hours before they arrived from Kowloon, but better late than never.

When Virgil Cole designed the Sergeant York units, he realized that the volume of data flowing from the sensors would require that each unit be individually monitored. Since a network was only as good as the data its sensors fed into it, he didn't trust a computer to make life-or-death decisions. The U.S. Army planners didn't want people completely removed from the loop, either. Consequently, part of the York system was a mobile command and control trailer where the people who monitored each unit sat at individual stations. Here a mainframe computer checked the sensor data and suggested possible courses of action to the human operators.

The trailer had also been on the C-5 Galaxy that delivered the York units and was now parked in an alley three blocks from the Bank of the Orient. Despite the fact that power cables led to it from mobile power units parked nearby, the trailer was gaily painted with surprisingly good graphic art. A sign on the side proclaimed the trailer to be a mobile museum exhibiting the latest in computer technology, sponsored by a well-known philanthropic organization dedicated to the education of the world's children.

Cole had huddled with the Scarlet Team members this morning, telling them what he knew of other team efforts throughout China. He repeated the litany of woes that the minister in Beijing had recited to Governor Sun, ticking them off on his fingers. 'The government is inundated with troubles this morning,' he said in summation. 'The population is getting out of control in most of the major Chinese cities. Beijing is beginning to suspect that revolution is in the wind. When the people see how fragile the government's control is, the rebellion will spread.'

'Wu Tai Kwong has done his work well,' someone commented.

'We must do ours equally well,' Cole shot back and went to check the sensor data feeds from each York unit. Six monitors were arranged in a row, all six labeled from left to right: Alvin, Bob, Charlie ...

Kerry Kent stood beside him, comparing her handheld tactical controller with the main monitor.

Satisfied, she stood back, took a deep breath.

'Worried?' Cole asked.

'Only about Wu,' she replied. 'This will go fine. You'll see. You built good stuff.'

Cole waved the compliment away. 'I won't authorize a transfer of money to Wong's account until Jake Grafton sees Wu and Callie Grafton in the flesh and calls me — they leave together when the Swiss have got the loot.'

'Does Wong know that?'

'I told him when he called earlier. The bastard threatened to hack off more fingers, but we have no choice. We must be tough, insist on fair dealing, or the son of a bitch will take the money and kill them, sure as shootin'.'

Kerry Kent took a deep breath. 'When?'

'Tomorrow night is the earliest I could set up the wire transfer. We have to do it while the Swiss bank is open; they don't stay late for anybody.'

The two-way radio had been busy all morning. Now the man monitoring it signaled to Cole. 'The convoy has cleared the harbor tunnel.'

'Cleared the tunnel, aye,' Cole acknowledged.

He keyed the intercom mike on his headset. 'The convoy has cleared the harbor tunnel. All units check in.'

The operator at each monitor sang out, 'Alvin ready,' 'Bob ready,' and so on, in order.

Kerry Kent took control. 'We are ready, Mr. Cole.'

Since Kerry Kent was going to be fighting a revolution this morning and her boyfriend was a guest of Sonny Wong's, this should be a good time to search Kent's apartment, Tommy Carmellini thought. He used the stairs for this visit — the elevator was out of service — and picked the lock to get in.

He checked the small bathroom and closet to ensure that he was the only person there, then strolled slowly through the place taking inventory.

He had no idea what he was looking for. Kerry Kent, SIS double agent, revolutionary, anti-Communist warrior ... maybe she had Mao's little red book under her pillow. He picked up the pillow and looked.

Well, no book, but a businesslike little automatic. He picked it up, checked the caliber: .380. She didn't use this on China Bob Chan.

The bed was as good a place as any to start. He put the pistol on the dresser, began stripping sheets. He examined the mattress inch by inch to see if it had a compartment for documents or the like. Apparently not. Nothing under the mattress, in the box springs, in the frame of the bed.

He piled the mess in the center of the bed and worked around it. Kerry's dresser was next.

The sea breeze and swells running in the strait this morning distracted Jake Grafton for a moment and made him smile. The salty wind cooled the perspiration on his forehead and filled his nostrils with the pungent scent of the Pearl River, flowing from deep in China. The pitching, bucking little tour boat was a handful and forced him to think about how he was going to bring the boat into the pier on Hong Kong Island.

Just which pier he should use was a problem. Who were the men on the sidewalk? Who hired them? Whom did the man call on the cell phone? They were undoubtedly watching him now, waiting to see where he landed.

He wanted to go back to the consulate, avoid the disaster that was about to happen in the Central District. When the shooting started the crowd might stampede, killing hundreds of people, perhaps thousands. Cole, you damned fool, getting smack in the middle of someone else's war!

The engine of the tour boat hummed sweetly. That was a lucky break. Thinking about possible observers, Jake took the boat in close to the shore and turned east. He motored along for five minutes before he found what he wanted, a low pier with empty cleats. Someone used this boat to make a living; Jake Grafton didn't want to deprive him of it.

He brought the boat in smartly toward the pier. Although he didn't own a boat, he had watched sailors handle small boats for years. With the prop engaged and the engine idling, he leaped onto the pier with a rope in his hand and dropped it over a cleat. Back onto the bucking boat as it kissed the tire hanging at the waterline, reverse the prop, let the bowline spring the boat in . . . When he had the boat tied up fore and aft, he killed the engine.

The rock-solid pier felt good under his feet. He walked off the pier thinking about the thugs in Kowloon, wondering if they had been working for Sonny Wong.

15

Sergeant Loo Ping was told to search the Bank of the Orient tower, which stood on the north side of the square. He picked four men and went to the front door, which was locked. With his face against the glass, shielding his eyes with both hands, he could see that the bank lobby was empty.

He fired his rifle into the door lock. After three shots he pushed experimentally on the door. It gave, but a piece of the deadbolt still held it. He had two of the men put their shoulders against the door and push. The glass cracked, the broken lock gave way, and the door opened.

Sergeant Loo led his men inside. Of course the major hadn't told him what to look for. 'Search the building,' was all the major said, as if the object of the search was self-evident.

'People,' Loo Ping told his squad now. 'Look for people. If we find anyone, we will take him outside to the command vehicle for interrogation.'

The soldiers moved off. One went to the basement, the others went to the elevators and pushed the button. Nothing.

Loo Ping led them to the staircase and they started up.

'What if we find money?' the youngest soldier asked, which amused the others.

'You think they leave money lying around?'

'This is a bank, isn't it? Perhaps there is money. They must keep it somewhere.'

Loo Ping was a rice farmer's son himself and had never had a bank account. Of course there was money in a bank, even a failed one. Perhaps the major really wanted the soldiers to search for money.

'Money would be locked away in safes,' one of the soldiers remarked now, which made sense to Loo Ping. The bankers certainly wouldn't leave money lying around.

The second floor was a huge open room, carpeted, full of desks, with a computer on each of them. The lights were off, so the only illumination came through the windows on the sides of the grand room. The soldiers stood at the door, marveling. Imagine what the room must be like when the lights were on and people were seated at every desk, counting money!

This morning there were no people, so after a bit the soldiers let the door close – amazing how the door silently closed by itself – and climbed another flight of stairs.

The third floor was like the second, a vast office full of desks and computers and wonderful white machines that did God knows what, and . . .

Something was standing in the center of the room, near the window overlooking the square.

It looked like a big man.

Loo led the way, the other three behind. All had their rifles in their hands so that anyone could see they were men with authority who must be obeyed.

The man at the window was huge! He turned to watch the soldiers walk between the rows of desks toward him. He had dark skin and was completely naked.

Loo Ping's steps slowed.

It wasn't a man.

No.

A machine? Nearly seven feet tall, the neck consisted of three flexible stalks. The head was narrow at the chin and top, widest at the eyes, with a stalk or flexible tube coming out the top. The legs reminded Loo Ping of the hind legs of a dog; he thought the feet looked like those of a chicken, with three prominent toes. And that tail! Something from a movie?

No!

A *robot*! That is what it must be!

One of the men whispered to Loo, tugged at his sleeve. 'It has a weapon,' the man said.

'Hey!' Loo Ping called, still walking forward, but slower.

He halted ten feet from the thing and looked it over. The letter C was visible high on its shoulders. Its hands were claws, and they held a launch tube for a wire-guided antitank missile. Another launch tube lay on the floor.

Now Loo realized the head was lowered a few degrees, so the eyes – they were really some kind of lenses – were looking right at him. One of them had a circular lens turret in front of it, and now the turret rotated, stopped with a click, then rotated again.

Nervous, Loo took a few steps sideways.

The head followed.

For the first time Loo Ping noticed that a multibarreled weapon of some kind was mounted on the right side of the robot's torso. Now the barrels began spinning, emitting a high-pitched whine, barely audible in this quiet room.

Loo Ping tightened the grip on his rifle, glanced at his three troops. They were still there, although they looked like they were going to run.

'Hey!' Loo Ping said again, facing the robot and moving the barrel of his rifle a little, so it pointed more at the robot. He searched for the safety with his right thumb.

'The gun is pointed right at you,' the closest soldier whispered to Loo Ping. He was right. The spinning barrels of the weapon were pointed at Loo Ping's chest. He took another step to the right. The barrels followed.

'Ooooo . . .' he began, but he never completed the sound.

The robot's weapon fired, and Loo Ping felt the impact of the bullet as it hit him dead center in the heart. His blood pressure dropped to zero, and he was dead seconds after he hit the floor.

The robot swung its weapon and fired one bullet at the nearest soldier, then the next, and the next. Four individual aimed shots in less than a second.

The four empty cartridges ejected from the minigun's breech rattled like hail against the window glass, then fell to the carpeted office floor while the barrels of the minigun freewheeled to a stop.

The soldier Loo Ping had sent to search the basement walked through the door just as the minigun fired. As the reports echoed through the room, he dove back through the door and scrambled down the staircase.

'Someone is escaping,' Kerry Kent said. She was watching the monitor intently, listening to Charlie York's audio in her headset.

'Let him go,' Cole said. 'He's no threat.' He wiped his mouth with the back of his hand. Four uneducated kids dead in a heartbeat. His mouth was watering badly, like he was going to puke.

Charlie York turned back to the window. The turret on his right camera clicked to another lens, bringing the video of the plaza below into focus on Kent's monitor.

She checked with the other units. All okay, all ready.

Jimmy Lee, the King of Cool, was still babbling incoherently about Wu Tai Kwong and treason and not wanting to be executed. Lee's producer and the government censor stood wringing their hands.

Governor Sun hadn't called and in truth the producer doubted if he would. Still, Jimmy Lee was a celebrity of sorts, so he might.

The censor tried to place a call to Beijing but the operator said the lines were down. 'This is a government emergency,' the censor shouted, then wished he hadn't. The possibility that Jimmy Lee had gone off his nut and was babbling nonsense crossed his mind for the first time. He wondered just how hard he should press to get though to someone important.

He didn't have to worry. The operator told him that government business or not, the telephone lines out of Hong Kong were still out of order.

'Call army headquarters,' the producer suggested.

'Why don't we just broadcast the news?' the censor replied. 'Everyone will hear. What better way is there to warn the authorities of the plot?'

'What if Jimmy is crazy? Huh? Have you considered that? Maybe he's on drugs. The fool has used them before, remember?'

'All the telephone lines out of Hong Kong are down,' the censor retorted. 'The banks are closed, the subway isn't running, the airport is closed ... Jimmy says the rebels are attacking the computers. There is going to be an attack on the troops in the Bank of the Orient square. That sounds like truth to me.'

'Okay, okay,' the producer said. He eyed Jimmy, tried to decide if he was up to talking coherently. No.

He went into the studio and sat on the stool in front of Jimmy's mike. As he waited for the current song to end, he thought about what he was going to say. Tell it straight, he decided. Don't try to jazz it up like Jimmy would. Just act like a man with all his marbles.

Don't panic, people, but this is a rumor that may have some truth to it. Authorities, take action. You heard it first, folks, right here on the Jimmy Lee show.

The song came to an end. The producer flipped the switch to make his microphone hot and began speaking.

The people in the mobile museum trailer parked three blocks from the Bank of the Orient had a radio tuned to the Jimmy Lee show and a television showing the only station left on the air. Popular music had been coming from the radio and a Chinese soap opera from the television.

Someone called Kerry Kent's attention to the voice that came over the radio. A male voice, talking about the revolution that was just beginning, a revolution to overthrow the People's Republic. Troops were going to be attacked this morning in the Central District by armed rebels, who were trying to cause a major riot, a riot that was supposed to engulf City Hall and lead to the arrest of the authorities there.

'That isn't Jimmy Lee's voice,' the man told Kerry ominously.

She looked at her watch. This wasn't supposed to be happening now.

'Have the people who are to guard the radio and television stations reached there yet?' These people could not be armed until the weapons came through the Cross-Harbor Tunnel.

'They are on their way. They haven't called in.'

'What is going on at the radio station?'

No one could answer that.

Virgil Cole was watching now. Kerry Kent called Hu Chiang, who was still circling over the Central District in a helicopter. The feed from the chopper's television camera was displayed on a monitor in the trailer.

'You're over the bank square?' Kerry asked.

'Yes. I'm ready when you are.'

864

Kerry turned to Cole. 'The television and radio station guards are not yet in position, but a premature announcement is coming over the radio.'

'Anything on television?'

'No.'

'Are we ready?'

'We are waiting for the television and radio guards. When the hammer falls, we have to deny the government use of the media and keep it for ourselves.'

'Is the army listening to Jimmy Lee?'

Kerry Kent stared at the monitors, which showed her what each of the Sergeant York units was seeing. Then she checked the computer-generated composite. 'If they are, they haven't taken alarm yet,' she said.

'Call the people on the way to the TV and radio stations. Get an estimated time of arrival. All they have to do is get there before the PLA does.'

Kerry Kent nodded at one of the computer technicians, who picked up a WB phone and began dialing.

'Two hours,' the radio operator told Moon Hok. That was how long the colonel at the barracks in the New Territories estimated it would take for the troops Moon requested to be loaded on trucks and transported to the Bank of the Orient square. Neither the barracks colonel nor Moon Hok yet knew that the Cross-Harbor Tunnel no longer belonged to the army, nor were they factoring in the gridlock conditions that prevailed in the streets of southern Kowloon. Still, Moon Hok knew the estimate was optimistic.

From where he stood he could hear the crowd chanting an antigovernment slogan, something about no more stealing.

Once again, Moon Hok thought bitterly, Tang and the governor had placed the army in an impossible situation. The crowd was definitely hostile and growing with each passing minute. In the streets leading to the square the people were packed to standing-room-only density.

Should they be allowed to remain where they were, or should he push them back and expand his perimeter?

While he was mulling his options, the radio traffic continued about the helicopter in which General Tang had been riding. It had crashed, according to an army officer who said he had witnessed the disaster from a vehicle a half-mile away. The helicopter had fallen near the Kowloon entrance to the Cross-Harbor Tunnel. Another officer chimed in, claiming he saw the missile that downed the chopper.

'It was shot down,' he said on the radio net.

Shot down!

If the hostile population was now shooting at PLA helicopters, the entire situation had changed. This bank square was militarily indefensible. Perhaps he should load the troops in the trucks and get them out of here. Of course, that move would have political repercussions.

He decided to dump the whole mess in the governor's lap. He directed the radio operator to get Governor Sun on the radio.

But time had run out. Some of the civilians in the crowd outside the military perimeter were listening to the only radio station in Hong Kong that was on the air. These people were being entertained by Jimmy Lee's producer, who was describing the horrible, treasonous uprising that was about to take place in the Bank of the Orient square.

At first the people who were listening laughed. Then they stood looking at each other, wondering if this diatribe were true.

To a crowd that was already rowdy, the radio voice seemed to be describing the perfect way to vent their anger at the myriad of frustrations and injustices that were their lot in life.

The shouts became loud, angry, and the people began pushing forward toward the soldiers in the square.

Virgil Cole saw the crowd surge on the monitors. He pushed a button on his control panel so that the audio from the York units was in his headset. Now he could hear the angry chants.

'If the soldiers feel threatened, they'll fire tear gas or bullets, and the crowd will panic,' he said to Kent, who was mesmerized by the unfolding spectacle. 'Let's do it now.'

The soldier who had witnessed Loo Ping's death at the hands of Charlie York stood now in front of General Moon, pointing at the Bank of the Orient building. He explained about the robot.

'A monster ten feet tall shot my sergeant and the other three men in my squad. Up there, on the third floor.'

The general listened to this drivel, then walked away. The junior officers could handle the man. Monsters!

The man kept pointing at the third floor.

When he heard glass breaking, Moon Hok involuntarily glanced in the direction the soldier was pointing. He saw glass showering down ... from a third-floor window.

Moon was about to tell one of the staff officers to have the soldier lead him to the monster in the bank when the nearest tank exploded. The explosion burned the general and tossed him through the air. He landed in a heap on the pavement, too stunned to move.

The York robot called Charlie dropped the empty launch tube for the wire-guided antitank missile and picked up another. While it was bringing the weapon into firing position, the second tank exploded. Dog York, in the building on the south side of the square, had fired that round.

866

Charlie aimed this missile at the command vehicle, then squeezed the trigger.

The missile pulverized the van, showering the men lying on the pavement with sheet metal and radio parts.

Having fired both the antitank missiles Charlie York had carried into the Bank of the Orient, Kerry Kent decided to have Dog York fire a rocket-propelled grenade at the machine gun nest on the far right side of the square. The York control screen was a Windows-based system – point and click – so in seconds she had a rocket screaming across the square. It struck the ammo feed on the side of the tripod-mounted heavy machine gun and destroyed it.

Seconds later Dog destroyed another machine gun on the far side of the square.

The tanks and two machine guns were out of action. Thirty seconds had passed, and every PLA soldier in the square was flat on his face or huddled behind a concrete planter wall.

The sounds of the explosions echoed through the urban canyons and were heard by more than a hundred thousand people standing and sitting in the streets. The energy level in the crowd soared as people craned their necks, trying to see in the direction of the square.

When the truck screeched to a halt outside the Victoria Peak television station, Wei Luk was standing in the doorway. With a huge sigh of relief, he watched a dozen university students with assault rifles pile out of the back of the truck and pass down a machine gun. They set up the machine gun where it had an excellent field of fire along the main street leading to the station, then took up positions around the building.

Wei Luk went back inside. The receptionist stared at him in wide-eyed amazement when he pulled a pistol from his pocket and directed her to unlock the door. Dazed, she pushed the button.

Wei Luk and his colleagues walked down the hallway toward the main studio, where they saw Peter Po and gave him the high sign.

Less than two minutes later the station had the feed from the camera in Hu Chiang's helicopter on the air. Peter Po began a voice-over, explaining to the television audience that the first battle of the revolution had begun.

In the museum trailer three blocks from the Bank of the Orient square, a cheer went up when the television began playing the aerial feed.

Virgil Cole turned to the shortwave radio that sat on a bench behind him. In less than a minute he began receiving reports from revolutionaries in television stations all across China that had picked up the Hong Kong signal from the satellite and were rebroadcasting it the length and breadth of the nation. With the program on the air, the revolutionaries would then abandon the stations, forcing all the personnel out and locking the doors of the buildings. When the authorities reacted, as they eventually would, they would have to break into the buildings to stop the broadcasts. And there would be no one there to arrest.

By then the damage would be done. The news would be out, the credibility of the government severely damaged.

Virgil Cole leaned back in his chair with a sigh of relief. *Finally,* he thought, *we have crossed the threshold. There can be no turning back.*

Alvin and Bob York were in a locked room in the basement of the building that stood on the west side of the square. The door was locked to discourage any soldiers who might be ordered to search the building. Now Alvin broke the lock with a twist of the door handle. Both units climbed the stairs toward the street level. The staircase was narrow with a low ceiling, with barely enough room for the robots when they tucked in their appendages and curled their backs.

Kerry Kent checked the video feed as the two units climbed the stairs to ensure all was well, then used the mouse to activate Easy and Fred.

Behind her Virgil Cole helped himself to another cup of coffee. He had spent five years of his life overseeing the design of the York units and had a huge financial stake in the company that manufactured them, so he should have been nervous about the Yorks' first operational trial. He wasn't. He had used up all his juice fretting the success of the nationwide television broadcast, which he thought more critical than the performance of the York units to the eventual success of the revolution.

He sipped the coffee and glanced at the monitors and wondered if he should have absolutely refused Wu Tai Kwong's demand to confront the PLA in front of an audience. He had confidence in the York units, but crowd psychology was a huge unknown – a stampede could kill thousands.

As he watched he remembered Wu's words: 'Revolutions are made by people – the Yorks are just things. The people of China must see that others are willing to fight. We can give them something to fight for, but they must find the courage in their own hearts.'

As the four York units that had been in hiding came running from the buildings, Charlie and Dog leaped through the broken glass of their respective third-floor windows. They used their hands and feet to cushion the shock of their landing on the concrete street, then they began running toward the center of the square.

Now all six Yorks were transmitting video and audio to the central computer in the museum trailer; in seconds the computer had transformed the six data streams into a three-dimensional picture of the square, the trucks, the decorative planters, trees, light poles, smoldering hulks of tanks ... and the armed men who were rising from the pavement with their weapons in hand, staring wild-eyed at the huge, running robots, which attacked the crews of the two remaining machine guns.

Inevitably a few of the soldiers snapped their rifles to their shoulders to shoot, and instantly the system directed a York to engage. An onboard CPU slewed the minigun onto the target and triggered a round. Just one round per target, because unlike humans, the Yorks didn't miss.

The ring-laser gyros inside each York fed data to a separate maneuvering computer that kept it upright and balanced, the onboard sensors gathered data that was processed internally by the weapons-control computer and passed to the mainframe via UWB, and threats were identified and engaged in the order set by the controller before the battle began. In addition, the weapons-control computer passed information to the maneuvering computer so that it could move the unit to minimize the danger posed by low-priority threats, or threats the York had not yet had time to engage.

The computers and sensors operated seamlessly. Each unit engaged targets that threatened it and ran, leaped, swerved, and bounded to throw off the aim of opponents it had yet to engage.

The result was mass confusion. Officers shouted and pointed, gesturing wildly at the Yorks, which were leaping from truck to truck, running across the square, leaping up on the sides of the buildings and executing turns in midair while their miniguns hammered out aimed shots.

Soldiers who raised their rifles to aim at the sprinting Yorks were shot down, those who did nothing were not harmed.

One soldier threw down his rifle and stood erect in the center of the square with his hands in the air. One of the junior officers drew a pistol and pointed it at the erect soldier. He was immediately shot by two Yorks.

Other soldiers threw down their rifles, first a few, then many.

The firing slowed to an occasional shot, then stopped altogether.

The running Yorks slowed to a walk, then came to rest. Each one stood with its head turning, its sensors scanning, and the barrels of its minigun spinning, ready to fire. They were ominous, fearsome.

A cheer went up from the watching civilians, who ran into the square.

Burned and groggy from the concussion of the tank that had exploded nearby, General Moon Hok managed to get to his feet. He stood swaying, looking uncomprehendingly at his soldiers with their hands up. Then he took his first good look at the closest York, Alvin, whose sensors were scrutinizing him in return. The minigun followed his every move, but the shot didn't come.

The helicopter carrying Hu Chiang settled into the center of the bank square and Hu stepped out. The cameraman, his camera still going, piled out the back and focused his camera on Hu, who looked around, then walked over to General Moon Hok and demanded that he surrender his command to the revolutionary forces of China.

The civilians were running into the square now, many of them armed with weapons liberated from the Kowloon police barracks. They were taking weapons from soldiers and passing them to unarmed civilians. A few of the newly armed revolutionaries aimed their weapons skyward and pulled the trigger, just to see if they would shoot.

The Yorks nearly shot these people. Cole suspected what was coming and warned Kerry Kent, who safetied the Yorks' firing circuits just in time.

Moon Hok was in no mood to do or say anything to the people who had killed his soldiers and humiliated him, and Hu Chiang wisely decided that Moon's silence was good enough. He ordered one of the armed revolutionaries who had appeared nearby to jail Moon and his officers.

All this made excellent television. It got even better: From his hip pocket Hu removed a written speech that he and Wu Tai Kwong had drafted for Wu to give at this moment. Since Wu wasn't here, Hu read the speech to the unseen audience behind the camera as the cheering crowd gathered around him.

'We hereby proclaim the goals of the revolution: China shall become a free and democratic nation with a written constitution guaranteeing the rule of law, with leaders regularly elected by popular vote, a nation free of graft and corruption, a nation that protects its citizens from criminals, a nation where everyone shall have an equal opportunity to earn a living, a nation with free speech and freedom of religion, a nation that can take its place as a proud member of the world's family of nations . . .'

The last half of the battle in the square was broadcast all over Hong Kong and mainland China. In Canton and Shanghai, in Beijing and Hunan Province and in villages all over the nation, people who happened to be near a television saw the Yorks standing in the center of the bank square surrounded by PLA troops with their hands in the air. Then the cheering crowd flowed into the square as if a dam had burst.

In Hong Kong City Hall someone called Governor Sun to the television. He was not in time to see the Yorks in action, but he watched as Hu Chiang landed in the square in the television station's helicopter and walked over to General Moon. He saw Hu accept General Moon's sidearm and he saw the first of the deliriously happy civilians stream into the square, hugging Hu Chiang and the surrendered soldiers and each other and gazing in awe at the York units.

'Radio Beijing,' Governor Sun ordered peremptorily. 'A revolution is underway in Hong Kong and we need more troops immediately to stabilize the situation.'

The aide went off to do as he was told, leaving Governor Sun rooted to the spot, still staring at the television.

Nothing happened instantly in China, Sun well knew. It would take days for the government to reinforce the division of troops that were already here. Perhaps several weeks.

For the first time, Sun admitted to himself that he had misjudged the situation here.

His next epiphany followed immediately: The rebels would probably execute him if they could catch him. Chinese revolutions had never been bloodless affairs. This one wouldn't be either.

Jimmy Lee's producer stopped talking into the radio microphone when he realized that someone was standing beside him with a pistol, a pistol that was pointed at his head. He stopped talking in midword.

The pistol jerked, ordering him out of the chair.

A young woman of eighteen or nineteen years, an inch over four feet tall, took his place and began speaking into the microphone. 'The Chinese revolution,' she announced simply, 'has begun. The island of Hong Kong has been liberated from Communist control.'

Lin Pe watched the celebration in the Bank of the Orient square on the small television the Shatin grocer kept above his soft drink cooler. She watched as the cameraman inspected a York unit at close range – the thing towered a foot over everyone there and its head never stopped scanning – and the smoking hulk of a tank.

Hu Chiang appeared on television, behind him the crowd milled around, every now and then someone fired a shot into the air ... the scene was festive, gay. No one even bothered to guard the unarmed PLA soldiers, who wandered through the crowd aimlessly, without direction.

Wu should have been here to see this, Lin Pe thought. He worked for a dozen years to make this happen, this *first step*!

The long journey had finally begun. She didn't know whether she should be happy or sad. She went back outside and sat down on the orange crate where she could see the gate of the army base and thought about everything.

She would tell Wu of this. In this life or the next.

In City Hall the governor and his staff were mesmerized by the televised spectacle, by the aerial shots of the crowd surging into the plaza, and by the simple, infectious joy that was apparent on every face.

They huddled around the television, which alternated between shots from the square taken with a handheld camera and aerial shots from the helicopter, which had taken off again. Through it all Peter Po gave the voice-over, as calm and collected as though revolutions were a weekly occurrence.

Hu Chiang's speech broke the spell in City Hall. Never known for an even temper, Sun exploded as he listened. He cursed Tang and Moon and the other PLA officers as incompetent, defeatist traitors. A call was put forth to the navy base. Sun demanded that all the gunboats steam up the strait and use their guns on the rebels celebrating in the Bank of the Orient square. The commander had caught the tail end of the televised debacle, and he agreed. Without much enthusiasm, Sun noted darkly.

Next he called the Su-27 squadron at Lantau. He got the squadron commander on the phone and demanded that armed sorties be flown against the rebels in the square.

'Drop bombs, strafe, shoot rockets ... *kill the rebels! Stop the rot right here, before it spreads.*'

The colonel made him repeat the order to ensure he understood. 'We will use a cannon to kill mosquitoes, eh?'

'Will you obey or must I call Beijing and have you court-martialed?'

'Bombs in the square will do a lot of damage, Governor. I just want to ensure you understand that. Afterward will be too late to complain.'

'Kill the rebels.'

'Bombs don't care whom they kill, Governor. Rebels, bankers, children, women, tourists, soldiers, policemen, whomever. That is what I am trying to explain.'

'Obey my order!'

Next he called the chief of the metropolitan police and demanded he muster his officers and engage the rebels in armed combat. The police chief wasn't enthusiastic. Unlike the navy and air force commanders, he knew his men would be face-to-face with the robots he had seen on television.

'What are those things, Governor? What are their capabilities?'

'I do not know. Bullets will stop them, however.'

'The army didn't seem to have much luck with bullets. What makes you think the police will do any better?'

'I have given the order,' Sun said icily.

'So you have. But I tell you now, my men are police, not soldiers. They are trained in traffic control, not armed combat. I make no promises.'

'Lead them yourself, coward!'

'If I am killed, whom will you blame for our defeat?'

Before Sun could give that disrespectful question the answer it deserved, he discovered that the chief of police had hung up.

Sun slammed down the phone. His chief aide was right there by the desk.

'Governor, you must report this matter to Beijing, but first, you must think of getting off this island.'

'What are you saying?'

'Sir, the rebels will come for you, walk in the front door. The three or four policemen on duty out front cannot hold off armed rioters. You must not be here. You must not let them make a spectacle of you.'

'You're right,' Sun said, with more than a little gratitude in his voice. He telephoned the army base in the New Territories, asked for a helicopter to pick up him and his key aides on the roof of City Hall as soon as possible.

On the way to the roof, he stopped in the radio room. The operator called Beijing on the scrambled voice net.

Sun tried to quickly summarize the events of the morning. He told Beijing of his orders to the army and navy. 'We need military reinforcements now,' he pleaded with the minister.

The minister made no promises. 'You must resist with the forces you have at your disposal,' the minister said. 'The rocket forces have had a horrible disaster, the trains cannot run until the computer systems get sorted out, the nation's electrical grid is experiencing spot failures, the telephone system is sporadic at best. We cannot get troops to you for some days.'

'Air support? Could we have two more squadrons of MiGs or Sukhois?'

'The maintenance personnel, spare parts, and weapons all must be moved by road,' the minister in Beijing informed Sun. 'The move will take several weeks. I will give the order, but until they arrive, you must hold out with what you have.'

Hold out with what we have.

Perhaps that is possible, Sun thought as he made his way up the stairs to the roof of City Hall. *If we can hurt the rebels in the square, then keep the remnants of the rebel forces on this island, prevent them from crossing the strait, perhaps it can be done.*

The chief of police was too old a dog to go running after every stick. He sat behind his desk at police headquarters watching the rebels celebrate on television.

After he read the flyer this morning, he ordered his policemen to stay away from the heart of the Central District. Apparently they had obeyed him, because he didn't see a single police officer on any of the camera's sweeps of the crowd.

A cop learns many things about the people he serves: who drinks to excess, who has a drug-addicted son or a pregnant teenage daughter, who takes bribes, who doesn't . . . who is fucking whom. In a society in which everything is for sale, everything has a price. A cop quickly learns to survive or he is eaten by the sharks.

The chief was busy surviving right now.

He tried to ignore politics when he could. Sonny Wong told him a year ago that rebellion was brewing in Hong Kong. Of course Sonny wanted to profit from that fact – that was a given. The rebels wanted change, Governor Sun and the Communists wanted to keep the status quo. One would win, one would lose.

Whoever won would need the police. And the police would need a chief.

This chief had no intention of ending up like China Bob Chan, with a fresh hole in his head and everyone in town breathing sighs of relief. Sure, China Bob made lots of money, got rich, had the big house and hot women and all the trimmings . . . and now he was sleeping in a hole in the ground because he knew too much about too many things.

Actually Sun wasn't a bad sort. The chief wondered now if he should have told the governor to get out of Hong Kong; the rebels would kill him if they caught him. Surely the man is bright enough to figure that out for himself.

The chief reached for the telephone, then thought better of it. He owed the governor nothing.

Michael Gao was on the roof of the building near the entrance to the Cross-Harbor Tunnel when he spotted the PLA helo running low, at treetop level, headed for City Hall on Hong Kong Island. He had a Strella launcher at his feet, so he lifted it, squeezed the trigger to the first notch to try for a heat lock-on.

And got one. He squeezed the trigger and the missile roared out of the launcher.

Away it went in a plume of fire. Straight across the street into the top story of the next building over.

He had another launcher, but he waited. Perhaps he would get a better shot. If he could get onto the sea wall . . .

The chopper settled onto the roof of City Hall. Sun and three aides came running out. When they were aboard, the chopper rose into the air just enough to clear the railing on top of the building, then tilted into the wind.

The pilot turned to fly out over the strait, then he turned east.

Michael Gao ran with the missile launcher in his arms. People scurried to clear a path. He came to the sidewalk on the sea wall and hurriedly threw the launcher to his shoulder. The helo was speeding east over the strait, at least two miles away and low, no more than fifty feet above the water.

The missile's guidance unit refused to lock on to the helo's exhaust. The distance was just too great, the angle too large.

Gao lowered the launcher and watched the helo fly away.

Tommy Carmellini systematically examined every item in Kerry Kent's apartment, disassembled the lamps and clocks, took the television from its shell, examined the works. Did the same with the clock radio. Tapped along the floorboards, scrutinized the light fixtures, used a knife to slice the stuffing from the easy chair near the window, picked through every single item in her dresser . . .

Tommy Carmellini knew how to search an apartment and he searched this one. He found absolutely nothing that shouldn't be there.

Two hours later, discouraged and tired, he dropped his trousers and lowered himself onto Kent's commode. Before he did so, however, he lifted the lid on the back and examined the workings. Looked precisely like a commode should. Then he felt behind the tank to ensure that nothing was taped to the back.

As he sat answering nature's call, he picked up a magazine that Kent had arranged on a nearby stand. Flipped through the pages, looking to see if anything had been inserted. No.

A newspaper. He picked it up, shook it. Nothing fell out. He was about to put it back on the stand when he paused, looked again. *The Financial Times*, a week-old edition. Kent had it folded to the stock listings.

Idly, Carmellini ran his eye down the listings. Column one, two . . .

Huh! There was a tiny spot of ink under the Vodafone listing, as if she rested the tip of her pen there for a moment.

He held the page up, scrutinized it carefully. Here was another spot, and another. Six in all.

Stocks. Investments. A portfolio. Well, even civil servants had portfolios these days. Hell, he had a little money in the market himself.

But he couldn't recall seeing anything about her portfolio in the apartment. Not a monthly statement, a letter from her broker, nothing.

Odd.

There should be something, shouldn't there?

16

Major Ma Chao and his three co-conspirators were standing in the back of the ready room when the commanding officer and his department heads came in. Someone called the people in the room to attention.

'We have orders,' the CO announced. 'Governor Sun has directed us to bomb the rebels in the Bank of the Orient square in the Central District, and headquarters in Beijing has confirmed. We will launch four airplanes with four two-hundred-and-fifty-kilogram bombs each. Fortunately, the weather is excellent. We will coordinate the attack with a shelling by two naval vessels, putting maximum pressure on the rebels.'

In the silence that followed this announcement the television audio could be heard throughout the room. The pilots had watched Hu Chiang make his speech, had seen the York units and the happy, joyous crowd that filled the square. They had listened to Peter Po explain the significance of the revolution, why the overthrow of the Communists was of the gravest national importance.

Now this.

There was certainly much to think about, including the fact that no pilot in the squadron had ever dropped bombs from a J-11. Although the plane was a license-built copy of one of the world's premier fighters, it had no all-weather attack capability; visual dive-bombing was the only option. Unfortunately the Beijing brass thought the risks of dive-bombing training too high, so it had been forbidden.

Major Ma turned sideways so his right side was partially hidden and drew his sidearm, a semiautomatic. He held it low, beside his leg.

'Sir,' Ma asked, 'did you verify the governor's identity? Agents provocateurs may be giving false orders.'

This comment was grossly insubordinate and the commanding officer treated it as such. '*I* am completely satisfied that the governor issued these orders and that headquarters concurred,' he said, daring anyone to contradict his statement. 'The time has come to separate the patriots from the traitors,' he added ominously. 'I intend to follow orders, to bomb the rebels as directed by the government. Who will fly with me?'

The senior officers raised their hands, but not a single junior.

'You traitors are under arrest,' the commanding officer snarled. 'Now clear the room.'

Ma Chao raised his pistol, pointed it at the CO. 'It is you who are under arrest, Colonel. Drop your sidearm.'

The CO was a true fighter pilot. He grinned broadly, then said, 'We thought something like this might happen, Ma Chao, but we never suspected you. Some of these other little dicks, yes, but you surprise me. Too bad.' He raised his voice. 'Come in, Sergeant, come in,' he called and gestured through the open door to people waiting in the hallway.

Three senior noncommissioned officers walked in. They were carrying assault rifles in the ready position.

The CO gestured toward the rear of the room. 'Major Ma and those junior officers. Lock them up until we can interrogate them and find how far the rot has spread.'

The NCOs pointed their rifles at Ma.

This was *it*! Now or never. Use your best judgment, Wu had said.

Ma steadied the front sight of his automatic and pulled the trigger. The bullet knocked the CO down.

'Anyone else?' Ma said, looking around.

The senior NCO grinned at Ma, then pointed his rifle at the department heads. 'Your pistols, please. You are under arrest.'

The lieutenant beside Ma couldn't contain himself. 'I thought the sergeant was going to shoot you!'

Ma Chao thought the sergeant was on his side. He said he was last week, yet every week the earth turns seven times. Ma breathed a sigh of relief and walked toward the front of the room to see how badly the CO was hurt and to take charge.

When the trucks filled with troops left the PLA base, Lin Pe telephoned a number she had memorized. She recognized the voice that answered, a nice young girl who attended Hong Kong University. 'Seven trucks have left the base.'

Five minutes later Lin Pe called again. 'Ten trucks filled with troops. They drove away through Shatin.'

'Very good. Thank you for the report. We would like you to go back to Nathan Road and walk along it. Report any strong points that you see under construction.'

Lin Pe said good-bye to the grocer, who had let her use his restroom, and walked through Shatin toward the bus stop. Her bag was heavy and she was tired, so she made slow progress.

Her son, Wu, had told her of the dangers of spying on the PLA. 'They will shoot you if they catch you talking about them on the cell phone. They may arrest you because they are worried. They will be frightened, fearful men, and very dangerous.'

'I understand,' she replied.

'They may beat you to death trying to make you talk. They may kill you regardless of what you say.'

'I understand,' she had repeated.

'You do not have to do this,' Wu told her.

'Someone has to.'

'Ah . . .' he said, and dropped the subject.

Where in the world could Kerry Kent hide the information about her stock portfolio? Tommy Carmellini stood in the middle of Kent's kitchen thinking about that problem. He could have sworn he had searched everything there was to search, peered in every cubbyhole and cranny, pried loose every baseboard, looked in all the vents. . . .

The pots and pans were piled carefully against one wall. He had even peeled up the paper she had used to line her shelves.

Her attaché case wasn't here. Must be at the consulate.

The notebook . . . a spiral notebook had lain on her bedroom table. He had flipped through it, but . . .

He found it again, sat down in the middle of the bathroom floor in the only open space and went through it carefully. Halfway through the notebook, there it was. A page of multiplication problems, seven in all, and a column where she added the seven answers together. She hid it in plain sight.

He compared the numbers in the problems to the stock listings in *The Financial Times*. Okay, this stock closed at 74.5, and here was the problem, 74.5×5400. Answer, 402,300.

He checked every problem. The correlation with the six stocks highlighted with a tiny spot of ink was perfect. One stock he couldn't find; only six were marked.

The total . . . £1,632,430.

A pound was worth what, about a buck fifty?

Wheee! She wasn't filthy rich, but Kerry Kent was certainly a modestly well-off secret agent, which was, as any self-respecting gentleman would tell you, the very best kind.

Almost two and a half million dollars.

On a civil servant's salary.

Perhaps her grandparents were loaded and left her a bundle. Perhaps she had a rich first husband. Then again, perhaps she was the world's finest stock picker and had done more than all right with her lunch money.

Or perhaps, Tommy Carmellini thought as he pocketed the worksheet and financial page, just perhaps, Kerry Kent was crooked.

Elizabeth Yeager's apartment was a walk-up in a small village setting on the south side of the island. As the taxi driver settled in to wait, Jake Grafton made his way past the craft shops that catered to the tourist trade, only some of which were open today, to the stairs of Yeager's building. Ivy and creeping vines covered the walls.

There were four mailboxes. Yeager's was Apartment Three. He pushed the button.

'Yes.' An American woman's voice, tired and angry.

'Elizabeth Yeager, I have a message for you.'

'What?'

'For you personally.'

'Come on up.' She buzzed the lock open.

The former consular employee opened her door just a crack. Jake Grafton slammed the door with his shoulder, and it flew open, nearly bowling her over. There was another woman sitting by the couch, a dumpy, middle-aged woman with graying hair.

'Who are you? What do you want?'

Yeager's eyes were red from crying.

'You're Yeager?'

'Yes.'

'Some questions for you.' He looked at the other woman. 'If you wouldn't mind.'

Yeager nodded at the woman, who glared at Jake as she swept past.

'It's a crime to break into people's apartments,' Yeager said as she perched on the edge of a chair. 'Don't forget, my neighbor, Mrs. O'Reilly, can identify you.'

'That was the woman who was just here?'

'That's right.'

'Ms. Yeager, I wouldn't be talking about crimes if I were you. Stealing passports, forgery, treason, kidnapping . . . If you ever go back to the states you may wind up spending the rest of your life in a cell.'

'You're Grafton, aren't you?'

Jake nodded.

'I've nothing to say, so get out.'

'Or what? You'll call the police?'

She merely glared at him.

'Perhaps you'll call Sonny Wong and he'll send someone over to run me off. There's the phone – call anyone you like.'

He sat in the chair facing her.

'Bastard.'

'Where's my wife?'

'I don't know.' Yeager hitched her bottom back in the chair and looked obstinately away.

Jake Grafton tried to hold his temper, which was getting more and more difficult. If Yeager only knew. 'My wife has been kidnapped,' he explained patiently. 'Her life is at stake. I think you know a great deal about Sonny

Wong, where he can be found, where he stays, where his men operate from. I want to know all that. I'm not going to tell anyone what you tell me. I won't report it to the United States government. It'll be strictly between us, absolutely confidential.'

She turned to face him again. 'You're an officer in the United States Navy. You can't touch me. *I know my rights!* I have nothing to say!'

He pulled the Colt .45 from under his sports jacket, pointed it at her head, and thumbed off the safety. As she blanched, he turned the muzzle a few inches and pulled the trigger. The report was like an explosion, overpowering in that enclosed space. The bullet smacked into the wall behind her.

He leaped for her, grabbed a handful of hair, put the muzzle against her nose.

'Your rights don't mean shit! Where is my wife, goddamn it?'

She swallowed hard. 'I don't know.' That came out a squeak.

'We're having a revolution in Hong Kong, Ms. Yeager. The police have crawled into holes and the army has its hands full. No one cares about you. I can break every bone in your miserable body. I can shoot you full of holes and leave you here to bleed to death and nobody on this green earth will give a good goddamn. Now I'm going to ask you one more time, and if you give the wrong answer, we're going to find out how many bullets it takes to kill you. *Where is my wife?*'

Elizabeth Yeager's eyes got big as half-dollars and the color drained from her face. She tried to speak; the words came out a croak. Then she passed out cold. At first Jake thought she was faking it, but she went limp as linguine.

'Shit!' said Jake Grafton, more than a little disgusted with himself. Scaring a woman half to death.

'Shit,' he said again, and released his hold on Yeager. She slid off the chair onto the floor like a bundle of old rags.

He kicked the coffee table. It skittered away.

He had his chance last night. He should have stuck that revolver up Wong's nose and told him he was going to blow his fucking head off if he didn't produce Callie in a quarter of an hour.

Yeah.

He slammed the door to the apartment on his way out.

He had the taxi take him back to the consulate so he could watch the revolution on television. Since Cole had submitted his resignation and was technically no longer an employee of the United States government, Grafton probably shouldn't be in his office. In any event, no one had suggested he leave. He turned on the television and settled behind Cole's desk.

The thought that he should be doing something to find Callie gnawed at him. Just what that something was he didn't know.

When the time came, Sonny would produce Wu and Callie to collect his money, but once he got it, he had to kill them all. Wu, Callie, Jake, Cole, everyone who had firsthand knowledge of the kidnapping. If he didn't he was a dead man.

Sonny Wong would have enough shooters in the area to ensure no one escaped. You could bet your life on that.

Jake's thoughts wandered. Callie had a brother in Chicago, married with two kids in college. Her mother was in an independent living facility near her brother, and her father was dead.

Her father had spent his career on the faculty at the University of Chicago. Professor McKenzie. What a piece of work he was! It wasn't that the old man believed in Marxism, with its dubious theories of social change and mind-numbing economic twaddle – the feature he liked was the dictatorship of the elite. The professor was an intellectual snob. The great failing of the common man, in McKenzie's opinion, was that he was common.

Jake wondered just what the prof would have thought of the collapse of communism all over the world.

He snapped off the television and sat down behind the consul general's desk in the padded leather executive chair that usually held Tiger Cole's skinny rump. There was a yellow legal pad on the desk, so he helped himself to a pen and began writing a report to the National Security staff on the situation in Hong Kong. Fortunately the consulate had radio communications with the State Department, so the staff could encrypt the report and put it on the air as soon as Jake finished it.

He was scrawling away when the secretary stuck his head in. 'Ahh ... Admiral.' He frowned, perhaps offended that Jake was using Cole's office.

'Yes,' Jake replied, and kept going on the sentence he was writing.

'There's a telephone call, sir. Mr. Carmellini.'

Jake picked up the instrument. 'Grafton.'

'Carmellini, Admiral. I'm over here at Kerry Kent's apartment checking her cupboard. It seems she has a sizable stock portfolio somewhere.'

Jake stopped writing. He had the telephone in a death grip. 'Tell me about it.'

Carmellini did. He gave Jake the names of the companies he thought she owned shares in, the number of shares, and the values. He also gave Jake the information on the seventh stock, though he didn't know the name of the company.

'Anything else?' Jake asked.

'That's about it, unless you are interested in the brands of her clothes.'

'Should I be?'

'Well, they strike me as expensive duds, better than I am used to seeing on government employees, but she's British and a hell of a lot richer than me ...'

'Better come on back to the consulate.'

'Is the ferry still running? I know the subway is dead and the tunnel is closed.'

'Hire or steal a boat,' Jake said, and hung up.

He pushed the intercom button to summon the secretary. When he appeared, Jake told him, 'I want to call the Pentagon on the satellite phone.'

'Those circuits are all in use by the staff, sir, for official business. They are giving the National Security Council and State real-time feeds on the situation here.'

'Terrific. I want to use a line.'

'Who are you, sir? Really? I mean, I know you are an admiral on active duty in the navy, but using the consul general's office and – '

'I don't have time for this,' Jake snapped. 'Get me a line, and now. After you do that you call the Secretary of State's office and complain to them.'

The secretary was offended. 'I'll have the call put through. You can use the phone on the desk. Wait until it rings.'

Okay: China Bob Chan was smuggling money and high-tech war equipment into Hong Kong. And he was a conduit for Communist money being given or donated to American politicians in the hopes of getting favorable export licenses. Sonny Wong was a professional criminal with ties to criminal gangs all over China. Cole was an American agent supplying money and highly classified weapons systems to the rebels.

And Kerry Kent? A British SIS agent, either covertly assigned or playing hooky. Cole's weapons system operator, WSO, wizzo in U.S. Air Force terminology. Screwing the head rebel. With money in the bank . . .

Cole didn't trust China Bob, so a CIA agent bugged his office and was killed before he could retrieve the tape. Then somebody shot China Bob Chan, and the whole tangled skein became a mare's nest.

Callie listened to the tape and heard . . . nothing.

She heard hours of conversation, much of it one-sided because Chan was on the phone, and probably all of it relevant if one knew more about Chan's business . . . but not otherwise. For Callie it was just noise.

Then she was kidnapped.

Money?

Wong threatened Cole. Callie could convict him with her testimony, he said.

How would he know? He didn't hear the tape.

What if he were assuming the tape contained something it didn't?

Ahhh . . . !

The phone rang.

Jake picked it up and found himself talking to the Pentagon war room duty officer. He identified himself and asked for Commander Tarkington.

Twenty seconds later Toad was on the line.

'Are you sleeping there?'

'Up in the office. I was down here loafing, hoping you'd call.'

'Got a job for you.'

'Yes, sir. Fire away.'

Jake gave Toad all the information he had on Kent's stock portfolio. 'This is a straw we are trying to build with,' he told Toad. 'See what the NSA computer sleuths can come up with. The account probably won't be under her name. I would think it's probably with a London brokerage or the Hong Kong office of a London brokerage. This woman may have had access to stolen American passports from this consulate. If she has contacts in the Hong Kong underworld, she may have passports from anywhere, genuine or faked.' Jake gave Toad a physical description of Kent.

When Toad had finished writing down the description, he told his boss, 'I've been talking to the CIA. They say SIS is well aware of Kent's status with the rebels, though they refuse to admit anything. Officially the Brits say they never even heard of her.'

'Forget that. Find the money. Find where it came from. An inheritance, divorce settlement, whatever.'

'Heard anything from Callie?'

'No.'

'I asked for permission to come over there to help you, but the President nixed it. Said he doesn't want any military personnel going in-country for any reason.'

'I figured he'd say that.'

'I've talked to the chairman.' The chairman of the Joint Chiefs, Toad meant. 'We shouldn't have a problem getting cooperation. When I find out anything, I'll call you.'

'I'll be sitting right here,' Jake Grafton said.

At that moment Callie Grafton was telling Wu Tai Kwong, 'We need an escape plan.' She had inspected every inch of the small stateroom where they were being held, as well as the tiny bathroom. She had looked at the door hinges, the window, the air vent, the beds, and didn't have a glimmer of an idea.

'Yes,' Wu agreed after a moment's reflection, 'a plan would be good.'

'Do you have any ideas?'

'No.' Wu raised his hands, then lowered them. The sheet strips around his arm were blood-soaked, but the bleeding seemed to have stopped.

She found the situation infuriating. She balled up her fists and shook them. 'I don't understand you. You say they will kill you, yet you don't seem to be worried. You aren't figuring out how to get out of here. You're just sitting there.'

'What else is there to do?'

She made an exasperated noise. She had been married so long she judged all men by her husband. Jake Grafton wouldn't be sitting calmly, waiting for the inevitable. Not Jake. He would be scheming and planning until he drew his very last breath.

She missed him terribly.

'Figure a way to get us out of here,' Callie told her fellow prisoner. 'There must be a way. We're on a ship, a small one I think, docked I believe, maybe anchored. When they come for me again – or you – we'll both jump them. Fight, claw, do whatever we have to. Get out. Get free. Stay alive. Let's find something we can use as a weapon. Anything.'

Wu waited a while before he spoke. He had that habit, she noticed, and she didn't much care for it. He said, 'You would like my mother, I think. She is much like you. She struggles with life, seeks to conquer it.'

'And you don't?'

'We all do to some degree. My mother more than me. You are more like her, I think.'

'You are supposed to be a revolutionary. By definition, revolution is struggle.'

'Quite so. I struggle to change the world as man has made it. But life? When the rain comes, it does not matter whether you welcome it or hate it – the rain falls upon your head regardless.'

'Everyone dies, too,' Callie said acidly. 'I don't know about you, but I'm not ready. I have a lot of good years left in me. I'm not going to be robbed of life by some hoodlum, not if I can do anything to prevent it.'

'That's the rub,' Wu said softly. 'Preventing it.'

The Luda-class destroyer, Number 109, came steaming west through Victoria Strait between the island of Hong Kong and the Kowloon peninsula. She had been ordered by the commanding officer of the naval base to sortie immediately and shell the rebels in the Bank of the Orient square, pursuant to the orders of Governor Sun.

Lieutenant Tan was the officer of the deck when the order was received, and he protested. The commanding officer was not aboard, the ship was not ready for sea. His protests fell on deaf ears. 'Sail with the men you have aboard and shell the rebels as ordered,' the base commander said.

Of course, the base commander was having his own troubles. A riot had broken out in the enlisted mess hall, probably instigated by the rebels. The officers who attempted to turn off the base television system had been met with sticks and garbage pail lids. The rioting sailors were making threats against the officers' lives.

Actually two destroyers had sailed, but Number 105 had gone dead in the water with an engine room casualty before it cleared the base breakwater. Sabotage, Lieutenant Tan suspected, but he didn't say so with the quartermaster and helmsmen within earshot. These two were surly, doing their duty with the minimum acceptable professional courtesy. No doubt they sympathized with their rioting mates and perhaps with the rebels in the bank square.

Number 109 steamed on alone.

Lieutenant Tan began thinking about the professional problem he faced. The gun to use for surface bombardment was the twin 130-millimeter dual-purpose mount on the bow. There was a similar mount on the stern, but it was out of service for some critical parts.

The bow gun would do very well. Unfortunately in this ship the Sun Visor fire control radar that was designed for this gun was never mounted, so the gun had to be aimed visually. The gun had an effective range of eight or nine miles; that was no problem. In fact, the ship was within maximum gun range now.

The problem, Lieutenant Tan told himself as he stared at the chart of Hong Kong on the navigator's table, was going to be putting the shells into the square. He was going to have to lob them in with the gun elevated to a high angle. Maximum elevation angle was eighty-two degrees.

If he missed the square and started scattering 130-millimeter, 33.5-kilogram high-explosive shells around the downtown, there would be hell to pay later. Regardless of what they said now, the governor and base commander would want pieces of his hide then.

Of course the designated gunnery officer was not aboard. Lieutenant Tan was the only officer qualified to lay the gun, and he also had to con the ship.

He was so nervous his hands shook. He laid the chart on the table so it wouldn't rattle and consulted the range and elevation charts for the gun. Shooting at a hidden urban target was going to be a challenge, perhaps an impossible one.

He put the binoculars to his eyes and studied the buildings in the Central District. The ship was about five miles from the downtown, he estimated. Needless to say, the buildings did not appear on his chart of the area's waters. If he could remember which buildings were which . . .

He asked the helmsman for the speed.

'Eight knots, sir.'

He was studying the chart, measuring, when he heard the lookout.

'Bogey on the starboard bow.'

What?

'Jet airplane, sir, looks like he's lining us up for a low pass.'

Lieutenant Tan looked.

A fighter, two of them. They were completing the turn to pass the length of the ship, bow to stern. Dropping down, one trailing the other, not going too quickly, maybe three hundred knots . . .

Suddenly he knew. '*Air attack!*' he screamed. 'Open fire!'

Flashes on the wing root of the lead fighter . . . the water in front of the ship erupted. Quick as thought, the shells began pounding the ship, cutting, smashing.

The glass in the bridge windows shattered, the helmsman went down, shrapnel and metal flew everywhere.

The attack ended in a thunderous roar as the jet pulled out right over the ship, and the next fighter began shooting.

Screaming ... someone was screaming amid the hammering of the cannon shells ...

Fire! Smoke and flame.

When the shooting stopped, Lieutenant Tan tried to stand. The ship was turning to port, out of the channel. The helmsman was lying on the deck, his head gone. Tan spun the helm to center the rudder, bring the ship back under control.

'Arm the see-whiz,' he shouted, meaning the CIWS, the close-in weapons system that the Chinese navy had purchased from the Americans.

Behind him he heard the talker repeat the order. The talker was huddled on the floor, bleeding badly from a wound that Tan couldn't see.

Tan looked aft. Something was burning, putting out smoke. He rang for full speed on the engine telegraph, a bell that was answered. The ship seemed to accelerate noticeably as the gas turbine engines responded.

The jets were on a downwind leg, high out to the right over Kowloon. 'Forward turret, fire at will at the enemy planes,' Tan ordered. 'CIWS on automatic fire.'

This time as the planes dove, the ship was going faster, perhaps twelve knots. The forward turret opened fire unexpectedly. Of course the gun crew was shooting visually, using an artillery piece to shoot at a fly, but the noise and concussion helped steady Tan. He huddled down behind the helm station as the fighter's cannon shells slammed into the base of the mast and bridge area.

The noise had become beyond human endurance – the twin 130-millimeter mount was hammering off a shell every two seconds. There was a pause as the first jet roared overhead, then the gun began again. Despite that racket Tan clearly heard the chain-saw roar of the 20-millimeter Gatling gun of the Phalanx close-in weapons system when it lit off, spitting out fifty tungsten bullets per second.

Then, suddenly, the guns fell silent. Only the roar of a jet engine changing pitch, then nothing. Tan rushed to the side of the bridge in time to see a man ejecting from a stricken fighter. Then the fighter rolled inverted and dove into the choppy water of the strait.

Pulling out, climbing away after his second strafing run, Major Ma Chao also saw his wingman eject and the plane go into the water.

The destroyer was on fire, smoking badly from the area behind the bridge.

The crew would probably forget about the mission to shell the square as they fought to save the ship.

That was enough.

Ma Chao's commanding officer had a bullet hole in a lung, and one of the squadron's planes had been shot down – status of the pilot unknown.

And so we begin.

'A good beginning.' Rip Buckingham used those words as the title for the story he wrote for the Buckingham newspapers. He told the story as completely as he could, leaving out the Sergeant York robots, concluding with the surrender of General Moon Hok in the bank square. When the story was finished he printed it out, then went to his den. He had an antique cabinet in one corner, one that he hinted to the maid contained liquor, which was why he kept it locked.

Inside the cabinet was a shortwave radio, an unlicensed ham set, the existence of which was unknown to the Chinese authorities.

Rip plugged the radio into a wall socket and connected the antenna lead. He used the wire that held up the awning on the roof patio for an antenna. Rip checked the time and ensured that the radio was tuned to the proper frequency.

He plugged in a hand microphone, then pushed the key and transmitted. 'Hey, Joe? You there?'

'I'm here.'

'Got a story for you.'

'Wait until I get a pen and paper.'

The man who monitored the radio would take down the story in shorthand, transcribe it, and send it via E-mail to Rip's father, Richard. Tomorrow it would be in the Buckingham newspapers worldwide.

'I'm ready.'

'Okay,' Rip said, and began reading aloud.

The televised celebration in the bank square was still going on hours after General Moon's surrender. Jake Grafton wondered why the giant block party had gone on so long because he knew that Cole and the rebels must prepare for the next battle, the real Battle of Hong Kong. What he didn't realize was that the rebels had lost control of the crowd. It was now a mob.

Beyond the range of the television cameras, the mob began seeping away down the side streets, flowing toward City Hall, which was on the waterfront.

The four policemen in front of City Hall stood their ground when the rioters first appeared by the dozens. By the time the crowd numbered several hundred, they were nervous. Not a single soldier was in sight.

As the crowd swelled into the thousands and began packing the streets, the four policemen walked away. They merely took off their hats and gloves and walked into the crowd.

The jets diving on destroyer 109 and the thunder of the guns galvanized the crowd, which had a ringside seat. When the pilot of one of the jets ejected the crowd fell silent, but when the destroyer, smoking badly and in obvious distress, turned and limped away to the east, the crowd cheered wildly.

As fishing boats along the shore rushed to rescue the pilot in the water, the television helicopter circled low over City Hall, transmitting the scene to the station on Victoria Peak, which broadcast it. Television stations in at least a dozen southern Chinese cities were still retransmitting the broadcast. Pictures of the mob around City Hall and the wounded destroyer retreating after an aerial attack, accompanied by Peter Po's professional voice-over, stunned audiences that had been allowed to hear nothing of the civil troubles in Hong Kong.

An hour and a half into the pirate show the mob stormed City Hall. No one led it, no one advocated it, it just happened.

Governor Sun was not there, of course, but three prominent Communists were. One was a Beijing appointee to the Court of Appeals, the other two were officials in the government of the Hong Kong Special Administrative Region. All three were dragged out of City Hall and beaten to death in the street as the camera filmed it from a hundred feet overhead.

Hu Chiang, Cole, Kerry Kent, and the rebel leaders were holding a council of war in the trailer in the alley when they were called to witness the storming of City Hall on television.

No one had much to say when they realized the crowd was beating the Communist officials to death.

'I hope the world gets a good look,' Cole said to no one in particular.

'What do you mean?' Kent asked.

'That mob has just driven a stake through the argument that the Chinese are happier and better off under communism. We've heard the last of that crap.'

The defeat of Moon Hok meant that the PLA had to temporarily abandon all hope of reinforcing its forces on Hong Kong Island. PLA radio traffic revealed that they were well aware that the Cross-Harbor Tunnel was in rebel hands.

The New Territories garrison was frantically appealing to Beijing for help. The government had plenty of problems of its own, most of which had been created by Cole's cybertroops. Still, given enough time the Communists would move additional troops from mainland China to Hong Kong. Eventually overwhelming military power would be brought to bear on the rebellious population of the former British colony. Obviously the rebels could not allow time to become their enemy's ally.

'We are in a life-or-death struggle,' Hu Chiang told the rebel leaders when they gathered again around the map of Hong Kong mounted on the wall of the trailer. 'We must never lose sight of that fact even for a moment, or all is lost.

'As we speak the PLA is constructing fortified positions and strong points beyond our perimeter at the tunnel exit. Our watchers report that tanks are being arranged as a defense in depth.

'Despite this, we still expect the PLA to assault the tunnel entrance to see how strongly it is held. If the resistance is weak, we anticipate they will press until we crack. On the other hand, should resistance be stronger than anticipated, we believe they will drop back and wait for us to shatter ourselves on their strong points.'

Hu Chiang paused here, surveyed the faces of his audience. 'The government in Beijing is pressing the local commanders for immediate action. The Communists see the revolt in Hong Kong as a political disaster that must be crushed before it spreads. Nor can we afford to wait. The government has an overwhelming military advantage and given enough time to marshal its forces, would crush us. We must convince the Communists that the real crisis is political, induce them to rush into action and fail to properly employ their military advantage.

'The fighter squadron at Lantau will keep the Chinese air force and navy off us for a few hours. While we enjoy air superiority, we will attack. Tonight, as planned.'

No one objected.

'Let us proceed,' Hu Chiang continued. 'The York units will be moved through the tunnel and take up hidden positions outside our perimeter.' He indicated those on the map that hung behind him on the wall. 'We have weapons for almost a thousand soldiers now, counting those captured today. We have a dozen heavy machine guns and several trucks full of tear gas canisters, if we need it.

'We are organizing our supporters into military units and using these units to reinforce our tunnel perimeter in Kowloon. When we are ready to push our entire force through the tunnel, we will open our assault by attacking the strong points with the York units. Are there any questions?'

Cole broke the silence. 'The PLA might attack before we are ready.'

'They could. If a fireball like Wu Tai Kwong were leading them, they would. Fortunately, the division commander is dead and the deputy commander is our prisoner. I listened to their radio traffic, and I did not sense a burning desire to fight. They are being ordered to fight. Beijing is making dire threats.'

'How would you characterize the morale of the common soldier?'

Hu Chiang paused a moment before he spoke. 'We have interrogated some of the soldiers captured this afternoon. They are not Communists. They want the same things every Chinese person wants – a job, money to feed and raise a family, a better life. Make no mistake, many will fight fiercely, and others will refuse to fight or defect. We hope the Sergeant York units sapped some of their fighting ardor. They are confused. Too much has happened too quickly.'

Cole grinned, and so did the others. 'Let's keep them confused, shall we?'

For Jake Grafton the tension was nearly unbearable, the waiting hell. Soon the sun would go down behind Victoria Peak and all of the Central District would be in shadow.

He paced like a caged lion and paid partial attention to the television while he worried about Callie. Was she still alive? Would Sonny Wong release her tomorrow when Cole paid off? Was hunting her tonight the right thing to do?

When Tommy Carmellini knocked on the consul general's office door, Jake waved at him to come in. He sat on the couch.

'Did you swim the strait or what?'

'I persuaded a ferry captain to bring a whole boatload of folks over, kids wanting to enlist, mostly.'

'Did you bribe him?'

'A little bit. I think he would have done it for nothing, but I wanted him to have some drinking money.'

'Have you been through her desk and files downstairs?'

'A cursory look, yes.'

'Go look again. I want to know everything there is to know about that woman.'

Fifteen minutes later the telephone rang, and Jake jumped for it. Almost two hours had passed since he spoke to his aide, Toad Tarkington, in America over the satellite circuits.

'Grafton.' He spit out the word.

'You were right, Admiral,' Toad said with triumph in his voice. 'There is an account belonging to an American woman, same age and physical description as Kent, at the Hong Kong office of a London brokerage. Turns out the American woman has been dead for six months, but her passport has never been turned in.'

'How'd she die?'

'Traffic accident in Hong Kong.'

'Her name?'

'Patricia Corso Parma.' Toad spelled it, gave Jake the social security number, date of birth, and passport number. 'She may be dead, but she opened the account four months ago and has been depositing money in hundred-thousand-American-dollar chunks.'

'The way I figure this,' Jake said, 'Kerry Kent is somehow tied in with Sonny Wong. He's the guy who kidnapped Callie and Wu Tai Kwong, the rebel leader. I'm going to sweat her, see if she knows where Wong might be holding Callie. If she doesn't know, she might know somebody who does.'

'Okay, boss,' Toad said.

Jake looked up and realized that Tommy Carmellini was standing near the desk, looking out the window. He must have just reentered the room.

'If anything happens to me,' Jake said into the telephone, 'I want you to make damned sure Wong and Kent don't have fun spending any of this money. Have the CIA screw with their bank records. Okay?'

'You got it, boss,' the Toad-man replied. 'But you be careful, will ya?'

'Yeah.'

'When you see Callie, tell her that she's been in my thoughts, mine and Rita's.'

'Yeah.'

'Take care,' was Toad's good-bye.

When Jake replaced the telephone on its cradle, Carmellini tossed a passport on the desk in front of Jake. American, with the blue cover. He opened it. Patricia Corso Parma. Staring at him from the page, however, was an excellent picture of Kerry Kent.

'Where did you find this?'

'Taped inside the air return ducting in Kent's cube, downstairs. I found a screwdriver in her desk and went looking for something to unscrew.'

17

'We need to talk,' Jake said to Tiger Cole. He and Carmellini had just gotten through two circles of armed guards around the museum exhibit trailer and had been allowed to enter. Cole was watching the video from the York units, which were being positioned in preselected hiding places in Kowloon. Kent was at the main control panel. Beside her sat a Chinese student from Hong Kong University whom Cole thought brilliant.

'Give me two more minutes,' Cole said.

'Where are you putting those things?'

Cole kept his eyes on the computer monitors. 'In shops and basements, just getting them out of sight.'

'This will be the acid test, huh?'

'They were designed for night fighting in urban areas. The official designation is AVSPU, for Assault Vehicle, Self-Propelled, Urban. The army put them in a class with hummers and armored personnel carriers.'

When the last York was in place, Cole turned to Jake. 'What can I do you for?'

'A short talk with you and Ms. Kent. Got a private place?'

'There's a tiny office at the end of this trailer.'

'That'll do.'

Cole spoke to Kent, and she got up from the control panel and followed Cole and Jake. Carmellini hung back, then followed her.

She glanced around at him, didn't say anything. She was wearing tennis shoes, jeans, and a pullover today; Carmellini had never seen her in anything but a dress or skirt. Her abundant hair was pulled back in a ponytail, making her look like the girl next door.

The office was small, with just a desk and two chairs. Jake snagged one and motioned Kent into the other. Cole stood. Carmellini waited until the door closed on the three of them, then went looking for Kent's purse.

Jake laid the passport on the small desk. 'Explain this,' he said to Kerry Kent.

She didn't reach for it. Jake passed it to Cole, who opened it, flipped through it, then tossed it back on the desk.

She nipped on her lower lip, but not a trace of emotion showed on her face.

After about ten seconds, she reached for the passport. She spent at least half a minute examining it, then laid it back on the desk.

'I never saw it before,' she said.

'Wrong answer,' Jake Grafton said sourly. 'I know a lot and can guess at a lot more. Believe me, your future depends on how clean you come, right now.'

'I'm a British citizen. I work for the SIS. I don't have to tell you anything.'

'Another wrong answer,' Jake said.

They were interrupted by a knock on the door. Cole opened it and Carmellini passed in a shoulder purse. Cole made room for him.

With another glance at Kent, Jake opened the purse, looked in. 'Aha.' From its depths he removed a Derringer, a small two-barrel single-action .22 caliber. 'Would you look at this.'

He opened the action. Loaded. Snapped it shut and passed it to Cole. 'Want to talk now?'

'Why?' she said. 'You don't know anything.'

'You should have gotten rid of the gun. Do the British still hang people?'

'It was given to me.'

'By whom?'

'Wu Tai Kwong.'

'Wrong answer again. How about Sonny Wong?'

She leaned back in her chair and looked in every face. 'You don't have proof of anything,' she said. 'Carmellini must have planted that gun in my purse.'

Jake stood. 'Tommy, stay here with Ms. Kent. Don't let her touch anything, call anyone, speak to anyone. We'll be back.'

He walked through the door and Cole followed him.

'What was it about the pistol?' Cole asked as they walked to the York control console.

'Wasn't that CIA agent, Harold Barnes, shot with a twenty-two?'

A look of surprise crossed Cole's face. 'I can't recall.'

'I can,' Jake Grafton said. He paused behind the York master control panel. 'I read the report. Twenty-two slug at point-blank range above the right ear. The Hong Kong police turned the bullet over to the FBI.'

'Kent?' He sounded skeptical.

'Perhaps. I'm guessing, but it fits. Now tell me, what would happen if someone changed some of the lines of the code that the Yorks use to separate the good guys from the bad guys?'

Cole pursed his lips thoughtfully. He went over to the keyboard and began typing. He spent two minutes studying lines of software code. 'Looks okay,' he muttered and came back to the control menu.

'But if one of the Yorks started shooting our guys, I would see it. I'm right here.'

'That problem could be easily solved with a bullet.'

'We've got to trust people,' Cole responded. 'There's no other way to do it.'

'Wake up, Tiger. Kerry Kent and Sonny Wong aren't on the same sheet of music that you and Wu have been singing from. A wise man surrounds himself with people he trusts and checks on 'em constantly.'

'You're right, of course.'

'Where's your television helicopter?' Jake asked. 'You and I need to take a ride.'

'It's back at the TV station. The PLA would gladly pot it over Kowloon tonight.'

'Call the station and have the pilot fly it down here. You and I need to borrow it.'

'Want to tell me what's going on?'

'Not yet. Like she said, we need some proof. Call the station and get us a chopper.'

The helicopter, a Bell 206 JetRanger, landed in the street. The pilot was a small man in his mid-twenties. As the chopper was making its approach, Jake turned to Tiger Cole and said, 'We better take assault rifles, just in case.'

'Okay.' He borrowed rifles from two of the men guarding the trailer.

The pilot flew the helicopter between the office towers of Victoria, then dropped to fifteen feet above the waters of the strait. They flew over the trucks and armed rebels who were guarding the tunnel and kept going. Cole pointed to a building, and the pilot slowed to a hover over the street in front of it. He let the chopper descend straight down, cushioning it at the bottom, until the skids kissed. Cole got out and led the way.

They were in front of a laundry. Not many civilians around, although heads peered out windows all along the block. With Cole leading, the two men went through the laundry, out the back, and down an alley. Forty feet or so down the alley, they knocked on a back door. It opened a crack.

Cole said something in Chinese, and the door opened.

A York unit, Alvin, stood near the front of the building, which was a shoe shop. A curtain hung between it and the shop door. It stood facing the curtain, a belt-fed machine gun in its hands and an electric cord hanging from its back. 'We're charging the battery,' Cole explained, gesturing at the cord.

'Yeah. Are there any access panels on this thing?'

'Yes. Three, actually. One in his abdomen under the UWB radar, one in his back above the electrical socket, and one in the back of his head.'

'Open 'em up. Let's take a look.'

Cole didn't hesitate. From a trouser pocket he produced a small cloth bundle. He unrolled it, revealing four tools. One looked to Jake like a plain Phillips screwdriver. Cole used it to open the panels.

From his shirt pocket he produced a penlight. 'This is a regular flashlight or a red-light laser. I use it to check the sensors. Use the white light.' He showed Jake the control.

Jake peered into the back of Alvin's head. It was full of wires, contacts, and component connections. 'Take a look,' Jake told Cole and held the penlight for him.

'What are we looking for?'

'Anything that isn't supposed to be there.'

'Looks okay to me.'

'Next panel.'

Of course, they found what they were looking for in the last panel, the one on the abdomen. Cole almost missed it. A tiny bare wire, no more than an inch long, protruded from the top of a solid black plug-in component.

Cole used his fingers to remove the connection, then began tugging on the bare wire. It turned out to be six inches long, a small antenna, and was connected to a small radio receiver, a AAA battery, and a blasting cap buried in about three ounces of malleable plastic explosive.

'A bomb.'

'If it went off, what would it do?'

'Destroy the main power supply. The York will just stop, wherever it is. Think Kent did this?'

'She had access and motive.'

'How did you know it was here?'

'Someone paid Kent a lot of money in the last four months,' Jake replied. 'A million and a half pounds. I'm betting it was Sonny Wong. He then kidnapped Wu and Callie and demanded fifty million American from you and ten from Rip, Wu's brother-in-law. He's your security chief, and he's dirty.'

Cole used a pocketknife to cut the wires leading to the head of the blasting cap, which protruded from the plastic.

Jake continued. 'Either Sonny Wong is going to kill you, Wu Tai Kwong, and the folks loyal to Wu, then take over the rebellion and lead it himself, or he sold the rebellion to the Communists. They pay him, he wipes out the rebel leadership – at a profit, which he pockets – and disables the Yorks. The PLA defeats the rebel army and hangs a couple hundred traitors as an example to everyone. Voilá! everything is once again copacetic in Communist heaven.'

'We've kept a tight rein on everything.'

'You're planning a goddamn revolution involving hundreds – for all I know thousands, maybe tens of thousands – of people all over China and you think the Communist leadership didn't get wind of it? Maybe in Oz, baby, but not in the real world. Hell, man, the folks in Silicon Valley are selling high-tech secrets to anyone with money. You know that! Cash is king! Sonny Wong may be a patriot, but he can be bought. Kent's a chippie; you could buy her for pocket change.'

'Okay, okay.' Cole shook his head. 'Yeah. Okay.'

'You better visit all these Yorks and see what Ms. Kent was up to in her spare time. I'll take the chopper back to the barn and have a little chat with our lady friend from SIS.'

'Okay,' Cole said. 'Send the chopper back for me. I'll meet him where it is.'

'Give me the bomb.' Jake held out his hand. Cole handed it to him. 'When you get back, Carmellini and I are going to need some weapons. What have you guys got in inventory?'

'A little bit of everything for the Yorks.'

'I need two silenced submachine guns, a couple of silenced pistols, and two fighting knives.'

'You going to get Kent to tell you where Callie is?'

'Uh-huh.'

'Don't do anything you'll regret.'

'I intend to get my wife back alive,' Jake Grafton said. 'Whatever happens to anybody who gets in the way is their tough luck.'

Tommy Carmellini and Kerry Kent were still seated in the small office at the end of the museum exhibit trailer. 'Any problem?' Jake asked.

'She offered me some money.'

Kent was staring at a spot on the wall, her face a mask.

'Anybody talk to her, she talk to anybody?'

'No, sir.'

Carmellini got out of the chair and Jake sat. 'I don't have a lot of time,' he said to Kent. 'I'm not going to fool around. I want the truth and I want it now.'

She didn't say a word.

'You understand that you're never going to see a dollar of that money. It's history. Forget about it. The SIS will confiscate the account. What we're talking about now is your life.'

Jake Grafton leaned forward and stared across the desk into Kerry Kent's eyes. In spite of herself, she found she couldn't look away. 'Tell me where my wife is. If I get her back safe and sound, you live. If I don't, you die. It's that simple.'

She said nothing.

'Carmellini,' Jake said. 'Get me a roll of duct tape.'

The CIA officer went through the door.

Almost too quickly for the eye to follow, Kent lashed out at Jake Grafton's throat with the cutting edge of her hand. Jake took the blow on his forehead and went for her with both hands. He got his left hand around her neck, his thumb on her windpipe, and squeezed for all he was worth while he used his right to pop her hard in the nose.

Cartilage shattered and blood spattered everywhere.

The fight went out of her. Grafton released his grip.

She sat dazed, bleeding freely, then her eyes focused again.

She held her shirttail to her nose, exposing her bra. Jake didn't take his eyes off her. Amazingly, he felt better.

'Asshole,' she hissed. 'Hitting a woman.'

Carmellini opened the door, then paused. Jake stood up and took the tape.

'We'll tape her to this chair. Put her in it.'

That didn't take much wrestling. Jake began wrapping tape around her. 'Put her hands behind her.'

'What about her nose?'

'Never heard of anyone dying of nosebleed. If she croaks we'll put her in the medical textbooks.'

Kent screamed. Jake punched her again, medium hard, and she stopped.

'One more time,' he told her. 'I enjoyed that.'

He used almost the whole roll of tape on her. 'Now,' he said, removing the bomb that had been in Alvin York from his pocket. 'Here's how we're going to do this. You are going to tell me where my wife is, and Mr. Carmellini and I will go get her. If we return with Mrs. Grafton, we'll come in here and disarm this bomb. If we don't return . . . well, I guess you'll die when Sonny pushes the button to pop the Sergeant Yorks.'

Carefully, with her watching, he twisted the wires that ran to the blasting cap back together. 'There.'

'You're an American naval officer,' she whispered. 'You can't do this to me.'

'Everyone keeps telling me that. Actually, I was thinking of taping this bomb to your head. What do you think, Tommy?'

'Asshole,' she hissed. The blood covered her mouth and shirt. She was a hell of a mess.

'Get the WB phone out of her bag.'

Carmellini did as he was told.

'I doubt if she memorized the phone number. Look for something with phone numbers written on it, a little pad, her checkbook, anything.'

Kent's eyes widened.

'You were supposed to blow the Yorks with the cell phone, weren't you?'

She lost control of her face.

Jake continued. 'We'll just tape the bomb to your head. If anything happens to Callie, I'll call you. How's that?'

Her eyes narrowed. She wiped the blood on her mouth off onto her shoulder.

'She doesn't think you'll really kill her,' Carmellini said.

'I won't have to,' Jake told him. 'All I have to do is tell these people how she betrayed Wu and them. If Wu dies, she won't live another ten minutes. They'll kill her with their bare hands.'

Her head was down now. Blood still flowed from her nose.

'He's holding them on a yacht, the *China Rose*.' Her voice was a husky whisper. 'It's at the Kowloon docks.'

Jake Grafton lifted her head. He looked straight into her eyes. 'You'd better pray we find them alive and get back here. Without me you're dead. Understand?'

They put tape over her mouth and punched a small hole in it so she could breathe. Then they left her, locking the door behind them.

'Sorry about that,' Jake said to Tommy Carmellini as he used a rag to wipe blood from his hands. 'When you left the room she turned wildcat, so I punched her in the nose.'

'Glad it was you and not me. I knew Harold Barnes. He didn't deserve what he got.'

'Cole is going to give me some weapons. I don't know what is on that ship. Maybe two people, maybe fifty. You want to come along?'

'Yeah.'

'Ain't in your job description. When you're dead the story is all over; the movie ends right there. If you've got a woman somewhere and big plans, I understand.'

Carmellini shrugged. 'Going places people don't want me to go is what I do.'

Jake tossed the bloody rag in a corner. 'I'm going to kill anybody who gets in my way,' he said. 'No questions asked, no hesitation.'

Carmellini glanced at the closed office door. 'And Kerry Kent gets off with a busted nose.'

'Oh, I doubt it,' Jake said, sighing. He gestured to the people conferring in front of the map and checking the computer monitors. 'She betrayed these people. If they don't kill her, Wu Tai Kwong will.'

When the helo brought Tiger Cole back from Kowloon, he had five more small bombs with him. 'Okay,' he told Jake Grafton, 'you've convinced me. She sold us out. There was a radio-controlled bomb in every one of the Yorks.'

'Only one?'

'God, I hope so. I inspected them as carefully as I could. We could take them out of service for a week or so and disassemble each of them into a pile of parts and check every goddamn nut, bolt, and screw, but . . .'

'She says Callie and Wu are being held in a yacht tied up at the Kowloon docks.'

'She being cooperative now?'

'That's probably not an accurate statement.'

Cole snarled, 'By God, I have a few things I'd like to ask her.'

'Hey, she isn't going to tell you anything you don't already know. She did it for the money.'

Virgil Cole shook his head, rubbed his eyes. 'I just don't understand people like that. Maybe I've had too much money for too long . . .'

'You were never that poor, believe me,' Jake said. He handed Cole the sixth bomb.

'You said you wanted weapons?'

'And the use of your helicopter. I want to find this yacht before the light fades.'

'Wong has a yacht?'

'Kent says he does. *China Rose.*'

Cole's eyes lit up. 'I've seen it! An older ship, steel, about two hundred and fifty, maybe three hundred feet long, with a little bridge and a massive salon aft. White with red trim.' He looked at his watch. 'The sun sets in about ten minutes. Go find that thing while I round up some weapons and clothes.'

'Black.'

'Today's your lucky day. Black is our uniform. I've got a truckful of black shirts and trousers. I'm trying to convince my friends that night is the time to fight.'

Jake settled into the copilot's seat of the Bell and the pilot immediately lifted it into a hover. When he was above the power lines, the pilot eased the nose over and let the machine fly between the buildings toward the harbor.

They stayed low, the skids almost in the dark water, as they worked their way northwest up the Kowloon docks. Scanning the ships with binoculars, Jake fought down the sense of panic that welled up within him as the sun dipped below the horizon. Time was running out.

Coasters, tankers, container ships, tramps, fiber-optic cable layers . . . ships of every kind and description. They were Russian, Chinese, Japanese, Greek, American, and flag-of-convenience ships from all over the globe. Grafton hunted through them as the light faded slowly, inexorably.

Lin Pe worked her way along the nearly deserted streets of Kowloon. She was very tired and her feet dragged.

Unable to go farther, she sat on the sidewalk against a building, her bag clutched in her hand.

She had never seen the streets this empty. Those people who were out walked purposefully, determined, with quick glances up and down the street.

There were soldiers, of course. PLA trucks drove along the streets with soldiers sitting on the fenders, rifles in hand. At street corners soldiers directed traffic, waving civilian cars off the streets to make way for trucks.

And tanks.

Three tanks rumbled by Lin Pe, huge beasts with long, clumsy barrels protruding from their turrets. Their treads chewed up the pavement.

She got up and followed them, walking as quickly as she could. The tanks were faster than she was, but they didn't disappear from sight.

The three of them came to a halt at the intersection of Nathan and Waterloo roads. The intersection was about a mile north of the southern tip of the peninsula. One tank went through the intersection, then turned in the street. Gingerly the drivers maneuvered. One tank came to rest in the intersection, its nose and the cannon pointed south. One tank was parked on each side of the intersection, slightly back. The tankers on each flank pushed the barrels of their cannons through the glass windows of the corner buildings so they could also command the street and remain half hidden by the buildings. Two trucks stopped to discharge soldiers, who took up positions behind the tanks and the parked cars that lined the side streets.

Owners of parked cars came pouring from adjacent buildings. They scrambled to move their vehicles, some of which were already blocked in by the tanks. Shouting and pleading with the soldiers did no good. One officer pointed his rifle at several civilians and ordered them to leave. In seconds the last car that could be moved was gone, and the sidewalks were empty.

Lin Pe walked another block and found a store whose owner had yet to lock the door. He protested as she entered, but she insisted, talking loudly, refusing to leave. When the owner went back in the store to summon his wife, Lin Pe took out her WB cell phone and dialed the number she had memorized. It took her but thirty seconds to report the location of the tanks.

'Climb,' Jake said to the helicopter pilot. He was desperate. There was little light left, and the *China Rose* was eluding him.

'If we climb the PLA may knock us out of the sky.'

'Climb,' Jake repeated, his voice hard and urgent.

The pilot hoisted the collective and the helo bounced upward; Jake fought against the downward G-force to hold the binoculars steady. The pilot leveled at a thousand feet above the water. 'Fly the whole waterfront again,' Jake Grafton ordered, 'especially the area by the amusement park.'

But *China Rose* wasn't there. The haystack contained no needle.

Just when he was ready to admit defeat, he saw it.

'*There!*' He pointed. 'Closer. Go closer.'

The pilot turned the Bell and closed the distance.

Yes. There was just enough light to see the red trim, the small bridge, and the windows of the salon. A small boat hung on davits behind the stack. The yacht's name . . . he couldn't make it out. It must be *China Rose!*

The yacht – actually a small ship – was moored to a pier, the last of three large yachts on the north side. Three more were moored against the south side of the pier, which was at least two hundred yards long.

At the head of the pier stood a wire fence with a closed gate. On the quay itself were pallets of boxes, some dumpsters, stacks of fifty-five-gallon drums, forklifts, trucks, some people walking . . . Oceangoing general cargo ships were berthed at piers to the north and south.

'Over the quay.' Grafton pointed out the direction he wanted to the pilot. He had to see how he was going to get onto the quay from the street.

In the last of the light he got his landmarks.

It was completely dark when he tapped the pilot on the shoulder and jerked a thumb toward Victoria. The helo turned and dropped the nose and accelerated out over the harbor. The pilot didn't turn on the exterior lights until he was approaching the shoreline of Hong Kong Island.

'Where did you see *China Rose*?' Jake Grafton asked Tiger Cole as they hunted through the clothes littering the floor of the truck for a pair of pants that might fit him.

'At a pier in Kowloon. Across from the yacht of a friend of mine, the *Barbary Coast*.'

'For Christ's sake, why didn't you say so two hours ago? I damned near didn't find it before the light faded.'

'It just slipped my mind, until you asked. I saw it but paid little attention.'

'Well, it's still there, on the end of a pier. If we had the time we could get a delivery truck, fake up some invoices, drive through the gate at the head of the pier and motor right up to Wong's gangway. No time, though. We gotta go as fast as we can get there.'

'Why don't you land on my friend's yacht? Nikko Schoenauer. He's right across the pier. Has a helo pad on top of the salon.'

'This guy German?'

'American as a hot dog.'

'It must be nice having all these filthy rich friends.'

'Nikko Schoenauer flew A-4s in Vietnam. He told me that he decided to get into a business that would always be popular, didn't pollute or use up scarce resources, with a product that people paid for with discretionary income, something nice to have but not necessary. His yacht's a whorehouse. He fills it with Japanese businessmen and sails off for weeklong parties and writes a fat check to a bank on the first of every month.'

Jake glanced at Cole, who looked absolutely serious. 'Whores 'n' More, eh? Tiger, you never cease to surprise me.'

Jake pulled the shoulder holster containing the Colt on over the black shirt. Tommy Carmellini was waiting outside the truck with two silenced submachine guns and five magazines of ammo for each. He also produced a couple of marine fighting knives, one for each of them, and two sets of night-vision goggles. 'First-class stuff,' Jake said to Cole after he gave them a quick brief on the goggles.

Jake and Tommy put on the goggles, turned on the power. Idly, Jake asked Tiger, 'So you were visiting Schoenauer last week?'

'Yeah. The girls are kinda cute.'

'I thought you were dating China Bob's sister?'

'Naw! China Bob was a snob. He wanted his sister married off to a decent husband. I was just another dude he was doing business with.'

'Schoenauer's got a floating whorehouse, huh?' Carmellini asked. He had been standing outside the truck listening to Grafton and Cole.

'California girls mostly,' Cole said. 'They come and go. Refugees from suburbia and bad marriages. When they've gotten their batteries recharged, off they go back across the pond.'

'Live in a yacht at the side of the road and be a friend of man.'

'Something like that.'

'We'll land on his boat and troop across the pier,' Jake said, 'if you don't think we'll be interrupting anything.'

'I'm sure he won't mind,' Tiger rejoined. 'He can't get underway until he gets another load of clients, which won't happen until the airport reopens. Tell him I sent you.'

Jake Grafton looked at his watch. 'You ready?' he asked Tommy Carmellini.

'Yes, sir. Let's do it.'

They stowed the weapons, ammo, and night-vision goggles in a drawstring bag, which they slung over their shoulders.

'When does the war start?' Jake asked Cole.

'In about two hours,' Tiger replied, 'unless the PLA kicks off the ball sooner.'

'We'll be back by then,' Jake muttered.

'Or dead,' Carmellini added.

'You still got a handle on the electrical grid?'

'Yep.'

'How about killing all power to that pier, or that area, in twenty minutes?'

'Sure. Hang tough, shipmate.' Cole shook both their hands, then went back into the museum exhibit trailer.

'You scared?' Carmellini asked Jake as they walked to the helicopter, which was sitting in the street with the engine off.

'Hell, yes, I'm scared,' Jake shot back. 'That's a fool question. Why'd you ask it?'

'I wanted to make sure I wasn't the only one.'

The helo pilot made sure both men were strapped in, then he pushed the starter, and the Bell's engine wound up with a whine.

Jake lied to Carmellini; he wasn't scared. He had been too busy worrying about Callie to be scared.

'Rip, Mother isn't here.'

Rip Buckingham looked up from his PC. He was doing an in-depth piece on the revolution for the Buckingham Sunday editions.

'The maid said she left this morning and hasn't come back,' Sue Lin said.

'Maybe she's at the cookie company.'

'I called there. No one answers.'

'Well . . .'

'Rip! She could be killed out there. If the government finds out she is Wu's mother, they'll throw her in prison. She'd die there. *Rip!*'

'For God's sake, Sue Lin, she's a grown woman, this is her town. She can take care of herself.'

'But she can't!' Sue Lin sagged into a sitting position and began weeping. First her brother, now her mother. She was trying to be brave, but she just couldn't.

Rip cradled her head in his hands. 'Sue Lin, your mother wanted to help. She wanted to be a part of what was happening.'

'Why didn't you tell me? Why didn't you say no?'

'What right did I have to tell her no? She's Chinese – this is her country. These are her people.'

'I'm your *wife*.' She struck his hands away.

'Indeed. And it's time you realized that the future of China is more important than we are.'

'What do you mean by that?'

'I mean it's time you realized that your happiness is not the most important thing in your mother's or brother's life.'

'Is it the most important thing in your life, Rip? Answer me that.'

'Don't ask me a foolish question, woman. You may not like the answer.'

She rose from the floor and walked to the window. With her back to Rip she said, 'You had no right to let her go without telling me.'

'You would have said no. She wanted to go. What would you have me do?'

'If you love me, you will find my mother and bring her home.'

He turned off the computer and stood. 'You don't understand what love is. You think it is possessive, and it isn't. Sometimes you have to let go of the things you love the most.'

He took a few steps toward her, then changed his mind. 'I will try to find Lin Pe and help her do the job she volunteered to do. When it's over, if we're alive I'll bring her here.'

Sue Lin didn't turn around.

He walked from the room and headed for the stairs.

903

This, Governor Sun Siu Ki thought, was without a doubt the worst afternoon of his life. His friends in Beijing had shouted, sworn, second-guessed, cajoled, and threatened him. He had been accused of being a dupe, a fool, a liar, and an incompetent imbecile. He tried to explain that the afternoon debacle was the fault of General Tang, now dead, and General Moon Hok, now a prisoner, but to no avail. The truth was that if those two soldiers had obeyed his orders to vigorously enforce the law and lay the wood to the outlaws, these riots would not have gotten out of control. They were afraid to use the military power the nation gave them. They were cowards.

Then the television showed the mob beating government officials to death. If that wasn't bad enough, the ministry in Beijing said that treasonous criminal spectacle had been seen by a large percentage of the urban population of China. It had even run on a television station in Beijing, the outraged minister told him, as if the failure of the media officials was Sun's fault.

So when his aide passed him a note saying Sonny Wong was on the phone, Sun Siu Ki was in a savage mood.

'Carrion-eater. Double-crosser. Traitor.' He used all three of these phrases on Sonny when he picked up the telephone.

'Whoa, Governor. I know you're having a bad day, but there is a way out. I've told you that. I couldn't single-handedly stop these criminal combinations, but I can save the day.'

'For money?'

'Of course, for money. I have a large organization that I support at my own expense, and we have done what the government could not – we have penetrated the rebel organization. Pay me the money and I will give you their heads.'

'Beijing has not authorized the payment,' Sun protested.

'I find their attitude beyond understanding. They are faced with a genuine rebellion that is getting worldwide press and inciting treason throughout China. The rebels are waging cyberwar against the nation. Government officals are being beaten to death by mobs, a spectacle played on every television on the planet' – this was only a small exaggeration – 'and the government dithers over whether or not to pay me one hundred million American dollars to put a stop to all this. What are you people thinking?'

'Beijing has faith in the PLA,' Sun explained. 'Beijing is a long way from Hong Kong; from there they see the backs of ten million soldiers. Ten million soldiers are ten million soldiers. These traitors are causing huge problems, of course, but no ragtag mob is going to crush the PLA.'

'You saw the robots on television today. Those robots are not a ragtag mob.'

'Beijing was not impressed. You cannot extort money from them with movie props.'

'Sun, you are as stupid as a snail. Wait until tonight. Tonight the robots will be in action. Tonight is the Battle of Hong Kong. When the PLA is losing, think of me. You know the telephone number.' And Sonny hung up.

18

Callie Grafton awoke with a start. She had been dozing, lost in despair, and suddenly she *knew*. The knowledge brought her wide awake. She sat up in her bunk.

'He's coming for me,' she said to Wu, who was also awake. She said it first in English, then had to translate.

'Who is?' Wu asked.

'My husband. He is coming. I know it.'

Wu didn't believe her, of course, but he had grown to like this strange American woman and her delicious accent.

'Us. He's coming for us.' The faux pas of excluding Wu occurred to her now, and automatically she spoke again, correcting her error.

'How do you know he is coming?'

'I just know.' She searched for words. 'I can feel it. I can feel his presence, the fact that he is thinking of me, the fact that he is coming.'

'Soon?'

'I do not know.'

'Tell me of your husband,' Wu said, to humor her.

Callie looked at him sharply. 'You don't believe me and I don't expect you to, because I wouldn't if I were you. But Jake is coming. Perhaps I know it because I know the man.'

She wrapped her arms around her legs. 'All this time I have been worried because I didn't have an escape plan. Ha! I've got Jake Grafton.'

'The knight in shining armor,' Wu said.

'Laugh if you like. He'll come.'

She was still sitting like that when they heard someone outside the door, then a key in the lock. Two men entered with weapons drawn.

'Come with us, Wu. Time to do some more work on your confession.'

They handcuffed his hands behind him and took him away.

Two minutes later the key turned again.

The Russian, Yuri Daniel, stood in the open doorway looking at her. 'You too, Mrs. Grafton. Your statement is ready to sign.'

'I gave no statement.'

'That wasn't a problem. I wrote it for you. Come.'

Since he knew where he was going this time, the helicopter pilot kept the Bell JetRanger low, just above the water. He weaved around several junks and a fishing boat, then flew parallel to the coast for several miles. When he was on the extended centerline of the pier that held the *China Rose* and *Barbary Coast*, he turned for it.

'Wind's out of the north, a bit east,' the pilot told Jake. 'I'll land into the wind on the helo pad on the *Coast*.'

'Yeah.'

'Guns in or out?' Carmellini wanted to know.

'In the bags, I think. Don't want to scare 'em to death. But be ready, just in case.'

The pilot kept the chopper so low that he actually had to climb to land on the *Barbary Coast*. A night landing on a tiny platform on a small ship, even one tied to a pier, was certainly not routine. The pilot's expertise was obvious.

As the helicopter settled onto its skids, Jake was looking across the pier at the *China Rose*. A few lights were on: on the bridge, over the gangway, and in a few of the portholes. The main salon aft was dark.

Safely on deck, the helicopter pilot shut down his engine. Jake and Carmellini got out, bags in hand.

Just in time to meet a man coming out the hatch from the bridge. He was about Jake's age, tan and graying.

'My name is Jake Grafton. Virgil Cole said you wouldn't mind if we landed on your boat.'

When he heard Cole's name, the man extended his hand. 'Name's Schoenauer. How long you going to be with us, Mr. Grafton?'

'Not long, I hope. Let's get off this weather deck and I'll explain.'

Nikko Schoenauer led them to the bridge. He poured them coffee while Jake talked. Carmellini went straight to the pierside corner of the bridge and stood looking at *China Rose* through binoculars.

'Sonny Wong is rather a nefarious character, but this is the first time I've heard he indulged in kidnapping.'

'I heard him ask for the ransom, so there is no doubt he's in it.'

'I believe you, Mr. Grafton.'

'It's Admiral Grafton,' Carmellini said without turning around. 'I'm just the civilian help.'

Jake reached into his bag for the silenced submachine gun. 'We're going over to get my wife back, if she's there. If it goes well, we'll return and ride the chopper off the pier. If it doesn't, friend Wong may pay you a visit.'

'Hmm,' Schoenauer said, looking at the submachine gun.

'If you have any weapons aboard, you might want to dig them out.'

'Well, we do keep some old AKs, just in case we run into pirates. Pay off customs with a few bucks and they let us by. They know me, of course.'

'Say, would you have any Vaseline and shoe polish around? Black shoe polish.'

'I buy Vaseline by the quart. Shoe polish is another thing entirely – these days everyone wears tennis shoes – but I'll check.'

While Schoenauer was gone the lights went out on *Barbary Coast, China Rose*, and the pier. In fact, the lights went off all along the waterfront.

Jake and Tommy got out their night-vision goggles and studied the *Rose*. 'They had an electric eye rigged at the top of the gangway. Probably have a pressure pad too, so an alarm rings somewhere when you step on it. They're off until someone starts a generator.'

'How many guys do you think?'

'I saw two before the lights went out. One was on the bridge. One walked along the main deck.'

'I'd bet my pension there're more than two.'

'Probably closer to twenty.'

'Can we get aboard without using the gangway?'

'How about that stern mooring rope? It's in shadow. That'll be about it from the pier.'

'Okay.'

'I got this creepy feeling,' Carmellini said, 'that those sons of bitches know we're coming.'

'Maybe. Just shoot first and it won't matter.'

Schoenauer returned with two women. Jake couldn't tell much about them in the dark, but they were definitely Americans. He also had Vaseline and shoe polish. Jake smeared Vaseline over his face, neck, and hands, then applied the black shoe polish.

'Jake Grafton,' one woman said as he smeared away. 'It's a pleasure to meet you. Virgil told me about you. He said you were his very best friend on this earth.'

Jake didn't know quite how to respond to that. 'I'm sure he was just being polite.'

'Oh, he didn't mean that he was your best friend, but that you were his, if that makes sense. He said you saved his life once.'

'Long ago,' Jake muttered, more than a little embarrassed.

'He said that Jake Grafton was the one man on this earth he would trust always to do the right thing, regardless of the stakes or the consequences.'

Cole said all that? The crazy bastard!

'Hurry up,' Jake urged Carmellini, who was also smearing himself with shoe polish. 'They'll start an engine or generator to get power while we're standing here socializing.'

As they were leaving, Carmellini asked Schoenauer, 'You got an address or something where I can write to you?'

'Got a Web site,' Schoenauer replied and told him the name.

'When I get some time off . . .'

They paused under a sheltered overhang on the main deck and used the night-vision goggles to check out *China Rose*. The small ship was dark, without a single light. Not even a battle lantern on the bridge. And no one was visible.

Due to the widespread power outage, only a glow of light from the sky enlivened the darkness.

'What if your wife isn't aboard?' Carmellini asked.

'We'll cross that bridge when we come to it,' Jake said, trying not to panic. The CIA officer had hit squarely on the problem.

If she wasn't there, they would probably kill her unless he got to her quickly. And how would he ever find her in this city?

'So what do you want to do?' Carmellini asked.

'What I'd like to do is march straight across the pier and up the gangway and shoot anyone we meet, just go right on through them.'

'Well, hell, why not?'

'Because we don't know where they are holding Callie or Wu, and Sonny Wong just might have someone guarding them with orders to kill them at the first sign of a commotion.'

'Double ditto for Wu,' Carmellini remarked. 'Okay, what's your second option?'

'Walk down the gangway, turn right, go aft to their stern line, and up it. I'll climb it while you watch, then I'll watch while you climb. How's that?'

'I'll go first up the rope,' Carmellini said. 'I don't know what they told you about me, but sneaking around is my thing. I'm a burglar by trade.'

'How in the world did you get in the CIA?'

'It was the CIA or prison. I'll tell you all about it sometime over a beer.'

'Let's go,' Jake said, and led the way down the gangway.

They walked along the pier, in no apparent haste, their weapons in bags over their shoulders. This was the most difficult part so far, Jake thought, as he willed his feet not to run.

When they reached the stern line bollard, Jake squatted behind it and donned the night-vision goggles. He saw no one on the *Rose*. Two people were visible on the bridge of the ship moored nose-to-stern of the *Rose*, but they didn't seem to be looking this way.

'Go,' he whispered to Tommy Carmellini. The CIA officer already had the straps of his weapons bag over his shoulders, so he immediately crouched under the line, which was Manila hemp about three inches in diameter, and launched himself up it hand over hand. He kept his heels hooked over it behind him. In seconds he reached the rat guard, a platelike metal dish that surrounded the line and was supposed to constitute an insurmountable obstacle for rats trying to go up the line from the pier. Hanging on the line with one hand, Carmellini used the other to explore the catch that held the guard on the line, then release it. He dropped the guard in the water and continued up the line to the rail, grabbed it with both hands, swung a heel up, and clambered over.

Jake was taking his goggles off when the *China Rose*'s lights came on. The pier was still dark, as were the other ships. Someone had started an emergency generator, probably in the *Rose*'s engine room.

With the goggles back in the bag and the bag looped over his shoulders, Jake Grafton took a deep breath, then grabbed the line and swung out. As he suspected, the physical effort required was very high. Heart thudding, breathing like a racehorse, he was stymied by the rail and probably wouldn't have gotten over it if Carmellini hadn't grabbed him with hands like steel bands and literally lifted him over the rail onto the deck of the *Rose*. It was then Jake realized that Carmellini's buff physique was indeed rock-solid muscle; the thought had just not occurred to him before.

'You take the port side, work your way forward to the bridge,' Jake whispered as they huddled out of sight under the rail. 'I'll find a way down. Meet me below.'

Carmellini's head bobbed.

Jake removed the submachine gun from his bag, made sure it was cocked and ready, then took the safety off. He pulled another magazine from the bag and held it against the forearm of the gun with his left hand. Carmellini already had his weapon in his hands. Now he went forward along the port side of the ship.

The little ship seemed deathly quiet. Almost too much so. Jake listened intently and heard the faint sounds of television. At least it sounded like television – a male voice, racing along in the up-and-down lilt of Chinese, allowing no breaks for conversation. He slipped up to the salon entrance and put his ear against the bulkhead.

A slight vibration – perhaps the generator?

He went forward along the starboard rail, walking as quietly as he could.

The first hatch he came to was a ladder down. He could hear television coming up the ladderway.

He looked down as much as he could without sticking his head down the hole. There didn't seem to be a passageway, so the ladder probably dropped right into a lounge of some kind. And that was where the people were.

Well, he could drop a grenade down the hole – he still had a couple the marines had given him – then go charging down after it went off, but everyone aboard would hear the explosion.

There had to be another way.

He walked on forward, looking for another ladder.

A lit cigarette arced out of the open bridge window toward the pier below. Tommy Carmellini saw it go and knew instantly what it was. The butt hit the concrete pier in a shower of tiny sparks.

He couldn't see the man who had tossed it. No, wait! He was walking in front of the open door at the top of the ladder. Now he was gone, back toward the helm in the center of the bridge.

Carmellini moved forward, almost a dark shadow.

He took a deep breath and exhaled slowly, silently.

You had to admit, this was living! Others could have the eight-hour days and houses in the suburbs; Carmellini liked living on the edge. He was certainly in his element now, although if he weren't very careful he could end up a corpse. That didn't worry him much. In fact, it added to the danger, so it added to the thrill.

He was thinking about the thrill when he got to the bridge ladder. He examined it for alarms, then experimentally put his weight on the lower step. Now the next.

The door at the top of the ladder was open, which Carmellini decided was a lucky break.

Or a trap.

He had had that feeling earlier, that they knew someone was coming. Was that just nerves?

Whatever, there was the open door, the dark bridge, and the man waiting up there.

He thought about sticking his head around the corner, then rejected that. If the man was expecting him, he would be in no position to shoot. He thought about jumping through the door, hoping he was faster on the draw. That option didn't seem so great, either. If the man was waiting for him he was dead meat.

Ah, I've watched too many movies, read too many thrillers. These guys are smugglers, thugs.

He decided to go in the third way, the tried-and-true Tommy Carmellini special way. He would sneak in, glacially slow, his weapon at the ready. And shoot the smuggler dude when he got a shot.

Up the last step, ever so carefully, weight balanced, weapon in left hand, so the barrel went around the edge at the same instant the eye passed it. . . .

There he was, by the navigator's table on the far side, bent over something. . . .

Slow as melting ice, Tommy Carmellini stepped onto the bridge, the gun leveled, his finger on the trigger. Carefully, purposefully, he scanned his eyes to ensure there was no one else on the bridge.

Just the one man.

Shoot him now or move closer?

Less chance to break a window with the bullets if I get closer.

Step . . . step . . .

Close enough. Sorry, pal!

He pulled the trigger. The gun coughed a short burst. Three shots in the lower back, to ensure he didn't punch one through the bridge window, breaking glass.

The man half turned and fell. Carmellini stepped forward to shoot him again in the head to finish it.

Something smashed him across the arms, ripping the gun from his grasp. His arms were numb! He couldn't feel his hands.

Another blow, this time across the back. The bag containing the night-vision goggles and spare ammo helped cushion the blow, but still he fell forward, sprawling on the deck. There was a room off the bridge, the captain's cabin. This guy must have been there!

'That twit!' a man's voice said conversationally. 'I told him you'd be along sooner or later, and the fool wouldn't listen.' The lights snapped on.

That voice . . .

'I heard about you, Carmellini. Harold Barnes told me.'

Carson Eisenberg.

Another mighty blow across the shoulders. A pipe or a baseball bat. Eisenberg smashed Tommy across the ribs, over the head, almost broke his arm when he raised it to protect himself.

Carson Eisenberg was going to kill him. He was going to beat him to death with the pipe.

'You . . . cost . . . me . . . my . . . life . . . fucker!' Eisenberg accented every word with a blow.

Tommy Carmellini fell to the floor, reached for the gun, but his hands were too numb to hold it.

Whack! '*Bastard!*'

Desperate, Carmellini lashed out with a foot. And caught Eisenberg on a knee.

The ex–CIA officer lost his balance, and the pipe made a metallic ring as it struck something.

The knife! Carmellini realized he had it on his belt! Could he hold it with his numb hands?

He forced his right hand to curl around the handle. He got it out of the scabbard. And lost it.

Eisenberg was trying to scramble up from the deck. Carmellini kicked him again, this time with more force behind it. And again. Now Carmellini levered himself erect and aimed a kick at the man's chin.

He caught Eisenberg with his head coming forward and bobbing down as he prepared to shift his weight aft, over his legs. Eisenberg's head snapped back from the force of the kick. He went over backward and lay still.

Sobbing, Carmellini sank to his knees. His hands . . . he kneaded one with the other, felt along the forearms where the pipe had struck him. It was a miracle bones weren't broken. His shoulders, ribs, on fire . . . Eisenberg had given him a hell of a beating.

Can't stay here . . . Gotta get the gun, get the knife, move on. To stay here is to die. Can't stay, can't stay, can't stay . . .

He got the gun in both hands, checked it over as well as he could, then picked up the knife.

His forearms felt like they were broken, but they weren't.

Carson Eisenberg lay absolutely still, the back of his head touching his spine, his eyes open wide.

Carmellini wiped his eyes on his sleeve, smearing shoe polish, Vaseline, and blood, and staggered to the bridge door.

There was a light switch on the bulkhead, and he snapped it off. He waited until his eyes adjusted to the gloom before he stuck his head around the bulkhead and looked at the deck below.

Empty.

Where was Grafton?

The blood flowing from Kerry Kent's smashed nose gradually slowed to a drip. Her shirt and jeans were covered with it. She was thinking of all the things she would like to do to Jake Grafton when the door opened and one of the Chinese York controllers stuck his head in. He looked the situation over, then stepped into the room and pulled the door shut behind him.

She tried to talk, but all she got past the tape were grunts.

The man squatted in front of her and ripped the tape from her mouth. She almost screamed.

'Wow,' the man said, staring at her nose and the blood.

'Cut me loose, goddamn it. Hurry.'

As the controller slashed with a penknife at the tape that held her to the chair, she demanded, 'Where in hell have you been? Why did you leave me sitting here bleeding?'

'Cole just stepped out to the porta-potty. He's been in front of the monitors continuously.'

'Do you have a gun?'

'In my pocket.'

'Hurry. Before he decides to ask more questions.'

The controller jerked the tape away in great wads. Everywhere it touched her skin it tore the tiny hairs out. She bit her lip until it bled.

'What did you tell them?' the controller asked.

'Nothing. I told them nothing. They knew a lot without a word from me.'

When the last of the tape came clear, she stood. There was not a rag in the room, nothing made of cloth. She pulled off her shirt and used it to wipe the worst of the blood from her face, then threw it on the floor.

'Give me the gun.' She held out a bloodstained hand.

The controller passed it over. It was a 9-millimeter automatic, a fairly small one.

Kent checked the chamber to ensure it had a cartridge in it, then let the slide close. She pointed it up and thumbed off the safety.

'We're leaving,' she said and jerked open the door.

Cole had just reentered the trailer and was standing ten feet away in front of the master York console when, out of the corner of his eye, he saw the office door fly open and Kerry Kent come boiling out. When he saw she had a pistol he dove behind the only desk in the place, so Kent's shot at him missed.

She knew that everyone in the place was armed. A shootout in here could end only one way, and Kerry Kent had no intention of dying for anybody's cause except her own. She ran. As she charged past the York control equipment she snapped off a shot into the main monitor and saw glass shatter, then she was flying out the door as fast as her legs would take her, the controller right behind.

One of the guards with an assault rifle tried to block her exit. She shot him in the chest and ran into the crowd before anyone else could get off a shot.

The main ladder to the belowdeck spaces in *China Rose* was in a thwartship passageway abeam the gangway. It was more of a staircase than a ladder. Jake Grafton eased himself down to the deck and looked as far as he could along the passageway. There were lights on down there and he could hear that television coming up the stairwell. It seemed to him probable that this passageway ran aft to the lounge where the television was located. Stateroom doors opened off both sides.

On the other side of the thwartship passageway was a closed hatch with a porthole in it. That probably was a ladder that led belowdeck to the crew's quarters and engine room spaces.

Okay.

He stood, grasped the long handle that rotated the dogs of the forward hatch, and put pressure on it.

The dogs rotated and the hatch came loose, ready to open.

As carefully and quietly as he could, he opened it, took it to its full one hundred and eighty degrees of travel, and hooked it over the latch that held it open. Yes, there was a regular ladder down.

He listened.

Voices.

And he was going to have to go down this damn ladder feet first!

He grasped the submachine gun with sweaty hands.

Maybe he should do the other side first.

Come on, decide, goddamn it! Callie is on this boat and her life – and yours – is on the line.

Forward. Then aft.

He stepped in, put his right foot on the first rung of the ladder.

The good news was that he had climbed ships' ladders all his adult life.

With his heart in his mouth, he went down as quickly as he could, swinging the gun barrel as he dropped below the overhead.

914

A short passageway with two doors off it, one port, one starboard, then another ladder down, and a door leading forward. He went to the open hatch and looked. Lights. Voices. The engine room spaces.

But first these compartments. Callie just might be in one of them.

The port door opened as he twisted the knob. A small stateroom, empty. The door to a tiny head stood open and he could see in. Also empty.

He tried the starboard door.

Locked.

He put the silencer right against the doorknob and pulled the trigger once. A ripping sound as the bullet smashed through the innards of the door lock.

He twisted the knob savagely, and it opened.

Another empty compartment. But wait!

The bunks were made up in this one.

He went back to the port compartment. Two messy bunks, wadded-up blankets . . . blood!

Had they held Callie here?

The door leading forward, this had to lead to the owner's stateroom. *Please God, let Sonny Wong be there right this very second.*

Grafton put his ear to the door and heard nothing.

Now he turned the doorknob.

Locked.

He used the gun on the lock. Instead of one shot, he accidentally triggered three.

This was the master stateroom, all right, complete with four portholes – two on each side of the ship – a king-sized bed, and Jacuzzi, but the stateroom and adjoining bathroom were empty.

Goddamn these sons of bitches.

He sensed that time was running out.

Hurrying, he descended the waiting ladder into the engine room.

Two men were fifteen feet aft, and they turned their heads as he came down the ladder. He hosed half a magazine at them, dropping them both.

Turning, going forward, hustling along, through a door into the accessories compartment.

Empty!

Aft again, running, checking for people . . .

There were another two men working on something on a workbench between the large diesel engines in the extreme after end of the ship. They saw him running toward them between the fuel tanks. One dove sideways to cover and the other pulled a pistol.

Jake managed to drop the gunman before he pulled the trigger.

A burst of Chinese came from the alcove where the other man had taken shelter.

Grafton didn't hesitate. He couldn't leave people alive behind him, or he and Callie and Wu and Carmellini would not leave this ship alive. He squirted a burst into the alcove as he ran by, then stopped and fired again, emptying the magazine in the gun.

Changing the magazine, he stalked forward, back through the engine room, past the bodies of the first two men he had killed. Even though he didn't want to, he looked to ensure they were dead. His stomach churned as if he were going to vomit.

Up the ladder he went, gun at the ready.

Jake Grafton saw the shadowy figure in the thwartship passageway as he climbed the ladder and almost shot him. At the last second he realized he was looking at Carmellini, who was swaying as if he were drunk.

'What happened?'

'Ran into an old colleague. He damn near killed me.'

Blood was running down Carmellini's blackened face from a cut on his scalp.

'I've been forward and into the engineering spaces,' Jake whispered. 'Callie has got to be aft, down this staircase.'

Carmellini wiped at the blood flowing from his scalp, then used a bloody hand against a bulkhead to steady himself. 'Let's go,' he muttered.

They descended the staircase together. The passageway at the bottom led aft to a swinging door, two actually, hinged on each side, with windows in each. There were doors – probably to staterooms or storage compartments – on each side of the passageway.

Motioning for Carmellini to hold his position, Jake walked the length of the passageway and peered through the window. He was looking into the dining facility. Four men sat there over bowls of Chinese food, smoking and watching a television mounted high in one corner. Beside Jake was a door to a refrigerated compartment. On the aft end of the dining hall was the door to the galley.

She had to be in one of these rooms off this passageway. Jake turned, went to the first stateroom door, and put his ear to it.

Nothing.

Voices at the next one, speaking in Chinese, it sounded like.

The next one nothing.

Carmellini motioned to him. He was checking the starboard doors. He was pointing to one. He came to Jake, whispered right in his ear. 'English, a woman's voice.'

'Chinese in this one,' Jake said and pointed.

He went to the door Carmellini pointed out, and Carmellini took the door with the Chinese speaker. They looked at each other, then both turned the knobs at the same time and opened the doors.

The first thing Jake saw was Callie, facing him across a table. A man sat facing her with his back to the door. Otherwise the room was empty.

He couldn't shoot the man in the back because he might hit Callie.

The look on her face galvanized Yuri Daniel into action. He rose, spinning, reaching for a pistol in his belt, all at the same time. And found himself staring into Jake Grafton's face.

The Russian got the pistol clear of his belt when a burst from the submachine gun caught him under his chin and knocked him backward. Another burst, this time full in the chest, caused Yuri Daniel to collapse across the table.

'Oh, Jake, *thank God*! They have Wu in the – '

He had her then, jerking her through the door into the passageway, in time to see Tommy Carmellini empty a magazine through the open doorway of his compartment.

Carmellini charged through the doorway. Jake pushed Callie forward toward the staircase and ran aft, toward the dining hall, the gun leveled at his waist.

A glance through the door – three of the men were still watching television, though one was looking toward Jake. Perhaps he heard something.

Jake dug in his pocket, pulled out a grenade. He pulled the pin and let the lever fly off. He pushed the swinging door open a couple of inches and tossed the grenade.

The explosion made the doors swing on their hinges.

Then Jake stepped in and emptied the magazine at the men sprawled amid the tables.

As he changed magazines, the cook came running from the kitchen, shooting with a pistol.

The first shot thudded into the bulkhead as Jake was going down, the second hit a chair while he struggled to get the Colt .45 out of his shoulder holster.

Before the cook could fire a third shot, Tommy Carmellini killed him with a burst of submachine gun fire.

'Let's go, Admiral,' he roared from the doorway. 'We got 'em. Let's get outta here.'

Jake finished changing magazines, then scrambled up. 'Go, go, go!' he yelled.

Tommy Carmellini led the way with Callie and Wu right behind. Jake Grafton followed.

Jake called to Tommy, 'Get them aboard the other ship and warm up the chopper. I'll be right along.'

He ran up the nearest ladder to the topmost deck, above the salon, and went to the lifeboat, which had a canvas cover protecting it. Jake used his knife on the cover.

Sure enough, in the bottom of the boat was a can of gasoline that might contain two or three gallons. He shook it. Full, or nearly so.

Jake went to the hatch that led down to the engine room and emptied the gasoline can into the compartment.

From the foot of the ladder leading topside, he tossed a grenade, then scrambled upward.

He was nearly up when a jet of hot gases tore at him, almost causing him to lose his grip, as the explosion shook the ship.

Trying not to breathe the flames that singed his feet and hands, Jake scrambled for the gangway.

He was across the pier and up the gangway on the *Barbary Coast* when another explosion tore through the *China Rose* and flames jetted from her hatches.

'Are you all right?' Jake demanded of Callie.

'Yes, yes! Are you all right?'

Before he could answer the adrenaline aftershock hit him like a hammer and he vomited. He leaned against the passageway bulkhead aboard *Barbary Coast* and whispered, 'Sorry about that,' to Nikko Schoenauer, who was standing guard with an AK-47.

'Hey, forget it,' said Nikko, who had overdosed on adrenaline a few times himself.

'Oh, Jake, I love you.' Callie hugged him as tightly as she could while staying away from the shoe polish. She drew back. 'You look like the wrath of God.'

He took a good look at Callie under the *Barbary Coast*'s lights, which were brilliantly lit by the ship's emergency generator. 'They really pounded on you,' he said bitterly.

'It's over. Get me to a hot bath.'

Wu and Schoenauer had a short conversation in Chinese. 'Why not take a bath here?' Schoenauer asked the Graftons. 'The helicopter can take these two – ' he jerked a thumb at Wu and Carmellini – 'to the Central District and come back for you in an hour.' He turned to Carmellini and examined the cut on his head. 'You need to have that stitched up.'

Jake nodded his agreement.

Wu paused and rested a hand on Jake's shoulder. 'Your wife save my life, maybe,' he said in heavily-accented English. 'She very strong woman.'

He smiled at Callie and nodded once, then turned to follow Tommy Carmellini.

When Callie was up to her neck in bathwater, Jake told her, 'For a while there I thought I might never see you again. When I saw the blood smears in that stateroom, I thought I was too late.'

'I knew you'd come, Jacob Lee. I've never been so happy in my life as I was when that door flew open and I realized that terrible blackface apparition standing there was you.'

While the Graftons cleaned up in *Barbary Coast*'s owner's stateroom,

China Rose burned at the pier. No one came to fight the fire, although the crews of nearby ships gathered on deck to watch her burn.

Flames gradually spread throughout the ship. Finally the aftermost line securing her to the pier burned through, and wave action and the tide swung the stern well away from the pier.

When she sank an hour later in a welter of steam there wasn't a whole lot left. The black water of the harbor extinguished the last of the flames.

19

The Cross-Harbor Tunnel was jammed when Rip Buckingham picked his way through it. People by the hundreds lounged against the wall and sat in the traffic lanes. Most were armed with weapons taken from the police barracks armory or soldiers who had surrendered in the afternoon, but there weren't enough weapons to go around.

Appointed officers were busy trying to organize the crowd into military units. To facilitate this process members of each unit were issued distinctive badges that attached to their clothes with Velcro. The plastic badges were in a variety of solid colors and simple shapes, such as circles, squares, triangles, and the like. The rebel organizers, Rip noted, stood in front of their groups and emphasized that everyone in the group must wear the group's badge, although they never told the volunteers why.

Rip knew. The badges allowed the York units to quickly recognize the wearer as a good guy, thereby freeing up York processing capability for other things.

The enemy would eventually catch on, of course, but by then the recognition patterns would have been routinely changed.

The tension in the air was palpable; it was impossible not to feel it. As Rip walked and listened to the excited conversations, which were echoed and magnified into an infinite chorus by the walls of the tunnel, the power of the moment almost overwhelmed him.

There was nothing these people could not do. They would pound at the rocks and shoals of the tyrant's forces like an angry sea and sweep them away, winning in the end, as inevitably as the spinning of the earth.

He reached the mouth of the tunnel and walked into the black night. The rebels had killed all electrical power in Kowloon. Looking north one could see the occasional glow of lantern light in a window, but that was all. The Kowloon skyline had completely disappeared. Members of the Scarlet Team were here at the mouth of the tunnel, working by flashlight with items on a long table.

Rip walked over for a closer look. Michael Gao was preparing a tiny radio-controlled airplane, a 'bat,' for flight. He held it in his hand, a black toylike thing with a wingspan of eight inches. With a two-bladed prop driven by a minuscule electric motor, the four-ounce bat could fly at about thirty miles per hour for several hours.

Gao nodded at a colleague in front of a control panel, who pushed a button, starting the bat's engine.

The controller waggled a stick; the ailerons, elevators, and rudder of the plane wriggled in sync. As Gao held the bat at arm's length, both men studied a monitor on the control panel.

Inside the bat was a miniature infrared television camera that continuously broadcast its signal. This signal gave the controller a real-time look at what lay beneath the bat. The signal was also processed by the York network, increasing the situation awareness of the York units.

When all was ready, Gao tossed the bat upward into the air at a thirty-degree angle. In seconds it disappeared into the darkness, and he reached for another one of the dozen that sat on the table.

'How close is the enemy?' Rip asked.

'They have a few scouts within a couple hundred yards,' Gao told him, 'but their combat units are about a mile back. They are building fortified positions in depth across the peninsula. We are trying to learn what is behind the leading edge of their forces. Are they or are they not going to attack us?'

'What do you think?'

'I don't know. The bats should tell us soon, then the brain trust will make some decisions.'

'Okay.'

'Have you heard? Wu Tai Kwong is back!'

Rip Buckingham hadn't heard. Relief flooded through him. His legs felt weak. He grinned and slapped Gao on the back.

'Did Sonny Wong release him?'

'No. He was rescued. I don't know much more than that. He landed in a helicopter moments ago.'

'My mother-in-law is out there,' Rip said, gesturing beyond the perimeter. 'I am going to go find her.'

'The PLA is out there, too. Do you want a weapon?'

'Have they started shooting civilians yet?'

'I don't know.'

'I'll take my chances.'

'Good luck,' Michael Gao said, and held out his hand.

Rip Buckingham shook it, then walked away into the darkness.

'Losing the main monitor is no big deal,' one of the controllers told Virgil Cole. 'We'll just use another monitor for the primary display. I can't understand why she wasted a bullet on it.'

Cole took a deep breath and exhaled carefully. He consciously tried to think like Jake Grafton. 'She just wanted us to keep our heads down while she got the hell out of here, that's all.'

'She might have caused real trouble if she'd taken the time to empty a clip into the CPU.'

'And someone would have shot her,' Cole muttered. 'She ain't sacrificing any goddamn skin for the cause. Sonny Wong doesn't have enough money to buy that epidermis.'

Wu Tai Kwong stood in the corner surrounded by his lieutenants, the Scarlet Team. He listened as they all tried to talk at once, smiled and said a few words now and then, then finally sent them back to their posts. Then he came over to Virgil Cole. A few minutes sufficed to tell the American of his adventures. The cuts on his arm had been stitched and bandaged, and he had been given an antibiotic for the infection. The stump of his finger seemed to be healing properly.

'We couldn't stop the revolution to turn Hong Kong upside down trying to find you,' Cole explained.

Wu waved it away. 'You did precisely the right thing, the same thing I would have done in your place.'

'Your return saved me fifty million dollars.'

'And I know you need the money,' Wu said with a grin.

'Is Callie Grafton okay?'

'She is bruised but intact. Her spirit is unbroken. She is a warrior's wife. They wanted her to sign statements implicating you in many crimes, and she refused.'

Cole didn't understand. 'Why did she refuse?'

'She thought she was protecting you, doing the honorable thing. She would not have signed to save her life.' Wu Tai Kwong's head bobbed as he thought of Callie. 'With a thousand like her I could conquer the world.'

'Jake Grafton and Carmellini?'

'Bloody but still on their feet.'

Cole passed a hand across his forehead, then moved on. He gestured toward the monitors. 'We are intercepting PLA radio traffic. Beijing has approved the use of heavy artillery. Governor Sun wanted a barrage laid on the tunnel entrance. We think the PLA is now positioning the guns at the army base preparatory to a barrage. We have launched bats to see where the guns are and estimate when they might open fire, but the question is: Should we keep our forces in the Cross-Harbor Tunnel while the barrage is underway or move them out now?'

The two men studied the computer presentations of enemy positions and the locations of the York units, then referred to the map on the wall. They were joined by a half dozen of the key lieutenants, who listened silently to the discussion.

'The PLA will probably attack after the barrage,' Wu said after he had looked at everything. 'Let's get the people out of the tunnel and position them in front of the PLA strong points. If we can do it without the PLA learning of the movement, they will think we are in the tunnel entrance rubble when they attack.'

The orders went out immediately on the WB cell phones, and the volunteers in the tunnel began walking forward, into Kowloon.

Wu continued to study the map. 'The winner of this battle,' he said, 'will be the side that controls the subway tunnel.'

Cole looked at Wu with raised eyebrows. 'That's very perceptive. I couldn't agree more. Your colleagues have been arguing with me about it.'

'What do they say?'

'That the tunnel is too narrow and dark to get many people through, that the PLA won't bother with it.'

'It will be difficult, certainly, but it is key. Most of the PLA officers are good soldiers – they will think of the subway. That is why I want them on our side.'

Cole nodded vigorously. 'We put a York in the tunnel at the Central Station. It's got four or five dozen men with it, which was about all that can follow efficiently. I was afraid to give them rocket-propelled grenades or antitank weapons for fear they might hit the York.'

'You have done well, Cole,' Wu said and bowed a millimeter. 'I will go through the subway tunnel behind the York. I will have a WB cell phone, so keep me advised.'

The artillery barrage, when it came an hour later, fell like Thor's hammer on the area around the entrance to the Cross-Harbor Tunnel, which was east of the Tsim Sha Tsui East reclamation project, a district of luxury hotels, restaurants, entertainment, and shopping complexes designed to profit from the tourist trade.

Nearby buildings absorbed direct hits from major-caliber shells, which began reducing them to rubble. Shells tore at concrete streets and abutments and gouged huge chunks from the levee. What the shells didn't do, however, was kill anyone. The rebels were no longer there.

Everyone in Kowloon heard the guns and felt the earth tremble from the impact of the shells. Windows rattled and broke, crockery fell from shelves, dust sifted from every nook and cranny.

Lin Pe was sitting in the entrance to an alleyway on Waterloo Road, a block west of the three-tank strong point at the Nathan Road intersection. Parked cars lined the side streets, including the one Lin Pe was on.

Ten minutes into the barrage a long column of troops marched south on Nathan Road and came to a halt behind the tank that sat in the intersection. The soldiers were eight abreast, all wearing steel helmets and carrying assault rifles and magazine containers.

The men stood nervously in line, peering about them in the darkness at the storefronts, looking up at the blank windows looking down on them, looking at each other and the tanks and the officers, who huddled together for a moment as they gestured and pointed at the buildings around them. The officers broke up their meeting in about a minute and began pulling squads of troops out of line and pointing to various buildings. The troops trailed off under NCOs. Then at least a hundred men peeled off and trooped down the steps into the Yau Ma Tei subway station, which was dark, without power.

Lin Pe removed her WB cell phone from her bag. When it synched up, she dialed the number she had memorized.

Whispering, she told the person who answered of the troops, where they were and what they were doing, how many she estimated there were. 'They are going into the buildings, up on the rooftops, and down into the subway,' she told the woman on the other end of the line.

Then she hung up.

An officer was staring at her.

She palmed the cell phone, pretended not to notice him.

He was wearing a pistol. Continuing to stare at her, he began toying with the holster flap as artillery shells rumbled overhead and the earth shook from their impact.

The man couldn't hold his feet still. All that dancing brought him a few steps closer, and he continued to toy with the holster. Now he pulled the pistol, took his eyes off her long enough to check it over.

When he looked again at Lin Pe, the officer still had the pistol in his hand. He seemed to be trying to make up his mind about something.

Would he search her? Shoot her?

She stood, turned to the nearest garbage can, took off the lid, and began rummaging through it as the artillery continued to pound.

Several minutes later she half turned so she could see him. His pistol was in his holster and he had his back to her as he talked to another officer.

Lin Pe bent over the next garbage can.

As the barrage hammered the entrance to the Cross-Harbor Tunnel, Bob York led Wu Tai Kwong and fifty other men through the subway tunnel under the strait. They had entered at the Central District Station; now they walked as quickly as they could given the unevenness of the rails and ties and the fact that the only light came from flashlights.

The third rail was not hot, which was a blessing since people occasionally stumbled against it. Wu had almost refused to let them use the flashlight, but with the York leading the way, no PLA soldier was going to surprise this little band.

The impact of the artillery shells could be felt rather than heard, a series of thuds that made the rails vibrate.

'What will we do if the electric power comes back on?' one soldier asked Wu.

'We have it turned off. It will not come on.'

'But if it does, a train might come through here.'

'You must trust me,' Wu told the nervous man, 'as I trust you. We hold our lives in each other's hands.'

Ironically, no one mentioned what Wu knew to be the worst aspect of the small, narrow tunnel: Any bullets fired in here would ricochet viciously. With its concrete sides and dearth of hiding places, this tunnel was a horrible place to fight.

Moving along, carrying two machine guns and a half dozen antitank rocket launchers, the rebels made good time. Still, Wu breathed easier when he felt the floor of the tunnel tilt upward and they began the climb to Kowloon.

They passed the southernmost subway station on Kowloon, Tsim Sha Tsui, and kept going. The next station was Jordan Road, and there they would stop. Beyond that was the station at the intersection of Nathan and Waterloo roads, Yau Ma Tei. Wu thought that PLA troops were somewhere between those two stations.

Twenty minutes after the barrage began, it was over. The rubble around the tunnel entrance was covered by a dense cloud of dirt and concrete particles, and there had been one casualty: a woman near the Tsim Sha Tsui East shopping development who went outside to watch and was hit by a sliver of flying metal. None of the other spectators was even scratched.

Breaking the silence following the barrage was the sound of running feet pounding the pavement. Four thousand troops of the People's Liberation Army charged through the streets toward the tunnel as fast as they could run.

The Alvin York robot stood behind the curtain in the shoe shop where it had been placed. In its hands it held a water-cooled machine gun. Belt after belt of ammo was draped over its shoulders. All of its sensors were in operation at the moment, but only three were feeding data to the network: the UWB radar in its chest and the infrared sensor in its face, both of which looked through the curtain that obscured it and the glass of the shop window, and the audio sensor. The main York processing unit used data from all the Yorks to update the tactical situation. In addition, the net was receiving data from the ten reconnaissance bats that were still circling unseen over Kowloon and feeding real-time infrared video into the system.

All this information was displayed in two- and three-dimensional form on the master control monitors. Cole and the York technicians watched intently and waited. The waiting was growing more difficult by the second. Cole wanted to hit the troops after the leading edge of the assault was well past in the hope that the Yorks could disrupt the rear, which would panic the people in the lead.

'They are coming down Nathan and the Wylie-Chatham roads,' one technician said. 'No doubt they will push down Austin, aiming for the tunnel.'

'We've got the Yorks positioned well enough,' Cole said. 'They can't win the battle for us, though they will help. We're going to have to win it for ourselves.' He turned to the man at another panel and said, 'Call the field commanders and tell them where the enemy is.'

Finally he touched the York operator on the shoulder. 'Okay,' he said. 'Do it.'

The operator slid the mouse over the Alvin York icon and clicked once.

Alvin reached out its left hand and tore the curtain down that hid it from people in the street. Only when the curtain was completely out of the way did it put its left hand back on the machine gun. Then it pulled the trigger, sweeping the gun back and forth, hosing bullets at the soldiers in the street, shattering window glass and knocking them down.

Alvin moved forward, right through the remains of the window to the street.

When it hit the sidewalk it turned north, away from the southern tip of the peninsula, and broke into a run. Alvin ran like a halfback. In seconds the York's erratic, shifting pace was up to twenty miles per hour, a terrific dash against the bulk of the running soldiers, who were still flowing down the street toward it.

The York fired the machine gun as it ran, a shot for each target, its titanium claw working the gun so quickly that many of the soldiers thought the York was firing a continuous burst. In addition, the 5.56-millimeter weapon in the chest turret was engaging targets, different targets, in aimed single-shot rapid fire.

Several times the robot shot at soldiers that were too close to fall by the time it got to them, so it ran over them, hitting them like a speeding truck, causing their bodies to bounce away.

Here and there soldiers managed to fire shots at Alvin. A bounding York running erratically at twenty miles per hour along a totally dark street packed with humanity was an extremely difficult target, so most of the shots missed. The few full-metal-jacket bullets that hit the York spanged away after striking titanium or Kevlar.

Fred York's nearest major threat was a machine gun nest in the third floor of a building on the corner of Nathan and Jordan roads. It left the apartment where it had been stationed and climbed the stairs to the roof of the building. In addition to the built-in weapon, Fred carried two antitank rocket launchers.

Children and householders stuck their heads out of their apartments to silently watch the robot pass, its machinery softly whining and the minigun barrel on the chest mount spinning ominously. Instinctively the civilians knew to say nothing, to make no noise, and to refrain from touching, but they could not resist the opportunity to see a York up close and personal.

Fred kept its legs flexed, so by bending its head it could get through the doors. When it straightened its head, the stalk on top dragged along the ceiling.

Once on the dark roof the robot moved quickly. It crossed the roof in three strides, saw that the next roof was only one story lower, and jumped.

An alley barred the way to the next building, which was two stories taller than the one the York unit was on. Without breaking stride Fred leaped the alley and went through a window of the taller building. Shards of glass cascaded to the street below.

Without electricity or the glow of city lights outside, the office building the York had leaped into was stygian. This mattered not a whit to the York, which went through the nearest door and made its way along the hall, looking for the stairs.

Down the stairs, whining ever so gently, the hulking machine moved along the hallway toward the office suite that held the machine gun nest.

It found the people and the gun with its UWB radar. There were four men behind an office wall. One man was leaning out the window, looking at the street below, and the others were loading the gun. Fred detected the metallic sounds of the ammo belt being inserted in the gun and the chamber being charged.

'How thick is that wall?' Cole asked the operator who was monitoring Fred's progress. Cole was standing behind him, looking over his shoulder.

'A few inches, I think. Typical commercial construction.'

'Have him shoot through it. If that doesn't work, have him punch a hole in it and shoot through the hole.'

The robot's minigun moved to slave itself to the aiming point, then fired. The soldier leaning out the window fell forward until he was lying across the sill.

Three more shots followed in less than a second. The other men around the machine gun fell to the floor.

'We're going to need that gun,' Cole said. 'Have Fred bring it along.'

'It won't be able to maneuver very well carrying the launchers, the machine gun, and some ammo belts,' the operator objected.

'If it needs to move quickly, it can drop anything that hinders it.'

Dog and Easy York fought their way along the tops of the buildings toward the tank strongpoint at the Nathan-Waterloo roads intersection, one on each side of Nathan Road. On top of the buildings the fighting machines were at peak efficiency – there were no civilian spectators and no friendly soldiers, so everyone they saw they shot.

Running, leaping from roof to roof, scrambling up or down, shooting at – and hitting – every target that the sensors detected, the Yorks covered six blocks quickly.

Each York carried an antitank rocket, so when they were in range they stepped to the edge of the buildings and brought the launch tubes to firing position. The Yorks fired their rockets simultaneously.

Flames jetted from the open hatches of the tanks as the rockets penetrated the relatively thin upper deck armor and exploded inside.

The one tank that survived was half buried inside a corner store, with its gun punched through the store and pointing down Nathan Road. When the other two tanks were hit, the commander of this tank screamed at his driver, 'Go, go, go!'

The driver popped the clutch and the tank leaped forward, collapsing the corner of the building that sheltered it. It accelerated across the sidewalk and bulled through a line of parked cars.

The tank crossed Nathan at an angle and rode up on the cars parked on the left side of the road, crushing them, as the driver struggled to turn the tank to the right to keep it in the road. The turn kept his left tread on top of the parked cars, which were squashed and ejected backward as the tread fought for purchase. PLA soldiers hiding in shop doorways and behind cars ran for their lives.

Into this bedlam the Yorks began tossing grenades. One of the grenades ignited fuel trickling from a crushed gasoline tank, and soon the car was burning in the street and casting an eerie glow on the storefronts and the wreckage.

Dog York was throwing its last grenade when it was hit in the back by two bursts of rifle bullets. It spun and found two PLA soldiers running toward it, shooting. They probably intended to push or throw it over the edge of the building, but they had no chance. With bullets bouncing off its torso, the robot leaped and grabbed each by the neck with its powerful titanium claws, killing them instantly. Then it tossed the bodies off the roof.

Easy and Dog descended the stairs in their respective buildings, hunting for PLA soldiers. There was a machine gun nest in a third-floor apartment of Easy's building. It tore its way through walls, killed the soldiers, and picked up the gun. With ammo belts draped over its shoulders, the York unit went into the hallway and descended the stairs.

Someone dropped a grenade down the staircase. The thing exploded a few feet from Easy, showering it with shrapnel, but it kept going.

Out in the street it attacked the soldiers there with the machine gun and the few rounds remaining in the minigun. The tank was long gone, careening south on Nathan Road, leaving a trail of crushed and damaged vehicles in its wake.

Dog came out of a building on the other side and began working in tandem with Easy, killing every enemy soldier they detected.

One soldier huddled behind a car heard a running York coming at him and threw down his rifle. He stood with his hands in the air.

The Yorks ignored him.

Seeing this, more and more soldiers threw down their weapons and stood, almost two hundred of them.

The shooting stopped. The two Yorks came to a halt in the center of the intersection back-to-back, one holding a machine gun, their heads turning back and forth, the barrels of their miniguns spinning silently.

In the control room, Virgil Cole looked the situation over, then ordered the operator to stop the spinning miniguns to save battery power.

The runaway tank tore south on Nathan Road, forcing the PLA soldiers in the street to scurry for cover or get run over. The panicked tank commander kept the hatch open so he could look up at the buildings, spot enemies with antitank weapons.

Alvin York, running north up the street, saw the tank coming and got between two parked vehicles, out of the way. As the tank passed, Alvin chased it.

The York was capable of a sustained pace of twenty miles per hour and even higher speeds in short, battery-draining bursts. Alvin used that speed now to catch the tank.

The tanker must have sensed the York coming, for he turned and looked back just as Alvin leaped onto the back of the machine and aimed the minigun at the tanker's head. One shot in the head killed the man.

Alvin pulled the body from the hatch and threw it backward into the street.

Then the robot climbed up on the turret and descended into the tank.

The driver pulled a pistol and emptied it at Alvin. Bullets ricocheting inside the steel compartment killed the gunner, who slumped in his seat.

The out-of-control tank smashed over a line of cars, crossed a sidewalk, and buried itself inside a shop selling electronic gadgets. With the treads still spinning, the tank tore out the building's supports, causing it to collapse.

Inside the tank Alvin York reached for the screaming driver and tore his head from his body.

'*Jesus H. Christ!*' Virgil Cole exclaimed as he witnessed the gruesome scene on the computer monitor, two miles away. 'Couldn't you just have the York shoot the guy?'

'He's on full automatic, sir,' the controller responded. 'The program is designed to allow him to conserve as much ammunition as possible.'

'Sweet Jesus,' Cole said, then turned away so he wouldn't have to look.

The Bob York robot saw the PLA soldiers advancing south in the subway tunnel toward the Jordan Road station and opened fire. It was standing in total darkness, partially hidden behind a pillar between the two train tracks. Wu had his men on the platforms on each side where they could not be hit by ricocheting bullets.

When the York opened fire, Wu shoved the muzzle of the machine gun he was manning around the edge of the platform and triggered a long burst. On the other platform another rebel did the same. The muzzle flashes lit the scene in a ghastly flickering light.

Wu waggled the barrel of the weapon, hosing the bullets into the tunnel. Up tunnel he glimpsed showers of sparks where the bullets bounced off concrete.

In that dark, closed space the din of the hammering machine guns and the strobing muzzle flashes were almost psychedelic.

Wu stopped firing when he saw Bob York leave its hiding place and begin advancing. He would like to know what the York was seeing, but the only way to find out would be by calling the command center – and the wide-band cell phones did not work in this tunnel. Wu knew because he had already tried it.

The York fired several more individual shots, then ceased. With his eyes closed, waiting for them to adjust to the darkness, Wu listened to the York until he could hear it no more. As the seconds passed he thought he could hear someone sobbing.

Well, there was no way around it. He was going to have to put his men on the track and advance.

'Let's go,' he whispered and lowered himself over the edge of the platform. Two other rebels passed down the machine gun.

He had advanced fewer than fifty yards before he stumbled over the first body. He stumbled over six more bodies before he came to his first live man, who was moaning softly, begging not to be shot. Wu flipped on his flashlight. In the beam he found a PLA soldier on his knees with his hands in the air. The man's eyes were shut and he had blood flowing from a gash on his forehead.

One of the men with Wu Tai Kwong picked up the soldier's weapon and told him to follow along behind the rebels.

On the streets above the subway tunnel the PLA had ceased to be a fighting force. The soldiers were no longer under military control; they were either running for their lives, trying to find a place to hide, or surrendering.

After conferring with Virgil Cole on the WB cell phone, Michael Gao ordered the rebel assault force to advance northward up the avenues.

The firing was sporadic and dying down. Soon each rebel was carrying an armful of rifles and being trailed by a half dozen PLA soldiers.

Gao met Wu Tai Kwong at the street entrance to the Yau Ma Tei subway station near the Nathan-Waterloo intersection. They conferred briefly, decided to hold the prisoners in the center of the intersection with a few guards while the main force advanced with the Yorks up Waterloo Road toward the army base. Wu called Cole on the cell phone and told him what they wanted to do.

While the leaders conferred, people began coming out of the apartment buildings on the side streets and avenues. They were in a festive mood and proved hard to handle.

When Wu finally got his men moving toward the army base, the civilians followed. Indeed, they mixed freely with his troops, as if everyone were out for an evening stroll.

Another force of two hundred rebels, accompanied by Charlie York, advanced northeastward toward the entrance to the naval base. The rebels advanced cautiously. The command center had informed them that the naval base personnel had dug a trench near the gate to the base and were in it with machine guns, grenade launchers, and antitank rockets.

After consultation, the rebels decided to appear in front of the position and threaten it while Charlie York worked its way over the buildings to a flanking position. When it was in position, it could pin the enemy with a machine gun while the rebels made an assault.

Charlie York had no trouble getting into position. The building contained enemy soldiers, but fighting in a dark building was the forte of the Yorks. Using infrared sensors and UWB radar, the Charlie robot quickly found the enemy and exterminated them.

Standing in a fourth-floor window looking the length of the trench, Charlie opened fire with the machine gun that it held cradled in its arms. Each round was aimed, each round found a target.

The people in the trench saw only the muzzle flashes on the side of the building. With people dying all around him, one man pointed an antitank rocket launcher at the muzzle flashes and squeezed it off.

The rocket hit Charlie in the right arm. The impact ripped the arm from its socket and knocked the robot off its feet. Shrapnel from the shaped charge in the warhead damaged the minigun, rendering it useless.

'Damn!' said an exasperated Virgil Cole. 'That's what happens when we sacrifice mobility, put a York in a fixed position and let people whale away at him. *Damnation!* We're going to lose a bunch of our guys carrying this trench if we don't get with the program, people! Don't let a York stand there like a statue until someone blows it into a thousand pieces! Now have Charlie jump down into the trench and get on with it.'

Charlie leaped ... forty feet into soft earth. It fell when it landed, its left hand ending up six inches under the ground.

The robot scrambled to its feet and charged the nearest live man with a weapon. Fortunately it didn't have far to go, because without the right arm to assist in balancing it lurched badly.

The melee that followed was short and vicious. Using only its left claws, Charlie York tore at living human flesh. One man had an arm ripped off at the shoulder and began screaming, a high-pitched wail that lasted until Charlie hit him in the head, fatally fracturing his skull.

The darkness, the screaming, the maniacal superhuman thing that killed by hitting, ripping, or tearing – the nerve of many of the sailors broke. They dropped their weapons and ran, either back onto the naval base or over the lip of the trench toward the rebels.

In less than a minute it was over.

The man leading the assault group didn't learn that for another thirty seconds, when his WB cell phone rang. 'You can advance now,' the controller said.

Governor Sun Siu Ki listened to the radioed reports from the units in the field and watched the headquarters staff mark the positions on a table map of Hong Kong. The senior officer was Colonel Soong, a practical, down-to-earth military professional who had spent forty years in the army. He had tried to advise Sun of the reality of the military situation earlier in the evening but the governor refused to listen, replied with bombast and party slogans and quotes from Chairman Mao about being one with the people.

As the Yorks cut a swath through his combat forces and demoralized the rest, Soong suggested that Sun confer with Beijing, which he did via the radiotelephone.

The fall of the naval base was the turning point for Colonel Soong. It was then that he realized that he could not defeat the rebels with the forces he had at his disposal. He made this statement to Sun, who turned deadly pale.

After one more hurried conversation with Beijing, Sun got out his cell phone and made a local call.

'Sonny Wong.'

'Governor Sun here, Wong.' He took the time to exchange the usual pleasantries, perhaps as a way of composing himself.

With that over, he said, 'I am calling to inform you that Beijing has decided to accept your offer. They are wiring one hundred million American dollars to your account in Switzerland.'

'Rather late in the game, don't you think, Sun?'

'Governments are not like businesses – some things take time.'

'I understand.' Sonny let the silence build, then said, 'I should wait until the money is in my account before I act, but since the hour is so late, I'll trust the government's good faith and move ahead expeditiously.'

'Good! Good!' Sun said, genuinely grateful. 'The government has committed to pay; it will honor its commitment, as it does all its obligations.'

'Of course,' said Sonny, a bit underwhelmed. 'I'll let you get back to your pressing duties while I get on with mine.'

When he severed the connection, for some reason Sun Siu Ki felt better.

Sonny Wong tossed the cell phone on his desk and broke into a roaring belly laugh.

Kerry Kent was sitting across from Wong. Her broken nose had been set, filled with packing, and taped into position. If she could have frowned, she would have.

'What's so funny?'

'We've *won*! That idiot Sun has talked Beijing into paying me a hundred million American.'

'I told you Cole took the bombs out of the Yorks,' Kent said. 'We can't sabotage them. There is nothing we can do even to slow the rebels.'

Sonny grinned pleasantly. 'I know that and you know that,' he said, 'but the ministers in Beijing don't. By the time they figure out that we have done nothing to earn the money it will be too late. The money will be in my bank and they will be unable to reverse the transaction.'

Sonny Wong laughed awhile, then poured himself a drink of good single-malt Scotch whiskey and lit a cigarette.

Damn, he felt good.

Too bad about Yuri. Too bad about the restaurant and the yacht. Grafton and Cole had screwed everything up and cost him some serious money. Before he left Hong Kong tomorrow he should probably settle that score.

But tonight, a drink. A laugh. One hundred million from the Communists in Beijing and ten million from their archenemy, Rip Buckingham's old man down under.

A good score, any way you looked at it.

Ha ha ha!

'Here's to revolution, wherever and whenever,' Sonny Wong said and lifted his glass.

Rip Buckingham accompanied the rebels following the Yorks north on Nathan Road. He stopped to watch technicians service the Yorks, replace batteries, replenish ammo, oil and lubricate them. He looked over the herd of prisoners sitting in the center of the street – they didn't seem unhappy – then he went looking for Lin Pe.

He found his mother-in-law just where the controller said she was, in the entrance to the alley a block west of the Nathan-Waterloo intersection. The street was filled with a happy, joyous crowd, everyone talking at once. The glare of numerous small fires that the celebrants had built in the center of the streets lit the scene.

Rip sat down beside her. The old woman looked exhausted.

'We have won,' he told her. 'The PLA soldiers are surrendering by the hundreds, by the thousands.'

'They really did not want to fight,' Lin Pe said. 'I could see that in their faces. Their officers made them fight.'

They sat together watching the rebels stream up Nathan Road and turn east, heading for the army base. From where they sat they could see one of the still-smoking tank hulks. When the breeze gave them a whiff, the smoke smelled of burning diesel fuel and rubber, a nauseating combination.

'Why are you here?' Lin Pe demanded. 'Why are you not writing this story for the world? That is your job.'

'Sue Lin was worried. She wanted me to come. Since I love you both, I could not refuse.'

After a moment to collect his thoughts, Rip said, 'Wu was rescued earlier this evening. He is leading the rebels now. He was just here a little while ago, organizing the rebel forces. He led them up Waterloo Road toward the army base.'

Lin Pe nodded. She had heard the news that Wu was alive and with the rebels earlier this evening from the girl taking cell phone calls. She didn't say that to Rip, though; she was so tired. And content.

In the midst of this raucous, happy crowd she could feel the common thread of humanity that ran down the long centuries of Chinese history from the unknowable past, through the present, into the unknowable future. Dynasties, wars, famines, babies born, and old people buried – these living people surrounding her now, filling the streets, were the sum of all that had ever been, and in their spirits and bodies they carried the future, all that would ever be.

She rested her head on her knees. With her eyes closed she could see her parents' faces as they were when she was very young, could remember the wonder she felt when she saw the sun rise on a misty morning, with the earth pungent and fresh after a night's rain. She remembered her husband, his face, the way he touched her, the feeling she had that their children were life the way it should be – these memories washed over her now, swept her along.

Lin Pe got out her notebook and wrote, 'You are mankind.'

She stared at the words, trying to decide if she had captured the nub of it. Beside the first sentence she wrote, 'You are the past and the future.'

She gave it one last try: 'Do not despair – life is happening as it should.'

Sun Siu Ki's mood was just the opposite of Lin Pe's. His world was crashing in on him. The rebels owned Hong Kong Island. They had the only television and radio stations still operating in the S.A.R. and were filling the airways with their capitalist, imperialist filth. Rebels were in control at the airfield on Lantau and at the naval base. With six robots and an armed mob, they defeated the trained troops Colonel Soong had put in the field. In fact, the only real estate the government still controlled in the Hong Kong S.A.R. was the army base.

All this, Sun reflected, was a local disaster, like a fire or an earthquake. It was just his bad fortune to be here when it happened. Certainly his friends in Beijing would understand.

The only ray of sunshine in this miasma of doom was the certain knowledge that the huge Chinese army, armed with weapons featuring the latest technology – some of it purchased from the Russians and the rest stolen from the Americans – would in the fullness of time crush these rebels like a tidal wave coming ashore, overwhelming all in its path.

Six robots? Untrained civilians with captured rifles and limited ammunition? Amateur officers? They didn't stand a chance.

The sky to the east was pink with the coming dawn when Colonel Soong faced the brooding governor.

'The base is surrounded,' the colonel said. 'The rebels have completely encircled the perimeter of the base.'

Sun got out of his chair and made his way to the map table. Grease marks on the map told the story.

'I have been begging Beijing to launch an air strike,' Sun said. 'Perhaps our comrades will deliver us.'

The colonel didn't reply. He was fed up with wishful thinking.

'Will they attack?' Sun asked, referring to the rebels.

'Unless we surrender.'

'Surrender?'

'They have not yet demanded our surrender, but we must consider it. They may attack without asking, or they ask and attack if we refuse.'

'Why not use your artillery? You know where they are – hammer them into the earth.'

'While we are hammering they will attack. There are too many people out there, Governor, for us to stop them.'

Sun was incredulous. 'What? A few thousand armed civilians against your trained soldiers?'

'We have about three thousand fighting men left on the base, counting every able-bodied man. My officers estimate there are more than two hundred thousand people outside the fence just now. Even if we set about slaughtering them with machine guns and artillery, they can push the fence down and overwhelm us before we kill them all.'

Sun didn't believe it and said so. Soong took him to an observation tower to see for himself.

With the sun peeping over the earth's rim, Sun forced his tired legs to climb the stairs. From three stories up on the open-air platform near the parade ground – a structure normally used to train paratroops and review military parades – one could see the main gate and the road beyond and several hundred yards of the base fence.

The situation was as the colonel had presented it. Sun found himself staring at a sea of humanity. The people weren't under cover – they were standing and sitting almost shoulder-to-shoulder. People! In every direction, as far as he could see.

A soft moan of despair escaped the governor. He closed his eyes, swayed as he hung on to the railing.

He took time to compose himself, then said, 'It would be a political and propaganda disaster if the rebels were to capture me. We mustn't take that risk. Order a helicopter warmed up.'

'Governor, I don't think you understand. The rebels have the base completely surrounded. Yesterday they fired missiles at the helicopter you were in. If you try to leave, Governor, they will shoot you down.'

A breathless messenger from the command center brought a ray of hope. 'Bombers are inbound, sir. They have radioed for instructions. What targets do you wish them to attack?'

'The rebels around the army base?' The pilot of the leading Sian H-6 bomber asked this question of his radio operator.

'Yes, sir. That is the order. Here is the chart.' The radio operator passed it forward to the copilot, who held it so the pilot could see.

The Sian H-6 was a twin-engine subsonic medium bomber, an unlicensed Chinese version of the Russian Tupolev Tu-16 Badger. First flown in 1952, the Badger was used only as a target drone or engine test bed in Russia these days. However, in China the H-6 was still a front-line aircraft in the air force of the PLA. This morning four of them were on their way to Hong Kong.

'The rebels are just outside the base perimeter,' the radio operator said.

As the implications of the target assignment sank in, the pilot and copilot looked at each other without enthusiasm. To ensure the bombs fell on the rebels and not inside the base, they would have to bomb from a very low altitude. Since the navigation-bombing radar was useless at low levels, the bombardier at his station in the glass nose would merely release the bombs as the plane flew over the enemy. As long as the rebels lacked antiaircraft missiles or radar-directed artillery, the bombers should be able to strike their target. If the weather was good enough.

'What did you tell the base commander?' the pilot asked the radio operator.

'That we would try for the assigned target, sir.'

'Tell the other airplanes to follow us in single file. We shall make a pass to locate the target, then bomb on the second pass.'

'Yes, sir.'

'We should be bombing on the first pass,' the copilot objected on the ICS.

'I want to see what's there.'

'We have been ordered to bomb – a first pass without bombing will merely wake up the rebels.'

'When you are the pilot in command you can do it your way. Today we do it my way.'

After he squashed the copilot, the pilot reminded his gunners to keep a sharp lookout. Alas, the Sian H-6 lacked a radar-warning receiver. The plane contained a single forward-firing 23-millimeter cannon and three twin 23-millimeter mounts: a remote on the top of the fuselage, one on the belly, and a manned mount in the tail. Only the tail turret was aimed by a fire-control radar.

The bombers were three miles high when they flew across the city of Hong Kong and turned eastward, out to sea, still descending. No low clouds this morning, the pilot noted, visibility five or six miles. He and the bombardier stared down into the haze as the planes flew over the city.

'I see the base,' said the bombardier on the intercom.

'They should have sent fighters to escort us,' the copilot said nervously as he searched the wide, empty sky.

'They did!' the tail gunner sang out. 'At four o'clock, high.'

The pilot looked in the indicated direction with a sense of foreboding. The briefing officer had specifically said there would be no escorting fighters. Rumor had it that the fighter pilots were politically unreliable. A civil war, the pilot told himself, was mankind's worst fear realized.

'Shengyang J-11s. Two of them.' The tail gunner again.

'Uh-oh,' said the copilot, who had also been told that the J-11 squadron at Hong Kong had joined the rebels. 'What do we do now?'

'Those fighters may be hostile,' the pilot told the tail gunner. 'If they shoot a missile or line us up for a gunshot, be ready.'

'Aye,' said the gunner, his voice rising in pitch. Like everyone in the bomber, he knew he had little chance of hitting an incoming missile with his gun. In fact, he had never been allowed to fire his gun with real ammunition.

Ensuring he was out of 23-millimeter range, Major Ma Chao turned to get behind the four bombers, which were strung out in trail. His wingman stayed in a loose cruise formation several hundred feet behind Ma and slightly above the plane of Ma's turn.

Ma Chao was well aware of the fact that the bombers were defenseless against the two fighters, each of which was armed with four air-to-air missiles and one hundred and forty-nine 30-millimeter cannon shells. The fact that each plane was flown by a crew of his countrymen also weighed heavily on him.

937

'What do we do?' his wingman asked over the radio.

'Let's try the radio,' Ma Chao replied.

'Think they know we're back here?'

'If they don't, we'll tell them.' The radios in Chinese warplanes could transmit and receive on only four frequencies, so it was a simple matter to try each of them.

Making a long, slow, descending turn in smooth air, the bombers dropped to a thousand feet above the water before they began their run westward toward the army base. Once in level flight the four bombers descended still farther, until they were only four hundred feet above the water.

Ma Chao locked up the trailing bomber with his radar and readied a missile.

'Bomber lead over Kowloon, this is fighter lead, over.' The pilot and copilot of the H-6 heard the call in their headphones.

'What do we do?' the copilot asked, panic evident in his voice. 'If we talk to them the authorities will call it treason.'

'Bomber lead, this is fighter lead. If any of the bombers open your bomb bay doors, we will shoot you down. Please acknowledge.'

The bomber pilot didn't know what to say, so he said nothing. He led the bombers around an island, then they straightened on course for the army base.

They crossed the waterline at about two hundred fifty knots, four hundred feet high.

There was no flak, of course, and no missiles. The planes flew in and out of splotchy sunshine over an immense, sprawling city. Ma Chao and the bomber pilots each wondered what the other would do as the tension ratcheted tighter and tighter.

'Target one mile,' the bombardier of the lead bomber sang out on the ICS. He readied the bombsight so that he could designate his aim point as he passed over it; the sight would track that location mechanically and give him steering back to it.

Crossing rooftops, racing along a few hundred feet up with the rising sun behind them and the buildings casting long shadows ahead, the string of planes thundered toward the army base. Automatically the pilot retarded the throttles slightly, causing the speed to bleed off still more.

Then they saw the people. A horde of people, an endless sea of humanity extending for miles completely surrounded the base.

'Those must be the rebels,' the bombardier said disgustedly as the lead plane swept overhead. 'They aren't even armed.'

'A few of them are,' the copilot offered.

The pilot, also looking, said nothing. He had never seen so many people in one place at one time in his life.

When they were past the base the pilot trimmed the nose a bit higher and pushed the power levers forward. With the two engines developing ninety-five percent r.p.m., he stabilized in a cruise climb. Passing three thousand feet, he said to the copilot, 'I think it's time we went home.'

'They will shoot us for disobeying orders,' the copilot objected.

'I saw no rebels, merely civilians.'

'Those *were* the rebels,' the copilot said obstinately. He was something of a fool, the pilot thought.

'You would bomb them, would you?'

'I have a wife and son at Quangzou,' the copilot replied, naming the town near the airbase they left before dawn.

'Life is full of shitty choices,' the pilot shot back. 'Are you suicidal? If we open the bomb bay doors those fighters will swat us out of the sky.'

Before the copilot could think of an answer to that verity, the tail gunner sang out on the ICS, 'Number two has dropped his landing gear! He's turning out of formation. And there goes number four! They must be going to land at Lantau.'

There it is! the pilot told himself. *Make up your mind.*

He retarded the throttles; with the nose in a climb attitude, the speed bled off sharply. Now he reached for the gear handle and moved it to the down position. As the hydraulics hummed and the gear extended, the pilot said to the copilot, 'Better hope it's a short war.'

Three of the bombers dropped their landing gear and turned for the airfield at Lantau. Only one continued to climb away to the northeast. Ma Chao's wingman went with the landing bombers while Ma Chao followed the one climbing out. As it passed twenty thousand feet he broke away.

He did a large 360-degree turn while he watched the lone H-6 disappear into the haze. When it was completely gone, he checked his compass, then dropped the fighter's nose.

Down he went toward the city below, accelerating rapidly. In seconds the plane was supersonic. He kept the nose down, let it accelerate.

Passing five thousand feet, Ma Chao engaged his afterburners. The airspeed slid past Mach two.

The tail of the fighter was hidden by a moisture disk condensing in the supersonic shock wave as Ma Chao flew across the PLA base below a thousand feet. Then he lifted his fighter's nose and rode his afterburner plumes straight up into the gauzy June morning.

Wu Tai Kwong and the members of the Scarlet Team were standing outside the closed main gate in plain sight of the PLA troops behind the gate and perimeter fence and in the observation tower when the shock wave of the racing fighter hit them like an explosion. When the crowd realized what it was, they cheered lustily.

Every person in the crowd looked up to watch the fighter disappear into the haze over their heads.

Wu listened to the fading roar of the engines and glanced at the hands of his watch, which were creeping toward seven o'clock.

At two minutes before the appointed hour, Wu nodded at Virgil Cole, who had a portable York control unit hanging from a strap around his neck. He used the unit to walk Alvin York forward and stop it next to Wu, who examined the robot with interest. This was the first time he had seen a York up close in the daylight.

When the Scarlet Team had looked it over, they stood aside, giving the soldiers on the other side of the fence their first good look. Cole walked the York to the closed metal gate, stopping it just a few feet short.

As the seconds ticked away, the crowd gradually fell silent. All that could be heard was the buzzing of the television helicopter overhead. Looking around, Cole tried to guess how many people were there. A quarter million, he thought, more or less. Most were unarmed, of course, but that was not the point. In human affairs numbers matter.

At precisely seven o'clock, Wu Tai Kwong nodded at Cole and he clicked on an icon.

Alvin York stepped forward, seized the gate, and tore it from its hinges. The robot threw the gate off to one side, then walked through the opening with its head scanning and minigun barrel spinning. Behind it walked the Scarlet Team, and behind them, all the people in the world.

The waiting soldiers threw down their rifles and stood aside. Alvin York and the Scarlet Team walked on by.

The Scarlet Team was not around when the crowd found Governor Sun hiding in a storage closet in a barracks. They dragged him outside and stripped him naked.

By the time Wu and Cole fought their way through the packed humanity, it was too late for Sun. The crowd used their fingernails to rip the flesh from his bones, then they pulled his limbs from their sockets and wrenched them from his body. He screamed some, then succumbed. Even if Wu could have reached Sun's person, it is doubtful that anyone could have stopped the mob.

The blood riot was captured by the television camera a few hundred feet overhead. Fortunately the human wave that swarmed over the base was fairly well-behaved and Wu's armed men were able to prevent wholesale looting of the military stores.

By noon the crowd had thinned considerably, and by midafternoon Wu's lieutenants began herding civilians off the base so they could see what was left.

Wu and Cole departed soon after Sun's death. They had much to accomplish and very little time.

20

Jake and Callie Grafton went to bed in the consul general's suite in the U.S. consulate while the rebels were fighting the PLA in Kowloon. After the television chopper brought them back to the consulate from the *Barbary Coast*, Jake merely nodded at the marines at the gate, who snapped him smart salutes, and walked through. He informed the consulate duty officer that he was expecting a call from Washington, which was an untruth of a low order of magnitude.

The duty officer was juggling telephones as he tried to coordinate the efforts of the staff, which was trying desperately to keep Washington informed of the progress of the battle in Kowloon as they learned of it. The duty officer muttered 'Yessir' at Jake, who wandered off with Callie in hand. When the duty officer was out of sight, Jake made a beeline for Cole's bedroom.

They were under the covers with glasses of champagne on the nightstand ten minutes after they locked the door.

'I have a serious question to ask and I want a serious answer,' Callie said.

Jake sipped champagne and wriggled his toes under the silk sheets. *Silk sheets!* God, how these billionaires lived! 'Sure,' he said, to humor her.

'Okay, here goes: If you were asked, would you accept an appointment as an officer in the Free Chinese Navy?'

'Have you been mulling that for the last two days?'

'I just wondered. What's your answer?'

'Hell, no. They might not make me an admiral. I'm not going to join anybody's navy unless they make me an admiral.'

'What if they offer to make you an admiral?'

'I'd have to think about it.'

'Really?'

'No. I'm pulling your leg. Turn out the lights and let's snuggle.'

'I'm too sore to make love,' she said.

'And I'm too tired. Turn out the lights, lover, and let's pretend until we collapse.'

She reached and got the lights. 'Do you mean it? If Wu Tai Kwong asks, you'll say no?'

941

'He won't ask, but if he does, I'll say what an honor it is to be asked, blah blah blah, but unfortunately blah blah blah.'

'You're absolutely sure?'

'You and I are hitting the road the first chance we get. We are going back to the land of Coke and hot dogs as fast as we can get there.'

'Level with me, Jake.'

'You're really serious, aren't you?'

'Yes.'

He thought about how he should say it. 'If you hadn't been kidnapped, I wouldn't have had to kill those guys tonight. I'm not blaming you; I just don't want to have to fight this fight. This is a Chinese civil war – it's *their* problem. I'm willing to fight for my country and my family, and that's it. Sure, those guys tonight got what they had coming, but I'm not God, don't want His job. If we go home we're out of it. Do you understand?'

'Yes.' She *did* understand, and she felt relieved.

'I was damned worried about you, Callie. Staring at the spectre of life without you was not pleasant. Maybe it's post-traumatic shock – I don't want you out of my sight, not for the foreseeable future.'

'I was pretty worried, too,' she whispered. 'I kept thinking there was something I should be doing to get out, and I finally calmed down when I realized you'd come for me if you could. Jake Grafton was my ticket out.'

'You're one tough broad, Callie Grafton.'

'It's crazy to tell you this: I *knew* you'd come. I could feel your presence.' She was going to say more, but he lowered his mouth on hers and the thought got lost somewhere.

It turned out he wasn't too tired and she wasn't too sore.

Afterward, as they lay back-to-back, she remarked, 'That's the first time I ever took a bath in a whorehouse,' but her husband didn't respond. He was already asleep.

An hour later the telephone rang. After he grappled with the thing, Jake managed to get it up to his ear.

'Grafton.'

'That call you were expecting from the states is on line two, sir. Before you answer it ... we just received a flash message appointing you the American chargé d'affaires in Hong Kong. Orders are coming via satellite now – tomorrow afternoon the American and British navies are bringing a half dozen ships to evacuate non-Chinese citizens who wish to leave.'

Jake took a few seconds to digest all that, then said, 'Who is on line two?'

'The Secretary of State, sir.'

'Thanks.' Jake sat up in bed, turned on the light, then pushed the button for line two.

He gave Callie the news while he dressed.

'Oh, Jake, I wanted to go home, too.'

'It'll be a few weeks, at least, the Secretary said. The main thing is to get out the non-Chinese people who want to leave.'

'Will that be many people?'

'Who knows?' he said as he strapped on the ankle holster. 'The real question is what the Communists will do. I assume the rebels will leave Hong Kong soon. Maybe the Communists will try to retake the city. Maybe they'll sail their navy down here and assault the place. I don't know and neither does anyone in Washington. On the other hand, if the Chinese try something big the recon satellites will pick it up and Washington will give us a warning – a few hours, anyway – for whatever that's worth.' He reached for the shoulder holster, decided he didn't want to wear the heavy Colt, then changed his mind and put it on.

'Some of the Americans won't leave,' Callie said. 'And you know that a lot of the British and Australians will refuse to go. This is their home.'

'They stay at their own risk. They're betting Wu Tai Kwong and Tiger Cole can protect them. In my opinion, that isn't a very good bet.'

He bent over and kissed her. 'Get some sleep. If I'm going to be responsible for the way the consulate staff performs, I'd better find out what they're up to.'

'I'm not leaving this city without you,' she told him as he started out the door.

Jake grinned at her. 'I didn't figure you would.'

Callie didn't think she could get back to sleep, but she was so exhausted she soon drifted off.

The sun was up and Jake Grafton was drinking coffee at Tiger Cole's desk in the consul general's office when the rebels walked into the army base. He was on the satellite telephone to the State Department when the television showed Governor Sun Siu Ki being torn to pieces by the mob.

The power was on throughout the city, so everyone in Hong Kong who wasn't in the streets got to watch the rebels' final victory.

When the conversation with Washington was over, Jake Grafton went to the window and pulled back the drapes so that the morning sun shone full in the office. He was standing at the window looking out when he heard a voice at the door. Tommy Carmellini, sporting a bandage on his head.

'Just the man I wanted to see. Come in and drink a cup of coffee.'

'I hear you're now the head hoo-ha around here.'

'Yep. You're still working for me.'

'I dunno, Admiral, if I'm up to it. Another night like the last one and I'll be a hospital case.'

'Thanks, Tommy, for everything. You saved my wife's life when you figured out that Kent was up to her eyeballs in this mess.'

Carmellini was still there when Callie came in.

'Did you get some sleep?' she asked her husband.

'No.'

He kissed her and held her awhile before he told her that the rebels had won in Hong Kong. The city was theirs. 'At least for a little while,' he added under his breath.

The three of them were eating breakfast when the secretary buzzed and announced Cole.

He breezed in, dirty and tired and elated.

'We've won the first campaign,' he told them.

'Congratulations.'

'And congratulations to you,' he said to Jake. 'The secretary said you are now the chargé d'affaires.'

'I'm moving right up the ladder. Who knows how high I'll go? How about some breakfast?'

'I'm starved. Order me some while I tell you all about it.'

Jake picked up the telephone and dialed the kitchen. When he hung up, he waited for Cole to finish his summation of the night's adventures, then told him, 'A federal grand jury in Washington has issued a warrant for your arrest. Washington announced it an hour ago. You are officially a fugitive.'

Cole shrugged. 'I volunteered. I'll live with it.'

'So where do you guys go from here?'

'Shenzhen, which is a special economic zone right across the border. It's actually sort of a suburb of Hong Kong. We'll cross the bridge this evening and try to take the town. If all goes well, we'll head for Canton in a day or so.'

'How are you going to get there?'

'The old-fashioned way – we're walking. We'll move the York units and our heavy weapons and ammo by truck, but the people will have to hoof it. We've got ten thousand men and women under arms, about half of them former soldiers who volunteered. With the trains out of commission, walking is our only viable option.'

'Can you win?' Callie asked. 'Can you really topple the Communists?'

'If we can convince the people that the Communists have lost the mandate of heaven, the right to rule, then, Yes. Mao Tse Tung always said political power grows from the barrel of a gun, and he couldn't have been more wrong. Every dictator who ever lived believed that fallacy. The truth is that power comes from the consent of the governed. So far the public reaction to the rebellion, at least in Hong Kong, has been better than anyone hoped. Wu always argued that the people were ready – events seem to be proving him correct.'

'You've bet your life that he was correct,' suggested Tommy Carmellini.

'Life is meant to be lived,' Cole replied and helped himself to a cup of coffee.

He grinned – a rarity for Tiger Cole – then offered a coffee toast, 'To life and good friends, wherever they are.'

They were finishing their breakfast at the conference table by the window, enjoying the morning sun and their last hour together, when the secretary burst through the door. 'Admiral, I'm sorry, but – '

He was knocked out of the way by Charlie York. The one-armed robot limped into the room and took up a position near the window, facing the three people around the breakfast table. A few wires hung from the robot's shoulder where its arm had been attached, and the minigun turret was visibly damaged. The skin was spattered with a dark substance, probably a mixture of blood and mud.

Behind the robot came Sonny Wong and Kerry Kent. Kent's nose was taped in position on her face. A portable York control unit hung from a strap around her neck.

Sonny Wong had a pistol in his hand, a nasty-looking automatic. He pointed it at Cole, then at Grafton, as he said, 'Sorry to interrupt your breakfast, my friends, but we owed you a social call.'

'The marines let them in, sir,' the secretary squeaked, 'because they thought they were with Mr. Cole.'

Sonny pointed the pistol at the secretary. 'If anybody comes through that door I'm going to shoot these people and turn loose the York. Tell that to the marines. Now get out!'

The man went, pulling the door closed behind him.

Kerry Kent sat in the consul general's desk chair and put the control unit on the desk. Jake saw that she was stirring the cursor around while Wong talked.

'We have both won, Mr. Cole. You have conquered Hong Kong and I have relieved the Chinese government of a great deal of money.' Sonny parked his rump on the edge of the desk, one leg dangling, the pistol negligently pointed in their direction.

'What do you want?'

'I owe this man here' – he gestured with the pistol at Grafton – 'some serious pain. He killed more than a dozen of my associates and destroyed several major assets of mine, a floating restaurant and a large yacht. Capital assets worth twelve million American dollars burned or went to the bottom, Admiral, thanks to you. You are a real pain in the ass.'

'You should have left my wife alone,' Jake said calmly.

'Nothing personal, but I was trying for a lever to pry some money from Mr. Cole, who has more than is good for any man. He couldn't spend it in five lifetimes. I merely wished to help him with that chore.'

'I should have killed you when I had the chance,' Jake said, still speaking in a conversational tone.

Sonny Wong grinned. The truth was he felt damned good. 'Too late now, Grafton. Too late, too late.'

'Where did you get the York?' Cole asked Sonny.

'It was being repaired. Miss Kent had to shoot several of the technicians when they proved uncooperative, but the York seemed glad to see her.'

Cole finished the last bite of his breakfast and put the knife and fork on the plate. Carmellini moved his feet back under his chair.

He truly is evil, Callie thought, staring at Sonny. She had never seen him in the flesh; he wasn't anything like she had imagined. Short, pudgy, a round, youthful-looking face – he didn't look like anyone's idea of a career criminal. He was, though.

'I'm ready,' Kerry Kent announced triumphantly. She smiled at Carmellini. It wasn't a nice smile. 'After Charlie does the admiral, he's going to do you, Carmellini, you sneaky bastard.'

The coffeepot, creamer, and sugar bowl sat on a highly polished silver tray. Jake reached for the edge of the tray with his left hand, pulled it a little closer so he could reach the coffeepot better. The York unit was about fifteen feet away, staring at him.

Jake poured himself a cup of coffee and set the pot on the table, away from the tray. He then looked again at Wong, who was saying, 'Tell you what, Cole. I will give you a chance to save yourself and your friends. Use the satellite telephone. Call your banker in California. Tell him to wire the fifty million to my Swiss account. There's been enough violence in Hong Kong. Pay me the money and get on with your quest.'

'I don't have that kind of cash available at a moment's notice,' Cole remarked evenly.

'Perhaps your banker can be persuaded to find some lying around somewhere. Miss Kent has programed the York. I am out of patience and time. We have played the game and you have lost. Step over here and pick up the phone.'

Callie was staring at her husband. *He's going to kill that man,* she thought, *and regret it for the rest of his life.*

'We just want to go home,' Callie said, causing Wong to look at her.

Jake reached for his coffee cup with his left hand and knocked the cup over. As he started to rise to avoid the coffee splashing across the table, he drew the Colt .45 from its shoulder holster with his right hand. He thumbed off the safety as he swung the barrel and shot at Sonny Wong.

Sonny was looking the wrong way when Jake drew and he wasn't ready, so he was a second behind, which was just enough. His shot missed Jake's head by three inches and smacked into the wall behind him.

Jake Grafton didn't miss. His shot hit Sonny in the middle of the chest. His second hit him high in the throat, snapping his head back, and his third went through Sonny's heart.

When the first bullet hit Sonny, Kerry Kent screamed and lifted the York control unit up in front of her face.

She was still screaming when Jake Grafton put his fourth shot through the control unit and hit her in the forehead, tearing off the top of her head and spraying a blood mist.

The York unit lurched forward as Kent's corpse toppled to the floor.

Jake tilted the edge of the silver tray with his left hand. The creamer and sugar bowl fell over. Jake turned the tray to catch the sun, then shined the brilliant reflection into the sensors of Charlie York. The robot froze, blinded.

Jake concentrated on keeping the reflected sunbeam in the lenses of the York's visual and infrared sensors.

'Oh, Jake,' Callie murmured.

'Now what?' Jake said to Cole as he slowly holstered the pistol.

'Jesus, man, you shouldn't have shot a hole in the damned control unit.'

Cole scrambled for it, picked it up, and turned it over in his hands, inspecting it.

'Oh, boy!' said Tommy Carmellini, who had dashed around the table and was checking Wong's pulse. 'I don't think Mr. Wong expected that.'

'Ruined the bastard's day,' Jake muttered.

'Is he dead?' Callie asked.

'Pretty much,' Carmellini replied, and went to take a squint at Kent. A glance was enough.

'Ruined,' Cole said disgustedly, and tossed the control unit on the desk.

'Well, don't just stand there, Dr. Frankenstein,' Jake said, his voice tightly controlled. 'Turn the son of a bitch off.'

'That's just it, Jake. Without the control unit, I can't.'

'Isn't there an on-off switch or something?'

'Ah, no. The thinking was that the enemy could flip a switch as well as we could. The control unit is the only way to communicate with a York.'

'Go get another one.'

'Okay, but I don't think it'll do any good. Kent probably slaved the York to this unit so no one else could give it extraneous commands.'

The sun was moving. In a couple of minutes Jake was going to lose it. As the beam wavered on Charlie York's face, he steadied the tray with both hands.

'Start thinking!' he said to Cole. 'Gimme a plan!'

'Maybe you'd better get the hell out of here!'

'What if the damn thing then kills you people?'

'Kent said – '

'She lied to everyone – her whole life was a lie.' He stared at Charlie York, trying to think. 'What are the York's shortcomings, its vulnerabilities?'

'We just started the testing process when we had to stop. We ran out of time.'

'No shit!' Jake took a deep breath, then exhaled. 'Okay, everyone out of the room. All you people clear out, now! Go down the hall and get in one of the offices and close the door.'

One by one they went around behind him and out. Callie was last.

'Jake . . .'

'Go on, Callie. I want to know you're safe.'

'Jake!'

'Go! Let me think for a minute.'

There it stood, a big, massive mechanical monster with one arm and a damaged minigun, blinded by the sun.

It *was* going to kill him.

Perhaps he should just sit still, refuse to be a threat.

But Kent said she had told the York to kill *him*! As the York was looking at his face, she probably designated him as a target, bypassing the threat recognition program. Or was she merely using a figure of speech? Or just flat lying?

He was about to find out. In a few seconds the sunbeam would be gone and . . .

Holding the tray as steady as he could with his left hand, he drew the Colt .45 again. The distance to the York was about ten or twelve feet. God, the thing was intimidating!

With his elbow on the table, he aimed at the York's visual light sensor behind the lens turret. Got the sights lined up, held them as still as humanly possible, and squeezed the trigger.

The gun bucked in his hand.

The York's head snapped back from the impact of the heavy .45 slug, but the sensor lens appeared intact. So did the lens in the turret.

Bulletproof glass! Of course!

He had two more rounds left, so he aimed at the left sensor, the infrared one.

The York jerked again from the impact of the bullet, yet when its head came erect the lens still appeared to be okay.

The last shell.

Another hit. Again to no apparent effect.

He gently laid the empty Colt on the table, trying not to disturb the beam of light reflected from the tray.

On the table was a squeeze bottle of ketchup. Jake picked it up with his right hand. Still pretty full.

Now!

He flipped the tray at the York and ran for the door.

The York was right behind him.

As he went through the outer office, he grabbed a chair and hurled it at the York's feet.

Like a champion hurdler, Charlie York launched itself up and over. And lost its balance on landing and fell in a crash.

Inertia caused the unit to do a somersault.

And it rolled forward onto its feet and kept coming!

Jake dashed along the hallway as fast as he could go. He risked a glance over his shoulder. The York was twenty feet back, lurching along, touching the wall occasionally with its left hand to steady itself.

Callie opened a door, pushing a chair on rollers. 'In here,' she urged Jake as she sent the chair flying along the corridor toward the York, who again attempted to hurdle it. This time the chair caught one foot while it was in the air, and the York landed in a thunderous crash on its head and good shoulder.

Jake slammed the door closed. Carmellini, Cole, and Callie were there along with five or six consulate personnel. 'I told you people to get outta here,' Jake protested.

'In line, quick,' Cole said. 'It'll look through the wall.'

A half dozen of the quickest thinkers got into a tight knot, then they separated.

The door shook from the impact of Charlie York's fist.

'Where's the nearest swimming pool?' Jake demanded of Cole.

'The hotel, three doors down the street.'

'Meet me there,' he shouted as the York's left fist smashed through the door. 'Bring extension cords.'

He jerked open the door to the adjacent room and dashed through it just as the York ripped the door to the room he had left completely off its hinges.

The robot charged into the room, then examined the features of each person there. Clearly it was unsure which of the humans was the designated target.

Grafton was not there. With its UWB radar the York had seen one person leave, so after no more than a four-second delay, it turned and charged after Grafton, lurching as it went, slightly off balance.

As he left the adjacent office Jake had locked the door behind him. He ran down the corridor as the York smashed at the wall, punching holes in the dry wall with its fist, ramming it, making dust come out in clouds.

Jake was going for the stairs when he reconsidered. He pushed the button for the elevator and stood there waiting while the York tore at the wall behind him. A leg came through, the head, now the arm.

He could hear an elevator coming, a high-pitched whine. There were two elevators, so he looked at the floor numbers over the doors. The elevator on the left was a floor away . . . stopping on this floor . . . the doors opened as the York crashed completely through the wall into the corridor.

Jake wormed his way between the opening doors and jabbed the down button as the York came tearing down the hall, each leg driving hard.

The elevator door took its own sweet time closing.

If it gets its claws in the door, the door won't close!

The elevator closed in the York's face, with the hand reaching . . .

949

The York slammed its fist into the exterior door, making the whole elevator shake.

Jake's eyes went to the floor indicator. The elevator had been going up, so the up arrow was there. Before his eyes the arrow flipped to a down indication, and the elevator doors began opening.

Jake pulled out the emergency stop button. An alarm rang somewhere.

The door opened about two inches and stopped.

The York got its two claws into the opening and began tugging.

The door creaked.

If Charlie York had had two hands, the door would probably have failed. With only one hand, the robot could get insufficient leverage.

The ringing alarm bell only added to Jake's adrenaline level.

The York was right there in front of him, its head only inches away.

He pointed the plastic bottle of ketchup at the York's face and squeezed with all his strength. The ketchup squirted out, covering the York's sensor lenses.

When its vision clouded, the York withdrew its claws from the crack in the elevator door and brought its hand in front of its face. Fluid squirted from an opening in its wrist onto the sensor lenses. The doors remained frozen open about two inches, so Jake could still see the York.

With the alarm ringing steadily, Jake opened the emergency escape door on top of the elevator car and grabbed it with both hands. He swung his feet, wriggled wildly, and got one shoulder through.

The York tore at the door again. It got its hand through and used the middle joint of its arm for leverage.

It's learning, he thought. *The damn thing is learning!*

Jake got both shoulders through the opening, now his chest, then he was sitting on the side of the hole. The York had the doors open a foot now.

He swung his feet up just as the York lunged for him.

His sports coat was torn and inhibiting his movements. He jerked it off. He was about to throw it away when the stalk on the top of the York's head came up through the hole.

He tossed the coat over the stalk, forcing the York to lower itself down and use its hand to pull the coat away.

Meanwhile Jake was climbing the ladder in the elevator shaft.

He pushed the emergency exit button by the door two floors above. The door slowly opened. Jake dashed through the door, paused and looked back, just in time to see the stalk on top of the York's head disappear into the exit hole.

The York is coming!

The York will undoubtedly use the stairs, the door to which was twenty feet away.

Jake pushed the button for the elevator. He went over to the stair door, opened it a crack, and listened.

The damn elevator alarm was still going off, masking the sound of the climbing York.

Jake heard the other elevator arrive and the door open.

He turned . . .

And found himself staring at the York, which was charging him as fast as its legs would churn.

He tore open the stair door and dashed downward, taking the stairs three at a time. Charlie York was right behind.

Goddamn Cole! This fucking machine is too smart by half.

Even crippled, the agility of the York was awe-inspiring.

Jake vaulted a rail to gain a little distance, then did it again.

He slammed open the door at the bottom of the stairwell and charged through, right past two marines with assault rifles.

They turned and knelt.

As the York blasted through the door the marines opened fire in full-automatic mode.

The impact of the bullets staggered the York and gave Jake another second of lead, but that was all.

Fortunately the York didn't attack the marines. It ignored them and ran by, limping slightly, using its hand on whatever was handy to help stay balanced.

Jake ran through the metal detector at the main entrance, blasted through a group of American tourists waiting to talk to consulate personnel about leaving Hong Kong, and on out the front door.

The York was four seconds behind him.

'Jesus!' one tourist exclaimed to a marine guard. 'What in hell was that?'

'A York unit,' the sergeant replied.

'Who was it chasing?' the tourist's wife asked.

'He is our new chargé d'affaires.'

'Oh, Lord,' the woman moaned. 'Why in the world did we ever leave Moline?'

There wasn't much traffic, so Jake sprinted across the street without breaking stride and ran into the next building, a huge office tower. The entire first floor consisted of a variety of shops, the interior walls of which were floor-to-ceiling glass. The effect was stunning.

Jake Grafton glanced over his shoulder, checking that the York wasn't too close, then dashed into a shop that had an exterior exit.

Sure enough, the York attempted to cut the corner and smashed into the glass, which literally exploded from the impact.

Shards of glass flew everywhere as screaming shop girls dove for cover. The York stumbled, went to its knees. Jake hit the bar for the outside door, triggering an alarm, and blasted on through.

In the center of the reception area of the next building was a large pool filled with giant Japanese goldfish. Water trickled in from a slime-covered waterfall. The whole thing was ringed with a variety of stunning tropical flowers.

Jake leaped to a small rock in the center of the pool, then leaped on across to the other side.

Charlie York tried to make the same leap . . . and fell into the pool.

With legs and arm churning, it rose, slime dripping from the barrels of its minigun, and splashed wildly after Grafton, who gained three or four seconds on the York.

The next building was the hotel. The doorman shouted at Jake as he ran toward him, but the uniformed man cleared out of the way when he saw the York coming, still decorated with green pond slime.

People in the hotel lobby ran for cover, screaming, shouting, getting behind whatever was handy as Jake ran by, looking for a sign or symbol that might indicate the pool's location.

He slowed as he went by the front desk. 'Where's the pool?' he roared at the little squad of clerks in their bright red blazers.

One of them pointed toward the rear of the hotel.

Jake ran that way.

He saw a short stairs, then a double door. Aha! A sign.

Two turns, one more door, and he found himself on the edge of a large swimming pool. He went around one side, slowed to a walk. His chest was heaving. Fortunately there was no one in the pool.

The York blasted through the door, slamming it open.

It saw Jake, started for him, then slowed, its head turning back and forth, scanning.

It came to a halt two yards past the shallow end, on the side opposite Grafton.

'Smart,' Jake muttered. 'The damned thing is too smart.'

Obviously the York appreciated the dilemma. Regardless of which way it chose to approach Grafton, he could escape by going in the other direction. He could even escape by jumping in the water.

Unless the York could swim.

Naw! Four hundred-plus pounds of titanium and hydraulic fluid, Kevlar and computer chips?

The York began moving forward, toward the deep end of the pool. It removed a pole the maintenance personnel used to vacuum the bottom of the pool from its hook on the wall.

The pole was far too short to reach. Apparently the York realized that fact, for it cocked its arm to throw the pole like a javelin. The butt end of the pole hit the wall behind the York.

Charlie York moved toward the shallow end, where there was more room to throw the thing.

Jake retreated toward the deep end. He suspected the York could heave that light pole with excellent velocity, and he wanted all the distance he could get.

He was right. The pole came like a Zulu spear and nearly got him.

When it realized the pole had missed, the York bent down and began breaking off tile with its claws. Then it backhanded the pieces the length of the pool at Jake.

He misjudged the first one, which almost got him on the arm.

The odds were with the York. It had him trapped.

How long would it keep this up? How much of a charge was on its battery?

Enough, apparently.

Jake dodged piece after piece of tile.

Then the door flew open and Tommy Carmellini and Tiger Cole came blasting through. They had power cords in their arms.

Callie was right behind them.

The two men stopped dead, sized up the situation, then began looking around for a place to plug in the cords.

The York half turned, watched them, waiting – probably – for threatening behavior, which didn't seem to be coming.

As it turned its head to check Jake's location, Callie charged the thing. She hit it in the side with her shoulder, her legs driving as if she were an all-pro tackle taking out a nose guard. She heard Jake's shout, then the force of her charge carried her and the York into the pool, where they hit with a mighty splash.

Foam welled up, obscuring the water.

Jake ran around the pool toward them. If the York got hold of her . . .

He hit the water in a running dive.

He was stroking toward them when he saw Callie's head break water.

The York had used its hand to get itself erect, its feet on the bottom.

As it stood it saw Jake swimming toward it.

And went for him.

'Get out of the damn pool,' Cole shouted.

Grafton managed to turn, to stroke toward the deep end. Over his shoulder he caught a glimpse of Callie climbing from the water.

The York followed Jake, walking on the bottom.

It went deeper and deeper, reaching for the man, who couldn't see how far behind the York was.

Terror flooded him. He was so tired.

'Get out of the damn pool!' It was Cole, shouting again.

Jake got to the end, reached up for the edge with both hands, and heaved himself up, out of the water.

The York was only ten feet behind. Its stalk was the only part that protruded above the water.

As Grafton got his feet out of the water, Cole threw one end of a plugged-in extension cord into the pool.

The York kept coming. There was just too much water and too little current.

It reached the end of the pool, turned, and started for the ladder in the corner.

'The damned thing is going to climb outta there,' Jake shouted. 'Get that cord out of the water and bring me a female end.'

Carmellini ran down the side, meeting Jake halfway. The hundred-foot cord was plugged into a socket near the door to the room and appeared to be long enough.

Jake ran back toward the York, which was slowly and laboriously trying to climb the ladder with one hand.

It slipped and fell back in.

Jake slowed, walked the rest of the way.

The York grasped the top of the ladder railing with its only hand and climbed the first two steps. Now it needed to release its hold on the top of the railing while it balanced itself and got a new hold farther back so it could complete its climb. This was where it fell the last time.

This time it slid its hand along the railing . . .

The damn thing had an uncanny ability to learn.

It was going to get up the ladder, onto the concrete . . .

Jake leaned in from the right side, the side with the missing arm, and jabbed the female end of the extension cord into the receptacle on its back.

The York froze, half in, half out of the water.

It had gone into its rest cycle.

Callie ran toward him. Jake turned and caught her as she threw herself into his arms.

21

'You guys have a way to go to perfect those York units,' Jake Grafton told Virgil Cole as they drove through Kowloon on their way to the railroad station at Lo Wu, a mile or so from the border. The army was gathering there.

'If they were any better you wouldn't be here.'

'I grant you that, but still . . .'

'Write a letter to my company, a guy named Harvey Keim. Tell him what you observed, what you think. He'll be pleased that you took the time to help.'

Callie was sitting in the middle of the limo's backseat, between her husband and Cole.

'Is that all you two have to talk about? Those damn robots?'

'Well – ' Cole said, coloring slightly. 'I'm sorry it wasn't much of a vacation for you folks.'

'I didn't mean that,' Callie stated emphatically. 'You guys haven't seen each other in twenty-eight years.' She made a gesture of exasperation.

'It's been an exciting visit,' Cole agreed.

Callie opened her mouth to speak, then closed it when she felt Jake squeeze her hand.

As they rode they watched the people walking beside the road. Many carried army weapons on their shoulders and a makeshift pack on their back. There were so many of them . . .

'Looks to me like you have more than ten thousand troops,' Jake commented.

'I was thinking the same thing.'

'Be honest. How would you rate the chances of overthrowing the Communists?'

Tiger Cole thought a moment. 'Fair. I think a majority of the Chinese people are ready for a change, and a revolution is the only way they're going to get it. Rebellion has busted out all over. There's fighting in every major city, units of the armed forces are refusing to fight the rebels, people are thinking seriously about what comes next. If the Chinese want change badly enough, they can accomplish anything. We'll just have to live the tale and hope it turns out well.'

The driver pulled the limo to a stop as near to the station as he could. The passengers got out and stretched their legs.

The aroma of shark cooking in a deep-fat fryer wafted across them. A street vendor had set up business nearby.

The driver opened the trunk and passed out a sleeping bag and a small backpack. Jake had given Cole the Colt in the shoulder holster, which he was wearing. Now Jake helped Cole put on the backpack.

'This is ridiculous, you know,' Jake said to Cole. 'You're on the *Fortune* magazine list of the five hundred richest Americans, and you boil your earthly possessions down to a pistol, a backpack, and a sleeping bag?'

'In the age of hypocrisy a man has to travel light.'

'I've heard there is such a thing as underpacking,' Callie remarked, 'though I've never gone there myself.'

'After a couple hundred miles I'll be down to a toothbrush and one extra pair of socks,' Cole replied. 'I'll give the backpack to some lucky soul who wants to make it into a hat.'

Another car drove up. Rip Buckingham and Wu Tai Kwong got out, along with two women, one old and one in her thirties.

The younger woman had been crying. Rip took her in his arms and held her tightly as he swayed ever so slightly back and forth. He didn't seem to care who was watching.

'I wish you would stay,' she whispered.

'I'm a newspaperman, Sue Lin. This is the story of a lifetime. I have to go.'

'I know,' she whispered.

Wu hugged the old woman, bent down and whispered something to her, then picked up his backpack and walked away. He looked back once, paused, then continued on into the crowd, which swallowed him.

Rip lingered. 'I want you and Lin Pe to go to Australia,' he said to his wife. 'I mean it. No ifs, ands, or buts. I don't want to walk all over China worrying about you.'

'We'll worry about you.'

'That'll be enough worry for the whole family. Lin Pe, will you and Sue Lin do as I ask?'

Both women nodded.

He put them back in the car finally, murmured something to the driver. The car pulled into a gap in the passing traffic and crept away.

Rip came over to where Cole and the Graftons were standing. 'Hello, Admiral. I owe you a debt of gratitude for rescuing my brother-in-law.'

Jake just nodded and shook the outstretched hand. 'Good luck, Mr. Buckingham. Don't be too harsh in your stories on the archcriminal Virgil Cole.'

'I'll try to be objective and fair.'

'I'll hold you to that,' Cole said, serious as always. Buckingham winked at Grafton, shook Callie's hand, then shouldered his packs and walked away.

'How long will you stay in Hong Kong?' Cole asked Jake.

'A couple of weeks, according to the weenie at State. He's probably lying so I won't squawk too much. You know how it is – I'll leave when they tell me to go back to the states, and not before.'

'I love Hong Kong,' Cole said, quite unnecessarily. He stood looking around, breathing in the sights and smells and sounds. 'It's a unique, magical place. Nowhere else quite like it.'

Callie Grafton found herself nodding in agreement. She too found Hong Kong fascinating. 'When you get back to America,' she told Cole, 'come see us. If you're broke, call and we'll wire you the price of a bus ticket.'

That remark brought a shadow of a grin to Cole's features. 'I'll remember the invitation,' he said, offering his hand. Callie shook it, then Jake.

'There is one thing I still don't know,' Jake said as Cole picked up his bags. 'Who shot China Bob Chan?'

'Ooh,' Cole said, grunting a little as he hefted his pack. 'I did, of course. He knew too much.'

'Why didn't the CIA tape pick up a conversation?'

'I knew the office was bugged, so I stopped in the secretary's office, and Chan stopped because I did. We discussed our business right there. He decided he wanted to show me a letter he had received, so he opened the door and walked across to his desk, me tagging along behind.

'You see, he knew everything and he wanted money, a lot of it. Even if I paid him off, I thought it probable that he'd tattle to the authorities with specifics they could check. So as I followed him to the desk I drew the pistol from my pocket and shot him in the head when he turned around. Bob didn't even see it coming. Not a bad way to check out, if you gotta go, and he did. Then I ditched the pistol in a trashcan and went downstairs and got on with the mixing and mingling.'

'So you knew there was nothing on the tape that would implicate you?'

'I was pretty sure there wasn't, but the truth was that I didn't care. Still don't. I wouldn't pay ten cents for a videotape of me doing the shooting, if one existed. Sonny Wong never understood that simple fact, which tells you how bright he really was. You can tell State I shot Chan if you want to – now that the revolution has begun, it just doesn't matter.'

'Doesn't sound like you're planning on returning to the states any time soon.'

'I'm not.' Cole sucked in a bushel of air and let it out. 'Life's an adventure. I've been a high-tech exec long enough, been a diplomat, been rich, been to all the black-tie parties I can stand. Now I'm going in this direction, going wherever the road leads.'

'Keep the faith, shipmate.'

'Yeah, Jake Grafton. I'll do that. For you and me and all of those guys who fought the good fight in their time.'

They shook hands, then Tiger Cole walked out of Jake Grafton's life.

Jake turned to Callie. 'I hate to say this, but I'm up to my ears in work at the consulate. Want to have the kitchen make us a pizza and help me tackle the paperwork?'

'Yes,' she said and put her arm around his waist as they walked back to the car.

Author's Note

Alas, there is no 'correct' way to render the Chinese language into English. Prior to the Communist takeover of China, the widely used Wade-Giles system of transliteration gave us Hong Kong, Peking, Mao Tse Tung, Chiang Kai Shek, etc. The Communist bureaucracy spawned a new system, Pinyin, to transliterate Mandarin, which the bureaucrats decreed would be *putonghua*, or 'common speech,' i.e., the 'official' language of China. (Mandarin is the language of northern China; the language of southern China is Cantonese.)

Unlike Wade-Giles, Pinyin often fails to present phonetic clues to English speakers, or, amazingly, the speakers of any language that uses the Roman alphabet. For example, *qi* in Pinyin is pronounced *chee*. We anglicize or transliterate Paris, Rome, and Moscow, and the French, Italians, and Russians seem unruffled. Why must Hong Kong become Xianggang?

For reasons we can only speculate about, in the last two decades American and British newspaper editors have embraced Pinyin with remarkable fervor, which leads to nonsense such as 'The President ate Peking duck in Beijing.'

In his excellent book, *The Making of Hong Kong Society* (Oxford: Clarendon Press, 1991), Dr. W.K. Chan points out that there are at least fifty-four different ways of presenting any Cantonese name in English. Faced with this plethora of choices, the author has spelled the names in this book in a way that seemed to him easiest for an English speaker to pronounce. Any complaints should be addressed to the Pinyin troglodyte in Peking, or Beijing, or wherever.